W9-BXE-252

THE MIDNIGHT CAFE

THE MIDNIGHT CAFE

The Lunatic Cafe
Bloody Bones
The Killing Dance

Laurell K. Hamilton

Published by arrangement with Ace Books
A Division of The Berkley Publishing Group
200 Madison Avenue
New York, New York 10016

ISBN 1-56865-765-X

PRINTED IN THE UNITED STATES OF AMERICA

Contents

THE LUNATIC CAFE

To Trinity Dianne Hamilton,
who has the most beautiful smile in the world,
even at three o'clock in the morning

Acknowledgments

Gary, my beloved husband. I wouldn't have made it through the last year without you. Dr. Keith Nunnelee, who helped bring Trinity into the world. No small task that. Sarah Sumner for food, comfort, and emergency runs to the doctor. Mark Sumner for the same. I can't wait to see *Range* on the shelves. John Sumner for worrying. Nobody has better neighbors or better friends. Deborah Millitello, who took time out of her own writing schedule to help with the baby so I could get this book finished. Marella Sands, congrats on selling your own series. I am going to take you up on that baby-sitting offer.

To all the rest of the Alternate Historians: Tom Drennan, N. L. Drew, and Rett McPherson, who made sure this book stood alone. New friends, new writers, who could ask for anything more.

1

It was two weeks before Christmas. A slow time of year for raising the dead. My last client of the night sat across from me. There had been no notation by his name. No note saying zombie raising or vampire slaying. Nothing. Which probably meant whatever he wanted me to do was something I wouldn't, or couldn't, do. Pre-Christmas was a dead time of year, no pun intended. My boss, Bert, took any job that would have us.

George Smitz was a tall man, well over six feet. He was broad shouldered, and muscular. Not the muscles you get from lifting weights and running around indoor tracks. The muscles you get from hard physical labor. I would have bet money that Mr. Smitz was a construction worker, farmer, or something similar. He was shaped large and square with grime embedded under his fingernails that soap would not touch.

He sat in front of me, crushing his toboggan hat, kneading it in his big hands. The coffee that he'd accepted sat cooling on the edge of my desk. He hadn't taken so much as a sip.

I was drinking my coffee out of the Christmas mug that Bert, my boss, had insisted everyone bring in. A personalized holiday mug to add a personal touch to the office. My mug had a reindeer in a bathrobe and slippers with Christmas lights laced in its antlers, toasting the merry season with champagne and saying, "Bingle Jells."

Bert didn't really like my mug, but he let it go, probably afraid of what else I might bring in. He'd been very pleased with my outfit for the evening. A high-collared blouse so perfectly red I'd had to wear makeup to keep from looking pale. The skirt and matching jacket were a deep forest green. I hadn't dressed for Bert. I had dressed for my date.

The silver outline of an angel gleamed in my lapel. I looked very Christmasy. The Browning Hi-Power 9mm didn't look Christmasy at all, but since it was hidden under the jacket, that didn't seem to matter. It might have bothered Mr. Smitz, but he looked worried enough to not care. As long as I didn't shoot him personally.

"Now, Mr. Smitz, how may I help you today?" I asked.

He was staring at his hands and only his eyes rose to look at me. It was a little-boy gesture, an uncertain gesture. It sat oddly on the big man's face. "I need help, and I don't know who else to go to."

"Exactly what kind of help do you need, Mr. Smitz?"

"It's my wife."

I waited for him to continue, but he stared at his hands. His hat was wadded into a tight ball.

"You want your wife raised from the dead?" I asked.

He looked up at that, eyes wide with alarm. "She's not dead. I know that."

"Then what can I possibly do for you, Mr. Smitz? I raise the dead, and am a legal vampire executioner. What in that job description could help your wife?"

"Mr. Vaughn said you knew all about lycanthropy." He said that as if it explained everything. It didn't.

"My boss makes a lot of claims, Mr. Smitz. But what does lycanthropy have to do with your wife?" This was the second time I'd asked about his wife. I seemed to be speaking English, but perhaps my questions were really Swahili and I just didn't realize it. Or maybe whatever had happened was too awful for words. That happened a lot in my business.

He leaned forward, eyes intense on my face. I leaned forward, too, I couldn't help myself. "Peggy, that's my wife, she's a lycanthrope."

I blinked at him. "And?"

"If it came out, she'd lose her job."

I didn't argue with him. Legally, you couldn't discriminate against lycanthropes, but it happened a lot. "What sort of work is Peggy in?"

"She's a butcher."

A lycanthrope that was a butcher. It was too perfect. But I could see why she'd lose her job. Food preparation with a potentially fatal disease. I don't think so. I knew, and the health department knew, that lycanthropy can only be transferred by an attack in the animal form. Most people don't believe that. Can't say I blame them entirely. I don't want to be fuzzy, either.

"She runs a specialty meat store. It's a good business. She inherited it from her father."

"Was he a lycanthrope, too?" I asked.

He shook his head. "No, Peggy was attacked a few years back. She survived . . ." He shrugged. "But, you know."

I did know. "So your wife is a lycanthrope and would lose her business if it came out. I understand that. But how can I help you?" I fought the urge to glance at my watch. I had the tickets. Richard couldn't go in without me.

"Peggy's missing."

Ah. "I am not a private detective, Mr. Smitz. I don't do missing persons."

"But I can't go to the police. They might find out."

"How long has she been missing?"

"Two days."

"My advice is to go to the police."

He shook his head stubbornly. "No."

I sighed. ''I don't know anything about finding a missing person. I raise the dead, slay vampires, that's it.''

''Mr. Vaughn said you could help me.''

''Did you tell him your problem?''

He nodded.

Shit. Bert and I were going to have a long talk. ''The police are good at their job, Mr. Smitz. Just tell them your wife is missing. Don't mention the lycanthropy. See what they turn up.'' I didn't like telling a client to withhold information from the police, but it beat the heck out of not going at all.

''Ms. Blake, please, I'm worried. We've got two kids.''

I started to say all the reasons I couldn't help him, then stopped. I had an idea. ''Animators, Inc., has a private investigator on retainer. Veronica Sims has been involved in a lot of preternatural cases. She might be able to help you.''

''Can I trust her?''

''I do.''

He stared at me for a long moment, then nodded. ''All right, how do I get in touch with her?''

''Let me give her a call, see if she can see you.''

''That would be great, thank you.''

''I want to help you, Mr. Smitz. Hunting missing spouses just isn't my specialty.'' I dialed the phone as I talked. I knew Ronnie's number by heart. We exercised at least twice a week together, not to mention an occasional movie, dinner, whatever. Best friends, a concept that most women never outgrow. Ask a man who his best friend is and he'll have to think about it. He won't know right off the top of his head. A woman would. A man might not even be able to think of a name, not for his best friend. Women keep track of these things. Men don't. Don't ask me why.

Ronnie's answering machine clicked in. ''Ronnie, if you're there, it's Anita, pick up.''

The phone clicked, and a second later I was talking to the genuine article. ''Hi, Anita. I thought you had a date with Richard tonight. Something wrong?''

See, best friends. ''Not with the date. I've got a client here who I think is more up your alley than mine.''

''Tell me,'' she said.

I did.

''Did you recommend he go to the police?''

''Yep.''

''He won't go?''

''Nope.''

She sighed. ''Well, I've done missing persons before but usually after the police have done everything they can. They have resources I can't touch.''

''I'm aware of that,'' I said.

''He won't budge?''

''I don't think so.''

''So it's me or . . .''

"Bert took the job knowing it was a missing person. He might try giving it to Jamison."

"Jamison doesn't know his butt from a hole in the ground on anything but raising the dead."

"Yeah, but he's always eager to expand his repertoire."

"Ask him if he can be at my office . . ." She paused while she leafed through her appointment book. Business must be good. "At nine tomorrow morning."

"Jesus, you always were an early riser."

"One of my few faults," she said.

I asked George Smitz if nine o'clock tomorrow was all right.

"Couldn't she see me tonight?"

"He wants to see you tonight."

She thought about that for a minute. "Why not? It's not like I have a hot date, unlike some people I could mention. Sure, send him over. I'll wait. Friday with a client is better than Friday night alone, I guess."

"You've just hit a dry spell," I said.

"And you've hit a wet spell."

"Very funny."

She laughed. "I'll look forward to Mr. Smitz's arrival. Enjoy *Guys and Dolls*."

"I will. See you tomorrow morning for our run."

"You sure you want me over there that early in case dream boat wants to stay over?"

"You know me better than that," I said.

"Yeah, I do. Just kidding. See you tomorrow."

We hung up. I gave Mr. Smitz Ronnie's business card, directions to her office, and sent him on his way. Ronnie was the best I could do for him. It still bothered me that he wouldn't go to the police, but hey, it wasn't my wife.

I've got two kids, he'd said. Not my problem. Really. Craig, our nighttime secretary, was at the desk, which meant it was after six. I was running late. There really wasn't time to argue with Bert about Mr. Smitz, but . . .

I glanced at Bert's office. It was dark. "Boss man gone home?"

Craig glanced up from his computer keyboard. He has short, baby-fine brown hair. Round glasses to match a round face. He's slender and taller than I am, but then who isn't? He's in his twenties with a wife and two babies.

"Mr. Vaughn left about thirty minutes ago."

"It figures," I said.

"Something wrong?"

I shook my head. "Schedule me some time to talk to the boss tomorrow."

"I don't know, Anita. He's booked pretty solid."

"Find some time, Craig. Or I'll barge in on one of the other appointments."

"You're mad," he said.

"You bet. Find the time. If he yells about it, tell him I pulled a gun on you."

"Anita," he said with a grin, as if I were teasing.

I left him riffling through the appointment book trying to squeeze me somewhere. I meant it. Bert would talk to me tomorrow. December was our slowest season for raising zombies. People seemed to think you couldn't do it close to

Christmas, as if it were black magic or something. So Bert scheduled other things to take up the slack. I was getting tired of clients with problems I could do nothing about. Smitz wasn't the first this month, but he was going to be the last.

With that cheerful thought I bundled into my coat and left. Richard was waiting. If traffic cooperated, I might just make it before the opening number. Traffic on a Friday night, surely not.

2

The 1978 Nova that I'd been driving had died a sad and tragic death. I was now driving a Jeep Cherokee Country. It was a deep, deep green that looked black at night. But it had four-wheel drive for winter and enough room to carry goats in the back. Chickens were what I used for zombie raising most of the time, but occasionally you needed something bigger. Carrying goats in the Nova had been a bitch.

I pulled the Cherokee into the last parking space in the lot on Grant. My long, black winter coat billowed around me because I had only buttoned the bottom two buttons. If I buttoned all the buttons I couldn't get to my gun.

My hands were shoved into the coat pockets, arms huddling the cloth around me. I didn't wear gloves. I've never been comfortable shooting with gloves on. The gun is a part of my hand. Cloth shouldn't interfere.

I ran across the street in my high-heeled pumps, careful on the frosty pavement. The sidewalk was cracked, with huge sections broken out of it, as if someone had taken a sledgehammer to it. The boarded-up buildings were as dilapidated as the sidewalk. I'd missed the crowd, being nearly late, so I had the shattered street to myself. It was a short but lonely walk on a December night. Broken glass littered the ground and in heels I had to be very careful where I stepped. An alley cut the buildings. It looked like the natural habitat of *Muggerus americanus*. I watched the darkness carefully. Nothing moved. With the Browning I wasn't too worried, but still . . . You didn't have to be a genius to shoot someone in the back.

The wind gusted cold enough to take my breath away as I neared the corner and relative safety. I wore a lot of sweaters in the winter, but tonight I'd wanted something dressier, and I was freezing my patooties off, but I was hoping that Richard would like the red blouse.

At the corner there were lights, cars, and a policeman directing traffic in the middle of the street. You never saw this many police in this section of St. Louis unless the Fox was on. A lot of wealthy people came down here in their furs, diamonds, Rolex watches. Wouldn't do for a friend of the city council to get mugged. When Topol came to reprise his role in *Fiddler on the Roof,* the audience was very crème de la crème and the place crawled with cops. Tonight there was just the usual. Mostly in front of the theater, mostly doing traffic, but also taking peeks at the seedy backs of buildings in case someone with money wondered away from the light.

I went through the glass doors into the long, narrow entryway. It was brightly lit, shiny somehow. There's a little room to the right where you can pick up your tickets. People streamed out of it, hurrying to the inner glass doors. I wasn't as late as I thought if there were this many people still getting tickets. Or maybe everyone else was as late as I was.

I caught a glimpse of Richard standing in the far right corner. At six foot one he is easier to spot across a crowded room than I am, at my own five foot three. He stood quietly, eyes following the crowd's movement. He didn't seem bored or impatient. He seemed to be having a good time watching the people. His eyes followed an elderly couple as they walked through the glass doors. The woman used a cane. Their progress was painfully slow. His head turned slowly with them. I scanned the crowd. Everyone else was younger, moving with confident or hurried stride. Was Richard looking for victims? Prey? He was, after all, a werewolf. He'd gotten a bad batch of lycanthropy vaccine. One of the reasons I never get the shots. If my flu shot accidentally backfires, that's one thing, but being furry once a month . . . No, thanks.

Did he realize he was standing there searching the crowd like a lion staring at a bunch of gazelles? Or maybe the elderly couple had reminded him of his grandparents. Hell, maybe I was giving him motives that were only in my suspicious little brain. I hoped so.

His hair was brown. In sunlight it gleamed with strands of gold, hints of copper. I knew the hair was shoulder length, nearly my length, but he'd done something to it, pulled it back somehow so it gave the illusion of being very short and close to his head. Not easy with hair as wavy as his.

His suit was some rich shade of green. Most men would have looked like Peter Pan in a green suit, but on him it looked just right. As I walked closer, I could see his shirt was a pale almost gold, tie a darker green than the suit, with tiny Christmas trees done in red. I would have made a smart remark about the tie, but dressed in red and green with a Christmas angel on my lapel, who was I to complain?

He saw me and smiled. The smile was very bright against his permanently tanned skin. His last name, Zeeman, is Dutch, but somewhere back in his ancestry was something not European. Not blond, not fair, not cold. His eyes were a perfect, chocolate brown.

He reached out and took my hands, gently, drawing me to him. His lips were soft against my mouth, a brief, nearly chaste kiss.

I stepped back, taking a breath. He kept hold of my hand, and I let him. His skin was very warm against my cold hand. I thought about asking him if he'd been thinking about eating that elderly couple, but didn't. Accusing him of murderous intent might spoil the evening. Besides, most lycanthropes weren't aware of doing nonhuman things. When you pointed it out, it always seemed to hurt their feelings. I didn't want to hurt Richard's feelings.

As we went through the inner doors into the crowded lobby, I asked, ''Where's your coat?''

''In the car. Didn't want to carry it, so I made a dash for it.''

I nodded. It was typical Richard. Or maybe lycanthropes didn't get cold. From the back I could see he'd braided his hair tight to his scalp. The tip of the braid trailed over his collar. I couldn't even figure out how he'd done it. My idea of fixing my hair is to wash, smear a little hair goop through it, then let it dry. I was not into high-tech hair design. Though it might be fun to figure out the knots in a leisurely fashion after the show. I was always willing to learn a new skill.

The main lobby of the Fox is a cross between a really nice Chinese restaurant and a Hindu temple, with a little Art Deco thrown in for flavor. The colors are so dazzling, it looks like the painter ground up stained glass with bits of light trapped in them. Pit bull–size Chinese lions with glowing red eyes guard a sweep of stairs that lead up to the Fox Club balcony, where for fifteen thousand dollars a year you can eat wonderful meals and have a private box. The rest of us peons mingled nearly shoulder to shoulder in the carpeted lobby, with offerings of popcorn, pretzels, Pepsi, and on some nights, hot dogs. A far cry from chicken cordon bleu or whatever they were serving up above.

The Fox treads that wonderfully thin line between gaudiness and the fantastic. I've loved the building since I first saw it. Every time I come, there is some new wonder. Some color, or carving, or statue that I didn't notice before. When you realize that it was originally built to be a movie theater, you realize how much things have changed. Movie theaters now have the souls of unwashed socks. The Fox is alive as only the best buildings are alive.

I had to let go of Richard's hand to unbutton my coat the rest of the way, but hey, we weren't attached at the hip. I stood close to him in the crowd without touching, but I could feel him, like a line of warmth against my body.

''We're going to look like the Bobsey twins when I take my coat off,'' I said.

He raised his eyebrows.

I spread the coat like a flasher, and he laughed. It was a good laugh, warm and thick like Christmas pudding.

'' 'Tis the season,'' he said. He gave me a one-armed hug, quick like you'd give a friend, but his arm stayed over my shoulders. It was still early enough in our dating that touching each other was new, unexpected, exhilarating. We kept looking for excuses to touch each other. Trying to be nonchalant about it. Not fooling each other. Not sure we cared. I slipped my arm around his waist and leaned just a bit. It was my right arm. If we were attacked now, I'd never draw my gun in time. I stayed there for a minute thinking it just might be worth it. I moved around him, offering my left hand to him.

I don't know if he caught a glimpse of the gun or just figured it out, but his eyes widened. He leaned close to me, whispering against my hair. ''A gun here, at the Fox? You think the ushers will let you in?''

''They did last time.''

He got a strange look on his face. ''You always go armed?''

I shrugged. ''After dark, yes.''

His eyes were puzzled, but he let it go. Before this year I'd sometimes gone out after dark unarmed but it had been a rough year. A lot of different people had tried to kill me. I was small even for a woman. I jogged, lifted weights, had a black belt in judo, but I was still outclassed by most professional bad guys. They tended to also lift weights, know martial arts, and outweigh me by a hundred pounds or more. I couldn't arm-wrestle them, but I could shoot them.

Also a lot of this year I'd been up against vampires, and other preternatural creepie-crawlies. They could lift large trucks with a single hand or worse. Silver bullets might not kill a vampire, but it certainly slowed them down. Enough for me to run like hell. To get away. To survive.

Richard knew what I did for a living. He'd even seen some of the messy parts. But I still expected him to blow it. To start playing the male protector and bitch about the gun or something. It was almost a permanent tightness in my gut, waiting for this man to say something awful. Something that would ruin it, destroy it, hurt.

So far, so good.

The crowd started flowing towards the stairs, parting on either side to the corridors leading into the main theater. We shuffle-stepped with the crowd, holding hands to keep from being separated. Sure.

Once free of the lobby, the crowd flowed towards the different aisles like water searching for the quickest route downstream. The quickest route was still pretty slow. I dug the tickets out of the pocket of my suit jacket. I didn't have a purse. There was a small brush, a lipstick, lipliner, eye shadow, ID, and my car keys stuffed in my coat pockets. My beeper was tucked in the front of my skirt, discreetly to one side. When not dressed up, I wore a fanny pack.

The usher, an older woman with glasses, shone a tiny flashlight on our tickets. She took us to our seats, motioned us in, and went back up to assist the next group of helpless people. The seats were good, near the middle, sort of close to the stage. Close enough.

Richard had scooted in to sit on my left without being asked. He's a quick study. It's one of the reasons we're still going out. That and the fact that I lust after his body something terrible.

I spread my coat over the seat, spreading it out so it wouldn't be bulky. His arm snaked across my chair, fingers touching my shoulder. I fought the urge to lay my head on his shoulder. Too hokey, then thought, what the hell. I snuggled into the bend of his neck, just breathing in the scent of his skin. His aftershave was clean and sweet, but underneath was the smell of his skin, his flesh. It made it so the aftershave would never smell the same on anyone else. Frankly, without a drop of aftershave I loved the smell of Richard's neck.

I straightened up, pulling just a little away from him. He looked at me questioningly. ''Something wrong?''

''Nice aftershave,'' I said. No need to confess that I'd had an almost irresistible urge to nibble his neck. It was too embarrassing.

The lights dimmed and the music began. I'd never actually seen *Guys and Dolls* except in the movies. The one with Marlon Brando and Jean Simmons. Richard's idea of a date was caving, hiking, things that required your oldest clothes and a pair of good walking shoes. Nothing wrong with that. I like the outdoors, but I wanted to try a dress-up date. I wanted to see Richard in a suit and let him see me in something frillier than jeans. I was after all a girl, whether I liked to admit it or not.

But having proposed the date, I didn't want to do the usual dipsy-duo of dinner and a movie. So I'd called up the Fox to see what was playing and asked Richard if he liked musicals. He did. Another point in his favor. Since it was my idea, I bought the tickets. Richard had not argued, not even to pay half. After all, I hadn't offered to pay for our last dinner. It hadn't occurred to me. I was betting paying for the tickets occurred to Richard, but he'd let it go. Good man.

The curtain came up and the opening street scene paraded before us, bright colors, stylized, perfect and cheerful, and just what I needed. ''The Fugue for Tinhorns'' filled the bright stage and flowed out into the happy dark. Good music, humor, soon to be dancers, Richard's body next to mine, a gun under my arm. What more could a girl ask for?

3

A trickle of people had slipped out before the end of the musical, to beat the crowd. I always stayed until the very end. It seemed unfair to slink away before you could applaud. Besides, I hated missing the end of anything. I was always convinced that the bit I'd miss would be the best part.

We joined in enthusiastically with a standing ovation. I've never lived in any city that gives so many standing Os. Admittedly sometimes, like tonight, the show was wonderful, but I've seen people stand on productions that didn't deserve it. I don't stand unless I mean it.

Richard sat back down after the lights came up. "I'd rather wait until the crowd thins out. If you don't mind." There was a look in his brown eyes that said he didn't think I would.

I didn't. We'd driven separate cars. When we left the Fox, the evening was over. Apparently, neither of us wanted to leave. I knew I didn't.

I leaned on the seats in front of us, gazing down at him. He smiled up at me, eyes gleaming with lust, if not love. I was smiling, too. Couldn't seem to help myself.

"You know this is a very sexist musical," he said.

I thought about that a moment, then nodded. "Yep."

"But you like it?"

I nodded.

His eyes narrowed a bit. "I thought you might be offended."

"I have better things to worry about than whether *Guys and Dolls* reflects a balanced worldview."

He laughed—a short, happy sound. "Good. For a minute there I thought I'd have to get rid of my Rodgers and Hammerstein collection."

I studied his face, trying to decide if he was teasing me. I didn't think so. "You really collect Rodgers and Hammerstein sound tracks?"

He nodded, eyes bright with laughter.

"Just Rodgers and Hammerstein, or all musicals?"

"I don't have them all, but all."

I shook my head.

''What's wrong?''

''You're a romantic.''

''You make it sound like a bad thing.''

''That happy-ever-after shit is fine on stage, but it doesn't have a lot to do with life.''

It was his turn to study my face. Evidently, he didn't like what he saw, because he frowned. ''This date was your idea. If you don't approve of all this happy stuff, why'd you bring me?''

I shrugged. ''After I asked you on a dress-up date, I didn't know where to take you. I didn't want to do the usual. Besides, I like musicals. I just don't think they reflect reality.''

''You're not as tough as you pretend to be.''

''Yes,'' I said, ''I am.''

''I don't believe that. I think you like that happy-ever-after shit as much as I do. You're just afraid to believe in it anymore.''

''Not afraid, just cautious.''

''Been disappointed too many times?'' He made it a question.

''Maybe.'' I crossed my arms on my stomach. A psychologist would have said I was closed off, uncommunicative. Fuck them.

''What are you thinking?''

I shrugged.

''Tell me, please.''

I stared into his sincere brown eyes and wanted to go home alone. Instead. ''Happy ever after is just a lie, Richard, and has been since I was eight.''

''Your mother's death,'' he said.

I just looked at him. I was twenty-four years old and the pain of that first loss was still raw. You could deal with it, endure it, but never escape it. Never truly believe in the great, good place. Never truly believe that the bad thing wasn't going to come swooping down and take it all away. I'd rather fight a dozen vampires than one senseless accident.

He pried my hand from its grip on my arm. ''I won't die on you, Anita. I promise.''

Someone laughed, a low chuckle that brushed the skin like fingertips. Only one person had that nearly touchable laugh—Jean-Claude. I turned, and there he was, standing in the middle of the aisle. I hadn't heard him come. Hadn't sensed any movement. He was just there like magic.

''Don't make promises you can't keep, Richard.''

4

I pushed away from the seats, taking a step forward to give Richard room to stand. I felt him at my back, a comforting presence if I hadn't been more worried about his safety than my own.

Jean-Claude was dressed in a shiny black tux, complete with tails. A white vest with minute black dots bordered the gleaming whiteness of his shirt. The collar was high and stiff, with a cravat of soft black cloth tied around it and tucked into the vest as if ties had never been invented. The stickpin in his vest was made of silver-and-black onyx. His shoes had spats on them, like the ones Fred Astaire used to wear, though I suspected the entire outfit was of a much older style.

His hair was fashionably long, the nearly black curls edging the white collar. I knew what color his eyes were, but I didn't look at them now. They were midnight blue, the color of a really good sapphire. Never look a vampire in the eyes. It's a rule.

With the master vampire of the city standing there, waiting, I realized how empty the theater was. We'd waited out the crowd, all right. We were alone in the echoing silence. The distant murmur of the departing crowd was like white noise. It meant nothing to us. I stared at the shiny mother-of-pearl buttons on Jean-Claude's vest. It was hard to be tough when you couldn't meet someone's eyes. But I'd manage.

"God, Jean-Claude, don't you ever wear anything but black and white?"

"Don't you like it, *ma petite*?" He gave a little spin so I could get the whole effect. The outfit suited him beautifully. Of course, everything he wore seemed made to order, perfect, lovely, just like him.

"Somehow I didn't think *Guys and Dolls* would be your cup of tea, Jean-Claude."

"Or yours, *ma petite*." The voice was rich like cream, with a warmth that only two things could give it: anger or lust. I was betting it wasn't lust.

I had the gun, and silver bullets would slow him down, but it wouldn't kill him. Of course, Jean-Claude wouldn't jump us in public. He was much too civilized for that. He was a business vampire, an entrepreneur. Entrepreneurs, dead or alive, didn't go around tearing people's throats out. Normally.

"Richard, you're unusually quiet." He stared past me. I didn't glance back to see what Richard was doing. Never take your eyes off the vampire in front of you to glance at the werewolf in back of you. One problem at a time.

"Anita can speak for herself," Richard said.

Jean-Claude's attention flicked back to me. "That is certainly true. But I came to see how the two of you enjoyed the play."

"And pigs fly," I said.

"You don't believe me?"

"Not hardly," I said.

"Come, Richard, how did you enjoy your evening?" There was an edge of laughter to his voice but under that was still the anger. Master vampires are not good to be around when they're angry.

"It was wonderful until you showed up." There was a note of warmth to Richard's voice, the beginnings of anger. I'd never seen him angry.

"How could my mere presence spoil your . . . date?" The last was spit out, scalding hot.

"Why are you so pissed tonight, Jean-Claude?" I asked.

"Why, *ma petite,* I never get . . . pissed."

"Bullshit."

"He's jealous of you and me," Richard said.

"I am not jealous."

"You're always telling Anita how you can smell her desire for you. Well, I can smell yours. You want her so bad you can"—Richard gave an almost bitter sound—"taste it."

"And you, Monsieur Zeeman, you don't lust after her?"

"Stop talking like I'm not here," I said.

"Anita asked me out on a date. I said yes."

"Is this true, *ma petite*?" His voice had gone very quiet. Scarier than anger, that quietness.

I wanted to say no, but he'd smell a lie. "It's true. What of it?"

Silence. He just stood there utterly still. If I hadn't been looking right at him, I wouldn't have known he was there. The dead make no noise.

My beeper went off. Richard and I jumped as if we'd been shot. Jean-Claude was motionless as if he hadn't heard it.

I hit the button, and the number that flashed made me groan.

"What is it?" Richard asked. He laid his hand on my shoulder.

"The police. I've got to find a phone." I leaned back against Richard's chest. His hand squeezed my shoulder. I stared at the vampire in front of me. Would Jean-Claude hurt him after I'd gone? I wasn't sure.

"You got a cross on you?" I didn't bother to whisper. Jean-Claude would have heard me anyway.

"No."

I half turned. "No! You're out after dark without a cross?"

He shrugged. "I'm a shapeshifter. I can take care of myself."

I shook my head. "Getting your throat ripped out once wasn't enough?"

"I'm still alive," he said.

"I know you heal from almost anything, but for God's sake, Richard, you don't heal from everything." I started pulling the silver chain of my crucifix out of my blouse. "You can borrow mine."

"Is that real silver?" Richard asked.

"Yes."

"I can't. I'm allergic to silver, remember."

Ah. Stupid me. Some preternatural expert offering silver to a lycanthrope. I tucked the chain back in my blouse.

"He's no more human than I am, *ma petite*."

"At least I'm not dead."

"That can be remedied."

"Stop it, both of you."

"Have you seen her bedroom, Richard? Her collection of toy penguins?"

I took a deep breath and let it out. I was not going to stand here and explain how Jean-Claude had managed to see my bedroom. Did I really have to say, out loud, that I didn't sleep with the walking dead?

"You're trying to make me jealous, and it won't work," Richard said.

"But there is that worm of doubt in you, Richard. I know it. You are my creature to call, my wolf, and I know you doubt her."

"I don't doubt Anita." But there was a defensiveness in his voice that I didn't like at all.

"I don't belong to you, Jean-Claude," Richard said. "I'm second in line to lead the pack. I come and go where I please. The alpha rescinded his orders about obeying you, after you nearly got me killed."

"Your pack leader was most upset that you survived," Jean-Claude said sweetly.

"Why would the pack leader want Richard dead?" I asked.

Jean-Claude looked past me at Richard. "You haven't told her that you're in a battle of succession?"

"I will not fight Marcus."

"Then you will die." Jean-Claude made it sound very simple.

My beeper sounded again. Same number. "I'm coming, Dolph," I muttered.

I glanced at Richard. Anger glittered in his eyes. His hands were balled into fists. I was standing close enough to feel the tension coming off him like waves.

"What's going on, Richard?"

He gave a quick shake of his head. "My business, not yours."

"If someone's threatening you, it is my business."

He stared down at me. "No, you aren't one of us. I won't involve you."

"I can handle myself, Richard."

He just shook his head.

"Marcus wants to involve you, *ma petite*. Richard refuses. It is a . . . bone of contention between them. One of many."

"How do you know so much about it?" I asked.

"We leaders of the preternatural community must deal with each other. For everyone's safety."

Richard just stood staring at him. It occurred to me for the first time that he seemed to look Jean-Claude in the eyes, with no ill effects. "Richard, can you meet his eyes?"

Richard's eyes flicked down to me, then back to Jean-Claude. "Yes. I'm a monster, too. I can look him in the eyes."

I shook my head. "Irving can't look him in the eyes. It's not just being a werewolf."

"As I am a master vampire, so our handsome friend here is a master werewolf. Though they do not call them that. Alpha males, is it not? Pack leaders."

"I prefer pack leader."

"I'll just bet you do," I said.

Richard looked hurt, his face crumbling like a child's. "You're angry with me, why?"

"You've got all this heavy shit going on with your pack leader, and you don't tell me. Jean-Claude keeps hinting your leader wants you dead. That true?"

"Marcus won't kill me," Richard said.

Jean-Claude laughed. The sound had a bitter undertaste to it, as if it hadn't been laughter at all. "You are a fool, Richard."

My beeper went off again. I checked the number, and turned it off. It wasn't like Dolph to call this many times, this close together. Something bad was happening. I needed to go. But . . .

"I don't have time to get the full story right this second." I poked a finger into the middle of Richard's chest. I gave Jean-Claude my back. He'd already done the damage he'd intended. "You are going to tell me every last bit of what's going on."

"I don't . . ."

"Save it. You either share this problem, or we don't date anymore."

He looked shocked. "Why?"

"Either you kept me out to protect me, which I'm going to hate. Or you have some other reason. It better be a damn good reason and not just some male ego shit."

Jean-Claude laughed again. This time the sound wrapped me around like flannel, warm and comforting, thick and soft next to naked skin. I shook my head. Just Jean-Claude's laughter was an invasion of privacy.

I turned to him, and there must have been something in my face because the laughter died as if it had never been. "As for you, you can get the hell out of here. You've had your fun for the night."

"Whatever do you mean, *ma petite*?" His beautiful face was as pure and blank as a mask.

I shook my head and stepped forward. I was leaving. I had work to do. Richard's hand gripped my shoulder.

"Let me go, Richard. I'm mad at you right now." I didn't look at him. I didn't want to see his face. I was afraid if he looked hurt, I'd forgive him anything.

"You heard her, Richard. She doesn't want you touching her." Jean-Claude had taken a gliding step closer.

"Leave it alone, Jean-Claude."

Richard's hand squeezed gently. "She doesn't want you, Jean-Claude." There was anger in his voice, more anger than should have been there. As if he were trying to convince himself more than Jean-Claude.

I stepped forward, shaking his hand off. I wanted to reach for it, but didn't. He'd been keeping major shit from me. Dangerous shit. It wasn't allowed. Worse yet, he thought in some dark corner of his soul that I might have given in to Jean-Claude. What a mess.

"Fuck you both," I said.

"So you have not had that pleasure?" Jean-Claude said.

"That's Anita's question to answer, not mine," Richard said.

"I would know it if you had."

"Liar," I said.

"No, *ma petite*. I would smell him on your skin."

I wanted to slug him. The desire to smash that beautiful face was physical. It tightened my shoulders, made my arms ache. But I knew better. You don't volunteer for slugfests with vampires. It shortens your life expectancy.

I walked up very close to Jean-Claude, bodies nearly touching. I stared him in the nose, which ruined some of the effect, but his eyes were drowning pools and I knew better.

"I hate you." My voice was flat with the effort not to scream. In that moment I meant it. And I knew Jean-Claude would sense it. I wanted him to know.

"*Ma petite . . .*"

"No, you've done enough talking. It's my turn. If you harm Richard Zeeman, I'll kill you."

"He means that much to you?" There was surprise in his voice. Great.

"No, you mean that little." I stepped away from him, around him. Gave him my back and walked away. Let him sink his fangs into that bit of truth. Tonight, I meant every word.

5

The number on my beeper was the car phone of Detective Sergeant Rudolf Storr. A Christmas present from his wife last year. I'd sent her a thank-you note. Police radio made everything sound like a foreign language. Dolph picked up on the fifth ring. I knew he'd get to it eventually.

"Anita."

"What if I'd been your wife?" I asked.

"She'd know I was working."

I let it go. Not every wife would appreciate her husband answering the phone with another woman's name. Maybe Lucille was different.

"What's up, Dolph? This was supposed to be my night off."

"Sorry the murderer didn't know that. If you're too busy, we'll muddle through without you."

"What's got your panties in a twist?"

I was rewarded with a small sound that might have been a laugh. "Not your fault. We're out towards Six Flags on Forty-four."

"Where exactly on Forty-four?"

"Out near the Audubon Nature Center. How soon can you get here?"

"Problem, I don't know where the hell you are. How do I get to the nature center?"

"It's across the road from the St. Ambrose Monastery."

"Don't know it," I said.

He sighed. "Hell, we're out in the middle of fucking nowhere. Those are the only landmarks."

"Just give me directions. I'll find it."

He gave me directions. There were too many of them, and I didn't have pen and paper. "Hold on, I've got to get something to write with." I laid the phone down and snatched a napkin from the concession area. I begged a pen from an older couple. The man was wearing a cashmere overcoat. The woman wore real diamonds. The pen was engraved, and might have been real gold. He did not make me promise to bring it back. Trusting, or above such petty concerns. I was going to have to start stocking my own writing materials. It was getting embarrassing.

"I'm back, Dolph, go ahead."

He didn't ask what took so long. Dolph isn't big on extraneous questions. He gave the directions again. I read them back to him to be sure I had them right. I did.

"Dolph, this is at least a forty-five minute drive." I'm usually the last expert to be called in. After the victim has been photographed, videotaped, poked, prodded, etc. . . . After I come, everyone gets to go home, or at least leave the murder scene. People were not going to like cooling their heels for two hours.

"I called you as soon as I figured out nothing human did it. It'll take us at least forty-five minutes to finish up and be ready for you."

I should have known Dolph would have planned ahead. "Okay, I'll be there as soon as I can."

He hung up. I hung up. Dolph never said good-bye.

I gave the man back his pen. He accepted it graciously as if he'd never doubted its return. Good breeding.

I went for the doors. Neither Jean-Claude nor Richard had made it to the lobby. They were in public so I didn't really think they'd have a fistfight, angry words but not violence. So the vampire and the werewolf could take care of themselves. Besides, if Richard wasn't allowed to worry about me when I was off on my own, the least I could do was return the favor. I didn't think Jean-Claude really wanted to push me that far. Not really. One of us would die, and I was beginning to think, just maybe, it wouldn't be me.

6

The cold wrapped around me outside the doors. I hunched my shoulders, tucking my chin inside my collar. A laughing foursome walked a few yards ahead of me. They hung on each other, huddling against the cold. The women's high heels made a sharp theatrical clatter. Their laughter was too high, too shrill. A first double date that had gone well, so far. Or maybe they were all deeply in love and I was feeling bitchy. Maybe.

The foursome parted like water around a stone, revealing a woman. The couples came back together on the other side of her, laughing as if they hadn't seen her. Which they probably hadn't.

I felt it now, a faint stirring in the cold air. A sensation that had nothing to do with the wind. She was pretending to be unseen. Until the couples had noticed her, by not noticing her, I hadn't noticed her, either. Which meant she was good. Very, very good.

She stood under the last streetlight. Her hair was butter yellow and thick with waves. Longer than mine, nearly to her waist. The coat she wore, buttoned all the way up, was black. The color was too harsh for her. It bleached the color from her skin even with makeup.

She stood in the center of the sidewalk, arrogant. She was about my size, not physically imposing. So why did she stand there as if nothing in the world could hurt her? Only three things give you that kind of confidence: a machine gun, stupidity, or being a vampire. I didn't see a machine gun, and she didn't look stupid. She did look like a vampire now that I realized what I was looking at. The makeup was good. It made her look almost alive. Almost.

She caught me staring at her. She stared back, trying to catch my eyes with her own, but I was an old hand at this little dance. Staring at someone's face while not staring at their eyes is a trick that gets easier with practice. She frowned at me. Didn't like the eyes not working.

I stood about two yards from her. Feet apart, as balanced as I was going to get in high heels. My hands were already out in the cold, ready to go for my gun if I had to.

Her power crept over my skin like fingers touching here and there, trying to find a weakness. She was very good, but she was also only a little over a hundred. A hundred years wasn't old enough to cloud my mind. All animators had a partial natural immunity to vampires. Mine seemed to be higher than most.

Her pretty face was blank with concentration like a china doll's. She flung a hand outward as if throwing something at me. I flinched, and her power caught me like an invisible wave, slamming into my body. It staggered me.

I pulled my gun. She didn't try and jump me. She tried to concentrate me out of it. She was at least two hundred years old. I'd underestimated her age by a century. I didn't make mistakes like that often. Her power beat along my skin like tiny clubs, but it never came close to touching my mind. I was almost as surprised as she looked when I pointed the gun at her. It had been too easy.

"Hey," came a voice from behind us. "Put the gun down, now!" A policeman, just when I needed one. I pointed the gun at the sidewalk.

"Put the gun on the sidewalk, right now," his voice growled out, and without turning around I knew his own gun was out. Cops take guns very seriously. I held the Browning out to my right, one-handed, left hand in the air, and squatted to lay the gun gently on the sidewalk.

"I do not need this interruption," the vampire said. I glanced up at her as I stood, slowly, putting my hands atop my head, fingers laced. Maybe I'd get points for knowing the drill. She was staring past me at the approaching cop. It wasn't a friendly look.

"Don't hurt him," I said.

Her eyes flicked back to me. "We are not allowed to attack the police." Her voice was thick with scorn. "I know the rules."

I wanted to say, "What rules?" but didn't. It was a good rule. The policeman could live with a rule like that. Of course, I wasn't a cop, and I was betting the rules didn't apply to me.

The cop came into view out of the corner of my eye. His gun was pointing at me. He kicked my gun out of reach. I saw it hit the building. A hand shoved into my back, getting my attention. "You don't need to know where the gun went."

He was right, for now. He frisked me one-handed. It wasn't very thorough, and I wondered where his partner was.

"Enough," the vampire said.

I felt the cop step back from me. "What's going on here?"

Her power slithered past me, like a great beast had brushed me in the dark. I heard the policeman gasp.

"Nothing is happening here," the vampire said. There was a flavoring of accent in her voice. German or Austrian, maybe.

I heard his voice say, "Nothing is happening here."

"Now go back to directing traffic," she said.

I turned, slowly, hands still on my head. The cop was standing there, face empty, eyes wide. His gun was pointed at the ground, as if he'd forgotten he was holding it.

"Go away," she said.

He stood there frozen. He was wearing his cross tie tack. He was wearing his blessed cross, just like he was supposed to, and it wasn't doing much good.

I backed away from both of them. If she stopped paying attention to the cop, I wanted to be armed. I lowered my arms slowly, watching the cop. If she took her control off suddenly, and I wasn't where I was supposed to be, he might shoot me. Probably not, but maybe. If he saw me with the gun in my hand a second time, almost certainly.

"I don't suppose you would remove his cross so I could order him about?"

My eyes flicked to the vampire. She was looking at me. The cop stirred, struggling like a dreamer in the grip of a nightmare. She turned her eyes back to him, and the struggles ceased.

"I don't think so," I said. I knelt, trying to keep my attention on both of them. I touched the Browning, and wrapped cold fingers around it. My hands were stiff from being exposed to the cold for so long. I wasn't sure how fast I could draw right at that moment. Maybe I should look into some gloves. Maybe ones with the fingertips cut out.

I shoved the Browning in my coat pocket, hand still gripping it. My hand would warm up, and I could shoot through my coat if I had to.

"Without the cross I could make him go away. Why can't I control you like that?"

"Just lucky, I guess."

Her eyes flicked to me. Again, he stirred. She had to stare at him while she talked to me. It was interesting to see how much concentration it took. She was powerful but it had its limits.

"You are the Executioner," she said.

"What of it?"

"I didn't believe the stories. Now I believe some of the stories."

"Bully for you. Now, what do you want?"

A slight smile curled her lipsticked mouth. "I want you to leave Jean-Claude alone."

I blinked, not sure I'd heard right. "What do you mean, leave him alone?"

"Don't date him. Don't flirt with him. Don't talk to him. Leave him alone."

"Glad to," I said.

She turned to me, startled. You don't get to surprise a two-hundred-year-old vamp often. Her face looked very human with its wide eyes and little *o* of surprise.

The cop gave a snort and looked around wildly. "What the hell?" He looked at both of us. We looked like two petite women out for the evening. He glanced down at his gun and seemed embarrassed. He didn't remember why it was out. He put the gun away, muttering apologies and backing away from us. The vampire let him go.

"You'd leave Jean-Claude alone, just like that?" she asked.

"You bet."

She shook her head. "I do not believe you."

"Look, I don't care what you believe. If you have the hots for Jean-Claude, more power to you. I've been trying to get him off my back for years."

Again that shake of the head, sending her yellow hair flying about her face. It was a very girlish gesture. It would have been cute if she hadn't been a corpse.

''You are lying. You desire him. Anyone would.''

I couldn't argue that. ''You got a name?''

''I am Gretchen.''

''Well, Gretchen, I wish you joy of the Master. If you need any help sinking your fangs into him, let me know. I would love for him to find a nice little vampire to settle down with.''

''You mock me.''

I shrugged. ''A little, but it's habit, nothing personal. I mean what I said. I don't want Jean-Claude.''

''You don't think he's beautiful?'' Her voice was soft with surprise.

''Well, yeah, but I think tigers are beautiful. I still don't want to sleep with one.''

''No mortal could resist him.''

''This one can,'' I said.

''Stay away from him, or I'll kill you,'' she said.

Gretchen wasn't listening to me, not really. She heard the words, but the meaning didn't sink in. Reminded me of Jean-Claude.

''Look, he chases me. I'll stay away from him if he'll let me. But don't threaten me.''

''He's mine, Anita Blake. Come against me at your peril.''

It was my turn to shake my head. Maybe she didn't know I had a gun pointed at her. Maybe she didn't know it had silver-plated bullets in it. Maybe she had lived for a couple of centuries and had grown arrogant. Yeah, that was probably it.

''Look, I don't have time for this right now. Jean-Claude is yours, great, fine. I'm thrilled to hear it. Keep him away from me, and I will be the happiest woman alive or dead.'' I didn't want to turn my back on her, but I had to go. If she wasn't going to jump me here and now, Dolph was waiting at a murder scene. I had to go.

''Gretchen, what are you and Anita talking about?'' Jean-Claude stalked towards us. He was wearing, I kid you not, a black cape. It was a Victorian style with a collar. A top hat with a white silk band completed the look.

Gretchen gazed at him. It was the only word for it. The naked adoration in her face was sickening, and very human. ''I wanted to meet my rival.''

I wasn't her rival, but I didn't think she'd believe that.

''I told you to wait outside so you would not meet her. You knew that.'' The last three words were spat out, thrown at her like rocks.

She flinched. ''I meant no harm this night.''

That was almost a lie, but I didn't say anything. I could have told him that she'd threatened me, but somehow it seemed like tattling. She'd gone to a lot of trouble to get me alone. To warn me off. Her love for him was so naked. I could not enlist his help against her. Foolish, but true. Besides, I didn't like owing Jean-Claude favors.

''I'll leave you two lovebirds alone.''

''What lies did you tell her about us?'' His words scalded the air. I could feel myself choking on his rage. Jesus.

She fell to her knees, hands held upward, not to avoid a blow, but beseeching, reaching for him. ''Please, I only wanted to meet her. To see the mortal that would steal you from me.''

I did not want to see this, but it was like a car crash. I couldn't quite bring myself to leave.

''She steals nothing. I have never loved you.''

The pain was raw on her face, and even under the makeup she looked less human. Her face was thinning out, bones growing more apparent, as if her skin were shrinking.

He grabbed her arm and pulled her roughly to her feet. His white-gloved fingers dug into her arm. If she'd been human, there would have been bruises. ''Get hold of yourself, woman. You are losing control.''

Her thinning lips drew back from fangs. She hissed at him, jerking free of his hand. She covered her face with hands that were almost claws. I'd seen vampires show their true form, but never by accident, never in the open, where anyone might see. ''I love you.'' The words came out muffled and twisted, but the feeling in those three words was very real. Very . . . human.

''Get out of sight before you disgrace us all,'' Jean-Claude said.

She raised a face to the light that was no longer human. The pale skin glowed with an inner light. The makeup sat on that glowing surface. The blush, eye shadow, lipstick seemed to float above the light, as if her skin would no longer absorb them. When she turned her head, I could see the bones in her jaws like shadows inside her skin. ''This is not over between us, Anita Blake.'' The words fell out from between fangs and teeth.

''Leave us!'' Jean-Claude's words were an echoing hiss.

She launched herself skyward, not a leap, not levitation, just upward. She vanished into the darkness with a backwash of wind.

''Sweet Jesus,'' I whispered it.

''I am sorry, *ma petite*. I sent her out here so this would not happen.'' He walked towards me in his elegant cape. A gust of icy wind whistled around the corner, and he had to make a grab for the top hat. It was nice to know that at least his clothing didn't obey his every whim.

''I've got to go, Jean-Claude. The police are waiting for me.''

''I did not mean for this to happen tonight.''

''You never mean for anything to happen, Jean-Claude. But it happens anyway.'' I put a hand up to stop his words. I didn't want to hear any more of them.

''I've got to go.'' I turned and walked towards my car. I transferred my gun back to its holster when I was safely across the icy street.

''I am sorry, *ma petite*.'' I whirled to tell him to get the hell away from me. He wasn't there. The streetlight glowed down on empty sidewalk. I guess he and Gretchen hadn't needed a car.

7

There is a glimpse of stately old homes to the right just before you turn onto Highway 44. The houses hide behind a wrought-iron fence and a security gate. When the homes were built, they were the height of elegance and so was the neighborhood. Now the town houses are an island in a rising flood of project housing and dead-eyed children who shoot each other over a scuffed sneaker. But the old money stayed, determined to be elegant, even if it kills them.

In Fenton the Chrysler plant is still the largest employer. A side road runs past fast-food restaurants and local businesses. But the highway bypasses them all. A straight line going onward and not looking back. The Maritz building spans the highway with a covered crosswalk that looks big enough to hold offices. It gets your attention like an overly aggressive date, but I know the name of the business, and I can't say that about many other buildings along 44. Sometimes aggressive works.

The Ozark Mountains rise on either side of the road. They are soft and rounded. Gentle mountains. On a sunny autumn day, with the trees blazing color, the mountains are startling in their beauty. On a cold December night with only my own headlights for company, the mountains sat like sleeping giants pressing close to the road. There was just enough snow to gleam white through the naked trees. The black shapes of evergreens were permanent shadows in the moonlight. A limestone cliff shone white where the mountains had been cracked open for a gravel pit.

Houses huddled at the base of the mountains. Neat farmhouses with front porches just made for sitting on. Not-so-neat houses made of unpainted wood with rusty tin roofs. Corrals sat in empty fields without a farmhouse near. A single horse stood in the icy cold, head down searching the tops of the winter-killed grass. A lot of people kept horses out past Eureka—people who couldn't afford to live in Ladue or Chesterfield, where houses cost over half a mil a piece, but you did get barns, exercising pens, and a corral in your backyard. Here all you got was a shed, a corral, and miles to drive to visit your horse, but at least you had one. A lot of trouble to go to for a horse.

The white head of a road sign flashed in the headlights. I slowed down. A car had run into the pole and crumbled it like a broken flower stem. The sign was hard to read from a sixty-degree angle. Which was probably why Dolph had told me to look for the smashed sign rather than the street name.

I pulled onto the narrow road. In St. Louis we'd gotten about a three-inch snowfall. Here it looked more like six. The road hadn't been plowed. It angled sharply upward, climbing into the hills. Tire tracks like wagon wheels made two lines through the snow. The police cars had gotten up the hill. So could my Jeep. In my old Nova I might have been wading fresh snow in high heels. Though I did have a pair of Nikes in the trunk. Still, jogging shoes weren't a big improvement. Maybe I should buy a pair of boots.

It just didn't snow that much in St. Louis. This was one of the deepest snowfalls I'd seen in four years. Boots seemed sort of unnecessary.

The trees curled over the road, naked branches bouncing in the headlights. Wet, icy trunks bent towards the road. In summertime the road would be a leafy tunnel, now it was just black bones erupting from the white snow.

At the crest of the hill there was a heavy stone wall. It had to be ten feet tall, and effectively hid anything on the left-hand side of the road. It had to be the monastery.

About a hundred yards further there was a plaque set in the wall next to a spiked gate. St. Ambrose Monastery was done in raised letters, metal on metal. A driveway curved up and out of sight around a curve of hill. And just across from the entrance was a smaller gravel road. The car tracks climbed into the darkness ahead of me and vanished over the next hill. If the gate hadn't been there for a landmark, I might have missed it. It was only when I turned the Jeep to an angle that my lights caught the tire tracks leading off to the right.

I wondered what all the heavy traffic was up ahead. Not my problem. I eased onto the smaller road. Branches scraped at the Jeep, scratching down the gleaming paint job like fingernails on a chalkboard. Great, just great.

I'd never had a brand-new car before. That first ding, where I'd run over a snow-covered tombstone, had been the hardest. After the first damage the rest was easy to take. Riiight.

The land opened up to either side of the narrow road. A large meadow with winter-killed weeds waist high, weighted down with snow. Lightning flashes of red and blue strobed over the snow, chasing back the darkness. The meadow stopped abruptly in a perfect straight line where the mower had cut it. A white farmhouse, complete with screened-in porch, sat at the end of the road. Cars were everywhere, like a child's spilled toys. I hoped the road formed a turn around under the snow. If not, the cars were parked all over the grass. My grandmother Blake had hated it when people parked on the grass.

A lot of the cars had their motors running, including the ambulance. There were people sitting in the cars, waiting. But for what? By the time I got to a crime scene, all the work was usually done. Someone would be waiting to take the body away after I'd finished looking at it, but the crime-scene people should have been done and gone. Something was up.

I pulled in next to a St. Gerard County Sheriff car. One policeman was standing in the driver's side door, leaning on the roof. He'd been staring at the knot of men near the farmhouse, but he turned to stare at me. He didn't look happy with what he saw. His Smokey Bear hat shielded his face but left his ears and the back of his head open to the cold. He was pale and freckled and at least six foot two. His shoulders were very broad in his dark winter jacket. He looked like a large man who had always been large, and thought that made him tough. His hair was some pale shade that absorbed the colors of flashing lights, so his hair looked alternately blue and red. As did his face, and the snow, and everything else.

I got out of the car very carefully. Snow spilled in around my foot, soaking my hose, filling the leather pump. It was cold and wet, and I kept a death grip on the car door. High heels and snow do not mix. The last thing I wanted to do was fall on my ass in front of the St. Gerard County Sheriff Department. I should have just grabbed my Nikes from the back of the Jeep and put them on in the car. It was too late now. The deputy sheriff was walking very purposefully towards me. He had boots on and was having no trouble with the snow.

He stopped within reach of me. I didn't let strange men get that close to me normally but to back up I'd have to let go of the car door. Besides he was the police, I wasn't supposed to be afraid of the police. Right?

"This is police business, ma'am, I'll have to ask you to leave."

"I'm Anita Blake. I work with Sergeant Rudolf Storr."

"You're not a cop." He seemed very certain of that. I sort of resented his tone.

"No, I'm not."

"Then you're going to have to leave."

"Can you tell Sergeant Storr that I'm here . . . please." Never hurts to be polite.

"I've asked you real nice twice now to leave. Don't make me ask a third time."

All he had to do was reach out and grab my arm, shove me into the Jeep, and away we went. I certainly wasn't going to draw my gun on a cop with a lot of other cops within shouting distance. I didn't want to get shot tonight.

What could I do? I shut the car door very carefully and leaned against it. If I was careful and didn't move around too much, I might not fall down. If I did, maybe I could claim police brutality.

"Now, why did you do that?"

"I drove forty-five minutes and left a date to get here." Try to appeal to his better nature. "Let me talk to Sergeant Storr and if he says I need to leave, I'll leave."

"I don't care if you flew in from outta state. I say you leave. Right now."

He didn't have a better nature.

He reached for me. I stepped back, out of reach. My left foot found a patch of ice and I ended up on my ass in the snow.

The deputy looked sort of startled. He offered me a hand up without thinking about it. I climbed to my feet using the Jeep's bumper, moving farther away from Deputy Sullen at the same time. He figured this out. The frown lines on his forehead deepened.

Snow clung in wet clumps to my coat and glided in melting runnels down my legs. I was getting pissed off.

He strode around the Jeep.

I backpedaled using my hands on the car as traction. "We can play ring-around-the-Rosie if you want to, Deputy, but I'm not leaving until I've talked to Dolph."

"Your sergeant isn't in charge here." He stepped a little closer.

I backed away. "Then find someone who is."

"You don't need to talk to anyone but me," he said. He took three rapid steps towards me. I backed up faster. If we kept this up we'd be running around the car like a Marx brothers movie, or would that be the Keystone Kops?

"You're running from me."

"In these shoes, you've got to be kidding."

I was almost around the back of the Jeep, we'd be back where we started soon. Over the crackle of police radios you could hear angry voices. One of them sounded like Dolph. I wasn't the only one having trouble with the local cops. Though I seemed to be the only one being chased around a car.

"Stop, right where you are," he said.

"If I don't?"

He unclicked the flap on his holster. His hand rested on the butt of his gun. No words necessary.

This guy was crazy.

I might be able to get to my gun before he could draw his, but he was a cop. He was supposed to be one of the good guys. I try not to shoot the good guys. Besides, try explaining to other cops why you shot a cop. They get testy as hell about stuff like that.

I couldn't draw my gun. I couldn't outrun him. Arm wrestling seemed to be out. I did the only thing I could think of. I yelled "Dolph, Zerbrowski! Get your butts over here."

The shouting stopped as if someone had clicked a switch. Silence and the crackle of radios were the only sounds. I glanced towards the men. Dolph was glancing my way. At six foot eight inches, Dolph towered over everyone else. I waved a hand at him. Not frantically, but I wanted to be sure he saw me.

The deputy drew his gun. It took everything I had not to go for mine. But this bugnut was looking for an excuse. I wasn't going to give it to him. If he shot me anyway, I was going to be pissed.

His gun was a .357 Magnum, great for whale hunting. It was overkill for anything on two legs. That was human. I felt very human staring down that gun barrel. My eyes flicked up to his face. He wasn't frowning anymore. He looked very determined, and very sure of himself, as if he could pull the trigger and not get caught.

I wanted to yell for Dolph again, but didn't. The fool might pull the trigger. At this distance with that caliber of weapon I was dead meat. All I could do was stand there in the snow, my feet going slowly numb, hands gripping the car. At least he hadn't asked me to put my hands up. Guess he didn't want me to fall down again until he splattered my brains all over the new paint job.

It was Detective Clive Perry who walked towards us. His dark face reflected the lights like ebony. He was tall, though not as tall as the deputy from hell. His slender frame was enclosed in a pale camel's hair coat. A hat that matched it perfectly sat atop his head. It was a nice hat and couldn't be pulled low enough to cover his ears. Most nice hats couldn't be. You had to get a toboggan hat, something knit that would ruin your hair to keep your ears warm. Not stylish. Of course, I wasn't wearing a hat at all. Didn't want to muss my hair.

Dolph had gone back to yelling at someone. I couldn't tell exactly what color uniform he was yelling at, there were at least two flavors to choose from. I caught a glimpse of a wildly gesturing arm, the rest of the man lost behind the small crowd. I'd never seen anybody wave their fists in Dolph's face. When you're six foot eight and built like a wrestler, most people are a little afraid of you. Probably wise.

"Ms. Blake, we're not quite ready for you," Perry said.

He always called everyone by title and last name. He was one of the most polite people I'd ever met. Soft-spoken, hardworking, courteous, so what had he done to end up on the Spook Squad?

The squad's full title was the Regional Preternatural Investigation Team. They handled all preternatural-related crime in the area. A sort of permanent floating special task force. I don't think anyone planned on the squad actually solving cases. Their success rate was high enough that Dolph had been invited to lecture at Quantico. Lecturing to the FBI's preternatural research branch was not shabby.

I kept staring at the deputy and his gun. I wasn't going to glance away a second time. I didn't really believe he'd shoot me, but I wasn't sure. There was something in his face that said he'd do it, that maybe he wanted to do it. You give some people a gun and they turn into bullies. Legally armed bullies.

"Hello, Detective Perry. The deputy here and I seem to have a problem."

"Deputy Aikensen, do you have your gun out?" Perry's voice was soft, calm, a voice to talk jumpers off of ledges, or madmen out of hostages.

Aikensen turned his head, glancing back at Perry. "No civilians allowed at a murder scene, sheriff's orders."

"I don't think Sheriff Titus meant for you to shoot the civilians, Deputy."

He glanced back at Perry. "You making fun of me?"

There was enough time. I could have pulled my gun. I wanted to shove it in his ribs. I wanted him disarmed, but I behaved myself. It took more willpower than was pretty, but I didn't draw my gun. I wasn't ready to kill the son of a bitch. If you draw guns, there is always the chance someone will end up dead. Unless you want someone dead, you don't draw, simple as that. But it hurt something deep down inside when the deputy turned back to me with his gun still out. So far my ego was taking a lot of bruising, but I could live with that, and so could Deputy Aikensen.

"Sheriff said I wasn't to let anybody but police into the perimeter."

"Perimeter" was a pretty fancy word for someone this stupid. Of course, it was a military term. He'd probably been dying to use it in conversation for years.

"Deputy Aikensen, this is our preternatural expert, Anita Blake."

He shook his head. "No civvies, unless the sheriff okays it."

Perry glanced back towards Dolph, and what I now assumed was the sheriff.

''He's not even allowing us near the body, Deputy. What do you think the chances are of Sheriff Titus saying a civilian can see the body?''

Aikensen grinned then, most unpleasant. ''Slim and none.'' He still held the gun very steady on the middle of my body. He was enjoying himself.

''Put the gun away and Ms. Blake will leave,'' Perry said.

I opened my mouth to say, The hell I will, but Perry gave a small shake of his head. I kept quiet. He had a plan, better than what I had.

''I don't take orders from no nigger detective.''

''Jealous,'' I said.

''What?''

''That he's a big city detective and you're not.''

''I don't have to take crap from you, either, bitch.''

''Ms. Blake, please, let me handle this.''

''You can't handle shit,'' Aikensen said.

''You've been totally uncooperative and rude, you and your sheriff. You can call me all the names you like, if that makes you feel better, but I can't let you point a gun at one of our people.''

A look passed over Aikensen's face. I could see the thought flicker into life. Perry was a cop, too. He probably had a gun, and Aikensen had his back to him. The deputy whirled, bringing the gun up as he moved. His hand flexed.

I went for my gun.

Perry's empty hands were held out from his body, showing he was unarmed.

Aikensen was breathing hard. He raised the gun to head level, two-handed, steady, no hurry.

Someone noticed us and yelled, ''What the fuck?'' Indeed.

I pointed the Browning at Aikensen's back. ''Freeze, Aikensen, or I will blow you away.''

''You're not armed.''

I clicked the hammer back. On a double-action you don't need to do that before you fire, but it makes a nice dramatic sound. ''You didn't frisk me, asshole.''

People were running towards us, shouting. But they wouldn't get here in time. It was just the three of us in the psychedelic snow, waiting.

''Put the gun down, Aikensen, now.''

''No.''

''Put it down or I'll kill you.''

''Anita, you don't need to shoot. He's not going to hurt me,'' Perry said. It was the only time he'd ever used my first name.

''I don't need no nigger protecting me.'' His shoulders tensed. I couldn't see his hands well enough to be sure, but I thought he was pulling the trigger. I started to squeeze the trigger.

A bellowing voice yelled, ''Aikensen, put that damn gun down!''

Aikensen pointed the gun skyward, just like that. He hadn't been pulling the trigger at all. He was just jumpy. I felt a giggle at the back of my throat. I'd almost shot him for being twitchy. I swallowed the laugh and eased off the trigger. Did Deputy Numb-nuts know how close he'd come? The only thing that had saved him was the Browning's trigger. It was stiff. There were a lot of guns out there where a tiny squeeze was all you needed.

He turned towards me, gun still out, but not pointed. Mine was still pointed. He started to lower his weapon to point it back at me. "If that barrel drops another inch, I'm going to shoot you."

"Aikensen, I said put the damn gun up. Before you get somebody killed." The man that went with the voice was about five foot six and must have weighed over two hundred pounds. He looked perfectly round like a sausage with arms and legs. His winter jacket strained over his round little tummy. A clear, grey stubble decorated his double chins. His eyes were small, nearly lost in the doughiness of his face. His badge glittered on his jacket front. He hadn't left it inside on his shirt. He'd pinned it outside, where the big city detectives couldn't miss it. Sort of like unzipping your fly so company could see you were well-endowed.

"This nigger . . ."

"We don't hold with talk like that, Deputy, you know that."

From the look on Aikensen's face you'd have thought the sheriff had told him there was no Santa Claus. I was betting the sheriff was a good ol' boy in the worst sense of the word. But there was intelligence in those beady little eyes, more than you could say for Aikensen.

"Put it away, boy, that's an order." His southern accent was getting thicker, either for show, or because he was getting teed off at Aikensen. A lot of people's accents got stronger under stress. It wasn't a Missouri accent. Something further south.

Aikensen finally, reluctantly, put up the gun. He didn't snap the holster closed, though. He was cruising for a bruising. I was just glad I hadn't been the one to give it to him. Of course if I'd pulled the trigger before Aikensen had raised his gun skyward, I'd never have known he wasn't pulling his trigger, too. If we'd all been cops with Aikensen as a criminal, it would have gone down as a clean shoot. Jesus.

Sheriff Titus put his hands in the pockets of his jacket and looked at me. "Now, miss, you can put your gun away, too. Aikensen here isn't going to shoot nobody."

I just stared at him, gun pointed skyward, held loose. I had been ready to put the gun away until he told me to do it. I'm not big on being told anything. I just stared at him.

His face still looked friendly, but his eyes lost their shine. Angry. He didn't like being defied. Great. Made my night.

Three other deputies gathered at Titus's back. They all looked sullen and ready to do anything their sheriff asked them to do. Aikensen stepped over to them, hand hovering near his freshly holstered gun. Some people never learn.

"Anita, put the gun away." Dolph's usual pleasant tenor was harsh with anger. Like what he wanted to say was shoot the son of a bitch, but it would be hard to explain to his superiors.

Though not officially my boss, I listened to Dolph. He'd earned it.

I put the gun away.

Dolph was made up of blunt angles. His black hair was cut very short, leaving his ears naked to the cold. His hands were plunged into the pockets of a long black trench coat. The coat looked too thin for the weather, but maybe it was lined. Though he was a little too bulky to leave room for him and a lining in the same coat.

He beckoned Perry and me to one side, and said softly, "Tell me what happened."

We did.

"You really think he was going to shoot you?"

Perry stared down at the trampled snow for a moment, then looked up. "I'm not sure, Sergeant."

"Anita?"

"I thought he was, Dolph."

"You don't sound sure now."

"The only thing I'm sure of is that I was going to shoot him. I was squeezing down on him, Dolph. What the hell is going on? If I end up killing a cop tonight, I'd like to know why."

"I didn't think anybody was stupid enough to pull a weapon," Dolph said. His shoulders hunched, the cloth of his coat straining to hold the movement.

"Well, don't look now," I said, "but Deputy Aikensen has still got his hand right over his weapon. He's just aching to draw it again."

Dolph drew a large breath in through his nose and let it out in a white whoosh of breath from his mouth. "Let's go talk to Sheriff Titus."

"We've been talking to the sheriff for over an hour," Perry said. "He isn't listening."

"I know, Detective, I know." Dolph kept walking towards the waiting sheriff and his deputies. Perry and I followed. What else could we do? Besides, I wanted to know why an entire crime-scene unit was standing around twiddling their thumbs.

Perry and I took a post to either side of Dolph, like sentries. Without thinking about it we were both a step back from him. He was, after all, our leader. But the automatic staging irked me. Made me want to step forward, be an equal, but I was a civvie. I wasn't equal. No matter how much I hung around or did, I wasn't a cop. It made a difference.

Aikensen's hand was gripping the butt of his gun tight. Would he actually draw down on all of us? Surely, even he wasn't that stupid. He was glaring at me, nothing but anger showed in his eyes. Maybe he was that stupid.

"Titus, tell your man there to get his hand away from his gun," Dolph said.

Titus glanced at Aikensen. He sighed. "Aikensen, get your damned hand away from your damn gun."

"She's a civilian. She drew on a policeman."

"You're lucky she didn't shoot your ass," Titus said. "Now, fasten the holster and tone it down a notch, or I'm going to make you go home."

Aikensen's face looked even more sullen. But he fastened his holster and plunged his hands into the pockets of his coat. Unless he had a derringer in his pocket, we were safe. Of course, he was just the sort of yahoo that would carry a backup weapon. Truthfully, sometimes so did I, but only when the alligator factor was high. Neck deep instead of ass deep.

Footsteps crunched through the snow behind us. I turned halfway so I could keep an eye on Aikensen and see the new arrivals.

Three people in navy blue uniforms came to stand on the other side of us. The tall man in front had a badge on his hat that said police chief. One of his deputies was tall, so thin he looked gaunt, and too young to shave. The second deputy was a woman. Surprise, surprise. I'm usually the only female at a crime scene. She was small, only a little taller than I, thin, with close-cropped hair hidden under her Smokey Bear hat. The only thing I could tell in the flashing lights was that everything on her was pale, from her eyes to her hair. She was pretty in a pixielike way, cute. She stood with her feet apart, hands on her Sam Brown belt. She was carrying a gun that was a little too big for her hands. I was betting she wouldn't like being called cute.

She was either going to be another pain in the ass, like Aikensen, or a kindred spirit.

The police chief was at least twenty years older than either deputy. He was tall, not as tall as Dolph, but then who was? He had a salt-and-pepper mustache, pale eyes, and was ruggedly handsome. One of those men who might not have been very attractive as a young man, but age had given his face character, depth. Like Sean Connery who was better looking at sixty than he had been at twenty.

''Titus, why don't you let these good people get on with their work? We're all cold and tired and want to go home.''

Titus's small eyes flared to life. A lot of anger there. ''This is county business, Garroway, not city business. You and your people are out of your jurisdiction.''

''Holmes and Lind were on their way into work when the call came over the radio that somebody had found a body. Your man Aikensen here said he was tied up and couldn't get to the body for at least an hour. Holmes offered to sit with the body and make sure the crime scene stayed pure. My deputies didn't touch anything or do anything. They were just baby-sitting the crime scene for your people. What is wrong with that?'' Garroway said.

''Garroway, the murder was found on our turf. It was our body to take care of. We didn't need any help. And you had no right to call in the Spook Squad without clearing it with me first,'' Titus said.

Police Chief Garroway spread his hands in a push-away gesture. ''Holmes saw the body. She made the call. She thought the man hadn't been killed by anything human. Protocol is we call in the Regional Preternatural Investigation Team anytime we suspect supernatural activity.''

''Well, Aikensen and Troy here don't think it was anything supernatural. A hunter gets eaten up by a bear and your little lady there jumps the gun.''

Holmes opened her mouth but the chief held up a hand. ''It's all right, Holmes.'' She settled back down, but she didn't like it.

''Why don't we ask Sergeant Storr here what he thinks killed the man?'' Garroway said.

I was close enough to hear Dolph sigh.

''She had no right to let people near the body without us there to supervise,'' Titus said.

Dolph said, ''Gentlemen, we have a dead body in the woods. The crime scene is not getting any younger. Valuable evidence is being lost, while we stand here and argue.''

''A bear atttack is not a crime scene, Sergeant,'' Titus said.

''Ms. Blake is our preternatural expert. If she says it was a bear attack, we'll all go home. If she says it was preternatural, you let us do our job, and treat it as a crime scene. Agreed?''

''Ms. Blake, Ms. Anita Blake?''

Dolph nodded.

Titus squinted at me, as if trying to bring me into focus. ''You're the Executioner?''

''Some people call me that, yeah.''

''This little bit of a girl has over a dozen vampire kills under her belt?'' There was laughter in his voice, disbelief.

I shrugged. It was actually higher than that now, but a lot of them were unsanctioned kills. Not something I wanted the police to know about. Vampires have rights, and killing them without a warrant is murder. ''I'm the legal vampire executioner for the area. You got a problem with that?''

''Anita,'' Dolph said.

I glanced at him, then back at the sheriff. I wasn't going to say anything more, honest, but he did.

''I just don't believe a little thing like yourself coulda done all the things I've heard.''

''Look, it's cold, it's late, let me see the body and we can all go home.''

''I don't need a civilian woman to tell me my job.''

''That's it,'' I said.

''Anita?'' Dolph said. That one word told me not to say it, not to do it, whatever it was.

''We have licked enough jurisdictional butt for one night, Dolph.''

A man appeared, offering us steaming mugs on a tray. The smell of coffee mingled with the scent of snow. The man was tall. There was a lot of that going around tonight. A lock of white-blond hair obscured one eye. He wore round metal-framed glasses that made his face look even younger than it was. A dark toboggan hat was pulled low over his ears. Thick gloves, a multicolored parka, jeans, and hiking boots completed his outfit. He didn't look fashionable but he was dressed for the weather. My feet had gone numb in the snow.

I took a mug of coffee gratefully. If we were going to stand out here and argue, hot anything sounded like a great idea. ''Thanks.''

The man smiled. ''You're welcome.'' Everybody was taking a mug but not everybody was saying thank you. Where were their manners?

''I've been sheriff of this county since before you were born, Ms. Blake. It's my county. I don't need any help from the likes of you.'' He sipped his coffee. He had said thank you.

''The likes of me? What's that supposed to mean?''

''Let it go, Anita.''

I looked up at Dolph. I didn't want to let it go. I sipped at the coffee. The smell alone made me feel less angry, more relaxed. I stared into Titus's little piggy eyes and smiled.

"What's so funny?" he asked.

I opened my mouth to say, you, but the coffee man interrupted. "I'm Samuel Williams. I'm the caretaker here. I live in the little house behind the nature center. I found the body." He held his now-empty tray down at his side.

"I'm Sergeant Storr, Mr. Williams. These are my associates, Detective Perry, and Ms. Blake."

Williams dunked his head in acknowledgment.

"You know all of us, Samuel," Titus said.

"Yes, I do," Williams said. He didn't seem too excited about knowing them all.

He nodded at Chief Garroway and his deputies. "I told Deputy Holmes that I didn't think it was a natural animal. I still don't, but if it is a bear, it slaughtered that man. Any animal that'll do that once will do it again." He looked down at the snow, then up, like a man rising from deep water. "It ate parts of that man. It stalked him and treated him like a prey animal. If it really is a bear, it needs to be caught before it kills somebody else."

"Samuel here has a degree in biology," Titus said.

"So do I," I said. Of course, my degree was in preternatural biology, but hey, biology is biology, right?

"I'm working on my doctorate," Williams said.

"Yeah, studying owl shit," Aikensen said.

It was hard to tell, but I think Williams blushed. "I'm studying the feeding habits of the barred owl."

I had a degree in biology. I knew what that meant. He was collecting owl shit and regurgitated pellets to dissect. So Aikensen was right. Sort of.

"Will your doctorate be in ornithology or strigiology?" I asked. I was proud of myself for remembering the Latin name for owls.

Williams looked at me with a sense of kinship in his eyes. "Ornithology."

Titus looked like he'd swallowed a worm. "I don't need no college degree to know a bear attack when I see it."

"The last reported bear sighting in St. Gerard County was in 1941," Williams said. "I don't think there's ever been a bear attack reported." The implication just sat there. How did Titus know a bear attack from beans if he'd never seen one?

Titus threw his coffee out on the snow. "Listen here, college boy—"

"Maybe it is a bear," Dolph said.

We all looked at him. Titus nodded. "That's what I've been saying."

"Then you better order up a helicopter and get some dogs out here."

"What are you talking about?"

"An animal that'd slice up a man and eat him might break into houses. No telling how many people the bear might kill." Dolph's face was unreadable, just as serious as if he believed what he was saying.

"Now, I don't want to get dogs down here. Start a panic if people thought there was a mad bear loose. Remember how crazy everyone got when that pet cougar got loose about five years ago. People were shooting at shadows."

Dolph just looked at him. We all looked at him. If it was a bear, he needed to treat it like a bear. If it wasn't . . .

Titus shifted uncomfortably in his heavy boots in the snow. ''Maybe Ms. Blake ought to have a look.'' He rubbed the cold tip of his nose. ''Wouldn't want to start a panic for the wrong reasons.''

He didn't want people to think there was a rampaging bear on the loose. But he didn't mind people thinking there was a monster on the loose. Or maybe Sheriff Titus didn't believe in monsters. Maybe.

Whatever, we were on our way to the murder scene. Possible murder scene. I made everyone wait while I put on my Nikes and the coveralls that I kept for crime scenes and vampire stakings. Hated getting blood on my clothes. Besides, tonight the coveralls were warmer than hose.

Titus made Aikensen stay with the cars. Hoped he didn't shoot anybody while we were gone.

8

I didn't see the body at first. All I saw was the snow. It had pooled into a deep drift in one of those hollows that you find in the woods. In spring the holes fill with rain and mud. In fall they pile deep with leaves. In winter they hold the deepest snow. The moonlight carved each footprint, every scuff mark into high relief. Every print filled like a cup with blue shadows.

I stood at the edge of the clearing staring down at the mishmash of tracks. Somewhere in all this were the murderer's tracks, or a bear's tracks, but unless it was an animal I didn't know how anyone was going to figure out which tracks were significant. Maybe all crime scenes were tracked up this much, the snow just made it obvious. Or maybe this scene had been screwed over. Yeah.

Every track, cop or not, led to one thing—the body. Dolph had said the man had been sliced up, eaten. I didn't want to see it. I'd been having a very good time with Richard. A pleasant evening. It wasn't fair to end the night by looking at partially eaten bodies. Of course, the dead man probably thought being eaten hadn't been much fun either.

I took a deep breath of the cold air. My breath fogged as I exhaled. I couldn't smell the body. If it'd been summer, the dead man would have been ripe. Hurrah for the cold.

''You planning to look at the body from here?'' Titus said.

''No,'' I said.

''Looks like your expert is losing her nerve, Sergeant.''

I turned to Titus. His round, double-chinned face was smug, pleased with itself.

I didn't want to see the body, but losing my nerve, never. ''You better hope this isn't a murder scene . . . Sheriff, because it has been fucked twenty ways to Sunday.''

''You're not helping anything, Anita,'' Dolph said softly.

He was right, but I wasn't sure I cared. ''You got any suggestions for preserving the crime scene, or can I just march straight in like the fifty billion people before me?''

''There were only four sets of footprints when I was ordered to leave the scene,'' Officer Holmes said.

Titus frowned at her. ''When I determined it was an animal attack, there was no reason to keep it secure.'' His southern accent was getting thicker again.

''Yeah, right,'' I said. I glanced at Dolph. ''Any suggestions?''

''Just walk in, I don't think there's much to preserve now.''

''You criticizing my men?'' Titus said.

''No,'' Dolph said, ''I'm criticizing you.''

I turned away so Titus wouldn't see me smile. Dolph doesn't suffer fools gladly. He'll put up with them a little longer than I will, but once you've reached his limit, run for cover. No bureaucratic ass will be spared.

I stepped into the hollow. Dolph didn't need my help to hand Titus his head on a platter. The snow collapsed at the edge of the hole. My feet slid on the leaves underfoot. I ended on my butt for the second time tonight. But I was on a slope now. I slid almost all the way to the body. Laughter bubbled up behind me.

I sat on my ass in the snow and stared at the body. They could laugh all they wanted; it was funny. The dead man wasn't.

He lay on his back in the snow. The moonlight shone down on the body, reflecting on the snow, and giving the luster of midday to objects below. I had a penlight in one of the coverall's pockets, but I didn't need it. Or maybe didn't want it. I could see enough, for now.

Ragged furrows ran down the right side of his face. One claw had sliced over the eye, spilling blood and thick globs of eyeball down his cheek. The lower jaw was crushed, as if some great hand had grabbed it and squeezed. It made the face look unfinished, only half there. It must have hurt like hell, but it hadn't killed him. More's the pity.

His throat had been torn out; that had probably killed him. The flesh was just gone. His spine shone a dull white, like he'd swallowed a ghost and it hadn't gotten away. His camouflage coveralls were ripped away from his stomach. Some trick of the moonlight threw a thick shadow inside that ripped cloth. I couldn't see the damage inside. I needed to.

I prefer night kills. Darkness steals the color. Somehow it just isn't as real at night. Shine some light on it and the colors explode: the blood is crimson; the bone sparkles; fluids are not just dark but green, yellow, brown. Light lets you differentiate. A mixed blessing, at best.

I slipped the surgical gloves on. They were a cool second skin. Even riding in my inner pocket, the gloves were cooler than my skin. The penlight snapped on. Its tiny yellowish beam was dimmed by the bright moonlight, but cut through the shadows like a knife. The man's clothing had been peeled away like the layers of an onion; coveralls, pants and shirt, thermal underwear. The flesh was torn. The light glinted on frozen blood and gobbets of icy flesh. Most of the internal organs were gone. I shone the light on the surrounding snow, but there was nothing to see. The flesh, organs, were gone.

The intestine had leaked dark fluid all over the cavity, but it was frozen solid. I smelled no odor as I leaned over. Cold was a wonderful thing. The edges of the wound were ragged. No knife had done this. Or if it had, it was like no blade I'd ever seen. The medical examiner could tell for sure. A rib had been broken. It pointed upward like an exclamation mark. I shone the light on the bone. It was chipped, but not claws, not hands . . . teeth. I would have bet a week's pay that I was looking at tooth marks.

The throat wound was crusted with frozen snow. Reddish ice crystals had frozen to his face. The remaining eye was frozen shut with bloody ice. There were tooth marks at each side of the throat wound, not claws. The crushed jaw bore clear imprint of teeth. It certainly wasn't human teeth. Which meant it wasn't ghouls, vampires, zombies, or any other human undead. I had to hike my coat up to fish the tape measure out of the coverall pocket. It would have looked better if I'd taken the time to unbutton my coat, but, hey, it was cold.

The claw marks on the face were wide ripping things. Wider than a bear's claws, wider than anything natural. Monstrously large. There was a nearly perfect imprint of teeth on either side of the jaw. As if the creature had bitten down hard, but not tried to tear. Biting to crush, biting to . . . stop the screaming. Can't make a lot of noise with the entire bottom half of your mouth crushed. There was something very deliberate about that one bite. The throat was torn away, but again not as bad as it could be. Just enough to kill. It was only when you got to the stomach that the creature had lost control. The man was dead before the stomach was opened. I'd have bet on that. But the creature took the time to eat the stomach. To feed. Why?

There was an imprint in the snow, near the body. The imprint showed where people had knelt in it, me included, but the light picked up blood drained into the snow. He'd been facedown when someone rolled him over.

The footprints had tracked through nearly every inch of snow except for the blood splatters. Given a choice, people won't walk through blood. Crime scene or not. There wasn't nearly as much blood as you'd expect. Slicing a throat is messy business. But, of course, this throat hadn't been sliced. It had been ripped out by teeth. The blood had gone into the mouth, not onto the snow.

The blood had soaked into the clothing. If we could find our creature, it would be covered in blood, too. The snow was surprisingly clean for the amount of carnage. There was a thick pool of blood to one side, at least a yard from the body, but right next to the body-size impression. The dead man had lain by that stain long enough to bleed quite a bit, then been rolled over on its stomach, where it had lain long enough for the skin to freeze to the snow. More blood had pooled underneath the body while it lay facedown. Now here the body lay faceup, but no fresh blood. The body hadn't been turned over the last time until after he was very dead.

I called up, "Who rolled the body over?"

"It was just like that when I came on the scene," Titus said.

"Holmes?" Chief Garroway made her name a question.

"He was faceup when we got here."

"Did Williams move the body?"

"I didn't ask," she said.

Great. "Someone moved him. It'd be good to know if it was Williams."

"I'll go ask him," Holmes said.

"Patterson, you go with her," Titus said.

"I don't need . . ."

"Holmes, just go," Garroway said.

The two deputies left.

I went back to looking at the body. Had to think of it as a body, couldn't call it a "him." If I did that, I'd begin to wonder if he had a wife, kids. I didn't want to know. It was just a body, so much meat. Don't I wish.

I shone the penlight on the mishmashed snow. I stayed on my knees, nearly crawling on the snow. Me and Sherlock Holmes. If the creature had come up behind the man, there should have been some mark in the snow. Maybe not a whole print but something. Every print I found wore shoes. Whatever had done this hadn't worn shoes. Even with a herd of squabbling cops trampling through there should have been some imprint of claws and animal tracks. I couldn't find any. Maybe the crime techs would have better luck. I hoped so.

If there were no prints, could it have flown in? A gargoyle, maybe? It was the only large winged predator that attacked man. Except for dragons, but they weren't native to this country, and it would have been a hell of a lot messier. Or maybe a lot neater. A dragon would simply have swallowed the man whole.

Gargoyles will attack and kill a man, but it's rare. Besides the nearest pack was in Kelly, Kentucky. The Kelly gargoyles were a small subspecies that had attacked people but never killed. They were mostly carrion eaters. In France there were three species of gargoyles that were man-sized or better. They'd eat you. But there'd never been anything that large in America.

What else could it be? There were a few lesser eastern trolls in the Ozarks, but not this close to St. Louis. Besides I'd seen pictures of troll kills, and this wasn't it. The claws were too curved, too long. The stomach looked like it had been cleaned out by something with a muzzle. Trolls looked frightfully human, but then they were primates.

A lesser troll wouldn't attack a human if it had a choice. A greater mountain troll might have, but they had been extinct for more than twenty years. Also they had a tendency to snap off trees and whap people to death, then eat them.

I didn't think it was anything as exotic as trolls or gargoyles. If there'd been tracks leading up to the body, I'd have been sure it was a lycanthrope kill. Trolls had been known to wear castoff clothing. So a troll could have tramped through the snow, or a gargoyle could have flown up, but a lycanthrope . . . they had to walk on naked feet that wouldn't fit any human shoe. So how?

I would have slapped my forehead, but didn't. If you do that at murder scenes, you got blood in your hair. I looked up. Humans almost never look up. Millions of years of evolution had conditioned us to ignore the sky. Nothing was big enough to take us from above. But that didn't mean something couldn't jump on us.

A tree branch snaked out over the hollow. The penlight picked out fresh white scars against the black limb. A shapeshifter had crouched on the bark, waiting for the man to walk underneath. Ambush, premeditation, murder.

"Dolph, could you come down here a minute?"

Dolph walked carefully down the snow-covered slope. Didn't want to repeat my performance, I guess. "You know what it is?"

"Shapeshifter," I said.

"Explain." He had his trusty notebook out, pen poised. I explained what I'd found. What I thought.

"We haven't had a rogue lycanthrope since the squad was formed. Are you sure about this?"

"I'm sure it's a shapeshifter, but I didn't say it was a lycanthrope."

"Explain."

"All lycanthropes are shapeshifters by definition, but not all shapeshifters are lycanthropes. Lycanthropy is a disease that you catch from surviving an attack or getting a bad batch of lycanthropy vaccine."

He looked at me. "You can get it from the vaccine?"

"It happens."

"Good to know," he said. "How can you be a shapeshifter and not a lycanthrope?"

"Most often an inherited condition. The family guardian dog, beast, giant cat. Mostly European. One person a generation has the genes and changes."

"Is that tied to the moon like normal lycanthropy?"

"No. A family guardian comes out when the family needs it. War, or some kind of physical danger. There are swanmanes. They are tied to the moon, but it's still an inherited condition."

"That it?"

"You can be cursed, but that's really rare."

"Why?"

I shrugged. "You've got to find a witch or something with magic powerful enough to curse somebody with shapeshifting. I've read spells for personal shapeshifting. The potions are so full of narcotics that you might believe you were an animal. You might also believe you were the Chrysler building, or you might just die. Real spells for it are a lot more complex and usually require a human sacrifice. A curse is a step up from a spell. It's not really a spell at all."

I tried to think how to explain it. In this area Dolph was the civvie. He didn't know the lingo. "A curse is like the ultimate act of will. You just gather all your power, magic, whatever, and focus it on one person. You will them to be cursed. You always do it in person, so they know it's been done. Some theories think it takes the victim's belief to make a curse work. I'm not sure I buy that."

"Are witches the only people that can curse people?"

"Occasionally somebody will run afoul of a fairy. One of the old Daoine sidhe, but you'd have to be in Europe for that. England, Ireland, parts of Scotland. In this country it'd be a witch."

"So a shapeshifter, but we don't know what kind or even how they got to be a shapeshifter."

"Not from a few marks and tracks, no."

"If you saw the shifter face-to-face could you tell what kind they were?"

"What animal?" I asked.

"Yeah."

"Nope."

"Could you tell if they'd been cursed or if it was a disease?"

"Nope."

He just looked at me. "You're usually better than this."

"I'm better with the dead, Dolph. Give me a vamp or a zombie and I'll tell you their Social Security number. Some of that is natural talent, but a lot of it is practice. I haven't had as much experience with shapeshifters."

"What questions can you answer?"

"Ask and find out," I said.

"You think this is a brand-new shapeshifter?" Dolph asked.

"Nope."

"Why not?"

"The first time you change on the night of the full moon. It's too early for a brand-new shifter. But it could be a second, or third month, but . . ."

"But what?"

"If this is still a lycanthrope that can't control itself, that kills indiscriminately, it should still be here. Hunting us."

Dolph glanced out into the darkness. He held his notebook and pen in one hand, right hand free for his gun. The movement was automatic.

"Don't sweat it, Dolph. If it was going to eat more people, it would have taken Williams or the deputies."

His gaze searched the darkness, then came back to me. "So the shapeshifter could control itself?"

"I think so."

"Then why kill the man?"

I shrugged. "Why does anyone kill? Lust, greed, rage."

"The animal form used as a murder weapon then," Dolph said.

"Yeah."

"Is it still in animal form?"

"This was done by a half-and-half form, sort of a wolfman."

"A werewolf."

I shook my head. "I can't tell what sort of animal it is. The wolfman was just an example. It could be any sort of mammal."

"Just a mammal?"

"These wounds, yeah. I know there are avian weres, but they don't do this sort of damage."

"So werebirds?"

"Yeah, but that's not what did this."

"Any guesses?"

I squatted beside the body, stared at it. Willed it to tell me its secrets. Three nights from hence, when the soul had finally flown far away, I might have tried to raise the man and ask what did this. But his throat was gone. Even the dead can't talk without the proper equipment.

"Why did Titus think it was a bear kill?" I asked.

Dolph thought about that for a minute. "I don't know."

"Let's ask him."

Dolph nodded. "Be my guest." He sounded just a wee bit sarcastic. If I'd been arguing with the sheriff for hours, I'd have been a large chunk o' sarcastic.

"Come on, Dolph. We can't know less than we do right now."

"If Titus has any say in it, we might."

"Do you want me to ask him or not?"

"Ask."

I called up to the waiting men. "Sheriff Titus."

He looked down at me. He'd gotten out a cigarette but hadn't lit it yet. He paused with a lighter halfway to his mouth. "You want something, Ms. Blake?" The cigarette bobbed in his lips as he spoke.

"Why do you think this is a bear attack?"

He snapped the lid on his lighter, and took the unlit cig out of his mouth with the same hand. "Why do you want to know?"

I wanted to say, just answer the damn question, but I didn't. Brownie point for me. "Just curious."

"It wasn't a mountain lion. A cat would have used its claws more. Scratched him up some."

"Why not a wolf?"

"Pack animal. Looks like only one animal to me."

I had to agree with all the above. "I think you've been holding out on us, Sheriff. You seem to know a lot about animals that aren't native to this area."

"I go hunting now and then, Ms. Blake. Need to know the habits of your prey if you want to bag one."

"So a bear by process of elimination?" I asked.

"You might say that." He put the cig back in his mouth. Flame flared, pulsing against his face. When he flipped the lighter closed, the darkness seemed thicker.

"What do you think it was, Ms. Expert?" The smell of his cigarette carried on the cold air.

"Shapeshifter."

Even in the darkness I could feel the weight of his eyes. He blew a ghostly cloud of smoke moonward. "You think so?"

"I know so," I said.

He gave a sharp *hmph* sound. "Awful sure of yourself, ain't ya?"

"You want to come down here, Sheriff. I'll show you what I've found."

He hesitated, then shrugged. "Why not?" He came down the slope like a bulldozer, heavy boots forming snowy wakes. "Okay, Ms. Expert, dazzle me."

"You are a pain in the ass, Titus."

Dolph sighed a white cloud of breath.

Titus thought that was real funny, laughed, doubled over, slapping his leg. "You are just a laugh a minute, Ms. Blake. Now, tell me what you got."

I did.

He took a long drag on his cig. The end flared bright in the darkness. "Guess it wasn't a bear, after all."

He wasn't going to argue. Bliss. "No, it wasn't."

"Cougar?" he said, sort of hopefully.

I stood carefully. "You know it wasn't."

"Shapeshifter," he said.

"Yeah."

''There hasn't been a rogue shapeshifter in this county for ten years.''

''How many did it kill?'' I asked.

He took in a lungful of smoke and blew it out slowly. ''Five.''

I nodded. ''I missed that case. It was before my time.''

''You'da been in junior high when it happened?''

''Yeah.''

He threw his cigarette in the snow and ground it out with his boot. ''I wanted it to be a bear.''

''Me, too,'' I said.

9

The night was a hard, cold darkness. Two o'clock is a forsaken time of night, no matter what the season. In mid-December two o'clock is the frozen heart of eternal night. Or maybe I was just discouraged. The light over the stairs leading up to my apartment shone like a captured moon. All the lights had a frosted, swimming quality. Slightly unreal. There was a haze in the air, like an infant fog.

Titus had asked me to stick around in case they found someone in the area. I was their best bet for figuring out if the person was a lycanthrope or some innocent schmuck. Beat the heck out of cutting off a hand to see if there was fur on the inside of the body. If you were wrong, what did you do, apologize?

There had been some lycanthrope tracks leading up to the murder scene. Plaster casts had been made, and at my suggestion, copies were being sent to the biology department at Washington University. I had almost addressed it to Dr. Louis Fane. He taught biology at Wash U. He was one of Richard's best friends. A nice guy A wererat. A deep, dark secret that might be jeopardized if I started addressing lycanthrope paw prints to him. Addressing it to the entire department pretty much guaranteed Louie would see it.

That had been my greatest contribution of the night. They were still searching when I drove off. I had my beeper on. If they found a naked human in the snow, they could call. Though if my beeper went off before I got some sleep, I was going to be pissed.

When I shut my car door, there was an echo. A second car door slammed shut. I was tired, but it was automatic to search the small parking lot for that second car. Irving Griswold stood four cars down, bundled in a Day-Glo orange parka with a striped muffler trailing around his neck. His brown hair formed a frizzy halo to his bald spot. Tiny round glasses perched on a button nose. He looked jolly and harmless, and was a werewolf, too. Seemed to be my night for it.

Irving was a reporter on the *St. Louis Post-Dispatch*. Any story about me and Animators, Inc., usually had his byline on it. He smiled as he walked towards me. Just your friendly neighborhood reporter. Yeah, right.

"What do you want, Irving?"

"Is that any way to greet someone who has spent the last three hours in his car waiting for you?"

"What do you want, Irving?" Maybe if I just kept repeating the question over and over, I'd wear him down.

The smile faded from his round little face. He looked solemn and worried. "We've got to talk, Anita."

"Will this be a long story?"

He seemed to think about that for a moment, then nodded. "Could be."

"Then come upstairs. I'll fix us both some real coffee."

"Real coffee as opposed to fake coffee?" he asked.

I started for the stairs. "I'll fix you a cup of java that'll put hair on your chest."

He laughed.

I realized I'd made a pun and hadn't meant to. I know Irving is a shapeshifter. I've even seen his wolf form. But I forget. He's a friend and doesn't seem the least preternatural in human form.

We sat at the small kitchenette table, sipping vanilla nut creme coffee. My suit jacket was draped over the back of the kitchen chair. It left my gun and shoulder holster exposed. "I thought you were on a date tonight, Blake."

"I was."

"Some date."

"A girl can never be too careful."

Irving blew on his cup, sipping it delicately. His eyes had flicked from side to side, taking in everything. Days from now he'd be able to describe the room completely, down to the Nike Airs and jogging socks in front of the couch.

"What's up, Irving?"

"Great coffee." He wouldn't meet my eyes. It was a bad sign.

"What's wrong?"

"Has Richard told you anything about Marcus?"

"Your pack leader, right?"

Irving looked surprised. "He told you?"

"I found out tonight that your alpha is named Marcus. There's a battle of succession going on. Marcus wants Richard dead. Richard says he won't fight him."

"Oh, he fought him, all right," Irving said.

It was my turn to be surprised. "Then why isn't Richard pack leader?"

"Richard got squeamish. He had him, Blake, claws at Marcus's throat." Irving shook his head. "He thought when Marcus recovered they could talk, compromise." He made a rude sound. "Your boyfriend is an idealist."

Idealist. It was almost the same thing as fool. Jean-Claude and Irving agreed. They didn't agree on much.

"Explain."

"You can move up in the pack hierarchy by fighting. You win, you go up a notch. You lose, you stay where you are." He took a long sip of coffee, eyes closed as if drinking in the warmth. "Until you fight for pack leader."

"Let me guess. It's a fight to the death."

''No killie, no new leader,'' he said.

I shook my head, coffee sitting untouched in front of me. ''Why are you telling me all this, Irving? Why now?''

''Marcus wants to meet you.''

''Why didn't Richard tell me that himself?''

''Richard doesn't want you involved.''

''Why not?'' Irving kept answering my questions, but the answers weren't helping much.

Irving shrugged. ''Richard won't give Marcus a freaking inch. If Marcus said black, Richard would say white.''

''Why does Marcus want to see me?''

''I don't know,'' Irving said.

''Yeah, right.''

''Honest, Blake, I don't know what's going on. Something big is up, and no one's talking to me.''

''Why not? You're a shapeshifter.''

''I'm also a reporter. I made the mistake years back of printing an article. The lycanthrope I talked to lied, said he never gave me permission to quote him. He lost his job. Some of the others wanted to out me, too, let me lose my job.'' He huddled around his coffee mug. Eyes distant with remembering. ''Marcus said no, said I was more valuable to them as a reporter. No one's really trusted me since.''

''Not a forgiving bunch,'' I said. I sipped my coffee and found it cooling. If I drank it fast enough, it would be drinkable, barely.

''They never forgive and they never forget,'' Irving said.

Sounds like a bad character trait, but it's one of my founding principles, so I couldn't complain much. ''So Marcus sent you out here to talk to me. About what?''

''He wants to meet you. To talk some kind of business.''

I got up and refilled my mug. A little less sugar this time. I was beginning to wake up just from frustration. ''Let him make an appointment to come to my office.''

Irving shook his head. ''Marcus is some hotshot surgeon. You know what would happen if even a hint of what he is got out?''

I could understand that. You might get away with being a shapeshifter on some jobs. Doctor was not one of them. There was still the dentist in Texas that was being sued by a patient. Said she contracted lycanthropy from him. Nonsense. You didn't get it from having human hands in your mouth. But the case hadn't been thrown out. People didn't have a lot of sympathy for fur balls treating their kid's sparkling teeth.

''Okay, send someone else to the office. Surely, Marcus must trust someone.''

''Richard has forbidden anyone to contact you.''

I just looked at him. ''Forbidden?''

Irving nodded. ''Anyone lower in the pack order contacts you at their peril.''

I started to smile and stopped. He was serious. ''You're not kidding.''

He raised a three-fingered salute. ''Scout's honor.''

''So how come you're here? You looking to move up in the pack?''

He paled. Honest to God, he paled. ''Me? Fight Richard? Hell no.''

''Then Richard won't mind you talking to me?''

''Oh, he'll mind.''

I frowned. ''Is Marcus going to protect you?''

''Richard gave a specific order. Marcus can't interfere.''

''But he ordered you to come see me,'' I said.

''Yep.''

''What's to stop Richard from busting your chops about this?''

Irving grinned. ''I thought you'd protect me.''

I laughed. ''You son of a bitch.''

''Maybe, but I know you, Blake. You won't like that Richard's been keeping things from you. You certainly won't like him protecting you. Besides, I've been your friend for years. I don't think you'll stand by while your boyfriend beats the hell out of me.''

Irving knew me better than Richard did. It was not a comforting thought. Had I been fooled by a handsome face, a nice sense of humor? Had I not seen the real Richard? I shook my head. Could I be fooled that completely? I hoped not.

''Do I have your protection?'' He was still smiling, but there was something in his eyes. Fear, maybe.

''You need me to say it out loud for it to be official?''

''Yeah.''

''That a rule in the lycanthrope underground?''

''One of them,'' he said.

''You have my protection, but I want information in return.''

''I told you I don't know anything, Blake.''

''Tell me what it's like to be a lycanthrope, Irving. Richard seems determined to keep me in the dark. I don't like being in the dark.''

Irving smiled. ''I heard that.''

''You be my guide to the world of the furry, and I'll keep Richard off your back.''

''Agreed.''

''When does Marcus want to meet?''

''Tonight.'' Irving had the grace to look embarrassed.

I shook my head. ''No way. I'm going to bed. I'll meet with Marcus tomorrow, but not tonight.''

He looked down into his coffee, fingertips touching the mug. ''He wants it to be tonight.'' He looked up at me. ''Why do you think I've been camped out in my car?''

''I am not at the beck and call of every monster in town. I don't even know what Fur Face wants to meet about.'' I leaned back in the chair and crossed my arms. ''No way am I going out tonight to play with shapeshifters.''

Irving squirmed in his chair, rotating the coffee cup slowly on the table. He wouldn't meet my eyes again.

''What's wrong now?''

''Marcus told me to set up a meeting with you. If I refused, he'd have me . . .

punished. If I come here, Richard gets pissed. I'm trapped between two alpha males, and I ain't up to it.''

''Are you asking me to protect you from Marcus, as well as Richard?''

''No,'' he said, shaking his head, ''no. You're good, Blake, but you aren't in Marcus's league.''

''Glad to hear it,'' I said.

''Will you meet with Marcus tonight?''

''If I say no, do you get in trouble?''

He stared into his coffee. ''Would you believe no?''

''Nope.''

He looked at me, brown eyes very serious. ''He'll get mad, but I'll live.''

''But he'll make you hurt.'' It wasn't a question.

''Yeah.'' That one word so soft, so tentative. It wasn't like Irving.

''I'll see him on one condition. That you're present at the meeting.''

His face bloomed into a grin that spread from pole to pole. ''You are a true friend, Blake.'' All the sadness was gone, washed away in the rosy glow of finding out what the hell was going on. Even ass deep in alligators, Irving was a reporter. It was who and what he was, more than the lycanthropy.

The smile alone was worth a meeting. Besides, I wanted to know if Richard was really in danger. Meeting the man who was threatening him was the only real way to find out. Also, I didn't really care for someone threatening one of my friends. Silver-plated bullets only slowed down a vampire, unless you can take out the head and heart. Silver bullets will kill a werewolf, no second chances, no healing, just dead.

Marcus might remember that. If he pushed it, I might even remind him.

10

Irving had called Marcus from my apartment. Again Irving didn't know why, all he did know was Marcus said to call before we came. I went into the bedroom. Hung up my dry-clean-only suit, and changed clothes. Black jeans, red polo shirt, black Nikes with a blue swoosh, and real socks. I abandoned jogging socks for everyday wear once winter set in.

I reached for the bulky green sweater I had laid out on the bed. I hesitated. It wasn't the fact that the sweater had stylized Christmas trees on it, and it might not be the coolest thing to wear. I didn't give a damn about that. I was debating on whether to carry a second gun. A fashion accessory nearer and dearer to my heart than any piece of clothing.

No lycanthrope had threatened me yet, but ol' Gretchen the vamp had. She might not be a master vampire but she was close. Besides, the memory of the cop taking the Browning away was still fresh. I had too many preternatural enemies to go unarmed. I got out my Uncle Mike's sidekick inner-pants holster. A comfy fit that didn't ruin the line of your jeans unless someone was really looking.

My main backup gun is a Firestar 9mm. Small, light, pretty to look at, and I could wear it at my waist and still be able to sit down. The sweater hung to midthigh. The gun was invisible unless you frisked me. The gun was set in front, ready for a cross-draw. Probably wouldn't need it. Probably.

The sweater bulked up around the straps of the shoulder holster. I've seen people wear shoulder rigs underneath bulky sweaters or sweatshirts, but you lose a few seconds groping under the cloth. I'd rather look less than fashion perfect and live.

The sweater was too long for my leather jacket, so I was back in my black trench coat. Me and Phillip Marlowe. I didn't take any extra ammo. I figured twenty-one rounds was enough for one night. I even left my knives at home. I almost talked myself out of the Firestar. I usually didn't start carrying two guns until after people had tried to kill me. I shrugged. Why wait? If I didn't need it, I'd feel silly tomorrow. If I did need it, I wouldn't feel silly at all.

Irving was waiting for me. Sitting on the couch like a good little boy. He looked like a schoolboy whom the teacher had made stand in the corner.

"What's wrong?"

"Marcus wanted me to just give you directions. He doesn't want me at the meeting. I said, you wouldn't come without me. That you didn't trust him." He looked up at me. "He's pretty pissed."

"But you stood your ground," I said.

"Yeah."

"Why don't you sound happier about that?"

He shrugged. "Marcus in a bad mood is not a pleasant experience, Blake."

"I'll drive, you give directions."

"Marcus said we both should drive. He said that I'd need to stay after the meeting, for a little talk."

"Come on, Irving, I'm driving, you're giving directions, and when I leave, you leave."

"I appreciate the offer, Blake, but you don't want Marcus mad at you."

"If I'm protecting you from Richard, I might as well throw in Marcus."

He shook his head. "No, you follow my car." He held up a hand. "No more arguing, Blake. I am a werewolf. I have to live in the community. I can't afford to make a stand against Marcus, not over one little talk."

I wanted to argue some more, but I didn't. Irving knew his problems better than I did. If fighting Marcus over this would make things worse, then I'd let it go. But I didn't like it.

The Lunatic Cafe was located in University City. Its sign was a glowing crescent moon with the restaurant name done in soft blue neon. Except for the name, and the nifty sign, the place didn't look much different from all the other shops and restaurants in the college district.

It was Friday night and there was no parking. I was beginning to think Marcus would have to come out to my car, when a wine dark Impala pulled out of the two spaces it had been hogging. My Jeep slipped in with room for a second car on one side.

Irving waited in front of the restaurant. His hands were shoved deep into his pockets. The ridiculous muffler trailed nearly to the ground. He looked distracted and not a bit happy.

I walked towards him with the trench coat flapping around me like a cape. Even like this, most people wouldn't see the gun. They'd see a small woman with a bright Christmas sweater. People see what they expect to see most of the time. The people that I was wearing the gun for would notice, and know I was armed.

Irving pushed the door in without a word. Irving, quiet? I didn't like seeing him subdued, almost beaten, like a kicked dog. It made me not like Marcus, and I hadn't even met him.

Noise poured around us just inside the door. A murmur of voices so thick it was like ocean noise. Silverware clinked, someone laughed high and bright like a hand rising from the noise, to be swallowed back again and lost. There was a bar along one wall, polished dark wood, old and lovingly cared for. The rest of the room held small, round tables that could comfortably seat about four. Every seat was full, and then some. Three doorways opened up; one beside the bar, one to the right, one in the middle. More tables were shoved into the smaller rooms.

The cafe had started life as someone's home. We were standing in the living room. Through the doorways leading to the other rooms were open archways, as if someone had knocked down a few walls. Even with that, the place was claustrophobic. People were three deep at the bar waiting for a table. The place was jammed to bursting with happy, smiling people.

One of the women behind the bar came around, wiping her hands on a towel tucked into the tie of her apron. She gave a wide, welcoming smile. She had a pair of menus in her one hand.

I started to say, but we don't need . . . when Irving gripped my arm. Tension vibrated through his hand. He'd grabbed my right arm. I turned to tell him not to do that, but the look on his face stopped me. He was staring at the smiling woman as if she had sprouted a second head. I turned back to the woman, and looked at her. Really looked at her.

She was tall, slender, with long, straight hair. It was a rich, reddish auburn that gleamed under the lights. Her face was a soft triangle, chin maybe a little too pointed, but overall she was lovely. Her eyes were a strange amber-brown that matched her hair perfectly.

Her smile widened, just a lift of lips. I knew what I was looking at. Lycanthrope. One that could pass for human. Like Richard.

I looked out over the room, and realized why it felt so tight. It wasn't just the crowd. A majority of the happy, smiling people were shapeshifters. Their energy burned in the air like the weight of a thunderstorm. I had thought the crowd was boisterous, too loud, but it was the shapeshifters. Their energy boiled and filled the room, masquerading as the energy of any crowd. As I stood there at the door, a face lifted here and there. Human eyes looked at me, but the glance wasn't human.

The glance was considering, testing. How tough was I? How good would I taste? It reminded me of the way Richard had been watching the crowd at the Fox. I felt like a chicken at a coyote convention. I was suddenly glad of the second gun.

''Welcome to the Lunatic Cafe, Ms. Blake,'' the woman said. ''I'm Raina Wallis, proprietor. If you'll follow me. Your party is waiting for you.'' She said it all with a smile and a warm glow in her eyes. Irving's grip on my arm was nearly painful.

I leaned into him, and whispered, ''That's my right arm.''

He blinked at me. His eyes flicked to the Browning, and he let go, muttering, ''Sorry.''

Raina leaned closer. Irving flinched. ''I won't bite, Irving, not yet.'' She gave a low laugh that was rich and bubbling. The kind of laugh that was meant for bedrooms and private jokes. The laugh gave her eyes and body a different look. She suddenly seemed more voluptuous, more sensual than just a second ago. Nicely weird.

''Mustn't keep Marcus waiting.'' She turned and began threading her way through the tables.

I glanced at Irving. ''Something you want to tell me?''

"Raina's our alpha female. If the punishment's going to be really bad, she does it. She's a lot more creative than Marcus."

Raina was motioning to us by the archway near the bar. Her lovely face was frowning, looking a little less lovely, and a lot more bitchy.

I patted his shoulder. "I won't let her hurt you."

"You can't stop it."

"We'll see," I said.

He nodded, but not as if he believed me. He started between the tables. I followed. A woman touched his hand as he walked past. Gave him a smile. She was about my size, and dainty, with straight black hair cut short that framed her face like black lace. Irving squeezed her fingers and kept walking. Her large, dark eyes met mine. The eyes told me nothing. They had smiled at Irving; for me they were neutral. Like the eyes of a wolf I'd seen once in California. I'd walked around a tree and there it had stood. I had never really understood what neutral meant until that moment. Those pale eyes stared at me, waiting. If I threatened it, it would attack. If I left it alone, it would run. My choice. The wolf hadn't given a damn which way it turned out.

I kept walking, but the space between my shoulder blades was itching. I knew if I turned around that nearly every eye would be on me, on us. The weight of their gaze was physical.

I had an urge to whirl and say boo, but fought it off. I had a feeling they were all staring at me with neutral inhuman eyes, and I didn't want to see it.

Raina led us to a closed door at the back of the dining room. She pushed it open and motioned us through with a theatrical wave of her arm. Irving just walked through. I walked through but kept my eyes on her. I was nearly close enough for her to have hugged me. Close enough that with her reflexes she could probably take me.

Lycanthropes are just faster than a normal human. It isn't mind tricks like with vampires. They are just flat out better. I wasn't sure how much better in human form, though. Staring up into Raina's smiling face, I wasn't sure I wanted to find out.

We stood in a narrow hallway. There was a door at either end, one showing the cold night through its glass window, the other closed, a question mark.

Raina closed the door behind us, leaning on it. She seemed to collapse against it, head hanging down, hair spilling forward.

"Are you all right?" I asked.

She took a deep, shuddering breath and looked up at me.

I gasped. I couldn't help myself.

She was gorgeous. Her cheekbones were high and sculpted. Her eyes wider and more centered in her face. She looked like what might have been her sister, a family resemblance but not the same person.

"What did you just do?"

She gave that rich, bedroom laugh again. "I am alpha, Ms. Blake. I can do a great many things that most shifters cannot."

I was willing to bet that. "You moved your bones around, on purpose, like do-it-yourself cosmetic surgery."

''Very good, Ms. Blake, very good.'' Her amber-brown eyes flashed to Irving. The smile left her face. ''Do you still insist on this one being at the meeting?''

''Yes, I do.''

Her lips pursed, as though she'd tasted something sour. ''Marcus said to ask, then to bring you.'' She shrugged, and stood away from the door. She was taller by about three inches. I wished I'd paid more attention to her hands. Had they changed, too?

''Why the body sculpting?'' I asked.

''The other form is my day form. This is real.''

''Why the disguise?''

''In case I have to do something nefarious,'' she said.

Nefarious?

She stalked down the hall towards the other closed door. Her walk was a gliding, athletic movement like a big cat's. Or would that be big wolf's?

She knocked on the door. I heard nothing, but she opened the door. She stood there, arms crossed over her stomach, cradling her breasts, smiling at us. I was beginning not to like Raina's smiles.

The room was a banquet hall with cloth-covered tables grouped in a horseshoe. A raised platform with four chairs and a lectern closed the mouth of the horseshoe. Two men stood on the platform. One was at least six feet tall, slender but muscled like a basketball player. His hair was black, cut short with a matching finger-thin mustache and goatee beard. He stood with one hand gripping his opposite wrist. A jock pose. A bodyguard pose.

He wore a skintight pair of black jeans, and a sweater with a black-on-black design clung to wide shoulders. There was a fringe of dark chest hair just above the scooped neckline. Black tooled cowboy boots and a large blocky watch completed the badass look.

The other man was no more than five foot seven. His hair was that funny shade of blond that has brown highlights in it, but still manages to be blond. The hair was short but styled and blow-dried, and would have been lovely to look at if it had been a little longer. His face was clean-shaven, square jawed, with a dimple in his chin. The dimple should have made the face look fun, but it didn't. It was a face for rules. Those thin lips were built for saying, my way or else.

He wore a pale blue linen suit jacket over black pants. A pale blue turtleneck that matched the jacket to perfection completed the outfit. His shoes were black and polished to a shine.

It had to be Marcus. ''Alfred.'' One word, but it was an order. The bigger man stepped-leaped off the platform. It was a graceful, bounding movement. He moved in a cloud of his own vitality. It rolled and boiled around him almost like heat rising off pavement. You couldn't see it with the naked eye, but you could sure as hell feel it.

Alfred came at me as though he had a purpose. I put my back to the wall, keeping Raina in sight, along with everybody else. Irving moved back with me. He stood a little away from all of us, but closer to me than anyone.

I put the trench coat back so the gun showed plainly. ''Your intentions better be friendly, Alfred.''

''Alfred,'' the other man said. One word, even the tone sounded the same, but this time Alfie stopped in his tracks. He stood, staring at me. His eyes weren't neutral, they were hostile. People don't usually dislike me on sight. But hey, I wasn't too thrilled with him, either.

''We have not offered you violence, Ms. Blake,'' Marcus said.

''Yeah, right. Alfie there is contained violence in motion. I want to know what his intentions are before he comes closer.''

Marcus looked at me as if I'd done something interesting. ''A very apt description, Ms. Blake. You can see our auras, then?''

''If that's what you want to call it,'' I said.

''Alfred's intentions are not hostile. He will merely search you for weapons. It is standard procedure for nonshifters. It is nothing personal, I assure you.''

The very fact that they didn't want me armed made me want to keep my weapons. Stubbornness, or a strong survival instinct.

''Maybe I'd agree to being searched if you explained why I'm here first.'' Stall, until I could decide what to do.

''We don't discuss business in front of the press, Ms. Blake.''

''Well, I'm not talking to you without him.''

''I will not jeopardize all of us to satisfy idle curiosity.'' He was still standing on the platform like a general surveying his troops.

''The only reason I'm here at all is because Irving is a friend. Insulting him isn't going to endear you to me.''

''I do not wish to endear myself to you, Ms. Blake. I wish your aid.''

''You want my help?'' I didn't try to keep the surprise out of my voice.

He gave a brief nod.

''What kind of help?''

''He must leave.''

''No,'' I said.

Raina pushed away from the wall and stalked around us, just out of reach, but circling like a shark. ''Irving's punishment could begin now.'' Her voice was low and purring around the edges.

''I didn't know wolves purred,'' I said.

She laughed. ''Wolves do a lot of things, as I'm sure you're aware.''

''I don't know what you mean.''

''Oh, come now, woman to woman.'' She leaned one shoulder against the wall, arms crossed, face friendly. I was betting she could bite my finger off and smile just like that the entire time.

She bent close as if we were sharing secrets. ''Richard is as good as he looks, isn't he?''

I stared into her amused eyes. ''I don't kiss and tell.''

''I'll tell you my juicy tidbit, if you'll tell me yours.''

''Raina, enough.'' Marcus had moved forward to the edge of the stage. He didn't look happy.

She gave him a lazy smile. She was baiting him more than me, and enjoying it very much.

"Irving must leave, and Alfred must search you for weapons. There is no negotiating those two points."

"I'll make you a deal," I said. "Irving leaves now, but he goes home. No punishment."

Marcus shook his head. "I have decreed he will be punished. My word is law."

"Who died and made you king?"

"Simon," Raina said.

I blinked at her.

"He fought and killed Simon. That's who died and made him pack leader."

Ask a silly question . . . "You want my help, Irving goes free and untouched. No punishment."

"Don't do this, Anita," Irving said. "You'll just make things worse."

Raina stayed leaning beside me. Just a little girl talk. "He's right, you know. Right now he's mine to play with, but if you make Marcus really angry he'll give him to Alfred. I'll torture his mind and body. Alfred will break him."

"Irving goes free, no punishment. I stay and let Alfred search me for weapons. Otherwise we walk."

"Not we, Ms. Blake. You are free to go, but Irving is mine. He will stay, and with or without you he will be taught his lesson."

"What did he do wrong?" I asked.

"That is our business, not yours."

"I'm not going to help you do shit."

"Then go," he leaped gracefully off the stage, walking towards us as he spoke, "but Irving stays. You are only among us for this one night. He must live with us, Ms. Blake. He cannot afford your bravado."

The last sentence brought him just a little behind Alfred. Close up there were fine lines around his eyes and mouth, a slackness to the skin of his neck and jaws. I added ten years to his age. Fifties.

"I can't leave Irving here, knowing what you'll do to him."

"Oh, you have no idea what we'll do to him," Raina said. "We heal so well." She pushed away from the wall and walked to Irving. She paced round him in a tight circle, shoulder, hip, brushing against him, here and there as she moved. "Even the weakest of us can take so very much damage."

"What do you want to guarantee Irving's safety?" I asked.

Marcus looked at me, face careful, neutral. "You promise to aid us, and let Alfred frisk you. He is my bodyguard. You must let him do his job."

"I can't promise to help you without knowing what it is."

"Then we have no bargain."

"Anita, I can take it, whatever they dish out. I can take it. I've done it before."

"You asked for my protection from Richard, just call it a package deal," I said.

"You asked her for her protection?" Raina stepped away from him, surprise plain on her pretty face.

"Just against Richard," Irving said.

"It's clever," Raina said, "but it does have certain implications."

"She's not a pack member. It only works on Richard because they're dating," Irving said. He looked a little worried.

"What implications?" I asked.

Marcus answered, "To ask pack members for their protection is to acknowledge they are of higher rank without having to fight them. If they give their protection, then you have agreed to help them fight their battles. If they are challenged you are honor bound to aid them."

I glanced at Irving. He looked ill. "She's not one of us. You can't hold her to the law."

"What law?" I asked.

"Pack law," Marcus said.

"I forfeit her protection," Irving said.

"Too late," Raina said.

"You place us in a quandary, Ms. Blake. A pack member has acknowledged you as higher rank than he is. Acknowledged you as dominant. By our laws we must accept that as binding."

"I can't be a pack member," I said.

"No, but you can be dominant."

I knew what the word meant in the real world. Marcus was using it as if it meant more. "What does it mean to be dominant?"

"It means you can stand as Irving's protector against all comers."

"No," Irving said. He brushed past Raina and stood in front of Marcus. He stood tall and stared him in the eye. It was not a submissive display.

"I won't let you use me like this. It's what you intended all along. You knew I'd ask her protection from Richard. You counted on it, didn't you, you smug bastard."

A low growl trickled out from between Marcus's perfect white teeth. "I would watch my tongue if I were you, youngling."

"If it offends you, I will cut it out." Alfred's first words were not comforting.

This was getting out of hand. "Irving is under my protection, Alfred. If I understand the law. You have to go through me to hurt Irving, is that right?"

Alfred turned cold, dark eyes to me. He nodded.

"If you kill me, then I can't help Marcus."

This seemed to puzzle the big fella. Great, confusion to my enemies.

Marcus smiled. "You have found a flaw in my logic, Ms. Blake. If you truly intend to protect Irving, to the letter of the law, then you would indeed die. No mere human could withstand one of us. Even the lowliest would kill you."

I let that comment go. Why argue when I was winning anyway?

"Since you cannot accept challenges, and you won't let us harm Irving, he is safe."

"Great, now what?"

"Irving can go, and he will not be harmed. You stay and hear our plea. You may decide to aid us or not, Irving will not suffer for your choice."

"That's mighty generous of you."

"Yes, Ms. Blake, it is." There was a look in his eyes that was very serious.

Raina might play sadistic games. Alfred might hurt you in an eager rush. But Marcus, it was just business. He was a mob boss with fur.

"Leave us, Irving."

"I won't leave her."

Marcus turned on him with a snarl. "My patience is not endless!"

Irving dropped to his knees, head bowed, spine bent low. It was a submissive display. I grabbed Irving's arm, and lifted him to his feet. "Get up, Irving. The nice werewolf isn't going to hurt you."

"And why is that, Ms. Blake?"

"Because Irving's under my protection. If Alfred can't fight me, then you sure as hell can't."

Marcus threw back his head, and gave a sharp, barking laugh. "You are clever, and brave. Traits we admire." The laughter died from his face, lingering in his eyes like a pleasant dream. "Do not challenge me too openly, Ms. Blake. It wouldn't be healthy."

The last of the laughter died out of his eyes. I was left staring into human eyes, but there was no one home to talk to. It looked like a human being, talked like a human being, but it wasn't one.

I dug my fingers into Irving's parka-clad shoulder. "Go on, Irving. Get out of here."

He touched my arm. "I would never leave you in a tough spot."

"I'm safe tonight, you're not. Now go, please, Irving."

I watched the struggle on his face. But finally after another dirty look from Marcus, he left. The door closed and I was alone with three werewolves. Down from four. The night was looking up.

"Alfred must search you now."

So much for the night looking up. "Then do it," I said. I just stood there. I didn't put my arms out. I didn't lean against the wall. I wasn't going to help him, not unless he asked.

He took the Browning, then patted down my arms, legs, even the small of my back. He didn't pat down the front center of my body. Maybe he was being a gentleman, or maybe he was just careless. Whatever, he missed the Firestar. I had eight silver bullets and they didn't know it. The night was looking up.

11

Marcus took a seat on the platform. Alfred stood just behind him like a good bodyguard. ''Join us, Ms. Blake. It may be a long meeting to stand through.''

I didn't want to sit with Alfred at my back, so I moved to the last chair. The empty chair between us looked unsociable, but I was out of Alfred's reach. Safety before good manners.

Raina sat on Marcus's right, hand on his knee. Marcus sat in the same manner he did everything—rigid. Posture that would have made my Aunt Mattie proud. But he didn't move Raina's hand. In fact, he laid his hand over hers. Love? Solidarity? They didn't strike me as a really compatible couple.

A woman came through the door. Short blond hair styled and held in place with gel. Her business skirt suit was red with pinkish undertones, like a rose petal. Her white blouse had one of those blousy ties that made the suit seem feminine, and a little silly.

''Christine, it's good of you to come,'' Marcus said.

The woman nodded, and took the seat at the end of the horseshoe of tables, nearest the stage. ''What choice did I have? What choice did you give any of us?'' she asked.

''We must have a united front on this, Christine.''

''As long as you're in charge, right?''

Marcus started to say more but the crowd was growing. People drifted through the door in ones, twos, threes. He let the argument go. They could argue later, and I was betting they would. The woman's complaint sounded like an old one.

I recognized one person. Rafael the Rat King. He was tall, dark, and handsome with short-cut black hair, strong Mexican features, and an arrogant expression. He would have looked as stern as Marcus except for his lips. They were soft and sensuous, and ruined some of the effect.

Rafael nodded at me. I nodded back. He had two wererats with him, in human form. I didn't recognize either of them.

There were about a dozen people sitting along the tables when Marcus stood and walked to the podium. "My friends, I have asked you here tonight to meet Anita Blake. The vampires call her the Executioner. I believe she can help us."

"What can a vampire hunter do for us?" This from a tall man who sat alone, chairs on either side acting as walls. He had short white hair, cut in a strange Mia Farrow sixties cut, but gentler. He wore a white dress shirt, pale pink tie, white sport jacket, and cream-colored pants. He looked like the Good Humor man with money. But he had a point.

"We don't need a human to help us." This from a man who sat with one other. He had hair cut just above his collar, so curly it looked like fur, or maybe . . . Naw. He had thick eyebrows over dark eyes, with heavy, sensual features. The Rat King's lips may have seemed kissable, but this man seemed made for nefarious deeds done in dark places.

His clothing matched his face. The boots that he had propped on the table were of soft, velvety leather. His pants were of shiny black leather. The shirt he was almost wearing was a muscle tank top that left most of his upper body bare. His right arm was covered from elbow to fingers in leather straps. The knuckles had spikes coming out of them. The hair on his chest was as curly and dark as the hair on his head. A black duster coat was thrown across the table beside him.

The woman on his right rubbed her cheek along his shoulder as if it were a cat scent marking. Long, dark hair formed waves around her shoulders. What I could see of her outfit looked tight, black, and mostly of leather.

"We are human here, Gabriel," Marcus said.

Gabriel made a rude noise. "You believe what you want to, Marcus. But we know what we are, and what she isn't." He pointed at me with his gauntleted fist. It didn't seem a particularly friendly gesture.

Rafael stood. The gesture stopped the argument. There was something about the way he stood there in his ordinary street clothes that made you stare at him as if he were wearing a crown. His presence was more commanding than that of a ton of black leather. Marcus made the lowest of growls. Too many kings in this room.

"Does Marcus speak for Anita Blake as he speaks for the wolves?"

"Yes," Marcus said. "I speak for Ms. Blake."

I stood up. "I don't know what's going on, but I can speak for myself."

Marcus turned like a small blond storm. "I am pack leader. I am law."

Alfred moved to face me, big hands flexing.

"Chill out, fur face. You're not my leader, and I'm not a pack member."

Alfred stalked forward. I hopped off the stage. I had the gun, but I might need it more later. If I drew it now, I might not have it later. He leaped off the stage, a high bounding as if he'd had a trampoline to jump from. I dropped to the ground and rolled. I felt the air of his passage. I ended up against the stage. I went for the Firestar, and he was on me. Faster than a speeding bullet, faster than anything I'd ever seen.

His hand gripped my throat and squeezed. His lips drew back from his teeth, and made a low, rolling growl, like the sound a Rottweiler would make.

My hand was on the Firestar, but I still had to lift up, point it, and pull the trigger. I'd never make it. He'd rip my throat out long before I could manage it.

He drew me to my feet using my throat as a handle. His fingers dug in just enough to let me feel the strength in his hands. All he had to do was clench his fist, and the front of my throat would come with it. I kept my hand on the Firestar. I'd be clinging to it when I died.

''Does Alfred fight your battles for you now?'' It was Christine of the blousy tie. ''Pack leaders must fight all challenges to their dominance personally or forfeit leadership. It's one of your own laws, Marcus.''

''Do not quote my laws back to me, woman.''

''She challenged your authority over her, not Alfred's. If he kills her, is he the new pack leader?'' There was soft derision in her voice.

''Release her, Alfred.''

Alfred's eyes flicked to Marcus, then back to me. His fingers tensed, digging in and raising me to my tiptoes.

''I said, let her go!''

He dropped me. I staggered back against the stage and aimed Firestar in one movement. It wasn't pretty, but the gun was out and pointed at Alfred. If he tried me again, I was going to kill him, and I'd enjoy it.

''I thought you checked her for weapons,'' Marcus said.

''I did.'' Alfred was backing away, hands held in front of him as if to ward off a blow.

I scooted along the stage so I could keep an eye on Marcus. I caught sight of Raina, still sitting, looking amused.

I backed away from everyone, working to put a wall at my back. If Marcus was faster than Alfred, I needed distance, like a hundred miles, but I'd have to settle for the far wall.

''Have him disarm her,'' Raina said. She sat there, legs crossed, hands resting on her knee, smiling. ''It was Alfred's oversight. Let him correct it.''

Marcus nodded. Alfred turned his eyes back to me.

I pressed my back more solidly into the wall, as if I could make a door if I pressed hard enough. Alfred stalked towards me, slow, like a movie maniac. I pointed the gun at his chest. ''I will kill him,'' I said.

''Your little bullets cannot hurt me,'' Alfred said.

''Silver-plated Glaser safety rounds,'' I said. ''It'll blow a hole in your chest big enough to put a fist through.''

He hesitated. ''I can heal any wound, even silver.''

''Not if it's a killing blow,'' I said. ''I take out your heart and you're dead.''

He glanced back at Marcus. Marcus's face was all squeezed down with anger. ''You let her bring a gun among us.''

''If you're afraid of the gun, Marcus, take it away from her yourself.'' Christine again. This time I wasn't sure she was helping me.

''We intend you no harm, Ms. Blake. But I promised the others you would bring no weapons among us. I gave my word. If you will give Alfred your gun, this can end.''

''No way.''

''You are defying me, Ms. Blake. I cannot let anyone contest my authority.''

He had come to stand at the end of the stage, closest to me. He was closer to me than Alfred. I wasn't sure it was an improvement.

"You step off that stage and I'll shoot."

"Alfred." Just the name again, but it was enough. Alfred moved up beside him, eyes on Marcus's face. "Master?"

"Take it from her, Alfred. She cannot defy us."

"You're going to get him killed, Marcus."

"I don't think so."

Alfred took a step forward, in front of Marcus. His face was neutral, eyes unreadable. "This is a stupid thing to die over, Alfie."

"He gives orders. I obey. It is the way of things."

"Don't do this," I said.

Alfred took a step forward.

I took a slow, steadying breath. I had a peripheral sense of everyone else, but I was looking only at Alfred. At a spot in the center of his chest. "I am not bluffing."

I felt him tense, knew he was going to do it. He was confident that he could move faster than I could pull the trigger. Nothing was that fast. I hoped.

He leaped in that wide, arching roll that he'd used earlier. I dropped to one knee, aiming as I moved. The bullet hit him in midair. He jerked and crumbled to the floor.

The gunshot echoed into silence. I got to my feet, the gun still pointed at him. I eased forward. He never moved. If he was breathing, I couldn't see it. I knelt until the gun was shoved into the back of his spine. No movement. I felt for a pulse in his neck. Nothing. I pulled the Browning out of his waistband left handed. I kept the Firestar pointed at everybody. I wasn't as good left handed, and I didn't want to take the time to switch hands.

Marcus stepped off the stage. "Don't," I said. He froze, staring at me. He looked shocked, as if he hadn't thought I'd do it.

Rafael came up through the tables. "May I look at him?"

"Sure." But I backed away. Theoretically out of reach.

Rafael turned him over. Blood had pooled on the floor from the hole in his chest. Bright crimson rivulets trailed down his lips to mingle with his beard. Not faster than a speeding bullet, after all.

Marcus looked at me over the body. I had expected to see anger, but all I saw was pain. He mourned Alfred's passing. I may have pulled the trigger, but he had pushed Alfred into it. He knew it, I knew it. We all knew it.

"You didn't have to kill him," he said, softly.

"You gave me no choice," I said.

He glanced down at Alfred's body, then back to me. "No, I suppose I didn't. We killed him together, you and I."

"For future reference, so there will never be another misunderstanding between us, Marcus. I never bluff."

"So you said."

"But you didn't believe me."

He watched the blood spread across the floor. "I believe you now."

12

We had a body on the ground. The age-old question remained. What do you do with a dead body? There was the traditional approach. "I'll call the cops," I said.

"No," Marcus said. That one word had more force in it than anything he'd said since Alfred hit the ground.

"He's dead, folks. If I'd hit him with a regular bullet he'd heal, but it was silver. We've got to call the cops."

"Are you so eager to go to jail?" This from Rafael.

"I don't want to go to jail, but I killed him."

"I think you had a little help on that." Christine had moved up beside us. She stood there in her rose-petal suit with her sensible black pumps, staring down at the body. A line of blood trickled towards her shoes. She had to see it, snaking its way towards her. She didn't move out of the way. The blood seeped around the toe of her shoe and kept going.

Raina came up behind Marcus. She put her arms around his shoulders, leaning her face against his neck, close enough to whisper in his ear. Those lips did not move, but it had been her one needling comment that had pushed things over the edge. One little remark.

Marcus rubbed his hand along her arm, lowering his face to kiss her wrist.

I looked around at them. Rafael was still kneeling by the body. A line of blood was making for the knee of his slacks. He stood up quickly, fingertips brushing the bloody floor. He raised the fingers to his mouth. I wanted to say, don't, but didn't. He stuck the fingers in his mouth and sucked them clean.

His dark eyes flicked to me. He lowered his hand as if he were embarrassed, as if I'd caught him in an intimate bodily function. Maybe I had.

The two leather-clad shapeshifters drifted up behind the tables, as if they'd circle me. I backed away. I still had the guns naked in my hands. The one with the spiked glove looked at me, a smile playing at the edge of his mouth. His eyes were a strange liquid grey. His curly black hair had fallen in a tangle over his eyes. They bore a startling luminosity peering from behind that black hair. He made no move to push his hair from his eyes. It would have driven me nuts. But then maybe I wasn't accustomed to staring out through fur.

He stepped closer to the body, which was closer to me. I raised the guns. At this range you didn't really have to aim. I did not feel more confident with a gun in each hand. Fact was, I felt silly, but I didn't want to lose the time to holster one of them. To holster the Firestar, I had to scoot my sweater up and shove the gun in the inner-pants holster. I could probably do it without glancing down, but I wasn't sure. Habit might take over. Like driving a car. You don't realize how long you glanced down until that semi truck looms into view. If Gabriel was as fast as Alfred, a fraction of a second would be enough.

His smile widened, the tip of his tongue traced his full lips. His gaze had heat in it. Nothing magical, just the heat that any man could put into his eyes. That look that said they were wondering what you looked like naked, and if you'd give a good blow job. Crude, but accurate. That look was not wanting to make love to anyone. The look was pure fucking. Even sex was too mild a term.

I fought the urge to turn away. I didn't dare take my eyes off of him. But I wanted to. My skin crawled under his gaze. I felt heat creeping up my face. I couldn't meet his eyes and not blush. My Daddy'd raised me better than that.

He took a step forward, a small movement, but it put him almost in arm's reach. With Alfred's body still warm, he was playing with me. I raised the guns a little more firmly, pointed at him. "Let's not do this again," I said.

"Gabriel, leave her alone," Christine said.

He glanced back at her. " 'Tyger! Tyger! burning bright/ In the forests of the night/ What immortal hand or eye/ Could frame thy fearful symmetry?' "

"Stop it, Gabriel," she said. She was blushing. One stanza of Blake and she was embarrassed. Why that poem? A weretiger maybe? But who was the kitty cat? Maybe both.

He turned back to me. I watched something slide behind his eyes. Some streak of perversity that made him want to take that next step.

"Try me tonight, and you're going to join your friend on the floor."

He laughed, mouth wide, exposing pointed canines, top and bottom like a cat. Not fangs, but not human, either.

"Ms. Blake is under my protection," Marcus said. "You will not harm her."

"You let Alfred nearly throttle me, then you goad him into attacking me. I don't think much of your protection, Marcus. I think I do just fine on my own."

"Without those little guns you wouldn't be so tough." This from the brunette biker chick. Brave words, but she was standing on the other side of the little crowd.

"I'm not going to offer to arm wrestle you. I know I'm outclassed without a gun. That's why I've got them."

"You refuse my protection?" Marcus asked.

"Yeah," I said.

"You are a fool," Raina said.

"Maybe, but I'm still the one with the guns."

Gabriel laughed again. "She doesn't believe you can protect her, Marcus, and she's right."

"You question my dominance?"

Gabriel turned, giving me his back, staring at Marcus. "Always."

Marcus moved forward, but Raina tightened her grip on him. "We've aired enough dirty laundry in front of Ms. Blake for one night. Don't you think?"

He hesitated. Gabriel just stared at him. Finally Marcus nodded.

Gabriel gave a purring laugh and knelt down by the body. He smeared his fingers through the blood. "It cools so fast." He wiped his hand on Alfred's sweater and touched the open chest wound. He ran his hand around the edge as though he were scooping icing from a bowl. His hand came out crimson. He raised it to his mouth, blood dripping down his arm. His tongue licked along his bloody fingers.

"Stop it," Marcus said.

The woman knelt on the other side of the body. She knelt, lowering her torso, butt in the air, like lions drinking at watering holes. She lapped up the blood from the floor with quick, sure movements of her tongue.

"Jesus," I whispered.

There was movement in the room like a wind over a field of wheat. They were all out of their seats. They were all moving towards the body.

I stepped back, put the wall at my back, and began working my way towards the door. If there was going to be a feeding frenzy, I didn't want to be the only non-shapeshifter in the room. Didn't seem healthy.

"No!" Marcus's voice roared through the room. He stalked to the body, pushing everyone back without a gesture. Even Gabriel rolled back onto his left side, propped up, sitting in the blood. The woman crawled back, out of reach. Gabriel stayed within touching distance of the master werewolf. He gazed up at Marcus, but there was no fear on his face.

"We are not animals to feed on our dead."

"We are animals," Gabriel said. He raised his bloody hand towards Marcus. "Smell the blood, and tell me you don't want it."

Marcus jerked his head away, swallowing hard enough for me to hear it. Gabriel rose to his knees, pressing the blood close to Marcus's face.

He slapped the hand away, but stepped away from the body, too. "I smell the blood." His voice was very harsh when he said it, every word squeezed out through a low growl. "But I am a human being. That means I do not have to give in to my urges." He turned his back on the body, pushed his way through the crowd, having to step up on the stage to find a clear place to stand. His breathing was hard and fast, as if he'd been running as fast as he could.

I was about halfway behind the podium. I could see his face. Beads of sweat touched his skin. I had to get out of here.

The white-haired man who had spoken first, wondering what good a vampire executioner would be to them, was standing apart from the others. He was leaning against a table, arms crossed. He was watching me. From across the room, he could watch all he wanted to. I had the guns out and pointed at everybody. There wasn't anyone in this room that I wanted to be around unarmed.

I was almost at the door. I needed a free hand for the door. I was nearly the length of the room away from them. It was as far away as I could get without opening the door. I holstered the Firestar. Transferred the Browning to my right hand. I slid my left hand behind me along the wall, until I touched the doorknob. I turned the knob and opened the door a crack. I was far enough away from all of them, that I gave the room my back and opened the door wide. And stopped.

The hallway was four deep with lycanthropes. They were all staring at me with wide, haunted eyes. I pressed the Browning into the chest of the nearest one. ''Back up.''

He just stared at me as if he didn't understand what I'd said. His eyes were brown and perfectly human, but it reminded me of the look a dog gets when it's trying to understand English. It wants to understand, but just doesn't quite get it.

There was movement behind me. I slammed my back against the door, pressing it flat to the wall, gun scanning the room. If the shapeshifters in the hallway surged forward, I was gone. I could shoot some of them, but not all of them.

It was the man who'd been leaning against the table. He put his hands up to show himself unarmed, but that didn't really help. What helped was there was no sweat on his face. He didn't look glassy eyed, like the ones in the hall. He looked very . . . human.

''My name is Kaspar Gunderson. Do you need a little help?''

I glanced at the waiting horde and back to him. ''Sure.''

Kaspar smiled. ''You'll take my help, but not Marcus's?'' He seemed amused.

''Marcus doesn't offer help. He gives orders.''

''Too true.''

Rafael moved up beside him. ''None of us takes orders from Marcus. Though he would like us to.''

A sound somewhere between a moan and a howl broke from the crowd in the hall. I scooted a little farther down the wall, pointing the gun at the crowd. There were too many possible dangers, I had to pick someone to trust. Rafael and the other man seemed a better choice than the crowd.

A high ragged scream broke from inside the room. I shoved my back into the wall, and turned back to the room. What now?

I caught a glimpse of thrashing limbs through the huddled lycanthropes. The dark-haired woman threw back her head and shrieked.

''She's fighting it,'' the pale man said.

''Yes, but she will not win unless a dominant steps in to help her,'' Rafael said.

''Gabriel won't help.''

''No,'' Rafael said, ''he enjoys the show.''

''It's not full moon yet, what the hell's happening?'' I said.

''The scent of blood started it. Gabriel fed it. He and Elizabeth. Now, unless Marcus can control them, they may all turn and feed,'' Rafael said.

''And this is a bad thing?'' I asked.

Rafael just looked at me. His hands gripped his forearms so tightly the skin paled. His short-clipped fingernails bit into the skin, and tiny little half circles of blood formed under his hands. He took a deep, cleansing breath and nodded. He removed his fingers from his arms. The cuts filled with blood but only a few trickled. Minor cuts, minor pain. Pain sometimes helped keep a vamp from controlling your mind.

His voice came out strained, but clear, each word pronounced with great care, as if it took great effort just to speak. "One of the old wives' tales that is true is that a lycanthrope has to feed after shapeshifting." His eyes stared at me, drowning deep. The black had eaten all the white. His eyes sparkled like jet buttons.

"Are you about to go all furry on me?"

He shook his head. "The beast does not control me. I control myself."

The other man stood there, calmly.

"Why aren't you having problems?"

"I'm not a predator. Blood doesn't bother me."

A whimper came in from the hallway. A young man who couldn't have been more than twenty was crawling on hands and knees into the room. A low whimper was rising from his throat like a mantra.

He raised his head, sniffing the air. His head turned with a jerk, eyes staring at me. He crawled towards me. His eyes were the color of spring skies, innocent as an April morning. The look in them was not. He looked at me as if he were wondering what I tasted like. In a human I'd have thought he was thinking of sex, now . . . maybe he was just thinking of food.

I pointed the gun at his forehead. His eyes looked past the gun, at me. I wasn't even sure he saw the gun. He touched my leg. I didn't shoot him. He hadn't offered to hurt me. I wasn't sure what the hell was going on, but I couldn't shoot him for touching me. Not just for that. He had to do something to deserve a bullet in the brain. Even from me.

I moved the gun slightly from side to side in front of his eyes. They didn't track.

His hands gripped my jeans, pulling him to his knees. His head was a little above my waist, blue eyes staring up at my face. His arms wrapped around my waist. He buried his face in my stomach, sort of nuzzling.

I tapped his head with the barrel of the gun. "I don't know you well enough for you to nuzzle me, fella. Get up."

His head buried under my sweater. His mouth bit gently into my side. He stiffened, arms rigid. His breathing was suddenly ragged.

And I was suddenly afraid. One man's foreplay was another man's appetizer. "Get him off of me before I hurt him."

Rafael yelled, voice roaring over the mounting chaos, "Marcus!" That one word rang out and silence fell. Faces turned to him. Faces smeared with blood. Elizabeth, the dark-haired woman, was nowhere in sight. Only Marcus remained clean. He stood on the stage rigid, but there was a vibration to him like a struck tuning fork. His face was gaunt with some great effort. He looked at us with the eyes of a drowning man, who was determined not to scream on the last trip down.

"Jason is having some difficulty controlling himself," Rafael said. "He is your wolf. Call him off."

Gabriel stood up, his face coated in blood. He bared his flashing teeth with a laugh. "I'm surprised Ms. Blake hasn't killed him yet."

Raina stood from the kill, a patch of blood on her chin. "Ms. Blake refused Marcus's protection. She is dominant. Let her discover what it means to refuse our help."

Jason was still rigid against me. His arms locked tight, face pressed against my stomach. I could feel his breath through my shirt, hot and too heavy for what was happening.

''You asked me here for my help, Marcus. Your hospitality sucks.''

He glared at me. But even from across the room I could see a nervous tic jumping in his face. A twitching, as though something alive were trying to come out.

''It is too late for business tonight, Ms. Blake. Things are out of hand.''

''No joke. Get him off of me, Marcus. One dead tonight is enough.''

Raina went to him, holding up a bloody hand to him. ''Let her acknowledge your dominance over her. Acknowledge that she needs your help.''

Marcus stared at me. ''Acknowledge my dominance, and I will call Jason off.''

''If he starts to shapeshift, I'll kill him. You know I'll do it, Marcus. Call him off.''

''If I am to give you my protection, you must acknowledge me.''

''Fuck you, Marcus. I'm not asking you to save me. I'm asking you to save him. Or don't you care about your pack members?''

''Rafael is a king,'' Raina said, ''let him save you.''

A shudder ran through the man. His grip tightened painfully. He stood, arms still locked behind my back. If he'd held me any closer, I'd have come out the other side. He was about my height, which put our faces very close. His eyes were full of a great hunger, a need. He bent his head as if to kiss me, but another shudder ran through him. He buried his face in my hair, lips touching my neck.

I pressed the barrel of the Browning into his chest. If he tried to take a bite out of me, he was dead. But where Alfred had been a bully, this one, Jason, seemed unable to help himself, like a compulsion. If I waited too long I'd be just as dead. But until he hurt me it made me not want to hurt him. Besides, I was feeling a wee bit gun happy for killing Alfred. Not a lot, but a little. It cut Jason some slack.

His teeth brushed along my neck, drawing an edge of skin into his mouth. He had just about reached the end of my patience even if he didn't turn furry.

A low, rumbling growl vibrated along my skin. My pulse thudded into my throat. I squeezed down on the trigger. I couldn't wait for him to bite my throat out.

I heard Kaspar say, ''Rafael, no!''

Jason's head jerked up, eyes wild. Rafael stood beside us, holding his arm in front of Jason's face. Blood ran down it from deep scratches.

''Fresh blood, my wolf,'' Rafael said.

Jason jerked away from me so fast, he threw me into the wall. My head smacked the wall after my shoulders made impact, which was the only thing that saved me from passing out. I ended up with my butt on the floor, gun in my hand only by instinct. The strength in that one movement left my gut hollow with fear. I had let him nuzzle my neck, as if he were human. He could have torn me apart with his human hands. I might have killed him first, but I'd have been just as dead.

Jason crouched in front of Rafael. A ripple ran through his back like a wave of water driven by wind. Jason fell into a little ball, his back pulsing under his shirt.

Rafael stood over him, blood dripping onto the floor. ''I hope you understand what I have done for you,'' he said.

I had enough air back to speak. ''You want me to shoot him?''

A strange look came over his face, leaving his black button eyes dead. ''You offer your protection.''

''Protection, smetection. You helped me. I'll help you.''

''Thank you, but I have started it, and I must finish it, but I think you must go before you run out of silver bullets.''

Kaspar offered me a hand up; I took it. His skin was unusually warm, but that was all. He didn't seem to have the urge to touch me or eat me. A nice change.

The crowd was coming in the door, in twos and threes and tens. Some moved like sleepwalkers towards the body at the far side of the room. That was dandy. Some went for Rafael and the writhing Jason. He'd said he could handle himself. But about six of them turned to me and Kaspar.

They stared at us with hungry eyes. One, a girl, dropped to her knees and began to crawl towards me. ''Can you do anything about this?'' I asked.

''I'm a swan, they consider me food.''

It took every ounce of self-control not to glance at him. I stared at the crawling lycanthrope, and said, ''A swan, great. You got any suggestions?''

''Wound one of them. They respect pain.''

The girl was reaching out for me. I stared at her slender arm and didn't fire. Glazer safety rounds could take off an arm. I wasn't sure lycanthropes could heal amputations. I pointed over her head at the large male behind her. I gut-shot him. He fell screaming to the floor, blood pouring between his fingers. The girl turned on him, burying her face in his stomach.

He slapped her away. The others surged forward.

''Let's get out while we can,'' Kaspar said. He motioned for the door.

Didn't have to ask me twice. Marcus was suddenly there. I hadn't seen him come, too busy concentrating on the immediate threat. He pulled two men off the wounded one, tossing them like toys. He drew a manila file folder from under his blue linen jacket and handed it to me. In a voice that was more growl than anything, he said, ''Kaspar can answer your questions.''

He turned with a snarl, tearing into the lycanthropes, protecting the one I'd wounded. Kaspar pushed me out the door, and I let him.

I had one last glimpse of Jason. He was a mass of flowing fur and naked dripping bones. Rafael was once again the slick, black ratman I'd met months ago. The crown-shaped burn in his forearm, the mark of kingship for the rats, showed clean. He was no longer bleeding. The change had healed him.

The door slammed shut. I wasn't sure who had done it. Kaspar and I stood in the hallway, alone. There were no sounds from behind the door. The silence was so heavy, it thrummed in my head.

''I can't hear them?''

''Soundproof room,'' he said.

Logical. I stared down at the file folder. There was a bloody handprint on it. I held it gingerly at the edge, waiting for the blood to dry.

''Are we supposed to sit down and have a business meeting?''

"Knowing Marcus, the information will be complete. He's a very good bureaucrat."

"But not a very good pack leader."

He glanced at the door. "I'd say that somewhere else if I were you."

He had a point. I stared up at him. His baby-fine hair was nearly white, almost feathery. I shook my head. It couldn't be.

He grinned at me. "Go ahead. Touch it."

I did. I brushed fingers through his hair, and it was soft and downy like the under feathers on a bird. Heat rose from his scalp like fever. "Jesus."

Something heavy smacked into the door. I felt the vibrations through the floor. I backed away, hesitating about putting the Browning away. I compromised and put my hand in the pocket of my trench coat. It was the only coat I owned with pockets deep enough to swallow the Browning.

Kaspar opened the door to the dining rooms. There were still people eating. Humans out for a night on the town. Carving their steaks, eating their veggies, oblivious to the potential destruction just two doors away.

I had a horrible urge to yell, Flee, flee for your lives. But they wouldn't have understood. Besides the Lunatic Cafe had been here for years. I'd never heard of an incident here. Of course, I'd killed one man, werewolf, whatever. I didn't think there was going to be enough evidence to turn over to the cops. Maybe a few well-gnawed bones.

Who knew what disasters had been covered up here?

Kaspar handed me a business card. It was white and shiny with Gothic script that said, KASPAR GUNDERSON, ANTIQUES AND COLLECTIBLES.

"If you have any questions, I will try to answer them."

"Even if the questions are about what the hell you are?"

"Even that," he said.

We were walking as we talked. He offered me his hand beside the bar in the outer dining room. The outside door was in sight, fun almost over for the night. Thank God.

My smile froze on my face. I knew one of the men at the bar. Edward was sitting there sipping a tall, cold drink. He never glanced at me, but I knew he saw me. Kaspar cocked his head to one side. "Is anything wrong?"

"No," I said, "no." My words were too fast, even I didn't believe myself. I tried my best professional smile. "It's just been a long night."

He didn't believe me, and I didn't care. I wasn't good at spur-of-the-moment lying. Kaspar let it go, but his eyes scanned the crowd as he walked out, looking for whatever or whoever had bothered me.

Edward looked like a nice, ordinary man. He was five foot eight, of slender build, with short blond hair. He had on a nondescript black winter jacket, jeans, and soft-soled shoes. He looked a little like Marcus, and in his own way, was just as dangerous.

He was ignoring me, effortlessly, which meant he might not want to be noticed. I walked past him, wanting to ask what the hell he was doing here, but not wanting to blow his cover. Edward was an assassin who specialized in vampires, lycanthropes, and other preternatural humanoids. He'd started out killing humans, but it had been too easy. Edward did love a challenge.

I stood in the cold dark wondering what to do. I had the bloody file folder in one hand. The other was still gripping the Browning. Now that the adrenaline was seeping away, my hand was cramping around the gun. I'd held it too long without firing it. I tucked the folder under my arm and put the gun away. All the shapeshifters were busy eating each other. I could probably walk to my car without having a gun naked in my hands.

Edward didn't come out. I had half expected him to. He was hunting someone, but who? After what I'd seen tonight, I wasn't sure hunting them was such a bad idea.

Of course, Richard was one of them. I didn't want anyone hunting him. I would have to ask Edward what he was doing, but not tonight. Richard wasn't inside. The rest of them could take their chances. I had a momentary thought about Rafael, but let it go. He knew what Edward looked like, if not exactly what he did for a living.

I stopped halfway down the sidewalk. Should I warn Edward that Rafael might recognize him and tell the others? My head hurt. For this one night let Death take care of himself. The vampires called me the Executioner, but they called Edward Death. After all, I'd never used a flamethrower on them.

I kept walking. Edward was a big, scary boy. He could take care of himself. And everyone else in the back room certainly didn't need my help.

Even if they did, I wasn't sure I wanted to give it to them. Which brought me back to the file folder. What could they need my help for? What could I do that they couldn't? I almost didn't want to know. But I didn't throw the folder in the nearest trash can. Truth was, if I didn't read it, it would bug me. Curiosity killed the cat. Here was hoping it didn't do the same for animators.

13

At 5:35 that morning I was tucked in bed with the file folder. My favorite stuffed toy penguin, Sigmund, was sitting next to me. It used to be that I used Sigmund only when people were trying to kill me. Lately, I'd been sleeping with him most of the time. It'd been a rough year.

The Browning Hi-Power was in its second home, a holster on the headboard of the bed. I sometimes slept without the penguin, but never without the gun.

The folder consisted of a half dozen sheets of paper. All neatly typed, double spaced. The first was a list of eight names with an animal designation beside them. The last two pages were an explanation of the names. Eight lycanthropes had gone missing. Vanished. No bodies, no signs of violence. Nothing. Their families knew nothing. None of the lycanthropes knew anything.

I went back over the names. Margaret Smitz was number seven. Designation wolf. Could it be George Smitz's wife? Peggy was a nickname for Margaret. Don't ask me how you get Peggy from Margaret, but you do.

The last few pages were suggestions about who Marcus thought I should talk to. Controlling little bastard. He did offer an explanation for why he asked me for help. He thought that the other shapeshifters would talk more freely to me than to him or any of his wolves. No joke. I was sort of a compromise. They didn't trust the police. And who else do the lunarly disadvantaged go to for help? Why, your friendly neighborhood animator.

I wasn't sure what I could do for them. I had sent George Smitz to Ronnie for a reason. I was not a detective. I'd never handled a missing-person case in my life. When I met Ronnie the next day, cancel that, that morning, I'd fill her in. George's wife missing was one thing, but eight lycanthropes missing was a pattern. They needed to go to the police. But they didn't trust human law. As late as the 1960s, lycanthropes were still being mobbed and burned at the stake. Couldn't blame them for being leery.

I put the folder in the drawer of the nightstand. I got a plain white business card out of the drawer. The only thing on it was a phone number. Edward had given me the card only two months ago. It was the first time I'd ever been able to contact him. Before he'd just shown up. Usually when I didn't want him to.

The number was a twenty-four-hour phone message service. A mechanized voice said, "At the tone leave your message." A long, low beep sounded. "This is Anita. What the hell are you doing in town? Call me soon." I wasn't usually that blunt on a phone message, but hey, it was Edward. He knew me. Besides, he didn't appreciate social niceties.

I set the alarm, turned off the light, and cuddled into the blankets, my faithful penguin at my side. The phone rang before I'd gotten warm. I waited for the machine to pick up; after the eighth ring I gave up. I'd forgotten to turn on the machine. Great.

"This better be important," I said.

"You said to call soon." It was Edward.

I pulled the receiver under the blankets with me. "Hi, Edward."

"Hi."

"Why are you in town? And why were you at the Lunatic Cafe?"

"Why were you?"

"It is nearly six in the freaking morning, I haven't been to sleep yet. I don't have time for games."

"What was in the folder you had? There was fresh blood on it. Whose blood was it?"

I sighed. I wasn't sure what to tell him. He might be a great deal of help, or he could kill people that I was supposed to be helping. Choices, choices.

"I can't tell you shit until I know if I'm endangering people."

"I never hunt people, you know that."

"So you are on a hunt."

"Yes."

"What this time?"

"Shapeshifters."

Figures. "Who?"

"I don't have any names yet."

"Then how do you know who to kill?"

"I've got film."

"Film?"

"Come to my hotel room tomorrow and I'll show you the film. I'll tell you everything I know."

"You're not usually this obliging. What's the catch?"

"No catch. You might be able to identify them, that's all."

"I don't know a lot of shapeshifters," I said.

"Fine, just come, see what I have."

He sounded so sure of himself, but then he always did. "Okay, where are you staying?"

"Adams Mark. Do you need directions?"

"No, I can get there. When?"

"Do you work tomorrow?"

"Yeah."

"Then at your convenience, of course."

He was being too damn polite. "How long will your little presentation take?"

"Two hours, maybe less."

I shook my head, realized he couldn't see it, and said, "It'll have to be after my last zombie appointment. I'm booked until then."

"Name the time."

"I can be there between twelve-thirty and one." Even saying it made me tired. I wasn't going to get any sleep again.

"I'll be waiting."

"Wait. What name are you registered under?"

"Room 212, just knock."

"You do have a last name, don't you?"

"Of course. Good night, Anita." The phone line went dead, buzzing in my hand like an unquiet spirit. I fumbled the receiver into its cradle and switched on the answering machine. I turned the sound down as low as it would go and snuggled back under the covers.

Edward never shared information unless forced to. He was being too helpful. Something was up. Knowing Edward, it was something unpleasant. Lycanthropes disappearing without a trace. It sounded like a game that Edward would enjoy. But somehow I didn't think it was him. He liked taking credit for his kills as long as the police couldn't tie him to them directly.

But somebody was doing it. There were bounty hunters who specialized in rogue lycanthropes. Edward might know who they were and if they'd condone murder. Because if all eight were dead, then it was murder. None of them was wanted, as far as I knew. The police would know, but I wasn't going to involve the police. Dolph should know if lycanthropes were disappearing in his territory.

I felt sleep sucking at the edges of the world. I flashed on the murder victim. I saw his face frozen in the snow, one eye ripped open like a grape. The crushed jaw tried to move, to speak. One word hissed out of his ruined mouth: "Anita." My name, over and over. I woke up enough to roll over, and sleep washed over me in a heavy, black wave. If I dreamed again, I never remembered.

14

Every year I wondered what to buy Judith, my stepmother, for Christmas. You'd think after fourteen years I'd get better. Of course, you'd think she'd get better at buying for me. Judith and I always end up staring at each other across this chasm of misunderstanding. She wants me to be this perfect feminine daughter, and I want her to be my dead mother. Since I can't have what I want, I've made sure Judith doesn't get her wish, either. Besides, she's got Andria, who is perfect. One perfect kid in the family is enough.

Ronnie and I were Christmas shopping. We had jogged on the slick wintery streets at nine that morning. I'd managed about three hours of sleep. The running helped. The freezing wind slapping my face helped even more. I was wide awake and temporarily energized when we hit the mall, hair still damp from the shower.

Ronnie is five foot nine. Her short blond hair is cut in a sort of pageboy. It's the same haircut she's had since I met her, but then my hairstyle hasn't changed, either. She was wearing jeans, cowboy boots with purple tooling, a short winter coat over a lilac crewneck sweater. She was not wearing a gun. Didn't think the mall elves would get that out of hand.

I was dressed for the office, because I'd need to go straight there from shopping. The skirt was a standard navy blue, with a black belt for my shoulder holster to slip through. The skirt was about two inches higher than I was comfortable with, but Ronnie had insisted. She's a tad more fashion conscious than I am. Then, who isn't? The jacket was a rich midnight blue, the color of Jean-Claude's eyes. Darker blue designs, nearly black, traced it in a vaguely Oriental pattern. The open-necked blouse was a blue that matched the jacket. With black high-heel pumps, I looked pretty snazzy. Ronnie had picked out the jacket, too. Its only fault was that it didn't hide the Browning as well. You got little flashes of it as I moved. So far no one had run screaming to the mall cops. If they'd had known I was wearing a knife on each forearm under the pretty jacket, maybe they would have.

Ronnie was staring into a jewelry case at Krigle's, and I was staring at her eyes. They were grey. The same color that Gabriel's eyes had been last night, but there was something different. Her eyes were human. Even in human form Gabriel's eyes weren't human.

''What's wrong?''

I shook my head. ''Thinking about last night.''

''How do you feel about loverboy after last night?'' The jewelry store was three deep in people. We'd forced our way to the case, but I knew I wasn't buying anything here, so I sort of stood beside Ronnie, scanning the crowd. All the faces looked hostile, but it was nothing personal. They were Christmas shopping with two weeks to the big day. Ho, ho, ho.

The store was a mass of shoving, jostling people. I was getting claustrophobic. ''Are you going to buy something?''

Ronnie looked up at me. ''You never answered my question.''

''Get me out of this mess and maybe I will.''

She stood up and motioned me forward. I cleared us a path to the open mall. I'm small and was dressed too pretty to be intimidating, but people cleared a path. Maybe they saw the gun. When we were in the main open space, I took a deep breath. It was crowded but nothing like the stores. At least here, people weren't actually brushing against me. If they did it out here, I could yell at them.

''You want to sit down?'' There were miraculously two seats open on a bench. Ronnie had made the offer because I was dressed for work, which meant heels. In her comfy jogging shoes she didn't need to sit. My feet didn't hurt yet. Maybe I was getting used to wearing heels. Eeek.

I shook my head. ''Let's hit the Nature Company. Maybe I'll find Josh something there.''

''How old is he now, thirteen?'' Ronnie asked.

''Fifteen,'' I said. ''My baby brother was my height last year. He'll be gigantic this year. Judith says he's outgrowing his jeans faster than she can buy them.''

''A hint to buy him jeans?'' Ronnie said.

''If it is, I'm ignoring it. I'm buying Josh something fun, not clothes.''

''A lot of teenagers would rather have clothes,'' Ronnie said.

''Not Josh, not yet anyway. He seems to have taken after me.''

''What are you going to do about Richard?'' she asked me.

''You're not going to let it go, are you?''

''Not a chance.''

''I don't know what I'm going do. After what I saw last night. After what Jean-Claude told me. I just don't know.''

''You know that Jean-Claude did it deliberately,'' she said. ''To try and drive a wedge between you.''

''I know, and it worked. I feel like I don't know Richard. Like I've been kissing a stranger.''

''Don't let fang-face break you up.''

I smiled at that. Jean-Claude would love being referred to as fang-face. ''I won't.''

She punched my shoulder softly. ''I don't believe you.''

''It won't be Jean-Claude that breaks us up, Ronnie. If Richard's been lying to me for months . . .'' I didn't finish the sentence. I didn't have to.

We were outside the Nature Company. It was crawling with people like a jar of lightning bugs abuzz with activity, but not half as bright.

"What exactly has Richard lied about?"

"He didn't tell me about this battle he's got going with Marcus."

"And you tell him everything," she said.

"Well, no."

"He hasn't lied to you, Anita. He just didn't tell you. Let him explain. Maybe he's got a good reason."

I turned and looked full at her. Her face was all soft with concern. It made me look away. "He's been in danger for months, and didn't tell me. I needed to know."

"Maybe he couldn't tell you. You won't know until you ask him."

"I saw lycanthropes last night, Ronnie." I shook my head. "What I saw last night wasn't human. It wasn't even close."

"So he's not human. No one's perfect."

I looked at her then. She was smiling at me. I had to smile back. "I'll talk to him."

"Call him before we leave the mall and set up a dinner for today."

"You are so pushy," I said.

She shrugged. "I've learned from the best."

"Thanks," I said. "What have you learned from George Smitz?"

"Nothing new to add to the folder you showed me. Except he doesn't seem to know that his wife is one of eight missing shapeshifters. He thinks she's the only one. I got a picture of her. You need pictures of the others. First thing you need in a missing-person case is a picture. Without a picture you could pass them on the street and not know it."

"I'll ask Kaspar about pictures."

"Not Richard?"

"I'm sort of mad at him. I don't want to ask him for help."

"You're being petty."

"It's one of my best traits."

"I'll check out the usual channels for a missing person, but if they're all lycanthropes, I bet it isn't a missing person."

"You think they're dead?"

"Don't you?"

"Yeah."

"But what could take out eight shapeshifters without a trace?" she asked.

"That's got me worried, too." I touched her arm. "You wear your gun from now on."

She smiled. "I promise, Mommy."

I shook my head. "Shall we brave one more store? If I can get Josh's gift, I'll be halfway done."

"You'll have to buy Richard a present, you know."

"What?"

"You have to buy your steady a gift. It's traditional."

"Shit." I was halfway mad at him, but she was right. Fighting or not, I had to buy him something. What if he bought me something, and I didn't? I'd feel guilty. If I bought something and he didn't, then I could feel superior. Or angry. I was almost hoping he wouldn't buy me anything.

Was I looking for an excuse to dump Richard? Maybe. Of course, maybe after we talked he'd give me a good excuse on a silver, excuse me, golden platter. I was ready for a knock-down, drag-out fight. It did not bode well.

15

My one o'clock appointment was with Elvira Drew. She sipped her coffee, elegant fingernails curled around the mug. Her nail polish was clear, making her fingertips glint like abalone shell; colorless until the light hit it. The rest of her was just as tasteful. Her dress was that interesting color that looked blue one minute and green the next. Blue-green they called it, but it wasn't accurate. The dress was almost green. For cloth to have that shimmer, almost a life of its own like fur, it had to be expensive. The dress was probably worth more than my entire wardrobe.

Her long yellow hair spilled down her back in an elegant line. It was the only thing that didn't match. That dress, the manicure, the dyed-to-match shoes, the nearly invisible makeup should have gone with a tasteful but complicated hairdo. I liked her better for the hair being free and nearly untouched.

When she raised her eyes to meet mine, I knew why she'd spent so much on the dress. Her eyes were the same startling blue-green. The combination was breathtaking.

I sat across from her, sipping my coffee, happy I'd dressed up. Most days she'd have made me feel like a country cousin. Today I could hold my own.

"What can I do for you today, Ms. Drew?"

She smiled, and the smile was all it should have been. She smiled like she knew the effect it had on most people. I was almost afraid to see her near a man. If she lit up this much for me, the thought of what she'd do around Jamison or Manny was kind of frightening.

"I'm a writer. I'm working on a book about shapeshifters."

My smile wilted around the edges. "Really. And what brings you to the offices of Animators, Inc.?"

"The book is set up with each chapter being a different animal form. I give history, any well-known shapeshifters of that form from history, then a personal profile of a present-day shapeshifter."

My face was beginning to hurt, and I knew my smile was more a baring of teeth than anything else. "Sounds like an interesting book. Now, how can I help you?"

She blinked gorgeous eyes at me and looked puzzled. She was good at looking puzzled. I'd seen the intelligence in her eyes a moment ago. The dumb-blonde routine was an act. Would it have worked if I were a man? I hoped not.

"I'm missing one interview. I need to find a wererat. The interview can be strictly confidential." The dumb blonde was gone as quickly as it had come. She'd seen I wasn't buying it.

The interview can be—not would—be confidential. I sighed and gave up on the smile. "What made you think I could find you a wererat?"

"Mr. Vaughn assured me that if anyone in this area could help me, it would be you."

"Did he really?"

She smiled, eyes glittering. "He seemed very sure you could help me."

"My boss promises a lot of things, Ms. Drew. Most of which he doesn't have to deliver." I stood. "If you could wait here for just a moment, I want to confer with Mr. Vaughn."

"I'll wait right here for you." Her smile was just as sweet, but something in her eyes let me know she knew exactly what kind of conferring I had in mind.

The outer office was done in pale greens, from the wallpaper, with its thin Oriental designs, to the foamy carpet. Plants flourished in every unoccupied niche. Bert thought the plants gave the office a homey touch. I thought it looked like a cheap jungle set.

Mary, our daytime secretary, glanced up from her computer keyboard with a smile. Mary was over fifty, with blond hair that was a little too yellow to be natural. "You need something, Anita?" Her smile was pleasant. I'd almost never seen her in a bad mood. It was a good personality trait for a receptionist.

"Yeah, to see the boss."

She cocked her head to one side, eyes suddenly wary. "Why?"

"I should have an appointment to see Bert today, anyway. I told Craig to schedule it."

She glanced through the appointment book. "Craig did, and Bert canceled it." The smile was gone. "He really is very busy today."

That was it. I went for Bert's door.

"He's with a client right now," Mary said.

"Peachy," I said. I knocked on the door and opened it without waiting for permission.

Bert's desk took up most of the pale blue office. It was the smallest of the three offices, but it was permanently his. The rest of us had to rotate. He'd played football in college and it still showed. Broad shoulders, strong hands, six feet four inches tall and aware of every inch. His boater's tan had washed away with the winter weather. His white crew cut seemed a little less dramatic against the paler skin.

His eyes are the color of dirty window glass, sort of grey. Those eyes glared at me now. "I'm with a client, Anita."

I spared a glance for the man sitting across from him. It was Kaspar Gunderson. He was dressed all in white today, and it emphasized everything. How I could have ever looked at him and thought him human was beyond me. He smiled. ''Ms. Blake, I presume.'' He put out a hand.

I shook it. ''If you could wait outside for just a few moments, Mr. . . .''

''Gunderson,'' he said.

''Mr. Gunderson, I need to speak with Mr. Vaughn.''

''I think it can wait, Anita,'' Bert said.

''No,'' I said, ''it can't.''

''Yes,'' he said, ''it can.''

''Do you want to have this particular talk in front of a client, Bert?''

He stared at me, his small grey eyes looking even smaller as he squinted at me. It was his mean look. It had never worked on me. He gave a tight smile. ''Are you insisting?''

''You got it.''

He took a long, deep breath and let it out slowly, as if he were counting to ten. His flashed his best professional smile on Kaspar. ''If you will excuse us for a few minutes, Mr. Gunderson. This won't take long.''

Kaspar stood, nodded at me, and left. I closed the door behind him.

''What the hell are you doing coming in here while I'm talking to a client?'' He stood up, and his broad shoulders nearly touched from wall to wall.

He should have known better than to try and intimidate me with size. I've been the smallest kid on the block for as long as I can remember. Size hadn't been impressive for a very long time.

''I told you no more clients that are outside my job description.''

''Your job description is anything I say it is. I'm your boss, remember?'' He leaned over his desk, palms flat.

I leaned into the desk on the other side. ''You sent me a missing person's case last night. What the fuck do I know about missing persons?''

''His wife's a lycanthrope.''

''And that means we should take his money?''

''If you can help him, yes.''

''Well, I gave it to Ronnie.''

Bert leaned back. ''See, you did help him. He would never have found Ms. Sims without your help.''

He was looking all reasonable again. I didn't want him reasonable. ''I've got Elvira Drew in my office right now. What the hell am I supposed to do with her?''

''Do you know any wererats?'' He had sat down, hands crossed over his slightly bulging middle.

''That's beside the point.''

''You do, don't you?''

''And if I say yes?''

''Set up an interview. Surely one of them wants to be famous.''

''Most lycanthropes go to a lot of trouble to hide what they are. Being outed endangers their jobs, marriages. There was that case in Indiana last year where a father lost his kids to his ex-wife after five years, because she found out he was a shapeshifter. No one wants to risk that kind of exposure.''

''I've seen shifters interviewed on live television,'' he said.

''They're the exceptions, Bert, not the rule.''

''So you won't help Ms. Drew?''

''No, I won't.''

''I won't try and appeal to your sense of greed, though she has offered us a lot of money. But think what a positive book on lycanthropy would do to help your shapeshifting friends. Good press is always welcome. Before you turn her down, talk to your friends. See what they say.''

''You don't give a damn about good exposure for the lycanthrope community. You're just excited about the money.''

''True.''

Bert was an unscrupulous bastard and didn't care who knew it. It was hard to win a fight when you couldn't insult someone. I sat down across from him. He looked pleased with himself, like he knew he'd won. He should have known better.

''I don't like sitting down across from clients and not knowing what the hell they want. No more surprises. You clear clients with me first.''

''Anything you say.''

''You're being reasonable. What's wrong?''

His smile widened, setting his little eyes sparkling. ''Mr. Gunderson has offered us a lot of money for your services. Twice the normal fee.''

''That's a lot of money. What does he want me to do?''

''Raise an ancestor from the dead. He's under a family curse. A witch told him if he could talk to the ancestor that the curse originated with, she might be able to lift it.''

''Why double the fee?''

''The curse started with one of two brothers. He doesn't know which one.''

''So I have to raise them both.''

''If we're lucky, only one.''

''But you keep the second fee anyway,'' I said.

Bert nodded vigorously, happy as a greedy clam. ''It's even your job description, and besides, even you wouldn't let a fellow go through his life with feathers on his head if you could help him, now would you?''

''You smug bastard,'' I said, but my voice sounded tired even to me.

Bert just smiled. He knew he'd won.

''You'll clear clients with me that aren't zombie raisings or vampire slayings?'' I said.

''If you have the time to read up on every client I see, then I certainly have time to write up a report.''

''I don't need to read about every client, just the ones you're sending my way.''

''But, Anita, you know it's just luck of the draw which of you is on duty on any given day.''

''Damn you, Bert.''

''You've kept Ms. Drew waiting long enough, don't you think?''

I stood up. It was no use. I was outmaneuvered. He knew it. I knew it. The only thing left was a graceful retreat.

''Your two o'clock canceled. I'll have Mary send Gunderson in.''

"Is there anything you wouldn't schedule in as a client, Bert?"

He seemed to think about that for a minute, then shook his head. "If they could pay the fee, no."

"You are a greedy son of a bitch."

"I know."

It was no use. I wasn't winning this one. I went for the door.

"You're wearing a gun." He sounded outraged.

"Yeah, what of it?"

"I think you can meet clients in broad daylight at our offices without being armed."

"I don't think so."

"Just put the gun in the desk drawer like you used to."

"Nope." I opened the door.

"I don't want you meeting clients armed, Anita."

"Your problem, not mine."

"I could make it yours," he said. His face was flushed, voice tight with anger. Maybe we were going to get to fight after all.

I closed the door. "You mean fire me?"

"I am your boss."

"We can argue about clients, but the gun is not negotiable."

"The gun frightens clients."

"Send the squeamish ones to Jamison," I said.

"Anita"—he stood up like an angry storm—"I don't want you wearing the gun in the office."

I smiled sweetly. "Fuck you, Bert." So much for a graceful exit.

16

I closed the door and realized I had accomplished nothing but pissing Bert off. Not a bad hour's work, but not a great accomplishment. I was going to tell Ms. Drew that I might be able to help her. Bert was right about good press. I nodded at Gunderson as I passed him. He smiled back. Somehow I didn't think he really wanted me to raise the dead. I'd find out soon enough.

Ms. Drew was sitting legs crossed, hands folded in her lap. The picture of elegant patience.

"I may be able to help you, Ms. Drew. I'm not sure, but I may know someone who can help you."

She stood up, offering me a manicured hand. "That would be wonderful, Ms. Blake. I certainly appreciate your help."

"Does Mary have a number where I can reach you?"

"Yes." She smiled.

I smiled. I opened the door, and she walked past me in a cloud of expensive perfume. "Mr. Gunderson, I can see you now."

He stood, laying the magazine he'd been leafing through on the small table beside the *Ficus benjium*. He didn't move with that dancelike grace that the other shapeshifters had. But then swans weren't particularly graceful on land.

"Have a seat, Mr. Gunderson."

"Please, Kaspar."

I leaned on the edge of the desk, staring down at him. "What are you doing here, Kaspar?"

He smiled. "Marcus wants to apologize for last night."

"Then he should have come in person."

His smiled widened. "He thought that offering a sizable monetary reward might make up for our lack of hospitality last night."

"He was wrong."

"You aren't going to give an inch, are you?"

"Nope."

"Are you not going to help us?"

I sighed. ''I'm working on it. But I'm not sure what I can do. What or who could take out eight shapeshifters without a struggle?''

''I have no idea. None of us do. That is why we have come to you.''

Great. They knew less than I did. Not comforting. ''Marcus gave me a list of people to question.'' I handed it to him. ''Any thoughts, or additions?''

He frowned, eyebrows arching together. The white eyebrows were not hair. I blinked, trying to concentrate. The fact that he was feathery seemed to bother me a lot more than it should have.

''These are all rivals for Marcus's power. You met most of them at the cafe.''

''Do you really think he suspects them, or is he just making trouble for his rivals?'' I asked.

''I don't know.''

''Marcus said you could answer my questions. Do you actually know anything that I don't?''

''I would say that I know a great deal more about the shapeshifting community than you do,'' he said. He sounded a trifle offended.

''Sorry, I think it's just wishful thinking on Marcus's part that his rivals are the bad guys. Not your fault he's playing games.''

''Marcus often tries to manage things. You saw that last night.''

''His management skills haven't impressed me so far.''

''He believes that if there were one ruler for all shapeshifters, we would be a force to rival the vampires.''

He might be right on that. ''He wants to be that ruler,'' I said.

''Of course.''

The intercom buzzed. ''Excuse me a minute.'' I hit the button. ''What is it, Mary?''

''Richard Zeeman on line two. He says he's returning your message.''

I hesitated, then said, ''I'll take it.'' I picked up the phone, very aware that Kaspar was sitting there listening. I could have asked him to step outside, but I was getting tired of playing musical clients.

''Hi, Richard.''

''I got your message on my answering machine,'' he said. His voice was very careful, as if he were balancing a glass of water filled to the very brim.

''I think we need to talk,'' I said.

''I agree.''

My, weren't we being cautious this afternoon. ''I'm supposed to be the one that's mad. Why does your voice sound so funny?''

''I heard about last night.''

I waited for him to say more, but the silence just stretched to infinity. I filled it. ''Look, I have a client with me right now. You want to meet and talk?''

''Very much.'' He said it as though he weren't really looking forward to it.

''I have a dinner break around six. You want to meet at the Chinese place on Olive?''

''Doesn't sound very private.''

''What did you have in mind?''

''My place.''

''I only get an hour, Richard. I don't have time to drive that far.''

''Your place, then.''

''No.''

''Why not?''

''Just no.''

''What we need to say to each other isn't going to go over well in public. You know that.''

I did. Dammit. ''All right, we'll meet at my place a little after six. Do you want me to pick up something?''

''You're at work. It'll be easier for me to pick up something. You want mooshu pork and crab ragoon?''

''Yeah.'' We'd dated enough that he could order food for me without asking. But he asked anyway. Brownie point for him.

''I'll see you at about six-fifteen then,'' he said.

''See you.''

''Bye, Anita.''

''Bye.'' We hung up. My stomach was one hard knot of dread. If we were going to have ''the'' fight, the breakup fight, I didn't want to have it at my apartment, but Richard was right. We didn't want to be screaming about lycanthropes and killing people in a public restaurant. Still, it was not going to be a good time.

''Is Richard angry about last night?'' Kaspar asked.

''Yeah.''

''Is there anything I can do to help?''

''I need the complete stories about the disappearances: struggles, who last saw them, that sort of thing.''

''Marcus said all questions directly about the disappearances should be answered only by him.''

''You always do what he says?''

''Not always, but he's quite adamant about this, Anita. I am not a predator. I cannot defend myself against Marcus at his worst.''

''Would he really kill you for going against his wishes?''

''Perhaps not kill me, but I would be hurting for a very, very long time.''

I shook my head. ''He doesn't sound any better than most master vampires I know.''

''I don't personally know any master vampires. I am forced to take your word for that.''

I had to smile. I knew more monsters than the monsters did. ''Would Richard know?''

''Perhaps, and if not, he could help you find out.''

I wanted to ask him if Richard was as bad as Marcus. I wanted to know if my sweetie was really a beast at heart. I didn't ask. If I wanted to know about Richard, I should ask Richard.

''Unless you have more information, Kaspar, I have work to do.'' It sounded grumpy even to me. I smiled to try to soften it but didn't take it back. I wanted this whole mess to go away, and he was a reminder of it.

He stood. ''If you need any assistance, please call.''

"You'll only be able to give me the assistance Marcus okays, right?"

A slight flush colored his pale skin, a pink glow like colored sugar. "I am afraid so."

"I don't think I'll be calling," I said.

"You don't trust Marcus?"

I laughed, but it was harsh, not amused. "Do you?"

He smiled, and gave a slight nod of his head. "I suppose not." He moved for the door.

I had my hand on the doorknob when I turned and asked, "Is it really a family curse?"

"My affliction?"

"Yeah."

"Not a family one, but a curse, yes."

"Like in the fairy tale?" I said.

"Fairy tale sounds like such a gentle thing. The original stories are often quite gruesome."

"I've read some of them."

"Have you read *The Swan Princess* in its original Norse?"

"Can't say I have."

"It's even worse in the original language."

"Sorry to hear that," I said.

"So am I." He stepped closer to the door, and I had to open it to let him go. I dearly wanted to hear the story from his own lips, but there was a pain in his eyes that was raw enough to cut skin. I couldn't press against that much pain.

He stepped past me. I let him go. I was really going to have to find my textbook on fairy tales as truth from that comparative literature class. It had been a long time since I'd read *The Swan Princess*.

17

It was more like six-thirty by the time I walked down the hallway to my apartment. I had half expected to see Richard sitting in the hall, but it was empty. The tightness in my stomach eased just a bit. A reprieve, even of a few minutes, was still a reprieve.

I had my keys in the door when the door behind me opened. I dropped the keys, leaving them dangling. My right hand went for the Browning. It was instinct, not something I thought about. My hand was on the butt, but I hadn't drawn it when Mrs. Pringle appeared in the door. I eased my hand away from the gun and smiled. I don't think she realized what I was doing because her smile never faltered.

She was tall and thin with age. Her white hair was wrapped in a bun at the nape of her neck. Mrs. Pringle never wore makeup and never apologized for being over sixty. She seemed to enjoy being old.

''Anita, you're running a little late tonight,'' she said. Custard, her Pomeranian, yapped in the background like a stuck record.

I frowned at her. Six-thirty was early for me to get home. Before I could say anything, Richard appeared behind her in the doorway. His hair fell around his face in a mass of rich brown waves. He was wearing one of my favorite sweaters. It was solid forest green and squishy soft to the touch. Custard was barking at him, inches away from his leg, as if working up courage for a quick nip.

''Custard, stop that,'' Mrs. Pringle said. She looked up at Richard. ''I've never seen him behave like this around anyone. Anita can tell you that he likes almost everyone.'' She looked to me for support, embarrassed about her dog being rude to a guest.

I nodded. ''You're right. I've never seen him act like this before.'' I was looking at Richard. His face was as closed and careful as I'd ever seen it.

''He acts like this around other dogs sometimes, tries to boss them,'' she said. ''Do you have a dog, Mr. Zeeman? Maybe Custard smells him on you.''

''No,'' Richard said, ''I don't have a dog.''

''I found your beau sitting in the hall with his sack of food. I thought he might like to wait inside. I'm sorry that Custard has made the visit so unpleasant.''

"I always enjoy talking shop with another teacher," he said.

"So polite," she said. Her face had broken into a wonderful smile. She'd only met Richard once or twice in the hall, but she liked him. Even before she found out he was a teacher. Snap judgment.

Richard stepped around her into the hall. Custard followed him, yipping furiously. The dog looked like an overly ambitious dandelion. But it was a pissed dandelion. The dog bounced forward on tiny feet, giving a little hop with each bark.

"Custard, get back in here."

I held the door open for Richard. He had a white take-out sack and a coat in his arms. The dog gave a running bound, darting in to nip his ankle. Richard looked down at the dog. Custard stopped a nose away from his pants leg. He rolled eyes upward, a look in his doggy eyes that I'd never seen before. A considering look as if he wondered if Richard really would eat him.

Richard slipped through the door. Custard just stood there in the hallway, as subdued as I'd ever seen him. "Thanks for looking after Richard, Mrs. Pringle."

"My pleasure. He's a nice young man," she said. Her tone of voice said more than the words. "Nice young man" meant marry him. My stepmother, Judith, would agree with her. Except that Judith would have said it out loud, no hinting.

I smiled and closed the door. Custard started yapping at the door. I locked the door out of habit and turned to face the music.

Richard had draped his leather coat across the back of the couch. The take-out sack was sitting on the small kitchenette table. He lifted out cartons of food. I put my coat on the back of the couch by his and slipped off the high heels. I lost about two inches of height and felt much better.

"Nice jacket," he said. His voice was still neutral.

"Thanks." I had been going to take the jacket off, but he liked it, so I kept it on. Silly, but true. We were both being so careful. The tension in the room was choking.

I got plates out of the cabinet. I got a cold Coke from the fridge for me and poured a glass of water for Richard. He didn't like carbonated beverages. I'd taken to keeping a jug of cold water in the fridge just for him. My throat felt tight as I set the drinks on the table.

He set out silverware. We moved around my minuscule kitchen like dancers, knowing where each would be, never bumping unless it was on purpose. Tonight there was no touching. We left the lights off. The only light was from the living room, leaving the kitchen in semidarkness like a cave. It was almost as if neither one of us wanted to see clearly.

We sat down at last. We stared at each other over the food on the plates: mooshu pork for me, cashew chicken for Richard. The smell of hot Chinese food filled the apartment. Warm and comforting on most occasions. Tonight it nauseated me. A double order of crab ragoon sat on a plate between us. He had filled a saucer with sweet-and-sour sauce. It was the way we always ate Chinese, sharing a bowl of sauce.

Damn.

His chocolate brown eyes stared at me. I was the one who looked away first. I didn't want to do this. ''So, do all dogs react like that to you?''

''No, just the dominant ones.''

I looked up at that. ''Custard is dominant to you?''

''He thinks so.''

''Unhealthy,'' I said.

He smiled. ''I don't eat dogs.''

''I didn't mean . . . oh, shit.'' If we were going to do this, might as well do it right. ''Why didn't you tell me about Marcus?''

''I didn't want to involve you.''

''Why not?''

''Jean-Claude involved you with Nikolaos. You told me how much you hated that. Resented it. If I brought you in to help me with Marcus, what would be the difference?''

''It's not the same,'' I said.

''How? I won't use you like Jean-Claude did. I won't do it.''

''If I volunteer, you're not using me.''

''What are you going to do? Kill him?'' There was a bitterness in his voice, anger.

''What's that supposed to mean?''

''You might as well take your jacket off. I saw the gun.''

I opened my mouth to protest and closed it. Explaining in the middle of a fight that I wanted to look good for him sounded silly. I stood up and took the jacket off. I draped it carefully over the back of the chair, taking a lot of time with it. ''There. Happy?''

''Is that gun your answer to everything?''

''Why do you suddenly have a problem with me carrying a gun?''

''Alfred was my friend.''

That stopped me. It hadn't even occurred to me that Richard might like Alfred. ''I didn't know he was your friend.''

''Would it have made a difference?''

I thought about that. ''Maybe.''

''You didn't have to kill him.''

''I had this conversation with Marcus last night. They left me no choice, Richard. I warned him, more than once.''

''I heard all about it. The pack's buzzing with it. How you wouldn't back down. You rejected Marcus's protection. You shot another one of us.'' He shook his head. ''Oh, everyone's real impressed.''

''I didn't do it to impress them.''

He took a deep breath. ''I know, that's what scares me.''

''You're scared of me?''

''For you,'' he said. The anger was seeping out of his eyes, what was replacing it was fear.

''I can handle myself, Richard.''

''You don't understand what you did last night.''

"I am sorry if Alfred was your friend. Frankly, he didn't strike me as someone you'd hang out with."

"I know he was a bully, and Marcus's dog to call, but he was mine to protect."

"Marcus wasn't doing a lot of protecting last night, Richard. He was more interested in his little power struggle than in keeping Alfred safe."

"I stopped by Irving's place this morning." He let the statement hang there in the air between us.

It was my turn to get angry. "Did you hurt him?"

"If I did, it was my right as beta male."

I stood up, hands pressed on the tabletop. "If you hurt him, we are going to have more than just words."

"Are you going to shoot me, too?"

I looked at him, with his wonderful hair, looking scrumptious in his sweater, and nodded. "If I had to."

"You could kill me, just like that."

"No, not kill, but wound, yeah."

"To keep Irving safe, you'd pull a gun on me." He was leaning back in the chair, arms crossed on his chest. His expression was amazed and angry.

"Irving asked for my protection. I gave it."

"So he told me this morning."

"Did you hurt him?"

He stared at me for a long time, then finally said, "No, I didn't hurt him."

I let out a breath I hadn't known I was holding and eased back into my chair.

"You'd really pit yourself against me to protect him. You really would."

"Don't sound so amazed. Irving was caught in the middle of the two of you. Marcus would have hurt him if he didn't contact me, and you said you'd hurt him if he did. Didn't seem very fair."

"A lot of things in the pack aren't fair, Anita."

"So is life, Richard. What of it?"

"When Irving told me that he was under your protection, I didn't hurt him, but I didn't really believe you'd hurt me."

"I've known Irving a lot longer than I've known you."

He leaned forward, hands on the tabletop. "But he's not dating you."

I shrugged. I didn't know what else to say. Nothing seemed like a safe bet.

"Am I still your sweetie or did your baptism by fire last night make you not want to date me anymore?"

"You're in a life-or-death struggle and you didn't tell me. If you hide things like that from me, how can we have a relationship?"

"Marcus won't kill me," he said.

I just stared at him. He seemed sincere. Shit. "You really believe that, don't you?"

"Yes."

I wanted to call him a fool, but I closed my mouth and tried to think of something else to say. Nothing came to mind. "I've met Marcus. I've met Raina." I shook my head. "If you really believe that Marcus doesn't want you dead, you're wrong."

"One night and you're an expert," he said.

"Yeah, on this I am."

"That's why I didn't tell you. You'd kill him, wouldn't you? You'd just kill him."

"If he was trying to kill me, yeah."

"I have to handle this myself, Anita."

"Then handle it, Richard. Kill his ass."

"Or you'll do it for me."

I sat back in my chair. "Shit, Richard, what do you want from me?"

"I want to know if you think I'm a monster."

The conversation was moving too fast for me. "You're accusing me of being a murderer. Shouldn't that be my question?"

"I knew what you were when we first met. You thought I was human. Do you still think I'm human?"

I stared at him. He looked so uncertain. In my head I knew he wasn't human. But I'd still never seen him do any of the otherworldly stuff. Looking at him here in my kitchen, brown eyes brimming with sincerity, he just didn't seem very dangerous. He believed that Marcus wouldn't kill him. It was too naive for words. I wanted to protect him. To keep him safe somehow.

"You're not a monster, Richard."

"Then why haven't you touched me tonight, not even a hello kiss."

"I thought we were mad at each other," I said. "I don't kiss people that I'm mad at."

"Are we mad at each other?" His voice was soft, hesitant.

"I don't know. Promise me something."

"What?"

"No more hiding. No more lying, not even by omission. You tell me the truth, and I'll tell you the truth."

"Agreed, if you promise not to kill Marcus."

I stared across at him. How could anybody be a master werewolf and be so goody-two-shoes? It was both charming and liable to get him killed. "I can't promise that."

"Anita . . ."

I held up a hand. "I can promise not to kill him unless he attacks me, or you, or a civilian."

It was Richard's turn to stare at me. "You could kill him, just like that?"

"Just like that."

He shook his head. "I don't understand that."

"How can you be a lycanthrope and never have killed anybody?"

"I'm careful."

"And I'm not?"

"You're almost casual about it. You killed Alfred last night, and you don't seem sorry."

"Should I be?"

"I would be."

I shrugged. Truth was, it did bother me a little. There might have been a way out without Alfred ending up in a body bag. Or in the stomachs of his friends. But I'd killed him. There it was. No going back. No changing it. No apologizing.

"It's the way I am, Richard. Live with it or get out. I'm not going to change."

"One of the reasons I wanted to date you to begin with was I thought you could take care of yourself. You've seen them now. I think I can get out of it alive, but a regular person—an ordinary human being—what chance would they have?"

I just looked at him. I flashed on him with his throat torn out. Dead. But he hadn't been dead. He'd healed. He'd lived. There'd been another man. Another human being that hadn't healed. I never wanted to love anyone and lose them like that. Ever.

"So you got what was advertised. What's the problem?"

"I still want you. I still want to hold you. Touch you. Can you stand to touch me after what you saw last night?" He wouldn't meet my eyes. His hair fell forward, hiding his face.

I stood up and took the step that left me looking down at him. He raised his face to me, his eyes glittered with unshed tears. The fear in his face was raw. I had thought that what I saw last night would make a difference between us. I flashed on Jason's unnatural strength, the sweat on Marcus's face, Gabriel with his blood-coated mouth. But staring into Richard's face, with him close enough to touch, none of that was real. I trusted Richard. Besides, I was armed.

I leaned over him, bending down to kiss his lips. The first kiss was gentle, chaste. He made no move to touch me, hands in his lap. I kissed his forehead, hands combing through his long hair, so I could feel the warmth of him against my fingers. I kissed his eyebrows, the tip of his nose, each cheek, finally his lips again. He sighed, the breath pouring into my mouth, and I pressed my lips against his like I'd eat him from the mouth down.

His arms wrapped around my back, hands hesitating at my waist, fingers slightly lower. His hands jumped to my thighs, skipping all those questionable areas. I put one leg on either side of his knees, and found the short skirt did have its uses. I straddled his lap, didn't have to raise the skirt an inch. Richard made a small sound of surprise. He stared at me, and his eyes were drowning deep.

I raised his sweater off his stomach, running hands against his bare flesh. "Off," I said.

He raised the sweater over his head in one movement, dropping it to the floor. I sat in his lap, staring at his bare chest. I should have stopped right there, but I didn't want to.

I pressed my face in the bend of his neck, breathing in the smell of his skin, his hair covering my face like a veil. I ran just the tip of my tongue in a thin line of wetness down his neck, across his collarbone.

His hands kneaded the small of my back, sliding downward. His fingers danced over my buttocks, then up to my back. Point for him. He hadn't groped me.

"The gun, can you take it off?" He asked with his face buried in my hair.

I nodded, slipping out of the shoulder straps. I couldn't get the rest off without removing the skirt's belt. My hands didn't seem to want to work.

Richard took my hands and placed them gently to either side. He undid the buckle and began to slide the belt out a loop at a time. Each pull made me move just a little. I held the holstered gun while he drew the belt free. He let the belt drop to the floor. I folded the shoulder holster carefully and laid it on the table behind us.

I turned back to him. His face was startingly close. His lips were soft, full. I licked the edges of his mouth. The kiss was quick and messy. I wanted to run my mouth over other things. Down his chest. We'd never let it go this far. Not even close.

He pulled my blouse out of the skirt, running hands over my bare back. The feel of his naked skin on places he'd never touched before made me shudder.

"We have to stop now." I whispered it into his neck, so it wasn't completely convincing.

"What?"

"Stop." I pushed a little back from him, enough to see his face. Enough to breathe just a little. My hands were still playing with his hair, touching his shoulders. I dropped my hands. Made myself stop. He was so warm. I raised my hands to my face, and could smell him on my skin. I did not want to stop. From the look on his face, the feel of his body, neither did he. "We should stop now."

"Why?" His voice was almost a whisper.

"Because if we don't stop now, we might not stop at all."

"Would that be such a bad thing?"

Staring into his lovely eyes from inches away, I almost said, no. "Maybe, yes."

"Why?"

"Because one night is never enough. You either have a regular diet of it or you go cold turkey."

"You can have this every night," he said.

"Is that a proposal?" I asked.

He blinked at me, trying to draw himself back up. To think. I watched the effort and struggled with it myself. It was hard to think sitting in his lap. I stood up. His hands were still under my shirt, on my bare back.

"Anita, what's wrong?"

I stood looking down at him, hands on his shoulders for balance, still too close for clear thinking. I backed away, and he let me go. I leaned my hands against the kitchen counter, trying to think enough to make sense.

I tried to think how to say a couple of years' worth of pain in one mouthful. "I was always a good girl. I didn't sleep around. In college I met someone, we got engaged, we set a date, we made love. He dumped me."

"He'd done all that just to get you in bed?"

I shook my head and turned to look at him. He was still sitting there with his shirt off, looking scrumptious. "His family disapproved of me."

"Why?"

"His mother didn't like my mother being Mexican." I leaned my back against the cabinets, arms crossed, hugging myself. "He didn't love me enough to go against his family. I missed him in a lot of ways, but my body missed him, too. I promised myself I'd never let that happen again."

"So you're waiting for marriage," he said.

I nodded. "I want you, Richard, badly, but I can't. I promised I'd never let myself get hurt like that again."

He stood up and came to stand in front of me. He stood close but didn't try to touch me. "Then marry me."

I looked up at him. "Yeah, right."

"No, I mean it." He put his hands on my shoulders, gently. "I've thought about asking before, but I was afraid. You hadn't seen what a lycanthrope could do, what we could be. I knew you needed to see that before I could ask, but I was afraid for you to see it."

"I still haven't seen you change," I said.

"Do you need to?"

"Standing here like this, I say no, but realistically, if we're serious, probably."

"Now?"

I stared up at him in the near dark and hugged him. I folded against him and shook my head, cheek sliding along his naked chest. "No, not now."

He kissed the top of my head. "Is that a yes?"

I raised my head to look at him. "I should say no."

"Why?"

"Because life is too complicated for this."

"Life is always complicated, Anita. Say yes."

"Yes." The minute I said it, I wanted it back. I lusted after him a lot. I even loved him maybe more than a little. Did I suspect him of eating Little Red Riding Hood? Hell, he couldn't even bring himself to kill the Big Bad Wolf. Of the two of us, I was the more likely to slaughter people.

He kissed me, his hands pressing against my back. I drew back enough to breathe, and said, "No sex tonight. The rule still stands."

He lowered his mouth and spoke with our lips almost touching. "I know."

18

I was late to my first zombie appointment. Surprise, surprise. Being late to the first meeting made me late to the other two. It was 2:03 by the time I got to Edward's room.

I knocked. He opened the door and stepped to one side. "You're late."

"Yeah," I said. The room was nice but standard. A single king-sized bed, nightstand, two lamps, a desk against the far wall. The drapes were closed over the nearly wall-to-wall windows. The bathroom light was on, door open. The closet door was half-open, showing that he'd hung up his clothes. He planned to stay for a while.

The television was on, sound turned off. I was surprised. Edward didn't watch television. A VCR sat on top of the TV. That was not standard hotel issue.

"You want something from room service before we get started?"

"A Coke would be great."

He smiled. "You always did have champagne tastes, Anita." He went to the phone and ordered. He asked for a steak, rare, with a bottle of burgundy.

I took off my coat and laid it on the desk chair. "I don't drink," I said.

"I know," he said. "You want to freshen up while we wait for the food?"

I glanced up and caught a distant look at myself in the bathroom mirror. Chicken blood had dried to a sticky, brick color on my face. "I see your point."

I shut the bathroom door and looked at myself in the mirror. The lighting was that harsh, glaring white that so many hotel bathrooms seem to have. It's so unflattering that even Ms. America wouldn't look good in it.

The blood stood out like reddish chalk against my pale skin. I was wearing a white Christmas sweatshirt that had Maxine from the Shoebox Hallmark commercials on it. She was drinking coffee with a candy cane in hand, saying, "This is as jolly as I get." Bert had asked us to wear Christmasy-type things for the month. Maybe the sweatshirt wasn't exactly what he had in mind, but hey, it was better than some of the ones I had at home. There was blood on the white cloth. Figures.

I took the sweatshirt off, draping it on the bathtub. There was blood smeared over my heart. I'd even gotten a little on my silver cross. I'd put the blood there along with the stuff on my face and hands. I'd killed three chickens tonight. Raising zombies was a messy job.

I got one of the white washrags from the little towel rack. I wondered how Edward would explain the bloodstains to the maid. Not my problem, but sort of amusing anyway.

I ran water into the sink and started scrubbing. I caught a glimpse of myself with blood running down my face in watery rivulets. I stood up and stared. My face looked fresh scrubbed and sort of surprised.

Had Richard really proposed? Had I really said yes? Surely not. I had said yes. Shit. I wiped at the blood on my chest. I played with monsters all the time. So I was engaged to one. That stopped me. I sat down on the closed lid of the stool, bloody washrag gripped in my hands. I was engaged. Again.

The first time he'd been so white bread that even Judith had liked him. He'd been Mr. All-American, and I hadn't been good enough for him, according to his family. What had hurt most was that he hadn't loved me enough. Not nearly as much as I'd loved him. I'd have given up everything for him. Not a mistake to make twice.

Richard wasn't like that. I knew that. Yet there was that worm of doubt. Fear that he'd blow it. Fear he wouldn't blow it. Damned if you do, damned if you don't.

I looked down and realized I was dripping bloody water on the linoleum. I knelt and wiped it up. I was scrubbed as clean as I was going to get until I showered at home. If I'd brought clean clothes, I might have done it here, but I hadn't thought of it.

Edward knocked on the door. "Food's here."

I got dressed, put the rag in the sink, and ran cold water over it. I made sure the cloth wasn't blocking the drain and opened the door. The smell of steak hit me. It smelled wonderful. I hadn't eaten for more than eight hours, and truthfully I hadn't eaten all that much then. Richard had distracted me.

"Do you think room service would shoot us if we asked for another order?"

He made a small hand motion at the room-service cart. There were two orders on the cart.

"How did you know I'd be hungry?"

"You always forget to eat," he said.

"My, aren't we being mother of the year."

"The least I can do is feed you."

I looked at him. "What's up, Edward? You're being awfully considerate."

"I know you well enough to know you won't like this. Call the meal a peace offering."

"Won't like what?"

"Let's eat, watch the movie, and all will be revealed."

He was being cagey. It wasn't like him. He'd shoot you, but he wouldn't be cute about it. "What are you up to, Edward?"

"No questions until after the movie."

"Why not?"

"Because you'll have better questions." With that inscrutable answer he sat down on the edge of the bed and poured a glass of red wine. He cut his meat, which was raw enough to bleed in the center.

"Please tell me my steak isn't bloody."

"It isn't bloody. You like your meat well dead."

"Ha, ha." But I sat down. It seemed odd sharing a meal in Edward's hotel room, like we were two business people traveling together, just a working dinner. The steak was well done. Thick house fries suitably spiced took up almost as much room as the steak. There was a side order of broccoli, which could be slid to one side and ignored.

The Coke came in a chilled wineglass, which seemed a little excessive, but it looked nice.

"The movie's going to start near the end. I don't think you'll have any trouble picking up the plot." He hit the remote control, and the TV screen flickered, jumping from a game show to a bedroom.

A woman with long brown hair lay on her back in a round bed. She was nude, or at least what I could see of her was nude. Below the waist she was hidden behind the furiously pumping buttocks of a dark-haired man.

"This is pornography." I didn't even try to keep the disbelief from my voice.

"It certainly is."

I glanced at Edward. He was cutting his steak with neat, precise hand movements. He chewed a bite of steak, sipped his wine, and watched the screen.

I glanced back at the "movie." A second man had joined the couple on the bed. He was taller than the first man, with shorter hair, but beyond that it was a little hard to tell, mainly because I was trying not to look.

I sat on the edge of Edward's bed with our nice steak dinners, and for the first time felt awkward around Edward. There had never been any sexual tension between us. We might kill each other someday, but we'd never kiss. But I was still in a man's hotel room watching a porno movie, and good girls just didn't do that.

"Edward, what the hell is going on?"

He hit the remote control. "Here, a face shot."

I turned back to the screen. The frozen image stared out at me. It was the second man. It was Alfred.

"Oh, my, God," I said.

"You know him?" Edward asked.

"Yeah." No sense denying it. Alfred was dead. Edward couldn't hurt him anymore.

"Name?"

"Alfred. I don't know the last name."

He hit fast forward. The images on the screen moved at a furious pace, doing intimate things that would have been obscene at any speed. At fast forward it seemed sadder. Ridiculous as well as degrading.

He hit the pause again. The woman was full face to the camera, mouth open, eyes heavy lidded with sexual languor. Her hair was spread artfully over the silken pillow. It should have been provocative. It managed not to be.

"Do you know her?"

I shook my head. "No."

He hit the button again. "We're near the end."

"What about the other man?"

"He wears a face mask throughout."

The masked man had mounted the woman from behind. His hips cupped her butt, the line of his thigh matching hers. He leaned his upper body over her nude torso, hands massaging the flesh of her upper arms. He seemed to be draping himself on top of her more than anything else. There seemed to be very little sex going on.

She was supporting his full weight on her hands and knees. Her breath came in pants. A low growl trickled through the room. The camera did a close-up of the man's back. The skin was rippled, as if a hand had rubbed the under surface of his skin, then vanished. More ripples, as if something small were trying to punch its way out.

A wider-angle shot showed him still draped over the woman. The ripples on his back were growing. You could see things pushing against his skin, movements large enough you could have seen them even if he'd been dressed. Like those I had seen on Jason last night.

I had to admit this part was fascinating. I'd seen people shapeshift, but never like this. Not in minute detail, not with the loving eye of a camera on it.

The skin split along his back, and he reared upward, hands hugging her waist, screaming. Clear liquid flowed down his back in a wash that soaked the bed and the woman underneath him.

The woman gave a little encouragement, moving her buttocks against him, thrusting against him, head bowed to the bed.

Black fur flowed outward from his back. His hands shot to his sides, spasming. He leaned over her again, hands digging into the bed. The hands were just hands, then those human fingers sliced into the bed, ripping white stuffing from great clawed furrows.

The man seemed to shrink. The fur flowed faster and faster, almost liquid in its speed. The mask dropped away. The face was the wrong shape for it now. The camera did a close shot of the fallen mask. A bit of art in all this . . . oh, hell. I didn't have a word for it.

The man was gone. A black leopard mounted the woman and seemed very happy with the arrangement. The leopard bent over the woman, lips spread to reveal glistening teeth. The leopard nipped her back, drawing a small amount of blood. She gave a low moan, a shudder sweeping her body.

Alfred came back into view. He was still in human form. He crawled up to the bed and kissed the woman. It was a long, complete kiss, full of probing tongues. He rose on his knees, still kissing her, rocking his body with the movements. He seemed very excited to see her.

His back rippled, and he tore away from her, hands clutching the sheets. The change seemed to go a lot faster for him. The camera did a close-up of one of his hands. Bones slid out of the skin with wet, sucking noises. Muscles and ligaments crawled and rearranged. The skin tore and that same clear liquid poured out. The hand changed into a naked claw before the dark fur flowed over it.

He stood on bent legs, half wolf, half man, but all male. He threw back his head and howled. The sound had a deep, resonating quality that filled the room.

The woman looked up at him, eyes wide. The leopard jumped off her, rolling on the bed, for all the world like a big kitten. It rolled itself in the silken sheet, until only its black-furred face peeked out.

The woman lay on her back, legs spread-eagled. She held out her hands to the wolfman, tongue flicking out along her lips as if she were really enjoying herself. Maybe she was.

The werewolf thrust into her, and it wasn't gentle. She gave a gasping moan, as if it were the best thing she'd ever felt.

The woman was making noises. Either she was a very good actor or she was coming close to climax. I wasn't sure which I preferred. Good acting, I think.

She came with a sound between a scream and a shout of joy. She lay back gasping on the bed, body liquid. The werewolf gave one last shuddering thrust and drew claws down the length of her naked body.

She screamed then, no acting required. Blood poured down her body in scarlet rivulets. The leopard gave a startled scream and jumped off the bed. The woman put her hands up in front of her face, and the claws smashed her arms to one side. Blood poured, and there was a glimpse of bone in one arm where the claws had torn all the flesh away.

Her screams were high and continuous, one loud ragged shriek after another, as fast as she could draw air. The werewolf's pointed muzzle lowered towards her face. I had an image of the murder victim's crushed jaw. But he went for her throat. He bit her throat out, spraying a great gout of blood.

Her eyes stared sightless at the camera, wide and shiny, dull with death. The blood had somehow left her face untouched. The werewolf reared back, blood dripping from its jaws. A gob of blood fell on her staring face, running between her eyes.

The leopard leaped back onto the bed. It licked her face clean with long, sure strokes of its tongue. The werewolf licked its way down her body, stopping over her stomach. It hesitated, one yellow eye staring at the camera. It began to feed. The leopard joined the feast.

I closed my eyes, but the sounds were enough. Heavy, wet, tearing sounds filled the room. I heard myself say, "Turn it off." The sounds stopped, and I assumed that Edward had turned the tape off, but I didn't look up to see. I didn't look up until I heard the whir of the tape rewinding.

Edward cut a bite of steak.

"If you eat that right now, I will throw up on you."

He smiled, but he put down his silverware. He looked at me. His expression was neutral, as it was most of the time. I couldn't tell if he'd enjoyed the film or been disgusted by it. "Now you can ask me questions," he said. His voice was like it always was, pleasant, unaffected by external stimuli.

"Jesus, where did you get that thing?"

"A client."

"Why give it to you?"

"The woman was his daughter."

"Oh, God, please, tell me he didn't watch this."

"You know he saw it. You know he watched it to the end or why hire me? Most men don't hire people to kill their daughter's lovers."

"He hired you to kill the two men?"

Edward nodded.

"Why did you show this to me?"

"Because I knew you'd help me."

"I'm not an assassin, Edward."

"Just help me identify them. I'll do the rest. Is it all right if I drink some wine?"

I nodded.

He sipped his wine. The dark liquid rolled around the glass, looking a lot redder than it had before the movie. I swallowed hard and looked away. I would not throw up. I would not throw up.

"Where can I find Alfred?"

"Nowhere," I said.

He set his wineglass carefully on the tray. "Anita, you disappoint me. I thought you'd help me after seeing what they did to the girl."

"I'm not being uncooperative. That film is one of the worst things I've ever seen, and I've seen a hell of a lot. You're too late to find Alfred."

"How too late?"

"I killed him last night."

A smile spread across his face, beautiful to behold. "You always make my job easier."

"Not on purpose."

He shrugged. "Do you want half the fee? You did do half the work."

I shook my head. "I didn't do it for money."

"Tell me what happened."

"No."

"Why not?"

I looked at him. "Because you hunt lycanthropes and I don't want to give someone to you by accident."

"The wereleopard deserves to die, Anita."

"I'm not arguing that. Though, technically, he didn't kill the girl."

"The father wants them both. Do you blame him?"

"No, I guess I don't."

"Then you'll help me identify the other man?"

"Maybe." I stood up. "I need to call someone. I need for someone else to see this film. He might be able to help you more than I could."

"Who?"

I shook my head. "Let me see if he'll come first."

Edward gave a long nod, almost a bow with just his neck. "As you like."

I dialed Richard's number by heart. I got his machine. "This is Anita, pick up if you're there. Richard, pick up. This is important." No one picked up the phone.

"Damn," I said.

"Not home?" Edward asked.

''Do you have the number for the Lunatic Cafe?''

''Yes.''

''Give it to me.''

He repeated the number slowly, and I dialed it. A woman picked up the phone. It wasn't Raina. I was thankful for that. ''Lunatic Cafe, Polly here, how may I help you.''

''I need to speak with Richard.''

''I'm sorry we don't have any waiters by that name.''

''Look, I was a guest of Marcus's last night. I need to speak with Richard. It's an emergency.''

''I don't know. I mean, like, they're all busy in the back room.''

''Look, get Richard on the phone now.''

''Marcus doesn't like to be disturbed.''

''Polly, is it? I have been on my feet for over thirteen hours. If you do not put Richard on the phone right now, I am going to come down there personally and bust your ass. Am I making myself clear?''

''Who is this?'' She sounded a little miffed, and not in the least afraid.

''Anita Blake.''

''Oh,'' she said. ''I'll get Richard for you, right away, Anita, right away.'' There was an edge of panic to her voice that hadn't been there before. She put me on hold. Someone with a sick sense of humor had compiled the Muzak. ''Moonlight and Roses,'' ''Blue Moon,'' ''Moonlight Sonata.'' Every song was a moon theme. We were halfway through ''Moon over Miami'' when the phone clicked back to life.

''Anita, it's me. What's wrong?''

''I'm all right, but I've got something you need to see.''

''Can you tell me what it is?''

''I know this sounds corny, but not over the phone.''

''You sure you're not just looking for an excuse to see me again?'' There was a note of teasing in his voice.

It had been too long a night. ''Can you meet me?''

''Of course. What's wrong? Your voice sounds awful.''

''I need a hug and to erase the last hour of my life. The first you can take care of when you get here, the second I'll just have to live with.''

''Are you home?''

''No.'' I glanced at Edward, putting my hand over the mouthpiece. ''Can I give him the hotel room?''

He nodded.

I gave Richard the hotel room, and directions. ''I'll be there as soon as I can.'' He hesitated, then said, ''What did you say to Polly? She's nearly hysterical.''

''She wouldn't put you on the phone.''

''You threatened her,'' he said.

''Yeah.''

''Was it an idle threat?''

''Pretty much.''

''Dominant pack members don't make idle threats to subordinates.''

''I'm not a pack member.''

''After last night you're a dominant. They're treating you like a rogue dominant lycanthrope.''

''What does that mean?''

''It means when you say you're going to bust someone's ass, they believe you.''

''Oh, sorry.''

''Don't apologize to me, apologize to Polly. I'll be there before you get her calmed down.''

''Don't put her on, Richard.''

''That's what you get for being trigger happy. People get scared of you.''

''Richard . . .'' A sobbing female voice came on the line. I spent the next fifteen minutes convincing a crying werewolf that I wasn't going to hurt her. My life was getting too strange, even for me.

19

Richard was wrong. He didn't knock on the door while I was on the phone calming Polly down. She was so grateful that I had forgiven her for her rudeness, that it was embarrassing. Waves of submissiveness poured out of the phone. I hung up.

Edward was grinning at me. He had moved to one of the soft chairs. "Did you just spend nearly twenty minutes convincing a werewolf that you weren't going hurt her?"

"Yes."

He laughed, a wide, abrupt sound. The smile vanished, leaving a sort of shimmering glow to his face. His eyes glittered with something darker than humor. I wasn't sure what he was thinking, but it wasn't pleasant.

He slid down in the chair, base of his skull resting on the back, hands clasped over his stomach, ankles crossed. He looked utterly comfortable. "How did you come to be the terror of good little werewolves everywhere?"

"I don't think they're used to people shooting and killing them. At least not on first acquaintance."

His eyes simmered with some dark joke. "You went in there and killed someone your first night? Hell, Anita, I've been down three times and haven't killed anyone yet."

"How long have you been in town?"

He looked at me for a long moment. "Is that an idle question or do you need to know?"

It had occurred to me that Edward could take out eight lycanthropes and leave no trace. If any human could do it, it was him.

"I need to know," I said.

"A week, tomorrow." His eyes had gone empty. They were as cool and distant as any of the shapeshifters' last night. There's more than one way to become a predator. "Of course, you'll have to take my word for it. You can check with registration, but I could have changed hotels."

"Why would you lie to me?"

"Because I enjoy it," he said.

"It's not the lie you enjoy."

"What do I enjoy?"

"Knowing something I don't."

He gave a small shrug, not easy for him, slid down in the chair as he was. He made it look graceful. "Egotistical of you."

"It's not just from me. You like keeping secrets for the pure hell of it."

He smiled then, a slow, lazy smile. "You do know me well."

I started to say, we're friends, but the look in his eyes stopped me. His stare was a little too intense. He seemed to be studying me as if he'd never really seen me before.

"What are you thinking, Edward?"

"That you might be able to give me a run for my money."

"What's that supposed to mean?"

"You know how I like a challenge."

I stared at him. "You're talking about coming against me, seeing who's better?" I made it a question. He didn't give me the answer I wanted.

"Yes."

"Why?"

"I won't do it. You know me—no money, no killing—but it would be . . . interesting."

"Don't go all spooky on me, Edward."

"It's just for the very first time I'm wondering if you would win?"

He was scaring me. I was armed, and he didn't seem to be, but Edward was always armed. "Don't do this, Edward."

He sat up in one liquid movement. My hand jumped to my gun. The gun was halfway out of its holster when I realized he hadn't done anything but sit up. I let out a shaky breath and eased the gun back into the holster. "Don't play with me, Edward. One of us will get hurt if you do."

He spread his hands wide. "No more games. I would like to know which of us was best, Anita, but not enough to kill you."

I let my hand relax. If Edward said he would kill me tonight, he meant it. If we ever did do this for real, he'd tell me first. Edward liked to be sporting about these things. Surprising your victim made things too easy.

There was a knock on the door. I jumped. Nervous—who, me? Edward sat there as though he hadn't heard, still staring at me with his spooky eyes. I went to the door. It was Richard. He put his arms around me, and I let him. I folded against his chest and was very aware that I couldn't pull a gun very fast clasped to Richard's body.

I drew back first and pulled him into the room. He looked questioningly at me. I shook my head. "You remember Edward?"

"Anita, you didn't tell me you were still dating Richard." Edward's voice was pleasant, normal, as if he hadn't been wondering what it would be like to kill me. His face was open, friendly. He walked across the room with his hand outstretched. He was a superb actor.

Richard shook his hand, looking a little puzzled. He glanced at me. "What's happening, Anita?"

"Can you set up the movie?"

"If you'll let me eat during it. My steak is getting ice cold," Edward said.

I swallowed hard. "You've seen the movie before, and you still ordered steaks. Why?"

"Maybe to see if you could eat after watching it."

"You competitive bastard."

He just smiled.

"What movie?" Richard asked.

"Eat your steak, Edward. We'll watch after you're done."

"It bothered you that much?"

"Shut up and eat."

He sat down on the edge of the bed and started cutting meat. The meat was red. Blood oozed out of it. I walked towards the bathroom. I wasn't going to be sick, but if I watched him eat that piece of meat I would be.

"I'm going to hide in the bathroom. You want an explanation, come join me," I said.

Richard glanced at Edward, then back to me. "What is going on?"

I pulled him into the bathroom and shut the door behind us. I ran cold water in the sink and splashed it on my face.

He gripped my shoulders, massaging. "Are you all right?"

I shook my head, water dripping down my face. I fumbled a towel and pressed it to my face, holding it there a minute. Edward hadn't warned me because he liked to shock people. And a warning would have lessened the impact. How much impact did I want Richard to endure?

I turned to him, towel still clutched in my hands. He looked worried, all tender concern. I didn't want him to look like that. Had I really said yes, just eight hours ago? It seemed less and less real.

"The movie is a porno flick," I said.

He looked startled. Good. "Porno? Are you serious?"

"Deadly," I said.

"Why do I need to see it?" A thought seemed to occur to him. "Why did you watch it with him?" There was the tiniest bit of anger in his voice.

I laughed then. I laughed until tears ran down my face, and I was too breathless to speak.

"What's so funny?" He sounded a little indignant.

When I could speak without gasping, I said, "Be afraid of Edward, but never be jealous of him."

The laughter had helped. I felt better, less dirty, less embarrassed, even a little less horrified. I stared up at him. He was still wearing the green sweater that had ended up on my kitchen floor earlier. He looked wonderful. I realized I didn't. In my oversize sweatshirt, complete with bloodstain, jeans, and sneakers, I had lost several notches in the cuteness game. I shook my head. Did it matter? No, I was delaying. I didn't want to go back out there. I didn't want to watch the movie again. I certainly didn't want to sit in the same room with the man I might marry and watch him watch a porno film. Should I spoil the ending?

Would it excite him before it went wrong? I looked at his very human face, and wondered.

"It's lycanthropes and a human in the film."

"They're already for sale?" he said.

It was my turn to look surprised. "You know about the film? You said 'they.' There are more of them?"

"Unfortunately," he said. He leaned against the door, sliding down to sit Indian fashion on the floor. If he'd stretched his legs out, there wouldn't have been room for both of us.

"Explain this, Richard."

"It was Raina's idea," he said. "She convinced Marcus to order some of us to participate."

"Did you . . ." I couldn't even say it.

He shook his head. Something tight in my chest eased. "Raina tried to get me in front of the cameras. For those that need to hide their identity they use masks. I wouldn't do it."

"Did Marcus order you to?"

"Yes. These damn films are one of the main reasons I started rising in the pack. Everyone higher in the structure could order me around. If Marcus okays it, they can order you to do almost anything, as long as it's not illegal."

"Wait. The films aren't illegal?"

"Bestiality is against the law in some states, but we sort of slip through the cracks on the law."

"Nothing else illegal goes on in these films?" I asked.

He stared up at me. "What's on that film that makes you look so scared?"

"It's a snuff film."

He just stared at me, no change of expression, as if waiting for me to say more. When I didn't, he said, "You cannot be serious."

"I wish I wasn't."

He shook his head. "Even Raina wouldn't do that."

"Raina wasn't in the film as far as I saw."

"But Marcus wouldn't approve of that, not that." He stood up, using only his legs and the wall. He paced to the edge of the bathtub and back. He brushed past me, slamming his hand into the wall. It gave a resounding thunk.

He turned, and I'd never seen him so angry. "There are other packs around the country. It doesn't have to be us."

"Alfred was in it."

He leaned his back against the far wall, and slammed his palms into the wall again. "I can't believe it."

Edward knocked on the door. "The film's ready."

Richard yanked the door open and poured into the other room like a crackling storm. For the first time I felt some of that otherworldly energy radiating from him.

Edward's eyes widened. "You gave him a preview?"

I nodded.

The room was in darkness except for the television. "I'll give you two lovebirds the bed. I'll sit over here.'' He sat down in the chair again, upright, watching us. ''Don't mind me if the mood strikes you.''

''Shut up and start the movie,'' I said.

Richard had sat down on the edge of the bed. The room-service cart was gone, along with its offending meat. Great, one less reason to upchuck. Richard seemed to have calmed down. He seemed normal enough sitting there. That wash of energy was gone so cleanly that I wondered if I'd imagined it. I glanced at Edward's face. He was watching Richard as if he had done something interesting. I hadn't imagined it.

I thought about turning on the lights but didn't. Darkness seemed better for this.

''Edward.''

''Showtime,'' he said. He hit the button, and it began again.

Richard stiffened at the first image. Did he recognize the other man? I didn't ask, not yet. Let him see it, then questions.

I didn't want to sit on the bed with my sweetie while this filth played. Maybe I hadn't really thought about what sex might mean to Richard. Did it mean shape-shifting? Bestiality? I hoped not, and wasn't sure how to find out without asking, and I didn't want to ask. If the answer was yes to the bestiality, the wedding was off.

I finally walked across the screen and sat down in the other chair, beside Edward. I didn't want to see the film again. Apparently neither did Edward. We both watched Richard watch the film. I wasn't sure what I expected to see, or even what I wanted to see. Edward's face gave nothing away. His eyes closed about halfway through. He'd slid down in the chair again. He looked asleep, but I knew better. He was aware of everything in the room. I wasn't sure Edward ever really slept.

Richard watched alone. He sat on the very edge of the bed, hands clasped together, shoulders hunched. His eyes were bright, reflecting the light of the television set. I could almost watch the action playing over his face. Sweat glistened on his upper lip. He wiped it away, catching me looking at him. He looked embarrassed, then angry.

''Don't watch me, Anita.'' His voice was choked tight with something more than emotion, or less.

I couldn't pretend sleep like Edward. What the hell was I supposed to do? I got up and walked towards the bathroom. I studiously did not look at the screen, but I had to cross in front of it. I felt Richard track me as I moved. His eyes on my back made my skin itch. I wiped suddenly sweating palms on my jeans. I turned, slowly, to look at him.

He was looking at me, not the movie. There was rage on his face—anger was too mild a word—and hatred. I didn't think it was me he was angry with. That left who? Raina, Marcus . . . himself?

The woman's scream jerked his head around to the film. I watched his face while his friend killed her. The rage blossomed on his face, spilling out his mouth in an inarticulate cry. He slid off the bed to his knees, covering his face with his hands.

Edward was standing. I caught the movement on the edge of my vision and found him holding a gun that had magically appeared. I was holding the Browning. We stared at each other over Richard's kneeling body.

Richard had rolled into an almost fetal position, rocking slowly back and forth on his knees. The sounds of tearing flesh came from the screen. He raised a shocked face, caught one glimpse of the screen, and scrambled towards me. I stepped out of the way and he let me. He was going for the bathroom.

The door slammed shut, and a few seconds later the sound of his retching came through the door.

Edward and I stood out in the room, looking at each other. We still had our guns out. "You go for your gun as quickly as I do. That wasn't true two years ago."

"It's been a rough two years," I said.

He smiled. "Most people wouldn't have seen me move in the dark."

"My night vision is excellent," I said.

"I'll remember that."

"Let's call a truce tonight, Edward. I'm too tired to screw with it tonight."

He gave one nod, and tucked the gun at the small of his back. "That wasn't where the gun started out," I said.

"No," he said, "it wasn't."

I holstered the Browning and knocked on the bathroom door. Admittedly, I didn't turn completely around. I just wasn't easy with Edward at my back right that moment.

"Richard, are you all right?"

"No." His voice sounded deeper, hoarse.

"Can I come in?"

There was a long pause, then, "Maybe you better."

I pushed the door open carefully, didn't want to smack him with it. He was still kneeling over the toilet, head down, long hair hiding his face. He had a bunch of toilet paper crumbled in one hand. The sharp, sweet smell of vomit hung in the air.

I closed the door and leaned against it. "Can I help?"

He shook his head.

I smoothed his hair back on one side. He jerked away from me as if I'd burned him. He ended up huddled in the corner, trapped between the wall and the bathtub. The look on his face was wild, panicked.

I knelt in front of him.

"Don't touch me, please!"

"Okay, I won't touch you. Now what's wrong?"

He wouldn't look at me. His eyes wandered the room, not settling on anything, but definitely avoiding me.

"Talk to me, Richard."

"I can't believe Marcus knows. He can't know. He wouldn't allow it."

"Could Raina do it without his knowing?"

He nodded. "She's a real bitch."

"I noticed."

"I have to tell Marcus. He won't believe it. He might need to see the film." His words were almost normal, but his voice was still breathy, thin, panicked. If he kept this up, he was going to hyperventilate.

"Take a slow, deep breath, Richard. It's all right."

He shook his head. "But it isn't. I thought you'd seen us at our worst." He gave a loud, spitting laugh. "Oh, God, now you really have."

I reached for him, to comfort, to do something. "Don't touch me!" He screamed it at me. I backed up and ended sitting with my back pressed against the far wall. It was as far away as I could get without leaving the room.

"What the hell is wrong with you?"

"I want you, right now, here, after seeing that."

"It excited you?" I made it a question.

"God help me," he said.

"Is that what sex means to you, not the killing but before?"

"It can, but it isn't safe. In animal form we're contagious. You know that."

"But it's a temptation," I said.

"Yes." He crawled towards me, and I felt myself recoil. He sat back on his knees and just looked at me. "I am not just a man, Anita. I am what I am. I don't ask you to literally embrace the other half, but you have to look at it. You have to know what it is or it's not going to work between us." He studied my face. "Or have you changed your mind?"

I didn't know what to say. His eyes didn't look wild anymore. They had gone dark and deep. There was a heat to his gaze, to his face, that had nothing to do with horror. He rose on all fours, the movement was enough to bring him close to me. I stared at his face from inches away. He gave a long, shuddering sigh, and energy prickled along my skin. I was left gasping. His otherness beat against my skin like a crashing wave. The wash of it pressed me against the wall like an invisible hand.

He leaned into me, lips almost touching, then moved past. His breath was hot against the side of my face. "Think how it could be. Making love like this, feeling the power crawl over your skin while I was inside you."

I wanted to touch him, and I was afraid to touch him. He drew back enough to look me in the face, close enough to kiss. "It would be so good." His lips brushed mine. He whispered the next words into my mouth like a secret. "And all this lust comes from me seeing blood and death and imagining her fear."

He was standing, as if someone had pulled him upright with strings. It was magically quick. It made Alfred last night look slow. "This is what I am, Anita. I can pretend to be human. I'm better at it than Marcus, but it's just a game."

"No." But my voice was just a whisper.

He swallowed hard enough for me to hear it. "I've got to go." He offered me his hand. I realized he couldn't open the door with me sitting there, not without banging me with it.

I knew if I refused his hand that that would be it. He would never ask again, and I would never say yes. I took his hand. He let out a long breath. His skin was hot to the touch, almost burning hot. His skin sent little shock waves through my arm. Touching him with all his power loose in the room was too amazing for words.

He raised my hand to his mouth. He didn't so much kiss my hand as nuzzle it, rub it along his cheek, trace his tongue over my wrist. He dropped it so abruptly, I stumbled back. "I have to get out of here, now." There was sweat on his face again.

He stepped out into the room. The lights were on this time. Edward was sitting in the chair, hands loose in his lap. No weapon in sight. I stood in the bathroom door, feeling Richard's power swirl out and fill the outer room like water too long imprisoned. Edward showed great restraint, not going for a gun.

Richard stalked to the door and you could almost feel the waves of his passing in the air. He stopped with his hand on the doorknob. "I'll tell Marcus if I can get him alone. If Raina interferes, we'll have to think of something else." He gave one last glance at me, then he was gone. I almost expected him to run down the hallway, but he didn't. Self-restraint at its best.

Edward and I stood in the doorway and watched him vanish around the corner. He turned to me. "You're dating that."

Minutes ago I would have been insulted, but my skin was vibrating with the backwash of Richard's power. I couldn't pretend anymore. He'd asked me to marry him, and I'd said yes. But I hadn't understood, not really. He wasn't human. He really, truly wasn't.

The question was, how big a difference did that make? Answer: I hadn't the foggiest.

20

I slept Sunday morning and missed church. I hadn't gotten home until nearly seven o'clock in the morning. There was no way to make a ten o'clock service. Surely God understood the need for sleep, even if he didn't have to do it himself.

Late afternoon found me at Washington University. I was in the office of Dr. Louis Fane, Louie to his friends. The early-winter evening was filling the sky with soft purple clouds. Strips of sky like a lighted backdrop for the clouds showed through his single office window. He rated a window. Most doctorates didn't. Doctorates are cheap on a college campus.

Louie sat with his back to the window. He had turned on the desk lamp. It made a pool of golden warmth against the coming night. We sat in that last pool of light, and it seemed more private than it should have. A last stand against the dark. God, I was melancholy today.

Louie's office was suitably cluttered. One wall was ceiling-to-floor bookshelves, filled with biology textbooks, nature essays, and a complete set of James Herriot books. The skeleton of a Little Brown Bat was laid behind glass and hung on his wall by his diploma. There was a bat identification poster on his door like the ones you buy for bird feeders. You know, ''Common Birds of Eastern Missouri.'' Louie's doctoral thesis had been on the adaptation of the Little Brown Bat to human habitation.

His shelves were lined with souvenirs; seashells, a piece of petrified wood, pinecones, bark with dried lichen on it. All the bits and pieces that biology majors are always picking up.

Louie was about five foot six, with eyes as black as my own. His hair was straight and fine, growing a little below his shoulders. It wasn't a fashion statement as it was with Richard. It sort of looked as though Louie had just not gotten around to cutting his hair in a while. He had a square face, a slender build, and looked sort of inoffensive. But muscles worked in his forearms as he tented his fingers and looked at me. Even if he hadn't been a wererat, I might not have offered to arm-wrestle him.

He had come in specially to talk to me on a Sunday. It was my day off, too.

It was the first Sunday that Richard and I hadn't at least talked to each other in months. Richard had called and canceled, saying it was pack business. I hadn't been able to ask questions because you can't argue with your answering machine. I didn't call him back. I wasn't ready to talk to him, not after last night.

I felt like a fool this morning. I'd said yes to a proposal from someone I didn't know. I knew what Richard had shown me, his outward face, but inside was a whole new world that I had just begun to visit.

"What did you and the rest of the professors think of the footprints the police sent over?"

"We think it's a wolf."

"A wolf? Why?"

"It's certainly a big canine. It isn't a dog, and other than wolves that's about it."

"Even allowing for the fact that the canine foot is mixed with human?"

"Even allowing."

"Could it be Peggy Smitz?"

"Peggy could control herself really well. Why would she kill someone?"

"I don't know. Why wouldn't she kill someone?"

He leaned back in his chair. It squeaked under his weight. "Fair question. Peggy was as much a pacifist as the pack would let her be."

"She didn't fight?"

"Not unless forced into it."

"Was she high in the pack structure?"

"Shouldn't you be asking Richard these questions? He is next in line to the throne, so to speak."

I just looked at him. I wouldn't look away as if I were guilty of something.

"I smell trouble in paradise," he said.

I ignored the hint. Business, we had business to discuss. "Peggy's husband came to see me. He wanted me to look for her. He didn't know about the other missing lycanthropes. Why wouldn't Peggy have told him?"

"A lot of us survive in relationships by pretending as hard as we can that we aren't what we are. I bet Peggy didn't talk pack business with her husband."

"How hard is it to pretend?"

"The better you control, the easier it is to pretend."

"So it can be done."

"Would you want to go through your life pretending you didn't raise zombies? Never talking about it? Never sharing it? Having your husband embarrassed by it, or sickened by it?"

I felt my face burn. I wanted to deny it. I wasn't embarrassed by Richard, or sickened, but I wasn't comfortable, either. Not comfortable enough to protest. "It doesn't sound like a very good way to live," I said.

"It isn't."

There was a very heavy silence in the room. If he thought I was going to spill the beans, he was wrong. When all else goes to hell, concentrate on business. "The police were all over the area where the body was found today. Sergeant Storr said they didn't find anything but a few more footprints, a little blood." Truth was, they had found some fresh rifle slugs in the trees near the kill area, but I wasn't sure I was free to share that with the lycanthrope community. It was police business. I was lying to both sides. It didn't seem like a good way to run a murder investigation, or a missing-person case.

"If the police and the pack would share information, we might be able to solve this case."

He shrugged. "It's not my call, Anita. I'm just an Indian, not a chief."

"Richard's a chief," I said.

"Not as long as Marcus and Raina are alive."

"I didn't think Richard had to fight her for pack dominance. I thought it was Marcus's fight."

Louie laughed. "If you think Raina would let Marcus lose without helping him, you haven't met the woman."

"I have met her. I just thought her helping Marcus was against pack law."

He shrugged again. "I don't know about pack law, but I know Raina. If Richard would play footsie with her, she might even help him defeat Marcus, but he's made it very clear that he doesn't like her."

"Richard said she had this idea about lycanthrope porno movies?"

Louie's eyes widened. "Richard told you about that?"

I nodded.

"I'm surprised. He was embarrassed about the whole idea. Raina was hot and heavy to have him be her costar. I think she was trying to seduce him, but she misjudged her boy. Richard is too private to ever have sex for a camera."

"Raina's starred in some of the movies?"

"So I'm told."

"Have any of the wererats appeared in the flicks?"

He shook his head. "Rafael forbid it. We're one of the few groups that refused it flat."

"Rafael's a good man."

"And a good rat," Louie said.

I smiled. "Yeah."

"What's up with you and Richard?"

"What do you mean?"

"He left a message on my answering machine. Said he had big news concerning you. When I saw him in person, he said it was nothing. What happened?"

I didn't know what to say. Not a new event lately. "I think it has to be Richard's news."

"He said something about it being your choice and he couldn't talk about it. You say it's his business and you can't talk about it. I wish one of you would talk to me."

I opened my mouth, closed it, and sighed. I had questions that I needed answers to, but Louie was Richard's friend before he was mine. Loyalty and all that. But who the hell else could I ask? Irving? He was in enough trouble with Richard.

"I've heard Richard and Rafael talk about controlling their beasts. Does that mean the change?"

He nodded. "Yes." He looked at me, eyes narrowing. "If you've heard Richard talk about his beast, you must have seen him close to changing. What happened last night?"

"If Richard didn't tell you, Louie, I don't think I can."

"The grapevine says you killed Alfred. Is that true?"

"Yes."

He looked at me as if waiting for more, then shrugged. "Raina won't like that."

"Marcus didn't seem too pleased, either."

"But he won't jump you in a dark alley. She will."

"Why didn't Richard tell me that?"

"Richard is one of the best friends I have. He's loyal, honest, caring, sort of the world's furriest boy scout. If he has a flaw, it's that he expects other people to be loyal, honest, and caring."

"Surely after what he's seen from Marcus and Raina, he doesn't still think they're nice people?"

"He knows they aren't nice, but he has trouble seeing them as evil. When all is said and done, Anita, Marcus is his alpha male. Richard respects authority. He's been trying to work out some sort of compromise with Marcus for months. He doesn't want to kill him. Marcus doesn't have the same qualms about Richard."

"Irving told me Richard defeated Marcus, could have killed him, and didn't. Is that true?"

" 'Fraid so."

"Shit."

"Yeah, I told Richard he should have done it, but he's never killed anyone. He believes all life is precious."

"All life *is* precious," I said.

"Some life is just more precious than others," Louie said.

I nodded. "Yeah."

"Did Richard change for you last night?"

"God, you are relentless."

"You said it was one of my better qualities."

"It is normally." It was like being picked at by Ronnie. She never gave up, either.

"Did he change for you?"

"Sort of," I said.

"And you couldn't handle it." It was a flat statement.

"I'm not sure, Louie. I'm just not sure."

"Better to find out now," he said.

"I guess so."

"Do you love him?"

"None of your damn business."

"I love Richard like a brother. If you're going to slice his heart up and serve it on a platter, I'd like to know now. If you leave, I'll be the one helping him pick up the pieces."

"I don't want to hurt Richard," I said.

"I believe you." He just looked at me. There was a great peacefulness to his expression, as if he could wait all night for me to answer the question. Louie had more patience than I would ever have.

"Yes, I love him. Happy?"

"Do you love him enough to embrace his furry side?" His eyes were staring at me as if they'd burn a hole through my heart.

"I don't know. If he were human . . . Shit."

"If he were human, you'd marry him maybe?" He was kind enough to make it a question.

"Maybe," I said. But it wasn't a maybe. If Richard had been human, I'd be a very happily engaged woman right now. Of course, there was another male that wasn't human that had been trying to get me to date him for a while. Jean-Claude had said that Richard wasn't any more human than he was. I hadn't believed him. I was beginning to. It looked like I owed Jean-Claude an apology. Not that I would ever admit it to him.

"A writer came to my office yesterday, Elvira Drew. She's doing a book on shapeshifters. It sounds legit and could be good press." I explained the format of the book.

"Sounds good, actually," he said. "Where do I come in?"

"Guess."

"She's missing a wererat interview."

"Bingo."

"I can't afford to be exposed, Anita. You know that."

"It doesn't have to be you. Is there anyone among you that would be willing to meet with her?"

"I'll ask around," he said.

"Thanks, Louie." I stood.

He stood and offered me his hand. His grip was firm but not too strong, just right. I wondered how fast he really was, and how easy it would be for him to crush my hand into pulp. It must have shown on my face, because he said, "You might want to stop dating Richard. Until you get this sorted out."

I nodded. "Yeah, maybe."

We stood there in silence for a moment. There didn't seem to be anything left to say, so I left. I was all out of clever repartee, or even a good joke. It was barely dark, and I was tired. Tired enough to go home and crawl into bed and hide. Instead, I was on my way to the Lunatic Cafe. I was going to try and convince Marcus to let me talk to the police. Eight missing, one dead human. It didn't have to be connected. But if it was a werewolf, then Marcus would know who did the killing, or Raina would know. Would they tell me? Maybe, maybe not, but I had to ask. They'd come closer to telling me the truth than they would to the police. Funny how all the monsters talked to me and not to the police. You had to begin to wonder why the monsters were so damn comfortable around me.

I raised zombies and slew vampires. Who was I to throw stones?

21

I walked along the campus sidewalk towards my car. I walked from one pool of light to the next. My breath fogged in the glow of the streetlights. It was my night off so I was dressed all in black. Bert wouldn't let me wear black to work. Said it gave the wrong impression—too harsh—associated with evil magic. If he'd done any research, he'd have found that red, white, and a host of other colors are used in evil rituals. It depends on the religion. It was very Anglo-Saxon of him to outlaw only black.

Black jeans, black Nike Airs with a blue swoosh, a black sweater, and a black trench coat. Even my guns and holsters were black. I was just monochrome as hell tonight. I was wearing silver, but it was hidden under the sweater; a cross, and a knife on each forearm. I was headed for the Lunatic Cafe. I was going to try to persuade Marcus to let me share information with the police. The missing lycanthropes, even the ones like Peggy Smitz who didn't want their secret known, were safe from bad publicity now. They were dead. They had to be. There is no way to hold eight shapeshifters against their will for this long. Not alive.

It couldn't hurt them to tell the cops, and it might save any other shapeshifters from going missing. I had to talk to the people who had last seen the missing ones. Why had none of them put up a fight? That had to be a clue. Ronnie was better at this sort of thing than I was. Maybe we could go out detecting tomorrow.

Would Richard be there? If so, what was I supposed to say to him? It made me stop walking. I stood in the cold dark, trapped between streetlights. I wasn't ready to see Richard again. But we had a dead body, maybe more. I couldn't chicken out just because I didn't want to see Richard. It would be pure cowardice.

Truth was, I would rather have faced down a herd of vampires than one would-be fiancé.

The wind whistled at my back as if a blizzard were moving up behind me. My hair streamed around my face. The trees were icy still, no wind. I whirled, Browning in my hand. Something slammed into my back, sending me smashing into the sidewalk. I tried to save myself, arms slamming into the concrete first. My arms went numb and tingling. I couldn't feel my hands. My head snapped downward.

There is that moment after a really good head blow that you can't react. A frozen moment when you wonder if you'll ever be able to move again.

Someone was sitting on my back. Hands jerked my coat on the left side. I heard the cloth rip. The feeling was coming back in my arms. I'd lost the Browning. I tried to roll over on my side to go for the Firestar. A hand slammed my head into the sidewalk again. Light exploded inside my head. My vision went dark, and when I could see again, I caught Gretchen's face rearing above me.

She had a handful of my hair, pulled painfully to one side. My sweater was ripped away from my shoulder. Gretchen's mouth was stretched wide, fangs shimmering in the dark. I screamed. The Firestar was trapped under my body. I went for one of the knives, but it was under the sleeve of my coat, the sleeve of my sweater. I wasn't going to get there in time.

There was a high scream, and it wasn't me. A woman was standing at the end of the sidewalk screaming. Gretchen raised her head and hissed at them. The man with her grabbed her shoulders and pushed her off the path. They ran. Wise.

I plunged the knife into her throat. It wasn't a killing blow and I knew it, but I thought she'd rear. Give me a chance at the Firestar. She didn't. I shoved the knife in to its hilt; blood poured down my hand, splattered my face. She darted downward, going for my throat. The knife had done as much damage as it could. There was no time to go for the second blade. I was still pinned over the gun. I had forever to watch her mouth coming for me, to know I was going to die.

Something dark smashed into her, rolling her off me with the impact. I was left gasping on the sidewalk, blinking. I had the Firestar in my hand. I didn't remember getting it out. Practice, practice, practice.

There was a wererat on top of Gretchen. The dark muzzle darted downward, teeth glimmering. Gretchen grabbed his muzzle, holding those snapping teeth from her throat. A furred claw slashed her pale face. Blood flowed. She screamed, punching one hand into his stomach. It raised him in the air, just enough for her to get her legs under him. She lifted with her legs and shoved him into the air. The wererat went tumbling like a thrown ball.

Gretchen was on her feet like magic. I sighted down the barrel of the gun, still on the ground. But she was gone into the bushes, after the wererat. I'd missed my chance.

Snarls and snapping branches came from the darkness. It had to be Louie. I didn't know that many wererats that would come to my rescue.

I stood up and the world swam. I stumbled, and it took everything I had to stay standing. For the first time I wondered how badly I was hurt. I knew I was scraped up some because I could feel that sharp, stinging pain that taking off the first layer of skin will get you. I raised a hand to my head and it came away with blood. Some of it was mine.

I tried another step, and I could do it. Maybe I'd just tried to stand too fast. I hoped so. I didn't know if a wererat could take a vampire or not. But I wasn't standing out here in the clear and waiting to find out.

I was at the edge of the trees when they rolled out of the darkness and over me. I lay on the pavement for the second time, but there was no time to get my wind back. I rolled onto my right side, sighting down my arm towards the noise.

The movement was too sudden, my vision swam. When I could focus again, Gretchen had sunk fangs into Louie's neck. He gave a high, wild squeal. I couldn't shoot her lying down, all I could see from here was the rat's body, her arms and legs riding him, but the only shot I had that might kill her was a line of her blond head. I didn't dare try it. I might kill Louie, too. Even clear-headed, it would have been an iffy shot.

I got to my knees. The world shifted, and nausea rolled at the back of my throat. When the world was still again, there was still nothing to shoot at. Some trick of a distant streetlight flashed on the blood pouring from his throat. If she'd had the teeth Louie had, he'd be dead.

I fired into the ground near them, hoping it would scare her off. It didn't. I aimed at a tree just above her head. It was as close to Louie as I dared get. The bullet exploded in the tree. One blue eye looked at me while she fed off of him. She was going to kill him while I watched.

''Shoot her,'' it was Louie's voice twisted around furry jaws, but his voice. His eyes glazed and closed, while I watched. Last words.

I took a deep, steadying breath and aimed two-handed, one hand cupping the other in a teacup grip. I sighted on that one pale eye. Darkness swam over my vision. I waited on my knees, blind, for my vision to clear and me to pull that trigger. If my vision went while I was firing, I'd hit Louie. I was out of options.

Or maybe not. ''Richard asked me to marry him and I said yes. You can smell a lie. I said yes to marrying someone else. We don't have to do this.''

She hesitated. I stared into her eye. My vision was clear. Arm steady, I pressed on the trigger. She released his throat, sliding her head into his neck fur, hiding. Her voice came muffled but clear enough: ''Put down your little gun, and I will let him go.''

I took a breath and raised the gun skyward. ''Let him go.''

''The gun first,'' she said.

I didn't want to give up my only gun. That seemed like a really bad idea. But what choice did I have? If I were Gretchen, I wouldn't want me armed. I did still have the second knife, but from this distance it was useless. Even if I could throw well enough to put it through her heart, it would have to be a very solid blow. She was too old for a glancing blow to do much good. I'd shoved a knife hilt-deep into her throat and it hadn't slowed her down. It had impressed me.

I laid the Firestar on the sidewalk and raised my hands to show myself unarmed. Gretchen rose slowly from behind Louie's limp body. Without her propping him up, his body rolled onto its back. There was a looseness to the movement that unnerved me. Was it too late? Could a vampire's bite kill like silver?

The vampire and I stared at each other. My knife was sticking out of her throat like an exclamation mark. She hadn't even bothered to take it out. Jesus. I must have missed the voice box or she wouldn't have been able to talk. Even vampirism has its limits. I was meeting her eyes. Nothing was happening. It was like looking into anyone's eyes. That shouldn't have been. Maybe she was holding her power in check? Naw.

''Is he still alive?''

''Come closer and see for yourself.''

"No, thanks." If Louie was dead, my being dead wouldn't help that.

She smiled. "Tell me again, this news of yours."

"Richard asked me to marry him, and I said yes."

"You love this Richard?"

"Yes." This was no time for hesitation. She accepted it with a nod. I guess it was true, surprise, surprise.

"Tell Jean-Claude and I will be content."

"I plan on telling him."

"Tonight."

"Fine, tonight."

"Lie. When I leave you will tend your wounds, and his, and not tell Jean-Claude."

I couldn't even get away with a little white lie, shit. "What do you want?"

"He is at Guilty Pleasures tonight. Go there and tell him. I will be waiting for you."

"I have to tend to his wounds before I do anything," I said.

"Tend his wounds, but come to Guilty Pleasures before dawn, or our truce is over."

"Why not tell Jean-Claude yourself?"

"He would not believe me."

"He could tell you were telling the truth," I said.

"Just because I believed it was truth would not make it so. But he will smell the truth on you. If I am not there, wait for me. I want to be there when you tell him you love another. I want to see his face fall."

"Fine, I'll be there before dawn."

She stepped over Louie's body. She had the Browning in her right hand, held palm over the barrel and grip, not to fire but to keep me from it. She stalked to me and picked up the Firestar, eyes never leaving me.

Blood dripped down the knife hilt in her throat. The blood fell in a heavy, wet splat. She smiled as my eyes widened. I knew it didn't kill them, but I'd thought it hurt. Maybe they only took the blades out from habit. It certainly didn't seem to bother Gretchen.

"You can have these back after you tell him," she said.

"You're hoping he kills me," I said.

"I would shed no tears."

Great. Gretchen took a step backwards, then another. She stopped at the edge of the trees, a pale form in the dark. "I await you, Anita Blake. Do not disappoint me this night."

"I'll be there," I said.

She smiled, flashing bloody teeth, stepped back again, and was gone. I thought it was a mind trick, but there was a backwash of air. The trees shook as if a storm were passing. I looked up and caught a glimpse of something. Not wings, not a bat, but . . . something. Something my eyes couldn't or wouldn't make sense of.

The wind died, and the winter dark was as still and quiet as a tomb. Sirens wailed in the distance. I guess the coeds had called the cops. Couldn't say I blamed them.

22

I stood, carefully. The world didn't spin. Great. I walked to Louie. His rat-man form lay very still and dark on the grass. I knelt, and another wave of dizziness took me. I waited on all fours for it to pass. When the world was steady once more, I put my hand on his fur-covered chest. I let out a sigh when his chest rose and fell under my palm. Alive, breathing. Fantastic.

If he'd been in human form, I'd have checked his neck wound. I was pretty sure that just touching his blood in animal form wouldn't give me lycanthropy, but I wasn't one hundred percent. I had enough problems without turning furry once a month. Besides, if I had to pick an animal, a rat wouldn't be it.

The sirens were getting closer. I wasn't sure what to do. He was badly hurt, but I'd seen Richard worse off and he had healed. But had he needed some medical attention to get healed? I didn't know. I could hide Louie in the bushes, but would I be leaving him to die? If the cops saw him like this, his secret was out. His life would be in a shambles around him, just because he'd helped me. It didn't seem fair.

A long sigh rose from his pointed muzzle. A shudder ran through his body. The fur began to recede like the tide pulling back. The awkward, ratlike limbs began to straighten. His bent legs straightened. I watched his human form rise from the fur like a shape caught in ice.

Louie lay there on the dark grass, pale and naked and very human. I'd never seen the process in reverse before. It was just as spectacular as the change to animal form, but it wasn't as frightening, maybe because of the end product.

The wound on his neck was more like an animal bite than a vampire, skin torn, but two of the marks were deeper, fangs. There was no blood on the wound now. As I watched, blood started to flow. I couldn't tell for sure in the dark, but it looked like the wound was already beginning to heal. I checked his pulse. It was steady, strong, but what did I know? I wasn't a doctor.

The siren was silent, but lights strobed the darkness just over the trees like colored lightning. The cops were coming, and I had to decide what to do. My head was feeling better. My vision was clear. The dizziness seemed to be gone. Of course, I hadn't tried to stand again. I could carry him in a fireman's carry; not too fast and not too far, but I could do it. The bite marks were shrinking. Hell, he'd be healed by morning. I couldn't let the cops see him, and I couldn't leave him here. I didn't know if lycanthropes could freeze to death, but I didn't feel lucky tonight.

I covered him with my coat, wrapping it around him as I lifted. Wouldn't do for him to get frostbite on certain delicate places. You lose a toe and there you are.

I took a deep breath and stood with him across my shoulders. My knees didn't like lifting him. But I got to my feet, and my vision wavered. I stood there, bracing against a suddenly moving world. I fell to my knees. The extra weight made it hurt.

The police were coming. If I didn't get out of here right now, I might as well give it up. Giving up wasn't one of my better things. I got to one knee and gave that last push. My knees screamed at me, but I was standing. Black waves passed over my eyes. I just stood there letting it sway over me. The dizziness wasn't as bad this time. The nausea was worse. I'd throw up later.

I stayed on the sidewalk. I didn't trust myself in the snow. Besides, even city cops could follow prints in the snow. A planting of trees hid me from the direction of the flashing lights. The sidewalk led around a building. Once around that I could backtrack to my car. The thought of driving while my vision kept sweeping in and out was a bad idea, but if I didn't get some distance between me and the cops, all this effort would be wasted. I had to get to the car. I had to get Louie out of sight.

I didn't look back to see if there were flashlights sweeping the area. Looking back wouldn't help, and with Louie on my shoulders it was a lot of effort to turn. I put one foot in front of the other, and the edge of the building curved around us. We were out of sight, even if they cleared the trees. Progress. Great.

The side of the building stretched like some dark monolith to my left. The distance around the building seemed to be growing. I put one foot in front of the other. If I just concentrated on walking, I could do this. Louie seemed to be getting lighter. That wasn't right. Was I about to pass out and just didn't know it yet?

I looked up and found the edge of the building right beside me. I'd lost some time there. It was a bad sign. I was betting I had a concussion. It couldn't be too bad or I'd pass out, right? Why didn't I believe that?

I peered around the corner, concentrating on not whacking Louie's legs into the building. It took a lot more concentration than it should have.

The police lights strobed the darkness. The car was parked on the edge of the lot with one door open. The radio filled the night with garbled squawking. The car looked empty. Squinting at something that far away brought a wave of blackness across my eyes. How the hell was I going to drive? One problem at a time. Right now, just get Louie to the Jeep, out of sight.

I stepped away from the sheltering building. It was my last refuge. If the cops came now with me walking across the parking lot, it was over.

On a Sunday night there weren't a lot of cars in the visitors' parking lot. My Jeep sat under one of the streetlights. I always parked under a light if I could. Safety rule number one for women traveling alone after dark. The Jeep looked like it was in a spotlight. The light was probably not that bright. It just looked that way because I was trying to be sneaky.

Somewhere about halfway to the Jeep, I realized that the head injury wasn't the only problem. Sure I could lift this much weight, even walk with it, but not forever. My knees were trembling. Every step was getting slower and took more effort. If I fell down again, I wasn't going to be able to pick Louie back up. I wasn't even sure I'd be able to get me back up.

One foot in front of the other, just one foot in front of the other. I concentrated on my feet until the Jeep's tires came into view. There, that wasn't so hard.

The car keys were, of course, in the coat pocket. I hit the button on the key chain that unlocked the doors. The high-pitched beeping noise that signaled them open only sounded loud enough to wake the dead. I opened the middle doors, balancing Louie one handed. I let him fall into the backseat. The coat fell open, revealing a naked line of body. I must have been feeling better than I thought because I took the time to fling the coat over his groin and lower chest. It left one arm flung outward, limp and awkward, but that was all right. My sense of propriety could live with a naked arm.

I closed the door and caught a glimpse of myself in the sideview mirror. One side of my face was a bloody mask, the clean parts had bloody scrapes. I slid into the Jeep, and got a box of aloe and lanolin baby wipes from the floorboard. I'd started carrying the wipes to help with the blood from zombie raisings. It worked better than the plain soap and water that I had been carrying. I wiped enough blood off that I wouldn't get stopped by the first cop that drove by, then slid behind the wheel.

I glanced in the rearview mirror. The police car still stood there alone, like a dog waiting for its master. The motor kicked. I put the car in gear and hit the gas. The Jeep weaved towards a streetlight as if it were a magnet. I slammed the brakes on and was glad I'd worn my seat belt.

Okay, so I was just a bit disoriented. I hit the light on my sunshade that's supposed to let you check your makeup, and checked my eyes instead. The pupils were even. If one pupil had been blown, that might have meant I was bleeding inside my head. People died from things like that. I'd have turned us in to the cops and gotten a ride to the hospital. But it wasn't that bad. I hoped.

I clicked the light off and eased the Jeep forward. If I drove very slowly, the car wouldn't want to kiss the streetlight. Great. I inched out of the parking lot, expecting to hear shouts behind me. Nothing. The street was dark and lined with cars on either side. I crawled down the street at about ten miles per hour, afraid to go faster. It looked like I was driving through cars on one side. Illusion but unnerving as hell.

A bigger street and headlights stabbed at my eyes. I put my hand up to shield my eyes and nearly ran into a parked car. Shit. I had to pull over before I hit something. Four more blocks before I found a gas station with pay phones outside. I wasn't sure how rough I looked. I didn't want some overzealous clerk to call the police after I'd gone to all the trouble of getting away undetected.

I eased the Jeep into the parking lot. If I overcorrected and took out the gas pumps, they might call the cops anyway. I pulled the Jeep in front of the phone bank. I put it in park and was very relieved to be standing still.

I fumbled a quarter out of the ashtray. It had never held anything but change. When I left the car, for the first time I was aware of how cold it was without my coat. There was a line of cold going down my back where the sweater had been ripped away. I dialed Richard's number without thinking about it. Who else could I call?

The answering machine kicked in. ''Dammit, be home, Richard, be home.''

The beep sounded. ''Richard, this is Anita. Louie's hurt. Pick up if you're there. Richard, Richard, dammit, Richard, pick up.'' I leaned my forehead against the cool metal of the phone booth. ''Pick up, pick up, pick up. Richard. Dammit.''

He picked up, sounding out of breath. ''Anita, it's me. What's wrong?''

''Louie got hurt. His wound's healing. How do you explain that to a hospital emergency room?''

''You don't,'' he said. ''We have doctors that can tend him. I'll give you an address to go to.''

''I can't drive.''

''Are you hurt?''

''Yeah.''

''How bad?''

''Bad enough that I don't want to drive.''

''What happened to the two of you?''

I gave him a very abbreviated version of the night's events. Just a vampire attack, no specific motive. I wasn't ready to tell him I had to tell Jean-Claude about our engagement, because I wasn't sure we still had one. He'd asked, I said yes, but now I wasn't sure. I wasn't even sure Richard was sure anymore.

''Give me the address.'' I did. ''I know the gas station you're talking about. I stop there when I visit Louie sometimes.''

''Great. When can you be here?''

''Are you going to be all right until I can get there?''

''Sure.''

''Because if you're not, call the police. Don't risk your life just to keep Louie's secret. He wouldn't want that.''

''I'll keep that in mind.''

''Don't get macho on me, Anita. I don't want anything to happen to you.''

I smiled with my forehead pressed against the phone. ''Macho's the only way I got this far. Just get here, Richard. I'll be waiting.'' I hung up before he could get mushy on me. I was feeling too pitiful to withstand much sympathy.

I got back into the Jeep. It was cold inside the car. I'd forgotten to turn on the heater. I turned the heater on full blast. I knelt on the seat and checked on Louie. He hadn't moved. I touched the skin of his wrist, checking for the pulse. It was strong and steady. For the heck of it, I lifted his hand and let it flop back. No reaction. I hadn't really expected one.

Usually, a lycanthrope stayed in animal form for eight or ten hours. Changing back early took a lot of energy. Even if he hadn't been hurt, Louie would be asleep for the rest of the night. Though sleep was too mild a word for it. You couldn't wake them from it. It wasn't a great survival method. Just like sleeping during the day didn't help vampires much. Evolution's way of helping us puny humans out.

I slid down in my seat. I wasn't sure how long it would take for Richard to get here. I glanced at the station building. The man behind the counter was reading a magazine. He wasn't taking any notice of us at the moment. If he'd been watching, I would have moved out of the lights. Didn't want him wondering why I was sitting here, but if he wasn't paying attention, we'd just sit here.

I leaned back, putting my head against the headrest. I wanted to close my eyes, but didn't. I was pretty sure I had a concussion. Going to sleep wasn't a good idea. I'd had one head injury worse than this, but Jean-Claude had cured it. But a vampire mark was a little harsh for a mild concussion.

This was the first time I'd been badly hurt since I lost Jean-Claude's marks. They had made me harder to hurt, faster to heal. Not a bad side effect. One of the other effects had been an ability to meet a vampire's eyes without them being able to bespell me. Like I had met Gretchen's eyes.

How had I met her eyes with impunity? Had Jean-Claude lied to me? Was there some lingering mark? Another question to ask him when I saw him. Of course, after I told him the news bulletin, all hell would break loose and there would be no more questions. Well, maybe one question. Would Jean-Claude try to kill Richard? Probably.

I sighed, closing my eyes. I was suddenly tired, so tired I didn't want to open my eyes. Sleep sucked at me. I opened my eyes and slid up in the seat. Maybe it was just tension, adrenaline draining away, or maybe it was a concussion. I clicked on the overhead light and checked on Louie again. Breathing and pulse were steady. His head was to one side, neck stretched in a long line that showed the wound. The bite marks were healing. I couldn't see it happening, but every time I looked it was better. Like trying to watch a flower bloom. You see the effect, but you never actually see it happening.

Louie was going to be all right. Would Richard be all right? I'd said yes because in the heat of the moment I meant it. I could see spending my life with him. Before Bert found me and showed me how to use my talent for money, I'd had a life. I'd gone hiking, camping. I'd been a biology major and thought I'd go on for my master's and doctorate and study preternatural creatures for the rest of my life. Sort of the preternatural Jane Goodall. Richard had reminded me of all that, of what I'd originally thought my life would be like. I hadn't planned on spending my life ass deep in blood and death. Really.

If I gave in to Jean-Claude, it would be admitting that there was nothing but death, nothing but violence. Sexy, attractive, but death all the same. I'd thought with Richard I had a chance at life. Something better. After last night I wasn't even sure of that.

Was it too much to ask for someone who was human? Hell, I knew a lot of women in my age bracket that couldn't get a date at all. I'd been one of them until Richard. All right, Jean-Claude would have taken me out, but I was avoiding him. I couldn't imagine dating Jean-Claude as if he were an ordinary guy. I could imagine having sex with him, but not dating. The thought of him picking me up at eight, dropping me off, and being satisfied with a good-night kiss seemed ridiculous.

I stayed kneeling in the seat, staring down at Louie. I was afraid to turn around and get comfortable, afraid I'd fall asleep and not wake up. I wasn't really afraid, but I was worried. A trip to the hospital might not be a bad idea, but first I had to tell Jean-Claude about Richard. And keep him from killing him.

I laid my face on my arms, and a deep, throbbing pain started behind my forehead. Good. My head should hurt after the beating it had taken. The fact that it hadn't been hurting had worried me. A good headache I could live with.

How was I going to keep Richard alive? I smiled. Richard was an alpha wolf. What made me think he couldn't take care of himself? I'd seen what Jean-Claude could do. I'd seen him when he wasn't human at all. Maybe after I saw Richard change I'd feel differently about him. Maybe I wouldn't feel so protective. Maybe hell would freeze over.

I did love Richard. I really did. I'd meant that yes. I'd meant it before last night. Before I felt his power creep over my skin. Jean-Claude had been right about one thing. Richard wasn't human. The snuff film had excited him. Was Jean-Claude's idea of sex any stranger than that? I'd never let myself find out.

Someone knocked on the window. I jumped and whirled. My vision swam in black streamers. When I could see again, Richard's face was outside the window.

I unlocked the doors, and Richard opened one. He started to reach for me and stopped. The hesitation on his face was painful. He wasn't sure I'd let him touch me. I turned away from the hurt on his face. I loved him, but love isn't enough. All the fairy tales, the romance novels, the soap operas; they're all lies. Love does not conquer all.

He was very careful not to touch me. His voice was neutral. "Anita, are you all right? You look awful."

"Nice to know I look like I feel," I said.

He touched my cheek, fingers sliding just over the skin, a ghost of a touch that made me shiver. He traced the edge of the scrape. It hurt and I jerked away. A spot of blood decorated his fingertips, gleaming in the dome light. I watched his eyes stare at the blood. I saw the thought trail behind his true brown eyes. He almost licked his fingers clean, as Rafael had done. He wiped his fingers on his coat, but I'd seen the hesitation. He knew I'd seen it.

"Anita . . ."

The back door opened, and I whirled, going for the last knife I had on me. The world swam in waves of blackness and nausea. The movement had been too abrupt. Stephen the Werewolf stood in the half-open door staring at me. He was sort of frozen there, blue eyes wide. He was looking at the silver knife in my hand. The fact that I'd been blind and too sick to use it seemed to have escaped him. It might have been that I was kneeling, moving towards him. I'd been willing to strike blind as a bat, not considering that whoever it was had a right to be there.

"You didn't tell me you brought someone with you," I said.

"I should have mentioned that," Richard said.

I relaxed, easing back to kneel in the seat. "Yeah, you should have mentioned that.'' The knife gleamed in the dome light. It looked razor sharp and well tended. It was.

''I was just going to check on Louie,'' Stephen said. He sounded a little shaky. He had a black leather jacket with silver studding snapped tight around his throat. His long, curling blond hair fell forward over the jacket. He looked like an effeminate biker.

''Fine,'' I said.

Stephen looked past me to Richard. I felt more than saw Richard nod. ''It's okay, Stephen.'' There was something in his voice that made me turn slowly to look at him.

He had a strange look on his face. ''Maybe you are as dangerous as you pretend to be.''

''I don't pretend, Richard.''

He nodded. ''Maybe you don't.''

''Is that a problem?''

''As long as you don't shoot me, or my pack members, I guess not.''

''I can't promise about your pack.''

''They're mine to protect,'' he said.

''Then make sure they leave me the hell alone.''

''Would you fight me over that?'' he asked.

''Would you fight me?''

He smiled, but it wasn't happy. ''I couldn't fight you, Anita. I could never hurt you.''

''That's where we're different, Richard.''

He leaned in as if to kiss me. Something on my face stopped him. ''I believe you.''

''Good,'' I said. I slipped the knife back in its sheath. I stared at his face while I did it. I didn't need to look to put the knife away. ''Never underestimate me, Richard, and what I'm willing to do to stay alive. To keep others alive. I never want us to fight, not like that, but if you don't control your pack, then I will.''

He moved away from me. His face looked almost angry. ''Is that a threat?''

''It's out of control, and you know it. I can't promise not to hurt them unless you can guarantee that they'll behave. And you can't do that.''

''No, I can't guarantee that.'' He didn't like saying it.

''Then don't ask me to promise not to hurt them.''

''Can you at least try not to kill them, as a first option?''

I thought about that. ''I don't know. Maybe.''

''You can't just say, 'Yes, Richard, I won't kill your friends'?''

''It would be a lie.''

He nodded. ''I suppose so.''

I heard the rustle of leather from the backseat as Stephen moved around. ''Louie's out of it, but he'll be okay.''

''How did you get him into the Jeep?'' Richard asked.

I just stared at him.

He had the grace to look embarrassed. ''You carried him. I knew that.'' He touched the cut on my forehead, gently. It still hurt. ''Even with this, you carried him.''

''It was either that or let the cops have him. What would have happened if they'd piled him into an ambulance and he'd started healing like that?''

''They'd have known what he was,'' Richard said.

Stephen was leaning on the back of the seat, chin resting on his forearms. He seemed to have forgotten that I'd nearly stabbed him, or maybe he was used to being threatened. Maybe. Up close his eyes were the startled blue of cornflowers. With his blond hair spilling around his face he looked like one of those china dolls that you buy in exclusive shops, that you never let children play with.

''I can take Louie to my place,'' he said.

''No,'' I said.

They both looked at me, surprised. I wasn't sure what to say, but I knew that Richard could not come with me to Guilty Pleasures. If I had any hope of keeping us all alive, Richard could not be on the spot when I broke the news.

''I thought I'd drive you home,'' Richard said, ''or to the nearest hospital, whichever you need.''

It would have been my preference to, but not tonight. ''Louie's your best friend. I thought you might want to take care of him.''

He was staring at me, lovely brown eyes narrowed into suspicious squints. ''You're trying to get rid of me. Why?''

My head hurt. I couldn't think of a good lie. I didn't think he'd buy a bad one. ''How much do you trust Stephen?''

The question seemed to throw him off balance. ''I trust him.''

His first reaction was to say yes, I trust him, but he hadn't thought about it first. ''No, Richard, I mean do you trust him not to talk to Jean-Claude or Marcus?''

''I wouldn't tell Marcus anything you didn't want me to,'' Stephen said.

''And Jean-Claude?'' I asked.

Stephen looked uncomfortable, but said, ''If he asked a direct question, I'd have to give a direct answer.''

''How can you owe more allegiance to the Master of the City than to your own pack leader?''

''I follow Richard, not Marcus.''

I glanced at Richard. ''A little palace revolt?''

''Raina wanted him in the movies. I stepped in and stopped it.''

''Marcus must really hate you,'' I said.

''He fears me,'' Richard said.

''Even worse,'' I said.

Richard didn't say anything. He knew the situation better than I did, even if he wasn't willing to do the ultimate deeds.

''Fine, I'd planned to tell Jean-Claude that you proposed.''

''You proposed,'' Stephen said. His voice held a lilt of surprise. ''Did she say yes?''

Richard nodded.

A look of delight swept over Stephen's face. ''Way to go.'' His face fell into sadness. It was like watching wind over a grassy field, everything visible on the surface. ''Jean-Claude is going to go ape-shit.''

''I couldn't have said it better myself.''

''Then why tell him tonight?'' Richard asked. ''Why not wait? You're not sure about marrying me anymore. Are you?''

''No,'' I said. I hated saying it, but it was the truth. I loved him already, but if it went much further it would be too late. If I had any doubts I needed to work them out now. Staring into his face, smelling the warm scent of his aftershave, I wished I could have thrown caution to the wind. Falling into his arms. But I couldn't. I just couldn't, not unless I was sure.

''Then why tell him at all? Unless you're planning to elope and didn't tell me, we have some time.''

I sighed. I told him why it had to be tonight. ''You can't go with me.''

''I won't let you go alone,'' he said.

''Richard, if you are Johnny-on-the-spot when he finds out, he'll try to kill you, and I'll try to kill him to protect you.'' I shook my head. ''If the shit hits the fan, this could end up like *Hamlet*.''

''How like *Hamlet*?'' Stephen asked.

''Everybody dead,'' I said.

''Oh,'' he said.

''You'd kill Jean-Claude to protect me, even after what you saw last night?''

I stared at him. I tried to read behind his eyeballs to know if there was anybody home I could really talk to. He was still Richard. With his love of the outdoors, any activity that would get you messy, and a smile that warmed me to my toes. I wasn't sure I could marry him, but I was positive I couldn't let anybody kill him.

''Yes.''

''You won't marry me, but you'll kill for me. I don't understand that.''

''Ask me if I still love you, Richard. That answer's still yes.''

''How can I let you face him alone?''

''I've been doing just fine without you.''

He touched my forehead, and I winced. ''You don't look fine.''

''Jean-Claude won't hurt me.''

''You don't know that for sure,'' he said.

He had a point there. ''You can't protect me, Richard. Your being there will get us both killed.''

''I can't let you go alone.''

''Don't go all manly on me, Richard. It's a luxury that we can't afford. If saying yes to marriage is going to make you behave like an idiot, it can be changed.''

''You took back your yes.''

''It's not a definite no, either,'' I said.

''Just trying to protect you would make you say no?''

''I don't need your protection, Richard. I don't even want it.''

He leaned his head against the headrest and closed his eyes. ''If I play the white knight, you'll leave me.''

''If you think you need to play the white knight, then you don't know me at all.''

He opened his eyes and turned his head to look at me. ''Maybe I want to be your white knight.''

''That's your problem.''

He smiled. ''I guess so.''

''If you can drive the Jeep back to my apartment, I'll take a cab.''

''Stephen can drive you,'' he said. He volunteered him without even wondering what Stephen would say about it. It was arrogant.

''No, I'll take a cab.''

''I don't mind,'' Stephen said. ''I'm due back at Guilty Pleasures tonight anyway.''

I glanced at him. ''What do you do for a living, Stephen?''

He laid his cheek on his forearm and smiled at me. He managed to look winsome and sexy at the same time. ''I'm a stripper,'' he said.

Of course he was. I wanted to point out that he'd refused to be in a pornographic movie, but he still stripped. But taking your clothes off down to tasteful undies was not the same thing as having sex on screen. Not even close.

23

Lillian was a small woman in her mid-fifties. Her salt-and-pepper hair was cut short and neat in a no-nonsense style. Her fingers were as quick and sure as the rest of her. The last time she'd treated my wounds, she'd had claws and greying fur.

I was sitting on an examining table in the basement of an apartment building. A building that housed lycanthropes and was owned by a shapeshifter. The basement was the makeshift clinic for the lycanthropes in the area. I was the first human they'd ever allowed to see the place. I should have been flattered, but managed not to be.

"Well, according to X-rays you don't have a skull fracture."

"Glad to hear it," I said.

"You may have a mild concussion, but a mild one won't show up on tests, at least nothing we have the equipment for here."

"So I can go?" I started to hop down.

She stopped me with a hand on my arm. "I didn't say that."

I eased back on the table. "I'm listening."

"Grudgingly," she said, smiling.

"If you want grace under pressure, Lillian, I'm not your girl."

"Oh, I don't know about that," she said. "I've cleaned the scrapes and taped up your forehead. You were very lucky not to need stitches."

I didn't like stitches, so I agreed with her.

"I want you to wake up every hour for twenty-four hours." I must not have looked happy, because she said, "I know it's awkward, and probably unnecessary, but humor me. If you go to sleep and are injured more severely than I think you are, you might not wake up. So humor an old rat lady. Set the alarm or have someone wake you every hour for twenty-four hours."

"Twenty-four hours from the injury?" I asked hopefully.

She laughed. "Normally I'd say from now, but you can do it from the time of the injury. We're just being cautious."

''I like being cautious.'' Richard pushed away from the wall. He came to stand with us under the lights. ''I volunteer to wake you every hour.''

''You can't go with me,'' I said.

''I'll wait for you at your apartment.''

''Oh, no driving for the night,'' Lillian said. ''Just as a precaution.''

Richard's fingertips touched the back of my hand. He didn't try to hold my hand, just that touch. Comforting. I didn't know what to do. If I was going to say no, eventually, it didn't seem fair to flirt. Just the weight of his fingers was a line of warmth all the way up my arm. Lust, just lust. Don't I wish.

''I'll drive your Jeep to your apartment, if you agree. Stephen can drive you to Guilty Pleasures.''

''I can take a cab.''

''I'd feel better if Stephen took you. Please,'' he said.

The ''please'' made me smile. ''All right, Stephen can drive me.''

''Thank you,'' Richard said.

''You're welcome.''

''I would recommend you go straight home and rest,'' Lillian said.

''I can't,'' I said.

She frowned at me. ''Very well, but rest as soon as you can. If this is a mild concussion and you abuse yourself, it could worsen. And even if it isn't a concussion, rest will do you more good than gallivanting around.''

I smiled. ''Yes, Doctor.''

She made a small umph sound. ''I know how much attention you're going to pay to my orders. But go along with you, both of you. If you won't listen to good sense, then be gone.''

I slid off the table, and Richard did not offer to help me. There were reasons why we had been dating this long. A moment of dizziness and I was fine.

Lillian didn't look happy. ''You promise me that this dizziness is less than it was.''

''Scout's honor.''

She nodded. ''I'll take your word for it.'' She didn't look really pleased about it, but she patted my shoulder and walked out. She had made no notes. There was no chart to check. Nothing to prove I'd ever been here, except for some bloody cotton swabs. It was a nice setup.

I had gotten to lie back and relax in the car on the way here. Just not having to tote around naked men or drive helped a lot. I really was feeling better, which was great since I had to see Jean-Claude tonight regardless of how I felt. I wondered whether Gretchen would have given me a night of grace if she had put me in the hospital. Probably not.

I couldn't put it off any longer. It was time to go. ''I've got to go, Richard.''

He put his hands on my shoulders. I didn't pull away. He turned me to look at him, and I let him. His face was very solemn. ''I wish I could go with you.''

''We've been over this,'' I said.

He looked away from my eyes. ''I know.''

I touched his chin and raised his eyes to mine. ''No heroics, Richard, promise me.''

His eyes were too innocent. "I don't know what you mean."

"Bullshit. You can't be waiting outside. You have to stay here. Promise me that."

He dropped his arms and stalked away from me. He leaned against the other examining table, palms flat, all his weight on his arms. "I hate you doing this alone."

"Promise me you will wait here, or wait at my apartment. Those are the only choices, Richard."

He wouldn't look at me. I walked over to him, and touched his arm. Tension sang through it. There was none of that otherworldly energy, yet, but it was there below the surface, waiting.

"Richard, look at me."

He stayed with his head bent, hair falling like a curtain between us. I ran my hand through that wavy hair, grabbing a handful close to the warmth of his skull. I used the hair like a handle and turned his face to me. His eyes were dark with more than just their color. Something was home in his eyes that I'd seen only last night. The beast was rising through his eyes like a sea monster swimming upward through dark water.

I tightened my grip on his hair, not to hurt, but to get his attention. A small sound escaped his throat. "If you fuck this up through some misguided male ego thing, you're going to get me killed." I drew his face towards me, hand tangled in his hair. When his face was only inches from mine, almost close enough to kiss, I said, "If you interfere, you will get me killed. Do you understand?"

The darkness in his eyes wanted to say no. I watched the struggle on his face. Finally he said, "I understand."

"You'll be waiting for me at home?"

He nodded, pulling his hair against my grip. I wanted to pull his face to me. To kiss him. We stood there frozen, hesitating. He moved to me. Our lips touched. It was a soft, gentle brush of lips. We stared at each other from an inch away. His eyes were drowning deep, and I could suddenly feel his body like an electric shock through my gut.

I jerked away from him. "No, not yet. I don't know how I feel about you anymore."

"Your body knows," he said.

"If lust was everything, I'd be with Jean-Claude."

His face crumbled as if I'd slapped him. "If you really aren't going to date me anymore, then don't tell Jean-Claude. It's not worth it."

He looked so hurt. That was one thing I'd never meant to do. I laid my hand on his arm. The skin was smooth, warm, real. "If I can get out of telling him, I will, but I don't think Gretchen will make that one of my choices. Besides, Jean-Claude can smell a lie. You did propose, and I said yes."

"Tell him you changed your mind, Anita. Tell him why. He'll love it. That I'm not human enough for you." He pulled away from my hand. "Jean-Claude will just eat that up." His voice was bitter, angry. The bitterness was strong enough to walk on. I'd never heard him like that.

I couldn't stand it. I came up behind him and wrapped my arms around his waist. I buried my face in the line of his spine. Cheek cradled between the swell of his shoulders. He started to turn, but I held tighter. He stood very still in my arms. His hands touched my arms tentatively at first, then he hugged them to him. A shudder ran through his back. His breath came in a long gasp.

I turned him around to face me. Tears glistened on his cheeks. Jesus. I'd never been good around tears. My first instinct was to promise them anything if they would only stop crying.

"Don't," I said. I touched a fingertip to one tear. It clung to my skin, trembling. "Don't let this tear you up, Richard. Please."

"I can't be human again, Anita." His voice sounded very normal. If I hadn't seen the tears, I wouldn't have known he was crying. "I'd be human for you if I could."

"Maybe human isn't what I want, Richard. I don't know. Give me a little time. If I can't handle you being furry, better to find out now." I felt awful, mean and petty. He was gorgeous. I loved him. He wanted to marry me. He taught junior high science. He loved hiking, camping, caving. He collected sound tracks of musicals, for God's sake. And he was next in line to rule the pack. An alpha werewolf. Shit.

"I need time, Richard. I am so sorry, but I do." I sounded like a chump. I'd never sounded so indecisive in my life.

He nodded, but didn't look convinced. "You may end up turning me down but you're going to risk your life confronting Jean-Claude. It doesn't make sense."

I had to agree. "I have to talk to him tonight, Richard. I don't want another run-in with Gretchen. Not if I can avoid it."

Richard wiped the palms of his hands over his face. He ran his hands through his hair. "Don't get yourself killed."

"I won't," I said.

"Promise," he said.

I wanted to say, "Promise," but I didn't. "I don't make promises I can't keep."

"Couldn't you be comforting and lie to me?"

I shook my head. "No."

He sighed. "Talk about painful honesty."

"I've got to go." I walked away before he could distract me again. I was beginning to think he was doing it on purpose to delay me. Of course, I was letting him do it.

"Anita." I was almost to the door. I turned back. He stood there under the harsh lights, hands at his sides, looking . . . helpless.

"We've kissed good-bye. You've told me to be careful. I've warned you not to play hero. That's it, Richard. There is no more."

He said, "I love you."

Okay, so there was more. "I love you, too." It was the truth, damn it. If I could just get over his being furry, I would marry him. How would Jean-Claude take the news? As the old saying goes, only one way to find out.

24

Guilty Pleasures is in the heart of the vampire district. Its glowing neon sign bled into the night sky, giving the blackness a crimson tint like a distant house fire. I hadn't come to the district unarmed after dark for a very long time. Okay, I had the knife, and it was better than arm wrestling, but against a vampire, not much better.

Stephen was beside me. A werewolf wasn't a bad bodyguard, but somehow Stephen didn't look scary enough. He was only an inch or two taller than me, slender as a willow with just enough shoulder definition to make him look masculine. To say his pants were tight wasn't enough. They were leather and looked painted on like a second skin. It was hard not to notice that his derriere was tight and firm. The leather jacket cut him off at the waist, so the view was unobstructed.

I was wearing my black trench coat again. It had a little bit of blood on it, but if I cleaned it, it would be wet. Wet would not keep me warm. My sweater, one of my favorite sweaters, was torn off one shoulder down to the line of my bra. Too cold without a coat. Gretchen owed me a sweater. Maybe after I got my guns back, we'd talk about that.

Three broad steps led up to closed doors. Buzz the Vampire was guarding them. It was the worst vampire name I'd ever heard. It wasn't great if you were human, but Buzz seemed all wrong for a vampire. It was a great name for a bouncer. He was tall and muscle-bound with a black crew cut. He seemed to be wearing the same black T-shirt he'd worn in July.

I knew vampires couldn't freeze to death, but I hadn't known they didn't get cold. Most vampires tried to play human. They wore coats in the winter. Maybe they didn't need them the same way Gretchen hadn't needed to take the knife from her throat. Maybe it was all pretend.

He smiled, flashing fangs. My reaction seemed to disappoint him. ''You missed a set, Stephen. The boss is pissed.''

Stephen sort of shrank in on himself. Buzz seemed to get larger, pleased with himself. ''Stephen was helping me. I don't think Jean-Claude will mind.''

Buzz squinted at me, really seeing my face for the first time. ''Shit, what happened to you?''

''If Jean-Claude wants you to know, he'll tell you,'' I said. I walked past him. There was a large sign on the door: No Crosses, Crucifixes, or Other Holy Items Allowed Inside. I pushed the doors open and kept walking, my cross securely around my neck. They could pry it from my cold dead hands if they wanted it tonight.

Stephen stayed at my heels, almost as if he were afraid of Buzz. Buzz wasn't that old a vampire, less than twenty years. He still had a sense of ''aliveness'' to him. That utter stillness that the old ones have hadn't touched the bouncer yet. So why was a werewolf afraid of a new vampire? Good question.

It was Sunday night and the place was packed. Didn't anyone have work tomorrow? The noise washed over us like a wave of nearly solid sound. That rich murmurous sound of many people in a small space determined to have a good time. The lights were as bright as they ever got. The small stage empty. We were between shows.

A blond woman greeted us at the door. ''Do you have any holy items to declare?'' She smiled when she said it. The holy-item check girl.

I smiled when I said, ''Nope.''

She didn't question me, just smiled and walked away. A male voice said, ''Just a moment, Shelia.'' The tall vampire that strode towards us was lovely to look at. He had high, sculpted cheekbones, and short blond hair styled to perfection. He was too masculine to be beautiful, and too perfect to be real. Robert had been a stripper last time I was here. It looked as though he'd moved up into management.

Shelia waited, looking from Robert to me. ''She lied to me?''

Robert nodded. ''Hello, Anita.''

''Hello. Are you the manager here now?''

He nodded.

I didn't like it, him being manager. He'd failed me once, or rather failed Jean-Claude's orders. Failed to keep someone safe. That someone had died. Robert hadn't even gotten bloody trying to stop the monsters. He should at least have gotten hurt trying. I didn't insist he die to keep people safe, but he should have tried harder. I'd never completely trust him or forgive him.

''You are wearing a holy item, Anita. Unless on police business, you must give it to Shelia.''

I glanced up at him. His eyes were blue. I glanced down, then up, and realized I could meet his eyes. He was over a hundred years old, not nearly as powerful as Gretchen, but I shouldn't have been able to meet his eyes.

His eyes widened. ''You have to give it up. Those are the rules.''

Maybe being able to look him in the eyes had given me courage, or maybe I had had enough for one night. ''Is Gretchen here?''

He looked surprised. ''Yes, she's in the back room with Jean-Claude.''

''Then you can't have the cross.''

''I can't let you in then. Jean-Claude is very clear on that.'' There was a hint of unease in his voice, almost fear. Good.

"Take a good look at my face, Bobby-boy. Gretchen did it. If she's here, I keep the cross."

Frown lines formed between his perfect brows. "Jean-Claude said no exceptions." He stepped closer, and I let him. He lowered his voice as much as he could and be heard above the noise. "He said if I ever fail him again in anything large or small, he'll punish me."

Normally, I thought statements like that were pitiful or cruel. I agreed with this one.

"Go ask Jean-Claude," I said.

He shook his head. "I cannot trust you to stay here. If you get past me with the cross, I will have failed."

This was getting tiresome. "Can Stephen go ask?"

Robert nodded.

Stephen sort of hung by me. He hadn't recovered from Buzz's remarks. "Is Jean-Claude mad at me for missing my set?"

"You should have called if you couldn't make your set," Robert said. "I had to go on in your place."

"Good to be useful," I said.

Robert frowned at me. "Stephen should have called."

"He was taking me to a doctor. You got a problem with that?"

"Jean-Claude may."

"Then bring the great man out and let's ask him. I'm tired of standing in the door."

"Anita, how good of you to grace us with your presence." Gretchen was practically purring with anticipation.

"Robert won't let me pass."

She turned her eyes to the vampire. He took a step back. She hadn't even unleashed any of that impressive magic yet. Robert scared easy for a century-old corpse.

"We have been awaiting her, Robert. Jean-Claude is most anxious to see her."

He swallowed hard. "I was told that no one came inside with a holy item other than the police. No exceptions were to be made."

"Not even for the master's sweetheart." She put a lot of irony in that last part.

Robert either didn't get it or ignored it. "Until Jean-Claude tells me differently, she doesn't go through with a cross."

Gretchen stalked around us all. I wasn't sure who looked more worried. "Take off the little cross and let us get this over with."

I shook my head. "Nope."

"It didn't do you a lot of good earlier tonight," she said.

She had a point. For the first time I realized I hadn't even thought of bringing out my cross earlier. I'd gone for my weapons, but not my faith. Pretty damn sad.

I fingered the cool silver of the chain. "The cross stays."

"You are both spoiling my fun," she said. The way she said it made that sound like a very bad thing. "I'll give you one of your weapons back."

A moment before I'd have agreed, but not now. I was embarrassed that I had not gone for my cross earlier. It wouldn't have kept her from jumping me at the beginning. She was too powerful for that. But it might have chased her off Louie. I was going to have to stop skipping church even if I didn't get to sleep at all.

"No."

"Is this your way of getting out of our bargain?" Her voice was low and warm with the first stirrings of anger.

"I keep my word," I said.

"I will escort her through, Robert." She raised a hand to stop his complaining. "If Jean-Claude blames you, tell him I was going to tear your throat out." She stepped into him until only a breath separated their bodies. It was only standing that close that you realized that Robert was taller by a head and a half. Gretchen seemed bigger than that. "It isn't a lie, Robert. I think you're weak, a liability. I would kill you now if our master did not need us both. If you still fear Jean-Claude, remember that he wants you alive. I do not."

Robert swallowed hard enough that it had to hurt. He didn't back up. Brownie point for him. She moved that fraction closer, and he jumped back as if he'd been shot. "Fine, fine, take her through."

Gretchen's lip curled in disgust. One thing we agreed on: we didn't like Robert. If we had one thing in common, maybe there'd be more. Maybe we could be girlfriends. Yeah, right.

The noise level had dropped to a background murmur. We had everybody's attention. Nothing like a floor show. "Is there supposed to be an act on stage right now?" I asked.

Robert nodded. "Yes, I need to introduce him."

"Go do your job, Robert." The words were thick with scorn. Gretchen gave good scorn.

Robert left us, obviously relieved. "Wimp," I said softly.

"Come, Anita, Jean-Claude is waiting for us." She stalked away, long pale coat swinging out behind her. Stephen and I exchanged glances. He shrugged. I followed her and he trailed behind as if he were afraid of losing me.

Jean-Claude's office was like being inside a domino. Stark white walls, white carpet, black lacquer desk, black office chair, black leather couch against one wall, and two straight-backed chairs sat in front of the desk. The desk and chairs were Oriental, set with enamel pictures of cranes and Oriental women in flowing robes. I'd always liked the desk, not that I would admit it out loud.

There was a black lacquer screen in one corner. I'd never seen it before. It was large, hiding one entire corner. A dragon curled across the screen in oranges and reds, with huge bulbous eyes. It was a nice addition to the room. It was not a comfortable room, but it was stylish. Like Jean-Claude.

He sat on the leather couch dressed all in black. The shirt had a high, stiff collar that framed his face. It was hard to tell where his hair left off and the shirt began. The collar was pinned at his throat, with a thumb-size ruby pendant. The shirt was open down to his belt, leaving a triangle of pale, pale skin showing. Only the pendant kept the shirt from opening completely.

The cuffs were as wide and stiff as the collar, nearly hiding his hands. He raised one hand and I could see the cuffs were open on one side so he could still use his hands. Black jeans and velvet black boots completed the outfit.

I'd seen the pendant before, but the shirt was certainly new. "Spiffy," I said.

He smiled. "Do you like it?" He straightened the cuffs, as if they needed it.

"It's a nice change from white," I said.

"Stephen, we were expecting you earlier." His voice was mild enough, but there was an undertaste of something dark and unpleasant.

"Stephen took me to the doctor."

His midnight blue eyes turned back to me. "Is your latest police investigation getting rough?"

"No," I said. I glanced at Gretchen. She was looking at Jean-Claude.

"Tell him," she said.

I didn't think she was referring to my accusing her of trying to kill me. It was time for a little honesty, or at least a little drama. I was sure Jean-Claude wouldn't disappoint us.

"Stephen needs to leave now," I said. I didn't want him getting killed trying to protect me. He wasn't up to being anything but cannon fodder. Not against Jean-Claude.

"Why?" he asked. He sounded suspicious.

"Get on with it," Gretchen said.

I shook my head. "Stephen doesn't need to be here."

"Get out, Stephen," Jean-Claude said. "I am not angry with you for missing your set. Anita is more important to me than your being on time to your job."

That was nice to know.

Stephen gave a sort of bob, almost a bow to Jean-Claude, flashed a look at me, and hesitated. "Go on, Stephen. I'll be all right."

I didn't have to reassure him twice. He fled.

"What have you been up to, *ma petite*?"

I glanced at Gretchen. She had eyes only for him. Her face looked hungry, as if she'd waited for this a long time. I stared into his dark blue eyes and realized that I could without vampire marks; I could meet his eyes

Jean-Claude noticed it, too. His eyes widened just a bit. "*Ma petite,* you are full of surprises tonight."

"You ain't seen nothing yet," I said.

"By all means, continue. I do love a surprise."

I doubted he'd like this one. I took a deep breath and said it fast, as if that would make it go down better, like a spoonful of sugar. "Richard asked me to marry him, and I said yes." I could have added, "But I'm not sure anymore," but I didn't. I was too confused to offer up anything but the bare facts. If he tried to kill me, maybe I'd add details. Until then . . . we'd wait it out.

Jean-Claude just sat there. He didn't move at all. The heater clicked on, and I jumped. The vent was above the couch. The air played along his hair, the cloth of his shirt, but it was like watching a mannequin. The hair and clothes worked but the rest was stone.

The silence stretched and filled the room. The heater died, and the quiet was so profound I could hear the blood rushing in my ears. It was like the stillness before creation. You knew something big was coming. You just didn't know quite what. I let the silence flow around me. I wouldn't be the one to break it, because

I was afraid of what came next. This utter calmness was more unnerving than anger would have been. I didn't know what to do with it, so I did nothing. A course of action I seldom regret.

It was Gretchen who broke first. "Did you hear her, Jean-Claude? She is to wed another. She loves another."

He blinked once, a long, graceful sweep of lashes. "Ask her now if she loves me, Gretchen."

Gretchen stepped in front of me, blocking Jean-Claude from view. "What does it matter? She's going to marry someone else."

"Ask her." It was a command.

Gretchen whirled to face me. The bones in her face stood out under the skin, lips thin with rage. "You don't love him."

It wasn't exactly a question, so I didn't answer it. Jean-Claude's voice came lazy and full of some dark meaning that I didn't understand. "Do you love me, *ma petite*?"

I stared into Gretchen's rage-filled face and said, "I don't suppose you'd believe me if I said no?"

"Can you not simply say yes?"

"Yes, in some dark, twisted part of my soul, I love you. Happy?"

He smiled. "How can you marry him if you love me?"

"I love him, too, Jean-Claude."

"In the same way?"

"No," I said.

"How do you love us differently?"

The questions were getting trickier. "How am I supposed to explain something to you that I don't even understand myself?"

"Try."

"You're like great Shakespearean tragedy. If Romeo and Juliet hadn't committed suicide, they'd have hated each other in a year. Passion is a form of love, but it isn't real. It doesn't last."

"And how do you feel about Richard?" His voice was full of some strong emotion. It should have been anger, but it felt different from that. Almost as if it were an emotion I didn't have a word for.

"I don't just love Richard, I like him. I enjoy his company. I . . ." I hated explaining myself. "Oh, hell, Jean-Claude, I can't put it into words. I can see spending my life with Richard, and I can't see it with you."

"Have you set a date?"

"No," I said.

He cocked his head to one side, studying me. "It is the truth but there is some bit of lie to it. What are you holding back, *ma petite*?"

I frowned at him. "I've told you the truth."

"But not all of it."

I didn't want to tell him. He'd enjoy it too much. I felt vaguely disloyal to Richard. "I'm not completely sure about marrying Richard."

"Why not?" There was something in his face that was almost hopeful. I couldn't let him get the wrong idea.

"I saw him go all spooky. I felt his . . . power."

"And?"

"And now I'm not sure," I said.

"He's not human enough for you, either." He threw back his head and laughed. A joyous outpouring of sound that coated me like chocolate. Heavy and sweet and annoying.

"She loves another," Gretchen said. "Does it matter if she doubts him? She doubts you. She rejects you, Jean-Claude. Isn't that enough?"

"Did you do all that to her face?"

She stalked a tight circle like a tiger in a cage. "She does not love you as I do." She knelt in front of him, hands touching his legs, face staring up into his. "Please, I love you. I've always loved you. Kill her or let her marry this man. She doesn't deserve your adoration."

He ignored her. "Are you all right, *ma petite*?"

"I'm fine."

Gretchen dug fingers into his jeans, grabbing at him. "Please, please!"

I didn't like her, but the pain, the hopeless pain in her voice was horrible to hear. She'd tried to kill me and I still felt sorry for her.

"Leave us, Gretchen."

"No!" She clutched at him.

"I forbade you to harm her. You disobeyed me. I should kill you."

She just stayed kneeling, gazing up at him. I couldn't see her expression and was glad of it. I wasn't big on adoration. "Jean-Claude, please, please, I only did it for you. She doesn't love you."

His hand was suddenly around her neck. I hadn't seen him move. It was magic. Whatever was letting me look him in the eyes, it didn't stop him playing with my mind. Or maybe he was just that fast. Naw.

She tried to talk. His fingers closed, and the words came out as small, choked sounds. He stood, drawing her to her feet. Her hands wrapped around his wrist, trying to keep him from hanging her. He kept lifting until her feet dangled in the air. I knew she could fight him. I'd felt the strength in those delicate-seeming hands. Except for her hand on his wrist she didn't even struggle. Would she let him kill her? Would he do it? Could I stand here and just watch?

He stood there in his wonderful black shirt, looking elegant and scrumptious, and holding Gretchen with one arm, straight up. He walked towards his desk still holding her. He kept his balance effortlessly. Even a lycanthrope couldn't have done it, not like that. I watched his slender body walk across the carpet and knew he could pretend all he wanted to, but it wasn't human. He wasn't human.

He set her feet on the carpet on the far side of the desk. He relaxed his grip on her throat but didn't let her go.

"Jean-Claude, please. Who is she that the Master of the City should beg for her attention?"

He kept his hand resting on her throat, not squeezing now. He pushed the screen back with his free hand. It folded back to reveal a coffin. It sat up off the ground on a cloth-draped pedestal. The wood was nearly black and polished to a mirrorlike shine.

Gretchen's eyes widened. "Jean-Claude, Jean-Claude, I'm sorry. I didn't kill her. I could have. Ask her. I could have killed her, but I didn't. Ask her. Ask her!" Her voice was pure panic.

"Anita." That one word slithered across my skin, thick and full of forboding. I was very glad that that voice was not angry with me.

"She could have killed me with the first rush," I said.

"Why do you think she did not do it?"

"I think she got distracted trying to draw it out. To enjoy it more."

"No, no, I was just threatening her. Trying to frighten her away. I knew you wouldn't want me to kill her. I knew that, or she'd be dead."

"You were always a bad liar, Gretel."

Gretel?

He raised the lid on the coffin with one hand, drawing her nearer to it.

She jerked away from him. His fingernails drew bloody furrows on her throat. She stood behind the office chair, putting it between her and him, as if it would help. Blood trickled down her throat.

"Do not make me force you, Gretel."

"My name is Gretchen and has been for over a hundred years." It was the first real spirit I'd seen in her against Jean-Claude anyway. I fought the urge to applaud. It wasn't hard.

"You were Gretel when I found you, and you are Gretel still. Do not force me to remind you of what you are, Gretel."

"I will not go into that cursed box willingly. I won't do it."

"Do you really want Anita to see you at your worst?"

I thought I already had.

"I will not go." Her voice was firm, not confident, but stubborn. She meant it.

Jean-Claude stood very still. He raised one hand in a languid gesture. There was no other word for it. The movement was almost dancelike.

Gretchen staggered, grabbing at the chair for support. Her face seemed to have shrunk. It wasn't the drawing down of power that I had seen on her earlier. Not the ethereal corpse that would tear your throat out and dance in the blood. The flesh squeezed down, wrapping tight on the bones. She was withering. Not aging, dying.

She opened her mouth and screamed.

"My God, what's happening to her?"

Gretchen stood clutching bird-thin hands on the chair back. She looked like a mummified corpse. Her bright lipstick was a gruesome slash across her face. Even her yellow hair had thinned, dry and brittle as straw.

Jean-Claude walked towards her, still graceful, still lovely, still monstrous. "I gave you eternal life and I can take it back, never forget that."

She made a low mewling sound in her throat. She held out one feeble hand to him, beseeching.

"Into the box," he said. His voice made that last word dark and terrible, as if he'd said "hell" and meant it.

He had beaten the fight out of her, or maybe stolen was the word. I'd never seen anything like this. A new vampire power that I'd never even heard whispered in folklore. Shit.

Gretchen took a trembling step towards the coffin. Two painful, dragging steps and she lost her grip on the chair. She fell, bone-thin arms catching her full weight, the way you're not supposed to. A good way to get your arm broken. Gretchen didn't seem to be worried about broken bones. Couldn't blame her.

She knelt on the floor, head hanging as if she didn't have the strength to rise. Jean-Claude just stood there, staring at her. He made no move to help her. If it had been anyone but Gretchen, I might have helped her myself.

I must have made some movement towards her because Jean-Claude made a back-away gesture to me. "If she fed on a human at this moment, all her strength would return. She is very frightened. I would not tempt her right now, *ma petite*."

I stayed where I was. I hadn't planned on helping her, but I didn't like watching it.

"Crawl," he said.

She started to crawl.

I'd had enough. "You've made your point, Jean-Claude. If you want her in the coffin, just pick her up and put her there."

He looked at me. There was something almost amused in his face. "You feel pity for her, *ma petite*. She meant to kill you. You know that."

"I'd have no problem shooting her, but this . . ." I didn't have a word for it. He wasn't just humiliating her. He was stripping her of herself. I shook my head. "You're tormenting her. If it's for my benefit, I've seen enough. If it's for your benefit, then stop it."

"It is for her benefit, *ma petite*. She has forgotten who her master is. A month or two in a coffin will remind her of that."

Gretchen had reached the foot of the pedestal. She had grabbed handfuls of the cloth but couldn't drag herself to her feet.

"I think she's been reminded enough."

"You are so harsh, *ma petite*, so pragmatic, yet suddenly something will move you to pity. And your pity is as strong as your hate."

"But not nearly as fun," I said.

He smiled and lifted the lid of the coffin. The inside was white silk, of course. He knelt and lifted Gretchen. Her limbs lay awkwardly in his arms as if they didn't quite work. As he lifted her over the lip of the coffin, her long coat dragged against the wood. Something in her pocket clunked, solid and heavy.

I almost hated to ask—almost. "If that's my gun in her pocket, I need it back."

He laid her almost gently in the silk lining, then rifled her pockets. He held the Browning in one hand and began to lower the lid. Her skeletal hands raised, trying to stop its descent.

Watching those thin hands beat at the air, I almost let it go. "There should be another gun and a knife."

He widened his eyes at me, but nodded. He held the Browning out to me. I walked forward and took it. I was standing close enough to see her eyes. They were pale and cloudy, like the eyes of the very old, but there was enough expression left for terror.

Her eyes rolled wildly, staring at me. There was a mute appeal in that look. Desperation was too mild a word for it. She looked at me, not Jean-Claude, as if she knew that I was the only person in the room that gave a damn. If it bothered Jean-Claude, you couldn't tell it by his face.

I tucked the Browning under my arm. It felt good to have it back. He held the Firestar out to me. "I cannot find the knife. If you want to search her yourself, feel free."

I stared down at the dry, wrinkled skin, the lipless face. Her neck was as skinny as a chicken's. I shook my head. "I don't want it that bad."

He laughed, and even now the sound curled along my skin like velvet. A joyous sociopath.

He closed the lid, and she made horrible sounds, as though she were trying to scream and had no voice to do it with. Her thin hands beat against the lid.

Jean-Claude snapped the locks in place and leaned over the closed coffin. He whispered, "Sleep." Almost immediately the sounds slowed. He repeated the word once more, and the sounds ceased.

"How did you do that?"

"Quiet her?"

I shook my head. "All of it."

"I am her master."

"No, Nikolaos was your master, but she couldn't do that. She'd have done it to you if she could have."

"Perceptive of you, and very true. I made Gretchen. Nikolaos did not make me. Being the master vampire that brings someone over gives you certain powers over them. As you saw."

"Nikolaos had made most of the vampires in her little entourage, right?"

He nodded.

"If she could have done what you just did, I'd have seen it. She'd have shown it off."

He gave a small smile. "Again perceptive. There are a variety of powers that a master vampire can possess. Calling an animal, levitation, resistance to silver."

"Is that why my knife didn't seem to hurt Gretchen?"

"Yes."

"But each master has a different arsenal of gifts."

"Arsenal, it is an appropriate word. Now, where were we, *ma petite*? Ah, yes, I could kill Richard."

Here we go again.

25

"*Did you hear* me, *ma petite*? I could kill your Richard." He pulled the screen back into place. The coffin and its terrible contents gone just like that.

"You don't want to do that."

"Oh, but I do, *ma petite.* I would love to tear out his heart and watch him die." He walked past me. The black shirt fanned around him, exposing his stomach as he moved.

"I told you, I'm not sure I'm going to marry him. I'm not even sure I'm going to be dating him anymore. Isn't that enough?"

"No, *ma petite*. You love him. I can smell his scent on your skin. You have kissed him tonight. With all your doubts, you have held him close."

"Hurt him and I'll kill you, simple as that." My voice was very matter-of-fact.

"You would try to kill me, but I am not so easily killed." He sat down on the couch again, shirt spreading out around him, leaving most of his upper body exposed. The cross-shaped burn scar was a shiny imperfection on his flawless skin.

I stayed standing. He hadn't offered me a seat anyway. "Maybe we'd kill each other. It's your choice of music, Jean-Claude, but once we start this dance, it doesn't stop until one of us is dead."

"I am not allowed to harm Richard. Is he allowed to harm me?"

Good question. "I don't think it'll come up."

"You have dated him for months, and I have said little. Before you marry him, I want equal time."

I looked at him. "What do you mean, 'equal time'?"

"Date me, Anita, give me a chance to woo you."

"Woo me?"

"Yes," he said.

I just stared at him. I didn't know what to say. "I've been trying to avoid you for months. I'm not just going to give in now."

"Then I will start the music, and we will dance. Even if I die, and you die.

Richard will die first, that I can promise you. Surely dating me is not a fate worse than that.''

He had a point, and yet . . . ''I don't give in to threats.''

''Then I appeal to your sense of fair play, *ma petite*. You have allowed Richard to win your heart. If you had dated me first, would it be my heart you hold so dear? If you had not fought our mutual attraction, would you even have given Richard a second glance?''

I couldn't say yes, and be honest. I wasn't sure. I had refused Jean-Claude because he wasn't human. He was a monster and I didn't date monsters. But last night I'd had a glimpse of what Richard might be. I'd felt a power that rivaled Jean-Claude's creep along my skin. It was getting harder to tell the humans from the monsters. I was even beginning to wonder about myself. There are more roads to monsterdom than most people realize.

''I don't believe in casual sex. I haven't slept with Richard, either.''

''I am not blackmailing you into sex, *ma petite*. I am trying to get equal time.''

''If I agree, then what?''

''Why, I pick you up on Friday night.''

''Like a date-date?''

He nodded. ''We might even discover how you are meeting my eyes with impunity.''

''Let's just stick to as normal a date as we can.''

''As you like.''

I stared at him. He looked at me. He would pick me up on Friday. We had a date. I wondered how Richard would feel about that.

''I can't date both of you indefinitely.''

''Allow me a few months, as you have given Richard. If I cannot win you from him, then I will retire from the field.''

''You'll leave me alone and you won't harm Richard?''

He nodded.

''You give me your word?''

''My word of honor.''

I took it. It was the best offer I was going to get. I wasn't sure how much his word of honor was worth, but it gave us time. Time to work something else out. I didn't know what else, but there had to be something. Something besides dating the freaking Master of the City.

26

There was a knock on the door. It opened without Jean-Claude's giving permission. Somebody was pushy. Raina stalked in through the door. Pushy was one word for it.

She was wearing a rust-collared trench coat with the belt tied very tight at her waist. The buckle flopped loosely as she glided into the room. She undid a multicolored scarf and shook her auburn hair. It shimmered in the light.

Gabriel followed at her back in a black trench coat. His-and-her outfits. His hair and strange grey eyes looked as good with his coat as Raina's did with hers. Earrings glittered from the earlobe to the curl at the top of his ear. Every piece of metal was silver.

Kaspar Gunderson followed at their heels. He was wearing a pale tweed coat and one of those hats with a little feather in the band. He looked like an elegant version of everybody's 1950s dream dad. He didn't look happy to be here.

Robert stood sort of hovering in the doorway. "I told them you were busy, Jean-Claude. I told them you didn't want to be disturbed." He was practically wringing his hands with anxiety. After what I'd seen done to Gretchen I didn't blame him for being afraid.

"Come in, Robert, and close the door behind you," Jean-Claude said.

"I really need to oversee the next act. I . . ."

"Come in and close the door, Robert."

The century-old vampire did as he was told. He closed the door and leaned against it, one hand on the doorknob as if that would keep him safe. The right sleeve of his white shirt was sliced up, and blood trickled out of fresh claw marks. His throat showed more blood, as if a clawed hand had lifted him by the throat. Like Jean-Claude had done to Gretchen, but with talons.

"I told you what would happen if you failed me again, Robert. In anything, large or small." Jean-Claude's voice was a whisper that filled the room like wind.

Robert dropped to his knees on the white carpet. "Please, master, please." He extended his hands towards Jean-Claude. A thick drop of blood plopped from his arm to the carpet. The blood seemed very red against the white, white carpet.

Raina smiled. I was betting I knew whose claw marks Robert was sporting. Kaspar went to sit on the couch, distancing himself from the show. Gabriel was looking at me. ''Nice coat,'' he said.

We were both wearing black trench coats. Great. ''Thanks,'' I said.

He grinned flashing, pointy teeth.

I wanted to ask him if the silver earrings hurt but Robert made a low whimpering noise, and I turned back to the main show.

''Come to me, Robert.'' Jean-Claude's voice had heat to it, enough to scald.

Robert went nearly prone on the carpet, abasing himself. ''Please, master. Please don't.''

Jean-Claude stalked towards him, fast enough to have his black shirt sweeping behind him like a miniature cape. His pale skin flashed against the black cloth. He stopped beside the cowering vampire. Jean-Claude's shirt swirled around the suddenly quiet body. Jean-Claude stood utterly still. The cloth had more life to it than he did.

Jesus. ''He tried, Jean-Claude,'' I said. ''Leave him alone.''

Jean-Claude stared at me, his eyes a bottomless blue. I looked away from those eyes. Maybe I could meet his gaze with impunity, but then again . . . He was always full of surprises.

''I was under the impression, *ma petite,* that you did not like Robert.''

''I don't, but I've seen enough punishment for one night. They bloodied him just because he wouldn't let them in your office a few minutes early. Why aren't you mad about that?''

Raina walked over to Jean-Claude. The spiked heels of her metallic copper pumps made indents in the carpet. A trail of stab wounds.

Jean-Claude watched her come. His face was neutral but there was something about the way he held himself. Was he afraid of her? Maybe. But there was a wariness to his body as she moved closer. He wasn't happy. More and more curious.

''We had an appointment with Jean-Claude. It would have hurt my feelings to be turned away at the door.'' She stepped over Robert, flashing a lot of leg. I wasn't sure she was wearing anything under the trench coat. Robert did not try to sneak a peek. He froze, flinching as her coat brushed his back.

Raina stood with her shapely calves, nearly touching Robert. He didn't move away from her. He seemed to just freeze as if he could pretend he wasn't there and everyone would forget about him. He wished.

She was standing so close to Jean-Claude that the length of their bodies touched. She was sort of wedged between the two vampires. I expected Jean-Claude to step back, give her a little room. He didn't.

She ran her fingers under his shirt, laying her hands on either side of his naked waist. Her lipsticked mouth parted and she leaned into him. She kissed him, and he stood like a statue under her hands. But he didn't tell her to go to hell.

What the hell was going on?

Raina raised her face enough to speak. ''Jean-Claude doesn't wish to offend Marcus. He needs the pack's backing to hold the city. Don't you, love?''

He put his hands on her slender waist and stepped back. Her hands trailed along his skin until he was completely out of reach. She watched him the way snakes watch small birds. Hungry. You didn't have to be a vampire to feel her lust. Obvious was putting it kindly.

"Marcus and I have an arrangement," Jean-Claude said.

"What sort of arrangement?" I asked.

"Why do you care, *ma petite*? You are going to be seeing Monsieur Zeeman. Am I not allowed to see other people? I have offered you monogamy and you have turned me down."

I hadn't thought about it. It did bother me. Damn. "It's not the sharing that bothers me, Jean-Claude."

Raina walked up behind him, long painted nails tracing his skin. Hands curling up his chest until her chin rested on his shoulder. Jean-Claude relaxed in her arms this time. He leaned his back against her, pale hands caressing her arms. He stared at me while he did it.

"What does bother you, *ma petite*?"

"Your choice of playmates."

"Jealous?" Raina asked.

"No."

"Liar," she said.

What was I supposed to say? That it bothered me to see her hanging all over him? It did. Which bothered me more than her groping him.

I shook my head. "Just wondering how far you'll go to secure the pack's favor."

"Oh, all the way," Raina said. She moved around to stand in front of him. She was taller than he was in her heels. "You are going to come play with me." She kissed him, one quick movement. She dropped to her knees in front of him, gazing upward.

Jean-Claude stroked her hair. His pale graceful hands raising her face upward. He bent towards her as if to kiss her, but he stared at me while he did it.

Was he waiting for me to say, no, don't? He'd seemed almost afraid of her at first. Now he was utterly comfortable. I knew he was taunting me. Trying to make me jealous. It was sort of working.

He kissed her long and lingering. He looked up from it with her lipstick smeared on his lips. "What are you thinking, *ma petite*?"

He couldn't read my mind anymore, one point for not having vampire marks. "That I think less of you for having sex with Raina."

Gabriel gave a warm, rolling laugh. "Oh, he hasn't had sex with her, not yet." He walked towards me in a long, gliding stride.

I flashed the trench coat showing the Browning. "Let's not get crazed."

He undid the trench coat's belt, and raised his hands in surrender. He wasn't wearing a shirt. He had a silver ring through his left nipple, and the edge of his belly button.

It made me wince just to see it. "I thought silver hurt a lycanthrope, like an allergy."

"It burns," he said. His voice had a soft huskiness to it.

"And this is a good thing?" I asked.

Gabriel put his hands down slowly and shrugged the coat off his shoulders. He turned slowly as the cloth fell like a striptease. I didn't see any other silver rings. He whirled as it came off his arms, and at the apex of the turn he flung it on me. I batted at the coat, knocking it away from me. That was the mistake.

He was on me, body flattening me to the floor. My arms ended up pinned to my chest, trapped under his coat. His waist had the Firestar trapped. I went for the Browning and his hand tore through the coat like paper, ripped the gun out from under my arm. He damn near took the holster and my arm with it. For a second my left arm was just one raw pain. When I could feel my arm again the Browning was gone and I was staring up into Gabriel's face from three inches away.

He wriggled his hips, grinding the Firestar into both of us. It had to hurt him more than it hurt me.

''Doesn't that hurt?'' I asked. My voice was surprisingly calm.

''I like pain,'' he said. He put the tip of his tongue on my chin and licked across my mouth. He laughed. ''Struggle harder. Push those little hands.''

''You like pain?'' I said.

''Yeah.''

''You're gonna love this.'' I shoved the knife into his upper stomach. He gave a small sound between a grunt and a sigh. A shudder ran the length of his body. He reared up over me, still pinning me from the waist down, like he was doing girl's push-ups.

I raised myself up with him, shoving the knife in deeper, drawing the blade upward through the meat of his body.

Gabriel ripped the coat into pieces but didn't try to grab the knife. He braced an arm on either side of me, staring downward at the knife and my bloody hands.

He rested his face in my hair, slumping just a little. I thought he'd pass out. He whispered, ''Deeper.''

''Oh, Jesus.'' The blade was almost at the bottom of his sternum. When I got to it one upward thrust would give me his heart.

I lay back on the floor to get a better angle for the killing blow.

''Don't kill him,'' Raina said. ''We need him.''

We? The knife was on its way to his heart when he rolled off me in a blinding blur of speed. He ended up lying on his back not too far away. He was breathing very fast, his chest rising and falling. Blood poured down his naked skin. His eyes were closed, lips curled in a half smile.

If he'd been human he might have died later tonight. Instead he lay on the carpet smiling. He rolled his head to one side and opened his eyes. His strange grey eyes looked at me. ''That was wonderful.''

''Jesus H. Christ,'' I said. I got to my feet using the couch for support. I was covered in Gabriel's blood. The knife was thick with it.

Kaspar was sitting on the corner of the couch staring at me. He huddled in his coat, eyes wide. I didn't blame him.

I wiped my hands and blade on the black couch. ''Thanks for the help, Jean-Claude.''

''I was told that you are a dominant now, *ma petite*. Struggles of internal dominance are not to be interfered with.'' He smiled. ''Besides, you did not need my help.''

Raina knelt beside Gabriel. She lowered her face to his bleeding stomach and began to lick it. Long, slow movements of her tongue. Her throat convulsed as she swallowed.

I would not be sick. I would not be sick. I looked at Kaspar. ''What are you doing with these two?''

Raina raised a blood coated face. ''Kaspar is our sample.''

''What's that supposed to mean?''

''He can shapeshift back and forth as often as he wants to. He doesn't pass out. We use him to test potential stars of our movie productions. To see how they react to somebody changing shape in the middle of things.''

I was going to be sick. ''Please tell me you don't mean he changes in the middle of sex as a sort of screen test.''

Raina cocked her head to one side. Her tongue rolled around her mouth, licking the blood clean. ''You know about our little films?''

''Yeah.''

''I'm surprised Richard told you. He doesn't approve of our fun.''

''Are you in the movies?''

''Kaspar won't play on film,'' Raina said. She stood up and walked towards the couch. ''Marcus won't force anybody to be on film. But Kaspar helps us audition people. Don't you, Kaspar?''

He nodded. He was staring at the carpet, working very hard at not looking at her.

''Why are you all here tonight?'' I asked.

''Jean-Claude promised us some vampires for our next movie.''

''That true?'' I asked.

Jean-Claude's face was blank, lovely but unreadable. ''Robert needs to be punished.''

I frowned at the change of subject. ''The coffin's full.''

''There are always more coffins, Anita.''

Robert crawled forward. ''I'm sorry, master. I'm sorry.'' He didn't touch Jean-Claude, but he crept close to him. ''I can't bear the box again, master. Please.''

''You're afraid of Raina, Jean-Claude. What do you expect Robert to do with her?''

''I am not afraid of Raina.''

''Fine, but Robert was overmatched. You know he was.''

''Perhaps you are right, *ma petite*.''

Robert looked up. A moment of hope flashed across his handsome face. ''Thank you, master.'' He looked at me. ''Thank you, Anita.''

I shrugged.

''You can have Robert for your next film,'' Jean-Claude said.

Robert grabbed his leg. ''Master, I . . .''

''Oh, come on, Jean-Claude, don't give him to her.''

Raina plopped down on the couch between Kaspar and me. I stood up. She put an arm over Kaspar's shoulders. He flinched.

"He's handsome enough. Any vampire can take a great deal of punishment. Most acceptable," she said.

"You saw them here tonight," I said. "Do you really want to do that to one of your own people?"

"Let Robert decide," Jean-Claude said. "The box, or Raina?"

Robert looked up at the lycanthrope. She smiled at him with her bloody mouth.

Robert lowered his head so he could see her, then nodded. "Not the box. Anything is better than that."

"I'm out of here," I said. I'd had all the interpreternatural politics that I could stand for one night.

"Don't you want to see the show?" Raina said.

"I thought I'd seen the show," I said.

She tossed Kaspar's hat across the room. "Strip," she said.

I'd sheathed the knife and retrieved the Browning from the carpet where Gabriel had thrown it. I was armed. For what good it did me.

Kaspar sat there on the couch. There was a pink flush to his white skin. His eyes glittered. Angry, embarrassed. "I was a prince before your ancestors discovered this country."

Raina propped her chin on his shoulder, still hugging his shoulders. "We know how blue your pedigree is. You were a prince and you were such a big, bad hunter, such a wicked boy that a witch cursed you. She turned you into something beautiful and harmless. She hoped you'd learn how to be gentle and kind." She licked his ear, running her hands through his feathery hair. "But you aren't gentle or kind. Your heart is just as cold and your pride just as impervious as it was centuries ago. Now, take off your clothes and turn into a swan for us."

"You don't need me to do it for the vampire," he said.

"No, do it for me. Do it so Anita can see. Do it so Gabriel and I don't hurt you." Her voice was going lower. Each word more measured.

"You can't kill me, not even with silver," he said.

"But we can make you wish you could die, Kaspar."

He screamed, a low, ragged cry of frustration. He stood up abruptly and pulled on his coat. The buttons snapped and fell to the carpet. He flung the coat into Raina's face.

She laughed.

I started for the door.

"Oh, don't leave yet, Anita. Kaspar may be a pain in the ass, but he's really quite beautiful."

I glanced back.

Kaspar's sport jacket and tie lay on the carpet. He unbuttoned his white dress shirt with quick, angry movements. There was a line of white feathers down the middle of his chest. Soft and downy as an Easter duck.

I shook my head and kept going for the door. I did not run. I did not walk faster than normal. It was the bravest thing I'd done all night.

27

I took a taxi home. Stephen stayed behind to strip or just to lick Jean-Claude's boots, I wasn't sure which and I wasn't sure I cared. I'd made sure Stephen wasn't in trouble. It was the best I could do. He was Jean-Claude's creature, and I'd had about enough of the Master of the City for one night.

Killing Gretchen was one thing, tormenting her was another. I kept flashing on the sound of her frantically beating hands. I'd like to believe that Jean-Claude would keep her asleep, but I knew better. He was a master vampire. They ruled, in part, through fear. Gretchen seemed like a real good threat. Displease me and I'll do that to you. Worked for me.

I was standing outside my apartment when I realized I didn't have a key to it. I'd given Richard my car keys, which had my house keys on the ring.

It felt silly standing out in the hallway about to knock on my own front door. The door opened without me touching it. Richard stood in the doorway. He smiled. ''Hi,'' he said.

I found myself smiling back. ''Hi, yourself.''

He stepped back to one side, giving me room. He hadn't tried to kiss me in the door like Ozzie meeting Harriet after work. I was glad. It was too intimate a ritual. If we ever did this for real, he could molest me at the door, but not tonight.

He closed the door behind me, and I half expected him to take my coat. Wisely, he did not.

I took off my own coat and laid it across the couch, where all good coats go. The warm smell of cooking food filled the apartment. ''You've been cooking,'' I said, not entirely pleased.

''I thought you might be hungry. Besides, all I had to do was wait. I cooked. It filled the time.''

I could understand that. Though cooking would never have occurred to me unless forced.

The only lights were in the kitchen. It looked like a lighted cave from the darkened living room. If I wasn't mistaken, there were candles on the table.

''Are those candles?''

He laughed. It had an embarrassed edge to it. "Too hokey?"

"It's a two-seater breakfast table. You can't possibly serve a fancy dinner on it."

"I thought we'd use the divider as a buffet and just have plates on the table. There's room if we're careful where we put our elbows." He walked past me into the light. He started puttering with a saucepan, sloshing something around in it.

I stood there staring at my kitchen, watching my possible fiancé cooking my dinner. My skin felt tight and itchy. I couldn't draw a complete breath. I wanted to go right back out the door. This was more intimate than a kiss at the door. He'd moved in, made himself at home.

I didn't leave. It was the bravest thing I'd done all night. I checked the lock on the door automatically. He'd left it unlocked. Careless.

I didn't know what to do next. My apartment was my refuge. I could come here and just kick back. I could be alone. I liked being alone. I needed some time to unwind, regroup, think how to tell him Jean-Claude and I had a date.

"Will dinner be spoiled if I clean up first?"

"I can reheat everything when you're ready. I planned the meal so it wouldn't ruin no matter how late you were."

Great. "I'm going to go clean up then."

He turned to me, framed by the light. He'd tied his hair back, but it was coming loose in long, curling strands. His sweater was a burnt orange that made his skin look golden highlighted. He was wearing an apron that said, Mrs. Lovett's Meatpies on it. I didn't own an apron, and I certainly wouldn't have chosen one with a logo from *Sweeney Todd.* A musical about cannibalism seemed inappropriate for an apron. Delightfully so, but still . . .

"I'm going to go clean up."

"You said that."

I turned on my heel and walked to the bedroom. I did not run, though the temptation was great. I closed the door to my bedroom and leaned against it. My bedroom was untouched. No signs of invasion.

There was a love seat under the room's only window. Stuffed toy penguins sit on the love seat and spill down onto the floor. The collection was threatening to take over half the floor like a creeping tide. I grabbed the nearest one and sat on the corner of the bed. I hugged it tight, burying the upper half of my face in its fuzzy head.

I'd said I would marry Richard, so why was I so bugged about his sudden domestic turn? We downgraded the yes to a maybe, but even if it had still been a yes it would have bugged me. Marriage. The implications of that hadn't really sunk in. It wasn't fair to ask questions like that when he was half-naked and looking yummy. If he'd dropped to one knee over a fancy restaurant dinner, would my answer have been different? Maybe. But we'd never know, would we?

If I'd been alone, I wouldn't have eaten at all. I'd have taken a shower, thrown on an oversize T-shirt, and gone to bed surrounded by a few select penguins.

Now I had a fancy dinner to eat, by candlelight nonetheless. If I said I wasn't hungry, would he be insulted? Would he pout? Would he yell about all the work going to waste and tell me about starving kids in Southeast Asia?

"Shit," I said softly and with feeling. Well, hell, if we ever were going to cohabitate, he'd have to know the truth. I was unsociable, and food was something you ate so you wouldn't die.

I decided to do what I'd have done if he hadn't been here, sort of. I really disliked feeling uncomfortable in my own home. If I'd known it was going to feel like this, I'd have called Ronnie to wake me every hour. I was fine. I didn't need the help, but Ronnie would have been more comfy, less threatening. Of course, if Gretchen got out of her box, I trusted Richard would survive an attack, but wasn't so sure about Ronnie. One good point in Richard's favor. He was damn hard to kill.

I put the Browning in the holster built into the bed. I stripped off the sweater and let it fall to the floor. It was ruined and sweaters didn't wrinkle anyway. I laid the Firestar on the back of the toilet. Then I stripped off and got in the shower. I didn't lock the bedroom door. It would seem insulting, as if, if I didn't lock the door, he'd be naked in the bed with a rose in his teeth when I came out.

I locked the bathroom door. I'd done it when I was home with my father. Now I did it so if someone busted down the door, I'd have time to grab the Firestar off the toilet.

I turned the shower on as hot as it would go and stayed under it until my fingers started to prune. I was scrubbed clean and had delayed as long as I could.

I wiped the steam from the mirror with a towel. The top layer of skin was gone from my right cheek. It would heal just fine, but a scrape looks like hell until it heals. There was a small scrape on my chin and the side of my nose. A knot was blossoming into brilliant color on my forehead. I looked as though I'd been hit by a train. It was amazing that anyone wanted to kiss me.

I peeked out the door into the bedroom. No one was waiting for me. The room was empty and full of the whir of the heater. It was quiet, peaceful, and I couldn't hear any noises from the kitchen. I let out a long sigh. Alone, for a little while.

I was vain enough that I didn't want Richard to see me in my usual nighttime attire. I had had a nice black robe that matched a tiny black teddy. An overly optimistic date had given it to me. He never got to see me wear it. Fancy that. The robe had died a sad death covered in blood and other bodily fluids.

Wearing the teddy seemed cruel since I didn't plan on having sex with him. I stood in front of my closet and didn't have a thing to wear. Since I consider clothes something you wear so you won't be naked, that was pretty sad.

I put on an oversize T-shirt with a caricature of Mary Shelley on it, a pair of grey sweatpants—not the fancy ones, either, the kind with a drawstring in them. The way God intended sweatpants to be. A pair of white jogging socks, the closest thing I owned to slippers, and I was ready to go.

I looked at myself in the mirror and wasn't happy. I was comfortable, but it wasn't very flattering. But it was honest. I've never understood those women who wear makeup, do their hair, and dress wonderfully until after they're married. Suddenly, they forget what makeup is and lose all their thin clothes. If we did marry, he should see what he'd be sleeping beside every night. I shrugged and walked out.

He'd combed his hair out. It foamed around his face, soft and inviting. The candles were gone. So was the apron. He stood in the entryway between kitchen and living room. His arms were crossed over his chest, shoulder leaning against the doorjamb. He smiled. He looked so scrumptious, I wanted to go back in and change, but I didn't.

"I'm sorry," he said.

"What about?"

"I'm not completely sure, but I think for presuming I could take over your kitchen."

"I think it's the first meal that's ever been cooked in it."

His smile widened, and he pushed away from the door. He walked towards me. He moved in the circle of his own energy. Not that otherworldly power, but just Richard. Or was it? Maybe a lot of his drive was from his beast.

He stood staring down at me, close enough to touch but not doing it. "I was going crazy waiting for you. I got this idea to cook a fancy meal. It was stupid. You don't have to eat it, but it kept me from running down to Guilty Pleasures and defending your honor."

It made me smile. "Damn you, I can't even pout around you. You always jolly me out of it."

"And this is a bad thing?"

I laughed. "Yes. I enjoy my bad moods, thank you very much."

He traced fingers down my shoulders, kneading the muscles in my upper arms. I pulled away from him. "Please, don't." Just like that, the cozy domestic scene was ruined. All my fault.

His hands dropped to his sides. "I'm sorry." I didn't think he meant the meal. He took a deep breath and nodded. "You don't have to eat a bite." I guess we were going to pretend he had meant the meal. Fine with me.

"If I said I wasn't hungry at all, you wouldn't be mad at me?"

"I fixed the meal to make me feel better. If it bothers you, don't eat it."

"I'll drink a cup of coffee and watch you eat."

He smiled. "It's a deal."

He stayed standing, looking down at me. He looked sad. Lost. If you love someone, you shouldn't make them miserable. It's a rule somewhere, or should be.

"You combed your hair out."

"You like it loose."

"Just like this is one of my favorite sweaters," I said.

"Is it?" His voice held a teasing edge to it. I could have the lightness back. We could have a nice relaxing evening. It was up to me.

I looked up into his big brown eyes and wanted it. But I couldn't lie to him. That would be worse than cruel. "This is awkward."

"I know. I'm sorry."

"Stop apologizing. It's not your fault. It's mine."

He shook his head. "You can't help how you feel."

"My first instinct is to cut and run, Richard. Stop seeing you. No more long conversations. No touching. Nothing."

"If that's what you want." His voice sounded sort of strangled, as if it cost him dearly to say those words.

"What I want is you. I just don't know if I can handle all of you."

"I shouldn't have proposed until you'd seen what I really was."

"I saw Marcus and the gang."

"It's not the same as seeing me go beastly on you, is it?"

I took a deep breath, and let it out slowly. "No," I said, "it isn't."

"If you have someone else you can call to wait with you tonight, I'll go. You said you needed time and I practically move in. I'm pushing."

"Yeah, you are."

"I'm scared that I'm losing you," he said.

"Pushing won't help," I said.

"I guess not."

I stood there staring at him. The apartment was dark. The only light from the kitchen. It could have been, should have been, very intimate. I told everybody that lycanthropy was just a disease. It was illegal and immoral to discriminate. I didn't have a prejudiced bone in my body, or so I told myself. Staring up into Richard's handsome face, I knew it wasn't true. I was prejudiced. I was prejudiced against monsters. Oh, they were good enough to be my friends, but even my closest friends, Ronnie and Catherine, were human. Good enough to be friends, but not good enough to love. Not good enough to share my bed. Is that really what I thought? Was that who I was?

It wasn't who I wanted to be. I raised zombies and slew vampires. I wasn't clean enough to throw stones.

I moved closer to him. "Hold me, Richard. Just hold me."

His arms enfolded me. I wrapped my arms around his waist, pressing my face against his chest. I could hear his heartbeat, fast and strong. I held him, listening to the beat of his heart, breathing his warmth. For just an instant I felt safe. It was the way I'd felt before my mother died. That childish belief that nothing can hurt you while Mommy and Daddy hold you tight. That utter faith that they can make everything all right. In Richard's arms, for brief moments, I had that again. Even though I knew it was a lie. Hell, it had been a lie the first time. My mother's death had proven that.

I pulled away first. He didn't try and hold on. He didn't say anything. If he'd said anything remotely sympathetic I might have cried. Couldn't have that. Down to business. "You haven't asked how it went with Jean-Claude."

"You were almost mad at me when you came through the door. I thought if I started questioning you right off the bat, you might yell at me."

He'd made coffee all on his own. That earned him at least two brownie points. "I wasn't mad at you." I poured coffee into my baby penguin mug. Regardless of what I take to work, it is my favorite mug.

"Yes, you were," he said.

"You want some coffee?"

"You know I don't like it."

How do you trust a man that doesn't like coffee? "I keep hoping you'll come to your senses."

He started dishing out his meal. "Sure you don't want some?"

"No, thanks." It was some small brown meat in a brown sauce. Looking at it made me nauseous. I'd eaten later than this with Edward, but tonight, food just didn't sound good. Maybe getting my head bashed into concrete had something to do with that.

I sat down in one of the chairs, one knee drawn up to my chest. The coffee was Viennese cinnamon, one of my favorites. Sugar, real cream, and it was perfect.

Richard sat down opposite me. He bowed his head and said grace over his meal. He's Episcopalian, did I mention that? Except for the furry part, he really is perfect for me.

"Tell me what happened with Jean-Claude, please," he asked.

I sipped my coffee and tried to think of a short version. Okay, a short version Richard wouldn't mind hearing. Okay, maybe just the truth.

"He took the news better than I thought he would, actually."

Richard looked up from his meal, silverware poised. "He took it well?"

"I didn't say that. He didn't burst through a wall and try to kill you immediately. He took it better than I expected."

Richard nodded. He took a sip of water and said, "Did he threaten to kill me?"

"Oh, yeah. But it was almost like he saw this coming. He didn't like it, but it didn't catch him by complete surprise."

"Is he going to try and kill me?" He asked it very calmly, eating his meat and brown sauce.

"No, he isn't."

"Why not?"

It was a good question. I wondered what he'd think of the answer. "He wants to date me."

Richard stopped eating. He just looked at me. When he could speak, he said, "He *what*?"

"He wants a chance to woo me. He says that if he can't win me from you in a few months, he'll give up. He'll let us go our merry way, and he won't interfere."

Richard sat back in his chair. "And you believe him?"

"Yeah. Jean-Claude thinks he's irresistible. I think he believes that if I let him use all his charms on me, I'll reconsider."

"Will you?" His voice was very quiet when he asked.

"No, I don't think so." It wasn't a rousing endorsement.

"I know you lust after him, Anita. Do you love him?"

The conversation was becoming déjà-vuish. "In some dark, twisted part of my heart, yeah. But not the way I love you."

"How is it different?"

"Look, I just had this conversation with Jean-Claude. I love you. Can you see me setting up house with the Master of the City?"

"Can you see setting up house with an alpha werewolf?"

Shit. I stared across the table at him, and sighed. He was pushing, but I didn't blame him. If I'd been him, I'd have dumped me. If I didn't love him enough to accept all of him, then who the hell needed me? I didn't want him to dump me. I wanted to be indecisive but I didn't want to lose him. Talk about having your cake and eating it, too.

I leaned across the table and held my hand out to him. After a moment he took it. ''I don't want to lose you.''

''You won't lose me.''

''You are a hell of a lot more tolerant than I would be.''

He didn't smile. ''I know I am.''

I would have liked to argue, but truth is truth. ''I'd be bigger about this if I could.''

''I understand your having reservations about marrying a werewolf. Who wouldn't? But Jean-Claude . . .'' He shook his head.

I squeezed his hand. ''Come on, Richard. This is the best we can do right now. Jean-Claude won't try and kill either of us. We still get to date and see each other.''

''I don't like you being forced into dating him.'' He rubbed his fingers across my knuckles, caressing. ''I like it even less that I think you'll enjoy it. In that small dark part of yourself, you'll be having a very good time.''

I wanted to deny it, but it would be a total lie. ''You can smell it if I lie?''

''Yep,'' he said.

''Then it's intriguing and terrifying.''

''I want you safe so the terrifying part bothers me, but the intriguing part bothers me more.''

''Jealous?''

''Worried.''

What could I say? So was I.

28

The phone rang. I groped for it and found nothing. I raised my head and found the nightstand empty. The phone was gone. It had even stopped ringing. The radio clock was still there, glowing red. It read 1:03. I stayed propped on my elbow blinking at the empty space. Was I dreaming? Why would I dream that someone had stolen my phone?

The bedroom door opened. Richard stood framed in the light beyond. Ah. Now I remembered. He'd taken the phone into the living room so it wouldn't wake me. Since he was having to wake me every hour, I'd let him do it. When you're only sleeping an hour, even a short phone call can screw things up.

''Who is it?''

''It's Sergeant Rudolf Storr. I asked him to wait until I had to wake you, but he was pretty insistent.''

I could imagine. ''It's all right.''

''Would fifteen minutes have killed him?'' Richard asked.

I swung my legs out from under the covers. ''Dolph's in the middle of a murder investigation, Richard. Patience isn't his strong suit.''

Richard crossed his arms over his chest, leaning against the doorjamb. The light from the living room made strong shadows on his face. The shadows cut huge square shapes on his orange sweater. He radiated displeasure. It made me smile. I patted his arm as I went past. I seemed to have inherited a watchwolf.

The phone was sitting just inside the front door, where the other phone jack was. I sat down on the floor, putting my back to the wall, and picked up the phone. ''Dolph, it's me. What's up?''

''Who's this Richard Zeeman that's answering your phone in the middle of the night?''

I closed my eyes. My head hurt. My face hurt. I hadn't had a hell of a lot of sleep. ''You're not my father, Dolph. What's up?''

A moment of silence. ''Defensive, aren't we?''

''Yeah, want to make something of it?''

''No,'' he said.

"You call just to catch up on my personal life or is there a reason you woke me up?" I knew it wasn't another murder. He was being too cheerful for that, which made me wonder if it couldn't have waited a few hours.

"We found something."

"What exactly?"

"I'd rather you just come and see it for yourself."

"Don't do this to me, Dolph. Just tell me what the fuck it is."

Another silence. If he was waiting for me to apologize, he was in for a long wait. Finally. "We found a skin."

"What kind of skin?"

"If we knew what the hell it was, would I be calling you at one o'clock in the freaking morning?" He sounded angry. I guess I couldn't blame him.

"I'm sorry, Dolph. I'm sorry I snapped at you."

"Fine."

He hadn't exactly accepted my apology. Fine. "Is it connected to the murder?"

"I don't think so, but I'm not some hotshot preternatural expert." He still sounded pissed. Maybe he wasn't getting much sleep, either. Of course, I bet no one had smashed his head into a sidewalk.

"Where are you?"

He gave me the address. It was down in Jefferson County, far away from the murder scene.

"When can you be here?"

"I can't drive," I said.

"What?"

"Doctor's orders, I'm not to get behind the wheel of a car tonight."

"How bad are you hurt?"

"Not too bad, but the doctor wanted me woken up every hour, and no driving."

"That's why Mr. Zeeman is there."

"Yeah."

"If you're too hurt to come tonight, it can wait."

"Is the skin where it was found? Nothing disturbed?"

"Yeah."

"I'll come. Who knows? There might be a clue."

He let that go. "How are you going to get here?"

I glanced at Richard. He could drive me, but somehow I didn't think it was a good idea. He was a civvie, for one thing. He was a lycanthrope, for another. He answered to Marcus, and to a degree to Jean-Claude. Not a good person to bring into a preternatural murder investigation. Besides, if he'd been human, the answer would have been the same. No deal.

"Unless you can send a squad car, I guess I'll take a taxi."

"Zerbrowski didn't answer his first page. He lives in St. Peters. He'll have to come right by you. He can pick you up."

"Is that okay with him?"

"It will be," Dolph said.

Great. Trapped in a car with Zerbrowski. "Fine, I'll be dressed and waiting."

"Dressed?"

''Don't even start, Dolph.''

''Touchy, very touchy.''

''Stop it.''

He laughed. It was good to hear him laugh. It meant not many people had died this time. Dolph didn't laugh much during serial-killer cases.

He hung up. So did I.

''You have to go out?'' Richard asked.

''Yeah.''

''Do you feel well enough to go?''

''Yes.''

''Anita . . .''

I leaned my head against the wall and closed my eyes. ''Don't, Richard. I'm going.''

''No debate allowed?''

''No debate,'' I said. I opened my eyes and looked at him.

He was staring down at me, arms crossed.

''What?'' I said.

He shook his head. ''If I told you that I was going to do something, no debate, you'd be mad.''

''No, I wouldn't.''

''Anita.'' He said my name the way my father use to say it.

''I wouldn't, not if your reasons were valid.''

''Anita, you'd be pissed, and you know it.''

I wanted to deny it but couldn't. ''All right, you're right. I wouldn't like it.'' I stared up at him. I was going to have to give him reasons why I was going to go out and do my job. It wasn't a pretty sight.

I stood. I wanted to say I didn't have to explain myself to anyone, but if I meant this marriage thing, it wasn't true anymore. I didn't like that much. His being a werewolf was not the only hurdle to domestic bliss.

''This is police business, Richard. People die when I don't do my job.''

''I thought your job was raising zombies and executing vampires.''

''You sound like Bert.''

''You've told me enough about Bert that I know that is an insult.''

''If you don't want to be compared, then stop saying one of his favorite things.'' I walked past him towards the bedroom. ''I've got to get dressed.''

He followed me. ''I know that helping the police is very important to you.''

I turned on him. ''I don't just help the police, Richard. The spook squad is just over two years old. The cops on it didn't know shit about preternatural creatures. It was a garbage detail. Do something to piss off your superiors and you get transferred.''

''The newspapers and TV said it was an independent task force like the major task force. That's an honor.''

''Oh, yeah, right. The squad gets almost no extra funding. No special training in preternatural creatures or events. Dolph, Sergeant Storr, saw me in the paper and contacted Bert. There was no training in preternatural crime for law officers in this country. Dolph thought I could be an adviser.''

"You're a heck of a lot more than an adviser."

"Yes, I am." I could have told him that earlier in the summer Dolph had tried not calling me in right away. It had seemed like a clear-cut case of ghouls in a cemetery getting a little ambitious and attacking a necking couple. Ghouls were cowards and didn't attack able-bodied people, but exceptions to the rule and all that. By the time Dolph called me in, six people were dead. It hadn't been ghouls. So lately Dolph had started calling me at the beginning before things got too messy. Sometimes I could diagnose a problem before it got out of hand.

But I couldn't tell Richard that. There might have been a lower kill count if I'd been called in this summer, but that was no one's business but Dolph's and mine. We'd spoken of it only once, and that was enough. Richard was a civvie, werewolf or not. It wasn't any of his business.

"Look, I don't know if I can explain this so you'll understand, but I have to go. It may head off a larger problem. It may keep me from having to go to a murder scene later on. Can you understand that?"

He looked perplexed, but what came out of his mouth wasn't. "Not really, but maybe I don't have to. Maybe seeing it's important to you is enough."

I let out a deep breath. "Great. Now I've got to get ready. Zerbrowski will be here any time. He's the detective giving me a ride."

Richard just nodded. Wise of him.

I went into the bedroom and closed the door. Gratefully. Would this be a regular occurrence if we married? Would I be forever explaining myself? God, I hoped not.

Another pair of black jeans, a red sweater with a cowl neck, so soft and fuzzy that it made me feel better just to wear it. The Browning's shoulder holster looked very dark and dramatic against the crimson of the sweater. The red sweater also brought out the raw-meat color of the scrapes on my face. I might have changed it, but the doorbell rang.

Zerbrowski. Richard was answering the door while I stared at myself in the mirror. That thought alone was enough. I went for the door.

Zerbrowski was standing just inside the door, hands in the pockets of his overcoat. His curly black hair with its touches of grey was freshly cut. There was even hair-goop in it. Zerbrowski was usually lucky if he remembered to comb his hair. The suit that showed from his open coat was black and formal. His tie was tasteful and neatly knotted. I glanced down, and yes indeed, his shoes were shined. I'd never seen him when he didn't have food stains on him somewhere.

"Where were you all dressed up?" I asked.

"Where were you all undressed?" he asked. He smiled when he said it.

I felt heat rush up my face and hated it a lot. I hadn't done anything worth blushing for. "Fine, let's go." I grabbed my trench coat from the back of the couch and touched dried blood. Shit.

"I've got to get a clean coat. I'll be right back."

"I'll just talk to Mr. Zeeman here," Zerbrowski said.

I was afraid of that, but I went for my leather jacket anyway. If we ended up engaged, Richard would have to meet Zerbrowski sooner or later. Later would have been my preference.

''What do you do for a living, Mr. Zeeman?''

''I'm a schoolteacher.''

''Oh, really.''

I lost the conversation then. I grabbed the jacket from the closet and walked back out. They were chatting along like old buddies.

''Yes, Anita is our preternatural expert. Wouldn't know what to do without her.''

''I'm ready. Let's go.'' I walked past them and opened the door. I held the door for Zerbrowski.

He smiled at me. ''How long have you two been dating?''

Richard looked at me. He was pretty good at picking up when I wasn't comfortable. He was going to let me answer the question. Good of him. Too good. If he would only be completely unreasonable and give me an excuse to say no. This isn't worth it. But damn if he didn't work really hard at keeping me happy. Not an easy task.

''Since November,'' I said.

''Two months, not bad. Katie and I were engaged two months after our first date.'' His eyes sparkled, his grin was mocking. He was pulling my leg, he didn't know it was coming off in his hands.

Richard looked at me. The look was long and serious. ''Two months isn't very long, really.''

He'd given me an out. I didn't deserve him.

''Long enough if it's the right one,'' Zerbrowski said.

I tried to get Zerbrowski through the door. He was grinning. He had no intention of being hurried. My only hope was for Dolph to page him again. That'd light a fire under his butt.

Dolph didn't call. Zerbrowski grinned at me. Richard looked at me. His big brown eyes were deep and wounded. I wanted to take his face in my hands and wipe that hurt from his eyes. Oh, hell.

He was the right one—probably. ''I've got to go.''

''I know,'' he said.

I glanced at Zerbrowski. He was grinning at us, enjoying the show.

Was I supposed to kiss him good-bye? We weren't engaged anymore. Quickest engagement in history. But we were still dating. I still loved him. That deserved a kiss if nothing else.

I grabbed the front of his sweater and pulled him down to me. He looked surprised. ''You don't have to do this for show,'' he whispered.

''Shut up and kiss me.''

That earned me a smile. Every kiss was still a pleasant shock. No one's lips were this soft. No one else tasted this good.

His hair fell forward and I grabbed a handful of it, pressing his face to mine. His hands slid around my back, underneath the leather jacket, hands kneading the sweater.

I pushed away from him, breathless. I didn't want to go now. With him staying overnight maybe it was a good thing I had to leave for a while. I meant it about no premarital sex, even if he hadn't been a lycanthrope, but the flesh was more than willing. I wasn't sure the spirit was up to the fight.

The look in Richard's eyes was drowning deep and worth anything in the world. I tried to hide a rather sappy smile but knew it was too late. I knew I would pay for this in the car with Zerbrowski. I would never hear the end of it. Staring up into Richard's face, I didn't care. We'd work out everything, eventually. Surely to God we could work it out.

"Wait 'til I tell Dolph we were late because you were smooching with some guy."

I didn't rise to bait. "I may not be home for hours. You might want to go home instead of waiting here."

"I drove your Jeep here, remember? I don't have a ride home."

Oh. "Fine, I'll be back when I can."

He nodded. "I'll be here."

I walked out into the hallway, not smiling anymore. I wasn't sure how I felt about coming home to Richard. How was I ever going to come to a real decision if he kept hanging around, making my hormones run amok?

Zerbrowski chuckled. "Blake, I have seen everything now. The heap-big vampire slayer in luuv."

I shook my head. "I don't suppose it would help to ask you to keep this to yourself?"

He grinned. "Makes the teasing more fun."

"Damn you, Zerbrowski."

"Loverboy seemed sort of tense, so I didn't say anything before, but now that we're alone, what the hell happened to you? You look like someone took a meat cleaver to your face."

Actually, I didn't. I'd seen that done once and it was a lot messier. "Long story. You know my secret. Where were you tonight all dressed up?"

"Married ten years tonight," he said.

"You're kidding?"

He shook his head.

"Big congrats," I said. We clattered down the stairs.

"Thanks. We hired a baby-sitter and everything. She made me leave my beeper home."

The cold bit into the sores on my face and made my head ache worse.

"Door's not locked," Zerbrowski said.

"You're a cop. How can you leave your car unlocked?" I opened the door and stopped. The passenger seat and floorboard were full. McDonald's take-out sacks and newspapers filled the seat and flowed onto the floorboards. A piece of petrified pizza and a herd of pop cans filled the rest of the floorboard.

"Jesus, Zerbrowski, does the EPA know you're driving a toxic waste dump through populated areas?"

"See why I leave it unlocked. Who would steal it?" He knelt in the seat and began shoveling armfuls of garbage into the backseat. It looked like this wasn't the first time he'd cleaned out the front seat by shoveling things in back.

I brushed crumbs from the empty seat onto the empty floorboard. When it was as clean as I could get it, I sat down.

Zerbrowski slid into his seat belt and started the car. It coughed to life. I put on my seat belt, and he pulled out of the parking lot.

''How does Katie feel about your job?'' I asked.

Zerbrowski glanced at me. ''She's okay with it.''

''Were you a cop when she met you?''

''Yeah, she knew what to expect. Loverboy didn't want you to come out tonight?''

''He thought I was too hurt to go out.''

''You do look like shit.''

''Thanks.''

''They love us, they want us to be careful. He's a junior high school teacher, for God's sake. What does he know about violence?''

''More than he'd like to.''

''I know, I know. The schools are a dangerous place nowadays. But it isn't the same, Anita. We carry guns. Hell, you kill vampires and raise the dead, Blake. Can't get much messier than that.''

''I know that.'' But I didn't know that. Being a lycanthrope was messier. Wasn't it?

''No, I don't think you do, Blake. Loving someone who lives by violence is a hard way to go. That anybody'll have us is a miracle. Don't get cold feet.''

''Did I say I was getting cold feet?''

''Not out loud.''

Shit. ''Let's drop it, Zerbrowski.''

''Anything you say. Dolph is going to be so excited that you've decided to tie the noose . . . ah, knot.''

I sank down into the seat as far as the belt would let me. ''I am not getting married.''

''Maybe not yet, but I know that look, Blake. You are a drowning woman, and the only way out is down the aisle.''

I would have liked to argue, but I was too confused. Part of me believed Zerbrowski. Part of me wanted to stop dating Richard and be safe again. Okay, okay, I wasn't exactly safe before, what with Jean-Claude hanging around, but I wasn't engaged. Of course, I still wasn't engaged.

''You okay, Blake?''

I sighed. ''I've lived alone a long time. A person gets set in her ways.'' Besides he's a werewolf. I didn't say that part out loud, but I wanted to. I needed a second opinion, but a police officer, especially Zerbrowski, wasn't the person to ask.

''He crowding you?''

''Yeah.''

''He want marriage, kids, the whole nine yards?''

Kids. No one had mentioned children. Did Richard have this domestic vision of a little house, him in the kitchen, me working, and kids? Oh, damn, we were going to have to sit down and have a serious talk. If we did manage to get engaged like normal people, what did that mean? Did Richard want children? I certainly didn't.

Where would we live? My apartment was too small. His house? I wasn't sure I liked that idea. It was his house. Shouldn't we have our house? Shit. Kids, me? Pregnant, me? Not in this lifetime. I thought furriness was our biggest problem. Maybe it wasn't.

29

The river swirled black and cold. Rocks stuck up like the teeth of giants. The bank behind me was steep, thick with trees. The snow between the trees was trampled and slicked away to show the leaves underneath. The opposite bank was a bluff that jutted out over the river. No way down from there unless you were willing to jump. The water was less than five feet deep in the center of the river. Jumping from thirty feet wasn't a good idea.

I stood carefully on the crumbling bank. The black water rushed just inches from my feet. Tree roots stuck out of the bank, tearing at the earth. The combination of snow, leaves, and nearly vertical bank seemed destined to send me into the water, but I'd fight it as long as I could.

The rocks formed a low, broken wall into the river. Some of the stones were barely above the swirling water, but one near the center of the river stuck up about waist high. Draped over that rock was the skin. Dolph was still the master of understatement. Shouldn't a skin be smaller than a breadbox, not bigger than a Toyota? The head hung on the large rock, draped perfectly as if placed. That was one of the reasons the thing was still in the middle of the river. Dolph had wanted me to see it in case there was some ritual significance to the placement.

There was a dive team waiting on the shore in dry suits, which are bulkier than wet suits and better at keeping you warm in cold water. A tall diver with a hood already pulled up over his hair stood by Dolph. He'd been introduced as MacAdam. "Can we go in after the skin now?"

"Anita?" Dolph asked.

"Better them in the water than me," I said.

"Is it safe?" Dolph asked.

That was a different question. Truth. "I'm not sure."

MacAdam looked at me. "What could be out there? It's just a skin, right?"

I shrugged. "I'm not sure what kind of skin it is."

"So?" he asked.

"So, remember the Mad Magician back in the seventies?"

"I'd think you wouldn't remember it," MacAdam said.

"I studied it in college. Magical Terrorism, senior year. The Magician specialized in leaving magical booby traps in out-of-the-way places. One of his favorite traps was an animal skin that would attach itself to whomever touched it first. Took a witch to remove it."

"Was it dangerous?" MacAdam asked.

"One man suffocated when it attached itself to his face."

"How the hell did his face touch it first?"

"Hard to ask a dead man. Animating wasn't a profession in the seventies."

MacAdam stared off across the water. "Okay, how do you find out if it's dangerous?"

"Has anyone been in the water yet?"

He jerked a thumb at Dolph. "He wouldn't let us, and Sheriff Titus said to leave everything for some hotshot monster expert." He looked me up and down. "That you?"

"That's me."

"Well, make like an expert so my people and I can get in there."

"You want the spotlight now?" Dolph asked. They'd had the place lit up like an opening night at Mann's Chinese Theatre. I'd made them turn off the lights after I'd gotten the first glance. There were some things that you needed light to see, other things only showed themselves in the dark.

"No light yet. Let me see it in the dark first."

"Why no light?" Dolph asked.

"Some things hide from light, Dolph, and they might still take a chunk out of one of the divers."

"You're really serious about this, aren't you?" MacAdam asked.

"Yeah, aren't you glad?"

He looked at me for a moment, then nodded. "Yeah. How are you going to get a closer look? I know the weather just got cold the last few days, so the water should be about forty degrees, but that's still cold without a suit."

"I'll stay on the rocks. I might dip a hand in to see if anything rises to bait, but I'll stay as dry as I can."

"You take the monsters serious," he said, "I take the water serious. You'll get hypothermia in about five minutes in water this cold. Try not to fall in."

"Thanks for the advice."

"You're going to get wet," Aikensen said. He stood just above me, leaning against a tree. His Smokey Bear hat was pulled low over his head, thick woolly collar pulled up near his chin. His ears and most of his face were still bare to the cold. I hoped he got frostbite.

He put his flashlight under his chin like a Halloween gag. He was smiling. "Didn't move a thing, Miss Blake. Left it just where we found it."

I didn't correct him on the "miss." He'd done it just to irritate me. Ignoring it irritated him. Great.

The Halloween smile faded, leaving him frowning in the light.

"What's the matter, Aikensen? Didn't want to get your delicate toes wet?"

He pushed away from the tree. The movement was too abrupt. He slid down the bank, arms windmilling, trying to slow his fall. He fell to his butt and kept scooting. He was coming straight for me.

I took a step to one side and the bank crumbled underfoot. I gave a hop and ended up on the nearest stone in the river. I huddled on it, nearly on all fours to keep from falling into the water. The stone was wet, slick, and bone-deep cold.

Aikensen landed in the river with a yell. He sat on his butt, freezing water swirling to nearly the middle of his chest. He beat at the water with his gloved hands, as if punishing it. All he was doing was getting wetter.

The skin didn't slide off the rock and cover him. Nothing grabbed him. I couldn't feel any magic on the air. Nothing but the cold and the sound of water.

''Guess nothing's going to eat him,'' MacAdam said.

''Guess not,'' I said. I tried to keep the disappointment out of my voice.

''God's sake, Aikensen, get out of the water,'' Titus's voice boomed from the top of the hill. The sheriff, along with most of the other policemen, were at the top of the bank, along the gravel road that led back to the place. Two ambulances were sitting up there, too. Since Gaia's law went into effect three years ago, an ambulance had to be on the scene if there was any chance the remains were humanoid. There were ambulances being called to take away coyote carcasses, as if they were dead werewolves. The law had gone into effect, but no extra money had been put into the emergency systems across the country. Washington did like to complicate things.

We were in the backyard of someone's summer house. Some of the houses had landings or even small boathouses, if they had deep enough water at the base of their land. The only boat you were taking off through this rocky channel was a canoe, so no landing, no boathouse, just the cold black water and a very wet deputy.

''Aikensen, get your butt up on one of those rocks. Help Ms. Blake out, since you're already wet.''

''I don't need his help,'' I called back to Titus.

''Well, now, Ms. Blake, this is our county. Wouldn't want you getting eaten by some beastie while we stayed nice and safe on shore.''

Aikensen stood, nearly falling again when his boots slid on the sandy bottom. He turned to glare at me as if it were all my fault, but he scrambled up on the rock on the side opposite the skin. He'd lost his flashlight. He was dripping wet in the dark, except for his Smokey Bear hat which he'd managed to keep above water. He looked as sullen as a wet hen.

''Notice you're not offering to climb out on this particular limb,'' I said.

Titus started down the bank. He seemed to be a lot better at it than I had been. I'd staggered like a drunk from tree to tree. Titus kept his hands out ready to catch himself, but he pretty much walked down. He stopped beside Dolph.

''Delegation, Ms. Blake. What made the country great.''

''What do you think of that, Aikensen?'' I said more softly.

He glared at me. ''He's the boss.'' He didn't sound like he was happy with it, but he believed it.

''Get on with it, Anita,'' Dolph said.

Translation, stop yanking everybody's chain. Everybody wanted out of the cold. Couldn't blame them. Me, too.

I stood ever so carefully on the slick rock. My flashlight reflected off the choppy water like a black mirror, opaque and solid.

I shone the flashlight on the first stone. It was pale and shining with water, and probably ice. I stepped onto it carefully. The next stone, still okay. Who knew Nike Airs were good for icy rocks?

MacAdam's warning about hypothermia ran through my head. Just what I'd need, to be hospitalized from exposure. Didn't I have enough problems without having to fight the elements?

There was a gap between the next two stones. It was a tempting distance. Almost stepping distance but just an inch out of comfort range. The stone I was on was flat, low to the water, but solid underfoot. The next one was sort of curved on one side with a point.

''Afraid you're going to get your feet wet?'' Aikensen flashed a smile that was more a baring of white teeth in the dark.

''Jealous that you're wet and I'm not?''

''I could get you wet,'' he said.

''Only in my nightmares,'' I said. I had to leap for it and hope some miracle of balance kept me safe. I glanced back at the bank. I thought about asking the divers if they had an extra dry suit for me, but it seemed cowardly with Aikensen shivering on the rocks. Besides, I could probably make the jump. Probably.

I backed to the edge of the rock I was standing on, and jumped. There was a second of being airborne, then my foot hit the rock. My foot slid off to one side. I collapsed onto the rock hugging it with both hands and one leg. The other leg ended up thigh deep in ice cold water. The shock of it left me cursing.

I struggled back up on the rock, water streaming from the jeans' pants leg. My foot hadn't touched bottom. The water on either side of the rocks would come up to my waist, if Aikensen's little wading show was a good indication. I'd found a sinkhole deep enough to have doused every inch of me. Lucky it was just my leg.

Aikensen was laughing at me. If it had been anyone else, we might have laughed together at how ridiculous all this was, but it was him, and he laughed at me.

''At least I didn't drop my flashlight,'' I said. It sounded childish even to me, but he stopped laughing. Sometimes childish will get you what you want.

I was beside the skin now. Up close, it was even more impressive. I'd known it was reptilian from the bank. Standing next to it, I could see it was definitely a snake. The largest scales were the size of my palm. The empty eye sockets were the size of golf balls. I reached out to touch it. Something swirled against my arm as I reached for it. I screamed before I realized it was the undulating snakeskin spreading out in the water. When I could breathe again, I touched the skin. I expected it to be light, a sloughed skin. It was heavy, meaty.

I turned the edge of it to the light. It wasn't a sloughed skin. The snake had been skinned. Whether it had been alive when the skinning started was a moot point. It was dead now. Very few creatures can survive being skinned alive.

There was something about the scales and shape of the head that reminded me of a cobra, but the scales, even in the light of a flashlight, gleamed with opalescence. The snake wasn't any one color. It was like a rainbow or an oil slick. The color changed depending on the angle of the light.

"You going to play with it, or can the divers come and get it?" Aikensen asked.

I ignored him for the moment. There was something on the snake's forehead, almost between the eyes. Something smooth and round and white. I ran my fingers over it. It was a pearl. A pearl the size of a golf ball. What the hell was a giant pearl doing embedded in the head of a snake? And why hadn't whoever skinned the creature taken the pearl with him?

Aikensen leaned forward running a hand over the skin. "Yuck. What the hell is it?"

"Giant snake," I said.

He jerked back with a yell. He started scraping at his arms as if he could wipe off the feel of it.

"Afraid of snakes, Aikensen?"

He glared at me. "No."

It was a lie, and we both knew it.

"The two of you enjoy being out on those rocks?" Titus asked. "Get a move on."

"You see anything significant about the placement of the skin, Anita?" Dolph asked.

"Not really. The thing might have just gotten hooked on the rocks. I don't think it was purposefully placed here."

"We can move it then?"

I nodded. "Yeah, the divers can come in. Aikensen's already tested the water for predators."

Aikensen looked at me. "What the hell does that mean?"

"It means there might have been creepy-crawlies in the water, but nothing tried to eat you, so it's safe."

"You used me for bait."

"You fell in."

"Ms. Blake say we can move the thing?" Titus asked.

"Yes," Dolph said.

"Go to it, boys."

The divers all looked at each other. "Can we have the spotlight now?" MacAdam asked.

"Sure," I said.

The light smashed into me. I put a hand up to shield my eyes and nearly slipped off the rock. Jesus it was bright. The water was still opaque, black, and choppy, but the rocks glistened and Aikensen and I were suddenly center stage. The bright light washed all the color from the snakeskin.

MacAdam slipped his face mask on, regulator secure in his mouth. Only one other diver followed his lead. Guess they didn't need four to go in after the skin.

"Why're they putting on tanks just to wade out here?" Aikensen asked.

"Insurance in case the current gets them, or they find a sinkhole."

"Current's not that bad."

"Bad enough that if it catches the skin, the skin's gone. With tanks you can follow something in the water all the way down, wherever it goes."

"You sound like you've done it."

"I'm certified."

"Well, aren't you multitalented," he said.

The divers were almost out to us. Their tanks looked like the backs of whales sticking out of the water. MacAdam raised his face mask out of the water, and put a gloved hand on the rocks. He took the regulator out of his mouth, hugging the rock and paddling with his legs to keep free of the current. The other diver moved over by Aikensen.

"There a problem if we tear the skin?" MacAdam asked.

"I'll unhook it from this side of the rock."

"You'll get your arm wet."

"I'll live, right?"

I couldn't see his face well enough under all the equipment, but I'd bet he was frowning at me.

"Yeah, you'll live."

I moved my hand down the front of the skin until I hit water. The cold made me hesitate, but only for a heartbeat. I reached down, soaking myself to the shoulder to untangle it. My hand touched something slick and solid that wasn't skin. I gave a small yip and jerked back, nearly falling. I got my balance and went for my gun.

I had time to say, "Something's down there." It surfaced.

A round face, with a screaming lipless mouth, shot upward, hands reaching for MacAdam. I had a glimpse of dark eyes before it fell back into the water.

The divers got the hell out of there, swimming with strong sure strokes for shore.

Aikensen had stumbled back, falling into the water. He came up sputtering, gun in hand.

"Don't shoot it," I said. The thing surfaced again. I slid in beside it. It shrieked, its human-shaped hand groping for me. It grabbed a handful of jacket and pulled itself to me. My gun was in my hand, but I didn't shoot.

Aikensen was aiming at it. Shouts from the shore. The other cops coming, but there was no time. There was just Aikensen and me in the river.

The creature clung to me, not screaming now, just clinging as if I were the last thing in the world. It buried its earless face into my chest. I pointed my gun at Aikensen's chest.

That seemed to get his attention. He blinked, focusing on me. "What the hell are you doing?"

"Point it somewhere else, Aikensen."

"I'm tired of looking down the barrel of your gun, bitch."

"Ditto," I said.

Voices shouting, movement on the bank, people coming, almost there. Only seconds left until someone came. Someone saved us. Seconds too late.

A shot exploded next to Aikensen. Close enough to spray him with water. He jumped, and his gun fired. The creature went wild, but I was already moving, diving for the rocks. It clung to me as if attached. We floated by the big rock, swirling in snakeskin, but I managed to point the Browning at Aikensen. The sound of his Magnum vibrated in the air, echoing down my bones. If Aikensen had turned towards us, I'd have fired.

"Goddamn it, Aikensen, put that damn gun away!" The splashing was heavy, and it was probably Titus wading into the water, but I couldn't look away from Aikensen.

Aikensen was looking away from me towards the splashing. Dolph got there first. He loomed over Aikensen like the vengeance of God.

Aikensen's gun started to swing towards him, as if he sensed his danger.

"You point that gun at me and I will feed it to you," Dolph said. His voice was low and reverberated even through the ringing in my ears.

"If he points it at you," I said, "I'll shoot him."

"Nobody's shooting him but me." Titus waded up. He was shorter than everyone but me, so he was struggling in the water. He grabbed Aikensen by the belt and pulled him off his feet, tearing the gun from his hand as he fell into the water.

Aikensen surfaced choking and mad. "What the hell did you do that for?"

"Ask Ms. Blake why I did it. Ask her, ask her!" He was short and wet, and still managed to browbeat Aikensen.

"Why?" Aikensen said.

I'd lowered the Browning, but hadn't put it away. "Trouble with carrying a big gun, Aikensen, is that it goes through a hell of a lot of flesh."

"What?"

Titus pushed him, making him stumble. Aikensen struggled to stay on his feet. "If you'd pulled that trigger, boy, with the creature pressed right up against her, you'd have killed her, too."

"I thought she was just protecting it. She said not to shoot it. Look at it!"

Everyone turned to me then. I used the rocks to leverage to my feet. The creature was dead weight, as if he'd passed out with his hands locked in my jacket. I had more trouble putting the gun away than I had getting it out. Cold, adrenaline, and the man's hand stuck on my jacket, covering the holster.

Because that's what I was holding. A man, a man who had been skinned alive, but somehow wasn't dead. Of course, it wasn't exactly a man.

"It's a man, Aikensen," Titus said. "It's a hurt man. If you weren't so damn busy pulling your gun and shooting at things, you might see what's in front of ya."

"It's a naga," I said.

Titus didn't seem to hear me. Dolph asked, "What did you say?"

"He's a naga."

"Who is?" Titus asked.

"The man," I said.

"What the hell is a naga?"

"Everybody out of the water now," a voice from shore yelled. It was a paramedic with an armload of blankets. "Come on folks, let's not have to run everybody into the hospital tonight." I wasn't sure, but I thought I heard the paramedic mutter under his breath, "Damn fools."

"What the hell is a naga?" Titus asked again.

"I'll explain if you can help me get him to shore. I'm freezing my ass off out here."

"You're freezing more than your ass off," the paramedic said. "Everybody to shore, now. Move it people."

"Help her," Titus said. Two uniformed deputies were in the water. They splashed up. They lifted the man, but his fists had locked into my jacket. It was a death grip. I checked the pulse in his throat. It was there, faint but steady.

The medic was folding blankets around everybody as they hit shore. His partner, a slender woman with pale hair was staring at the naga, glistening like an open wound in the spotlight.

"What the hell happened to him?" one of the deputies asked.

"He's been skinned," I said.

"Jesus Christ," the deputy said.

"Right thought, wrong religion," I said.

"What?"

"Nothing. Can you pry his hands loose?" They couldn't, not easily. They ended up carrying him cradled between them. I sort of stumbled to the shore with his fingers still locked in my clothes. None of us fell. A second miracle. The first was that Aikensen was still alive. Staring at the raw bluish skin of the man, maybe the miracle count was higher than just two.

The medic with the pale hair knelt by the naga. She let out her breath in a great whoosh of air. The other medic threw blankets around me and the two deputies.

"When you get him pried off of you, you get your butt up to the ambulances. Get out of those wet clothes, ASAP."

I opened my mouth and he pointed a finger at me. "Clothes off and sit in a warm ambulance, or a trip to the hospital. Your choice."

"Aye, aye, Captain," I said.

"And don't you forget it," he said. He moved off to spread blankets and orders to the rest of the cops.

"What about the skin?" Titus asked. He had a blanket wrapped around him.

"Bring it to shore," I said.

MacAdam said, "You sure this is the only surprise out there in that sinkhole?"

"I think this is our only naga for the night."

He nodded and slipped back into the water with his partner. It was nice not to be argued with. Maybe it was the naked ripped body of the naga.

The paramedics had to pry the naga's hands from my jacket a finger at a time. His fingers didn't want to uncurl. They stayed bent like the fingers of the dead after rigor had set in.

"Do you know what he is?" the paramedic with pale hair asked.

"A naga."

She exchanged glances with her partner. He shook his head. "What the hell is a naga?"

"A creature out of Hindu legend. They're mostly pictured in serpent form."

"Great," he said. "Will he react like a reptile or a mammal?"

''I don't know.''

The medics from the other ambulance were setting up a pulley system and directing everybody up to the warmth of the ambulances. We needed more medics.

The paramedics spread a warm saline solution on a soft cotton sheet and wrapped the naga in it. His whole body was an open wound with all that that implied. Infection was the big threat. Could immortal beings get infections? Who knew? I knew about preternatural creatures, but first aid for the immortal? That wasn't my area.

They bundled him in layers of blankets. I looked at the drill sergeant paramedic. ''Even if he's reptilian blankets can't hurt.''

He had a point.

''His pulse is weak but steady,'' the woman said. ''Should we risk trying an IV or . . .''

''I don't know,'' her partner answered. ''He shouldn't be alive at all. Let's just move him. We'll keep him alive and get him to the hospital.''

The distant whoop of more ambulances sounded. Reinforcements were on the way. The medics put the naga on a long spine-board and fit it in a Stokes basket, attached to the ropes the other paramedics had set up at top of the hill.

''You got any other information that'll help us treat him?'' the paramedic asked. His eyes were very direct.

''I don't think so.''

''Then get your butt up to an ambulance, now.''

I didn't argue. I was cold, and my clothes were beginning to freeze to my body even under the blanket.

I ended up in a warm ambulance wearing nothing but a blanket while more paramedics and EMTs forced heated oxygen on me. Dolph and Zerbrowski ended up in the ambulance with me. Better them than Aikensen and Titus.

While we waited for the medics to tell us we would all live, Dolph got back to business.

''Tell me about nagas,'' Dolph said.

''Like I said, they're creatures from Hindu legend. They're mostly pictured as snakes, particularly cobras. They can take human form. Or appear as snakes with human heads. They're the guardians of raindrops and pearls.''

''Say the last again?'' Zerbrowski asked. His neatly combed hair had dried in messy curls. He'd jumped in the river to save little ol' me, even though he couldn't swim.

I repeated it. ''There's a pearl embedded in the head of the skin. I think the skin was the naga's. Someone skinned him, but he didn't die. I don't know how the skin ended up in the river, or how he did.''

Dolph said, ''You mean he was a snake and they skinned him, but it didn't kill him.''

''Apparently not.''

''How is he in man form now?''

''I don't know.''

''Why isn't he dead?'' Dolph asked.

''Nagas are immortal.''

"Shouldn't you tell the paramedics that?" Zerbrowski said.

"He's been completely skinned and is still alive. I think they're going to figure it out on their own," I said.

"Good point."

"Which of you fired the shot at Aikensen?"

"Titus did it," Dolph said.

"He cussed him out, and took his gun away," Zerbrowski said.

"Hope he doesn't give it back. If anyone shouldn't be armed, it's Aikensen."

"You got an extra change of clothes with you, Blake?" Zerbrowski asked.

"Nope."

"I've got two pairs of sweats in the trunk of my car. I want to get back to what's left of my anniversary."

The thought of wearing a used pair of sweats that had been sitting in Zerbrowski's car was too much for me. "I don't think so, Zerbrowski."

He grinned at me. "They're clean. Katie and I were going to exercise today but never got around to it."

"Never made it to the gym, huh," I said.

"No." Color crept up his neck. It must have been something really good, or really embarrassing to get to Zerbrowski that quickly.

"What kind of exercise were you two doing?" I asked.

"A man needs exercise," Dolph said solemnly.

Zerbrowski looked at me, eyebrows going up. "And how much of a workout is your sweetie giving you?" He turned to Dolph. "Did I tell you that Blake's got herself a boyfriend? He's sleeping over."

"Mr. Zeeman answered the phone," Dolph said.

"Isn't your phone right beside your bed, Blake?" Zerbrowski asked. He was giving me his best wide innocent brown eyes.

"Get the sweats and get me out of here," I said.

Zerbrowski laughed, and Dolph joined him.

"These are Katie's sweats so don't get anything on them. If you really want to work out, do it nude."

I flashed him a one-fingered salute.

"Oh, do that again," Zerbrowski said, "your blanket gaped."

I was just amusing the hell out of everyone.

30

I was standing in my hallway at four o'clock. I was dressed in a very pink sweatsuit. My wet clothes were held sort of gingerly in a bundle under my left arm. Even with the new pink sweats, I was cold. The paramedics had only let me go because I promised to drink hot fluids and take a hot bath. I'd run up the stairs in a pair of gym socks. I could wear Katie's sweats, but not her shoes.

I was cold, tired, and my face hurt. The headache was gone, though. Maybe it was being dunked in ice-cold water. Maybe it was the touch of a naga. I couldn't recall any stories associating them with spontaneous healing, but it had been a long time since I read up on nagas. They'd been on the final in preternatural bio class. The big clue had been the pearl and the cobra skin. I was going to have to dig up my textbook and reread the section. Though the doc on call at whatever hospital they went to was going to have to read up faster than I was. Would nagas be in their computers? By law, they'd better be. Would the naga have anyone to sue for him if they didn't? Would he rise from his deathbed and sue himself?

I stood in front of my apartment for the second time in six hours and had no key. I leaned my head against the door for just a second and felt sorry for myself. I didn't want to see Richard again tonight. We had a lot to talk about that had nothing to do with his shapeshifting. I wished I hadn't thought of children. I didn't want to discuss the little tykes tonight. I didn't want to discuss anything. I wanted to drag off to bed and be alone.

I took a deep breath and stood straight. No need to look as woebegone as I felt. I rang my own doorbell and vowed to get an extra set of keys made. No, one of them wasn't for Richard. They were both for me.

Richard opened the door. His hair was sleep tousled, falling in a heavy, wavy mass around his face. He was shirtless and barefoot. The top button of his jeans was undone. I was suddenly glad to see him. Lust is a wonderful thing.

I grabbed the top edge of his jeans and drew him to me. He jumped when my wet clothes touched his bare chest, but he didn't pull away. His body was almost fever warm from sleep. I warmed my hands along his spine and he twitched, writhing against the cold but never pulling away. I dropped the wet clothes on the floor.

We kissed. His lips were gentle. My hands traced the edge of his waistband, fingers dangerously low. He spoke low and soft next to my ear. I expected sweet nothings or dirty promises. What I got was, "We have company."

I sort of froze. I had this image of Ronnie, or worse Irving, sitting on the couch while we groped each other. "Shit," I said softly and with feeling.

"Home at last, *ma petite*." It was much worse than Irving.

I stared up at Richard with my mouth hanging open. "What's going on?"

"He came in while I was asleep. I woke up when the door opened."

I was suddenly cold again, down to my sodden toes. "Are you all right?"

"Do you really want to discuss this in the hall, *ma petite*?" Jean-Claude's voice was oh so reasonable.

I wanted to stand in the hall just because he'd said not to, but that was childish. Besides, it was my apartment.

I stepped through the door, Richard a warm presence at my side. I kicked my wet clothes through the door, keeping my hands free. The gun was in plain sight over the sweats. The holster flapped loose without a belt, but I could draw the gun if I needed it. I probably didn't need it, but it was good to keep reminding the master that I meant business.

Richard closed the door and leaned against it, hands behind his back. His face was nearly hidden by a spill of hair. The muscles in his stomach bunched and just seemed to invite caressing, which was what we'd probably have been doing if there hadn't been a vampire in my living room.

Jean-Claude sat on my couch. The black shirt was spread around his naked torso. His arms were straight out along the back of the couch, raising the shirt, revealing nipples that were only two shades darker than his white skin. A slight smile curled his lips. He was dramatic and perfect on the white couch. He matched the decor. Shit. I was going to have to buy new furniture, something not white, not black.

"What are you doing here, Jean-Claude?"

"Is that any way to greet your new suitor?"

"Don't be a pain in the ass tonight, please. I'm too tired and too sore to mess with it. Tell me why you're here and what you want, then get out."

He rose to his feet as if pulled by strings, all boneless ease. At least the shirt closed on most of the pale perfection of his body. That was something.

"I am here to see you and Richard."

"Why?"

He laughed, and the sound rolled over me like a wave of fur, soft and slick, tickling, and dead. I took a deep breath and stripped the holster off. He wasn't here to hurt. He was here to flirt. I walked past both of them and draped the holster on the back of a kitchen chair. I felt their eyes follow me as I moved. It was both flattering and uncomfortable as hell.

I glanced back at them. Richard was still by the door, looking unclothed and inviting. Jean-Claude stood by the couch utterly still, like a three-dimensional picture of a wet dream. The sexual potential in the room was astronomical. The fact that nothing was going to happen was almost sad.

There was still coffee in the pot. If I drank enough hot coffee and took a really hot bath, maybe I'd thaw out. My preference would have been a hot shower, quicker at four o'clock in the morning. But I'd promised the paramedics. Something about my core temperature.

''Why did you want to see Richard and me?'' I poured coffee into my freshly washed penguin mug. Richard was good at being domestic.

''I was told that Monsieur Zeeman planned to spend the night.''

''If he did, what of it?''

''Who told you?'' Richard asked. He'd pushed away from the door. He'd even buttoned the top button of his pants. Pity.

''Stephen told me.''

''He wouldn't have volunteered the information,'' Richard said. He was standing very close to Jean-Claude. Physically, he was looming above him, just a bit. Half-dressed. He should have looked uncertain, hesitant. He looked completely at home. The first time I'd met Richard, he'd been naked in a bed. He hadn't been embarrassed then, either.

''Stephen did not volunteer it,'' Jean-Claude said.

''He is under my protection,'' Richard said.

''You are not pack leader yet, Richard. You can protect Stephen within the pack, but Marcus still rules. He has given Stephen to me, as he gave you to me.''

Richard was just standing there. He hadn't moved, yet suddenly, the air around him swam. If you blinked, you'd have missed it. A creeping edge of power fanned out, prickling along my skin. Shit.

''I belong to no one.''

Jean-Claude turned to him. Face pleasant, open, voice conversational. ''You do not acknowledge Marcus's leadership?'' It was a trick question, and we all knew it.

''What happens if he says no?'' I asked.

Jean-Claude turned back to me. His face was carefully blank. ''He says no.''

''And you tell Marcus, and then what?''

He smiled then, a slow curve of lips that left his perfect blue eyes glittering. ''Marcus would see it as a direct challenge to his authority.''

I set down the cup of coffee and came around the island. Standing nearly between them, Richard's energy crawled over my skin like insects on the march. From Jean-Claude there was nothing. The undead make no noise. ''If you get Richard killed, even indirectly, the deal is off.''

''I don't need you to protect me,'' Richard said.

''If you get yourself killed fighting Marcus, that's one thing, but if you get killed because Jean-Claude is jealous of you, that's my fault.''

Richard touched my shoulder. His power was like a rush of electricity down my body. I shivered, and he dropped his hand. ''I could just give in to Marcus, just acknowledge his leadership, then I'd be safe.''

I shook my head. ''I've seen what Marcus considers acceptable. It's not even close to being safe.''

"Marcus didn't know they filmed two endings," Richard said.

"So you have talked to him about it?"

"Are you referring to the delightful little films that Raina masterminded?" Jean-Claude asked.

We both looked at him. A brush of power lashed out, growing stronger. It was hard to breathe standing next to him, like trying to swallow a thunderstorm.

I shook my head. One problem at a time. "What do you know about the films?" I asked.

Jean-Claude looked at us, one and then the other. He ended staring into my eyes. "Your voice makes it sound more important than it should be. What has Raina done now?"

"How do you know about the films?" Richard asked. He moved a step closer. His chest touched my back, and I gasped. The skin up and down my back tingled as if someone had touched a live wire to the skin, but it didn't hurt. It was just an almost overwhelming sensation. Pleasurable, but you knew if it didn't stop soon, it would begin to hurt.

I stepped away from him, standing between both of them, giving my back to neither. They both looked at me. Almost identical expressions on their faces. Alien, as if they were thinking thoughts that I'd never dreamed of, listening to music that I could not dance to. I was the only human in this room.

"Jean-Claude, just tell me what you know about Raina's movies. No games, okay."

He stared at me for a heartbeat, then gave a graceful shrug. "Very well. Your alpha female invited me to join her in a dirty movie. I was offered a starring role."

I knew he'd turned her down. He was an exhibitionist, but he liked a certain decorum to his sideshow. Dirty movies would have been beyond the pale for him.

"Did you enjoy having sex with her on screen?" Richard asked. His voice was low, and that energy flooded into the room.

Jean-Claude turned to him, anger dancing in his eyes. "She brags about you, my furry friend. Says you were magnificent."

"Cheap shot, Jean-Claude," I said.

"You don't believe me. You are that sure of him?"

"That he wouldn't have sex with Raina, yeah."

A strange look crossed Richard's face.

I stared at him. "You didn't?"

Jean-Claude laughed.

"I was nineteen. She was my alpha female. I didn't think I had a choice."

"Yeah, right."

"She has her pick of the new males. It's one of the things I want to stop."

"You're still sleeping with her?" I asked.

"No, not once I had a choice," Richard answered.

"Raina speaks so fondly of you, Richard. In such loving detail. It can't have been that long ago."

"It's been seven years."

"Really?" That one word held a universe of doubt.

"I don't lie to you, Anita," said Richard.

Richard took a step forward. Jean-Claude moved towards him. The testosterone was rising higher than the supernatural powers. We were going to drown in both.

I stepped between them, bodily, putting a hand on each chest. The minute my hand touched Richard's bare skin, the power poured down my arm, like some cool electric liquid. My hand touched Jean-Claude a second later. Some trick of cloth, or vampire, put my hand on his bare skin, too. The skin was cool and soft, and I felt Richard's power cross my body and smash into that perfect skin.

The moment it touched, an answering roll of power spilled out of the vampire. The two energies did not fight each other, they mingled inside me, spilling back on each of them. Jean-Claude's power was a cool, rushing wind. Richard was all warmth and electricity. Each one fed the other like wood and flame. And under it all I could feel myself, that thing inside me that allowed me to call the dead. Magic for lack of a better word. The three powers melded into one skin-curling, heart-pumping, stomach-clenching rush.

My knees buckled, and I was left gasping on the floor on all fours. My skin felt as if it were trying to pull away from my body. I could taste my heart in my throat and couldn't breathe past it. Everything was sort of golden around the edges, and spots of light danced before my eyes. I was in danger of passing out.

''What the hell was that?'' It was Richard. His voice seemed to come from farther away than it should have. I'd never heard him cuss before.

Jean-Claude knelt beside me. He didn't try to touch me. I looked into his eyes from inches away. The pupils were gone, nothing but that lovely midnight blue remained. It was the way his eyes looked when he was getting all vampiric on me. I didn't think he'd done it on purpose this time.

Richard knelt on the other side. He started to reach out to touch me. When his hand was an inch away, a little jump of power ran between us, like static electricity. He jerked his hand back. ''What is that?'' He sounded a little scared. Me, too.

''*Ma petite*, can you speak?''

I nodded. Everything was in hyperfocus, the way the world gets on an adrenaline high. The shadows on Jean-Claude's chest where his shirt spilled around him were solid and touchable. The cloth looked almost metallic black, like the back of a beetle.

''Say something, *ma petite*.''

''Anita, are you all right?''

I turned in almost slow motion to Richard. His hair had fallen over one eye. Each strand was thick and perfect like a line drawn apart. I could see every eyelash around his brown eye in startling contrast.

''I'm all right.'' But was I?

''What happened?'' Richard asked. I wasn't sure who he was asking. I hoped it wasn't me because I didn't know.

Jean-Claude sat beside me on the floor, back against the island. He closed his eyes and took a deep, shuddering breath. When he let it out, his eyes opened. They were still that drowning deep color as if he were about to feed on something. His voice came out normal, or as normal as it ever got. ''I have never tasted such a rush of power without spilling blood first.''

''Trust you to think of the perfect thing to say,'' I said.

Richard sort of hovered over me as if he'd like to help but was afraid to touch me. He glared at Jean-Claude. "What did you do to us?"

"I?" Jean-Claude's beautiful face was nearly slack, eyes half-closed, lips parted. "I did nothing."

"That's a lie," Richard said. He sat Indian fashion a little ways from me, far enough away to make sure we didn't accidentally touch but close enough that that lingering power crawled between us. I inched away and found that closer to Jean-Claude wasn't much better. Whatever it was, it wasn't a one-time deal. The potential was still there in the air, under our skins.

I looked at Richard. "You sound awfully sure that he's up to something. I'm willing to believe it. But what do you know that I don't?"

"I didn't do it. You didn't do it. I know magic when I smell it. It had to be him."

Smell it? I turned back to Jean-Claude. "Well?"

He laughed. The sound trailed down my spine like the brush of fur, soft, slick, startling. It was too soon after the rushing power we'd shared. I shuddered, and he laughed harder. It hurt and you knew you shouldn't be doing it, but it felt too good to stop. His laughter was always dangerously delicious, like poisoned candy.

"I swear by whatever oath you would trust that I did nothing on purpose."

"What did you do by accident?" I asked.

"Ask yourself the same question, *ma petite.* I am not the only master of the supernatural in this room."

Well, he had me there. "You're saying one of us did it."

"I am saying that I do not know who did it, nor do I know what *it* is. But Monsieur Zeeman is correct it was magic. Raw power to raise the hackles on any wolf."

"What's that supposed to mean?" Richard asked.

"If you could harness such power, my wolf, even Marcus might bow to it."

Richard pulled his knees up, hugging them to his chest. His eyes looked distant, thoughtful. The thought intrigued him.

"Am I the only person in this room not trying to consolidate my kingdom?"

Richard looked at me. He looked almost apologetic. "I don't want to kill Marcus. If I could make a great enough show of power, he might back down."

Jean-Claude smiled at me. It was a very satisfied smile. "You admit he is not human, and now he wants power, so he can be leader of the pack." His smile widened just this short of a laugh.

"I didn't know you were a fan of sixties music," I said.

"There are many things you do not know about me, *ma petite.*"

I just stared at him. The image of Jean-Claude boogying down to the Shangri-Las was stranger than anything I'd seen tonight. After all I believed in nagas, I didn't believe that Jean-Claude had hobbies.

31

A hot bath. Once more in the oversize T-shirt, sweatpants, and socks. I was going to be the worst-dressed person in the room. I was planning to replace that black robe at the first opportunity.

They were sitting on the couch, each as far away from the other as they could get. Jean-Claude was sitting like a mannequin, one arm on the back of the couch, the other on the arm of the couch. One foot rested atop his knee showing his soft boots to perfection. Richard was curled on his side of the couch, one knee clutched to his naked chest, the other knee curled on the couch.

Richard looked comfortable. Jean-Claude looked as if he were waiting for a roving photographer to come by. The two men in my life. I could barely stand it.

''I've got to get some sleep, so everybody who isn't staying, out.''

''If you are referring to me, *ma petite*, I have no intention of leaving. Unless Richard goes with me.''

''Stephen told you why I'm here,'' Richard said. ''She's hurt and doesn't need to be alone.''

''Look at her, Richard. Does she look hurt?'' He held up a graceful hand. ''I admit she has sustained some damage. But she does not need your help. Perhaps she doesn't even need mine.''

''I invited Richard to stay over. I did not invite you.''

''But you *did* invite me, *ma petite*.''

''First, please stop calling me that. Second, when did I invite you?''

''The last time I was here. In August I believe.''

Shit, I'd forgotten. It was beyond careless. I'd endangered Richard. Things were working out, but I hadn't known that when I left him here alone, alone in a place where Jean-Claude could come and go at will.

''I can take care of that right now,'' I said.

''If a dramatic gesture will please you, then be my guest. But Richard must not spend the night.''

''Why not?''

''I think you are one of those women that where you give your body, there, too, is your heart. If you sleep with our Monsieur Zeeman, I think it might be the point of no return.''

''Sex isn't a commitment,'' I said.

''For most people, no, but for you, I think it is.''

The fact that he knew me that well brought heat in a rush up my face. Damn him. ''I don't plan on sleeping with him.''

''I believe you, *ma petite,* but I see the way your eyes follow him. He sits there looking luscious and warm and very alive. If I had not been here when you came home, would you have resisted?''

''Yes.''

He shrugged. ''Perhaps. Your strength of will is frightening, but I cannot take that chance.''

''You don't trust me not to molest him?''

Again that shrug that could have meant anything. His smile was inviting and condescending.

''Why? You got the hots for him yourself?''

The question caught him off guard. The surprise on his face was worth the outraged look on Richard's face. Jean-Claude looked at Richard. He gave him his full attention. He stared at Richard, eyes roaming his body in a slow, intimate dance. His gaze ended not on his groin or his chest, but on his neck. ''It is true that the blood of shapeshifters can be sweeter than human blood. It is a wild ride if you can manage it without getting torn apart.''

''You sound like a rapist,'' I said.

His smile blossomed in a surprised flash of fangs. ''It is not a bad comparison.''

''That was an insult, you know,'' I said.

''I know it was meant as such.''

''I thought we had an agreement,'' Richard said.

''We do.''

''You can sit there and talk about taking me for food, and we've still got an agreement.''

''It would be enjoyable to take you for many reasons, but we have an agreement. I won't go back on it.''

''What agreement?'' I asked.

''We are exploring our mutual powers,'' Jean-Claude said.

''What does that mean exactly?'' I asked.

''We're not sure,'' Richard said. ''We haven't worked out the details yet.''

''We've just agreed not to kill each other, *ma petite.* Give us a little time to plan beyond that.''

''Fine. Then both of you get out.''

Richard sat up straighter on the couch. ''Anita, you heard Lillian. You need to be woken every hour just in case.''

''I'll set an alarm. Look, Richard, I'm fine. Get dressed and go.''

He looked puzzled and a little hurt. ''Anita.''

Jean-Claude didn't look hurt or puzzled. He looked smug.

''Richard's not spending the night. Happy?''

''Yes.''

''And you're not spending the night, either.''

''I had not planned to.'' He stood, turning to face me. ''I will leave as soon as I've had my good-night kiss.''

''Your *what*?''

''My kiss.'' He came around the couch to stand in front of me. ''I will admit I had envisioned you wearing something a little more''—he tugged on my sleeve—''salacious, but one takes what one can get.''

I jerked the sleeve out of his fingers. ''You haven't gotten anything yet.''

''True, but I am hopeful.''

''I don't know why,'' I said.

''The agreement between Richard and me is predicated on the fact that we are all dating. You date Richard, and you date me. We both woo you. One cozy little family.''

''Can you speed this up? I want to get to bed.''

A slight frown appeared between his eyes. ''Anita, you are not making this easy.''

''Hurrah,'' I said.

The frown smoothed out as he sighed. ''You would think I would give up on you ever being easy.''

''Yes,'' I said, ''you would.''

''A good-night kiss, *ma* . . . Anita. If you truly intend to date me, it will not be the last.''

I glared up at him. I wanted to tell him to go to hell, but there was something about the way he stood there. ''If I say no kiss, what then?''

''I go away for tonight.'' He took that step closer to me that put us almost touching. The cloth of his shirt brushed the front of my T-shirt. ''But if you give Richard kisses and do not allow me such privileges, then the agreement is off. If I cannot touch you, and he can, it is hardly fair.''

I'd agreed to the dating because it seemed like a good idea at the time, but now . . . I hadn't really thought through all the implications. Dating, kissing, making out. Yikes! ''I don't kiss until after the first date.''

''But you have already kissed me, Anita.''

''Not willingly,'' I said.

''Tell me you did not enjoy it, *ma petite*.''

I'd have loved to lie, but neither of them would have bought it. ''You are an intrusive bastard.''

''Not as intrusive as I would like to be,'' he said.

''You don't have to do anything you don't want to do,'' Richard said. He was on his knees on the couch, hands gripping the back.

I shook my head. I wasn't sure I could explain it out loud, but if we were really going to do this, Jean-Claude was right. I couldn't hold Richard's hand and not his. Though it did give me a real incentive not to go all the way with Richard. Tit for tat and all that.

''After our first date you can have a willing kiss, not before,'' I said. I was going to give it the old college try.

He shook his head. ''No, Anita. You yourself told me you liked Richard, not just loved him. That you could see spending your life with him, but not with me. Perhaps he is a more likable fellow. I cannot compete in niceness."

"That's certainly gospel," I said.

He stared down at me with his blue, blue eyes. No drag of power, but there was a weight to his gaze. Not magic, but dangerous all the same.

"But in one area I can compete." I could feel his gaze on my body as if he'd touched me. The weight of his gaze made me shiver.

"Stop it."

"No." One word, soft, caressing. His voice was one of his best things. "One kiss, Anita, or we can end it here, tonight. I will not lose you without a struggle."

"You'd fight Richard tonight, just because I won't kiss you."

"It is not the kiss, *ma petite*. It is what I saw tonight when you met him at the door. I see you forming a couple before my eyes. I must interfere now, or all is lost."

"You'll use your voice to trap her," Richard said.

"I promise, no tricks tonight."

If he said no tricks, he meant it. Once he gave his word he kept it. Which also meant he would fight Richard tonight over a kiss. I'd left both guns in the bedroom. I thought we were safe for tonight. I was too damn tired to do this tonight.

"Okay," I said.

"You don't have to do anything you don't want to, Anita," Richard said.

"If we are all going to go down in a bloody mess, let it be over something more important than a kiss."

"You want to do it," Richard said. "You want to kiss him." He didn't sound pleased.

What was I supposed to say? "What I want most right this moment is to go to bed, alone. I want some sleep." That at least was the truth. Maybe not all of the truth, but enough to earn me a puzzled frown from Richard, and an exasperated sigh from Jean-Claude.

"Then if it is such a distasteful duty, let it be done quickly," Jean-Claude said.

We were standing so close, he didn't have to make a full step to press the line of his body against mine. I tried to put my hands up, to keep our bodies apart. My hands slid over the bare skin of his stomach. I jerked back from him, balling my hands into fists. The feel of his skin clung to my hands.

"What is it, *ma petite*?"

"Leave her alone," Richard said. He was standing beside the couch, hands in loose fists. Power prickled along my skin. His power creeping outward like a slow-moving wind. His hair had spilled over one side of his face. He looked out through a curtain of hair. His face had fallen into shadows. Light gleamed along his naked skin, painting it in shades of grey, gold, and black. He stood there looking suddenly primal. A low, spine-brushing growl trickled through the room.

"Stop it, Richard."

"He is using his powers on you." His voice was unrecognizable. A low, bass growl that was sliding away from human. I was glad for the shadows. Glad I couldn't see what was happening to his face.

I'd been so worried about Jean-Claude starting a fight, it hadn't occurred to me that Richard might pick one. "He isn't using powers on me. I touched his bare skin. That's all."

He stepped forward into the light, and his face was normal. What was happening inside that smooth throat, behind those kissable lips, to make his voice sound monstrous?

"Get dressed and get out."

"What?" His lips moved but that growling voice rolled out. It was like watching a badly dubbed movie.

"If Jean-Claude isn't allowed to attack you, then you sure as hell aren't allowed to attack him. I thought he was the only monster I had to deal with. If you can't behave like a human being, Richard, get out."

"What of my kiss, *ma petite*?"

"You have both pushed it about as far as it's going to go tonight," I said. "Everybody out."

Jean-Claude's laugh filled the shadowed dark. "As you like, Anita Blake. I am suddenly not so worried about you and Monsieur Zeeman."

"Before you start congratulating yourself, Jean-Claude—I revoke my invitation."

There was a sound like a low sonic pop. A great roaring filled the room. The door smashed open, banging against the wall. A wind rushed in like an invisible river, tugging at our clothes, flinging our hair across our eyes.

"You don't have to do this," Jean-Claude said.

"Yes," I said, "I do."

It was as if an invisible hand shoved him through the door. Slamming the door shut behind him.

"I'm sorry," Richard said. The growl was slipping away. His voice was almost normal. "It is too close to the full moon to get this angry."

"I don't want to hear it," I said. "Just go."

"Anita, I am sorry. I don't usually lose control like this. Even this close to the full moon."

"What was different tonight?"

"I've never been in love before. It seems to break my concentration."

"Jealousy will do that to you," I said.

"Tell me I don't have reason to be jealous, Anita. Make me believe it."

I sighed. "Go away, Richard. I've still got to clean my guns and knife before I can go to bed."

He smiled and shook his head. "I guess tonight didn't reassure you about how human I am." He walked around the couch and bent over, retrieving his sweater from the floor, where it lay neatly folded.

He pulled the sweater over his head. He pulled a ponytail holder from his jeans pocket, and tied his hair back. I could see the muscles in his arms work even through the sweater. He slipped his shoes on, bending over to tie them.

His coat was long, falling to his ankles. In the half light it looked like a cape.

"I don't suppose I get a kiss, either."

"Good night, Richard," I said.

He took a deep breath and let it out slowly. ''Good night, Anita.''

He left. I locked the door. I cleaned my weapons and went to bed. After the show that Richard and Jean-Claude had put on, the Browning was about the only thing I wanted in bed with me tonight. All right, the gun and one stuffed penguin.

32

The phone was ringing. It seemed to have been ringing a long time. I lay in bed listening to it ring, wondering when the hell the machine would pick up. I rolled over, reaching for the phone. It was missing. The ringing was coming from the other room. Shit. I'd forgotten to bring it back in last night.

I crawled out of the warm covers and staggered into the living room. The phone must have rung fifteen times before I got to it. I sank to the floor with the receiver clutched to my ear. "Who is it?"

"Anita?"

"Ronnie?"

"You sound awful."

"I look worse," I said.

"What's up?"

"Later, why are you calling at"—I glanced at my wristwatch—"seven o'clock in the freaking morning. This better be good, Ronnie."

"Oh, it's good, all right. I thought we should catch George Smitz before he goes to work."

"Why?" My face was throbbing. I lay down on the carpet, cradling the phone against my ear. The carpet was very soft.

"Anita, Anita, are you there?"

I blinked and realized I'd fallen asleep. I sat up and leaned against the wall. "I'm here, but I didn't hear a word you said after something about needing to talk to Smitz before work."

"I know you're not a morning person, Anita, but you've never fallen asleep on me before. How much sleep did you get last night?"

"About an hour."

"Oh, God, I am sorry. But I knew you'd want to know. I've found the smoking gun."

"Ronnie, please, what are you talking about?"

"I have pictures of George Smitz with another woman." She let that sink in for a moment or two. "Anita, are you there?"

"I'm here. I'm thinking." The last was harder to do than I wanted it to be. I am never at my best first thing in the morning. After an hour's sleep I wasn't even close to my best. "Why do you say it's a smoking gun?"

"Well, a lot of times a spouse will report the other spouse missing to divert suspicion."

"You think Smitz offed his wife?"

"How poetically you put it, but yes, I do."

"Why? A lot of men cheat on their wives, most of them don't kill them."

"Here's the clincher. After I took the pictures, I talked to a few gun stores in the area. He'd bought some silver bullets at a store near the butcher shop."

"Not very bright," I said.

"Most murderers aren't."

I nodded, realized she couldn't see it, and didn't care. "Fine, looks like Mr. Smitz isn't the grieving widower he pretended to be. What do you want to do about it?"

"Confront him at home."

"Why not go to the cops?"

"The store clerk isn't exactly positive it was George."

I closed my eyes. "Great, just great. You think he'll confess to us?"

"He might. He's shared a bed with her for fifteen years. Mother of his children. There's got to be a lot of guilt there."

I don't think real well on an hour's sleep. "Cops, we should have the cops waiting in the wings, at least."

"Anita, he's a client of mine. I don't turn clients over to the cops unless I have to. If he confesses, I'll bring them in. If he doesn't confess, I'll hand over what I have. But I've got to try it my way first."

"Fine, do you call him and tell him we're coming or do you want me to?"

"I'll do it. I just thought you'd like to be there."

"Yeah, let me know when."

"He hasn't gone to work yet. I'll call him and be over to pick you up."

I wanted to say, "No, I have to go back to sleep," but what if he had killed her? What if he'd taken the others? George hadn't struck me as dangerous enough to take out shapeshifters, but then I'd thought he was genuinely grieving. Genuinely worried about his wife. What the hell did I know?

"I'll be ready," I said. I hung up without saying good-bye. I was getting as bad as Dolph. I'd apologize when Ronnie got here.

The phone rang before I could crawl to my feet. "What is it, Ronnie?"

"Anita, it's Richard."

"Sorry, Richard, what's up?"

"You sound awful."

"You don't. You didn't get much more sleep than I did. How come you sound so much better? Please tell me you aren't a morning person."

He laughed. "Sorry, guilty as charged."

Furry I could forgive; a morning person, I'd have to think about that. "Richard, don't take this wrong, but what do you want?"

"Jason's missing."

''Who's Jason?''

''Young male, blond, crawled all over you at the Lunatic Cafe.''

''Ah, I remember him. He's missing.''

''Yes. Jason is one of our newest pack members. Tonight is the full moon. He wouldn't risk going out alone today of all days. His sponsor went over to his house, and he was gone.''

''Sponsor like in AA?''

''Something like that.''

''Any signs of a struggle?''

''No.''

I stood up dragging the phone in one hand. I tried to think past the leaden tiredness. How dare Richard sound so cheerful. ''Peggy Smitz's husband—Ronnie caught him with another woman. A clerk may have sold him silver bullets.''

There was silence on the other end of the phone. I could hear his soft breathing, but that was all. The breathing was a little fast.

''Talk to me, Richard.''

''If he killed Peggy, then we'll handle it.''

''Has it occurred to you that he could be behind all the disappearances?'' I asked.

''I don't see how.''

''Why not? A silver bullet will take care of any shapeshifter. No great skill involved. You just need to be someone that the shapeshifter trusts.''

More silence finally. ''Okay, what do you want to do?''

''Ronnie and I were going to confront him this morning. With Jason missing we don't have time to pussy-foot around. Can you supply me with a shapeshifter or two to help threaten Smitz? Maybe with a little muscle power we can get to the truth faster.''

''I have to teach school today, and I can't afford for him to know what I am.''

''I didn't ask for you to come. Just for some of you to come. Make sure they look intimidating, though. Irving may be a werewolf, but he isn't very scary.''

''I'll send someone. To your apartment?''

''Yeah.''

''When?''

''Soon as you can. And, Richard.''

''Yes.''

''Don't tell anybody what we suspect about George Smitz. I don't want to find him clawed up when we get there.''

''I wouldn't do that.''

''You wouldn't, but Marcus might, and I know Raina would.''

''I'll tell them you have a suspect and want some backup. I won't tell them who.''

''Great, thanks.''

''If you find Jason before they kill him, I'll owe you one.''

''I'll take the payment in carnal favors,'' I said. The minute I said it, I wished I hadn't. It was sort of true, but after last night, not down to my toes.

He laughed. ''Done. I've got to go to work. I love you.''

I hesitated just a second. ''I love you, too. Teach the kiddies well today.''

He was quiet for a space of heartbeats. He'd heard the hesitation. ''I will. Bye.''

''Bye.'' When I'd hung up, I stood there for a minute. If someone was just walking up and shooting shifters, then Jason was dead. The best I'd be able to do would be to locate the body. It was better than nothing, but not much.

33

We pulled up in front of George Smitz's house at a little after nine that morning. Ronnie was driving. I was riding shotgun. Gabriel and Raina were in the backseat. If asked, I would have chosen different people for backup. I also wouldn't have chosen my boyfriend's old lover for backup. What had Richard been thinking? Or maybe Raina hadn't given him a choice. Her coming today, not the sex. I still wasn't sure how I felt about that. All right. I knew how I felt. I was pissed. But I'd slept with someone else. Glass houses and all. In any case, Richard had given me exactly what I'd asked for: scary, intimidating shapeshifters. I wasn't used to getting exactly what I asked for. Next time I'd be more specific.

Gabriel was dressed in black leather again. It could almost have been the same outfit I'd first seen him in, down to the metal-studded gauntlet on his right hand. Maybe his whole closet was one great big leather fest. The earrings were gone. The holes even in the harder cartilage of the ears had healed.

Raina was dressed normally enough. Sort of. She was wearing an ankle-length fur coat. Fox. Cannibalism is one thing, but wearing the skin of your dead? It seemed a little cold blooded even for the psycho bitch from hell. All right, she was a wolf, not a fox, but heck, I didn't wear fur on moral grounds. She flaunted it.

She leaned over the back of the seat. "What are we doing in front of Peggy's house?"

It was time to spill the beans. Why didn't I want to do it? I undid the seat belt and turned to face her. She was looking at me, face pleasant enough. On her lycanthrope bone structure she had all high cheekbones and a luscious mouth. Maybe she planned on doing something nefarious today.

Gabriel had draped himself over the backseat. The gauntleted hand trailed down Ronnie's arm. Even through her suede coat she shivered. "Touch me again, and I am going to feed you that hand." She'd scooted away from him as far as the steering wheel would allow, which wasn't far. Gabriel had touched her several times on the drive over. Teasing, nothing embarrassing, but it was bothersome.

"Hands are very bony. I prefer a more tender cut of meat. Breast or thigh is my preference," Gabriel said. His grey eyes were startling even in sunlight, maybe more so. They had a quality of light to the grey that was almost luminous. I'd seen eyes like that before, but I still couldn't place it.

"Gabriel, I know you are a pain in the ass. I know you're enjoying the hell out of teasing Ronnie, but if you don't stop it we're going to see just how good your recuperative powers are."

He slid across the seat, closer to me. Not necessarily an improvement. "I'm yours anytime you want me."

"Is coming that close to dying really your idea of sex?"

"As long as it hurts," Gabriel said.

Ronnie looked at us with wide eyes. "You have got to tell me about your evening."

"You really don't want to know," I said.

"Why are we here?" Raina asked again. She wasn't going to be distracted by Mr. Leather. Good for her. Bad for me. Her gaze was intense, as if my face were the most important thing in the world. Was this what Marcus saw in her? A lot of men are very flattered by undivided attention. Then aren't we all?

"Ronnie?"

She got the pictures out of her purse. They were the kind of pictures that didn't need any explanation. George had left his drapes up, very careless.

Gabriel curled back into the seat, flipping through the shots, a big smile on his face. He got to one particular shot, and laughed. "Very impressive."

Raina's reaction was very different. She wasn't amused. She was angry. "You brought us out here to punish him for cheating on Peggy?"

"Not exactly," I said. "We think he is responsible for her disappearance. If he's responsible for one disappearance, he could be responsible for more."

Raina looked at me. The concentration was just as pure but now I had to fight an urge to squirm. Her rage was pure and simple. George had hurt a pack member. He would pay for that. There was no uncertainty in her gaze, only an instant rage.

"Let Ronnie and I do the talking. The two of you are here to intimidate him if we need it."

"If there is any chance he has Jason, we don't have time to be subtle," Raina said.

I agreed with her, but not out loud. "We talk, you stay in the background and look menacing. Unless we ask. Okay?"

"I'm here because Richard asked me," Raina said. "He's an alpha male. I obey his orders."

"Somehow I don't picture you obeying anybody's orders," I said.

She flashed me a very nasty smile. "I obey the orders I want to obey."

That I believed. I jerked a thumb at Gabriel. "Who called in him?"

"I chose him. Gabriel is very good at intimidation."

He was big, leather clad, metal studded, and had sharp, pointy teeth. Yeah, I'd say that was intimidating.

"Your word that you'll stay in the background unless we need you."

"Richard said we are to obey you as we would obey him," Raina said.

"Great. Since you obey Richard only when it suits you, what does that mean?"

Raina laughed. It had a hard, brittle edge to it. The kind of laughter that made you think of mad scientists and people locked too long in solitary. ''I will let you handle it, Anita Blake, as long as you are doing a good job. Jason is my pack member. I will not let your squeamishness endanger him.''

I was liking this less and less. ''I'm not squeamish.''

She smiled. ''That is true. My apologies.''

''You're not a wolf,'' I said. ''What are you getting out of this?''

Gabriel smiled, flashing sharp, pointy teeth. He was still flipping through the pictures. ''Marcus and Richard will owe me a favor. The whole damn pack will owe me one.''

I nodded. It was a motive I believed. ''Give the pictures back to Ronnie. No smart remarks, just do it.''

He pouted, sticking out his lower lip. It would have worked better without the fangs. But he handed the pictures to Ronnie. His fingertips brushed her hand, lingering a little, but he didn't say anything. That had been what I asked. Were all shapeshifters so damn literal?

His strange eyes stared at me. I suddenly remembered where I'd seen those eyes. Behind a mask in a film that I'd rather not have seen. Gabriel was the other man in the snuff film. I hadn't had enough sleep to hide the shock. I felt my face crumble with it and couldn't stop it.

Gabriel turned his head to one side, like a dog. ''Why are you looking at me like I just sprouted a second head?''

What could I say? ''Your eyes. I just figured out where I've seen them.''

''Yes.'' He moved closer, putting his chin on the back of the seat, letting me have a good look at those luminous eyes. ''Where?''

''The zoo. You're a leopard.'' Liar, liar, pants on fire, but I couldn't think of a better one, not this quick.

He blinked, staring at me. ''Meow, but that wasn't what you were thinking.'' He sounded very sure of himself.

''Believe it or not, I don't give a damn. It's the best answer you're getting.''

He stayed there, chin indenting the upholstery. You couldn't see his shoulders, so his head looked disembodied, like a head on a pike. Accurate, if Edward found out who he was. And Edward would find out. I'd tell him, gladly, if it would stop any more of those films from being made. Of course, I wasn't sure it would stop them. They were Raina's brainchild. Supposedly, she didn't know about the alternate ending. Yeah, right, and I moonlighted as the Easter Bunny.

Ronnie was staring at me. She knew me too well. I hadn't told her about the snuff film. Now I'd introduced her to two of the stars. Shit. We got out of the car into the bright, chilly winter sunlight. We walked up the sidewalk with a shapeshifter following at our backs that I had seen murder a woman on screen and feed from her still-twitching body. God help George Smitz if he was guilty. God help us all if he wasn't. Jason was missing. One of the newest pack members, Richard had said. If George Smitz didn't have him, who did?

34

Raina grabbed my hand before it could touch the doorbell. Her grip had been very fast. I hadn't had time to react at all. Her nails were long and perfectly manicured with nail polish the color of burnt pumpkins. Those orange-brown nails dug into my wrist just enough to indent the skin. She let me feel the strength in that delicate hand. She didn't hurt me, but the smile on her face said she could. I smiled back. She was strong, but she wasn't a vampire. I was betting I could get to a gun before she could finish crushing my wrist.

She didn't crush my wrist. She let go. "Perhaps Gabriel and I should go in the back way. You did say you wanted us to stay in the background." She was smiling and looking oh, so reasonable. The nail marks in my skin hadn't filled out yet.

"I mean, look at us, Ms. Blake. Even if we say nothing, he can't ignore us."

She had a point. "How will the two of you get in the back door if it's locked?"

Raina gave me a look worthy of Edward, as if I'd asked a very stupid question. Was I the only one who didn't know how to pick a lock? "Fine, go to it."

Raina smiled and walked off through the snow. Her auburn hair gleamed against the fox fur coat. Her high-heeled brown boots left sharp little prints in the melting snow. Gabriel trailed after her. The chains on his leather jacket jingled as he walked. His metal-studded cowboy boots smashed over Raina's daintier prints almost as if it were purposeful.

"Nobody's going to mistake them for door-to-door salespeople," Ronnie said.

I glanced at our jeans, my Nikes, her snow boots, my leather jacket, her long suede coat. "Us either," I said.

"Good point."

I rang the bell.

We stood on the little front porch listening to the eaves drip. We were having one of those strange winter thaws that Missouri is famous for. The snow was all soft and fading like a snowman in the sunshine. But it wouldn't last. Getting this much snow at all in December was unusual here. We usually didn't get real snow until January or February.

It was taking a long time for Mr. Smitz to come to the door. Finally I heard movement. Something heavy enough to be a person moving toward the door. George Smitz opened the door in a bloodstained apron over jeans and a pale blue T-shirt.

There was a bloodstain on one shoulder, as if he'd lifted a side of beef and it had bled on him. He wiped his hands on his apron, palms flat, skin stretching along the fabric as if he couldn't get them clean. Maybe he just wasn't used to being covered in blood. Or maybe his palms were sweating.

I smiled and offered him my hand. He took it. His palm was sweaty. Nervous. Great. "How are you, Mr. Smitz?"

He shook hands with Ronnie and ushered us inside. We were standing in a little entryway. There was a closet to one side, a mirror on the opposite wall with a low table. A vase full of yellow silk flowers sat on the table. The walls were pale yellow and matched the flowers.

"May I take your coats?"

If he was a murderer, he was the most polite one I'd ever met. "No, thanks, we'll keep them with us."

"Peggy always got on to me if I didn't ask for people's coats. 'George, you weren't raised in a barn, ask them if you can take their coats.' " The imitation sounded accurate.

We stepped out into the living room. It was wallpapered in pale yellow with brown flowers done very small. The couch, the love seat, the recliner were all a pale, pale yellow, almost white. There were more silk flowers on the pale wood end table. Yellow.

The pictures on the wall, the knickknacks on the shelves, even the carpet underfoot was yellow. It was like being inside a lemon drop.

Either it showed on my face or George was used to it. "Yellow was Peggy's favorite color."

"Was?"

"I mean is. Oh, God." He collapsed on the pale lemon couch, face hidden in his big hands. He was the only thing in the room that didn't match the yellow lace curtains. "It's been so awful, wondering." He looked up at us. Tears glistened in his eyes. It was Academy Award caliber.

"Ms. Sims said she had news about Peggy. Have you found her? Is she all right?" His eyes were so sincere it hurt to look into them. I still couldn't tell he was lying. If I hadn't seen the pictures of him with another woman, I wouldn't have believed it. Of course, adultery wasn't murder. He could be guilty of one and not the other. Sure.

Ronnie sat on the couch, as far away from him as she could get but still rather companionable. Cozier than I was willing to be with the son of a bitch. If I ever managed to get married and my husband cheated on me, it wouldn't be me to go missing.

"Please sit down, Ms. Blake. I'm sorry, I'm not being a very good host."

I perched on the edge of the yellow recliner. "I thought you worked construction, Mr. Smitz. What's with the apron?"

"Peggy's dad can't run the store by himself. He deeded it to her years ago. I may have to quit working construction. But you know, he's family. I can't leave him in the lurch. Peggy did most of the work. Dad's almost ninety-two. He just can't do it all.''

''Do you inherit the butcher shop?'' I asked. We'd automatically gone into good cop, bad cop. Guess which one I was.

He blinked at me. ''Well, yes. I suppose so.''

He didn't ask if she was all right this time. He just looked at me with his soulful eyes.

''You love your wife?''

''Yes, of course. What kind of question is that?'' He looked less sad and more angry now.

''Ronnie,'' I said softly.

She took the pictures out of her purse and gave them to him. The front picture showed him embracing the dark-haired woman. Peggy Smitz had been a blond.

Color crept up his face. Not so much red as purplish. He slammed the pictures down on the coffee table without looking at the rest. They slid across the table, images of him and the woman in various states of undress. Kissing, groping, nearly doing it standing up.

His face went from red to purplish. His eyes bulged. He stood up, his breath coming in fast, harsh gasps. ''What the hell are these?''

''I think the pictures are self-explanatory,'' I said.

''I hired you to find my wife, not to spy on me.'' He turned on Ronnie, towering over her. His big hands balled into even bigger fists. The muscles in his arms bulged, veins standing out like worms.

Ronnie stood up, using her five feet and nine inches to good advantage. She was calm. If she was worried about facing down a man that outweighed her by a hundred pounds, it didn't show.

''Where's Peggy, George?''

He glanced at me, then back to Ronnie. He raised a hand as if he would strike her.

''Where'd you hide the body?''

He whirled on me. I just sat there and looked at him. He'd have to come over or around the coffee table to get to me. I was pretty sure I could be out of reach. Or have a gun. Or put him through a window. That last was sounding better and better.

''Get out of my house.''

Ronnie had stepped back out of reach. He stood there like a purple-faced mountain, swaying between us.

''Get out of my house.''

''Can't do that, George. We know you killed her.'' Maybe *know* was too strong a word, but ''we're pretty sure you killed her'' didn't have the right ring. ''Unless you really plan to start swinging, I'd sit down, Georgie-boy.''

''Yes, by all means sit down, George.'' I didn't look behind me to see where Raina was. I didn't think George would really hurt me, but better to be cautious. Taking my eyes off a guy who weighed over two hundred pounds sounded like a bad idea.

He stared at Raina. He looked confused. ''What the hell is this?''

Ronnie said, ''Oh, my God.'' She was staring behind me with her mouth open.

Something was going on behind my back, but what? I stood, eyes all for George, but he wasn't looking at me anymore. I stepped away from him just to be safe. When I had enough distance to be safe. I could see the doorway.

Raina was wearing a brown silk teddy, high heeled boots and nothing else. The fur coat was held open, the bloodred lining outlining her body dramatically.

''I thought you were going to stay in the background unless I called for you.''

She dropped the fur into a fuzzy puddle on the floor. She stalked into the room, swaying everything that would move.

Ronnie and I exchanged glances. She mouthed the words, ''What's going on?'' I shrugged. I didn't have the faintest idea.

Raina bent over the silk flowers on the coffee table, giving George Smitz a long, thorough view of her slim backside.

The color was draining from his face. His hands were slowly unclenching. He looked confused. Join the club.

Raina smiled up at him. She stood up very slowly, giving George a good view of her high, tight breasts. His eyes were glued to her décolletage. She stood up, running her hands down the teddy, ending with a pass over her groin. George seemed to be having a little trouble swallowing.

Raina walked up to him until she was just a finger's pull away from him. She looked up at him and whispered out of full, sensuous lips, ''Where's Jason?''

He frowned. ''Who's Jason?''

She caressed his cheek with her painted nails. The nails slid out of her skin long and longer, until they were great hooking claws. The tips were still the color of burnt pumpkins.

She hooked those claws under his chin, putting them just enough in not to break the skin. ''The tiniest bit of pressure and you'll have a howling good time once a month.''

It was a lie. She was still in human form. She wasn't contagious. All the color had drained from his face. His skin was the color of unbleached paper.

''Where's your wife's body, Mr. Smitz?'' I asked. It was a good threat worth more than one question.

''I don't . . . don't know what you mean.''

''Don't lie to me, George, I don't like it.'' She raised her other hand in front of his face, and the claws slid out like unsheathed knives.

He whimpered.

''Where's Peggy, George?'' She whispered it. The voice was still seductive. She might have been whispering, I love you, instead of a threat.

She kept her claws under his jaw and lowered the other hand slowly. His eyes followed that hand. He tried to move his head down, but the claws stopped him. He gasped.

Raina sliced through the bloody apron. Two quick, hard slices. The clothes underneath were untouched. Talent.

''I . . . killed her. I killed Peggy. Oh, God. I shot her.''

"Where's the body?" I asked that. Raina seemed to be enjoying her game too much to pay attention to all the details.

"Shed out back. It's got a dirt floor."

"Where's Jason?" Raina asked. She touched claw tips to his jeans, over his groin.

"Oh, God, I don't know who Jason is. Please, I don't know. I don't know." His voice was coming in breathy gasps.

Gabriel walked into the room. He'd lost the jacket somewhere and wore a tight black T-shirt with his leather pants and boots. "He doesn't have the guts to have taken Jason or the others."

"Is that right, George? You don't have the guts?" Raina pressed her breasts against his chest, claws still at his jawline and groin. The lower claws pressed into the jean fabric, not quite tearing.

"Please, please don't hurt me."

Raina put her face very close to his. Claws forcing him to stand on tiptoes or have his chin spitted. "You are pathetic." She shoved the claws into his jeans, tearing into the fabric.

George fainted. Raina had to pull her hands away to keep from slicing him up. She kept a near perfect circle of jeans. His white briefs showed through the hole in his pants.

Gabriel knelt by the body, balancing on the balls of his feet. "This human did not take Jason."

"Pity," Raina said.

It was a pity. Somebody had taken eight, no seven shapeshifters. The eighth had been Peggy Smitz. We had her murderer on the carpet with his fly torn out. Who had taken them, and why? Why would anybody want seven lycanthropes? Something clicked. The naga had been skinned alive. If he'd been a lycanthrope instead of a naga, a witch could have used the skin to become a snake. It was a way to be a shapeshifter with all the advantages and none of the bad stuff. The moon didn't control you.

"Anita, what is it?" Ronnie asked.

"I have to go to the hospital and talk to someone."

"Why?" A look was enough for Ronnie to say, "Fine, I'll call the cops. But I drove."

"Damn." I glanced up and caught sight of a car driving by on the street. It was a Mazda, green. I knew that car.

"I may have a ride." I opened the door and walked down the sidewalk, waving. The car slowed, then double-parked beside Ronnie's car.

The window whirred down at the press of a button. Edward sat behind the wheel, a pair of dark glasses covering his eyes. "I've been following Raina for days. How'd you spot me?"

"Dumb luck."

He grinned. "Not so dumb."

"I need a ride."

"What about Raina and her little leather friend?"

It occurred to me to tell him that Gabriel was the other lycanthrope in the snuff film, but if I did that now, he'd go in and kill him. Or at least wouldn't want to take me to the hospital. Priorities.

"We can either give them a ride home or they can take a taxi."

"Taxi," he said.

"My preference, too."

Edward drove around the block to wait for me. Raina and Gabriel were persuaded to call a taxi to pick them up in front of another house. They didn't want to talk to the police. Fancy that. George Smitz came to, and Raina convinced him to confess to the police when they arrived. I apologized to Ronnie for deserting her and walked down the block to meet Edward. We were off to the hospital to talk to the naga. Here's hoping he'd gained consciousness.

35

There was a uniformed officer standing outside the naga's room. Edward had stayed in the car. After all, he was wanted by the police. One of the bad things about working with Edward and the cops is that you can't necessarily work with them at the same time.

The cop at the door was a small woman with a blond ponytail. There was a chair beside the door, but she was standing, one hand on her gun butt. Her pale eyes squinted suspiciously at me.

She gave a curt nod. ''You Anita Blake?''

''Yeah.''

''See some ID?'' she said, real tough, no nonsense. Had to be a rookie. Only a rookie had that hard-on attitude. Older cops would have asked for ID, but they wouldn't have tried to make their voices lower.

I showed her my plastic ID badge. The one I clipped to my shirt when I had to cross a police line. It wasn't a police badge, but it was the best I had.

She took it in her hand and looked at it for a long time. I fought the urge to ask if she was going to be tested later. It never helps to piss the police off. Especially over trivialities.

She finally gave the badge back to me. Her eyes were blue and cold as a winter sky. Very tough. Probably practiced that look in the mirror every morning. ''No one can question the man without police being present. When you called up to ask to speak with him, I contacted Sergeant Storr. He's on his way.''

''How long will I have to wait?''

''I don't know.''

''Look, a man's missing, any delay could cost him his life.''

I had her attention now. ''Sergeant Storr didn't mention a missing person.''

Shit. I'd forgotten that the cops didn't know about the missing shapeshifters. ''I don't suppose that you'd buy time is of the essence. How about lives are at stake?''

Her eyes went from hard to bored. She was impressed. ''Sergeant Storr was very specific. He wants to be present when you question the man.''

''Are you sure you spoke with Sergeant Storr, and not Detective Zerbrowski?'' It would be like Zerbrowski to screw this up for me, just to irritate.

''I know who I spoke with, Ms. Blake.''

''I didn't mean to imply that you didn't, Officer. I just meant that Zerbrowski could have gotten confused about how much access I'm allowed to the . . . ah, witness.''

''I talked to the sergeant, and I know what he told me. You're not going in until he gets here. Those are my orders.''

I started to say something unpleasant and stopped. Officer Kirlin was right. She had her orders, and she wasn't going to budge from them.

I glanced at her nameplate. ''Fine, Officer Kirlin. I'll just wait around the corner in the patient waiting room.'' I turned and walked away before I said something not so nice. I wanted to push my way into the room, pull rank. But I didn't have any rank. It was one of those times when I was forcibly reminded that I was a civilian. I didn't like being reminded.

I sat down on a multicolored couch that backed a raised area of real plants. The chest-high planting area gave the illusion of walls, dividing the waiting room into three pseudo rooms. The illusion of privacy if you needed it. A television set was mounted high on one wall. No one had bothered to turn it on yet. It was hospital quiet. The only noise was the heater coming through the wall registers.

I hated waiting. Jason was missing. Was he dead? If he were alive, how much longer would he be alive? How long would Dolph keep me waiting?

Dolph came around the corner. Bless his little heart, he hadn't kept me waiting long at all.

I stood. ''Officer Kirlin says you mentioned a missing person to her. Are you holding out on me?''

''Yeah, but not by choice. I've got a client that won't go to the police. I've tried to persuade them . . .'' I shrugged. ''Just because I'm right and they're wrong doesn't mean I can spill their secrets without clearing it with them first.''

''There's no client-animator privilege, Anita. If I asked for the information you're legally obligated to give it to me.''

I hadn't had enough sleep to deal with this. ''Or what?''

He frowned. ''Or you go to jail for obstruction of justice.''

''Fine, let's go,'' I said.

''Don't push me, Anita.''

''Look, Dolph, I'll tell you everything I know when they give me the okay. I may tell you anyway because they're being stupid, but I won't tell you shit because you bullied me.''

He took a deep breath through his nose and let it out slow. ''Fine, let's go talk to our witness.''

I appreciated the naga still being ''our'' witness. ''Yeah, let's go.'' Dolph motioned me out of the waiting room. We walked down the hallway together in silence. But the silence was companionable. No need to fill it with idle chitchat or accusations.

A doctor in a white coat with a stethoscope draped over his shoulders like a feather boa opened the door. Officer Kirlin was still at her post, ever vigilant. She gave me her best flinty steel look. It needed work. But when you're small, blond, female, and a cop, you have to at least try to look tough.

"He can talk for a very short time. It's a miracle that he's alive, let alone talking. I'll monitor the questioning. If he gets upset, I'll stop the interview."

"That's fine with me, Dr. Wilburn. He's a victim and a witness, not a suspect. We don't mean him any harm."

The doctor didn't look completely convinced but he stepped back into the room, and held the door for us.

Dolph loomed up behind me. He was like an immovable force at my back. I could see why the doctor thought we might browbeat the witness. Dolph couldn't look harmless if he tried, so he just didn't try.

The naga lay in the bed, thick with tubes and wires. His skin was growing back. You could see it spreading in raw, painful patches, but it was growing back. He still looked as though he'd been boiled alive, but it was an improvement.

He turned his eyes to look at us. He moved his head very slowly, the better to see us. "Mr. Javad, you remember Sergeant Storr. He's brought some people to talk with you."

"The woman . . . ," he said. His voice was low and sounded painful. He swallowed carefully and tried again. "The woman at the river."

I walked forward. "Yes, I was at the river."

"Helped me."

"I tried."

Dolph stepped forward. "Mr. Javad, can you tell us who did this to you?"

"Witches," he said.

"Did you say 'witches'?" Dolph asked.

"Yes."

Dolph looked at me. He didn't have to ask. This was my area. "Javad, did you recognize the witches? Names?"

He swallowed again and it sounded dry. "No."

"Where did they do this to you?"

He closed his eyes.

"Do you know where you were when they . . . skinned you?"

"Drugged me."

"Who drugged you?"

"Woman . . . eyes."

"What about her eyes?"

"Ocean." I had to lean forward to hear that last. His voice was fading.

He opened his eyes suddenly, wide. "Eyes, ocean." He let out a low guttural sound, as if he were swallowing screams.

The doctor came up. He checked his vitals, touching the ruined flesh as gently as he could. Even that touch made him writhe with pain.

The doctor pressed a button on the bedside. "It's time for Mr. Javad's medication. Bring it now."

"No," Javad said. He grabbed my arm. He gasped, but held on. His skin felt like warm raw meat. "Not first."

"Not first? I don't understand."

"Others."

"They did this to others?"

"Yes. Stop them."

"I will. I promise."

He slumped back against the bed but couldn't hold still. It hurt too much for that. Every movement hurt, but he couldn't hold still against the pain.

A nurse in a pink jacket came in with a shot. She put the needle into his IV. Moments later he began to ease. His eyes fluttered shut. Sleep came and something in my chest loosened. That much pain was hard to endure, even if you were only just watching.

"He'll wake up and we'll have to sedate him again. I've never seen anyone that could heal like this. But just because he can heal the damage doesn't mean it doesn't hurt."

Dolph took me to one side. "What was all that about eyes and others?"

"I don't know." Half-true. I didn't know what the eye comment meant, but I suspected the others were the missing shapeshifters.

Zerbrowski came in. He motioned to Dolph. They walked out into the hall. The nurse and doctor were fussing with the naga. No one had invited me out into the hall, but it was only fair. I wasn't sharing with them, why should they share with me?

The door opened, and Dolph motioned me out into the hall. We went. Officer Kirlin wasn't at her post. Probably told to leave for a little while.

"Can't find any missing-person case that has your name associated with it," Dolph said.

"You had Zerbrowski check me out?"

Dolph just looked at me. His eyes had gone all cool and distant—cop eyes.

"Except for Dominga Salvador," Zerbrowski said.

"Anita said she didn't know what happened to Mrs. Salvador," Dolph said. He was still giving me his hard look. It was a hell of a lot better than Officer Kirlin's.

I fought the urge to squirm. Dominga Salvador was dead. I knew that because I'd seen it happen. I'd pulled the trigger, metaphorically speaking. Dolph suspected I had something to do with her disappearance but he couldn't prove it, and she had been a very evil woman. If she'd been convicted of everything she was suspected of doing, it would have been an automatic death penalty. The law doesn't like witches much better than it likes vampires. I'd used a zombie to kill her. It was enough to earn me my own trip to the electric chair.

My beeper sounded. Saved by the bell. I checked the number. I didn't recognize the number, but no need sharing that. "An emergency, I've got to find a phone." I walked off before Dolph could say anything else. Seemed safer that way.

They let me use the phone at the nurses' station. Kind of them. Richard picked up the phone on the first ring. "Anita?"

"Yeah, what's up?"

"I'm at school. Louie never showed up for his morning classes." He lowered his voice until I had to plug one ear just to hear him. "Tonight is full moon. He wouldn't miss classes. It raises suspicions."

"Why call me?"

"He said he was going to meet your writer friend, Elvira something."

"Elvira Drew?" As I said her name, I could picture her face. Her green-blue eyes the color of ocean water. Shit.

"I think so."

"When was he supposed to meet her?"

"This morning."

"Did he make the meeting?"

"I don't know. I'm at work. I haven't been by his place yet."

"You're afraid something happened to him, aren't you?"

"Yes."

"I didn't set up the meeting. I'll call work and find out who did. Will you be at this number?"

"I've got to get back to class. But I'll check back with you as soon as I can."

"Okay. I'll call you as soon as I know anything."

"I've got to go," he said.

"Wait, I think I know what happened to the missing shapeshifters."

"What!"

"This is an ongoing police investigation. I can't talk about it, but if I could tell the police about the missing shapeshifters, we might find Louie and Jason faster."

"Marcus said not to tell?"

"Yeah."

He was quiet for a minute. "Tell them. I'll take the responsibility."

"Great. I'll get back with you." I hung up. It wasn't until I heard the dial tone that I realized I hadn't said, I love you. Oh, well.

I dialed work. Mary answered. I didn't wait for her to get through her greeting. "Put me through to Bert."

"Are you all right?"

"Just do it."

She didn't argue. Good woman. "Anita, this better be important. I've got a client with me."

"Did you speak with someone about finding a wererat today?"

"As a matter of fact, I did."

My stomach hurt. "When and where was the appointment set up?"

"This morning, about six. Mr. Fane wanted to get it in before he had to go to work."

"Where?"

"Her house."

"Give me the address."

"What's wrong?"

"I think Elvira Drew may have set him up to be killed."

"You are kidding me, right?"

"Address, Bert."

He gave it to me.

"I may not be in for work tonight."

''Anita . . .''

''Save it, Bert. If he gets killed, we set him up.''

''Fine, fine. Do what you have to.''

I hung up. It was a first, Bert giving in. If I hadn't known that visions of lawsuits were dancing in his head, I'd have been more impressed.

I went back to our little group. No one was talking to anyone. ''There have been seven shapeshifters taken in this area.''

''What are you talking about?'' Dolph asked.

I shook my head. ''Just listen.'' I told him everything about the disappearances. Ending with, ''Two more shifters have gone missing. I think whoever skinned the naga thought he was a lycanthrope. It is possible by magic to take a shifter's skin and use it to shapeshift yourself. You get all of the advantages, greater strength, speed, etc. . . . and you are not tied to the moon.''

''Why didn't it work with the naga?'' Zerbrowski asked.

''He's immortal. The shifter has to die at the end of the spell.''

''We know why. Now, where the hell are they?'' Dolph asked.

''I've got an address,'' I said.

''How?''

''I'll explain on the way. The spell doesn't work until dark, but we can't take the chance they'll keep them alive. They have to be worried that the naga healed enough to talk.''

''After seeing him last night, I wouldn't be,'' Zerbrowski said.

''You're not a witch,'' I said.

We left. I would have liked Edward at my back. If we did find renegade witches and a few shapeshifters on the night of the full moon, Edward at my back was not a bad idea. But I couldn't figure out how to manage it. Dolph and Zerbrowski were no slouches, but they were cops. They aren't allowed to shoot people without giving them every opportunity to give up. Elvira Drew had skinned a naga. I wasn't sure I wanted to give her an opportunity. I wasn't sure we'd survive it.

36

Elvira Drew's house was a narrow two-story set off from the road by a thick line of bushes and trees. You couldn't even see the yard before you turned into the driveway. Woods stretched out all around the small yard, as if someone had put the house here and forgotten to tell anybody.

A patrol car followed us down the gravel driveway. Dolph parked behind a vivid green Grand Am. The car matched her eyes.

There was a For Rent sign in the yard. Another lay beside it, waiting to be stuck in the ground. It would probably go out by the road.

Two clothes bags hung inside the car. The backseat was packed with boxes. A quick getaway was in the offing.

''If she's a murderer, why'd she give you her actual address?'' Zerbrowski asked.

''We check out clients. They have to have a place of residence or some way of proving who they are. We demand more ID than most banks.''

''Why?''

''Because every once in a while we get a crazy. Or a tabloid reporter. We have to know who we're dealing with. I bet she tried to pay cash with no ID and when asked for three forms of it, she wasn't prepared.''

Dolph led the way to the door. We followed behind like good soldiers. Officer Kirlin was one of the uniforms. Her partner was an older guy with greying hair and a round little belly. I bet it didn't shake like a bowlful of jelly. He had a sour expression on his face that said he'd seen it all and didn't like any of it.

Dolph knocked on the door. Silence. He knocked harder. The door trembled. Elvira opened the door. She was wearing a brilliant green robe, tied at the waist. Her makeup was still perfect. The polish on her fingernails matched the robe. Her long blond hair was combed straight back, held from her face with a scarf that was just a touch bluer green than the robe. Her eyes blazed with the color.

Dolph muttered, ''Eyes like the ocean.''

''Excuse me, what's all this about?''

''May we come in, Ms. Drew?''

''Whatever for?''

There hadn't been time to get a warrant. Dolph wasn't even sure we could have gotten one with what we had. The color of someone's eyes wasn't exactly proof.

I sort of peeked around Dolph, and said, ''Hello, Ms. Drew, we need to ask you a few questions about Louis Fane.''

''Ms. Blake, I didn't know you were with the police.''

She smiled, I smiled. Was Louie here? Was she stalling while someone killed him? Dammit. If the police hadn't been here, I'd have pulled the gun and gone in. There are disadvantages to being law abiding.

''We're checking into the disappearance of Mr. Fane. You were the last one to see him.''

''Oh, dear.'' She didn't back away from the door.

''May we come in and ask you a few questions?'' Dolph asked.

''Well, I don't know what I can tell you. Mr. Fane never made our meeting. I didn't see him at all.''

She stood there like a pretty smiling wall.

''We need to come in and look around, Ms. Drew, just in case.''

''Do you have a warrant?''

Dolph looked at her. ''No, Ms. Drew, we do not.''

Her smile was dazzling. ''Then I'm sorry, but I can't let you in.''

I grabbed the front of her robe, yanking it tight enough to know she wasn't wearing a bra. ''We either go past you or through you.''

Dolph's hand descended on my shoulder. ''I'm sorry, Ms. Drew. Ms. Blake gets a little overzealous.'' The words were squeezed out between his teeth, but he said them.

''Dolph . . .''

''Let her go, Anita, right now.''

I looked up into her strange eyes. She was still smiling but there was something else there now. Fear. ''If he dies, you die.''

''They don't put you to death for suspicions,'' she said.

''I wasn't talking about a legal execution.''

Her eyes widened. Dolph jerked back on my shoulder. He pushed me down the steps. Zerbrowski was already apologizing for my faux pas.

''What the hell do you think you're doing?'' Dolph asked.

''He's in there, I know it.''

''You don't know it. I've called in for a warrant. Until we get it, unless she lets us in or he comes to a window and yells for help, we can't go in. That's the law.''

''Well, it sucks.''

''Maybe, but we're the police. If we don't obey the law, then who else will?''

I hugged myself, fingers digging into my elbows. It was either that or run up and smash Elvira Drew's perfect face in. Louie was in there, and it was my fault.

''Take a walk, Anita, cool off.''

I looked up at him. He could have told me to sit in the car, but he hadn't. I tried to read his face, but it had gone cop blank. ''A walk, good idea.''

I walked towards the trees. No one stopped me. Dolph didn't call me back. He had to know what I'd do. I walked into the winter-bare trees. Melt fell in droplets onto my head and face. I walked out until I couldn't see them clearly anymore. In winter you can catch glimpses of things for yards, but it was far enough for our little game of pretend.

I angled back for the back of the house. The melting snow soaked into my Nikes. The leaves were a soggy mat underfoot. I had both guns and two knives. I'd replaced the one that Gretchen never returned. They were a set of four that I'd had made for me. Hard to find a knife with a high enough silver content to kill monsters and still take a hard edge.

But I couldn't kill anyone. My job was to get inside, find Louie, and yell for help. If someone in the house yelled for help, the police could come in. Those were the rules. If Dolph hadn't been scared they'd kill Louie, he wouldn't have let me do this. But law or no law, sitting outside while your suspect kills her next victim was hard to swallow.

I hunkered down at the tree line looking at the back of the house. A back door led onto an enclosed porch. There was a door with glass in it that led into the house, and a second door off to one side. Most houses in St. Louis have basements. Some of the older houses originally had only outside access to them. Add a little porch, add a little door. If I was hiding somebody, a basement sounded like a good place. If it was a broom closet, I just wouldn't go in.

I checked the upper-story windows. The drapes were closed. If there were people up there watching, I couldn't see them. Here was hoping they couldn't see me.

I crossed the open ground without getting out a gun. They were witches. Witches didn't shoot you, as a general rule. In fact, witches, real witches, didn't practice a lot of violence. A Wiccan wouldn't have had anything to do with human sacrifice. But the word *witch* means a lot of different things. Some of them can get pretty scary, but they seldom shoot you.

I knelt by the screen door that led onto the porch. I held my hand as close to the door handle as I could without touching it. No heat, no . . . hell there's no word for it. But there was no spell on the handle. Even good witches will sometimes bespell their outer doors so they're either alerted to a burglar's presence or some attachment occurs. Say, you break in and don't take a thing. The spell will stick to you and let the witch and friends find you. Bad witches can put worse things on their doors. We'd already established what sort of witches were inside, so caution seemed best.

I slipped the tip of my knife through the edge of the door. A little jiggling and the door opened. No breaking yet, but I had definitely entered. Would Dolph arrest me for it? Probably not. If Elvira forced me to shoot her out of sight of witnesses, he might.

I went to the second door. The one I hoped led to the basement. I ran my hand over it, and there it was. A spell. I'm not a witch. I don't know how to decipher spells. Sensing them is about my limit. Oh, one other thing. I can break them. But it's a raw burst of power directed at the spell. I just call up whatever it is that allows me to raise the dead and grab the doorknob. It's worked up to this point, but it's like kicking in a door without knowing what's on the other side. Eventually, you're going to get a shotgun blast in your face.

The real problem was even if I got past it safely, whoever laid the spell would know it. Hell, a good witch would feel the buildup of power before I touched it. If Louie was behind this door, great. I'd go in and keep him safe until my screams brought the cavalry. If he wasn't behind this door, they might panic and kill him.

Most witches, good or bad, are nature worshipers to a certain extent. If it had been Wiccans, their ceremonial area would have been outside somewhere. But for this, darkness and an enclosed space might suffice.

If I had a human sacrifice lying about, I'd want him stored as close to the ceremonial area as possible. It was a gamble. If I was wrong and they killed Louie . . . No. No dwelling on worst-case scenarios.

It was still daylight. It was afternoon. The winter sunlight was grey and soft, but it wasn't dark. My abilities don't come out until after dark. I can sense the dead and certain other things in daylight, but I'm limited. The last time I did this, it had been dark. I approached magic the same way I did everything else. Straight ahead, brute force. What I was really gambling on was that my powers were greater than whoever laid the spell. Sort of the theory that I could take a better beating than she or he could dish out.

Was that true in daylight? We'd find out. Question, was the spell just on the doorknob? Maybe. I'd have locked the door, spell or no spell. Why not just cut out the middle man?

I drew the Browning and backed up. I centered myself, concentrating on a point near the lock but not on it. I waited until that piece of wood was all there was. There was a quality of silence in my ears. I kicked it with everything I had. The door shuddered but did not open. Two more kicks and the wood splintered. The lock gave.

It wasn't a burst of light. If someone had been watching, they wouldn't have seen a damn thing but me falling backwards. My whole body tingled as if I'd put my finger in an electric socket.

I heard running footsteps in the house. I crawled to the open door. I dragged myself to my feet using the banister. A wash of cool air swept against my face. I started down the steps before I was sure I could walk. I had to find Louie before Elvira caught me. If I didn't find proof, she could have me arrested for breaking and entering and we'd be worse off than we were before.

I stumbled down the stairs, one hand in a death grip on the banister, gun in the other. The darkness was velvet black. I couldn't see a damn thing beyond the finger of daylight. Even my night vision needs some light. I heard footsteps behind me.

"Louie, are you down here?"

Something moved in the darkness below me. It sounded big. "Louie?"

Elvira was standing at the head of the stairs. She was framed by the light, as if standing in a body-sized halo. "Ms. Blake, I must insist you get off my property this moment."

My skin was still twitching with whatever had been on the lock. Only my hand on the banister kept me standing. "You do the spell on the door?"

"Yes."

"You're good."

"Not good enough apparently. Now, really I must insist you come up the stairs and get off my property."

A low growl came up from the darkness. It didn't sound much like a rat, and it certainly didn't sound human.

"Come out, come out, wherever you are," I said.

The growling got louder, closer. Something large and furry darted across the pale band of light. The glimpse was enough. I could always say I thought it was Louie. I leaned against the banister and screamed. I screamed for help with every ounce of sound I could make.

Elvira darted a look behind her. I heard the distant yells of police coming in the front door.

"Curse you."

"Words are cheap," I said.

"It will be more than words when I have the time."

"Knock yourself out."

She ran into the house, not away. Was I wrong? Had Louie been inside all along, and I was down here with a different fur ball? Was it Jason?

"Jason?"

Something came to the stairs and peered up into the dim light. It was a dog. A big, furry mutt dog, the size of a pony, but it wasn't a shapeshifter.

"Damn."

It growled at me again. I got up and started to back up the stairs. I didn't want to hurt it if I didn't have to. Where was Dolph? He should have been back here by now.

The dog let me ease back up the steps. Apparently it was only supposed to protect the basement. Fine with me.

"Nice doggy."

I eased up until I could touch the broken door. I slammed it shut, holding the doorknob. The dog hit it with a roaring crash. Its own weight kept the door closed.

I opened the back door, slowly. The kitchen was long, narrow, and mostly white. Voices came from farther in the house. A low growl filled the house, reverberating. The sound raised the hair on my neck.

"No one has to get hurt here," Dolph said.

"That's right," Elvira said. "Leave now, and no one gets hurt."

"We can't do that."

A hallway made up of one wall and the stairs led out of the kitchen towards the living room and the voices. I checked the stairs, empty. I kept going, easing towards the voices. The growl came again, closer.

Dolph yelled, "Anita, get your butt up here!"

It made me jump. He couldn't have seen me yet. The entrance to the living room was an open doorway. I went to one knee and peered around the wall. Elvira stood facing them. A wolf the size of a pony was at her side. If you just glanced at them, you might mistake it for the big dog. It was a good cover. Neighbors see it and think the wolf is a dog.

The other one was a leopard. A black leopard that put every Halloween kitty-cat to shame. It had backed Zerbrowski into a corner. Its slick, furred back came to his waist. Big as a hellcat. Jesus.

Why hadn't they shot? Police were allowed to shoot for self-protection.

"Are you Louie Fane or Jason?" Dolph asked. I realized he was asking the shapeshifters. I hadn't told him what kind of shifter Louie was, and Jason was a wolf. The wolf could be Jason. Though why he'd be helping Elvira I did not know. Maybe I didn't have to know.

I stood up and came around the corner. Maybe the movement was too sudden. Maybe the cat had just grown impatient. The leopard leaped at Zerbrowski. His gun fired.

The wolf turned on me. It all slowed down. I had forever to look down the barrel and pull the trigger. Every gun in the room fired. The wolf went down with a bullet in its brain from me. I wasn't sure who else had gotten a piece of it.

Zerbrowski's screams filled the echoing silence. The leopard was on him, slashing at him.

Dolph fired one more time, then threw the gun to the floor and waded in. He grabbed for the cat and it turned on him, slashing with daggerlike claws. He screamed but didn't back off.

"Dolph, down, and I'll nail it." He tried to get out of the way but the cat leaped on him, carrying them both to the floor. I walked forward, gun extended. They were a rolling mass. If I shot Dolph, he'd be just as dead as the leopard would make him.

I knelt by them and shoved the gun into that warm, furred body. Claws slashed my arm, but I pulled the trigger twice. The thing slumped, twitched, and died.

Dolph blinked up at me. There was a bloody slash on his cheek. But he was alive. I got to my feet. My left arm was numb, which meant it was really hurt. When the numbness wore off, I'd want to be somewhere with doctors.

Zerbrowski lay on his back. There was a lot of blood. I fell to my knees beside him. I laid the Browning on the ground and searched for the big pulse in his neck. It was there, thready, but there. I wanted to cry with relief, but there was no time. There was a black stain of blood near the lower center of his body. I pulled his coat back and nearly threw up on him. Wouldn't he laugh at that? The cat had damn near eviscerated him. His intestines bulged out at the tear.

I tried to pull my jacket off to hold over the wound, but my left arm didn't want to work. "Someone help me." No one did.

Officer Kirlin had Ms. Drew handcuffed. Her green robe was gaping open and it was clear she had nothing on under it. She was crying, crying for her fallen comrades.

Dolph said, "He alive?"

"Yeah."

"I've called for an ambulance," the male uniform said.

"Get over here and help me stop the bleeding."

He just looked at me, sort of shamefaced but neither he nor Kirlin moved to help.

"What the fuck is the matter with you two? Help them."

"We don't want to get it."

"It?"

"The disease," he said.

I crawled back to the leopard. It looked big, even dead. Nearly three times the size of a natural cat. I fumbled at its belly, and found the catch. Not a button, not a belt, but a catch where the fur peeled away. Inside was a naked human body. I pulled the skin back so they could see. "They're shapeshifters but not lycanthropes. It's a spell. It's not contagious, you chicken-shit son of a bitch."

"Anita, don't pick on him," Dolph said. His voice sounded so strange, so distant that I minded him.

The man pulled off his own jacket and sort of laid it on top of Zerbrowski. He pressed down, but gingerly, as if he still didn't trust the blood.

"Get away from him." I leaned on the coat, using my body weight to hold his intestines inside. They moved under my hand like something alive, squishy and so warm they were hot.

"When the hell are you going to get some silver bullets for your squad?" I asked.

Dolph almost laughed. "Soon, I hope."

Maybe I could buy them a few boxes for Christmas. Please, dear God, let there be a Christmas for all of us. I stared at Zerbrowski's pale face. His glasses had fallen off in the struggle. I looked around and couldn't see them. It seemed important to find his glasses. I knelt there in his blood and cried because I couldn't find his damn glasses.

37

Zerbrowski was being sewn back together. None of the doctors were telling us anything. Guarded. His condition was guarded. Dolph was also in the hospital. Not as bad off but enough to stay for a day or so. Zerbrowski hadn't regained consciousness before they took him away. I waited. Katie, his wife, arrived sometime in the middle of all that waiting.

It was only the second time we'd ever met. She was a small woman with a mane of dark hair tied in a loose ponytail. Without a spot of makeup she was lovely. How Zerbrowski had managed to snag her I'd never figured out.

She walked towards me, dark eyes wide. She was clutching her purse like a shield, fingers digging into the leather. "Where is he?" Her voice was high and breathy, like a little girl's. It always sounded like that.

Before I could say anything, the doctor came out of the swinging doors at the end of the hall. Katie stared at him. All the blood had drained from her face.

I stood up and moved to stand beside her. She stared at the approaching doctor like he was some monster in her worst nightmare. Probably more accurate than I wanted it to be.

"Are you Mrs. Zerbrowski?" the doctor asked.

She nodded. Her hands where they gripped the purse were mottled, trembling with tension.

"Your husband is stable. It looks good. He's going to make it."

Christmas was coming after all.

Katie gave a small sigh and her knees buckled. I caught her and stood there supporting her dead weight. She couldn't have weighed ninety pounds.

"We've got a lounge in here if you can . . ." He looked at me, then shrugged.

I lifted Katie Zerbrowski in my arms, got the balance of it, and said, "Lead on."

I left Katie sitting by Zerbrowski's bedside. His hand wrapped around hers, like he knew she was there. Maybe he did. Lucille, Dolph's wife, was there now to hold her hand just in case. Staring down at Zerbrowski's pale face, I prayed that there was no "just in case."

I wanted to wait until Zerbrowski woke up, but the doctor told me it would probably be tomorrow. I couldn't go without sleep that long. My new stitches made the cross-shaped burn scar on my left arm crooked. The claw marks twisted to one side, missing the mound of scar tissue at the bend of my arm.

Carrying Katie had broken some of my stitches, and they bled through the bandage. The doctor who had operated on Zerbrowski resewed it personally. He looked at the scars a lot.

My arm hurt and was bandaged from wrist to elbow. But we were all alive. Yea.

The taxi dropped me off at my apartment building at what would have been a decent hour. Louie had been drugged and tied in the basement. Elvira had admitted to taking the skins of a werewolf, a wereleopard, and trying for the naga. Jason hadn't been in the house. She denied ever having seen him. What did she need with another werewolf skin? The wererat skin would have been for her, she said. When asked who the snakeskin would have been for, she said her. There was at least one other person involved that she wasn't willing to give up.

She was a witch and had used magic to kill. It was an automatic death sentence. Once convicted, the sentence would be carried out within forty-eight hours. No appeals. No pardons. Dead. The lawyers were trying to get her to admit to the other disappearances. If she'd admit to it they might commute her sentence. Might. A killer witch. I didn't believe they'd lighten her sentence, but maybe they would.

Richard was sitting outside my apartment door. I hadn't expected to see him, night of the full moon and all. I'd left a message on his answering machine about finding Louie and him being all right.

The police were trying to keep it all quiet, especially Louie's secret identity. I hoped they could manage it. But at least he was alive. Animal control had the dog.

"I got your message," he said. "Thanks for saving Louie."

I put my key in the lock. "You're welcome."

"We haven't found Jason. Do you really think the witches took him?"

I opened the door. He followed me in and closed the door. "I don't know. That's been bothering me, too. If she'd taken Jason. He should have been there." The wolf, once out of its skin, had been a woman that I didn't know.

I walked into the bedroom as if I'd been alone. Richard followed me. I felt light and distant and faintly unreal. They'd cut off the sleeve of my jacket and sweater. I'd tried to save the jacket but I guess it had been ruined anyway. They'd also cut through the left arm sheath. I had it and the knife shoved in my jacket pocket. Why do they always cut everything off in the emergency room?

He came up behind me, not touching, hands hovering over my arm. "You didn't tell me you were hurt."

The phone rang. I picked it up without thinking.

A man's voice said, "Anita Blake?"

"Yes."

"This is Williams, the naturalist at the Audubon Center. I played back some of my owl tapes that I'd recorded at night. One of them has what I'd swear was hyenas on it. I told the police, but they didn't seem to understand the significance. Do you understand what it might mean to have hyena sounds out here?''

''A werehyena,'' I said.

''Yes, I thought so, too.''

No one had told him the killer was probably a werewolf. But one of the missing shifters was a hyena. Maybe Elvira really didn't know what happened to all the missing lycanthropes.

''Did you say you told the police?''

''Yes, I did.''

''Who'd you tell?''

''I called Sheriff Titus's office.''

''Who'd you speak to?''

''Aikensen.''

''Do you know if he told Titus?''

''No, but why wouldn't he?''

Why indeed.

''Someone's at the door. Can you hold on a minute?''

''I don't think . . .''

''I'll be right back.''

''Williams, Williams, don't answer the door.'' But I was talking to empty air. I heard him walk across the floor. The door opened. He made a surprised sound. Heavier footsteps came back across the floor.

Someone picked up the phone. I could hear them breathing. They didn't say anything.

''Talk to me, you son of a bitch.''

The breathing got heavy.

''If you hurt him, Aikensen, I will feed you your dick on knife point.''

He laughed and hung up. And I'd never be able to testify in court who was on the other end of that phone.

''Dammit, damn it, damn it.''

''What's wrong?''

I called information to get the number for the Willoton Police Department. I pressed the button that dialed it automatically for a small fee.

''Anita, what is it?''

I held up a hand, telling him to wait. A woman answered. ''Is this Deputy Holmes?''

It wasn't. I got Chief Garroway after impressing on the dispatcher that this was a matter of life and death. I did not scream at her. I deserved mucho brownie points for that.

I gave Garroway the *Reader's Digest* version. ''I can't believe even Aikensen would be involved in something like this, but I'll send a car.''

''Thanks.''

''Why didn't you just call 911?'' Richard asked.

''They'd call the county police. Aikensen might even be assigned the call.''

I was struggling out of my butchered jacket. Richard eased it off my left shoulder or I might never have gotten it off. When it was off, I realized I was out of coats. I'd ruined two in as many days. I grabbed the only coat I had left. It was crimson, long and full. I'd worn it twice. The last time was Christmas. The red coat would show up even at night. If I needed to sneak up on anybody, I could take it off.

Richard had to help me get my left arm in the sleeve. It still hurt.

"Let's go get Jason," he said.

I looked at him. "You're not going anywhere but wherever lycanthropes go when there's a full moon."

"You can't even put your own coat on. How are you going to drive?"

He had a point.

"This may put you in danger."

"I'm a full-grown werewolf and tonight is the full moon. I think I can handle it." He had a faraway look in his eyes as if he were hearing voices I would never know.

"All right. Let's go, but we're going to save Williams. I think the weres are close to his place, but I don't know exactly where."

He was standing there with his long duster coat on. He was wearing a white T-shirt, a pair of jeans with one knee gone, and a pair of less than reputable shoes.

"Why the scuffy clothes?"

"If I shift in my clothes, they're always torn apart. Precaution. You ready?"

"Yeah."

"Let's go," he said. There was something about him that was different. A waiting tension like water just before it spills over the edge. When I looked into his brown eyes, something slid behind them. Some furred shape was inside there, waiting to get out.

I realized what I was sensing from him. Eagerness. Richard's beast was looking out of his true brown eyes, and it was eager to be about its business.

What could I say? We went.

38

Edward was leaning against my Jeep, arms crossed, breath fogging in the air. The temperature had dropped by twenty degrees with the dark. The freeze was back on. All the meltwater had turned to ice. The snow crunched underfoot.

''What are you doing here, Edward?''

''I was about to come up to your apartment when I saw you coming down.''

''What do you want?''

''I want to play,'' he said.

I stared at him. ''Just like that. You don't know what I'm involved in, but you want a piece of it.''

''Following you around lets me kill a lot of people.''

Sad, but true. ''I don't have time to argue. Get in.''

He slid in the backseat. ''Who exactly are we going to kill tonight?''

Richard started the engine. I buckled up. ''Let's see. There's a renegade policeman, and whoever's kidnapped seven shapeshifters.''

''The witches didn't do it?''

''Not all of it.''

''You think I'll get to kill any lycanthropes tonight?'' He was teasing Richard, I think.

Richard wasn't offended. ''I've been thinking about who could have taken them all without a struggle. It had to be someone they trusted.''

''Who would they trust?'' I asked.

''One of us,'' he said.

''Oh, boy,'' Edward said, ''lycanthrope on the menu for tonight.''

Richard didn't correct him. If it was all right with him, it was all right with me.

39

Williams lay crumpled on his side. He'd been shot at close range through the heart. Two shots. So much for the doctorate.

One hand was wrapped around a .357 Magnum. I was even betting that there would be powder on his skin, as though he'd really fired the gun.

Deputy Holmes and her partner, whose name I couldn't remember, were lying in the snow dead. The Magnum had taken most of her chest. Her pixielike features were slack and not half so pretty. With her eyes staring straight up she didn't look asleep. She just looked dead.

Her partner was missing most of his face. He was collapsed in the snow, blood and brains melting through the frozen snow. His gun was still gripped in his hand.

Holmes had gotten her gun out, too. For what good it did her. I doubted either one of them had shot Williams, but I'd have bet a month's pay that one of their guns had.

I knelt in the snow and said, ''Shit.''

Richard stood by Williams. He was staring at him as if he'd memorize him. ''Samuel didn't own a gun. He didn't even believe in hunting.''

''You knew him?''

''I'm in Audubon, remember.''

I nodded. None of it seemed real. It looked staged. Would he get away with it? No. ''He's dead,'' I said, softly.

Edward came to stand beside me. ''Who's dead?''

''Aikensen. He's still walking and talking but he's dead. He just doesn't know it yet.''

''Where do we find him?'' Edward asked.

Good question. I didn't have a good answer. My beeper went off, and I screamed. One of those little yip screams that are always so embarrassing. I checked the number with my heart thundering in my chest.

I didn't recognize the number. Who could it be, and could it possibly be important enough to call back tonight? I'd left my beeper number with the hospital. I didn't know their number, either. I had to answer it. Hell, I needed to call Chief

Garroway and tell him his people had walked into an ambush. I could make both calls from Williams's house.

I trudged towards the house. Edward followed. We were on the porch before I realized that Richard wasn't with us. I turned back. He had knelt down beside Williams. I thought at first he was praying, then realized he was touching the bloody snow. Did I really want to know? Yeah.

I walked back over. Edward stayed on the porch without being asked. Point for him. "Richard, are you all right?" It was a stupid question with a man he knew dead at his feet. But what else was I supposed to ask?

His hand closed over the bloody snow, crushing it. He shook his head. I thought he was just angry, or grief stricken, until I saw the sweat on his face.

He turned his face upward, eyes closed. The moon rode full and bright, heavy and silver white. The light was almost daylight bright this far away from the city. Wisps of cloud rode the sky, made luminous with moonshine.

"Richard?"

"I knew him, Anita. We've gone birding together. We talked about his doctorate thesis. I knew him, and now all I can think of is the smell of blood and how warm he still is."

He opened his eyes and looked at me. There was sorrow in his eyes, but mostly there was darkness. His beast was looking out through his eyes.

I turned away. I couldn't hold his gaze. "I've got to make this phone call. Don't eat any of the evidence." I walked away across the snow. It had been too long a night.

I called from the phone in Williams's kitchen. I called Garroway first, told him what we'd found. Once he could breathe, he cursed a bit and said he'd come himself. Probably wondering if things would have turned out differently if he'd come in the first place. Command decisions are always hard.

I hung up and dialed the number on my beeper. "Hello."

"This is Anita Blake. This number was left on my beeper."

"Anita, this is Kaspar Gunderson."

The swan man. "Yes, Kaspar, what is it?"

"You sound awful. Has something happened?"

"Lots, but why did you beep me?"

"I found Jason."

I stood a little straighter. "You're kidding."

"No, I found him. I've got him at my house now. I've been trying to contact Richard. Do you know where he is?"

"With me."

"Perfect," he said. "Can he come take charge of Jason before he changes?"

"Well, yeah, I guess so, why?"

"I'm just a bird, Anita. I'm not a predator. I can't control an inexperienced werewolf."

"Okay, I'll tell him. Where's your house?"

"Richard knows where it is. I've got to get back to Jason, keep him calm. If he loses it before Richard arrives, I'm running for cover. So if I don't answer the doorbell, you'll know what happened."

"Are you in danger from him?"

"Just hurry." He hung up.

Richard had come inside. He was standing in the doorway looking bemused, as if listening to music only he could hear.

"Richard?"

His head moved slowly towards the sound of my voice like a video running on slow speed. His eyes were pale golden yellow, the color of amber.

"Jesus," I said.

He didn't look away. He blinked his new eyes at me. "What is it?"

"Kaspar called. He found Jason. He's been trying to get you. Says he can't control him once he changes."

"Jason's all right," he said. He gave it that questioning lilt.

"Yes, are you all right?"

"No, I have to change soon or the moon will pick the time for me."

I didn't exactly understand that statement, but he could explain in the car. "Edward can drive, in case the moon picks going down Highway Forty-four as the perfect time."

"Good idea, but Kaspar's house is just up the mountain."

"What do you mean?"

"Kaspar lives just up the road."

"Great, let's go."

"You'll have to leave Jason and me up there," he said.

"Why?"

"I can make sure he doesn't hurt anybody, but he has to hunt. I'll take him out here. There are deer in the woods."

I stared at him. He was still Richard. Still my sweetie, but . . . His eyes were the color of pale amber, startling in his dark face.

"You're not going to change in the car, are you?" I asked.

"No. I would never endanger you. I have complete control over my beast. It's what being an alpha wolf means."

"I wasn't worried about being eaten," I said. "I just didn't want you to get that clear junk all over my new seats."

He flashed a smile. It would have been more comforting if his teeth hadn't been just a little pointier than usual.

Jesus H. Christ.

40

Kaspar Gunderson's house was made of stone, or at least sided with it. Pale chunks of granite formed the walls. The trim was white, the roof shingles pale grey. The door was white as well. It was clean, neat, and still managed to be rustic. It sat in a clearing at the top of the mountain. The road stopped at his house. There was a turnaround but the road didn't go past.

Richard rang the bell. Kaspar opened it. He looked very relieved to see us. "Richard, thank God. He's managed to hold on to human form so far, but I don't think he can last much longer." He held the door for us.

We walked in and found two strange men sitting in his living room. The man to the left was short, dark, and had wire-framed glasses on. The other man was taller, blond, with a reddish beard. They were the only things that didn't match the decor. The entire living room was white—carpet, couch, two chairs, walls. It was like standing in the middle of a vanilla ice-cream cone. He had the same couch that I did. I needed new furniture.

"Who are they?" Richard asked. "They aren't one of us."

"You could say that." It was Titus. He stood in the doorway leading to the kitchen, a gun in his hand. "Don't anybody move," he said. His southern accent was thick as corn pone.

Aikensen stepped out of the door leading to the rest of the house. He had another big Magnum in his hand.

"You buy those by the caseload?" I asked.

"I liked your threat on the phone. It got me hot."

I took a step forward, hadn't meant to. "Please," Aikensen said. He was pointing the big gun at my chest. Titus was pointing at Richard. The two men in the chairs had guns out now, too. One big happy party.

Edward was very still at my back. I could almost feel him weighing the odds. A bolt action on a rifle shot back behind us. We all jumped, even Edward. Another man was behind us in the door. His solid grey hair was balding. The grey man had a rifle in his hands, pointed at Edward's head. There wouldn't be enough left to pick up in a baggie.

''Hands up, y'all.''

We put our hands up. What else could we do?

''Lace your fingers atop your head,'' Titus said.

Edward and I did it like we'd done it before. Richard was slower.

''Now, wolfman, or I will drop you where you stand, and your little girlfriend might get all shot up in the bargain.''

Richard laced his fingers. ''Kaspar, what's going on?''

Kaspar was sitting on the couch, no, reclining was the word. He looked comfortable, happy as a well-fed cat . . . er, swan.

''These gentlemen here have paid a small fortune to hunt lycanthropes. I supply them prey and a place to hunt.''

''Titus and Aikensen make sure that no one finds out, right?''

''I told you I did a little hunting, Ms. Blake,'' Titus said.

''The dead man one of your hunters?''

His eyes flicked, not exactly looking away but flinching. ''Yes, Ms. Blake, he was.''

I looked at the two men with their guns out. I didn't turn around to see Grey Hair at the door. ''You three think that hunting shapeshifters is worth dying over?''

The dark-haired one looked at me from behind his round glasses. His eyes were distant, calm. If it bothered him to be pointing a gun at fellow human beings, it didn't show.

The bearded man's eyes flicked around the room, never settling on anything. He wasn't having a good time.

''Why didn't you and Aikensen clean up the mess before Holmes and her partner saw the body?''

''We were out hunting werewolf,'' Aikensen said.

''Kaspar, we're your people,'' Richard said.

''No,'' Kaspar said. He stood. ''You aren't. I am not a lycanthrope. I'm not even an inherited condition. I was cursed by a witch so long ago that I don't care to remember how long.''

''Is that supposed to make us feel sorry for you?'' I asked.

''No. In fact, I don't suppose I have to explain myself. You have both been decent to me. I suppose I feel guilty about that.'' He shrugged. ''This will be our last hunt. One big gala event.''

''If you had slaughtered Raina and Gabriel, I could almost understand it,'' I said. ''But what did the lycanthropes you helped murder ever do to you?''

''When the witch told me what she had done, I remember thinking that being a great ravening beast would be a fine thing. I could still hunt. I could even slay my enemies. Instead she made . . .'' He spread his hands wide.

''You kill them because they are what you want to be,'' I said.

He gave a small smile. ''Jealousy, Anita, envy. They are very bitter emotions.''

I thought about calling him a bastard, but it wouldn't help. Seven people had died because this son of a bitch didn't like being a bird. ''The witch should have killed you, slowly.''

''She wanted me to learn my lesson and repent.''

''I'm not real big on repentance,'' I said. ''I like revenge better.''

''If I wasn't confident you would die tonight, that might worry me.''

''Worry,'' I said.

''Where's Jason?'' Richard asked.

''We'll take you to him, won't we, boys,'' Titus said.

Edward hadn't said a word. I wasn't sure what he was thinking, but I hoped he didn't go for a gun. If he did, most of the people in this room were dead. Three of them would be us.

''Pat 'em down, Aikensen.''

Aikensen grinned. He holstered his big gun. That left one revolver, two automatics, and a high-powered rifle. It was enough. Dream team that we are, Edward and I had our limits.

He patted Richard down, a quick search. He was having a good time until he got up to where he could see Richard's eyes. He paled just a little looking into those wolf eyes. Nervous was good.

He kicked my legs farther apart. I glared at him. His hands hovered over my breasts, not where you start a search. ''If he does anything but search me for weapons, I am going to draw a gun and take my chances.''

''Aikensen, you treat Ms. Blake here like a lady. No hanky-panky.''

Aikensen dropped to his knees in front of me. He ran just the palm of his hand over my breast, lightly just over the nipples. I smashed my right elbow into his nose. Blood sprayed outward. He rolled around on the ground, hands to his busted nose.

The dark-haired man was standing. He was pointing his gun very steadily at me. His glasses reflected the light hiding his eyes.

''Everybody calm down, now,'' Titus said. ''Aikensen deserved that, I guess.''

Aikensen came up off the floor, blood covering the lower half of his face. He fumbled for his gun.

''If that gun clears your holster, I will shoot you myself,'' Titus said.

Aikensen was breathing fast and heavy through his mouth. Little bubbles of blood showed at his nose when he tried to breathe through it. It was definitely broken. It wasn't as good as eviscerating him, but it was a start. He kept his hands on his gun, but he didn't pull it. He stayed on his knees for a long time. You could see the struggle in his eyes. He wanted to shoot me almost enough to try for it. Great. The feeling was mutual.

''Aikensen,'' Titus said softly. His voice was very serious, as if he were just realizing that Aikensen might go for it. ''I mean what I say, boy. Don't you be toying with me.''

He got to his feet, spitting blood, trying to get it away from his mouth. ''You're going to die tonight.''

''Maybe, but it won't be you.''

'Ms. Blake, if you could refrain from teasing Aikensen long enough for me to get him away from you, I'd appreciate it.''

''Always glad to cooperate with the police,'' I said.

Titus laughed. The bastard. ''Well, now the criminals pay better, Ms. Blake.''

''Fuck you.''

''No need to get abusive.'' He tucked his own gun into his side holster. ''Now,

I'm not going to do a thing but search you for weapons. Any more of this nonsense and we're going to have to shoot one of you to prove we're serious. You don't want to lose your sweetheart here. Or your friend here.'' He smiled. Just good ol' Sheriff Titus. Friendly. Jesus.

He found both guns, then patted me down a second time. I must have winced, because he said, ''How'd you hurt your arm, Ms. Blake?''

''I was helping the police on another case.''

''They let a civvie get hurt?''

''Sergeant Storr and Detective Zerbrowski are in the hospital. They were injured in the line of duty.''

Something passed over his chubby face. It might have been regret. ''Heroes don't get anything but dead, Ms. Blake. You best remember that.''

''Bad guys die, too, Titus.''

He pushed the sleeve of the red coat up and took the knife. He hefted it, testing its balance. ''Custom made?''

I nodded.

''I do admire good equipment.''

''Keep it. I'll get it later.''

He chuckled. ''You have guts, girl, I'll give you that.''

''And you're a fucking coward.''

The smile vanished. ''Always needing to have the last word is a bad trait, Ms. Blake. Pisses people off.''

''That's the idea.''

He moved to Edward. I'd give Titus one thing, he was thorough. He took two automatics, a derringer, and a knife big enough to pass for a short sword from Edward. I had no idea where he'd been hiding the knife.

''Who do the two of you think you are? The freaking cavalry?''

Edward didn't say a thing. If he could be quiet, so could I. There were too many guns to make one of them angry and try to jump the rest. We were outnumbered and outgunned. It was not a good way to start the week.

''Now we are all going to go downstairs,'' Titus said. ''We want you all to join us in the hunt. You will be let out into the woods. If you can get away from us, then you are free. You can run to the nearest police and turn us in. You try anything funny before we let you go, and we will just kill you. You all understand that?''

We just looked at him.

''I can't hear you.''

''I heard what you said,'' I said.

''How 'bout you, blondie?''

''I heard you, too,'' Edward said.

''Wolfman, you hear me?''

''Don't call me that,'' Richard said. He didn't sound particularly scared, either. Good.

If you're going to die, at least die brave. It pisses your enemies off.

''Can we put our hands down now?'' I asked.

''No,'' Titus said.

My left arm was beginning to throb. If that was the most painful thing that happened to me tonight, I'd be ahead of the game.

Aikensen went first. Richard next with the dark-haired man and his calm eyes at his back. The bearded man. Then me. Titus. Edward. Grey Hair and his rifle next. Kaspar brought up the rear. It was a parade.

The stairs led into a natural cavern below the house. It was about sixty by thirty feet, with a ceiling that wasn't higher than twelve feet. A tunnel led out the far wall. Electric lights gave a harsh yellow glow to everything. Two cages were set into the granite walls. In the far cage Jason was huddled into a fetal ball. He didn't move as we all trooped in.

''What have you done to him?'' Richard said.

''Tried to get him to change for us,'' Titus said. ''Birdie here said he'd be an easy mark.''

Kaspar looked uncomfortable. Whether it was the Birdie remark or Jason's stubbornness, it was hard to tell. ''He will change for us.''

''So you say,'' Grey Hair said.

Kaspar frowned at him.

Aikensen opened the empty cage. His nose was still bleeding. He had a wad of Kleenex held to it, but it wasn't helping much. The Kleenexes were crimson.

''In ya go, Wolfie,'' Titus said.

Richard hesitated.

''Mr. Carmichael, the boy, if you please.''

Dark Hair put up his 9mm, and got out a .22 from his waistband. He pointed it at Jason's huddled form.

''We'd been discussing putting a bullet in him anyway. See if it would help persuade him to change for us. Now get in the cage.''

Richard stood there.

Carmichael pointed the gun through the bars, sighting down his arm.

''Don't,'' Richard said. ''I'll do it.'' He walked into the cage.

''Now you, Blondie.''

Edward didn't argue. He just walked in. He was taking this a lot better than I thought he would.

Aikensen shut the door. He locked the door, then walked across to the second cage. He didn't unlock it. He waited with the soggy Kleenex pressed to his nose. A drop of blood fell to the floor.

''You get to share accommodations with our young friend.''

Richard gripped the bars of his cage. ''You can't put her in there. When he changes, he'll need to feed.''

''Two things help the change happen,'' Kaspar said, ''sex and blood. I saw how much Jason likes your lady friend.''

''Don't do this, Kaspar.''

''Too late,'' he said.

If I went in the cage, I was going to end up eaten alive. That was actually one of my top five ways not to die. I wasn't going in the cage. I'd make them shoot me first.

''Aikensen is going to open the cage, then you step inside, Ms. Blake.''

"No," I said.

Titus looked at me. "Ms. Blake, Mr. Fienstien here will shoot you, won't you Mr. Fienstien?"

The bearded man, uncertain eyes and all, pointed a 9mm Beretta at me. A nice gun, if you didn't insist on buying American. The barrel looked very big, and solid from the wrong end.

"Fine, shoot me."

"Ms. Blake, we are not joking."

"Neither am I. My choices are being eaten alive or being shot. So shoot me."

"Mr. Carmichael, if you will point your .22 over here." Carmichael did. "We can wound you, Ms. Blake. Put a bullet in your leg and then shove you in that cage."

I looked into his beady little eyes and knew he would do it. I didn't want to go into the cage, but I really didn't want to go in wounded.

"I'm going to count to five, Ms. Blake, then Carmichael here is going to wound you and we will drag you into that cage. One . . . two . . . three . . . four . . ."

"All right, all right, damn you. Unlock the damn door."

Aikensen did. I walked in. The door clanged shut behind me. I stood there near the door. Jason was shivering as if he had a fever, but he never moved otherwise.

The men outside seemed disappointed. "We paid good money to hunt a werewolf," Grey Hair said. "We are not getting our money's worth."

"We've got all night, gentlemen. He won't resist this luscious tidbit forever," Kaspar said.

I didn't like being called a tidbit. Luscious or otherwise. "I called Garroway before we drove up here. I told him about his deputies getting ambushed. I told him it was Aikensen."

"Liar."

I looked straight at Titus. "You think I'm lying."

"Maybe we'll just shoot all of you now, and flee, Ms. Blake."

"You going to give these gentlemen their money back?"

"We want a hunt, Titus." The three armed men didn't look like leaving before the fun was an option. "The police don't know about the birdman's involvement," Carmichael of the .22 said. "He can stay upstairs. If they come asking questions, he can answer them."

Titus wiped his palms against his pants. Sweating palms, nerves? I hoped so.

"She didn't call. She's just bluffing," Aikensen said.

"Make him change," Carmichael said.

"He's not paying any attention to her," Grey Hair said.

"Give it time, gentlemen."

"You said we don't have time."

"You're the expert, Kaspar. Thinka something."

Kaspar smiled, staring at something behind me. "I don't think we'll have to wait much longer."

I turned around slowly, looking behind me. Jason was still huddled on the ground but his face was turned to me. He rolled onto all fours in one easy motion.

His eyes flicked to me, then stared at the men on the outside of the cage. "I won't do it. I won't change for you." His voice was strained but normal. Human sounding.

"You've held out a long time, Jason," Kaspar said, "but the moon is rising. Smell her fear, Jason. Smell her body. You know you want her."

"No!" He bowed his head to the ground, hands and arms flat to the floor, knees drawn up. He shook his head, face pressed into the rock. "No." He raised his face up. "I won't do it like some sideshow freak."

"Do you think giving Jason and Ms. Blake here a little privacy would help matters along?" Titus asked.

"It might," Kaspar said. "He doesn't seem to like an audience."

"We'll just give you a little breathin' space, Ms. Blake. If you aren't alive when we get back, well, it's been nice meetin' ya."

"I can't say the same, Titus," I said.

"Well, now that is the God's honest truth. Good-bye, Ms. Blake."

"Rot in hell, bitch," was Aikensen's parting shot.

"You'll remember me every time you look in a mirror, Aikensen."

His hand went to his nose. Even that touch hurt. He scowled at me, but it's hard to look tough with Kleenex sticking out of your nose. "I hope you die slow."

"Same to you," I said.

"Kaspar, please," Richard said. "Don't do this. I'll change for you. I'll let you hunt me. Just get Anita out of there."

The men stopped and looked at him.

"Don't help me, Richard."

"I'll give you the best hunt you've ever had." He was pressed against the bars, hands wrapped around them. "You know I can do it, Kaspar. Tell them."

Kaspar looked at him for a long moment. He shook his head. "I think you'd kill them all."

"I'd promise not to."

"Richard, what are you saying?"

He ignored me. "Please, Kaspar."

"You must love her a great deal."

Richard just stared at him.

"No matter what you do, Richard, they're not going to let me go."

He wasn't listening to me.

"Richard!"

"I'm sorry," Kaspar said. "I trust you, Richard, but your beast . . . I think your beast isn't so trustworthy."

"Come on, we're wasting time. Garroway doesn't know where to look but he might come up here. Let's give 'em some privacy," Titus said.

They all trooped out after the chubby sheriff. Kaspar was last up the stairs. "I wish it were Gabriel and Raina in the cages. I am sorry about that." The swan man disappeared into the rock tunnel.

"Kaspar, don't leave us like this. Kaspar!" Richard's yells echoed in the cavern. But nothing answered the echoes. We were alone. Scuffling sounds made me whirl. Jason was on his knees again. Something moved behind his pale blue eyes, something monstrous and not friendly at all. I wasn't half as alone as I wanted to be.

41

Jason took one crawling step towards me and stopped. "No, no, no." Each word was a low moan. His head fell forward. His yellow hair swept forward not long enough to touch the ground, but thick. He was wearing an oversize blue dress shirt and jeans. Clothes you wouldn't mind ruining if you happened to shapeshift in them.

"Anita," Richard said.

I moved so I could see the other cage, without losing sight of Jason.

Richard was reaching through the bars. One hand stretching out towards me as if he could bridge the space and somehow drag me to him.

Edward crawled to the door and began running hands over the lock. He couldn't really see the lock from inside the cage. He pressed his cheek to the bars and closed his eyes. When you can't use your eyes they become a distraction.

He leaned back and drew a slender leather case from his pocket. He unzipped it to reveal tiny tools. From this distance I couldn't really see them clearly but I knew what they were. Edward was going to pick the lock. We could be out in the woods before they knew we were missing. The night was looking up.

Edward settled back against the bars, one arm on either side of the lock, a pick in each hand. His eyes were closed, his face blank, all concentration to his hands.

Jason made a small sound low in his chest. He crawled towards me, two slow, dragging steps. His head flung upward. His eyes were still the innocent blue of spring skies but there was nobody home now. He looked at me as though he could see inside my body, watch my heart thudding in my chest, smell the blood in my veins. It was not a human look.

"Jason," Richard said, "hold on. We'll be free in a few minutes. Just hold on."

Jason didn't react. I don't think he heard.

I thought the few minutes was being overly optimistic, but hey, I was willing to believe it if Jason would.

Jason crawled towards me. I plastered my back against the cage bars. "Edward, how are you coming with that lock?"

"These are not the tools I would have chosen for this particular lock, but I'll get it."

There was something in the way Jason crawled towards me, as if he had muscles in places that he shouldn't have. "Make it soon, Edward."

He didn't answer me. I didn't have to look to know that he was working at the lock. I had every faith that he'd unlock the door. I backed down the bars, trying to keep an even distance between me and the werewolf. Edward would get the door open, but would it be in time? That was the $64,000 question.

A sound at the entrance caused me to glance back. Carmichael stepped into the cavern. He had the 9mm in his hand. He smiled. It was the happiest I'd seen him.

Edward ignored him, working at the lock as if an armed man hadn't stepped into the room.

Carmichael raised the gun and pointed it at Edward. "Get away from the lock, now." He cocked the hammer back, not necessary, but always dramatic. "We don't need you alive. Stop . . . working . . . on . . . the . . . lock." He stepped closer with each word.

Edward looked up at him. His face was still blank, as if his concentration were still in his hands, not quite focused on the gun being pointed at him.

"Throw the tools away from you. Right now."

Edward stared at him. His expression never changed but he tossed the two small tools away.

"Take the complete kit out of your pocket and toss it out of the cage. Don't even try to say you don't have one. If you've got those two pieces, you've got the rest."

I wondered what Carmichael did in the real world. Something not nice. Something where he knew what tools would be in a professional lock-picking kit.

"I won't warn you again," Carmichael said. "Throw it out or I pull the trigger. I am tired of screwing with this mess."

Edward threw out the slim leather pouch. It made a small slapping sound on the rock. Carmichael made no move to pick up the lock picks. They were out of our reach. That was what counted. He walked backwards, keeping us all in sight. He directed some of his attention to Jason and me. Oh, joy.

"Our little werewolf's awake. I was hoping he would be."

A low, ragged growl crawled up Jason's throat.

Carmichael gave a delighted bark of laughter. "I wanted to see him change. Good thing I checked back in."

"I'm thrilled that you're here," I said.

He came to stand just out of reach of our cage bars. He was staring at Jason. "I've never seen one of them change."

"Let me out and we'll watch him together."

"Now, why would I do that? I paid to see the whole show."

His eyes were sparkling with anticipation. Bright and shiny as a kid on Christmas morning. Shit.

A growl brought my attention completely back to Jason. He was crouched on the rock floor, hands and legs bunched under him. Watching that growl trickle from between his human lips raised the hair on the back of my neck.

He wasn't looking at me. "I think he's growling at you, Carmichael."

"But I'm not in the cage," he said. He had a point.

"Jason, don't get angry at him," Richard said. "Anger will feed the beast. You can't afford to get angry." Richard's voice was amazingly calm, even soothing. He was trying to talk Jason down, or out, or in, or whatever word you used for keeping a werewolf from shifting.

"No," Carmichael said, "get angry, wolf. I'm going to cut your head off and mount it on my wall."

"He'll revert back to human form after he's dead," I said.

"I know," Carmichael said.

Jesus. "Police find you with a human head in your possession, they may get a little suspicious."

"I've got a lot of trophies that I wouldn't want the police to find," he said.

"What do you do in the real world?"

"This is as real as it gets."

I shook my head. It was hard to argue with him, but I wanted to.

Jason crawled towards the bars, in a sort of monkey crouch. It wasn't as graceful but it had an energy to it, as if he were about to launch himself into the air. As if when he jumped he could fly.

"Calm, Jason, easy," Richard said.

"Come on, boy, try it. Rush the bars and I'll pull the trigger."

I watched him bunch every muscle and launch himself at the bars. He clung to the bars, hands clawing between them. Arms stretched as far as they would go. He wedged a shoulder between the bars as if he'd slip through. For one moment Carmichael looked uncertain, then he laughed.

"Shoot me," Jason said. His voice was more growl than words. "Shoot me."

"I don't think so," Carmichael said.

Jason gripped the bars with his hands and slid down to his knees, forehead pressed to the bars. His breathing was fast, panting, as if he'd run a mile in a minute flat. If he'd been human he'd have hyperventilated and passed out. His head turned slowly towards me, painfully slow, as if he didn't want to do it. He'd tried to force Carmichael to shoot him. Risked being killed to keep from turning on me. He didn't know me well enough to risk his life. It got him a lot of points in my book.

He looked at me, and his face was naked, raw with need. Not sex, not hunger, both, neither, I didn't understand the look in his eyes, and didn't want to.

He scrambled towards me. I backed away, almost running backwards.

"Don't run," Richard called. "It excites him."

Staring into Jason's alien expression, it took everything I had to stand still. My hands gripped the bars behind me hard enough to hurt, but I stopped running. Running was bad.

Jason stopped when I did. He crouched just out of reach. He put one hand on the ground and crawled towards me. It was slow, as if he didn't want to, but he kept coming.

"Any more bright ideas?" I asked.

"Don't run. Don't struggle. It's exciting. Try to be calm. Try not to be afraid. Fear is very exciting."

"Speaking from personal experience?" I asked.

"Yes," he said.

I wanted to turn, see his face, but I couldn't. I had eyes only for the werewolf that was crawling towards me. The werewolf in the other cage could take care of himself.

Jason knelt on all fours by my legs, like a dog awaiting a command. He raised his head and looked at me. A spot of pale green color spilled into his eyes. The blue of his irises drowned in a swirl of new color. When it was done his eyes were the color of new spring grass, pale, pale green, and not human at all.

I gasped. I couldn't help it. He moved closer, sniffing the air around me. His fingertips brushed my leg. I jerked. He let out a long sigh and rubbed his cheek against my leg. He'd done more than this at the Lunatic Cafe, but his eyes had still been mostly human. And I had been armed. I'd have given nearly anything for a gun right now.

Jason grabbed the hem of my coat, balling his hands into fists, tugging at the cloth. He was going to pull me to the ground. No way. I shrugged the coat off my shoulders. Jason pulled it off me. I stepped out of the circle of cloth. He bundled the coat to his face with both arms. He rolled on the ground with it pressed to his body like a dog with a piece of carrion. Wallowing in the scent.

He came to his knees. He stalked towards me, moving with a liquid grace that was unnerving as hell. Human beings did not crawl gracefully.

I backed up, slowly, no running. But I didn't want him to touch me again. He moved faster, each movement precise. Pale green eyes locked on me as if I were all that existed in the world.

I started backing up faster. He moved with me.

"Don't run, Anita, please," Richard said.

My back thunked into the corner of the cage. I gave a little yelp.

Jason covered the distance between us in two smooth movements. His hands touched my legs. I swallowed a scream. My pulse was threatening to choke me.

"Anita, control your fear. Calm, think calm."

"You think fucking calm." My voice sounded strident, panicked.

Jason had his fingertips hooked in my belt. He pressed his body into my legs, pinning me to the bars. I made a small gasp and hated it. If this was going to be it, then dammit, I wasn't going to go out whimpering.

I listened to my heart pounding in my ears, and took slow, even breaths. I stared into those spring green eyes and relearned how to breathe.

Jason pressed his cheek against my hip, hands sliding around my waist. My heart gave a little pitty-pat and I swallowed it. I concentrated on my own heart until my pulse slowed. It was the kind of concentration that let you do that new throw in judo. The concentration that fed a zombie raising.

When Jason lifted his head and looked at me again, I gave him calm eyes. I felt my face blank, neutral, calm. I wasn't sure how long it would last but it was the best I could do.

His fingers slid under my sweater, up my back. I swallowed and my heartbeat sped up. I tried to slow it down, tried to concentrate, but his hands slid around my waist over my skin. His fingers traced my ribs moving upward. I grabbed his wrists, stopping his hands short of my breasts.

As he rose, my hands stayed on his arms. Standing with his hands still under my sweater raised the cloth, baring my stomach. Jason seemed to like the sight of bare skin. He knelt again, letting me keep hold of his arms. I felt his breath almost burning warm on my bare stomach. His tongue flicked out, a quick touch to one side of my belly button. His lips brushed my skin, soft, caressing.

I felt him take a deep, shaking breath. He pressed his face into the soft flesh of my belly. His tongue lapped my stomach, mouth pressing hard. His teeth grazed my waist. It made me squirm, and not with pain. His hands balled into fists under my sweater, hands convulsing. I didn't really want to let go of his wrists but I wanted him away from me.

"Is he going to eat me or . . ."

"Fuck you," Carmichael added. I'd almost forgotten him. Careless forgetting the man with the gun. Maybe it was the realization that he wasn't a danger to me. The danger was kneeling at my feet.

"Jason's only been one of us for a few months. If he can channel the energy into sex instead of violence I'd take it. I'd try to keep him away from killing zones."

"What's that supposed to mean?"

"Keep him away from your throat and your stomach."

I stared down at Jason. He looked up at me, rolling his eyes. There was a darkness in those pale eyes, a darkness deep enough to drown in.

I drew Jason's hands out from under my sweater. He slid his hands into mine, fingers interlocking. He nuzzled my stomach, trying to bury his face where the sweater had slid over my skin. I raised him up with our hands still locked together.

He raised our hands upward, pressing my arms backwards against the bars. I fought the urge to struggle, to jerk away. Struggling was exciting, and that was a bad thing.

We were almost the same height. His eyes were too startling from an inch away. His lips parted and I caught a glimpse of fangs. Jesus.

He rubbed his cheek along mine. His lips moved down my jawline. I turned my head, trying to keep him away from the big pulse in my neck. He came up for air, and brushed his mouth against mine. He pressed his body against mine hard enough that I knew he was glad to be there. Or at least his body was. He buried his face in my hair and stood there pressed against me, our hands on the bars of the cage.

I could feel the pulse in his neck thudding against the bone of my jaw. His breathing was too fast, his chest rising and falling as if he were doing a lot more than foreplay. Was I about to move from foreplay to appetizer?

Power prickled along my skin but it wasn't Jason. I'd tasted this particular power before. Was the show exciting Richard? Would watching me die like this be a thrill like the woman on the film?

"She's mine, Jason." It was Richard's voice but with a bass undertone. The change was coming.

Jason whimpered. It was the only word for it.

Richard's power rode the air like distant thunder, drawing close. "Get off her, Jason. Now!" That last word lunged out in something close to a scream. But it was the kind of scream that cougars gave; no fear, but warning.

I felt Jason shake his head against my hair. His hands convulsed against mine. The strength of it made me gasp. It was the wrong thing to do.

He let go of my hands so suddenly I would have stumbled, but the line of his body kept me upright. He jerked away from me and I did stumble. He grabbed me around the thighs and lifted me into the air, too fast for me to stop even if I could have. He smacked me back against the bars. I took most of the blow on my back. Bruised, but alive.

He supported me with one arm and shoved my sweater upward with the other. I shoved the sweater back down. He made a sound low in his throat and slammed me into the floor. Hitting the rock took all the fight out of me for just a minute. He ripped the sweater as if it were paper, spreading it away from my stomach. He threw his head skyward and screamed, but the mouth he opened wasn't human anymore.

If I'd had enough air I'd have screamed.

"Jason, no!" The voice wasn't human anymore. Richard's power flooded the cage, thick enough to choke on. Jason struggled almost as if the power were thicker than air. He swiped at nothing that I could see with hands that had claws for fingers.

"Back off," the words were a snarl, barely recognizable.

Jason snarled back, teeth snapping the air, but not at me. He rolled off me, crawling along the rock, growling.

I just lay there on my back, afraid to move. Afraid that any movement would tip the balance and make him finish what he'd started.

"Shit," Carmichael said. "I'll be right back, folks, and the birdman better think of something to make one of you change." He marched off, leaving us to a silence that was replaced with a low, steady growl. I realized that it wasn't Jason anymore.

I rose up slowly on my elbows. Jason didn't try to eat me. Richard was still standing by the bars of his cage, but his face had lengthened. He had a muzzle. His thick brown hair was longer. The hair seemed to have flowed down his back, as if attached to the spine. He was holding onto his humanity with a string. A weak, shiny string.

Edward was standing very still near the door. He hadn't tried to run when Richard went all spooky. Edward always did have nerves of steel.

42

Titus was the first one through the door. ''I am mighty disappointed in you all. Carmichael here tells me you almost had it, and this one interfered.''

Kaspar stared at Richard as if he'd never seen him before. Maybe he'd never seen half-human, half-wolf before, but something about the way he was staring said that wasn't it. ''Marcus couldn't have done what you did.''

''Jason didn't want to hurt her,'' Richard said. ''He wanted to do the right thing.''

''Well, Birdman,'' Carmichael said, ''what next?''

I stayed sitting on the rock floor. Jason was huddled against the far wall on his hands and knees, rocking back and forth, back and forth. A low, moaning sound crawled out of his throat.

''He's near the edge,'' Kaspar said. ''Blood will push him over. Not even an alpha can hold him in the presence of fresh blood.''

I did not like the sound of that.

''Ms. Blake, could you come over to the bars, please.''

I moved so I could keep an eye on the moaning werewolf and the armed camp outside. ''Why?''

''Either do it or Carmichael will shoot you. Don't make me start counting again, Ms. Blake.''

''I don't think I want to come over to the bars.''

Titus took out his .45 and walked over to the other cage. Edward was sitting down. He looked at me across the room, and I knew that if we ever got out, they were all dead. Richard was still standing at the bars, hands wrapped around them.

Titus stared up at Richard's animalistic face and gave a low whistle. ''Good lord.'' He pointed the gun at Richard's chest. ''These are silver bullets, Ms. Blake. If you called Garroway, we don't have time for two hunts anyway. Garroway doesn't know you're here, so we have a little time, but we don't have all night. Besides, I think the wolfman here might be too dangerous. So if you keep pissing me off, I'll kill him.''

I met Richard's new eyes. ''They're going to kill us anyway. Don't do it,'' he said. His voice was still a growl that was such a deep bass that it crawled down my spine.

They were going to kill us. But I couldn't stand there and watch, not if I could prolong the inevitable. I walked to the bars nearest them. "Now what?"

Titus stayed with the gun pointed at Richard. "Put your arms through the bars, please."

I wanted to say no, but we'd already established that I wasn't willing to watch Richard die just yet. It made saying no sort of hollow. I slipped my arms through the bars, which put my back to the werewolf. Not good.

"Grab her wrists, gentlemen."

I balled my hands into fists but didn't pull back. I was going to do this, right.

Carmichael grabbed my left wrist. The bearded Fienstien took my right. Fienstien wasn't holding on very hard. I could have pulled away, but Carmichael's hand was like warm steel. I stared into his eyes, and found no pity there. Fienstien was getting squeamish. Grey Hair, with his rifle, was in the middle of the room, distancing himself from it. Carmichael was here for the whole ride.

Titus came over and started unwrapping the bandage on my arm. I fought the urge to ask what he was doing. I had an idea. I hoped I was wrong.

"How many stitches did you get, Ms. Blake?"

I wasn't wrong. "I don't know. I stopped counting at twenty." He let the bandages fall to the ground. He got out my own knife and held it up where it would catch the light. Nothing like a little showmanship.

I pressed my forehead to the cage bars and took a deep breath.

"I'm going to reopen some of this wound. Cut out your stitches."

"I figured that out," I said.

"No struggles?"

"Get on with it."

Aikensen came over. "Let me do it. I owe her a little blood."

Titus looked at me, almost as if asking permission. I gave him my best blank look. He handed the knife to Aikensen.

Aikensen held the point just over the first stitch near my wrist. I felt my eyes widen. I didn't know what to do. Looking seemed a bad idea. Not looking seemed worse. Begging them not to do it seemed futile and humiliating. Some nights there are no good choices.

He cut the first stitch. I felt it snap, but surprisingly it didn't really hurt all that much. I looked away. The stitches went snip, snip, snip. I could do this.

"We need blood," Carmichael said.

I looked back in time to see Aikensen put the point of the knife against the wound. He was going to reopen the wound, slowly. That was going to hurt. I caught a glimpse of Edward in his cage. He was standing now. Looking at me. He was trying to tell me something. His eyes slid right.

Grey Hair had walked away from the show. He was standing close to the other cage. Evidently, he could shoot you, but he didn't like torture.

Edward looked at me. I thought I knew what he wanted. I hoped so.

The knife bit into my skin. I gasped. The pain was sharp and immediate, like all shallow wounds, but this one was going to last a long time. Blood flowed in a heavy line down my skin. Aikensen pulled the point down a fraction of an inch. I pulled suddenly on my arms. Fienstien lost his grip. He grabbed for my flaying arm. Carmichael tightened his grip. I couldn't get free but I could drop to the floor and make my arm move too much to use a knife on it.

I started to scream and fight in earnest. If Edward needed a diversion, I could give him one.

"One woman in a cage and the three of you can't handle her." Titus waddled up. He grabbed my left arm while Carmichael had my wrist. My right hand was back in the cage with me.

Fienstien was sort of hovering near the cage, not sure what to do. If you were going to pay money to hunt monsters, you should be better at violence than this. His holster was close to the bars.

I screamed over and over, jerking at my left arm. Titus held my arm under his, pinned next to his body. Carmichael's grip on my wrist was bruising. They had me at last. Aikensen put the knife to the wound and started to cut.

Fienstien bent down as if to help. I screamed and leaned into the bars. I didn't draw his gun. I grabbed the trigger and pushed it into his body. The shot took him in the stomach. He fell backwards.

A second shot echoed in the cavern. Carmichael's head exploded all over Titus. His Smokey Bear hat was covered in blood and brains.

Edward was standing with the rifle to his shoulder. Grey Hair was slumped against the cage bars. His neck was at an odd angle. Richard knelt by the body. Had he killed him?

There was a sound behind me. A low guttural cry. Titus had his gun out. He still had my arm pinned. Fienstien was rolling around on the ground. His gun was out of reach.

There was a low growl coming from behind me. I heard movement. Jason was coming back to play. Great.

Titus jerked my arm forward, nearly wrenching it out of the socket. He shoved his .45 against my cheek. The barrel was cold.

"Put down the rifle or I pull this trigger."

My face was pressed into the bars and the gun. I couldn't look behind me, but I could hear something crawling closer.

"Is he changing?"

"Not yet," Richard said.

Edward still had the rifle up, sighted on Titus. Aikensen seemed frozen, standing there with the bloody knife.

"Put it down, blondie, right now, or she's dead."

"Edward."

"Anita," he said. His voice sounded like it always did. We both knew he could drop Titus, but if the man's finger twitched while he died, I died, too. Choices.

"Do it," I said.

He pulled the trigger. Titus jerked back against the bars. Blood splattered over my face. A glob of something thicker than blood slid down my cheek. I breathed in shallow gasps. Titus slumped along the bars, gun still gripped in his hands.

''Open her cage,'' Edward said.

Something touched my leg. I jerked and whirled. Jason grabbed my bleeding arm. The strength was incredible. He could have crushed my wrist. He lowered his face to the wound and lapped at the blood like a cat with cream.

''Open her door now, or you're dead, too.''

Aikensen just stood there.

Jason licked my arm. His tongue caressed the wound. It hurt, but I swallowed the gasp. No sounds. No struggles. He'd done damn good not to jump me while I fought the men outside. But a werewolf's patience isn't endless.

''Now!'' Edward said.

Aikensen jumped, then went for the door. He dropped my knife by the door and fumbled at the lock.

Jason bit into my arm, just a little. I did gasp. I couldn't help it. Richard screamed, wordless and thundering.

Jason jerked away from me. ''Run,'' he said. He buried his face in a puddle of blood on the floor, lapping at it. His voice was strangled, more growl than word. ''Run.''

Aikensen opened the door. I crab-walked backwards.

Jason threw his head skyward and shrieked, ''Run!''

I got to my feet and ran. Aikensen slammed the door shut behind me. Jason was writhing on the floor. He fell to the ground in convulsions. Foam ran from his mouth. His hands spasmed, reaching for nothing that I could see. I'd seen people shift before but never this violently. It looked like a bad *grand mal* seizure or someone dying of strychnine.

The wolf burst out of his skin in a nearly finished product, like a cicada pulling out of its old skin. The wolfman raced for the bars. Claws grabbed for us. We both backed up. Foam fell from the wolf jaws. Teeth snapped the air. And I knew that he'd kill me and eat me afterwards. It was what he did, what he was.

Aikensen was staring at the werewolf. I knelt and picked up the dropped knife. ''Aikensen?''

He turned to me, still startled and pale.

''Did you enjoy shooting Deputy Holmes in the chest?''

He frowned at me. ''I let you go. I did what he asked.''

I stepped up close to him. ''Remember what I told you would happen if you hurt Williams?''

He looked at me. ''I remember.''

''Good.'' I drove the knife upward into his groin. I shoved it hilt deep. Blood poured over my hand. He stared at me, eyes going glassy.

''A promise is a promise,'' I said.

He fell and I let his own weight pull the knife up through his abdomen. His eyes closed and I pulled the knife out.

I wiped the knife on his jacket and took the keys from his limp hand. Edward had the rifle slung over his shoulder by the strap. Richard was watching me as if he'd never seen me before. Even with his odd-shaped face and amber eyes I could tell he disapproved.

I unlocked their door. Edward walked out. Richard followed but he was staring at me. ''You didn't have to kill him,'' he said. The words were Richard's even if the voice wasn't.

Edward and I stood there looking at the alpha werewolf. ''Yes, I did.''

''We kill because we have to, not for pleasure and not for pride,'' Richard said.

''Maybe you do,'' I said. ''But the rest of the pack, the rest of the shifters, aren't so particular.''

''The police may be on their way,'' Edward said. ''You don't want to be here.''

Richard glanced at the ravening beast in the other cage. ''Give me the keys. I'll take Jason out through the tunnel. I can smell the outside.''

I handed him the keys. His fingertips brushed my hand. His hand convulsed around the keys. ''I can't last much longer. Go.''

I looked into those strange amber eyes. Edward touched my arm. ''We've got to go.''

I heard sirens. They must have heard the gunshots.

''Be careful,'' I said.

''I will be.'' I let Edward pull me up the stairs. Richard fell to the ground, face hidden in his hands. His face came up, and the bones were longer. They flowed out of his face as if it were clay.

I tripped on the stairs. Only Edward's hand kept me from falling. I turned around and we ran up the stairs. When I glanced back, Richard wasn't in sight.

Edward dropped the rifle on the stairs. The door burst open, and the police came through the door. It was only then that I realized Kaspar was gone.

43

Neither Edward nor I had to go to jail, even though the cops found the people we killed. Everyone pretty much thought it was a miracle that we had gotten away with our lives. People were impressed. Edward surprised me by showing ID for a Ted Forrester, bounty hunter. Slaughter of a bunch of illegal lycanthrope hunters enhanced the reputation of all bounty hunters, Ted Forrester's in particular. I got a lot of good press out of it, too. Bert was pleased.

I asked Edward if Forrester was his real last name. He just smiled.

Dolph was released in time for Christmas. Zerbrowski had to stay longer. I bought them both a case of silver bullets. It was only money. Besides, I never wanted to watch one of them drip their life away through tubes.

I made one last visit to the Lunatic Cafe. Marcus told me that Alfred had killed the girl all on his own. Gabriel hadn't known it was going to happen, but once she was dead, waste not, want not. Lycanthropes are nothing if not practical. Raina had distributed the film for the same reason. I didn't really believe them. Awful damn convenient to blame a dead man. But I didn't tell Edward. I did tell Gabriel and Raina that if any other snuff films surfaced, they could kiss their furry asses good-bye. I'd sic Edward on them. Though I didn't tell them that.

I got Richard a gold cross and made him promise to wear it. He got me a stuffed toy penguin that played ''Winter Wonderland,'' a bag of black-and-white gummy penguins, and a small velvet box, like one for a ring. I thought I would swallow my heart. There was no ring in it, just a note that said, ''Promises to keep.''

Jean-Claude got me a glass sculpture of penguins on an ice floe. It's beautiful and expensive. I'd have liked it better if Richard had gotten it.

What do you get the Master of the City for Christmas? A pint of blood? I settled for an antique cameo. It'd look great at the neck of one of his lacy shirts.

Sometime in February a box arrived from Edward. It was a swan skin. The note read, ''I found a witch to lift his curse.'' I lifted the feathered skin from the box, and a second note fluttered to the ground. This one said, ''Marcus paid me.''

I should have known he'd find a way to make a profit from a kill he'd have made for free.

Richard doesn't understand why I killed Aikensen. I've tried to explain, but saying I killed a man because I said I'd do it does sound like pride. But it wasn't pride. It was for Williams, who would never finish his doctorate or see his owls again. For Holmes, who never got to be the first female chief of police. For all the people he killed who never got a second chance. If they couldn't have one, neither could he. I haven't lost any sleep over killing Aikensen. Maybe that should bother me more than the killing—the fact that it doesn't bother me at all. Naw.

I had the swan skin mounted in a tasteful frame, behind glass. I hung it in the living room. It matched the couch. Richard doesn't like it. I like it just fine.

BLOODY BONES

In loving memory of my mother,
Susie May Gentry Klein.
Would that we had had more time.

Miss you.

Acknowledgments

As always to my husband, Gary, more precious to me now than ever. To my editor, Ginjer Buchanan, whose input changed Serephina for the better. Paty Cockrum, who you can blame for the bathtub scene. Marella Sands, who was right about our reaction to Stirling. Mark Sumner for emergency reading, and questions. Who else can I call at midnight and know I won't wake them? Deborah Millitello as always for emergency phone calls and hand-holding. Rett MacPherson, who heard parts of this book over the phone. To Tom Drennan and N. L. Drew, new talent in the group. Alternate Historians forever. Jean-Claude, truce at last. Sergeant St. Clair, Public Information and Education Officer for the Missouri State Highway Patrol, who answered my last-minute questions. Brynda Mitchell, thanks for the penguin. Thanks to everyone who has written to us.

1

It was St. Patrick's Day, and the only green I was wearing was a button that read, ''Pinch me and you're dead meat.'' I'd started work last night with a green blouse on, but I'd gotten blood all over it from a beheaded chicken. Larry Kirkland, zombie-raiser in training, had dropped the decapitated bird. It did the little headless chicken dance and sprayed both of us with blood. I finally caught the damn thing, but the blouse was ruined.

I had to run home and change. The only thing not ruined was the charcoal grey suit jacket that had been in the car. I put it back on over a black blouse, black skirt, dark hose, and black pumps. Bert, my boss, didn't like us wearing black to work, but if I had to be at the office at seven o'clock without any sleep at all, he would just have to live with it.

I huddled over my coffee mug, drinking it as black as I could swallow it. It wasn't helping much. I stared at a series of 8-by-10 glossy blowups spread across my desktop. The first picture was of a hill that had been scraped open, probably by a bulldozer. A skeletal hand reached out of the raw earth. The next photo showed that someone had tried to carefully scrape away the dirt, showing the splintered coffin and bones to one side of the coffin. A new body. The bulldozer had been brought in again. It had plowed up the red earth and found a boneyard. Bones studded the earth like scattered flowers.

One skull spread its unhinged jaws in a silent scream. A scraggle of pale hair still clung to the skull. The dark, stained cloth wrapped around the corpse was the remnants of a dress. I spotted at least three femurs next to the upper half of a skull. Unless the corpse had had three legs, we were looking at a real mess.

The pictures were well done in a gruesome sort of way. The color made it easier to differentiate the corpses, but the high gloss was a little much. It looked like morgue photos done by a fashion photographer. There was probably an art gallery in New York that would hang the damn things and serve cheese and wine while people walked around saying, ''Powerful, don't you think? Very powerful.''

They were powerful, and sad.

There was nothing but the photos. No explanation. Bert had said to come to his office after I'd looked at them. He'd explain everything. Yeah, I believed that. The Easter Bunny is a friend of mine, too.

I gathered the pictures up, slipped them into the envelope, picked my coffee mug up in the other hand, and went for the door.

There was no one at the desk. Craig had gone home. Mary, our daytime secretary, didn't get in until eight. There was a two-hour space of time when the office was unmanned. That Bert had called me into the office when we were the only ones there bothered me a lot. Why the secrecy?

Bert's office door was open. He sat behind his desk, drinking coffee, shuffling some papers around. He glanced up, smiled, and motioned me closer. The smile bothered me. Bert was never pleasant unless he wanted something.

His thousand-dollar suit framed a white-on-white shirt and tie. His grey eyes sparkled with good cheer. His eyes are the color of dirty window glass, so sparkling is a real effort. His snow-blond hair had been freshly buzzed. The crewcut was so short I could see scalp.

"Have a seat, Anita."

I tossed the envelope on his desk and sat down. "What are you up to, Bert?"

His smile widened. He usually didn't waste the smile on anybody but clients. He certainly didn't waste it on me. "You looked at the pictures?"

"Yeah, what of it?"

"Could you raise them from the dead?"

I frowned at him and sipped my coffee. "How old are they?"

"You couldn't tell from the pictures?"

"In person I could tell you, but not just from pictures. Answer the question."

"Around two hundred years."

I just stared at him. "Most animators couldn't raise a zombie that old without a human sacrifice."

"But you can," he said.

"Yeah. I didn't see any headstones in the pictures. Do we have any names?"

"Why?"

I shook my head. He'd been the boss for five years, started the company when it was just him and Manny, and he didn't know shit about raising the dead. "How can you hang around a bunch of zombie-raisers for this many years and know so little about what we do?"

The smile slipped a little, the glow beginning to fade from his eyes. "Why do you need names?"

"You use names to call the zombie from the grave."

"Without a name you can't raise them?"

"Theoretically, no," I said.

"But you can do it," he said. I didn't like how sure he was.

"Yeah, I can do it. John can probably do it, too."

He shook his head. "They don't want John."

I finished the last of my coffee. "Who's they?"

"Beadle, Beadle, Stirling, and Lowenstein."

"A law firm," I said.

He nodded.

"No more games, Bert. Just tell me what the hell's going on."

"Beadle, Beadle, Stirling, and Lowenstein have some clients building a very plush resort in the mountains near Branson. A very exclusive resort. A place where the wealthy country stars that don't own a house in the area can go to get away from the crowds. Millions of dollars are at stake."

"What's the old cemetery have to do with it?"

"The land they're building on was in dispute between two families. The courts decided the Kellys owned the land, and they were paid a great deal of money. The Bouvier family claimed it was their land and there was a family plot on it to prove it. No one could find the cemetery."

Ah. "They found it," I said.

"They found an old cemetery, but not necessarily the Bouvier family plot."

"So they want to raise the dead and ask who they are?"

"Exactly."

I shrugged. "I can raise a couple of the corpses in the coffins. Ask who they are. What happens if their last name is Bouvier?"

"They have to buy the land a second time. They think some of the corpses are Bouviers. That's why they want all the bodies raised."

I raised my eyebrows. "You're joking."

He shook his head, looking pleased. "Can you do it?"

"I don't know. Give me the pictures again." I set my coffee mug on his desk and took the pictures back. "Bert, they've screwed this six ways to Sunday. It's a mass grave, thanks to the bulldozers. The bones are all mixed together. I've only read about one case of anyone raising a zombie from a mass grave. But they were calling a specific person. They had a name." I shook my head. "Without a name it may not be possible."

"Would you be willing to try?"

I spread the pictures over the desk, staring at them. The top half of a skull had turned upside down like a bowl. Two finger bones attached by something dry and desiccated that must once had been human tissue lay next to it. Bones, bones everywhere but not a name to speak.

Could I do it? I honestly didn't know. Did I want to try? Yeah. I did.

"I'd be willing to try."

"Wonderful."

"Raising them a few every night is going to take weeks, even if I can do it. With John's help it would be quicker."

"It will cost them millions to delay that long," Bert said.

"There's no other way to do it."

"You raised the Davidsons' entire family plot, including Great-Grandpa. You weren't even supposed to raise him. You can raise more than one at a time."

I shook my head. "That was an accident. I was showing off. They wanted to raise three family members. I thought I could save them money by doing it in one shot."

"You raised ten family members, Anita. They only asked for three."

"So?"

"So can you raise the entire cemetery in one night?"

"You're crazy," I said.

"Can you do it?"

I opened my mouth to say no, and closed it. I had raised an entire cemetery once. Not all of them had been two centuries old, but some of them had been older, nearly three hundred. And I raised them all. Of course, I had two human sacrifices to ride for power. It was a long story how I ended up with two people dying inside a circle of power. Self-defense, but the magic didn't care. Death is death.

Could I do it? "I really don't know, Bert."

"That's not a no," he said. He had an eager, anticipatory look on his face.

"They must have offered you a bundle of money," I said.

He smiled. "We're bidding on the project."

"We're what?"

"They sent this package to us, the Resurrection Company in California and the Essential Spark in New Orleans."

"They prefer Élan Vital to the English translation," I said. Frankly, it sounded more like a beauty salon than an animating firm, but nobody had asked me. "So what? The lowest bid gets it?"

"That was their plan," Bert said.

He looked entirely too satisfied with himself. "What?" I asked.

"Let me play it back to you," he said. "There are what, three animators in the entire country that could raise a zombie that old without a human sacrifice? You and John are two of them. I'm including Phillipa Freestone of Resurrection in this."

"Probably," I said.

He nodded. "Okay. Could Phillipa raise without a name?"

"I don't have any way of knowing that. John could. Maybe she could."

"Could either she or John raise from the mass bones, not the ones in the coffin?"

That stopped me. "I don't know."

"Would either of them stand a chance of raising the entire graveyard?" He was staring at me very steadily.

"You're enjoying this too much," I said.

"Just answer the question, Anita."

"I know John couldn't do it. I don't think Phillipa is as good as John, so no, they couldn't do it."

"I'm going to up the bid," Bert said.

I laughed. "Up the bid?"

"Nobody else can do it. Nobody but you. They tried treating this like any other construction problem. But there aren't going to be any other bids, now are there?"

"Probably not," I said.

"Then I'm going to take them to the cleaners," he said with a smile.

I shook my head. "You greedy son of a bitch."

"You get a share of the fee, you know."

''I know.'' We looked at each other. ''What if I try and can't raise them all in one night?''

''You'll still be able to raise them all eventually, won't you?''

''Probably.'' I stood, picking up my coffee mug. ''But I wouldn't spend the check until after I've done it. I'm going to go get some sleep.''

''They want the bid this morning. If they accept our terms, they'll fly you up in a private helicopter.''

''Helicopter—you know I hate to fly.''

''For this much money you'll fly.''

''Great.''

''Be ready to go at a moment's notice.''

''Don't push it, Bert.'' I hesitated at the door. ''Let me take Larry with me.''

''Why? If John can't do it, then Larry certainly can't.''

I shrugged. ''Maybe not, but there are ways to combine power during a raising. If I can't do it alone, maybe I can get a boost from our trainee.''

He looked thoughtful. ''Why not take John? Combined, you could do it.''

''Only if he'd give his power willingly to me. You think he'd do that?''

Bert shook his head.

''You going to tell him that the client didn't want him? That you offered him to the client and they asked for me by name?''

''No,'' Bert said.

''That's why you're doing it like this; no witnesses.''

''Time is of the essence, Anita.''

''Sure, Bert, but you didn't want to face Mr. John Burke with yet another client that wants me over him.''

Bert looked down at his blunt-fingered hands clasped on the desktop. He looked up, grey eyes serious. ''John is almost as good as you are, Anita. I don't want to lose him.''

''You think he'll walk if one more client asks for me?''

''His pride's hurt,'' Bert said.

''And there's so much of it to hurt,'' I said.

Bert smiled. ''You needling him doesn't help.''

I shrugged. It sounded petty to say he'd started it, but he had. We'd tried dating, and John couldn't handle me being a female version of him. No; he couldn't handle me being a better version of him.

''Try to behave yourself, Anita. Larry's not up to speed yet; we need John.''

''I always behave myself, Bert.''

He sighed. ''If you didn't make me so much money, I wouldn't put up with your shit.''

''Ditto,'' I said.

That about summed up our relationship. Commerce at its best. We didn't like each other, but we could do business together. Free enterprise at work.

2

At noon Bert called and said we had it. ''Be at the office packed and ready to go at two o'clock. Mr. Lionel Bayard will fly up with you and Larry.''

''Who's Lionel Bayard?''

''A junior partner in the firm of Beadle, Beadle, Stirling, and Lowenstein. He likes the sound of his own voice. Don't give him a rough time about it.''

''Who, me?''

''Anita, don't tease the help. He may be wearing a three-thousand-dollar suit, but he's still the help.''

''I'll save it up for one of the partners. Surely Beadle, Beadle, Stirling, or Lowenstein will appear in person sometime this weekend.''

''Don't tease the bosses either,'' he said.

''Anything you say.'' My voice was utterly mild.

''You'll do whatever you want no matter what I say, won't you?''

''Gee, Bert, who says you can't teach an old dog new tricks?''

''Just be here at two o'clock. I called Larry. He'll be here.''

''I'll be there, Bert. I've got one stop to make, so if I'm a few minutes late, don't worry.''

''Don't be late.''

''Be there as soon as I can.'' I hung up before he could argue with me.

I had to shower, change, and go to Seckman Junior High School. Richard Zeeman taught science there. We had a date set up for tomorrow. At one point Richard had asked me to marry him. That was sort of on hold, but I did owe him more than a message on his answering machine, saying sorry, honey, can't make the date. I'm going to be out of town. A message would have been easier for me, but cowardly.

I packed one suitcase. It was enough for four days and then some. If you pack extra underwear and clothes that mix and match, you can live for a week out of a small suitcase.

I did add a few extras. The Firestar 9mm and its inner pants holster. Enough extra ammo to sink a battleship and two knives plus wrist sheaths. I'd had four knives. All handcrafted for little ol' *moi*. Two of them had been lost beyond recovery. I was having them replaced, but hand forging takes time, especially when you insist on the highest silver content possible in the steel. Two knives, two guns should be enough for one weekend business trip. I'd wear the Browning Hi-Power.

Packing wasn't a problem. What to wear today was the problem. They'd want me to raise them tonight if I could. Hell, the helicopter might fly directly to the construction site. Which meant I'd be walking over raw dirt, bones, shattered coffins. It didn't sound like high-heel territory. Yet, if a junior partner was wearing a three-thousand-dollar suit, the people who'd just hired me would expect me to look the part. I could either dress professionally or in feathers and blood. I'd actually had one client who was disappointed that I didn't show up nude smeared with blood. There could have been more than one reason for his disappointment. I don't think I've ever had a client that would have objected to some kind of ceremonial getup, but jeans and jogging shoes didn't seem to inspire confidence. Don't ask me why.

I could pack my coverall and put it over whatever I wore. Yeah, I liked that. Veronica Sims—Ronnie, my very best friend—had talked me into buying a fashionably short navy skirt. It was short enough that I was a little embarrassed, but the skirt fit inside the coverall. The skirt didn't wrinkle or bunch up after I'd worn the outfit to vampire stakings or murder scenes. Take the coverall off, and I was set to go to the office or out for the evening. I was so pleased, I went out and bought two more in different colors.

One was crimson, the other purple. I hadn't been able to find one in black yet. At least not one that wasn't so short that I refused to wear it. Admittedly, the short skirts made me look taller. They even made me look leggy. When you're five-foot-three, that's saying something. But the purple didn't match much that I owned, so crimson it was.

I'd found a short-sleeved blouse that was the exact same shade of red. Red with violet undertones, a cold, hard color that looked great with my pale skin, black hair, and dark brown eyes. The shoulder holster and 9mm Browning Hi-Power looked very dramatic against it. A black belt cinched tight at the waist held down the loops on the holster. A black jacket with rolled-back sleeves went over everything to hide the gun. I twirled in front of the mirror in my bedroom. The skirt wasn't much longer than the jacket, but you couldn't see the gun. At least not easily. Unless you're willing to have things tailor-made, it's hard to hide a gun, especially in women's dress-up clothes.

I put on just enough makeup so the red didn't overwhelm me. I was also going to be saying good-bye to Richard for several days. A little makeup couldn't hurt. When I say makeup, I mean eye shadow, blush, lipstick, and that's it. Outside of a television interview that Bert talked me into, I don't wear base.

Except for the hose and black high heels, which I would've had to wear no matter what skirt I wore, the outfit was comfortable. As long as I remembered not to bend directly at the waist, I was safe.

The only jewelry I wore was the silver cross tucked into the blouse, and the watch on my wrist. My dress watch had broken and I just had never gotten around to getting it fixed. The present watch was a man's black diving watch that looked out of place on my small wrist. But hey, it glowed in the dark if you pressed a button. It showed me the date, what day it was, and could time a run. I hadn't found a woman's watch that could do all that.

I didn't have to cancel running with Ronnie tomorrow morning. She was out of town on a case. A private detective's work is never done.

I loaded the suitcase into my Jeep and was on the way to Richard's school by one o'clock. I was going to be late to the office. Oh, well. They'd wait for me or they wouldn't. It wouldn't break my heart to miss the helicopter ride. I hated planes, but a helicopter . . . scared the shit out of me.

I hadn't been afraid of flying until I was on a plane that plunged several thousand feet in seconds. The stewardess ended up plastered against the ceiling, covered in coffee. People screamed and prayed. The elderly woman beside me recited the Lord's Prayer in German. She'd been so scared, tears had come down her face. I offered her my hand, and she gripped it. I knew I was going to die and there was nothing I could do to prevent it. But we would die holding on to human hands. Die covered in human tears, and human prayers. Then the plane straightened out and suddenly we were safe. I haven't trusted air transportation since.

Normally in St. Louis there is no real spring. There's winter, two days of mild weather, and summer heat. This year spring had come early and stayed. The air was soft against your skin. The wind smelled of green growing things, and winter seemed to have been a bad dream. Redbuds bent from the trees on either side of the road. Tiny purple blossoms like a delicate lavender mist here and there through the naked trees. There were no leaves yet, but there was a hint of green. Like someone had taken a giant paintbrush and tinted everything. Look directly at them and the trees were bare and black, but look sideways, not at a particular tree but at all the trees, and there was a touch of green.

270 South is about as pleasant as a highway can be; it gets you where you're going fairly fast, and it's over quickly. I exited at Tesson Ferry Road. The road is thick with strip malls, a hospital, and fast-food restaurants, and when you leave the commerce behind you hit new housing developments so thick they nearly touch. There are still stands of woods and open spaces, but they won't last.

The turn to Old 21 is at the crest of a hill just past the Meramec River. It is mostly houses with a few gas stations, the area water district office, and a large gas field to the right. Where the hills march out and out.

At the first stoplight I turned left past a little shopping area. The road is a curving narrow thing that snakes between houses and woods. There were glimpses of daffodils in the yards. The road dips down into a valley, and at the bottom of a steep hill is a stop sign. The road climbs quickly to the crest of a hill, to a T, turn left and you're almost there.

The one-story school sits on the floor of a wide, flat valley surrounded by hills. Having been raised in Indiana farm country, I'd have called them mountains once. The elementary school sits separate, but close enough to share a playground. If you got recess in junior high. When I was too little to go to junior high, it seemed you did get recess. By the time I got there, you didn't. The way of the world.

I parked as close to the building as I could. This was my second visit to Richard's school, and my first during the actual school day. We'd come once to get some papers he'd forgotten. No students then. I entered the main entrance and ran into a crowd. It must have been between classes when they moved the warm bodies from one room to another.

I was instantly aware that I was about the same height as or shorter than everyone I saw. There was something claustrophobic about being jostled by the book-carrying, backpack-wearing crowd. There had to be a circle of Hell where you were eternally fourteen, eternally in junior high. One of the lower circles.

I flowed with the crowd towards Richard's room. I admit I took comfort in the fact that I was better dressed than most of the girls. Petty as hell, but I had been chunky in junior high. There isn't a lot of difference between chunky and fat when it comes to teasing. I'd had my growth spurt and never been fat again. That's right; I'd been even tinier once. Shortest kid in school for years and years.

I stood to one side of the doorway, letting the students come and go. Richard was showing something in a textbook to a young girl. She was blonde, wearing a flannel shirt over a black dress that was three sizes too big for her. She was wearing what looked like black combat boots with heavy white socks rolled over the tops of them. The outfit was very now. The look of adoration on her face was not. She was shiny and eager just because Mr. Zeeman was giving her some one-on-one help.

I had to admit that Richard was worth a crush or two. His thick brown hair was tied back in a ponytail that gave the illusion that his hair was very short and close to his head. He has high, full cheekbones and a strong jaw, with a dimple that softens his face and makes him look almost too perfect. His eyes are a solid chocolate brown with those thick lashes that so many men have and women want. The bright yellow shirt made his permanently tanned skin seem even darker. His tie was a dark, rich green that matched the dress slacks he wore. His jacket was draped across the back of his desk chair. The muscles in his upper arms worked against the cloth of his shirt as he held the book.

The class was mostly seated, the hallway nearly silent. He closed the book and handed it to the girl. She smiled and scrambled for the door, late to her next class. Her eyes flicked over me as she passed, wondering what I was doing there.

She wasn't the only one. Several of the seated students were glancing my way. I stepped into the room.

Richard smiled. It warmed me down to my toes. The smile saved him from being too handsome. It wasn't that it wasn't a great smile. He could have done toothpaste commercials. But the smile was a little boy's smile, open and welcoming. There was no guile to Richard, no deep, dark plan. He was the world's biggest Boy Scout. The smile showed that.

I wanted to go to him, have him wrap his arms around me. I had a horrible urge to grab his tie and lead him out of the room. I wanted to touch his chest underneath the yellow shirt. The urge was so strong, I put my hands in the pockets of my jacket. Mustn't shock the students. Richard affects me like that sometimes. Okay, most of the time when he's not furry, or licking blood off his fingers. He's a werewolf. Did I mention that? No one at the school knows. If they did, he'd be out of a job. People don't like lycanthropes teaching their precious kiddies. It's illegal to discriminate against someone for a disease, but everyone does it. Why should the educational system be different?

He touched my cheek, just his fingertips. I turned my face into his hand, brushing lips against his fingers. So much for being cool in front of the kiddies. There were a few oohs and nervous laughs.

''I'll be right back, guys.'' More oohs, louder laughter, one ''Way to go, Mr. Zeeman.'' Richard motioned me out the door and I went, hands still in my pockets. Normally, I'd have said I wasn't going to embarrass myself in front of a bunch of eighth-graders, but lately I wasn't entirely trustworthy.

Richard led me a little ways from his classroom into the deserted hallway. He leaned up against the wall of lockers and looked down at me. The little-boy smile was gone. The look in his dark eyes made me shiver. I ran my hand down his tie, smoothing it against his chest.

''Am I allowed to kiss you, or would that scandalize the kiddies?'' I didn't look up at him as I asked. I didn't want him to see the raw need in my eyes. It was embarrassing enough that I knew he sensed it. You can't hide lust from a werewolf. They can smell it.

''I'll risk it.'' His voice was soft, low, with a warm edge that made my stomach clench.

I felt him bend over me. I raised my face to his. His lips were so soft. I leaned against his body, palms flat against his chest. I could feel his nipples harden under my skin. My hands slid to his waist, smoothing along the cloth of his shirt. I wanted to pull his shirt out of his pants and run my hands over bare skin. I stepped back from him feeling just a little breathless.

It was my idea that we wouldn't have sex before marriage. My idea. But damn, it was hard. The more we dated, the harder it got.

''Jesus, Richard.'' I shook my head. ''It gets harder, doesn't it?''

Richard's smile didn't look innocent or Boy Scoutish in the least. ''Yes, it does.''

Heat rushed up my face. ''I didn't mean that.''

''I know what you meant.'' His voice was gentle, taking the sting out of the teasing.

My face was still hot with embarrassment, but my voice was steady. Point for me. ''I've got to go out of town on business.''

''Zombie, vampire, or police?''

''Zombie.''

''Good.''

I looked up at him. ''Why good?''

''I worry more when you go away on police business, or vampire stakings. You know that.''

I nodded. ''Yeah, I know that.'' We stood there in the hallway, staring at each other. If things had been different, we'd be engaged, maybe planning a wedding. All this sexual tension would have been coming to some kind of conclusion. As it was . . .

''I'm going to be late as it is. I've got to go.''

''Are you going to tell Jean-Claude bye in person?'' His face was neutral when he asked, but his eyes weren't.

''It's daylight. He's in his coffin.''

''Ah,'' Richard said.

''I didn't have a date planned with him this weekend, so I don't owe him an explanation. Is that what you wanted to hear?''

''Close enough,'' he said. He took a step away from the lockers, bringing our bodies very close together. He bent to kiss me good-bye. Giggles erupted down the hall.

We turned to see most of his class huddled in the doorway gazing at us. Great.

Richard smiled. He raised his voice enough so they'd hear him. ''Back inside, you monsters.''

There were catcalls, and one small brunette girl gave me a very dirty look. I think there must have been a lot of girls that had a crush on Mr. Zeeman.

''The natives are restless. I've got to get back.''

I nodded. ''I'm hoping to be back by Monday.''

''We'll go hiking next weekend, then.''

''I put Jean-Claude off this weekend. I can't not see him two weeks in a row.''

Richard's face clouded up with the beginnings of anger. ''Hike during the day, see the vampire at night. Only fair.''

''I don't like this any better than you do,'' I said.

''I wish I believed that.''

''Richard.''

He gave a long sigh. The anger sort of leaked out of him. I never understood how he did that. He could be furious one minute and calm the next. Both emotions seemed genuine. Once I was angry, I was angry. Maybe it's a character flaw?

''I'm sorry, Anita. It's not like you're dating him behind my back.''

''I would never do anything behind your back; you know that.''

He nodded. ''I know that.'' He glanced back at his classroom. ''I've got to go before they set the room on fire.'' He walked down the hallway without looking back.

I almost called after him, but I let him go. The mood was sort of spoiled. Nothing like knowing your girlfriend is dating someone else to take the wind out of your sails. I wouldn't have put up with it if it was the other way around. A double standard that, but one we could all three live with. If living was the term for Jean-Claude.

Oh, hell, my personal life was too confusing for words. I walked off down the hall, having to pass by his open classroom door. My high heels made loud, rackety echoes. I didn't try to catch a last glimpse of him. It would make me feel worse about leaving.

It hadn't been my idea to date the Master of the City. Jean-Claude had given me two choices; either he could kill Richard, or I could date both of them. It had seemed a good idea at the time. Five weeks later I wasn't so sure.

It had been my morals that had kept Richard and me from consummating our relationship. Consummating, nice euphemism. But Jean-Claude had made it clear that if I did something with Richard, I had to do it with him too. Jean-Claude was

trying to woo me. If Richard could touch mc but hc couldn't, it wasn't fair. IIe had a point, I guess. But the thought of having to have sex with the vampire was more likely to keep me chaste than any high ideals.

I couldn't date both of them indefinitely. The sexual tension alone was killing me. I could move. Richard might even let me do that. He wouldn't like it, but if I wanted free of him, he'd let me go. Jean-Claude, on the other hand . . . He'd never let me go. The question was, did I want him to let me go? Answer: hell, yes. The real trick was how to break free without anybody dying.

Yeah, that was the $64,000 question. Trouble was, I didn't have an answer. We were going to need one sooner or later. And later was getting closer all the time.

3

I huddled against the side of the helicopter, one hand in a death grip on the strap that was bolted to the wall. I wanted to use both hands to hold on, as if by holding very tightly to the stupid strap it would save me when the helicopter plummeted to earth. I used one hand because two hands looked cowardly. I was wearing a headset, sort of like ear protection for the shooting range, but with a microphone so you could talk above the teeth-rattling noise. I hadn't realized that most of a helicopter was clear, like being suspended in a great buzzing, vibrating bubble. I kept my eyes closed as much as possible.

''Are you all right, Ms. Blake?'' Lionel Bayard asked.

The voice startled me. ''Yeah, I'm fine.''

''You don't look well.''

''I don't like to fly,'' I said.

He gave a weak smile. I don't think I was inspiring confidence in Lionel Bayard, lawyer and flunkie of Beadle, Beadle, Stirling, and Lowenstein. Lionel Bayard was a small, neat man with a tiny blond mustache that looked like it was as much facial hair as he would ever get. His triangular jaw was as smooth as my own. Maybe the mustache was glued on. His brown suit with a thin yellow tweed fit his body like a well-tailored glove. His thin tie was brown-and-yellow striped with a gold tie tack. The tie tack was monogrammed. His slender leather briefcase was monogrammed as well. Everything matched, down to his gold-tasseled loafers.

Larry twisted in his seat. He was sitting beside the pilot. ''You're really afraid of flying?'' I could see his lips move, but all the sound came out of my headset; without them we'd never have been able to talk over the noise. He sounded amused.

''Yes, Larry, I'm really afraid of flying.'' I hoped sarcasm traveled the headsets as clearly as amusement did.

Larry laughed. Evidently, sarcasm traveled. Larry looked freshly scrubbed. He was dressed in his other blue suit, his white shirt—which was one of three he owned—and his second-best tie. His best tie had blood all over it. He was still in college, working weekends for us until he graduated. His short hair was the color of a surprised carrot. He was freckled and about my height, short, with pale blue eyes. He looked like a grown-up Opie.

Bayard was working hard at not frowning at me. The effort showed enough that he shouldn't have bothered. ''Are you sure you're up to this assignment?''

I met his brown eyes. ''You better hope I am, Mr. Bayard, because I'm all you got.''

''I am aware of your specialized skills, Ms. Blake. I spent the last twelve hours contacting every animating firm in the United States. Phillipa Freestone of the Resurrection Company told me she couldn't do what we wanted, that the only person in the country who might be able to do it was Anita Blake. Élan Vital in New Orleans told us the same thing. They mentioned John Burke but weren't confident that he could do all we wanted. We must have all the dead raised or it's useless to us.''

''Did my boss explain to you that I am not a hundred percent sure that I can do it?''

Bayard blinked at me. ''Mr. Vaughn seemed very confident that you could do what we asked.''

''Bert can be as confident as he wants. He doesn't have to raise this mess.''

''I realize the earthmoving equipment has complicated your task, Ms. Blake, but we did not do it deliberately.''

I let that go. I'd seen the pictures. They'd tried to cover it up. If the construction crew hadn't been local with some Bouvier sympathizers, they'd have plowed up the boneyard, poured some concrete, and voilá, no evidence.

''Whatever. I'll do what I can with what you've left me.''

''Would it have been that much easier if you had been brought in before the graves were disturbed?''

''Yeah.''

He sighed. It vibrated through the headphones. ''Then my apologies.''

I shrugged. ''Unless you did it personally, you're not the one who owes me an apology.''

He shifted a little in his seat. ''I did not order the digging. Mr. Stirling is on site.''

''*The* Mr. Stirling?'' I asked.

Bayard didn't seem to get the humor. ''Yes, that Mr. Stirling.'' Or maybe he really expected me to know the name.

''You always have a senior partner looking over your shoulder?''

He used one finger to adjust his gold-framed glasses. It looked like an old gesture from a time before new glasses and designer suits. ''With this much money at stake, Mr. Stirling thought he should be in the area in case there were more problems.''

''More problems?'' I asked.

He blinked at me rapidly, like a well-groomed rabbit. ''The Bouvier matter.''

He was lying. ''What else is going wrong with your little project?''

''Whatever do you mean, Ms. Blake?'' His manicured fingers smoothed down his tie.

''You've had more problems than just the Bouviers.'' I made it a statement.

"Any problems we may or may not be having, Ms. Blake, are not your concern. We hired you to raise the dead and establish the identity of said deceased persons. Beyond that, you have no duties here."

"Have you ever raised a zombie, Mr. Bayard?"

He blinked again. "Of course not." He sounded offended.

"Then how do you know the other problems won't affect my job?"

Small frown lines formed between his eyebrows. He was a lawyer and was earning a good living, but thinking seemed to be hard for him. Made you wonder where he'd graduated from.

"I don't see how our little difficulties could affect your job."

"You've just admitted you don't know anything about my job," I said. "How do you know what will affect it and what won't?" Alright, I was fishing. Bayard was probably right. The other problems probably wouldn't affect me, but you never know. I don't like being kept in the dark. And I don't like being lied to, not even by omission.

"I think Mr. Stirling would have to make the call about whether you are enlightened or not."

"Not senior enough to make the decision," I said.

"No," Bayard said, "I am not."

Geez, some people you can't even needle. I glanced at Larry. He shrugged. "Looks like we're going to land."

I glanced out at the rapidly growing land. We were in the middle of the Ozark Mountains, hovering over a blasted scar of reddish naked earth. The construction site, I presume.

The ground swelled up to meet us. I closed my eyes and swallowed hard. The ride was almost over. I would not throw up this close to the ground. The ride was almost over. Almost over. Almost over. There was a bump that made me gasp.

"We've landed," Larry said. "You can open your eyes now."

I did. "You are enjoying the hell out of this, aren't you?"

He grinned. "I don't get to see you out of your element often."

The helicopter was surrounded by a fog of reddish dirt. The blades began to slow with a thick *whump, whump* sound. As the blades stopped, the dirt settled down and we could see where we were.

We were in a small, flat area between a cluster of mountains. It looked like it had once been a narrow valley, but bulldozers had widened it, flattened it, made it a landing pad. The earth was so red it looked like a river of rust. The mountain in front of the helicopter was one red mound. Heavy equipment and cars were clustered to the far side of the valley. Men were clustered around the equipment, shielding their eyes from the dust.

When the blades came to a sliding stop, Bayard unbuckled his seat belt. I did, too. We lifted off the headsets and Bayard opened his door. I opened mine and found that the ground was farther away than you'd think. I had to expose a long line of thigh to touch the ground.

The construction workers were appreciative. Whistles, catcalls, and one offer to check under my skirt. No, those weren't the exact words used.

A tall man in a white hard hat strode towards us. He was wearing a pair of tan coveralls, but his dirt-covered shoes were Gucci and his tan was health-club perfect. A man and a woman followed at his back.

The man looked like the real foreman. He was dressed in jeans and a work shirt with the sleeves rolled over muscular forearms. Not from racquetball or a little tennis, but from plain hard work.

The woman wore the traditional skirt suit complete with little blousy tie at her throat. The suit was expensive, but was an unfortunate shade of puce that did nothing for the woman's auburn hair but did match the blush that she'd smeared on her cheeks. I checked her neckline, and yes, she did have a pale line just above her collar where the base had not been blended in. She looked like she'd been made up at clown school.

She didn't look that young. You'd think someone somewhere would have clued her in to how bad she looked. Of course, I wasn't going to tell her either. Who was I to criticize?

Stirling had the palest grey eyes I'd ever seen. The irises were only a few shades darker than the whites of his eyes. He stood there with his entourage behind him. He looked me up and down. He didn't seem to like what he saw. His strange eyes flicked to Larry in his cheap, wrinkled suit. Mr. Stirling frowned.

Bayard came around, smoothing his jacket into place. "Mr. Stirling, this is Anita Blake. Ms. Blake, this is Raymond Stirling."

He just stood there, looking at me like he was disappointed. The woman had a clipboard notebook, pen poised. Had to be his secretary. She looked worried, as if it was very important that Mr. Raymond Stirling like us.

I was beginning not to care if he liked us or not. What I wanted to say was, "You got a problem?" What I said was, "Is there a problem, Mr. Stirling?" Bert would have been pleased.

"You're not what I expected, Ms. Blake."

"How so?"

"Pretty, for one thing." It wasn't a compliment.

"And?"

He motioned at my outfit. "You're not dressed appropriately for the job."

"Your secretary's wearing heels."

"Ms. Harrison's attire is not your concern."

"And my attire is none of yours."

"Fair enough, but you're going to have a hell of time getting up that mountain in those shoes."

"I've got a coverall and Nikes in my suitcase."

"I don't think I like your attitude, Ms. Blake."

"I know I don't like yours," I said.

The foreman behind him was having trouble not smiling. His eyes were getting shiny with the effort. Ms. Harrison looked a little scared. Bayard had moved to one side, closer to Stirling. Making clear whose side he was on. Coward.

Larry moved closer to me.

"Do you want this job, Ms. Blake?"

"Not enough to take grief about it, no."

Ms. Harrison looked like she'd swallowed a bug. A big, nasty, squirming bug. I think I'd missed my cue to fall down and worship at her boss's feet.

The foreman coughed behind his hand. Stirling glanced at him, then back to me. "Are you always this arrogant?" he asked.

I sighed. "I prefer the word 'confident' to 'arrogant,' but I'll tell you what. I'll tone it down if you will."

"I am so sorry, Mr. Stirling," Bayard said. "I apologize. I had no idea . . ."

"Shut up, Lionel," Stirling said.

Lionel shut up.

Stirling was looking at me with his strange pale eyes. He nodded. "Agreed, Ms. Blake." He smiled. "I'll tone it down."

"Great," I said.

"All right, Ms. Blake, let's go up to the top and see if you're really as good as you think you are."

"I can look at the graveyard, but until full dark I can't do anything else."

He frowned and glanced at Bayard. "Lionel." That one word had a lot of heat in it. Anger looking for a target. He'd stop picking on me, but Lionel was fair game.

"I did fax you a memo, sir, as soon as I realized that Ms. Blake would be unable to help us until after dark."

Good man. When in doubt, cover your ass with paper.

Stirling glared at him. Bayard looked apologetic but he stood his ground, safe behind his memo.

"I called Beau and had him bring everybody down here on the understanding we could get some work done today." His gaze was very steady on Bayard. Lionel wilted just a little; evidently one memo was not protection enough.

"Mr. Stirling, even if I can raise the graveyard in one night, and that's a big if, what if the dead are all Bouviers? What if it is their family plot? My understanding is that construction will stop until you rebuy the land."

"They don't want to sell," Beau said.

Stirling glared at him. The foreman just smiled softly.

"Are you saying that the entire project is off if this is the Bouvier family plot?" I asked Bayard. "Why, Lionel, you didn't tell me that."

"There was no need for you to know," Bayard said.

"Why wouldn't they want to sell the land for a million dollars?" Larry asked. It was a good question.

Stirling looked at him like he'd just appeared out of thin air. Evidently, the flunkies weren't supposed to talk. "Magnus and Dorcas Bouvier have only a restaurant, called Bloody Bones. It is nothing. I have no idea why they wouldn't want to be millionaires."

"Bloody Bones? What kind of name is that for a restaurant?" Larry asked.

I shrugged. "It doesn't exactly say bon appetit." I looked at Stirling. He looked angry but that was all. I would have bet a million dollars that he knew exactly why the Bouviers didn't want to sell. But it didn't show on his face. His cards were close to his chest and unreadable.

I turned to Bayard. There was an unhealthy flush to his cheeks, and he avoided my gaze. I'd play poker with Bayard any day. But not in front of his boss.

"Fine. I'll change into something more bulky and we'll go take a look." The pilot handed out my suitcase. The coverall and shoes were on top.

Larry came up to me. "Gee, I wished I'd thought of the coverall. This suit's not going to survive the trip."

I pulled out two pairs of coveralls. "Be prepared," I said.

He grinned. "Thanks."

I shrugged. "One good thing about being nearly the same size." I slipped off the black jacket, which left the gun in plain sight.

"Ms. Blake," Stirling said. "Why are you armed?"

I sighed. I was tired of Raymond. I hadn't even gone up the hill and I didn't want to go. The last thing I wanted to do was stand here and debate whether I needed a gun. The red blouse was short-sleeved. Visual aids are always better than lectures.

I walked over to him with my arms bent outward, exposing the inside of both forearms. There's a rather neat knife scar on my right arm, nothing too dramatic. My left arm is a mess. It had only been a little over a month since a shapeshifting leopard had opened my arm. A nice doctor had stitched it back together, but there is only so much you can do with claw marks. The cross-shaped burn scar that some inventive vampire servants had put on me was now a little crooked because of the claws. The mound of scar tissue at the bend of my arm where a vampire had bitten through the flesh and gnawed the bone dribbled white scars like water.

"Jesus," Beau said.

Stirling looked a touch pale but he held up well, like he'd seen worse. Bayard looked green. Ms. Harrison paled so that the makeup floated on her suddenly pale skin like impressionist water lilies.

"I don't go anywhere unarmed, Mr. Stirling. Live with it, because I have to."

He nodded, eyes very serious. "Fine, Ms. Blake. Is your assistant armed as well?"

"No," I said.

He nodded again. "Fine. Change, and when you're ready we'll go up."

Larry was zipping up his coverall when I walked back. "I could have been armed, you know," he said.

"You brought your gun?" I asked.

He nodded.

"Unloaded in your suitcase?"

"Just like you told me."

"Good." I let it go. Larry wanted to be a vampire executioner as well as an animator, which meant he needed to know how to use a gun. A gun with silver-plated bullets that could slow a vampire down. We'd work up to shotguns, which could take out a head and heart from a relatively safe distance. Beat the hell out of staking.

I'd gotten him a carry permit on the condition he didn't carry it concealed until I thought he was a good enough shot not to blow a hole in himself or me.

I'd gotten him the permit mainly so we could carry it around in the car and go to the range in any spare moments.

The coverall went over the skirt like magic. I took off the heels and put the Nikes on. I left the coverall unzipped enough that I could go for the gun if needed, and I was set to go.

''Are you going up with us, Mr. Stirling?''

''Yes,'' he said.

''Then lead the way,'' I said.

He walked past me, glancing at the coveralls. Or maybe visualizing the gun under it. Beau started to follow but Stirling said, ''No, I'll take her up alone.''

Silence among the three flunkies. I'd expected Ms. Harrison to stay behind in her high-heeled pumps, but I'd been sure the two men would come along. So, from the looks on their faces, had they.

''Wait a minute. You said 'her.' You want Larry to wait down here, too?''

''Yes.''

I shook my head. ''He's in training. You can't learn if you don't see it done.''

''Will you be doing anything that he needs to see today?''

I thought about that for a minute. ''I guess not.''

''I do get to come up after dark?'' Larry asked.

''You'll get to see the down and dirty, Larry. Don't worry.''

''Of course,'' Stirling said. ''I have no problem with your associate doing his job.''

''Why can't he come along now?'' I asked.

''At the price we're paying, humor me, Ms. Blake.''

He was being strangely polite, so I nodded. ''Okay.''

''Mr. Stirling,'' Bayard said, ''are you sure you should go up alone?''

''Why ever not, Lionel?''

Bayard opened his mouth, closed it, then said, ''No reason, Mr. Stirling.''

Beau shrugged. ''I'll tell the men to go home for the day.'' He started to turn away, then stopped. ''Do you want the crew back tomorrow?''

Stirling looked at me. ''Ms. Blake?''

I shook my head. ''I don't know yet.''

''What's your best guess?'' he asked.

I looked over at the waiting men. ''Do they get paid whether they show up or not?''

''Only if they show up,'' Stirling said.

''Then no work tomorrow. I can't guarantee they'll have anything to do.''

Stirling nodded. ''You heard her, Beau.''

Beau looked at me, then back to Stirling. He had a strange look on his face, half amused, half something I couldn't read. ''Anything you say, Mr. Stirling, Ms. Blake.'' He turned and strode off over the raw ground, waving at the men as he moved. The men began to leave long before he got to them.

''What do you want us to do, Mr. Stirling?'' Bayard asked.

''Wait for us.''

''The helicopter, too? It has to leave before dark.''

''Will we be down before dark, Ms. Blake?''

"Sure. I'm just going to take a quick look around. I'll need to get back in here after dark, though."

"I'll give you a car and driver for your stay."

"Thanks."

"Shall we, Ms. Blake?" He motioned me forward. Something had changed in the way he was treating me. I couldn't put my finger on it, but I didn't like it.

"After you, Mr. Stirling."

He nodded and took the lead, striding over the red earth in his thousand-dollar shoes.

Larry and I exchanged glances. "I won't be long, Larry."

"Us flunkies aren't going anywhere," he said.

I smiled. He smiled. I shrugged. Why did Stirling want it to be just the two of us? I watched the senior partner's broad back as he marched across the torn earth. I followed him. I'd find out what the secrecy was all about when we got to the top. I was betting I wouldn't like what I'd hear. Just me and the big cheese on top of the mountain with the dead. What could be better?

4

The view from the top of the mountain was worth the hike. Trees stretched out and out to the horizon. We stood in a circle of forest that showed no hand of man as far as the eye could see. That first blush of green was more pronounced here. But the thing you noticed most was the lavender color of redbuds through the dark trees. Redbuds are such delicate things that if they came out in the height of summer they'd get lost in all the leaves and flowers, but here with nothing but naked trees the redbuds were eye-catching. A few dogwoods had started to bloom, adding their white to the lavender. Spring in the Ozarks, ah.

"The view is magnificent," I said.

"Yes," Stirling said, "it is, isn't it?"

My black Nikes were covered in rust-colored dirt. The raw, wounded earth filled the mountaintop. This hilltop had probably been just as pretty as the rest once. There was an arm bone sticking out of the dirt next to my feet. The lower arm, judging from the length. The bones were slender and still connected by a dry remnant of tissue.

Once I'd seen one bone, my eyes found more to look at. It was like one of those magic-eye pictures where you stare and stare and suddenly see what's there. I saw them all, studding the ground like hands reaching up through a river of rust.

There were a few splintered coffins, their broken halves spilling out into the air, but mostly it was just bones. I knelt and put my hands palm down on the ruined earth. I tried to get some sense of the dead. There was something faint and far-off like a whiff of perfume, but it was no good. In the bright spring sunlight I couldn't work my . . . magic. Raising the dead isn't evil, but it does require darkness. I don't know why.

I stood up, brushing my hands against the coverall, trying to clean the red dust away. Stirling was standing at the edge of the naked dirt staring off into space. There was a distance to his gaze that said he wasn't admiring the trees.

He spoke without looking at me. "I can't bully you, can I, Ms. Blake?"

"Nope," I said.

He turned to me with a smile, but it left his eyes empty, haunted. "I invested everything I had into this project. Not just my money, but clients' money. Do you understand what I am saying, Ms. Blake?''

''If the bodies up here are Bouviers, you're screwed.''

''How eloquently you put it.''

''Why are we up here alone, Mr. Stirling? Why all the skullduggery?''

He took a deep breath of the gentle air and said, ''I want you to say they aren't Bouvier ancestors even if they are.'' He looked at me when he said it. Watched my face.

I smiled and shook my head. ''I won't lie for you.''

''Can't you make the zombies lie?''

''The dead are very honest, Mr. Stirling. They don't lie.''

He took a step towards me, face very sincere. ''My entire future is riding on you, Ms. Blake.''

''No, Mr. Stirling, your future rides on the dead at your feet. Whatever comes out of their mouths will decide it.''

He nodded. ''I suppose that is fair.''

''Fair or not, it's the truth.''

He nodded again. Some light had gone out of his face, like someone had turned down the power. The lines in his face were suddenly clearer. He aged ten years in a few seconds. When he met my gaze, his dramatic eyes were woeful.

''I'll give you a piece of the profits, Ms. Blake. You could be a billionaire in a few years.''

''You know bribing won't work.''

''I knew it wouldn't work just a few minutes after we met, but I had to try.''

''You really do believe this is the Bouvier family plot, don't you?'' I asked.

He took a deep breath and walked away from me to gaze off at the trees. He wasn't going to answer my question, but he didn't have to. He wouldn't be so desperate if he didn't believe he was screwed.

''Why won't the Bouviers sell?''

He glanced back at me. ''I don't know.''

''Look, Stirling, there are just the two of us up here, nobody to impress, no witnesses. You know why they won't sell. Just tell me.''

''I don't know, Ms. Blake,'' he said.

''You're a control freak, Mr. Stirling. You've overseen every detail of this deal. You have personally seen that every 'i' was dotted, every 't' crossed. This is your baby. You know everything about the Bouviers and their problem. Just tell me.''

He just looked at me. His pale eyes were opaque, empty as a window with no one home. He knew, but he wasn't going to tell me. Why?

''What *do* you know about the Bouviers?''

''The locals think they're witches. They do a little fortune-telling, a few harmless spells.'' There was something about the way he said it, too casual, too offhand. Made me want to meet the Bouviers in person.

''They any good at magic?'' I asked.

''How am I supposed to know?''

I shrugged. ''Just curious. Is there a reason why it had to be this mountain?''

''Look at it.'' He spread his arms wide. ''It's perfect. It is perfect.''

''It is a great view,'' I said. ''But wouldn't the view be equally good over on that mountaintop? Why did you have to have this one? Why did you have to have the Bouviers' mountain?''

His shoulders slumped; then he straightened and glared at me. ''I wanted this land, and I got it.''

''You got it. Trick is, Raymond, can you keep it?''

''If you are not going to help me, then don't taunt me. And don't call me Raymond.''

I opened my mouth to say something else and my beeper went off. I fished under the coverall for it, and checked the number. ''Shit,'' I said.

''What's wrong?''

''I'm being paged by the police. I've got to get to a phone.''

He frowned at me. ''Why would the police be calling you?''

So much for being a household name. ''I'm the legal vampire executioner for a three-state area. I'm attached to the Regional Preternatural Investigation Team.''

He was looking very steadily at me. ''You surprise me, Ms. Blake. Not many people do that.''

''I need to find a phone.''

''I have a portable with a battery pack at the bottom of this damned hill.''

''Great. I'm ready to head down if you are.''

He did one last turn, taking in that breath-stealing billion-dollar view. ''Yes, I'm ready to go down.''

It was an interesting choice of words, a Freudian slip you might say. Stirling had wanted this land for some perverse reason. Maybe because he was told he couldn't have it. Some people are like that. The more you say no, the more they want you. It reminded me of a certain master vampire I knew.

Tonight I'd walk the land, visit with the dead. It would probably be tomorrow night before I actually tried to raise them. If the police matter was pressing enough, it might be longer. I hoped it wasn't pressing. Pressing usually meant dead bodies. When the monsters are involved, it's never just one dead body. One way or another, the dead multiply.

5

We got back to the valley. The construction crew was gone except for Beau the foreman. Ms. Harrison and Bayard stood next to the helicopter, as if huddling against the wilderness. Larry and the pilot stood to one side, smoking, sharing that comradery of all people who are determined to blacken their lungs.

Stirling walked towards them all, his stride firm and confident once more. He'd left his doubts on top of the mountain, or so it seemed. He was the impervious senior partner once more. Illusion is all.

''Bayard, get the phone. Ms. Blake needs to use it.''

Bayard gave a startled little jump, like he'd been caught doing something he shouldn't have. Ms. Harrison looked a little flushed. Was there romance in the air? And was that not allowed? No fraternizing among the flunkies.

Bayard ran off across the dirt towards the last car. He fetched what looked like a small, black leather backpack with a handle. He pulled a phone out and handed it to me. It looked like an antennaed walkie-talkie.

Larry walked over smelling of smoke. ''What's up?''

''I got beeped.''

''Bert?''

I shook my head. ''Police.'' I walked a little ways from our group. Larry was polite enough to stay with them, though he didn't have to. I dialed Dolph's number. Detective Sergeant Rudolf Storr was head of the Regional Preternatural Investigation Team.

He answered on the second ring. ''Anita?''

''Yeah, Dolph, it's me. What's up?''

''Three dead bodies.''

''Three? Shit,'' I said.

''Yeah,'' he said.

''I can't be there soon, Dolph.''

''Yes, you can,'' he said.

There was something in his voice. ''What's that supposed to mean?''

''The victims are right near you.''

''Near Branson?''

''Twenty-five minutes east of Branson,'' he said.

''I'm already forty miles from Branson in the middle of freaking nowhere.''

''The middle of nowhere is where this one is,'' Dolph said.

''Are you guys flying up?'' I asked.

''No, we got a vampire victim in town.''

''Jesus, are the other three vamp victims?''

''I don't think so,'' he said.

''What do you mean, you don't think so?'' I asked.

''Missouri State Highway Patrol has this one. Sergeant Freemont is the investigator in charge. She doesn't think it was a vampire because the bodies are cut up. Pieces of the bodies are missing. I had to do a lot of tap dancing to get that much information out of her. Sergeant Freemont seems convinced that RPIT is going to come in and steal all the glory. She was particularly worried about our headline-stealing pet zombie queen.''

''It's the pet part that I mind the most,'' I said. ''But she sounds charming.''

''I'll bet she's even more charming in person,'' Dolph said.

''And I get to meet her?''

''Given the choice between a large chunk of the squad coming down later and just you right now, she chose you. I think she sees you alone, without us to back you up, as the lesser evil.''

''Nice to be the lesser evil for a change,'' I said.

''You might get upgraded,'' Dolph said. ''She doesn't know you too well yet.''

''Thanks for the vote of confidence. Let me test my understanding here. None of you are coming up to the scene?''

''Not right away. You know we're shorthanded until Zerbrowski gets back on duty.''

''What does the Missouri State Highway Patrol think about a civilian helping them in a murder investigation?''

''I made it clear that you are a valuable member of my squad.''

''Thanks for the compliment, but I still don't have a badge to flash.''

''You may if that new federal law goes into effect,'' Dolph said.

''Don't remind me.''

''Don't you want to be a federal marshal?'' His voice was very mild. Nah, amused.

''I agreed they should license us, but giving us what amounts to federal marshal status is ridiculous.''

''You could handle it.''

''But who else? John Burke with the power of the law behind him? Give me a break.''

''It won't get passed, Anita. The pro-vampire lobby is too strong.''

''From your lips to God's ear. Unless they revoke the need for court orders of execution, it won't make killing them any easier, and they won't do that. I've already gone out of state to execute vamps. I don't need no stinking badge.''

Dolph laughed. ''If you run into trouble, give a yell.''

''I really don't like this, Dolph. I'm out here investigating a murder without any official status.''

"See, you do need a badge." I heard him sigh over the phone. "Look, Anita, I wouldn't leave you solo if we didn't have problems of our own. I've got a body on the ground here. When I can, I'll send somebody. Hell, I'd like you to come take a look at our corpse. You're our resident monster expert."

"Give me some details and I'll try to play Kreskin."

"Male, early twenties, rigor hasn't set in."

"Where's the body?"

"His apartment."

"How'd you get there so soon?"

"Neighbor heard a fight, called 911. They called us."

"Give me his name."

"Fredrick Michael Summers, Freddy Summers."

"He got any old vampire bites on his body? Healed bites?"

"Yeah, quite a few. Looks like a damn pincushion. How'd you know?"

"What's the first rule of a homicide?" I said. "You check the nearest and dearest. If he had a vamp lover, there'd be healed bite marks. The more of them, the longer the relationship has gone on. No vamp can bite a victim three times within a month without running the risk of killing them and raising them as a vamp. You can have different vamps bite somebody, but that would make Freddy a vampire junkie. Ask the neighbors if there were a lot of different guys or girls going in and out at night."

"It never occurred to me that a vampire could be someone's nearest and dearest," Dolph said.

"Legally, they're people. Means they get to have sweethearts, too."

"I'll check the bite radiuses," Dolph said, "If they match one vamp, a lover; different ones, and our boy was doing groups."

"Hope for a lover," I said. "If it's all one vamp, he might even rise from the dead."

"Most vamps know enough to slit the throat or take the head," he said.

"Doesn't sound well planned. Crime of passion, maybe."

"Maybe. Freemont is holding the bodies for you. Eagerly awaiting your expertise."

"I bet."

"Don't bust Freemont's balls on this, Anita."

"I won't start anything, Dolph."

"Be polite," he said.

"Always," I said in my mildest voice.

He sighed. "Try to remember that the staties may never have seen bodies with pieces missing."

It was my turn to sigh. "I'll be good, scout's honor. Do you have directions?" I got a small notebook with a pen stuck in its spiral top out of a pocket of the coverall. I'd started carrying notebooks just for such occasions.

He gave me what Freemont had given him. "If you see anything fishy at the crime scene, keep the scene intact and I'll try to send some people down. Otherwise, look over the victim, give the staties your opinion, and let them do their job."

"You really think Freemont would let me close up her shop and force her to wait for RPIT?"

Silence for a second; then, "Do the best you can, Anita. Call if we can do anything from this end."

"Yeah, sure."

"I'd rather have you on a murder than a lot of the cops I know," Dolph said.

That was a very big compliment coming from Dolph. He is the world's ultimate policeman. "Thanks, Dolph."

I was talking to empty air. Dolph had hung up. He was always doing that. I hit the button, turning the phone off, and just stood there for a minute.

I didn't like being out here in unfamiliar territory with unfamiliar police, and partially eaten victims. Hanging around with the Spook Squad legitimized me. I'd even pulled that "I'm with the squad" at crime scenes. I had a little ID badge that clipped to my clothes. It wasn't a police badge, but it did look official. But pretending on home turf, where I knew I could run to Dolph if I got in trouble for it, was one thing; out here with no backup was another story.

The police have absolutely no sense of humor about civilians meddling in their homicide cases. Can't really blame them. I wasn't really a civilian, but I had no official status. No clout. Maybe the new law would be a good thing.

I shook my head. Theoretically, I'd be able to go into any police station in the country and demand help, or involve myself uninvited in any case. Theoretically. In the real world, the cops would hate it. I'd be as welcome as a wet dog on a cold night. Not federal, not local, and there weren't enough licensed vamp executioners in the country to fill a dozen slots. I could only name eight of us; two of those were retired.

Most of them specialized in vampires. I was one of the few who would look at other types of kills. There was talk of the new law being expanded to include all preternatural kills. Most of the vampire executioners would be out of their depth. It was an informal apprenticeship. I had a college degree in preternatural biology, but that wasn't common. Most of the rogue lycanthropes, occasional trolls run amok, and other more solid beasties were taken out by bounty hunters. But the new law wouldn't give special powers to bounty hunters. Vampire executioners, most of them, worked very strictly within the confines of the law. Or maybe we just had better press.

I'd been screaming about vamps being monsters for years. But until a senator's daughter got herself attacked just a few weeks ago, nobody did shit. Now suddenly it's a cause celebre. The legitimate vampire community delivered the supposed attacker in a sack to the senator's home. They left his head and torso intact, which meant even without arms and legs he wouldn't die. He confessed to the attack. He'd been the new dead and just got carried away on a date, like any other twenty-one-year-old red-blooded male. Yeah, right.

The local hitter, Gerald Mallory, had done the execution. He's based out of Washington, D.C. He has to be in his sixties now. He still uses a stake and hammer. Can you believe it?

There had been some talk that cutting off their arms and legs would allow us to keep vamps in jail. This was vetoed mainly on the grounds of cruel and unusual punishment. It also wouldn't have worked, not for the really old vampires. It isn't just their bodies that are dangerous.

Besides, I didn't believe in torture. If cutting someone's arms and legs off and putting them in a little box for all eternity isn't torture, I don't know what is.

I walked back to the group. I handed the phone to Bayard. "I hope it isn't bad news," he said.

"Not personally," I said.

He looked puzzled. Not an uncommon occurrence for Lionel.

I talked directly to Stirling. "I've got to go to a crime scene near here. Is there someplace to rent a car?"

He shook his head. "I said you'd have a car and driver while you were here. I meant it."

"Thanks. I'm not so sure about the driver, though. This is a crime scene they won't want civilians hanging around."

"A car, then; no driver. Lionel, see that Ms. Blake gets anything she wants."

"Yes, sir."

"I'll meet you back here at full dark, Ms. Blake."

"I'll be here at dusk if I can, Mr. Stirling, but the police matter takes precedence."

He frowned at me. "You are working for me, Ms. Blake."

"Yes, but I'm also a licensed vampire executioner. Cooperation with the local police takes precedence."

"So it's a vampire kill?"

"I am not free to share police information with anyone," I said. But I cursed myself. By bringing up the word "vampire," I'd started a rumor that would grow with the telling. Damn.

"I can't leave the investigation early just to come look at your mountain. I'll be here when I can. I'll definitely look the dead over before daylight, so you won't really lose any time."

He didn't like it, but he let it go. "Fine, Ms. Blake. I will wait here for you even if it takes all night. I'm curious about what you do. I've never seen a zombie raised before."

"I won't raise the dead tonight, Mr. Stirling. We've been over that."

"Of course." He just looked at me. For some reason it was hard to meet his pale eyes. I made myself meet his gaze and didn't look away, but it was an effort. It was like he was willing me to do something, trying to compel me with his eyes like a vampire. But a vampire, even a little one, he was not.

He blinked and walked away without saying another word. Ms. Harrison toddled after him in her high heels on the uneven ground. Beau nodded at me and followed. I guess they'd all come in the same car. Or maybe Beau was Stirling's driver. What a joyous job that must be.

"We'll fly you to the hotel where we booked your rooms. You can unpack, and I'll have a car brought around for you," Bayard said.

"No unpacking, just a car. Murder scenes age fast," I said.

He nodded. "As you like. If you'll get back into the helicopter, we'll be off."

It wasn't until I was taking off the coveralls and repacking both of them that I realized I could have gone with Mr. Stirling. I could have driven out of here, instead of flying. Shit.

6

Bayard had gotten us a black Jeep with black-tinted windows and more bells and whistles than I could even guess at. I'd been worried they'd saddle me with a Cadillac or something equally ridiculous. Bayard had given me the keys with the comment, "Some of these roads are not even paved. I thought you might need something more substantial than just a car."

I resisted the urge to pat him on the head and say "Good flunkie." Hell, he'd made a great choice. Maybe he'd make full partner someday after all.

The trees made long, thin shadows across the road. In the valleys between mountains, the sunlight had softened to a late-afternoon haze. We might make it back to the graveyard by full dark.

Yes, we. Larry sat beside me in his wrinkled blue suit. The cops wouldn't mind his cheap suit. My outfit, on the other hand, might raise a few eyebrows. There aren't many female cops out in the boonies. And fewer who wear short red skirts. I was beginning to really regret my choice of clothes. Insecure: who, me?

Larry's face was shiny with excitement. His eyes sparkled like a kid's on Christmas Day. He was drumming his fingers on the armrest. Nervous tension.

"How you doing?"

"I've never been to a murder scene before," he said.

"There's always a first time."

"Thanks for letting me come along."

"Just remember the rules."

He laughed. "Don't touch anything. Don't walk through the blood. Don't speak unless spoken to." He frowned. "Why the last? I understand all the others, but why can't I talk?"

"I'm a member of the Regional Preternatural Investigation Team. You're not. If you go around saying golly gee whiz a dead body, they may catch on."

"I won't embarrass you." He sounded insulted; then a thought occurred to him. "Are we impersonating police officers?"

"No. Keep repeating I'm a member of the Spook Squad, I'm a member of the Spook Squad, I'm a member of the Spook Squad."

''But I'm not,'' he said.

''That's why I don't want you talking.''

''Oh,'' he said. He settled back into his seat, a little of the shine dimming around the edges. ''I've never actually seen a freshly dead body before.''

''You raise the dead for a living, Larry. You see corpses all the time.''

''It's not the same thing, Anita.'' He sounded grumpy.

I glanced at him. He had slumped down as far into the seat as the seat belt would allow, arms crossed over his chest. We were at the crest of a hill. A band of sunlight fell like an explosion over his orange hair. His blue eyes looked translucent for a moment as we passed from light into shadow. He looked all scrunched and sulky.

''Have you ever seen a dead person outside of a funeral or a freshly raised zombie?''

He was quiet for a minute. I concentrated on driving, letting the silence fill the Jeep. It was a comfortable silence, at least for me.

''No,'' he said at last. He sounded like a little boy who had been told he couldn't go outside and play.

''I'm not always good around fresh bodies either,'' I said.

He looked at me sort of sideways. ''What do you mean?''

It was my turn to scrunch into the seat. I fought the urge and sat up straighter. ''I threw up on a murder victim once.'' Even saying it very fast, it was still embarrassing.

Larry scooted up in his seat, grinning. ''You're just telling me that to make me feel better.''

''Would I tell a story like that about myself if it wasn't true?'' I asked.

''You really threw up on a body at a crime scene?''

''You don't have to sound so happy about it,'' I said.

He giggled. I swear he giggled. ''I don't think I'll throw up on the body.''

I shrugged. ''Three bodies, with parts missing. Don't make promises you can't keep.''

He swallowed loud enough for me to hear it. ''What do they mean, parts missing?''

''We'll find out,'' I said. ''This isn't part of your job description, Larry. I get paid for helping the cops; you don't.''

''Will it be awful?'' His voice was low, uncertain.

Chopped-up bodies. Was he kidding? ''I don't know until we get there.''

''But what do you think?'' He was staring at me very earnestly.

I glanced back at the road, then at Larry. He looked very solemn, like a relative who'd asked the doctor for the truth. If he would be brave, I could be truthful. ''Yeah, it'll be awful.''

7

It was awful. Larry had managed to stagger from the crime scene before he threw up. The only comfort I could offer him was that he wasn't the only one. Some of the cops were looking a little green around the edges, too. I hadn't thrown up yet, but I was keeping it as an option for later.

The bodies lay in a small hollow near the base of a hill. The ground was nearly knee-deep with leaves. Nobody rakes in the woods. The drought had dried the leaves to a fine, biting crunch underfoot. The hollow was ringed by naked trees and bushes with branches like thin brown whips. When the leaves came out, the hollow would be hidden on all sides.

The body nearest to me was a blond man with hair cut so short it looked like an old-fashioned butch. Blood pooled around the eyeballs, flowing from them down the face. There was something wrong with the face, besides the eyes, but I couldn't quite figure out what. I knelt in the dry leaves, glad that the leg of the coverall was protecting my hose from the leaves and the blood. Blood had pooled to either side of the boy's face, soaking into the leaves. The blood had dried to a tacky maroon substance. It looked like the teenager's eyes had been crying dark tears.

I touched the tip of my gloved fingers to the blond's chin. It moved in a boneless, wiggling movement that chins were not meant to do.

I swallowed hard and tried to take shallow breaths. I was glad it was still spring. If the bodies had been sitting this long in full summer heat, they'd have been ripe in more ways than one. Cool weather was a blessing.

I put my hands in the leaves and bent from the waist in an awkward sort of push-up motion. I was trying to see under his chin without moving the body again. There, nearly lost in the blood on the neck, was a puncture mark. A puncture mark wider than my outspread hand. I'd seen knife wounds and claw marks that could make a similar wound, but it was too big for a knife and too clean for a claw. Besides, what the hell had a claw that big? It looked like a massive blade had been shoved under the blond's chin, close enough to the front of his face to slice the eyes up from inside the head. That's why the eyes were bleeding, but still looked intact. The sword had nearly pulled the blond's face off his skull.

I ran my gloved fingers over the blond's short hair and found what I was looking for. The tip of the sword, if that's what it was, had come out the top of his head. Then the blade had been withdrawn and the blond had dropped to the leaves. Dead, I hoped, but dying I was sure of.

His legs were missing just below the hip joint. There was almost no blood where the legs had been bisected. They'd been cut off after he'd died. Small blessing, that. He'd died relatively quickly, and had not been tortured. There were worse ways to die.

I knelt by the stubs of his legs. The left bone had been cut clean with one blow. The right bone had splintered, as if the sword struck from the left side, cut the left cleanly, but only got a piece of the right leg. A second blow had been needed to sever the right leg.

Why take the legs? A trophy? Maybe. Serial killers took trophies, clothing, personal items, a body part. Maybe a trophy?

The other two boys were shorter, neither of them over five feet. Younger maybe, maybe not. They were both small and dark-haired, slender. Probably the kind of boys who looked pretty rather than handsome but, frankly, it was hard to tell.

One lay on his back almost opposite from the blond. One brown eye stared up at the sky, glassy and immobile, somehow unreal like the eyes of a taxidermy animal. The rest of his face was sliced in two huge gaping furrows, as if the tip of the sword had been used coming and going like a backhand slap. The third slice had taken out his neck. It was a very clean wound; they all were. The damn sword, or whatever it was, was incredibly sharp. But it was more than a good blade. No human could have been fast enough to take them all without a struggle. But most beasties that will kill a human being won't pick up a weapon to do it.

A lot of things will claw us apart, or eat us alive, but the list of preternatural beings that will cut us up with weapons is pretty small. A troll may tear up a tree and whap you to death, but it won't use a blade. Not only had this thing used a sword, not a common weapon, but it had some skill.

The blows to the face hadn't killed the boy. Why didn't the other two run? If the blond was killed first, why didn't this one run? Nothing was fast enough that it could take out three teenage boys with a sword before any of them could run. These were not quick blows. Whoever, or whatever, had done this had taken some time with each kill. But they all acted as if they'd been hit by surprise.

The boy had fallen onto his back in the leaves, hands clutching at his throat. The leaves had been scuffed away where his feet had kicked them. I took a shallow breath. I didn't want to probe the wounds, but I was beginning to have a nasty idea.

I knelt and traced the neck wound with my fingertips. The edges of the skin were so smooth. But it was still human flesh, human skin, blood dried to a thick stickiness. I swallowed hard and closed my eyes and let my fingers search for what I thought I'd find. The edge of the wound had two lips, starting about midway. I opened my eyes and traced the double wound with my fingers. My eyes still couldn't see it. There was too much blood. Once the wound was clean, you'd see it, but not here, not like this. The neck had been sliced twice, deeply. One cut was enough to kill. Why twice? Because they were hiding something on the neck.

Fang marks, maybe? Being killed by a vampire would explain why he hadn't tried to crawl away. He'd just lain in the leaves and kicked until he died.

I stared at the last teenager. He was crumpled on his right side. Blood had pooled under him. He was so cut up that at first my eyes didn't want to make sense of what I was seeing. I wanted to look away before my brain caught up to my eyes, but I didn't.

Where the face should have been was just a ripped, gapping hole. The creature had done the same thing to this one as to the blond, but it had been more thorough. The front of the skull had been ripped away. I glanced around, searching the leaves for the piece of bone and flesh, but didn't see it. I had to look back then, at the body. I knew what I was looking at now. I liked it better when I didn't.

The back of the skull was full of blood and gore, like a gruesome cup, but the brain was gone. The blade had sliced him open across the chest and stomach. His intestines spilled out in a thick, rubbery mass. What I thought was his stomach had spilled out from the wound like a balloon half-inflated. The left leg had been chopped off at the hip joint. The ragged cloth of his jeans clung to the hole like the petals of an unopened flower. The left arm had been ripped out just below the elbow. The bone of the humerus was dark with dried blood, sticking up at an odd angle as if the entire arm had been broken at the shoulder and no longer moved. More violent. Had this one struggled a little?

My eyes flicked back to his face. I didn't want to look again, but I hadn't really examined it. There was something horribly personal about disfiguring a person's face. If it had been humanly possible to do all this, I'd have said check their nearest and dearest. As a general rule, only people who love you will cut up your face. It implies passion that you can't get from strangers. One exception is serial killers. They're working through a pathology in which the victims can represent someone else. Someone that the killer has a personal passion for. When cutting up the faces of strangers they'd be symbolically cutting up, say, a hated father figure.

The fine bones of the boy's sinus cavities had been cracked open. The maxillary was gone, making the face look incomplete. Part of the mandible was still there, but it had been cracked apart back to the rear molars. Some trick of blood flow had left two teeth white and clean. One of the teeth had a filling in it. I stared at that ruined face. I'd been doing pretty good at thinking of it as so much meat, just dead meat. But dead meat didn't get cavities, didn't go to dentists. It was suddenly a teenager, or maybe even younger. I was only judging on height and the apparent age of the other two. Maybe this one with no face was a child, a tall child. A little boy.

The spring afternoon wavered around me. I took a deep breath to steady myself, and it was a mistake. I got a big whiff of bowels and stale death. I scrambled for the side of the hollow. Never throw up on the murder victims. Pisses off the cops.

I fell to my knees at the top of the small rise where all the cops were gathered. I hadn't exactly fallen so much as thrown myself down. I took deep, cleansing breaths of the cool air. It helped. A small breeze was blowing up here, thinning out the smell of death. It helped more.

Cops of all shapes and sizes were huddled at the top of the rise. Nobody was spending more time than they had to down among the dead. There were ambulances waiting on the distant road, but everybody else had had their piece of the bodies. They had been videotaped and trooped through with the crime scene technicians. Everybody had done their job, except me.

''Are you going to be sick, Ms. Blake?'' The voice was that of Sergeant Freemont, Division of Drug and Crime Control, DD/CC—affectionately known as D2C2. Her tone was gentle but disapproving. I understood the tone. We were the only two women at the crime scene, which meant we were playing with the big boys. You had to be tougher than the men, stronger, better, or they held it against you. Or they treated you like a girl. I was betting Sergeant Freemont hadn't gotten sick. She wouldn't have allowed it.

I took another cleansing breath and let it out. I looked up at her. From my knees she looked every inch of her five-foot-eight. Her hair was straight, dark, cut just below her chin. The ends were curled under to frame her face. Her pants were a bright sunny yellow, jacket black, blouse a softer yellow. I had a good view of her polished black loafers. There was a gold wedding band on her left hand, but no engagement ring. Deep smile lines put her on the far side of forty, but she wasn't smiling now.

I swallowed once more, trying not to taste that smell on the back of my tongue. I got to my feet. ''No, Sergeant Freemont, I'm not going to be sick.'' I was glad that it was true. I just hoped she didn't make me go back down into the hollow. I'd toss my cookies if I had to look at the bodies again.

''What did that?'' she asked. I didn't turn and look where she pointed. I knew what was down there.

I shrugged. ''I don't know.''

Her brown eyes were neutral and unreadable, good cop eyes. She frowned. ''What do you mean, you don't know? You're supposed to be the monster expert.''

I let the ''supposed to be'' go. She hadn't called me a zombie queen to my face; in fact she'd been very polite, correct, but there was no warmth to it. She wasn't impressed, and in her quiet way, with a look or the slightest inflection, she let me know. I was going to have to pull a very big corpse out of my hat to impress Sergeant Freemont, DD/CC. So far I wasn't even close.

Larry walked up to us. His face was the color of yellow-green tissue paper. It clashed with his red hair. His eyes were red-rimmed where his eyes had teared while he threw up. If it's violent enough, sometimes you cry while you vomit.

I didn't ask Larry if he was okay; the answer was too obvious. But he was on his feet, ambulatory. If he didn't faint, he'd be fine.

''What do you want from me, Sergeant?'' I asked. I'd been more than patient. For me, I'd been downright conciliatory. Dolph would be proud. Bert would have been amazed.

She crossed her arms over her stomach. ''I let Sergeant Storr talk me into letting you see the crime scene. He said you were the best. According to the newspapers, you just do a little magic and figure it all out. Or maybe you can just raise the dead and ask them who killed them.''

I took a deep breath and let it out. I didn't use magic to solve crimes, as a general rule; I used knowledge, but saying so would be defending myself. I didn't need to prove anything to Freemont. "Don't believe everything you read in the papers, Sergeant Freemont. As for raising the dead, it won't work with these three."

"Are you telling me you can't raise zombies, either?" She shook her head. "If you can't help us then go home, Ms. Blake."

I glanced at Larry. He gave a small shrug. He still looked shaky. I don't think he had the energy yet to tell me to behave myself. Or maybe he was as tired of Freemont as I was.

"I could raise them as zombies, Sergeant, but you have to have a mouth and a working throat to talk with."

"They could write it down," Freemont said.

It was a good suggestion. It made me think better of her. If she was a good cop, I could put up with a little hostility. As long as I never had to see another set of bodies like the ones below, I could put up with a lot of hostility.

"Maybe, but the dead often lose higher brain function faster after a traumatic death. They might not be able to write, but even if they could, they might not know what killed them."

"But they saw it," Larry said. His voice sounded hoarse, and he coughed gently behind his hand to clear it.

"None of them tried to run away, Larry. Why?"

"Why are you asking him?" Freemont said.

"He's in training," I said.

"Training? You brought a trainee in on my murder case?"

I stared up at her. "I don't tell you how to do your job. Don't tell me how to do mine."

"You haven't done a damn thing yet. Except for your assistant throwing up in the bushes."

An unhealthy flush crept up Larry's neck. Embarrassed when he was almost too nauseated to stand.

"Larry wasn't the only one upchucking in the weeds, just the only one without a badge." I shook my head. "We don't need this shit." I brushed past Freemont. "Come on, Larry."

Larry followed, obedient to the last.

"I don't want any of this leaked to the press, Ms. Blake. If the media gets hold of it, I'll know where it came from." She wasn't yelling, but her voice carried.

I turned. I wasn't yelling either, but everyone could hear me. "You have an unknown preternatural creature that uses a sword, and is faster than a vampire."

Something flickered across her face, like maybe I'd finally done something interesting. "How do you know it's faster than a vampire?"

"None of the boys tried to get away. All of them died where they stood. Either it's faster, or it has some amazing mind control."

"It's not a lycanthrope, then?"

"Even a lycanthrope isn't that fast, and they don't have the ability to cloud men's minds. If a lycanthrope came in there with a sword, the boys would have screamed and run. There would have at least been signs of a struggle."

Freemont just stood there looking. It was a very serious look, like she was weighing and measuring me. She still wasn't happy with me, but she was listening.

''I can help you, Sergeant Freemont. I can help you figure out what did this, maybe, before it does it again.''

Her quiet, confident mask crumbled around the edge for a second. If I hadn't been staring at her neutral brown eyes, I'd have missed it.

''Shit,'' I said, loud. I walked back over to her and lowered my voice. ''That's it, isn't it? These aren't the first killings.''

She glanced down at the ground, then met my eyes, jaw sort of thrust forward. Her eyes weren't neutral now; they were just a little bit scared. Not for herself, but for what she'd done, or not done.

''The State Highway Patrol can handle a homicide.'' Her voice was the gentlest I'd heard it.

''How many?'' I asked.

''Two before. A couple of teenagers, boy and a girl. Probably necking in the woods.'' Her voice was soft, almost tired.

''What's the M.E. say?''

''You're right,'' she said. ''It was a blade, probably a sword. The monsters don't use weapons, Ms. Blake. I thought it was the girl's ex-boyfriend. He's got a collection of Civil War memorabilia, including swords. It seemed pretty cut-and-dried.''

I nodded. ''Sounds logical.''

''None of his swords matched the blows, but I thought he'd ditched the murder weapon. I didn't think . . .'' She looked away from me, hands shoved so hard into her pants pockets I thought they'd split the cloth. ''The first scene wasn't like this. They were killed with the first blow; it pinned them through the chest into the ground. A human being could have done that.'' She looked back at me as if wanting me to agree with her. I did.

''Were their bodies cut up beyond the death wound?''

She nodded. ''Disfigured faces, her left hand missing. The one that had worn the ex-boyfriend's ring.''

''Were their throats cut?''

She frowned, thinking, then nodded. ''Hers was. Not much blood either, like it'd been done after she died.''

My turn to nod. ''Great.''

''Great?'' Larry asked.

''I think you've got a vampire on your hands, Sergeant Freemont.''

They both frowned at me. ''Look at the body parts that are missing. The legs of the one boy were cut off after he died. The femoral artery is in the thigh near the groin. I've seen vamps take blood from that in preference to the neck. Cut off the legs, and no fang marks.''

''What about the other two?'' Freemont asked.

''Maybe the smallest boy was bitten. His neck was sliced twice for no reason. Maybe it was just a little extra violence like the disfigurement of the face. I don't know. But a vamp can take blood from the wrist, the bend of the arm. All parts that are missing.''

"One of their brains is missing," Freemont said.

Larry swayed gently beside me. He wiped a hand over his suddenly sweating face.

"You going to be alright?" I asked.

He nodded, not trusting his voice. Brave Larry.

"What better way to throw us off the track than to take something a vamp wouldn't be interested in?" I said.

"Okay, say it makes some sense. Why this way? This is . . ." She spread her hands wide, staring down at the carnage. She was the only one of the three of us still looking at it. "This is nuts. If it was human, I'd say we had a serial killer on our hands."

"We may have," I said softly.

Freemont stared at me. "What the hell do you mean?"

"A vampire was a person once. Just being dead doesn't cure you of any problems you had as a live human being. If you have a violent pathology before death, that won't change just because you're dead."

Freemont looked at me like I was the one who was crazy. I think it was the word "dead" that was bothering her. Once her suspects were dead, they weren't suspects anymore. I tried again. "Say Johnny is a serial killer. He becomes a vampire. Why should being a vampire make him suddenly less violent? Why not more violent?"

"Oh, my God," Larry said.

Freemont took a deep breath in through her nose and let it out slow. "Okay, maybe you're right. I'm not saying you are. I've seen pictures of vampire victims and they don't look like this, but if you are, what do you need from me?"

"The pictures from the first crime scene. And a look at where it happened."

"I'll send the file to your hotel," she said.

"Where was the couple killed?"

"Just a few hundred yards from here."

"Let's go take a look."

"I'll have one of the troopers take you over," she said.

"This is a damn small geographic area. I assume you searched it."

"With a fine-tooth comb. But frankly, Ms. Blake, I wasn't sure what we were looking for. The leaves and the dry weather make it almost impossible to find tracks."

"Yeah," I said. "Tracks would help." I glanced back the way I'd come. The leaves were disturbed coming up the hill. "If it is a vampire . . ."

Freemont cut me off. "What do you mean, if?"

I met her suddenly accusing eyes. "Look, Sergeant, if it is a vampire it has more mind control than I've ever seen. I've never met a vampire, even a master vampire, that could hold three humans in thrall while he killed them. Until I saw this, I'd have said it couldn't be done."

"What else could it be?" Larry asked.

I shrugged. "I think it's a vamp, but if I said I was a hundred percent sure, I'd be lying. I try not to lie to the police. There may be no tracks up the hill even if the ground was soft, because the vampire could have flown in."

''Like a bat?'' Freemont asked.

''No, they don't change shape into a bat, but they can . . .'' I searched for a word and there wasn't one. ''They can levitate, sort of fly. I've seen it. I can't explain it, but I've seen it.''

''A serial killer vampire.'' She shook her head, the lines near her mouth deepening. ''The Feds are going to be all over this.''

''No joke,'' I said. ''Did you find the missing body parts?''

''No, I thought maybe it had eaten them.''

''If it ate that much, why not more? If it ate, why no teeth marks? If it ate, why not some scattered body parts, like crumbs?''

She clenched her hands into fists. ''You've made your point. It was a vampire. Even a dumb cop knows they don't eat flesh.'' She turned her brown eyes to me, and there was a lot of anger in them. Not at me, exactly, but I might make a good target. I stared back at her, not flinching. She looked away first. Maybe I wouldn't make a good target.

''I don't like having a civilian contractor in on a homicide investigation, but you spotted things down there that I missed. You're either very good, or you know something that you aren't telling me.''

I could have just said I'm good at my job, but I didn't. Didn't want the police thinking I was holding out information when I wasn't. ''I've got one advantage over a normal homicide detective, I expect it to be a monster. No one ever calls me in if it's just a stabbing, or a hit-and-run. I don't spend a lot of time trying to come up with nice, normal explanations. It means I get to ignore a lot of theories.''

She nodded. ''Alright, if you help me catch this thing, I don't care what you do for a living.''

''Glad to hear it,'' I said.

''But no reporters, no media. I am in charge here. This is my investigation. I decide when we go public. Is that clear?''

''Sure.''

She stared at me like she didn't believe me. ''I mean it about the media, Ms. Blake.''

''I don't have a problem with no media, Sergeant Freemont. I prefer it that way.''

''For a person who doesn't want the media around, you get a lot of attention.''

I shrugged. ''I'm involved in only sensational cases, detective. Cases that make good press, good sound bites. I slay vampires, for God's sake; it makes great headlines.''

''As long as we understand each other, Ms. Blake.''

''No media; it's not a hard concept,'' I said.

She nodded. ''I'll have someone walk you over to the first crime scene. I'll see you get the file at your hotel.'' She started to turn away.

''Sergeant Freemont?''

She turned back, but it was not a friendly look. ''What is it now, Ms. Blake? You've done your job.''

''You can't treat this like a human serial killer.''

"I'm in charge of this investigation, Ms. Blake. I can do what I damn well please."

I stared up at her, met her hostile eyes. I wasn't feeling too friendly myself. "I am not trying to steal your thunder here. But vampires aren't just people with fangs. If the vamp could catch their minds and hold them while he slaughtered each of them in turn, he could capture your mind, anyone's mind. A vampire that talented could make you think black was white. Do you understand me?"

"It's daylight, Ms. Blake; if it's a vampire then we find it and stake it."

"You'll need a court order of execution."

"We'll get one."

"When you get it, I'll come back and finish the job."

"I think we can handle it."

"You ever stake a vampire?" I asked.

She just looked at me. "No, but I've shot a man. It can't be that much harder."

"It's not harder in the way you mean," I said. "But it's a hell of a lot more dangerous."

She shook her head. "Until the Feds get here, I'm in charge, and not you or anyone else is taking over. Is that clear, Ms. Blake?"

I nodded. "Crystal, Sergeant Freemont." I stared at the cross-shaped pin in the lapel of her suit jacket. Most plainclothesmen had a cross-shaped tie tack. Standard police issue across the country. "You do have silver ammo, right?"

"I'll take care of my men, Ms. Blake."

I raised my hands slightly. So much for girl talk. "Fine, we're leaving. You've got my beeper number. Use it if you need it, Detective Freemont."

"I won't need it."

I took a deep breath and swallowed a lot of words. Picking a fight with the cop in charge of a murder investigation was not the way to get invited back to play. I walked past her without saying good-bye. If I opened my mouth, I wasn't sure what would come out. Nothing pleasant, and nothing useful.

8

People who don't camp much think darkness falls from the sky. It doesn't. Darkness slides from the trees and fills them first, then spreads outward to the open places. It was so dark under the trees that I wished for a flashlight. When we stumbled to the road, and our waiting Jeep, it was only dusk.

Larry looked up at the coming night, and said, "We can get back and walk the graveyard for Stirling."

"First let's eat," I said.

He looked at me. "You wanting to stop for food, that's a first. I usually have to beg for drive-up."

"I forgot to eat lunch," I said.

He grinned. "That I believe." The smile faded slowly from his face. "The first time you offer me food voluntarily, and I don't think I can eat." He stared at me. There was enough light left for me to see him search my face. "Could you really eat after what we just saw?"

I looked at him. I didn't know what to say. Not so long ago, the answer would have been no. "Well, I wouldn't want to face a plate of spaghetti, or steak tartare, but yeah, I could eat."

He shook his head. "What the heck is steak tartare?"

"Raw beef, pretty much," I said.

He swallowed hard, looking just a little paler than he had a second ago. "How can you even think of stuff like that so soon after . . ." He let the words trail off. We'd both seen it; no words were needed.

I shrugged. "I've been going to murder scenes for nearly three years, Larry. You learn to survive. Which means you learn to eat after seeing cut-up bodies." I didn't add that I'd seen worse. I'd seen human bodies reduced to a roomful of blood and gobbets of unrecognizable flesh. Not enough left to fill a gallon-size baggie. I hadn't gone out for Big Macs after that one.

"Are you up to at least trying to eat?"

He was looking at me sort of suspiciously. "Where did you have in mind?"

I untied the Nikes and stepped carefully on the gravel road. Didn't want to snag the hose. I unzipped the coverall and stepped out of it. Larry did the same, but he tried to keep his shoes on. He managed to work his feet through, but it required some hopping on one leg.

I folded my coverall carefully so the blood wouldn't touch the Jeep's immaculate interior. I tossed the Nikes into the back floorboard and got the high heels out.

Larry was trying to brush wrinkles from his suit pants, but some things only a dry cleaner could fix.

''How would you like to go to Bloody Bones?'' I asked.

He looked up at me, hands still patting at the wrinkles. He frowned. ''Where?''

''It's the restaurant that Magnus Bouvier owns. Stirling mentioned it.''

''Did he tell us where it was?'' Larry said.

''No, but I asked one of the local cops for restaurants, and Bloody Bones isn't that far from here.''

Larry squinted suspiciously at me. ''Why do you want to go there?''

''I want to talk to Magnus Bouvier.''

''Why?'' he asked.

It was a good question. I wasn't sure I had a good answer. I shrugged and climbed into the Jeep. Larry had no choice but to join me, unless he didn't want to continue the conversation. When we were all settled in the Jeep, I still didn't have a really good answer.

''I don't like Stirling. I don't trust him.''

''I got the impression you didn't like him,'' Larry said, his voice very dry. ''But why not trust him?''

''Do you trust him?'' I asked.

Larry frowned and thought about it. He shook his head. ''Not as far as I could throw him.''

''See?'' I said.

''I guess so, but you think talking to Bouvier will help?''

''I hope so. I don't like raising the dead for people I don't trust. Especially something this big.''

''Okay, so we go eat dinner at Bouvier's restaurant and talk to him; then what?''

''If we don't learn anything new, we go see Stirling and walk the graveyard for him.''

Larry was looking at me like he wasn't sure he trusted me. ''What are you up to?''

''Don't you want to know why Stirling had to have that mountain? Why the Bouviers' mountain and not someone else's?''

Larry looked at me. ''You've been hanging around the police too long. You don't trust anybody.''

''The cops didn't teach me that, Larry; it's natural talent.'' I put the Jeep in gear and off we went.

The trees made long, thin shadows. In the valleys between mountains, the shadows formed pools of coming night. We should have driven straight to the graveyard. Just walking the cemetery wouldn't hurt anything. But if I couldn't go vampire hunting, I could question Magnus Bouvier. That part of my job nobody could chase me out of.

I didn't really want to go vampire hunting. It was almost dark. Hunting vamps after dark was a good way to get killed. Especially one that could control minds like this one could. A vampire can cloud your mind and even hurt you, if its control is good enough, and you won't mind. But once its concentration is off you, onto someone else, and that person starts screaming, you'll wake up. You'll run. But the boys hadn't run. They hadn't woken up. They'd just died.

If this thing wasn't stopped, other people would die. I could almost guarantee it. Freemont should have let me stay. They needed a vampire expert with them on this one. They needed me. Okay, they really needed police with expertise in monsters, but they didn't have that. It had only been three years since Addison v. Clark made vampires legally alive. Three years ago Washington had made the bloodsuckers living citizens with rights. Nobody had thought what that meant for the police. Before the law changed, preternatural crime was handled by bounty hunters, vampire hunters. Those private citizens with enough experience to keep them alive. Most of us had some sort of preternatural power that helped give us an edge against the monsters. Most cops didn't.

Ordinarily human beings didn't fare well against the monsters. There have always been a few of us who had a talent for taking out the beasties. We've done a good job, but suddenly the cops are expected to take over. No extra training, no extra manpower, nothing. Hell, most police departments wouldn't even spring for the silver ammunition.

It had taken this long for Washington, D.C., to realize they might have been hasty. That maybe, just maybe, the monsters were really monsters and the police needed some extra training. It would take years to train the cops, so they were going to short-circuit the process, just make cops out of all the vampire hunters and monster slayers. For myself, personally, it might work. I would've loved to have a badge to shove in Freemont's face. She couldn't have chased me off then, not if it was federal. But for most vampire hunters, it was going to be a mess. You needed more than preternatural expertise to work a homicide case. You sure as hell needed more than vampire expertise to carry a badge.

There were no easy answers. But out there in the coming darkness were a bunch of police hunting a vampire that could do things I never thought they could do. If I had a badge, I could be with them. I wasn't an automatic safety zone, but I knew a damn sight more than a state cop who had "seen" pictures of vampire victims. Freemont had never seen the real thing. Here was hoping she survived her first encounter.

9

Bloody Bones bar and grill lay up a red gravel road. Someone had butchered the trees back to either side, so the Jeep climbed upward towards a black blanket of sky, sprinkled with a million stars. The shine of stars was the only light in sight.

"It is really dark out here," Larry said.

"No streetlights," I said.

"Shouldn't we see the lights from the restaurant by now?"

"I don't know." I was staring at the broken trees. The trunks gleamed white and ragged. It had been done recently, as if someone had gone mad with an axe, or maybe a sword, or something big had ripped off the trunks.

I slowed down, scanning the darkness. Was I wrong? Was it trolls? Was there a Greater Ozark Mountain Troll left in these mountains? One that would use a sword? I was a big believer in a first time for everything.

I brought the Jeep almost to a stop.

"What's wrong?" Larry asked.

I hit the emergency flashers. The road was narrow, barely two cars wide, but it was going uphill. Anybody coming down wouldn't see the Jeep right away. The lights helped, but if someone was speeding . . . Hell, I was going to do it; why quibble? I put the Jeep in park and got out.

"Where are you going?"

"I'm wondering if a troll ripped the trees apart."

Larry started to get out on his side. I stopped him. "Slide over on my side if you want to get out."

"Why?"

"You're not armed." I got the Browning out. It was a solid, comforting weight, but truthfully, against something the size of one of the great mountain trolls, it wasn't too useful. Maybe with exploding bullets, but short of that a 9mm wasn't the gun for hunting something the size of a small elephant.

Larry closed his door and slid across. "You really think there's a troll out here?"

I stared off into the darkness. Nothing moved. "I don't know." I moved to a dry gully that cut the edge of the road. I stepped very carefully into it. The heels sank in the dry, sandy soil. I grabbed a handful of weeds with my left hand and levered myself up the slope. I had to grab one of the butchered trunks to keep from sliding backwards in the loose leaves and pine needles.

My hand came up against thick sap. I fought the urge to jerk away, forcing myself to keep hold of the sticky bark.

Larry scrambled up the bank, slick-soled dress shoes sliding in the dry leaves. I didn't have a free hand to offer him. He caught himself in a sort of half push-up, and used the weeds to move up beside me. ''Damn dress shoes.''

''At least you're not in heels,'' I said.

''And don't think I'm not grateful,'' he said. ''I'd break my neck.''

Nothing moved in the dark, dark night except us. There was the sound of spring peepers close by, musical, but nothing bigger. I let out a breath I hadn't realized I was holding. I pulled myself up to more solid footing and looked at the trees.

''What are we looking for?'' Larry asked.

''An axe makes a wide, smooth stroke. If a troll snapped the trunks, they'll be ragged and full of jagged points of wood.''

''Looks smooth to me,'' he said. He ran his fingertips over the naked wood. ''But it doesn't look like an axe.''

The wood was too smooth. An axe will come in at an angle. This was almost flat, like each tree had been felled with a single stroke, two at most. Some of the trees had been nearly a foot in diameter. No human could do that, even with an axe.

''Who could have done this?''

I searched the darkness, fighting an urge to aim the gun into the dark, but I kept it skyward. Safety first. ''A vampire with a sword, maybe.''

He stared off into the darkness. ''You mean the one that killed the guys? Why would the vampire chop down a bunch of trees after he killed them?''

It was a good question. A great question. But like with so many questions today, I didn't have a good answer. ''I don't know. Let's get back to the car.''

We scrambled back the way we'd come. Neither of us fell down this time. A record.

When we were at the car I put the gun away. I probably hadn't needed it at all, but then again . . . something cut down those trees.

I used the aloe and lanolin baby wipes that I kept in the car to wipe off blood, to wipe the sap from my hand. The wipes worked nearly as well on tree blood as it did on human.

We drove on, searching for lights. We had to be close to Bloody Bones, unless the directions were way off. Here's hoping they weren't.

''Is that a torch?'' Larry asked.

I stared into the darkness. There was a flicker of fire, too high off the ground to be a campfire. Two torches on long poles illuminated a wide gravel turnaround to the left of the road. The trees had been pushed back here, too, but years ago. It was an old, established clearing. The trees formed a backdrop for a one-story building. A wooden sign hung from the eaves. It was hard to read by torchlight, but it might have read ''Bloody Bones.''

Dark wooden shingles covered the roof and climbed down the walls, so that the entire building looked like a natural growth that had sprung from the red clay soil. About twenty cars and trucks were parked haphazardly on the dark gravel.

The sign swung in the wind, the torchlight reflecting off the deeply carved words. "Bloody Bones" was carved in smooth, curving letters.

I walked carefully over the gravel in my high heels. Larry's dress shoes worked better on gravel than mine did. "Bloody Bones is a strange name for a bar and grill."

"Maybe they serve ribs," I said.

He made a face at me. "I could not face barbecue anything right now."

"It wouldn't be my first choice either."

The door swung inward directly into the bar. The door swung shut and we were plunged into a fire-shot twilight. Most bars are gloomy places to drink and hide. A place of refuge from the noisy shiny world outside. But as refuges went, this was a good one. There was a bar along one side of the room, and a dozen small tables scattered on the dark polished wood floor. There was a small stage to the left and a jukebox near the back wall where a small hallway probably led to bathrooms and the kitchen beyond.

Every surface was dark wood and polished 'til it shone. Candles with chimney glass over them shone from the walls. A chandelier with more chimney glass and candles hung from the low, dark wood ceiling. The wood was the darkest of mirrors, glowing in the light rather than reflecting it.

The beams that supported the ceiling were carved with fruiting vines and stray leaves that looked like oaks. Every face was turned towards us like a bad western. A lot of the faces were male; the eyes slid over me, saw Larry, and most went back to their drinks. A few stayed hopeful, but I ignored them. It was too early in the night for anybody to be drunk enough to give me grief. Besides, we were armed.

The women were grouped three deep at the bar. They were dressed for a Friday night, if you planned to spend Friday night on a street corner propositioning strangers. They stared at Larry like they wondered if he'd be good to eat. Me, they seemed to hate on sight. If I knew any of them, I'd have said they were jealous, but I'm not the kind of woman to elicit jealousy on sight. Not tall enough, not blonde enough, not Nordic enough, not exotic enough. I'm pretty, but I'm not beautiful. The women looked at me like they saw something I didn't. It made me glance behind me to see if someone had come in behind us, even though I knew no one had.

"What's going on?" Larry whispered.

That was another thing. It was quiet. I'd never been in a bar on a Friday night that you could whisper in and be heard.

"I don't know," I said softly.

The women at the bar parted like someone had asked, giving us a clear view of the bar. There was a man behind the bar. I thought what beautiful hair *she* had when I first saw him. The hair fell to his waist like thick, chestnut-colored water. The candle flames gleamed in his hair the same way they shone in the polished wood of the bar.

He raised startling blue-green eyes, like deep sea water, to us. He was dark and lovely rather than handsome, androgynous as a cat. He was exotic as hell and I suddenly understood why the bar was three deep in women.

He sat an amber-filled glass down on a tiny napkin and said, ''You're up, Earl.'' His voice was surprisingly low, like he'd sing deep bass.

A man got up from the tables, Earl probably. He was a large, lumbering man, formed of soft squares like a gentler version of Boris Karloff's monster. Not a cover boy. He reached for his drink, and his arm brushed the back of one of the women. The woman turned, angry. I expected her to tell him to go to hell, but the bartender touched her arm. She was suddenly very still, as if listening to voices I couldn't hear.

The air wavered. I was suddenly very aware that Earl smelled of soap and water. His hair was still damp from the shower. I could lick the water from his skin, feel those big hands on my body.

I shook my head and stepped back into Larry. He caught my arm. ''What's wrong?''

I stared at him, clutching his arm, my fingers digging through the cloth of his suit, until I could feel his arm solid under my hand. I turned back to the bar.

Earl and the woman had gone to sit at a table. She was kissing the palm of his calloused hand.

''Jesus,'' I said.

''What's wrong, Anita?'' Larry asked.

I took a deep breath and stood away from him. ''I'm okay; it was just unexpected.''

''What was?''

''Magic.'' I stepped up to the bar.

Those amazing eyes stared back at me, but there was no power to them. It wasn't like dealing with a vampire. I could gaze into those beautiful eyes forever, and they would still just be eyes. Sort of.

I placed my hands on the gleaming wood of the bar. More vines and leaves curved around the edge of the heavy wood. I ran my fingers over the deep set carvings. Hand-carved, all of it.

His fingertips caressed the wood like it was skin. It was a proprietal touch, the way some men touch their girlfriends when they're into ownership. I was betting that he'd carved every inch of it.

A brunette in a dress two sizes smaller than it should have been touched his arm. ''Magnus, you don't need a stranger.''

Magnus Bouvier turned to the brunette. He trailed those caressing fingertips down her arm. She shivered. He raised her hand gently from his arm, pressing his lips to the back of her hand. ''Pick anyone you want, darlin'. You are too beautiful to be denied tonight.''

She wasn't beautiful. Her eyes were small and muddy brown, her chin too sharp, nose too large for a thin face. I was staring right at her from not a foot away, and her face smoothed. Her eyes were suddenly large and sparkling, her thin lips full and moist. It was like seeing her through one of those soft filters they used during the sixties, except more.

I glanced at Larry. He looked like he'd been hit by a truck. A slim, lovely truck. I stared out over the bar, and every other male in the place except Earl was staring at the woman in exactly the same way, as if she'd just appeared before them like Cinderella transformed by her fairy godmother. Not a bad analogy.

I turned back to Magnus Bouvier. He was not staring at the woman. He was staring at me.

I leaned into the bar, meeting his gaze. He smiled slightly. I said, "Love charms are illegal."

The smile widened. "You're much too pretty to be the police." He reached out to touch my arm.

"Touch me and I'll have you arrested for using undue preternatural influence."

"It's a misdemeanor," he said.

"Not if you're not human, it isn't," I said.

He blinked at me. I didn't know him well enough to be sure, but I think I surprised him, like I should have believed he was human. Yeah, right.

"Let's talk at a table," he said.

"Fine with me."

"Dorrie, can you take over for a few minutes?"

A woman came behind the bar. She had the same thick chestnut hair, but it was tied back from her face in a severe ponytail, high and tight on her head. The long, shining tail of hair swung as she moved, like it was alive. Her face, free of hair and makeup, was triangular, exotic, catlike. Her eyes were the same startling seawater green as Magnus's.

The men nearest the bar watched her out of the corners of their eyes, as if afraid to look directly at her. Larry stared at her open-mouthed.

"I'll watch the bar, but that's all," she said. She turned those eyes to Larry and said, "What are you staring at?" Her voice was harsh, thick with scorn.

Larry blinked, closed his mouth, and stuttered. "N-nothing."

She glared at him like she knew he was lying. I got an inkling why the men weren't staring at her.

"Dorcas, be nice to the customers."

She glared at Magnus; he smiled, but he backed down. Magnus stepped out from behind the bar. He was wearing a soft blue dress shirt untucked over jeans so faded they were almost white. The shirt hit him at nearly mid-thigh; he'd had to roll the sleeves over his forearms. Black and silver cowboy boots completed the outfit. Everything but the boots looked borrowed. He should have looked sloppy, too casual among everyone else duded up for a Friday night, but he didn't. His utter confidence made the outfit seem perfect. A woman at one of the tables grabbed the hem of his shirt as he moved past. He pulled it out of her hands with a playful smile.

Magnus led us to a table near the empty stage. He stood, letting me choose my seat; very gentlemanly of him. I sat with my back to the wall so I could see both doors and the room. It was sort of cowboyish, but magic rode the air. Illegal magic.

Larry sat to my right. He'd watched me and scooted his chair a little back from the table so he could see the room too. It was almost frightening how seriously Larry watched what I did. It would keep him alive, but it was like being followed around by a three-year-old with a carry permit. Kind of intimidating.

Magnus smiled at us both, indulgently, like we were doing something cute or amusing. I wasn't in the mood to be amusing.

''Love charms are illegal,'' I said.

''You said that already,'' Magnus said. He flashed me a smile that I think was meant to be charming and harmless. It wasn't. There wasn't anything he could do to make himself less than exotic. He sure as hell wasn't harmless.

I stared at him until the smile wilted around the edges, and he swallowed. He spread his long-fingered hands on the tabletop, staring at them. When he looked up, the smile was gone. He looked solemn, a little nervous even. Good.

''It's not a charm,'' he said.

''The hell it isn't,'' I said.

''It isn't. A spell, but nothing as mundane as a charm.''

''You're splitting hairs,'' I said.

Larry was staring at us intently. ''Was that stuff at the bar a love charm?''

''What stuff at the bar?'' Magnus's face was incredibly mild, as if he thought Larry would believe him.

Larry looked at me. ''Is he kidding? The woman went from a three to a twenty-three. It had to be magic.''

Magnus turned his attention to Larry for the first time, excluding me—and I felt excluded. It was like a ray of sunshine had moved away from me, and I was just a little colder, a little more in the dark.

I shook my head. ''Cut the glamor crap.''

Magnus turned back to me, and for a minute I felt that warmth. ''Stop it.''

''What?''

I stood up. ''Fine; let's see how funny you think you are in jail.''

Magnus encircled my wrist with his hand. His skin should have been work-roughened, but it wasn't. His skin was unnaturally soft, like living velvet. Of course, that could have been illusionary, too.

I tried to pull my hand away, but his grip tightened. I kept pulling, and he kept tightening with that certainty of someone who knew that I couldn't get away. He was wrong. It wasn't just a matter of strength, it was a matter of leverage.

I turned my wrist towards his fingers in a quick turning motion, jerking at the same time. His fingers slid over my skin trying to dig in, but it was over. My wrist felt rubbed raw where his finger had scraped along the skin. It wasn't bleeding, but it hurt anyway. It would have felt better if I rubbed it, but I wouldn't give him the satisfaction. I was, after all, a tough-as-nails vampire slayer. Besides, it would have ruined some of the effect, and I liked the surprise on Magnus's face.

''Most women don't pull away once I've touched them.''

''You use magic on me one more time, and I'll feed you to the cops.''

He stared up at me, a thoughtful look on his face. He nodded. ''You win. No more magic on you or your friend.''

''Or anyone else,'' I said. I sat back down carefully, putting a little more distance between me and him. I angled the chair just a little to one side so the grab for my gun would be smoother. I didn't think I'd have to shoot him, but my wrist was aching where he'd squeezed. I had arm wrestled with vampires and shapeshifters. I knew preternatural strength when I felt it. He had it. He could have squeezed until my bones popped out of my skin, but he hadn't squeezed fast enough. He hadn't really wanted to hurt me. His mistake.

"Oh, my customers wouldn't like the magic going away," he said.

"You can't manipulate them like this. It is illegal, and I will turn you in for it."

"But everyone knows that Friday night is lovers' night at Bloody Bones," Magnus said.

"What's lovers' night?" Larry asked.

Magnus smiled, already regaining some of his easy charm, but that flicker of warmth was gone. He was being true to his word, as far as I could tell. Even vampires couldn't work mind control on me without my knowing it. That Magnus could make me nervous.

"I make everyone beautiful or handsome, or sexy, tonight. For a few hours you can be the lover of your own dreams, and someone else's. Though I wouldn't spend the night. The glamor doesn't last that long."

"What are you?" Larry asked.

"What looks like *Homo sapiens*, can breed with *Homo sapiens*, but isn't *Homo sapiens*?" I asked.

Larry's eyes widened. "*Homo arcanus*. He's a fairie?"

"Please keep your voice down," Magnus said. He glanced around at the near tables. No one was playing much attention to us. They were too busy gazing into each other's magically enhanced eyes.

"You can't be passing for human," I said.

"The Bouviers have told the future and made love charms for centuries around here."

"You said it wasn't a love charm," I said.

"They think it is, but you know what it is."

"Glamor," I said.

"What's glamor?" Larry asked.

"It's fairie magic. It's what allows them to cloud our minds, make things seem better or worse than they are."

Magnus nodded, smiling, as if pleased that I knew so much. "Exactly; it's really a minor magic compared to some."

I shook my head. "I've read about glamor, and it doesn't work this well unless you're high court, *Daoine Sidhe*. The seelie court of fairyland doesn't interbreed with mortals often. At least not commoners. The unseelie court, on the other hand, does."

He stared at me with his beautiful eyes, looking, even without glamor, so gorgeous you wanted to touch him. Wanted to see if his hair was as luxuriant as it looked. He was like a really fine sculpture; you wanted to run your hands over it and feel the lines.

Magnus smiled gently. "The unseelie court is evil, cruel. What I do here is not evil. For one night these people can come here and be their own fantasies. They think it's love charms, and I let them. We all keep the secret of this small illegal act. The local police know. They even come down once in a while and join in."

"But it's not love charms."

"No, it's natural talent on my part. Using my own homegrown magic isn't illegal if everyone knows I'm doing it."

"So you pretend it's love charms, and everyone looks the other way because they're having a good time, but it's really fairie glamor, which isn't illegal with permission of the participants."

"Exactly," he said.

"Which makes it all legal."

He nodded. "Now if I was descended from the dark side of fairie, would I do anything to bring pleasure to so many?"

"If it suited your needs, yeah."

"Isn't there a ban on unseelie court moving to this country?" Larry asked.

"Yeah," I said.

"Not if my family moved here before the ban went into effect. The Bouviers have been here for nearly three hundred years."

"Not possible," I said. "Nobody but the Indians have been here that long."

"Llyn Bouvier was a French fur trapper. He was the first European to set foot on this land. He married into the local tribe, Christianized them."

"Bully for him. So how come you didn't want to sell to Raymond Stirling?"

He blinked at me. "It would disappoint me greatly to find out you are working for him."

"Sorry to disappoint you," I said.

"What are you?"

He hadn't asked who, he'd asked what. It was a very different question. It sort of stopped me for a second.

"I'm Anita Blake; this is Larry Kirkland. We're animators."

"I take it you don't draw cartoons," he said.

It made me smile. "No. We raise the dead; 'animate' from the Latin, to give life."

"Is that all you do?" He was staring at me very intently, like there was something written on the inside of my skull and he was trying to read it.

It was an uncomfortable level of scrutiny, but I've been stared at by the best. I met his eyes and answered. "I'm a licensed vampire executioner."

He shook his head gently. "I didn't ask what you did for a living. I asked what you were."

I frowned. "Maybe I don't understand the question."

"Perhaps you don't, but your friend asked what I was. You said I was a fairie. I ask you what you are, and you describe your job. It would be like me saying I'm a bartender."

"I don't know how to answer you, then," I said.

He was still staring at me. "Yes, you do. I can see a word in your eyes. One word."

When he said it, a word did come to mind. "Necromancer. I'm a necromancer."

Magnus nodded. "Does Mr. Stirling know what you are?"

"I doubt he'd understand even if I told him."

"Do you really have the ability to control all types of undead?" Magnus asked.

"Can you really make a hundred shoes in a single night?" I asked.

Magnus smiled. ''Wrong kind of fairie.''

''Yeah,'' I said.

''If you're working for Stirling, why are you here? I hope you didn't come here to try to persuade me to sell. I'd hate to have to say no to such a lovely woman.''

''Can the compliments, Magnus. It won't get you anywhere.''

''What would get me somewhere?''

I sighed. ''I've got too many men on my plate now.''

''That's the God's honest truth,'' Larry muttered.

I frowned at him.

''I'm not asking you out on a date. I'm asking you into my bed.''

I frowned at Magnus. No, glared was a better word. ''Not in this lifetime.''

''Sex between supernatural beings is always amazing, Anita.''

''I'm not a supernatural being.''

''Now who's splitting hairs?''

I didn't know what to say to that, so I said nothing. I rarely get in trouble with silence.

Magnus smiled. ''I've made you uncomfortable. I am sorry, but I'd never have forgiven myself if I hadn't asked. It's been a long time since I was with anyone who wasn't straight human. Let me buy you both drinks, to make up for my rudeness.''

I shook my head. ''Menus would be fine. We haven't eaten yet.''

''The meals will be on the house.''

''No,'' I said.

''Why not?''

''Because I don't particularly like you, and I don't take favors from people I don't like.''

He sat back in his chair, a strange, almost startled expression on his face. ''You are direct.''

''You have no idea,'' Larry said.

I resisted the urge to kick Larry under the table and said, ''Can we have some menus?''

He raised a hand and called, ''Two menus, Dorrie.''

Dorrie brought them over. ''I'm part owner of this place, not your waitress, Magnus. Hurry it up.''

''Don't forget that appointment I've got tonight, Dorrie.'' His voice was mild. She wasn't fooled.

''You aren't leaving me alone with these people. I will not . . .'' She glanced at us. ''I don't approve of lovers' night. You know that.''

''I'll take care of everybody before I leave. You won't have to sully your morals.''

She glared at all of us in turn. ''You're leaving with them?''

''No,'' he said.

She turned on her heel and stalked back to the bar. The men who weren't paired off watched her swaying back, carefully, not staring until she couldn't see them.

"Your sister doesn't approve of abusing glamor?" I asked.

"Dorrie doesn't approve of a lot of things."

"She has morals."

"Implying I don't," he said.

I shrugged. "You said it, not me."

"She always this judgmental?" he asked Larry.

Larry nodded. "Usually."

"Let's just order our food," I said.

Larry smiled, but he looked down at the menu.

It was a laminated piece of paper printed on both sides. I ordered a cheeseburger, well done, house fries, and a large Coke. I hadn't had caffeine in several hours; I was running low.

Larry was frowning at the menu. "I don't think I could eat a hamburger right now."

"They've got salads," I said.

Magnus laid his fingertips against the back of Larry's hand. "Something swims up behind your eyes. Something . . . awful just behind your eyes."

Larry stared at him. "I don't know what you mean."

I grabbed Magnus's wrist and pulled him away from Larry. He turned his eyes to me, but there was more than just their color to make them hard to stare at. The pupil of his eyes had spiraled down like the eye of a bird. Human eyes just didn't do that.

I was suddenly very aware that I was still holding his wrist. I drew my hand away. "Stop reading us, Magnus."

"You wore gloves, or I'd be able to tell what you'd touched," he said.

"It's an ongoing police investigation. Anything you discern by psychic means must be held confidential, or you're liable just as if you stole information out of our files."

"Do you always do that?" he asked.

"What?"

"Quote the law when you're nervous."

"Sometimes," I said.

"I saw blood, that's all. My gifts are rather limited in the area of far-seeing. You should shake Dorrie's hand. Far-seeing is her strong suit."

"Thanks, but no thanks," Larry said.

He smiled. "You are not police, or you wouldn't have threatened me with the police, but you were with them earlier. Why?"

"I thought all you saw was blood," I said.

He had the grace to look embarrassed; nice to know he could be embarrassed. "A little bit more, perhaps."

"Touch clairvoyance isn't a traditional fey power."

"Our many-times-great-grandmother was the daughter of a shaman, so the story goes."

"Getting magic from both sides of the family tree," I said. "Dirty pool."

"Clairvoyance isn't magic," Larry said.

"A really good clairvoyant will make you think it is," I said. I stared at

Magnus. The last clairvoyant who had touched me and seen blood had been horrified. He hadn't wanted to touch me again. He hadn't wanted me anywhere near him. Magnus didn't look horrified, and he'd offered to have sex with me. Different strokes for different folks.

"I'll take your order through to the kitchen myself, if you'll just decide what you want," he said.

Larry stared at the menu. "A salad, I guess. No dressing." He thought about it some more. "No tomatoes."

Magnus started to stand.

"Why won't you sell to Stirling?" I asked.

Magnus cocked his head to one side, smiling. "The land has been in our family for centuries. It's our land."

I looked at him and couldn't read his face. It could have been the absolute truth, or a bold-faced lie.

"So the only reason you don't want to be a millionaire is because of what . . . family tradition?"

The smile deepened. He leaned closer, long hair spilling forward. He whispered, and it was quiet enough that he needed to whisper. "Money is not everything, Anita. Though Stirling seems to think it is."

His face was very close, just barely far enough away for me not to complain. I could smell his aftershave, faint as if you'd have to get very near his skin to smell it, but it would be worth the effort.

"What do you want, Magnus, if it's not money?" I stared at him from too close. His long hair trailed over my hand.

"I told you what I wanted."

Even without the glamor he was trying to sweet-talk me, distract me. "What happened to the trees out by your road?" I didn't distract that easily.

He blinked long lashes. Something slid behind his eyes. "I happened."

"You cut down those trees?" Larry asked.

Magnus turned to him, and I was glad not to be staring at him from inches away. "Sadly, yes."

"Why?" I asked.

He straightened up, suddenly businesslike. "I got drunk and went on a little rampage." He shrugged. "Embarrassing, isn't it?"

"That's one word for it," I said.

"I'll go get your food. One naked salad coming up."

"You remember what I'm getting?" I asked.

"Meat burned to death; I remember."

"You sound like a vegetarian."

"Oh, no," he said. "I eat all sorts of things."

He walked away through the crowd before I could decide if I'd been insulted or not. Just as well. For the life of me, I couldn't think of a good comeback line.

10

Dorcas brought our food without a word. She seemed angry—maybe not at us, but with us. Or with everything. I sympathized. Magnus went behind the bar, spreading his own special brand of magic to his customers once more. He glanced our way and smiled but didn't come back to finish our talk. Of course; we'd been finished. I was all out of questions.

I took a bite of my cheeseburger. It was almost crispy around the edges, not a smidgen of pink in the center. Perfect.

"What's wrong?" Larry asked. He was nibbling at a lettuce leaf.

I swallowed. "Why should something be wrong?"

"You're frowning," he said.

"Magnus didn't come back to the table."

"So? He answered all our questions."

"Maybe we just don't know the right questions to ask."

"You suspect him of something now?" Larry shook his head. "You have been hanging around with cops too long, Anita. You think everyone's up to something."

"They usually are." I took another bite of burger.

Larry squinched his eyes tight.

"What's wrong with you?" I asked.

"There's juice coming out of your burger. How can you eat that after what we just saw?"

"I guess this means you don't want me to put ketchup on my fries."

He looked at me with something near physical pain on his face. "How can you make jokes?"

My beeper went off. Had they found the vampire? I hit the button, and Dolph's number flashed at me. Now what?

"It's Dolph. Eat hearty. I'll phone from the Jeep and be back."

Larry stood up with me. He put a tip on the table and left his salad nearly untouched. "I'm done."

"Well, I'm not. Have Magnus pack my meal to go." I left him staring forlornly down at my half-eaten burger.

"You're not going to eat it in the car, are you?"

"Just have it packed up." I went for the Jeep and its fancy phone.

Dolph answered on the third ring. "Anita?"

"Yeah, Dolph, it's me. What's up?"

"Vampire victim out near you."

"Shit, another one."

"What do you mean another one?"

That stopped me. "Freemont didn't call you after I talked to her?"

"Yeah, she said good things about you."

"That surprises me; she wasn't too friendly."

"How not friendly?"

"She wouldn't let me hunt vampires with her."

"Tell me," Dolph said.

I told him.

Dolph was quiet for a very long time after I finished.

"You still there, Dolph?"

"I'm here. I wish I wasn't."

"What's going on, Dolph? Why would Freemont call and tell you what a good job I'm doing, but not ask for the squad's help on something this big?"

"I bet she hasn't called the Feds either," Dolph said.

"What's going on, Dolph?"

"I think Detective Freemont is pulling a Lone Ranger on us."

"The federal boys are going to want a piece of this. The first vampire serial killer in recorded history. Freemont can't keep it to herself."

"I know," Dolph said.

"What are we going to do?"

"The body on the ground this time sounds like a straightforward vampire kill. It's classic, bite marks, no other damage to the body. Could it be a different vamp?"

"Could be," I said.

"You sound doubtful."

"Two rogue vamps in this small a geographical area, this far from a city, doesn't seem likely."

"The body wasn't cut up."

"There is that," I said.

"How sure are you that the first killer is a vamp? Is there anything else it could be?"

I opened my mouth to say no, and closed it. Anybody who could cut down all those trees in one drunken brawl could certainly cut up people. Magnus had his glamor. I wasn't sure it was capable of doing what I'd seen in the clearing, but . . .

"Anita?"

"I might have an alternative."

"What?"

"Who," I said. I hated giving Magnus up to the cops. He'd kept his secret so long, but . . . what if the question I should ask was, had he killed five people? I'd felt the strength in his hands. I remembered the clean trunks of the trees, cut by just one blow, two at most. I flashed on the murder scene. The blood, the naked bone. I couldn't rule Magnus out, and I couldn't afford to be wrong.

I gave him up to Dolph. "Can you keep the part about him being fairie out of it for a while?"

"Why?"

"Because if he didn't do it, then his life is ruined."

"A lot of people have fey blood in them, Anita."

"Tell that to the college student last year whose fiance beat her to death when he found out he was about to marry a fairie. He protested in court that he hadn't meant to kill her. The fey were supposed to be hard to kill, weren't they?"

"Not everyone is like that, Anita."

"Not everyone, but enough."

"I'll try, Anita, but I can't promise."

"Fair enough," I said. "Where's the new victim?"

"Monkey's Eyebrow," he said.

"What?"

"That's the name of the town."

"Jesus. Monkey's Eyebrow, Missouri. Let me guess. It's a small town."

"Big enough to have a sheriff and a murder."

"Sorry. Do you have directions?" I fished my small, spiral-bound notebook out of the pocket of the black jacket.

He gave me directions. "Sheriff St. John is holding the body for you. He called us first. Since Freemont wants to go it alone, we'll let her."

"You're not going to tell her?"

"No."

"I don't suppose Monkey's Eyebrow has a crime scene unit, Dolph. If we don't have Freemont come in with her people, we're going to need somebody. Can you guys come down yet?"

"We're still working our own murder. But since Sheriff St. John called us in for his murder, we'll be in the area as soon as we can get there. Not tonight, but tomorrow."

"Freemont's supposed to send over crime-scene photos from the first couple that was killed. I bet if I asked she might send over photos from the second scene, too. Show-and-tell tomorrow when you get here."

"Freemont may be suspicious about you asking for more pictures," Dolph said.

"I'll tell her I want them for comparison. She may be trying to hog the case for herself, but she wants it solved. She just wants to solve it herself."

"She's a glory hound," Dolph said.

"Looks that way."

"I don't know if I'll be able to keep Freemont out of the second case or not, but I'll try to give you some lead time, so you can look around without her breathing down your neck."

"Much appreciated."

"She said you had your assistant with you at the crime scene. Had to be Larry Kirkland, right?"

"Right."

"What are you doing bringing him to crime scenes?"

"He'll have a degree in preternatural biology this spring. He's an animator and a vampire slayer. I can't be everywhere, Dolph. If I think he can handle it, I thought it might be nice to have two monster experts."

"It might. Freemont said Larry lost his lunch all over the crime scene."

"He didn't throw up on the crime scene, just near it."

There was a moment of silence. "Better than throwing up on the body."

"I'm never going to live that down, am I?"

"No," Dolph said, "you aren't."

"Great. Larry and I will get out there as soon as we can. It's about a thirty-minute drive, maybe more."

"I'll tell Sheriff St. John you're on your way." He hung up.

I hung up. Dolph was training me never to say good-bye over the phone.

11

Larry slumped in the seat as far as the seat belt would let him. His hands were clenched tight in his lap. He stared out into the dark like he was seeing something besides the passing scenery. Images of butchered teenagers dancing in his head, I bet. They weren't dancing in mine. Not yet. I might see them in my dreams, but not awake, not yet.

"How bad will this one be?" he asked. His voice sounded quiet, strained.

"I don't know. It's a vampire victim. Could be neat, just a couple of puncture wounds; could be carnage."

"Carnage like the three boys?"

"Dolph said no, said it's classic, just bite marks."

"So it won't be messy?" His voice was squeezed down to a near whisper.

"Won't know until we get there," I said.

"You couldn't just comfort me?" His voice sounded so small, so uncertain that I almost offered to turn the Jeep around. He didn't have to see another murder scene. It was my job, but it wasn't his job, not yet.

"You don't ever have to see another murder scene, Larry."

He turned his head and looked at me. "What do you mean?"

"You've had your quota of blood and guts for one day. I can turn around and drop you back at the hotel."

"If I don't come tonight, what happens next time?"

"If you aren't cut out for this kind of work, you aren't cut out for it. No shame in that."

"What about next time?" he asked.

"There won't be a next time."

"You aren't getting rid of me that easy," he said.

I hoped the darkness hid the smile on my face. I kept it small.

"Tell me about vampires, Anita. I thought a vampire couldn't drink enough blood in one night to kill somebody."

"Pretty to think so," I said.

"They told us in college that a vampire couldn't drain a human being with one bite. Are you saying that's not true?"

"They can't drink a human dry with one bite, in one night, but they can drain one with one bite."

He frowned at me. "What's that supposed to mean?"

"They can pierce the flesh and drain the blood without drinking it."

"How?" he asked.

"Just put the fangs in, start the blood flow, and let the blood fall down your body onto the ground."

"But that's not taking blood for food, that's just murder," Larry said.

"And your point is?" I said.

"Hey, isn't that our turnoff?"

I caught a glimpse of the road sign. "Damn." I slowed down, but couldn't see over the crest of the hill. I didn't dare U-turn until I was sure there were no cars coming the other way. It was another half mile before we came to a gravel road. There was a row of mailboxes beside the road.

Trees grew so close to the road that even winter-bare they covered the one-lane road in shadows. There was no place to turn around. Hell, if a second car had come, one of us would have had to back up.

The road rose up and up, as if it were going to go straight into the sky. At the crest of the hill I could see nothing in front of the car. I had to simply trust that there was more road in front of us, rather than some endless precipice.

"Jesus, this is steep," Larry said.

I eased the Jeep forward and the tires touched road. My shoulders loosened just a little. There was a house just up ahead. The porch light was on, like they were expecting company. The bare light bulb was not kind. The house was unpainted wood with a rusting tin roof. Its raised porch sagged under the weight of the front seat of a car that was sitting by the screen door. I turned around in the dirt in front of the house that passed for a front yard. It looked like we weren't the first car to do it. There were deep wheel ruts in the powder-dry dirt from years of cars turning in and out.

By the time we got down to the end of the road, the darkness was pure as velvet. I hit the Jeep's high beams, but it was like driving in a tunnel. The world existed only in the light; everything else was blackness.

"I'd give a lot for a few streetlights right now," Larry said.

"Me, too. Help me spot our road. I don't want to drive past it twice."

He leaned forward in his seat, straining against the shoulder belt. "There." He pointed as he spoke. I slowed and turned carefully onto the road. The headlights filled the tunnel of trees. This road was just bare red earth. The dirt rose in a mist around the Jeep. For once I was glad of the drought. Mud would have been a real bitch on a dirt road.

The road was wide enough that if you had nerves of steel, or were driving someone else's car, you could drive two cars abreast. A stream cut across the road, with a ditch at least fifteen feet deep. The bridge was nothing but planks laid across some beams. No rails, no nothing. As the Jeep crept over the bridge, the planks rattled and moved. They weren't nailed in. God.

Larry was staring at the drop, his face pressed against the tinted glass. ''This bridge isn't much wider than the car.''

''Thanks for telling me, Larry. I'd have never noticed on my own.''

''Sorry.''

Past the bridge, the road was still wide enough for two cars. I guess if two cars met at the bridge they took turns. There was probably some traffic law to cover it. First car on the left gets to go first, maybe.

At the crest of the hill, lights showed in the distance. Police lights strobed the darkness like muticolored lightning. They were farther away than they looked. We had two more hills to go up and down before the lights reflected off the bare trees, making them look black and unreal. The road spilled into a wide clearing. A lawn spread up from the road, surrounding a large white house. It was a real house with siding and shutters and a wraparound porch. It was two-storied and edged with neatly trimmed shrubs. The driveway was white gravel, which meant someone had shipped it in. Narcissus edged the driveway in two thick stripes.

A uniformed policeman stopped us in the foot of the sloping drive. He was tall, big through the shoulders, and had dark hair. He shined a flashlight into the car. ''I'm sorry, miss, but you can't go up there right now.''

I flashed my ID at him and said, ''I'm Anita Blake. I'm with the Regional Preternatural Investigation Team. I was told Sheriff St. John is expecting me.''

He leaned into the open window and flashed his light at Larry. ''Who's this?''

''Larry Kirkland. He's with me.''

He stared at Larry for a few seconds. Larry smiled, doing his best to look harmless. He's almost as good at it as I am.

I had a good view of the cop's gun as he leaned into the window. It was a Colt .45. Big gun, but he had the hands for it. I caught a whiff of his aftershave; Brut. He'd leaned too far into the window to look at Larry. If I'd had a gun hidden in my lap, I could have fed it to him. He was big, and I bet sheer size saw him through a lot, but it was careless. Guns don't care how big you are.

He nodded and pulled out the car. ''Go on up to the house. Sheriff's expecting you.'' He didn't sound particularly happy about that.

''You got a problem?'' I asked.

He gave a smile, but it was sour. He shook his head. ''It's our case. I don't think we need any help; that includes you.''

''You got a name?'' I asked.

''Coltrain. Deputy Zack Coltrain.''

''Well, Deputy Coltrain, we'll see you up at the house.''

''I guess you will, Miss Blake.''

He thought I was a cop and deliberately didn't call me ''officer'' or ''detective.'' I let it go. If I really had a professional title I'd have demanded it, but getting into an argument because he wouldn't call me ''detective'' when I wasn't one seemed counterproductive.

I drove up and parked between the police cars. I clipped my ID to my lapel. We walked up the pale curve of sidewalk, and no one stopped us. We stood outside the door in a silence that was almost eerie. I'd been to a lot of murder scenes. One thing they weren't was silent. There was no static crackle of police radios, no men milling around. Murder scenes were always thick with people: plainclothes detectives, uniforms, crime scene techs, people taking photographs, video, the ambulance waiting to take the body away. We stood on the freshly swept porch in the cool spring night with the only sounds the calls of frogs. The high-pitched, peeping sound played oddly with the swirling police lights.

"Are we waiting for something?" Larry asked.

"No," I said. I rang the glowing doorbell. The sound gave a rich *bong* deep within the house. A small dog barked furiously, somewhere deep in the house. The door opened. A woman stood framed in the light from the hall, placing most of her in shadow. The police lights strobed across her face, painting in neon Crayola flashes. She was about my height with dark hair that was either naturally curly or had a really good perm. But she'd done more with it than I did, and it framed her face neatly. Mine always looked sort of unruly. She was wearing a button-down shirt with long sleeves untucked over jeans. She looked about seventeen, but I wasn't fooled. I looked young for my age, too. Heck, so did Larry. It can't just be being short, can it?

"You aren't the state police," she said. She seemed very sure of that.

"I'm with the Regional Preternatural Investigation Team," I said. "Anita Blake. This is my colleague Larry Kirkland."

Larry smiled and nodded.

The woman moved back out of the door, and the light from the hallway fell full on her face. It added five years to her age, but they were a good five years. It took me a minute to realize she was wearing very understated makeup. "Please come in, Miss Blake. My husband, David is waiting with the body." She shook her head. "It's awful."

She peered out into the colored darkness before she closed the door. "David told him to turn off those lights. We don't want everyone for miles to know what's happened."

"What's your name?" I asked.

She blushed slightly. "I'm sorry; I'm not usually this scattered. I'm Beth St. John. My husband is the sheriff. I've been sitting with the parents." She made a small motion towards a set of double doors to the left of the main entrance.

The dog was still barking behind those doors like a small furry machine gun. A man's voice said, "Quiet Raven." The barking stopped.

We were standing in an entryway that had a ceiling that soared up to the roof, as if the architect had cut a piece out of the room above us to create the sweeping space. A crystal chandelier sparkled light down on us. The light cut a rectangle out of the darkened room to our right. There was a glimpse of a cherrywood dining room set so polished it gleamed.

The hallway cut straight back to a distant door that probably led to the kitchen. Stairs ran along the wall with the double doors. The bannister and door edges were white, the carpet was pale blue, the wallpaper white with tiny blue flowers and tinier leaves. It was open and airy, bright and welcoming, and utterly quiet. If we could have found a piece of uncarpeted floor, we would have dropped a pin and listened to it bounce.

Beth St. John led us up the blue-and-white stairway. In the center of the hallway on the right-hand side was a series of family portraits. They began with a smiling couple; smiling couple and smiling baby; smiling couple and one smiling baby, one crying baby. I walked down the hallway, watching the years pass by. The babies became children, a girl and a boy. A miniature black poodle appeared in the pictures. The girl was the oldest, but only by about a year. The parents grew older, but didn't seem to mind. The parents and the girl smiled; sometimes the boy did, sometimes he didn't. The boy smiled more on the other wall, where the camera had caught him tanned with a fish, or with hair slicked back from just coming out of the pool. The girl smiled everywhere you looked. I wondered which of them was dead.

There was a window at the end of the hallway. The white drapes framed it; no one had bothered to draw them. The window looked like a black mirror. The darkness pressed against the glass like it had weight.

Beth St. John knocked on the last door to the right, next to that pressing darkness. ''David, the detectives are here.'' I let that slide. The sin of omission is a many-splendored thing.

I heard movement in the room, but she stepped back before the door could open. Beth St. John backed up into the middle of the hallway so there would be no chance of her seeing inside the room. Her eyes flicked from one picture to another, catching glimpses of smiling faces. She put a slender hand to her chest, as if she was having trouble breathing.

''I'm going to go make coffee. Do you want some?'' Her voice was strained around the edges.

''Sure,'' I said.

''Sounds good,'' Larry said.

She gave a weak smile and marched down the hallway. She did not run, which got her a lot of brownie points in my book. I was betting it was Beth St. John's first murder scene.

The door opened. David St. John was wearing a pale blue uniform that matched the one his deputy wore, but there the resemblance ended. He was about five-foot-ten, thin without being skinny, like a marathon runner. His hair was a paler, browner version of Larry's red. You noticed his glasses before you noticed his eyes, but the eyes were worth noticing. A perfect pale green like a cat's. Except for the eyes it was a very ordinary face, but it was one of those faces you wouldn't grow tired of.

He offered me his hand. I took it. He barely touched my hand, as if afraid to squeeze. A lot of men did that, but at least he offered to shake hands; most don't bother.

''I'm Sheriff St. John. You must be Anita Blake. Sergeant Storr told me you'd be coming.'' He glanced at Larry. ''Who's this?''

''Larry Kirkland.''

St. John's eyes narrowed. He stepped fully into the hallway, closing the door behind him. ''Sergeant Storr didn't mention anyone else. Can I see some ID?''

I unclipped my badge ID. He looked at it and shook his head. ''You're not a detective.''

''No, I'm not.'' I was mentally cursing Dolph. I'd known it wouldn't work.

"How about him?" He jerked his chin at Larry.

"All I have on me is a driver's license," Larry said.

"Who are you?" the sheriff asked.

"I am Anita Blake. I am part of the Spook Squad. I just don't happen to have a badge. Larry is a trainee." I fished my new vampire executioner's license out of my jacket pocket. It looked like a glorified driver's license, but it was the best I had.

He peered at the license. "You're a vampire hunter? It's a little early for you to be called in. I don't know who did it yet."

"I'm attached to Sergeant Storr's squad. I come in at the start of a case instead of the end. It tends to keep the body count down that way."

He handed back the license. "I didn't think Brewster's law had gone into effect."

Brewster was the senator whose daughter got eaten. "It hasn't. I've been working with the police for a long time."

"How long?"

"Nearly three years."

He smiled. "Longer than I've been sheriff." He nodded, almost as if he'd answered a question for himself. "Sergeant Storr said if anybody could help me solve this, it was you. If the head of RPIT has that much confidence in you, I'm not going to refuse the help. We've never had a vampire kill out here, ever."

"Vampires tend to stay near cities," I said. "They can hide their victims better that way."

"Well, no one tried to hide this one." He pushed the door open and made a little arm gesture, ushering us in.

The wallpaper was all pink roses, big old-fashioned cabbage roses. There was an honest-to-God vanity, with a raised mirror and everything, that looked like it might be an antique, but everything else was white wicker and pink lace. It looked like the room for a much younger girl.

The girl lay on the narrow bed. The bedspread matched the wallpaper. The sheets twisted up underneath her body were jellybean pink. Her head lay on the edge of the pillows, as if it had slipped to one side after she was laid on them.

The pink curtains fanned against the open window. A cool breeze crawled through the room, ruffling her thick black hair. It had been curled and styled with hair gel. There was a small red stain under her face and neck where the sheets had soaked up some blood. I was betting there was a bite mark on that side of the neck. She wore makeup not nearly as well applied as Beth St. John's, but the attempt had been made. The lipstick was badly smeared. One arm hung off into space, the hand half-cupped as if reaching for something. The nails were shiny with fresh red nail polish. Her long legs were spread-eagled on the bed. There were two fang marks high on her inner thigh—not fresh, though. Her toenails were painted to match her fingers.

She was still almost wearing the black teddy she'd started the night in. The straps had been pushed down her shoulders, exposing small, well-formed breasts. The crotch had been ripped out, or was one of the ones that snapped open, because the bottom was pushed up nearly to her waist until the teddy was little more than a belt. With her legs spread wide, she was completely exposed.

That, more than anything, pissed me off. He could have at least covered her up, not left her like some whore. It was arrogant and cruel.

Larry was standing across the room at the other window. It was open too, spilling cool air into the room.

"Have you touched anything?"

St. John shook his head.

"Have you taken any photos?"

"No."

I took a deep breath, reminding myself that I was a guest here and had no official status. I could not afford to piss him off. "What have you done?"

"Called you, and the state cops."

I nodded. "How long ago did you find the body?"

He checked his watch. "An hour ago. How did you get here so fast?"

"I wasn't ten miles away," I said.

"Lucky for me," he said.

I looked at the girl's body. "Yeah."

Larry was hugging the windowsill, gripping it with his hands. "Larry, why don't you run down to the Jeep and get some gloves out of my bag?"

"Gloves?"

"I've got a box of surgical gloves in with my animating stuff. Bring the box."

He swallowed hard and nodded. Every freckle stood out on his face like ink spots. He moved very quickly to the door and shut it behind him. I had two sets of gloves in my jacket pocket, but Larry needed air.

"This his first murder?"

"Second," I said. "How old is the girl?"

"Seventeen," he said.

"Then it's murder even if she consented."

"Consented? What are you talking about?" There was the very first hint of anger in his voice.

"What do you think happened here, Sheriff?"

"A vampire climbed in her window while she was getting ready for bed and killed her."

"Where's all the blood?"

"There's more blood under her neck. You can't see the mark, but that's where he drained her."

"That's not enough blood to kill her."

"He drank the rest." He sounded a little outraged.

I shook my head. "No single vampire can consume the entire blood supply of an adult human in one sitting."

"Then there was more than one," he said.

"You mean the bites on her thighs?"

"Yeah, yeah." He paced the pink shag carpet in quick, nervous strides.

"Those marks are at least a couple of days old," I said.

"So he hypnotized her twice before, but this time he killed her."

"It's awfully early for a teenager to be going to bed."

"Her mother said she wasn't feeling well."

That I believed. Even if you want it to happen, that much blood loss can take the sparkle out of your step.

"She fixed her hair and makeup before she went to bed," I said.

"So?"

"Did you know this girl?"

"Yes, hell yes. This is a small town, Miss Blake. We all know each other. She was a good kid, never in any trouble. You never found her parked with a boy, or out drinking. She was a good girl."

"I believe she was a good girl, Sheriff St. John. Being murdered doesn't make you a bad person."

He nodded, but his eyes were sort of wild, too much white showing. I wanted to ask how many murders he'd seen, but didn't. Whether this was his first or his twenty-first, he was sheriff.

"What do you think happened here, Sheriff?" I'd asked the question once, but I was willing to try it again.

"A vampire raped and killed Ellie Quinlan, that's what happened here." He said it almost defiantly, like he didn't believe it either."

"This wasn't rape, Sheriff. Ellie Quinlan invited her killer into this room."

He paced to the far window and stood like Larry had, staring out into the darkness. He wrapped his arms around himself like he was hugging himself. "How am I going to tell her parents, her kid brother, that she let some . . . thing make love to her? That she'd been letting it feed off her? How can I tell them that?"

"Well, in three nights, two counting tonight, Ellie can rise from the dead and tell them herself."

He turned back to me, his face pale with shock. He shook his head slowly. "They want her staked."

"What?"

"They want her staked. They don't want her to rise as a vampire."

I stared down at the still-warm body. I shook my head. "She'll rise in two more nights."

"The family doesn't want it."

"If she was a vampire, it would be murder to stake her just because her family doesn't want her to be one."

"But she's not a vampire yet," St. John said. "She's a corpse."

"The coroner will have to certify death before she can be staked. That can take a little time."

He shook his head. "I know Doc Campbell; he'll speed it along for us."

I stood there, staring down at the girl. "She didn't plan to die, Sheriff. This isn't a suicide. She's planning on coming back."

"You can't know that."

I stared at him. "I do know that, and so do you. If we stake her before she can rise from the dead, it's murder."

"Not according to the law."

''I am not going to take out the head and heart of a seventeen-year-old girl just because her parents don't like the lifestyle she's chosen.''

''She's dead, Miss Blake.''

''It's Ms. Blake, and I know she's dead. I know what she'll become. Probably better than you do.''

''Then you understand why they want it done.''

I looked at him. I did understand. There was a time when I could have done it and felt good about it. Felt like I was helping the family, freeing her soul. Now, I just wasn't sure anymore.

''Let her parents think about it for twenty-four hours. Trust me on this. They're horrified right now, and grief-stricken; are they really in a position to decide what happens to her?''

''They're her parents.''

''Yeah, and two days from now would they rather have her on her feet, talking to them, or dead in a box?''

''She'll be a monster,'' he said.

''Maybe, probably, but I think we should hold off for just a little while until they've had some time. I think the immediate problem is the blood-sucker that did this.''

''I agree, we find him and kill him.''

''We can't kill him without a court order of execution,'' I said.

''I know the local judge. I can get you a court order.''

''I bet you can.''

''What's the matter with you? Don't you want to kill him?''

I looked at the girl. If he'd really wanted her to rise as a vampire, he'd have taken the body with him. He'd have hidden her until she rose to keep her safe from people like me. If he cared for her. ''Yeah, I'll kill him for you.''

''Alright, what can we do?''

''Well, first, the killing took place just after dark, so his daytime resting place had to be very near here. Are there any old houses, caves, some place where you could hide a coffin?''

''There's an old homestead about a mile from here, and I know there's a cave down along the stream. I used to go there when I was little. We all did.''

''Here's the deal, Sheriff. If we go out into the dark after him now, he'll probably kill some of us. But if we don't try it tonight, he'll move his coffin. We might not find him again.''

''We'll look for him tonight. Now.''

''How long have you and your wife been married?'' I asked.

''Five years; why?''

''You love her?''

''Yes, we were high school sweethearts. What kind of question is that?''

''If you go out after the vampire, you may never see her again. If you've never hunted one out there at night in its own territory, you don't know what we're up against, and nothing I can tell you will prepare you for it. But think about never seeing Beth again. Never holding her hand. Never hearing her voice. We can go out in the morning. The vampire may not move its coffin tonight, or it might move from the cave to the homestead, or vice versa. We might catch it tomorrow without risking anybody's life.''

''Do you think it won't move tonight?''

I took a deep breath and wanted to lie. God knows I wanted to lie. ''No, I think it'll leave the immediate area tonight. That's probably why he came just after full dark. It gives him all night to run.''

''Then we go after him.''

I nodded. ''Okay, but we have to have some ground rules here. I'm in charge. I've done this before and I'm still alive; that makes me an expert. If you do everything I say, maybe, just maybe, we can all live until morning.''

''Except for the vampire,'' St. John said.

''Yeah, sure.'' It had been a long time since I had gone up against a vampire at night in the open. My vampire kit was at home in my closet. It was illegal to carry it with me without a specific court order of execution. I had the cross I was wearing, the two handguns, the two knives, and that was it. No holy water, no extra crosses, no shotgun. Hell, no stake and mallet.

''Do you have silver bullets?''

''I can get some.''

''Do it, and find me a shotgun and silver ammo for that too. Is there a Catholic or Episcopalian church around here?''

''Of course,'' he said.

''We need some holy water and holy wafer, the host.''

''I know you can throw the holy water on the vampire, but I didn't know you could throw the host.''

I had to smile. ''They aren't like little holy grenades. I want the host to give to the Quinlans so they can put one at every windowsill, every doorsill.''

''You think it'll come for them?''

''No, but the girl invited it in, only she can revoke the invitation, and she's dead. Until we get the bastard, better safe than sorry.''

He hesitated, then nodded. ''I'll go to the church. I'll see what I can do.'' He went for the door.

''And, Sheriff?''

He stopped and turned to me.

''I want that court order in my hands before we leave. I'm not going to be up on murder charges.''

He nodded, sort of nervously, head bobbing like one of those dogs you see in the backs of cars. ''You'll have it, Ms. Blake.'' He left, closing the door behind him.

I was left alone with the dead girl. She lay there pale and unmoving, growing colder, deader. If her parents had their way, it would be permanent. And it would be my job to make it happen. There were schoolbooks scattered beside the bed, as if she had been studying in bed before he came. I pushed one of the book covers closed with my toe, careful not to rearrange it. Calculus. She'd been studying calculus before she put on her makeup and black teddy. Shit.

12

While we waited for the court order, I talked to the family. Not my favorite thing to do, but necessary. This hadn't been a random attack, which meant they probably knew the vampire, or had known him before he died.

The living room continued the pastel theme, blue predominating. Beth St. John had made coffee. She'd shanghaied Larry into carrying up a tray. I guess she didn't want to see the body again. Couldn't say I blamed her. I'd seen bloodier murder scenes, a lot bloodier, but each death has its own peculiar poignancy. There was something very piteous about Ellie Quinlan stretched across her pink candy sheets, and I hadn't known her. Beth St. John had. Made it hard.

The family sat huddled on the white sofa. The man was broad, not fat, but square like a linebacker. He had short black hair that was going nicely grey at the sideburns. Very distinguished. His complexion was ruddy, not tanned, but colorful just the same. He was dressed in a white dress shirt unbuttoned at the neck, but sleeves still sporting their cuff-links. His face was very tight, immobile like a mask, as if underneath something entirely different was going on. He looked calm, composed, but the effort thrummed along his skin. Anger glittered in his dark eyes.

His arm was around his wife's shoulders. She leaned into him crying softly, eyes closed as if that would make it better. Her eye makeup had smeared in long, multicolored streaks like an oil slick down her cheeks. She had thick black hair done in some short, complicated style that looked too stiff to touch. She wore a long-sleeved, button-down blouse with a delicate flower pattern on it, pink predominating. Her slacks were a matching pink. Her feet were bare except for dark hose. A delicate gold cross and wedding rings were her only jewelry.

The boy was only about my height and slender as a willow. He hadn't hit his growth spurt yet, and it made him look younger than he was. His face had that soft, perfect skin that said he'd never had a pimple and shaving was a distant dream. If the girl was seventeen, he had to be at least fifteen, maybe sixteen. He could have passed for twelve. A perfect victim, except for his eyes and the way he held himself. Even in the midst of grief with the lines of tears drying on his face, he looked sure of himself, self-possessed. His eyes held a quick intelligence and a rage that would hold the bullies at bay.

His hair was the perfect black of his father's, but it was baby fine, probably the natural texture of Mrs. Quinlan's before she styled it to death.

A little black poodle was in his lap. It had barked like a machine gun, rat-a-tat-tat, yip-yip-yip until he'd picked it up and held it. A soft growl tickled out of its curly jaws.

"Hush, Raven," the boy said. He petted the dog as he said it, thus rewarding the growling. The dog growled again; he petted it again. I decided to ignore it. If the poodle got loose, I figured I could take it. I was armed.

"Mr. and Mrs. Quinlan, my name's Anita Blake. I need to ask you a few questions."

"Have you staked the body yet?" the man asked.

"No, Mr. Quinlan, the sheriff and I agreed to wait twenty-four hours."

"Her immortal soul is in jeopardy. We want it done now."

"If you still want it done tomorrow night, I'll do it."

"We want it done now." He was holding his wife very tight, fingers digging into her shoulder.

She opened her eyes and blinked at him. "Jeffrey, please, you're hurting me."

He swallowed hard and loosened his grip. "I'm sorry, Sally. I'm sorry." The apology seemed to take some of the anger out of him. The lines in his face softened. He shook his head. "We must save her soul. Her life is gone, but her soul remains. We must save that at least."

There had been a time when I believed that, too. Down to my toes I thought all vampires were evil. Now, I wasn't so sure. I knew too many of them who didn't seem that bad. I knew evil when I felt it, and that wasn't what they were. I didn't know what they were, but were they damned? According to the Catholic Church, yes, they were, and so was the girl upstairs. But then, according to the Church, so was I. I'd become Episcopalian when the church declared all animators excommunicates.

"Are you Catholic, Mr. Quinlan?"

"Yes; what difference does that make?"

"I was raised Catholic. So I understand your beliefs."

"They are not beliefs, Miss . . . What is your name?"

"Blake, Anita Blake."

"They are not beliefs, Miss Blake. They are facts. Ellie's immortal soul is in danger of eternal damnation. We must help her."

"Do you understand what you're asking me to do?" I asked.

"To save her."

I shook my head. Mrs. Quinlan was looking at me. Her eyes were very intent. I was betting I could cause a little family disagreement.

"I will put a stake through her heart and chop off her head." I left the fact out that most of my executions were done with a shotgun now, at close range. It was messy and you needed a closed coffin, but it was a lot easier on me and a quicker death for the vampire.

Mrs. Quinlan started to cry again, huddling against her husband. She buried her face against him, smearing makeup on his clean white shirt.

''Are you trying to upset my wife?''

''No, sir, but I want you all to realize that two nights from now Ellie will rise as a vampire. She'll walk and talk. Eventually, she'll be able to be around you. If I stake her, all she'll be is dead.''

''She is already dead. We want you to do your job,'' he said.

Mrs. Quinlan wouldn't look at me. Either she believed as strongly as her hubby, or she wouldn't fight him. Not even for her daughter's continued existence.

I let it go. I could stall for twenty-four hours. I doubted that Mr. Quinlan was going to change his mind. I had hopes for Mrs. Quinlan.

''Does the poodle always bark at strangers?''

They all three blinked at me like rabbits caught in headlights. The change of subject was too abrupt for their grief.

''What has that got to do with anything?'' he asked.

''There is a murderous vampire out there somewhere. I'm going to catch him, but I need your help. So please just answer my questions as best you can.''

''What does the dog have to do with it?''

I sighed and sipped my coffee. He had just found his daughter dead, murdered, raped, I'm sure he'd told himself. The horror of it cut him some slack, but he was beginning to use it up.

''The poodle barked its head off when I came to the door. Does it bark every time a stranger comes to the house?''

The boy saw what I was getting at. ''Yeah, Raven always barks at strangers.''

I ignored his parents and talked to the most reasonable person in the room. ''What's your name?''

''Jeff,'' he said. God, Jeffrey Junior, of course.

''How many times would I have to come to the house before Raven stopped barking at me?''

He thought about that, rolling his lower lip under, really thinking about it.

Mrs. Quinlan sat up, a little apart from her husband. ''Raven always barks when someone comes to the door. Even if she knows you.''

''Did she bark tonight?''

The parents frowned at me. Jeff said, ''Yeah. She barked like crazy until Ellie let her in her room just after dark. Ellie let her in, then a few minutes later Raven came back downstairs.''

''How'd you find the body?''

''Raven started barking again and wouldn't stop. Ellie didn't let her in. Ellie always lets her in. I mean, I'm not allowed in her room, but Raven gets to go in even when Ellie wants her privacy.'' He made that last word sound like he usually said it with a lot of eye-rolling.

''I knocked at the door and she didn't answer. Raven was scratching at the door. It was locked. She locked her door a lot, but she wouldn't answer.'' A tear escaped from his wide eyes. ''I went and got Dad.''

''You unlocked the door, Mr. Quinlan?''

He nodded. ''Yes, and she was just lying there. I couldn't bear to touch her.

She's unclean now. I . . ." He was choking on tears, trying so hard not to cry that his face was turning purple.

Jeff came and put his arm around his dad, leaning against his mother, the poodle still gripped in his other arm. The dog whined softly, licked the makeup from Mrs. Quinlan's face. The woman looked up and gave a choked laugh, petting the curly fur.

I wanted to leave. I wanted to let them huddle together and grieve. Hell, the death was so fresh, they hadn't gotten to grieving yet. They were still in shock. But I couldn't leave. Sheriff St. John would be back with the warrant, and I needed as much information as I could get before we braved the darkness.

Larry was sitting in the corner in a pale blue chair. He was being so quiet you'd almost forget he was there. But his eyes were eager, noticing everything, filing it all away. When I first realized he damn near memorized everything I said and did, it was intimidating. Now I counted on it.

Beth St. John came into the room with a tray of sandwiches, coffee, and soft drinks. I didn't remember anybody asking for them, but I think Beth was needing something to do besides sit here and watch the Quinlans cry. Me, too.

She set the tray on the coffee table between the couch and the love seat. The Quinlans ignored it. I took a fresh mug of coffee. Grilling grieving families always goes down better with caffeine.

The group huddle broke up. The poodle was transferred to the wife's arms, and the two men sat on either side of her. Jeffrey and Jeff looked at me with identical eyes. It was almost eerie. Genetics at work.

"The vampire had to be in the room with Ellie when she let the dog in at full dark," I said.

"My daughter would not have let in her murderer."

"If she was eighteen, Mr. Quinlan, it wouldn't be murder."

"Being made a vampire against your will is still murder, Miss Blake."

I was getting tired of everyone calling me "Miss," but the grieving father could do it a few more times. "I believe your daughter knew the vampire. I believe she let him in willingly."

"You are crazy. Beth, go get the sheriff. I want this woman out of my house."

Beth stood up uncertainly. "David's gone to get some things, Jeffrey. I . . . Deputy Coltrain's upstairs with the body, but . . ."

"Then get him down here."

Beth looked at me, then back to him. She gripped her small hands together, almost wringing them. "Jeffrey, she's a licensed vampire hunter. She's done this a lot. Listen to her."

He stood up. "My daughter was raped and murdered by some soulless, blood-sucking animal, and I want this woman out of my house, now." If he hadn't been crying at the same time, I'd have been pissed.

Beth looked at me. She was willing to stand up to him if I needed her to. Mucho points for her. "Has anyone you know vanished or died recently?" I asked.

Quinlan squinted at me. He looked confused. The change of subject again was just too abrupt. I was hoping I could distract him from throwing me out long enough to learn something.

"What?"

"Has anyone you know gone missing or died recently?"

He shook his head. "No."

"Andy's missing," Jeff said.

Quinlan shook his head again. "That boy is no concern of ours."

"Who's Andy?" I asked.

"Ellie's boyfriend."

"He is not her boyfriend," Quinlan said.

I caught Jeff's gaze. The look said it all. Andy had been a boyfriend, and dear old dad hadn't liked him one little bit.

"Why didn't you like Andy, Mr. Quinlan?"

"He was a criminal."

I raised my eyebrows. "In what way?"

"He was arrested for drug abuse."

"He smoked some pot," Jeff said.

I was beginning to wish I could just go off and talk with Jeff. He seemed to know what was going on and wasn't trying to hide it. Trick was how to manage it.

"He was a corrupting influence on my daughter, and I put a stop to it."

"And he's missing?" I asked.

"Yes," Jeff said.

"I will answer Miss Blake's questions, Jeff. I am the man of the house."

Jesus, man of the house. Hadn't heard that in a while. "I'd like to see the rest of the house in case the vampire entered somewhere other than her room. If Jeff could show me the doors, I'd appreciate it."

"I can show you around, Miss Blake," Quinlan said.

"I'm sure your wife needs you right now, Mr. Quinlan. Jeff can show me around, but only you can comfort your wife."

Mrs. Quinlan looked up at him, then at me, as if she wasn't sure she wanted to be comforted, but I knew the image would appeal to him.

He nodded. "Perhaps you're right." He touched his wife's shoulder. "Sally needs me right now."

Sally cooperated with fresh crying, using the poodle as a sort of impromptu handkerchief. The poodle squirmed and whined. Quinlan sat down and took his wife in his arms. The dog squirmed free and trotted over to Jeff.

I stood. Larry stood. I moved toward the door and looked back at the boy. Jeff stood and the poodle trotted at his side. I opened the doors and ushered us all outside. Raven the poodle eyed me suspiciously, but she came along.

I caught a last glimpse of Beth St. John gazing at the door as if she wanted to go with us, but she sat down beside the unwanted sandwiches and the cooling coffee. She sat like a good soldier. She would not abandon her post.

I closed the door, feeling cowardly. I was glad it wasn't my job to hold the Quinlans' hands. Facing the vampire even in the dark didn't seem so bad by comparison. Of course, I was still safe inside the house. Out there in the dark with the vampire, I might feel different.

13

We stood out in the entryway. The air felt cooler out here, easier to breathe. Had to be my imagination. The poodle was sniffing at my foot. She gave a low growl and Jeff picked her up, tucking her under one arm, in a familiar gesture like he'd done it a hundred times before.

''You don't really want to see the doors, do you?'' he asked.

''No,'' I said.

''Dad's all right. He's just . . .'' He shrugged. ''He's just right, and everyone else is wrong. He doesn't mean anything by it.''

''I know. He's scared right now, too. That makes everyone bitchy.''

Jeff grinned. I wasn't sure if it was the ''scared'' comment or the word ''bitchy.'' Probably didn't hear many people saying either about his dad.

''How serious were Andy and your sister?''

He glanced at the closed doors and lowered his voice just a little. ''Dad'll say not very, but they were serious. Real serious.'' He glanced at the door again.

''We can go somewhere else to talk,'' I said. ''Your choice of rooms.''

He looked at me. ''You're really a vampire hunter?'' If the circumstances had been different, he would have been enjoying himself. It's hard not to think it's cool to put stakes through people's chests.

''Yeah, and we raise zombies, too.''

''Both of you?'' He sounded surprised.

''I'm a full-fledged animator,'' Larry said.

Jeff shook his head. ''We can talk in my room.'' He led the way up the stairs. We followed.

If I'd been a cop, questioning a juvenile without a guardian or lawyer present would have been illegal, but I wasn't a cop. And he wasn't a suspect. Just gathering information, folks. Just grilling a sixteen-year-old boy about his sister's sex life. Murder investigations are never pleasant, and some of that unpleasantness has nothing to do with the corpse.

Jeff hesitated at the head of the stairs, peering down the hallway. Deputy Coltrain was standing outside Ellie's room, back stiff, hands behind his back, alert for intruders. The door was open. Too hard to stand in the room with the body, I guess. He saw Jeff and closed the door, still standing in front of it. Nice of Coltrain to make sure Jeff didn't see the body. But standing outside the closed door was not the best idea. A vampire, if it was old enough, could have come in the room behind him and opened the door before he could have drawn his gun. The undead make no noise.

I debated on whether to tell him that. I let it go. If the vamp had meant to take out more people, it could have. He could have taken out the entire family. Instead, when the dog barked he panicked and ran. This was not an ancient bloodsucker. This was someone who was new at the job. I was betting on the boyfriend, Andy, but I'd keep an open mind. Andy might have just driven to California to find fame and fortune, but I doubted it.

Jeff opened the door near the head of the stairs and went in. His room was smaller than his sister's. Being firstborn does have its advantages. The wallpaper was tan with cowboys and Indians on it. The bed had a matching spread. It was the room of a much younger person, just like his sister's. The walls were bare, no pinups, no sports figures. There was a desk stacked high with books. A small pile of clothes lay near the closet door. Raven the poodle sniffed the clothes. Jeff shooed her away and kicked the clothes into the closet and closed the door.

"Sit down anywhere you can." He pulled the desk chair out a little, then stood near the window, not sure what to do. I doubted he had many adults up to his room for a talk. Parents didn't count. Though frankly I couldn't imagine either of the Quinlans coming in for a quiet chat.

I took the chair. I figured Jeff would feel more comfortable lounging on his bed with Larry than with me. Besides, I wasn't used to wearing skirts this short yet, and every once in a while I forgot. The chair seemed safer.

Larry sat down on the bed with his back pressed against the wall. Jeff sat down next to him, propping some of the pillows into the corner for a back rest. Raven jumped up on the bed, circled his lap twice, and lay down. Cozy.

"How hot an item were Andy and your sister?" No prelims; off with the clothes.

He glanced at both of us. Larry gave him an encouraging smile. He shifted more securely against his mound of pillows and said, "Pretty hot. I mean, they hung all over each other at school."

"Embarrassing," I said.

"Yeah. I mean, she was my sister. She's only a year older than me, and there's this guy pawing her." He shook his head. He rubbed the poodle's ears, hands moving down her small curly body. He petted her like it was habit, a comfort measure.

"Did you like Andy?"

He shrugged. "He was older and sort of cool, but no, I thought Ellie could have done better."

"How so?"

"He did smoke pot and didn't have any plans for college. Andy wasn't going anywhere. It was like the fact that he loved my sister was everything. Like they'd live on love or something stupid like that."

I agreed that that was stupid. "When your dad put a stop to it, did it stop?"

He grinned at me. "No. They just started sneaking around. I think if anything, telling Ellie she couldn't see him made it worse."

"It usually does," I said. "When did Andy disappear?"

"About two weeks ago. His car went missing, too, so everybody thought he'd run off, but he wouldn't have left Ellie behind. He was sort of creepy, but he wouldn't have left her."

"Was Ellie upset at being left behind?"

He frowned, hugging the dog against his chest. Raven licked his chin with her small pink tongue. "That was the weird part. I mean, I know she had to pretend not to care in front of Mom and Dad, but even at school or out with our friends she didn't seem to care. I was kinda glad. I mean, Andy was a loser, but it was like she didn't believe he was gone or knew something the rest of us didn't. I thought he'd just gone off to find like an out-of-town job and was going to send for her."

"Maybe he did," I said.

The frown deepened between his smooth, unblemished brows. "What do you mean?"

"I think Andy may be the vampire that did your sister."

A look of disgust crumbled his face even further. "I don't believe that. Andy loved Ellie; he wouldn't kill her."

"If he's a vampire, Jeff, he wouldn't think turning her into the undead is killing her. He'd probably think of it as bringing her over."

Jeff shook his head. Raven wiggled out of his grasp as if he was squeezing too hard. She hopped off his lap and lay down on the covers. "Andy wouldn't hurt Ellie. Doesn't it hurt to die?"

"Probably," I said.

"The bushes underneath her end window are all crushed," Larry said.

I looked at him. "Say again."

He smiled, pleased with himself. "I took a look around outside. That's what took me so long when you sent me out for gloves that you didn't need. The bushes under the end window to the girl's room are all smashed like something heavy fell on them."

I had a moment to visualize Larry out in the dark all alone, unarmed except for his cross. The thought made my skin cold. I opened my mouth to yell at him and closed it. Never dress anyone down in public unless it's an object lesson. I said, "Any tracks?" I gave myself a dozen brownie points for not yelling.

"Do I look like Tonto? Besides, the ground is just grass and it's been so dry lately. I don't think there'd be any tracks." He frowned at me. "Can you track vampires?"

"Not normally, but if this one is as new as I think he is, then maybe." I nodded. "Yeah." I stood up. "I've got to go ask the deputy something. Thank you for your help, Jeff." I offered him my hand to shake. He took it. His handshake was a little uncertain, as if he wasn't used to it.

I went for the door and Larry followed.

"You will find him and kill him, even if it's Andy?" Jeff asked.

I turned back and looked at him. His dark eyes were still intelligent, still full of purpose, but there was also a little boy needing reassurance.

''Yeah, we'll find him.''

''And kill him?''

''And kill him,'' I said.

''Good,'' he said. ''Good.''

I wasn't sure if ''good'' was the word I would have chosen, but it wasn't my sister lying dead in the other room.

''You got a cross?'' I asked.

He frowned, but said, ''Yeah.''

''You wearing it?''

He shook his head.

''Get it and wear it until we catch him. Okay?''

''You think he'll come back?'' Fear glittered at the edge of his eyes.

''No, but you never know, Jeff. Just humor me.''

He got up and went to his bureau. There was a line of glittering chain on one corner of the mirror. When he picked it up, a tiny gold cross dangled from it. I watched him put it on. The dog watched it all with anxious eyes.

I smiled. ''We'll see you later.''

He nodded, fingering the cross, scared now underneath the shock. We left him in the tender care of Raven.

''You really think the vamp will come back to the house?'' Larry asked.

''No,'' I said, ''but just in case your little visit out into the dark gives him ideas, I want Jeff to at least have a cross on.''

''Heh,'' he said. ''I found a clue.''

Deputy Coltrain was watching us, but we were running out of privacy. I kept my voice down and hoped that was enough. ''Yeah, and you went out, alone, unarmed, in the dark with a vampire that had already killed once on the loose.''

''You said it was a really new vampire.''

''Not before you went out after the gloves.''

''Maybe I figured out that it was a new one all on my own,'' he said. He was looking stubborn, like far from taking my warning to heart, he just might do it again.''

''New vampires can still kill you, Larry.''

''With a cross on?''

He had a point. Very few of the new dead could get past the pain of a cross, or play enough head games to get you to take it off voluntarily.

''Fine, Larry, but where's the vampire that made him? That one may be a couple of centuries old, and it's out in the dark, too.''

He went a little pale around the edges. ''I never thought of that.''

''I did.''

He gave a shrug and had the grace to look embarrassed. ''That's why you're the boss.''

''That's right,'' I said.

''All right, all right. I promise to be good.''

"Great; now let's go ask Deputy Coltrain if he knows anyone who could track our vampire."

"Can you really track a vampire like that?"

"I don't know, but with one less than two weeks old, one that falls out a window and into some shrubs, you might be able to. They at least might be able to narrow down where we should look first."

He was grinning very broadly at me.

"Yeah, knowing it fell out the window is useful information. It might not have occurred to me to check for tracks outside the window."

If he grinned any wider, he was going to pull something.

"And if a vampire old enough to get past your cross had eaten your face, I'd have never known about the shrubs."

"Ah, Anita. I done good."

I shook my head. For all that Larry had seen of vampires, it wasn't enough. He still didn't fully appreciate what they were. He didn't have any scars yet. If he stayed in the business long enough to get his license, that would change.

God help him.

14

The wind was cool and smelled of rain. I turned my face to the soft touch of it. The air smelled of green growing things. It smelled clean and new. I stood on the grass looking upward. Ellie Quinlan's window shone like a soft yellow beacon. Ellie had opened the windows, but her father had turned on the lights. She had met her vampire lover in darkness. The better not to see him for the walking corpse he was.

I had the coverall back on, unzipped halfway so I could get to the Browning. I'd only brought an inner pants holster for the Firestar, so I shoved it into a pocket of the coveralls. Not handy for a quick draw, but better than not having it. An inner pants holster just doesn't work well with a skirt on.

Larry had his very own gun in a shoulder rig. He stood beside me shrugging his shoulders, trying to get the straps more comfortable. It isn't really uncomfortable if it's a good fit, but it isn't really comfortable either. It's sort of like a bra. They fit and they are necessary, but they are never completely comfortable.

He was wearing the extra coverall unzipped and flapping nearly to his hips. A flashlight flicked over us, glinting on Larry's cross. The light swept over me, glaring in my eyes. ''Now that you've ruined my night vision, get that damn thing out of my eyes.''

Deep masculine laughter came from behind the brilliant beam of light. Two state cops had arrived just in time to join us on the hunt. Oh, joy.

''Wallace,'' a man's voice said, ''do what the lady says.'' The voice was deep and vaguely threatening. A voice to say, ''lean on the hood of the car and spread 'em.'' And you'd do it or else.

Officer Granger walked up to us, his flashlight pointed at the ground. He wasn't as tall as Wallace, and a gut was beginning to creep over his belt, but he moved through the dark like he knew what he was doing. Like maybe he'd hunted in the dark before. Maybe not vampires but something. Maybe men.

Wallace walked over to us, flashlight swimming around us like an oversized firefly. It wasn't in my eyes, but it was still not helping my night vision.

''Turn off the flashlight . . . please,'' I said.

Wallace took a step closer, looming over me. He was tall, built like a football player, with long legs. A running back, maybe. He and Deputy Coltrain could arm wrestle later. Right now I just wanted him to back the fuck off me.

"Turn it off, Wallace," Granger said. He'd already clicked off his own.

"I won't be able to see a damn thing," he protested.

"Afraid of the dark?" I asked, smiling up at him.

Larry laughed. It was the wrong thing to do.

Wallace turned on him. "You think that's funny?" He stepped up to Larry until they were almost touching, using his size to intimidate. But Larry's like me; he's been small all his life. He'd been bullied by the best. He stood his ground.

"Are you?" Larry asked.

"Am I what?" Wallace asked.

"Afraid of the dark?"

Animating wasn't the only thing Larry was learning from me. Unfortunately for Larry, he was a boy. I could get away with being a pain in the ass and most people wouldn't take a swing at me. Larry wasn't so lucky.

Wallace balled his hands into Larry's coverall and lifted him to tiptoes. His flashlight fell to the grass, rolling around spotlighting our ankles.

Officer Granger stepped up close to them but didn't touch Wallace. Even in the dark you could see the tension in his shoulders and arms. Not from lifting Larry, but from wanting to hit him and resisting the urge.

"Ease down, Wallace. He didn't mean anything."

Wallace didn't say anything, he just pulled Larry closer to him, leaning over to put his face next to Larry's. A square of yellow light fell across his face. The muscle along the edge of his jaw was jutting out, throbbing like it would pop out of his face. There was a scar under the bone of his jawline. A scar that disappeared into the collar of his jacket.

Wallace nearly put his face nose to nose with Larry. "I-am-not-afraid-of-anything." Each word was squeezed out.

I stepped up close to him. He was bent down to intimidate Larry, so I could whisper in his ear. "Nice scar, Wallace."

He jumped like I'd bit him. He released Larry so suddenly that Larry stumbled. He whirled, one big hand raised to smash my face. At least he'd let go of Larry.

He swung at me. I swept his arm to one side and past me. He stumbled. I brought my knee up into his stomach hard. It took a lot not to follow through and really hurt him. He was a cop. One of the good guys. You don't beat up on them. I stepped back, out of reach, and hoped that one near miss had cooled him down. I could have hurt him badly in the initial rush, but now he'd be ready. Harder to hurt.

He was nearly a foot taller than me and outweighed me by more than a hundred pounds. If the fight turned serious, I was in trouble. I hoped I wouldn't regret my gallant gesture.

Wallace ended on all fours near the shrubs by the house. He got to his feet quicker than I wanted him to, but he stayed half bent over, hands on his knees. He looked up at me. I wasn't sure what his expression meant, but it wasn't completely hostile. It was more a considering sort of look, as if I'd surprised him. I get that look a lot.

"You all right now, Wallace?" Granger asked.

Wallace nodded. Hard to talk after a good gut shot.

Granger glanced at me. "You all right, Ms. Blake?"

"I'm fine."

He nodded. "Yes, you are."

Larry moved up beside me. He was standing too close. If Wallace came back at me, I would need more room to maneuver. I knew that Larry meant it as a show of support. After we got Larry's shooting up to speed, we'd have to work on some basic hand-to-hand techniques.

Why was I training him to shoot before I taught him to fight? Because you don't arm wrestle vampires. You shoot them. He would live through a beating from Officer Wallace. He wouldn't live through a vampire attack. Not if he couldn't shoot.

"Were you with him when he got that scar?" I asked.

Granger shook his head. "His first partner didn't make it."

"Vampire got him?"

He nodded.

Wallace stood up sort of slow. He arched his back just a bit, as if working the kinks out. "Nice shot," he said.

I shrugged. "It was my knee, not my fist."

"Still a good shot. I don't have any excuses good enough for what I just did."

"No," I said, "you don't."

He just looked down at the ground, then up. "I don't know what made me do it."

"Let's take a little walk." I started off into the dark without looking back, as if I had no doubt he'd follow me. This technique works more often than you think it would.

He followed me. He had stopped to pick up his flashlight, but bravely turned it off.

I stopped just short of the woods and stared off into the trees, letting my eyes adjust to the dark. I didn't look at anything in particular. I let my eyes just sort of see everything. I was looking for movement. Any movement. The tree limbs moved fitfully in the spring wind, but it was a general movement like ocean waves. The trees weren't what worried me.

Wallace tapped the darkened flashlight against his thigh. A soft *whap, whap.* I wanted to tell him to stop but didn't. If it comforted him, I could live with it.

I let the silence stretch between us. The wind picked up, filling the night with a rushing, hurrying sound. You could smell the rain on the wind.

He gripped the flashlight in both hands. I could hear his intake of breath above the wind. "What was that?"

"The wind," I said.

"Are you sure?"

"Pretty much."

"What do you want?" he asked.

"Is this the first vamp you've gone after since your partner's death?"

He looked at me. "Granger told you?"

"Yeah, but I saw your neck. I was pretty sure what had done it."

I wanted to tell him it was okay to be scared. Hell, I was scared, but he was a cop and a man, and I didn't know him well enough to know how he'd take a pep talk from me. But I had to know if he'd follow me into those woods. I had to know if I could depend on him. If he stayed this scared, I couldn't.

"What happened?" I asked. Maybe talking about it right now was the wrong thing to do, but ignoring it wasn't working very well.

He shook his head. "Headquarters says you're in charge, Ms. Blake. Fine, I'll do what I'm told. But I don't have to answer personal questions."

It was too much trouble to shrug out of the overall, and I really didn't want my arms trapped. I undid one button on my blouse and spread the cloth.

"What are you doing?"

"How good's your night vision?"

"Why?"

"Can you see the scar?"

"What are you talking about?" He sounded suspicious. Suspicious that I was crazy, maybe.

My night vision would have picked it up, but most people don't have my eyes. "Give me your hand."

"Why?"

"I am about to give you a once-in-a-lifetime offer. Just give me your damn hand."

He did, sort of hesitatingly, glancing back at the waiting men.

His hand was cold to the touch. He was one scared puppy. I traced his large, blunt fingers along my collarbone. The moment he touched the scar tissue, his hand jerked like he'd had an electric shock. I pulled my hand away, and he traced the scar again on his own.

He took his hand back, slowly, rubbing his fingers together like he was remembering the feel of my skin. "What did that?"

"Same thing that did your neck. A vampire that wasn't neat with its food."

"Jesus," he said.

"Yeah," I said. I rebuttoned my blouse. "Tell me what happened, Wallace. Please."

He looked at me for a moment longer, then nodded. "Harry, my partner, and me, we got a call that someone had found a body with its throat torn out." He made the words very bland, ordinary, but I knew he was seeing it in his head. Watching it all happen again behind his eyeballs.

"It was a construction site. Just us in the middle of the place with our flashlights. There was a sound like wind whistling, and something hit Harry. He went down with a man on top of him. He screamed, and I had my gun out. I fired into the man's back. I hit him solid three, four times. He turned on me and his face was bloody. I didn't have time to wonder why, 'cause he jumped me. I emptied my gun into him before I hit the ground."

He took a deep breath, big hands twisting back and forth on the flashlight. He was looking off into the trees, too, but not for vampires, or at least not for this one.

"He ripped my jacket and shirt like they were paper. I tried to fight him, but . . ." He shook his head. "He caught me with his eyes. He caught me with his eyes, and when he tore into my neck, I wanted him to do it, wanted it worse than I've ever wanted anything in my life."

He turned a little away from me, as if not meeting my eyes wasn't enough. "When I woke up, he was just gone. Harry was dead. The girl was dead. I was alive."

He turned to me finally, looked me straight in the eyes and said, "Why didn't he kill me, Ms. Blake?"

I looked into his earnest eyes and didn't have a good answer. "I don't know, Wallace. He wanted to make you one of them, maybe. I don't know why you and not Harry. You ever catch him?"

"The local master sent his head in a box to the station. The note apologized for his uncivilized behavior. That's what the note said, 'uncivilized behavior.' "

"It's hard to look at it as murder when you feed off humans yourself."

"Do they all do that? Feed off people?"

"I've never met one that didn't."

"Can't they eat animals?"

"Theoretically, yes. In practice it seems to lack certain nutrients." Truth was, feeding was too close to sex for most vamps. They weren't into bestiality, so they didn't feed off animals. I didn't think the sex analogy would go over well with Officer Wallace.

"Can you do this, Wallace?"

"What do you mean?"

"Can you go out into the dark and hunt vampires?"

"It's my job."

"I didn't ask if it was your job. I asked if you can go out into that darkness and hunt vampires."

"You think there's more than one?"

"Always best to assume so," I said.

He nodded. "Yeah, I guess so."

"Scared?" I asked.

"Are you?"

I looked off into the windswept night. The trees tossed and moaned in the wind. There was movement everywhere. Soon there would be rain, and what light the stars gave would be gone.

"Yeah, I'm scared."

"But you're a vampire hunter," he said. "How can you do this night after night if it scares you?"

"Doesn't it scare you to know that every time you pull over some yahoo for a traffic violation that he could be armed? You walk up on that car and never know."

"It's my job."

"And this is my job."

"But you're scared?"

"Down to my toes."

Larry called, "The sheriff's back. He's got the warrant."

Wallace and I looked at each other. "You got silver bullets?" I asked.

"Yes."

I smiled. "Then let's go. You'll be fine," I said. I believed it. Wallace would do his job. I would do my job. We would all do our jobs. And come morning, some of us would be alive and some of us wouldn't. Of course, maybe there was just the one newly dead vampire to deal with. If so, we might all see the sunrise. But I hadn't lived this long assuming the best. Assuming the worst was always safer. And usually truer.

15

I'd gotten used to the sawed-off shotgun that I had at home. Yeah, it is illegal, but it's easy to carry and makes mincemeat out of vampires. What more could a modern vampire hunter want? The Ithaca pump action 12 gauge was close.

"Why don't I get a shotgun?" Larry asked.

I just looked at him. He looked serious. I shook my head. "When you can handle the nine, we'll talk about shotguns."

"Great."

Oh, for the enthusiasm of youth. Larry was only four years younger than I was. Sometimes it seemed like a million.

"He's not going to shoot us in the back by accident, is he?" Deputy Coltrain asked.

I smiled, not sweetly. "He promised not to."

Coltrain looked at me like he wasn't sure I was kidding.

Sheriff St. John joined us at the edge of the woods. He had a shotgun, too. I had to trust that he knew how to use it. Wallace had the shotgun from their unit. His partner Granger had a wicked-looking rifle like something a sniper would carry. It looked like the wrong tool for tonight's job, and I had said so. Granger had just looked at me. I'd shrugged and let it go. It was his neck and his gun.

I looked around at them. They looked at me. Waiting for me to give the word.

"Everybody got their holy water?" I asked.

Larry patted his coverall pocket. Everyone else nodded, or mumbled yes.

"Remember the three rules of vampire hunting. One: Never, ever look them in the eyes. Two: Never, ever give up your cross. Three: Aim for the head and heart. Even with silver ammo, it won't be a killing blow anywhere else." I felt like a kindergarten teacher sending her kiddies off to a hostile playground. "Don't panic if you get bitten. The bite can be cleansed. As long as they don't mesmerize you with their eyes, you can still fight."

I looked at them, all silent, all taller than me, even Larry by an inch or two. They could all arm wrestle me and win. So why did I want to order them all into the house where'd they'd be safe? Heck, we could all go inside. Have a nice cup of hot cocoa. Tell the Quinlans their little girl would be fine. I mean, liquid diets are in with teens. Right?

I took a deep breath and let it out slow. "Let's do it, boys. We're wasting starlight." Either nobody got my John Wayne reference, or nobody thought it was funny. Hard to tell which.

I had to let St. John lead the way into the black trees. I didn't know the area. He did. But I didn't like him taking point. I didn't like it at all. I wanted to bring him back to his wife. His high school sweetheart. Five years married and still in love. Jesus, I didn't want to get him killed.

The trees closed around us. St. John threaded his way through them like he knew what he was doing. There was very little undergrowth this time of year. It made it easier, but there is still an art to going through thick woods, especially in the dark. You can't really see even with a flashlight. You have to sort of give yourself over to the trees the way you give yourself to water when you swim. You don't really concentrate on the water, or even on your own body. You concentrate on the rhythm of your body cutting, sliding through the cool liquid. For the forest you find a rhythm, too. You concentrate on sliding your body through the natural openings. Finding the place where the forest itself will let you through. If you fight it, it will fight you back. And, just like water, it can kill you. Anyone who doesn't believe that the forest is a deadly place has never been lost in one.

St. John knew how to move, and so did I. I was pretty pleased at that, actually. I'd been a city girl for a long time. Larry stumbled into me. I had to brace, or we'd have both gone down.

"Sorry," he said, pushing himself away from me.

"How ya doing up there, vampire hunter?" Coltrain called. He was bringing up the rear. I had to go second to back up St. John, and I wouldn't let Larry take rear. Coltrain had wanted it. Said he and the sheriff would guard our ass. Fine with me.

"Yell a little louder," Wallace said. "I don't think the vampire heard you."

"I don't need no statie telling me how to do my job."

"It knows we're here," I said.

That stopped them. They both looked at me. Granger, who was just ahead of Wallace, looked at me, too. I had everyone's attention.

"Even if the vampire is only a few weeks old, its hearing is incredibly acute. It knows we're here. It knows we're coming. It doesn't matter if we're quiet or have a brass band. It's all the same. We won't surprise it in the dark." It would probably surprise us, but I didn't add that part aloud. We were all thinking it anyway.

"We are wasting time here, Deputy," St. John said.

Coltrain didn't apologize or even look sorry. Wallace did. "I'm sorry, Sheriff. It won't happen again."

St. John nodded and turned without another word and led us farther into the woods.

Coltrain made a small humphing sound but let it go. Whatever he said, I didn't think Wallace would rise to bait again. At least I hoped not. I didn't care if he was scared; we had enough problems without fighting among ourselves.

The trees rustled and swayed around us. Last year's dead leaves crunched underfoot. Someone cursed softly behind me. The wind blew in a wild gust, streaming my hair back from my face. Up ahead the quality of darkness was different. We were approaching the clearing.

St. John stopped just short of the tree line. He glanced back at me. "How do you want to do this?"

I could taste the rain on the wind coming closer. If possible, I wanted us out of here before it came. Visibility sucked as it was.

"We kill it, and we get the hell back to the house. It's not a hard plan."

He nodded, as if I'd said something profound.

Wish I had.

A figure stepped in front of us. One minute nothing, the next there he was. Darkness and shadows, magic. He grabbed St. John as he went for his gun and threw him out into the clearing in a high looping arch.

I shot the vampire in the chest at almost point-blank range. He collapsed to his knees. I caught a glimpse of the whites of his eyes, like he couldn't believe it. I had to pump the shotgun to jack another shell in place.

Granger's rifle exploded behind me like a cannon. Someone screamed. I shot the vampire between the eyes. His head splattered into the leaves. I turned with the shotgun to my shoulder before the body hit the ground.

Larry was on the ground with a vamp on top of him. I had a glimpse of long brown hair before his cross flared to life in a brilliant flash of blue-white fire. She flung herself backwards with a scream, scrambling into the dark. Gone.

A vamp with long blonde hair held Granger in her slender arms, head pressed to his neck. I couldn't use the shotgun. They were pressed too close together. At this range I'd kill them both.

I dropped the shotgun into Larry's surprised lap. He was still lying on the ground, blinking. I drew the Browning and fired into the vampire's broad chest. She jerked but didn't let go of Granger. The vampire looked at me, the man still clasped to her chest. She hissed at me. I fired a round into her gaping mouth. It blew the back of her head out.

The vamp shuddered. I fired a second round into her head. She let go of Granger and fell to the leaves in convulsions. Granger just lay there. In the dark I couldn't see his face or neck. Dead or alive, I'd done all I could.

Larry was on his feet, shotgun awkward in his hands.

There was a scream, low and pain-filled. Wallace was on the ground with a slender-bodied vamp on top of him. Fangs sunk in his arm. The bone broke with a loud, brittle snap. He screamed again.

I had a glimpse of Coltrain standing, frozen, just beyond. There was movement behind him. I stared straight at it, waiting for the vampire to take shape from the shadows, but something gleamed. A dull silver blade flashed into sight. I stared straight at it, but I lost a second somehow. The next thing I knew the blade tip exploded from Coltrain's throat. I lost another second, blinking at shadows, and the vampire tore the blade from his throat and was gone. It scuttled through the trees like nothing human, unbelievably fast, like a nightmare seen from the corner of your eye.

Larry raised the shotgun to his shoulder, aimed in Wallace's direction. I grabbed it from him, and something smashed into my back and rode me into the leaves. A hand pressed my face into the dry, crackling leaves. A second hand ripped the back of my coverall so violently it wrenched one shoulder. There was an explosion just behind my head, and the vampire was gone. I rolled over, ears ringing.

Larry was standing over me with his arm extended, gun out. Whatever he'd shot was gone out in the dark.

My left shoulder was hurt, but not as badly as it might be if I didn't get up. I struggled to my feet. The vampires were gone.

Wallace was sitting up, cradling his arm. Coltrain lay on the ground without moving. A sound behind us. I turned, Browning pointed. Larry was turning too, but too slow. I sighted down the barrel, and it was St. John.

"Don't shoot. It's me."

Larry held his gun two-handed pointed at the ground. "Sweet Jesus," he said.

Amen. "What happened to you?"

"The fall knocked me out. I followed the sound of shots," St. John said.

A gust of wind slapped against us. It smelled so strongly of rain I almost felt it on my skin.

"Check Granger's pulse, Larry," I said.

"What?" Larry looked shell-shocked.

"See if he's alive." It was a messy job, and I'd have done it myself, but I trusted me more than Larry to keep the vampires away. He'd saved me once tonight, but I still trusted me more.

St. John walked past us. He touched Wallace, who nodded. "My arm's broke, but I'll live." St. John went to Coltrain's still form

Larry knelt by Granger. He switched his gun to his left hand, not the best thing to do, but I understood. Hard to check for a pulse in the dark on a throat warm with blood; better to use your dominant hand.

"I've got a pulse." He looked up, his broad smile a dim whiteness in the dark.

"Coltrain's dead," St. John said. "God help me, he's dead." He raised a hand and the skin glistened with blood, black in the dim light. "He's nearly decapitated. What did this?"

"Sword," I said. I'd seen it. Watched it happen. But all I could remember was a black shape larger than a human being. Or larger than most. A shadow with a sword was all I'd seen, and I'd been looking right at it.

Something flowed across my skin, and it wasn't the wind. Power filled the spring night like water. "There's something old out here," I said.

"What are you talking about?" St. John said.

"An ancient vampire. It's here. I can feel it." I searched the darkness, but nothing moved but the trees, the wind. There was nothing to see. Nothing to fight. But it was here and it was close. Sword in hand, maybe.

Granger sat up so suddenly that Larry fell back into the leaves with a squeak.

The big man's eyes turned to me. I saw his hand go for his gun, and I knew what the vampire was doing.

I pointed the Browning at his head and waited. I had to be sure.

Granger didn't hunt for his dropped rifle. He drew his sidearm and pointed it very slowly, as if he didn't want to do it. He pointed it at Larry from less than a foot away.

Wallace yelled, ''Granger, what the fuck are you doing?''

I fired.

Granger jerked; the gun wavered, then his hand came back up. I fired again, and again. His hand fell slowly to the ground, gun still in it. He fell straight back into the leaves.

''Granger!'' Wallace was screaming, crawling toward his partner. Shit.

I got there first and kicked the gun out of his hand. If he'd twitched, I'd have shot him again. He didn't twitch. He just lay there, dead.

Wallace tried to cradle him one-handed. ''Why'd you shoot him? Why?''

''He was going to kill Larry. You saw it.''

''Why?''

''The vamp that bit him. His master is out here. And he's a powerful son of a bitch. He used him.''

Wallace had Granger's bloody head in his lap, his own ravaged arm pressed to Granger's chest. He was crying.

Shit.

A sound rode the rising wind. A sharp, furious barking. A woman's scream, high and clear, cut across the sound.

''Oh, God,'' I whispered.

''Beth.'' St. John was on his feet running before I could say anything.

I grabbed Wallace's shoulder, pulling on his jacket. He looked up.

''What's happening?''

''They're in the house,'' I said. ''Can you walk?''

He nodded. I helped him to his feet.

Another scream came. It wasn't the same scream. A man this time, or a boy.

''Stay with him, Larry. Get to the house as soon as you can.''

''What if they're trying to split us up?'' Larry asked.

''Then it's going to work,'' I said. ''Shoot anything that moves.'' I touched his arm, as if that would make him more real, keep him safe. It wouldn't, but it was all I had. I had to go for the house. Larry had signed up to be a monster slayer. The Quinlans and Beth St. John hadn't.

I holstered the Browning, kept a two-handed grip on the shotgun, and threw myself into the trees. I ran, not trying to see where I was going. Rushing through openings in the trees that I wasn't sure were there, but they were. I jumped over a log and nearly fell but caught myself and kept running. A branch slashed my face, bringing tears to my eye. The forest that had seemed passable before was now a maze of roots and branches that grabbed and tripped. I was running blind. It was not a good way to stay alive with vampires in the dark. I spilled out onto the Quinlans' lawn on my knees, shotgun tightly gripped.

The front door was open. Light spilled in a warm rectangle. Shots sounded from inside the house. I got to my feet and ran for the light.

The poodle lay broken by the door, crumpled like someone had tried to force it into a ball.

The doors to the living room were open. A second shot sounded. I went in to the left of the door, wall at my back, shotgun ready.

Mr. and Mrs. Quinlan were huddled in the far corner with their crosses held out before them. The metal glowed with a white-hot light like burning magnesium.

The thing in front of them didn't look much like a vampire. It looked like a skeleton with muscle and flesh stretched over a bone frame. It was stretched impossibly thin and tall. A sword rode its back, gleaming and wide as a scimitar. Coltrain's killer?

St. John was firing into the brown-haired vamp from the woods. She had long brown hair parted in the middle, straight and lovely, framing a face that was blood-smeared and stretched wide over fangs.

I had a glimpse of Beth St. John on the floor behind her. She wasn't moving.

St. John kept firing into the vampire's body. She just kept coming. Blood blossomed on the front of her jean jacket. His gun clicked, empty. The vampire staggered, then fell to her knees. She fell forward on all fours, and you could see that her back was so much raw meat. She lay gasping on the floor while St. John reloaded.

I got to my feet, trying to keep an eye on the door just in case this wasn't all. I walked towards the Quinlans and the thing that stood in front of them. I needed a better angle before I used the shotgun. Didn't want to catch them in the shot pattern.

The thing turned on me. I had a glimpse of a face that was neither human nor animal, but stretched thin and alien with fangs and blind, glowing eyes. It shrank, and skin flowed over the bare flesh, covered the nearly naked bone. I'd never seen anything like it. When I aimed the shotgun, I was looking into what could have passed for a human face. Long white hair framed a fine-boned face, and it ran—if running was the word for that blur of motion. It ran like some of them flew, almost like it was doing something else altogether, but I had no better word for it. Some of them flew; this one ran. It was gone before I could pull the trigger.

I was left staring at the open door where the barrel had followed its movement. Could I have fired? Had I hesitated? I didn't think so, but I wasn't sure. It was like in the woods when Coltrain died, like I'd missed a few seconds. The vampire had to be our killer, but the only thing I'd seen clearly in the woods had been the sword.

St. John shot into the fallen vampire. He fired until his gun clicked empty again. The gun went click, click, click.

I walked over to him. The vampire's head was bloody meat and heavier, wetter things. There was no face left. ''It's dead, St. John. You killed it.''

He just stared at it, down the barrel of his empty gun. He was shaking. He collapsed to his knees suddenly, as if he just couldn't stand any longer. He crawled over to his wife, gun left behind him on the carpet. He cradled her in his arms, half-lifting, rocking her. She was soaked with blood. Her throat was so much raw meat on one side.

St. John was making a high, keening sound deep in his throat.

The Quinlans's crosses had stopped glowing. They stood still clinging to each other, blinking as if blinded by the light.

"Jeff—he took Jeff," Mrs. Quinlan said.

I looked at her. Her eyes were too wide. "He took Jeff."

"Who took Jeff?" I asked.

"The big one," Mr. Quinlan said. "That thing, that thing told Jeff to take his cross off, and Jeff did it." He looked at me with startled eyes. "Why did he do that? Why did he take it off?"

"The vampire caught him with his eyes," I said. "He couldn't help himself."

"If his faith had been stronger, he wouldn't have given in," Quinlan said.

"It wasn't your son's fault."

Quinlan shook his head. "He wasn't strong enough."

I turned away from him. Which put me staring at St. John. He had folded as much of his wife's body into his lap and arms as he could. He rocked her, eyes distant. He wasn't seeing this room. He'd gone somewhere deep inside. Someplace better. I hoped.

I went for the door. I didn't have to see this. Watching St. John rock his wife's body was not part of my job description. Honest.

I sat down on the stairs where I could see the door, the hallway, and the stairs as far as the landing. St. John started singing in a strange, broken voice. It took me a few minutes to figure out what he was singing. It was "You Are So Beautiful." I got up and went for the outer door. Larry and Wallace were just limping up onto the porch.

I just shook my head and kept walking. I was almost to the driveway before I couldn't hear the singing. I stood there taking deep breaths, letting them out slowly. I concentrated on my breathing, concentrated on the sound of frogs and wind. I concentrated on anything but the sound that was building in my throat. I stood there in the dark, in the open, knowing it was dangerous, and not sure I cared. I stood there until I was sure I wasn't going to start screaming. Then I turned and went back to the house.

It was the bravest thing I'd done all night.

16

Detective Freemont sat on one end of the Quinlans' couch and I perched on the other. We were as far away from each other as we could get and share it. Only pride kept me from taking a chair. I wouldn't flinch under her cool cop eyes. So I stayed nailed to my end of the couch, but it was an effort.

Her voice was low and careful, every word enunciated, as if she thought she might yell if she rushed the words. ''Why didn't you call and tell me you had a second vampire kill?''

''Sheriff St. John called the state cops. I assumed you'd be told.''

''Well, I wasn't.''

I stared up into her cool eyes. ''You're twenty minutes away with a crime scene unit looking into a possible vampire kill. Why wouldn't they send you over to a second vampire scene?''

Freemont's eyes shifted to one side, then back to me. Her cool cop eyes had melted just a little. It was hard to read for sure, but she looked uneasy. Maybe even scared.

''You haven't told them it was a vampire kill, have you?''

Her eyes flinched.

''Shit, Freemont. I know you don't want the Feds to steal your case, but withholding information from your own people . . . Bet your superiors aren't happy with you.''

''That's my business.''

''Fine. Whatever plan you've got, more power to you, but why are you pissed at me?''

She took a deep, shaking breath and blew it out like a runner trying to get that extra kick. ''How sure are you the vampire used a sword?''

''You saw the body,'' I said.

She nodded. ''A vampire could have ripped the neck apart.''

''I saw a blade, Freemont.''

''The ME will either back you up, or not.''

''Why don't you want this to be vampires?''

She smiled. ''I thought I had this case all solved. Thought I'd make an arrest this morning. I didn't think it was vampires.''

I stared at her. I wasn't smiling. ''If it wasn't vamps, then what was it?''

''Fairies.''

I stared at her for a heartbeat. ''What do you mean?''

''Your boss, Sergeant Storr, called me. Told me what you'd found out about Magnus Bouvier. He's got no alibi for the time of the killings, and even you think he could have done it.''

''Because he could have done it, doesn't mean he did,'' I said.

Freemont shrugged. ''He ran when we tried to question him. Innocent people don't run.''

''What do you mean, he ran? If you were there questioning him, how could he run?''

Freemont settled back into the couch, hands clasped together so tightly her fingers were mottled. ''He used magic to cloud our minds, and made his escape.''

''What sort of magic?''

Freemont shook her head. ''What do you want me to say, Ms. Preternatural Expert? Four of us sat there in his restaurant like idiots while he just walked out. We didn't even see him get up from the table.''

She looked at me, no smiles. Her eyes were back to that neutral coolness. You could stare all day at someone with eyes like that and keep all your secrets safe.

''He looked human to me, Blake. He looked like a nice, normal guy. I wouldn't have picked him out of a crowd. How did you know what he was?''

I opened my mouth, and closed it. I wasn't exactly sure how to answer the question. ''He tried to use glamor on me, but I knew what was happening.''

''What's glamor, and how did you know he was using a spell on you?''

''Glamor isn't exactly a spell,'' I said. I always hated explaining preternatural things to people who had no skill in the area. It was like having quantum physics explained to me. I could follow the concepts, but I had to take their word for it on the math. The math was beyond me, hated to admit it, but it was. But not understanding quantum physics wouldn't get me killed. Not understanding preternatural creatures might get Freemont killed.

''I'm not stupid, Blake. Explain it to me.''

''I don't think you're stupid, Detective Freemont. It's just hard to explain. I was riding with two uniforms in St. Louis. They were transporting me from a crime scene, playing taxi. The driver spotted this guy just walking along. He pulled over, put him up against a car. The guy was carrying a weapon, and was wanted in another state for armed robbery. If I'd been in a room with him, I'd have noticed the gun, but just passing by in a car, no way. I wouldn't have seen it. Even his partner asked him how he spotted him. He couldn't explain so that we could do it, but he knew how to do it.''

''So it's practice?'' Freemont said.

I sighed. ''In part, but hell, Detective, I raise the dead for a living. I have some preternatural abilities. It gives me a leg up.''

''How the hell are we supposed to police creatures, Ms. Blake? If Bouvier had pulled a gun, we'd have sat there and let him shoot us. We just sort of woke up and he wasn't there anymore. I've never seen anything like it."

"There are things you can do to protect yourself from fairie glamor," I said.

"What?"

"A four-leaf clover will break glamor, but it won't keep the fey from killing you by hand. There are other plants you can wear, or carry that break glamor: Saint-John's-wort, red verbena, daisies, rowan, and ash. My choice would be an ointment made of either four-leaf clovers or Saint-John's-wort. Spread it on your eyelids, mouth, ears, and hands. It'll make you proof against glamor."

"Where do I get this stuff?"

I thought about that for a second. "Well, in St. Louis I'd know where to go. Here, try health-food stores and occult shops. Any fairie ointment will be hard to find because we don't have any fairies native to this country. Ointment from four-leaf clovers is very expensive, and rare. Try for the Saint-John's-wort."

She sighed. "Will this ointment work on any mind control, like for vamps?"

"Nope," I said. "You could drop a vamp in a whole tub of Saint-John's-wort and it wouldn't give a damn."

"What do you do against vampires, then?"

"Keep your cross, avoid eye contact, pray. They can do things that'll make Magnus look like an amateur."

She rubbed her eyes, smearing eye shadow on the ball of her thumb. She suddenly looked tired. "How do we protect the public against something like that?"

"You don't," I said.

"Yes, we do," she said. "We have to; it's our job."

I didn't know what to say to that, so I didn't try. "So you thought it was Magnus because he ran, and he doesn't have an alibi?"

"Why else would he run?"

"I don't know," I said. "But he didn't do it. I saw the thing in the woods. It wasn't Magnus. Hell, I've only heard about vampires forming from shadows. I'd never seen it before."

She looked at me. "You've never seen it before. That's not comforting."

"It wasn't meant to be. But since it wasn't Magnus, you can call off the warrant."

She shook her head. "He used magic on police officers while committing a crime. That's a class C felony."

"What was his crime?"

"Escaping."

"But he wasn't under arrest."

"I had a warrant for his arrest," she said.

"You didn't have enough for a warrant," I said.

"Helps to know the right judge."

"He didn't kill those kids, or Coltrain."

"You pointed the finger at him," she said.

"Just an alternate possibility. With five people dead, I couldn't afford to be wrong."

She stood. ''Well, you got your wish. It was vampires, and I don't know why the hell Magnus Bouvier ran from us. But just using magic on a police officer is a felony.''

''Even if he was innocent of the original crime you were trying to bring him in on?'' I asked.

''Felonious use of magic is a serious crime, Ms. Blake. There's a warrant for his arrest. You see him, you remember that.''

''I know Magnus isn't nice people, Detective Freemont. I don't know why he ran, but if you put out the word that he used magic on cops, someone'll shoot him.''

''He's dangerous, Ms. Blake.''

''Yeah, but so are a lot of people, Detective. You don't hunt them down and arrest them for it.''

She nodded. ''We've all got prejudices, Ms. Blake; makes us all wrong once in a while. At least here we know what did it.''

''Yeah,'' I said. ''We know what did it.''

''Do you know when the girl's body was taken?'' she asked. She got a notebook out of her coat pocket. Down to business.

I shook my head. ''No. It was just gone when I went up.''

''What made you think to check on the body?''

I looked at her. Her eyes were pleasant and unreadable. ''They'd gone to a lot of trouble to make her one of them. I thought they might try to get her. They did.''

''The father's making noises that he asked you to stake her body before you went out after the vampires. Is that true?'' Her voice was soft, matter-of-fact. But she was paying attention to the answers. She didn't take as many notes as Dolph did. The notebook seemed to be more something to do with her hands than anything else. I was finally seeing Freemont doing her job. She seemed good at it. That was reassuring.

''Yeah, that's true.''

''Why didn't you stake the girl when the parents requested it?''

''I had a father. A widower. His daughter and only child got bit. He wanted her staked. I did it that night, right away. Next morning he's in my office crying, wanting me to undo it. Wanting me to bring her back as a vampire.'' I leaned back into the couch, hugging myself. ''You put a stake through a new vamp's heart, and it's dead for good.''

''I thought you had to take a vampire's head to be sure.''

''You do,'' I said. ''If I had staked the Quinlan girl, I would have taken out her heart, cut off her head.'' I shook my head. ''There isn't much left.''

She drew something on her note pad. I couldn't see what. I was betting it was a doodle and not a word. ''I see why you wanted to wait, but Mr. Quinlan is talking about suing you.''

''Yeah, I know.''

Freemont raised her eyebrows. ''Just thought you'd want to know.''

''Thanks.''

''We haven't found the boy's body yet.''

''I don't think you will,'' I said.

Her eyes didn't look pleasant anymore. They looked narrow and suspicious. ''Why?''

''If they wanted to kill him, they could have done it here, tonight. I think they want to make him one of them.''

''Why?''

I shrugged. ''I don't know. But usually when a vampire takes this personal an interest in a family, there's a reason for it.''

''You mean a motive?''

I nodded. ''You've seen the Quinlans. They're devout Catholics. The church sees vampirism as suicide. Their children will be damned for all eternity if they become vampires.''

''Worse than just killing them,'' she said.

''To the Quinlans, I think so.''

''You think the vampires will be back to get the parents?''

I thought about that for a minute. ''Hell, I don't know. I mean, before vampires were legal you had some cases where a master vamp would take out entire families. Sometimes befriend them first. Sometimes just for revenge for some slight. But since they've been legal, I don't know why the vamp would do it. I mean, the vampire can take them to court. What could the Quinlans have done that was bad enough for this?''

The doors opened. Freemont turned, a frown already in place. Two men appeared in the doorway. They were both dressed in dark suits, dark ties, white shirts. Standard federal issue. One was short and white, the other tall and black. That alone should have made them look different, but there was a sameness to them, like the same cookie cutter had been used no matter how well cooked the outside was.

The shorter of the two flipped his badge at us. ''I'm Special Agent Bradford, this is Agent Elwood. Which one of you is Detective Freemont?''

Freemont walked towards them with her hand out. Showing she was unarmed and friendly. Yeah, right. ''I'm Detective Freemont. This is Anita Blake.''

I appreciated being included in the introductions. I stood up and joined the foursome.

Agent Bradford looked at me for a long time. Long enough that it got on my nerves. ''Is there something wrong, Agent Bradford?''

He shook his head. ''I attended Sergeant Storr's lectures at Quantico. The way he talked about you, I thought you'd be bigger.'' He smiled when he said it, halfway between friendly and condescending.

A lot of scathing comebacks came to mind, but never get in a pissing contest with the Feds. You'll lose. ''Sorry to disappoint you.''

''We've already talked with Officer Wallace. He makes you sound taller, too.''

I shrugged. ''Hard to make me sound shorter.''

He smiled. ''We'd like to speak with Detective Freemont in private, Ms. Blake. But don't go far; we'll want a statement from you and your associate, Mr. Kirkland.''

''Sure.''

"I took Ms. Blake's statement personally," Freemont said. "I don't think we need her any more tonight."

Bradford looked at her. "I think we'll be the judge of that."

"If Ms. Blake had called me in when there was only one body on the ground, there wouldn't be two dead policemen, and a dead civilian," Freemont said.

I just looked at her. Somebody's ass was going to be in a sling, and Freemont didn't want it to be hers. Fine.

"Don't forget the missing boy," I said. Everyone looked at me. "You want to start pointing fingers, fine; there's enough blame to go around. If you hadn't chased me off earlier, I might have called you in, but I did call the state police. If you'd told your superiors everything I told you, they'd have connected the two cases, and you'd have been here anyway."

"I had enough men with me to cover the house and the civilians," Freemont said. "Not including me cost lives."

I nodded. "Probably. But you'd have come down here and kicked me out again. You'd have taken St. John and his people out in the dark with five vampires, one of them ancient, when all you've seen is pictures of vampire kills. They'd have slaughtered you, but maybe, just maybe, Beth St. John would be alive. Maybe Jeff Quinlan would still be here."

I stared up at her, and watched the anger drain from her eyes. We looked at each other. "It took both of us to fuck this one up, Sergeant." I turned back to the two agents. "I'll wait outside."

"Wait," Bradford said. "Storr said that sometimes the legal vampire community will help on a case like this. Who do I talk to down here?"

"Why would they hunt down one of their own?" Agent Elwood asked.

"This kind of shit is bad for business. Especially right now with Senator Brewster's daughter getting killed. Vampires don't need any more bad publicity. Most of them like being legal. They like the fact that killing them is murder."

"So who do I talk to?" Bradford asked.

I sighed. "In this area, I don't know. I'm not a hometown girl."

"How do I go about finding out who to talk to?"

"I might be able to help you there."

"How?"

I shook my head. "I know someone who might know a name. I'm not trying to give you a hard time here, but a lot of the monsters don't like dealing with cops. It just hasn't been that long ago that the police shot them on sight."

"So you're saying the vampires will talk to you and not to us?" Elwood said.

"Something like that."

"That makes no sense. You're a vampire executioner. Your job is to kill them. Why would they believe you and not us?" he asked.

I didn't know how to explain it, and wasn't sure I wanted to. "I also raise zombies, Agent Elwood. I think they sort of consider me one of the monsters."

"Even though you're their version of an electric chair."

"Even though."

"That's not logical."

I laughed then; I couldn't help it. ''God, has anything that happened here tonight been logical?''

Elwood gave a very small smile. I pegged him as the newer of the two. I don't think he'd gotten over the thought that FBI agents don't smile.

''You wouldn't be withholding information from the FBI, would you, Ms. Blake?'' Bradford asked.

''If I come up with a vampire in this area that will talk to you, I'll give you the name.''

Bradford stared at me. ''How about if you come up with any vampires in this area, you give us the names. Let us worry about whether they'll talk to us or not.''

I looked at him for a heartbeat and lied. ''Sure.'' If I expected the monsters to help me, I couldn't give them all over to the cops. Only a select few.

He looked like he didn't believe me, but couldn't quite call me a liar to my face. ''When we find the vampires responsible, we'll be sure to call you in for the kill.''

That was more than Freemont had been willing to do. The night was looking up. ''Beep me any time.''

''We'll talk to Sergeant Freemont now, Ms. Blake.'' I was dismissed. Fine with me. He offered his hand. I took it. We shook. Agent Elwood and I shook. Everyone smiled. I left.

Larry was waiting out in the entryway. He got up off the stairs where he'd been sitting. ''What now?''

''I need to make a phone call.''

''Who to?''

Two more men with ''Federal Agent'' tattooed on their foreheads walked up the hallway from the direction of the kitchen. I shook my head and went out the door into the cool windy night. The place was swarming with cops. I'd never seen so many federal agents in my life. But hey, the very first vampire serial killer was news. Everyone would want a piece. Watching everyone mill around on the carefully tended lawn, I suddenly wanted to go home. To just pack up and go home. It was still early. Hours and hours left of darkness. It only seemed like it had been an eternity since we left the graveyard. Hell, there'd be time to go back and look at Stirling's boneyard before dawn.

I got in the jeep that Bayard had loaned us. I'd use the nifty portable phone it came with.

Larry got in the passenger side.

''Private call.''

''Come on, Anita.''

''Out, Larry.''

''Out in the dark with the vampires.'' He blinked his big blue eyes at me.

''The place is lousy with cops. I think you'll be safe. Out.''

He got out, grumbling under his breath. He could grumble all he wanted to. Larry wanted to be a vampire hunter, fine; but he didn't have to be as intimately involved with the monsters as I was. I was trying to keep him as out of it as I could. Not easy, but worth the effort.

I'd lied to the nice agents. It wasn't the fact that I raised zombies that got me in good with the vampires. It was the fact that the Master of the City, of St. Louis, had the hots for me. Was maybe in love with me, or at least thought he was.

I knew the number by heart, which was a bad sign all on its own. "Guilty Pleasures, where your darkest fantasies come true. This is Robert. How may I help you?"

Great; Robert, one of my least favorite vampires. "Hi, Robert, this is Anita. I need to speak to Jean-Claude."

He hesitated, then said, "I'll transfer you to his office phone. It's a new system, so if I disconnect you, call back."

The phone clicked before I could answer. A moment of silence, and the voice came on the line. You can criticize a lot about Jean-Claude, but he gives good phone.

"Good evening, *ma petite*." That was it, all he said, but even over the buzzing phone his voice was like fur inside my skull.

"I'm near Branson. I need to contact the Master of the City down here."

"No 'Good evening, Jean-Claude, how are you doing?'? Just down to business. How terribly rude, *ma petite*."

"Look, I don't have time for games right now. Some vampires down here are on the rampage. They've kidnapped a young boy. I want to find him before they can make him one of them."

"How young is the boy?"

"Sixteen."

"In centuries past, *ma petite*, that was not considered a child."

"It isn't legal age right this minute."

"Did he go willingly?"

"No."

"You know that for a fact, or were you merely told he was kidnapped?"

"I talked to him before. He didn't go willingly."

Jean-Claude sighed. The sound slithered down my skin like cool fingers. "What do you want of me, *ma petite*?"

"I want to talk to the Master of the City down here. I need the name. I'm assuming you do know who the Master is down here?"

"Of course, but it is not that simple."

"We only have three nights to save him, and a hell of a lot less if they just want a snack."

"The Master will not talk to you without a guide to take you in."

"Send someone, then."

"Who? Robert? Willie? Neither of them is powerful enough to be your escort."

"If you mean they can't protect me, I can protect myself."

"I know you can take care of yourself, *ma petite*. You have made that abundantly clear. But you do not look as dangerous as you are. You might have to shoot one or two to teach them their place. If you got out alive, they would not help you."

"I want to get this boy back intact, Jean-Claude. Work with me here."

"*Ma petite* . . ."

I had an image of Jeff Quinlan's brown eyes. His room with its cowboy wall-paper. "Help me, Jean-Claude."

He was silent for a moment. "I am the only one powerful enough to be your escort. Do you wish me to drop everything and rush down to you?"

It was my turn to be quiet. Put like that, it didn't sound right. It sounded like a big favor. I didn't want to be indebted to him. But I'd probably live through owing him a favor. Jeff Quinlan might not.

"Fine," I said.

"You want me to come help you?"

I gritted my teeth and said, "Yes."

"I will fly down tomorrow night."

"Tonight."

"*Ma petite*, *ma petite*, what am I to do with you?"

"You said you'd help me."

"And I will, but these things take time."

"What things?"

"It might be helpful if you thought of Branson as a foreign country. A potentially hostile foreign country where I am working to get us safe passage. There are customs to be observed. If I barge in, it will be seen as a declaration of war."

"Isn't there any way to start tonight?" I asked. "Short of starting a war?"

"Perhaps, but if you wait one more night, *ma petite*, we can enter much more safely."

"We can take care of ourselves. Jeff Quinlan can't."

"That is his name?"

"Yeah."

He took a deep breath and let it out in a sigh that made me shiver. I would have told him to stop that, but it would have amused him, so I didn't.

"I will fly down tonight. How do I contact you?"

I gave him the name of my hotel and then, with a sigh, my beeper number.

"I will call you when I arrive."

"How long will it take you to fly this far?"

"Anita, do you think I am going to fly myself down, as a bird would?"

I didn't like the faint amusement in his voice, but I answered truthfully. "It was a thought."

He laughed, and it raised goose-bumps on my arms. "Oh, *ma petite*, *ma petite*, you are precious."

Just what I wanted to hear. "So how are you getting here?"

"My private jet."

Of course, he had a private jet. "When can you be here?"

"I will be there as soon as I can, my impatient flower."

"I prefer *ma petite* to flower."

"As you like, *ma petite*."

"I want to see the Master of Branson tonight before dawn."

"You have made that abundantly clear, and I will try."

"Do more than try."

"You are feeling guilty about this boy; why?"

"I'm not feeling guilty."

"Responsible, then," he said.

I sat there, not sure what to say. He was right. "I don't suppose you read my mind just then?"

"No, *ma petite*, just your voice and your impatience."

I hated that he knew me that well. Hated it. "Yeah, I feel responsible."

"Why?"

"I was in charge."

"Did you do all you could to keep him safe?"

"I had hosts put at every entrance."

"Someone let them in, then?"

"They had a doggie door that exited through the garage, into the house wall. They didn't want to cut a hole through any of the outer doors."

"Was there a child vampire among them?"

"No."

"Then how?"

I described the thin, skeletal vampire. "It was almost a form change. He changed back in seconds. Once he changed back, he could have passed for human in dim light. I've never seen anything like it."

"I've only seen the ability once," he said.

"You know who it is, don't you?"

"I will be with you as soon as I am able, *ma petite*."

"You sound serious all of a sudden; why?"

He gave a small laugh, but this one was bitter, like swallowing broken glass. It hurt just to hear it. "You know me too well, *ma petite*."

"Just answer the question."

"Did the boy who was taken look younger than his years?"

"Yeah; why?"

Silence thick enough to slice was the only answer.

"Talk to me, Jean-Claude."

"Have there been any other young boys gone missing?"

"Not to my knowledge, but I haven't asked."

"Ask," he said.

"How young?"

"Twelve, fourteen, older if they look young enough."

"Like Jeff Quinlan," I said.

"I fear so."

"Is this vampire into more than just kidnapping?"

"What do you mean, *ma petite*?"

"Murder, not just biting them, but murder."

"What sort of murder?"

I hesitated. I didn't discuss ongoing police investigations with the monsters.

"I know you do not trust me, *ma petite*, but it is important. Tell me of these deaths, please."

He didn't say please very often. I told him. Not in great detail, but enough.

"Were they violated?"

"What do you mean, violated?" I asked.

"Violated, *ma petite*, violated. There are other words for it, but none better for children."

"Oh," I said. "I don't know if they were sexually assaulted. They were still clothed."

"There are things that can be done without removing clothing, *ma petite*. But the abuse would have happened before the killings. Systematic abuse over a period of weeks or months."

"I'll find out if they were assaulted." An idea occurred to me. "Would this vamp ever do a girl?"

"By 'do,' you mean sex?"

"Yeah."

"If pressed for company, he would take a young girl, prepubescent, but only if he could find nothing else."

I swallowed hard. We were talking about children like they were things, objects. "No, this girl looked like a woman. She didn't look young."

"Then, no, he would not willingly touch her."

"What do you mean, willingly? What other choice would there be?"

"His master could order him to do it, and he might, if he feared the master enough. Though I cannot think of many people that he would fear enough to do something he found repugnant."

"You know this vampire. Who is he? Give me a name."

"When I arrive, *ma petite*."

"Just give me the name."

"So you can give it to the police?"

"That is their job."

"No, *ma petite*. If it is who I think it is, it will not be a matter for the police."

"Why not?"

"Put simply, he is too dangerous and too exotic to be revealed to the general public. If mortals found out we could have among us such things, they might turn on us all together. You must be aware of that nasty law floating around the Senate."

"I'm aware."

"Then you must understand my caution."

"Maybe, but if more people die because of your caution, it's going to help Brewster's law get passed. You think about that."

"Oh, I am, *ma petite*. Trust that I am. Now farewell. I have much to do." He hung up.

I sat there staring at the phone. Damn him. What did he mean by exotic? What could this new vampire do that others couldn't? He could slim himself down enough to fit through a doggie door. Maybe it made Houdini jealous, but it was hardly a crime. But I remembered its face. Not human. Not even just a corpse's face. It had been something else altogether. Something different. And I remembered those few seconds I lost, twice. Me, the great vampire hunter, helpless as any civilian for just a heartbeat. With vampires, a heartbeat was enough.

Visions of such things would get you talking of demons, which Quinlan had done briefly. The police ignored him, and I didn't back up his story. Quinlan had never met a real demon, or he wouldn't have made the mistake. Once you've been in the presence of demons, you never forget it. I'd rather fight a dozen vampires than one demonic presence. They don't give a shit about silver bullets.

17

It was after 2:00 a.m. before we got back to the graveyard. The Feds had kept us forever, like they didn't believe we were telling them the whole truth. Fancy that. I hated being accused of concealing evidence when I wasn't. Made me want to lie to them just so they wouldn't be disappointed. I think Freemont had painted a less than charitable picture of me. That'll teach me to be generous. But it seemed petty to point fingers at each other, and say she did it, when Beth St. John's blood was still wet on the carpet.

The wind that had all but promised rain had drifted away. The thick clouds that had obscured the woods while we were playing tag with vampires were suddenly gone. The moon rode high and two days past full. Since dating Richard, I'd paid more attention to the lunar cycles. Fancy that.

The moon sailed the shining night sky, gleaming like it had been polished. The moonlight was so strong it cast faint shadows. You didn't need a flashlight, but Raymond Stirling had one. A big freaking halogen torch that filled his hand like a captive sun.

I watched him start to point it at Larry and me. I raised an arm and said, "Don't point it at us. You'll ruin our night vision." It wasn't very diplomatic, but I was tired, and it had been a long night.

He hesitated in mid-motion. I didn't have to see his face to know he didn't like it. Men like Raymond give orders better than they take them.

He clicked off the light. Good for him. He waited with Ms. Harrison, Bayard, and Beau gathered around him. He was the only one with a flashlight. I bet that his entourage wasn't worried about night vision, and would have liked to have had a light.

Larry and I were still wearing the coveralls. I was getting tired of mine. What I really wanted to do was go back to the hotel and sleep. But once Jean-Claude arrived I wouldn't be sleeping anyway; might as well work. Besides, Stirling was my only paying client. Well, yeah I do get money for killing vampires if it's a legal kill, but it's not a lot of money. Stirling was financing this trip. He deserved his money's worth, I guess.

''We've been waiting for a very long time, Ms. Blake.''

''I'm sorry that the death of a young girl inconvenienced you, Mr. Stirling. Shall we go up?''

''I am not unsympathetic to another's loss, Ms. Blake, and I resent the implication that I am.'' He stood there in the moonlit dark, very straight, very commanding. Ms. Harrison and Bayard moved a little closer, showing support. Beau just stood there, looking sort of amused behind Stirling's back. He was wearing a black slicker with a hood. He looked like a phantom.

I looked up at the clear, sparkling sky. Looked at Beau. He grinned broadly enough for his teeth to flash in the moonlight. I just shook my head and let it go. Maybe he'd been a Boy Scout, always prepared and all that.

''Fine, whatever you say. Let's get this over with.'' I didn't wait for them. I just walked past them and started up.

Larry, at my side, said, ''You're being rude.''

I glanced at him.

''Yeah, I am.''

''He is a paying client, Anita.''

''Look, I don't need you to chastise me, okay?''

''What's wrong with you?''

I stopped. ''What we just left is what's wrong with me. I'd think it'd bother you a little more, too.''

''It bothers me, but I don't have to take it out on everyone else.''

I took a deep breath and let it out slow. He was right. Damn. ''Alright, you've made your point. I'll try to be nicer.''

Stirling marched up to us, entourage in tow. ''Are you coming, Ms. Blake?'' He walked past us, his back ramrod-straight.

Ms. Harrison stumbled, and only Bayard's grab on her elbow kept her from falling flat on her butt. She was still wearing her high heels. Maybe it was against the executive secretary code to wear tennis shoes.

Beau followed with his black slicker flapping around his long legs. It made a distinctive *slap-slap* sound that was most irritating.

Okay, maybe everything was irritating right now. I was feeling decidedly grumpy. Jeff Quinlan was out there somewhere. He was either already dead or had one bite by now. It wasn't my fault. I'd told his father to put a piece of the host in front of every entrance. I would have thought of the doggie door if I'd seen it, but I'd never gone that far into the house. Even I would have thought it was paranoid to guard the doggie entrance. But I would have done it, and Beth St. John would be alive.

I'd dropped the ball. I couldn't bring Beth St. John back, but I could save Jeff. And I would. I would. I didn't want to avenge him by killing the vampire that killed him. For once I wanted to be in time. For once I wanted to save someone and leave revenge for someone else.

Was Jeff being violated, right this minute? Was that thing I'd seen in the Quinlans' living room doing more than just biting his neck? God, I hoped not. I was pretty sure I could bring Jeff back from a vampire bite, but combine that with rape by a monster, and I wasn't so sure. What if I found him and there wasn't much left to save? The mind is a surprisingly fragile thing sometimes.

I prayed as we walked up the hill. I prayed and felt a measure of calm return. No visions. No angels singing. But a feeling of peace flowed over me. I took a deep breath, and something hard and tight and ugly in my heart let go. I took it as a good sign that I'd get to Jeff in time. But part of me was skeptical. God doesn't always save someone. Often He just helps you live through the loss. I guess I don't entirely trust God. I never doubt Him, but His motives are too beyond me. Through a glass darkly and all that. Just once I'd like to see through the damn glass clearly.

The moon shone down on the top of the hill like silver fire. The air was almost luminescent. The rain was gone, giving its blessing somewhere else. Heaven knows we could have used the rain, but personally I was just as glad I didn't have to walk the raw dirt in a downpour. Mud would have been just too perfect.

''Well, Ms. Blake, shall we begin?'' Stirling asked.

I glanced at him. ''Yeah.'' I took a breath and swallowed the blunt things I wanted to say. Larry was right. Stirling was a pain in the ass, but he wasn't who I was mad at. He was just a convenient target.

''Mr. Kirkland and I will walk the graveyard. But you need to stay here. Other people moving around are very distracting.'' There; that was diplomatic.

''If you were going to make us stand here like an audience, you could have said so at the bottom of this mountain. And saved us the walk.''

So much for diplomacy. ''Would you have liked me telling you to stay at the bottom of the hill where you couldn't see what we were doing?''

He thought about that for a minute. ''No, I suppose I wouldn't have liked it.''

''Then what are you complaining about?''

''Anita,'' Larry said very softly under his breath.

I ignored him. ''Look, Mr. Stirling, it has been a really rough night. I am just out of niceness right now. Please, just let me do my job. The faster I get this done, the sooner we go home. Okay?''

Honesty. I was hoping profound honesty would work. It was about all I had left.

He hesitated a minute, then nodded. ''All right, Ms. Blake. Do your job, but know this. You have been decidedly unpleasant. It better be pretty spectacular.''

I opened my mouth, and Larry touched my arm. He gripped my arm not too hard, but hard enough. I swallowed what I was going to say and walked away from all of them. Larry trailed after me. Brave Larry.

''What's the matter with you tonight?'' he asked when we were out of earshot of Stirling and Co.

''I told you.''

''No,'' he said, ''it isn't just the murder tonight. Hell, I've seen you kill people and be less upset afterwards. What's wrong?''

I stopped walking and just stood there for a minute. He'd seen me kill people and be less upset. Was that true? I thought about it for a heartbeat. It was true. That was pretty damn sad.

I knew what was wrong. I'd seen too many slaughtered people in the last few months. Too much blood. Too much killing. I'd done some of the killing. Not all of it had been sanctioned by the state. I also wanted to be looking for Jeff Quinlan. I couldn't do anything until Jean-Claude arrived. I really couldn't. But I felt like my job was interfering with my police work. Was that a bad sign? Or a good one?

I took a deep breath of the cool mountain air. I let it out very slowly, concentrating on just breathing, in and out, in and out. When I felt calm again, I looked at Larry.

"I'm just a little on edge tonight, Larry. I'll be alright."

"If I said a little on edge with a surprised lilt in my voice, would you get mad?"

I smiled. "Yeah, I would."

"You've been in a blacker mood than usual since you talked to Jean-Claude. What's up?"

I stared into his smiling face and didn't want to tell him. He wasn't that much older than Jeff Quinlan, four years. He could still have passed for a high-schooler. "Fine," I said, and told him.

"A vampire pedophile; isn't that against the rules?"

"What rules?"

"That you can only be one kind of monster at a time."

"It kind of caught me off guard, too."

A strange look flashed across his face. "Sweet Jesus, Jeff Quinlan is with that thing." He looked at me, all the horror, all the pain, or as much as he could imagine, flowing across his face. "We have to do something, Anita. We have to save him." He turned as if to go back down the mountain.

I grabbed his arm. "We can't do anything until Jean-Claude arrives."

"But we can't just do nothing."

"We aren't doing nothing. We're doing our job."

"But how can we . . ."

"Because we can't do anything else right now."

Larry looked at me for a second, then nodded. "Okay; if you can be calm, so can I."

"Good man."

"Thanks. Now show me this nifty trick you've been talking about. I've never heard of anyone who could read the dead without raising them first."

Truthfully, I didn't know if Larry could do it. But telling him he might not be able to was not going to help his confidence. Magic, if that was the right word, often rises and falls on your own belief in your abilities. I've seen very powerful people completely crippled by self-doubt.

"I'm going to walk the cemetery." I tried to think of how to put it into words. How do you explain something that you don't fully understand yourself?

I have always had an affinity with the dead. Even as a small child, I always knew if the soul had fled the body. I remember my great-aunt Katerine's funeral. I'm named after her, my middle name. She was my father's favorite aunt. We went early to view the body and make sure everything was ready. I felt her soul hovering above the coffin. I looked up expecting to see it, but there was nothing for my eyes to hold onto. I've never seen a soul. I've felt them, but I've never seen one.

I know now that Aunt Katerine's soul hung around a long time. Most souls leave within three days, some leave instantly, some don't. My mother's soul was gone by the time the funeral arrived. I didn't feel her there. There was nothing but a closed coffin and a blanket of pink roses over the coffin, as if the coffin would get cold.

It was at home where I felt my mother hovering close. Not her soul, not really, but some piece of her that couldn't let go immediately. I would hear her footsteps in the hall outside my bedroom as if she was coming to kiss me good night. She moved through the house for months, and I found it comforting. When she finally left, I was ready to let her go. I never told my father. I was only eight, but even then I knew that he couldn't hear her. Maybe he heard other things. I don't know. My father and I never talked much about my mother's death. It made him cry.

I'd been able to sense ghosts long before I could raise the dead. What I was about to do was just an extension of that, or maybe a combination of both skills. I don't know. But it was like trying to explain that there was a soul hovering over Aunt Katerine's coffin. Either you knew the soul was there or you didn't. Words didn't quite cover it.

"Can you see ghosts?"

"You mean right now?"

I smiled and shook my head. "No, just in general."

"Well, I knew the Calvin house wasn't haunted, no matter how many stories people made up. But there was a little cave near town that had something in it. Something not nice."

"Was it a ghost?"

He shrugged. "I never tried to find out, but nobody else seemed able to feel it."

"Do you know when the soul leaves the body? I mean, can you tell it?"

"Sure." He said it like, Couldn't everybody do that?

I had to smile. "Good enough. I'm just going to do it. I don't know what you'll see, if anything. I know that Raymond is going to be disappointed because he won't see anything, unless he's a lot more talented than he looks."

"What are you going to do, Anita? They never talked about 'walking a cemetery' in college."

"It's not like a magic spell, a few words or gestures and it works. It isn't anything like that." I struggled to put into words something that we had no vocabulary for. "It's closer to psychic ability than magic. It's not physical. It's not a muscle to move, or even a thought. It's . . . I just do it. Let me get started; then if I can, I'll bring you in or try and talk to you while I do it. Okay?"

He shrugged. "I guess so. I still don't understand what the heck you're doing, but that's okay. I usually don't know what's going on."

"But you always figure it out," I said.

He grinned. "I do, don't I?"

"You bet."

I stood in nearly the dead center of the raw earth. Not so long ago I was afraid of what I was about to do. It wasn't really frightening in and of itself. I was scared of the fact that I could do it at all. It wasn't a very human thing to be able to do.

But then, lately I'd been rethinking exactly what made you human, and what made you one of the monsters. Once I'd been very sure of myself, and everyone else. I wasn't so sure anymore. Besides, I'd been practicing.

Of course, I'd been practicing in empty graveyards where there was nothing but me and the dead. Okay, night insects, but arthropods never bothered my concentration. People did.

Even with my back turned, I could feel Larry like a warm presence behind me. It bugged me. "Can you move back farther?"

"Sure; how far?"

I shook my head. "As far as you can get and still be in sight."

He raised his eyebrows. "Do you want me to go over and wait with Mr. Stirling?"

"If you can stand it."

"I can stand it. I schmooze clients better than you do."

That was the God's honest truth. "Great. When I call you over, come slowly. I've never tried to talk to someone while I do this."

"Whatever you say." He gave a laugh that was almost nervous. "I can't wait to see this."

I let that go, and turned away. I walked away from him. When I glanced back, he was walking to the others. I hoped Larry wouldn't be disappointed. I still wasn't sure if he'd be able to even sense anything. I turned my back on all of them. Seeing them huddled there would distract me, that much I was sure of.

The top of the mountain had been stripped. It was like standing on the edge of the world looking down. The moonlight bathed everything in a soft glow. It was so bright up here near the sky without any trees to hide it that the air itself glowed with diffused light. A gentle wind traced just about head-high. It smelled green and fresh, almost as if the rain had actually fallen. I closed my eyes and let the wind touch my skin, ruffle my hair. There was almost no sound but the singing of insects from below. Nothing but the wind, me, and the dead.

I couldn't tell Larry exactly how to do it, because I wasn't completely sure myself. If it was a muscle, I would move it. If it was a thought, I would think it. If it was a magic word, I would say it. It is none of those things. It is like my skin opens up. All my nerve endings naked to the wind. My skin grew cool. It's like a cool wind emanates from my body. It isn't really wind. You can't see it. You can't feel it, or no one else can. But it's there. It's real.

The cool fingers of "wind" stretched outward from me. Within a ten- to fifteen-foot radius I would be able to search the graves. As I moved, the circle would move with me, searching.

I raised my arm and waved. I didn't turn around to see if Larry saw me. I stayed tight inside my private circle. I was holding it in, trying not to start searching the dead until Larry got over here. I was hoping he'd be able to sense what was going on. Seemed logical that it would be easier to figure out if he saw it from the beginning.

I heard his footsteps on the dry earth. They seemed thunderously loud, as if I could hear every grain of dirt under his shoes.

He stopped behind me. "Jesus, what is that?"

"What?" My voice sounded distant and loud at the same time.

"Wind, a cold wind." He sounded a little scared. Good. You should always be a little afraid when you do magic. It's when you start taking it for granted that you get in trouble.

"Come closer, but don't touch me." I wasn't sure on that last, but it sounded like a good idea. Better cautious than not.

He came slowly, one hand held out like he was feeling the wind against his skin. "Jesus, Mary, and Joseph. Anita, it's coming from you. The wind is coming from you."

"Yes," I said.

His eyes were wide. He looked like his voice sounded, a little scared.

"If I stood right next to Stirling, he wouldn't feel a thing. None of them would."

Larry shook his head. "How could they miss it?" His hand hovered just off my body, almost touching but not quite. "It's colder, or stronger, or something the closer I get to your body."

"Interesting," I said.

"What now?" he asked.

"Now, I touch the dead." I let go of it, like unclenching a hand. The fingers of "wind" stretched downward. How does it feel to go through solid earth and touch the dead beneath? Like nothing human. It was as if the invisible fingers could melt through the dirt searching for the dead. This time we didn't have to search far. The earth was disturbed, and the dead lay on top of the raw land.

I'd never tried this in anything but a well-organized cemetery. Where each grave, each body, was distinct. The wind touched Larry like a stone in a stream. The power rippled around him. He was alive, and it disturbed us. But we'd been practicing, and we could work around him.

I was standing on top of bones. Under the earth where eyes could not see. I tried to step off them, and only stepped on more. The earth was thick with bodies, like raisins in a pudding. No eating around them.

I stood on top on a raft of bones in a sea of dry, red earth. Everywhere I touched was a body—a piece of bone. There was no clear space. No breathing space. I stood there, huddled in on myself, trying to sort through what I was sensing.

The rib cage just to the left belonged with the thighbone yards away. The wind leaked out and touched piece after piece. I could have put the skeleton back together like a giant jigsaw puzzle. That was what my power would do if I tried to raise it.

I moved, stepping on the dead, and everywhere I walked I put bodies together. The pieces stayed separate, but I remembered.

Larry moved with me. He moved surprisingly smoothly through the power, like a swimmer leaving the smallest possible ripples behind.

A ghost flared to life like a pale, dancing flame. I walked towards it. It rose like a swaying snake, watching me without eyes. There was that thread of hostility that some ghosts seem to feel towards the living. A jealousy. But if I'd been tied to some forsaken piece of earth for a hundred years or more, I might be hostile, too.

''What is that?'' Larry whispered.

''What do you see?'' I asked.

''I think it's a ghost. I've just never seen one materialize before.'' He reached out as if to touch it.

I grabbed his wrist before he could ever have reached. I felt his power flare to life in a rush of wind that should have poured my hair back from my face.

The circle suddenly widened, like a camera lens spreading wide. The dead awoke under our combined power like twigs touched by fire. Our power spread over them, and they gave up their secrets. Bits of muscle withered to bone, gaping skulls, all the pieces were there. All we had to do was call them forth. Two more ghosts rose from the ground like smoke. It was a lot of active ghosts for this small and this old a cemetery. And they were all angry at being disturbed. The level of hostility was unusual.

Combining our powers hadn't doubled the circle—it had quadrupled it.

The nearest ghost stood like a white pillar of flame. It was strong, powerful. A full-blown ghost in a graveyard that hadn't seen a burial in over two hundred years.

I stared at it. Larry stared at it. As long as we didn't touch it, we were safe. Heck, we were safe even if we did touch it. Ghosts can't cause physical harm, not really. They can grab you, but if you ignore them they fall away. If you pay attention, they can be bothersome. Frightening, but if a spirit causes real harm it isn't just a ghost. Demon, evil sorcerous dead, but not a normal ghost.

Staring at the wavering shape, I wasn't at all sure this was a normal ghost. Ghosts wear out. They fade to haunts, which don't usually materialize, hot spots that can give you a jolt, then just shivery places. Ghosts do not last forever. These looked pretty damn solid. For ghosts.

''Stop!'' a man's voice yelled.

Larry and I turned towards the voice. Magnus Bouvier scrambled up the side of the mountain opposite from where we had walked up. His hair fell across his face, hiding everything but his eyes from the moonlight. His eyes glowed in the dark, reflecting lights I could not see.

''Stop!'' He was waving his hands. His long-sleeved shirt was untucked over jeans. He hit the circle of wind and froze. He put his hands up as if he was trying to touch it.

Two people in one night who could sense the power. Unusual, but sort of cool. If Magnus hadn't been on the run from the police, we could have sat down and had a nice talk about it.

''We told you to stay off this land, Mr. Bouvier,'' Stirling said.

Bouvier looked at him, turning his head slowly as if concentrating on anything besides the feel of power was hard.

''We've tried being nice about this,'' Stirling said. ''We are not going to be nice any longer. Beau.''

The pump action on a shotgun is a very distinctive sound. I turned towards the sound, gun in hand. I don't remember thinking about it. I was just looking down the barrel of a gun at Beau. He was cradling a shotgun in his arms, not aimed at anything. That saved him. I know if it had been pointed near us, I'd have shot him.

I was still seeing double. I could see the graveyard behind my eyes where there is no optic nerve. The cemetery was mine. I knew the bodies. I knew the ghosts. I knew where all the pieces lay. I stared down the gun, seeing Beau and the shotgun, but inside my head the dead still reached out for their scattered parts.

The ghosts were still real. The power had agitated them. They'd dance and sway on their own for a while. But they'd fade back into the ground. There was more than one way to raise the dead, but not permanently.

I couldn't look away from the shotgun to see what Bouvier was doing. "Anita, please don't raise the dead." His surprisingly deep voice held a note of pleading.

I fought an urge to glance at him. "Why not, Magnus?"

"Get off my land," Stirling said.

"This is not your land."

"Get off my land or you will be shot for trespassing."

Beau glanced my way. "Mr. Stirling?" He was being very careful that the shotgun stayed loose, and harmless, in his hands.

"Beau, show him we mean business."

"Mr. Stirling," he said again, with a little more urgency in his voice.

"Do what I pay you for," Stirling said.

He started to raise the shotgun to his shoulder, but slowly, watching me.

"Don't do it," I said. I let my breath out all the way until my body was still and quiet. There was nothing but the gun and what I was aiming at.

Beau lowered the shotgun.

I took a breath and said, "Put it on the ground, now."

"Ms. Blake, this is none of your business," Stirling said.

"You are not going to shoot someone for trespassing on a piece of land while I watch."

Larry had his gun out too, now. It wasn't pointed at anybody in particular, which I was grateful for. Pointed guns have a tendency to go off if you don't know what you're doing.

"On the ground, Beau, now. I won't ask a third time."

He laid the shotgun on the ground.

"I pay your salary."

"You don't pay me enough to get killed."

Stirling made an exasperated sound and moved forward as if he would pick up the gun himself.

"Don't touch it, Raymond. You'll bleed just as easy as anybody else."

He turned to me. "I cannot believe that you would hold me at gunpoint on my own property."

I lowered my gun arm just a touch; it gets shaky if you hold a shooting pose too long. "I cannot believe that you had Beau come up here armed. You knew my little show would attract Bouvier. You knew it and planned for it. You cold-blooded son of a bitch."

"Mr. Kirkland, are you going to let her talk to me like that? I am a client."

Larry shook his head. "I'm with her on this one, Mr. Stirling. You were going to ambush that man. Murder him. Why?"

"Good question," I said. "Why are you so afraid of the Bouvier family? Or is it just him that you're afraid of?"

"I am afraid of no one. Come along; we will leave you to your new friend." He marched away, and the others followed. Beau sort of hesitated.

"I'll bring the shotgun down for you," I said.

He nodded. "Figured that."

"And you better not be waiting down there with another gun."

He looked at me for a long minute. At both of us. He shook his head. "I'm going home to my wife."

"You do that, Beau," I said.

He walked away, black slicker flapping against his legs. He hesitated, then said, "I'm out of it from now on. Money doesn't spend if you're dead."

I knew a few vampires that would argue with him, but I said, "Glad to hear it."

"I just don't want to get shot," he said. He walked away down the slope, out of sight.

I stood there with the Browning pointed skyward. I turned in a slow circle, surveying the mountaintop. We were alone, the three of us. So why didn't I want to put my gun up?

Magnus took a step up the slope and stopped. He raised slender hands towards the power-charged air. He trailed fingertips down it, like it was water. I felt the ripples of his touch shiver down my skin, tremble through my magic.

No, I wasn't putting my gun up yet.

"What was that?" Larry asked. His gun was still out, pointed at the ground.

Bouvier moved his gleaming eyes to Larry. "He is not a necromancer, Anita, but he is more than he seems."

"Aren't we all," I said. "Why didn't you want me to raise the dead, Magnus?"

He stared up at me. His eyes were full of glinting lights like reflections in a pool, but the reflections were of things that were not there.

"Answer me, Magnus."

"Or what?" he asked. "You'll shoot me?"

"Maybe," I said.

The slope made him shorter than I was, so I was looking down on him. "I didn't believe anyone could raise dead this old without a human sacrifice. I thought you'd take Stirling's money, try, fail, and go home." He took a step forward, trailing his hands through the power again, as if he were testing it. As if he weren't sure he could cross into it. The touch made Larry gasp.

"With this power you can raise some of them, maybe enough of them," Magnus said.

"Enough for what?" I asked.

He stared up at me, as if he hadn't meant to speak aloud. "You mustn't raise the dead on this mountain, Anita, Larry. You must not."

"Give us a reason not to," I said.

He smiled up at me. ''I don't suppose just because I asked.''

I shook my head. ''Not hardly.''

''This would be so much easier if glamor worked on you.'' He took another step up the slope. ''Of course, if glamor worked on you, we wouldn't be here, would we?''

If he wouldn't answer one question, I'd try another one. ''Why'd you run from the police?''

He took another step closer, and I backed up. He'd done nothing overtly threatening, but there was something about him as he stood there, something alien.

There were images in his eyes that made me want to glance behind to see what was reflecting in his eyes. I could almost see trees, water . . . It was like the things you see out of the corner of your eye, except in color.

''You told the police my secret; why?''

''I had to.''

''You really think I did those awful things to those boys?'' He took another step, moving into the flow of power, but he didn't slip easily as Larry had. Magnus was like a mountain, huge, forcing the power to go wide around him, as if he filled more space magically than could be seen with the naked eye.

I pointed the Browning two-handed at his chest. ''No, I don't.''

''Then why point a gun at me?''

''Why all this fey magic shit?''

He smiled. ''I performed a lot of glamor tonight. It's like a high.''

''You feed off your customers,'' I said. ''You don't just do it for business. You siphon them; that's fucking unseelie court.''

He gave a graceful shrug. ''I am what I am.''

''How'd you know the victims were boys?'' I asked.

Larry moved to my left, gun pointed carefully at the ground. I'd yelled at him for pointing guns at people too soon.

''The police said so.''

''Liar.''

He smiled gently. ''One of them touched me. I saw it all.''

''Convenient,'' I said.

He reached out towards me. ''Don't even think it.''

Larry pointed his gun at Magnus. ''What's going on, Anita?''

''I'm not sure.''

''I can't allow you to raise the dead here. I am sorry.''

''How are you going to stop us?'' I asked.

He stared at me, and I felt something push against my magic, like something large swimming just out of sight in the dark. It made me gasp.

''Freeze, right there, or I will pull this trigger.''

''I haven't moved a muscle,'' he said softly.

''No games, Magnus; you're too damn close to being dead.''

''What did he just do?'' Larry asked. There was a fine tremor in his two-handed grip.

''Later,'' I said. ''Clasp your hands on top of your head, Magnus, slowly, very slowly.''

"Are you going to take me in, as they say on television?"

"Yeah," I said. "You've got a better chance of getting to the jail alive with me than with most of the cops."

"I don't think I'll go with you." Staring down two guns, and he still sounded sure of himself. He was either stupid or knew something I didn't. I didn't think he was stupid.

"Tell me when to shoot him," Larry said.

"When I shoot him, you can shoot him, too."

"Okay," Larry said.

Magnus looked from one to the other of us. "You would take my life for such a small thing?"

"In a heartbeat," I said. "Now clasp your hands slowly on top of your head."

"If I don't?'

"I don't bluff, Magnus."

"Do you have silver bullets in those guns?"

I just stared at him. I could feel Larry shift slightly beside me. You can only point a gun so long without getting tired, or antsy.

"I'll bet they're silver. Silver isn't very effective against fairies."

"Cold iron works best," I said. "I remember."

"Even normal lead bullets would be better than silver. The metal of the moon is a friend to the fey."

"Hands, now, or we find out how fairie flesh holds up to silver bullets."

He raised his hands slowly, gracefully upward. His hands were above shoulder level when he threw himself backwards, falling down the slope. I fired, but he kept on rolling down the earth, and somehow I couldn't quite see him. It was like the air blurred around him.

Larry and I stood at the top of the slope and fired down on him, and I don't think either of us hit him.

He scrambled down the raw earth faster than he looked because he got harder to see even in the moonlight until he vanished into the underbrush left near the midpoint on that side.

"Please tell me he didn't just go poof," Larry said.

"He didn't just go poof," I said.

"What did he do, then?"

"How the hell do I know. This wasn't covered in Fairies 301." I shook my head. "Let's get out of here. I don't know what's going on, but whatever it is, I think we lost our client."

"You think we lost our hotel rooms?"

"I don't know, Larry. Let's go find out." I clicked the safety on the Browning but left it out in my hand. I'd have left the safety off, but that didn't seem wise while stumbling down a rocky mountainside even in the moonlight.

"I think you can put the gun up now, Larry." He hadn't put his safety on.

"You aren't."

"But I've got the safety on."

"Oh." He looked a little sheepish, but he clicked the safety on and holstered it. "You think they would have really killed him?"

"I don't know. Maybe. Beau would have shot at him, but see how much good it did us."

"Why does Stirling want Magnus dead?"

"I don't know."

"Why did Magnus run from the police?"

"I don't know."

"It makes me nervous when you keep answering all my questions with 'I don't know.' "

"Me, too," I said.

I glanced back once just before we lost sight of the mountaintop. The ghosts twisted and flared like candle flames, cool white flames. I knew something else I hadn't known before tonight. Some of the bodies were nearly three hundred years old. A hundred years older than Stirling had told us they were. A hundred years makes a lot of difference in a zombie raising. Why had he lied? Afraid I'd refuse, maybe. Maybe. Some of the bodies were Indian remains. Bits and pieces of jewelry, animal bone, stuff that wasn't European. The Indians in this area didn't bury their dead, at least not in simple graves. And this wasn't a mound.

Something was going on, and I didn't have the faintest idea what it was. But I'd find out. Maybe tomorrow after we got new hotel rooms, gave back the nifty jeep, rented a new car, and told Bert we no longer had a client. Maybe I'd let Larry break the news to him. What are apprentices for if they can't do some of the grunt work?

Okay, okay, I'd tell Bert myself, but I wasn't looking forward to it.

18

Stirling and Co. were gone when we trudged down off the mountain. We drove the Jeep back to the hotel. I was frankly surprised they hadn't taken the Jeep with them and left us to walk. Stirling didn't strike me as a man who liked having guns pointed at him. But then, who does?

Larry's room was first down the hall. He hesitated with his room card in the lock. "You think the rooms are paid for tonight, or do we pack?"

"We pack," I said.

He nodded, and shoved the card in its little slot. The door handle turned, and in he went. I went to the next door and put in my own card. There was a connecting door between the rooms. We hadn't unlocked it, but it was there. Personally I liked my privacy, even from my friends. And especially from my coworkers.

The room's silence flowed around me. It was wonderful. A few minutes of quiet before I faced Bert and told him all that money had just flown the coop.

The room was a suite with an outer room and a separate bedroom. My apartment wasn't much bigger. There was a bar set into the left-hand wall. Being a teetotaler, that was a real plus for me. The walls were a soft pink with a delicate pattern of gilt-edged leaves, the carpet a deep burgundy. The full-sized couch was a purple so dark it looked nearly black. A love seat matched it. Two armchairs were done in a purple, burgundy, and white floral pattern. All exposed wood was very dark and highly polished. I had suspected I had some kind of honeymoon suite until I saw Larry's room. It was nearly a mirror of mine, but done in shades of green.

A cherrywood desk that looked like a genuine antique sat against the far wall. The connecting door was beside it but opened opposite so you wouldn't accidentally bump the desk. Monogrammed stationery graced the desk, along with a second telephone line for your modem I guess.

I don't know if I'd ever stayed in a room this expensive. I doubted seriously if Beadle, Beadle, Stirling, and Lowenstein would want to pick up the tab now.

A sound jerked me around. The Browning sort of materialized in my hand. I was staring down the barrel at Jean-Claude. He stood in the doorway leading to the bedroom. The shirt had long, full sleeves that had been gathered in three puffs down the length of the arm to end in a spill of cloth that framed his long, pale fingers. The collar was high and tied with a white cravat that spilled lace down the front of him tucked into a vest. It was black and velvety with pinpricks of silver on it. Thigh-high black boots fit his legs like a second skin.

His hair was nearly as black as the vest, making it hard to tell where the curls ended and the velvety cloth began. A silver and onyx stickpin that I'd seen before pierced the white lace at his chest.

''Well, *ma petite*, are you going to shoot me?''

I was still standing there with the gun pointed at him. He had not moved. He had been very careful to do nothing that could be taken as threatening. His blue, blue eyes stared at me. Serious, waiting.

I pointed the gun at the ceiling and let out a breath I hadn't realized I was holding. ''How the hell did you get in here?''

He smiled then, and pushed away from the doorjamb. He walked into the room with that wonderful gliding motion of his. Part cat, part dancer, part something else. Whatever the ''else'' was, it wasn't human.

I put the gun away, though I wasn't sure I wanted to. It made me feel better having it in my hand. Trouble was, a gun wouldn't help me against Jean-Claude. Oh, if I was going to kill him it would, but that's not what we were doing lately. Lately we were—dating. Can you stand it? I wasn't sure I could.

''The desk clerk let me in.'' His voice was very mild, amused, whether with himself or with me it was hard to tell.

''Why would he do that?''

''Because I asked him to.'' He walked around me like a shark circling its prey.

I didn't turn with him. I stared straight ahead and let him circle me. It would only amuse him if I kept him in sight. The hairs at the back of my neck stood up. I took a step forward and felt his hand fall back. He'd been about to touch my shoulder. I didn't want him to touch me.

''You used mind tricks on the desk clerk?''

''Yes,'' he said. That one word was full of so much more. I turned towards him so I could see his face.

He was staring at my legs. He raised his face to mine, and somehow that one quick gaze took in my entire body. His midnight blue eyes looked even darker than usual. We weren't sure how I was able to meet his gaze. I was beginning to suspect that being a necromancer had more fringe benefits than just being good with zombies.

''Red becomes you, *ma petite*.'' His voice had grown softer, deeper. He moved closer to me, not touching. He knew better than that, but somehow his eyes showed where his hands wanted to be. ''I like this very much.''

His voice was soft and warm, and far more intimate than his words. ''Your legs are wonderful.'' His words were growing softer. A whisper in the dark that hovered around my body like a line of warmth. His voice was always like that, touchable. He still had the best voice I'd ever heard.

''Stop it, Jean-Claude. I'm too short to have wonderful legs.''

''I do not understand this modern obsession with height.'' He ran his hands just above my hose, so close I could almost feel it like a breath of warmth against my skin.

"Stop it," I said.

"Stop what?" His voice was utterly mild, harmless. Ri—ight.

I shook my head. Asking Jean-Claude not to be a pain in the ass was like asking rain not to be wet. Why try?

"Fine, flirt all you want, but keep in mind that you're here to save the life of a young boy. A young boy who may be being raped while we sit here and waste time."

He sighed deeply and walked towards me. Something must have shown on my face because he sat down in the other chair, not trying to come closer. "You have a habit, *ma petite*, of taking all the fun out of seducing you."

"Yippee," I said. "Now, can we get down to business?"

He smiled his lovely, perfect smile. "I had arranged to meet with the Master of Branson tonight."

"Just like that," I said.

"Isn't that what you wanted me to do?" he asked. His voice held that amused edge again.

"Yeah. I'm just not used to you giving me exactly what I ask for."

"I would give you anything you wanted, *ma petite*, if you would only let me."

"I wanted you out of my life. You don't seem to want to do that."

He sighed. "No, *ma petite*, I do not want to do that." He let it go at that. No accusations about me wanting to be with Richard instead of him. No vague threats on Richard's life. It was sort of odd.

"You're up to something," I said.

He turned, eyes wide, long fingers pressed to his heart. "*Moi?*"

"Yeah, you," I said. I shook my head and let it go. He was up to something. I knew him well enough to know the signs, but I also knew him well enough to know that he wouldn't tell me until he was good and ready. Nobody kept a secret like Jean-Claude, and nobody else had as many of them. There was no deceit in Richard. Jean-Claude lived and breathed it.

"I've got to change and pack before we can leave."

"Change your lovely red skirt, why? Because I like it?"

"Not just that," I said, "though admittedly it's a plus. I can't wear my inner pants holster with the skirt."

"I will not argue that having a second gun will help our show of force tomorrow night."

I stopped and turned. "What do you mean, tomorrow night?"

He spread his hands wide. "It is too close to dawn, *ma petite*. We cannot even drive to the master's lair before the sun rises."

"Dammit," I said softly and with feeling.

"I did my part, *ma petite*. But even I cannot stop the sun from rising."

I leaned against the back of the love seat, hands gripping the edge hard enough to hurt. I shook my head. "We're going to be too late to save him."

"*Ma petite, ma petite*." He knelt in front of me, staring up at me. "Why does this boy bother you so very much? Why is his life so precious to you?"

I stared down into Jean-Claude's perfect face, and had no answer. "I don't know."

He laid his hands on top of my hands. "You're hurting yourself, *ma petite*."

I moved my hands out from under his, crossing my arms over my stomach. Jean-Claude remained kneeling, a hand on either side of me. He was entirely too close to me, and I was suddenly very aware of how short the skirt was.

"I have to go pack," I said.

"Why? Don't you like your room?" Without moving, he seemed closer somehow. I could feel the line of his body against my legs like heat.

"Move," I said.

He leaned backwards, sitting on his heels, forcing me to move past him. The hem of my skirt brushed his cheek as I walked past. "You are such a pain in the ass."

"So nice of you to notice, *ma petite*. Now, why are you leaving this lovely room?"

"A client's paying for the room, and he's not a client anymore."

"Why ever not, *ma petite*?"

"I pulled a gun on him."

His eyes widened, his face a perfect mask of surprise. The mask slipped and he stared at me with ancient eyes. Eyes that had seen much but still didn't know what to make of me. "Why would you do that?"

"They were going to shoot a man for trespassing."

"Was he trespassing?"

"Technically, yeah."

Jean-Claude just looked at me. "Does he not have the right to protect his own land?"

"No, not if it means killing people. A piece of land isn't worth killing over."

"Protecting our lands has been a valid excuse for slaughter since the beginning of time, *ma petite*. Did you suddenly change the rules?"

"I wasn't going to stand there and watch them kill a man for walking on a piece of ground. Besides, I think it was a setup."

"A setup? You mean a plot to kill the man."

"Yeah."

"Were you part of this plot?"

"I may have been bait. He could feel my power over the dead. It called to him."

"Now that is interesting. What is this man's name?"

"You give me the name of the mystery vampire first."

"Xavier," he said.

"Just like that. Why wouldn't you give me the name earlier?"

"I do not want the police to have it."

"Why not?"

"I explained all that. Now, the name of the man you saved tonight."

I stared at him, and didn't want to give it to him. I didn't like how interested he was in the name. But a deal was a deal. "Bouvier, Magnus Bouvier."

"I do not know the name."

"Should you?"

He just smiled at me. It meant nothing and everything.

"You are an irritating son of a bitch."

"Ah, *ma petite*, how can I resist you when you whisper such sweet endearments to me?"

I glared at him, which made him smile wider. There was just the faintest hint of fang peeking into view.

Someone knocked on the door. Probably the manager telling me to get out. I walked to the door. I didn't bother looking through the peephole, so I was caught off guard by who was outside. It was Lionel Bayard.

Had he come to throw us out in person?

I stood there for a second, looking at him. He spoke first, clearing his throat nervously. "Ms. Blake, may I speak with you for a moment?"

He was being awfully polite for someone who had come to kick us out. "I'm listening, Mr. Bayard."

"I really don't think the hallway is the place to discuss this."

I stepped to one side, ushering him into the room. He stepped past me, hands smoothing his tie. His gaze flicked to Jean-Claude, who was standing now. Jean-Claude smiled at Bayard. Pleasant, charming.

"I didn't realize you had company, Ms. Blake. I can come back."

I closed the door. "No, Mr. Bayard, it's all right. I told Jean-Claude about our misunderstanding this evening."

"Ah, yes, uh . . ." Bayard looked from one to the other of us, as if not sure what to say.

Jean-Claude didn't so much sit in the chair as fold his body around it. The movement was almost catlike. "Anita and I have no secrets from one another, Mr. . . ."

"Bayard, Lionel Bayard." He walked over and offered his hand to Jean-Claude. Jean-Claude raised an eyebrow but took the offered hand.

The handshake seemed to make Bayard feel better. A normal gesture. He didn't know what Jean-Claude was. How he could look at him and think him human was beyond me. I'd only seen one vampire that could have passed for human, and he hadn't been human at all. Bayard turned back to me, adjusting his glasses, which didn't need adjusting. That nervous little gesture again. Something was up.

"What's up, Bayard?" I asked. I'd closed the door and was leaning to one side of it, arms crossed over my stomach.

"I'm here to offer our most sincere apologies for earlier tonight."

I just stared at him. "You're apologizing to me?"

"Yes. Mr. Stirling was overzealous. Why, if you had not been there to bring us all to our senses, a great tragedy might have occurred."

I tried to keep my face blank. I wanted to frown at him, or look confused. "Stirling's not mad at me?"

"On the contrary, Ms. Blake. He's grateful to you."

I didn't believe that. "Really," I said.

"Oh, yes. In fact, I've been authorized to offer you a bonus."

"Why?"

''To make up for our behavior tonight.''

''Your behavior was fine,'' I said.

He smiled modestly. His act was about as sincere as faux pearls, but not half so realistic.

''How much is the bonus?''

''Twenty thousand,'' he said.

I stayed leaning against the wall, staring at him. ''No.''

He blinked at me. ''Excuse me?''

''I don't want the bonus.''

''I'm not authorized to go higher than twenty thousand, but I could speak with Mr. Stirling. Perhaps he would go higher.''

I shook my head and pushed away from the wall. ''I don't want more money. I don't want the bonus at all.''

''You aren't quitting on us, are you, Ms. Blake?'' He was blinking so fast I thought he'd pass out. Me quitting bothered him. A lot.

''No, I'm not quitting. But you're already paying an enormous fee. You don't need to pay more.''

''Mr. Stirling is just very anxious that he has not offended you.''

I let that one go. Too easy. ''Tell Mr. Stirling I'd have thought better of his apology if it had been delivered in person.''

''Mr. Stirling is a very busy man. He would have come himself, but he had pressing business.''

I wondered how often Bayard had to apologize for the big man. I wondered how often the apology was for telling a fellow flunkie to shoot someone. ''Fine, you've delivered the message. Tell Mr. Stirling that it isn't the gunfight that's going to make me bail. I read the cemetery tonight. Some of the corpses are closer to three hundred than two hundred. Three hundred years, Lionel; that's an old zombie.''

''Can you raise them?'' He had stepped closer, hands fidgeting with his lapels. He was close to invading my space. I'd have rather had Jean-Claude next to me.

''Maybe. The question isn't can I, but will I, Lionel.''

''What do you mean?''

''You lied to me, Lionel. You underestimated the age of the dead by nearly a century.''

''Not deliberately, Ms. Blake, I assure you. I merely repeated what our research department told me. I did not deliberately mislead you.''

''Sure.''

He reached out almost like he wanted to touch me. I moved back, just enough. He seemed terribly intense. He let his hand drop. ''Please, Ms. Blake, I did not lie on purpose.''

''The problem, Lionel, is that I'm not sure I can raise zombies this old without a human sacrifice. Even I have my limits.''

''So nice to know,'' Jean-Claude said softly.

I frowned at him. He smiled.

''You will try, won't you, Ms. Blake?''

''Maybe. I haven't decided yet.''

He shook his head. ''We will do anything to make this oversight up to you, Ms. Blake. It is entirely my fault that I did not double-check the research department's findings. Is there anything that I can do personally to make it up to you?''

''Just leave. I'll call your office tomorrow to discuss details. I may need some extra . . . paraphernalia to attempt the raising.''

''Anything, anything at all, Ms. Blake.''

''Fine; I'll call.'' I opened the door and stood by it. I thought it was enough of a hint. It was. Bayard went to the door and almost backed out, apologizing as he went.

I closed the door and stood there for a minute.

''That little man is up to something,'' Jean-Claude said.

I turned and looked at him. He was still curled in the chair, looking scrumptious.

''I didn't need vampiric powers to tell me that.''

''Neither,'' he said, ''did I.'' He rose from the chair easily. If I'd curled up in a chair like that, I'd have been stiff.

''I've got to tell Larry that he can stop packing. I don't understand why we're still hired, but we are.''

''Can anyone else raise the graveyard?''

''Not without a human sacrifice, maybe not even then,'' I said.

''They need you, *ma petite*. From the little man's anxiety, they must need the dead raised very badly.''

''Millions of dollars are at stake.''

''I do not think money is all that is at stake,'' he said.

I shook my head. ''Me either.''

He came to join me by the door. ''What extra paraphernalia will you need to raise a three-hundred-year-old corpse, *ma petite*?''

I shrugged. ''A bigger death. I'd originally thought to use a couple of goats.'' I opened the door.

''What are you thinking about using now?''

''An elephant, maybe,'' I said.

We were out in the hall and he was staring at me.

''I'm kidding. Honest. Besides, elephants are an endangered species. I was thinking maybe a cow.''

Jean-Claude stared down at me for a long space of moments, his face very serious. ''Remember, *ma petite*, I can tell if you are lying.''

''What's that supposed to mean?''

''You meant the elephant comment.''

I frowned up at him. What could I say? ''Okay, but just for a minute. I wouldn't really do in an elephant. I'm telling the truth.''

''Yes, *ma petite*, I know.''

I hadn't really meant the crack about the elephant. Not really. It was just the biggest animal I could think of on short notice. And if I was going to attempt to raise several three-hundred-year-old corpses, I was going to need something big. I didn't think a cow would do. Hell, I didn't think a herd of cows would do it. I just hadn't thought of a good alternative yet.

But no elephants, I promise. Besides, can you imagine trying to slit the throat of an elephant? The logistics of just getting one to hold still while you killed it were mind-boggling. There's a reason why most sacrifices are our size or smaller. Makes it easier to hold them down.

"We can't just leave Jeff with that monster," Larry said. He was standing in the middle of his forest green carpet. Jean-Claude was sitting in the corner of the green patterned couch. He was looking amused, like a cat that had found a very interesting mouse.

"We aren't leaving him," I said. "We just can't go looking for him tonight."

He whirled and pointed a finger at Jean-Claude. "Why, because he says so?"

Jean-Claude's smile widened. Definitely amused.

"Check the time, Larry. It'll be dawn soon. All the vampires will be asnooze in their coffins."

Larry shook his head. The look on his face reminded me of me. Stubborn, not wanting to accept it. "We have to do something, Anita."

"We can't talk to vampires during daylight hours, Larry. That's just the way it is."

"And what happens to Jeff today, while we wait for the sun to go down?" His pale skin had gone almost white. His freckles looked like brown ink spots. His pale blue eyes glittered like angry glass. I'd never seen Larry so mad. Hell, I'd never seen him angry.

I glanced at Jean-Claude; he just looked at me. I was on my own. Wasn't I always. "Xavier will have to sleep. He won't be able to harm Jeff once the sun rises."

Larry shook his head. "Will we get him back in time?"

I wanted to say "Sure," but I wouldn't lie. "I don't know. I hope so."

His soft, Howdy-Doody face was set in very stubborn lines. I looked at him and understood why so many people underestimate me. He looked so harmless. Hell, he was sort of harmless, but he was armed now, and learning how to be dangerous. And in his face for the first time I saw a grim purpose building. I'd planned on leaving him behind when I went to talk to the Master of Branson. Looking at him now, I wasn't sure he was going to let me do that. He'd had his first vampire hunt tonight. I'd managed to keep him out of the rough stuff until now. But it wasn't going to last. I'd been hoping he'd give up the idea of hunting vampires. Staring into his glittering eyes, I realized I was the one who was fooling myself. In his own way Larry was as stubborn as I was. Frightening thought, that. But for tonight he was safe.

"You couldn't just comfort me? Tell me we'll find him?" Larry asked.

I smiled. "I try not to lie to you, if I can avoid it."

"For once," Larry said, "I'd have liked to have heard the lie."

"Sorry," I said.

He took in a deep breath and let it out slow. His anger was gone just like that. Larry didn't know what it was to hold onto his rage. He didn't brood over things. One of the main differences between us. I never forgave anyone for anything. A character flaw to be sure, but hell, everyone's got to have at least one.

There was a knock on the door. Larry went for the door.

Jean-Claude was suddenly standing by me. I hadn't seen him move. Hadn't heard his leather boots slither over the carpet. Nothing. Magic. My heart was suddenly thudding in my throat.

''Stomp your feet or something when you do that.''

''Do what, *ma petite*?''

I glared up at him.''That wasn't a mind trick, was it?''

''No,'' he said. That one word slithered across my skin like a low creeping breeze.

''Damn you,'' I said softly and with feeling.

He smiled. ''We've been over that, *ma petite*; you are too late.''

Larry had closed the door. ''There's a guy out in the hall says he's with Jean-Claude.''

''A guy or a vampire?'' I asked.

Larry frowned. ''Not a vampire, but if you mean human I wouldn't go that far.''

''You expecting company?'' I asked.

''Yes, I am.''

''Who?''

He stalked to the door and put a hand on the doorknob. ''Someone I believe you've already met.'' He opened the door with a flourish, stepping to one side to let me have a clear view.

Jason stood in the open door, smiling, relaxed. He was my height exactly, not something you find in a man often. Straight blond hair barely touched the top of his collar; his eyes were the innocent blue of spring skies. The last time I'd seen him he'd been trying to eat me. Werewolves will do that sometimes.

He was dressed in an oversized black sweater that hit him almost at mid-thigh. He'd had to roll the sleeves over his wrists. His pants were leather, laced up the side from waist to mid-calf, where the laces vanished into boots. The lacings were loose enough that there was a pale line of flesh all the way down.

''Hello, Anita.''

''Hi, Jason. What are you doing here?''

He had the grace to look embarrassed. ''I'm Jean-Claude's new pet.''

He said the last word like it was alright. Richard wouldn't have said it that way.

''You didn't tell me you brought company,'' I said.

''We are going to be calling on the Master of the City. We must make a good show of it.''

''So a werewolf, and what . . . me?''

He sighed. ''Yes, *ma petite*, whether you bear my marks or not, most consider you my human servant.'' He raised a hand. ''Please, Anita, I know you are not my human servant in the technical sense. But you have helped me defend my territory. You have killed to protect me. That is the best definition of what a human servant does.''

''So, what? I have to pretend to be your human servant on this visit?''

''Something like that,'' he said.

''Forget it.''

''Anita, I need a show of strength here. Branson was part of Nikolaos's territory. I gave it up because the population density could support another group. But it was still my land, and now it's not. Some view that as weakness rather than practicality.''

''So without any marks at all you've finally got me to play servant for you. You manipulative son of a bitch.''

''You asked me down here, *ma petite*.'' A thread of warmth cut through his words. He stalked towards me. ''I am doing you a favor, do not forget that.''

''I don't think you'll let me forget,'' I said.

He made a harsh sound, as if he had no words for his anger. ''Why do I put up with you? You insult me at every turn. There are many who would give their souls for what I offer you.''

He stood in front of me, eyes like dark sapphires, skin white as marble. His skin glowed like there was a light inside him. He looked like some kind of live sculpture made of light, jewels, and stone.

He was impressive and scary, but I'd seen it before. ''Cut the vampire powers shit, Jean-Claude. It's almost dawn; don't you have a coffin to crawl into somewhere?''

He laughed, but it wasn't pleasant, it was bitter like the touch of steel wool. Something to irritate rather than entice. ''Our luggage has not arrived, has it, my wolf?''

''No, master,'' Jason said.

''Your coffin hasn't arrived?'' I asked.

''Either I have chosen a very lax skycab, or . . .'' He let the words trail off, face bland and pleasant.

''Or what?'' Larry asked.

''*Ma petite*.''

''You think the local master took your coffin,'' I said.

''A punishment for entering her territory without observing all the social niceties.'' He looked at me when he said it.

''I suppose that's my fault,'' I said.

He gave that infuriating shrug. ''I could have said no, *ma petite*.''

''Stop being so civilized about it.''

''Would you be happier if I was angry?'' His voice was very mild when he said it.

''Maybe,'' I said. It would have made me feel less guilty, but I didn't say that out loud.

''Go to the airport and find our luggage if you can, Jason. Bring it back to Anita's room.''

''Wait a minute. You are not moving into my room.''

''It is nearly dawn, *ma petite*. I have no choice. Tomorrow we will find other accommodations.''

''You planned this.''

He gave a short, bitter laugh. ''Even my deviousness knows some bounds, *ma petite*. I would not willingly be without my coffin this close to dawn.''

''What are you going to do without your coffin?'' Larry asked. He looked anxious.

Jean-Claude smiled. ''Do not fear, Lawrence, all I need is darkness, or rather lack of sunlight. The coffin itself is not absolutely necessary, simply more secure.''

''I've never known a vampire that didn't sleep in a coffin,'' I said.

''If I am underground in a secure place, I forego my coffin. Though truthfully, once daylight finds me I am insensible and could sleep on a bed of nails and not know it.''

I wasn't sure I believed him. He worked harder than most at passing for human.

''You will see the truth of my words soon enough, *ma petite*.''

''That's what I'm afraid of,'' I said.

''You can sleep on the couch if you prefer, but I am telling you truly that once full daylight arrives I will be harmless, helpless if you like. I would be unable to molest you even if I wanted to.''

''And what other fairy tales am I supposed to believe? I've seen you move around after dawn, hidden from light, but you worked just fine.''

''After eight hours or so of sleep, if it is still daylight I can move around, true, but I doubt you will stay abed for eight hours. You have clients or something, a murder investigation, some business that will take you out and about.''

''If I leave you alone, who'll see that some maid doesn't come in, pull the curtains back and French fry you?''

The smile widened. ''Concern over my well-being. I am touched.''

I looked at him. He looked pleasant, amused, but it was a mask. His expression when he didn't want you to know what he was thinking, but didn't want you to know that he didn't want you to know. ''What are you up to?''

''For once, *ma petite*, nothing.''

''Yeah, right.''

''If I find the coffin, I'll need to rent a truck,'' Jason said.

''You can use our Jeep,'' Larry said.

I glared at him. ''No, he can't.''

''Think of it as expediency, *ma petite*. If Jason must rent a truck, then I may have to spend another day in your bed. I know you do not want that.'' There was amusement in his voice, and an undercurrent of something else. It might have been bitterness.

''I'll drive,'' Larry said.

''No, you won't,'' I said.

''It's almost dawn, Anita. I'll be alright.''

I shook my head. ''No.''

''You can't treat me like a kid brother forever. I can drive the Jeep.''

''I promise not to eat him,'' Jason said.

Larry held out his hand for the keys. ''You have to trust me sometime.''

I just looked at him.

''I promise to shoot anything, human or monster, that threatens me while I'm gone.'' He made the Boy Scout sign, three fingers to heaven. ''You can bail me out of jail and explain that I was just following orders.''

I sighed. ''Alright, dammit.'' I gave him the keys.

He grinned at me. ''Thanks.''

I shook my head. ''Just hurry back, okay?''

''Anything you say.''

''Just get out of here, and be careful.''

Larry left with Jason trailing behind. I stared at the door after it closed, wondering if I should have gone with them. Knowing that Larry would have gotten mad, but mad was better than dead. Hell, it was a simple errand; go to the airport and pick up a coffin. What could go wrong with less than an hour of darkness left? Shit.

''You cannot protect him, Anita.''

''I can try.''

Jean-Claude gave that infuriating shrug that meant anything you wanted it to mean, and nothing at all. ''Shall we retire to your room, *ma petite*?''

I opened my mouth to tell him he could bunk with Larry, but didn't say it. I didn't really believe he'd munch on Larry, but I was sure he wouldn't munch on me. ''Sure,'' I said.

He looked a little surprised, as if he'd expected an argument. But I was all out of argument tonight. He could have the bed. I'd take the couch. What could be more innocent? Biker Nuns from Hell, but besides that.

19

I could feel dawn pressing against the windows like a cool hand when we got back to my room. It was very near. Jean-Claude smiled at me. "The first time I manage to share a hotel room with you, and there is no time." He gave an elaborate sigh. "Things never work as I plan with you, *ma petite*."

"Maybe that's a hint," I said.

"Perhaps." He glanced at the closed drapes. "I must go, *ma petite*. Until darkness." He shut the bedroom door a little hurriedly. I could feel the coming light pressing around the building. I'd noticed over the years of hunting vamps that I'd become aware of dawn, and sunset. There had been times when I'd struggled from disaster to disaster just to stay alive until that soft growing pressure of light could sweep the sky and save my cookies. For the first time I wondered what it would be like to see it as a danger instead of a blessing.

After he'd closed the door I realized my suitcase was in the bedroom. Damn. I hesitated, and finally knocked. No answer. I opened the door just a crack, then farther. He wasn't in there. Water ran in the bathroom. A line of light showed under the door. What did vampires do in bathrooms? Better not to know.

I grabbed my suitcase from the floor and carried it out before the bathroom door could open. I did not want to see him again. I did not want to see what happened to him when the sun rose.

When the sun had risen enough to pulse against the closed drapes like pale lemon liquid, I changed into a t-shirt and jeans. I had a robe with me, but if I was going to greet both Larry and Jason I wanted to be wearing some pants.

I called down for extra blankets and a pillow. No one bitched that it was a quarter past dawn, and a strange time to need bedclothes. They just brought the stuff. True class. The maid didn't even glance at the closed bedroom door.

I spread the blanket on the couch and stared at it. It was a pretty couch but didn't look terribly comfortable. Oh, well, virtue had its punishments. Of course, maybe it wasn't virtue that kept me out of the bedroom. If it had been Richard curled up in the next room, then only moral fortitude would have kept me out. With Jean-Claude . . . I had never seen him after dawn when he was dead to the world. I wasn't sure I wanted to see. I knew I didn't want to cuddle up next to him while the warmth left his body.

There was a knock on the door. I hesitated. It was probably Larry, but then again . . . I went to the door with the Browning naked in my hand. Beau had had a shotgun last night. Paranoia, or caution; hard to tell the difference sometimes.

I stood to one side of the door and said, "Yes."

"Anita, it's us."

I hit the safety and put the barrel of the Browning down the front of my jeans. It was too big a gun to wear in an inner pants holster, but for temporary holding, that worked.

I opened the door.

Larry leaned against the doorjamb, looking rumpled and tired. He had a McDonald's sack in one hand, and four cups shoved into one of those Styrofoam holders. Two of the cups held coffee, the other two sodas.

Jason had a large leather suitcase under each arm, a battered, much smaller suitcase in his right hand, and a second McDonald's bag in his left. He didn't look the least bit tired. A morning person, even after no sleep at all. It was disgusting. His eyes flicked to the gun shoved in my waistband. He noticed, but he didn't comment. Point for him.

Larry never even blinked at the gun.

"Food?" I asked.

"I didn't eat much last night. Besides, Jason was hungry, too," Larry said. He came inside, putting the drinks and food on the wet bar. None of us drank; good to use the bar for something.

Jason walked through the door sideways with the suitcases and food, but there was no effort to it. He wasn't straining one little bit to carry it all.

"Showoff," I said.

He sat the luggage on the floor. "This isn't even close to showing off," he said.

I locked the door behind them. "I suppose you can bring the coffin up single-handedly."

"No, but not because it's heavy. It's just too long. The balance isn't right."

Great. Super werewolf. Though for all I knew, all lycanthropes could lift that much weight. Maybe Richard could lift coffins with one arm. It was not a comforting thought.

Jason started laying food out on the bar. Larry had already climbed onto one of the bar stools. He was pouring sugar into one of the coffees.

"Did you just leave the coffin in the lobby?" I asked. I had to lay the Browning on the bar to sit down. I was just too short-waisted to have it down my pants.

Larry sat the unopened coffee in front of me. "It's missing."

I stared at him. "You found the suitcases but not the coffin?"

"Yep," Jason said, as he finished dividing the food into three piles. He'd pushed some of it in front of both of us, but the lion's share was in front of him.

"How can you eat this early in the morning?"

"I'm always hungry," he said. He looked at me sort of expectantly.

I let it slide. It was too easy.

"Come on, I fed you that one," he said.

"You don't seem particularly worried," I said.

He shrugged, and slid onto a bar stool. "What do you want me to say? I've seen some weird shit since I became a werewolf. If I got hysterical every time something went wrong, every time someone I knew died, I'd be in the loony bin by now."

"I thought fights for dominance in the pack, except for pack leader, weren't to the death," I said.

"People forget," he said.

"I'll have to talk to Richard when I get back in town. He hasn't been mentioning any of this."

"Nothing to mention," Jason said. "Just business as usual."

Great. "Did anybody see who took the coffin?"

Larry answered, his voice sluggish even with the caffeine and sugar. There's only so much you can do on no sleep at all. "No one saw anybody take it. In fact, the only guy left from the night shift said, 'I just turned away for a second, and it wasn't there. Just the luggage standing there by itself.' "

"Shit," I said.

"Why take the coffin?" he asked. He drank most of his coffee. His Egg McMuffin sat untouched in front of him. They'd put hotcakes in front of me with a little tub of syrup beside it.

"Your breakfast is getting cold," Jason said.

He was enjoying himself too much. I frowned at him, but I opened my coffee. I didn't want the food. "I think the master is flexing a little muscle. What do you think, Jason?" I kept my voice casual.

He smiled at me around a mouthful of food, swallowed, and said, "I think whatever Jean-Claude wants me to think."

Maybe my voice had been too casual. I should really give up on subtlety; I just wasn't good enough at it. "Did he tell you not to talk to me?"

"No, just to be careful what I said."

"He says jump, and you say how high; is that it?"

"That's it." He ate a bite of scrambled egg, his face peaceful.

"Doesn't that bother you?"

"I don't make the rules, Anita. I'm not an alpha anything."

"And it doesn't bother you?" I asked.

He shrugged. "Sometimes, but there's nothing I can do about it. Why fight it?"

"I don't understand that at all," Larry said.

"Me either."

"You don't have to understand it," he said. He couldn't have been more than twenty, but the look in his eyes wasn't young. It was the look of someone who'd seen a lot, done a lot, and not all of it nice. It was the look I was dreading to see on Larry's face someday. They were nearly the same age; what had people been doing to Jason to give him such jaded eyes?

"What do we do now?" Larry asked.

"You're the vampire experts. I'm just Jean-Claude's pet."

He said it like it didn't bother him. It would have bothered me. I shook my head. ''I'm going to call the cops, then get some sleep.''

''What are you going to tell them?'' Jason asked.

''I'm going to tell them about Xavier.''

''Did Jean-Claude say you could tell the cops?''

I looked at him. ''I didn't ask for permission.''

''Jean-Claude wouldn't like you bringing in the police.''

I just stared at him.

He blinked at me. ''Don't do it just because I said that, please.''

''He knows you pretty well for someone who's only met you twice,'' Larry said.

''Three times,'' I said. ''Two out of three times, he's tried to eat me.''

Larry's eyes widened a little. ''You're kidding.''

''She just looks so tasty,'' Jason said.

''I've had about enough of you,'' I said.

''What's wrong? Jean-Claude and Richard both tease you.''

''I'm dating both of them,'' I said. ''I'm not dating you.''

''Maybe you've got a thing for monsters. I can be just as scary as the next guy.''

I stared at him. ''No,'' I said, ''you can't. That's why you're not alpha. That's why you're Jean-Claude's pet, because you aren't scary enough.''

Something flowed through his pale blue eyes. Something angry and dangerous. Sitting there with his forkful of scrambled eggs, and a Coke in one hand, he was suddenly different. It was hard to put into words, but it raised the hair on the back of my neck.

''Ease down, wolf-boy,'' I said. My voice was soft, careful. I was sitting less than a foot away from him. At this distance he could jump me easy. The Browning was an inch away from my right hand, but I knew better. I might grab the gun, but I'd never get it pointed in time. I'd seen him move before, and I wasn't quick enough. Lack of sleep was making me trusting, or stupid. Same thing.

A low, trickling growl rumbled out of him. My pulse beat a little faster.

Larry's gun was suddenly pointing past my nose at the werewolf's face. ''Don't,'' Larry said. His voice was low and even, and very damn serious.

I eased back off the bar stool, bringing the Browning with me. Didn't really want Larry's gun to go off right next to my face.

I pointed my gun at Jason's chest, one-handed, almost casual. ''Don't ever threaten me again.''

Jason stared at me. His beast lurked just behind his eyes like a wave rushing towards the shore.

''You start going furry, and I won't wait to find out if you're bluffing,'' I said.

Larry had one knee on the bar stool, gun still pointed nice and steady. I hoped he didn't fall off the bar stool and accidentally shoot Jason. If he shot him, I wanted it to be on purpose.

Jason's shoulders relaxed. His hands unclenched, leaving the fork and the drink on the bar. He closed his eyes and sat very still for nearly a full minute. Larry and I waited, guns still pointed. Larry's eyes flicked to me. I shook my head.

Jason opened his eyes and let out a deep, sighing breath. He looked normal again, that tension drained away. He grinned. ''I had to try.''

I took another step back, putting my back to the wall. Out of reach, I lowered the gun. Larry hesitated, but followed my lead.

''So you tried; now what?''

He shrugged. ''You're dominant to me.''

''Just like that,'' I said.

''Would you be happier if I made you fight me?''

I shook my head.

''But I backed her up,'' Larry said. ''She didn't do it alone.''

''Doesn't matter. You're loyal to her, would risk your life for her. There's more to being dominant than just muscle, or guns.''

Larry looked puzzled. ''What do you mean, dominant? I feel like I'm missing part of the conversation.''

''Why are you working so damn hard at not being human, Jason?'' I asked.

He smiled and went back to his breakfast.

''Answer me, Jason.''

He finished off his eggs and said, ''No.''

''What's going on?'' Larry said.

''Mind games,'' I said.

Larry made an exasperated noise. ''Someone explain to me why we had to pull a gun on someone who's supposed to be on our side.''

''Jean-Claude keeps telling me Richard isn't any more human than he is. Jason's little display helps emphasize that. Doesn't it, wolf-boy?''

Jason ate the rest of his food like we weren't there.

''Answer me,'' I said.

He turned on the bar stool, putting his elbows behind him. ''I have too many masters now, Anita. I don't need another one.''

''And I've got too many monsters messing with me right now. Don't add yourself to the list, Jason.''

''Is it a short list?'' he asked.

''Gets shorter all the time,'' I said.

He smiled and slid off the bar stool. ''Is anybody tired but me?''

Larry and I stared at him. The werewolf didn't look tired—more than I could say for us mere humans.

Jason wasn't going to answer my questions, and they weren't important enough to shoot him over. Stalemate.

''Fine; where are you sleeping?'' I asked.

''If you trust me not to eat him, in Larry's room.''

''No way,'' I said.

''You want me here, with you?''

''I told him he could stay in my room on the ride over,'' Larry said.

''That was before he pulled the werewolf crap,'' I said.

Larry shrugged. ''You've got the Master of the City tucked into your bed. I think I can handle one werewolf.''

I didn't think so. But I didn't want to discuss it in front of the werewolf. ''No, Larry.''

He was instantly angry. ''What do I have to do to prove myself to you?''

''Stay alive,'' I said.

''What's that supposed to mean?''

''You're not a shooter, Larry.''

''I was willing to shoot him.'' Larry pointed to the smiling werewolf.

''I know.''

''Because I'm not trigger-happy, you don't trust me to handle myself?''

I sighed. ''Larry, please. If Jason turned furry in the middle of the day and killed you, I couldn't live with myself.''

''And if he kills you?'' Larry said.

''He won't.''

''Why not?'' Larry asked.

''Because Jean-Claude would kill him. If he hurt you, I'd kill him, but I don't know if Jean-Claude would avenge you. Jason's more frightened of Jean-Claude than he is of me. Aren't you, Jason?''

Jason had sat down on the end of the couch on my blanket. ''Oh, yes.''

''I don't know why,'' Larry said. ''You're the one who kills for Jean-Claude. He never seems to kill anyone on his own.''

''Larry, who would you be more afraid of, Jean-Claude or me?''

''You wouldn't hurt me,'' he said.

''If you had to face one of us, which would you prefer?''

Larry looked at me for a long time. The anger drained away, replaced by something tired and old in his eyes. ''Him.''

''For God's sake, why?'' I asked.

''I've seen you kill a lot of people, Anita. A lot more than Jean-Claude. He might try to frighten me to death, but you'd just kill me.''

My mouth was open, just a little. ''If you really believe that I'm more dangerous than Jean-Claude, then you haven't been paying attention.''

''I didn't say you were more dangerous. I said you'd kill me quicker.''

''That's why I'm not as afraid of Anita as I am of Jean-Claude,'' Jason said.

Larry looked at him. ''What do you mean?''

''All she'll do is kill me, quick, neat. Jean-Claude wouldn't kill me quick, or easy. He'd make sure it hurt.''

The two men stared at each other. Each one's logic was sound as far as it went. I was with Jason. ''If you really believe what you're saying, Larry, then you haven't seen enough vampires.''

''How am I ever going to see enough vampires if you keep me at arm's length, Anita?''

Had I really kept him out of it that much? Had I overprotected him? Let him see my ruthlessness but not Jean-Claude's?

''And I'm going to the master's tomorrow night. You are not leaving me behind anymore.''

''You're right,'' I said. The answer seemed to surprise both of them.

''If you really believe that I'd kill someone quicker than Jean-Claude would,

I have overprotected you. You have to understand how dangerous they are, Larry. How deadly, or someday I won't be around and you'll get killed.''

I took a deep breath and let it out slowly. My stomach was tight with fear. Fear that Larry would get killed because I'd kept him out of it. It was something I hadn't anticipated.

''Come on, Jason,'' Larry said.

Jason stood up.

''No. Tomorrow you can be ass-deep in vampires with me watching. Until you understand how dangerous the monsters are, I don't want you alone with them.''

His eyes were angry and hurt. I'd undercut his confidence, his self-esteem. But . . . what else could I do?

Larry turned abruptly on his heel and left. He didn't argue. He didn't say goodbye. He slammed the door behind him, and I fought an urge to follow him. What could I say? I leaned my forehead against the door, and whispered, ''Damn.''

''Do I get the couch?'' Jason asked.

I turned and leaned against the door. I still had the Browning in my hand, though I wasn't sure why anymore. I was getting tired, sloppy. ''No, I get the couch.''

''Where do you want me, then?''

''I don't care; just not near me.''

He ran his hands down the edge of the blanket, running the cloth between his fingers. ''If you're really sleeping out here, I'd just as soon have the bed.''

''It's taken,'' I said.

''How big is the bed?''

''King-size, but what difference does it make?''

''Jean-Claude won't mind if I share with him. He'd prefer it was you, but . . .'' He shrugged.

I looked at him, at his tranquil, pleasant face. ''Is this the first time you've shared a bed with Jean-Claude?''

''No,'' he said.

It must have shown on my face, because he lowered the high neck of the sweater enough for me to see two fang marks. I pushed away from the wall and walked closer. Close enough to see that the bite was almost healed.

''Sometimes he likes a snack when he first wakes up,'' Jason said.

''Jesus,'' I said.

Jason let go of the collar, and it slid over the bite like it wasn't there. The same way you'd hide a hickey. Jason sat there looking harmless. He was exactly my height, and had the face of a knowledgeable angel.

''Richard didn't let Jean-Claude snack on him,'' I said.

''No,'' he said.

''No. That's all you have to say.''

''What do you want me to say, Anita?''

I thought about that for a second. ''I want you to be outraged. Angry.''

''Why?''

I shook my head. ''Go to bed, Jason. You're making me tired.''

He went into the bedroom without another word. I didn't peek to see if he changed into a wolf and curled up on the carpet, or if he crawled into bed beside the corpse. None of my business, or at least nothing I wanted to see.

20

I put the Browning under the pillow with the safety on. At home with the gun in the special holster I'd added to the headboard of the bed, the safety would have been off. But I'd look pretty silly if I accidentally shot myself during the night—day—trying to protect myself from werewolves.

The Firestar I put under the couch cushion, safety on. Normally it would have been in my luggage, but I was feeling just a little insecure.

The knives were in the luggage. Things weren't quite dangerous enough to wear the wrist sheaths to bed. Besides, they weren't very comfortable, not to sleep in, anyway.

I had just settled down for a long day's sleep when I realized I hadn't called Special Agent Bradford. Damn. I threw the blanket back and padded to the telephone in nothing but a t-shirt and undies. Yes, the Browning came with me. Doesn't do you a damn bit of good to have a weapon if it isn't with you.

I dialed the number and got no answer. Fancy that. Didn't everyone work twenty-four hours a day? I had his beeper number. Could the news about Xavier wait? Would even having the name help them? Agent Bradford had made it very clear that I was persona non grata. First, Freemont had blackballed me; second, the Quinlans were threatening to sue everybody unless I was kept away from the case. I'd done such a bang-up job protecting their family, they didn't want a repeat. They seemed to think I'd get their son killed. Fancy that.

I had Bradford's beeper number. He'd given strict orders that if I found out anything I was to tell him, and only him. Made me not want to tell him a bloody thing. But who was I to say the FBI didn't have a vampire file somewhere? Maybe the name would mean something to them. Maybe it would help them find Jeff. Besides, Jean-Claude hadn't told me not to give Xavier's name to the cops. I used the beeper number. I left my phone number. Now I could either go back to bed, and let his return call wake me, or I could sit in the chair for a few minutes and wait. I waited.

The phone rang in under five minutes. I like a man who returns his pages promptly. I said "Hello," in case it wasn't him. It was.

"Special Agent Bradford. This number was on my beeper." His voice was rough with sleep.

"This is Anita Blake."

A moment of silence, then, "Do you know what time it is?"

"I haven't been to bed yet, so yeah, I know what time it is."

Another silence. "What do you want, Ms. Blake?"

I took a deep breath and let it out slow. Getting mad would not be helpful. "I have a possible name for the vampire that's been slaughtering kids."

"What's the name?"

"Xavier."

"Last name?"

"Vampires don't have last names, as a general rule."

"Thank you for the name, Ms. Blake. How did you get it?"

I thought about that for a few seconds. I couldn't think of a really good answer. "It sort of fell into my lap."

"Why don't I believe that, Ms. Blake? I thought I'd made myself clear this evening. You are not to involve yourself in this case, in any way."

"Look, I didn't have to call, but I want Jeff Quinlan back alive. I thought the FBI might be able to use the name of the vampire who took him."

"I want to know how you got the name," he said.

"An informant."

"I'd like to talk to this informant," he said.

"No," I said.

"Are you withholding information from a federal investigation, Ms. Blake?"

"No, Agent Bradford, I am going out of my way to share information."

He was quiet again. "Alright, Ms. Blake, you're right. Thank you for the name. We'll run it in the computers."

"This vampire has a history of harming preadolescent boys. He's a pedophile."

"Good lord, a vampire pedophile." He finally sounded genuinely interested in what I was saying. "And he has the Quinlan boy."

"Yeah," I said.

"I would really like to talk to this source of yours," he said.

"He's a little shy around the police."

"I could insist, Ms. Blake. We've got reports that a private jet flew in last night, and a coffin got unloaded. It's registered to a J. C. Corporation. They seem to own a lot of vampire-related, St. Louis-based businesses. Do you know anything about that, Ms. Blake?"

Lying to the FBI seemed like a bad idea, but I wasn't sure what they'd do with the truth. The Feds were investigating vampire crime, and suddenly a new vamp shows up in town. The least they would do was question him. The worst . . . well, there was the vampire in Mississippi that had been accidentally transferred to a cell with a window. The sun rose, and . . . French fried vampire. An ACLU lawyer had sued the cops' asses, and won, but that didn't bring the vamp back. Admittedly the dead vamp was one of the newly dead. Jean-Claude would have escaped fairly easily, but just escaping from the law by using vampire powers would get a warrant for his arrest. Sort of like what was happening to Magnus.

Besides, a vampire had killed a cop last night. The police might not be terribly careful with any vampire right now. The police are only human, after all.

''You still there, Blake?''

''I'm here.''

''You didn't answer my question.''

''Where was the coffin delivered?'' I asked.

''It wasn't. It just disappeared.''

''So what do you want from me?''

''There was some luggage that went with it. The luggage was picked up a little while ago by two young men. The description of one of them sounds a lot like Larry Kirkland.''

''Is that so?''

''That's so.''

We both sat on our ends of the phone waiting for someone to say something.
''I could send some agents down to your hotel room.''

''There are no coffins in my hotel room, Agent Bradford.''

''You sure of that, Blake?''

''My hand to God.''

''Do you know who runs this J. C. Corporation?''

''No.'' It was the truth. Until Bradford told me about it, I'd never heard of the J. C. Corporation. It would only have been an educated guess if I'd said Jean-Claude owned it. Okay, I was fooling myself, but so what?

''Do you know where the coffin was delivered?'' he asked.

''Nope.''

''Would you tell me if you knew?''

''If it would help find Jeff Quinlan, you bet.''

''Alright, Blake, but no more helping. Stay the fuck out of this case. When we find the vampires we'll call you in, and you can do your job. You're a vampire hunter, not a cop. Try to remember that.''

''Fine,'' I said.

''Good. Now I'm going back to sleep. I suggest you do the same. We'll find the vampires today, Blake. And let's just say I don't believe everything Freemont said. We'll call you in for the kill.''

''Thanks.''

''Good night, Blake.''

''Good night, Bradford.''

We hung up. I sat there for a minute, just letting it all sink in. If they found Jean-Claude in my room, what would they do? I'd seen the cops pop a comatose vampire in a body bag, transport it to the station house, and wait for nightfall to question it. I'd thought it was a bad idea because the vamp would wake up pissed. It did. I ended up killing it. I've always felt bad about that particular kill. It was an out-of-state job. The local cops invited me in to advise them. Once we found the vamp, they stopped listening to my advice. Reminded me of now. That vampire had also just been brought in for questioning.

I was suddenly tired. It was like the entire night just hit me in one grinding wave. Sleep dragged at me. I had to go to sleep. I couldn't help Jeff Quinlan, or anybody else, until I'd had a few hours of sleep. Besides, maybe the Feds would find him. Stranger things had happened.

I left a wake-up call with the desk for noon, and cuddled under the blanket. The Browning was lumpy under the pillow. At least I couldn't feel the Firestar under the couch cushion. I half wished I'd packed Sigmund, my stuffed toy penguin, but somehow having Jean-Claude or Jason find me sleeping with a stuffed toy bothered me almost as much as them trying to eat me. What price machismo?

21

Someone was banging on the door. I opened my eyes to a room filled with soft, indirect sunlight. The curtains in here weren't nearly as thick as the ones in the bedroom. Which was why I was out here and Jean-Claude was in there.

I struggled into the jeans I'd left on the floor and yelled, ''I'm coming.''

The banging stopped, then it sounded like they kicked the door. Was this a federal wake-up call? I went to the door with the Browning in my hand. Somehow I didn't think the FBI would be so rude. I stood to the side of the door and asked, ''Who is it?''

''It's Dorcas Bouvier.'' She kicked the door again. ''Open this damn door.''

I peeked through the little peephole. It was Dorcas Bouvier, or her evil twin. She didn't have a weapon in sight. I was probably safe. I put the Browning under the t-shirt in the waistband of my pants. The t-shirt was a large and fell to mid-thigh. It hid the gun and then some.

I unlocked the door and stood to one side. Dorcas shoved the door open, leaving it swinging open behind her. I closed and locked the door, leaning against it watching her.

Dorcas stalked through the room like some sort of exotic cat. Her waist-length, chestnut hair swung like a curtain as she moved. She finally turned and glared at me with those sea-green eyes that were a mirror of her brother's. The pupil had spiraled downward to a pinpoint, leaving the irises floating and making her look almost blind.

''Where is he?''

''Where's who?'' I asked.

She glared at me and went for the bedroom door. I couldn't get there in time to stop her, and I wasn't willing to shoot her yet.

When I came up behind her she was two steps into the bedroom, back rigid, staring at the bed. It was worth staring at.

Jean-Claude lay on his back with the wine-dark sheets pulled up to mid-chest. One shoulder and a pale, pale arm were stretched across the dark sheets. In the semidarkness his hair blended with the pillow to leave his face white and nearly ethereal.

Jason lay on his stomach. The only things under the sheet were one leg and, barely, his buttocks. If he was wearing clothes, I couldn't tell. He raised up on his elbows and turned to us. His yellow hair had fallen into his face, and he blinked like he'd been deeply asleep. He smiled when he saw Dorcas Bouvier.

"It isn't Magnus," she said.

"No," I said, "it isn't. You want to talk outside?"

"Don't go on my account," Jason said. He rolled onto one elbow. The silken sheet slid across his hips as he moved.

Dorcas Bouvier turned on her heel and marched out of the room. I closed the door to the sound of Jason's laughter.

Dorcas looked shaken, embarrassed even. Good to see. I was embarrassed, too, but didn't know what to do about it. Trying to explain your way out of situations like this never works. People are always willing to believe the worst of you. So I didn't try. I just stood there looking at her. She wouldn't meet my eyes.

After a nice uncomfortable silence that caused heat to wash up her face, she said, "I don't know what to say. I thought my brother was in there. I . . ." She met my eyes finally. She was already regaining her composure, her surety of purpose. You could watch it solidify in her eyes. She was here for more than rousting her brother out of my bed.

"Why in the world would you think Magnus was here?"

"May I sit down?"

I motioned her to a seat. She sat in one of the chairs, spine very straight, perfect posture. My stepmother, Judith, would have been proud. I leaned on the arm of the couch because I couldn't sit down with the Browning down my pants. I wasn't sure how she'd take me being armed, so I didn't want to show the gun. Some people freeze up around firearms. Go figure.

"I know Magnus was with you last night."

"With me?" I said.

"I don't mean . . ." Heat crept up her face again. "I don't mean *with* you. I mean I know you saw him last night."

"He tell you that?"

She shook her head, making her hair slide like fur over her shoulders. It was eerily reminiscent of Magnus. "I saw you together."

I studied her face, trying to read past the embarrassment. "You weren't there last night."

"Where?" she asked.

I frowned at her. "How did you see us?"

"You admit you saw him last night, then," she said. Her eagerness came back in a rush.

"What I want to know is how you saw us together."

She took a deep breath. "That's my business."

"Magnus said his sister was better at visions than he was. Is that true?"

"What didn't he tell you?" she asked. She was angry again. Her emotions seemed to collide, spinning too fast over her face and voice.

''He didn't tell me why he ran from the police.''

She looked down at her hands, folded in her lap. ''I don't know why he ran. It doesn't make any sense.'' She looked back up at me. ''I know he didn't kill those children.''

''I agree,'' I said.

Surprise showed on her face. ''I thought you told the police he did it.''

I shook my head. ''No, I told them he could have done it. I never said he did it.''

''But . . . The detective was so sure. She said you'd told her.''

I cursed softly under my breath. ''Detective Freemont?''

''Yes.''

''Don't believe everything she tells you, especially about me. She doesn't seem to like me very much.''

''If you didn't tell them, then why are they so sure Magnus did these horrible things? He would have no reason to kill these people.''

I shrugged. ''Magnus isn't wanted for the killings anymore. Didn't anybody tell you that?''

She shook her head. ''No. You mean he can come back home?''

I sighed. ''It's not that simple. Magnus used glamor on the police to escape. That's a felony all on its own. The cops will kill him on sight, Ms. Bouvier. They don't mess around where magic is concerned. Can't say I blame them.''

''I saw the two of you talking outside under the sky.''

''I did see him last night.''

''Did you tell the police?''

''No.''

She stared at me. ''Why not?''

''Magnus is probably guilty of something, or he wouldn't have run, but he deserves better treatment than he's getting.''

''Yes,'' she said, ''he does.''

''What made you think he'd be in my bed?''

She looked down at her lap again. ''Magnus can be very persuasive. I can't remember the last time a woman told him no. I apologize for assuming that about you.'' She stopped, glanced towards the bedroom, then back to me. She blushed again.

I was not going to explain how I ended up with two males in my bed. Surely it was obvious from the blanket and pillow that I'd slept out here. Surely.

''What do you want from me, Ms. Bouvier?''

''I want to find Magnus before he gets himself killed. I thought you could help me. How could you have betrayed Magnus to the police? Surely you know what it's like to be different.''

I wanted to ask if it showed, if she could see ''Necromancer'' written across my forehead, but I didn't. If the answer was yes, I wasn't sure I wanted to know.

''If he hadn't run away, they would have simply questioned him. They didn't have enough to arrest him. Do you have any idea why he ran?''

She shook her head. ''I've tried to think of something, anything, but it doesn't make any sense to me, Ms. Blake. My brother is a little amoral, but he's not a bad man.''

I wasn't sure you could be a little amoral, but I let it slide. ''If he turns himself in to me, I'll walk him into the police station. But short of that, I don't know what I can do.''

''I've been everywhere I can think of, but he's just not there. I even checked the mound.''

''The mound?'' I asked.

She stared up at me. ''He didn't tell you about the creature?''

I thought about lying to see if I could get information, but the look in her eyes told me I'd blown it. ''He didn't mention any creature.''

''Of course; if he had told you, the police would be down there with dynamite. Dynamite won't kill it, but it would screw our magical wards six ways to Sunday.''

''What creature?'' I asked.

''Is there anything Magnus told you that you didn't tell the police?'' Dorcas asked.

I thought about that for a second. ''No.''

''He was right not to tell you.''

''Maybe, but I'm trying to help him now.''

''Do you have a guilty conscience?'' she asked.

''Maybe,'' I said.

She looked at me. Her pupils had resurfaced, and she looked almost normal. Almost. ''How can I trust you?''

''You probably can't. But I do want to help Magnus. Please talk to me, Ms. Bouvier.''

''I have to have your word that you won't tell the police. I am serious, Ms. Blake. If the police interfere, they could loose the thing and people would die.''

I debated but couldn't see any reason the police would need to know. ''Okay, I give you my word.''

''I may not have Magnus's way with glamor, but an oath to one of the fey is a serious matter, Ms. Blake. Lying to us tends to go badly.''

''Is that a threat?''

''Think of it as a warning.'' The air moved between us like heat rising off a road. Her eyes swirled like miniature whirlpools.

Maybe I should have shown her my gun. ''Don't threaten me, Dorcas. I'm not in the mood.''

The magic seemed to seep away like water running into a crack in the rocks. You knew it was still there, below the surface. But for someone who had been threatened by werewolves and vampires, she paled in comparison. Magnus seemed to have most of the talent in the family. On the scale of scariness, Magnus was up there.

''Just so we understand each other, Ms. Blake. If you tell the police and they let loose the creature, the deaths will be on your head.''

''Alright, I'm impressed; now tell me about it.''

''Did Magnus tell you about our ancestor, Llyn Bouvier?''

''Yeah, he was the first European in this area. He married into the local tribe. Converted them to Christianity. He was also fey.''

She nodded. ''He brought another fey with him.''

''A wife?'' I asked.

''No, he had captured one of the less intelligent fairies. He imprisoned it in a magically constructed box. It escaped and slaughtered nearly the entire tribe we're descended from. He finally managed to contain it with the help of an Indian shaman, or priest, but he never regained control over it. The best he could do was to imprison it.''

''What kind of fairie did he bring over?''

''Bloody Bones isn't just the name of our bar,'' she said. ''It's short for Rawhead and Bloody Bones.''

My eyes widened. ''But that's a nursery boggle; why would your ancestor want to capture one? They don't have any treasure, or wishes, to give out. Or am I wrong on that?''

''No, you're quite correct. Bloody Bones has no riches or gentle magic to grant wishes.''

''Then why capture it?''

''Most children born of human and fairie blood don't have a lot of magic.''

''That's what the legends say,'' I said, ''but Magnus proves that wrong.''

''Llyn Bouvier made a sort of pact for himself and his descendants. We would all have fey power, at a price.''

She was dragging this out, and I was tired. ''Just tell me, Ms. Bouvier. The suspense is getting irritating.''

''Has it ever occurred to you that this might be embarrassing for me to admit?'' she asked.

''No; if that's the case, I apologize.''

''My ancestor imprisoned Bloody Bones so he could make a potion of its blood. But the potion had to be remade periodically, retaken, or his magic deserted him.''

I stared at her. ''How did the other fey take this little idea?''

''He was forced to flee Europe, or they would have killed him. It is forbidden among us to use each other like that.''

''I can see why.''

''His barbaric act gave us glamor. Power. But it was still purchased by blood, Ms. Blake. After Rawhead and Bloody Bones was imprisoned, my ancestor gave up his potion. He finally saw it as evil. Though his power faded, his children had the power of fairie in their blood. So here we are,'' she said.

''So you've got Rawhead and Bloody Bones hidden in some magic box somewhere?'' I asked.

She smiled, and it made her face seem suddenly young and lovely. I had no way of judging her age. I couldn't see a line on her face. ''When the magic failed the first time, Rawhead and Bloody Bones grew to its full size. It is bigger than a person, almost as big as a giant. It is imprisoned in a mound of earth and magic.''

''You say it nearly wiped out an entire tribe way back when?''

She nodded.

I sighed. "I have to see where it's imprisoned."

"You promised . . ."

"I promised not to tell the police, but you've just told me there's a giant-sized creature capable of mass destruction imprisoned near here. I have to see that it's secure, that it's not going to break out and start slaughtering people."

"I assure you, Ms. Blake, our family has managed for centuries. We know what we're doing."

"If I can't tell the cops, I have to see for myself."

She stood up, trying to use her height to intimidate me. She wasn't even close. "And you'll bring the police, right? Do you think I'm that stupid?"

"I won't bring the cops, Ms. Bouvier, but I have to see it. If it does break out and I didn't warn the cops, then it would be my fault that no one was prepared."

"You can't prepare for Bloody Bones," she said. "It is immortal, Ms. Blake, truly immortal. It cannot die. You could cut off its head and it would not die. The police can do nothing but make things worse."

She had a point. "I still need to see for myself."

"You are a stubborn woman."

"Yeah, I can be a real pain in the ass, Ms. Bouvier. Let's not dance, just take me to see the prison, and if it's secure I'll leave you to it."

"If it's not secure enough for you?" she asked.

"We contact a witch and see what she recommends."

She frowned. "You wouldn't just go to the police?"

"If my home was robbed, I'd call the cops. If I need help with magic, I call somebody who can do magic."

"You are a strange woman, Ms. Blake. I don't understand you."

"There's a lot of that going around," I said. "Do I get to see where Rawhead and Bloody Bones is buried, or not?"

"Alright, I'll show you."

"When?"

"Without Magnus we're shorthanded at the bar, so not today. Come to the bar around three tomorrow. I'll take you from there."

"I have a coworker that I'd like to bring along," I said.

"One of those in the bedroom?"

"No."

"Why do you want to bring him?"

"Because I'm training him, and when will he ever get to see fey magic again?"

She seemed to think about it for a minute, then nodded. "Alright, you may bring one other person with you, but no more."

"Trust me, Ms. Bouvier, one is plenty."

"My friends call me Dorrie," she said. She held out her hand.

"I'm Anita." I shook her hand. She had a nice, firm grip for a woman. Sexist but true. Most women don't seem to know how to give a good handshake.

She held my hand longer than she had to. When she took her hand back, I remembered Magnus's clairvoyance. Dorrie turned those wide, eerie eyes to me. She held her hand to her chest like it hurt. "I see blood, and pain, and death. It follows you like a cloud, Anita Blake."

I watched horror seep into her eyes. Horror at the brief glimpse she'd had of me, my life, my past. I didn't look away. If you're not ashamed, you don't need to look away. Sometimes I would prefer a different line of work, but it's what I do, who I am.

The look faded from her eyes, and she blinked. "I won't underestimate you, Anita."

Dorrie looked normal again, or as normal as she had when she first came in, which wasn't very. Now for the first time I looked at her and wondered if I was seeing what was really there. Was she using glamor on me now, to appear normal? To appear less powerful than she was?

"I'll return the favor, Dorrie."

She flashed me that lovely smile again that made her seem young and vulnerable. Illusion, maybe? "Until tomorrow, then."

"Until tomorrow," I said.

She left, and I locked the door behind her. So Magnus's family were the guardians of a monster. Had that had something to do with why he ran? Dorrie didn't think it was a reason. She should know. But there was a feeling in the room of power gently moving on the air currents. A faint whiff of magic traced the air like perfume, and I hadn't known it until just before she left. Maybe Dorrie was just as good with glamor as Magnus, just more subtle. Could I really trust Dorrie Bouvier? Hmmm.

Why had I asked if Larry could go along? Because I knew it would please him. It might even make up for treating him so badly in front of Jason. But standing there, sensing Dorrie Bouvier's power hanging like a ghost in the air, I wasn't sure it was a good idea. Oh, hell, I knew it wasn't, but I was going, and Larry would go, too. He had a right to go. He even had a right to endanger himself. I couldn't keep him safe forever. He was going to have to learn to take care of himself. I hated it, but I knew it was true.

I wasn't ready to cut the apron strings, but I was going to have to lengthen them a bit. I was going to give Larry the proverbial rope. Here was hoping he didn't hang himself.

22

I slept most of the day, and when I woke up, I discovered that nobody would let me come play. Everybody was running scared of the Quinlan lawsuit, and I was persona non grata everywhere I tried to go. Agent Bradford sent me packing, and threatened to have me jailed for obstruction of justice and hampering a police investigation. That's gratitude for you. The day was a bust. The only person who would talk to me was Dolph. All he could tell me was that they hadn't found any sign of Jeff Quinlan, or his sister's body. No one had seen Magnus either. The cops were questioning people, searching for clues, while I twiddled my thumbs, but neither of us came up with anything useful.

I watched darkness fall with a sense of relief; at least now we could get on with it. Larry had gone back to his room. I hadn't asked. Maybe he wanted to give me some privacy with Jean-Claude. Scary thought, that. At least Larry was talking to me. Nice that someone was.

I opened the drapes and watched the glass turn black. I'd brushed my teeth in Larry's room today. My own bathroom was suddenly off limits. I just didn't want to see Jason naked, and I certainly didn't want to see Jean-Claude. So, I borrowed part of Larry's room for the day.

I heard the bedroom door open but didn't turn. Somehow I knew who it was. ''Hello, Jean-Claude.''

''Good evening, *ma petite*.''

I turned. The room was almost in darkness. The only light was from the street-lights outside, and the glowing sign of the hotel. Jean-Claude stepped into that faint glow. His shirt had a collar so high it covered his neck completely. Mother-of-pearl buttons fastened the high collar so that his face was framed by the white, white fabric. There must have been a dozen buttons gleaming down the pleated front of his shirt. A black waist-high jacket that was almost too black to be seen hid the sleeves. Only the shirt's cuffs showed; wide and stiff, covering half his hand. He raised a hand to the light and the cuffs bent back underneath to give his hand a full range of motion. His tight black pants were stuffed into another pair of black boots. They came all the way up his legs, so that he was encased in leather; black on black buckled straps held the soft leather in place.

"Do you like it?" he asked.

"Yeah, it's spiffy."

"Spiffy?" There was an edge of humor to that one word.

"You just can't take a compliment," I said.

"My apologies, *ma petite*. It was a compliment. Thank you."

"Don't mention it. Can we go get your coffin now?"

He stepped out of the light, so I couldn't see his face. "You make it sound so simple, *ma petite*."

"Isn't it?"

Silence then, so thick the room felt empty. I almost called out to him; instead I walked to the bar and turned on the track lighting above it. The soft white light glowed in the dark like a lighted cave. I felt better with the light. But with my back to where I thought he should be, I couldn't sense Jean-Claude. The room felt empty. I turned and there he was, sitting in one of the chairs. Even when I looked at him, there was no sense of movement. It was like a stop-action picture waiting for the switch to go on.

"I wish you wouldn't do that," I said.

He turned his head and looked at me. His eyes were solid darkness. The faint light picked up blue sparks from them. "Do what, *ma petite*?"

I shook my head. "Nothing. What's so complicated about tonight? I feel like you're not telling me everything."

He stood in one smooth motion almost like he skipped part of the process, and was just suddenly on his feet. "It is within our rules for Serephina to challenge me tonight."

"Is that the master's name, Serephina?"

He nodded.

"You don't think I'll tell the cops?"

"I will take you to her, *ma petite*. There will be no time for your impatience to make you foolish."

If I'd been stuck here all day with nothing much to do, but had had the name, would I have tried to find her on my own? Yeah, I would have.

"Fine, let's go."

He paced the room, smiling and shaking his head. "*Ma petite*, do you understand what it will mean if she challenges me tonight?"

"It means we fight them, right?"

He stopped pacing and came into the light. He slid onto one of the bar stools. "There is no fear in you, none."

I shrugged. "Being afraid doesn't help. Being prepared does. Are you afraid of her?" I looked at him, trying to read that lovely mask.

"I do not fear her power. I believe us to be near equals in that, but let us say I am wary. All things being equal, I am still in her territory with only one of my wolves, my human servant, and Monsieur Lawrence. It is not the show of force I would have chosen to confront her after two centuries."

"Why didn't you bring more people? More werewolves, anyway."

"If I had had time to negotiate more of an entourage I would have, but with the rush . . ." He looked at me. "There was no time to bargain."

"Are you in danger?"

He laughed, and it wasn't entirely pleasant. "Am I in danger, she asks. When the council asked me to divide my lands, they promised to set in place someone of power equal to or less than mine. But they did not expect me to enter her territory so unprepared."

"Who are they? What council?"

He cocked his head to one side. "Have you really come among us so long and not heard of our council?"

"Just tell me," I said.

"We have a council, *ma petite*. It has existed for a very long time. It is not so much a governing body as a court, or police, perhaps. Before your courts made us citizens with rights, we had very few rules, and only one law. Thou shalt not draw attention to yourself. That's the law that Tepes forgot."

"Tepes," I said, "Vlad Tepes? You mean Dracula?"

Jean-Claude just looked at me. His face was perfectly blank, no expression. He looked like a particularly lovely statue, if a statue's eyes could glitter like sapphires. I could not read that expressionless face, nor was I meant to.

"I don't believe you."

"About the council, our law, or Tepes?"

"The last part."

"Oh, I assure you we did kill him."

"You make it sound like you were around when it happened. He died in, what, the 1300s?"

"Was it 1476, or was it 1477?" He made a great show of trying to remember.

"You are not that old," I said.

"Are you sure, *ma petite*?" He turned that unnervingly blank face to me; even his eyes went dead and empty. It was like looking at a well-constructed doll.

"Yeah, I'm sure."

He smiled, and sighed. Life, for lack of a better word, rushed back into his face, his body. It was like watching Pinocchio spring to life.

"Shit."

"So nice to know that I can still unnerve you from time to time, *ma petite*."

I let that go. He knew exactly the effect he had on me. "If Serephina is your equal, then you take care of her, and I'll shoot everybody else."

"You know it will not be that simple."

"It never is."

He stared at me, smiling.

"Do you really think she'll challenge you?"

"No, but I wanted you to know that she could."

"Is there anything else I need to know?"

He smiled wide enough to flash a little bit of fang. He looked wonderful in the light. His skin was pale but not too pale. I touched his hand. "You're warm."

He glanced up at me. "Yes, *ma petite*; what of it?"

''You've slept an entire day. You should be cold to the touch until after you've fed.''

He just looked at me with his drowning eyes.

''Shit,'' I said. I went for the bedroom. He didn't try to stop me. He didn't even try. It made me nervous. I was half-running by the time I hit the door.

All I could see was a pale outline on the bed. I turned on the switch by the door. The overhead light was glaring, and merciless.

Jason lay on his stomach, blond hair bright against the dark pillows. He was naked except for a pair of vibrant blue bikini briefs. I walked towards the bed, staring at his back, willing him to breathe. When I was almost at the bed I could see him breathe. Something tight in my chest loosened.

I had to kneel on the edge of the bed to reach him. I touched his shoulder. He moved under my hand. I rolled him onto his side, and he didn't try to help. He was totally passive. He stared up at me with heavy-lidded eyes. Two thin crimson lines flowed down his neck. Not a lot of blood, at least not spilled onto the sheets. I had no way of knowing how much he'd lost. How much Jean-Claude had taken.

Jason smiled at me. It was a slow, lazy smile.

''Are you alright?''

His hand slid around my waist as he rolled onto his back.

''I'll take that as a yes.'' I tried to back off the bed, but his arm was firm around me, holding me. He pulled me down to his chest. I pulled the Browning on the way down. He could have stopped me, but he didn't try.

I shoved the gun against his ribs. My other hand was pressed to his bare chest, trying to hold my face a little above his. He raised his face towards mine.

''I will pull this trigger.''

He stopped with his face inches from mine. ''I'll heal.''

''Is one kiss worth getting a hole punched in your side?''

''I don't know,'' he said. ''Everyone else seems to think so.'' His face moved towards me slowly, giving me plenty of time to decide.

''Jason, release her, now.'' Jean-Claude's voice filled the room with whispers like tiny echoes.

Jason let me go. I slid off the bed, the gun still naked in my hand.

''I need my wolf tonight, Anita. Try not to shoot him until after we've seen Serephina.''

''Tell him to stop hitting on me,'' I said.

''Oh, I shall, *ma petite*, I shall.''

Jason lay back against the pillows. He raised one knee, his hands lying across his stomach. He looked relaxed, lascivious, but his eyes stayed on Jean-Claude.

''You are almost the perfect pet, Jason, but do not provoke me.''

''You never said she was off limits.''

''I am saying it now,'' Jean-Claude said.

Jason sat up on the bed. ''I'll be a perfect gentleman from now on.''

''Yes,'' Jean-Claude said, ''you will.'' He stood there in the doorway, still lovely to look at, but dangerous. You could feel it building in the room, whispering through his voice. ''Leave us for a moment, *ma petite*.''

''We don't have time for this,'' I said.

Jean-Claude looked at me. His eyes were still a solid midnight blue; the whites had drowned. "Are you protecting him?"

"I don't want him hurt because he got out of hand with me."

"Yet you would have shot him."

I shrugged. "I never said I was consistent, just serious."

Jean-Claude laughed. The abrupt change in mood made both Jason and me jump. His laughter was rich and thick as chocolate, as if you could pull it from the air and eat it.

I glanced at Jason. He was watching Jean-Claude the way a well-trained dog will watch its master, looking for clues to what its master wanted next.

"Get dressed, my wolf, and you, *ma petite*, you must change as well."

I was wearing black jeans and a royal blue polo shirt. "What's wrong with what I'm wearing?"

"We must make a show of it tonight, *ma petite*. I would not ask if it were not important."

"I am not wearing a dress tonight."

He smiled. "Of course not. Just something a little more stylish. If your young friend does not have anything suitable, I believe he and Jason are about the same size. I'm sure we could find something."

"You'll have to talk to Larry about that."

Jean-Claude looked at me for a heartbeat. "As you like, *ma petite*. Now, if you would leave Jason to dress? I will stay in here until you have chosen more appropriate attire."

I wanted to argue. I didn't like being told what to wear, or what not to wear. But I let it go. I'd been around vampires enough to know they admired the spectacular, or the dangerous. If Jean-Claude said we needed to make a show of it, maybe he was right. It wouldn't kill me to dress up a little. It might get us all killed to refuse. I just didn't know the rules in this situation. I suspected that there weren't any.

I hadn't packed with meeting a master vampire in mind, so my choices were sort of limited. I settled for a crimson blouse with a high collar and a spill of lace down the front. There was even a little frilly cuff at each sleeve. It looked like a cross between a Victorian blouse and a business shirt. It would have looked very conservative if it hadn't been screaming vermillion red. I hated the idea of wearing it, because I knew Jean-Claude would like it. Except for the color, it looked like something he might wear.

I put the all-purpose black jacket over the blouse. With both guns, both knives, and a cross around my neck inside the blouse, I was ready to go.

"*Ma petite*, may we come out?"

"Sure."

He opened the door and took it all in with a glance. "You look splendid, *ma petite*. I appreciate the makeup."

"I look pale in crimson without it."

"Of course; do you have other shoes?"

"I only have the Nikes and high heels. I move better in the Nikes."

"The blouse was more than I hoped for; keep your jogging shoes. They are black, at least."

Jason walked out of the bedroom. He was wearing black leather pants tight enough that I knew he wasn't wearing the underwear anymore. The top was vaguely oriental with one of those upright collars and one black button, the kind where a loop of thread comes over the button. The sleeves were full, and the collar was a soft shining blue that matched his eyes to perfection. It was embroidered in yellow so dark it looked gold, and darker blue thread. The sleeves, collar, and edge of the fabric were embroidered black on black. When Jason moved, the shirt gaped just a little, enough to show glimpses of his bare stomach. Soft black boots rode up over his knees.

"Well, I know who your tailor is," I said. I was going to be woefully underdressed.

"If you would fetch Monsieur Kirkland. When he is dressed, we can go."

"Larry may not want to change."

"Then he won't. I will not force him."

I looked at him, not quite sure I believed him, but I got Larry. He agreed to go into the bedroom and see what other goodies were in the luggage, but he didn't promise to change.

He came out still wearing dark blue jeans and Nikes. He had changed his T-shirt for a silk dress shirt that was a rich, vibrant blue. It made his eyes look even bluer than usual. A black leather jacket that was just a touch big in the shoulders hid his shoulder holster. I guess it was an improvement over the oversized flannel he'd been wearing. The collar of the shirt was spread over the jacket so that it framed his face.

"You should see some of the stuff in there," Larry said. He shook his head as if he still couldn't believe it. "I wouldn't even know how to get into some of it."

"You look nice," I said.

"Thanks."

"Can we go now?" I asked.

"Yes, *ma petite*, we can go. It will be interesting to meet Serephina after two centuries."

"I know this is old home week for you, but let's remember why we're here," I said. "Xavier has Jeff Quinlan. Who knows what he's doing to him? I want him home safe. It's the second night. We have to get to him tonight, or find someone else who can."

Jean-Claude nodded. "Then let us be off, *ma petite*. Serephina awaits us." He sounded almost eager, like he was looking forward to seeing her. For the first time I wondered if he and Serephina had been lovers. I knew Jean-Claude wasn't a virgin. I mean, get real. But knowing he had lovers and meeting one were two different things. I realized with a start that it would bother me.

He smiled at me, almost as if he knew what I was thinking. The whites of his eyes had reappeared. It made him look almost human. Almost.

23

Jean-Claude walked across the parking lot in his boots and jacket, looking like someone should be snapping his picture, or asking for an autograph. The rest of us followed like his entourage. Which was what we were, whether I liked it or not. But to save Jeff Quinlan I could do a little bootlicking. Even I will toady a little if it's in a good enough cause.

"You driving, or do I get directions to Serephina's house now?" I asked.

"I will tell you where to turn when it is time."

"You think I'm going to run to the cops with directions to her house?"

"No," he said. That was all he said.

I frowned at him, but we all got in the Jeep. Guess who got the front seat.

We drove out onto the main road, the Strip. The traffic was bumper-to-bumper. If traffic is bad, it can take a couple of hours to drive the four miles that make up the Strip. Jean-Claude had me turn on a small road. It looked like a driveway leading to yet another theater, but it turned out to be an access road. If you knew your way around the smaller roads, you could avoid most of the congestion.

You would never know from the main drag of Branson but just out of sight, over the next hill, is the real Ozarks. Mountains, forests, houses where people who don't make their living off tourists live. On the Strip it was all neon and artifice; within fifteen minutes we were surrounded by trees, on a road that wound through the Ozark Mountains.

Darkness closed around the Jeep. The only light was a spill of stars pressed against the blackness, and the tunnel of my own headlights.

"You seem to be looking forward to seeing Serephina, even with the coffin missing," I said.

Jean-Claude turned in his seat as far as the seat belt would allow. I'd insisted everybody wear seat belts, which amused the vampire. I guess it was silly to have a dead man buckle up, but hey, I was driving.

"I believe Serephina still thinks of me as the very young vampire she knew centuries ago. If she thought me a worthy opponent, she would have confronted me or my minions directly. She would not have simply stolen the coffin. She is overconfident.''

''Speaking as one of your minions,'' Larry called from the back seat, ''are you sure you're not the one who's overconfident?''

Jean-Claude glanced back at him. ''Serephina was centuries old when I met her. The limit of a vampire's powers is well established after two or three centuries. I know her limits, Lawrence.''

''Stop calling me Lawrence. The name's Larry.''

Jean-Claude sighed. ''You have trained him well.''

''He came that way,'' I said.

''Pity.''

Jean-Claude made this sound like a hostile family reunion, or is that an oxymoron? I hoped he was right, but one thing I've learned about vampires—they keep pulling new rabbits out of their cloaks. Big, fanged, carnivorous bunnies that'll eat your eyeballs if you're not paying attention.

''What's wolf-boy in the back going to do?''

''I do what I'm told,'' Jason said.

''Great,'' I said.

We drove in silence. Jean-Claude rarely sweats small talk, and I wasn't in the mood. We could all have a nice little visit, but out there somewhere Jeff Quinlan had woken to a second night in Xavier's tender care. Sort of ruined the mood for me.

''The turn is just ahead to your right, *ma petite*.'' Jean-Claude's voice made me jump. I had sunk into the silence and the dark hush of the highway.

I slowed the Jeep. Didn't want to miss the turnoff. A gravel road, like a hundred other gravel roads, spilled off the main road. There was nothing to make it stand out. Nothing special.

The road was narrow with trees growing so close on either side it was like driving through a tunnel. The naked branches of trees curved around us like interlocking pieces of a wall. The headlights slid over the nearly naked trees, bouncing when the Jeep eased over a pothole. Naked wooden fingers tapped the roof of the Jeep. It was damn near claustrophobic.

''Geez,'' Larry said. He had pressed his face to the dark glass as far as the seat belt would allow. ''If I didn't know there was a house down this road, I'd turn back.''

''That is the idea,'' Jean-Claude said. ''Many of the older ones value their privacy above almost all else.''

The headlights picked up a hole that stretched across the entire road. It looked like a gully wash where rainwater had eaten the road away over decades.

Larry leaned over the back of the seat, straining against his seatbelt. ''Where'd the road go?''

''The Jeep can make it,'' I said.

''Are you sure?'' he asked.

''Pretty sure,'' I said.

Jean-Claude had settled back into the seat. He seemed totally relaxed, almost detached, like he was listening to music I couldn't hear, thinking thoughts that I never would understand.

Jason leaned forward, putting a hand on the back of my seat. "Why wouldn't she pave the road? She's been here almost a year."

I glanced back at Jason. It was interesting to find out that he knew more about Jean-Claude's business than I did.

"This is her moat," Jean-Claude said. "Her barrier against the curious. Many find our new status hard to accept and still closet themselves away."

The wheels slid over the edge. It was like driving into a crater. Miraculously, the Jeep crawled out the other side. If we'd been in a car, we'd have had to walk.

The road climbed upward for about a hundred yards, and suddenly on the right-hand side of the road was an opening. It didn't look big enough to drive the Jeep through, not without scratching the paint job to hell. The only thing that really told you it was a clearing was the moonlight pulsing against the darkness of the trees. That much moonlight meant something was there. Grass had grown over a scattering of gravel that might once have been a driveway.

"Is this it?" I asked, just to make sure.

"I believe so," Jean-Claude said.

I eased the Jeep into the trees and listened to branches slap the sides. I hoped Stirling's company owned the Jeep, and wasn't just renting. We crawled free of the trees with a last metallic *scritch*. An acre of open land spread out before us, silver-edged with moonlight. The grass was butchered short like someone had bush-hogged it last fall, and left it naked and unfinished through the winter. There was a neglected orchard behind the house. The land rose in a gentle slope up towards the foot of a mountain. Just beyond the bush-hogged grass was forest, thick and untouched.

A house sat in the middle of the gentle rise. The house was silver-grey in the moonlight. Curling flecks of paint clung here and there, like the last sad remnants of an accident victim's clothes. A large stone porch graced the front of the house, hid the door and windows in a well of shadow.

"Turn off the lights, *ma petite*."

I looked at that dark porch and didn't want to hit the lights. The moonlight should have penetrated those shadows.

"*Ma petite*, the lights."

I hit the lights. The moonlight bathed us like a wash of visible air. The porch stayed dark and still like a cup of ink. Jean-Claude undid his seat belt and slid out. The boys followed suit. I got out last.

Large, flat stones were set in the grass, forming a curving sidewalk to the foot of the steps that led up to the porch. There was a large picture window to one side of the peeling door. The glass was jagged. Someone had nailed plywood behind the broken window to keep out the night air.

The smaller window on the other side of the door was intact, but so covered in grime it was blind. The shadows were viscous, and seemed thick enough to touch. It reminded me of the darkness that the sword had come swinging out of. But it wasn't as thick. I could see through this darkness. There was nothing there but shadows.

''What's with the shadows?'' I asked.

''A parlor trick,'' Jean-Claude said. ''Nothing more.'' He glided up the steps without a backward glance. If he was worried, it didn't show. Jason glided up the steps behind him. Larry and I just walked up. It was the best we could do. The shadows were colder than they should have been, and Larry shivered beside me. But there was no sense of power to it. As Jean-Claude had said, a parlor trick.

The screen door had been ripped off its hinges. It lay on the porch, torn and forgotten. Even with the protection the porch offered, the inner door was warped and peeling, exposed to too much weather. Leaves lay in piles at the edges of the porch railings where the wind had blown them.

''Are you sure this is it?'' Larry asked.

''I am sure,'' Jean-Claude said.

I understood the question. If it hadn't been for the shadows, I'd have said the house was deserted. ''The shadows would discourage any casual passersby,'' I said.

''Well, I wouldn't come trick-or-treating,'' Larry said.

Jean-Claude glanced back at us. ''Our hostess comes.''

The pitted, broken door opened. I had expected a haunted-house *screech* of rusty hinges but the door opened smoothly. A woman stood in the doorway. The room behind her was dark, her body silhouetted against the room and the night. But even in the dark I knew two things: she was a vampire, and she wasn't old enough to be Serephina.

The vampire was only a few inches taller than I was. She raised an unlit candle in one hand. The hairs on the back of my neck stood at attention, as a trickle of power slid through the room. The candle flared to life, leaving stars dancing across my night vision.

The vampire had brown hair, cut so short the hair on either side of her head had been shaved. Silver stud earrings glittered up the curve of her ears. One long earring dangled from her left ear. It was a green enamel leaf on a silver chain. She wore a red leather dress that was so tight on top, it was how I'd known in the dark she was a girl. The skirt of the dress fell to her ankles, loose once you got past the hips. A leather formal; wow.

She grinned at us, flashing fangs. ''I'm Ivy.'' Her voice had an edge of laughter to it, but unlike Jean-Claude's laugh that always felt vaguely sexual, or fattening, hers felt sharp as broken glass, meant to hurt, terrify, not titillate.

''Enter our dwelling, and be welcome.'' The words sounded too formal, like a rehearsed speech, or an incantation that you don't understand.

''Thank you, Ivy, for your most generous invitation,'' Jean-Claude said. He was suddenly holding her hand. I hadn't seen him reach for it. I hadn't seen him move. It was like I'd missed a frame of the film. From the look on Ivy's face, so had she. She looked pissed.

Jean-Claude raised her hand, very slowly, towards his lips. He never took his eyes off her. The way you bow to someone on the dojo mat, because if you look away they may spill you on your ass.

A line of wax trickled down the side of the white candle. She was holding it in her bare fist, no candle holder. Jean-Claude slowly raised her hand and laid his lips on the back of it. The wax dripped faster than it should have.

He released her hand in time for her to save herself, but she stood there and let the line of hot wax drip down her skin. Only the faintest flicker in her eyes showed that it hurt. She left the wax to harden on her hand. A faint redness spread from the line of wax. She ignored it.

No more wax dripped from the candle. Usually when a candle runs that soon, it keeps running. The wax made a little golden pool at the top of the candle, like a drop of water under tension.

I glanced from one vampire to the other and shook my head. Does the term ''childish'' mean anything to you? I didn't say it out loud, though. For all I knew, this was some kind of ancient vampire ritual. Though I doubted it pretty damn sincerely.

''Aren't your companions going to come inside?'' Ivy stepped aside with a swish of leather skirts, holding the candle high, lighting our way.

Jean-Claude stepped to the other side of the door so we would have to walk between the two vampires to get into the house. I trusted Jean-Claude not to munch on me. I even trusted him to keep Ivy from munching on me. But I didn't like how much fun Jean-Claude was having. Made me nervous. I've never been around vampires that were having a good time when it didn't get ugly.

Jason walked between them, into the house. Larry glanced at me. I shrugged and walked inside. He followed at my heels, trusting that if I went inside it would be okay. It probably would be. Probably.

24

The door closed behind us, and I don't think anybody closed it, not with hands anyway. Safe or not, these little displays of power were getting on my nerves.

The air in the room was utterly still, stale. It smelled musty, dry, with an undertaste of mildew. You knew even with your eyes closed that these rooms had been empty for a very long time. There was an open archway to the left that led into a smaller room. I could see a bed, complete with bedspread and pillows, so covered in dust it looked grey. A vanity sat in one corner with its mirror reflecting the empty room.

There was no furniture left in the living room. The wooden floor was dust-coated. The hem of Ivy's dress trailed in the thick dust as she moved towards a door in the far wall. A thin line of light showed under that door. Golden and thicker than electricity. I was betting on more candles.

The door opened before Ivy reached it. A rich wave of light spilled out, brighter than it should have been because we'd been in the dark so long. A male vamp stood framed in the light. He was short, slender, with a face too young to be handsome, more pretty. He was so newly dead that his skin still held the tan he'd picked up at the beach, or lake, or some other sun-soaked place. He looked frightfully young to be dead. He had to be eighteen, anything younger and it was illegal, but he still looked delicate and half-finished. Jailbait forever.

''I'm Bruce.'' He seemed vaguely embarrassed. Maybe it was the clothes. He was dressed in a pale grey tux complete with tails, and a charcoal grey strip down the outside leg of the pants. His gloves were white and matched what could be seen of his shirt. His vest was a silky grey. His bow tie and cummerbund were a red that matched Ivy's dress. They looked like they were going to the prom.

Two man-sized candelabra stood on either side of the door, filling the room with moving, golden light. The room beyond was twice the size of the living room, and had probably been the kitchen once upon a time. But unlike the front rooms, there'd been some redecorating.

A Persian carpet was spread across the floor. The colors were so bright it looked like stained glass. Wall hangings covered the two longest walls. On one wall a unicorn fled from a pack of hounds. The other hanging was a battle scene so dimmed with age that parts of the figures had vanished into the cloth. Bright silken drapes covered the far end of the room, hung from the ceiling with heavy cords. A door opened to the left of the drapes.

Ivy sat the candle she'd been holding in an empty sconce on the candelabra. She moved in front of Jean-Claude. She had to tilt her head up to look him in the eyes. ''You are beautiful.'' She ran her fingers along the edge of his jacket. ''I thought they'd lied. That nobody could be that beautiful.'' She fingered the mother-of-pearl buttons, starting at his neck and working down. Jean-Claude moved her hand when she reached the last button before the shirt disappeared into his pants.

Ivy seemed to find that amusing. She stood on tiptoe, leaning her hands and forearms on his chest. Her mouth was tilted towards him, kissable. ''Do you fuck as good as you look? They said you did. But you're sooo pretty. Nobody could be that good a lay.''

Jean-Claude laid his fingers on either side of her face, cradling her jawline. He smiled at her.

Her red lips curved into a smile. She pressed against him, letting her full weight rest against his body.

Jean-Claude kept his light touch on her face as if she wasn't leaning full out against him.

Her smile began to fade, slipping from her face like the sun sinking below the earth. She slid slowly down to stand flat-footed in front of him. Her face was blank and empty in the cradle of his hands.

Bruce the vampire jerked her back by one arm. Ivy stumbled and would have fallen if he hadn't caught her. She looked around bewildered, as if she expected to be elsewhere.

Jean-Claude wasn't smiling now. ''It has been a long time since I was anyone's meat that wanted me. A very long time.''

Ivy stood half-collapsed in Bruce's arms. Her face was harsh with fear. She pushed away from Bruce to stand straight and alone. She tugged at the red dress as if to settle it into place. The fear was mostly gone from her face; just a certain tightness remained around the eyes.

''How did you do that?''

''Centuries of practice, little one.''

Anger made her eyes dark. ''You aren't supposed to be able to capture another vampire with your gaze.''

''You aren't?'' he asked, his voice lilting with amazement.

''Don't you laugh at me.''

I had some sympathy for her frustration. Jean-Claude can be such a pain in the ass when he wants to be.

''You were told to lead us somewhere, children; do so.''

Ivy stood in front of him, hands balled into fists. Her anger spilled into her eyes, and the brown irises bled onto the whites of her eyes until she looked blind. Her power breathed through the room, creeping along the skin, raising the tiny hairs on my body as if a finger had been run just above them.

My hand started for the Browning. Old habits.

''No, Anita, that is not necessary,'' Jean-Claude said. ''This little one cannot hurt me. She shows her fangs, but unless she wishes to die on this lovely carpet she had best remember who and what I am.''

''I am the Master of the City!'' His voice thundered through the house, echoing in the room until the air was so thick with echoes that it was like breathing his words.

When the sound died, I was shaking. Ivy had pulled herself together. She still looked angry, but her eyes had bled back to normal.

Bruce had laid a hand on her shoulder, as if he wasn't sure she would listen to reason. She shook off his hand and motioned gracefully towards the open door.

''We are to take you downstairs. Others await you there.''

Jean-Claude gave a low theatrical bow, never taking his eyes from her. ''After you, my sweet. A lady should always walk before a gentleman, never behind.''

She smiled, suddenly pleased with herself again. ''Then your human lady can walk beside me.''

''I don't think so,'' I said.

She turned innocent brown eyes to me. ''Are you not a lady, then?'' She stalked towards me with an exaggerated sway of her hips. ''Did you bring us someone who is not a lady, Jean-Claude?''

I heard him sigh. ''Anita is a lady. Walk beside her, *ma petite*, but carefully.''

''What does it matter what these assholes think of me?''

''If you are not a lady, then you are a whore. You do not want to know what would happen to a human whore within these walls.'' He seemed tired as he said it, as if he'd been there, done that, and hadn't had a good time.

Ivy smiled at me, giving me a big dose of brown eyes. I met her gaze and smiled.

She frowned. ''You are human. You can't meet my gaze, not like that.''

''Surprise, surprise,'' I said.

''Shall we go?'' Jean-Claude said.

Ivy frowned again, but she stepped into that open door, and down a step or two, one hand on her dress to keep the hem from tripping her feet. She turned and looked back at me. ''Are you coming?''

I asked Jean-Claude, ''How careful do I need to be?''

Larry and Jason came to stand beside me.

''Defend yourself if they offer violence first. But do not shed the first blood, or strike the first blow. Defend, but do not attack, *ma petite*. We are playing games tonight, unless you make it more; the stakes are not that high.''

I scowled at him. ''I don't like this.''

He smiled. ''I know, but bear with us, *ma petite*. Remember the human you wish to save, and control that wonderful temper of yours.''

''Well, human?'' Ivy said. She was waiting for me on the steps. She looked like an impatient child, petulant.

''I'm coming,'' I said. I did not run to catch up with the waiting vampire. I walked at a normal pace, though the weight of her gaze made my skin itch. I stopped at the head of the stairs and peered downward. Cool, damp air pushed against my face. The smell was thick, enclosed, and mildewed. You knew there would be no windows, and somewhere water was eating the walls. A basement. I hated basements.

I took a deep breath of the fetid air and walked down the steps. They were the widest stairs I'd ever seen in a basement. The wood felt new and raw, like they hadn't taken time to stain or sand it. There was enough room for the two of us to share a step. I didn't want to share a step. Maybe she wasn't a threat to Jean-Claude, but I had no illusions about what she could do to me. She was a baby master, not full grown yet, but the power was there bubbling under the surface, crawling along my skin. I stopped a step above her, waiting for her to go down.

Ivy smiled. She could smell my fear. ''If we are both ladies, then we should walk together. Come, Anita.'' She held out a hand to me. ''Let us go down together.''

I didn't want to be that close to her. If she tried to jump me, there wouldn't be time to do much. I might get a weapon out in time, I might not. It irritated me that I wasn't supposed to show a weapon first. And scared me. One of the things that's kept me alive is shooting first and asking questions later. Doing it the other way around was no way to stay alive.

''Is Jean-Claude's human servant afraid of me?'' She stood there framed against the darkness beyond, smiling. The basement was like a great black pit behind her.

But she couldn't sense vampire marks, or she'd have known I wasn't his servant. She wasn't as hot as she thought she was. I hoped.

I ignored the outstretched hand, but walked down those two steps. My shoulder brushed her bare skin, and it felt like worms were crawling down my arm. I kept walking down the steps into the dark beyond, left hand in a death grip on the railing. I heard her high heels clattering down the steps to catch up with me. I could feel her irritation like heat rising from her skin. I heard the menfolk following us, but didn't look behind to check. We were playing chicken tonight. It was one of my best games.

We went down the steps together like horses pulling a carriage, my left hand on the railing, her hands lifting her dress. I kept up a pace that made gliding effortlessly impossible, unless she could levitate. She couldn't.

She grabbed my right arm and whirled me around to face her. I couldn't go for a gun. Because I was wearing wrist sheaths, I couldn't even go for a knife. I stood there nearly face to face with an angry vampire and couldn't reach a weapon. All that could save me was her not killing me. Trusting my life to Ivy's beneficence seemed like a bad bet.

Her anger spilled along my skin. Heat flowed down her body. I could feel her hand, hot, even through the leather jacket. I didn't try to pull away; things that can bench-press Toyotas don't let go. Her touch didn't burn, because it wasn't that kind of heat, but it was hard to convince my body that it wouldn't hurt eventually. Years of warnings, don't touch, it's hot. Heat flared along my body like I was standing next to a fire. If she hadn't been doing it unintentionally, it would have been impressive. Hell, it was still impressive. Give her a few centuries and she'd be scary as hell, as if she wasn't already.

I could still meet her eyes, drowning deep and glowing with their own light. That was going to do me a hell of a lot of good when she ripped my throat out.

"If you hurt her, Ivy, our truce is over." Jean-Claude glided down the steps to stand just above us. "You do not want the truce to be over, Ivy." He ran his fingertip along the edge of her jaw.

I felt the jolt of power jump from him, to her, to me. I gasped, but she let me go. My arm was numb at my side like it'd gone to sleep. I couldn't have held a gun. I wanted to ask what the hell he'd done, but didn't. As long as I got the use of my arm back, we could argue about it later.

Bruce pushed between us, hovering over Ivy like a worried boyfriend. Watching his face, I realized that was accurate. I was betting she'd brought him over.

Ivy pushed him away so hard that he went tumbling backwards down the stairs, lost in the thicker darkness. Everything seemed to be working on her just fine. I could barely feel my fingertips.

Heat rushed over me like a scalding wind, and swept outward into the dark. Torches flared to life in sconces along the walls with a *whoosh* and a shower of sparks. A large kerosene lamp suspended from the ceiling filled with fire. Its glass chimney exploded in a shower of glass, its flame burning naked on the wick.

"Serephina will make you clean up your mess," Jean-Claude said. He made it sound like she'd spilled her milk.

Ivy walked down the rest of the steps in a hip-swinging glide. "Serephina will not care. Broken glass and flame have so many uses." I didn't like the way she phrased that.

The basement was black. Black walls, black floors, black ceiling. It was like being in a great dark box. Chains hung from the walls, some with what looked like fur on the cuffs. Straps dangled from the ceiling like obscene decorations. There were . . . devices placed throughout the room. I recognized some of them. A rack, an iron maiden, but most of it was like looking at bondage paraphernalia. You were pretty sure what the point was, but not how it worked. There were always more holes than I could figure out what to do with, and nothing ever seemed to come with instructions.

There was a drain in the floor, and a thin trickle of water ran down it. But I was betting that the drain wasn't there just for water.

Larry moved down the steps to stand beside me. "Are those what I think they are?"

"Yeah, they're torture devices." I forced my hand to make a fist, and another one. The feeling was coming back.

"I thought they weren't going to harm us," he said.

"I think it's supposed to scare us."

"It's working," he said.

I didn't like the decor much either, but I could feel my hand. I could have held a gun if I had to.

A door that I hadn't even seen opened to the left. A secret panel. A vampire came through the door. He had to bend nearly double to make it through the door frame. He unfolded, impossibly tall and thin, cadaverous. He had not fed tonight, and was wasting no power on looking pretty. His skin was the color of old parchment and clung to the bones of his face like a thin film barely covering his skull. His eyes were sunken and dull in his head, the dead blue of fish eyes. His sickly hands were long and bony with impossibly long fingers, like white spiders sticking from the sleeves of his black coat.

He stalked into the room with the edges of his black coat sweeping behind him like a cloak. He was dressed entirely in black; only his skin and the short cut white hair on his head betrayed him. As he moved through the black room, it looked like his head and hands were floating on their own.

I shook my head to clear the image. When I looked back, he seemed a touch more normal. ''He's using his powers to make himself look frightening,'' I said.

''Yes, *ma petite*, he is.'' There was something in his voice that made me turn and look at him. His face was its usual lovely mask—but in his eyes, for just a second, I saw fear.

''What's going on, Jean-Claude?''

''The rules have not changed. Do not draw a weapon. Do not strike the first blow. They cannot harm us unless we break these rules.''

''Why are you suddenly scared?''

''That is not Serephina,'' he said. His voice was very bland when he said it.

''What's that supposed to mean?''

He threw back his head and laughed. The sound reverberated through the room, echoing and outwardly joyous. But I could taste it on the back of my tongue, and it was bitter. ''It means, *ma petite*, that I am a fool.''

25

Jean-Claude's laughter faded away in bits and pieces, like the sound was clinging to the walls. "Where is Serephina?" he asked.

Ivy and Bruce walked out of the room. I didn't know where they were going, but it had to be better than this. How many torture rooms could a house this size have? Don't answer that.

The tall vampire looked at us with his dead-fish eyes. There was no pull, nothing; it was like looking into the eyes of a corpse.

His voice, when it came, was almost shocking. It was rich and deep, resonant, but not with vampiric powers. It was the voice of an actor, or an opera singer. I watched it come out of the thin, lipless mouth and it still looked like a parlor trick, like the mouth should move out of sync with the words, but they didn't.

"You must pass through me before she will see you."

"You surprise me, Janos." Jean-Claude glided down the steps. I guess we were going down. Pity. "You are more powerful than Serephina. How is it you do her bidding?"

"When you have seen her, you will understand. Now come, all of you, join us. The night is young, and I want to see you all naked and bleeding before dawn."

"Who is this guy?" I asked. I could use my hand again; might as well smart off.

Jean-Claude stopped on the last step. Jason moved up, one step behind him. Larry and I stayed a little behind that. I don't think either of us was too eager to go down.

The vampire turned his dead eyes on me. "I am Janos."

"Dandy, but the rules say you can't bleed us, or anything else. Or did I miss something?"

"You miss very little, *ma petite*," Jean-Claude said.

"You will not be harmed against your will," Janos said. "You must all consent for any harm to befall you."

"Then we're safe," I said.

He smiled, the skin of his face stretching like paper. I half-expected bone to break through, but it didn't. The smile was nicely hideous.

"We shall see."

Jean-Claude took that last step, and moved farther into the room. Jason followed, and after a moment's hesitation so did I. Larry followed me like a trooper.

"This room is your idea, Janos," Jean-Claude said.

"I do nothing without my master's consent."

"She cannot be your master, Janos. She is not powerful enough."

"Yet, here I am, Jean-Claude. Here I am."

Jean-Claude walked around the dark wood of the rack, trailing a pale hand over it. "Serephina was never much for torture. She was many things, but not sadistic." Jean-Claude came to stand in front of Janos. "I think you are master here and she is your stalking horse. She is known as master so all the challenges come her way. When she dies, you will find another puppet."

"I promise you, Jean-Claude, she is my master. Think of this room as my reward for being a faithful servant." He looked around the room with a proprietary smile, like a storekeeper admiring well-stocked shelves.

"What do you plan for us in this room of yours?"

"But wait a few moments, my impatient boy, and all will be revealed."

It was odd to have someone call Jean-Claude "boy," as if he were a much younger cousin that Janos had watched grow up. Had Janos known him when he was a little vampire? Freshly dead?

A woman's voice: "Where are you taking me? You're hurting me." Ivy and Bruce dragged a young woman through the side door. Literally dragged her. She had let her legs collapse, trying to use them like a dog does when you try to take it to the vet. But she only had two legs and a vampire on each arm. She wasn't having much luck slowing them down.

She had straight blonde hair that barely touched the tops of her shoulders. Her eyes were large and blue, and the makeup she'd started the night with was smeared from crying.

Ivy seemed to be having a good time. Bruce had very wide eyes. He was afraid of Janos. Hard not to be, I guess.

The girl stared wordlessly at Janos for a second, then screamed. Ivy cuffed her absently like you'd swat a barking dog. The girl whimpered and fell silent, staring at the floor, fresh tears trailing down her cheeks.

There was only Janos and the two youngsters in the room with us. I was betting we could take them. Two more vampires came in, but they didn't drag in the next girl. She walked in, eyes glittering with anger, back very straight, hands in fists at her sides. She was short, a little heavy, but not quite fat, as if a good burst of growth would take care of the weight. Her hair was a nondescript brown, glasses framed small brown eyes, freckles dusted her face. The personality that radiated from that face was not nondescript. I liked her instantly.

"Oh, Lisa," she said, "get up." She sounded embarrassed as well as angry.

The blonde girl, Lisa, just cried harder.

The two vamps that were guarding the second girl were not young. They were both tall, around six feet, dressed in black leather, one with her long yellow hair in a braid down her back, the other with black hair falling free around her face. Their bare arms were muscled and firm. They looked like female bodyguards from some bad spy movie.

The power that radiated from the two of them was not a B movie effect. It crept through the room like a current of water, thick and cool. When the line of power poured over my body it took my breath away. The power crawled into my bones and made them ache. Larry gasped behind me.

I glanced at him just to make sure he was gasping for the same reason I was. No new monsters behind us, just the power of the two new vamps.

''What are you guys doing, running a halfway house for all vampires over five hundred years?'' I asked.

Everyone turned towards me. The two female vamps smiled, most unpleasantly. They looked at me like I was a piece of candy and they wondered what sort of center I had. Soft and gooey, or hard with a nut in the middle? I'd had men undress me with their eyes, but I'd never had anything trying to picture what I'd look like with my skin off. Yikes.

''Do you have something to add?'' Janos asked.

''You can't just drag a couple of underage girls in here and expect us to do nothing.''

''On the contrary, Anita, we expect you to do many things.''

I didn't like the phrasing of that. ''What's that supposed to mean?''

''First, the young women aren't underage, are you, girls?''

The second girl just glared at him. Lisa shook her head, still staring at the floor.

''Tell her your ages,'' Janos said.

Neither of them answered. Ivy yanked hard enough to make the blonde girl cry out.

''Eighteen. I'm eighteen.'' She collapsed on the floor in a sobbing heap, and the vampires let go of her so she could do it.

One of the female vamps said, ''Your age, now.'' Her voice was like quiet thunder, a warning of the coming storm.

The second girl's eyes widened behind her glasses. ''I'm nineteen.'' There was fear now peeking out from behind her anger.

''Fine; they're over eighteen, but an unwilling human is still an unwilling human, regardless of age,'' I said.

''Would you play policeman here, Anita?'' Janos asked. He sounded amused.

''I won't just stand here and watch you hurt them.''

''You have a high opinion of yourself, Anita. Confident. I like that. Always so much more entertaining to break someone strong. The weaklings fold and cry and snivel, but the brave ones, they almost demand that you hurt them.'' He stalked towards me, reaching out one white spider-hand. ''Do you want me to hurt you?''

I remembered Jean-Claude's warning not to use weapons, but fuck it, I was going for the Browning.

Jean-Claude was just suddenly there, holding Janos's wrist. Janos seemed impressed. Truthfully, so was I. I hadn't seen him move, and apparently neither had Janos. A nifty trick, that.

I let my hand relax away from the gun, though I was pretty sure that drawing it would make me feel better. But the purpose of tonight's exercise was not to make me feel better, it was to stay alive.

"No harm to any of us; that was the promise," Jean-Claude said.

Janos drew his wrist from Jean-Claude's grasp slowly, almost lingeringly, as if he enjoyed it. "Once Serephina's promise is given, she keeps it."

"Then why are the young women here?"

"Those two"—he motioned to Larry and me—"would truly not stand by and watch harm come to strangers?" He sounded surprised, but not unhappy about it.

"Sadly, yes," Jean-Claude said.

"And if they join the fray, you will come in to protect her?" Janos asked.

"If I must."

Janos smiled, and I could hear his skin creak with the strain of holding in his bones. "Splendid."

I saw a tremor run through Jean-Claude's back, as if he had been caught off guard. I was just plain confused.

"The two young women came willingly into our house. They knew what we were, and agreed to help us entertain guests."

I glanced at the second girl. "Is that true?"

One of her vampire guards touched her shoulder, lightly, but it was enough. "We came willingly, but we didn't know . . ." The vampire's hand squeezed. The girl's face crumbled in pain but she made no sound.

"They came of their own free will, and they are of the age of consent," Janos said.

"So what happens now?" I asked.

"Ivy, chain that one over there." He pointed as he said it to some fur-lined manacles to the left of the door. Ivy and Bruce picked up the girl, pulled her to her feet, and led her stumbling to the wall.

"Her back facing the room, please."

I stepped next to Jean-Claude and whispered, though I knew within reason they'd hear, "I don't like this."

"Nor I, *ma petite*."

"Can we stop it without breaking the truce?"

"Not unless they offer harm to us directly, no."

"What happens if I break the truce?"

"They will try to kill us, most likely."

There were five vampires in the room, three of them older than Jean-Claude. We would die. Dammit.

The blonde girl sobbed and struggled, pulling at her arms as the vampires chained her to the wall. She screamed and pulled so violently that without the fur lining she'd have bloodied her wrists.

A woman stepped into the room from the side door. She was tall, taller than Jean-Claude. Her skin was the color of coffee with two creams. Her dark hair fell in long cornrows to her waist. She was dressed in a black, patent leather body suit. It left very little to the imagination. She strode hard on her heels, a very human walk. But she wasn't human.

''Kissa,'' Jean-Claude said. ''You are still with Serephina.'' He sounded surprised.

''Not all of us have your luck.'' Her voice was thick like honey. There was a smell like spices in the air, and I wasn't sure if it was her perfume or illusion.

Her high-boned face was empty of makeup and still she was beautiful—though I wondered what she'd look like if she weren't clouding my mind. Because surely no human could have radiated the raw sexuality that clung to Kissa like a touchable cloud.

''I am sorry you are here, Kissa.''

She smiled. ''Don't pity me, Jean-Claude. Serephina has promised you to me, before Janos breaks that beautiful body of yours.''

Six vampires, four of them older than Jean-Claude. The odds were not going in our favor.

''Chain the other girl there.'' Janos motioned to a matching set of manacles to the right of the door.

The girl shook her head. ''No way.'' She just refused to go, and she struggled better than the blonde. She threw her body on the ground and used every inch of it, not to fight, just not to go.

Two vampires several centuries old, powerful enough to make my teeth hurt, and they had to pick her up from both ends and carry her to the wall. She'd finally started to scream, one loud, ragged, rage-filled sound after another. The dark-haired vamp pinned her to the wall, and the other one chained her.

''I can't just watch this,'' Larry said. He was standing very close to me; maybe he didn't know the vampires would hear his whispers.

It didn't really matter. ''Neither can I.''

We were going to get ourselves killed; might as well take as many of them with us as we could.

Jean-Claude turned around, as if he could smell us going for our guns. ''*Ma petite*, Monsieur Kirkland, do not go for your weapons. They are treading legalities. The women have come to help entertain. They will not kill them.''

''You're sure of that?'' I asked.

He frowned. ''I am sure of nothing anymore, but I believe that they will keep their word. The women are frightened and a little bruised, but they are not harmed.''

''This isn't harm?'' Larry asked. He looked outraged, and I couldn't blame him.

I answered him. ''Vampires have a very unique sense of what's harmful, don't they, Jean-Claude?''

He met my gaze. ''I see accusation in your eyes, but remember this, *ma petite*, you asked me to bring you here. So do not blame this particular problem on me.''

''Is our entertainment so boring?'' Janos asked.

''We were discussing whether to kill you all now, or later,'' I said, my voice very matter-of-fact.

Janos gave a low chuckle. ''Please do break the truce, Anita. I would love to have an excuse to get you on one of my novelties. I think you would take a long time to break. Then again, it is sometimes the braggarts who break first.''

''I don't brag, Janos. I tell the truth.''

''She believes what she says,'' Kissa said.

''Yes, she has a disturbing hint of truth to her,'' Janos said. ''Most tasty.''

The blonde, Lisa, had stopped struggling against the chains. She sagged in them, nearly incoherent with crying. The other girl, now that she was chained, stood very still, but a fine trembling had started in her arms and hands. She balled her hands into fists, but could not stop the trembling.

''The women came for a little adventure. They are certainly getting their money's worth,'' Janos said.

The two female vamps opened panels in the black walls. They each took out a long coil of whip. Neither of the girls could see. I was glad.

I couldn't stand and watch, I couldn't. It would kill something inside me to just stand and watch, even if it meant I died. I'd at least go down fighting, and I'd take some of them with me. Better than nothing. But before we all committed suicide, I'd try to talk. ''If you're not trying to goad us into breaking the truce, then what the hell do you want?''

''Want?'' Janos said. ''Want? Why, many things, Anita.''

I was beginning to hate the way he said my name, sort of half-amused, and intimate, like we were friends, or close enemies.

''What do you want, Janos?''

''Shouldn't you be negotiating for your people?'' he asked Jean-Claude.

''Anita does well enough on her own,'' Jean-Claude said.

Janos gave another rictus smile. ''Very well. What do we want?''

The vampires went to the girls. They held up the whips so the two girls could see them.

''What is that?'' the blonde asked. ''What is that?'' Her voice was high and bubbly with fear.

''It's a whip,'' the second girl said. Firm and clipped, her voice did not betray her the way her trembling body did.

The two vampires backed away, just enough for good whipping distance, I guess.

''What the bloody hell do you want?'' I asked.

''Are you familiar with the term 'whipping boy'?'' Janos asked.

''It was a person used by royalty to be beaten in the place of the royal heir.''

''Very good; so few young people have a sense of history.''

''What does the history lesson have to do with anything?''

''The girls are whipping boys for your two young men,'' Janos said.

The two vampires snaked the whips along the floor, and cracked them nearly in unison, but neither whip touched the girls. The second girl screamed, a short, clipped sound, when the whip whistled into the wall next to her. The blonde just sank against the wall, sobbing, ''Please, please, please,'' over and over in a ragged voice.

''Don't hurt them,'' Larry said. ''Please.''

''Would you take her place?'' Janos asked.

I finally understood where we were heading. ''You can't hurt us without our cooperation. You treacherous son of a bitch.''

He smiled. ''Answer me, lad. Would you take her place?''

Larry nodded.

I grabbed his arm. ''No.''

''Surely it is his choice,'' Janos said.

''Let go of my arm, Anita.''

I stared at his eyes, searching to see if he understood what he was doing. ''You don't know what a whip will do to human flesh. You don't know what you're offering.''

''We can remedy that,'' Janos said.

The vampires ripped the backs of the girls' blouses with a harsh, quick tearing.

The blonde screamed.

''We can't just watch,'' Larry said.

He was right; whether I liked it or not, he was right.

''I've seen what a whip can do,'' Jason said suddenly. ''Don't hurt them.''

I stared at him. ''You don't strike me as the self-sacrificing kind.''

He shrugged. ''We all have our moments.''

''Would it make this an easier choice if I swore that if your young man takes the girl's place we will not cripple him?''

''How about kill him?'' I said. ''You can die of shock from a whipping.''

''No killing, no crippling. We simply want our pound of flesh, and a quart of blood.''

Something must have shown on our faces, because he laughed. ''Figuratively speaking, of course. You will wear scars until you die, but no greater harm.''

''This is ridiculous,'' I said. ''We aren't going to do this.''

''If we pull our guns, can we take them?'' Larry asked.

I looked away from his earnest eyes. He touched my arm. ''Anita?''

''We can take some of them with us,'' I said.

''But we'll still be dead, and once we're dead who'll help the girls?''

I shook my head. ''There's got to be a better way.''

Larry looked at Jean-Claude. ''Will he keep his word? Will they not kill me?''

''Janos's word has always been reliable, or at least it was a couple of centuries ago.''

''Can we trust them?'' Jason asked.

''No,'' I said.

''Yes,'' Jean-Claude said.

I glared at him.

''I know you would rather shoot it out, but you would only succeed in getting us all killed. Or perhaps some of us made into vampires.''

Larry touched my shoulders. He made me look at him. ''It's alright.''

''It's not alright,'' I said.

''Fine, but it's the best we can do right now.''

''Don't do this.''

''I don't have a choice,'' he said. ''Besides, I'm a big boy, remember? I can take care of myself.''

I hugged him. I didn't know what else to do.

''I'll be alright,'' he whispered.

I just nodded. I didn't trust my voice, and I try never to lie to my friends. He would not be alright. I knew it. He knew it. We all knew it.

Jason walked away from us towards the vampires. "Oh, no, my good shapeshifter, we don't want you chained to a wall."

"But you said . . ."

"I said you could save the girls, but not like that. Let the human take his lashes. All you must agree to is satisfying the desires of my two helpers, Bettina and Pallas."

Jason stared at the two vampires. They'd turned to face us. I suddenly tried to see them from the viewpoint of a twenty-year-old male. They were chesty, slim waisted; if Pallas's face was a little too witchy-looking for my taste, and Bettina's eyes too small, that was just me. Neither of them was pretty, or even beautiful; they were handsome in the way that some tall, leggy women are. Handsome in a good way, if they had been human.

Jason frowned. "It seems I'm getting the better deal here."

"Would it make any difference if I said you had to do it here in this room, on the floor, in front of everyone?" Janos asked.

Jason thought about that for a minute. "If I say no, does the girl get whipped?"

Janos nodded.

"Then I agree," he said, but his voice was soft and uncertain. Being lascivious in private was one thing; doing it in public was different.

"Come then, shapeshifter, let the show begin." Janos made a sweeping motion with his white hands.

Jason glanced back at Jean-Claude like a kid on the first day of school wondering if the bullies were really going to hurt him. Jean-Claude gave no comfort. His face was as still and unreadable as a painting. He gave a small nod that could have meant anything from "It will be alright" to "Just do it."

I watched Jason's shoulders rise with a deep breath, and heard him blow it out like a runner before a race. Why is it that most things you might willingly do under other circumstances become distasteful when you have no choice?

"Have you ever been with one of us?" Janos asked.

Jason shook his head.

Janos put a long-fingered hand on Jason's shoulder. Jason didn't seem to enjoy that. Couldn't blame him. "There are many pleasures that await you, my young shapeshifter. Things that no human or wereanimal can give to you. Sensations that only the dead can offer."

The two female vampires had stepped to the far end of the room in a clear space on the black floor. The whips lay coiled at the feet of the two girls, as if they were a reminder of what would happen if anyone chickened out.

If Jason wanted to fuck a few vampires, that was fine with me. Besides, he wasn't mine to protect. But the sex wasn't going to last forever. I couldn't let them have Larry. I couldn't stand by and watch him be tortured. I just couldn't. But if I pulled down the room, then even if we got out of the basement—highly doubtful all on its own—we'd have every vamp in the place after our ass. There would be more; there were always more. But what had Jean-Claude said? If they broke the truce first, we could draw weapons. It had possibilities.

The one with long blonde hair had undone her braid. She shook out her hair like it was a thick curtain of yellow waves. It hid her face for a moment, and she seemed softer, more human. Maybe it was illusion. Whatever, Jason touched that thick hair, wadded his hands into it, then slid his hands around her waist. If he was going to have to do it, it looked like he was going to have fun while he did. Nice to see someone who enjoys his work.

The dark-haired vamp came in from behind, pressing her leather-clad body against him. Jason was short enough that his face was about breast level for both of them. He buried his face in the blonde's chest. She unlaced the front of her leather vest, peeling it back so he could suck her breasts.

I turned away. I was never much for voyeurism. Had an embarrassing tendency to blush. Ivy and Bruce moved along the wall to stand near the corner next to the threesome. Bruce was fascinated and embarrassed, but he kept looking. There was no embarrassment on Ivy's face. She moved along the wall, her back pressed to it, hands feeling their way along. Her red lipsticked mouth was partially open. She slid down the wall, the red dress bunching around her thighs as she went to all fours. Watching them move along the wall brought my gaze back to the entertainment.

Jason's shirt was gone. Wearing nothing but his leather pants and his black boots, he matched the two vampires. He was on his knees, his back arched so he was cradled against the brunette behind him. She smoothed her hands down his naked chest. He turned, giving her his lips. The kiss was long and deep, and full of more probing than anybody but your doctor should be doing.

The blonde was sitting with her legs wide open in front of them, undoing Jason's pants. She'd already done something to her leather pants so that the crotch was open. She was a natural blonde. Why was I surprised?

Ivy stretched out a hand to pull at the other vampire's long yellow hair.

"Ivy," Janos said, "you were not invited."

She pulled her hand back but didn't back away. She was as close to the action as she could get and not be part of it. Bruce was still pinned to the wall, open-mouthed and a little sweaty, but he didn't seem to want to come closer.

Janos stood very calmly watching. He had a tight grin on his face, and for the first time there was some light in those dead-fish eyes. He was enjoying himself.

Jean-Claude was half-leaning, half-sitting against a metal frame that held the rough outline of a body. He was watching the show, but his face was still unreadable, a beautiful mask.

He saw me looking at him, but there was no change in his eyes. He was as closed and solitary as if he were standing in an empty room. He wasn't breathing that I could see. Did he have a heartbeat when he held himself so still? Or did everything stop?

Kissa stood by the door that we hadn't been through. She had her arms crossed over her stomach. For someone that had wanted to jump Jean-Claude's bones so badly, she didn't seem to like the show much. Or maybe she was the guard to keep Larry and me from running screaming from the room.

Larry had backed as far away from the action as he could get. He was pressed up against the wall, trying to find something to look at, but his eyes kept being drawn back to the other end of the room. It was like trying not to watch a train wreck. You didn't want to see it happen, but if it was going to happen you didn't quite want to look away either. When would you ever get the chance to see it again? A ménage à trois made up of two vampires and a werewolf couldn't be that common a sight for Larry. It wasn't even a common sight for me.

The two girls still chained to the wall couldn't see what was going on. Probably just as well.

A low moan broke from the other side of the room. It made me glance back. Jason's pants had been pulled partially down to reveal most of the smooth expanse of his buttocks. His arms were braced, leaving only his lower body touching the woman. His body rose and fell rhythmically. The blonde vampire writhed under him, another low moan escaping her throat. Her breasts spilled out of her black leather vest like an offering as she did a sort of sit-up to meet Jason's mouth.

The brunette licked a slow, pink tongue along his spine. His back convulsed with the sensation, or maybe it was another sensation. The effect looked the same.

I turned away, but the image was burned on my mind. I felt heat crawl up my neck. Damn. Larry's eyes widened and I watched the color drain from his face, until his skin was the surprised white of paper and his eyes too big for his face.

I fought it for a minute, but I turned back to see, like Lot's wife risking it all for one last forbidden glimpse. Jason had collapsed, his face lost in the blonde's hair. Her face was turned to the room. Her skin had thinned until you could see every bone in her face. Her full lips had thinned back, making her teeth look longer. She no longer had enough lips to hide her fangs.

The brunette knelt just behind them, her knees between both their legs. She lowered her hands from her face, and one half of that handsome face rotted away. She ran her hand through her long dark hair and it came away in clumps.

She turned her face towards the rest of us. The skin sloughed off the bones on the left side of her face and fell to the floor with a thick wet plop.

I swallowed hard enough that it hurt going down and backed up to stand by Larry. He wasn't white anymore; he was green.

"My turn now," one of the vampires said. My face turned back to the scene at the end of the room, almost against my will. I couldn't stand to watch, and couldn't stand to look away.

Jason rose in a sort of push-up motion. He caught a glimpse of the blonde's face and his shoulders tensed, the line of his spine tightening. He pulled away from her slowly, coming to his knees.

The brunette ran her fingers down his naked back. Her flesh sloughed away, leaving a trail of greenish slime behind. A tremor ran through his body that had nothing to do with sex.

From across the room I could see Jason's chest rise and fall faster and faster, as if he was hyperventilating. He stayed staring straight ahead, making no move to turn and look behind him, as if it would go away if he didn't look.

The brunette wrapped her decaying arms around his shoulders, leaned her rotted face next to his, and whispered something.

Jason struggled away from them, crawling against the wall. His bare chest was covered in bits of her flesh. His eyes were impossibly wide, showing too much white. He couldn't seem to get enough air. A strand of something thick and heavy slid slowly down his neck onto his chest. He batted at it like you would swat at a spider that you found crawling along your skin. He was pressed into the black wall with his pants nearly to his thighs.

The blonde rolled off her back and crawled towards him, reaching a hand out that was nothing but bones with bits of dried flesh. She seemed to be decaying in dry ground. The brunette was wet. She lay back on the floor, and some dark fluid rushed out from her to pool beneath her body. She'd undone her own leather shirt, and her breasts were like heavy bags of fluid.

"I'm ready for you," the brunette said. Her voice was still clear and solid. No human voice should have come out of those rotting lips.

The blonde grabbed Jason's arm, and he screamed.

Jean-Claude sat there watching, motionless, unmoved.

I found myself walking towards them. It surprised even me. I kept waiting for the smell that should have accompanied the rotting flesh, but with every step the air was clean.

I stood beside Jean-Claude and said, "Is this illusion?"

He wouldn't look at me. "No, *ma petite*, it is not an illusion."

I poked him in the arm, and it was hard and firm as wood. It didn't feel like flesh at all. "Is this illusion?"

"No, *ma petite*." He looked at me at last, and his eyes were solid drowning blue. "Both forms were real." He stood, and even standing next to him I could not see him breathe.

The brunette was on all fours reaching for Jason with a hand that fell into wet pieces as it moved. Jason screamed and pressed himself into the wall as if he wanted to crawl through it. He hid his face like a child ignoring the monster under his bed, but this was no child, and he knew the monsters were real.

"Help him," I whispered, and I wasn't sure which of us I was talking to.

"I shall do what I can," Jean-Claude said. I was staring at him when I heard the next words in my head. His lips never moved. "If they break the truce first, *ma petite*, then you are free to slaughter everyone in this room."

I stared at him, but his face betrayed nothing. Only the echo of him inside my head told me I hadn't hallucinated it. There was no time to bitch about the fact that he'd invaded my head. Later; we could argue later.

"Janos." That one word reverberated through the room until it echoed up the soles of my feet like a deep bass drum.

Janos turned to look at Jean-Claude, his skeletal face set in a pleased expression. "You rang?"

"I challenge you." The three words were bland; they fell like off-key notes jangling along my nerves. If the tone bothered Janos, you couldn't tell it.

"You cannot prevail against me," Janos said.

"That remains to be seen, does it not?" Jean-Claude asked.

Janos smiled until the skin nearly snapped. "If by some miracle you best me, what do you want?"

"Safe passage for all my people." I cleared my throat. "And the two girls."

"And if I win," Janos said, "what do I get?"

''What do you want?''

''You know what we want.''

''Say it,'' Jean-Claude said.

''You give up your safe passage. We get you, to do with as we like.''

Jean-Claude gave a small nod. ''So be it.'' He pointed at the rotting vampires. ''Get them away from my wolf.''

Janos smiled. ''They will not hurt him, but if you fail . . . I'll make a gift of him to my two beauties.''

A low sound like a swallowed scream crawled from Jason's throat. The brunette's hand started the crawl down his stomach to his privates. He screamed and pushed her away, but unless he resorted to violence he was trapped. And if we broke the truce first we were dead, but if they broke the truce . . .

Jean-Claude and Janos had moved back to the center of the room. They stood a few yards apart. Jean-Claude stood with his feet spaced as if he was bracing for a fight. Janos stood with his feet together, easy, unconcerned.

''You will lose everything, Jean-Claude; what are you up to?''

Jean-Claude just shook his head. ''Challenge has been offered and accepted; what are you waiting on, Janos? Are you afraid of me at long last?''

''Afraid of you? Never, Jean-Claude. Not a hundred years ago, not a moment ago.''

''Enough talk, Janos.'' His voice had gone low and soft, yet it carried through the entire room, and crawled up the black walls to rain down in drops of sound that were dark and anger-filled.

Janos laughed, but the sound had none of the touchable qualities of Jean-Claude's voice. ''Let us dance.'' Silence fell so abruptly on the room I thought I'd gone deaf. Then I realized I could still hear my own heartbeat, the blood rushing in my own head. Waves of something rose between the two master vampires like heat rising off summer pavement. What poured along my skin wasn't heat, it was . . . power.

A whirling, rushing storm of power. I'd felt Jean-Claude go up against other vampires, and I'd never felt anything like this. My hair streamed in a wind that was coming from the two.

Jean-Claude's face was thinning down, his white skin glowing like polished alabaster. His eyes were blue flames that bled sapphire fire down every vein under his skin. His bones glowed gold. His humanity was folding away, and it wouldn't be enough. He would lose.

Unless they broke the truce first.

Kissa stood by the door, still guarding it. Her dark face was impassive. She was no help to me. The two rotted things still crawled over Jason. Only Ivy and Bruce were still standing. Bruce looked scared, Ivy looked excited. She watched the two master vamps with half-parted lips, her lower lip drawn under with concentration or excitement.

I'd been able to meet her eyes, and that had bothered her—a lot.

I crossed the room behind Jean-Claude. When I passed him, the current of power lashed out and curled around me like an arm. I kept walking and it slipped away, but my skin shivered where it had touched me. The shit was going to hit the fan unless I could stop it.

Kissa watched me move past her with narrowed eyes. I ignored her. One master vampire at a time. I walked past Bruce and stopped in front of Ivy. She stared past me at the two masters, ignoring me.

I opened my mouth. As I spoke, the silence split apart and sound came back to me ears with a nearly painful clap like a tiny sonic boom.

"I challenge you."

Ivy blinked at me as if I'd just appeared. "What did you say?"

"I challenge you," I said. I kept my face blank and tried very hard not to think about what I was doing.

Ivy laughed. "You are mad. I am a master vampire. You cannot challenge me."

"But I can meet your eyes," I said. I let a small smile play along my lips. I tried to keep my mind blank, no thought to betray me, no fear to leak out, but of course once I thought of fear it was there curling in my stomach.

She laughed, high and tinkling like broken glass. It nearly cut skin just to hear it. What the hell was I doing?

The wind rushed against my back, nearly flinging me into her. I glanced back in time to see Jean-Claude stagger and a splash of blood spill from his hand. Janos hadn't broken a sweat yet.

Whatever I was doing, I'd better do it fast.

"After Jean-Claude loses, I'm going to ask Janos to make him fuck me. Your master is going to be everybody's meat, and so will you."

My eyes flicked to the rotted things clawing at Jason. Incentive enough. I turned back to Ivy and met her brown eyes. "You won't do shit. You can't even outstare one puny human being."

She glared at me. Her anger was instantaneous, like fire springing out of a match. I watched the brown of her irises spread across her eyes from a space of less than ten inches. Her eyes were shining pools of dark light. My pulse threatened to choke me, and a little voice in my head was screaming, "Run away, run away." I stood there and stared her down.

She was a master vampire but a young one. A hundred years from now she'd have eaten me for breakfast, but right now, tonight, maybe, just maybe, she wouldn't.

She hissed at me, flashing her fangs.

"Oh, that's impressive," I said. "Like a dog showing its teeth."

"This dog could tear your throat out." Her voice had gone low and evil crawling along my spine, until I spent most of my effort not to shiver.

I didn't trust my voice not to shake, so I spoke low, and soft, and very clear. "Try it; see how far you get."

She darted forward, but I saw her move, felt her come for me. I threw myself backwards away from her, but she grabbed my arm and lifted me off my feet with her elbow braced so that she could hold me aloft. Her strength was incredible. She could have crushed my arm and I couldn't have done a damn thing about it.

Kissa was suddenly there. "Put her down, now!"

Ivy put me down. She threw me across the room. Air rushed past me, the world blurring so quickly it was like being blind. The air stopped rushing, and down I came.

26

Falling does not cover the speed and abruptness of being thrown from less than ten feet high. I smacked into the wall and tried to slam my arms and hands against it to take some of the momentum before my head smacked into it. I slid down the wall, though slid implies something slow, and there was nothing slow about it. I collapsed at the base of the wall in a crumbled, breathless heap, blinking at bright jarring images that didn't quite make pictures yet.

The first image that came clear was a rotted face with a patch of long, dark hair dangling from its scalp. The vamp's tongue rolled behind broken teeth; something black and thicker than blood spilled with a plop out of her mouth.

I pushed to my knees and found skeletal arms wrapped around my shoulders. The blonde's dried, fang-filled mouth whispered in my ear. ''Come to play.'' Something hard and stiff poked my ear. It was her tongue. I scrambled away, but claws caught in my jacket. Hands that should have been weak as dried sticks were like steel bands.

''They broke the truce, *ma petite*. I cannot hold him long.''

I had a moment to glance up and find Jean-Claude on his knees with both hands extended towards Janos. Janos still stood, but he did nothing else. I had a few moments, nothing more.

I stopped trying to get free of the two vampires. They swarmed over me, and in the mess of arms and legs and body fluids, I drew the Browning. I fired it point-blank into the rotted one's chest. She staggered, but didn't go down. Fangs sank into my back, and I screamed.

A gun exploded from across the room, but there was no time to look. Jason was suddenly there, pulling the blonde off me. I fired into the rotting skull of the brunette. She finally collapsed onto the floor in a puddle of liquid and jerking limbs.

I turned back to Jean-Claude and found him nearly prone on the floor, a pool of blood in front of him. He had one arm still held outward towards Janos.

Janos made a small, flicking motion, and blood flew in an arc from Jean-

Claude's body. He collapsed to the floor, and power rushed outward, blowing back my hair. The world suddenly stank of rotting corpses.

I gagged and pulled the trigger on that long black body.

Janos turned. It seemed like slow motion, as if I had all the time in the world to aim and fire again, but somehow he was facing me when I pulled the trigger the second time. The bullet took him squarely in the chest. He staggered, but didn't go down.

I sighted on that round, skeletal head. His white hand came up and slashed the air. And impossibly, I felt like some invisible claw had slashed my arm. I fired, but my aim was a little off. The bullet grazed the side of his face.

He slashed at me again, and I saw blood start to drip down my hands. Scare tactics. It didn't hurt that much, not nearly as much as it would hurt if he got his hands on me for real.

A second gun sounded, and Janos staggered as a bullet took him in the shoulder. Larry was behind him, gun out.

My vision faded, as if fog was rolling in behind my eyes. I lowered my aim to the larger target of his upper body and pulled the trigger again. I heard Larry's bullet go high and wide into the wall behind me.

A startled, "Hey!" let me know Jason was still back there.

I saw Janos go for the door, like watching slow motion through a fog so thick I could barely see. I fired twice more and knew I hit him at least once. When he was out of the room I fell forward onto all fours, and waited for my vision to clear. Hoped it would clear.

Through my ruined vision I saw Jean-Claude still lying motionless in a pool of his own blood. The question that came into my head was, Is he dead? A stupid question about a vampire, but it was still the first thing I thought of.

I glanced behind me and found Jason scattering bits of the two female vampires around the floor. He was tearing at them with his bare hands, cracking their bones and throwing them far away from each other, as if by sheer destruction he could wash away what they'd done to him.

Bruce lay on his back by the wall. Blood had soaked into his tuxedo. I couldn't tell for sure, but he looked dead. Ivy and Kissa were nowhere to be seen.

Larry was still standing across the room, gun extended, as if he didn't realize that Janos was gone. He was frowning. Everybody was up, everybody was moving except Jean-Claude. Shit.

I crawled towards him, not trusting myself to stand with my vision so spotty. It seemed to take a long time to reach him, as if more than my eyesight wasn't working quite right.

My vision was mostly clear by the time I got to him. I knelt in a thick pool of his blood and stared down at him. How do you tell if a vampire is dead? Sometimes he didn't have a pulse, or a heartbeat, or didn't breathe. Shit, again.

I holstered the Browning. There was nothing here right now to shoot, and I needed my hands. I bled on my shirt and looked at my hands for the first time. It looked like fingernails had scraped down both of them, a little deeper than normal, but they'd heal. Probably wouldn't even be a scar.

I touched Jean-Claude's shoulder and the flesh was soft, very human. I rolled him over onto his back. His hand flopped against the floor with a bonelessness that only the dead have. Some trick of the night had made his face beautiful again. The most human I'd ever seen it, except for the fact that no one was that pretty.

I checked for the big pulse in his neck. I held my fingers against his cooling skin, and felt nothing. Something like tears welled against my eyes, and my throat was tight. But I wouldn't cry, not yet. I wasn't even sure I wanted to.

When is dead, dead for a vampire? Is there such a thing as CPR for the undead? Hell, he breathed some of the time. He had a heart, and it beat most of the time. Not beating couldn't be a good thing.

I positioned his head, pinched his nose closed, and blew a breath into his mouth. His chest rose with it. I tried two more breaths, but he didn't breathe on his own. I unbuttoned his shirt and found the spot above his breastbone, and pressed, one, two, three, four, all the way to fifteen compressions. Two breaths.

Jason staggered over to me, then collapsed to his knees. ''Is he gone?''

''I don't know.'' I pumped with everything I had in me, hard enough to break ribs on a human being, but he wasn't human. He lay there, his body moving only when I moved it, as loose and boneless as only the dead can be. His lips were half-parted, his closed eyes edged with the black lace of his thick eyelashes. His curling black hair still framed his pale face.

I'd pictured Jean-Claude dead. I'd even thought about killing him myself once or twice, but now that his death was a fact I didn't know how to feel. It didn't seem fair somehow. I'd brought him here. I'd asked him to come, and he came. And now he was dead, well and truly dead. And it was partially my fault, partially my doing. If I killed Jean-Claude, I wanted to actually pull the trigger and watch his eyes as he died. Not like this.

I stared down at him. I thought about no more Jean-Claude. This beautiful body rotting at last in the grave it so richly deserved. I shook my head. I couldn't let that happen, not if I could save him. I only knew one thing that all dead respected, craved. Blood. I tried to breathe life into him one more time, with one difference. I smeared my blood on his mouth first. My lips touched his, and I tasted the sweet, metallic taste of my own blood.

Nothing.

Larry knelt beside us. ''Where did Janos go?''

He hadn't been able to see through the fog, but I didn't have time to explain. ''Watch the door; shoot anything that comes through.''

''Can I let the girls go?''

''Sure.'' I'd forgotten about the girls. I'd forgotten about Jeff Quinlan. I'd have traded them all for Jean-Claude to blink his eyes at me. Not if the choice had been offered to me as an either-or, but just now they were strangers. He wasn't.

''More blood, maybe,'' Jason said softly.

I looked at him. ''You offering?''

''Neither of us can feed him back to full strength without dying, but I'll help,'' he said.

''You fed him once tonight already. Can you donate twice?''

"I'm a werewolf. I heal quick. Besides, my blood has more kick to it than a human's, more power."

I really looked at him then. He was covered in slime. A big black smear covered most of one cheek. His blue eyes didn't look wolfish; they looked haunted, hurt. There are things that harm a lot more than physically.

I took a deep breath and slid one of my knives out of its sheath. I sliced my left wrist. The pain was sharp and immediate. I placed the wound against Jean-Claude's lips. Blood welled into his mouth. Blood filled his mouth like wine pouring into a cup. It seeped out the corner of his mouth and slid down his cheek. I stroked his throat to make him swallow the blood.

How he'd laugh to know I'd finally opened a vein for him. More blood spilled from his unresponsive lips. Dammit.

I breathed into his mouth and got a taste of my own blood. I made his chest rise, breathing in my own blood. I thought one word at him: Live, live, live.

A shudder ran through the body. The throat convulsed, swallowed. I pulled back from him. He caught my wrist as I moved it back from his chin. His grip hurt. I could feel that unnatural strength that could break bone. His eyes were still closed; only the grip on my wrist let me know we were making progress.

I put a hand on his chest. He wasn't breathing on his own yet. No heartbeat. Was that bad? Good? Indifferent? Hell, I didn't know.

"Jean-Claude, can you hear me? It's Anita."

He raised up in a small motion and pressed my bleeding wrist to his mouth. He bit me, and I gasped. He used both hands to press my wrist to his mouth and sucked me. In the middle of sex it might have felt good; now it just hurt.

"Damn," I said.

"What's wrong?" Larry asked.

"It hurts," I said.

"I thought it was supposed to feel good," the blonde girl said.

I shook my head. "Not unless you're under hypnotic control."

"How long will this take?" Larry asked.

"As long as it takes," I said. "Watch the door."

"Which one?"

"Oh, hell, just shoot anything that comes through it." I was feeling light-headed. How much had he drunk?

"Jason, I'm getting a little woozy here." I tried to pull my wrist free, but his hands were like iron forged to my skin. "I can't get him off."

Jason pulled at the pale hands, but couldn't budge them. "I could tear the fingers off one at a time and get you loose, but . . ."

"Yeah, Jean-Claude would be pissed." Dizziness was coming in waves, nausea starting to build in the pit of my stomach. I had to get him off me.

"Let go of me, Jean-Claude. Let go of me, dammit!"

His eyes were still closed, his face blank. He fed like a baby with single-minded determination, but this baby was draining my life away. I could feel it going down my arm. My heart was beginning to pound in my ears as if I'd been running, pumping the blood faster. Feeding him faster. Killing me faster.

Spots were dancing in front of my eyes. The darkness beginning to eat the light. I drew the Browning.

"What are you doing?" Jason asked.

"He's going to kill me."

"He doesn't know what he's doing."

"I'll still be dead."

"Something's moving around at the head of the stairs," Larry called.

Great. "Jean-Claude, let go of me, now!"

I pressed the barrel of the gun to the flawless skin of his forehead. Darkness was eating my vision in great moving bites. Nausea burned up my throat.

I leaned over him and whispered, "Please, Jean-Claude, let me go. It's your *ma petite*, let me go." I sat back up.

"Vampires coming," Larry said. "Hurry up."

I stared down at that beautiful face locked on my arm, eating me alive, and squeezed. His eyes flew open. I moved my whole finger to keep from squeezing down.

He lay his head back onto the floor, still holding my wrist but no longer feeding. His mouth was crimson with my blood. The gun was still pointed at him.

"Ah, *ma petite*, haven't we done this before?"

"The gun," I said, "but not this." I drew my wrist from his reluctant hands and sat back with the Browning cradled in my lap. Nausea and darkness flew inside my head like clouds driven by the wind.

I saw Larry crouched by the foot of the stairs, gun out. But it was like looking down a tunnel, distant and not as important as it should have been.

Jason lay down on the bloody floor. I blinked at him. "The neck hurts less," he said, just as if I'd asked. Jean-Claude crawled on top of him. Jason turned his head to one side without being asked. Jean-Claude pressed his bloodstained mouth over the big pulse in Jason's neck. I saw the muscles in his mouth and jaw as he sank fangs into the tender skin.

Even if I'd known the neck hurt less, I wouldn't have offered it. It looked too much like sex. The wrist at least let me pretend we weren't doing something intimate.

"Anita!"

I turned back to the stairs. Larry was crouched there, alone, with his gun. The two girls had moved back away from the door. The blonde was having hysterics again. Couldn't really blame her.

I shook my head, lifted the Browning in a teacup grip, and pointed it at the door. I needed the extra arm to steady me. There was a faint tremor to my arms that wasn't going to help my aim much.

Power breathed through the room, prickling along my skin. You could almost smell it like perfumed sheets in the dark. I wondered if Jean-Claude and I had given off that kind of power when he'd fed off me. I hadn't noticed it.

Something white appeared in the doorway. It took me a second to figure out what it was. A white handkerchief tied to a stick.

"What the fuck is that?" I asked.

"A flag of truce, *ma petite*."

I didn't look away from the stairs to that thick, honey-dipped voice. Jean-Claude sounded better, or worse, than ever, each word like fur rubbing along my tired body. His voice was thick enough to wrap around all the aches and pains. He could make them go away. I just knew it.

I swallowed and lowered the gun towards the floor. ''Stay the fuck out of my head.''

''My apologies, *ma petite*. I can taste you in my mouth, feel your frantic heartbeat like a treasured memory. I will curb my enthusiasm, but with effort, Anita, with great effort.'' He sounded like I had let him have just a little sex, and he wanted more.

I glanced at him. He was sitting beside Jason's half-naked body. Jason was staring at the ceiling, eyes heavy-lidded like he was half-asleep. Blood trickled from two new puncture wounds in his neck. He didn't look like he'd felt much pain. In fact, it looked like it had felt good. I'd taken the edge off Jean-Claude's need, and Jason had gotten a smoother ride. Bully for him.

''May we talk?'' A voice from the hallway, a man's. I couldn't place it. Hell, I was having trouble focusing on anything, let alone who the disembodied voices belonged to.

''Anita, what do you want me to do?'' Larry asked.

''It's a flag of truce,'' I said. My words felt slurred, though they sounded clear enough. I felt almost drunk, or drugged. It was a bad drunk, a dangerous downer.

Magnus stepped into the doorway. For a second I thought I was seeing things. It was so damned unexpected. He was dressed all in white from his tux to his shoes. The cloth seemed to shine against his dark skin. His long hair was tied back with a loose white ribbon. He had the handkerchief-coated stick gripped in one hand. He walked down the steps in a graceful, almost dancelike movement. It wasn't a vampire's glide, but it was close.

Larry kept his gun trained on him. ''Stay where you are,'' Larry said. He sounded a little scared, but like he meant it. The gun was pointed nice and steady.

''We've discussed the fact that silver bullets don't work on the fey.''

''Who says this gun has silver bullets?'' Larry said.

It was a good lie. I was proud of him. I was certainly too gone to have thought of it.

''Anita?'' Magnus looked past Larry like he wasn't there, but he didn't come down those last few steps.

''I'd do what he says, Magnus. Now what do you want?''

Magnus smiled and spread his arms away from his body. To show he was unarmed, I guess. But I knew, and Larry knew, that weapons weren't what made him dangerous. ''I mean you no harm. We know that Ivy broke the truce first. Serephina offers her most sincere apologies. She asks that you come directly to her audience chamber. No more tests. We have all been unforgivably rude to a visiting master.''

''Do we believe him?'' I asked of no one in particular.

''He speaks the truth,'' Jean-Claude said.

Great. ''Let him pass, Larry.''

''You sure that's a good idea?''

"No, but do it anyway."

Larry pointed his gun at the floor, but he didn't look happy. Magnus walked down the stairs, smiling, mostly at Larry. He walked past him and made a show of giving him his back. It was almost enough to make me wish Larry would shoot him.

He stopped a few feet in front of the rest of us. We were all still on the floor, sitting, or in Jason's case, lying. Magnus looked down at us, amused, or bemused.

"What the hell are you doing here?" I asked.

Jean-Claude glanced at me. "You seem to know each other."

"This is Magnus Bouvier," I said. "What are you doing here, with them?"

He loosened the tie at his collar and spread the stiff cloth. I was pretty sure what he was trying to show me, but I couldn't see from the floor. I wasn't at all sure I could stand without falling over. "If you want me to take a peek, you're going to have to come down here."

"With pleasure." He knelt in front of me less than two feet away. He had two healing bite marks on his neck.

"Shit, Magnus. Why?"

He looked at me, eyes flicking to my bloody wrist. "I might ask you the same thing."

"I donated blood to save his life. What's your excuse?"

He smiled. "Nothing half as nice as that." Magnus undid the ribbon and let his hair fall like a curtain around his shoulders. He looked at me with his turquoise blue eyes, and crawled on all fours towards Jean-Claude. He moved like he had muscles in places that people didn't. It was like watching a great cat move. People just didn't move like that.

He knelt in front of Jean-Claude, so close they were almost touching. He swept his hair to one side and offered his neck.

"No," Jean-Claude said.

"What's going on?" Larry asked.

It was a good question. I didn't have a good answer. I didn't even have a bad one.

Magnus slipped off his white jacket and let it slide to the floor. He undid the cuff to his right wrist and pushed the cloth back. He offered his bare wrist to Jean-Claude. The skin was smooth and unbroken. Jean-Claude took his hand and raised the skin to his lips.

I almost looked away, but in the end I didn't. Looking away is like lying to yourself. You pretend it isn't happening, but it is.

Jean-Claude brushed his lips across the skin, then released Magnus's hand. "The offer is generous, but I would be drunk indeed if I added your blood to theirs."

"Drunk?" I asked. "What the fuck are you talking about?"

"Ah, *ma petite*, you do have a way with words."

"Shut up."

"Losing a quantity of blood makes you grumpy," he said.

"Fuck off."

He laughed, and the sound was sweet. It had a taste just outside description, like some forbidden candy that was not just fattening but poisonous. But what a way to go.

Magnus stayed kneeling, staring at the laughing vampire. "You won't taste me?"

Jean-Claude shook his head, as if he didn't trust himself to speak. His eyes glittered with suppressed laughter.

"The blood has been offered." Magnus crawled back towards me. His hair had spilled forward on one side so one eye was lost, glittering like a jewel through his hair. Eyes just weren't supposed to be that color. He crawled up to me until our faces were inches apart. "A pint of blood, a pound of flesh." He whispered it, leaning in towards me as if for a kiss.

I leaned back, away from him, and overbalanced. I ended up on my back on the floor. It was not an improvement. Magnus crawled over me, still on all fours, hovering. I pressed the Browning into his chest.

"Back off, or bite it."

Magnus crawled backwards, but not very far. I sat up, keeping the gun on him one-handed. The barrel wavered a lot more than normal. "What was that all about?"

Jean-Claude said, "Janos spoke of taking blood and flesh from us this night. As an apology, Serephina offers us blood, and flesh."

I stared at Magnus, still on all fours, still looking feral and dangerous. I lowered the gun. "No, thanks."

Magnus sat back on the floor, smoothing his hands through his hair, brushing it back from his face. "You have refused Serephina's peace offerings. Do you refuse her apology as well?"

"Take us to Serephina, and you will have done what was asked of you," Jean-Claude said.

Magnus looked at me. "What of you, Anita? Are you content that I take you to Serephina? Do you accept her apology?"

I shook my head. "Why should I?"

"Anita is not a master," Jean-Claude said. "It is my vengeance, my pardon, you should be asking."

"I am doing what I was told," he said. "She challenged Ivy to a test of wills. Ivy lost."

"I didn't throw her across the room," I said.

Jean-Claude frowned. "She resorted to brute force, *ma petite*. She could not win by force of will or vampire wiles against a human being." He looked suddenly very serious. "She lost . . . to you."

"So?"

"So, *ma petite*, you declared yourself a master, and proved that claim."

I shook my head. "That's ridiculous; I'm not a vampire."

"I did not declare you a master vampire, *ma petite*. I said you were a master."

"A master what? Human being?"

It was his turn to shake his head. "I do not know, *ma petite*." He turned to Magnus. "What does Serephina say?"

"Serephina says to bring her."

Jean-Claude nodded and stood like he was pulled by strings. He looked fresh and new, if a little bloodstained. How dare he look so good when I felt like shit?

He looked down at Jason and me. His strange good humor had returned. He smiled down at me, and even with blood staining his mouth he was beautiful. His eyes glittered with some amusing secret. He was full of himself in a way I'd never seen before.

''I do not know if my companions are able to walk. They're feeling a little drained.'' He chuckled at his own joke, putting a hand in front of his eyes, as if it was too funny even for him.

''You are drunk,'' I said.

He nodded. ''I believe I am.''

''You can't be drunk on blood.''

''I've drunk deep of two mortals, but neither of you are human.''

I didn't want to hear this. ''What the hell are you talking about?''

''Necromancer with a chaser of werewolf; a drink to make any vampire giddy.'' He giggled. Jean-Claude never giggled.

I ignored him, if you can ignore an intoxicated vampire. ''Jason, can you stand?''

''I think so.'' His voice was thick, heavy but not sleepy, more the languor after sex. Maybe I was glad my bite had hurt.

''Larry?''

Larry walked over to us, glancing at Magnus, gun naked in his hand. He didn't look happy. ''Can we trust him?''

''We're going to,'' I said. ''Help me stand up, and let's get out of here before fangface busts a gut.''

Jean-Claude was doubled over with laughter. He seemed to think ''fangface'' was outrageously funny. Ye gods.

Larry helped me stand, and after a second of dizziness I was okay. He offered a hand to Jason without being asked. Jason swayed on his feet, but stayed standing.

''Can you walk?''

''If you can, I can,'' he said.

A man after my own heart. I took a step, another, and was on my way across the room. Jason and Larry followed. Jean-Claude staggered to his feet, still laughing softly.

Magnus was standing at the foot of the stairs, waiting for us. He had the jacket slung over one arm. He'd even found the ribbon to tie back his hair.

Jason walked wide around the torn bodies of his two would-be lovers and picked his shirt off the floor. The shirt covered the mess on his chest, but the goo was still on his face, and his hair was stiff and nearly as dark as his pants.

Even the back of Jean-Claude's clothes and hair were thick with congealing blood. I had my own share of blood and goop. Good thing I wore mostly black tonight; didn't show dirt as badly. The crimson blouse was looking a little worse for wear.

Larry was the only one without any blood or gore on him. Here was hoping he could keep up the good work.

The two girls had hidden under the stairs while we discussed things. I was betting it was the brown-haired girl's idea to hide. Lisa seemed too scared to think, let alone do anything smart. Not that I could blame her, but hysteria gets you nowhere but dead.

The brown-haired girl walked over to Larry. The blonde came along for the ride, her hands dug so tightly into the other one's torn blouse it would have taken surgery to remove them.

"We just want to go home now. Can we do that?" Her voice was a little breathy, but for the most part solid. I stared into her brown eyes and nodded.

Larry looked at me.

"Magnus," I said.

He raised his eyebrows, still waiting by the stairs like a tour guide, or a butler ready to escort us up. "You called?"

"I want the girls to leave now, safe."

He glanced at them. "I don't see why not. Serephina had us collect them mostly for your benefit, Anita. They've served their purpose."

I didn't like the way he said that last. "Safe, Magnus, no more harm. Are we clear on what that means?"

He smiled. "They walk out the door, and go home. Is that clear enough for you?"

"Why so cooperative all of a sudden?"

"Would letting them go be apology enough?" Magnus asked.

"Yeah, if they go free, unharmed. I'll accept her apology."

He nodded. "Then consider it done."

"Don't you have to check with your master first?"

"My master whispers sweetly to me, Anita, and I obey." He smiled while he said it, but there was a tightness around his eyes, an involuntary flexing of his hands.

"You don't like being her lap dog."

"Perhaps, but there's not much I can do about it." He started up the stairs. "Shall we go up?"

Jean-Claude paused at the bottom of the stairs. "Do you need some help, *ma petite*? I have taken quite a bit of your blood. You do not recover as quickly as my wolf."

Truthfully, the stairs looked longer going up than they had coming down. But I shook my head. "I can make it."

"Of that, *ma petite*, I have no doubt." He stepped close to me, but did not whisper; instead I felt him in my mind. "You are weak, *ma petite*. Let me help you."

"Stop doing that, dammit."

He smiled and sighed. "As you like, *ma petite*." He walked up the steps like he could have flown, barely touching them. Larry and the girls went up next; none of them seemed tired. I slogged up after them. Jason brought up the rear. He looked hollow-eyed. It may have felt good, but donating that much blood is still rough, even on the temporarily furry. If Jean-Claude had offered to carry him up the stairs, would he have agreed?

Jason caught me looking, but he didn't smile; he just stared back. Maybe he'd have said no, too. Weren't we all just being uncooperative tonight?

27

The silken drapes had been drawn aside. A throne sat in the far right-hand corner. There was no other word for it; ''chair'' just didn't cover that golden, bejeweled thing. Cushions were scattered on the floor around it, heaped like they should be covered with harem girls, or at least small pampered dogs. Nothing sat on them. It was like an empty stage waiting for the actors to appear.

A small wall-hanging on the back wall had been pushed aside to reveal a door. The door had been wedged open with a triangular piece of wood. The spring air poured through the open door, chasing back the smell of decay. I started to say ''Come on, girls,'' but the wind changed. It blew harder, colder, and I knew it wasn't wind at all. My skin prickled, the fine muscles along my arms and shoulders twitching with it.

''What is that?'' Larry asked.

''Ghosts,'' I said.

''Ghosts? What the hell are ghosts doing here?''

''Serephina can call ghosts,'' Jean-Claude said. ''It is a unique ability among us.''

Kissa appeared in the doorway. Her right arm hung loose at her side. Blood dripped down her arm in a slow, heavy line.

''Your handiwork?'' I asked.

Larry nodded. ''I shot her, but it didn't seem to slow her down much.''

''You hurt her.''

Larry widened his eyes. ''Great.'' He didn't sound great when he said it. Wounded master vampires get cranky as hell.

''Serephina bids you come outside,'' Kissa said.

Magnus dropped to the cushions, boneless as a cat. He looked like he'd curled up there before.

''You aren't coming?'' I asked.

''I've seen the show,'' he said.

Jean-Claude walked towards the door. Jason had moved up beside him, but back a couple of steps like a good dog.

The two girls were holding onto Larry's jacket. He had been the one who unchained them. They'd seen him shoot the bad guys. He was a hero. And like all good heroes, he'd get himself killed protecting them.

Jean-Claude was suddenly at my side. ''What is wrong, *ma petite*?''

''Can the girls go out the front?''

''Why?''

''Because whatever's out there is big and bad, and I want them out of it.''

''What's wrong?'' Jason asked. He stood a little to one side. He was flexing his hands, closed, open, closed, open. He'd seemed a lot more relaxed thirty minutes ago, but then, weren't we all?

Jean-Claude turned to Kissa. ''Was this one right?'' He motioned to Magnus. ''Are the girls free to go?''

''They may go; so says our master.''

He turned to the girls. ''Go,'' he said.

They looked at each other, then at Larry. ''Alone?'' the blonde said.

The brown-haired one shook her head. ''Come on, Lisa, they're letting us go. Come on.'' She looked at Larry. ''Thank you.''

''Just go home,'' he said. ''Be safe.''

She nodded and started for the far door with Lisa clinging to her. They left the door to the room open, and we watched them walk out the front. Nothing swooped down upon them. No screams cut the night. What do you know?

''Are you ready now, *ma petite*? We must pay our respects.'' He took a step forward, looking at me. Jason already stood at his side, nervous hands and all.

I nodded and fell into step behind Jean-Claude. Larry stayed at my side like a second shadow. I could feel his fear like a trembling against my skin.

I understood why he was scared. Janos had beaten Jean-Claude. Janos was afraid of Serephina, which meant she could take Jean-Claude without raising a sweat. If she could take the vampire that was on our side, she wouldn't find us much of a challenge. If I was smart, I'd shoot her as soon as I saw her. Of course, we were here to ask for her help. It sort of cut my options.

The cool wind played in our hair like it had little hands. It was almost alive. I'd never felt any wind that could make me want to brush it off, like an overly amorous date. But I wasn't afraid. I should have been. Not of the ghosts, but of whatever had called them up. But I felt distant and faintly unreal. Blood loss will do that to you.

We walked out the door and down two small stone steps. Rows of small, gnarled fruit trees decorated the back of the house. There was a wall of darkness just beyond the orchard. It was a thick wall of shadows, so black that I couldn't see through it. The naked tree branches were framed against the blackness.

''What is that?'' I asked.

''Some of us can weave shadows and darkness around us,'' Jean-Claude said.

''I know. I saw it when Coltrain was killed, but this is a freaking wall.''

''It is impressive,'' he said. His voice was very bland, matter-of-fact. I glanced at him, but even in the bright moonlight I couldn't read his face.

A sparkle of white light showed behind the blackness. Beams of cold, pale light pierced the darkness. The light ate away at the dark like paper burns, the blackness crumbling, vanishing as the light consumed it. When the last of the darkness had shredded away, a pale figure stood among the trees.

Even from this distance you wouldn't have mistaken her for human, but then she wasn't trying to pass. A pale, white luminescence swirled above her head, a glowing cloud, yards across like colorless neon. Vague figures darted out from it, then swirled back.

"Is that what I think it is?" Larry asked.

"Ghosts," I said.

"Shit," he said.

"My thoughts exactly."

The ghosts flowed out into the trees. They hung on the dead branches like a froth of early blossoms, if blossoms could move and writhe and glow.

The strange wind blew against my face, sending my hair streaming backwards. A long, thin line of phosphorescent figures whirled out. The ghosts came sweeping towards us, low to the ground.

"Anita!"

"Just ignore them, Larry. They can't actually hurt you as long as you keep moving and ignore them."

The first ghost was long and thin with a wide, screaming mouth that looked like a smoke ring. It hit me at mid-chest; the shock ran through me like electricity. The small muscles in my arms jerked with it. Larry gasped.

"What the hell was that?" Jason asked.

I took a step forward. "Keep walking and ignore them."

I didn't mean to, but my pace took me ahead of Jean-Claude. The next ghost swept over my face. There was a moment of smothering but I kept walking and it passed.

Jean-Claude touched my arm. I stared into his face and wasn't sure what I saw. He was definitely trying to tell me something. He stepped out in front of me, still staring at me.

I nodded, and let him lead. It didn't cost me anything.

"I don't like this," Larry said in a singsong voice.

"Me either," Jason said. He was batting at a tiny swirl of whiteness like a tame mist. The more he swatted at it, the more solid it became. A face was forming out of the mist.

I walked back to Jason and grabbed his arms. "Ignore it."

The small ghost perched on his shoulder. It had a large, bulbous nose and two half-formed eyes.

Jason's arms tensed under my hands. "Every time you notice them, you give them power to manifest themselves," I said. A ghost hit me in the back. It was like a lump of moving ice in the center of my body. It crawled out the front of my body like a cold rope being pulled through me. The sensation was unnerving as hell, but it wasn't permanent. It didn't even really hurt.

The ghost dived into Jason's chest, and he cried out. Only my grip on his arms kept him from clawing at the thing. Every muscle in Jason's body twitched like a horse being eaten alive by flies. He sagged when the ghost was through him, looking at me with horror-filled eyes. It was nice to know he could be scared. The vampires seemed to have taken some of his courage with their rotting arms. Couldn't blame him. I'd have had screaming fits, too.

Larry jumped when a ghost popped through him, but that was all. His eyes were a little wide, but he knew where the danger lay, and it wasn't the ghosts.

Jean-Claude came to stand near us. "What is wrong, my wolf?" There was an undercurrent of warning, anger. His pet was not living up to his reputation.

"We're fine," I said. I squeezed Jason's hand; his eyes were still wide, but he nodded. "We'll be fine."

Jean-Claude walked towards the distant white figure once more, his movement graceful, unhurried, as if he wasn't as scared as the rest of us. Maybe he wasn't. I pulled Jason with me. Larry had moved to my back. The three of us walked like normal human beings behind Jean-Claude. We looked like good little soldiers except for the fact that I was holding the werewolf's hand. His hand was sweating against my skin. Couldn't afford to have a hysterical werewolf. My right hand was still free to go for a gun, or a knife. We'd hurt them once; if they didn't behave themselves, we could finish the job. Or at least go down trying.

Jean-Claude led us among the naked trees with the ghosts crawling over the bare branches like phantom snakes. He stopped a few feet away from the vampire. I almost expected him to bow, but he didn't. "Greetings, Serephina."

"Greetings, Jean-Claude." She was dressed in a simple white dress that fell in folds of shining cloth over her feet. White gloves covered her arms almost completely. Her hair was grey with streaks of white, left unadorned save for a headband of silver and pearls. It wasn't a headband, probably called a coronet or something. Her face was lined with age. Delicate makeup had been added, but not enough to hide the fact that she was old. Vampires didn't age. That was the whole point, wasn't it?

"Shall we go inside?" she asked.

"If you like," he said.

She gave a faint smile. "You may escort me inside, as you did of old."

"But it is not olden days, Serephina. We are both masters now."

"I have many masters serving me, Jean-Claude."

"I serve only myself," he said.

She stared at him for a space of heartbeats, then nodded. "You have made your point. Now be a gentleman."

Jean-Claude took a deep enough breath that I heard it sigh from his lips. He offered her his arm, and she slid one gloved hand through it, her hand resting on his wrist.

The ghosts floated downward behind her like a great flowing train. They brushed past the rest of us with a skin-prickling rush, then floated upward, hovering about ten feet off the ground.

"You may walk with us," Serephina said. "They will not molest you."

"Comforting," I said.

She smiled again. It was hard to tell in the moonlight and ghostly glow, but her eyes were pale, maybe grey, maybe blue. You didn't need to see the color to not like the look in them.

"I have looked forward to meeting you, necromancer."

"Wish I could say the same."

The smile didn't widen, and didn't fade; it didn't move at all. It was like her face was a well-constructed mask. I raised my glance to her eyes, for just a moment. They didn't try to suck me under, but there was an energy in them, a deep burning that pushed at the surface of her being like a banked fire; move a log just wrong, and the flames would come licking out and burn us all up. I couldn't judge her age; she was stopping me. I'd never met anyone that could actually stop me—trick me into believing them younger, yes, but not just glare at me and keep me from doing it.

She turned and walked through the door. Jean-Claude helped her up the steps, as if she needed it. The easy distance of the blood loss was receding, leaving me real, and alive, and wanting to stay that way. Maybe it was Jason's hand warm in my own. The sweat on his palm. The reality of him. I was suddenly scared, and she hadn't done a damn thing to me.

The ghosts flowed into the house, some pouring through the door, some sliding through the walls. Watching them pull free of the wood, you almost expected a sound, like a plop, but it was utterly quiet. The undead make no noise.

The ghosts bounced along the ceiling like helium-filled balloons, poured down the walls in back of the throne like milky water. They were translucent near the candle flames, like bubbles.

Serephina sat down in the corner on her throne. Magnus curled in the cushions at her feet. There was a flash of anger in his eyes, there, and gone. He wasn't enjoying being Serephina's boy toy. That got him an extra point in my book.

"Come sit by me, Jean-Claude," Serephina said. She motioned to the cushions on the opposite side from Magnus. They'd have made an interesting pair.

"No," Jean-Claude said. That one word was warning enough. I drew my hand slowly from Jason's. If we really were going to fight, I'd need both hands.

Serephina laughed, and with that sound her power broke open and crashed on us poor humans.

The power rode down on me like pounding horses. My whole body vibrated with it. My mouth was too dry to swallow, and I couldn't quite get a full breath of air. She didn't have to touch me to hurt me. She could just sit on her throne and throw power at me. She could grind my bones into dust from a nice safe distance.

Something touched my arm. I jerked and turned, and it felt like slow motion. It has hard to focus on Jean-Claude's face, but once I did, the grinding power receded like the ocean pulling back from the shore.

I took a deep, shuddering breath, then another; every breath was firmer. "Illusion," I whispered. "Fucking illusion."

"Yes, *ma petite*." He turned from me and went to Larry and Jason, who were still standing spellbound.

I looked back at the throne. The ghosts had formed a glowing nimbus around her; most impressive. But not nearly as impressive as her eyes. I had one wild glimpse of eyes that seemed to go on forever, then I stared at the hem of her white dress as hard as I could.

"Can you not meet my gaze?"

I shook my head. "No."

"Can you really be that powerful a necromancer when you cannot even meet my eyes?"

I wasn't just not meeting her eyes. I was hunched over. I straightened but didn't move my eyes. "You're only about six hundred years old." I raised my eyes slowly, inch by inch up the white dress until I could see her chin. "How the hell did you get to be this powerful in that amount of time?"

"Such bravado. Meet my eyes and I will answer you."

I shook my head. "I don't want to know that badly."

She chuckled, and the sound was low and dark. It slid down my spine like something loathsome and half-alive. "Ah, Janos, Ivy, so good of you to join us."

Janos glided through the door with Ivy at his side. Janos looked more human than he had since I'd first met him. His skin was pale but fleshy. His face was still thin, and he couldn't have passed for completely human, but he looked less monstrous. He also looked healed.

"Shit."

"Is something wrong, necromancer?" Serephina asked.

"I hate to waste that many bullets."

She gave that low chuckle again. It made my skin feel tight. "Janos is very talented."

He walked past us. I could see bullet holes in his shirt. At least I'd ruined his wardrobe.

Ivy looked dandy. Had she run when the shooting started? Had she left Bruce to die?

Janos went down on one knee among the cushions. Ivy knelt with him. They stayed there, head bent, waiting for her to notice them.

Kissa moved to stand beside Magnus, bleeding, her arm held close to her side. But she glanced from the two kneeling vampires to Serephina, and back again. She looked . . . worried.

Something was up. Something unpleasant.

She left them kneeling, and said, "What business brings you to me, Jean-Claude?"

"I believe you have something that belongs to me," he said.

"Janos," she said.

Janos rose to his feet and went back out the door. He was out of sight only a moment, then came back carrying a large cloth sack like something Santa Claus would have carried. He untied the cord that held it shut and emptied the contents on the floor at Jean-Claude's feet. Splinters of wood, none of them big enough to make a decent stake, fell into a medium-sized pile. The wood was dark and polished where it wasn't white with new cuts.

"With my compliments," Janos said. He shook the last bits of wood out of the sack and knelt back on the steps.

Jean-Claude stared down at the splintered wood. "This is childish, Serephina. Something I would have expected from you centuries ago. Now . . ." He motioned at the ghosts, at everything. ''How have you managed to subdue Janos? You feared him once.''

''State your business, Jean-Claude, before I grow impatient and challenge you myself.''

He smiled and gave a graceful bow, arms out to his sides like an actor. When he raised up, the smile was gone. His face was like a beautiful mask. ''Xavier is in your territory,'' he said.

''Did you truly think I would feel the presence of your pet necromancer, and not sense Xavier? I know he is here. If he challenges me, I will deal with him. Speak the rest of your business, or was that it? Did you come all this way to warn me? How touching.''

''I realize you are more powerful than Xavier now,'' Jean-Claude said, ''but he is slaughtering humans. Not just the attack on the missing boy's home, but many deaths. He has gone back to cutting up his pets. He draws attention to us all.''

''Then let the council kill him.''

''You are master in this territory, Serephina; it is your task to police it.''

''Do not presume to tell me my duties. I was centuries old when you died. You were nothing but a catamite for any vampire that wanted you. Our beautiful Jean-Claude.'' She made beautiful sound like a bad thing.

''I know what I was, Serephina. Now I am Master of the City and follow the council's laws. We are not to allow humans to be slaughtered in our territories. It is bad for business.''

''Let Xavier kill hundreds. There are always more,'' she said.

''Nice attitude,'' I said.

She turned her attention to me, and I wished I hadn't said anything. Her power pulsed against me, like a great beating heart.

''How dare you disapprove of me,'' Serephina said. I heard the rustle of her silk dress as she stood. No one else moved, and I heard her dress slither across the cushions, sliding along the floor, as she came closer. I did not want her to touch me.

I stared up the line of her body, and saw her gloved hand strike outward. I gasped. Blood dripped down my hand.

''Shit!'' It was a deeper cut than Janos had managed, and it hurt more. I met her eyes, anger making me brave, or stupid. Her eyes were pure white, like captive moons shining from her face. Those eyes called to me. I wanted to fling myself into her pale arms, to feel the touch of those soft lips, the sharp sweet caress of her teeth. I wanted to feel her body cradling mine. I wanted her to hold me like my mother once had. She would take care of me forever, and never leave, never die, never desert me.

That stopped me. I stood very still. I was standing at the edge of the pillows. The hem of her dress spilled at my feet. I could have reached out a hand and touched her.

Fear pounded my heart in my head. I could taste my pulse on my tongue.

She spread her arms wide. ''Come to me, child, and I will always be with you. I will hold you forever.''

Her voice was everything good; warmth, food, shelter from all the things that hurt, all the disappointment. I knew in that moment that all I had to do was step into her arms and all the bad things would go away.

I stood there with my hands balled into fists. My skin ached to have her touch me, hold me. Blood still dripped down my hand from where she'd cut me. I rubbed my fingers into the cut, making the pain sharp.

I shook my head.

"Come to me, child. I will be your mother forever."

I found my voice. It sounded rusty, choked, but it came. "Everything dies, bitch. You aren't immortal, none of you are."

I felt her power waver like a pebble thrown in a pool, and I moved back a step, then another. It took everything I had left not to run from that room, and to keep running. To run and run and run. Away from her.

I didn't run. In fact, I stayed about two steps back, looking around. People had been busy. Janos stood next to Jean-Claude. They weren't trying their vampire wiles on each other, but the threat was open, and there. Kissa stood to one side, blood pooling on the pillows at her feet. There was a look on her face that I couldn't read. It was almost amazement. Ivy was standing now, staring at me, smiling, pleased that I'd nearly fallen into Serephina's arms.

I wasn't pleased. No one had ever come closer, not even Jean-Claude. I was beyond scared. My skin was cold. I had broken her hold over me, but it was temporary. She might not be able to trick me with her mind, but I'd felt her mind brush mine. If she wanted me, she could have me. It wouldn't be pretty. No illusions, no tricks, just brute fucking force and she could have me. I would never run into her arms, but she could crush my mind. That she could do.

The knowledge was almost calming. If there was nothing I could do to prevent it, might as well not worry about it. Worry about the things you can control; the rest will either work themselves out, or they'll kill you. Either way, no more worries.

"You are quite right, necromancer," Serephina said. "We are all mortal in this room. Vampires can live a long, long time. It makes us forget that we are mortal. But immortality eludes even us."

It wasn't a question, and I agreed with everything she said, so I just looked at her.

"Janos told me you had an aura of power, necromancer. He said he used it against you as he would another vampire. I did it just now when I slashed your hand. I have never known a human that could be harmed so."

"I don't know what you mean about an aura of power."

"It is what allowed you to slip my magic. No human could have withstood me, and few vampires."

"Glad I could do something to impress you."

"I never said I was impressed, necromancer."

I shrugged. "Fine, maybe you don't give a damn about humans, or keeping a low profile. I don't know about your council, or what they'll do to you for not helping us. But I do know what I'll do."

"What are you babbling about, human?"

"I am the vampire executioner for this state. Xavier and his crew took a young boy. I want him back, alive. You help me get him back alive, or I go to the courts and get a death warrant on you."

"Jean-Claude, talk to her, or I will kill her."

"She has the weight of human law behind her, Serephina."

"What is human law to us?"

"The council says that it rules us as it rules the humans. Refusing the human laws is the same as breaking with the council."

"I don't believe you."

"You can taste the truth of my words. I could never lie to you, not two hundred years ago, not now." His voice was very calm, very sure.

"When did this new law go into effect?"

"When the council saw the benefit of being mainstream. They want the money, the power, the freedom to walk the streets in safety. They don't want to hide anymore, Serephina."

"You believe what you say; that much is true," she said. She looked down at me, and the weight of that gaze even with me looking away was like a giant hand mashing me down. I stayed on my feet, but it was an effort. You should bow down to such power. Grovel before it. Worship it.

"Stop it, Serephina," I said. "Cheap mind tricks won't work, and you know it." The cold lump in my stomach wasn't so sure.

"You fear me, human. I can taste it on the back of my tongue."

Oh, goody. "Yeah, you scare me. You probably scare everybody in this room. So what?"

She drew herself up to every inch of her tall, thin frame. Her voice was suddenly soft, breathing down my skin like fur. "I will show you."

She gestured outward with one gloved hand. I tensed, waiting for another cut, but it never came. A scream cut the air and whirled me around.

Blood ran down Ivy's face. Another cut appeared on her bare arm. Two more on her face. Long, slicing wounds with every gesture that Serephina made.

Ivy shrieked. "Serephina, please!" She fell to her knees among the bright cushions, one hand outstretched towards the master vampire. "Serephina, master, please."

Serephina walked around her, one gliding movement at a time. "If you had held your temper, they would all be ours now. I knew their hearts, their minds, their deepest fears. We would have broken them all. They would have broken the truce and we could have feasted on them to our blood's content."

She was almost even with me. I wanted to move back away from her, but she might see it as a sign of weakness. Her dress brushed my leg, and I didn't care. I did not want her to touch me. I moved back, and she caught my wrist. I hadn't even seen her move.

I stared at that silk-gloved hand as if a snake had just coiled around my wrist. Hell, I'd have rather had the snake.

"Come, necromancer; help me punish this bad vampire."

"No, thanks," I said. My voice sounded shaky. It matched the fluttering in my gut. She hadn't done anything to me yet except touch me, but touch makes all powers stronger. If she tried a mind trick now, I was finished.

"Ivy would have taken great delight in your pain, necromancer."

"That's her problem, not mine." I was staring very hard at the silky cloth of Serephina's dress. I had a terrible urge to look upward, to meet her eyes. I didn't think it was her power, just my own morbid compulsion. It's hard to be tough when you're staring at someone's body and being led around by the hand like a child.

Ivy lay on the floor, half-propped on her arms. Her lovely face was a mass of deep cuts. Bone gleamed in the candlelight from one cheek. Her right arm had a cut that showed muscle twitching and bloody.

Ivy stared up at me, and behind the pain was a hatred strong enough to light a match. The anger rose from her in slapping waves.

Serephina knelt beside her, drawing me down with her. I glanced back at Jean-Claude. Janos had a white spider-hand on his chest. Larry mouthed the word "gun." I shook my head. She hadn't hurt me yet. Not yet.

The hand jerked my arm hard enough to wrench my head around to face her. We were eye to eye, suddenly, horribly. What I saw in her eyes wasn't horrible. Her eyes, which I would have sworn were some pale shade, looked solid wood brown. My mother's eyes.

I think she meant for it to be comforting, or seductive. It wasn't. My skin went cool with fear. "Stop it."

"You don't want me to stop," she said.

I tried to pull my arm out of her grasp. I might as well have tried to move the sun to a different part of the sky. "All you can offer me is death. My dead mother in your dead eyes." I stared into those brown eyes that I never thought to see this side of heaven. I yelled at my mother's eyes, because I couldn't look away. Serephina wouldn't let me, and I couldn't fight her on that, not while she touched me. "You're a walking corpse, and everything else is just lies."

"I am not dead, Anita." There was an echo of my mother's voice in her words. She raised her other hand as if to caress my cheek.

I tried to close my eyes. Tried to look away. I couldn't. A strange paralysis was sliding over my body, like the feeling you get just on the edge of sleep when your body weighs a thousand pounds and every movement is nearly impossible.

That hand came for me in slow motion, and I knew if she touched me I would fall into her arms. I would cling to her and cry.

I remembered my mother's face the last time I'd seen her. The coffin had been dark wood covered in a blanket of pink roses. I knew Mommy was in there, but they wouldn't let me see. No one could see. Closed coffin, they said, closed coffin. Every adult in my life was having hysterics. The room was full of screams, sobbing. My father collapsed to the floor. He was useless to me. I wanted my mother. The latches on the coffin were silver. I opened them, and I heard a cry behind me. I didn't have much time. The lid was heavy, but I shoved it upward and it moved. I got a glimpse of white satin, and shadows. I raised my arms over my head with every ounce of strength and got a glimpse of something.

My Aunt Mattie grabbed me back. The lid clanged shut, and she snapped the lock back in place, dragging me away. I didn't struggle; I'd seen enough. It was like looking at one of those pictures that you know must look like something, but your eyes can't make sense of it. It took me years to make sense of it. But what I saw wasn't my mother. Couldn't be my beautiful mother. It had been a husk, something left behind. Something to hide in a dark box and let rot.

I opened my eyes, and Serephina had pale grey eyes. I pulled my wrist from her suddenly loose grasp and said, ''Pain helps.''

I stood and stepped away from her, and she didn't stop me. Which was good, because I was shaking all over, and it wasn't from the vampire. Memories have teeth, too.

She stayed kneeling by Ivy, and said, ''Most impressive, necromancer. I will help you find this boy you seek.''

Her sudden cooperation was unnerving. ''Why?''

''Because since I attained my full powers, no one has ever slipped my illusions twice in one night. No one living or dead.''

She grabbed Ivy by one bloody arm and pulled her into her lap to bleed on the white dress. Ivy gasped. ''Remember this, young master vampire: This mortal did what you could not. She stood against me and won.'' She tossed her suddenly away, sending her sprawling across the floor. ''You are not worthy of my sight. Get out.''

Serephina stood. The fresh blood stood out in scarlet relief against her white dress and gloves. ''You have impressed us. Now go, all of you.'' She turned and walked back to her throne. She didn't sit down. She stood with her back to us, one hand on the chair arm. Perhaps it was my imagination, but she seemed tired. Her ghosts flowed down to meet her in a swirling white mist. There weren't as many individual shapes as before, as if the phantoms had lost some of their solidity.

''Go,'' she said without turning around.

The back door was open, but Jean-Claude walked to the doorway that led out the front. I wasn't going to argue. I just wanted out. I didn't give a damn which door we took.

We walked coolly, calmly towards the door. I wanted to run. Larry stood next to me, and I could see the pulse in his throat jumping with the effort not to bolt. Jason reached the door a little ahead of us, but he waited and turned and motioned us through like a doorman, or a butler.

I caught a glimpse of his eyes, too wide, scared, and knew what the gesture had cost him. We went through; he followed. Jean-Claude brought up the rear. The doors slammed behind us, and we walked out. Just like that.

But for the first time I knew that I'd been let go. I hadn't fought my way out, or bluffed my way out. She could be impressed all she wanted, but she had allowed us to go. Being allowed to leave was not the same thing as winning.

I would never go back into that house voluntarily. I would never be near her willingly. Because I'd been impressive tonight, but I couldn't keep it up. Even now I knew that she could have me. This vampire had my ticket. Had a lie almost worth my immortal soul.

Damn.

28

Jason walked past me into the hotel room. He headed straight for the bathroom. ''I'm taking a shower.'' It was pushy, but he did smell like a decayed corpse. We'd driven back with all the windows rolled down. Most of the time if you stink, you can't smell someone else. I had some of the rotted stuff on me, but I could still smell Jason. Some smells are too unique to ever really go away.

''Wait,'' Larry said.

Jason turned, but not like he was happy.

''Use my shower.'' He held up a hand before I could say anything. ''It's an hour until dawn. If we want everybody tucked in before that, it makes sense to use both bathrooms.''

''I thought we'd all sleep in this room tonight,'' I said.

''Why?'' he asked.

Jean-Claude stood by the love seat looking lovely and unhelpful. Jason just looked impatient.

''Safety in numbers,'' I said.

Larry shook his head. ''Alright, but I can take the werewolf next door and let him shower. Or don't you trust me to even do that?'' He was getting angry again.

''I trust you, Larry. You did good tonight.''

I expected a smile. I didn't get it. He looked very serious. ''I killed that vampire Bruce.''

I nodded. ''I thought we were going to have to kill everything in the room.''

''So did I.'' He sank into one of the chairs. ''I've never killed anyone before.''

''It was a vampire. It's not the same thing as killing a person.''

''Yeah, right. And how many corpses have you given CPR to lately?''

I glanced at Jean-Claude smiling at me. I shrugged. ''Just one. Can you give us some privacy here?'' I asked.

''I will hear what you are saying no matter where I stand in this room,'' Jean-Claude said.

''Illusion is all; just back off,'' I said.

Jean-Claude bowed his head slightly and took Jason to one side of the room, near the windows. I knew he'd hear everything, but at least he wouldn't be standing over us.

"You don't really believe he's dead, do you?" Larry asked.

"You saw what happened to those two vampires," I said. "They are just rotting corpses; everything else is illusion."

"You think he ever looks like that?"

I looked at Jean-Claude's back for a minute. "I'm afraid I do."

"How can you date him after seeing that?"

I shook my head. "I don't know."

"Corpse or not, you tried to keep him alive." He reacted to the look on my face. "Alive, undead, whatever you want to call it, you tried to preserve it. You were scared he was really dead."

I just looked at him. "So?"

"So, I killed another living being, or undead being. Hell, Anita, Bruce was so newly dead he seemed human."

"Probably why one bullet to the chest finished him."

"How am I supposed to feel about that?"

"Killing him, you mean?"

"Yeah."

"They are monsters, Larry. Some of them are prettier than others, but they are monsters. Never doubt that."

"You can honestly tell me that you think Jean-Claude is a monster." It was more statement than question.

I almost looked at the monster in question, but I didn't. I'd looked at him enough for one night. "Yeah, I do."

"Now, ask her if she thinks she's a monster." Jean-Claude leaned on the back of the love seat, his arms crossed over his chest.

Larry looked a little startled, but he said, "Anita?"

I shrugged. "Sometimes."

Jean-Claude smiled. "See, Lawrence? Anita thinks we're all monsters."

"Larry's not," I said.

"Give him time."

That was a little too close to the truth. "I asked for privacy, or did you forget?"

"I forget nothing, *ma petite*, but time grows short. My wolf is not the only one that needs a bath. Only our young friend is still fresh."

I looked at Larry. There wasn't a drop of blood on him. He was the only one who hadn't wrestled with vampires tonight. He shrugged. "Sorry; I just couldn't get anybody to bleed on me tonight."

"Don't joke, Larry," I said. "With Serephina I think you'll get another chance."

"Sadly, true, *ma petite*."

"How long can you go without a coffin?" I asked.

He smiled. "Concern over my well-being. I am touched."

"Don't give me crap. I opened a freaking vein for you tonight."

"If I have not thanked you for saving my life tonight, *ma petite*, my apologies."

I looked at him. He looked pleasant, amused, but it was a mask. His expression when he didn't want you to know what he was thinking, but didn't want you to know that he didn't want you to know. "Don't mention it."

"I will remember that you saved me, *ma petite*. You could have been free of me. Thank you."

It sounded sincere enough. "You're welcome."

"I need to get this crud off me," Jason said. He sounded just a touch frantic. I was betting he'd be trying to scrub off more than just dirt. But memories don't wash that easily. More's the pity.

"Go on, both of you. Jason can scrub up in Larry's room. It's only practical."

Larry grinned at me. "Thanks."

"I meant it when I said you did good tonight."

I finally got the smile I'd expected. "Come on, Jason, hot water and fresh towels await." Larry held the door for Jason and gave me a little salute. Geez.

Alone again with Jean-Claude. Would this night never end? "You never answered my question about the coffin," I said.

"I will be alright for another night or two."

"How did Serephina go from being your equal in power to being what we saw tonight?"

He shook his head. "I truly do not know, *ma petite*. She surprised me badly. She did not have to let us go tonight. As long as she did not harm us, we could have been her guests for the day."

"Are you surprised she let us go?" I asked.

"Yes," he said.

Jean-Claude pushed away from the love seat. "Take your shower, *ma petite*. I will await the young men's return."

"I thought you could go next, wash the blood out of your hair."

He put a hand up to the back of his hair. He grimaced at the feel of it. "Distasteful, but I want a bath, *ma petite*. It takes longer than a shower, so you go first."

I looked at him for a long moment.

"If you do not hurry, I will not have time for a bath before dawn. I would hate to sleep on your clean sheets covered in blood."

I took a deep breath and let it out slowly. "Fine; just be sure you stay out of the bathroom."

"My word of honor that I will not barge in on you."

"Yeah, right." Though, strangely enough, I believed him. Jean-Claude had been trying to seduce me for a long time. A frontal assault just wasn't his style. I went to take my shower.

29

Ronnie had dragged me into Victoria's Secret. I had pointed out that no one would see my underwear or my nightclothes except other women in the gym locker room. Ronnie had replied, ''You'll see them.'' The logic escaped me but she had talked me into a robe.

It was burgundy, the color of wine-dark peonies. It glowed against my pale skin and matched some of the bruises blossoming on my back. Nothing like getting thrown into a wall to give you a little color. The bite mark on my back wasn't very deep. Hard for humanoid fangs to sink in from that angle. The fang marks on my wrist were deeper. They were two neat little holes, almost dainty. It didn't hurt as much as it should have. Maybe vampires did have painkillers in their saliva, or maybe it was the fangs.

I still couldn't believe that I'd let him sink fangs into me. Shit.

I pulled the robe closer around me. The material was heavy enough to be cozy on a winter evening, and had wide silky cuffs, and more silk lining the edges. It looked vaguely Victorian, a little masculine. I looked delicate in it, like a Victorian doll that hadn't gotten completely dressed yet. I put on an oversized black t-shirt under the robe. It ruined some of the effect, but it beat the heck out of wearing nothing but a robe and underwear out to greet the boys.

I retrieved the Browning from the back of the stool where it had sat during my shower. I carried it with me to the bedroom, and hesitated. I always went armed. Hell, I slept with a gun, but I didn't feel like slipping on a holster. I put the Browning away and settled for slipping the Firestar into the robe pocket. Made the cloth hang funny, but if something nasty came through the door I was ready for it.

Jean-Claude was standing at the window when I opened the bedroom door. He had opened the drapes, and was leaning against the window's edge staring out into the darkness. He turned when the door opened, though I knew he'd heard me before that.

''*Ma petite*, you look lovely.''

''It's the only robe I own,'' I said.

''Of course,'' he said. His face had that amused mask on it again; this time I would have liked to know what he was thinking. His midnight blue eyes were very intense; they didn't match the nonchalant expression. Maybe I didn't want to know what he was thinking.

''Where are Larry and Jason?''

''They have come and gone,'' he said.

''Gone?''

''Jason had a sudden craving, and Larry drove him in the Jeep.''

I just looked at him. ''There is such a thing as room service.''

''It is the wee hours of the morning, *ma petite*. The room service menu is somewhat limited. Jason has donated blood twice to me tonight; he needed protein.'' Jean-Claude smiled. ''It was either take-out, or he could eat Larry. I thought you'd prefer take-out.''

''Very funny. You shouldn't have sent them alone.''

''We are safe from Serephina tonight, *ma petite*, and as long as they stay in town, safe from Xavier.''

''How can you be so sure?'' I crossed my arms over my stomach.

He leaned his back against the window and looked at me. ''Your Monsieur Kirkland handled himself well tonight. I think you worry unnecessarily about him.''

''One night of heroics doesn't keep you safe,'' I said.

''It will be dawn soon, *ma petite*; even Xavier cannot bear the light of day. All the vampires will be seeking shelter. They will have no time to chase our young men.''

I stared at him, trying to read past his pleasant face. ''I wish I was as sure as you seem to be.''

He smiled then, and pushed away from the wall. He slid out of his jacket and let it fall to the rose-colored carpet.

''What are you doing?''

''Undressing.''

I jerked a thumb at the bedroom. ''Undress in there.''

He began unbuttoning his shirt.

''In the other room, right now,'' I said.

He pulled the white shirt out of his pants, working the last few buttons as he walked towards me. The flesh of his chest and stomach had more color than the shirt. He was pumped up and human-looking on blood, part of it mine. The dried bloodstains that had soaked through the shirt marred the pale perfection of his body.

I expected him to try to kiss me, or something, but he walked past me. The back of the shirt was brownish with dried blood. He peeled it off his skin with a sound like tearing. He dropped the shirt on the carpet and walked into the bedroom.

I stood there staring after him. There had been white scars on his back. At least I thought that's what they were. Hard to tell through all the blood. He left the bedroom door open, and in a few minutes I heard water running in the bathtub.

I sat down in one of the straight-back chairs. I wasn't sure what else I was supposed to do. Water ran for a long time, then silence, then sloshing water. He was in the tub. He hadn't closed the bathroom door first. Great.

"*Ma petite*," he called.

I sat there for a minute, unwilling to move.

"*Ma petite*, I know you are there. I can hear you breathing."

I walked to the edge of the bedroom door, very careful not to look inside. I leaned my back against the wall and crossed my arms. "What do you want?"

"There seem to be no clean towels."

"What am I supposed to do about it?"

"Could you call down to housekeeping and have some sent up?"

"I guess so."

"Thank you, *ma petite*."

I stomped over to the phone, pissed. He'd known there were no clean towels before he got into the tub. Hell, I'd known there were no clean towels, but I'd been so busy listening to him splash around in the water I hadn't thought of it.

I was as mad at me as I was at him. He was always a tormenting son of a bitch. I was supposed to watch myself around him better than this. I was in a hotel room that looked like a freaking bridal suite with Jean-Claude all naked and soapy in the next room. After what I'd seen with Jason, there shouldn't have been this much sexual tension in the air, but there was. Maybe it was habit, or maybe Larry was right. I just didn't believe that Jean-Claude was a rotting corpse.

I called for more towels.

They would be happy to bring some up. No one bitched about the time. No one questioned. You can always tell how much you're paying for a room by how little they complain.

A maid brought me four big, soft towels. I looked at her for a full minute, hesitating. I could have her take the towels into Jean-Claude.

She said, "Ma'am?"

I took the towels, said thanks, and closed the door. I just couldn't let a strange woman see that I had a naked vampire in my tub. I wasn't even sure the vampire part was what made it embarrassing. Good girls do not end up with naked male anything in their bathtubs at four something in the morning. Maybe I wasn't a good girl. Maybe I never had been.

I hesitated at the bedroom door. The room was dark. The only light came from the bathroom, spilling in an oblong across the carpet.

I crushed the towels to my chest, took a deep breath, and stepped into the room. I could see the bathtub from here, but mercifully not all of it. I had a glimpse of white porcelain and a mound of white bubbles. Just seeing the bubble bath made the muscles in my shoulders relax a little. Bubbles can hide a multitude of sins.

I stopped at the bathroom door.

Jean-Claude lay back against the edge of the tub. His black hair was wet and had obviously been cleaned. Strands of it clung to his bare shoulders. His arms lay propped on the edge of the bathtub, his head resting against the dark tile of the wall. One pale hand was suspended in midair as if reaching for something, but the hand was utterly limp. His eyes were closed, making black half-moons against his pale cheeks. Beads of water clung to his face and what I could see of his body. He looked almost asleep.

His knee came up through the mound of bubbles, a surprising glimpse of bare wet skin. He turned his head and opened his eyes. The midnight blue of his eyes seemed darker. Maybe it was the way the water made his hair seem heavier, blacker.

I took a shallow breath and said, "Here are the towels."

"Could you place them here, please?" He gestured with that one half-suspended hand.

"Here" was the closed top of the toilet, which was close enough to the tub for grabbing. "I'll put them on the edge of the sink."

"I'll drip water all over the floor getting them from there," he said. His voice was neutral, no vampiric tricks, almost no tone at all.

He was right, and I was being silly. He wouldn't grab me and ravish me. If that'd been the plan, he could have done that years ago.

I placed the towels on the stool, eyes studiously anywhere but the tub.

"You must have questions about tonight," he said.

I glanced at him. The water on his naked torso caught the light like quicksilver. Suds clung to his chest, just under one nipple. I had a horrible urge to brush off the bubbles. I stepped back until I was standing by the far wall.

"It's not like you to offer answers," I said.

"I am feeling generous tonight." His voice had that quality that voices get when they are edging towards sleep.

"If you weren't naked in a tub of bubble bath, would you be offering to answer questions?"

He smiled then, a quick, familiar expression. "Perhaps not, but if I must answer your ravenous curiosity, isn't it more fun this way?"

"Fun for whom?"

"Both of us, if you would only admit it."

That got a smile from me, and I didn't want to smile. I didn't want to be enjoying watching him all soapy and wet. I wanted to be afraid of him, and I was, but I also wanted him. Wanted to run my hands down his wet flesh, wanted to touch what lay under those bubbles. I didn't want intercourse. I couldn't imagine that with him, but I wanted to do a little exploring. I hated that. He was a corpse; surely what I'd seen tonight convinced me of that.

"You're frowning, *ma petite*; why?"

"I asked you if the two rotting vampires were illusion, you said no. I asked if your form was real, you said yes. Both forms are real, you said."

"That is true," he said.

"Are you a rotting corpse?"

He settled lower in the warm, soapy water, drawing his arms into it, until only his head showed above the surface of the water. "That is not one of my forms."

"That isn't an answer."

He raised a pale hand from the water, a handful of bubbles cupped like a snowball. "There are different vampiric abilities, *ma petite*; you know that."

"What's that have to do with it?"

He raised his other hand and began to play with the bubbles, trailing them from hand to hand. "Janos and his two female companions are a different type of vampire than I am. Than most of us are. They are much rarer. If you ever see me as a rotted corpse, I will be well and truly dead. They can rot and reform, and it makes them much harder to kill. The only true surety is fire.''

''Volunteering an awful lot of information, aren't you?''

He lowered his hands in the water, washing the soap away. He sat up a little straighter; suds clung to his body. ''Perhaps I am afraid you will think that what happened with Jason would happen with us.''

''We will never test that theory,'' I said.

''You sound so sure of that,'' he said. ''Your lust perfumes the air, and yet you truly believe that we will never make love. How can you want me almost as much as I want you, yet be sure we will never know each other's bodies?''

I wasn't sure I had an answer for that one. I slid down the wall and sat with my knees drawn up to my chest. The pocket with the gun in it clunked against the wall. I moved the gun to a better position and said, ''We just won't, Jean-Claude, not ever. I just can't.'' A part of me regretted that, but only part.

''Why, *ma petite*?''

''Sex is about trust. I'd have to trust someone implicitly to have sex with them. I don't trust you.''

He stared at me with his blue, blue eyes, looking all scrumptious and wet. ''You mean that, don't you?''

I nodded. ''Yeah, I do.''

''I do not understand you, *ma petite*. I try, but still I do not.''

''You're pretty much a riddle to me, too. If that's any comfort.''

''It isn't. If you were a woman who had casual lusts, we would have been in bed long ago.'' He sighed and sat up even straighter in the water so it hit him just above the waist. ''Of course, if you were a woman of casual appetites, I don't think I would love you.''

''You enjoy the chase, the challenge,'' I said.

''True, but it is more than that with you, if only you would believe me.'' He leaned forward, drawing his knees to his naked chest, rounding his shoulders to hug himself. White scars dribbled down his back from his shoulders to vanish into the water, not a lot of them, but enough.

''What made the scars on your back? Unless it was a holy item, you should have been able to heal them.''

He laid his cheek on his knees so he could look at me. He looked younger, more human, vulnerable suddenly. ''Not if the injury occurred before I died.''

''Who whipped you?''

''I was the whipping boy for an aristocrat's son.''

I stared at him. ''You're telling me the truth, aren't you?''

''Yes.''

''Is that why Janos chose whips tonight, to remind you where you came from?''

''Yes.''

''You weren't born into the aristocracy?''

''I was born in a house with a dirt floor, *ma petite*.''

I looked at him. ''Yeah, right.''

He raised his head. ''If I was going to make something up, *ma petite*, it would be more romantic, more entertaining than being a French peasant.''

''So you were a servant in the castle?''

''I was their only son's constant companion. When he had clothes made, so did I. His tutor was my tutor. His riding instructor, mine. I learned swordplay and dancing and the proper way to eat at table. And when he was bad I was punished, because he was their only child, their only heir to an old family name. People speak of child abuse now.'' He leaned back in the tub, cuddling down into the warm water. ''They complain of spanking. They have no idea what true abuse is. When I was a boy, parents thought nothing of taking a horse whip to a misbehaving child, or beating them bloody. Even the aristocrats beat their children. It was normal.

''But he was the only heir, the only child. So they paid money to my parents and took me. The lady of the manor chose me because I was fair of face. When the vampire who made me sought me out, she said my beauty called to her.''

''Wait a minute.''

He turned his head to give me the full weight of those dark blue eyes. I worked hard at not looking away.

''This gorgeous body and face is all vampire illusion, right? I mean, no one's this beautiful.''

''I told you once that it was not my power that made you see me as you do, not most of the time at any rate.''

''Serephina said you were a catamite for any vampire that would have you. What did she mean?''

''Vampires kill for food, but they bring others over for many reasons. Some for money, wealth, even title, love, but I was brought over for lust. When I was young and weak, they passed me around among them. One would grow tired of me, but there was always another.''

I stared at him, horrified. ''You're right. If you were going to make up a story, this wouldn't be it.''

''The truth is so often disappointing, or ugly; don't you find that, *ma petite*?''

I nodded. ''Yeah. Serephina was old. I thought vampires weren't supposed to age.''

''Whatever age we die at is the age we remain.''

''Did you know Serephina when you were young?''

''Yes.''

''Did you sleep with her?''

''Yes.''

''How could you let her touch you?''

''I was given to her as a gift by a master that makes even her new and improved powers seem weak. I had very little choice.'' He stared at me. ''She knows what you want. Your greatest need, your most treasured wish, and she'll make it come true, or seem to. What did she offer you, *ma petite*? What could she offer you that nearly won you tonight?''

I looked away then; I didn't want to meet his eyes. ''What did she offer you all those years ago?''

''Power.''

I looked up at that. ''Power?''

He nodded. ''Power to escape them all.''

''But you had to have the ability to be a master vampire inside you from the beginning. No one can give that to you,'' I said.

He smiled, but it wasn't a happy smile. ''I know that now, but then I thought only she could save me from an eternity of . . .'' His words trailed off and he submerged, leaving only a few black locks floating on the top of the water. He sat up with a loud breath of air, blinking the water from his eyes. The water had clumped his thick, dark eyelashes. He ran his hands through his wet hair, and it trailed over his shoulders.

''Your hair wasn't this long when we first met.''

''You seem to prefer longer hair on your men.''

''If you're dead, how can your hair grow?''

''That is a question for you to answer,'' he said. He ran his hands through his hair again, squeezing the ends out. He reached out a hand for a towel.

I scrambled to my feet. ''I'll leave you to get dressed.''

''Have Jason and Larry returned?'' he asked.

''No.''

''Then I won't be getting dressed.'' He stood, drawing the towel towards him. I had a glimpse of one side of his pale naked body, water streaming from it. The towel moved into view just in time. I fled.

30

I huddled in the straight-back chair farthest from the bedroom. But I was staring at the doorway. Shit. I wanted to run from the room, but why? It wasn't Jean-Claude I didn't trust. It was me. Fuck.

I touched the gun in my robe pocket. It was smooth and hard and reassuring, but it wouldn't help me now. Violence I understood; sex gave me more problems.

I honestly didn't want to sleep with him, but part of me was hoping for another glimpse of naked flesh. A long line of naked thigh, perhaps. Or maybe . . . I put the palms of my hands over my eyes, as if I could get the image out of my head by just pressing.

"*Ma petite*?" His voice sounded closer than the bathroom.

I didn't want to look, as if, just as Grandma Blake had said, I'd be struck blind. I felt him standing in front of me. Felt the movement of air. I lowered my hands a millimeter at a time. He was kneeling in front of me, one of the thick white towels wrapped around his waist.

I lowered my hands to my lap. Beads of water still clung to his skin. He'd combed his hair, but it was wet, slicked back, leaving his face plainer, more unadorned than normal. His eyes seemed bluer without his hair to frame them.

He put a hand on each chair arm and raised himself up. His lips brushed mine in a soft, nearly chaste kiss. He moved back from me, letting go of the chair.

I could taste my heart in my throat, and it wasn't fear.

Jean-Claude touched my hands, lifted them up. He placed my hands on his bare shoulders. The skin was warm, smooth, wet. He held my wrists in his hands, lightly, very lightly. I could have pulled away at any time. He ran my hands down his slick body.

I pulled my hands free. He said nothing, did nothing. He stayed kneeling, looking at me. Waiting. I could see the pulse in his neck jumping against the skin, and I wanted to touch it.

I slid my hands across his shoulders and lowered my face to his. He started to move into me for a kiss, but I slid my hand along his jaw and turned his head away. I touched lips to his neck and slid my mouth down his skin, until I could taste his pulse beating against my tongue. He tasted of perfumed soap, water, and clean skin.

I slid from the chair to the floor, kneeling in front of him. He was taller now, but not too tall. I licked water off his chest, and let myself do something I'd wanted to do for months. I ran my tongue over his nipple, and he shuddered against me.

I licked water off the center of his chest and ran my hands along his waist up the damp curve of his back.

He pulled the sash of my robe, and I didn't protest. I let his hands slide under the robe, around my waist, with nothing but the t-shirt between his flesh and mine. He ran his hands up my sides, his thumbs playing over my rib cage. The gun swung heavily in the loose cloth. It was annoying.

I raised my face to his. His arms slid behind my back, pressing me against the long wet line of his body. The towel was perilously loose.

His lips brushed mine; then the kiss became something more. Harder, nearly bruising, with his arms locked behind my shoulders. My hands slid down his waist, rubbed the sliding top of the towel, and found it had already slipped. My hand touched the smooth top of his buttocks. Only the pressure of our bodies kept the towel in place.

He ate at my mouth and I felt something sharp, painful. I jerked back and tasted blood.

Jean-Claude let me go. He sat back on his heels, the towel gathered in his lap. "I am sorry, *ma petite*. I got carried away."

I touched my mouth and came away with a spot of blood. "You nicked me."

He nodded. "I am truly sorry."

"I'll just bet you are," I said.

"Do not go all self-righteous on me, *ma petite*. You have finally admitted to yourself, to me, that you feel the pull of my body."

I sat on the floor by the chair with my robe in disarray. The t-shirt had ridden up to my waist. I guess it was a little too late to protest my innocence.

"Fine, lust; you happy?"

"Almost," he said, and now there was something in his eyes. Something dark and drowning, and older than it should have been.

"I can offer you my mortal body, and more, *ma petite*. It can be between us much more than any human lover could offer."

"Would I lose a little blood each time?"

"That was an accident," he said.

I stared at him, all pale and damp, kneeling on the floor with the white towel bundled into his lap, leaving nearly every inch of him bare.

"This is the first time I've cheated on Richard," I said.

"You have been dating me for weeks," he said.

I shook my head. "But I haven't been cheating. *This* is cheating."

"Then have you been cheating on me, with Richard?"

I didn't know what to say to that. "Go get dressed."

"Do you really want me to dress?" he asked.

I looked away. I was embarrassed now and uncomfortable. "Yes, please."

He stood up, the towel gripped in his hands. I looked down at the floor and didn't have to see his face to picture the smile on it.

He walked away from me, and didn't bother moving the towel around behind him. Muscles moved under his skin from calf to waist. He walked naked into the bedroom, and I enjoyed the view.

I touched my finger to my tongue. It was still bleeding. That's what I got for French kissing a vampire. Even thinking about it made me nervous.

"*Ma petite*?" he called from the other room.

"Yeah."

"Do you have a blow dryer?"

"In my suitcase. Help yourself."

Thankfully, I'd dragged my suitcase into the bedroom beside the bathroom door. One point for laziness. I was spared another glimpse of his naked body. Now that hormones were receding, I was embarrassed.

I heard the dryer and wondered if he was standing naked in front of the bathroom mirror while he dried his hair. I was very aware that all I had to do was go to the doorway and I could see for myself.

I stood up, pulled my t-shirt down, tied my robe securely in place, and sat down on the couch. My back was to the bedroom. I wouldn't be seeing anything else. I took the Firestar out of my pocket and laid it on the coffee table in front of me. The gun sat there looking very solid, very black, and somehow accusatory.

The dryer stopped, and he called to me again. "*Ma petite*?"

"What?"

"Come talk to me as the sun rises."

I glanced up at the window he had opened. The sky outside was less black, not light yet, but not pure darkness anymore. I closed the drapes and went to the bedroom. I left the gun on the table. The Browning was in the bedroom anyway.

Jean-Claude had neatly folded the bedspread and blanket at the foot of the bed. Only the wine-dark sheet covered him. He lay with his black hair soft and curling over the dark pillows. The sheet was bunched at his waist. "You can join me if you like."

I leaned against the wall and shook my head.

"I'm not offering sex, *ma petite*; dawn is too close for that. I offer you your half of the bed."

"I'll take the couch; thanks anyway."

He smiled, a slow knowing curve of lips—his old arrogance peeking back out. It was almost comforting to know nothing had really changed. "It is not me that you do not trust. It is you."

I shrugged.

He raised the sheet in front of his chest, an almost protective gesture. "It comes." Fear in his voice.

"What comes?"

"The sun."

I glanced at the closed drapes against the far wall. They were double thick, but a line of greyish light edged them. "You'll be alright like this without your coffin?"

''As long as no one opens the drapes.'' He looked at me for a long moment. ''I love you, *ma petite*, as much as I'm able.''

I didn't know what to say. Saying I lusted after him didn't seem appropriate. Saying I loved him would be a lie.

The light grew stronger, a white edge around the curtains. His body slumped back against the bed. He rolled onto his side, one hand outstretched, the other curling the sheets against his chest. He stared at the growing light, and I could taste his fear.

I knelt beside the bed. I almost took his hand but didn't. ''What happens now?''

''You want the truth, then watch.'' I expected his eyes to flutter, his voice to grow sluggish as if he were falling asleep. It didn't happen that way. He closed his eyes all at once. Pain flashed across his face. He whispered, ''It hurts.'' His face went slack. I'd seen people die, watched the light fade from their bodies. Felt their souls slip away. That was what I saw. He died. The light grew against the drapes, and when it was a solid white line, he died. His breath went out of him in a long rattle.

I knelt beside the bed and stared. I knew dead when I saw it, and this was it. Shit.

I put my arms on the bed and propped my chin on them. I watched him, waiting for him to breathe, to twitch, something. But there was nothing. I reached out to his one outstretched arm. My fingers hovered above his skin, then I touched him. The skin was still warm, still human, but he did not move. I checked his wrist, and there was no pulse. No blood moved in this body.

Did he know I was here? Did he feel me touching him? I stared at him for what seemed like a long time. So this answered the question. Vampires were dead. Whatever animated them was like my own power, some sort of necromancy. But I knew death when I saw it. It gave necrophilia a whole new slant.

Had I only imagined that I felt the brush of his soul leave his body? Surely vampires had no souls—that was part of the point—but I'd felt something leave. If not a soul, what? If a soul, where did it go for the daylight hours? Who watched all the vampires' souls while they lay dead?

There was a knock at the door, probably the other boys. I stood up, pulling my robe in tight. I was cold, and wasn't sure why. I went to answer the door. The cut on my tongue had almost stopped bleeding.

31

I dreamed. In the dream, someone held me in their lap. Smooth dark arms wrapped around me. I looked up into my mother's laughing face. She was the most beautiful woman in the world. I snuggled against her body, and the clean smell of her skin was there. She'd always smelled of Hypnotique bath powder. She bent and kissed me on the lips. I had forgotten the taste of her lipstick, the way she brushed my mouth with her thumb, and laughed because she'd gotten bright red lipstick on my small mouth.

Her thumb came away with something brighter than lipstick. Blood dripped down her thumb. She'd pricked her skin with a safety pin. It was bleeding. She held her thumb out to me and said, "Kiss it, Anita, make it all better."

But there was too much blood. It ran down her hand. I stared up at her laughing face, and blood ran down it like rain. I woke sitting bolt upright on the velvet couch, gasping for breath. I could still taste her lipstick on my mouth, and the smell of Hypnotique bath powder clung to me.

Larry sat up on the love seat, rubbing at his eyes. "What's wrong? Did we get our wake-up call?"

"No, I had a bad dream."

He nodded, stretching, then frowned. "Do you smell perfume?"

I stared at him. "What do you mean?"

"Perfume or powder or something; do you smell it?"

I swallowed and nearly choked on my own pulse. "Yeah. I smell it."

I flung back the extra blanket and threw the lumpy pillow across the room.

Larry swung his legs off the love seat. "What is wrong with you?"

I went to the window and flung the drapes open. The bedroom door was closed, and Jean-Claude was safely inside. Jason was sleeping in there. I stood in the sunlight and let the heat sink into me. I leaned against the warm glass, and only then realized that I was wearing nothing but an oversized t-shirt and my undies. Oh, well. I stayed in the sunlight for a few minutes, waiting for my pulse to calm down.

"Serephina sent me a dream. The smell is my mother's perfume."

Larry came to stand beside me. He was wearing a pair of gym shorts and a green T-shirt. His curly red hair stuck up in all directions. His blue eyes squinted when he stepped into the light. ''I thought only a vampire that had a connection with you, a hold on you, could invade your dreams.''

''That's what I thought,'' I said.

''How could I smell perfume from your dream?''

I shook my head, forehead against the glass. ''I don't know.''

''Has she marked you?''

''I don't know.''

He touched my shoulder, squeezing. ''It'll be alright.''

I stepped away from him to pace the room. ''It won't be alright, Larry. Serephina invaded my dreams. No one but Jean-Claude has ever done that.'' I stopped, because that wasn't true. Nikolaos had done it. But that was after she'd bitten me. I shook my head. Either way, it was a very bad sign.

''What are you going to do?''

''Kill her.''

''Murder her, you mean.''

If Larry's earnest eyes hadn't been staring at me, I'd have said, ''You bet.'' But it's hard to contemplate murder with someone staring at you like you've kicked their favorite puppy.

''I'll try to get a warrant,'' I said.

''If you can't?''

''If it's her or me, Larry, then it's her. Okay?''

Larry looked at me sadly. ''What I did last night was murder. I know that, but I didn't go in planning to kill someone.''

''You stay in this business long enough and you will.''

He shook his head. ''I don't believe that.''

''Believe what you want, but it's still the truth. These things are too dangerous to play fair.''

''If you really believe that, then how can you date Jean-Claude? How can you let him touch you?''

I shook my head. ''I never said I was consistent.''

''You can't defend yourself, can you?''

''Defend which one? Killing Serephina or dating Jean-Claude?''

''Either, both. Hell, Anita, if you're one of the bad guys you can't be one of the good guys.''

I opened my mouth and closed it. What could I say? ''I am one of the good guys, Larry. But I'm not going to be a martyr. If that means breaking the law, so be it.''

''Are you going to get a warrant?'' His face was very neutral as he asked. He looked older suddenly. Even with his orangey curls sticking up, he looked solemn.

I was watching Larry grow older before my eyes. Not in age, but in experience. The expression in his eyes was older than it had been a few months ago. Seen too much, done too much. He was still trying to be Sir Galahad, but Galahad had had God on his side. All Larry had was me. It wasn't enough.

''The only way I could get a death warrant is to lie,'' I said.

''I know,'' he said.

I stared at him. ''Serephina hasn't broken any laws, yet. I won't lie about that.''

He smiled. ''Good. When do we meet Dorcas Bouvier?''

''Three.''

''Have you figured out what you can sacrifice to raise the zombies Stirling wants done?'' he asked.

''Nope.''

He stared at me. ''What are you going to tell Stirling?''

I shook my head. ''I don't know yet. I wish I knew why he's so hot and heavy to kill Bouvier.''

''He wants the land,'' Larry said.

''Stirling and Company have been saying the Bouvier family, not Magnus Bouvier. That means he's not the only one suing them. So killing Magnus won't solve their problems.''

''So why do it?'' Larry asked.

''Exactly,'' I said.

Larry nodded. ''We need to talk to Magnus again.''

''Preferably without Serephina around,'' I said.

''Amen to that,'' Larry said.

''I'd love to talk to Magnus, but before we tackle Mr. Bouvier again, I'd like to find some fairie ointment.''

''Some what?''

''Didn't you take any classes on fairies?''

''It was an elective,'' he said.

''Fairie ointment makes you proof against glamor. Just in case whatever else Magnus is hiding is nastier than Serephina.''

''Nothing nastier than that,'' he said.

''True, but just in case, he won't be able to work magic on us. In fact, it's not a bad precaution before we meet Dorrie. She may not be as scary as Magnus, but she shines, and I'd just as soon she didn't shine all over us.''

''You think Serephina will find Jeff Quinlan?''

''If anyone can, she can. She seemed pretty confident she could take Xavier, but then Jean-Claude had been pretty confident he could take her last night. He was wrong.''

He frowned. ''So we're rooting for Serephina?''

It sounded wrong, put that way, but I nodded. ''If it's a choice between a vampire that obeys most of the laws, and one that slaughters kids, yeah, we're on her side.''

''You were talking about killing her just a little bit ago.''

''I can stay out of her way until she saves Jeff, and kills Xavier.''

''Why would she kill him?'' Larry asked.

''He's killing people in her territory. She can say anything she wants, but that's a direct challenge to her authority. Besides, I don't think Xavier will give up Jeff without a fight.''

''What do you think happened to him last night?'' Larry asked.

I shook my head. "It doesn't do any good to dwell on it, Larry. We're doing all we can."

"We could tell the FBI about Serephina."

"One thing I've learned is that master vamps don't talk to the cops. Too many years of the cops killing them on sight, or trying to."

"Okay," he said, "but we've still got to come up with something big enough to kill for raising the cemetery tonight," he said.

"I'll think on it."

"You really have no idea what to do?" He sounded surprised.

"Short of a human sacrifice, Larry, I don't think I can raise several three-hundred-year-old corpses. Even I've got my limits."

He grinned. "Nice to hear you admit it."

I had to smile. "It'll be our little secret."

He put his hand out, and I slapped it. He slapped mine back, and I felt better. Larry had a way of making me smile. Friends will do that to you.

32

Dorcas Bouvier was leaning on a car in the parking lot. Her hair gleamed in the sunlight, swirling as she moved, like heavy water. In jeans and a green tank top, she was flawless.

Larry tried not to stare at her, but it was hard work. Larry was wearing a blue T-shirt, jeans, white Nikes, and an oversized checked flannel shirt to hide his shoulder holster.

I was in jeans and a navy blue polo shirt, black Nikes, and an oversized blue dress shirt. I'd had to borrow it from Larry after my black jacket had gotten covered in vampire goop. Had to have something to hide the Browning. Makes people nervous if you go around with a naked gun. Larry and I looked like we'd dressed from the same closet.

Dorrie pushed away from the car. "Shall we go?"

"We'd like to talk to Magnus."

"So you can turn him in to the cops?"

I shook my head. "So we can find out why Stirling is so hot to kill him."

"I don't know where he is," Dorcas said.

Maybe it showed on my face, because she said, "I don't know where he is, but if I did, I wouldn't tell you. Using magic on the police is a death penalty case. I won't turn him in."

"I'm not the police."

She looked at me, eyes narrowing. "Did you come to look at Bloody Bones, or to question me about my brother?"

"How did you know to be waiting here for us?" I asked.

"I knew you'd be on time." Her pupils swirled downward to pinpoints, like the eyes of an excited parrot.

"Let's go," I said.

She led us to the back of the restaurant where it nearly touched the woods. A path began at the edge of the clearing. It was barely wide enough for a man. Even though we walked single file, the branches whipped at my shoulders. The new green leaves rubbed like velvet along my cheek. The path was deep and rutted down to naked tree roots in places, but weeds were beginning to encroach on the path, as if it wasn't used as much as it once had been.

Dorrie moved down the uneven path with an easy, swinging stride. She was obviously familiar with the path, but it was more than that. The tree limbs that caught on my shirt didn't get caught in her hair. The roots that threatened to trip me didn't slow her down.

We'd found ointment at a health food store. So the bushes moving for her and not for us was real, not illusion. Maybe glamor wasn't the only thing to worry about. Which was why the Browning was loaded with nonsilver bullets. I'd had to go out and buy some special for the occasion. Larry was loaded up too, and for the first time I wished he had two guns. I still had the Firestar with silver ammo, but Larry was out of luck if a vamp jumped us. Of course, it was broad daylight. I was more worried about fairies than vamps right this minute. There was salt in our shirt pockets, not a lot, but you didn't need much, just enough to throw on the fey or the thing being magicked. Salt disrupted fey magic. Temporarily.

A breeze came up the path. It grew into a wind in one fitful gust. The air smelled clean and fresh. You hoped the beginning of time smelled like that; like fresh bread, clean laundry, childhood memories of spring. It probably smelled like ozone and swamp water. Reality almost always smells worse than daydream.

Dorrie stopped and turned back to us. "The trees across the path are just illusion. They're not solid."

"What trees?" Larry asked. I cursed silently. It would have been nice to keep the ointment a secret.

Dorrie took two steps back towards us. She stared at my face from inches away, then made a face like she'd seen something unclean. "You're wearing ointment." She made it sound like a very bad thing.

"Magnus did try to bedazzle us twice. Nothing wrong with being cautious," I said.

"Well, our illusions won't matter to you, then." She took off at a faster pace, leaving us to stumble after her.

The path led into a clearing that was nearly a perfect circle. There was a small mound in the center with a white stone Celtic cross in the middle of a mass of vibrant blue flowers. Every inch of ground was covered with bluebells. English bluebells, thick and fleshy, bluer than the sky. The flowers never grew in this country without help. They never grew in Missouri without more water than was practical. But standing in the solid mass of blue surrounded by trees, it seemed worth it.

Dorrie stood frozen nearly knee-deep in the flowers. She was staring open-mouthed, a look of horror on her lovely face.

Magnus Bouvier knelt in the flowers on top of the mound, near the cross. His mouth was bright with fresh blood. Something moved around him, in front of him. Something more felt than seen. If it was illusion, the ointment should have taken care of it. I tried looking at it out of the corner of my eye. Sometimes peripheral vision works better on magic than straight-on sight.

From the corner of my eye I could see the air swimming in something that was almost a shape. It was bigger than a man.

Magnus turned and saw us. He stood up abruptly, and the swimming air blinked out like it had never been. He wiped a sleeve across his mouth.

''Dorrie . . .'' His voice was soft and strangled.

Dorrie clawed her way up the hill. She screamed, ''Blasphemy!'' and smacked him. I could hear the slap all the way across the clearing.

''Ouch,'' Larry said. ''Why is she mad?''

She hit him again, hard enough to sit him down on his butt in the flowers. ''How could you? How could you do such a vile thing?''

''What did he do?'' Larry asked.

''He's been feeding off Rawhead and Bloody Bones just like his ancestor,'' I said.

Dorrie turned to me. She looked haggard, horrified, as if she had caught her brother molesting children. ''It was forbidden to feed.'' She turned back to Magnus. ''You knew that!''

''I wanted the power, Dorrie. What harm did it do?''

''What harm? What harm?'' She grabbed a handful of his long hair and pulled him to his knees. She exposed the bite marks on his neck. ''This is why that creature can call you. This is why one of the *Daoine Sidhe*, even a half-breed like you, is called by death.'' She let go so abruptly he fell forward on his hands and knees.

Dorrie sat down in the flowers and cried.

I waded into the flowers. They parted like water, but they didn't move. They were just never exactly where you were stepping.

''Jesus, are they moving out of the way?'' Larry asked.

''Not exactly,'' Magnus said. He walked down the mound to stand at its base. He was wearing the white tuxedo from last night, or what was left of it. The smear of blood on his shirtsleeve was very bright against the whiteness.

We waded through the flowers that were moving and not moving, to join him in front of the mound.

He'd shoved his hair back behind his ears so his face was visible. And no, his ears weren't pointed. Where do these rumors get started?

He met my eyes without flinching. If he was ashamed of what he'd done, it didn't show. Dorrie was still weeping in the bluebells like her heart would break.

''So now you know,'' he said.

''You can't bleed a fairie, in the flesh or not in the flesh, without ritual magic. I've read the spell, Magnus. It's a doozy,'' I said.

He smiled at that, and the smile was still lovely, but the blood at the corner of his mouth ruined the effect. ''I had to tie myself to the beastie. I had to give him some of my mortality in order to get his blood.''

''The spell isn't meant to help you gather blood,'' I said. ''It's to help the fairies kill each other.''

''If it got some of your mortality, did you get some of its immortality?'' Larry asked. It was a good question.

''Yes,'' Magnus said, ''but that wasn't why I did it.''

''You did it for power, you son of a bitch,'' Dorrie said. She came down the mound, sliding in the strange flowers. ''You just had to do real glamor, real magic.

My God, Magnus, you must have been drinking its blood for years, ever since you were a teenager. That's when your powers suddenly got so strong. We all thought it was puberty."

"Afraid not, sister dear."

She spit at him. "Our family was cursed, tied to this land forever in repentance for doing what you have done. Bloody Bones broke free last time someone tried to drink from his veins."

"It's been safely imprisoned for ten years, Dorrie."

"How do you know? How do you know that nebulous thing you called up hasn't been out scaring children?"

"As long as it doesn't hurt any of them, what's the harm?"

"Wait a minute," said Larry. "Why would it scare children?"

"I told you, it's a nursery boggle. It was supposed to eat bad children," I said. I had an idea, an awful idea. I'd seen a vampire use a sword, but was I absolutely sure of what I'd seen? No. "When the thing got out and started slaughtering the Indian tribe, did it use a weapon, or its hands?"

Dorrie looked at me. "I don't know. Does it matter?"

Larry said, "Oh, my God."

"It might matter a great deal," I said.

"You can't mean those killings," Magnus said. "Bloody Bones cannot manifest itself physically. I've seen to that."

"Are you sure, brother dear? Are you absolutely sure?" Dorrie's voice cut and sliced; she wielded scorn like a weapon.

"Yes, I'm sure."

"We'll have to have a witch look at this. I don't know enough about it," I said.

Dorrie nodded. "I understand. The sooner the better."

"Rawhead and Bloody Bones did not do those killings," Magnus said.

"For your sake, Magnus, I hope not," I said.

"What do you mean?"

"Because five people have died. Five people who didn't do a damn thing to deserve it."

"It's imprisoned by a combination of Indian, Christian, and fairie power," he said. "It's not breaking free of that."

I walked around the mound slowly. The fleshy flowers still moved out of the way. I'd tried watching my feet, but it was dizzying, because the flowers moved yet didn't, like trying to watch one of them bloom. You knew it did, but you could never watch the actual event.

I ignored the flowers and concentrated on the mound. I wasn't trying to sense the dead, so daylight was fine. There was magic here, lots of it. I'd never felt fairie magic before. There was something here that had a familiar taste to it, and it wasn't the Christianity. "Some kind of death magic went into this," I said. I walked around the mound until I could see Magnus's face. "A little human sacrifice, perhaps?"

"Not exactly," Magnus said.

"We would never condone human sacrifice," Dorrie said.

Maybe she wouldn't, but I wasn't so sure about Magnus. I didn't say it out loud. Dorrie was upset enough already.

"If it's not sacrifice, then what is it?"

"Three hills are buried with our dead. Each death is like a stake to hold old Bloody Bones down," Magnus said.

"How did you lose track of which hills belonged to you?" I asked.

"It's been over three hundred years," Magnus said. "There were no deeds back then. I wasn't a hundred percent sure the hill was the right hill myself. But when they raked up the dead, I felt it." He huddled in on himself as if the air had suddenly grown colder. "You can't raise the dead from that hillside. If you do it, then Bloody Bones will be loosed. The magic to stop it is complicated. Truthfully, I'm not sure I'm up to it myself. And I don't know any Indian shamans anymore."

"You have made a mockery of everything we stand for," Dorrie said.

"What did Serephina offer you?" I asked.

He looked at me, surprised. "What are you talking about?"

"She offers everyone their heart's desire. What was yours, Magnus?"

"Freedom and power. She said she'd find another guardian for Rawhead and Bloody Bones. She said she'd find a way for me to keep the power I'd borrowed from it without having to tend it."

"And you believed her?"

He shook his head. "I'm the only person in the family who has the power. We are the guardians forever as penance for stealing it, for letting it kill." He collapsed to his knees in the blue, blue flowers, his head bowed, hair spilling forward to hide his face. "I'll never be free."

"You don't deserve to be free," Dorrie said.

"Why did Serephina want you so badly?" I asked.

"She's afraid of death. She says drinking from something as long-lived as I am helps her keep death at bay."

"She's a vampire," Larry protested.

"But not immortal," I said.

Magnus looked up, strange aquamarine eyes glimmering out through his shining hair. Maybe it was the hair, or the eyes, or his being nearly covered in the strange moving, not moving flowers, but he didn't look very human.

"She fears death," he said. "She fears you." His voice was low and echoing.

"She nearly cleaned my clock last night. Why's she afraid of me?"

"You brought death among us last night."

"It can't be the first time," I said.

"She came to me for my long life, my immortal blood. Perhaps she will go to you next. Perhaps instead of running from death, she will embrace it."

The skin on my arms twitched, marching in gooseflesh up to my elbows. "She tell you that last night?"

"There is a power involved, hurting her old enemy Jean-Claude, but in the end, Anita, she wonders if your power would make the difference. If she drank you up, would she be immortal? Would you be able to keep death from her with your necromancy?"

''You could leave town,'' Larry said. I wasn't sure which of us he was speaking to.

I shook my head. ''Master vampires don't give up that easy. I'll tell Stirling that I won't be raising his dead, Magnus. No one else can do it but me, so it won't get done.''

''But they won't give back the land,'' Magnus said in his strange voice. ''If they simply blow up the mountain, the result might be the same.''

''Is that true, Dorrie?''

She nodded. ''It could be.''

''What do you want me to do?'' I asked.

Magnus crawled through the flowers, peering at me through the shining curtain of his hair. His eyes were swirling bands of green and blue, whirling until I was dizzy. I looked away.

''Raise a handful of the dead. Can you do that?'' he asked.

''No sweat,'' I said. ''But will everybody's lawyers agree to that?''

''I'll see that they do,'' he said.

''Dorrie?'' I asked.

She nodded. ''I'll see to it.''

I stared at Magnus for a moment. ''Will Serephina really rescue the boy?''

''Yes,'' he said.

I stared down at him. ''Then I'll see you tonight.''

''No, I'll be well and truly drunk again. It's not foolproof, but it helps drown her out.''

''Fine; I'll raise you a handful of dead. Keep your land safe.''

''You have our gratitude,'' Magnus said. He looked feral, frightening, beautiful crouched in the flowers. His gratitude might be worth something if Serephina didn't kill him first.

Hell, if she didn't kill me first.

33

I called Special Agent Bradford late in the day. They hadn't found Xavier. They hadn't found Jeff. They hadn't found any vampires that I needed to kill, and why the hell was I calling him? I was not on this case, remember? I remembered. And yes, the two youngest victims had been sexually assaulted, but not the same day they were killed. I probably should have brought Magnus in, but he was the only one who understood the spells on Bloody Bones. He wouldn't be any good to us locked up. Dorrie knew a local witch she trusted. I'd thought that maybe Bloody Bones was our killer. I'd never seen a vampire hide itself so completely from me as the one that killed Coltrain. I'd added it to my list of suspects, but hadn't told the cops. Now I was glad I hadn't. The sexual assault had Xavier written all over it. Besides, explaining that a nursery boggle from Scotland was committing murders on the ethereal plane sounded far-fetched even to me.

The sky was thick with clouds that glowed like jewels. They shimmered and stretched across the sky like a gigantic gleaming blanket that some great beast had shredded with massive claws. Through the holes in the clouds, the sky peeked through black with a few diamond-chip stars bright enough to compete with the gleaming sky.

I stood on the hilltop staring up at the sky, breathing in the cool spring air. Larry stood beside me, looking up. His eyes reflected the glowing light.

''Get on with it,'' Stirling said.

I turned and looked at him. Him, Bayard, and Ms. Harrison. Beau had been with them, but I'd made him wait at the bottom of the mountain. I'd even told him if he so much as showed his face up top, I'd put a bullet in it. I wasn't sure Stirling believed me, but Beau had.

''Not an appreciator of nature's beauty, are you, Raymond?''

Even by moonlight I could see his scowl. ''I want this over with, Ms. Blake. Now, tonight.''

Strangely enough, I agreed with him. It made me nervous. I didn't like Raymond. It made me want to argue with him, regardless of whether I agreed. But I didn't argue. Point for me.

"I'll get it done tonight, Raymond; don't sweat it."

"Please stop calling me by my first name, Ms. Blake." He made the request through clenched teeth, but he had said "please."

"Fine. It'll be done tonight, Mr. Stirling. Okay?"

He nodded. "Thank you; now get on with it."

I opened my mouth to say something smart, but Larry said very softly, "Anita."

He was right, as usual. As much fun as it was to yank Stirling's chain, it was just delaying the inevitable. I was tired of Stirling, of Magnus, and of everything. It was time to do this job and go home. Well, maybe not straight home. I wouldn't leave without Jeff Quinlan, one way or another.

The goat gave a high, questioning bleat. It was staked out in the middle of the boneyard. It was a brown-and-white-spotted goat with those strange yellow eyes they sometimes have. It had floppy white ears and seemed to like having the top of its head scratched. Larry had petted it in the Jeep on the drive over. Always a bad idea. Never get friendly with the sacrifices. Makes it hard to kill them.

I had not petted the goat. I knew better. This was Larry's first goat. He'd learn. Hard or easy, he'd learn. There were two more goats at the bottom of the hill. One of them was even smaller and cuter than this one.

"Shouldn't we have the Bouviers' lawyers present, Mr. Stirling?" Bayard said.

"The Bouviers waived having their attorney present," I said.

"Why would they do that?" Stirling asked.

"They trust me not to lie to them," I said.

Stirling looked at me for a long moment. I couldn't see his eyes clearly, but I could feel the wheels inside his head moving.

"You're going to lie for them, aren't you?" he said. His voice was cold, repressed, too angry for heat.

"I don't lie about the dead, Mr. Stirling. Sometimes about the living, but never about the dead. Besides, Bouvier didn't offer me a bribe. Why should I help him if he doesn't throw money at me?"

Larry didn't call me on that one. He was looking at Stirling, too. Wondering what he'd say, maybe.

"You've made your point, Ms. Blake. Can we get on with it now?" He sounded reasonable, ordinary suddenly. All that anger, all that mistrust, had had to go somewhere. But it wasn't in his voice.

"Fine." I knelt and opened the gym bag at my feet. It held my animating equipment. I had another one that held vampire gear. I used to just transfer whatever I wanted into the bag. I bought a second bag after I showed up once at a zombie raising with the wrong bag. It was also illegal to carry vampire slaying stuff if you didn't have a warrant of execution on you. Brewster's law might change that, but until then . . . I had two bags. The zombie was my normal burgundy one; the vampire bag was white. Even in the dark, it was easy to tell them apart. That was the plan.

Larry's zombie bag was a nearly virulent green with Teenage Mutant Ninja Turtles on it. I was almost afraid to ask what his vampire bag looked like.

"Let me test my understanding here," Larry said. My words fed back to me. He knelt and unzipped his bag.

"Go ahead, " I said. I got out my jar of ointment. I knew animators who had special containers for the ointment. Crockery, hand-blown glass, mystical symbols carved into the sides. I used an old Mason jar that had once held Grandma Blake's green beans.

Larry fished out a peanut butter jar with the label still on it. Extra-crunchy. Yum-yum.

"We have to raise a minimum of three zombies, right?"

"Right," I said.

He stared around at the scattered bones. "A mass grave is hard to raise from, right?"

"This isn't a mass grave. It's an old cemetery that was disturbed. That's easier than a mass grave."

"Why?" he asked.

I laid the machete down beside the jar of ointment. "Because each grave had rites performed that would tie the dead individual to the grave, so that if you call it you have a better chance of getting an individual to answer."

"Answer?"

"Rise from the dead."

He nodded. He laid a wicked curved blade on the ground. It looked like a freaking scimitar.

"Where did you get that?"

He dipped his head, and I would have bet he was blushing. Just couldn't see it by moonlight.

"Guy at college."

"Where'd he get it?"

Larry looked at me, surprise plain on his face. "I don't know. Is something wrong with it?"

I shook my head. "Just a little fancy for beheading chickens and slitting a few goats open."

"It felt good in my hand." He shrugged. "Besides, it looks cool." He grinned at me.

I shook my head, but I let it go. Did I really need a machete to behead a few chickens, no, but the occasional cow, yeah.

Why, you may ask, didn't we have a cow tonight? No one would sell Bayard one. He had the brilliant idea of telling the farmers why he wanted the cow. The God-fearing folk would sell their cows to be eaten, but not for raising zombies. Prejudiced bastards.

"The youngest of the dead here are two hundred years old, right?" Larry asked.

"Right," I said.

"We're going to raise a minimum of three of these corpses in good enough condition for them to answer questions."

"That's the plan," I said.

"Can we do that?"

I smiled at him. ''That's the plan.''

His eyes widened. ''Damn, you don't know if we can do it either, do you?'' His voice had dropped to an amazed whisper.

''We raise three zombies a night every night routinely. We're just doing them back to back.''

''We don't raise two-hundred-year-old zombies routinely.''

''True, but the theory's the same.''

''Theory?'' He shook his head. ''I know we're in trouble when you start talking about theories. Can we do this?''

The honest answer was no, but the thing that dictated more than anything else what you could raise and what you couldn't was confidence. Believing you could do it. So . . . I was tempted to lie. But I didn't. Truth between Larry and me.

''I think we can do it.''

''But you don't know for sure,'' he said.

''No.''

''Geez, Anita.''

''Don't get rattled on me. We can do this.''

''But you aren't sure.''

''I'm not sure we'll survive the plane ride home, but I'm still getting on the plane.''

''Was that supposed to be comforting?'' he asked.

''Yeah.''

''It wasn't,'' he said.

''Sorry, but this is as good as it gets. You want certainty, be an accountant.''

''I'm not good at math.''

''Me either.''

He took a deep breath and let it out slowly. ''Alright, boss, how do we combine powers?''

I told him.

''Neat.'' He didn't look nervous anymore. He looked eager. Larry may have wanted to be a vampire executioner, but he was an animator. It wasn't a career choice, it was a gift, or a curse. No one could teach you to raise the dead unless you had the power in your blood. Genetics is a wonderful thing: brown eyes, curly hair, zombie raising.

''Whose ointment you want to use?'' Larry asked.

''Mine.'' I'd given Larry the recipe for the ointment and told him which ingredients you couldn't mess with, like the graveyard mold, but there was room for experimentation. Every animator had their own special recipe. You never knew what Larry's ointment would smell like. For sharing powers you used the same ointment, so we were using mine.

For all I knew, we didn't have to use the same ointment, but I'd only shared my powers three times. Twice with the man who trained me as an animator. Each time we'd used the same ointment. I had acted as a focus all three times. Which meant I was in charge. Where I liked to be, right?

''Could I act as a focus?'' Larry asked. ''Not this time, but later?''

''If this comes up again, we'll try it,'' I said. Truth was, I didn't know if Larry had the power to be a focus. Manny, who taught me, couldn't do it. Very few animators could act as a focus. Those who could were mistrusted by the rest, and most wouldn't play with us. We would literally share our powers. A lot of animators wouldn't be willing to do that. There is a theory that you could permanently steal another's magic. But I don't buy it. Raising the dead isn't like a magic charm that someone can take with them, and leave you without. Animating is built into the cells of our bodies. It's part of us. You can't steal that.

I opened the ointment, and the spring air suddenly smelled like Christmas trees. I used a lot of rosemary.

The ointment was thick and waxy and always felt cool. Flecks of glowing graveyard mold looked like ground-up lightning bugs. I smeared ointment across Larry's forehead, down his cheeks. He untucked his t-shirt and raised it so I could dab it over his heart. Which is harder than it sounds with a shoulder holster on, but we'd both worn a gun apiece. I had left both knives and my backup gun in the Jeep. I touched his skin and could feel his heart pounding under my hand.

I handed Larry the Mason jar. He dipped two fingers into the thick ointment. He traced ointment over my face. His hand was very steady, face blank with concentration. Eyes utterly serious.

I unbuttoned the polo shirt and Larry slipped his fingers inside to touch my heart. His fingers rubbed the chain of my crucifix, spilling it out of my shirt. I slipped it back inside next to my skin. He handed the jar back to me, and I screwed the lid on tight. Wouldn't do to let it dry out.

I'd never heard of anyone doing exactly what we were about to attempt. Not the age part, but the scattered bodies. We only wanted three, but there weren't three intact bodies. Even doing them one at a time, it was chancy. How to raise just so much dead and no more when they were lying jumbled together? I had no names to use. No gravesite to encircle with power. How to do it?

It was a puzzlement.

But for now we just had to close the circle. One problem at a time.

''Make sure both of your hands have ointment on them,'' I said.

Larry rubbed his hands together like he was putting on lotion. ''Aye, aye, boss; what next?''

I drew a deep silver bowl out of my bag. It gleamed in the moonlight like another piece of sky.

Larry's eyes widened.

''It doesn't have to be silver. There are no mystical symbols on it. You could use a Tupperware bowl, but the life of another living creature is going in here. Use something nice to show some respect, but understand that it doesn't have to be silver, or this shape, or anything. It's just a container. Okay?''

Larry nodded. ''Why not have the other goats up here on top? It's going to be a trek to get them up here every time.''

I shrugged. ''First, they'd panic. Second, it seems cruel for them to watch their friends bite the dust, knowing they're next.''

''My zoology prof would say you're humanizing them.''

''Let him. I know they feel pain, and fear. That's enough.''

Larry looked at me for a long moment. ''You don't like doing it either.''

''No. You want to help hold or feed the carrot?''

''Carrot?''

I dug a carrot, complete with leafy green top, out of the bag.

''Was that what you got in the grocery store while I waited in the car with the goats?''

''Yeah.''

I held the carrot up in the air. The goat strained to the end of its picket line, towards the carrot. I let the goat lip the leafy top. It bleated and strained towards me. I let him get a little more leaf. His stubby little tail started wagging. Happy goat.

I handed Larry the silver bowl. ''Put it on the ground under the throat. When the blood starts coming, catch as much as you can.''

I had the machete behind my back in my right hand, carrot in my left. I felt like a child's dentist. No, nothing behind my back. Pay no attention to that huge needle. Except this needle was permanent.

The goat yanked most of the leaves off the carrot, and I waited while it snaked them up into its mouth. Larry knelt beside it, bowl on the ground. I offered the meat of the carrot to the goat. It got a taste of it, and I drew the carrot out, out, until the goat strained its neck out as far as it could, trying to get more of the hard orange flesh.

I laid the machete against the hairy throat, not cutting, gentle. The neck vibrated against the blade, straining for the carrot. I drew the blade across the neck.

The machete was sharp, and I had practice. There was no sound, only the shocked, widened eyes, and blood pouring from the neck.

Larry picked up the bowl, holding it under the wound. Blood splashed down his arms onto the blue t-shirt. The goat collapsed to its knees. Blood filled the bowl, dark and glinting, more black than red.

''There's bits of carrot in the blood,'' Larry said.

''It's alright,'' I said. ''Carrot's inert.''

The goat's head fell slowly forward until it touched the ground. The bowl sat under its throat, filling with blood. It had been nearly a perfect kill. Goats could be sort of pesky, but sometimes, like tonight, it all worked. Of course, we weren't done.

I laid the bloody knife against my left arm and sliced it open. The pain was sharp and immediate. I held the wound over the bowl, letting the thick drops mingle with the goat's blood.

''Give me your right arm,'' I said.

Larry didn't argue. He just held out his bare arm. I'd told him what would happen, but it was still a very trusting gesture. His face turned up to me was without any trace of fear. God.

I sliced his arm. He winced but didn't draw back. ''Let it drip into the bowl.''

He held his arm over the bowl. All the blood was red-black in the moonlight.

The beginnings of power trickled over my skin. My power, Larry's power, the power of a ritual sacrifice. Larry looked up at me with wide eyes.

I knelt beside him and laid the machete across the mouth of the bowl. I held out my left hand to him. He gave me his right. We clasped hands and pressed the wounds in our forearms together, letting the blood mingle. Larry held one side of the blood-filled bowl and I held the other. Blood trickled down our arms to drip off our elbows into the bowl, onto the bloody naked steel.

We stood still clasped together, still holding the bowl. I withdrew my hand from his slowly, then took the bowl from him. He followed my every movement like he always did. He'd be able to close his eyes and mimic me.

I walked to the edge of the circle I had in my mind and plunged my hand into the bowl. The blood was still amazingly warm, almost hot. I grasped the handle of the machete with my bloody hand and began using the blade to sprinkle blood as I walked.

I could feel Larry standing in the center of the circle that I walked like there was a rope stretched between us. As I walked, that rope stretched tighter and tighter like a rubber band being twisted. The power grew with each step, each drop of blood. The earth was hungry for it. I'd never raised the dead on ground that had seen death rituals before. Magnus should have mentioned that. Maybe he hadn't known. Charitable of me.

It didn't matter now. There was magic here for blood and death. Something that was eager for me to close the circle. Eager for me to raise the dead. Hungry.

I stood nearly where I'd begun. I was a sprinkle of blood away from closing the circle. The line of power between Larry and me was so tight it hurt. The potential power was frightening, and exhilarating. We'd awakened something old and long dormant. It made me hesitate. Made me not want to finish the circle. Stubbornness, and fear. I didn't completely understand what I was feeling. It was someone else's magic, someone's spell. We'd triggered it, but I didn't know what it would do. We could raise our dead, but it would be like walking a tightrope between the other spell and . . . something.

I felt old Bloody Bones in its barrow miles away. I felt it watching me, urging me to take that last step. I shook my head as if the fey creature could see me. I just didn't understand the spell well enough to risk it.

"What's wrong?" Larry asked. His voice sounded strangled. We were choking on unused power, and damned if I knew what to do with it.

I caught movement out of the corner of my eye. Ivy stood at the edge of the mountain. She was wearing hiking boots with thick white socks folded over them, baggy black shorts, and a skin-tight neon pink top, with a checked flannel shirt over it. The chain of her dangling earring gleamed in the moonlight. She'd dressed herself tonight.

All I had to do was drop that last bit of blood, and the circle would close. And I could hold this circle against her, against them all. Nothing would cross it that I didn't want to cross it. Well, within reason. Demons and angels could probably cross it, but vampires couldn't.

I felt a surge of triumph from the thing trapped in its mound. It wanted me to close the circle. I tossed the bowl and machete behind me towards the center of the circle, away from the outer edge so no blood would fall on it. Ivy started towards me in a faster-than-light display, a blur of speed. I went for my gun, felt it slide from the holster, and she smashed into me. The impact knocked the Browning out of my hand. I hit the ground with nothing in my hands but air.

34

Ivy reared backwards, fangs flashing. Larry screamed, "Anita!" I heard the gun go off, felt the bullet hit her body. It hit her in the shoulder, twisted her body, but she turned back to me with a smile. She dug fingers into my shoulders and rolled us over, putting me on top, with one of her hands leeched to the back of my neck. She squeezed until I gasped.

"I'll snap her spine unless you throw that toy away," she said.

"She'll kill me anyway. Don't do it."

"Anita . . ."

"Now, or I'll kill her while you watch."

"Shoot her!" But there wasn't a clear shot. He'd have to walk around me and fire point-blank. Ivy could kill me twice over before he got to us.

Ivy forced my neck lower. I braced my right arm on the ground. She'd have to break something to get me down to her. If she broke my neck, it'd be over; a broken arm would just hurt.

I heard something hit the ground, a dull, heavy thump. Larry's gun. Damn.

She pressed harder on the back of my neck. I dug the palm of my hand into the ground hard enough to leave an imprint.

"I can break that arm and bring you to me. Your choice: easy, or hard."

"Hard," I said between gritted teeth.

She grabbed for my arm, and I had an idea. I collapsed forward on top of her. It caught her off guard. I had a handful of seconds to pull the chain around my neck out of my shirt.

Her hand slid through my hair like a lover's, pressing my face against her cheek, not hard, almost gentle. "Three nights from now you'll like me, Anita. You'll worship me."

"I doubt that." The chain slid forward, the crucifix pooled against her throat. There was a blinding flash of white, white light. A rush of heat that singed my hair.

Ivy screamed and clawed at the cross, scrambling from underneath me.

I stayed on all fours with the cross dangling in front of me. The blue-white flames died away because it wasn't touching vampiric flesh anymore, but it glowed like a captive star, and she backed away from it.

I didn't know where my gun was, but the machete gleamed against the dark earth. I wrapped my hand around it and got to my feet. Larry was behind me with his own cross out, held in front of him to the length of its chain. The white light with its core of blue was almost painfully bright.

Ivy screamed, shielding her eyes. All she had to do was walk away. But she was frozen, immobile in the face of the crosses, and two true believers.

"Gun," I said to Larry.

"Can't find it."

Both guns were matte black so they wouldn't reflect light at night and make us a target; now it made them invisible.

We advanced on the vampire. She threw both arms up before her face and screamed, "Nooo!" She'd backed up nearly to the edge of the circle. If she ran, we wouldn't chase her, but she didn't run. Maybe she couldn't.

I shoved the machete up under her ribs. Blood poured down the blade onto my hands. I drove the blade upward into her heart. I gave it that last little wrench to slice it up.

Her arms fell away from her face slowly. Her eyes were wide, surprised. She stared down at the blade in her stomach, as if she didn't understand what it was doing there. The flesh of her neck was black where the cross had burned her.

She fell to her knees and I went with her, keeping my grip on the machete. She didn't die. I hadn't really expected her to. I jerked the blade out of her, doing more damage. She made a low gurgling sound, but stayed on her knees. Her hands touched the blood flowing out of her chest and stomach. She stared at the gleaming darkness as if she'd never seen blood before. The blood flow was already slowing; unless I killed her soon, the wound would close.

I stood over her and brought the machete back in a two-handed grip. I put everything I had into that downswing. The blade bit into her neck, down to the spine, catching on the bone.

Ivy stared up at me with blood streaming down her neck. I swung back for another chop, and she watched me do it, too hurt to run now. I had to struggle to get the blade out of the spine, and still she blinked up at me. If I didn't finish her, she'd heal even this.

I brought the blade down one last time and felt the last edge of bone give. The blade came out the other side, and her head slid off her shoulders in a spray of blood like a black fountain. That black blood poured over the circle and closed it.

Power filled the circle until we were drowning in it. Larry fell to his knees. The light from the crosses faded like dying stars. The vampire was dead, and the crosses couldn't help us now.

"What's happening?"

I could feel the power like water on every side, choking close. I was breathing it in, soaking it up through my skin.

I screamed wordlessly and fell to the ground. I fell through layers of power, and the moment I hit the ground I could feel the power below me, stretching downward, outward.

I was lying on top of bones. They twitched like something moving in its sleep. I crawled to my knees, hands digging into the earth. I touched a long, thin arm bone, and it moved. I scrambled to my feet, slow, too slow through the pressing air, and watched.

Bones slid through the earth like water, coming together. The earth heaved and rocked underfoot like giant moles were crawling.

Larry was on his feet now, too. ''What's happening?''

''Something bad,'' I said.

I'd never seen the dead coalesce. They always came to the surface of the grave all in one piece. I'd never realized it was like putting together a macabre jigsaw puzzle. A skeleton formed at my feet, and flesh began to crawl over it, flow like clay, molding itself back to the bones.

''Anita?''

I turned to Larry. He was pointing at a skeleton at the far edge of the circle. Half the bones were on the outside of the circle. Flesh crawled over this side of the bones and pushed against the blood circle. The earth gave one last heave, and the magic poured out over the ground. I heard it pop inside my head like a release of pressure. The air spread out, not so drowning-thick. It poured over the hillside like invisible flame, and everywhere it touched the dead formed bodies.

''Stop it, Anita. Stop it.''

''I can't.'' The killing magic in the ground had stolen the reins. All I could do was watch and feel the power spreading outward. Enough power to ride forever. Enough power to raise a thousand dead.

I knew when Rawhead and Bloody Bones burst its prison. I felt the power sag as the thing escaped. Then the power lashed back into this bit of ground and drove us to our knees. The dead struggled from the earth like swimmers dragging themselves to shore. When nearly twenty dead stood waiting with empty eyes, the power flowed outward. I felt it seeking more dead, something else to raise. This I could stop. The fairie was gone, out of the loop; he had what he wanted.

I called the power back. I drew it into me, back through the ground, like pulling a snake by its tail out of a hole. I flung it into the zombies. Flung it into them and said, ''Live.''

The wrinkled flesh filled out. The dead eyes gleamed. The tattered clothing mended itself. Dirt fell away from a long gingham dress. A woman with midnight hair, dark skin, and Magnus's startled eyes looked at me. They all looked at me. Twenty dead, all over two hundred years old, and they could have passed for human.

''My God,'' Larry whispered.

Even I was impressed.

''Very impressive, Ms. Blake.'' Stirling's voice was wrenching, as if he shouldn't have been there. He was a different part of reality from the near-perfect zombies. The fairie was out, but I'd do my job, for what good it would do any of us.

''Which of you is a Bouvier?''

There was a murmur of voices, most of them speaking French. Nearly all of them were Bouviers. The woman introduced herself as Anias Bouvier. She looked very alive.

"Looks like you'll have to move your hotel," I said.

"Oh, I don't think so," Stirling said.

I turned and looked at him.

He had a big shiny silver gun out. A nickel-plated .45. He held it like it was a movie, kind of out in front of him, waist-high. A .45 is a big gun; you don't hit much from a waist shot. Or that's the theory. With it pointed at us, I wasn't eager to try the theory.

Bayard was pointing a .22 automatic vaguely in our direction. It didn't look like he'd held a gun before. Maybe he forgot and left the safety on.

Ms. Harrison had a nickel-plated .38 pointed very steadily at me. She stood with her legs apart, balanced on her ridiculous high heels. She held the gun in a two-handed grip like she knew what she was doing.

I flashed on her face. Her eyes in her thick makeup were a little wide, but she was rock steady. Steadier than Bayard and a better stance than Stirling. I hoped Stirling paid her well.

"What's going on, Stirling?" I asked. My voice was even, but there was an edge of power to it. I was still riding the power, enough power to put the zombies back in the ground. Enough power to do a lot of things.

He smiled visibly in the bright reflected light. "You've released the creature; now we shall kill you."

"Why the hell do you care if Bloody Bones is out?" I saw the guns and still didn't know why.

"It came into my dreams, Ms. Blake. It promised me all the Bouvier land. All of it."

"The fey breaking out won't get you the land," I said.

"It will with Bouvier dead. The deed that got us this hillside will be found to include all the land, once there's no one to fight it."

"Even with Magnus dead, you won't get the land," I said, but my voice didn't sound so sure.

"You mean his sister?" Stirling said. "She'll die just as easily as Magnus."

My stomach was tight. "Her children?"

"Rawhead and Bloody Bones loves children best of all," he said.

"You son of a bitch." It was Larry. He took a step forward, and Ms. Harrison's gun swung to him. I grabbed his arm with my free hand. I still had the machete in my hand. Larry stopped, and the gun stayed on him. I wasn't sure that was an improvement.

Tension sang down Larry's arm. I'd seen him angry, but never like this. The power responded to that anger. The zombies all turned to us in a rustle of cloth. Their glittering eyes, so alive, were waiting for us.

"Move in front of us," I whispered. The zombies began walking towards us. The closest ones moved in front of us immediately. I lost sight of the gun toting trio. Here was hoping they'd lost sight of us.

"Kill them," Stirling said, loud, almost a yell.

I started to drop to the ground, still holding Larry's arm. He resisted. Gunfire exploded around us and he kissed dirt, flat.

With the side of his face pressed to the ground, he said, ''What now?''

Bullets were hitting the zombies. The bodies jerked and twitched. Some of the very alive faces stared down, alarmed as holes appeared in their bodies. But there was no pain. The panic was reflex.

Someone was yelling; it wasn't us. ''Stop it, stop it. We can't do this. We can't just kill them.''

It was Bayard.

''It is late for an attack of conscience,'' Ms. Harrison said. It may have been the first time I'd heard her voice. She sounded efficient.

''Lionel, you are either with me, or against me.''

''Shit,'' I muttered. I wormed forward, trying to see what was happening. I pushed aside a billowing skirt just in time to see Stirling shoot Lionel in the stomach. The .45 gave out a booming sound and nearly jerked itself out of Stirling's hand, but he held on. From less than ten inches away, you could shoot nearly anything with a .45.

Bayard collapsed to his knees, looking up at Stirling. He was trying to say something, but no sound came out.

Stirling took the gun from Bayard's hand and put it in his own jacket pocket. He turned his back on Bayard and walked out onto the hard, dry soil.

Ms. Harrison hesitated, but she followed her boss.

Bayard fell onto his side with a dark flood draining out of him. His glasses reflected the moonlight, making him look blind.

Stirling and Ms. Harrison were coming in after us. Stirling pushed among the dead as if they were trees and he was wading through. The dead didn't move for him. They stood there like stubborn, fleshy barriers. I hadn't told them to move, so they wouldn't.

Ms. Harrison had stopped trying to force her way through. Moonlight glinted on her shiny gun as she used a zombie's shoulder to sight on us.

''Kill her,'' I whispered.

The zombie she was using as a sighting post turned towards her. She made an exasperated sound, and the dead closed on her.

Larry looked at me. ''What did you tell them?''

Ms. Harrison was screaming now. High, frightened shrieks. She fired her gun again and again. It clicked empty. Slow, eager hands and mouths latched onto her body.

''Stop them,'' Larry said. He grabbed my arm. ''Stop them.''

I could feel the hands tearing bits of flesh from Ms. Harrison. Teeth sank into her shoulder, tore that tender neck, and I knew when blood flowed into that mouth.

Larry was along for the ride. ''Oh, God, stop it!'' He was on his knees pulling at me, begging.

Stirling hadn't fired a shot. Where was he?

''Stop,'' I whispered.

The dead froze like automatons, stopped in mid-action. Ms. Harrison slid to the ground in a moaning heap.

Stirling came in from one side, the big gun pointed very steadily at us, out in a two-handed grip like it was supposed to be held. He'd made his way behind us while the zombies worked over Ms. Harrison. He was standing nearly on top of us. It took a lot of nerve to come that close to the zombies.

Larry's fingers dug into my arm. "Don't, Anita; please don't." Even staring down the barrel of a gun, Larry stuck to his morals. Admirable.

"If you say a word, Ms. Blake, I will kill you."

I just stared up at him. I was so close to him I could have reached out and touched his pants leg. The .45 was pointed very solidly at my head. If he pulled the trigger, I was gone.

"Careless of you not to have the zombies attack both of us."

I agreed with him, but all I could do was stare up at him. I still had the machete in one hand. I tried not to tighten my grip on it. Not to draw attention to it.

I must have made some betraying motion because he said, "Take your hand away from the knife, Ms. Blake, slowly."

I didn't do it. I stared up at him and his gun.

"Now, Ms. Blake, or . . ." He thumbed back the hammer on the gun. Not necessary but always dramatic.

I let go of the machete.

"Hand away from it, Ms. Blake."

I moved my hand away. I didn't move away from him and the gun. I wanted to, but I made myself be still. A few inches wouldn't make the gun less deadly, but it might make a big difference if I tried to jump him. Not my first choice, but if we ran out of other options . . . I wouldn't go down without a fight.

"Can you lay these zombies to rest, Mr. Kirkland?"

Larry hesitated. "I don't know."

Good boy. If he'd said no, Stirling might have killed him. If he'd said yes, he'd have killed me.

Larry let go of my arm and moved just a little away from me. Stirling's eyes flicked to him, back to me, but the gun barrel never wavered. Damn.

Larry was on his knees, still moving away from me, forcing Stirling to keep an eye on both of us. The .45 moved an inch from the center of my forehead, towards Larry. I took a breath and held it. Not yet, not yet . . . If I tried something too soon, I'd be dead.

Larry lunged for something on the ground. The .45 swung towards him.

I did two things at once. I slipped my left hand behind Stirling's leg and pulled, and I grabbed his groin with my right and shoved with all I was worth. I was doing the wrong thing to cause a lot of pain, but it tipped him over. He fell flat on his back with the gun swinging back towards me.

I'd hoped he'd drop the gun, or be slower. He didn't, and he wasn't. So I only had a split-second to decide whether to try to pull his privates out of his body, and cause as much pain as possible, or go for the gun. I went for the gun, not trying to grab it, but sweeping my hands into his arms. If I could control his arms, I could control the gun.

The gun went off. I didn't look. No time. Larry was either hit, or he wasn't. If he wasn't, I had to get that gun. Stirling's arms were on the ground, my hands keeping them there, but I had no leverage. He raised his arms off the ground, and I couldn't stop him. I shoved my feet into the ground and forced his arms over his head, but it had become a wrestling match now, and he outweighed me by sixty pounds.

"Drop the gun." Larry's voice behind me. I couldn't look. Couldn't take my attention from the gun. We both ignored him.

"I will shoot you," Larry said.

That got Stirling's attention. His eyes flicked to Larry; for just a moment his body hesitated. I kept my grip on his wrists and shoved myself forward, up his body. I dug my knee into his groin, trying to reach the ground through him. He let out a strangled cry. His hands spasmed.

I moved my hands up and touched the gun. His grip tightened. He wasn't letting go.

I came up beside Stirling's arms and braced his arms against my hip. I pulled the arm against my body, just one quick movement, and snapped his arm at the elbow. The hand went numb, and the gun fell into my hand.

I crawled away from him, the gun in one hand.

Larry was standing over us with a gun pointed at Stirling. Stirling didn't seem to care. He was rocking back and forth over the ground, trying to cradle both injuries at once.

"I had a gun. You could have just moved away from him," Larry said.

I just shook my head. I trusted Larry to shoot Stirling. I just hadn't trusted Stirling not to shoot Larry. "I had my hands on the gun. Seemed a shame to let it go," I said.

Larry pointed the gun at the ground, but kept a nice two-handed grip on it. "It's yours; you want it?"

I shook my head. "Keep it until we get to the car."

I looked up at the zombies. They were watching me with calm eyes. There was blood on the mouth of the dark-haired woman. It had been her teeth that tore into Ms. Harrison's neck.

Ms. Harrison was lying very still on the ground. Passed out, at the very least.

The power was beginning to unravel at the edges. If I was going to put everybody back in the ground, it had to be now.

"Go back into the ground. Back to your graves. Go back, all of you, go back."

The dead walked upon the earth, moving among one another like children in a game of musical chairs. Then one by one they lay down upon the earth, and it swallowed them like water. The earth moved and buckled in waves, until they were all tucked out of sight.

There were no bones protruding from the earth. The earth was smooth and soft, as if the entire top of the mountain had been dug up and smoothed over.

The power shredded, flowing back into the ground, or wherever the hell it came from. We had to get down to the Jeep and start making phone calls. There was a rampaging fey on the loose. We at least had to get cops out to the Bouviers' place.

Larry knelt beside Ms. Harrison. He touched her neck. "She's alive." His hand came away stained with blood.

I looked at Stirling. He'd stopped rolling around and was just sort of huddled on his side, his arm held at an obscene angle. The look he gave me was part pain and part hate. If he ever got a second chance, I was dead.

"Shoot him if he moves," I said.

Larry got to his feet and pointed the gun dutifully at Stirling.

I went to check on Bayard. He lay on his side, half-crumpled around the wound in his belly. A wide black circle showed where his blood had soaked into the thirsty ground. I knew dead when I saw it, but I knelt on the far side of his body so I could keep an eye on Stirling. It wasn't that I didn't trust Larry. I just didn't trust Stirling.

There was no pulse in his neck. The skin was already cooling in the soft spring air. It hadn't been an instant death. Lionel Bayard had died while we were fighting. He'd died alone, and he'd known he was dying, and that he'd been betrayed. It was a bad way to die.

I stood up and looked at Stirling. I wanted to kill him for Bayard, for Magnus, for Dorrie Bouvier, for her kids. For being a heartless son of bitch.

He'd witnessed me using zombies as a weapon. Using magic as a killing weapon was punishable by death. Self-defense was not an acceptable plea.

I stared very calmly across at Stirling and the unconscious Ms. Harrison, and realized that I could have crossed that ground and put a bullet in both of them, and slept just fine.

Sweet Jesus.

Larry glanced my way, gun still steady, but he'd taken his eyes off Stirling for a second. Not fatal, tonight, but I'd have to break him of it. "Is Bayard dead?"

"Yeah." I started back towards them, wondering what I was going to do. I didn't think Larry would let me shoot them in cold blood. Part of me was glad. Part of me wasn't.

Wind blew against my face. There was a rustling sound in the wind, like that made by trees or cloth. There were no trees on top of this mountain. I turned with the big .45 in a two-handed grip, and Janos was just there, on the edge of the mountain. Staring at his skeletal face, I think I stopped breathing. He was dressed all in black; even his hands were hidden inside black gloves. For one wild moment he looked like a floating skull. "We have the boy," he said.

35

The crosses were still in plain sight. They glowed with a soft white radiance. No burning light, not yet. We weren't in active danger, but the cross grew warm even through my shirt.

Janos put a hand in front of his eyes, the way I would guard my eyes from the sun in the car. ''Please put those away, so we may talk.''

He hadn't asked us to take them off. I could live with tucking my cross in my shirt. It could come out again later. I spilled the chain back down my shirt one-handed, keeping the .45 ready. I realized then that I didn't know if the gun had silver ammo. Now was not the time to ask. Stirling would probably lie anyway.

Larry slipped his own cross out of sight. The glowing night was just a little dimmer.

''Alright, now what?'' I asked.

Kissa came up behind him, Jeff Quinlan in front of her like a shield. His glasses were gone, and he looked even younger without them. She had his arm behind his back, at an angle that could be painful with just a tug.

He was wearing a cream-colored tuxedo with a cummerbund done two shades darker to match the bow tie. Kissa was in black leather. Jeff stood out against her in wonderful contrast.

I swallowed; my pulse threatened to choke me. What was going on? ''You alright, Jeff?''

''I guess so.''

Kissa gave a little tug.

He winced. ''I'm okay.'' His voice was a little higher than it should have been, a little scared.

I held out my hand to him. ''Come here.''

''Not yet,'' Janos said.

I'd tried. ''What do you want?''

''First drop your guns.''

''If we don't?'' I thought I knew the answer, but I wanted him to say it.

''Kissa will kill the boy, and you will have done all this for nothing.''

''Help me,'' Stirling said. ''She's mad. She attacked Ms. Harrison with zombies. When we tried to defend ourselves, she nearly killed us.''

That was probably what he'd say in court, too. And a jury would believe him. They'd want to believe him. I would be the big, bad zombie queen, and he would be the innocent victim.

Janos laughed, his paper-thin skin threatening to split, but never quite doing it. ''Oh, no, Mr. Stirling, I watched from the darkness. I saw you murder the other man.''

Fear flashed across his face. ''I don't know what you mean. We hired him in good faith. He turned on us.''

''My master opened your mind to Bloody Bones. She freed him to whisper in your dreams about land, money, and power. All that you desire.''

''Serephina sent Ivy to kill me, or rather for me to kill her. So she'd be sure to have Bloody Bones free,'' I said.

''Yes,'' he said. ''Serephina told her she had to rid herself of the disgrace of losing to you.''

''By killing me.''

''Yes.''

''What if she'd succeeded?''

''My master had faith in you, Anita. You are death come among us. A breath of mortality.''

''Why'd she want the thing freed?'' I seemed to be asking that a lot tonight.

''She wishes to taste immortal blood.''

''This is all sort of elaborate for a little extra kick in your food.''

He gave another rictus grin. ''You are what you eat, Anita. Think upon it.''

I did, and my eyes widened. ''She thinks by drinking immortal blood, she'll be truly immortal?''

''Very good, Anita.''

''It won't work,'' I said.

''We shall see,'' he said.

''What do you get out it?'' I asked.

He cocked his skeletal head to one side, like a decaying bird. ''She is my master, and she shares her bounty.''

''You want immortality, too?''

''I want power,'' he said.

Great. ''And it doesn't bother you that the thing will kill children? That it's already killed some?''

''We feed, Bloody Bones feeds, what does it matter?''

''And Bloody Bones is going to just let you feed off it?''

''Serephina has found the spell that Magnus's ancestor used. She controls the fairie.''

''How?''

He shook his head and smiled. ''No more delays, Anita. Drop the gun, or Kissa will taste him before your eyes.''

Kissa ran a hand through Jeff's short hair, a caressing gesture. It pushed his head to one side, baring a long smooth line of neck.

''No!'' Jeff tried to pull away, and Kissa yanked on his arm hard enough that he cried out.

''I will break the arm, boy,'' she growled.

The pain held him immobile, but his eyes were wide and terrified. He looked at me. He wouldn't plead, no begging, but his eyes did it for him.

Kissa's lips pulled back from her teeth in a flashy snarl, fangs visible.

''Don't,'' I said, and hated it. I tossed the .45 to the ground. Larry threw my gun down. Disarmed twice in one night. It was a record even for me.

36

"Now what?" I asked.

"Serephina awaits us at the party. She sent suitable clothing for you. You can change in the limousine," Janos said.

"What party?" I asked.

"The one we have come to invite you to. She is delivering Jean-Claude's invitation in person."

That didn't sound good. "I think we'll pass on the party."

"I don't think so," Janos said.

Another vampire stepped out of the trees. It was the brunette that had tormented Jason. She stalked forward in a long black dress that covered her from neck to ankle. She slid her arms around Janos, nuzzling his neck, giving us a glimpse of her pale back. Only a fine webbing of black straps covered her back. The dress moved like it would slide down her body at the least movement, but somehow it stayed in place. Fashion-plate magic. Her dark hair was in a looping braid to one side of her face. She looked good for someone I'd seen ripped to rotting bits of flesh.

I couldn't keep the surprise off my face.

"I thought she was dead," Larry said.

"So did I."

"I would never have risked Pallas if I truly thought your werewolf could kill her," Janos said.

A second figure came out of the dark woods. Long white hair framed a thin, fine-boned face. His eyes glowed bloodred. I'd seen vampires with glowing eyes before, but they always glowed the color of their irises. No one who had ever been human had red irises. He wore a proverbial black tux and tails, complete with a nearly ankle-length cape.

"Xavier," I said softly.

Larry looked at me. "This is the vampire that's been killing everyone?"

I nodded.

"Then what's he doing here?"

''That's how you found Jeff so quickly. You're working with Xavier,'' I said. ''Does Serephina know?''

Janos smiled. ''She is master of all, Anita, even him.'' He said the last like it impressed him.

''You won't get to munch on your fairie for long if the cops trace Xavier to you.''

''Xavier was following orders. He was on a recruitment drive.'' Janos seemed to like saying that last bit like it was an in-joke.

''Why did you want Ellie Quinlan?''

''Xavier likes a bit of young boy now and then. It is his one weakness. He turned the girl's lover, and the boy wanted her with him forever. Tonight she will rise and feed with us.''

Not if I could help it. ''What do you want, Janos?''

''I was sent to make your life easier,'' he said.

''Yeah, right.''

Pallas uncurled herself from Janos. She glided over to Stirling.

Stirling stared up at her, cradling his broken arm. It had to hurt like hell, but it wasn't pain on his face now, it was fear. He stared up at the vampire; all the arrogance had slipped away. He looked like a kid who'd discovered the thing under the bed was really there.

A third vampire moved out of the trees. It was the blonde half of the pair. She looked fine, like she'd never rotted right before our eyes. I'd never known a vampire that could look so dead, and not be.

''You remember Bettina,'' he said.

Bettina wore a black dress that left her pale shoulders bare. A throw of black cloth went over one shoulder and down the front of the dress. A gold belt held it in place, cinching her waist tight. Her yellow braid was wound in a crown atop her head.

She walked towards us, and her face was perfect. The dry, rotting skin had been a bad dream, a nightmare. I wish. Fire, Jean-Claude had said, fire was the only surety. I thought he'd meant just Janos.

Janos reached over and grabbed Jeff from Kissa. He gripped the boy's shoulders with both black-gloved hands. His fingers were longer than they should have been, as though they had an extra joint. Against the white of Jeff's jacket, you could tell that the index finger was as long as the middle finger. Another myth that was true, at least for Janos. Those long, strange fingers dug into Jeff just a little.

Jeff's eyes were so wide it looked painful.

''What's going on?'' I asked.

Kissa was dressed in the same black vinyl outfit she'd had on in the torture room, though it couldn't be the exact same one, because the first one had Larry's bullet hole in it. She stood beside him, her hands in fists. She stood very still, as only the dead can, but there was a tension to her, a wariness. She wasn't happy. Her dark skin was strangely pale. She hadn't fed yet tonight. I could always tell . . . with most vampires. There are always exceptions.

Xavier moved in a shadow of that impossible blurring speed past Stirling, to stand beside the still unconscious Ms. Harrison. Larry shook his head. "Did he just appear there, or did I see him move?"

"He moved," I said.

I expected Janos to send Kissa out to join the others, but he didn't. A figure crawled over the lip of the hill, dragging itself into sight like it hurt to move. Pale hands dug into the naked dirt, pale arms bare to the spring night. The head drooped towards the ground, short dark hair hiding the face. With one upward motion, the face raised into the moonlight. Thin, bloodless lips drew back from fangs. The face was ravaged with hunger. I knew the eyes were brown only because I'd seen them staring lifelessly at the ceiling of Ellie Quinlan's bedroom. There was no pull to her eyes, but down in the dark depths a flicker of something burned. It wasn't sanity; hunger, maybe. An animal's emotion, nothing human. Maybe after they'd let her feed for the first time, she'd have time for emotions; now everything had narrowed down to one basic need.

"Is that who I think it is?" Larry asked.

"Yeah," I said.

Jeff tried to run to her. "Ellie!"

Janos jerked him tight against his chest, one arm around his shoulders like an embrace. Jeff struggled against that arm, tried to run to his dead sister. I was with Janos on this one. The newly risen have a tendency to eat first and ask questions later. The thing that had once been Ellie Quinlan would have gladly torn out her baby brother's throat. She'd have bathed in the blood, and minutes, or days, or weeks later, she would realize what she'd done. She might even regret it.

"Go, Angela; go to Xavier," Janos said.

"A new name won't change who she was," I said.

Janos looked at me. "She is two years dead, and her name is Angela."

"Her name is Ellie," Jeff said. He'd stopped struggling, but he looked at his dead sister with fresh horror, as if just beginning to really see her.

"People will recognize her, Janos."

"We shall be careful, Anita. Our new angel will see no one that we do not wish."

"Well, isn't that cozy?" I said.

"It will be," he said, "once she has drunk her fill."

"I'm impressed that you dragged her this far without feeding her first."

"I did it." Xavier's voice was surprisingly pleasant. It was disturbing hearing that voice coming from that pale, ghostly face.

I looked at him, careful to avoid his gaze. "Impressive," I said.

"Andy brought her over, and I brought Andy over. I am her master."

Since Andy hadn't shown up, I was betting I'd killed him in the woods with Sheriff St. John. Probably not a good time to bring that up. "And who is your master?"

"Serephina, for now," Xavier said.

I glanced at Janos. "You haven't worked out which of you is top dog, have you?" I smiled.

"You waste our time, Anita. Our master awaits you eagerly. Let us finish this. Call our angel."

Xavier held out one pale hand. Ellie made a noise low in her throat, and scrambled on all fours over the raw dirt. The long black dress tangled around her legs. She tore at it impatiently. The cloth ripped like paper in her hands, the skirt shredding around her bare legs. She grabbed Xavier's hand like it was a lifeline. She bent over his wrist, and only his hand in her hair kept her from trying to feed on him.

''There is no sustenance for you from the dead, Angela,'' Janos said. ''Feed on the living.''

Pallas and Bettina knelt on either side of Stirling. Xavier fell gracefully beside Ms. Harrison, his black cape spread out around him like a pool of blood. He kept hold of Ellie's hair the whole way down, forcing her snarling face to touch the dirt. Her hands dug at his hands, mewling sounds crawling from her throat. Nothing that was human should have made sounds like that.

''Ms. Blake,'' Stirling said, ''you're the law. You have to protect me.''

''I thought you were going to see me in court, Raymond. Something about me attacking you and Ms. Harrison with zombies.''

''I didn't mean it.'' He glanced up at the kneeling vampires, then back to me. ''I won't tell. I won't tell anyone. Please.''

I just looked at him. ''Begging for mercy, Raymond?''

''Yes, yes, I'm begging.''

''Like the mercy you showed Bayard?''

''Please.''

Bettina caressed Stirling's cheek. He jerked like it had burned. ''Please!''

Shit.

''We can't just watch,'' Larry said.

''You have another suggestion?''

''You never give anyone over to the monsters, not for any reason. It's a rule,'' he said.

It was my rule. I'd believed in it once, back when I'd been sure who the monsters were.

He was pulling the chain out from inside his shirt.

''Don't do this, Larry. Don't get us killed for Raymond Stirling.''

His cross spilled out in the open air. It glowed like Serephina's eyes. He just looked at me.

I sighed, and brought out my own cross. ''This is a bad idea.''

''I know,'' he said. ''But I can't just watch.''

I stared at his earnest face, and knew it was true. He couldn't just watch. I could have. I might not have enjoyed it, but I could have let it happen. More's the pity.

''What are you doing with your little holy objects?'' Janos asked.

''Stopping this,'' I said.

''You want them dead, Anita.''

''Not like this,'' I said.

''Would you have me let you use your gun and waste all this blood?''

He was offering to let me shoot them. I shook my head. ''I don't think that's an option anymore.''

''It was never an option,'' Larry said.

I let that go; no need to disillusion him. I walked towards Pallas and Bettina. Larry walked towards Ellie and Xavier, cross held outward to the length of its chain, as if that made it work better. Nothing wrong with a little dramatic gesture, but I'd have to clue him in that it didn't really help. But later.

The cross's glow grew until it was like wearing a 100-watt lightbulb naked around your neck. I saw the world as a black circle outside the glow.

Xavier was on his feet facing Larry, but the others had crawled away from their prey, beaten by the light.

''Thank you, Ms. Blake,'' Stirling said. ''Thank you.'' He grabbed my leg with his good hand, fawning over me. I fought an urge to shake him off.

''Thank Larry; I'd have let you die.''

He didn't seem to hear me. He was nearly crying with relief, slobbering all over my Nikes.

''Back away from them, please.'' The voice was female and honey-thick.

I blinked over the glow of the cross and saw Kissa holding a gun. A revolver that looked like a Magnum; hard to tell in the glow. Whatever it was, it'd make a big hole.

''Move away from them, now.''

''I thought Serephina didn't want me dead.''

''Kissa will shoot your young friend.''

I stopped in mid-breath and let it out. ''If you kill him, I won't cooperate with whatever you have in mind for tonight.''

''You misunderstand us, Anita,'' Janos said. ''My master does not require your cooperation. Everything she wants from you can be taken by force.''

I stared at him over the shining light. He had Jeff cuddled against him; most heartwarming.

''Take off your crosses and throw them far out into the trees,'' Janos said. He ran a gloved hand along both sides of Jeff's face, planting a kiss on his cheek.

''Now that we know you would give up your safety for both young men, we have one more hostage than is absolutely necessary.'' He put his hands on either side of Jeff's neck, just holding, not hurting, not yet.

''Take off your crosses and throw them into the woods. I will not ask a third time.''

I stared at him. I didn't want to give up my cross. I glanced at Larry. He was still facing off against Xavier, his cross glowing bravely. Shit.

''Kissa, shoot the man.''

''No,'' I said. I undid the chain. ''Don't shoot him.''

''Don't do it, Anita,'' Larry said.

''I can't watch them shoot you, not if I can stop it.'' I let the chain pool in my hand; the cross shone with a blue-white flame like burning magnesium. It was a bad idea to throw it away. A real bad idea. I tossed it into the woods. The cross glittered like a falling star and died out of sight in the dark.

''Now your cross, Larry,'' Janos said.

Larry shook his head. ''You'll have to shoot me.''

''We'll shoot the boy,'' Janos said. ''Or perhaps I'll feed upon him while you watch.'' He pinned Jeff against himself with one arm, while his other hand dug into the boy's hair, holding him immobile, neck exposed.

Larry looked at me. ''What do I do, Anita?''

''You have to decide this one for yourself,'' I said.

''They'll really kill him, won't they?''

''Yeah, they will.''

He cursed under his breath and let the cross fall against his chest. He undid the chain and threw it out into the woods with a lot of force to it, as if he could throw his anger with it.

When the light from his cross died away, we stood there in the darkness. The moonlight that had seemed so bright before was a dim substitute.

My night vision returned in stages. Kissa stepped closer, the gun still pointed at us. The first time I'd seen her, she had exuded sexuality, power; now she was docile, quiet, as though some of her power had been drained away. She looked pale and drawn. She needed to feed.

''Why haven't they let you feed tonight?'' I asked.

''Our master is not a hundred percent sure of Kissa's loyalty. It needed testing, didn't it, my dark beauty?''

Kissa didn't answer. She stared at me with large, dark eyes, but the gun never wavered.

''Feed, children, feed.''

Pallas and Bettina walked over to Stirling. They stared at me over him. I stared back.

Stirling grabbed my leg. ''You can't let them have me. Please, please.''

Pallas knelt by him. Bettina walked around to the side I was on. She pulled Stirling's hand off my leg. The vampire's lower back brushed my legs. I took a step back, and Stirling started screaming.

Xavier and Ellie had already started to feed on the blessedly unconscious Ms. Harrison. Larry looked at me, hands out, empty, helpless.

I didn't know what to say.

''Don't touch me, don't touch me!'' Stirling batted at Pallas with his good hand, and the vampire caught it easily, held it.

''At least put him under,'' I said.

Pallas looked up at me. ''After he tried to kill you? Why show him mercy?''

''Maybe I don't want to hear him scream.''

Pallas smiled. Her eyes flashed dark fire. ''For you, Anita, anything.''

She grabbed Stirling's chin, forcing him to meet her gaze.

''Ms. Blake, help me. Help . . .'' The words died in his mouth.

I watched everything slide out of his eyes, until they were empty and waiting.

''Come to me, Raymond,'' Pallas said. ''Come to me.''

Stirling sat up, his one good arm embracing the vampire. He tried to use the broken arm, but it wouldn't bend at the elbow.

Bettina bent the broken arm backward and forward, laughing. Stirling never reacted to the pain. He snuggled against Pallas. The look on his face was one of happiness, joy. Eagerness.

Pallas sank fangs into his neck. Stirling spasmed for a second, then relaxed and began making soft noises in his throat.

Pallas moved Stirling's head to one side, sucking on the wound but leaving enough room on the other side for someone else. Bettina sank fangs into the exposed flesh.

The two vampires fed, heads so close together their hair mingled, gold and black. And Raymond Stirling made happy noises while they killed him.

Larry walked away to the edge of the clearing, hugging his arms tight across his chest.

I stayed where I was. I watched. I had wanted Stirling dead. It would be cowardly to look away. Besides, I should have to watch. I needed to remember who the monsters were. Maybe if I forced myself not to look away, not to blink, I wouldn't forget again.

I stared at Stirling's happy, eager face, until his arm dropped away from Pallas's back, and his eyes closed. He passed out from blood loss and shock, and the vampires hugged him tight, and fed.

His eyes flew open wide, and a gurgling sound crawled out of his throat. Fear screamed out of his eyes. Pallas raised a hand and stroked Stirling's hair, a gesture you'd use on a frightened child. The fear died out of his eyes, and I watched the last light die with it. I watched Raymond Stirling die, and knew I would remember that last look of terror in my dreams for weeks to come.

37

There was a rush of wind that raised a fine cloud of dirt. Jean-Claude appeared as if conjured from the air itself. I had never been so happy to see him. I didn't run to his arms, but I moved to stand near him. Larry followed me. Jean-Claude wasn't always the safest refuge, but right now he looked pretty damn good.

He was dressed in one of his white shirts. This one had so much lace on the front it looked fluffy. A short white jacket hit him just at the waist. More lace peeked from the sleeves of the jacket. He wore tight white pants with a black belt. The belt matched his velvet black boots.

''I did not expect you here, Jean-Claude,'' Janos said. I couldn't tell for sure, but he sounded surprised. Goody.

''Serephina delivered her invitation in person, Janos, but it was not enough.''

''You surprise me, Jean-Claude,'' he said.

''I surprised Serephina, as well.'' He sounded terribly calm. If he was afraid standing outnumbered on the hilltop, it didn't show. I'd have loved to know how he'd surprised Serephina.

Jason walked up the far side of the hill, from the direction of the Jeep. He wore black leather pants that looked like they'd been poured on him, short black boots, and no shirt. There was what looked like a silver-studded dog collar around his neck, and a black glove on either hand, but other than that he was naked from the waist up. I hoped Jason had chosen his own outfit for tonight.

The right side of his face was bruised from chin to forehead as though something large had hit him.

''I see your pet joined the struggle,'' Janos said.

''He is mine in every way, Janos. They are all mine.''

Just this once I let it go. If my choice was belonging to Jean-Claude or to Serephina, I knew what my vote would be.

Larry moved so close to me that I could have taken his hand. Maybe he didn't like being included in Jean-Claude's menagerie.

''You have lost that air of humbleness that I found so appealing, Jean-Claude. Have you refused Serephina's invitation altogether?''

"I will come to Serephina's party, but on my own with my people around me."

I glanced at him. Was he crazy?

He frowned. "Serephina wanted you at the party in chains."

"We can all live with this choice, Janos."

"Are you saying you would challenge us all here and now?" There was an edge of laughter in his voice.

"I will not die alone, Janos. In the end you may have me, but it will cost you dearly."

"If you will truly come of your own free will, then come," Janos said. "Our master calls; let us answer that call." Janos, Bettina, and Pallas were just suddenly airborne. It wasn't flying, or levitation. I had no word for it. Larry whispered, "Dear God." The first time you see a vampire fly is a red-letter night.

The others scattered into the trees in that blurring motion that made them disappear almost as fast as flying. Ellie Quinlan had vanished with the rest of them. Her brother had been carried away by Janos. Until that moment I hadn't known a vampire could carry more than its own body weight while "flying." Learn something new every night.

We found our guns and walked down the mountainside. Our crosses were well and truly lost. Even Jean-Claude walked, and I knew he had other methods of transportation. Was it considered impolite to fly when others couldn't?

The Jeep was still where I'd parked it. The night was still thick. It was hours until dawn, and I just wanted to go home.

"I took the liberty of choosing clothes for you to wear tonight," Jean-Claude said. "They are in the Jeep."

"I locked the Jeep," I said.

He just smiled at me.

I sighed. "Fine." When I tried the handle it was unlocked. Clothes were folded in the passenger seat. They were black leather. I shook my head. "I don't think so."

"Your clothes, *ma petite*, are on the driver's side. Those are Lawrence's clothes."

Larry peered over my shoulder. "You've got to be kidding."

I walked around the Jeep and found a clean pair of black jeans. The tightest pair I owned. A bloodred tank top that I didn't remember buying. It felt like silk. There was a black duster coat that I had never seen. When I tried it for length it hit me at mid-calf, and billowed capelike when I moved. I liked the coat. The silk blouse I could have done without.

"Not bad," I said.

"Mine is bad," Larry said. "I don't even know how to get into these pants."

"Jason, help him dress." Jason picked up the bundle of leather and carried them to the back of the Jeep. Larry followed him but didn't look happy.

"No boots?" I said.

Jean-Claude smiled. "I didn't think you would give up your jogging shoes."

"Damn straight."

''Change quickly, *ma petite*; we must arrive at Serephina's before she decides to kill the boy just for spite.''

''Would Xavier let her kill his new toy?''

''If she is truly his master, he has no choice. Now, dress, *ma petite*, quickly.'' I walked towards the far side of the Jeep but that brought me within earshot, and nearly eyesight, of Larry. I stopped and sighed. What the hell.

I turned my back on Jean-Claude and slid out of my shoulder holster. ''How did you guys get away from Serephina?'' I slipped my shirt over my head. I fought the urge to look back. I knew Jean-Claude was watching; why check?

''Jason jumped her at a crucial moment. It was distraction enough for us to flee, but little else. I'm afraid the room is something of a mess.''

His voice was so mild I had to see his face. I slid the red tank top on and turned. He was standing closer than I'd thought, nearly within touching distance. He stood there in his white clothes, spotless and perfect.

''Step a few paces back, please. I'd like a little privacy.''

He smiled, but he did what I asked. A first.

''Had she underestimated you that badly?'' I asked. I changed jeans as quickly as I could. I tried not to think of him watching. It was too embarrassing.

''I was forced to flee, *ma petite*. Janos calls her master, and he defeated me. I cannot stand against her, not in a fair fight.''

I slipped the shoulder holster back on, threading the belt I'd been wearing back through it. The straps chafed a little with no sleeves but it was better than not having it. I got the Firestar from under my seat and tucked the inner pants holster down the front of my jeans. It would show, even with the duster. I finally put it at the small of my back, though it wasn't my first or even second choice of places. I got the silver knives out of the glove compartment and strapped them to my forearms. I also got out a small box. It held two extra crosses. Vampires seemed to always be taking them from me.

Jean-Claude watched it all with interest. His dark eyes followed my hands like he was memorizing the movements.

I put the duster on and walked a few steps to get the feel of everything. I drew both knives just to make sure the coat sleeves weren't too tight. I drew both guns and still didn't like the Firestar. I finally shifted the inner pants holster to one side. It dug into my side hard enough to bruise, but I could draw it in a reasonable time. That was more important than comfort tonight. I slipped an extra clip for both guns in the coat pockets. They were loaded with nonsilver bullets. It made me nervous to only have the silver bullets that were in the guns, but Rawhead and Bloody Bones was going to make his appearance sometime tonight. Magnus might even be there. I wanted ammo for everything I'd meet tonight.

Larry came out from behind the Jeep. I bit my lip to keep from laughing. It wasn't that he looked bad, he just looked so uncomfortable. He seemed to have trouble walking in the black leather pants.

''Just walk naturally,'' Jason said.

''I can't,'' Larry said. He had a silk tank top that was the twin of mine except it was blue instead of red. He had short black boots on. The black jacket he'd borrowed from Jason last night completed the outfit.

I looked at the boots.

"Black jogging shoes perhaps, *ma petite*, but white jogging shoes with black leather? I do not think so."

"I feel ridiculous," Larry said. "How can you wear this all the time?"

"I like leather," Jason said.

"We must be off," Jean-Claude said. "Anita, if you would drive?"

"I thought you might want to fly," I said.

"It is important we arrive together," he said.

Larry and I added salt to our pockets. With the extra ammo clips in one pocket and salt in the other, my coat hung a little crooked, but hey, we weren't going to a fashion show. We all slid into the Jeep. There was a lot of protesting from the back seat. "These pants are even more uncomfortable sitting down."

"I will remember your dislike of leather in the future, Lawrence."

"My name is Larry."

I drove the Jeep down the rutted road that led out of the construction site. "Serephina wants to be immortal." I turned onto the main road and headed back towards Branson, though of course we'd be stopping at Serephina's on the way.

Jean-Claude turned in his seat to stare at me. "What are you saying, *ma petite*?"

I told him. I told him about Rawhead and Bloody Bones, and Serephina's plan. "She's mad."

"Not entirely, *ma petite*. It might not give her immortality, but it would give her undreamt-of power. The question remaining is, how did Serephina grow powerful enough to snag Janos before she fed off Magnus and Bloody Bones?"

"What do you mean?"

"Janos was in the old country. He would not have left voluntarily. He followed her. Where did she get the power to subjugate him?"

"Maybe Magnus isn't the first fairie she's fed off," I said.

"Perhaps," he said, "or perhaps she has found other food."

"What other food?"

"That, *ma petite*, is the question that I would very much like answered."

"Thinking of changing diets?" I asked.

"Power is always tempting, *ma petite*, but for tonight I was thinking of more practical matters. If we can discover her source of power, we might be able to undo it."

"How?"

He shook his head. "I do not know, but unless we can find some trick to pull out of our hats tonight, *ma petite*, we are doomed." He sounded remarkably calm about it. I wasn't calm. My pulse was thundering so fast I could feel it in my throat and wrists. Hear it like a rushing in my ears. Doomed: it had a bad ring to it. With Serephina waiting at the other end, it had a very bad ring to it indeed.

38

We walked up the stone steps to the porch. Moonlight and soft darkness filled the porch. There were no thick, unnatural shadows, no hint of what lay inside. It was just an abandoned house, nothing special. The nervous flutter in my stomach didn't buy it either.

Kissa opened the door. Candlelight spilled behind her from the open door to the far room. No pretense tonight that the empty room was all there was. Sweat beaded on her face, golden drops in the warm light. She was still being punished. I wondered why, but it wasn't my biggest problem.

Kissa led us through that open door without a word. Serephina sat on her throne in the corner of the big room. She was dressed in a white ball gown like Cinderella, her hair piled atop her head. Diamonds like a string of fire glimmered in her hair as she nodded her greeting.

Magnus was curled at her feet in a white tux and tails. Gloves, a white top hat, and a cane were laid next to his knees. His long chestnut hair was the only color in the picture. Every master vamp I'd ever met had been into dramatic presentation. Janos and his two females stood in black behind the throne, like a living curtain of darkness. Ellie lay on her side in the cushions, looking almost alive. Even in her torn and stained black dress she looked content, like a cat that was full of cream. Her eyes sparkled, lips curled with a secret smile. Ellie, alias Angela, was enjoying being undead. So far. Kissa stalked to them, and knelt on the side away from Magnus. Her black leather blended with Janos's cloak. Serephina stroked Kissa's sweating face with a white-gloved hand.

Serephina smiled, and it was lovely until you glimpsed her eyes. They glowed with a pale phosphorescence. You could still get a hint of pupil, but it was sinking fast. Her eyes matched her dress. Now that was color-coordinating.

Jeff and Xavier were missing. I didn't like that. I opened my mouth to ask, and Jean-Claude looked at me. For just this once, the look was enough. He was the master; I was playing servant. Fine, as long as he asked the right questions.

"We have come, Serephina," Jean-Claude said. "Give us the boy, and we will leave you in peace."

She laughed. ''But I will not leave you in peace, Jean-Claude.'' She turned her softly glowing eyes to me. It was like being looked at by twin flashlights, and just as human. ''Niña, I am so happy to see you.''

I stopped breathing for a second. Niña: it had been my mother's nickname for me. Something flared in her eyes, like a distant glimpse of fire; then the light banked back to a cool wavering light. She wasn't trying to capture me with her eyes. Why? Because she was that sure of me.

My skin suddenly went cold. That was it. I would have said it was arrogance, but I believed it. She offered something better than sex, more fulfilling than power. Home. Lie or not, it was a good offer.

Larry touched my hand. ''You're shaking.''

I swallowed hard. ''Never admit how scared you are out loud, Larry; ruins the effect.''

''Sorry.''

I stepped away from him; no sense in huddling. I glanced at Jean-Claude, sort of silently asking if I was about to break vampire protocol.

''She has acknowledged you as she would another master. Answer as one.'' He didn't seem bothered by that; I was.

''What do you want, Serephina?'' I asked.

She stood, gliding across the carpeted floor. It looked like whatever was under that full skirt wasn't legs. Feet just didn't move like that. Maybe she was levitating. However she managed it, she kept coming closer. I wanted desperately to back away. I didn't want her close to me.

Larry moved a step behind me. Jason moved a step up to Jean-Claude's other side. I stood my ground. It was the best I could do.

Something flickered in her eyes, like a distant glimpse of movement through a fringe of trees. Eyes didn't do that. I looked away and realized I didn't remember looking at her eyes. So how was I looking away?

I felt her move towards me. Her gloved hand came into view. I jerked back and looked up at the same time. I barely glanced at her face, but it was enough. Her eyes had fire burning down a long dark tunnel, as if the inside of her head fell away into an impossible darkness, and some small creatures had lit a fire against that darkness. I could warm my hands by that flame forever.

I screamed. Screamed and covered my eyes with my hands.

A hand touched my shoulder. I jerked away and screamed again. ''*Ma petite*, I am here.''

''Then do something,'' I said.

''I am,'' he said.

''I will have this one by sunrise.'' She motioned to me. She took a gliding step towards Jason. She caressed her gloved hand down his bare chest. He stood there and took it. I wouldn't have let her touch me on a dare.

''I will give you to Bettina and Pallas. They will teach you to enjoy rotting flesh.''

Jason stared straight ahead, but his eyes widened just a little. Bettina and Pallas had moved from behind the throne to stand a few feet behind Serephina. Dramatic gestures are us.

"Or perhaps I will force you to change into wolf form until it becomes more natural than this human shell." She slid a finger under the collar on his throat. "I will chain you to my wall, and you will be my guard dog."

"Enough of this, Serephina," Jean-Claude said. "The night bleeds away. These petty torments are beneath one of your power."

"I am feeling petty tonight, Jean-Claude, and soon I will have the power to be as petty as I feel." She glanced at Larry. "He will join my flock." She stared up at Jean-Claude. I hadn't realized he was taller. "And you, my lovely catamount, will serve us all for all eternity."

Jean-Claude stared down at her, utterly arrogant. "I am Master of the City now, Serephina. We cannot torture each other. We cannot steal each other's possessions, no matter how attractive they are."

It took me a second to realize the possessions he was referring to were us.

Serephina smiled. "I will have your businesses, your money, your lands, and your people before the night is out. Did the council really think I would be content with the crumbs from your table?"

If she challenged him officially, we were all dead. Jean-Claude couldn't take her, and neither could I. Distraction, we needed a distraction. "You're wearing enough diamonds to buy your own businesses, your own house."

She turned those glowing eyes to me, and I half wished I had kept quiet. "Do you think I live in this house because I cannot afford better?"

"I don't know."

She glided back to her throne and settled onto it, smoothing her skirts. "I do not trust your human laws. I will remain the secret we have always been; let others walk in the spotlight. I will be here when such modern thinkers are no more." She suddenly slashed out with one hand.

Jean-Claude staggered. Blood flew from his face, splattering on his white shirt and jacket in bright crimson flecks. Drops of it clung to my hair and cheek.

She slashed again, and another cut exploded on the other side of his face, splashing Jason with Jean-Claude's blood.

Jean-Claude stayed on his feet. He never cried out. He didn't touch the wounds. He stood there utterly still; except for the blood there was no movement to him. His eyes were drowning pools of sapphire floating in a mask of blood.

Naked muscle twitched in his cheek. Bone glistened at jaw and cheek. It was a frighteningly deep wound. But I knew he could heal it. Horrible as it looked, it was a scare tactic. I kept telling that to the pounding of my heart. I wanted to go for a gun. To shoot the bitch. But I couldn't shoot them all. I wasn't even sure Janos could be shot.

"I don't have to kill you, Jean-Claude. Hot metal in your wounds, and they'll be permanent. Your beautiful face ravaged for all time. You can still pretend to be Master of the City, but I will rule. You will be my puppet."

"Say the word, Serephina," Jean-Claude said. "Say it and be done with these games." His voice was bland, as normal as it ever was. His voice gave nothing away, not pain, or fear, or terror.

"Challenge: is that the word you want to hear, Jean-Claude?"

"It will do." His power crawled over my skin like cool fire. The power lashed out suddenly; I felt it sweep past me like a giant fist. It slammed into Serephina, scattering the air currents. Kissa caught the edge of it and fell back from the throne, thrown nearly prone among the cushions.

Serephina threw back her head and laughed. The laughter died in mid-motion, gone like it had never been. Her face was a mask with eyes of white fire. Her skin seemed to grow paler, whiter until it was like translucent marble. Veins showed under her skin like lines of blue flame. Her power flowed through the room like rising water, deeper and deeper until when she released it we would all be drowned.

"Where are your ghosts, Serephina?" I asked.

I thought for a second she would ignore me, but that masklike face turned slowly, slowly towards me.

"Where are your ghosts?"

Even though she was looking straight at me, I couldn't tell if she heard. It was like trying to read the face of an animal; no, the face of a statue. There was no one home.

"Can't control Bloody Bones and your ghosts at the same time? Is that it? Did you have to give up one of them?"

Serephina rose to her feet, and I knew she was floating, rising on tiny currents of her own power to hover above the cushions. She floated slowly upward towards the ceiling, and it was impressive. I was babbling, trying to buy time, but time for what? What the hell could we do?

A voice echoed in my head. "Crosses, *ma petite*; do not be bashful on my account." I didn't argue or hesitate.

The cross spilled out of my shirt in a ball of light so bright it was painful. I squinted and looked away, only to find Larry's cross behind me blazing to life.

Jean-Claude cowered beside me, hunched away, arms shielding his face. Serephina shrieked and half-fell to the floor. She could stand before a cross, but she couldn't do tricks in front of one. She landed in a heap of silken skirts. The other vamps shielded their faces, hissing.

Magnus rose from the cushions. He stalked towards us. Jason stepped in front of Jean-Claude, moving to stand in front of me. He glanced at me with amber eyes; his beast stared at me over the glow of the cross, and had no fear. For a heartbeat I was glad I had silver bullets just in case.

Serephina said, "No, Magnus, not you."

Magnus hesitated, staring at Jason. A thin growl crawled out of Jason's throat. "I can take him," Magnus said.

There was a sound from the open door to the basement. Something was coming up the stairs. Something heavy. The stairs creaked in protest. A hand came out of the darkness, large enough to palm my head. The fingernails were long and dirty, almost clawlike. Ragged clothes clung to huge, square shoulders. The thing was at least ten feet tall. It had to bend sideways to come through the door, and when it stood, its head brushed the ceiling, and you couldn't pretend it was human anymore.

Its huge, oversized head had no skin. The flesh was raw and open like a wound. The veins pulsed and throbbed with blood flowing through them, but it didn't bleed. It opened a mouth full of broken yellow teeth and said, "I am here." It was shocking to hear words out of that mouth, that face. Its voice was like the sound at the bottom of a well; deep, and rough, and lost.

The room suddenly seemed small. Rawhead and Bloody Bones could have reached out one long arm and touched me. Not good. Jason had moved back a step to rejoin us. Magnus had moved back to Serephina's side. He was staring at the creature as wide-eyed as the rest of us. Had he never seen it in the flesh before?

"Come to me," Serephina said. She held out her hands to the creature, and it moved towards her, surprisingly graceful. It had a liquidness to its walk that was all wrong. Nothing that big and that ugly should move like quicksilver, but it did. In that movement I saw Magnus and Dorrie. It moved like something beautiful.

Serephina cradled its huge, dirty hand in her white-gloved hands. She pushed back the ragged sleeve, laying the thick, muscled wrist bare.

"Stop her, *ma petite*."

I glanced down at Jean-Claude, who was still cowering before the crosses' fire. "What?"

"If she drinks from it, the crosses may not work against her."

I didn't question him; there was no time. I drew the Browning and felt Larry draw his gun.

Serephina bent over the fairie's wrist, mouth wide, fangs glistening.

I pulled the trigger. The bullet smacked into the side of her head. The force rocked her, and blood dribbled down. She could be shot. Life was good. Janos threw himself in front of her, and it was like trying to hit Superman. I pulled the trigger twice, staring at his dead-eyed face from just over a yard. He smiled at me. Silver bullets just weren't going to do it.

Larry had stepped around Jean-Claude. He was firing at Pallas and Bettina. They kept coming. Kissa stayed on the floor. Ellie seemed frozen in the face of the crosses.

Bloody Bones stood there like it was waiting for orders, or didn't give a damn. It was staring at Magnus like it recognized him. It was not a friendly look.

Serephina's voice came from behind Janos's protective body. "Give me your wrist."

The fairie gave a ragged smile. "Soon I will be free to kill you." It looked at Magnus when it said it.

I didn't really want something the size of a small giant mad at me, but I didn't want Serephina to have its power either. I fired into its raw head, and I might as well have spit at it. The shot did earn me a dirty look. "I have no quarrel with you," the fairie said. "Do not make one."

Staring into its monstrous face, I agreed. But what could I do? "What'll we do?" Larry asked. He'd moved to stand nearly back to back with me. Bettina and Pallas had stopped just out of touching range, held at bay by the crosses, not the guns. Jean-Claude had gone to his knees, face cradled away from the glare of the crosses, but he didn't crawl away. He stayed within the protective touch of that light.

Silver bullets wouldn't hurt the fey, so . . . I hit the button on the Browning and popped the clip out. I fished in my pocket for the extra clip and slid it home. I aimed at the thing's chest, where I hoped the heart was, and pulled.

Bloody Bones bellowed. Blood blossomed on its ragged clothes. I knew when it felt Serephina bite into its flesh. Power whirled through the room, raising every hair on my body. For a heartbeat I couldn't breathe; there was too much magic in the room for something as mundane as breathing.

Serephina rose slowly from behind Janos's dark form. She levitated to the ceiling, bathing in the light of the crosses, smiling. The bullet wound in her head was healed. Her eyes licked white flame around her face, and I knew we were going to die.

Xavier appeared in the door to the basement. He held a sword in his hands, but it was heavier, softer-edged than any blade I'd ever seen. He stared at Serephina and smiled.

"I have fed you," Bloody Bones said. "Free me."

Serephina threw her hands skyward, caressing the ceiling. "No," she breathed, "never. I will drink you dry and bathe in your power."

"You promised," Bloody Bones said.

She stared at him, floating; her eyes of fire were even with his raw face. "I lied," she said.

Xavier cried, "No!" He tried to come closer, but the crosses kept him just out of reach.

I threw a handful of salt on Serephina and Bloody Bones. She laughed at me. "What are you doing, Niña?"

"Never break your word to the fey," I said. "It negates all bargains."

A sword appeared in Bloody Bones' hands, just appeared like the fey had grabbed it out of mid-air. It was the one I'd seen Xavier carrying at the Quinlans' house. How many scimitars as long as my upper body could there be? He stabbed it through Serephina's chest, spitting her in midair like a butterfly. Normal steel shouldn't have touched her, but backed by the fairie's magic, it could. He pinned her to the wall, driving the hilt into her chest. He tore the sword out of her, twisting it, doing as much damage as he could.

She shrieked and slid down, leaving a bloody trail on the naked wall.

Bloody Bones turned back to the rest of us. It touched fingers to its bleeding chest. "I will forgive you this wound, because you freed me. When he is dead, there will be no more wounds." He drove the sword into Magnus. The move was so quick, it looked like stop action. He was as fast as Xavier. Shit.

Magnus fell to his knees, mouth wide with a scream he had no breath to make. Bloody Bones drew the sword upward like he had with Serephina, and it reminded me of the wounds that the boys had had.

If Bloody Bones would help us escape Serephina and company, I had no problem with that, but then what? It drew the sword outward, and Magnus was still alive, staring up at me. He reached out to me, and I could have let him die. Bloody Bones raised the blade back for a final blow.

I pointed the Browning at it. "Don't move. Until you kill him, you're mortal, and bullets can kill you."

The fairie froze, staring at me. "What do you want, mortal?"

"You killed the boys in the woods, didn't you?"

Bloody Bones blinked at me. "They were wicked children."

''If you get out of here, will you kill more wicked children?''

Bloody Bones looked at me, blinked, then said, ''It is what I do. What I am.''

I fired before I could think. If it moved first, I was dead. The bullet took it between the eyes. It staggered backwards, but didn't go down.

''*Ma petite*, the crosses, or I cannot help you.'' Jean-Claude's voice was a harsh whisper.

I slipped the cross inside my shirt; a second later Larry followed suit. The room was suddenly darker, colder with just the candlelight. Bloody Bones raced forward, and it was just a blur. I fired into it and didn't know if I hit it or not.

The sword swung out to meet me, and Jean-Claude was suddenly there hanging onto the arm, sending it off balance. Larry moved up beside me, and we both fired into the fey's chest.

It shook Jean-Claude off, sending him skittering into a wall. Larry and I stood our ground, shoulder to shoulder. I saw the sword coming like a blur of silver, and knew I couldn't get out of the way in time.

Xavier was suddenly in front of me, the strange sword blocking Bloody Bones' blade. The steel blade stopped an inch from my face. Xavier's sword was notched where the steel had bit into it. The strange sword shoved upward through Bloody Bones' chest. The fairie bellowed, slicing at Xavier, but he was in too close for the fairie's giant sword.

Bloody Bones collapsed to its knees. Xavier twisted the sword as if hunting for the heart. He jerked the sword out in a wash of gore. The fairie collapsed on its stomach, shrieking. It tried to raise itself. I pressed the barrel of the Browning against its skull and fired as fast as I could. From point-blank range you didn't need to aim. Larry moved up beside me and fired. We emptied the clips into it, and it was still breathing. Xavier drove the sword through its back, pinning it to the floor. Its chest rose and fell, struggling for air.

I switched the Firestar and changed its clip to nonsilver. Three shots more, and as if a critical mass had been reached, the head exploded in a rush of bone and blood and thicker, wetter things.

Xavier was on its back when it blew. We stood there covered in bloody brains. Xavier drew the sword out of its back. The sword came out notched, dented from contact with bone. We stood there by the dead giant, the two of us isolated in one clear moment of understanding.

''The sword's cold iron, isn't it?'' I asked.

''Yes,'' he said. The pupils of his eyes were scarlet as a cherry, not the blood color of an albino, but truly red. Humans didn't have eyes like that.

''You're fey,'' I said.

''Don't be silly. The fairie can't become vampires, everyone knows that.''

I stared at him, and shook my head. ''You tampered with Magnus's spell. You did this to him.''

''He did this to himself,'' Xavier said.

''Did you help Bloody Bones kill the teenagers, the children, or did you just give him the sword?''

''I fed him my victims when I grew tired of them.''

I had eight shots left in the Firestar. Maybe he saw the thought move behind my eyes. ''Neither lead nor silver bullets will harm me. I am proof against both.''

''Where's Jeff Quinlan?''

''He's down in the basement.''

''Get him.''

''I don't think so.'' And suddenly there was sound again, movement again, besides us. He'd bespelled me, and bad things had been happening while I'd been caught.

Jason was coughing blood on the carpet. If he'd been human, I'd have said he was dying. Being a lycanthrope, he might live to see morning. One of the vampires had hurt him badly. I didn't know which one.

Jean-Claude was lying under a pile of vampires made up of Ellie, Kissa, Bettina, and Pallas. His voice came out in a thundering yell, echoing through the room. It was impressive, but not enough. ''Do not do it, *ma petite*.''

Janos stood near the throne with Larry. They'd tied his hands behind his back with one of the cords that held the drapes. A piece of cloth was shoved in his mouth. Janos had one pale spider hand around Larry's neck.

Serephina was propped on her throne, black blood pouring out of her. I'd never seen anyone lose so much blood so quickly. Her chest was torn open so wide I had a glimpse of a frantically beating heart.

''What do you want?'' I asked.

''No, *ma petite*.'' Jean-Claude struggled to move and couldn't. ''It is a trap.''

''Tell me something I don't know.''

''She wants you, necromancer,'' Janos said.

I let that sink in for a minute. ''Why?''

''You have stolen her immortal blood from her. You will take its place.''

''It wasn't immortal,'' I said. ''We proved that.''

''It was powerful, necromancer, as you are powerful. She will drink you up and live.''

''What about me?''

''You will live forever, Anita, forever.''

I let the ''forever'' part go; I knew better.

''She will take you and kill him anyway,'' Jean-Claude said.

He was probably right, but what could I do? ''She let the girls go.''

''You do not know that, *ma petite*. Have you seen them alive?'' He had a point.

''Necromancer.'' Janos's voice jerked me back to him. Serephina lay propped on the throne beside him. Blood had drenched the white dress, turning it black, plastering it to her thin body.

''Come, necromancer,'' Janos said. ''Come now, or the human suffers.''

I started forward and Jean-Claude yelled, ''No!''

Janos slashed outward with one pale spider-hand, just above Larry's body. Larry's white shirt sliced open, and blood soaked it. He couldn't scream with the gag, but if Janos hadn't held him, he'd have fallen.

''Drop all your weapons and come to us, necromancer.''

''*Ma petite*, do not do this. I beg you.''

"I have to do this, Jean-Claude. You know that."

"*She* knows that," he said.

I looked at him, struggling helplessly under three times his body weight in vampires. It should have been ridiculous, but it wasn't.

"She doesn't just want you for herself. She doesn't want me to have you. She will take you to spite me."

"I invited you to come play this time, remember?" I said. "It's my party."

I walked towards Janos. I tried not to look behind him, not to see what else I was moving towards.

"*Ma petite*, don't do this. You are an acknowledged master. She cannot take you by force. You must consent. Refuse."

I just shook my head and kept going.

"Your weapons first, necromancer," Janos said.

I laid both guns on the floor.

Larry was shaking his head furiously. He made little protesting noises. He struggled, falling to his knees. Janos had to release his grip on his neck to keep from strangling him.

"Now your knives," Janos said.

"I don't . . ."

"Do not try to lie to us here and now."

He had a point. I put the knives on the floor.

My heart was hammering so hard I could barely breathe. I stopped just in front of Larry. I stared into Larry's blue eyes. I pulled out the gag, somebody's silk scarf.

"Don't do it. God, Anita, don't do it. Not for me. Please!"

Fresh slashes cut his shirt; more blood flowed. He gasped, but didn't scream.

I looked up at Serephina. "You said this slashing only works with an aura of power."

"He has his own aura," Janos said.

"Let him go. Let them all go, and I'll do it."

"Do not do this for me, *ma petite*."

"I'm doing it for Larry; doesn't cost any more to throw everybody in."

Janos glanced at Serephina. She was slumped to one side, eyes half-closed. "Come to me, Anita. Let me touch your arm, and they will release them all, my word, one master to another."

"Anita, no!" Larry struggled not to get away but to come after me.

Janos slashed his hand through the air, and the sleeve of Larry's jacket flew with blood. Larry screamed.

"Stop it," I said. "Stop it." I stalked towards him. "Don't touch him again. Don't ever touch him again."

I spit the last words in his face, staring up into his dead eyes and feeling nothing. A hand brushed my arm, and I jerked, gasping. I'd let anger carry me those last few steps. What I was about to do scared me too much to think about it.

Serephina had lost a glove. It was her bare hand that encircled my wrist, not too tight, not painful in the least. I stared at her hand on my arm and couldn't talk past the beating of my own heart.

"Release him," she said.

The minute Janos let him go, Larry tried to come to me. Janos gave him a casual slap that knocked him to the floor and sent him skidding back a couple of yards.

I stayed frozen with her hand on my arm. For one awful moment I thought they'd killed him, but he moaned and tried to get back up.

I glanced past Larry, and met Jean-Claude's eyes. He'd been after me for years; now here I was letting another master vamp sink her fangs into me.

Serephina jerked me to my knees, squeezing the bones of my arm so hard I thought she'd broken it. The pain brought me up to meet her eyes. They were solid perfect brown, so dark they were nearly black. Those eyes smiled at me gently.

I smelled my mother's perfume, her hair spray, her skin. I shook my head. It was a lie. It was all a lie. I couldn't breathe. She knelt over me, and when her face came forward it was my mother's thick, black hair that fell against my cheek.

"No! It's not real."

"It can be as real as you want it to be, Niña." I stared up into those eyes, and I fell down the long black tunnel of her eyes. I fell towards that tiny flame. I reached towards it. It would warm my flesh, comfort my heart. It would be all things, all people, everything to me.

Distant and dreamlike I heard Jean-Claude scream my name, "Anita!" But it was too late. Her fire warmed me, made me feel whole. The pain was such a small price to pay.

The black tunnel collapsed behind me until there was nothing but the darkness and the flicker of Serephina's eyes.

39

I dreamed. I was very small. Small enough that I fit all in my mother's lap, only my feet stuck off the edge of her knees. When she wrapped her arms around me I was so safe, so sure that nothing could ever hurt me as long as Mommy was here. I laid my head against her chest. I could hear the beat of her heart against my ear. A strong, sure rhythm that pounded louder and louder against my face.

The sound woke me. But I wasn't awake. The darkness was so complete it was like being blind. I lay in my mother's arms in the dark. I'd fallen asleep in bed with her and Dad. Her heart pounded against my ear, and the rhythm was wrong. Mommy had a heart murmur. The beat of her heart was a fraction of a second slow, a hesitation, then two quick thumps to catch up. The heart beating against my skin was as regular as a clock.

I tried to raise up, off her, and bumped my head against something hard and firm. My hands slid over the body that I was pinned to. I touched a satin dress with smooth jewels sewn into it. I lay there in the absolute dark and tried to roll off her. I slid into the crook of her arm. Her naked flesh slid along my bare shoulders, boneless as the dead, but her heart filled the darkness even with me struggling not to touch her.

Our bodies were molded against each other. It was not a coffin built for two. Sweat broke out on my skin in a rush. The dark was suddenly chokingly close, hot. I couldn't breathe. I tried to roll onto my back. Tried to roll off her, and I couldn't. There wasn't room.

Every small struggle made her boneless body move, jiggling the soft, loose flesh. I couldn't smell my mother's perfume anymore. I smelled old blood, and a stale, neck-ruffling smell that I'd smelled before. Vampires.

I screamed and tried to do a push-up to get some distance, and the lid moved. I stayed on my arms, shoving my back into the satin and wood. The lid slammed backwards, and I was suddenly straddling her body, my upper body raised in a half push-up.

Dim light edged the lines in her face. The careful makeup looked wrong, like a badly made-up corpse. I scrambled out of the coffin, nearly falling to the floor.

Serephina's coffin sat on the stage in the Bloody Bones bar and grill. Ellie lay curled at the base of the stage. I stepped around her, half-expecting her to grab at my ankles, but she did not move. Not even to breathe. She was the newly dead, and with the sun up she was truly dead.

Serephina wasn't breathing either, but her heart was pounding, beating, alive. Why? For my comfort? Because of my touch? Hell, I didn't know. If I got out, I'd ask Jean-Claude. If he was alive. If she had kept her word.

Janos lay in the middle of the floor, on his back, hands folded on his chest. Bettina and Pallas were snuggled up against him, one on either side. A coffin lay on the floor. I had no way of knowing what time of day it was. I would have bet that Serephina didn't have to sleep all day. I was getting out of here.

"I told her you wouldn't sleep all day."

The voice jerked me around. Magnus was behind the bar, leaning his elbows on its smooth surface. He was slicing a lime with a very sharp-looking knife. He looked at me with his green-blue eyes. His long auburn hair spilled around his face. He straightened up suddenly, stretching his back. He was wearing one of those frilly shirts that you rent for wearing with a tux. The shirt was pale green and brought out the green in his eyes.

"You scared me," I said.

He leaped over the bar easily, landing on his feet light as a cat. He smiled, and it wasn't a friendly smile. "I didn't think you scared that easy."

I took a step back. "You recovered damn fast."

"I drank immortal blood; it helps." He stared at me with a heat in his eyes that I didn't like at all.

"What's wrong with you, Magnus?"

He swept his long hair to one side. He pulled the collar of his shirt until the first two buttons popped, spinning to the floor. There was a new bite mark on the smooth skin of his neck.

I took another step back towards the door. "So what?" I ran my hand over my neck and found my own bite marks. "So we've got a matching pair. So what?"

"She forbade me to drink. She said you'd sleep all day. That she'd keep you sleeping all day, but I thought she'd underestimated you."

I took another step towards the door.

"Don't, Anita."

"Why not?" But I was afraid I knew the answer.

"Serephina told me to keep you here until she wakes." He looked at me, and it was a sad, woebegone expression. "Just have a seat. I'll fix you something to eat."

"No, thanks."

"Don't run, Anita. Don't make me hurt you."

"Who's in the other coffin?" I asked.

The question seemed to surprise him. He let his hair fall back over his neck. The shirt gaped open over his chest. I didn't remember noticing his chest this much last time, or the way his hair swept over his shoulders. The ointment must have worn off.

"Stop it, Magnus."

''Stop what?''

''Glamor won't work on me.''

''Glamor would be a more pleasant alternative,'' he said.

''Who's in the coffin?''

''Xavier and the boy.''

I ran for the door. He was suddenly behind me, impossibly fast, but I'd seen faster. Most of them just happened to be dead. I didn't try to open the door. I turned into his body, and it surprised him. He fell into a shoulder roll almost textbook perfect. I tried to throw him three feet under the floor, everything I had.

He lay stunned for a second. I flung open the door. The spring sunlight poured in and fell on Janos and his women. Janos's face twisted away from the light. I didn't wait to see more. I ran.

Screams followed me out into the sunlight. I heard the door slam behind me, but didn't look back. I hit the gravel parking lot running with everything I had. I heard him pounding up behind me. I wasn't going to outrun him. I waited until the last second, stopped running, and kicked him. He saw it coming and dived under it, taking my other leg out from under me, sending us both to the ground. I threw a handful of gravel at his face, and he hit me in the jaw with his fist. There is a frozen moment after a really good shot to the face. A moment of shock, of paralysis where all you can do is blink. Magnus's face appeared over me. He didn't ask if I was alright; that had been the point. He picked me up and flung me over his shoulders. I got a nice view of the ground about the time I was able to move again.

I walked my hands up his back, trying to get enough leverage to swing a two-handed grip at his shoulders. I let him brace my lower body, but before I could try it, he kicked the door open and tossed me to the floor, none too gently. He leaned against the door and locked it.

''You just had to do it the hard way, didn't you?''

I got to my feet and backed away from him, which took me closer to the vampires. Not an improvement. I backed towards the bar. There had to be a back door. ''I don't know any other way, Magnus.''

He took a deep breath and pushed away from the door. ''It's going to be a long day, then.''

I put a hand on the smooth wood of the bar. ''Yeah,'' I said. The half-sliced lime and the knife lay just a few inches away. I stared at Magnus, trying very hard not to look at the knife again. To not draw attention to it. Which isn't nearly as easy as it sounds.

His eyes flicked to the knife. He smiled and shook his head. ''Don't do it, Anita.''

I put my hands on the bar and pushed myself up on it. I heard him coming, but I didn't look back. Never look back; something is always gaining on you. I grabbed the knife and rolled over the bar at the same time. Magnus's face appeared above the bar too fast. I wasn't ready. All I could do was look up at him with the knife gripped in my hand. If he'd been just a little slower, I'd have stabbed him in the throat, or that had been the plan.

Magnus crouched on the bar, staring down at me. His aquamarine eyes glittered. Lights and colors played in them, reflecting things that were not there. He stayed on the bar above me, swaying slightly on the balls of his feet, one hand on the bar for balance. His hair had fallen forward, trailing thick strands across his face. He was going all feral on me, like he had at the mound. But this time he wasn't trying to be one of the good guys. I expected him to leap down on me, but he didn't. Of course, he wasn't fighting me, he was just trying to keep me from leaving.

I glanced at what was under the bar. Liquor in bottles, clean glasses, a tub of ice, some clean towels, napkins. None of it looked helpful. Shit. I got slowly to my feet, back pressed to the wall, as far from Magnus as I could get. I began to inch my way towards the side of the bar towards the door. Magnus paced me, sidling on the bar, making the awkward movement graceful.

He was faster than me, stronger than me, but I was armed. The knife was good quality, made for slicing food, not people, but a good knife is a good knife. It's versatile. I had to force myself not to squeeze too tight on the handle, to relax. I'd get out of this. I would. My eyes flicked to Serephina's open coffin. I thought I saw her breathe.

Magnus jumped me. His body slammed into mine, and I drove the knife into his stomach. He grunted, and his weight rode me to the floor. I drove the knife in hilt-deep. His fist closed over my hand, and he rolled off me, taking the knife with him.

I scrambled around the edge of the bar on all fours. Magnus was there, yanking me to my feet by one arm. Blood had soaked the front of his shirt. He raised the bloody knife in front of my face. "That hurt," he said. He laid the edge of the blade against the side of my throat. It felt like my pulse was jumping out to meet the blade. He started backing up, pulling me with him.

"Where are we going?" I asked.

"You'll see," he said. I didn't like that he wouldn't tell me.

His feet bumped against Ellie's body. I could glimpse Serephina's coffin behind him, if I rolled my eyes. Hard to move your head when a knife's at your throat. He pulled on my arm, and I didn't go. I leaned back on my heels, just a little, aware of the knife, but I was more afraid of Serephina than any blade.

"Come on, Anita."

"Not until you tell me what we're doing." I spoke very carefully around the knife.

Ellie lay motionless, boneless, dead at our feet. Magnus's blood dropped onto her empty face. If it had been one of the others, they might have licked the blood off even in their slumber, but Ellie was well and truly dead. She was the newly risen, empty, waiting for her "personality" to rebuild, if it ever did. I'd seen vamps that never recovered. Never became close to the human being they'd once been.

"I'm going to put you in the coffin and lock it until Serephina wakes up."

"No," I said.

Magnus squeezed my arm like his fingers were searching for the bone. If he didn't break it, it would be a hell of a bruise. I didn't cry out, but it was an effort. "I can hurt you, Anita, in all sorts of ways. Just get in."

"Nothing you can do to me scares me as much as getting in that coffin again."

I meant it. Which meant unless he was really going to kill me, the knife didn't work anymore. I turned my head into the blade. He was forced to move it away from my skin before I drove it into myself.

I stared at him from about a foot away, and saw something in his eyes that I hadn't seen before. He was afraid.

"Bloody Bones died because he shared your mortality. Were you harder to kill before, Magnus? No immortality to draw from, is that it?"

"You are just too damn smart for your own good," he said softly.

I smiled. "Mortal just like the rest of us; poor baby."

He smiled, a quick baring of teeth. "I can still take more damage than you can dish out."

"If you really believed that, you wouldn't be putting me back in the coffin."

His hand moved in a blur of speed that was almost vampire-quick. He hit my arm, and it took a handful of seconds to realize he'd cut me. Blood welled from the cut and dripped down my arm. He switched his grip from my upper arm to my wrist, faster than I could take advantage of it.

I watched the blood drip down my arm towards my elbow. It wasn't much of a cut, might not even leave a scar; of course, on my left arm, who could tell? "Couldn't you have cut the right arm? I haven't got nearly as many scars on that one."

He made one quick slice downward and opened my right arm from my shoulder damn near to my elbow. "Always happy to oblige a lady."

The slice hurt and was deeper than the first one. Me and my big mouth. Blood ran down my arm in a thin crimson line. Blood on my left arm trembled on my elbow and fell with a soft *plop* onto Ellie's cheek. The blood slid down her skin, into her mouth. A tingle of magic went up my spine. I held my breath. I could feel it. I could feel the body at our feet.

It was broad daylight. I shouldn't have been able to raise even a zombie, let alone a vampire. It was impossible; yet I could feel the body feel the magic. I knew it was mine if I wanted it. I wanted it.

"What's wrong?" Magnus jerked my arm, bringing my eyes back to his face. I'd been staring at the vampire. Hadn't meant to, it was just so damn unexpected.

I could feel the magic just out of reach, almost there. But how to push it over the edge? How? I smiled at Magnus. "You planning to just whittle me down until I get in the coffin?"

"I could."

"The only way I'm going in that coffin is dead, Magnus, and Serephina doesn't want me dead." I stepped into him; he started to move back, but forced himself to stand his ground. Our bodies were nearly pressed against each other. Great. I ran my hand under his shirt, along his bare skin.

Magnus's eyes widened. "What are you up to?"

I smiled, and traced the trail of fresh blood upward to the wound. I trailed the edge of the wound, and he made a small sound like it had hurt. I smoothed my one free hand over his skin, smearing his blood across his flesh like finger paints.

"You saw the murder scene when you touched me and still wanted to have sex with me, remember?"

He took a breath, and it trembled when he let it out between his lips.

I drew my blood-coated hand out from under his shirt. I held it up to him, let him see it. His breath came just a little quicker. I knelt, slowly; he didn't let go, he didn't put down the knife, but he didn't stop me. I smeared the blood on Ellie's mouth. The magic flared, sparked down my skin like cool fire. It crawled up my arm and onto Magnus.

''Shit!'' Magnus swung the knife at me.

I blocked his wrist with my arm and came up under him, driving up from my knees. He was balanced across my shoulders, but he still had the knife. I flung him on top of Ellie.

I stood over him, breathing hard. ''Ellie, rise.''

The vampire's eyes flew open wide. Magnus started to push away from her.

''Grab him,'' I said.

Ellie wrapped her arms around his waist and held on. He stabbed her with the knife, and she screamed. God help me, she screamed. Zombies didn't scream.

I ran for the door.

Magnus came after me, dragging Ellie behind him. He was moving faster than I'd thought he would, but not fast enough. I flung open the door, and a long bar of sunlight spilled in through the door. I was a step out the door when the screaming started. I glanced back; I couldn't help it. Ellie was on fire. Magnus tried to loosen her arms, screaming. But nothing holds on like the dead.

I ran out into the parking lot.

''Niña, don't go.''

The voice stopped me at the edge of the parking lot. I looked back. Magnus had dragged himself out the door and onto the gravel. Ellie was burning white hot. Magnus's shirt and hair were burning.

I screamed, ''Go back, you son of a bitch!'' But the same voice that kept me pinned to the edge of the parking lot kept him coming out into the light.

The voice came again. ''Come back to bed, Anita. You're tired. You must rest.''

I was suddenly tired, so tired. I felt every cut, every bruise. She would make it all better. She would touch me with her cool hands and make it all better.

Magnus collapsed in the middle of the driveway, shrieking. The vampire was melting into him, burning him alive. Sweet Jesus.

He reached one hand out to me. He screamed, ''Help me!'' The vampire was melting into his flesh, eating it away.

I ran. I ran with Serephina's voice whispering in my ear: ''Niña, Mother misses you.''

40

I flagged a car down on the highway. I was covered in dried blood, cut, scraped, bruised, and still an elderly couple picked me up. Who says there are no more good Samaritans? They wanted to take me to the police, and I let them.

The nice policemen took one look at me and asked if I needed an ambulance. I said no, and could they page Special Agent Bradford, and tell him it was Anita Blake.

They tried to get me to go to the hospital, but there was no time. It was mid-afternoon. We had to move before dark. I asked the police to send a two-man car to make sure that no one moved the coffins. I told them there might be a hurt man in the parking lot and if he was still there to call an ambulance, but under no circumstances go inside the place.

Everybody nodded and agreed with me. Most of the cops in the area had been through Serephina's house last night and today. The cops told me Kirkland had brought the cops back to the vampire's lair after they took me. It took me a second to realize that Kirkland was Larry. Which meant Serephina had kept her word and let them go. The relief at knowing for sure that Larry was alive made me weak-kneed, and I was wobbly enough as it was.

The cops had found over a dozen bodies buried in the basement of Serephina's house. She should have buried them in the woods. For all I knew, she'd raised their ghosts. I didn't know. It didn't matter. All that mattered was that we had a warrant of execution, and the cops were listening to me today.

They sat me in an interrogation room with a cup of black coffee, thick enough to walk on, and a blanket to wrap around me. I was shivering and couldn't seem to stop.

Bradford came in and sat down across from me. He stared at me with eyes that were just a little too wide. ''The locals say you found the master vampire's lair.''

I laughed, and it came out wrong, almost like a sob. ''I wouldn't say I found Serephina's lair. More like I woke up in it.'' I raised the coffee to my mouth and had to stop in mid-motion. My hands were shaking so badly I was about to slosh coffee onto the table. I took a deep breath, blew it out, and concentrated on taking a drink of coffee. Just concentrated on the simple physical movement. It helped. I got coffee, and calmer at the same time.

"You need to go to the hospital," Bradford said.

"I need Serephina dead."

"We've got warrants for all of them. All the vampires involved. How do you want to do it?"

"Burn them out. Block off everything but the front door. If Magnus is inside, he'll come out."

"Magnus Bouvier?" he asked.

"Yeah." There was something about the way he said it that I didn't like.

"The cops found what's left of him in the parking lot. It looks like something melted the lower half of his body. Would you know anything about that?" He looked at me very steadily when he asked it.

I took another careful sip of coffee, and met his eyes without blinking. What was I supposed to say? "The vampires were controlling him. He was supposed to keep me in the bar until nightfall. Maybe they punished him for failing." What I'd done to Magnus and Ellie was enough to earn me a death sentence. I wasn't admitting that to the Feds.

"The vampires punished him?" He made it a question.

"Yeah."

He looked at me for a long time, then nodded and changed the subject. "Won't the vampires try to make a break when the fire starts?"

"Sunlight or fire," I said. "Just a choice of how well done you want your vampires to be." I finished the last of the coffee in my cup.

"Your protege, Mr. Kirkland, said you were kidnapped from the graveyard. Is that your story, too?"

"It happens to be the truth, Agent Bradford." It was the truth as far as it went. Omission is a wonderful thing.

He smiled and shook his head. "You are hiding more shit from me than you're telling me."

I stared at him until the smile wilted around the edges. "Truth is a mixed blessing, Agent Bradford, don't you think?"

He stared at me for a moment, then nodded. "Maybe, Ms. Blake, maybe."

I called the hotel, and no one answered in Larry's room. I tried my room, and got Larry there. There was a moment of stunned silence when he realized it was me.

"Anita, oh my God, oh my God. Are you alright? Where are you? I'll come get you."

"I'm at the police station in town. I'm alright, sort of. I need you to bring me some clothes to change into. The ones I have on smell like vampire. We're going after Serephina."

Another silence. "When?"

"Now, today."

"I'll be right there."

"Larry?"

"I'll bring the guns and the knives, and an extra cross."

"Thanks."

"I've never been so glad to hear anybody's voice in my entire life," he said.

"Yeah," I said. "Get here soon. Wait, Larry."

"You need something else?" he said.

"Are Jean-Claude and Jason alright?"

"Yeah. Jason's in the hospital, but he'll live. Jean-Claude's in the bedroom asleep. After Serephina bit you, she hit Jean-Claude with some kind of power, energy. I felt it, and it was awesome. She knocked him out and left. The others went with her."

Everyone was alive, or as alive as they had started out. It was more than I'd hoped for. "Great; I'll see you soon." I hung up the phone and had a horrible urge to cry, but I fought it off. I was afraid if I started to cry I wouldn't be able to stop. I couldn't have hysterics just yet.

As agent on site, Bradford was in charge. Special Agent Bradley Bradford, yes Bradley Bradford, seemed to think I knew what I was doing. Nothing like getting almost killed to give you credentials. For once, badge or no badge, nobody was arguing with me. A refreshing change, that.

I did not hug Larry when he brought my clothes; he hugged me. I pushed away sooner than I wanted to, because I wanted to collapse into his arms in tears. To just let a pair of friendly arms hold me while I melted down. Later, later.

A huge bruise had blossomed on the side of his face from jaw to mid-temple. It looked like he'd been hit by a baseball bat. He was lucky Janos hadn't broken his jaw.

Larry had brought me blue jeans, a red polo shirt, jogging socks, my white Nikes, an extra cross from my suitcase, the silver knives, the Firestar complete with inner pants holster, and the Browning and its shoulder holster. He'd forgotten a bra, but hey, except for that it was perfect.

The wrist sheaths stung going over the cuts, but it felt wonderful to be armed again. I didn't try to hide the guns. The cops knew who I was, and I wasn't fooling any of the bad guys.

Barely two hours after I'd crawled out of Serephina's coffin, we pulled up in front of Bloody Bones. There were ambulances, and more cops than you could shake a stick at. Local cops, state cops, federal cops; it was a smorgasbord of policemen. A fire truck plus fire emergency services completed the official list. Oh, Larry and me.

With Magnus dead, Serephina and company were unguarded. Not helpless. Oh, no. Nothing this side of Hell would have gotten me inside that building voluntarily. But there were alternatives.

The gas truck pulled around to the back and busted out a window. I watched them snake the hose into the window of the back door and turn on the juice.

I stood there in the warm sunlight, a cool breeze playing on my skin, and whispered, "May you rot in Hell."

"Did you say something?" Larry asked.

I shook my head. "Nothing important."

The hose shivered to life, and the sharp, sweet smell of gasoline filled the air.

I felt her wake up. I felt her eyes open wide in the dark. I breathed in the sweet smell of gasoline, felt my hands gripping the coffin edges.

I put my hands over my eyes. "Oh, God."

Larry touched my shoulder. "What is it?"

I kept my hands pressed to my face. "Take the guns, now."

"What . . ."

"Do it!" My hands came down and I looked at him. I looked at his familiar face, and Serephina saw him, too.

She whispered, "Kill him."

I ripped the knives out of the sheaths and let them fall to the ground. I started backing up towards the cops. I needed people with guns around me, right now.

The voice in my head said, "Anita, what are you doing to your mother? You don't want to hurt me. Niña, help Mommy."

"Oh, God." I ran and nearly collided with Bradford.

"Help me, Niña. Help me!"

My hand closed on the Browning. I balled my hands into fists at my side. "Bradford, disarm me now. Please."

He stared at me, but he took the guns from their holsters. "What's wrong, Blake?"

"Cuffs, you got cuffs?"

"Yeah."

I held my hands out to him. "Use them." My voice sounded squeezed, my throat so tight I couldn't breathe.

I smelled Hypnotique perfume, tasted my mother's lipstick on my mouth. The cuffs snapped into place. I jerked away from him, stared at the handcuffs. I opened my mouth to say "Take them off," and closed it.

I could feel my mother's hair tickling my face.

"I smell perfume," Larry said.

I looked at him with wide eyes. I couldn't speak, I couldn't move. I didn't trust myself to do anything at that moment.

"Oh, my God," Larry said. "You're going to feel her burn."

I just looked at him.

"What can I do?"

"Help me." My voice was squeezed down to a whisper.

"What's happening to her?" Bradford asked.

"Serephina's trying to get Anita to help save her."

"The vampire's awake in there?" he asked.

"Yes," I said.

Serephina was out of her coffin. The full skirt of her ball gown brushed the edges of the door that led to the kitchen. She couldn't go closer, because there was a spill of daylight from the window. Gasoline was pouring across the floor towards her.

"Anita, help Mommy."

"It's a lie," I said.

"What's a lie?" Bradford said.

I shook my head.

''Anita, help me, you don't want me to die. You don't want me to die, not when you can save me.''

I collapsed to my knees, cuffed hands digging into the gravel of the parking lot. ''Stop the gasoline.''

Larry knelt beside me. ''Why?''

It was a good question. Serephina had a good answer. ''Jeff Quinlan is in there. He's inside.''

''Shit,'' Larry said. He looked up at Bradford. ''We can't torch the place. There's a kid inside.''

''Stop the gas,'' Bradford said. He walked away from us, towards the truck, motioning them off.

And I felt a surge of triumph from Serephina. It was a lie. Xavier had brought Jeff over last night. There was nothing alive in that building.

I gripped Larry's arm with my cuffed hands. ''Larry, it's a lie. She's lying to me. Through me. Get me in the back of a squad car, now, and torch the place.''

He stared at me. ''But if Jeff . . .''

''Don't argue with me, just do it!'' I screamed it, burying my face between my arms, trying to ignore the voice in my head.

I could taste Hypnotique on my tongue. It was too much. Serephina was scared.

Larry called Bradford back, and they half-carried me to a marked car. I started to struggle when they tried to shove me in the back, but I did my best not to fight, and they closed the door. I was in a metal and glass cage. I gripped my fingers through the mesh in front of me, digging it into my skin until it hurt. But even pain didn't help.

The gasoline was everywhere, soaking into everything. Serephina was choking on it. ''Niña, don't do this. Don't hurt your Mommy. Don't lose me again.''

I started rocking back and forth, hands digging into the wire. Back and forth, back and forth. It'd be over soon. It'd be over soon.

I felt a gentle touch on my face, a memory so real it made me turn and look for someone. ''My death will be as real, Anita.''

Somebody lit it. The flames roared to life, and I screamed before they hit her. I slammed my cuffed hands against the glass and screamed, ''Nooo!''

Heat washed over her, crumbled the cloth of her dress like a melting flower, and ate her flesh.

I pounded my hands against the glass until I couldn't feel them anymore. I had to help her. I had to go to her. I fell to my back and kicked the window. I kicked it and kicked it, feeling the shock all the way up my back. I screamed and kicked the glass, and it cracked. The glass cracked and fell outward.

She was screaming my name. ''Anita! Anita!''

I was halfway out the window before somebody tried to grab me. I let them grab my arm, but pushed my legs free of the window. I had to get to her; nothing else mattered. Nothing.

I fell to the ground with someone holding my arm. I got halfway up and threw them in a shoulder roll onto the ground. I ran for the fire. I could feel the heat now, rippling along my skin. I could feel the heat inside eating us alive.

Someone tackled me, and I beat at them with my hands made into one fist.

The hands let go, and I scrambled to my feet. Shouting, and someone else holding me. He lifted me off the ground, arms wrapped around my waist, pinning my arms. I kicked backwards, and hit his knees. The arms loosened, but there were more arms. More hands. Someone lay on top of me. A hand the size of my head pressed the side of my face against the rocks. Hands pinned my hands against the rocks, his full body weight on just my wrists. Someone was sitting on my legs.

"Niña! Niña!"

I screamed with her. I screamed while I choked on the smell of burning hair and Hypnotique bath powder. I saw the needle coming in from the side, and started to cry, "No, no! Mommy! Mommy!"

The needle sank home, and darkness swallowed the world. A darkness that smelled like burning flesh, and tasted like lipstick, and blood.

41

I spent a few days in the hospital. Bruises, cuts, some stitches, but mainly the second-degree burns on my back and arms. The burns weren't that bad; there wouldn't be any scarring. The doctors just couldn't figure out how I'd gotten burned. I didn't feel like explaining, mainly because I wasn't sure I could.

Jason had broken ribs, a punctured lung, and other internal damage. He healed perfectly and in record time. There are benefits to being a lycanthrope.

Jean-Claude healed. His face was once again that perfection that had attracted Serephina to him so long ago.

Stirling's company rebought the land from Dorcas Bouvier, and made her wealthy. With Bloody Bones dead, she can leave the land. She's free.

The Quinlans are still suing me. Bert has lawyers that promise to keep us out of court, though I'm not sure how. If I'd walked the house personally, checked every inch of it myself, maybe . . . Hell, even I might not have protected the doggie door. Maybe I do deserve to be sued. I told the Quinlans Ellie was dead. They had to take my word for it; there wasn't anything left of Ellie to prove it. When vampires burn, they burn; no dental records, no nothing. Jeff was well and truly dead, too. Both their children were lost to them. It had to be somebody's fault; why not mine?

I'd raised a vampire like a zombie, which wasn't possible. Necromancers were supposed to be able to control all types of undead. But that was legend, not real. Right?

Serephina is dead, but the nightmares live on. The nightmares are tangled with the real memories of my mother's death. They are a bitch. For the first time in my life, I'm having insomnia.

What to do with the two men in my life? How the hell do I know? In Richard's arms, breathing in the warmth of his body, is the closest I've ever found to my mother's arms. It isn't the same, because I know that though Richard would give his life for me, even that might not be enough. When I was a child, I believed it would be. There is no real safety. Innocence lost can never be regained. But sometimes with Richard I want to believe in it again.

There is nothing comforting about Jean-Claude's arms. He doesn't make me feel safe in the least. He's like some forbidden pleasure that you know eventually you'll regret. I've decided not to wait; I'm regretting it now, but I'm still seeing him.

Somehow Jean-Claude has crossed that line that a handful of other vampires have crossed. I don't think of him as a monster anymore.

God have mercy on my soul.

THE KILLING DANCE

To Paty Cockrum,
fan, friend, fine artist.
You should see the pictures
she sends me of Jean-Claude.
She really is
the voice of temptation.

Acknowledgments

Ricia Mainhardt, my agent, who came up with the title.

Marion Stensgard who answered my questions.

The Wild Canid Survival and Research Center (Wolf Sanctuary) for letting me use their library.

Bonnee Pierson, who helped with a very different kind of research.

The Alternate Historians: Rett Macpherson who went above and beyond the call of duty for research, N. L. Drew who heard parts of this book over the phone, Tom Drennan, whose book is finally ready to make the rounds, Mark Sumner who says everything will be all right, even when he doesn't know, Marella Sands who reminded me we're supposed to be having fun, and Deborah Millitello who holds my hands.

My husband, Gary, who always tells me the truth whether I want to hear it or not.

Sarah Sumner for bitching sessions.

Joan-Marie Knappenberger who let me use her house.

The Saint Louis Bread Company for letting me take up a table for hours at a time.

The newsletter everyone's been asking about is here. Write to my publisher and I'll send you one. Find out where I'll be. Find out what Anita and the gang are doing. Questions answered, mysteries solved.

1

The most beautiful corpse I'd ever seen was sitting behind my desk. Jean-Claude's white shirt gleamed in the light from the desk lamp. A froth of lace spilled down the front, peeking from inside his black velvet jacket. I stood behind him, my back to the wall, arms crossed over my stomach, which put my right hand comfortably close to the Browning Hi-Power in its shoulder holster. I wasn't about to draw on Jean-Claude. It was the other vampire I was worried about.

The desk lamp was the only light in the room. The vampire had requested the overheads be turned out. His name was Sabin, and he stood against the far wall, huddling in the dark. He was covered head to foot in a black, hooded cape. He looked like something out of an old Vincent Price movie. I'd never seen a real vampire dress like that.

The last member of our happy little group was Dominic Dumare. He sat in one of the client chairs. He was tall, thin, but not weak. His hands were large and strong, big enough to palm my face. He was dressed in a three-piece black suit, like a chauffeur except for the diamond stickpin in his tie. A beard and thin mustache lined the strong bones of his face.

When he'd entered my office, I'd felt him like a psychic wind tripping down my spine. I'd only encountered two other people who had that taste to them. One had been the most powerful voodoo priestess I'd ever met. The second had been the second most powerful voodoo priest I'd ever met. The woman was dead. The man worked for Animators, Inc., just like I did. But Dominic Dumare wasn't here to apply for a job.

''Ms. Blake, please be seated,'' Dumare said. ''Sabin finds it most offensive to sit when a lady is standing.''

I glanced behind him at Sabin. ''I'll sit down if he sits down,'' I said.

Dumare looked at Jean-Claude. He gave a gentle, condescending smile. ''Do you have such poor control over your human servant?''

I didn't have to see Jean-Claude's smile to know it was there. ''Oh, you are on your own with *ma petite*. She is my human servant, so declared before the council, but she answers to no one.''

''You seem proud of that,'' Sabin said. His voice was British and very upper crust.

''She is the Executioner and has more vampire kills than any other human. She is a necromancer of such power that you have traveled halfway around the world to consult her. She is my human servant without a mark to hold her to me. She dates me without the aid of vampire glamor. Why should I not be pleased?''

Listening to him talk you'd have thought it was all his own idea. Fact was, he'd tried his best to mark me, and I'd managed to escape. We were dating because he'd blackmailed me. Date him or he'd kill my other boyfriend. Jean-Claude had managed to make it all work to his advantage. Why was I not surprised?

''Until her death you cannot mark any other human,'' Sabin said. ''You have cut yourself off from a great deal of power.''

''I am aware of what I have done,'' Jean-Claude said.

Sabin laughed, and it was chokingly bitter. ''We all do strange things for love.''

I would have given a lot to see Jean-Claude's face at that moment. All I could see was his long black hair spilling over his jacket, black on black. His shoulders stiffened, hands sliding across the blotter on my desk. Then he went very still. That awful waiting stillness that only the old vampires have, as if, if they held still long enough, they would simply disappear.

''Is that what has brought you here, Sabin? Love?'' Jean-Claude's voice was neutral, empty.

Sabin's laughter rode the air like broken glass. It felt like the very sound of it hurt something deep inside me. I didn't like it.

''Enough games,'' I said, ''let's get it done.''

''Is she always this impatient?'' Dumare asked.

''Yes,'' Jean-Claude said.

Dumare smiled, bright and empty as a lightbulb. ''Did Jean-Claude tell you why we wished to see you?''

''He said Sabin caught some sort of disease from trying to go cold turkey.''

The vampire across the room laughed again, flinging it like a weapon across the room. ''Cold turkey, very good, Ms. Blake, very good.''

The laughter ate over me like small cutting blades. I'd never experienced anything like that from just a voice. In a fight, it would have been distracting. Heck, it was distracting now. I felt liquid slide down my forehead. I raised my left hand to it. My fingers came away smeared with blood. I drew the Browning and stepped away from the wall. I aimed it at the black figure across the room. ''He does that again, and I'll shoot him.''

Jean-Claude rose slowly from the chair. His power flowed over me like a cool wind, raising goose bumps on my arms. He raised one pale hand, gone nearly translucent with power. Blood flowed down that gleaming skin.

Dumare stayed in his chair, but he, too, was bleeding from a cut nearly identical to mine. Dumare wiped the blood away, still smiling. ''The gun will not be necessary,'' he said.

''You have abused my hospitality,'' Jean-Claude said. His voice filled the room with hissing echoes.

''There is nothing I can say to apologize,'' Sabin said. ''But I did not mean to do it. I am using so much of my power just to maintain myself that I do not have the control I once did.''

I moved slowly away from the wall, gun still pointed. I wanted to see Jean-Claude's face. I needed to see how badly he was hurt. I eased around the desk until I could see him from the corner of my eye. His face was untouched, flawless and gleaming like mother of pearl.

He raised his hand, one thin line of blood still trailing down. ''This is no accident.''

''Come into the light, my friend,'' Dumare said. ''You must let them see, or they will not understand.''

''I do not want to be seen.''

''You are very close to using up all my good will,'' Jean-Claude said.

''Mine, too,'' I added. I was hoping I could either shoot Sabin or put the gun down soon. Even a two-handed shooting stance is not meant to be maintained indefinitely. Your hands start to waver just a bit.

Sabin glided towards the desk. The black cloak spilled around his feet like a pool of darkness. All vampires were graceful, but this was ridiculous. I realized he wasn't walking at all. He was levitating inside that dark cloak.

His power flowed over my skin like icy water. My hands were suddenly steady once more. Nothing like having several hundred years worth of vampire coming at you to sharpen your nerves.

Sabin stopped on the far side of the desk. He was expending power just to move, just to be here, as if like a shark, if he stopped moving he'd die.

Jean-Claude glided around me. His power danced over my body, raising the hair at the back of my neck, making my skin tight. He stopped almost within reach of the other vampire. ''What has happened to you, Sabin?''

Sabin stood on the edge of the light. The lamp should have cast some light into the hood of his cloak, but it didn't. The inside of the hood was as smooth and black and empty as a cave. His voice came out of that nothingness. It made me jump.

''Love, Jean-Claude, love happened to me. My beloved grew a conscience. She said it was wrong to feed upon people. We were once people, after all. For love of her, I tried to drink cold blood. I tried animal blood. But it was not enough to sustain me.''

I stared into that darkness. I kept pointing the gun, but I was beginning to feel silly. Sabin didn't seem at all afraid of it, which was unnerving. Maybe he didn't care. That was also unnerving. ''She talked you into going vegetarian. Great,'' I said. ''You seem powerful enough.''

He laughed, and with the laughter, the shadows in his hood faded slowly, like a curtain lifting. He threw it back in one quick flourish.

I didn't scream, but I gasped and took a step back. I couldn't help myself. When I realized I'd done it, I stopped and made myself take back that step, meet his eyes. No flinching.

His hair was thick and straight and golden, falling like a shining curtain to his shoulders. But his skin . . . his skin had rotted away on half his face. It was like late-stage leprosy, but worse. The flesh was puss-filled, gangrenous, and should have stunk to high heaven. The other half of his face was still beautiful. The kind of face that medieval painters had borrowed for cherubim, a golden perfection. One crystalline blue eye rolled in its rotting socket as if in danger of spilling out onto his cheek. The other eye was secure and watched my face

"You can put up the gun, *ma petite*. It was an accident, after all," Jean-Claude said.

I lowered the Browning, but didn't put it up. It took more effort than was pretty to say calmly, "This happened because you stopped feeding off of humans?"

"We believe so," Dumare said.

I tore my gaze away from Sabin's ravaged face and looked back at Dominic. "You think I can help cure him of this?" I couldn't keep the disbelief out of my voice.

"I heard of your reputation in Europe."

I raised my eyebrows.

"No modesty, Ms. Blake. Among those of us who notice such things, you are gaining a certain notoriety."

Notoriety, not fame. Hmmm.

"Put the gun away, *ma petite*. Sabin has done all the—what is your word—grandstanding he will do tonight. Haven't you Sabin?"

"I fear so, it all seems to go so badly now."

I holstered the gun and shook my head. "I honestly don't have the faintest idea how to help you."

"If you knew how, would you help me?" Sabin asked.

I looked at him and nodded. "Yes."

"Even though I am a vampire and you are a vampire executioner."

"Have you done anything in this country that you need killing for?"

Sabin laughed. The rotting skin stretched, and a ligament popped with a wet snap. I had to look away. "Not yet, Ms. Blake, not yet." His face sobered quickly; the humor abruptly faded. "You school your face to show nothing, Jean-Claude, but I read the horror in your eyes."

Jean-Claude's skin had gone back to its usual milky perfection. His face was still lovely, perfect, but at least he'd stopped glowing. His midnight blue eyes were just eyes now. He was still beautiful, but it was a nearly human beauty. "Is it not worth a little horror?" he asked.

Sabin smiled, and I wished he hadn't. The muscles on the rotted side didn't work, and his mouth hung crooked. I glanced away, then made myself look back. If he could be trapped inside that face, I could look at it.

"Then you will help me?"

"I would aid you if I could, but it is Anita you have come to ask. She must give her own answer."

"Well, Ms. Blake?"

"I don't know how to help you," I repeated.

"Do you understand how dire my circumstances are, Ms. Blake? The true horror of it, do you grasp it?"

"The rot probably won't kill you, but it's progressive, I take it?"

"Oh, yes, it's progressive, virulently so."

''I would help you if I could, Sabin, but what can I do that Dumare can't? He's a necromancer, maybe as powerful as I am, maybe more. Why do you need me?''

''I realize, Ms. Blake, that you don't have something specifically for Sabin's problem,'' Dumare said. ''As far as I can discover, he is the only vampire to ever suffer such a fate, but I thought if we came to another necromancer as powerful as myself—'' he smiled modestly ''—or nearly as powerful as myself, perhaps together we could work up a spell to help him.''

''A spell?'' I glanced at Jean-Claude.

He gave that wonderful Gallic shrug that meant everything and nothing. ''I know little of necromancy, *ma petite*. You would know if such a spell were possible more than I.''

''It is not only your ability as a necromancer that has brought us to you,'' Dumare said. ''You have also acted as a focus for at least two different animators, I believe that is the American word for what you do.''

I nodded. ''The word's right, but where did you hear I could act as a focus?''

''Come, Ms. Blake, the ability to combine another animator's powers with your own and thus magnify both powers is a rare talent.''

''Can you act as a focus?'' I asked.

He tried to look humble but actually looked pleased with himself. ''I must confess, yes, I can act as a focus. Think of what the two of us could accomplish together.''

''We could raise a hell of a lot of zombies, but that won't cure Sabin.''

''True enough.'' Dumare leaned forward in his chair. His lean, handsome face flushed, eager, a true convert looking for disciples.

I wasn't much of a follower.

''I would offer to teach you true necromancy, not this voodoo dabbling that you've been doing.''

Jean-Claude made a soft sound halfway between a laugh and a cough.

I glared at Jean-Claude's amused face but said, ''I'm doing just fine with this voodoo dabbling.''

''I meant no insult, Ms. Blake. You will need a teacher of some sort soon. If not me, then you must find someone else.''

''I don't know what you're talking about.''

''Control, Ms. Blake. Raw power, no matter how impressive, is not the same as power used with great care and great control.''

I shook my head. ''I'll help you if I can, Mr. Dumare. I'll even participate in a spell if I check it out with a local witch I know first.''

''Afraid that I will try and steal your power?''

I smiled. ''No, short of killing me, the best you or anyone else can do is borrow.''

''You are wise beyond your years, Ms. Blake.''

''You aren't that much older than I am,'' I said. Something crossed over his face, the faintest flicker, and I knew.

''You're his human servant, aren't you?''

Dominic smiled, spreading his hands. ''*Oui*.''

I sighed. "I thought you said you weren't trying to hide anything from me."

"A human servant's job is to be the daytime eyes and ears of his master. I am of no use to my master if vampire hunters can spot me for what I am."

"I spotted you."

"But in another situation, without Sabin at my side, would you have?"

I thought about that for a moment. "Maybe." I shook my head. "I don't know."

"Thank you for your honesty, Ms. Blake."

Sabin said, "I am sure our time is up. Jean-Claude said you had a pressing engagement, Ms. Blake. Much more important than my little problem." There was a little bite to that last.

"*Ma petite* has a date with her other beau."

Sabin stared at Jean-Claude. "So you are truly allowing her to date another. I thought that at least must be rumor."

"Very little of what you hear about *ma petite* is rumor. Believe all you hear."

Sabin chuckled, coughing, as if struggling to keep the laughter from spilling out his ruined mouth. "If I believed everything I heard, I would have come with an army."

"You came with one servant because I allowed you only one servant," Jean-Claude said.

Sabin smiled. "Too true. Come Dominic, we must not take more of Ms. Blake's so valuable time."

Dominic stood obediently, towering over us both. Sabin was around my height. Of course, I wasn't sure if his legs were still there. He might have been taller once.

"I don't like you, Sabin, but I would never willingly leave another being in the shape you're in. My plans tonight are important, but if I thought we could cure you immediately, I'd change them."

The vampire looked at me. His blue, blue eyes were like staring down into clear ocean water. There was no pull to them. Either he was behaving himself or, like most vampires, he couldn't roll me with his eyes anymore.

"Thank you, Ms. Blake. I believe you are sincere." He extended a gloved hand from the voluminous cloak.

I hesitated, then took it. His hand squished ever so slightly, and it took a lot not to jerk back. I forced myself to shake his hand, to smile, to let go, and not to rub my hand on my skirt.

Dominic shook my hand as well. His was cool and dry. "Thank you for your time, Ms. Blake. I will contact you tomorrow and we will discuss things."

"I'll be expecting your call, Mr. Dumare."

"Call me, Dominic, please."

I nodded. "Dominic. We can discuss it, but I hate to take your money when I'm not sure that I can help you."

"May I call you Anita?" he asked.

I hesitated and shrugged. "Why not."

"Don't worry about money," Sabin said, "I have plenty of that for all the good it has done me."

''How is the woman you love taking the change in your appearance?'' Jean-Claude asked.

Sabin looked at him. It was not a friendly look. ''She finds it repulsive, as do I. She feels immense guilt. She has not left me, nor is she with me.''

''You'd lived for close to seven hundred years,'' I said. ''Why screw things up for a woman?''

Sabin turned to me, a line of ooze creeping down his face like a black tear. ''Are you asking me if it was worth it, Ms. Blake?''

I swallowed and shook my head. ''It's none of my business. I'm sorry I asked.''

He drew the hood over his face. He turned back to me, black, a cup of shadows where his face should have been. ''She was going to leave me, Ms. Blake. I thought that I would sacrifice anything to keep her by my side, in my bed. I was wrong.'' He turned that blackness to Jean-Claude. ''We will see you tomorrow night, Jean-Claude.''

''I look forward to it.''

Neither vampire offered to shake hands. Sabin glided for the door, the robe trailing behind him, empty. I wondered how much of his lower body was left and decided I didn't want to know.

Dominic shook my hand again. ''Thank you, Anita. You have given us hope.'' He held my hand and stared into my face as if he could read something there. ''And do think about my offer to teach you. There are very few of us who are true necromancers.''

I took back my hand. ''I'll think about it. Now I really do have to go.''

He smiled, held the door for Sabin, and out they went. Jean-Claude and I stood a moment in silence. I broke it first. ''Can you trust them?''

Jean-Claude sat on the edge of my desk, smiling. ''Of course not.''

''Then why did you agree to let them come?''

''The council has declared that no master vampires in the United States may quarrel until that nasty law that is floating around Washington is dead. One undead war, and the anti-vampire lobby would push through the law and make us illegal again.''

I shook my head. ''I don't think Brewster's Law has a snowball's chance. Vampires are legal in the United States. Whether I agree with it or not, I don't think that's going to change.''

''How can you be so sure?''

''It's sort of hard to say a group of beings is alive and has rights, then change your mind and say killing them on sight is okay again. The ACLU would have a field day.''

He smiled. ''Perhaps. Regardless, the council has forced a truce on all of us until the law is decided one way or another.''

''So you can let Sabin in your territory, because if he misbehaves, the council will hunt him down and kill him.''

Jean-Claude nodded.

''But you'd still be dead,'' I said.

He spread his hands, graceful, empty. ''Nothing's perfect.''

I laughed. ''I guess not.''

''Now, aren't you going to be late for your date with Monsieur Zeeman?''

''You're being awfully civilized about this,'' I said.

''Tomorrow night you will be with me, *ma petite*. I would be a poor . . . sport to begrudge Richard his night.''

''You're usually a poor sport.''

''Now, *ma petite*, that is hardly fair. Richard is not dead, is he?''

''Only because you know that if you kill him, I'll kill you.'' I held a hand up before he could say it. ''I'd try to kill you, and you'd try to kill me, etc.'' This was an old argument.

''So, Richard lives, you date us both, and I am being patient. More patient than I have ever been with anyone.''

I studied his face. He was one of those men who was beautiful rather than handsome, but the face was masculine; you wouldn't mistake him for female, even with the long hair. In fact, there was something terribly masculine about Jean-Claude, no matter how much lace he wore.

He could be mine: lock, stock, and fangs. I just wasn't sure I wanted him. ''I've got to go,'' I said.

He pushed away from my desk. He was suddenly standing close enough to touch. ''Then go, *ma petite*.''

I could feel his body inches from mine like a shimmering energy. I had to swallow before I could speak. ''It's my office. You have to leave.''

He touched my arms lightly, a brush of fingertips. ''Enjoy your evening, *ma petite*.'' His fingers wrapped around my arms, just below the shoulders. He didn't lean over me or draw me that last inch closer. He simply held my arms, and stared down at me.

I met his dark, dark blue eyes. There had been a time not so long ago that I couldn't have met his gaze without falling into it and being lost. Now I could meet his eyes, but in some ways, I was just as lost. I raised up on tiptoe, putting my face close to his.

''I should have killed you a long time ago.''

''You have had your chances, *ma petite*. You keep saving me.''

''My mistake,'' I said.

He laughed, and the sound slid down my body like fur against naked skin. I shuddered in his arms.

''Stop that,'' I said.

He kissed me lightly, a brush of lips, so I couldn't feel the fangs. ''You would miss me if I were gone, *ma petite*. Admit it.''

I drew away from him. His hands slid down my arms, over my hands, until I drew my fingertips across his hands. ''I've got to go.''

''So you said.''

''Just get out, Jean-Claude, no more games.''

His face sobered instantly as if a hand had wiped it clean. ''No more games, *ma petite*. Go to your other lover.'' It was his turn to raise a hand and say, ''I know you are not truly lovers. I know you are resisting both of us. Brave, *ma petite*.'' A flash of something, maybe anger, crossed his face and was gone like a ripple lost in dark water.

''Tomorrow night you will be with me and it will be Richard's turn to sit at home and wonder.'' He shook his head. ''Even for you I would not have done what Sabin has done. Even for your love, there are things I would not do.'' He stared at me suddenly fierce, anger flaring through his eyes, his face. ''But what I do is enough.''

''Don't go all self-righteous on me,'' I said. ''If you hadn't interfered, Richard and I would be engaged, maybe more, by now.''

''And what? You would be living behind a white picket fence with two point whatever children. I think you lie to yourself more than to me, Anita.''

It was always a bad sign when he used my real name. ''What's that supposed to mean?''

''It means, *ma petite*, that you are as likely to thrive in domestic bliss as I am.'' With that, he glided to the door and left. He closed the door quietly but firmly behind him.

Domestic bliss? Who me? My life was a cross between a preternatural soap opera and an action adventure movie. Sort of *As the Casket Turns* meets *Rambo*. White picket fences didn't fit. Jean-Claude was right about that.

I had the entire weekend off. It was the first time in months. I'd been looking forward to this evening all week. But truthfully, it wasn't Jean-Claude's nearly perfect face that was haunting me. I kept flashing on Sabin's face. Eternal life, eternal pain, eternal ugliness. Nice afterlife.

2

There were three kinds of people at Catherine's dinner party: the living, the dead, and the occasionally furry. Out of the eight of us, six were human, and I wasn't sure about two of those, myself included.

I wore black pants, a black velvet jacket with white satin lapels, and an oversized white vest that doubled for a shirt. The Browning 9mm actually matched the outfit, but I kept it hidden. This was the first party Catherine had thrown since her wedding. Flashing a gun might put a damper on things.

I'd had to take off the silver cross that I always wore and put it in my pocket because there was a vampire standing in front of me and the cross had started glowing when he entered the room. If I'd known there were going to be vamps at the party, I'd have worn a collar high enough to hide the cross. They only glow when they're out in the open, generally speaking.

Robert, the vampire in question, was tall, muscular, and handsome in a model-perfect sort of way. He had been a stripper at Guilty Pleasures. Now he managed the club. From worker to management: the American dream. His hair was blond, curly, and cut quite short. He was wearing a brown silk shirt that fit him perfectly and matched the dress that his date was wearing.

Monica Vespucci's health club tan had faded around the edges, but her makeup was still perfect, her short auburn hair styled into place. She was pregnant enough for me to have noticed and happy enough about it to be irritating.

She smiled brilliantly at me. ''Anita, it has been too long.''

What I wanted to say was, ''Not long enough.'' The last time I'd seen her, she had betrayed me to the local master vampire. But Catherine thought she was her friend, and it was hard to disillusion her without telling the whole story. The whole story included some unsanctioned killing, some of it done by me. Catherine's a lawyer and a stickler for law and order. I didn't want to put her in a position where she had to compromise her morals to save my ass. So Monica was her friend, which meant I had been polite all through dinner, from appetizer all the way to dessert. I'd been polite mainly because Monica had been at the other end of the table. Now, unfortunately, we were mingling in the living room and I couldn't seem to shake her.

"It doesn't seem that long," I said.

"It's been almost a year." She smiled up at Robert. They were holding hands. "We got married." She touched her glass to the top of her belly. "We got knocked up." She giggled.

I stared at them both. "You can't get knocked up by a hundred-year-old corpse." Okay, I'd been polite long enough.

Monica grinned at me. "You can if the body temperature is raised for long enough and you have sex often enough. My obstetrician thinks the hot tub did us in."

This was more than I wanted to know. "Have you had the amnio yet?"

The smile faded from her face, leaving her eyes haunted. I was sorry I'd asked. "We've got another week to wait."

"I'm sorry, Monica, Robert. I hope the test comes back clean." I did not mention Vlad syndrome, but the words hung on the air. It was rare but not as rare as it used to be. Three years of legalized vampirism and Vlad syndrome was the highest rising birth defect in the country. It could result in some really horrible disabilities, not to mention death for the baby. With that much at stake, you'd think people would be more cautious.

Robert cradled her against him, and all the light had faded from her face. She looked pale. I felt like a heel.

"The latest news was that a vampire over a hundred was sterile," I said. "They should update their information, I guess." I meant for it to be comforting, like they hadn't been careless.

Monica looked at me, and there was no gentleness in her eyes when she said, "Worried?"

I stared at her all pale and pregnant and wanted to slap her anyway. I was not sleeping with Jean-Claude. But I was not going to stand there and justify myself to Monica Vespucci—or anyone else, for that matter.

Richard Zeeman entered the room. I didn't actually see him enter. I felt it. I turned and watched him walk towards us. He was six foot one, nearly a foot taller than me. Another inch and we couldn't have kissed without a chair. But it would have been worth the effort. He wove between the other guests, saying a word here and there. His smile flashed white and perfect in his permanently tanned skin as he talked to these new friends that he'd managed to charm at dinner. Not with sex appeal or power but with sheer good will. He was the world's biggest boy scout, the original hail fellow, well met. He liked people and was a wonderful listener, two qualities that are highly underrated.

His suit was dark brown, his shirt a deep orangey gold. The tie was a brighter orange with a line of small figures down the middle of it. You had to be standing right next to him to realize the figures were Warner Brothers cartoons.

He'd tied his shoulder-length hair back from his face in a version of a french braid, so the illusion was that his brown hair was very short. It left his face clean and very visible. His cheekbones were perfect, sculpted high and graceful. His face was masculine, handsome, with a dimple to soften it. It was the kind of face that would have made me shy in high school.

He noticed me watching him and smiled. His brown eyes sparkled with the smile, filling with heat that had nothing to do with room temperature. I watched him walk the last few feet, and felt heat rise up my neck into my face. I wanted to undress him, to touch his bare skin, to see what was under that suit. I wanted that very badly. I wouldn't, because I wasn't sleeping with Richard, either. I wasn't sleeping with the vampire or the werewolf. Richard was the werewolf. It was his only fault. Okay, maybe one other: he'd never killed anybody. That last fault might get him killed someday.

I slid my left arm around his waist, under the unbuttoned jacket. The solid warmth of him beat like a pulse against my body. If we didn't have sex soon, I was simply going to explode. What price morals?

Monica stared at me very steadily, studying my face. "That's a lovely necklace. Who got it for you?"

I smiled and shook my head. I was wearing a black velvet choker with a cameo, edged by silver filigree. Hey, it matched the outfit. Monica was pretty sure Richard hadn't given it to me, which meant, to Monica, that Jean-Claude had. Good old Monica. She never changed.

"I bought it to match the outfit," I said.

She widened her eyes in surprise. "Oh, really?" like she didn't believe me.

"Really. I'm not much into gifts, especially jewelry."

Richard hugged me. "That's the truth. She's a very hard woman to spoil."

Catherine joined us. Her copper-colored hair flowed around her face in a wavy mass. She was the only one I knew with curlier hair than mine, but its color was more spectacular. If asked, most people described her from the hair outward. Delicate makeup hid the freckles and drew attention to her pale, grey green eyes. Her dress was the color of new leaves. I'd never seen her look better.

"Marriage seems to agree with you," I said, smiling.

She smiled back. "You should try it sometime."

I shook my head. "Thanks a lot."

"I have to steal Anita away for just a moment." At least she didn't say she needed help in the kitchen. Richard would have known that was a lie. He was a much better cook than I was.

Catherine led me back to the spare bedroom where the coats were piled in a heap. There was one real fur coat draped over the pile. I was betting I knew who owned it. Monica liked being close to dead things.

As soon as the door was shut, Catherine grabbed my hands and giggled, I swear. "Richard is wonderful. My junior high science teachers never looked like that."

I smiled, and it was one of those big, dopey smiles. The silly kind that say you're in horrible lust if not love, maybe both, and it feels good even if it is stupid.

We sat down on the bed, pushing the coats to one side. "He is handsome," I said, my voice as neutral as I could make it.

"Anita, don't give me that. I've never seen you glow around anyone."

"I don't glow."

She grinned at me and nodded. "Yes, you do."

"Do not," I said, but it was hard to be sullen when I wanted to smile. "All right, I like him, a lot. Happy?"

"You've been dating him for nearly seven months. Where's the engagement ring?"

I did frown at her then. "Catherine, just because you're deliriously happily married doesn't mean everyone else has to be married, too."

She shrugged and laughed.

I stared into her shining face and shook my head. There had to be more to Bob than met the eye. He was about thirty pounds heavier than he should have been, balding, with small round glasses on a rather nondescript face. He did not have a sparkling personality, either. I'd been ready to give her the thumbs down until I saw the way he looked at Catherine. He looked at her like she was the whole world, and it was a nice, safe, wonderful world. A lot of people are pretty, and clever repartee is on every television set, but dependability, that's rare.

"I didn't bring Richard here to get your stamp of approval; I knew you'd like him."

"Then why did you keep him such a secret? I've tried to meet him a dozen times."

I shrugged. The truth was because I knew she'd get that light in her eyes. That maniacal gleam that your married friends get when you're not married and you're dating anyone. Or worse yet, not dating, and they're trying to fix you up. Catherine had the look now.

"Don't tell me you planned this entire party just so you could meet Richard?"

"Partly. How else was I ever going to?"

There was a knock on the door.

"Come in," Catherine said.

Bob opened the door. He still looked ordinary to me, but from the light in Catherine's face, she saw something else. He smiled at her. The smile made his whole face glow and I could see something shining and fine. Love makes us all beautiful. "Sorry to interrupt the girl talk, but there's a phone call for Anita."

"Did they say who it is?"

"Ted Forrester; says it's business."

My eyes widened. Ted Forrester was an alias for a man I knew as Edward. He was a hit man who specialized in vampires, lycanthropes, or anything else that wasn't quite human. I was a licensed vampire hunter. Occasionally, our paths crossed. We might even on some level be friends, maybe.

"Who's Ted Forrester?" Catherine asked.

"Bounty hunter," I said. Ted, Edward's alias, was a bounty hunter with papers to prove it, all nice and legal. I stood and went for the door.

"Is something wrong?" Catherine asked. Not much got past her, which was one of the reasons I avoided her when I was ass deep in alligators. She was smart enough to figure out when things were off-center but she didn't carry a gun. If you can't defend yourself, you are cannon fodder. The only thing that kept Richard from being cannon fodder was that he was a werewolf. Although refusing to kill people made him almost cannon fodder, shapeshifter or not.

''I was just hoping not to have to do any work tonight,'' I said.

''I thought you had the entire weekend off,'' she said.

''So did I.''

I took the phone in the home office they'd set up. They'd divided the room down the middle. One half was decorated in country with teddy bears and miniature gingham rockers, the other half was masculine with hunting prints and a ship in a bottle on the desk. Compromise at its best.

I picked up the phone and said. ''Hello?''

''It's Edward.''

''How did you get this number?''

He was quiet for a second. ''Child's play.''

''Why did you hunt me down, Edward? What's up?''

''Interesting choice of words,'' he said.

''What are you talking about?''

''I was just offered a contract on your life, for enough money to make it worth my while.''

It was my turn to be quiet. ''Did you take it?''

''Would I be calling you if I had?''

''Maybe,'' I said.

He laughed. ''True, but I'm not going to take it.''

''Why not?''

''Friendship.''

''Try again,'' I said.

''I figure I'll get to kill more people guarding you. If I take the contract, I only get to kill you.''

''Comforting. Did you say guard?''

''I'll be in town tomorrow.''

''You're that sure someone else will take the contract?''

''I don't even open my door for less than a hundred grand, Anita. Someone will take the hit, and it'll be someone good. Not as good as me, but good.''

''Any advice until you get into town?''

''I haven't given them my answer yet. That'll delay them. Once I say no, it'll take a little time to contact another hitter. You should be safe tonight. Enjoy your weekend off.''

''How did you know I had the weekend off?''

''Craig is a very talkative secretary. Very helpful.''

''I'll have to speak to him about that,'' I said.

''You do that.''

''You're sure that there won't be a hitter in town tonight?''

''Nothing in life is sure, Anita, but I wouldn't like it if a client tried to hire me and then gave the job to someone else.''

''You lose many clients at your own hands?'' I asked.

''No comment,'' he said.

''So one last night of safety,'' I said.

''Probably, but be careful anyway.''

''Who put the hit out on me?''

"I don't know," Edward said.

"What do you mean, you don't know? You have to know so you can get paid."

"I go through intermediaries most of the time. Keeps down the chance that the next client is a cop."

"How do you find wayward clients if they piss you off?"

"I can find them, but it takes time. Anita, if you've got a really good hitter on your tail, time is something you won't have."

"Oh, that was comforting."

"It wasn't supposed to be comforting," he said, "Can you think of anyone who hates you so badly and has this kind of money?"

I thought about that for a minute. "No. Most of the people that would fit the bill are dead."

"The only good enemy is a dead enemy," Edward said.

"Yeah."

"I heard a rumor that you're dating the master of the city. Is that true?"

I hesitated. I realized I was embarrassed to admit the truth to Edward. "Yeah, it's true."

"I had to hear you say it." I could almost hear him shake his head over the phone. "Damn, Anita, you know better than that."

"I know," I said.

"Did you dump Richard?"

"No."

"Which monster are you with tonight, bloodsucker or flesh-eater?"

"None of your damn business," I said.

"Fine. Pick the monster of your choice tonight, Anita, have a good time. Tomorrow we start trying to keep you alive." He hung up. If it had been anybody else, I'd have said he was angry about me dating a vampire. Or maybe disappointed would be a better word.

I hung up the phone and sat there for a few minutes, letting it all sink in. Someone was trying to kill me. Nothing new there, but this someone was hiring expert help. That was new. I'd never had an assassin after my butt before. I waited to feel fear wash over me, but it didn't. Oh, in a vague sort of way, I was afraid, but not like I should have been. It wasn't that I didn't believe it could happen. I did believe. It was more that so much else had happened in the last year that I couldn't get too excited yet. If the assassin jumped out and started shooting, I'd deal with it. Maybe later I'd even have an attack of nerves. But I didn't get many attacks of nerves anymore. Part of me was numbing out like a combat veteran. There was just too much to take in, so you stop taking it in. I almost wished I had been scared. Fear will keep you alive; indifference won't.

Somewhere out there, by tomorrow, someone would have my name on a to-do list. Pick up dry cleaning, buy groceries, kill Anita Blake.

3

I stepped back into the living room and caught Richard's eye. I was sort of ready to go home. Somehow, knowing an assassin was out there, or would be soon, had put a damper on the evening.

"What's wrong?" Richard asked.

"Nothing," I said. I know, I know, I had to tell him, but how do you tell your sweetie that people are trying to kill you? Not in a room full of people. Maybe in the car.

"Yes, there is. You've got that tension between your eyebrows that means you're trying not to frown."

"No, I'm not."

He smoothed his finger between my eyes. "Yes, you are."

I glared at him. "Am not."

He smiled. "Now you are frowning." His face sobered. "What's wrong?"

I sighed. I stepped closer to him, not for romance but for privacy. Vampires had incredibly good hearing, and I didn't want Robert to know. He'd tattle to Jean-Claude. If I wanted Jean-Claude to know, I'd tell him myself.

"It was Edward on the phone."

"What does he want?" Richard was frowning now, too.

"Someone tried to hire him to kill me."

A look of total astonishment blossomed on his face, and I was glad his back was to the room. He closed his mouth, opened it, and finally said, "I would say you're kidding, but I know you're not. Why would anyone want to kill you?"

"There are plenty of people who would like to see me dead, Richard. But none of them have the kind of money that's being put out for the hit."

"How can you be so calm about this?"

"Would it solve anything if I had hysterics?"

He shook his head. "It's not that." He seemed to think for a second. "It's that you're not outraged that someone's trying to kill you. You just accept it, almost like it's normal. It isn't normal."

"Assassins aren't normal, even for me, Richard," I said.

"Just vampires, zombies, and werewolves," he said.

I smiled. "Yeah."

He hugged me tightly and whispered, "Loving you can be very scary sometimes."

I wrapped my arms around his waist, leaning my face against his chest. I closed my eyes, and for just a moment I breathed in the smell of him. It was more than his aftershave; it was the smell of his skin, his warmth. Him. For just a moment, I sank against him and let it all go. I let his arms be my shelter. I knew that a well-placed bullet would destroy it all, but for a few seconds, I felt safe. Illusion is sometimes all that keeps us sane.

I pushed away from him with a sigh. "Let's give our regrets to Catherine and get out of here."

He touched my cheek gently, looking into my eyes. "We can stay if you want."

I nestled my cheek against his hand and shook my head. "If the shit hits the fan tomorrow, I don't want to spend tonight at a party. I'd rather go back to my apartment and cuddle."

He flashed me that smile that warmed me down to my toes. "Sounds like a plan to me."

I smiled back because I couldn't not smile back. "I'll go tell Catherine."

"I'll get the coats," he said.

We did our various tasks and left early. Catherine gave me a very knowing smile. I wished she was right. Leaving early to jump Richard's bones beat the heck out of the truth. Monica watched us leave. I knew that she and Robert would report back to Jean-Claude. Fine. He knew I was dating Richard. I hadn't lied to anybody. Monica was a lawyer at Catherine's firm—frightening thought all on its own—so she had a legitimate reason to be invited. Jean-Claude hadn't arranged it, but I didn't like being spied on, no matter how it came about.

The walk to the car was nerve-racking. Every shadow was suddenly a potential hiding place. Every noise a footstep. I didn't draw my gun, but my hand ached to do it. "Dammit," I said, softly. The numbness was wearing off. I wasn't sure it was an improvement.

"What is it?" Richard asked. He was suddenly scanning the darkness, not looking at me while he talked. His nostrils flared just a little, and I realized he was scenting the wind.

"Just jumpy. I don't see anyone out here, but I'm suddenly looking too damn hard."

"I don't smell anyone close to us, but they could be downwind. The only gun I smell is yours."

"You can smell my gun?"

He nodded. "You've cleaned it recently. I can smell the oil."

I smiled and shook my head. "You are so blasted normal, sometimes I forget you turn furry once a month."

"Knowing how good you are at spotting lycanthropes, that's quite a compliment." He smiled. "Do you think assassins would fall from the trees if I held your hand right now?"

I smiled. "I think we're safe for the moment."

He curved his fingers around my hand, and a tingle went up my arm like he'd touched a nerve. He rubbed his thumb in small circles on the back of my hand and took a deep breath. "It's almost nice to know that this assassin business has unnerved you, too. I don't want you afraid, but sometimes it's hard to be your guy when I think you may be braver than I am. That sounds like macho crap, doesn't it?"

I stared up at him. "There's a lot of macho crap out there, Richard. At least you know it's crap."

"Can this male chauvinist wolf kiss you?"

"Always."

He leaned his face downward, and I rose on tiptoe to meet his mouth with mine, my free hand against his chest for balance. We could kiss without me going on tiptoe, but Richard tended to get a crick in his neck.

It was a quicker kiss than normal because I had this itching in the middle of my back, right between the shoulder blades. I knew it was my imagination, but I felt too exposed out in the open.

Richard sensed it and pulled away. He went around to the driver's side of his car and opened his door, leaning across to unlock mine. He didn't open the door for me. He knew better than that. I could open my own bloody door.

Richard's car was an old Mustang, sixty something, a Mach One. I knew all this because he had told me. It was orange with a black racing stripe. The bucket seats were black leather, but the front seat was small enough that we could hold hands when he wasn't using the gear shift.

Richard pulled out onto 270 South. Friday night traffic spilled around us in a bright sparkle of lights. Everybody out trying to enjoy the weekend. I wondered how many of them had assassins after them. I was betting I was one of the few.

"You're quiet," Richard said.

"Yeah."

"I won't ask what you're thinking about. I can guess."

I looked at him. The darkness of the car wrapped around us. Cars at night are like your own private world, hushed and dark, intimate. The lights of oncoming traffic swept over his face, highlighting it, then leaving us in darkness.

"How do you know I'm not thinking about what you'd look like without your clothes on?"

He flashed me a grin. "Tease."

I smiled. "Sorry. No sexual innuendo unless I'm willing to jump your bones."

"That's your rule, not mine," Richard said. "I'm a big boy. Give me all the sexual innuendo you want, I can take it."

"If I'm not going to sleep with you, it doesn't seem fair."

"Let me worry about that," he said.

"Why, Mr. Zeeman, are you inviting me to make sexual overtures to you?"

His smile widened, a whiteness in the dark. "Oh, please."

I leaned toward him as far as the seat belt would allow, putting a hand on the back of his seat, putting my face inches from the smooth expanse of his neck. I took a deep breath in and let it out, slowly, so close to his skin that my own breath came back to me like a warm cloud. I kissed the bend of his neck, running my lips lightly up and down the skin.

Richard made a small, contented sound.

I curled my knees into my seat, straining against the seat belt so I could kiss the big pulse in his neck, the curve of his jaw. He turned his face into me. We kissed, but my nerves weren't that good. I turned his face away. "You watch the road."

He shifted gears, his upper arm brushing against my breasts. I sighed against him, putting my hand over his, holding it on the gear shift, keeping his arm pressed against me.

We stayed frozen for a second, then he moved against me, rubbing. I scooted out from under his arm, settling back into my seat. I couldn't breathe past the pulse in my throat. I shivered, hugging myself. The feel of his body against mine made places all over my body tighten.

"What's wrong?" he said, his voice low and soft.

I shook my head. "We can't keep doing this."

"If you stopped because of me, I was enjoying myself."

"So was I. That's the problem," I said.

Richard took in a deep breath and let it out, sighing. "It's only a problem because you make it one, Anita."

"Yeah, right."

"Marry me, Anita, and all this can be yours."

"I don't want to marry you just so I can sleep with you."

"If it was only sex, I wouldn't want you to marry me," Richard said. "But it's cuddling on the couch, watching *Singing in the Rain*. It's eating Chinese and knowing to get that extra order of crab Rangoon. I can order for both of us at most of the restaurants in town."

"Are you saying I'm predictable?"

"Don't do that. Don't belittle it," he said.

I sighed. "I'm sorry, Richard. I didn't mean to. I just . . ."

I didn't know what to say because he was right. My day was more complete for having been shared with Richard. I bought him a mug that I just happened to see in a store. It had wolves on it, and said, "In God's wildness lies the hope of the world—the great fresh, unblighted, unredeemed wilderness." It was a quote from John Muir. No special occasion, just saw it, knew Richard would like it, bought it. A dozen times a day I'd hear something on the radio or in conversation, and I'd think, I must remember and tell Richard. It was Richard who took me on my first bird-watching trip since college.

I had a degree in biology, preternatural biology. Once I'd thought I'd spend my life as a field biologist like a preternatural version of Jane Goodall. I'd enjoyed the bird-watching, partly because he was with me, partly because I'd enjoyed it years ago. It was like I'd forgotten that there was life outside of a gun barrel or a grave side. I'd been neck deep in blood and death so long; then Richard came along. Richard who was also neck deep in strange stuff, but who managed to have a life.

I couldn't think of anything better than waking up beside him, reaching for his body first thing in the morning, knowing I'd be coming home to him. Listening to his collection of Rodgers and Hammerstein, watching his face while he watched Gene Kelly musicals.

I almost opened my mouth and said, let's do it, let's get married, but I didn't. I loved Richard; I could admit that to myself, but it wasn't enough. There was an assassin after me. How could I involve a mild-mannered junior high teacher in that kind of life? He was one of the monsters, but he didn't accept it. He was in a battle for leadership of the local werewolf pack. He'd beaten the current pack leader, Marcus, twice, and twice refused the kill. If you didn't kill, you didn't get to be leader. Richard clung to his morals. Clung to values that only worked when people weren't trying to kill you. If I married him, his chance at any kind of normal life was gone. I lived in a sort of free-fire zone. Richard deserved better.

Jean-Claude lived in the same world that I did. He had no illusions about the kindness of strangers, or anyone else for that matter. The vampire wouldn't be shocked at the news of an assassin. He'd simply help me plan what to do about it. It wouldn't throw him, or not much. There were nights when I thought that Jean-Claude and I deserved each other.

Richard turned off onto Olive. We were soon going to be at my apartment, and the silence was getting a little thick. Silences don't usually bother me, but this one did. "I'm sorry, Richard. I am truly sorry."

"If I didn't know you loved me, this would be easier," he said. "If it wasn't for that damned vampire, you'd marry me."

"That damn vampire introduced us," I said.

"And he's regretting it, don't think he isn't," Richard said.

I looked at him. "How do you know that?"

He shook his head. "All you have to do is see his face when we're together. I may not like Jean-Claude, and I hate the thought of you with him, but we aren't the only two hurting here. It's a threesome, don't think it's not."

I huddled in my seat, suddenly miserable. I'd have almost welcomed a hit man appearing out of the darkness. Killing I understood. Relationships confused me. Admittedly, this relationship was more confusing than most.

Richard turned into the parking lot of my apartment building. He parked the car and turned off the engine. We sat there in the dark, the only illumination the distant glow of a street light.

"I don't know what to say, Richard." I stared out through the windshield, concentrating on the side of the building, too cowardly to look at him while I talked. "I wouldn't blame you for just saying to hell with it. I wouldn't put up with this kind of indecision from you, and I wouldn't share you with another woman." I finally looked at him. He was staring straight ahead, not looking at me.

My heart sped up. If I was truly as brave as I thought I was, I'd have let him go. But I loved him, and I wasn't that brave. The best I could do was not sleep with him. Not take the relationship that next step forward. That was hard enough. Even my self-control wasn't limitless. If we'd been planning a wedding, I could have waited. With an end in sight, my self-control would have appeared endless, but there was no end in sight. Chastity works better if you don't keep testing it quite so often.

I unbuckled the seat belt, unlocked and opened the door. Richard touched my shoulder before I could get out. ''Aren't you going to invite me up?''

I let out a breath I hadn't realized I was holding and turned back to him. ''Do you want to be invited up?''

He nodded.

''I don't know why you put up with me,'' I said.

He smiled. He leaned into me, a light brush of lips. ''Sometimes I'm not sure, myself.''

We got out. Richard held his hand out to me, and I took it.

A car pulled in behind us, beside my own Jeep. It was my neighbor, Mrs. Pringle. She had a huge television box tied into her trunk.

We walked to the sidewalk and waited for her to get out. She was a tall woman, stretched almost painfully thin with age. Her snow white hair was done in a bun at the back of her head. Custard, her Pomeranian, jumped out of the car and stood yapping at us. He looked like a golden powder puff with little cat feet. He bounced forward on stiff legs. He sniffed Richard's foot and looked up at him with a small growl.

Mrs. Pringle tugged on his leash. ''Custard, behave yourself.''

The dog quieted, but I think it was more Richard's steady glare than Mrs. Pringle's admonishments. She smiled at us. She had the same light in her eyes that Catherine had had. She liked Richard and made no bones about it.

''Well, now, this is advantageous. I need some strong young arms to carry that monstrous television up the stairs for me.''

Richard smiled at her. ''Happy to oblige.'' He walked around to the trunk and started trying to undo the knots.

''What'd you do with Custard while you shopped?'' I asked.

''I carried him with me. I've spent a great deal of money at that store before. The salesmen fairly salivate when I come through the doors, so they indulge me.''

I had to smile. There was a sharp twang as the ropes broke. ''I'll help Richard.'' I walked back to the trunk. The rope was an inch thick and flopped, broken, onto the pavement. I raised eyebrows at him and whispered, ''My, my, Grandma, what strong hands you have.''

''I could carry the television up alone, but it might arouse suspicions.''

It was a thirty-inch wide screen. ''You could really carry it up the stairs by yourself?''

''Easily,'' he said.

I shook my head. ''But you're not going to because you are a mild-mannered science teacher, not an alpha werewolf.''

''Which is why you get to help me,'' he said.

''Are you having trouble undoing the rope?'' Mrs. Pringle asked. She'd walked back to us with Custard in tow.

''No,'' I said, giving Richard a look. ''We've got the rope.'' If people found out Richard was a lycanthrope, he'd lose his job. It was illegal to discriminate, but it happened all the time. Richard taught children. He'd be branded a monster, and most people didn't let monsters near their children.

Mrs. Pringle and Custard led the way. I went up backwards, sort of steadying the box, but Richard took all the weight. He walked up the stairs like the box weighed nothing, pushing with his legs, waiting for me to go up another step. He made a face at me, soundlessly humming under his breath as if he was bored. Lycanthropes are stronger than your run-of-the-mill human being. I knew that, but it was still a little unsettling to be reminded.

We made it to the hallway, and he let me have some of the weight. The thing was heavy, but I held on, and we kept moving towards Mrs. Pringle's apartment, which was right across the hall from mine.

"I've got the door opened," she called.

We were at the door, starting to maneuver through, when Custard darted between us, underneath the box, trailing his leash. Mrs. Pringle was trapped behind the television. "Custard, come back here."

Richard lifted with his forearms, taking the weight. "Get him. I can get inside."

I let him pretend to struggle inside the apartment and went for the dog. I expected to have to chase him down the hall, but he was sniffing at my door, whining. I knelt and grabbed the end of his leash, pulling him back towards me.

Mrs. Pringle was at her door, smiling. "I see you caught the little rascal."

I handed her the leash. "I've got to get something out of my apartment. I'm sure Richard can help you set up the TV."

"Thanks a lot," he called from inside the apartment.

Mrs. Pringle laughed. "I'll give you both some iced tea, unless you have better things to do." There was a knowing look in her blue eyes that made me blush. She winked at me, I kid you not. When the door was safely closed with her and Richard on the other side, I walked toward my apartment. Three doors down, I crossed the hallway. I took the Browning out and clicked the safety off. I eased back towards my door. Maybe I was being paranoid. Maybe Custard hadn't smelled anybody in my apartment. But he'd never whined at my door like that before. Maybe Edward's phone call was making me jumpy. But better jumpy than dead. Paranoid it was.

I knelt by the door and took a breath, letting it out slowly. I took my keys out of my jacket pocket left-handed. I scrunched down as low as I could get and still have a decent shooting stance. If there was a bad guy in there, he'd probably shoot at chest level. On my knees I was a lot shorter than chest level. I pushed the key in the lock. Nothing happened. The apartment was probably empty, except for my fish wondering what the hell I was doing. I turned the knob, pushed the door inward, and a hole exploded out through the door, thundering over my head like a cannon shot. There was no sound for a second. The door swung closed with the force of the shot, and through the hole in the door I saw a man with a shotgun raised to his shoulder. I fired once through the hole. The door bounced open, still reverberating from the shotgun blast. I threw myself onto one side, gun pointed through the open door.

The shotgun fired again, showering the hallway with bits of wood. I fired twice more, hitting the man in the chest both times. He staggered, blood blossoming on his coat, and fell straight back. The shotgun fell to the carpet near his feet.

I got to my knees, back pressed to the wall near my kitchenette. All I could hear was a roaring in my ears, then dimly my own blood rushing through my head.

Richard was suddenly there in the doorway, like a target. ''Get down! He may not be alone!'' I wasn't sure how loud I was yelling. My ears were still ringing.

Richard crouched beside me. I think he said my name, but I didn't have time for it. I pushed upward, my back to the wall, gun in a two-handed grip. He started to stand. I said, ''Stay down.'' He did. Point for him.

I could see that there was no one in front of my apartment. Unless there was somebody hiding in the bedroom, the hit man had been alone. I approached him, slowly, gun pointed at him. If he'd twitched, I'd have shot again, but he didn't move. The shotgun was by his feet. I'd never seen anybody use a gun with their feet, so I left it where it was.

He lay on his back, one arm thrown up over his head, one down at his side. His face was slack with death, his eyes wide and unseeing. I didn't really need to check for a pulse, but I did it anyway. Nothing. There were three holes in his chest. I'd hit him with the first shot, but it hadn't been a killing blow. That had nearly cost me my life.

Richard came up behind me. ''There's no one else in the apartment, Anita.''

I didn't argue with him. I didn't ask if he knew this by smell or by hearing. I didn't bloody care. I checked the bedroom and bathroom just to be thorough and came back out to find Richard staring down at the dead man.

''Who is he?'' Richard asked.

It occurred to me that I could hear again. Bully for me. I still had a faint ringing in my ears, but it would pass. ''I don't know.''

Richard looked at me. ''Was he the . . . hitter?''

''I think so.'' There was a hole in the door big enough to crawl through. It was still open. Mrs. Pringle's door was closed, but the doorjamb was splintered like something had taken a big bite out of it. If she'd been standing there, she'd have been dead.

I heard the distant wail of police sirens. Couldn't blame the neighbors for calling them. ''I'm going to make some phone calls before the cops get here.''

''Then what?'' he asked.

I looked at him. He was pale, the whites of his eyes showing just a little too much. ''Then we go with the nice police officers down to the station to answer questions.''

''It was self-defense.''

''Yeah, but he's still dead on my carpet.'' I walked into the bedroom, searching for the phone. I was having a little trouble remembering where I'd left it, as if it ever moved from the nightstand. Shock is always fun.

Richard leaned in the doorway. ''Who are you going to call?''

''Dolph, and maybe Catherine.''

''A friendly policeman I understand, but why Catherine?''

''She's a lawyer.''

''Oh,'' he said. He glanced back at the dead man, who was bleeding all over my white carpet. ''Dating you is never boring, I'll give you that.''

"And it's dangerous," I said, "Don't forget dangerous." I dialed Dolph's number from memory.

"I never forget you're dangerous, Anita," Richard said. He stared at me and his eyes were amber, the color of a wolf's eyes. His beast slid behind those eyes, peering out. Probably the smell of fresh blood. I stared into those alien eyes and knew I wasn't the only dangerous thing in the room. Of course, I was armed. The dead man could vouch for that. Laughter tickled the back of my throat. I tried to swallow it, but it spilled out, and I was giggling when Dolph answered the phone. Laughing was better than crying, I guess. Though I'm not sure Dolph thought so.

4

I sat in a straight-backed chair at a small, scarred table in an interrogation room. Oh, sorry, interview room. That's what they were calling it now. Call it what you will, it still smelled like stale sweat and old cigarettes with an overlay of disinfectant. I was sipping my third cup of coffee, and my hands were still cold.

Detective Sergeant Rudolph Storr leaned against the far wall. His arms were crossed over his chest, and he was trying to be unobtrusive, but when you're six foot eight and built like a pro wrestler, that's hard. He hadn't said a word during the interview. (Just here to observe.)

Catherine sat beside me. She'd thrown a black blazer over the green dress, brought her briefcase, and sat wearing her lawyer face.

Detective Branswell sat across from us. He was in his mid-thirties, black hair, dark complected, with eyes as black as his hair. His name was English, but he looked Mediterranean, like he'd just stepped off the olive boat. His accent was pure middle Missouri.

''Now, Ms. Blake, go over it just one more time for me. Please.'' He poised his pen over his notebook as if he'd write it all down again.

''We'd helped my neighbor carry up her new television.''

''Mrs. Edith Pringle, yeah, she confirms all that. But why did you go to your apartment?''

''I was going to get a screwdriver to help install the television.''

''You keep a lot of tools, Ms. Blake?'' He wrote something on his notepad. I was betting it was a doodle.

''No, detective, but I've got a screwdriver.''

''Did Mrs. Pringle ask you to go get this screwdriver?''

''No, but she'd used it when she bought her stereo system.'' Which was true. I was trying to keep the lies to an absolute minimum.

''So you assumed she'd need it.''

''Yes.''

''Then what?'' He asked like he'd never heard the answer before. His black eyes were intense and empty, unreadable and eager at the same time. We were coming to the part that he didn't quite buy.

"I unlocked my door and dropped my keys. I squatted down to pick them up and the first shotgun blast roared over my head. I returned fire."

"How? The door was closed."

"I shot through the hole in the door that the shotgun had made."

"You shot a man through a hole in your door and hit him."

"It was a big hole, detective, and I wasn't sure I hit him."

"Why didn't the second shotgun blast take you out, Ms. Blake? There wasn't enough left of the door to hide behind. Where were you, Ms. Blake?"

"I told you, the blast rocked the door inward. I hit the floor, on my side. The second blast went over me."

"And you shot the man twice more in the chest," Detective Branswell said.

"Yes."

He looked at me for a long moment, studying my face. I met his eyes without flinching. It wasn't that hard. I was numb, empty, and distant. There was still a fine ringing in my ears from being so damn close to two shotgun blasts. The ringing would fade. It usually did.

"You know the man you killed?"

Catherine touched my arm. "Detective Branswell, my client has been more than helpful. She's told you several times that she did not recognize the deceased."

He flipped back through his notebook. "You're right, counselor. Ms. Blake has been helpful. The dead man was James Dugan, Jimmy the Shotgun. He's got a record longer than you are tall, Ms. Blake. He's local muscle. Someone you call when you want it cheap and quick and don't care how messy it is." He stared at me while he talked, studying my eyes.

I blinked at him.

"Do you know anyone who would want you dead, Ms. Blake?"

"Not right offhand," I said.

He closed his notebook and stood. "I'm going to recommend justifiable homicide to the DA. I doubt you'll see the inside of a courtroom."

"When do I get my gun back?" I asked.

Branswell stared at me. "When ballistics is done with it, Ms. Blake. And I'd be damn grateful that you're getting it back at all." He shook his head. "I've heard stories about you from some of the cops who answered the last call from your apartment. The one with the two killer zombies." He shook his head again. "Don't take this wrong, Ms. Blake, but have you considered moving to a new jurisdiction?"

"My landlord is probably going to suggest the same thing," I said.

"I'll just bet he is," Branswell said. "Counselor, Sergeant Storr."

"Thanks for letting me sit in on this, Branswell," Dolph said.

"You said she was one of yours. Besides, I know Gross and Brady. They were the first officers on scene for the zombies. They say good things about her. I've talked to half a dozen officers that say Ms. Blake saved their butt or stood shoulder to shoulder with them under fire and didn't blink. It cuts you a hell of a lot of slack, Blake, but that slack isn't unlimited. Watch your back, and try not to shoot up any innocent bystanders.'' With that, he left.

Dolph stared down at me. ''I'll drive you back to your place.''

''Richard's waiting for me,'' I said.

''What's going on, Anita?''

''I told Branswell everything I know.''

Catherine stood up. ''Anita has answered all the questions she's going to answer tonight.''

''He's a friend,'' I said.

''He's also a cop,'' Catherine said. She smiled. ''Isn't that right, Sergeant Storr?''

Dolph stared at her for a minute. ''That is certainly true, Ms. Maison-Gillette.'' He pushed away from the wall. He looked at me. ''I'll talk to you later, Anita.''

''I know,'' I said.

''Come on,'' Catherine said. ''Let's get out of here before they change their minds.''

''Don't you believe me?'' I asked.

''I'm your lawyer. Of course I believe you.''

I looked at her. She looked at me. I got up. We left. I wondered if Richard would believe me. Probably not.

5

Richard and I walked toward his car, through the police station parking lot. He hadn't said a word to me. He'd shaken hands with Catherine and headed for the car. He got into his side. I slid into the passenger side. Richard started the engine and backed out of the parking slot.

"You're mad about something," I said.

He eased out onto the street. He always drove carefully when he was angry. "What could I possibly be mad about?" The sarcasm was thick enough to eat with a spoon.

"You think I knew there was a hit man in my apartment?"

He flashed me a look that was pure rage. "You knew, and you let me go inside and set that damned TV up. You got me out of harm's way."

"I wasn't sure, Richard."

"I bet you had your gun drawn before he fired."

I shrugged.

"Dammit, Anita, you could have been killed."

"But I wasn't."

"That's your answer to everything. If you survive, it's all right."

"It beats the alternative," I said.

"Don't make jokes," Richard said.

"Look, Richard, I didn't go out hunting this guy. He came to me."

"Why didn't you tell me?"

"And you would have done what? Go through the door first? You'd have taken a chest full of buckshot and survived. How would you have explained that? You'd have been outed as a lycanthrope. You'd have lost your job, at the very least."

"We could have called the police."

"And told them what? That Custard sniffed at the door? If they had investigated, they'd have gotten shot. The guy was jumpy as hell. He shot through the door, remember? He didn't know who he was firing at."

He turned onto Olive, shaking his head. "You should have told me."

"What would it have changed, Richard? Except maybe you'd have tried to play hero, and if you survived, you'd have lost your career."

"Dammit, dammit." He smashed his hands into the steering wheel over and over. When he looked at me, his eyes had gone amber and alien. "I don't need you to protect me, Anita."

"Ditto," I said.

Silence filled the car like ice water. Nobody but the bad guy had died. I'd done the right thing. But it was hard to explain.

"It wasn't that you risked your life," Richard said, "it was that you got rid of me before you did it. You didn't even give me a chance. I have never interfered with you doing your job."

"Would you have considered this part of my job?"

"Closer to your job description than mine," he said.

I thought about that for a minute. "You're right. One of the reasons we're still dating is you don't pull macho crap on me. I apologize. I should have warned you."

He glanced at me with eyes that were still pale and wolfish. "Did I just win an argument?"

I smiled. "I admitted I was wrong. Is that the same thing?"

"Exactly the same thing."

"Then give yourself a point."

He grinned at me. "Why can't I stay mad at you, Anita?"

"You're a very forgiving person, Richard. One of us has to be."

He pulled into my parking lot for the third time that night. "You can't stay at your place tonight. The door is in pieces."

"I know." If I'd been kicked out of my apartment because it was being painted, I had friends I could stay with, or a hotel, but the bad guys had proven they didn't care who got hurt. I couldn't risk anybody, not even strangers in the next room at a hotel.

"Come home with me," he said. He parked in an empty space closest to the stairs.

"I don't think that's a good idea, Richard."

"The shotgun blast wouldn't have killed me. I'd have healed, because it wasn't silver shot. How many of your other friends can say that?"

"Not many," I said quietly.

"I've got a house set back in a yard. You won't be risking innocent bystanders."

"I know you have a yard, Richard. I've spent enough Sunday afternoons there."

"Then you know I'm right." He leaned towards me and his eyes had bled back to their normal brown. "I have a guest room, Anita. It doesn't have to be more than that."

I stared at him from inches away. I could feel his body like a force just out of reach. It wasn't his otherworldly wolf powers. It was simply sheer physical attraction. It was dangerous agreeing to go to Richard's house. Maybe not to my life, but to other things.

If Jimmy the Shotgun had had a partner inside the apartment tonight, I'd be dead now. I'd been so busy concentrating on killing him that a second perp could have blown me away. Edward had told his contact no by now, and it takes a little while to find another hitter of Edward's caliber. So, instead of waiting, they hired cheap and local, taking the chance that cheap might take me out and they'd be saved several hundred grand. Or maybe they wanted me dead really quickly for some reason that I didn't understand. Either way, they wanted me dead pretty damn badly. Usually, when someone wants you dead that badly, they succeed. Not tonight or tomorrow, but unless Edward and I could find out who had put the contract out on me, the line of talent would just keep coming.

I stared into Richard's face, almost close enough to kiss. I thought about never seeing him again. About never touching him again. About never satisfying that growing hunger that perfumed the air whenever I was with him. I touched his face, lightly running my fingertips down his cheek. "Okay."

"You look so serious. What are you thinking, Anita?"

I leaned in and kissed him. "Blood, death, and sex. What else is there?"

We got out of the car. I filled my automatic fish feeder full of enough food for a week. In a week's time, if the assassin was still after me, and if I was still alive, I'd have to come back. All the bad guys had to do was stake out my fish tank, and they had me if they were patient enough. Somehow I didn't think they would be.

I packed a few things, including my stuffed toy penguin, Sigmund, every weapon I owned, a few clothes, an outfit for tomorrow's date with Jean-Claude. Yeah, probably I wouldn't be going, but I didn't want to come back to the apartment, not for anything. I left a message on Ronnie's machine. We usually worked out together on Saturday morning, but I didn't want Ronnie in the line of fire. She was a private detective, but Ronnie wasn't a shooter, not like I was. She had a certain respect for life that could get you killed.

Richard waited while I changed. Black jeans, a royal blue polo shirt, white jogging socks with a blue stripe, black Nikes, and I felt more myself. I laid the Browning's shoulder holster in my suitcase. The Browning was my main gun, and I missed it. I'd have missed it under normal circumstances, but now my hand ached for the gun.

I guess that's what backup guns are for. The Firestar 9mm is a good gun and fits my hand well. My hands are small enough that a lot of 9mms are just too big. The Browning was about the limit of a comfortable grip. I wore the Firestar in an inter-pants holster, set for a forward cross draw, which meant you could see the gun. I wasn't sure I cared tonight.

I put on wrist sheaths and both knives. These were the last two of a foursome that I'd had custom made for my hands, with the highest silver content possible in the steel. I'd had to have two of them replaced; monsters ate them. I put the two new knives in the suitcase still in their felt-lined box. They were pretty and sharp enough to cut your skin if you ran a thumb along the edge.

While I was having the lost knives replaced, I'd ordered a new one. It was nearly a foot long, more a sword than a knife. I'd had a leather harness made that let me carry it down my spine, with the hilt under my hair. I hadn't used it before, but I'd seen it in a catalog and couldn't resist.

I had a Derringer, a sawed-off shotgun, two full-sized, pump-action shotguns, a twelve gauge, and a mini-Uzi. The Derringer, the Uzi, and the sawed-off shotgun were all gifts from Edward. Not Christmas or birthday gifts. No, we'd be out hunting vampires together, and he'd give me a new toy. I'd asked for the shotgun.

The full-sized shotguns wouldn't pack in either the suitcases or the gym bags. I put them in their individual carrying cases, with straps. The gym bags held my vampire hunting kit and my zombie paraphernalia. I put extra ammo in both bags for temporary keeping. Heck, I shoved extra ammo in the suitcase, too. You could never have too much.

I caught a glimpse of myself in the mirror. The gun was pretty obvious against the bright blue of the shirt. I finally put a black jacket over it, what they call a boyfriend's jacket, because it's sort of big through the shoulders and body. The sleeves rolled back to expose the silky lining. I liked the jacket, and with one button fastened, it hid the Firestar, though not completely. You'd still catch glimpses of it when I moved, but maybe people wouldn't run screaming.

I felt naked without the Browning, which was kind of funny, considering I had an Uzi in my suitcase. But hey, I slept with the Browning.

Richard never said a word about the two shotguns. Maybe he would have complained about the rest if he'd seen them, but he picked up one suitcase, put one gym bag over his shoulder, one shotgun carrying case on the same shoulder, and let me pick up my share.

"Can you carry both suitcases?" I asked.

"Yeah, but I'm shocked you asked. The last time I tried to carry something unasked, you nearly handed me my head in a basket."

"I want one hand free for my gun."

"Ah," he said, "of course." He took the other suitcase without another word. He really is a very wise man.

Mrs. Pringle stepped out of her door as we were leaving. She had Custard in her arms. He growled briefly at Richard, and she hushed him. "I thought I heard you out here. Are you all right, Anita?"

I glanced at the hole by her door. "I'm fine. How 'bout you?"

She hugged Custard, raising his tiny furry body near her face. "I'll be all right. Are you going to be charged?"

"It doesn't look like it."

"Good." She glanced at the suitcases. One for clothes, one for weapons. "Where are you going?"

"I think I'm a little too dangerous to be around right now."

She searched my face like she was trying to read my mind. "How bad is this mess, Anita?"

"Bad enough," I said.

She gently touched my hair, "You be very careful out there."

I smiled. "Always. You take care of yourself, too."

"Custard and I will take care of each other."

I petted Custard, rubbing his little fox ears. ''I owe you a box of doggie treats, furball.'' He licked my hand with a tiny, pink tongue.

''When you can, give me your new phone number,'' she said.

''When I can, I'll come back.''

She smiled, but her pale eyes stayed worried.

We left because we had to. My imagination has always been too good for my own peace of mind. I had a very clear image of Mrs. Pringle splattered against the wall, that lovely, aging face blown away. If she had opened the door at the wrong moment, I wouldn't be imagining it. Too close, too damn close.

6

Richard's house was a one-story, half-brick ranch. It looked like a house for children, and Mommy baking cookies in the kitchen. It wasn't even set that far back off the road, but it had plenty of yard on either side and the backyard was an acre of woods. You could look out both the sides and the back and not see a neighbor, except in winter when the bare trees revealed distant glimpses across the valley. From the front picture window, you could see the corner of the next house half obscured by overgrown shrubs. No one had lived in it the entire time I'd been visiting. The place was a little isolated. Richard liked that, and whether I did or not, I needed it now.

The place looked like an invitation for an ambush, but neighbors would have been cannon fodder. Most bad guys try not to take out innocent bystanders. It's not moral outrage, just bad for business. The cops tend to put the heat on if you waste a lot of bystanders.

Richard hit the garage door opener and eased the Mustang into the garage. His four by four was already inside. I followed him in my Jeep. I idled out on the street, waiting for him to move the four by four out so I could put the Jeep in. Parking my Jeep out in front of his house seemed like making the bad guys' job a little too easy. He pulled out. I pulled in. He parked behind me in the driveway and walked into the garage. I unloaded the suitcases, and he hit the button by the interior door.

The door opened into the kitchen. The walls were lined with Hogarth prints of dogs and more modern hunting scenes. A Warner Brothers canister set; Bugs to Tweety Bird sat on the off-white cabinets. The countertops were off white. The cabinets light honey colored oak. There were dishes draining on a towel by the sink, even though Richard had a dishwasher. A glass, a bowl, a spoon; he'd washed his breakfast dishes before he left for work this morning. I'd have poured water in them and left them in the sink. Of course, I never ate breakfast.

Richard walked through into the living room, carrying one suitcase. I followed, carrying the suitcase with the weapons in it. I also had the two gym bags.

The living room had deep forest green carpet and pale yellow walls. Cartoon lithographs took up the far wall. The near wall was taken up with a wooden entertainment center that Richard had built himself. There was a large-screen TV, a miniature stereo system that made mine sound like humming through a comb, shelves of books, and closed doors that hid part of his extensive video collection and a portion of his CDs. The rest of his books were in the basement, set in shelves along every wall. There were still boxes he hadn't unpacked because he ran out of shelf space.

There was a large couch and a heavy wood coffee table. The couch was green and brown, patterned with a yellow afghan thrown across it that his grandmother had made. A small antique armoire sat against the far wall. There was no other furniture in the room.

He'd set the suitcase in the smaller bedroom. It had a twin bed, a nightstand, and a lamp. The walls, the drapes, and the coverlet where all white, like he hadn't really decided what to do with the room yet.

I laid the gym bags on the bed, put the suitcase on the floor, and stared at it all. My life sitting in little bags on the carpet. Seemed like there should have been more.

Richard came up and hugged me from behind, arms wrapping around my shoulders. ''I think this is where I'm supposed to ask what's wrong, but I know the answer already. I'm sorry the bad guys invaded your house.''

That was it exactly. The bad guys were not supposed to come home with you. It should have been against the rules. I knew it wasn't, it had happened before, but not like this. Not where I knew I couldn't go back. Even when this was over, I couldn't risk Mrs. Pringle and my other neighbors again.

I turned in his arms, and he loosened them so I could do it. I hugged him around the waist. ''How did you know that was exactly what was bothering me?''

He smiled. ''I love you, Anita.''

''That's not an answer.''

He kissed me on the forehead. ''Yes, it is.'' He kissed me gently on the lips and stepped back. ''I'm going to get out of this tie. Change into your jammies if you want to.'' He left, closing the door behind him.

I opened the door and called after him. ''Can I use the phone?''

He answered from his bedroom. ''Make yourself at home.''

I took that for a yes, and went into the kitchen. The phone was on the wall. I got a card out of my fanny pack, which I'd been forced to carry like a purse. You couldn't fasten the jacket over the fanny pack, and the open jacket would have shown off the gun.

The card was white with a number printed in black script, nothing but the number. I dialed and got Edward's twenty-four-hour answering service. I left a message, saying to call me ASAP, and Richard's number.

Richard's answering machine sat on the counter, connected by wires to the wall-mounted phone. The message light was blinking, but it wasn't my machine, so I didn't check it.

Richard came into the kitchen. His hair fell around his shoulders in tight, foaming waves, curlier from the French braid. His hair was brown, but light of almost any kind brought out golden highlights, hints of bronze. He was wearing a flannel shirt, forest green, with the sleeves rolled above his elbows, showing the fine muscles in his forearms. I'd seen the shirt before. It was high-quality flannel, soft as a blanket to touch. He had on jeans and no socks. He padded barefoot towards me.

The phone rang. It was nearly one o'clock in the morning. Who else could it be but Edward? "I'm expecting a call," I said.

"Help yourself."

I picked it up, and it was Edward. "What happened?" he asked.

I told him.

"Somebody wants you dead quick."

"Yeah. When you said no, they went out and bought some cheap local talent."

"You get what you pay for," Edward said.

"If there'd been two of them, Edward, I wouldn't be here."

"You aren't going to like my news."

"How much worse could it get?" I asked.

"I answered a message just before yours. They upped the offer to five hundred thousand dollars, if you were dead within twenty-four hours."

"Sweet Jesus, Edward, I'm not worth that kind of money."

"They knew you blew away their hitter, Anita. They knew the hit had failed."

"How?" I asked.

"I don't know yet. I'm trying to find out who's putting up the money, but it'll take a little time. The safeguards that keep me out of it protect the client, too."

I was shaking my head back and forth. "Why twenty-four hours for the hit?"

"Something's happening that they want you out of the way for, something big."

"But what?"

"You know what it is, Anita. You may not be aware that you know, but you do. Something worth this kind of money that you could put a stop to. There can't be that many choices."

"I can't think of a single thing, Edward."

"Think harder," he said. "I'll be there as early as I can tomorrow. Watch your back. Don't drive your car."

"Why not?"

"Bombs," he said.

"Bombs," I repeated.

"For half a million dollars, Anita, they'll get someone good. A lot of professionals will do you from a nice, safe distance. A bomb, a high-powered rifle."

"You're scaring me," I said.

"Good, maybe you'll be careful."

"I'm always careful, Edward."

"I apologize. You're right, but be more careful. I didn't expect them to try a local hit."

"You're worried," I said.

He was quiet for a second. "We can keep taking out the hitters, but eventually we've got to get to the man with the money. As long as the contract's out there, somebody'll keep taking it."

''It's just too much damn money to pass up,'' I said.

''A lot of professionals won't take a hit with a time limit on it,'' he said. ''Some of the best are out of the running because of the deadline. I won't take a hit with special circumstances.''

''I hear a 'but' coming up,'' I said.

He laughed, quietly. ''For half a million dollars, people will break their rules.''

''Not comforting,'' I said.

''Not meant to be,'' he said. ''I'll be at Richard's tomorrow early.''

''Do you know where it is?''

''I could find it, but let's not play games. Give me directions.''

I did. ''I would tell you to stay indoors, but you've been dating Richard for months. A good hitter will be able to find you. I don't know if you're safer inside or on the move.''

''I'll pack extra firepower and be more paranoid than usual.''

''Good. See you tomorrow.'' He hung up, and I was left holding the buzzing phone.

Richard was staring at me. ''Did I hear you say twenty-four hours for the hit?''

I hung up the phone. ''I'm afraid so.'' I hit the message button on his machine out of habit. It whirred as it rewound.

''Why, for God's sake?'' Richard asked.

''I wish I knew.''

''You mentioned money twice. How much?''

I told him.

He sat down in one of the kitchen chairs, looking shocked. Couldn't blame him. ''Anita, don't take this wrong. To me you're worth any amount of money, but why would somebody pay half a million dollars to kill you?''

For someone who knew nothing about assassins, he'd grasped the big question quite nicely. I walked over to him. I ran my fingertips through his hair. ''Edward says I must already know what the big event is, that I wouldn't be worth this kind of money, with this kind of deadline, unless I was already intimate with the situation.''

He looked up at me. ''But you don't know, do you?''

''Not a clue.''

He laid his hands on either side of my waist, pulling me against him, wrapping his arms completely around my waist.

The message machine clicked to life and made us both jump. We laughed nervously, not just from fear. There was a heat to his eyes as he stared up at me that made me want to blush or kiss him. I hadn't decided which.

Two hang-ups, his younger brother Daniel, sorry Richard had canceled their rock climbing tomorrow.

I leaned towards Richard. His lips were the softest I'd ever kissed. The taste of him was intoxicating. How could I be thinking of giving him up?

The last message began playing: ''Richard, this is Stephen. Oh, God, pick up. Please pick up. Please be there.''

We froze, listening.

''They're trying to get me to do one of those movies. Raina won't let me leave.

Richard, where are you? They're coming. I've got to go. Oh, God, Richard.'' The phone clicked dead. A mechanical voice said, ''End of messages.''

Richard stood up, and I let him. ''I thought Raina had stopped making pornographic movies,'' I said.

''She promised not to make snuff films, that was all.'' He replayed the message. The time on it was 12:03.

''That's less than an hour ago,'' I said.

''I can't leave you alone here tonight. What if another killer comes?'' He paced in a tight circle. ''But I can't abandon Stephen.''

''I'll go with you,'' I said.

He shook his head, walking for the bedroom. ''I can survive the games that the pack plays, Anita. You're human, they'll tear you up.''

''They'll tear you up, too, Richard.''

He just kept walking. ''I can handle myself.''

''Are you at least going to call some of the pack that's on your side? Get some backup?''

He sat down on his bed, pulling on socks. He glanced up at me, then shook his head. ''If I take my army, this'll turn into a war. People will get killed.''

''But if you go in alone, you only endanger yourself, is that it?''

He glanced up at me. ''Exactly.''

I shook my head. ''And what happens to Stephen if you go out there and get killed? Who rescues him?''

That stopped him for a second. He frowned, fishing his shoes out from under the bed. ''They won't kill me.''

''Why not?'' I asked.

''Because if Marcus kills me outside the challenge circle, he doesn't retain leadership of the pack. It's like cheating. The pack would turn on him.''

''What if you accidentally died in a fight with someone else?''

He was suddenly very interested in tying his shoes. ''I can handle myself.''

''Meaning if someone else kills you in a legitimate fight, Marcus is off the hook, right?''

He stood up. ''I guess.''

''Raina is Marcus's mate, Richard. She's afraid you're going to kill him. This is a trap.''

He shook his head stubbornly. ''If I call in the wolves on my side and we go over there in a mass, they'll be slaughtered. If I go over there alone, I may be able to talk my way through it.''

I leaned against the doorjamb and wanted to yell at him, but bit it back. ''I'm going with you, Richard.''

''You have enough problems of your own.''

''Stephen risked his life to save mine once. I owe him. If you want to play politician, fine, but I want Stephen safe.''

''Going out where the assassin can find you isn't a smart idea, Anita.''

''We've been dating for months, Richard. If a professional assassin hits town, it won't take him long to find me here.''

He glared at me, jaw tight enough that I could see the small muscle on the side. ''You'll kill someone if I take you.''

''Only if they need killing.''

He shook his head. ''No killing.''

''Even to save my own life? Even to save Stephen's?''

He looked away from me, then back, anger turning his dark eyes almost black. ''Of course you can defend yourself.''

''Then I'm coming.''

''All right, for Stephen's sake.'' He didn't like saying it.

''I'll get my jacket.'' I got the mini-Uzi out of the suitcase. It was amazingly small. I could have shot it with one hand, but for accuracy, I needed two. Though accuracy and machine guns were sort of mutually exclusive. You pointed it a little lower than you meant to hit and held on. Silver ammo, of course. I slid the strap over my right shoulder. It had a little clip that attached to my belt at the small of my back. The clip kept the Uzi from sliding all over the place, but left enough play for me to slide the gun out and fire it. The gun rode at the small of my back, which was irritating, but no matter what I told Richard, I was scared, and I wanted at least two guns with me. The police had the Browning. I didn't have a holster big enough for the sawed-off, not to mention it was illegal. Come to think of it, wasn't the machine gun? I had a permit to own it, but they didn't hand out carry permits for fully automatic weapons, not to civilians, anyway. If I got caught with it, I might be going to court after all.

I put the jacket on and whirled around. The jacket was bulky enough that it didn't show. Amazing. The Firestar was more noticeable in its front-draw holster.

My pulse was beating hard enough that I could feel it thrumming against my skin. I was scared. Richard was going to play politics with a bunch of werewolves. Shapeshifters didn't play politics much, they just killed you. But I owed Stephen, and I didn't trust Richard to save him. I'd do whatever it took to see him safe; Richard wouldn't. Richard would hesitate. It would almost surely get him killed one day. Tonight, for the first time, I realized it might get me killed.

No way should we walk into one of Raina's little shows without more people. No way. Jean-Claude would never have tolerated Raina and Marcus's games. They'd be dead by now, and we'd all be safe. I would have trusted Jean-Claude at my back tonight. He wouldn't flinch. Of course, he'd have brought his own little army of vampires and made it a true battle. The shit could hit the fan tonight and be over before morning. Richard's way, we'd rescue Stephen, survive, escape, and Raina would still be alive. Nothing would be settled. It may have been civilized, but it was a bad way to stay alive.

Richard was waiting by the front door, keys in hand, impatient. Couldn't blame him.

''Stephen didn't say where he was. Do you know where they make the films?''

''Yeah.''

I looked a question at him. ''Raina took me to watch the filming a few times. She thought I'd overcome my shyness and join in.''

''You didn't.'' It wasn't a question.

''Of course not. Let's go get Stephen.'' He held the door for me, and just this once I didn't tell him not to.

7

I expected Richard to drive into the city, to some disreputable warehouse in a seedy section of town. Instead, he drove further into Jefferson County. We drove down Old Highway 21 between soft, rolling hills, silvered in the moonlight. It was early May, and the trees were already thick with leaves.

Woods hugged the sides of the road. An occasional house would break out of the trees, but for the most part, we were alone in the dark, as if the road stretched out forever and no other human had ever set foot on it.

''What's the plan?'' I asked.

Richard glanced at me, then back to the road. ''Plan?''

''Yeah, a plan. If Raina's there, she won't be alone, and she won't like you taking Stephen.''

''Raina's the alpha female, the lupa. I'm not allowed to fight her.''

''Why not?''

''An alpha male becomes Ultric, wolf king, by killing the old leader, but the winner chooses the lupa.''

''So Raina didn't have to fight for her place?''

''She didn't have to fight to be lupa, but she did have to fight to be the most dominant female in the pack.''

''You once told me that the pack considers me a dominant. What's the difference between being a dominant and being an alpha female? I mean, can I be an alpha?''

''Alpha is the equivalent to being a master vampire, sort of,'' he said.

''So what is a dominant?''

''Anyone not pack, not lukoi, that's earned our respect. Jean-Claude is a dominant. He can't be more unless he becomes pack.''

''So you're alpha, but you're not pack leader.''

''We have about half a dozen alphas, male and female. I was Marcus's second in command, his Freki.''

''Freki is the name of one of Odin's wolves. Why would second wolf be named after something out of mythology?''

''The pack is very old, Anita. Among ourselves, we are the lukoi. There can be two seconds, Freki and Geri.''

''Why the history lesson and the new vocabulary?''

''To outsiders, we keep it simple. But I want you to know who and what we are.''

''Lukoi is Greek, right?''

He smiled. ''But do you know where it's from?''

''No.''

''King Lykaon of Arcadia was a werewolf. He didn't try and hide it. We call ourselves the lukoi in his memory.''

''If you're not Freki anymore, what are you?''

''Fenrir, challenger.''

''The giant wolf that kills Odin at Ragnarok.''

''I'm impressed, not many people would know that.''

''Two semesters of comparative religion,'' I said. ''Can a woman be Ulfric?''

''Yes, but it's rare.''

''Why?''

''They'd have to win a knock-down drag-out physical battle. All the power in the world won't stop someone from pounding your face into the ground.''

I would have liked to argue, but I didn't. He was right. Not because I was female. Small men get their asses kicked, too. Size matters if both people are equally well trained.

''Why don't the female alphas have to duke it out to win the top spot?''

''Because the Ulfric and his lupa are a mating pair, Anita. He doesn't want to get stuck with a woman he can't stand.''

I looked at him. ''Wait a minute. You're next in line to lead the pack. If you succeed Marcus, do you have to sleep with your lupa?''

''Technically, yes.''

''Technically?'' I said.

''I won't choose one. I won't sleep with someone just so the pack can feel secure.''

''Glad to hear it,'' I said, ''but does that jeopardize your standing in the pack?''

He took a deep breath, and I heard it sigh outward. ''I have a lot of support among the pack, but some of them are bothered by my morals. They think I should pick a mate.''

''And you won't, because . . . of me?''

He glanced at me. ''That's a big part of it. It wouldn't be only one time, Anita. An alpha couple binds for life. It's like a marriage. They usually marry each other in real life, not just in the pack.''

''I can see why the pack leader gets to pick his mate.''

''I've picked my mate,'' Richard said.

''But I'm not a werewolf.''

''No, but the pack considers you a dominant.''

''Only because I killed a few of them,'' I said.

''Well, that does tend to impress them.'' He slowed down. There was a line of pine trees along the left-hand side of the road, too regular and too thick to be natural. He turned down a gravel driveway in the middle of them.

The driveway curved downhill, and at the bottom of a shallow valley was a farmhouse. Hills thick with trees poured out around the house. If there had ever been fields, the forest had reclaimed them.

The driveway opened into a small gravel lot that was crowded with cars, at least a dozen of them. Richard jerked the car into park and was out the door before I could unbuckle my seat belt. I had to run to catch up and was at his back just as he flung open the barn door. There was a thick wall of cloth hanging inside the door, not a curtain but more a barrier. Richard pulled it aside, and light flooded out around us. He stalked into that light, and I trailed after him.

There were lights everywhere, hanging from the rafters like large, ugly fruit. About twenty people stood around the open interior of the barn. Two cameras were trained on a set, made up of two walls and a king-size bed. Two cameramen were sort of draped on the cameras, waiting. A long table thick with take-out bags and cold pizza was set near the entrance. Over a dozen people were clustered around the food. They glanced at us as we entered. A handful of humans looked hurriedly away and began inching back. The lycanthropes stared, their eyes almost motionless, intent. I suddenly knew what it must feel like to be a gazelle near a lion pack.

At least two-thirds of the people in the barn were shape-shifters. Probably, they weren't all werewolves. I couldn't tell what animal they might be by looking, but I knew they were all shapeshifters. Their energy burned through the air like a hint of lightning. Even with the Uzi, if things went wrong, I was in trouble. I was suddenly angry with Richard. We shouldn't have come alone like this. It was too careless for words.

A woman stepped out of the group. She had what looked like an industrial-strength makeup kit on her shoulder. Her dark hair was shaved close to her head, leaving a very pretty face open and clean, without a drop of makeup on it.

She moved uncertainly towards us as if afraid she'd get bitten. The air vibrated around her, a tiny shimmer, as though reality was just a little less firm than it should be around her. Lycanthrope. I wasn't sure what flavor, but that really didn't matter. Whatever the flavor, they were dangerous.

''Richard,'' she said. She stepped away from the watching crowd, small hands running up and down the strap of her bag. ''What are you doing here?''

''You know why I'm here, Heidi,'' he said. ''Where's Stephen?''

''They aren't going to hurt him,'' she said. ''I mean, his brother's here. His own brother wouldn't let him get hurt, would he?''

''Sounds like you're trying to convince yourself, not us,'' I said.

Her eyes flicked to me. ''You must be Anita Blake.'' She glanced behind at the watchers at her back. ''Please, Richard, just go.'' The aura of energy around her was vibrating harder, almost a visible shimmer in the air. It prickled along my skin like ants.

Richard reached out towards her.

Heidi flinched but stood her ground.

Richard smoothed his hand just above her face, not quite touching her skin. As he moved his hand, the energy around her quieted, like water calming. ''It's all right, Heidi. I know the situation Marcus has put you in. You want to join another pack, but he has to give permission. To get his permission, you do what he says, or you're trapped. Whatever happens, I won't hold it against you.''

The anxiety seeped away. Her otherworldly energy quieted until it was barely there at all. She might have passed for human.

''Very impressive.'' A man stepped forward. He was at least six foot four, maybe an inch taller, his head bald as an egg, only his eyebrows showing dark above pale eyes. His black T-shirt strained over the muscles in his arms and chest, as if the shirt was the skin of an insect about to split and let loose the monster. Energy boiled off him like summer heat. He moved with the confident strut of a bully, and the power crawling over my skin said he might be able to back it up.

''He's new,'' I said.

''This is Sebastian,'' Richard said. ''He joined us after Alfred died.''

''He's Marcus's new enforcer,'' Heidi whispered. She stepped back, halfway between the two men, her back to the curtain we'd entered through.

''I challenge you, Richard. I want to be Freki.''

Just like that, the trap was sprung.

''We are both alpha, Sebastian. We don't have to do anything to prove that.''

''I want to be Freki, and I need to beat you to do it.''

''I'm Fenrir now, Sebastian. You can be Marcus's Freki without fighting me.''

''Marcus says no, says I have to go through you.''

Richard took a step forward.

''Don't fight him,'' I said.

''I have to answer challenge.''

I stared at Sebastian. Richard is not a small man, but he looked small beside Sebastian. Richard wouldn't back down to save himself. But for someone else . . . ''And if you get killed, where does that leave me?'' I asked.

He looked at me then, really looked at me. He turned back to Sebastian. ''I want safe passage for Anita.''

Sebastian grinned and shook his head. ''She's dominant. No safe passage. She takes her chances like the rest of us.''

''She can't accept challenge, she's human.''

''When you're dead, we'll make her one of us,'' Sebastian said.

''Raina has forbidden us to make Anita lukoi,'' Heidi said.

The glare that Sebastian gave her made her cringe against the curtain door. Her eyes were round with fear.

''Is that true?'' Richard asked.

''It's true,'' Sebastian growled. ''We can kill her, but we can't make her pack.'' He grinned, a brief flash of teeth. ''So we'll just kill her.''

I drew the Firestar, using Richard's body to shield the movement from the lycanthropes. We were in trouble. Even with the Uzi, I couldn't kill them all. If Richard would kill Sebastian, we might salvage the situation, but he'd try not to kill him. The other shapeshifters watched us with patient, eager eyes. This had been the plan all along. There had to be a way out.

I had an idea. ''Are all Marcus's enforcers assholes?''

Sebastian turned to me. ''Was that an insult?''

''If you have to ask, then indeedy-do, it was.''

''Anita,'' Richard said, low and careful, ''what are you doing?''

''Defending myself,'' I said.

His eyes widened, but he didn't take his glance from the big werewolf. Richard understood. There was no time to argue about it. Sebastian took a step forward, big hands balled into fists. He tried to step around Richard to get to me. Richard moved in front of him. He put out his hand, palm outward like he had with Heidi, and that roiling energy damped down, spilling out like water from a broken cup. I'd never seen anything like it. Calming Heidi was one thing. Forcing a lycanthrope to swallow such power was something else.

Sebastian took a step back, almost a stagger. ''You bastard.''

''You are not strong enough to challenge me, Sebastian. Don't ever forget that,'' Richard said. His voice was still calm, with the barest hint of anger underneath. It was a reasonable voice, a voice for negotiating.

I stood behind Richard with the Firestar held at my side, as unobtrusive as I could make it. The fight was off, and my little show of bravado hadn't been needed. I'd underestimated Richard's power. I'd apologize later.

''Now, where is Stephen?'' Richard asked.

A slender black man stalked towards us, moving like a dancer in a shimmering wash of his own energy. His hair was braided in shoulder-length cornrows with colored beads worked into them. His features were small and neat, his skin a rich solid brown. ''You may be able to control us one at a time, Richard, but not all at once.''

''You were kicked out of your last pack for being a troublemaker, Jamil,'' Richard said. ''Don't make the same mistake twice.''

''I won't. Marcus will win this fight because you are a fucking bleeding heart. You still don't get it, Richard. We aren't the Young Republicans.'' Jamil stopped about eight feet back. ''We are a pack of werewolves, and we aren't human. Unless you accept that, you are going to die.''

Sebastian stepped back to stand beside Jamil. The rest of the lycanthropes moved up behind the two men. Their combined energy flowed outward, filling the room like warm water with piranha in it. The power bit along my skin like tiny electric shocks. It rose in my throat until it was hard to breathe, and the hair on my head stood at attention.

''Will you be pissed if I kill some of them?'' I asked. My voice sounded squeezed and harsh. I moved closer to Richard, but had to step back. His power poured over me like something alive. It was impressive, but there were twenty lycanthropes on the other side, and it wasn't that impressive.

A scream shattered the silence, and I jumped.

''Anita,'' Richard said.

''Yeah.''

''Go get Stephen.''

''That was him screaming?'' I asked.

''Go get him.''

I looked at the mass of lycanthropes and said, ''You can handle this?''

''I can hold them.''

''You can't hold us all,'' Jamil said.

''Yes,'' Richard said, ''I can.''

The scream sounded again, higher, more urgent. The sound came from deeper in the barn where it had been divided into rooms. There was a makeshift hallway. I started towards it, then hesitated. ''Will you be pissed if I kill people?''

''Do what you have to do,'' he said. His voice had grown low, with an edge of growl to it.

''If she kills Raina with a gun, she still won't be your lupa,'' Jamil said.

I glanced at Richard's back. I hadn't known I was being considered for the job.

''Go, Anita; now.'' His voice was dying down to a growl. He didn't have to add, hurry. I knew that part. He might be able to stall, but he couldn't fight them all.

Heidi walked towards me, behind Richard's back. He didn't turn any attention to her, as if he didn't consider her a danger at all. She wasn't powerful, but you didn't have to be powerful or even strong to stab someone in the back, claw or knife, what did it matter? I pointed the gun at her. She passed within inches of Richard and he did nothing. My gun was the only thing guarding his back. Even now, he trusted Heidi. Right this minute, he shouldn't have trusted anyone but me. ''Gabriel's with Raina,'' she said. She said his name like she was afraid of him.

Gabriel wasn't even a member of the pack. He was a were-leopard. He was one of Raina's favorite actors, though. He'd appeared in her porno flicks and even one snuff film. I almost asked her who she feared most, Raina or Gabriel. But it didn't matter. I was about to confront them both.

''Thanks,'' I said to Heidi.

She nodded.

I went for the hallway and the sound of screams.

8

I entered the hallway and followed the sounds of voices to the second door on the left. I heard at least two different male voices, soft, murmuring. I couldn't make out the words. The screams changed to yelling. ''Stop, please, stop. No!'' It was a man, too. Unless they were torturing more than one person tonight, it had to be Stephen.

I took a deep breath, let it out, and reached for the door with my left hand, gun in my right. I wished I knew the layout of the room. Stephen yelled, ''Please, don't!''

Enough. I opened the door, shoving it against the wall so I'd know there was no one behind it. I meant to sweep the room, but what I saw on the floor stopped me cold, like some kind of flash-frozen nightmare. Stephen lay on his back, a white robe open, revealing his nude body. Blood trailed down his chest in thin scarlet ribbons, though there were no apparent wounds. Gabriel held Stephen's arms, pinned underneath his body, behind his back as if they might already be tied. Stephen's waist-length yellow hair spilled over Gabriel's leather-clad lap. Gabriel was naked from the waist up, a silver ring through his right nipple. His curly black hair had spilled over his eyes, and when he looked up at me, he looked blind.

A second man knelt on the far side of Stephen. Curling blond hair fell to his waist. He wore an identical white robe, fastened. When he looked at the door, his slender, nearly pretty face was a mirror of Stephen's. Had to be his brother. He was holding a steel knife. He was in midslice when I came through the door. Fresh blood welled from Stephen's skin.

Stephen screamed.

There was a naked woman curled over Stephen's body. She straddled his lower body, pinning his legs. Her long auburn hair fell like a curtain, hiding the last indignity from sight. Raina raised her head from Stephen's groin. Her full lips parted in a smile. She'd worked him to erection. Even with his protests, his body had gone on without him.

It took a heartbeat to see it all, a sort of slow-motion shorthand. I sensed movement to my right and tried to turn, but it was too late. Something furred and only half-human slammed into me. I hit the far wall hard enough to make it shudder. The Firestar went spinning, and I fell, stunned, to the floor. A wolf the size of a pony loomed over me. It opened jaws big enough to crush my face, and growled, a sound low and deep enough to stop my heart.

I could move again, but that face was an inch from my cheek; I could feel its breath on my face. A line of saliva fell from its mouth to glide down the edge of my mouth. It lowered its muzzle that last inch, lips drawn back like it was going to take a nibble. The Uzi was pinned between my back and the wall. I went for one of the knives, and knew I'd never make it.

Human arms curved around the wolf, tore it back, away from me. Raina stood holding the struggling wolf like it was no effort. Her beautiful naked body rippled with muscles that didn't show until they were used. ''Draw no blood from her, I told you that.'' She tossed the wolf into the other wall. The wall cracked and buckled. The wolf lay still, eyes rolled back into its skull.

It gave me the time I needed. I pulled the Uzi around on its strap. When Raina turned back to me, I was pointing it at her.

She stood over me, naked, perfect, slender where she was supposed to be slender, curved where she was supposed to be curved. But since I'd seen her sculpt her body at will, I wasn't that impressed. When you could manipulate your body like she could, who needed plastic surgery?

''I could have let her kill you, Anita. You don't seem very grateful.''

I sat on the floor, propped against the wall, not completely trusting that I could stand yet. But the Uzi was pointed nice and steady. ''Thanks a lot,'' I said, ''Now, back up, slowly, or I will cut you in half.''

Raina laughed, a low, joyous sound. ''You are so dangerous. So exciting. Don't you think so, Gabriel?''

Gabriel came to stand beside her. Both of them looking down at me was too much, so I used the wall to brace myself and stood. I could stand. Great. I was beginning to think I could even walk. Better.

''Back up,'' I said.

Gabriel stepped around her, bringing him almost close enough to have reached out and touched me. ''She's perfect for anyone who's into pain and has a death wish.'' He reached out, as if to run his fingers down my cheek. I pointed the machine gun at his waist, because it would kick upward. Aim too high and you can actually miss.

''The last time you pushed me, Gabriel, all I had on me was a knife. You survived having me gut you, but even you can't heal from a submachine gun burst. At this range, I'll cut you in half.''

''Would you really kill me just for trying to touch you?'' He seemed amused, his strange grey eyes almost fever bright as they peered out of the tangle of his hair.

''After what I just saw, you bet.'' I stood away from the wall. ''Back up or we'll find out how much damage you can take.''

They backed up. I was almost disappointed. The Uzi with silver ammo would do exactly what I'd said it would do. I could cut them down, kill them, no muss, no fuss, just a hell of a mess. I wanted them dead. I looked at them for a heartbeat and thought about it, thought about pulling the trigger and saving us all a lot of trouble.

Raina backed up, pulling Gabriel with her. She stared at me as she moved, back towards the wall where the pony-sized wolf was staggering to its feet. Raina looked at me and I saw the knowledge on her face of how close she'd come. I think until that moment she hadn't realized I could kill her and not lose sleep. Hell, leaving her alive would cost me more sleep.

A roaring scream came from the other room. Howling vibrated through the barn. There was a moment of breathless silence, then growls, shrieks. The floor shuddered with the impact of distant bodies. Richard was fighting without me.

Raina smiled at me. ''Richard needs you, Anita. Go to him. We'll take care of Stephen.''

''No thanks.''

''Richard could be dying while you waste time.''

Fear flowed over me in a cool wash. She was right. They'd lured him here to die. I shook my head. ''Richard told me to get Stephen, and that's what I'm going to do.''

''I didn't think you took orders that well,'' she said.

''I take the ones I like.''

Stephen had curled onto his side, pulling the robe over his body. His brother sat beside him, smoothing his hair and murmuring, ''It's all right, Stephen. You're not hurt.''

''You sliced him up, you son of a bitch.''

He spread Stephen's robe, exposing his chest. Stephen tried weakly to close his robe. His brother slapped his hands lightly. He wiped his hands across the bloody chest. The skin was perfect. The cut had healed already, which meant that all the blood was Stephen's.

''Get off of him, right now, or I will blow you away.''

He eased back from him, eyes wide. He believed me. That was good, because it was true.

''Come on, Stephen. We've got to go.''

He raised his head and looked at me, tears sliding down his cheeks. ''I can't stand.'' He tried to crawl to me, but collapsed on the floor.

''What did you give him?'' I asked.

''Something to relax him,'' Raina said.

''You bitch.''

She smiled. ''Exactly.''

''Go over and stand by them,'' I said to the brother.

The man turned a face to me so like Stephen's it was startling. ''I wouldn't let them hurt him. He'd enjoy it if he'd just let himself go.''

''He is hurt, you son of a bitch! Now get over there, right now, or I'll kill you. Do you understand me? I will kill you and be happy about it.''

He got to his feet and went to stand beside Gabriel. ''I made sure no one hurt him,'' he said softly.

The walls shuddered. There was a sound of splintering wood. Someone had been thrown through the wall of the room next to us. I had to get us out of there.

I had to get to Richard. But if I was careless, I'd never make it. Richard wasn't the only one in danger of getting his throat ripped out.

With this many lycanthropes in a room so small, they were too close. They could jump me if I went to help Stephen stand, but with a machine gun in my hand, I was betting most of them would be dead before they reached me. It was a comforting thought.

I spotted the Firestar in the far corner. I picked it up and holstered it without having to look. Practice, practice, practice. I kept the machine gun out. It just made me feel better.

I knelt by Stephen without taking my eyes off the others. It was hard not to at least glance down, but I was too damn close to them. The wolf had been unbelievably fast, and I didn't think Raina would save me a second time. I was lucky she didn't want me wounded. I got my arm around Stephen's waist, and he managed to throw his arms around my neck. I stood, and he was almost dead weight, but we both managed to stand, and with my help, Stephen kept his feet. I was glad he was about my size. Bigger would have been harder. His robe flapped open, and he took one arm from around my shoulders and tried to tie it closed, but he couldn't do it. He started to take his other arm off my shoulders.

''Leave it, Stephen, please. We've got to go now.''

''I don't want people to see me.'' He stared at me from inches away, his face vague and unfocused from the drugs, but a single tear trailed from the corner of one cornflower blue eye. ''Please,'' he said.

Shit. I braced him around the waist, and said, ''Go ahead.'' I stared at Raina while he tied his robe, clumsy and slow from the drug she'd slipped him. He was making a low whimpering sound deep in his chest by the time he got it closed.

''In some ways you are as sentimental as Richard,'' she said. ''But you could kill us, all of us, even Stephen's brother, and feel nothing.''

I met her honey brown eyes and said, ''I'd feel something.''

''What?'' she asked.

''Safer,'' I said.

I backed us towards the open door and had to glance behind to make sure nothing was coming up at me. When I looked back at them, Gabriel had moved forward, but Raina had a hand on his arm, stopping him. She was looking at me like she'd never really seen me before. Like I'd surprised her. I guess it was mutual. I'd known she was twisted, but not in my wildest dreams would I have accused her of raping one of her own people.

Stephen and I stepped out into the hall, and I took a deep breath, feeling something in my chest loosen. The sounds of fighting crashed over us. I wanted to run towards the fight. Richard was alive, or they wouldn't have still been fighting. There was time. There had to be.

I called to Raina, ''Don't show your face out here until after we're gone, Raina, or I'll shoot it off.'' There was no answer from the room. I had to get to Richard.

Stephen stumbled and nearly took us both down. He hung from my shoulders, his arms pressing into my neck, then he got his feet under him. ''You with me, Stephen?''

''I'm all right. Just get me out of here.'' His voice sounded weak, thready, like he was losing consciousness. I could not carry him and shoot, or at least I didn't want to try. I got a firmer grip on his waist and said, "Stay with me, Stephen, and I'll get you out."

He nodded, long hair spilling around his face. "Okay." The one word was almost too soft to hear above the fighting.

I stepped out into the main room, and it was chaos. I couldn't see Richard. There was just a mass of bodies, arms, legs, a clawed form rose above the rest, a man-wolf close to seven feet tall. He reached down and drew Richard out of the mess, claws digging into his body. Richard shoved a hand that was too long to be human, and not furry enough to be wolf, under the werewolf's throat. The creature gagged, spitting blood.

A wolf almost as long as Richard was tall leapt upon his back. Richard staggered, but didn't fall. The mouth sank teeth into his shoulder. Furred claws and human hands grabbed at him from every side. Fuck it. I fired the machine gun into the wooden floor. It would have looked more impressive if I'd fired into the overhead lights, but bullets come down at the same speed they go up, and I didn't want to catch my own ricochet. Holding the machine gun one-handed was a trip. I held on and sprayed a line from me to the bed. I ended with the gun pointing at the fight. Everyone had frozen, shocked. Richard crawled out of the mess, bleeding. He got to his feet, swaying a bit, but moving on his own power. I could never have carried both him and Stephen, let alone the machine gun.

He stopped in front of the curtain, waiting for me to come to him. Stephen sagged against me, arms limp. I think he'd passed out. It was an agonizingly slow walk to Richard. If I tripped and went down, they'd be on me. They watched me move with eyes, human and wolf, but nothing I could have talked to. They watched me like they wondered what I'd taste like and would enjoy finding out.

The giant man-wolf spoke, its furry jaws thick and strange around human words. "You can't kill us all, human."

He was right. I raised the machine gun a little. "True, but who's going to be first in line?"

No one else moved as I walked. When I reached Richard, he took Stephen from me, cradling him in his arms like he was a child. Blood seeped down his face from a cut on his forehead. It covered half his face like a mask. "Stephen is never to come back here, not ever," Richard said.

The man-wolf spoke again, "You are not a killer, Richard. That is your weakness. Even if we bring Stephen back here, you will not kill us for it. You will hurt us, but not kill us."

Richard didn't say anything. It was probably true. Damn.

"I'll kill you," I said.

"Anita, you don't understand what you're saying," Richard said.

I glanced at him, then back to the waiting masses. "Killing is all they understand, Richard. If you aren't willing to kill them, Stephen isn't safe. I want him safe."

"Enough to kill for it?" Richard asked.

"Yeah," I said, "enough to kill for it."

The wolfman stared at me. "You are not one of us."

''It doesn't matter. Stephen is off limits. Tell Raina if he gets dragged back here, I'll hold her personally responsible.''

''Tell me yourself.'' Raina stood in the hallway, naked, and totally comfortable as if she'd been wearing the finest silk. Gabriel was at her back.

''If anyone brings Stephen back here, tries to force him into the movies, I'll kill you.''

''Even if I have nothing to do with it.''

I smiled, like I would believe that. ''Even if, no matter who does it, or why, it'll be your ass on the line.''

She nodded her head, almost a bow. ''So be it, Anita Blake. But know this, you have challenged me in front of my pack. I cannot let that stand unanswered. If you were another shapeshifter, we would duel, but your being human poses a problem.''

''You know this, bitch. I am human, so if you expect me to drop my gun and fight you one on one, you're crazy.''

''That would hardly be fair, would it?''

''I didn't think you worried much about being fair, after what I saw in the back room.''

''Oh, that,'' she said, ''Stephen will never rise in the pack. There is no more challenge to him. He is anyone's meat that is higher in the pack.''

''Not anymore,'' I said.

''You offer him your protection?'' she asked.

I'd been asked this question once before and knew it meant more than it sounded like it did, but I didn't care. I wanted Stephen safe, and I'd do what it took, killing or making myself a target. Hell, the assassin would probably finish me soon, anyway. ''Yeah, he's under my protection.''

''He's already under *my* protection, Anita,'' Richard said.

''Until you're willing to kill to back it up, it doesn't mean a whole lot to these people.''

''You will kill to support Richard's claims of protection?'' Raina asked.

''She doesn't understand what you're asking,'' Richard said. ''It isn't a fair question unless she understands it.''

''Then explain it to her, Richard, but not tonight. It grows late, and if we are to get any filming done, we must hurry. Take your little human and explain the rules to her. Explain how deep a hole she's dug herself tonight. When she understands the rules, call me. And I will think of a way to make a duel between us as fair as possible. Perhaps I could blindfold myself or tie one arm behind my back.''

I started to say something, but Richard said, ''Come on, Anita. We have to go now.'' He was right. I could kill a lot of them, but not all. I hadn't brought a spare clip for the machine gun. I hadn't thought I'd need it. Silly me.

We got out the door with me walking backwards, ready to shoot anyone who stuck a head out. No one followed us. Richard carried Stephen through the late spring night and didn't look back, as if he knew they wouldn't follow.

I opened the door, and he laid Stephen in the backseat. ''Can you drive home?'' he asked.

''Yeah, how bad are you hurt?''

''Not bad, but I'd like to ride back here with Stephen in case he wakes up.''

I couldn't argue with that. I drove. We were safe. We were all actually still alive. But if they'd rushed us, we wouldn't be. Now that we were safe, I could be mad. ''Well, we survived. No thanks to your little plan,'' I said.

''And no one died, thanks to my little plan,'' Richard said.

''Only because I was better armed than usual.''

''You were right,'' he said, ''it was a trap. Happy?''

''Yeah, I'm happy,'' I said.

''Glad to hear it.'' Underneath the sarcasm he was tired. I could hear it in his voice.

''What are you supposed to explain to me, Richard?'' I glanced in the rearview mirror but couldn't see his face in the dark.

''Raina backs up Marcus's orders. She's his lupa. He uses her to do things he doesn't approve of, like torture.''

''So I set myself up as your lupa.''

''Yes, I'm the Fenrir. Normally, I'd already have a lupa picked out. The pack is divided, Anita. I've given my protection to my followers so that if Marcus tries to hurt them, I come after him, or my followers will act to protect each other with my blessing. Without a Fenrir or a pack leader to back you up, it's a sort of mutiny to go against the pack leader's orders.''

''What's the penalty for mutiny?''

''Death or mutilation.''

''I thought you guys could heal anything short of a death wound.''

''Not if you shove burning metal into it. Fire purifies and stops the healing process, unless you reopen the wound.''

''It works that way with vampires, too,'' I said.

''I didn't know that,'' he said, but not like he really cared.

''How have you risen to next in line to lead and not killed anyone? You had to fight a lot of duels to get to the top of the heap.''

''Only the fight for Ulfric has to be to the death. All I had to do was beat them all.''

''Which is why you take karate and lift weights, so you'll be good enough to beat them.'' We'd had this discussion before when I asked if lifting weights when you could bench press a small car was redundant. He'd replied, not if everyone you're fighting can lift a car, too. He had a point.

''Yes.''

''But if you won't kill, then your threat doesn't have much bite, no pun intended.''

''We're not animals, Anita. Just because this is the way it's always been in the pack doesn't mean things can't change. We are still people, and that means we can control ourselves. Dammit, there has to be a better way than slaughtering each other.''

I shook my head. ''Don't blame it on the animals. Real wolves don't kill each other for dominance.''

''Only werewolves,'' he said. He sounded tired.

''I admire your goals, Richard.''

"But you don't agree."

"No, I don't agree."

His voice came from the darkness out of the backseat. "Stephen doesn't have any wounds. Why was he screaming?"

My shoulders hunched, and I made myself sit up straight. I turned onto Old Highway 21, and tried to think of a delicate way to tell him, but there was nothing delicate about rape. I told him what I'd seen.

The silence from the backseat lasted a very long time. I was almost to the turnoff for his house when he said, "And you think if I'd killed a few people along the way, this wouldn't have happened?"

"I think they're more afraid of Raina and Marcus than they are of you, so yeah."

"If you back my threat with killing, it undermines everything I've tried to do."

"I love you, Richard, and I admire what you're trying to do. I don't want to undermine you, but if they touch Stephen again, I'll do what I said I'd do. I'll kill them."

"They're my people, Anita. I don't want them dead."

"They're not your people, Richard. They're just a bunch of strangers that happen to share your disease. Stephen is your people. Every shapeshifter who threw their support to you and risked Marcus's anger, they're your people. They've risked everything for you, Richard."

"When Stephen joined the pack, I was the one who told Raina she couldn't have him. I've always stood by him."

"Your intentions are good, Richard, but they didn't keep him safe tonight."

"If I let you kill for me, Anita, it's the same as doing it myself."

"I didn't ask your permission, Richard."

He leaned on the back of the seat, and I realized he wasn't wearing his seat belt. I started to tell him to put it on, but didn't. It was his car, and he could survive a trip through the windshield. "You mean if they take Stephen again, you'll kill them because you said you'd kill them, not for me."

"A threat's not worth anything if you aren't willing to back it up," I said.

"You'd kill for Stephen. Why? Because he saved your life?"

I shook my head. It was hard to explain. "Not just that. When I saw him tonight, what they were doing to him . . . He was crying, Richard. He was . . . Oh, hell, Richard, he's mine now. There are a handful of people that I'd kill for, kill to keep safe, kill to revenge. Stephen's name got added to the list tonight."

"Is my name on the list?" he asked. He rested his chin on my shoulder over the seat. He rubbed his cheek on my face and I could feel a faint beard stubble, scratchy and real.

"You know it is."

"I don't understand how you can talk about killing so casually."

"I know."

"My bid for Ulfric would be stronger if I were willing to kill, but I'm not sure it would be worth it."

"If you want to martyr yourself for high ideals, fine. I don't like it, but fine.

But don't martyr the people who trust you. They're worth more than any set of ideals. You nearly got yourself killed tonight.''

''You don't just believe in something when it's easy, Anita. Killing is wrong.''

''Fine,'' I said, ''but you also nearly got *me* killed tonight. Do you understand that? If they had rushed us, I wouldn't have made it out. I will not go down in flames because you want to play Gandhi.''

''You can stay home next time.''

''Dammit, that isn't what I'm saying, and you know it. You're trying to live in some Ozzie and Harriet world, Richard. Maybe life used to work like that, but it doesn't anymore. If you don't give up on this, you're going to get killed.''

''If I really thought I had to become a murderer to survive, I think I'd rather not survive.''

I glanced at him. His expression was peaceful, like a saint. But you only got to be a saint if you died. I looked back at the road. I could give Richard up, but if I left him, he was going to end up dead. He'd have gone in there tonight without anyone, and he wouldn't have made it out.

Tears burned at the back of my eyes. ''I don't know if I'd survive it if you died on me, Richard. Doesn't that mean anything to you?''

He kissed my cheek, and something warm and liquid seeped down my neck. ''I love you, too.''

They were only words. He was going to get killed on me. He was going to do everything short of suicide. ''You're bleeding on me,'' I said.

He sighed and leaned back into the darkness. ''I'm bleeding a lot. Too bad Jean-Claude isn't here to lick it up.'' He made a bitter sound low in his throat.

''Do you need a doctor?''

''Get me home, Anita. If I need a doctor, I know a wererat that makes house calls.'' He sounded tired, weary, as if he didn't want to talk anymore. Not about the wounds, or the pack, or his high ideals. I let the silence grow and didn't know how to break it. A soft sound filled the quiet dark, and I realized that Richard was crying. He whispered, ''I'm sorry, Stephen. I am so sorry.''

I didn't say anything because I didn't have anything good to say. Just lately I had noticed that I could kill people and not blink. No attack of conscience, no nightmares, nothing. It was like some part of me had turned off. It didn't bother me that I was able to kill so easily. It did bother me that it didn't bother me. But it had its uses, like tonight. I think every last furry one of them had believed I'd do it. Sometimes, it was good to be scary.

9

It was 4:40 in the morning when Richard carried the still unconscious Stephen into his bedroom. Blood had dried the back of Richard's shirt to his skin. "Go to bed, Anita. I'll take care of Stephen."

"I need to look at your wounds," I said.

"I'm all right."

"Richard . . ."

He looked at me, half of his face covered in dried blood, his eyes almost wild. "No, Anita, I don't want your help. I don't need it."

I took in a deep breath through my nose and let it out. "Okay, have it your way."

I expected him to apologize for snapping at me, but he didn't. He just walked into the other room and closed the door. I stood there in the living room for a minute, not sure what to do. I'd hurt his feelings, maybe even offended his sense of male honor. Fuck it. If he couldn't take the truth, fuck him. People's lives were at stake. I couldn't give Richard comforting lies when it could get people killed.

I went into the guest room, locked the door, and went to bed. I put on an oversized T-shirt with a caricature of Arthur Conan Doyle on it. I'd packed something a little sexier. Yes, I admit it. I could have saved myself the trouble. The Firestar was lumpy under the pillow. The machine gun went under the bed within reach. I laid an extra clip beside it. Never thought I'd need that much firepower, but between assassination attempts and packs of werewolves, I was beginning to feel a little insecure.

When I shoved the silver knives half under the mattress so I could get to them if I had to, I realized just how insecure I was feeling. But I left the knives out. Better insecure and paranoid than dead.

I got my stuffed toy penguin, Sigmund, out of the suitcase and cuddled under the covers. I'd had some vague idea that spending the night at Richard's house might be romantic. Shows how much I knew. We'd had three fights in one night, a record even for me. It probably wasn't a good sign for the longevity of the relationship. That last thought made my chest tight, but what was I supposed to do? Go into the other room and apologize? Tell him he was right when he wasn't? Tell him it was okay to get himself killed and take the rest of us down with him? It wasn't okay. It wasn't even close to okay. I hugged Sigmund until he was nearly squeezed in two. I refused to cry. Question: Why was I more worried about losing Richard than about the assassins? Answer: Killing didn't bother me; losing Richard did. I fell asleep holding my penguin and wondering if Richard and I were still dating. Who would keep him alive if I wasn't around?

Something woke me. I blinked up into the dark and reached under my pillow for the Firestar. When it was secure in my hand, I listened. A knock, someone was knocking at the locked bedroom door. Soft, hesitant. Was it Richard come to apologize? That would be too convenient.

I threw back the covers, spilling Sigmund to the floor. I put him back in the suitcase, lowering the lid without closing it, and padded barefoot to the door. I stood to one side of it, and said, ''Who is it?''

''It's Stephen.''

I let out a breath I hadn't known I was holding. I crossed to the other side of the door, gun still ready, and unlocked the door. I opened it slowly, looking, listening, trying to make sure it was just Stephen.

He stood outside the door wearing a pair of Richard's cut-off sweat pants. The shorts hung nearly to his ankles. A borrowed T-shirt covered his knees. His long yellow hair was tousled, like he'd been asleep.

''What's wrong?'' I lowered the gun to my side, and he watched me do it.

''Richard went out, and I'm afraid to be alone.'' His eyes wouldn't quite meet mine when he said the last, flinching like he was afraid of what he'd see on my face.

''What do you mean he went out? Where to?''

''The woods. He said he'd keep watch for assassins. Does he mean Raina?'' He did look up then, amazing blue eyes wide, the beginnings of panic sliding across his face.

I touched his arm, not sure it was the right thing to do. Some people don't want to be touched after a sexual molestation. It seemed to comfort Stephen. But he glanced behind him at the empty living room, rubbing his hands along his bare arms.

''Richard told me to stay in the house. He said I needed to rest.'' He wouldn't meet my eyes again. ''I'm afraid to be alone, Anita. I . . .'' He hung his head, long yellow hair spilling like a curtain to hide his face. ''I can't get to sleep. I keep hearing noises.''

I put a finger under his chin and lifted his face gently. ''Are you asking to sleep in here with me?''

His eyes stared at me, wide and pain-filled. ''Richard said I could.''

''Run that by me again,'' I said.

''I told him I couldn't stand to be alone. He said, Anita's here, she'll protect you. Go sleep with her.'' He looked at me, his face awkward. Something must have shown on my face. ''You're mad now. I don't blame you. I'm sorry . . . I'll . . .'' He started to turn away, and I caught his arm.

''It's okay, Stephen. I'm not mad at you. Richard and I had a . . . disagreement, that's all.'' I didn't want him to sleep in here with me. The bed was too small for two people, and if I was going to share it with anyone, I'd have preferred Richard, but that wasn't going to happen. Maybe not ever at the rate we were going.

''You can stay in here.'' I didn't add, keep your hands to yourself. His face was raw with a need that had nothing to do with sex. He needed to be held, to be told the monster under the bed wasn't really there. I couldn't help him on the last. The monsters were real. But the first, I might manage that. Cold-blooded killer that I am, maybe I could share my toy penguin with him.

''Could you get an extra pillow from Richard's room?'' I asked.

He nodded and fetched it. He clutched it to his chest like he'd have rather slept with it than on it. Maybe the penguin wasn't such a bad idea.

I locked the door behind us. I could have moved into Richard's room. It was a bigger bed, but it also had a picture window with a deck and bird feeders. The guest room only had one small window. Easier to defend. Unless I wanted to go out a window, they were both traps, so we stayed in the more secure room. Besides, I'd have had to move all the weapons and it would have been dawn before I finished.

I pulled the covers back and said, ''You first.'' If something came through the door, I wanted to be the first to greet it, but I didn't say that out loud. Stephen was jumpy enough.

He climbed into bed with his pillow, pressing it against the wall, because there really wasn't room for two full-sized pillows. He lay on his back, staring up at me, his curling yellow hair falling around his face and bare shoulders like Sleeping Beauty. You didn't see many men with hair longer than mine. He was one of those men who was pretty rather than handsome, lovely as a doll. Staring up at me with his blue eyes, he looked about twelve. The look on his face was what did it, like he was expecting me to kick him, and he'd let me because he couldn't stop me. I understood in that moment what Raina had meant about him being anyone's meat. There was nothing dominant about Stephen, and it made me wonder about his background. Abused children will sometimes have that raw look to their eyes. And they'll take abuse, because it's normal.

''What's wrong?'' Stephen said.

I'd been staring. ''Nothing, just thinking.'' Tonight was not the night to ask if his father had beat him. I thought about throwing on a pair of jeans, but it would have been uncomfortable, not to mention hot. It was late spring, the heat hadn't set in. It was only seventy degrees, but it wasn't cool enough to wear jeans, especially if you had someone else in bed with you. Besides, I wasn't sure how Stephen would take me getting dressed to lie down beside him. Maybe he'd be insulted. It was too complicated for me. I turned off the light and climbed into bed beside him. If either of us had been much bigger, we'd have never fit. Stephen had to roll onto his side as it was.

He curled against my back, spooning his body against mine, one arm flung across my waist, like I was the stuffed toy. I stiffened, but Stephen didn't seem to notice. He buried his face into my back, and let his breath out in a sigh. I lay there in the dark and couldn't sleep. Two months ago after I'd nearly ended up a vampire, I'd had trouble sleeping. Close brushes with death, I could handle. Close brushes with becoming the undead, that scared me. But I got over it. I was sleeping just fine, thank you very much, until now. I pushed the button on my watch that made it glow. It was only 5:30. I'd had about an hour's sleep. Great.

Stephen's breathing deepened, and his body relaxed against me a muscle at a time. He whimpered softly in his sleep, arm convulsing around me, then the dream passed and he lay still and warm.

I drifted off to sleep, cuddling Stephen's arm around my body. He was almost as good as a stuffed toy, though he did have a tendency to move at the odd moment.

Daylight spilled through the thin white drapes, and at first I thought the light had awakened me. I woke stiff, in the same position that I'd fallen asleep in, as if I hadn't moved at all during the night. Stephen was still curled around me, a leg over my legs along with one arm like he was trying to get as close to me as he could, even in his sleep.

I lay there for a moment with his body wrapped around me and realized I'd never awakened with a man before. I'd had a fiancé in college and I'd had sex with him, but I'd never spent the night. I'd never actually slept in the same bed with a man. It was kind of odd. I lay in the circle of warmth of Stephen's body and wished it was Richard.

I had a vague feeling that something had awakened me, but what? I eased out from the covers and Stephen's clinging body. He rolled over on his other side, sighing, making small protesting noises. I tucked the covers around him and took the Firestar out from under my pillow.

According to my watch, it was nearly 10:30. I'd had about five hours of sleep. I slipped on a pair of jeans, got my toothbrush and some clean undies and socks out of the suitcase. I folded everything in a clean polo shirt and unlocked the door. I kept the Firestar in my hand. I'd put it on the top of the toilet while I cleaned up. I'd have done the same thing at home.

Someone passed in front of the door, talking. Two voices, one of them female. I laid the clothes on the floor, unclicked the safety on the gun, and put my left hand on the doorknob.

''Was that the safety on a gun I heard?'' a man's voice said from the other side of the door. I recognized the voice.

I clicked the safety back in place, put the gun down the front of my pants, and slipped the T-shirt over it. Armed, but not visibly, I opened the door. Jason stood there, grinning at me. He was about my height. His blond hair was straight and baby fine, and cut just above his shoulders. His eyes were the innocent blue of spring skies, but the look in them wasn't innocent. He peered around me at Stephen still curled up in the bed.

''Is it my turn next?'' he asked.

I sighed, picked up my clothes, tucked them under my arm, and closed the door behind me. ''What are you doing here, Jason?''

''You don't sound happy to see me.'' He was wearing a fishnet T-shirt. His jeans were faded and soft with one knee completely out. He was twenty and had been a college student before he'd joined the pack. Now he was Jean-Claude's wolf, and playing bodyguard and breakfast entrée to the Master Vampire of the City seemed to be his only job.

''Isn't it a little early in the morning for fishnet?''

''Wait until you see what I'm wearing to tonight's gala opening of Jean-Claude's dance club.''

''I may not be able to make it,'' I said.

He raised his eyebrows. ''You spend one night under Richard's roof, and you break a date with Jean-Claude.'' He shook his head. ''I don't think that's a good idea.''

''Look, neither of them own me, okay?''

Jason backed up, hands held up in mock surrender. ''Hey, don't shoot the messenger. You know it will piss Jean-Claude off, and you know he'll think you slept with Richard.''

''I didn't.''

He glanced at the closed door. ''I know that, and I am shocked, Anita, at your choice of bed partners.''

''When you tell Jean-Claude that I slept with Stephen, you make absolutely sure he knows we just shared the bed and nothing else. If Jean-Claude gives Stephen a hard time because of your word games, I'll be angry. You don't want me angry, Jason.''

He looked at me for a heartbeat or two. Something slid behind his eyes, his beast stirring to life, just a touch. Jason had a small streak of what Gabriel had a big streak of. A fascination with danger, pain, and simply being an all round pain in the ass. Jason was tolerable, not a bad guy, all in all; Gabriel was perverted; but it was still the same personality flaw done small. After what I'd seen last night, I wondered what Jason would have thought of the entertainment. I was almost sure he'd have disapproved, but not a hundred percent sure, which told you something about Jason.

''Did you really draw a machine gun on Raina and Gabriel last night?''

''Yeah, I did.''

A woman stepped out of Richard's bedroom with an armful of towels. She was about five foot six, with short brown hair so curly it had to be natural. She wore navy slacks and a short-sleeved sweater. Open-toed sandals completed the outfit. She looked me up and down, sort of disapproving or maybe disappointed. ''You must be Anita Blake.''

''And you are?''

''Sylvie Barker.'' She offered a hand and I took it. The moment I touched her skin, I knew what she was. ''Are you with the pack?'' I asked.

She took her hand back and blinked at me. ''How could you tell?''

''If you're trying to pass for human, don't touch someone who knows what they're looking for. Your power prickles down my skin.''

''I won't waste time trying to pass then.'' Her power flooded over me, pouring like a blast of heat when you open an oven door.

''Impressive,'' I said, glad my voice was steady.

She gave a small smile. ''That's quite a compliment, coming from you. Now, I've got to get these towels to the kitchen.''

''What's happening?'' I asked.

Sylvie and Jason exchanged glances. She shook her head. "You knew Richard was hurt?" She made it a question.

My stomach clenched tight. "He said he'd be all right."

"He will be," she said.

I felt my skin go pale. "Where is he?"

"Kitchen," Jason said.

I didn't run, it wasn't that far, but I wanted to. Richard sat at the kitchen table, shirtless, his back to me. His back was a mass of fresh claw marks. There was a bite mark in his left shoulder where a piece of flesh was missing.

Dr. Lillian was blotting blood off his back with a kitchen towel. She was a small woman in her mid-fifties with salt-and-pepper hair cut in a short, no-nonsense style. She'd treated my own wounds twice before, once when she was furry and looked like a giant man-rat.

"If you had called for medical attention last night, I wouldn't be having to do this, Richard. I do not enjoy causing my patients pain."

"Marcus was on call last night," Richard said. "Under the circumstances, I thought it best to go without."

"You could have let someone clean and bandage the wounds."

"Yes, Richard, you could have let me help you," I said.

He glanced back over his shoulder, his hair spilling around his face. There was a bandage on his forehead. "I'd had enough help for one night."

"Why? Because I'm a woman, or because you know I'm right?"

Lillian took a small silver knife to the lower half of a claw mark. She sliced the blade down the wound, reopening it. Richard took in a deep breath and let it out.

"What are you doing?" I asked.

"Lycanthropes heal, but sometimes without medical attention, we can scar. Most of the wounds will heal, but a few of them are deep enough that he really needs some stitching before the skin starts to close, so I'm having to reopen some of the wounds and add a few stitches."

Sylvie handed Dr. Lillian the towels.

"Thank you, Sylvie."

"What are you two lovebirds fighting about?" Sylvie asked.

"Let Richard tell you, if he wants to."

"Anita agrees with you," Richard said. "She thinks I should start killing people."

I walked over to where he could see me without straining. I leaned against the cabinet island and tried to watch his face rather than Lillian's slicing knife. "I don't want you to start killing people indiscriminately, Richard. Just back your threat up. Kill one person and the rest will back down."

He glared up at me, outraged. "You mean make an example of one of them?"

Put that way, it sounded sort of cold-blooded, but truth was truth. "Yeah, that's what I mean."

"Oh, I like her," Sylvie said.

"I knew you would," Jason said. They exchanged a glance that I didn't quite get, but it seemed to amuse the hell out of them.

''Am I missing a joke here?''

They both shook their heads.

I let it go. Richard and I were still fighting, and I was beginning to think this fight had no end. He winced as the doctor sliced open another wound. She was only adding a stitch here and there, but it was still more than I'd have wanted in my flesh. I didn't like stitches.

''No painkillers?'' I asked.

''Anesthesia doesn't work well on us. We metabolize it too quickly,'' Lillian said. She wiped the silver knife on one of the clean towels and said, ''One of the claw marks drops below your jeans. Take them off so I can see.''

I glanced at Sylvie. She smiled at me. ''Don't mind me. I like girls.''

''That's what you two were laughing about,'' I said to Jason.

He nodded, smiling happily.

I shook my head.

''The others will be here soon for the meeting. I don't want my ass hanging out as everyone comes in the door.'' Richard stood up. ''Let's finish up in the bedroom.'' There were a ring of puncture wounds just below his collarbone. I remembered the man-wolf lifting with its claws last night.

''You could have been killed,'' I said.

He glanced at me. ''But I wasn't. Isn't that what you always say?''

I hated having my own words fed back to me. ''You could have killed Sebastian or Jamil and the rest wouldn't have jumped you.''

''You've already decided who I should kill.'' His voice was thick with anger.

''Yeah,'' I said.

''She's actually making pretty good choices,'' Sylvie said.

Richard turned his dark, dark eyes to her. ''You stay out of this.''

''If it was just a lovers' quarrel, Richard, I would,'' she said. She went to stand in front of him. ''But Anita's not saying anything that I haven't said. That most of us haven't begged you to do. For a few months, I was willing to try it your way. I hoped you were right, but it isn't working, Richard. Either you're alpha male or you're not.''

''Is that a challenge?'' he asked. His voice had grown very quiet. Power flowed through the room like a warm wind.

Sylvie backed up a step. ''You know it's not.''

''Do I?'' he said. The power in the room built, growing like a flash of electricity. The hairs on my arms stood to attention.

Sylvie stopped backing up, hands in fists at her sides. ''If I thought I could defeat Marcus, I'd do it. If I could protect us all, I would. But I can't do it, Richard. You're our only chance.''

Richard loomed over her. It wasn't just physical size. His power flowed over her, filled the room, until it was almost chokingly close.

''I won't kill just because you think I should, Sylvie. No one is going to force me into it. No one.''

He turned his gaze on me, and it took a lot to meet his eyes. There was a force to them, a burning weight. It wasn't a vampire's drowning power, but it was something. My skin shivered with his power, his energy, and I didn't turn away.

I stared at the wounds just below his neck and knew I'd come close to losing him. That was unacceptable.

I walked closer until I could have reached out and touched him. His otherworldly energy whirled over me until it was hard to draw a good breath. ''We need to talk, Richard.''

''I don't have time for this right now, Anita.''

''Make time,'' I said.

He glared down at me. ''Talk to me while Lillian finishes up. I've got people coming over for a meeting in about fifteen minutes.''

''What meeting?'' I asked.

''To discuss the Marcus situation,'' Sylvie said. ''He scheduled the meeting before last night's adventure.''

Richard stared at her, and it wasn't a friendly look. ''If I'd wanted her to know about the meeting, I'd have told her.''

''What else haven't you told me Richard?''

He turned those angry eyes to me. ''What haven't you told me?''

I blinked at him, genuinely puzzled. ''I don't know what you're talking about.''

''A shotgun fires over your head twice and you don't know what I'm talking about.''

Oh that. ''I did the right thing, Richard.''

''You're always right, aren't you?''

I looked at the floor and shook my head. When I looked back at him, he was still angry, but I was losing my anger. A first. This was going to be *the* fight. The one that ended it. I wasn't wrong. No amount of talking would change that. But if we were going to break up, we'd go down in flames. ''Let's finish this, Richard. You wanted to go into the bedroom.''

He stood up, body stiff with an anger that was deeper than I could comprehend. It was controlled rage, and I didn't understand where it was coming from. It was a bad sign. ''You sure you can stand to see me naked?'' His voice was utterly bitter, and I didn't know why.

''What's wrong, Richard? What did I do?''

He shook his head too vigorously, making him wince as his shoulder caught the movement. ''Nothing, nothing.'' He walked out of the room. Lillian looked at me, but followed him. I sighed and joined them. I wasn't looking forward to the next few minutes, but I wasn't going to chicken out. We'd say all the ugly things and make it as nasty as possible. Trouble was, I didn't have any nasty things to say. It made the fight a lot less fun for me.

Jason whispered as I walked by, very softly, ''Go, Anita, go, Anita.''

It made me smile.

Sylvie watched me with cool eyes. ''Good luck.'' It didn't sound completely sincere.

''Do you have a problem?'' I'd have much rather fought with her than Richard.

''If he wasn't dating you, then he might choose a mate. It would help things.''

''You want the job?'' I asked.

''Yes,'' she said, ''I do, but sex is integral and I'm not up for it.''

''Then I'm not standing in your way,'' I said.

''Not in mine, no,'' she said.

Which implied there were others, but I didn't give a shit, not today. I said, ''It is too damn early in the morning for furball politics. If someone wants a piece of me, tell them to go to the back of the line.''

She cocked her head to one side, like a curious dog. ''Is it a long line?''

''Lately, yeah.''

''I thought all your enemies were dead,'' Jason said.

''I keep making new ones,'' I said.

He smiled. ''Fancy that.''

I shook my head and walked towards the bedroom. I'd have rather faced Raina again than Richard. I almost hoped the assassin would jump out of the woodwork and give me something to shoot at. It would hurt less than breaking up with Richard.

10

Richard's bedroom was painted pale green, a vibrant rug thrown in front of the bed like a piece of stained glass. The bed was a heavy four-poster, and even hurt, he'd made the bed, pulling the solid red spread up over it. He had three solid spreads that he rotated on the bed; green, blue, and red. Each color picked up a different color in the rug and the painting over the bed. The painting was of wolves in a winter scene. The wolves were looking directly out of the picture as if you'd just come around a tree and surprised them. There was a deer bleeding on the snow, its throat torn out. It was an odd choice for a bedroom, but it fit somehow. Besides, I liked it. It had that quality that all fine paintings do, as if when you leave the room the painting will move, life suspended and captured on canvas. The green spread emphasized the evergreens, the blue spread caught the washed blue of the sky and the bluish shadows, the red caught the stain of blood on the snow.

Richard lay on his stomach across the crimson cloth. He was totally nude, his jeans thrown on the corner of the bed. His tanned skin looked dark and smooth and incredibly touchable against the red cloth. I felt heat rise up my face as my eyes followed the curve of his body, over the smooth expanse of his buttocks. Lillian had just finished sewing up a curve of claw that had spilled down from his buttocks. I looked away.

I'd seen Richard nude once when I first met him, but never since. We hadn't even been thinking about dating then. I had to look away, mainly because I wanted to look. I wanted to see him like that, and it was too embarrassing for words. I studied the contents of the built-in shelves on his bedroom wall like I'd memorize them. Bits of quartz, a small bird's nest. There was a lump of fossilized coral as big as my hand, a dark rich gold in color with streaks of white quartz. I'd found it on a camping trip and given it to him because he collected bits and pieces, and I didn't. I touched the bit of coral, and didn't want to turn around.

"You said you wanted to talk, then talk," Richard said.

I glanced back. Lillian snipped the black thread she was using to close his skin. "There," she said. "You shouldn't even have a scar."

Richard folded his arms on the bed, resting his chin on his forearms. His hair spread around his face, foaming and touchable. I knew it was as soft as it looked.

Lillian glanced from one to the other of us. "I believe I'll leave you two alone." She began putting things into her bag, which was brown leather and looked more like a fishing tackle box than anything else. She looked at Richard and back to me. "Take a piece of advice from an old lady. Don't screw up."

She left with Richard and me both staring after her.

"You can get dressed now," I said.

He glanced at his crumpled jeans, moving only his dark eyes. His eyes came back to me, and they were as angry as I'd ever seen them. "Why?"

I concentrated on meeting those angry eyes and tried not to stare at his body. It was harder than I would have admitted out loud. "Because it's hard to fight with you when you're naked."

He raised up on his elbows, hair falling down into his eyes, until he stared at me through a curtain of brown gold hair. It reminded me of Gabriel, and that was unnerving as hell.

"I know you want me, Anita. I can smell it."

Oh, that made me feel better. I blushed for the second time in five minutes. "So, you're gorgeous. So what? What the hell does that have to do with anything?"

He raised up on all fours, knees, and hands. I looked away so fast it made me dizzy. "Please put on your jeans."

I heard him slide off the bed. "You can't even look at me, can you?"

There was something about the way he said it that made me want to see his face, but I couldn't turn around. I just couldn't. If this was the last fight we ever had, I didn't want the memory of his body imprinted on my mind. It would be too cruel.

I felt him standing behind me. "What do you want from me, Richard?"

"Look at me."

I shook my head.

He touched my shoulder, and I jerked away.

"You can't even stand for me to touch you, can you?" For the first time, I heard pain in his voice, raw and hurting.

I turned then. I had to see his face. His eyes glittered with unshed tears, eyes wide so they wouldn't fall. He'd pushed his hair back from his face, but it was already spilling forward. My eyes traveled down his muscular chest, and I wanted to run my hands over his nipples, down his slender waist, and lower. I drew my eyes back up to his face with force of will alone, my face pale now, rather than blushing. I was having trouble breathing. My heart was beating so hard, it was hard to hear.

"I love it when you touch me," I said.

He stared down at me, his eyes filled with pain. I think I preferred the anger. "I used to admire you for saying no to Jean-Claude. I know you want him, and you keep refusing. I thought it was very moral of you." He shook his head, one tear slid from the corner of his eye, trailing in slow motion down his cheek.

I brushed the tear from his face with my fingertip. He caught my hand in his, holding it a little too hard, but not hurting, only surprising. It was also my right hand, and drawing the gun left-handed was going to be a bitch. Not that I really thought I'd need the gun, but he was acting so strangely.

Richard spoke, staring down at me. "But Jean-Claude's a monster and you don't sleep with monsters. You just kill them." Tears slid from both of his eyes and I let them fall. "You don't sleep with me, either, because I'm a monster, too. But you can kill us, can't you, Anita? You just can't fuck us."

I jerked away from him, and he let me. He could have bench pressed the heavy cherry wood bed, so he let me go. I didn't like that much. "That was an ugly thing to say."

"But it's true," he said.

"I want you, Richard, you know that."

"You want Jean-Claude, too, so that's not very flattering. You tell me to kill Marcus, like it would be easy. Do you think it wouldn't bother me to kill him because he's a monster, or because I am?"

"Richard," I said. This was an argument I hadn't seen coming. I didn't know what to say, but I had to say something. He was standing there with tears drying on his face. Even nude and gorgeous, he looked lost.

"I know it would bother you to kill Marcus. I never said it wouldn't," I said.

"Then how can you urge me to do it?"

"I think it's necessary," I said.

"Could you do it? Could you just kill him?"

I thought about that for a moment, then nodded. "Yeah, I could."

"And that wouldn't bother you?" he asked.

I stared straight at him, looked him right in his pain-filled eyes, and said, "No."

"If you really mean that, it makes you a bigger monster than I am."

"Yeah, I guess it does."

He shook his head. "It doesn't bother you, does it, knowing that you could take a human life?" He laughed, and it was bitter. "Or don't you consider Marcus human?"

"The man I killed last night was human," I said.

Richard stared at me, fresh horror growing in his eyes. "And you slept just fine didn't you?"

I nodded. "Pretty good, considering you sent Stephen to my bed."

A strange look passed through his eyes, and for a split second, I saw him wonder.

"Sweet Jesus, you know me better than that."

He looked down. "I know. It's just that I want you so badly, and you keep saying, no. It makes me doubt everything."

"Shit. I am not going to stroke your ego in the middle of a fight. You sent Stephen to me because you were mad. Said I could protect him. Had it occurred to you that I'd never slept—just slept—in the same bed with a man before?"

"What about your fiancé in college?"

"I had sex with him, but I didn't sleep over," I said. "The first time I woke up in the morning with a man curled around me, I wanted it to be you."

"I'm sorry, Anita. I didn't know. I . . ."

"You didn't think. Great. Now, what's with the no clothes? What's going on, Richard?"

"You saw the fight last night. You saw what I did, what I can do."

"Some of it, yeah."

He shook his head. "You want to know why I don't kill? Why I always stop just short of it?" The look in his eyes was almost desperate, wild.

"Tell me," I said, softly.

"I enjoy it, Anita. I love the feel of my hands, my claws ripping into flesh." He hugged himself. "The taste of fresh, warm blood in my mouth is exciting." He shook his head harder, as if he could erase the sensation. "I wanted to rip Sebastian apart last night. I could feel it, like an ache in my shoulders, in my arms. My body wanted to kill him, the way I want you." He stared at me, still hugging himself, but his body was speaking for him. The thought of killing Sebastian did excite him, really excite him.

I swallowed hard. "You're afraid that if you let go and killed, that you'd like that, too?"

He stared at me, and that was the horror in his eyes: the fear that he was a monster, the fear that I was right not to touch him, not to let him touch me. You don't fuck the monsters, you just kill them.

"Do you enjoy killing?" he asked.

I had to think about that for a second or two. Finally, I shook my head. "No, I don't enjoy it."

"What does it feel like?" he asked.

"Like nothing. I don't feel anything."

"You have to feel something."

I shrugged. "Relief that it wasn't me. Triumph that I was faster, meaner." I shrugged again. "It doesn't bother me to kill people, Richard. It just doesn't."

"Did it once?"

"Yes, it used to bother me."

"When did it stop bothering you?"

"I don't know. Not the first death, or the second, but when it gets to the point that you can't keep track of them all . . . It either stops bothering you or you find another line of work."

"I want it to bother me, Anita. Killing should mean something other than blood, and excitement, or even survival. If it doesn't, then I'm wrong, and we are just animals." His body reacted to the thought, too. And he did not find it exciting. He looked vulnerable and afraid. I wanted to tell him to get dressed, but I didn't. He'd chosen to be naked very deliberately, as if to prove once and for all that I didn't want him, or that I did.

I didn't much like tests, but it was hard to bitch with the fear in his eyes. He'd walked away to stand in front of the bed. He rubbed one hand up and down the opposite arm as if he were cold. It was May in Saint Louis. He wasn't cold, at least not that kind of cold.

"You aren't animals, Richard."

"How do you know what I am?" And I knew that he was asking the question more of himself than of me.

I walked over to him. I took the Firestar out of the front of my pants and laid it on the night stand beside his cut glass lamp. He watched me do it, eyes wary. Almost like he expected me to hurt him. I was going to try very hard not to do that.

I touched his arm, gently, where he was rubbing it. He froze under my touch. ''You are one of the most moral people I have ever met. You can kill Marcus and not become a ravening beast. I know that, because I know you.''

''Gabriel and Raina kill and look what they are.''

''You aren't like them, Richard. Trust me on that.''

''What if I kill Sebastian or Marcus, and I enjoy it.'' His handsome face was raw with terror at the thought.

''Maybe it will feel good.'' I gripped his arm tighter. ''But if it does, there's no shame in that. You are what you are. You didn't choose it. It chose you.''

''How can you say there's no shame in enjoying killing something. I've hunted deer and I love it. I love the chase, and the kill, and eating the warm meat.'' As before, the thought excited him. I kept my eyes on his face as much as possible, but it was distracting.

''Everyone has different things that flip their switch, Richard. I've heard worse. Hell, I've seen worse.''

He stared down at me like he wanted to believe me and was afraid to. ''Worse than this.'' He lifted his right hand from its grip on his arm, he held his hand in front of my face. His power prickled over my hand, down my arm, until I gasped. It was force of will alone that kept my hand on his arm.

His fingers elongated, stretching impossibly long and thin. The nails grew into heavy claws. It wasn't a wolf hand, rather his own grown into a claw. Nothing else had changed that I could see. Only that one hand.

I was having trouble breathing, for different reasons than before. I stared at the clawed hand and realized for the first time that he was right. Watching the bones in his hand stretch and pop sickened me, scared me.

I kept my hand on his arm, but I was shaking. I found my voice, and it shook, too. ''I saw Raina do that once. I thought it wasn't a common ability.''

''Only Raina, Marcus, and I can do it within our pack. We can partially change at will.''

''That's how you stabbed Sebastian last night.''

He nodded, eyes searching my face. I was fighting to keep it blank, but what he saw there wasn't reassuring enough. He turned away from me, and I didn't have to see his eyes to feel the pain.

I grabbed his hand and wrapped my fingers around those long, thin bones. I felt muscles under my hands that had never been in Richard's hand before. It took everything I had to hold that hand. To touch him like that. Everything. The effort left me shaking and unable to meet his eyes. I didn't trust what he'd see in them.

He touched my chin with his other hand and turned me slowly to face him. He stared down at me. ''I can taste your fear, and I like it. Do you understand? I like it.''

I had to clear my throat to talk. ''I noticed,'' I said.

He had the grace to blush. He bent slowly to kiss me. I didn't try to stop him, but I didn't help, either. I usually rose on tiptoe to meet him halfway. I stood there, too scared to move, forcing his tall body to bend at the shoulders, to fold down towards me. The long, thin-fingered hand that I was holding convulsed around me, the claws playing lightly on my bare forearm.

I tensed, and his power poured over me. I held onto his hand while the muscles and bones slid back into place. I held on with both hands while his hand re-formed under mine. My skin shuddered with the spill of power.

His lips brushed mine, and I kissed him back, almost swaying. I let go of his hand, my fingers brushed his bare chest, playing over his hardened nipples. His hands slid around my waist, fingers kneading upward, over my ribs, along my spine. He whispered into my mouth, "You're not wearing anything under this T-shirt."

"I know," I said.

His hands slid under the shirt, caressing my back, pressing our bodies together. His naked body touched me, and even through my jeans, it made me shudder. I wanted to feel his naked flesh against mine so badly, I could feel it like a hunger in my skin. I slipped the T-shirt off, and he made a sound of surprise.

He stared down at my bare breasts, and he wasn't the only one excited. He ran his hands over my breasts, and when I didn't stop him, he dropped to his knees in front of me. He looked up at me, his brown eyes filled with a dark light.

I kissed him while he knelt in front of me, as if I'd eat him from the mouth down. The feel of him against my naked flesh was almost too much.

He broke from the kiss and ran his mouth over my breasts. It brought a surprised moan from my throat.

There was a knock at the door. We froze. A woman's voice that I didn't recognize said, "I didn't come all this way to listen to you make out, Richard. I'd like to remind you that all of us have incredibly good hearing."

"Not to mention sense of smell." That was Jason.

"Damn," he said softly, head buried against me.

I leaned my head over him, burying my face in his hair. "I think I'll just climb out the window."

He hugged me around the waist and stood, passing his hands over my breasts one last time. "I can't tell you how long I've wanted to do that."

He reached for his jeans and underpants still lying on the bed. I touched his arm, bringing his attention back to me.

"I want you, Richard. I love you. I want you to believe that."

He stared at me, his face grew strange and solemn. "You haven't seen me change into a wolf yet. You need to see that before we go any further."

The thought did not excite me, and I was glad I was the girl, so it didn't show. "You're right, though if you'd played your cards right, we might have had sex first."

"It wouldn't be fair to you."

"So you're saying even if we'd been alone you'd have stopped and shape-shifted."

He nodded.

"Because it wouldn't be fair to sleep with me until I'd seen the whole package?"

"Exactly."

"You are such a boy scout, Richard."

"I think I just lost one of my merit badges," he said. The look on his face brought a rush of heat up my neck.

He grinned and slipped on his pants. He wore briefs. He pulled on his jeans and was careful zipping them up. I watched him get dressed with a proprietary air. An air of anticipation.

I picked the T-shirt up from the floor and pulled it back on. Richard came up behind me, sliding his hands under the shirt, cupping a hand around each breast, kneading them. I leaned back against him. He was the one who stopped, hugging me around the waist, picking me an inch off the floor. He turned me around and gave me a quick kiss. "When you make up your mind to do something, you really make up your mind, don't you?"

"Always," I said.

He took in a deep breath through his nose and out through his mouth. "I'd try to make it a quick meeting, but . . ."

"Edward should be here soon, so it doesn't matter."

He nodded, his face falling. "I almost forgot that someone was trying to kill you." He cupped my face in his hands and kissed me, eyes searching my face. "Be careful."

I touched the bandage on his shoulder. "You, too."

He pulled a black T-shirt from a drawer and slipped it on. He tucked it into his jeans, and I made myself stay away from him while he fumbled with his zipper. "Join us after you get dressed."

I nodded. "Sure." He left, closing the door behind him. I sighed and sat down on the edge of the bed. Damn. I didn't want to lose Richard. I really didn't. I wanted to sleep with him. I wasn't sure how I felt about seeing him change into full animal form. The hand thing had bothered me enough. What if I couldn't take it? What if it was too gross? Dear God, I hoped not. I hoped I was a better person than that. A stronger person than that.

Richard was afraid that if he started to kill, he'd just keep killing. It wasn't a completely unreasonable fear. I hugged myself tight. The feel of his body against mine clung to my skin. The feel of his mouth on me . . . I shivered, and it wasn't fear. It was stupid to love Richard. Having sex with him would make it worse. He was going to be dead soon if he didn't kill Marcus. Simple as that. Jean-Claude would never have endangered himself like that. Never. You could always trust Jean-Claude to survive. It was one of his talents. I was almost sure it wasn't one of Richard's. Last night should have proved to me beyond any doubt that I should dump him. Or that he should dump me. You could agree to disagree on politics, or even religion sometimes, but you either killed people or you didn't. Homicide was not something you could be neutral on.

Jean-Claude didn't mind killing people. Once upon a time, I'd thought that made him monstrous. Now I agreed with him. Will the real monster please stand up?

11

I'd finally gotten dressed, red polo shirt, black jeans, black Nikes, the Firestar 9mm in its inner-pants holster. The gun was very visible against the red shirt, but hey, why try to hide it? Besides, I could feel the roil of power just outside the door. Shapeshifters, not all of them happy. Strong emotions make it harder to hide their power. Richard was one of the best at hiding it that I'd ever met. He'd fooled me for a while, made me think he was human. No one else had ever been able to do that.

I looked at myself in the mirror and realized that it wasn't facing a room full of lycanthropes that bothered me, it was facing a room full of people who knew that Richard and I had been making out. I preferred danger to embarrassment any day. I was used to danger.

The bathroom was just off the living room, so when I opened the door, they were all there, clustered on or around the couch. They glanced at me as I stepped out, and I nodded. ''Hello.''

Rafael said, ''Hello, Anita.'' He was the Rat King, the wererats equivalent of pack leader. He was tall, dark, and handsome with strong Mexican features that made his face seem stern. Only his lips hinted that perhaps there were more smiles than frowns in him. He was wearing a short-sleeved dress shirt that left the brand on his arm bare. The brand was in the shape of a crown, and was the mark of kingship. There was no equivalent mark among the wolves. Being a lycanthrope meant different things, depending on the animal; different cultures as well as forms.

''I didn't know the wererats would be interested in the packs' internal squabbles,'' I said.

''Marcus is trying to unify all shapeshifters under one leader.''

''Let me guess,'' I said, ''he gets to be leader.''

Rafael gave a small smile. ''Yes.''

''So you've thrown in with Richard as the lesser evil?'' I made it a question.

''I've thrown in with Richard because he is a man of his word. Marcus has no honor. His bitch Raina has seen to that.''

''I still think if we killed Raina, Marcus might be willing to talk with us.''

This from a woman who I thought I'd seen before but couldn't place. She sat on the floor sipping coffee from a mug. She had short blond hair, and was wearing a pink nylon jogging suit, jacket open over a pink T-shirt. It was a jogging suit made for looking at, not working out in, and I remembered her. I'd seen her at the Lunatic Cafe, Raina's restaurant. Her name was Christine. She wasn't a wolf, she was a weretiger. She was here to speak on behalf of the independent shapeshifters. Those who didn't have enough people to have a leader. Not every kind of lycanthropy was equally contagious. You could get cut to pieces by a weretiger and not get it. A werewolf could barely cut you and you got furry. Almost none of the cat-based lycanthropy was as contagious as wolf and rat. No one knew why. It was just the way it worked.

Richard introduced me to about fifteen others, first names only.

I said hi and leaned against the wall by the door. The couch was full, and so was the floor. Besides, I liked being out of reach of any shapeshifter I didn't know. Just a precaution.

"Actually, I've met Christine before," I said.

"Yes," Christine said, "the night you killed Alfred."

I shrugged. "Yeah."

"Why didn't you kill Raina last night when you had the chance?" she said.

Before I could answer, Richard interrupted. "If we kill Raina," he said, "Marcus will hunt us all down."

"I don't think he's up to the job," Sylvie said.

Richard shook his head. "No, I still won't give up on Marcus."

No one said anything, but the looks on their faces were enough. They agreed with me. Richard was going to get himself killed and hang his followers out to dry.

Louie came out of the kitchen carrying two mugs of coffee. He smiled at me. Louie was Richard's best friend, and he'd gone on a lot of hiking dates with us. He was five foot six, with eyes darker than my own, true black, not just darkest brown. His baby-fine black hair had been cut recently. He'd worn it long for all the time I'd known him, not a fashion statement like Richard; he just never got around to getting it cut. Now it was short enough that his ears showed, and he looked older, more like a professor with a doctorate in biology. He was a wererat, and one of Rafael's lieutenants. He handed me one of the mugs.

"These meetings have been so much more pleasant since Richard bought that coffeemaker. Thanks to you."

I took a big breath of coffee, and felt better instantly. Coffee might not be a cure-all, but it was close. "I'm not sure everyone is happy to see me."

"They're scared. It makes them a little hostile."

Stephen came out of the guest room dressed in clothes that fit too well to be Richard's. A blue dress shirt, tucked into faded blue jeans. The only man in the room that was close to Richard's size was Jason. Jason never minded sharing his clothes.

"Why does everyone look so grim?" I asked.

Louie leaned against the wall, sipping coffee. "Jean-Claude withdrew his support of Marcus and threw in with Richard. I can't believe neither of them mentioned that.''

''They said something about having formed a bargain, but they didn't explain.'' I thought about what he'd just told me. ''Marcus must be pissed.''

The smile faded from his face. ''That is an understatement.'' He looked at me. ''You don't understand, do you?''

''Understand what?'' I asked.

''Without Jean-Claude's backing, Marcus doesn't stand a chance of forcing the rest of the shapeshifters under his control. His dreams of empire building are finished.''

''If he doesn't stand a chance, why is everyone so worried?''

Louie gave a sad smile. ''What Marcus can't control, he has a tendency to kill.''

''You mean he'd start a war?''

''Yes.''

''Not just with Richard and the pack, you mean, but an all-out war with all the other shapeshifters in town?''

Louie nodded. ''Except the wereleopards. Gabriel is their leader and he sides with Raina.''

I thought about it for a second or two. ''Sweet Jesus, it would be a bloodbath.''

''And there'd be no way of containing it, Anita. Some of it would spill over onto the normal world. There are still three states in this country that will pay hundreds of dollars in bounty for a dead shapeshifter, no questions asked. A war like this could make the practice look practical.''

''Do you two have something better to do?'' Christine asked. I was beginning not to like her. It was she that knocked on the door and interrupted Richard and me. Frankly, for that I was sort of grateful. The thought of everyone hearing us go further would have been too embarrassing for words.

Louie moved back to sit on the floor with the others. I stayed leaning against the wall, sipping my coffee.

''Are you going to join us?'' she asked.

''I'm fine where I am,'' I said.

''Too good to sit with us?'' a man in his late thirties with dark blue eyes asked. He was about five foot eight; it was hard to tell with him sitting on the floor. He was dressed in a suit, complete with tie, as if he was on his way to work. His name was Neal.

''Not good enough,'' I said, ''not good enough by half.''

''What the hell's that supposed to mean?'' he asked. ''I don't like having a normal here.''

''Leave it alone, Neal,'' Richard said.

''Why? She's laughing at us.''

Richard glanced back at me from his corner of the couch. ''Come join us, Anita?''

Sylvie was sitting beside Richard, not too close, but still, there was not enough room for me. Rafael sat on the end of the couch, spine straight, ankle propped on one knee.

"Couch looks full," I said.

Richard held out his hand to me. "We'll make room."

"She isn't even pack," Sylvie said. "I won't give up my seat to her. No offense to you, Anita, you don't know any better." Her voice was matter-of-fact, not hostile, but the look she gave Richard wasn't exactly friendly.

"No offense taken," I said. I wasn't sure I wanted to sit on the couch surrounded by lycanthropes anyway. Even supposedly friendly ones. Everyone in the room was stronger and faster than I was, just a fact. The only leg up I had was the gun. If I sat right beside them, I'd never get it out in time.

"I want my girlfriend to sit with me, Sylvie, that's all," Richard said. "It isn't meant as a challenge to your position in the lukoi." His voice sounded patient like he was talking to a child.

"What did you say?" Sylvie asked. She looked shocked.

"We are the lukoi. Anita knows that."

"You shared our words with her?" Neal said, outrage thick in his voice.

I wanted to say that it was just words, but I didn't. Who says I'm not getting smarter?

"There was a time when sharing our secrets with normals could get you a death sentence," Sylvie said.

"Even Marcus doesn't allow that anymore."

"How much of our secrets do you know, human?"

I shrugged. "A few words, that's all."

Sylvie stared at me. "You want your human girlfriend to cuddle up next to you, is that it, Richard?"

"Yes," he said. There was no trace of anger in his voice.

Personally, I didn't like the way she'd said "human."

Sylvie knelt on the couch, staring at me. "Come human, sit with us."

I stared at her. "Why the change of heart?"

"Not everything has to do with the pack hierarchy. That's what Richard is always telling us. Sit by your lover. I'll scoot over." She did, curling up on the couch, near Rafael.

The Rat King glanced at me. He raised an eyebrow, almost a shrug. I didn't trust Sylvie, but I trusted Rafael, and I trusted Richard, at least here, today. I realized that I would have trusted Rafael last night. He wouldn't have the moral qualms that Richard had. Poor Richard was like a lone voice crying in the wilderness. God help me, I agreed with the pagans.

Louie and Stephen were curled on the floor, close by. I was among friends. Even Jason, grinning up at me, wouldn't let me get hurt. Jason was Jean-Claude's wolf to call, as was Stephen. I think if they let me get killed, they might not survive much longer than I did.

"Anita?" Richard made it a question.

I sighed and pushed away from the wall. I was among friends, so why were the muscles in my back so tight it hurt to move? Paranoid? Who me?

I walked around the couch, coffee mug in my left hand. Sylvie patted the couch, smiling, but not like she meant it.

I sat beside Richard. His arm slid over my shoulders. My right arm was pressed against his side, not too tightly. He knew how much I hated having my gun hand impeded.

Leaning into the warmth of his body, I relaxed. The tightness in my shoulders eased. I took a sip of coffee. We were all being terribly civilized.

Richard put his lips against my face, and whispered, "Thank you."

Those two words earned him a lot of brownie points. He knew what it had cost me to sit down among the wolves, rats, and cats. Not sitting with him would have undermined him in front of the pack and the other leaders. I wasn't here to make the situation worse.

"Who saved you last night, Stephen?" Sylvie asked. Her voice was sweet, face pleasant. I didn't trust her at all.

Every eye turned to Stephen. He tried to huddle into the floor, as if he could go invisible, but it didn't work. He stared at Richard, eyes wide.

"Go ahead, Stephen, tell the truth. I won't be mad."

Stephen swallowed. "Anita saved me."

"Richard was fighting about twenty lycanthropes at the time," I said. "He told me to get Stephen, so I did."

Neal sniffed Stephen, running his nose just above the other man's face and neck, down his shoulder. It wasn't a human gesture, and it was unnerving in the well-dressed man. "He has her scent on his skin." Neal glared at me. "He's been with her."

I expected an outcry, but instead, the others crowded around Stephen, sniffing his skin, touching him, and bringing their fingers close to their own faces. Only Sylvie, Jason, Rafael, and Louie stayed sitting. One by one, the rest turned to Richard and me.

"He's right," Christine said. "Her scent clings to his skin. You don't get that much scent just by carrying someone."

Richard's hand tightened on my shoulder. I glanced at his face. It was calm, only a slight tightness around the eyes betrayed tension. "I was patrolling the woods for assassins," Richard said. "Stephen didn't want to be alone. I sent him to Anita."

"We know about the assassination attempts," Sylvie said.

I widened my eyes. "You do, do you?"

"Richard wants us to help protect you. If we're going to take a bullet for you, we need to know why."

I met her eyes. Her pretty face was harsh, the bones in her cheeks standing out.

"I'm not asking anyone to take my bullet," I said. I scooted out from under Richard's arm, which put me closer to Sylvie, not an improvement.

Richard didn't fight it. He drew his arm back. "I should have talked to you before I told them."

"Damn straight," I said.

Sylvie leaned her arms on the back of the couch, bringing her face inches from mine. "Are you going to chastise our would-be pack leader, human?"

"You say *human* like it's a bad thing, Sylvie. Jealous?"

She drew back like I'd hit her. A look that was part pain, part rage passed across her face. ''Most of us here survived an attack, human. We did not choose this.'' Her voice was chokingly harsh.

I'd expected a lot of things from her, but not the pain of a survivor. I was sorry I'd made the crack. ''I'm sorry. I didn't mean anything personal by it.''

''You have no idea how personal it is.''

''That's enough, Sylvie,'' Richard said.

She rose on her knees to meet Richard's face over my head. ''Don't you even have the balls to be angry that she slept with a subordinate male?''

''Wait a minute,'' I said. ''Stephen and I did not have sex. We literally slept together, nothing else.''

Neal plunged his face into Stephen's crotch and sniffed. It wasn't a human gesture. Stephen let him do it, and that wasn't very human, either.

Jason leaned in, sniffing my leg.

I put my coffee cup on my knee, in front of his face. ''Don't even think it,'' I said.

Jason grinned up at me. ''Can't blame a guy for trying.''

''I can,'' Richard said softly.

Jason smiled at him and scooted back.

Neal raised his face and shook his head. ''They didn't have sex.''

''He said she'd protect me,'' Stephen said. The silence grew so thick you could have walked on it.

''Is that what you said?'' Sylvie asked. She was staring at Richard like he'd done something very bad.

Richard took a deep enough breath that his shoulders shuddered. ''Yes, that's what I said.''

''Stephen,'' Sylvie said, ''Did you believe she'd protect you? If Raina had come through the door, would you have trusted Anita to save you?''

Stephen looked at the floor, then up, his eyes darted to Richard, then to me. His eyes finally stopped, staring at me. ''She had me sleep near the wall so she'd be in front in case anything came through the door.''

And I'd thought I'd been subtle.

''What would you have done if Raina *had* come?'' Sylvie asked.

Everyone was watching me, except Richard. Their eyes were very intent, and I knew the question meant more than it should have. ''I'd have killed her.''

''Not just shot her or wounded her?'' Christine asked.

I shook my head. ''She got her free pass last night. If she comes after Stephen again, I'll kill her.''

''You mean that, don't you?'' Sylvie said.

''Every word,'' I said.

There was a hum of energy in the room, almost as if they were all sharing some telepathic message. I don't think they were, but something was happening. The energy level in the room was rising, and I didn't like it. I sat the coffee mug on the floor. I wanted both my hands free.

Sylvie grabbed me around the waist and rolled us off the couch. We were on the floor with her riding my back before I could react. I went for the gun, and her hand was there first. She jerked the gun out of its holster and tossed it away. She wasn't fast, she was miraculous, and I was in deeper shit than I could get out of.

The bend of her arm was tucked under my chin like in a strangle hold, positioned just right so she could black me out without killing me. Her legs locked around my waist, as close as she could get and not climb down my shirt.

A half dozen werewolves flowed between her and Richard. He was standing, hands in fists at his side. His power poured through the room, deeper and higher, until it was like being buried alive in some kind of static charge.

''Don't,'' I whispered. I wasn't talking to Richard.

I felt something open inside Sylvie, a trembling, vibrating energy flowed from her skin across my body. It was almost hot, like opening the door to an oven. Where her skin touched me, I shivered. It was painful, like small electric shocks.

''What are you doing, Sylvie?'' Richard asked. His voice had gone low and growling deep; it didn't sound human. I expected his eyes to be amber, but they were the same solid brown as always. Human eyes, but the look in them was not. The beast stared out of Richard's eyes. I knew in that moment that he was truly dangerous. I also knew that all that impressive power wouldn't save me if Sylvie wanted to rip my head off.

My pulse thudded against her arm like a trapped butterfly. I forced my voice calm. ''What's going on?''

''I'm going to make you his mate.''

''You're not contagious in human form,'' I said.

''Really?'' she said. The arm around my throat grew warm, pulsing like a beating heart. I felt the muscles slide under her skin.

''Richard.'' My voice sounded high and wispy. Fear will do that to you.

Rafael and Louie were on their feet now. The werewolves that had joined Sylvie in this little protest fanned out to cover the rats, too.

I couldn't see Stephen. He was somewhere behind us, crouched on the floor, last I saw.

Jason crouched at Richard's feet, facing the other werewolves. But at least ten of them just sat there, watching, not taking sides. ''You've been holding out on us,'' Jason said.

Sylvie flexed the arm around my neck. I had a glimpse of a long-clawed hand. ''Only Raina is higher in the pack than I am, Jason.''

Richard faced the werewolves. He brought his hands upward, making a soothing gesture like he'd done at the movie set. The prickling energy in the room went down a notch. He was forcing their power back.

''All it takes is a scratch, Richard,'' Sylvie said. ''You'll never reach us in time.''

''I forbid this,'' Richard growled. ''No one is to be infected against their will. Especially Anita.''

''Why?'' Sylvie said. ''Because if she wasn't human, you wouldn't want her? Not taking the pack to your bed is just another way of denying what you are, Richard.''

Something passed over his face behind the anger and the power: uncertainty.

I knew in that moment she was right.

Sylvie whispered in my ear, her breath warm on my face. "See his face."

"Yeah," I said.

"He accuses you of not being able to sleep with him because you think he's a monster, but if I make you one of us, he won't want you. He thinks of all of us as monsters, but not good old Richard. He's better than the rest of us."

"I will hurt you, Sylvie. I'll bleed you, do you understand," Richard said.

"But you won't kill me, will you?" she said. Her arm flexed, long claws tickled down my face.

I put my hands on her arm, trying to hold it away from me, and not succeeding. "*I'll* kill you," I said.

She went very still against my body. "For changing you into one of us? For losing you Richard's love when he sees you monstrous and furry?"

I spoke very low, very carefully. "You hate what you are, Sylvie."

Her arm convulsed tight enough that I couldn't breathe for a second. "I don't hate what I am. I accept what I am." Her arm loosened.

I took a shaky breath and tried again. "I saw the look on your face when I accused you of being jealous. You are jealous of me being human, Sylvie. You know you are."

She held her other hand up in front of my face, letting me get a good look at the long, thin claws. The hand at my throat combed claws through my hair.

"You know that Raina has forbidden us to make you lukoi. She's afraid if you joined us, you'd be a better bitch than she is."

"How flattering," I whispered. I looked at Richard through the backs of the werewolves. His eyes had gone amber and alien. Even now, I knew, he wouldn't kill Sylvie. Even if she bled me, infected me, he wouldn't kill her. It was there in the pain on his face. The confusion replacing the fear.

Maybe Sylvie saw it. Maybe she'd made her point. Whatever, she uncurled herself from my body and stood carefully on the other side of me.

I scuttled away on all fours as fast as I could go. It wasn't pretty, it wasn't slick, but it was effective.

I crawled until I came to the far wall. I stayed sitting against it, as far away from everything in the room as I could get.

The other werewolves had faded away. Sylvie and Richard stood facing each other. Sylvie's eyes had gone a strange liquid grey, wolf eyes.

Richard flung his power outward. It ate along my skin, tore a gasp from my throat.

Sylvie stood in that flood of power and didn't flinch. "The power is impressive, Richard, but it means nothing as long as Marcus lives."

He backhanded her, in a blur of motion that was too fast to follow. Sylvie careened into the wall and slid to the floor, stunned.

"I am pack leader," Richard's voice roared, and he raised clawed hands to the sky. He fell to his knees, and I didn't go to help. I stayed huddled against the wall, wishing I'd packed an extra gun.

Richard crouched on the floor, rocking gently. He curled on his knees into a ball, and I felt him swallow the power back. I felt it drain away. He stayed crouched on the floor, hugging himself for a long time after the power vanished from the room, head down, his hair hiding his face.

Sylvie got to her knees and crawled towards him. She crouched beside him, smoothing his hair back on one side. ''We would follow you anywhere if you would kill for us. She will kill for us. If your mate, your lupa, will kill for us, it might be enough.''

Richard raised his head up with a shudder. ''No one is to be infected against their will, that is my word, and my order.'' He raised back on his knees.

Sylvie stayed crouched down, face near the floor, a sign of abasement. ''But you will not kill to enforce it.''

''I will kill to protect Anita,'' Rafael said.

Everyone looked at him.

He met their eyes and didn't back down. ''If anyone touches her against her will, I and mine will hunt them down.''

''Rafael,'' Richard said, ''don't do this.''

He stared at Richard. ''You bring a human among us, but you do not protect her. Someone has to.''

I wanted to say I could protect myself, but it wasn't true. I was good, but I was just human. It wasn't enough.

''I can't let you do my dirty work for me,'' he said.

''I am your friend, Richard,'' Rafael said. ''I do not mind.''

Sylvie hugged the ground at Richard's feet. ''Will you let the Rat King kill your pack? Is he our leader now?''

He stared down at her, and something happened to his face, not otherworldly, or wolf, but a hardness, almost a sadness passed over him. I watched it, and I didn't like it. If I'd had my gun, I might have shot Sylvie for making that look pass over his face. ''I will kill anyone who breaks my word. I have spoken, and it is law.''

Sylvie abased herself even lower, and the other wolves came crowding around, crawling on the floor, abasing themselves in front of him. Some of them licked his hands, touched his body. They moved around him until he was nearly hidden from sight.

Richard stood up, walking through them, their hands clinging to his legs. He bent down and picked up the Firestar from the floor and walked over to me. He looked normal enough, all the wolfish changes hidden away. He handed me the gun, butt first. ''Are you all right?''

I cradled the gun in both hands. ''Sure.''

''I value your humanity, Anita. Sylvie's right. How can I ask you to embrace my beast, when I can't do it myself?'' The pain on his face was heartrending. ''I will kill to keep you safe. Does that make you happy?''

I stared up at him. ''No,'' I said. ''I thought it would, but no.'' I felt like Rafael, I'd kill for him. I'd kill to keep the pain out of his eyes.

I holstered the gun and raised my right hand to him. His eyes widened. He understood the gesture. He took my hand and raised me to my feet. He drew me with him towards the waiting wolves.

I hung back, pulling on his hand.

"I said I'd kill for you, Anita." His voice was soft and harsh at the same time. "Don't you believe I'd do it?"

His eyes were utterly sad. It was like something inside of him that he'd kept alive all these years was dead now. I believed the look in his eyes. He would kill to protect me, and the decision had cost him dearly.

The werewolves closed around us. I would have said they crawled around us, but that didn't cover what they were doing. Crawling wasn't graceful, or sensuous, but this was. They moved like they had muscles in places that people didn't. They circled us and rolled their eyes up at us. When I met those eyes, they looked away, all except Sylvie. She met my gaze and held it. It was a challenge, but I wasn't sure what I was supposed to do about it.

A hand touched me, and I jerked away from it. Only Richard's hand on mine kept me from going for my gun. He held both my hands in his and drew me to him, our bodies not quite touching. He met my eyes and held them. He wasn't afraid. I tried to relax, but it wasn't working.

"This is my lupa. Know her scent, know her skin. She has shed our blood, and shed her blood for us. She stands as protector for those weaker than herself. She will kill for us, if we ask. She is your alpha."

Sylvie and Neal stood up. They both moved out of the circle. They stood, staring at me, at Richard. The others crouched on the floor, watching.

"She is not dominant to me," Sylvie said.

"She is not even one of us," Neal said, "I won't bow to her. I could break her in half with one hand." He shook his head. "She isn't my alpha."

"What's happening, Richard?" I asked.

"I tried to bring you into the pack, make you one of us without contaminating you."

"Why?" I asked.

"If you're going to protect Stephen, then you deserve the protection of the pack. If you're going to take risks for us, then you deserve to have the benefits of our protection."

"No offense," I said, "but I haven't been too impressed with your protection so far." The minute I said it, I wished I hadn't. His face fell.

"You made it personal last night with Raina, Anita. You have no idea how dangerous she is. I wanted you to have everyone's protection in case something happened to me."

I looked up at him. "You will kill Marcus if he jumps you, right? No more being squeamish." I touched his arm. I studied his face. "Answer me, Richard."

He nodded, finally. "I won't let him kill me."

"You will kill him; promise me."

His jaw tightened, the muscle thrumming. "I promise."

"Well, hallelujah," Sylvie said. She stared at me. "I withdraw my challenge. You aren't dominant to me, but you can be his alpha female. You're a good influence on him." She stepped back into the circle, but didn't kneel. "Come on Neal," she said, "let it go."

He shook his head. "No, she isn't one of us. She can't be. I won't acknowledge her as alpha."

''All you have to do is prove to Neal that you're serious,'' Sylvie said. ''You just have to make him hurt a little.''

''Since he could probably survive a direct hit with a mack truck, how am I supposed to hurt him?''

She shrugged.

''I didn't think anyone would challenge you. I'm sorry,'' Richard said.

''You expect people to be nice, Richard. It's one of your best qualities and greatest weaknesses,'' I said.

''Refuse the challenge, Anita.''

''If I refuse, then what?''

''It's over. You won't be a member of the pack, but I can order them to protect you from Raina. It's almost as good.''

''I told you, I don't want anyone being ordered to take a bullet for me. Besides, no way am I volunteering to go one on one with a lycanthrope. I'll keep my gun, thanks anyway.''

The doorbell rang. It was probably Edward. Damn. I looked at the little group, and even though they were in human form, he'd know what they were. He was better at smelling monsters than I was, at least live ones. ''If you guys can tone it down a bit, I'll get the door.''

''Edward?'' Richard made it a question.

''Probably,'' I said.

He stared around at the group. ''Everybody up off the floor. He's another normal.''

They got to their feet, slowly, almost reluctantly. They seemed almost intoxicated, as if the power in the room had done more for them than for me.

I went for the door. I was halfway to it when Richard yelled, ''No!''

I dropped to the ground, rolling, and felt the air whistling over me where Neal had swung. If he'd been any good at fighting, he'd have nailed me. The missed swing put him off balance, and I foot-swept him to the floor, but he got to his feet again before I could stand, like there were springs in his spine. It was impressive as hell.

''Stop it, Neal,'' Sylvie said.

''She didn't refuse the challenge. It's my right.''

I scuttled backwards, still on the ground, not sure what to do. The closed drapes of the picture window were at my back if I stood up. I wasn't sure standing up was my best bet. ''Give me the rules, quick,'' I said.

''First blood,'' Sylvie said. ''Human form only.''

''If he shapeshifts, you can shoot him,'' Richard said.

''Agreed,'' Sylvie said, others murmured their agreement.

Peachy. Neal leaped for me, leaving the ground completely, hands outstretched. I came up on one knee, grabbed his jacket, and rolled on my back, letting his amazing momentum carry us both. I shoved both feet into his stomach and pushed with everything I had. He flew over me in a near perfect arc. He'd set himself up for a textbook tomoe-nage throw.

He smashed through the window, taking the curtain with him. I rolled to my feet and stared at the gaping window. Broken shards of glass sprinkled onto the carpet and the yard beyond. Neal struggled out of the curtain, blood running down his face where the glass had cut him.

Edward was on the ground in a combat stance, gun out. He pointed it at Neal, as he struggled free of the curtain.

"Don't shoot him," I said. "I think the fight's over."

Neal stood, kicking free of the clinging curtain. "I'll kill you."

I drew the Firestar and pointed it at him. "I don't think so."

Richard stepped up beside me. "She drew first blood, Neal. The fight is over, unless you want to fight me, too."

"And me," Sylvie said. She stepped up on the other side of Richard. The rest of the pack stepped up behind us. Stephen crouched at my feet.

"She is pack now," Sylvie said. "You fight one of us, and you fight all of us."

Edward raised his eyebrows at me. "What is going on, Anita?"

"I think I've been adopted," I said.

Neal glared at me.

"Do it, Neal," Sylvie said.

Neal knelt in the glass and the curtain. The cuts were already beginning to heal on his face. Glass wasn't silver or the claws of another monster, so he healed almost magically.

"You are dominant. You are alpha." The words were dragged from his throat. "If this window hadn't been here, you couldn't have bloodied me."

"Why do you think I moved in front of it, Neal?" I asked.

His eyes squinted. "You planned this?"

I nodded and raised my gun skyward. "I'm not just another pretty face."

Richard took my left hand, squeezing it gently. "That's the God's honest truth."

I put up the Firestar.

Edward shook his head, smiling, but didn't put his gun up. He did stop pointing it at anyone. "You are the only person I know who leads a more interesting life than I do."

Jason patted me on the back. "Tomorrow night we'll take you out chasing deer."

"I thought you'd chase cars," I said.

He grinned. "What fun is that? Cars don't bleed."

I smiled, and then stopped. His eyes were as innocent as spring skies, as joyous, and staring into them, I wasn't sure if he was kidding me or not. I almost asked, but didn't. I wasn't sure I wanted to know.

12

Edward was five foot eight, with blond hair cut very short and close to his head. He was blue-eyed and the epitome of WASP breeding. He was also the most dangerous man I'd ever met, living or dead.

He was amused as hell by the gathering of lycanthropes. The group broke up soon after his arrival, mainly because all the business had been taken care of. The meeting had mainly been a last-ditch effort to convince Richard to compromise his morals and kill someone. Barring that, for him to pick a lupa who would kill for him. We'd sort of killed two birds with one stone, pun intended. But I was very aware that I'd gotten lucky with Neal. If he'd had a background in any martial art, if he'd known anything about fighting, I'd have been toast.

Richard had boarded up the broken window and had a call in to a glass repair shop that was willing, for an exorbitant fee, to come out and repair the damage immediately. I'd offered to pay for the damages since I made them.

Edward, Richard, and I sat around the kitchen table. Edward and I sipped coffee. Richard drank tea. One of his few serious faults was a total dislike of coffee. Hard to trust a man who won't drink coffee.

''What have you found out?'' I asked.

Edward sipped his coffee and shook his head. ''Not much. The contract has been picked up.''

''Even with the time limit?'' I asked.

He nodded.

''When is the twenty-four hours up?'' I asked.

''Let's say two o'clock. I got the offer about one o'clock last night, but we'll add an hour to be safe.''

''To be safe,'' Richard said. I think it was sarcasm.

''What's wrong with you?'' I asked.

''Am I the only one in this room who's worried?''

''Panicking won't help, Richard.''

He stood up, emptying his mug in the sink and rinsing it automatically. He turned, leaning his butt against the cabinets, arms crossed over his chest. "You need a clear head to plan?"

I nodded. "Yeah."

He stared at us. I watched him thinking about something serious. He finally said, "I don't understand how the two of you can be calm. I'm shocked that someone has put a contract out on Anita. Neither of you is shocked."

I looked at Edward, and he looked back at me. We had one of those moments of perfect understanding, and I knew I couldn't explain it to Richard. I wasn't even sure I could explain it to myself. "I've stayed alive this long because I don't react the way most people react."

"You've stayed alive because you're willing to do things other people aren't."

I nodded. "That, too."

His face was very serious, like a little boy asking about the facts of life. "Let me ask one stupid question; then I'll shut up."

I shrugged. "Ask away."

"Anita says she doesn't enjoy killing. That she feels nothing when she kills."

I realized then that the question was going to be for Edward. I wasn't sure how that would go over.

"Do you enjoy killing?"

Edward sat very still in his chair, drinking his coffee quietly. His blue eyes were as neutral and unreadable as any vampire's, and in some ways just as dead. I wondered for the first time if my eyes ever looked like that. "Why do you want to know?"

"I agreed to kill Marcus," Richard said. "I've never killed anyone."

Edward stared up at him. He set his coffee down carefully and met Richard's eyes. "Yes."

"Yes, you enjoy killing?" Richard asked.

Edward nodded.

Richard was waiting for him to explain. You could see it in his face.

"He's answered your question, Richard."

"But does he enjoy the sensation of killing? Is it physical? Or is it the planning that he enjoys?"

Edward picked up his coffee.

"The question and answer session is over, Richard," I said.

A look halfway between stubbornness and frustration crossed Richard's face. "But 'yes,' doesn't tell me anything."

"After you kill Marcus," Edward said, "you can ask the question again."

"And you'll answer it?" Richard asked.

Edward gave the barest of nods.

For the first time, I realized that Edward liked Richard. Not as a friend, maybe, but he didn't think Richard was a complete waste of time.

Richard stared into Edward's face for a long time, then shook his head. "Okay." He sat back down. "No more questions. What's the plan?"

I smiled at him. "To keep the hitter from killing me."

"That's your entire plan?" Richard asked.

''And to take out the man with the money,'' Edward said. ''As long as the money is out there, Anita won't be safe.''

''Any ideas how to accomplish this?'' Richard asked.

Edward nodded and up-ended his coffee mug, finishing the last of it. He went to the counter and refilled it, like he was at home. He sat back down. Good ol' Edward, comfortable wherever he was.

I sat waiting, watching him quietly. He'd tell us when he was ready and not before. Richard was practically dancing in place. ''What?'' he finally asked.

Edward smiled, I think at Richard, or maybe at that eternal music that only he could hear. The rhythm that kept him self-contained and alive.

''The assassin might come here today, and we'll take precautions for that. A herd of shapeshifters was perfect. I'd have passed on the hit myself until they cleared out.''

I glanced around the quiet kitchen. The spot between my shoulder blades was itching. ''You think we're in danger now?''

''Maybe.'' He didn't seem too worried. ''But I think they'll hit you tonight on your date with the Master of the City.''

''How did you know I had a date tonight?''

Edward just smiled. ''I know that the Master of the City is taking the Executioner to the opening of his dance club, Danse Macabre. I know that you'll be arriving in a limo.''

''I didn't even know that,'' I said.

He shrugged. ''It wasn't hard to find out, Anita.''

''I was going to cancel my date tonight and hide out.''

''If you stay here, the assassin will almost certainly come here.''

I glanced at Richard. ''Oh,'' I said.

''I can take care of myself,'' Richard said.

''Could you kill a human being?'' I asked.

He blinked at me. ''What do you mean?''

''I mean if someone came at you with a gun, could you kill them?''

''I said I'd kill to protect you.''

''That's not what I asked, Richard, and you know it.''

He stood up and paced a small circle in the kitchen. ''If it was standard ammunition, it couldn't kill me.''

''You wouldn't know whether it was silver ammo until it was too late,'' I said.

He hugged his arms, ran his hands through his long hair, and turned to me. ''Once you decide to start killing, it never stops, does it?''

''No,'' I said.

''I don't know if I could kill a human being.''

''Thanks for the honesty,'' I said.

''But that means you'll take an assassin into a club crowded with people? You'll endanger all of them to keep me safe?''

''I would endanger almost anyone to keep you safe.''

Edward made a small sound, almost a laugh. His face was pleasant and empty. He sipped coffee. ''Which is why I don't want Richard in the line of fire. You'll be so busy worrying about him, it might make you careless.''

''But all those people, you can't put them in danger,'' Richard said.

Edward looked at me and didn't say what he was thinking. I was grateful for that. ''I think Edward has a plan for that, too, Richard.''

''I think they'll hit you on the way home from the club. Why work in the middle of a crowd if they don't have to? Plant a bomb on the limo, or wait until you're alone on the drive back.''

''Is that what you would do?'' Richard asked.

Edward looked at him for a moment, then nodded. ''Probably. Not the bomb, but I'd hit the limo.''

''Why not the bomb?'' Richard asked.

I didn't ask, because I knew the answer. Edward's eyes flicked to me. I shrugged.

''Because I like to kill up close and personal. With a bomb there's no personal risk.''

Richard stared at him, studying his face. He finally said, ''Thank you for answering the question.''

Edward acknowledged him with a nod. Richard was gaining brownie points from both of us. But I knew that Richard had illusions. If Edward seemed to like him, Richard would assume Edward wouldn't kill him. I knew better. If the situation called for it, Edward could pull the trigger on anyone.

''Let's say you're right,'' I said. ''I go on the date and let the hitter make his move. Then what?''

''We take him out.''

''Wait a minute,'' Richard said. ''You're betting that the two of you are better than a professional assassin. That you'll get to him before he gets to Anita.''

We both nodded.

''What if you're not better?''

Edward looked at him like he'd said the sun wouldn't rise tomorrow.

''Edward will be better,'' I said.

''You'd bet your life on that?'' Richard asked.

''I am betting my life on that,'' I said.

Richard looked a touch pale. He nodded. ''I guess you are. What can I do to help?''

''You heard Edward,'' I said. ''You stay here.''

Richard shook his head. ''I heard, but surely in a crowd of people even Superman will need a few more eyes and ears. The pack can help watch your back.''

''It doesn't bother you to endanger them?''

''You said you'd risk almost anyone to keep me safe,'' Richard said. ''I feel the same way.''

''If they want to volunteer, that's one thing, but I don't want them ordered into it. People aren't good bodyguards if they resent doing it.''

Richard laughed. ''Very practical. For a second there, I thought you were really worried about my wolves.''

''Practical will keep me alive, Richard, sentimentality won't.''

''If we had some extra watchers, it'd free me up a little,'' Edward said.

I looked at him. ''You'd trust monsters to watch my back?''

He smiled, and it wasn't pleasant. ''Monsters make excellent cannon fodder.''

''They aren't cannon fodder,'' Richard said.

''Everyone's cannon fodder,'' Edward said, ''eventually.''

''If I really thought we were endangering innocent bystanders, I wouldn't go to the club. You know that, Richard.''

He stared at me for a second, then nodded. ''I know that.''

Edward made a small sound low in his throat. ''Innocent bystanders.'' He shook his head, smiling. ''Let's get dressed,'' Edward said. ''I bought some new toys for you to use tonight.''

I looked at him. ''Dangerous toys?'' I asked.

''Is there any other kind?'' We grinned at each other.

''You two are enjoying this,'' Richard said. It was almost accusatory.

''If we didn't enjoy it, we'd both do something else,'' Edward said.

''Anita doesn't kill people for money, and you do.''

I watched the humor drain from Edward's eyes like the sun sinking behind clouds, leaving them pitiless and empty. ''Think what you like, loverboy, but Anita could have chosen another line of work, one that wouldn't put her in harm's way. But she didn't. There's a reason for that.''

''She's not like you.''

Edward looked at me with empty eyes. ''Closer than she used to be.'' His voice was soft, almost neutral, but it made me shiver.

I met his eyes, and for the first time in a long time, wondered what I'd given up to be able to pull the trigger. The same thing Edward had given up inside himself to be able to kill so easily? I looked up at Richard and wondered if he could do it. If, when the fur flew, he could really kill anyone. Some people couldn't. No shame in that. But if Richard backed out, he was dead. Not tonight or tomorrow, but eventually, because Marcus would see to it. Richard had beaten Marcus twice and refused the kill. I doubted Marcus would let him have another shot at it. They'd taken Stephen last night, knowing what Richard would do. If I hadn't been with him, he might he dead now. Shit.

All I had to do was kill the assassin before he or she killed me. Trust Richard not to let Marcus kill him. Keep Raina from killing me. And let's see, I was sure there was something else. Oh, yeah, decide whether I'm going to sleep with Richard, and if I did, what that would mean for Jean-Claude and myself. There were days when my life was too complicated even for me.

13

Finding dress-up clothes that you can hide a gun in is a bitch. I actually hadn't planned to carry a gun on my date with Jean-Claude. Of course, that was before the assassin. Now I wasn't going out without one. If I'd known I'd be needing a gun tonight, I'd have worn the little black dress yesterday and saved the pants suit. But who knew, and now all I'd packed besides jeans was the dress. It was a little black dress with just enough strap to allow a bra, if you were careful. I'd bought a black bra to be safe. Flashing a white bra strap in a black dress always looked so tacky. The jacket was a deep black velvet, a bolero cut that hit me at the waist. Black beading edged the collar and hem.

The jacket was hanging on the doorknob of Richard's closet. He was sitting forlornly on the bed, watching me put the last touches on my lipstick. I was leaning forward, peering at myself in the mirror on his dresser. The skirt was short enough that I decided to wear a black teddy under it, not for underwear but to go over my panty hose, so everything matched. Ronnie hadn't trusted me not to end over at least once tonight. She was right. So even if I forgot, the teddy covered more than most bathing suits. I'd have never picked out something so short on my own. Ronnie was a bad influence on me. If she'd known I was planning to wear it for Jean-Claude, she'd have probably chosen something else. She called him fangface. Or worse. She liked Richard.

''Nice dress,'' Richard said.

''Thanks.'' I turned in front of the mirror to check the way the skirt hung. It was just full enough to swing when I moved. The black knife sheaths on my forearms actually matched the dress. The knives made a nice touch of silver. The wrist sheaths almost covered the scars on my arms. Only the mound of scar tissue at my left elbow was visible. A vampire had torn up my arm once upon a time. The same vamp had bitten through my collarbone. The scars were normal for me, but every once in a while I'd be out enjoying myself and catch someone looking, staring. They'd look hurriedly away, or meet my eyes. It wasn't that the scars were awful to look at. They weren't that bad—really. But they told a story of pain and something out of the ordinary. They said I'd been places that most people hadn't, and I'd survived. Worth a stare or two, I guess.

The black straps that held the new knife down along my spine showed a little at the shoulders, but more across the back. The hilt was hidden under my hair, but I wouldn't be taking the jacket off.

"Why didn't you wear this last night?" Richard asked.

"The pants suit seemed more appropriate."

He stared at me, eyes roving over my body more than my face. He shook his head. "For seeing someone you're not going to sleep with, that is a very sexy outfit."

I had never planned on Richard seeing the dress, at least not on the night I wore it for Jean-Claude. I wasn't sure what to say, but I'd try. "I trust myself with Jean-Claude more than I trust myself with you, so he gets the short skirt and you don't." That was the truth.

"You're saying I don't get the sexy outfit because I'm so irresistible?"

"Something like that."

"If I ran my hands up your legs, would I find panty hose or garters?" He looked so solemn, hurt. With everything else going down, I shouldn't have had to worry about my boyfriend's hurt feelings, but there it was. Life goes on, even if you're ass deep in alligators.

"Panty hose," I said.

"Will Jean-Claude find out what kind of hose you're wearing?"

"He could ask, like you did," I said.

"You know that's not what I meant," he said.

I sighed. "I don't know how to make this easier on you, Richard. If there's anything that would make you feel more secure about this, ask."

To his credit, he didn't ask me not to go. I think he knew he wouldn't like the answer. "Come here," he said and held out his hand to me.

I walked over to him and took his outstretched hand. He sat me on his lap, legs sideways like you'd sit on Santa. He encircled me with one arm, then laid his other hand on my thigh. "Promise me you won't sleep with him tonight."

"With assassins ready to jump out of the woodwork, I think that's a safe bet," I said.

"Don't joke, Anita, please."

I smoothed my hand through his hair. He looked so serious, so hurt. "I've said no for a very long time, Richard. Why should you be worried about tonight?"

"The dress," he said.

"I admit it's short, but . . ."

He smoothed his hand up my thigh until it vanished under the skirt. He rested his hand just below the lace of the teddy. "You're wearing lingerie, for God's sake; you never wear lingerie."

I would have explained about everything matching, but somehow I didn't think that would be comforting. "Okay, I won't sleep with him tonight. I hadn't planned on it to begin with."

"Promise me you'll come back and sleep with me." He smiled when he said it.

I smiled back and slid off his lap. "You'd have to shift first. I'd have to see your beast. Or so you keep telling me."

"I could shift when you get back."

"Could you take human form again quickly enough to do us any good to-night?"

He smiled. "I'm strong enough to be Ulfric, Anita. One of the things I can do is change form almost at will. I don't pass out when I change back to human form like most shapeshifters."

"Handy," I said.

He smiled. "Come back tonight, and I'll change for you. Sylvie's right. I have to accept what I am."

"Part of that is trying it out on me, huh?"

He nodded. "I think so."

Staring into his solemn eyes, I knew that if he changed for me tonight and I couldn't deal with it, it would destroy something inside of him. I hoped I was up to it. "When I come back tonight, I'll watch you shift."

He looked grim as if he expected that I'd run screaming. "Kiss me, and get out of here," he said.

I kissed him, and he licked his lips. "Lipstick." He kissed me again. "But underneath I can still taste you."

"Hmmm," I said. I stared down at him and almost didn't want to go. Almost. The doorbell rang, and I jumped. Richard didn't, as if he'd heard it before I had.

"Be careful. I wish I could be with you."

"There'll be media all over the place," I said. "Wouldn't do to get your picture taken with a bunch of monsters. It might blow your cover."

"I'd blow my cover if it would keep you safe."

He loved teaching, yet I believed him. He'd come out of the closet for me. "Thanks, but Edward's right. I'd be so worried about keeping you alive, I wouldn't be taking good care of myself."

"You don't worry about Jean-Claude?"

I shrugged. "He can take care of himself. Besides, he's already dead."

Richard shook his head. "You don't really believe that anymore."

"No, he's dead, Richard. That I know. Whatever keeps him alive is a form of necromancy, different than my own powers, but still magic."

"You can say it, but in your heart you don't believe it."

I shrugged again. "Maybe not, but it's still the truth."

There was a knock on the door. Richard said, "Your date's here."

"I'm coming. Now I have to fix my lipstick all over again."

He wiped fingers across his mouth, coming away with crimson stains. "At least I'll be able to tell if you've been kissing him. This stuff will show up like blood on his white shirt."

I didn't argue. Jean-Claude always wore black and white. I'd only seen him in one shirt that wasn't white. It had been black. I reapplied the lipstick and put it in the beaded black purse on the dresser. The purse was too small even for the Firestar. I did have a Derringer, but except at close quarters, it was pretty worthless. With an assassin I might not want to get that close. Edward had a solution. He'd loaned me his See-camps .32 autoloader. It was about the same size as a small .25, only a little wider than my own hand, and I had a small hand. It was a very nice gun, and for the caliber and the size, I'd never seen better. I wanted one. Edward informed me that he'd had to wait nearly a year for the gun to come in. It was pretty much a custom order. Otherwise, he'd have made it a gift. Fine, I'd order my own—if I survived the night. If I didn't, well, I wouldn't be ordering anything.

I'd managed not to think too much about that. I'd concentrated on dressing, putting the weapons in place, Richard, anything but that I was putting myself out as bait for someone good enough to earn 500,000 dollars a pop. I was having to trust that Edward would keep me alive. Because though Edward would have stopped the limo and fired only when he could see my face, most hit men wouldn't. Most professionals prefer to take you out from a nice, safe distance. A high-powered rifle could be yards or even miles away. Not much I, or even Edward, could do about that. I knew nothing about explosives. I was going to have to depend on Edward to take care of any bombs. I was putting myself in Edward's hands tonight, trusting him like I'd never trusted anyone before. Scary thought, that.

I checked the purse again; ID, lipstick, money, gun. I'd have normally carried a small travel hairbrush, but there wasn't room. I could live with messy hair for one night.

The thought made me check my hair in the mirror and run a brush through it one last time. I had to admit that it looked great. It was one of my best features. Even Ronnie couldn't improve on it. It was all natural curl. Even tonight I'd shoved hair goop in it after my shower and let it dry naturally. I'd had a woman get angry with me once in California because I wouldn't tell her where I'd gotten my hair permed. She wouldn't believe it was natural.

I slipped the purse over my shoulders so the thin strap went across my chest. It blended with the dress well enough that it looked almost as good with it as without. But the purse rode at my ribs, just a little lower than my shoulder holster. I tried drawing the gun a couple of times, and it wasn't too bad. Not as good as a holster, but what was? I slipped the jacket on and checked myself in the mirror for the umpteenth time. Neither the knives nor the gun showed. Great. I slipped my cross on last. I made sure the cross was inside the dress, then put a small piece of masking tape over it. This way I kept my cross, but it didn't spill out of my clothes and glow at Jean-Claude. I picked up the brush again and put it down without using it.

I was stalling. It wasn't just the assassin I was afraid of. I was dreading the moment Richard and Jean-Claude met tonight. I wasn't sure how they were going to react, and I wasn't up to an emotional confrontation. I rarely was.

I took a deep breath and went for the door. Richard followed me. It was his house. I couldn't ask him to hide in the bedroom.

Jean-Claude stood by the television, peering at the shelves of videos, as if studying the titles. He was tall and slender, though not as tall as Richard. He wore black pants and a short black jacket, cut just at the waist like my own. He had on high, leather boots that covered nearly his entire leg, the soft leather tops were held in place by black straps with small silver buckles. His black hair spilled over his shoulders, inches longer than when I first met him.

He turned at last, as if he hadn't known we were standing there. I made a small involuntary gasp as he faced me. His shirt was red, a pure, clear crimson that blazed inside his open jacket. The collar was high, held in place by three antique jet beads. The shirt gaped open below the collar, showing a large oval of his chest. The cross-shaped burn scar on his chest showed in the circle of red cloth as if it were framed for viewing. The circle of bare skin ended just above the black pants, where the shirt was safely tucked away.

The shirt looked splendiferous against his pale skin, the black wavy hair, his midnight blue eyes. I closed my gaping mouth, and said, ''Spiffy, very spiffy.''

He smiled. ''Ah, *ma petite*, always the perfect thing to say.'' He glided across the carpet in his nifty boots, and I found myself wanting him to take the jacket off. I wanted to see his hair spill over that shirt, black over red. I knew it would look wonderful.

Richard came up behind me. He didn't touch me, but I could feel him standing there. A warm, unhappy presence at my back. I couldn't blame him. Jean-Claude looked like an advertisement for Wet Dreams ''R'' Us. I couldn't blame anyone for being jealous.

Jean-Claude stood in front of me, close enough that I could have reached out and touched him. I stood between the two of them, and the symbolism wasn't lost on any of us.

''Where's Edward?'' I managed to ask. My voice sounded almost normal. Good for me.

''He is checking the car. I believe for incendiary devices,'' Jean-Claude said with a small smile.

My stomach clenched tight. Someone really wanted me dead by midnight tonight. Edward was sweeping the car for bombs. Even for me, it didn't seem quite real.

''*Ma petite*, are you well?'' Jean-Claude took my hand in his. ''Your hand is cold.''

''Nice complaint, coming from you,'' Richard said.

Jean-Claude looked over my shoulder at Richard. ''It was not a complaint but an observation.''

His hand was warm, and I knew that he had stolen that warmth from someone. Oh, they'd been willing enough. There were always people willing to donate to the Master of the City. But still, he was a blood sucking corpse, no matter what he looked like. Staring up at him, I realized part of me didn't buy that anymore. Or maybe I just didn't care anymore. Damn.

He raised my hand slowly to his lips, eyes watching not me but Richard. I drew my hand out of his. He looked at me. ''If you want to kiss my hand, fine, but don't do it just to get on Richard's nerves.''

''My apologies, *ma petite*. You are quite right.'' He looked past me to Richard. ''My apologies to you as well, Monsieur Zeeman. We are in a . . . ticklish position. It would be childish to make it worse with game playing.''

I didn't have to see Richard's face to know he was frowning.

Edward came in and saved us. We could all shut up and leave. Hopefully.

''The car's clean,'' he said.

"Glad to hear it," I said.

Edward was dressed for the evening. A brown leather coat hung to his ankles and moved like something alive as he came into the room. The coat hung strangely heavy in places. He'd shown me some of his toys that were positioned here and there. I knew there was a garotte hidden in the stiff white collar of his shirt. A garotte was a little too up-and-close even for me.

His eyes flicked to the two men in my life, but all he said was, "I'll follow the limo. Don't look around for me tonight, Anita. I'll be there, but we don't want the hitter alerted to the fact that you've got a bodyguard."

"A second bodyguard," Jean-Claude said. "Your, how do you say, hitter will know I will be by her side."

Edward nodded. "Yeah, if they hit the limo, you'll be there. They'll have to plan on taking you out, too, which means it's got to be serious firepower."

"I am both a deterrent and an invitation to up the stakes, is that it?" Jean-Claude asked.

Edward looked at him like the vampire had finally done something interesting. Edward didn't meet his eyes though. I was the only human I knew that could meet the Master's eyes and not be bespelled. Being a necromancer had its uses. "Exactly." He said it like he hadn't expected the vampire to grasp the situation. But if there was one thing Jean-Claude was good at, it was surviving.

"Shall we go then, *ma petite*? The party awaits us." He made a sweeping motion with his arms, directing me towards the door but not taking my hand. He glanced at Richard, then at me. He was behaving himself terribly well. Jean-Claude was a world-class pain in the ass. It wasn't like him to be a good boy.

I glanced at Richard. "Go on. If we kiss good-bye, it'll smear your lipstick again."

"You are wearing quite enough of her lipstick already, Richard," Jean-Claude said. For the first time tonight, I heard that warm edge of jealousy.

Richard took two steps forward, and the tension level in the room soared. "I could kiss her good night again, if that would make you happy."

"Stop it, both of you," I said.

"By all means," Jean-Claude said. "She is mine for the rest of the evening. I can afford to be generous."

Richard's hands balled into fists. The first trickle of power oozed through the room.

"I'm leaving now." I made for the door and didn't look back. Jean-Claude caught up with me before I reached the door. He reached for the doorknob first, and then released it, letting me get it.

"I do forget your penchant for doors," he said.

"I don't," Richard said softly.

I turned and looked at him standing there in his jeans, his T-shirt molded to the muscles of his arms and chest. He was still barefoot, his hair a wavy mass around his face. If I'd been staying here, we could have cuddled on the couch in front of one of his favorite movies. We were beginning to have our favorite movies, songs, sayings that were ours. Maybe a moonlight walk. His night vision was almost as good as my own. Maybe later we could finish what we'd started before the meeting.

Jean-Claude slid his fingers through mine, drawing my attention to him. I stared up into those blue, blue eyes like a sky before a storm, or seawater where the rocks lie deep and cold. I could touch those three black buttons and see if they were really antique beads. My gaze traveled downward to the pale glimpse of his chest. I knew that the cross-shaped burn scar was a rough slickness to the touch. Looking at him made my chest tight. He was so beautiful. Would my body always feel the pull of him, like a sunflower turning towards the light? Maybe. But standing there holding his hand, I realized it wasn't enough.

Jean-Claude and I could have had a glorious affair, but I could see spending my life with Richard. Was love enough? Even if Richard killed for self-preservation, could he really accept my body count? Could I accept his beast, or would I be as horrified by it as he was himself? Jean-Claude accepted me lock, stock, and gun. But I didn't accept him. Just because we both looked at the world through dark glasses, didn't mean I liked it.

I sighed, and it wasn't a happy sound. If this was the last time I ever saw Richard, I should have jumped his body and given him a kiss he would never forget, but I couldn't do it. Holding Jean-Claude's hand, I couldn't do it. It would have been cruel to all of us.

"Bye, Richard," I said.

"Be careful," he said. He sounded so alone.

"Louie and you are going to the movies tonight, right?" I asked.

He nodded. "He should be here soon."

"Good." I opened my mouth to say more, but didn't. There was nothing to say. I was going with Jean-Claude. Nothing I said would change that.

"I'll wait up for you," Richard said.

"I wish you wouldn't."

"I know."

I left, walking a little too fast out to the waiting limo. It was white. "Well, isn't this shiny and bright," I said.

"I thought black looked too much like a hearse," Jean-Claude said.

Edward had come out also. He closed the door behind us. "I'll be there when you need me, Anita."

I met his eyes. "I know you will."

He gave the briefest of smiles. "But just in case, watch your back like a son of a bitch."

I smiled. "Don't I always?"

He glanced at the vampire standing by the open limo door. "Not as well as I thought you did." Edward walked into the darkness towards his waiting car before I could think of a reply. It was just as well. He was right. The monsters had finally gotten me. Seducing me was almost as good as killing me, and nearly as crippling.

14

The name of the club, Danse Macabre, blazed in red neon letters nearly eight feet high. The letters were curved and flowed at an angle like some giant hand had just finished writing them. The club was housed in an old brewery warehouse. The place had stood on the Riverfront, boarded up and abandoned for years. It had been the only eyesore in a line of chic restaurants, dance clubs, and bars. Most of them were owned by vampires. The Riverfront was also known as The District, or Blood Square, though not in polite vampire company. For some reason, the nickname bugged them. Who knew why?

The crowd had spilled out from the sidewalk into the street, until the limo was stopped by the sheer weight of people. It was so bad that I spotted a uniformed cop trying to ease the people back enough for the cars to get through. I looked through the dark tinted windows at the press of people. Was the assassin out there? Was one of those well-dressed, smiling people waiting to kill me? I opened my purse and slipped the Seecamp out.

Jean-Claude eyed the little gun. ''Nervous, *ma petite*?''

''Yes,'' I said.

He looked at me, head to one side. ''Yes, you are nervous. Why does one human assassin unnerve you so much more than all the preternatural creatures you have faced?''

''Everyone else who's wanted to kill me, it was personal. I understand personal. Whoever this is wants to kill me because it's business. Just business.''

''But why is that more frightening to you? You will be just as dead, regardless of your assailant's motives.''

''Thanks a lot,'' I said.

He touched my hand, as it gripped the gun. ''I am trying to understand, *ma petite*, that is all.''

''I don't know exactly why it bothers me. It just does,'' I said. ''I like to put a face on my enemies. If someone kills you, it shouldn't be only for money.''

''So killing for hire offends your moral sensibilities?'' he asked. His voice was very bland, too bland, as if he were laughing silently to himself.

"Yes, dammit, it does."

"Yet you are friends with Edward."

"I never said I was consistent, Jean-Claude."

"You are one of the most consistent people I have ever known, *ma petite*."

"How consistent can I be if I'm dating two men?"

"Do you think being unable to choose between us makes you frivolous?" He leaned towards me as he said it, hand smoothing up the sleeve of my jacket.

The trouble was I had almost chosen. I almost told him, but I didn't. First, I wasn't a hundred percent sure. Second, Jean-Claude had blackmailed me into dating him. Date him or he'd kill Richard. He wanted a chance to woo me away from Richard. Which meant really dating him. As he put it, "If you allow Richard to kiss you, but not me, it is not fair." Supposedly, if I chose Richard, Jean-Claude would merely step aside. I think he was egotist enough to mean it. The Master of the City couldn't imagine anyone not being won over, eventually. Not if you had access to his lovely body. He kept offering it. I kept refusing. If I chose Richard over him, would he really bow out gracefully, or would he take us all down in a bloodbath?

I stared into his deep blue eyes and didn't know. I'd known him for years. Dated him for months. But he was still a mystery to me. I just didn't know what he would do. I wasn't willing to push that button, not yet.

"What are you thinking about so seriously, *ma petite*? Do not say it is the assassin. I would not believe you."

I didn't know what to say, so I just shook my head.

His hand slid over my shoulders until I was resting in the curve of his arm. The feel of his body that close to mine made my stomach flutter. He bent forward as if to kiss me, and I stopped him, the back of my left hand against his chest. Since I was now touching bare skin, I wasn't sure this helped.

"You behaved yourself the entire drive up here. What gives now?" I asked.

"I am trying to comfort you, *ma petite*."

"Yeah, right," I said.

He wrapped his other arm around my waist, turning my upper body against him. The gun was still in my hand, but it began to seem awkward. I wasn't going to use it on Jean-Claude, and the assassin wasn't coming through the locked doors. That much violence in a crowd this large with cops directing traffic seemed a little bold even for a professional.

I slid my arm across his back, the gun still in my hand. "If you kiss me, I'll have to redo my lipstick."

He leaned his face close enough to kiss, lips so close to mine he could have breathed me in. He whispered just above my mouth. "We mustn't have that." He kissed my cheek, running his lips down the edge of my jaw.

I touched his face with the edge of the gun, moving his face where I could see it. His eyes had gone drowning blue. "No necking," I said. I meant that. I'd only volunteered once for blood donation and that was when he was dying. I did not share bodily fluids with the Master of the City.

He rubbed his cheek against the gun. "I had something a bit lower in mind."

He ducked his head to my collarbone, licking down my skin. For a second I wondered how low he was planning on going, then I pushed him off of.me.

"I don't think so," I said, half-laughing.

"Do you feel better now, *ma petite*?"

I stared at him for a heartbeat, then laughed. I did. "You are a devious son of a bitch, did you know that?"

"I've been told that before," he said, smiling.

The police had pushed the crowd back, and the limo moved forward. "You did that just to cheer me up." I sounded almost accusatory.

He widened his eyes. "Would I do such a thing?"

I stared at him and felt the smile slide from my face. I really looked at him for a moment, not just as the world's greatest lust object, but as him, Jean-Claude. The Master of the City was worried about my feelings. I shook my head. Was he becoming nicer, or was I just fooling myself?

"Why so solemn, *ma petite*?"

I shook my head. "The usual, trying to figure out how sincere you are."

His smile widened. "I am always sincere, *ma petite*, even when I lie."

"Which is what makes you so good at it," I said.

He nodded his head once, almost a bow. "Exactly."

He glanced ahead of us. "We are about to embark on a sea of media, *ma petite*. If you could put the gun up? I think the press would find it a bit much."

"Press?" I said. "You mean local media?"

"Local, yes."

"What aren't you telling me?"

"When the door opens, take my arm and smile, please, *ma petite*."

I frowned at him. "What is about to happen?"

"You are about to be introduced to the world."

"Jean-Claude, what are you up to?"

"This is not my doing, *ma petite*. I do not like the limelight quite this much. The vampire council has chosen me to be their representative to the media."

"I know you had to come out of the casket to the local vampires after you won your last challenge, but isn't it dangerous? I mean you've been pretending to be some mysterious master's number-one flunkie. It's kept you safe from outside challengers."

"Most masters use a stalking horse, *ma petite*. It cuts down on challenges and human assassins."

"I know all that, so why are you going public?"

"The council believes that skulking in the shadows gives ammunition to our detractors. Those of us who would make good media fodder have been ordered into the light, as it were."

I stared at him. "How into the light?"

"Put the gun away, *ma petite*. The doorman will open the door and there will be cameras." I glared at him, but I slid the Seecamp into my purse.

"What have you gotten me into, Jean-Claude?"

"Smile, *ma petite*, or at least do not frown." The door opened before I could say anything else. A man in a tux held the door. The flash of lightbulbs was blinding, and I knew it had to bother his eyes more than mine. He was smiling as he held a hand back for me. If he could stare that much light in the face without blinking, I could be gracious. We could always fight later.

I stepped out of the limo and was glad I was holding his hand. Flashbulbs were everywhere like tiny suns blasting off. The crowd surged forward, microphones shoved at us like knives. If he hadn't been holding my hand tight, I'd have crawled back into the limo. I moved closer to him, just to be able to keep my feet. Where the hell was crowd control?

A microphone nearly touched my face. A woman's voice yelled from far too close, "Is he good in bed? Or would that be coffin?"

"What?" I said.

"Is he good in bed?" There was a moment of near silence, while everyone waited for my answer. Before I could open my mouth and say something scathing, Jean-Claude moved in, graceful as always.

"We do not kiss and tell, do we, *ma petite*?" His French accent was the thickest I'd ever heard it.

"*Ma petite*—is that your pet name for her?" a man's voice.

"*Oui*," he said.

I looked up at him, and he leaned down as if to kiss my cheek. He whispered, "Glare at me later, *ma petite*. There are cameras everywhere."

I wanted to say that I didn't give a damn, but I did. I mean, I think I did. I felt like a rabbit caught in headlights. If the assassin had jumped out with a gun at that moment, I'd have stood there and let him shoot me. That thought, more than anything else, brought me back to myself, helped me to think again. I started trying to see past the lights, the microphones, a few tape recorders, and video cameras. I caught at least two major network emblems on the cameras. Shit.

Jean-Claude was fielding questions like a pro, smiling, gracious, the perfect vampire cover boy. I smiled and leaned into him, standing on tiptoe, putting my lips so close to his ear that I could have licked it, but I was hoping the microphones wouldn't pick up what I was saying. I was sure it looked coy and girlish as hell, but hey, nothing was perfect. I whispered, "Get me out of here now, or I pull the gun and clear a path for myself."

He laughed, and it flowed down my skin like fur, warm, and ticklish, and vaguely obscene. The reporters ooohed and aahed. I wondered if Jean-Claude's laugh worked off a recorder, or on video. That was a frightening thought.

"Oh, *ma petite*, you naughty girl."

I whispered, "Don't ever call me that again."

"My apologies." He smiled, waved, and began escorting me through the press of reporters. Two vampire doormen had come out to help clear our path. They were both large and muscular, and neither of them had been dead long. They looked rosy-cheeked and almost alive. They'd fed on someone tonight. But then, so had Jean-Claude. It was getting harder and harder for me to throw stones at the monsters.

The door opened, and we slipped inside. The silence was wonderful. I turned on him. "How dare you drag me into that kind of media coverage."

"It does not endanger you, *ma petite*."

"Had it occurred to you that if I chose Richard over you, that I might not want everybody in the world to know I was dating a vampire?"

He gave a slight smile. "Good enough to date, but not good enough to go public with?"

"We've gone to everything from the symphony to the ballet together. I'm not ashamed of you."

"Really?" The smile was gone, replaced by something else, not anger exactly, but close. "Then why are you angry, *ma petite*?"

I opened my mouth, then closed it. Truth was that I would rather not have gone quite this public, because I guess I didn't really believe I could choose Jean-Claude. He was a vampire, a dead man. In that one moment I realized how prejudiced I still was. He was good enough to date. Good enough to hold hands with, and maybe a bit more. But there was a limit. Always a point where I knew I'd say stop because he was a corpse. A beautiful corpse, but a vampire is a vampire. You couldn't really fall in love with one. You couldn't have sex with one. No way. I'd broken Jean-Claude's one rule for dating both of the boys. I'd never really given Jean-Claude the same chance that I'd given Richard. And now, with national television coverage, the bat was out of the bag. It embarrassed me that anyone would think I might actually date him. That I might actually care for a walking dead man.

The anger washed away in the knowledge that I was a hypocrite. I don't know how much of it showed on my face, but Jean-Claude cocked his head to one side. "Thoughts are flying across your face, *ma petite*, but what thoughts?"

I stared up at him. "I think I owe you an apology."

His eyes widened. "Then this is a truly historic occasion. What are you apologizing for?"

I wasn't sure how to put it into words. "You're right; I'm wrong."

He put his fingers to his chest, face wide with mock surprise. "You admit that you have treated me like some guilty secret, hidden away. Exiled from your true feelings while you cuddle with Richard and his living flesh."

I frowned at him. "Enough already. See if I ever give you another apology for anything."

"A dance would suffice," he said.

"I don't dance. You know that."

"This is the grand opening of my dance club, *ma petite*. You are my date. Are you truly going to deny me even one dance?"

Put that way it sounded petty. "One dance."

He smiled, wicked, enticing. The smile that the serpent must have given Eve. "I think we will dance well together, *ma petite*."

"I doubt it."

"I think we would do many things well together."

"Give you one dance and you want the whole package. Pushy bastard."

He gave a small bow, smiling, eyes shining.

A female vamp strode towards us. She was inches taller than Jean-Claude, which made her at least six feet tall. She was blond and blue-eyed, and if she'd looked any more Nordic, she'd have been a poster girl for the master race. She was wearing a violet blue body suit with strategic holes cut out. The body that showed through was broad-shouldered, muscular, and still managed to be full-breasted. Leather boots in the exact same color rode her long, muscular legs all the way up to her thighs.

''Anita Blake, this is Liv.''

''Let me guess,'' I said. ''Jean-Claude chose the outfit.''

Liv looked at me from her considerable height as if simply being tall made her intimidating. When I didn't flinch, she smiled. ''He is the boss.''

I stared up at her. I almost asked why. I could feel her age pressing down on me like a weight. She was six hundred years old. Twice Jean-Claude's age or more. So why wasn't she the boss? I could feel the answer along my skin like a cool wind. Not enough power. She wasn't a master vampire, and no amount of age would change that.

''What are you staring at?'' she asked. She looked me right in the eyes and shook her head. ''She really is immune to our gaze.''

''To your gaze,'' I said.

She put her hands on her hips. ''What's that supposed to mean?''

''It means you don't have enough juice to do me,'' I said.

She took a step forward. ''How about I just pick you up and squeeze some juice out of you?''

Here was where not having a gun in a holster was going to get me killed. I could get one of the knives out, but unless I was willing for her to come very close, it wouldn't help. I could slip my hand in the purse; most people didn't expect a gun to come out of a purse so small. Of course, if Liv caught me going for the gun, she could get to me before I could draw it. With a holster I'd have tried it. From a purse hanging from a strap, I didn't think so. Vampires are just that fast.

''How many vampire kills do you have now, Anita?'' Jean-Claude asked.

The question surprised me, and my answer surprised me more. ''Over twenty legal kills.''

''How many kills altogether, *ma petite*?''

''I don't know,'' I said. It had to be over thirty now, but truthfully, I didn't remember anymore. I didn't know how many lives I'd taken. A bad sign, that.

''Liv is mine, *ma petite*. You may speak freely in front of her.''

I shook my head. ''Never admit to murder in front of strangers, Jean-Claude. Just a rule.''

Liv looked at me. She didn't seem to like what she saw. ''So this is the Executioner.'' She shook her head. ''She's a little on the small side, isn't she?'' She stalked around me like I was a horse for sale. When she was at my back, I opened the purse. By the time she came around again, I had the gun out, behind the purse, unobtrusive, though in a pinch I guess I could have shot through the purse. But why, if I didn't have to?

Liv shook her head. ''She's pretty, but she's not very impressive.'' She stood behind Jean-Claude, running her strong hands over his shoulders, his arms. She ended with her hands around his waist, fingers kneading his body.

I was getting very tired of Liv.

''I can do things that no human can do for you, Jean-Claude.''

''You are being rude to Anita. I will not remind you of it again.'' There was a cold, even threat in his voice.

Liv unwrapped herself from him and stood between us, hands on hips. ''The great Jean-Claude driven to celibacy by a human. People are laughing behind your back.''

''Celibacy?'' I asked.

Jean-Claude glanced at me, then sighed. ''Until you give up your nunnish ways, *ma petite*, I am playing monk.''

My eyes widened. I couldn't help it. I knew that Richard and I had each had one lover and chosen celibacy afterwards. But I'd never thought about Jean-Claude and what he might be doing to satisfy his needs. Abstinence would not have been one of my choices for him.

''You seem surprised, *ma petite*.''

''I guess anyone who exudes sex the way you do . . . I just never thought about it.''

''Yet if you discovered that I had been sleeping with another female, alive or dead, while we were dating, what would you do?''

''Drop you in a hot minute.''

''Exactly.''

Liv laughed, a loud, unattractive bray of sound. ''Even your human doesn't believe you.''

Jean-Claude turned to her, his eyes a blaze of sapphire flame. ''You say they laugh behind my back.''

She nodded, still laughing.

''But only you are laughing to my face.''

Her laughter died abruptly like a turned switch. She stared at him.

''A little more submissiveness, Liv, or is this a challenge to my authority?''

She looked startled. ''No, I mean . . . I never meant . . .''

He just looked at her. ''Then you had best ask my forgiveness, had you not?''

She dropped to one knee. She didn't look afraid, more as if she'd done some huge social gaffe and now had to make amends. ''I beg your forgiveness, Master. I forgot myself.''

''Yes, you did, Liv. Do not make it a habit.''

Liv got to her feet, all smiles, all forgiven. Just like that. The political maneuvering was thick in the air. ''It's only that she doesn't look nearly as dangerous as you painted her.''

''Anita,'' Jean-Claude said, ''show her what you have in your hand.''

I moved the purse to one side, flashing the gun.

''I could have your throat in my hands before you could point that toy,'' Liv said.

''No,'' I said, ''you couldn't.''

''Is that a challenge?'' she asked.

''Six hundred years of life, plus or minus a decade,'' I said. ''Don't throw it away for a little grandstanding.''

''How did you know my age?''

I smiled. ''I am really not in the mood to bluff tonight, Liv. Don't try me.''

She stared at me, her extraordinary eyes narrowing. ''You are a necromancer, not just a corpse-raiser. I can feel you inside my head, almost like another vampire.'' She looked at Jean-Claude. ''Why couldn't I feel her before?''

''Her power flares when she feels threatened,'' he said.

This was news to me. To my knowledge, I wasn't using any power right now. But I didn't say it out loud. Now was not the time to ask stupid questions or even smart ones.

Liv stepped to one side, almost as if she was afraid. ''We're opening in an hour. I've got work to do.'' She moved towards the door, never taking her eyes from me.

I watched her move, happy with her reaction but not understanding it.

''Come, Anita,'' Jean-Claude said, ''I want to show you my club.''

I let him lead me into the main area of the club. They had gutted the warehouse until it rose three stories straight up with railings around each floor. The main dance floor was huge, shining and slick, gleaming in the subdued light. Track lighting was hidden away so it was hard to tell where the light was coming from.

Things hung from the ceiling. At first glance I thought they were bodies, but they were mannequins, life-size rubber dolls, crash-test dummies. Some were naked, one wrapped in cellophane, some in black leather or vinyl. One rubber doll wore a metal bikini. They were hung from chains at different levels. It was a mobile.

''That's different,'' I said.

''A promising new artist did it especially for the club.''

I shook my head. ''It does make a statement.'' I slipped the gun back into my purse but kept the purse open. That way I was able to get to the gun surprisingly quickly. Besides, I couldn't walk around all night with a loaded gun in my hand. Eventually, your hand starts cramping, no matter how small the gun is.

Jean-Claude glided across the dance floor, and I followed. ''Liv was afraid of me. Why?''

He turned gracefully, smiling. ''You are the Executioner.''

I shook my head. ''She said she could feel me in her head like another vamp. What did she mean?''

He sighed. ''You are a necromancer, *ma petite*, and your power grows with use.''

''Why would that scare a six-hundred-year-old vampire?''

''You are relentless, *ma petite*.''

''It's one of my best things.''

''If I answer your question, will you enjoy my club with me, be my date until the assassin shows up?''

''Thanks for reminding me.''

''You had not forgotten.''

''No, I hadn't. So, yeah, answer my question and I'll play date.''

''Play?''

''Stop stalling and answer the question.'' I thought of one other question I wanted answered. ''Two questions.''

He raised his eyebrows, but nodded. ''Vampires are given powers in folklore and popular myth that we do not possess: controlling weather, shapeshifting into animals. Necromancers are supposedly able to control all types of undead.''

''Control? You don't mean just zombies, do you?''

''No, *ma petite.*''

''So Liv's afraid I'll take her over?''

''Something like that.''

''But that's crazy. I can't order vampires around.'' The moment I said it, I wished I hadn't. It wasn't true. I had raised a vampire once. Once. Once had been enough.

Something must have shown on my face, because Jean-Claude touched my cheek.

''What is it, *ma petite*? What fills your eyes with such . . . horror?''

I opened my mouth and lied. ''If I could order vampires around, Serephina wouldn't have cleaned my clock two months ago.''

His face softened. ''She is dead, *ma petite*. Well and truly dead. You saw to that.'' He leaned forward and kissed my forehead. His lips were silken soft. He brushed his lips across my forehead, moving his body in closer, comforting me.

It made me feel guilty as hell. I did still have nightmares about Serephina, that much was true. Just saying her name out loud made my stomach clench. Of all the vampires I'd faced, she'd come the closest to getting me. Not killing me, that would happen sooner or later. No, she had nearly made me one of them. Nearly made me want to be one of them. She had offered me something more precious than sex or power. She'd offered me peace. It had been a lie, but as lies go, it had been a good one.

Why not tell Jean-Claude the truth? Well, it was none of his damn business. Frankly, what I'd done frightened me. I didn't want to deal with it. Didn't want to think about it. Didn't want to know what the philosophical ramifications of raising a vampire during daylight hours might be. I was very good at ignoring things I didn't want to deal with.

''*Ma petite*, you are trembling.'' He pushed me back from him to search my face.

I shook my head. ''There's an assassin out to kill me, and you ask why I'm trembling.''

''I know you too well, *ma petite*. That is not why you tremble.''

''I don't like you using me like some kind of bogeyman for vampires. I'm not that scary.''

''No, but I have encouraged the illusion.''

I pushed away from him. ''You mean, you've been telling other vamps that I could control vampires?''

''A hint or two.'' He smiled, and in that one simple expression, you just knew he was thinking wicked thoughts.

''Why, for heaven's sake?''

''I have taken a lesson from our diplomatic Richard. He has won over many wolves by simply promising to treat them well, not to force them to do things they do not want to do.''

''So?'' I said.

''I have invited vampires to join my flock with the promise not of fear and intimidation but of safety.''

''Like Liv?''

He nodded.

''How do you make sure they don't stage a palace revolt?'' I asked.

''There are ways.''

''Like threatening them with a necromancer,'' I said.

He smiled. ''Indeed.''

''Not everyone will believe it.''

''I know I don't,'' a voice said.

15

I turned to find another new vampire. He was tall and slender with skin the color of clean white sheets, but sheets didn't have muscle moving underneath, sheets didn't glide down the steps and pad godlike across a room. His hair fell past his shoulders, a red so pure it was nearly the color of blood. The color screamed against his paleness. He was wearing a black frock coat like something out of the 1700s, but his chest gleamed lean and naked inside it. The heavy cloth was nearly covered in thick embroidery, a green so vivid it gleamed. The embroidery matched his eyes. Green as a cat's eyes, green as an emerald. From the waist down, he was wearing green lycra exercise pants that left little to the imagination. A sash was tied at his waist like a pirate belt, black with green fringe. Knee-high black boots completed the outfit.

I thought I knew all the bloodsuckers in town, but here were two new ones in less than two minutes. ''How many new vampires are in the city?'' I asked.

''A few,'' Jean-Claude said. ''This is Damian. Damian, this is Anita.''

''I feel silly in this outfit,'' he said.

''But you look splendid, doesn't he, *ma petite*?''

I nodded. ''Splendid is one way of putting it.''

Jean-Claude walked around the new vampire, flicking imaginary specks of lint from the coat. ''Don't you approve, Anita?''

I sighed. ''It's just . . .'' I shrugged. ''Why do you make everyone around you dress like they stepped out of a sexual fantasy with a high costume budget?''

He laughed, and the sound wrapped around me, tugged at things lower than he'd ever gotten to touch. ''Stop that,'' I said.

''You enjoy it, *ma petite*.''

''Maybe, but stop it anyway.''

''Jean-Claude has always had a killer fashion sense,'' Damian said, ''and sex was always one of his favorite pastimes, wasn't it?'' There was something about the way he said that last that made it not a compliment.

Jean-Claude faced him. ''And yet, for all my foppish ways, here you are, in my lands, seeking my protection.''

The pupils in Damian's eyes were swallowed by a rush of green fire. "Thank you so much for reminding me."

"Remember who is master here, Damian, or you will be banished. The council themselves interceded with your old master, rescued you from her. She did not want to give you up. I spoke for you. I ransomed you because I remember what it was like to be trapped. To be forced to do things you didn't want to do. To be used and tormented."

Damian stood a little straighter but didn't look away. "You've made your point. I am . . . grateful to be here." He looked away, then to the floor, and a shudder ran through him. "I am glad to be free of her." When he looked back up, his eyes had returned to normal. He managed a smile that didn't quite reach his eyes. "Wearing a few costumes is not the worst thing I've ever done."

There was a sorrow to his voice that made me want to ask Jean-Claude to let him change into a pair of pants, but I didn't. Jean-Claude was walking a very fine line here. Damian was over five hundred years old. He wasn't a master, but that was still a hell of a lot of power. Jean-Claude might be able to handle Liv and Damian, but if there were more, Master of the City or not, he wasn't up to the job. Which meant these little dominance games were necessary. The others couldn't be allowed to forget who was Master, because once they did, he was done for. If he'd asked for my vote before he put out the invitations, I'd have said no.

A door at the far side of the room opened. It was a black door in the black walls, and it seemed almost magical as a woman stepped out. She was about my own height, with wavy, waist-length brown hair that foamed over the shoulders of her ankle-length black coat. She was wearing a pair of hot turquoise exercise pants with a matching sports bra. Crisscrossing straps went from pants to the bra, emphasizing her small waist. Black vinyl boots reached to her knees, with a small projection that covered the knees. She walked down the steps and strode across the floor with a free-swinging walk that was almost a run. She entered the room like it was her room, or maybe she was her own room, comfortable wherever she went.

She stopped by us, smiling, pleasant, hazel eyes greener because of the strip of turquoise around her neck. "What do you think?"

"You look lovely, Cassandra," Jean-Claude said.

"You look better in yours than I do in mine," Damian said.

"That's a matter of opinion," I said.

The woman looked at me. Her eyes flicked down the length of Damian's body. She met my eyes, and we both laughed.

Damian looked puzzled. Jean-Claude looked at me. "Share your humor with us, *ma petite*, please."

I met Cassandra's eyes again, swallowed another laugh, and shook my head. I took a few deep breaths. When I was pretty sure I could speak without laughing, I said, "Girl humor, you wouldn't understand."

"Very diplomatic," Cassandra said. "I'm impressed."

"If you knew how hard diplomacy comes to *ma petite*, you would be even more impressed," Jean-Claude said. He had gotten the joke, as if there'd been any doubt.

Damian was frowning at us, still puzzled. It was just as well.

Jean-Claude looked from Cassandra to me and back again. "Do you two know each other?"

We shook our heads in unison.

"Cassandra, Anita. My newest wolf, meet the light of my life. Cassandra is one of your guards for the night."

"You're very good. I wouldn't have picked up on it."

Her smile widened. "Richard said you didn't know he was a werewolf at first, either."

Instantly, a little spark of jealousy flared. Of course, if she were a werewolf and with Jean-Claude, then she was one of Richard's followers. "You weren't at the meeting."

"Jean-Claude needed me here. He couldn't do without both Jason and me."

I looked at Jean-Claude. I knew what Jason did for him. He bled Jason when he woke, and sucking blood was damn close to sex for a vampire. "Really," I said.

"Don't worry, ma petite. Cassandra won't share blood with me, either. She and Richard have many similarities. I believe that Richard chose her for me because she bears a certain resemblance to you, not just physically, but a certain je ne sais quoi."

"*Je ne sais quoi* is French for nothing," I said.

"It means an indefinable something that is difficult to put into words, *ma petite*. A quality that transcends vocabulary."

"He does talk pretty, doesn't he?" Cassandra said.

"He has his moments," I said. "You can't be draining Jason every morning. Even a werewolf needs a little recoup time."

"Stephen is a willing donor."

"Why wasn't Stephen with you last night?" I asked.

"Is that an accusation?" Jean-Claude asked.

"Just answer the question."

"He had requested an evening off to spend time with his brother. Who am I to stand in the way of familial obligations?" He stared at me while he answered like he wasn't completely happy with the conversation. Tough. Neither was I.

Stephen's own brother had betrayed him, acted as bait for the trap. Damn. "Where is Stephen?"

"He's in the back room," Cassandra said. "He helped me get into this thing. I couldn't reach all the straps." She dropped the coat off her shoulders and turned so I could see her back. The straps formed a tight web, most of them in places you couldn't have fastened without help. She slipped the coat back on and turned, looking at me. "You're taking this alpha female thing seriously, aren't you?"

I shrugged. "I'm serious about Stephen's safety."

Cassandra nodded, face solemn, thoughtful. "I like that. Sometimes alpha female is just a token position. Just a word for the pack leader's lover. Most of them aren't as active as Raina." She made a face when she said the name, like she'd tasted something bitter.

Jean-Claude interrupted. "I will leave you two girls to your conversation. I have things to attend to before the club opens.'' He kissed the back of my hand and was gone, leaving us standing in the middle of the club, alone. Damian had gone at his heels as if he'd been asked.

For a moment, I was nervous. Cassandra and I were very much in the open. ''Let's go over there.'' I motioned to the steps that led to the next level. We sat down on them, me having to smooth my skirts down. Even that didn't help. I had to keep my feet and knees together or I would have flashed the room. Sigh.

''Let me guess,'' I said. ''Raina wanted you for her movies.''

''She wants everyone that is remotely attractive for her movies. Though sometimes sharing her bed for a tryout can get you out of it. She offered me to Gabriel for my tryout. That damn leopard is not even a pack member.''

''If he were, she'd make him pack leader,'' I said.

Cassandra shook her head. ''Gabriel couldn't defeat Marcus, let alone Richard. He's the leader of the wereleopards only because there's no one stronger. He's an alpha, but he's flawed. It makes him weak.''

''Sexual perversion doesn't always mean you'll lose a fight,'' I said.

''It's not that,'' Cassandra said. ''He's into dangerous sex. Lycanthropes can take a lot of damage.'' She shivered. ''The things he wanted to do to me.'' She looked at me, and the fear showed in her eyes. ''He says you nearly gutted him once while he had you pinned to the ground.''

I looked away. ''Yeah.''

Cassandra touched my arm, and there was no sense of power. She was every bit as good as Richard at hiding what she was. She made Sylvie look like an amateur. The touch made me turn back to her. ''He's hot for you, Anita. I didn't tell Richard because, well, I'm new in the pack. Got into town about two weeks ago. I was afraid that if I told him what Gabriel had said about you, he might do something stupid. But meeting you, maybe telling you is enough. You can decide whether Richard needs to know.''

She looked so serious. It scared me. ''What did Gabriel say?''

Cassandra took a deep breath. ''He has a fantasy about you. He wants to arm you with knives and let you try to kill him, on film, while he rapes you.''

I stared at her. I wanted to say, you're kidding, but I knew she wasn't. Gabriel was just that twisted. ''How does the movie end in his version?''

''With you dead,'' she said.

''While he rapes me?'' I said.

She nodded.

I hugged myself, running my hands down my arms, tensing my back, feeling the weapons I was carrying. I was armed. I was safe, but shit.

She touched my shoulder. ''You all right?''

''Well, isn't this touching,'' a man's voice on the stairs behind us. Cassandra was on her feet, facing it in an instant. I slid my hand into the open purse and drew the Seecamp out. The gun caught a bit on the cloth lining and cost me a couple of seconds, but it was out and ready. I felt better. I'd twisted on the steps, coming up on one knee, not bothering to stand. Sometimes, standing made you a better target.

Sabin stood about five steps above us. Frightfully close for neither of us to have sensed him. He was dressed as I'd seen him in the office; hooded cloak covering him from head to toe. I could see under the cloak now. There were no feet. He was floating above the step. "I wish you could see the look on your face, Ms. Blake."

I swallowed my pulse back into my mouth and said, "I didn't know you'd be here tonight, Sabin."

Cassandra took a step towards him, a soft growl oozing from her throat. "I don't know you," she said.

"Calm yourself, wolf. I am Jean-Claude's guest, aren't I, Ms. Blake?"

"Yeah," I said. "He's a guest." I stopped pointing the gun at him, but I didn't put it up. He was awfully damn good to have snuck up on me and a werewolf.

"You know him?" Cassandra asked. She was still standing above me, blocking the vampire's path. She was taking this bodyguard thing very seriously.

"I've met him."

"He safe?"

"No," I said, "but he's not here to hurt me."

"Who is he here to hurt?" Cassandra asked. She still hadn't given any ground.

Sabin eased down the steps, cloak billowing around him in an odd motion, like the sleeve of an amputee. "I have come to watch the night's entertainment, nothing more."

Cassandra backed up to stand a step ahead of me. I stood but still kept the gun out. I was jumpier than normal. I was also remembering how Sabin had bled me from a distance with his laughter. Keeping a gun handy seemed like a good idea.

"Where's Dominic?"

"He's here somewhere." His hood was a cup of darkness, smooth and empty, but I knew he was watching me. I felt his gaze like a weight.

He stayed on the step just above Cassandra, two steps above me. "Who is your lovely companion?"

"Sabin, this is Cassandra; Cassandra, Sabin."

A black-gloved hand slid out of the cloak. He reached towards Cassandra as if he'd caress her face.

She jerked back. "Don't touch me."

His hand froze in midmotion. A stillness washed over him. I'd seen other vampires fill with that utter quietness, but I'd thought it was made up of visual clues. There was no visual from Sabin, but that same emptiness flowed outward. The illusion was almost better this way as if it was just an empty cloak somehow hovering on the stairs.

His voice came out of that stillness. It was startling. "Is my touch so repulsive?"

"You smell of sickness and death."

Sabin drew his hand back inside his cloak. "I am a visiting master. It is within my rights to ask for a bit of . . . companionship. I could ask for you, wolf."

Cassandra growled at him.

"No one's forcing anyone into anyone's bed," I said.

"Are you so sure of that, Ms. Blake?" Sabin asked. He floated around Cassandra. The cloak brushed her, and she shuddered.

I couldn't smell him; I didn't have a werewolf's sense of smell. But I'd seen some of what was under that cloak. It was worth a shudder or two.

"Cassandra is only on loan to Jean-Claude. She belongs to the pack, so yeah, I'm sure."

Cassandra glanced back at me. "You'd protect me?"

"It's part of my job description now, isn't it?"

She studied my face. "Yes, I suppose it is." Her voice was soft, the growling like a distant dream. She looked terribly normal except for the outfit.

"You've seen what I am, Ms. Blake. Do you shudder at my touch?"

I moved down a step until I was on the floor. Better footing than the stairs. "I shook your hand earlier."

Sabin floated to the floor. The darkness faded from inside the hood. He pushed it back to reveal that golden hair and that ravaged face.

Cassandra let out a hiss. She backed up until she hit the banister. I think Sabin could have pulled a gun and shot her right that second, and she wouldn't have reacted in time.

He smiled at her. His beautiful mouth pulling the rotted flesh loose. "Have you never seen anything like this?"

She swallowed hard enough for me to hear, like she was trying not to throw up. "I've never seen anything so horrible."

Sabin turned back to me. His one eye was still a clear, pure blue, but the other had burst in the socket in a welter of pus and thinner liquid.

I did my own swallowing. "Your eye was fine yesterday."

"I told you it was virulent, Ms. Blake. Did you think I was exaggerating?"

I shook my head. "No."

His gloved hand came out of hiding once more. I remembered the way his hand had squished when I shook it yesterday. I did not want him to touch me, but there was a look in his beautiful eye, some pain on what was left of his face, that made me hold still. I wouldn't flinch. I felt sorry for him, pretty stupid, but true.

That black glove hovered beside my face, not quite touching me. The Seecamp was forgotten in my hand. Sabin's fingertips brushed my face. The glove was liquid-filled, like some kind of obscene balloon.

He stared at me. I stared back. He spread his hand over my lower jaw and pressed. There were solid things inside the glove, thicker pieces, and bone, but it wasn't a hand anymore. Only the glove gave it shape.

A small sound crawled out of my throat. I couldn't stop it.

"Perhaps I should ask for you?" he said.

I eased back out of his grip. I was afraid to move too quickly. Afraid that sudden movement might tear off the glove. I did not want to see him spill out in a flood of foul-smelling liquid. He was a horror show enough without that.

Sabin didn't try to hold me; maybe he was afraid of the same thing.

"Are you abusing my hospitality again?" Jean-Claude said. He stood on the dance floor, looking at Sabin. His eyes were pure blue light. His skin had gone pale and smooth like carved marble.

"You have not yet shown me true hospitality, Jean-Claude. It is customary to offer me companionship."

"I didn't think there was enough of you left to have such needs," Jean-Claude said.

Sabin grimaced. "It is a cruel illness. Not all of my body has rotted away. The need remains, though the vessel is so grotesque that no one will touch me, not by choice." He shook his head, and the skin split on one side. Something black and thicker than blood oozed down the side of his face.

Cassandra made a small sound. My bodyguard was about to be sick. Maybe it smelled bad to her.

"If one of my people angers me enough while you are in my territory, you may have them. But I cannot give someone to you just because you wish it. Not everyone's sanity would survive it."

"There are days, Jean-Claude, when my own sanity is in doubt." Sabin looked from Cassandra to me. "It would break your wolf, I think. But your servant, I think she would survive."

"She is off limits to you, Sabin. If you abuse my hospitality with such an insult, council edict or no council edict, I will destroy you."

Sabin turned to him. The two vampires stared at each other. "There was a time, Jean-Claude, when no one spoke to me like that, no one short of the council."

"That was before," Jean-Claude said.

Sabin sighed. "Yes, before."

"You are free to enjoy the show, but do not tempt me again, Sabin. I have no sense of humor where *ma petite* is concerned."

"You share her with a werewolf but not with me."

"That is our business," Jean-Claude said, "and we will never speak of this again. If we do, it will be a challenge between us, and you are not up to it."

Sabin gave a half bow, hard to get the leverage for it without legs. "You are Master of the City. Your word is law." The words were correct. The tone was mocking.

Liv came up to stand behind and to one side of Jean-Claude. "It is time to open the doors, Master." I think that last was deliberate. Jean-Claude usually chastised his flock for calling him master.

Jean-Claude said, "Everyone to their places then." His voice sounded strangled.

"I will find a table," Sabin said.

"Do so," Jean-Claude said.

Sabin raised the hood back into place. He glided back up the stairs, headed for the tables on the upper level. Or maybe he'd just float in the rafters.

"My apologies, *ma petite*. I believe the sickness has progressed to his mind. Be wary of him. Cassandra is needed for the show. Liv will remain with you."

I looked at the tall vampire. "She won't take a bullet for me."

"If she fails me, I will give her to Sabin."

Liv paled, which is a neat trick for a vampire, even one that's fed. "Master, please."

"Now I believe she'll take a bullet for me," I said. If the choices were sleeping with Sabin or getting shot, I'd take the bullet. From the look on Liv's face, she agreed.

Jean-Claude left to make his entrance.

Cassandra met my eyes. She wasn't just pale, she was green. She jerked her gaze from mine as if afraid of what I'd see. "I am sorry, Anita." She went for the door she'd first entered through. She seemed embarrassed. Guess I couldn't blame her.

Cassandra had failed the bodyguard test. She was a powerful lycanthrope, but Sabin had totally unnerved her. She'd have probably been just fine if the vampire had tried violence, but he'd just stood there and rotted at her. What do you do when the monsters start being piteous?

The doors opened, and the crowd flowed in like a tidal wave, spilling in a wash of thunderous noise. I slipped the gun back into the purse but didn't shut it.

Liv was at my elbow. "Your table is over here." I went with her because I didn't want to be alone in the jostling crowd. Besides, she was suddenly taking my safety very seriously. Couldn't blame her. Sabin's diseased body was a wonderful threat.

I'd have felt better if I hadn't believed Jean-Claude would do it. But I knew better. He'd give Liv to Sabin. He really would. There was a look in the vampire's eyes that said she knew it, too.

16

The table was the largest of a string of small, black lacquer tables. It blended nearly perfectly with the black walls. My dress matched the decor. I was really going to have to look into something in a different color scheme. The table was set away from the wall, near the railing so that the growing crowd couldn't block my view of the dance floor. It also meant that my back was exposed. I had scooted my chair so that the wall was at my back, but I was very aware that the edge of the railing curved around on my right side, so that someone could walk up and shoot me, relatively hidden from anyone else.

Of course, Liv was with me. She stood at my back, arms crossed over her stomach. All she needed was a sign over her head that flashed bodyguard.

Admittedly, my purse was open. The gun was within reach, and it was tempting to put it in my lap. I was spooked, but that wasn't the point. We had a plan. The plan did not include the assassin being scared away.

I touched Liv's arm.

She bent down.

''You're supposed to be unobtrusive.''

She looked puzzled. ''I'm supposed to keep you safe.''

''Then sit down and pretend to be my friend. The trap won't work if I look like I'm being guarded.''

She knelt by me; too far to bend down, I suppose. ''I will not risk being given to Sabin. I don't care if your assassin knows I'm here or not.''

It was hard to blame her, but I was willing to make the effort. I leaned into her. ''Look, either work with the program, or get away from me.''

''I obey Jean-Claude, not his strumpet.''

As far as I could remember, I'd never done anything in my life to deserve being called a strumpet. ''Jean-Claude said if you failed him, he'd give you to the rotting corpse, right?''

Liv nodded. Her eyes searched the crowd behind me. She really was trying to do the job, and the effort showed.

''He didn't say you'd be punished if I got hurt, did he?''

Liv's eyes flicked to me. "What are you saying?"

"If you scare away the hitter and spoil the plan, that's failure."

She shook her head. "No, that's not what he meant."

"He said never to fail him again."

I watched her try to work out the logic. I was betting that logic wasn't one of her strong points.

"Clever, Anita, but if you get killed, Jean-Claude will punish me. You know he will."

I was wrong. She was a lot smarter than she looked. "But if you spoil our plan, he'll punish you anyway."

Fear flashed through her eyes. "I'm trapped."

I felt sorry for her. Pity for two monsters—no three—in one night. I was losing my edge. "If I don't get killed, I'll make sure you don't get punished."

"You swear it?" She said the phrase like it meant more. Giving your oath was not a casual thing to her. A lot of vampires came from times when a man's or a woman's word was their bond.

"I give you my word."

She stayed kneeling for a moment longer, then stood. "Try not to get killed." She moved into the crowd, leaving me on my own, like I'd asked.

The rest of the tables filled up quickly. The crowd spilled around the edges of the room on the raised area around the dance floor. So many people stood at the fenced edges that if the table had been by the wall, I'd have lost my view of the dance floor. Under other circumstances, I'd have appreciated the thoughtfulness. Another bodyguard could come along at any time. I was ready for some company.

The crowd filled the two levels above, standing room only. I looked for Sabin's dark cloak, but didn't see him. The main dance floor was untouched. The way to the floor was barred by half a dozen vampires. They had quietly but firmly motioned everybody back to the sides of the room. Both male and female were dressed nearly identically, black lycra pants, boots, and black fishnet shirts. The women wore black bras under their shirts, but that was the only difference. I approved. Short little skirts or hot pants for the women would have pissed me off. The thought occurred that maybe Jean-Claude had dressed them with me in mind. He knew me too well in some ways and didn't have a clue in others.

I scanned the crowd for Edward and for anything suspicious, but it was hard to pick out any one person in the jostling, laughing crowd. I couldn't spot Edward. I had to just trust that he was there somewhere. And although I did trust him to be there, the tightness in my chest didn't ease.

Edward had cautioned me to be casual, not to look suspicious. Outwardly, I was trying. Inwardly, I was almost dizzy searching the crowd and that painful empty spot to the right and almost behind me where the railing went. I put my hands in my lap and forced myself to look down. If the assassin came now, I wouldn't be looking, but I had to get hold of myself. If I didn't, I was going to be so busy jumping at shadows, I wouldn't be ready when the real thing came. I was beginning to wish I'd let Liv stay.

I took deep, even breaths, in and out, concentrating on the rhythm of my own body. When I could hear the blood flowing inside my head, I raised my face slowly.

I stared calmly out at the crowd and the dance floor. I felt empty, distant, calm. Much better.

A vampire came up to the railing in front of my table. Willie McCoy was dressed in a suit so horribly green it could only be called chartreuse. Green shirt, and a wide tie with Godzilla crushing Tokyo on it. No one would ever accuse Willie of matching any decor.

I smiled. I couldn't help it. Willie had been one of the first vampires to ever cross that line from monster to friend. He scooted one of the chairs around so his back was to the open space. He sat down like he hadn't done it on purpose. I didn't have to pretend to be happy to see him.

He had to lean a bit into me to be heard over the crowd's rising murmur. I could smell the sweet scent of the goop he used to slick back his short hair. Him being this close didn't even make me tense. I trusted Willie more than I trusted Jean-Claude.

"How ya doing, Anita?" He grinned enough to show fang. Willie hadn't been dead three years yet. He was one of the few vamps I'd known before and after death.

"I've been better," I said.

"Jean-Claude said we were to bodyguard you, but to keep it casual. We'll drift in and out. But you looked spooked."

I shook my head, smiling. "That obvious?"

"To someone who knows ya, yeah."

We smiled at each other. Looking into Willie's face from inches away, I realized that he was on my list. The list that Stephen was on. If someone killed Willie, I'd hunt them down. It surprised me to realize that any vamp had made the list. But Willie had, and come to think of it, I guess, so had one other vampire.

Jean-Claude appeared on the far side of the club. Speak of the devil. A spotlight hit him from somewhere. It had to be coming from a fly loft, but it was hidden away so that it was hard to tell. A perfect place for a high-powered rifle. *Stop it, Anita. Stop tormenting yourself.*

I hadn't truly realized how crowded the opening would be. Edward by himself searching for one lone assassin in this mass of people would have been poor odds. Maybe the vamps and werewolves were amateurs, but their extra eyes couldn't hurt.

The lights began dimming until the only illumination was the spotlight on Jean-Claude. He seemed to glow. I wasn't sure if it was a trick or if he was making his own light from the skin outward. Hard to tell. Whichever, I was in the dark with an assassin, maybe, and I was not a happy camper.

Hell with it. I put the Seecamp in my lap. Better. Not perfect, but better. The fact that just the touch of a gun in my hand made me feel better was probably a bad sign. The fact that I missed my own guns was a worse one.

Willie touched my shoulder and made me jump enough that people near us glanced back. Shit.

He whispered, "I got your back covered. Easy."

Willie would make great cannon fodder, but he wasn't up to protecting me. He'd been a bit player before he died, and dying hadn't changed that. I realized if the shooting started and the bad guys were using silver bullets, I was worried about Willie. Worrying about your bodyguard is not good.

Jean-Claude's voice rose through the darkness, filling it with a sound that caressed my skin. A woman standing near the table shivered as if she'd been touched. Her date put his arm around her shoulders, and they huddled in the dark, surrounded by Jean-Claude's voice.

"Welcome to Danse Macabre. The night will be filled with surprises. Some wondrous." Two smaller spotlights hit the crowd. Cassandra appeared balanced on the railing on the second floor. She swept the coat back, revealing her body, stalking along the inches-wide iron bar like it was the floor, nearly dancing. Wild applause broke out. The second spot hit Damian on the first floor. He glided out of the crowd, swishing the embroidered coat around him like a small cape. If he felt silly in the outfit, it didn't show.

He moved through the crowd with the spotlight following him. He touched a shoulder here, ran his hands through waist-length hair, put his arm around one woman's waist. Each one, man or woman, didn't seem to mind. They leaned into him or whispered in his ear. He came to a woman with long brown hair parted in the middle. She was dressed rather modestly for the crowd. Navy blue business skirt and jacket. Her white blouse had one of those big bows that are supposed to look like a tie but never do. Of the women around Damian, she looked the most normal. He circled her so closely that his body brushed her. She jerked away from every touch, eyes wide with fear I could see, even from across the room.

I wanted to say, "Leave her alone," but I didn't want to yell. Jean-Claude wouldn't allow anything illegal, at least not in front of this many witnesses. Bespelling a group of people wasn't illegal. Mass hypnosis wasn't permanent. But one on one, it was permanent. Which meant that Damian could stand under the woman's window and call her out some dark night, no time limitation.

Willie was leaning forward in his chair, his dark eyes on the woman and Damian. He didn't seem to be looking for assassins right that second.

I watched the woman's face go blank of all expression, until she was like one asleep. Her empty eyes stared at Damian. He took her hand and leaned against the railing. He rolled both legs over, ending on his feet, still holding her hand. She took two hesitant steps to the railing edge. He put his hands on her waist, under her jacket, and lifted her high in the air, effortlessly, setting her down on the dance floor in her sensible black pumps.

The spotlights on Jean-Claude and Cassandra died until the only light was that on Damian and the woman. He led her to the center of the dance floor. She walked, looking only at him as if the rest of the world no longer existed.

Dammit. What Damian was doing was illegal. Most of the crowd wouldn't pick it up. Vampires were allowed to use their powers for entertainment purposes so even the media, if they were inside, would be okay with it. But I knew the difference; I knew the law. Jean-Claude had to know I'd recognize what was happening for what it was. Was she an actress? A plant for the show?

I leaned into Willie, close enough to brush the shoulder of his suit. "Is she an actress?"

He turned startled eyes to me, and I could see that the pupils had been swallowed by the brown of his eyes. Down a long dark tunnel there was a hint of fire.

I swallowed hard and eased back from him, glad of the gun in my lap. "It's real, isn't it?"

Willie licked his lips nervously. "If I say it is, you're going to do something to mess up the show. Jean-Claude will get mad at me. I don't want him mad at me, Anita."

I shook my head but didn't argue with him. I'd seen what Jean-Claude did to vamps that angered him. Torture was putting it mildly. I had to find out what was going on but without disrupting things and drawing more attention to myself than I wanted tonight.

Damian stood the woman in the center of the light. He focused her face on something we could not see. She stood there, empty and waiting for his commands. He stood behind her, folding his arms around her waist, rubbing his cheek against her hair. He undid the bow at her throat, and the first three buttons of her blouse. He rubbed his lips along her exposed neck, and I couldn't take any more. If she was an actress, fine; but if she was an unwilling victim, this had to stop.

"Willie?"

He turned to me slowly, reluctantly. His hunger made him want to watch. His fear of what I was about to ask made him slower.

"What's up?"

"Go tell Jean-Claude that the show is over."

Willie shook his head. "If I leave your side and you get wasted, Jean-Claude will kill me. Slow and painful. I'm not leaving your side until I'm supposed to."

I sighed. Fine. I leaned over the railing and motioned one of the vampire waiters over to me. He glanced off in the dark as if he could see Jean-Claude, even though I couldn't, then he walked over to me.

"What is it?" he whispered. He leaned in close enough that I could smell the mints on his breath. Nearly every vampire I knew used breath mints.

I still had the Seecamp naked in my hand. I figured I could afford to get up close and personal with the new dead, so I leaned in and whispered back, "Is she an actress?"

He glanced back at the little tableau. "Just a volunteer from the audience."

"She wasn't a volunteer," I said. There had been a half dozen people that would have volunteered, but the vampire had chosen the one who was afraid. That extra little bit of sadism—they just couldn't resist it.

"Tell Jean-Claude that if he doesn't stop this, I will."

He blinked at me.

"Just do it," I said.

He walked around the edge of the dance floor, vanishing into the darkness. I could sort of follow him, more an impression of movement than anything else. I couldn't see Jean-Claude at all.

Damian passed his hand above the woman's face, and when his hand came away, she blinked, awake at last. Her hands flew to her blouse, eyes frantic. "What's happening?" Her voice carried, thin with fear.

Damian tried to take her in his arms, but she drew away, and all he caught was a wrist. She strained against him, and he held her easily. "Let me go, let me go, please!" She reached out to someone in the crowd. "Help me!"

The crowd had gone very quiet, quiet enough that I could hear the voice of her supposed friend, "Enjoy it. It's just part of the show."

Damian jerked her around to face him, hard enough that there would be bruises. As soon as her eyes met his, her face went blank. She sagged to her knees, still held by one wrist.

He raised her to her feet, gently now. He clasped her against him and drew her hair to one side, exposing a long line of neck. He turned in a slow circle as if they were dancing, showing her bare flesh to all.

Willie leaned forward, tongue dancing over his lower lip as if he could taste her skin already. Willie was my friend, but it was good to remember that he was also a monster.

The vampire waiter was coming back. I could see him moving towards me.

Damian curled his lips, exposing fangs. He thrust his neck back giving everyone a view. I saw his neck muscles tense and we were out of time.

Willie looked up as if realizing the shit was hitting a different fan, but there was no time.

I shouted, "Don't do it, Damian." I pointed the gun at his back, about where the heart would be. When a vamp gets around five hundred, one shot to the chest, silver bullets or not, doesn't always guarantee a kill. But we would by God find out if he bit her.

Willie raised his hand toward me.

"Don't, Willie." I meant it. Just because nobody else was allowed to kill him, didn't mean I couldn't.

Willie sank back into his chair.

Damian relaxed enough to turn his head and look at me. He turned so that the girl was in front of him like a shield. Her hair was still back on one side, her neck still exposed. He stared at me, running one finger down her naked flesh. Daring me.

A dim spotlight shone on me, and the illumination built as I walked very carefully to the two steps that led down to the dance floor. Vaulting the railing might have looked better, but it made it damn hard to hold a target. I could probably have made the head shot from the railing, but with an unfamiliar gun, it was too risky. I didn't want to accidentally shoot the woman in the head. Killing the hostage is always frowned upon.

The vampire waiters and waitresses didn't know what to do. If I'd been some schmuck off the street, they might have tried to jump me, but I was their master's beloved, which made things a little sticky. I kept a sort of peripheral eye on them. "You guys back up and give me some room—right now."

They all glanced at each other.

"You don't want to crowd me, boys and girls, so move it!" They moved.

When I was close enough to feel confident that I could make the shot, I stopped. "Let her go, Damian."

"She will not be harmed, Anita. Just a little fun."

"She's unwilling. That's against the law, even for entertainment purposes, so let her go, or I'll blow your fucking head off."

"Would you really shoot me in front of all these witnesses?"

"You bet," I said. "Besides, you're over five hundred years old. I don't think one shot to the head will kill you, not permanently at least. But it'll hurt like hell and may leave scars. You wouldn't want to spoil that beautiful face, now would you?" I was getting tired of holding one arm out. It wasn't that the gun was heavy, but it was hard to hold a one-handed pose for long without starting to waver. I didn't want to waver.

He stared at me for a space of heartbeats. He very carefully, very slowly licked the side of the woman's neck, strange green eyes staring at me the whole time. It was a dare. If he thought I was bluffing, he'd picked the wrong girl.

I let my breath out until my body was quiet, and I could hear my pulse in my ears. I sighted down my arm, down the gun, and . . . he was gone. He'd moved so suddenly it startled me. I moved my finger off the trigger and pointed the gun skyward, waiting for my heart to stop pounding.

He was standing just at the edge of the light, leaving the woman empty-faced, waiting. Damian stared at me.

"Are you going to interrupt our entertainment every night?" he asked.

"I don't like it," I said, "but pick a volunteer, and I have no quarrel with you."

"A volunteer," he said, turning in a circle to view the audience. They all stared at him. He licked his lips, and hands went up.

I shook my head and put the gun up. I took the woman's hand. "Release her, Damian," I said.

He glanced back at her and did it. Her eyes flew open wide, searching frantically like someone awakened from a nightmare to find it real. I patted her hand.

"It's all right. You're safe now."

"What's happening? What's happening?" She caught sight of Damian and started sobbing hysterically.

Jean-Claude appeared on the edge of the light. "You have nothing to fear from us, fair lady." He glided towards us.

She started screaming.

"He won't hurt you," I said. "I promise. What's your name?"

She kept screaming. She was taller than me, but I touched her face, putting a hand on either side, forcing her to look at me. "What's your name?"

"Karen," she whispered, "my name's Karen."

"We're going to walk off this dance floor, Karen, and no one will hurt you. You have my word."

She nodded over and over, breath coming so fast I was afraid she was going to pass out.

Cassandra walked into the light, but stayed back. "Can I help?"

Jean-Claude had not moved since Karen started screaming. He just looked at me, and I still couldn't read his expression.

"Yeah," I said, "I could use some help."

Karen shied away from her. "She's not a vampire," I said.

She let Cassandra take her other arm, and we led her off the dance floor away from the light. Jean-Claude stepped onto center stage, and his voice followed us into the darkness. "Did you enjoy our little melodrama?" There was a puzzled silence. His voice was like fur wrapping the crowd in the dark, breathing in their fear, giving them back desire. "We do not tease here at Danse Macabre. Who would like to experience the reality of Damian's kiss?" Someone would take him up on it. Someone always did. If anyone could salvage the show after the woman's hysterics, Jean-Claude could.

Liv came to help, I think. Karen took one look at the muscle-bound vamp and fainted dead away. She was not a small woman, and it surprised both Cassandra and myself. She sagged to the floor. Liv started to come closer, but I waved her off.

A woman from the crowd came towards us, hesitantly. "Can I help?" she asked. She was about the same size as Cassandra and me, small, with long reddish hair that swung to her waist, straight and fine. She was dressed in a pair of dark brown dress slacks, the kind that run large and have cuffs and are usually linen. For a shirt she wore only a vest with a silk camisole under it.

I glanced at Cassandra. She shrugged. "Thanks, if you could take her feet." Cassandra could have flung the woman across her shoulders in a fireman's carry, but most lycanthropes didn't like to show off their strength. I could have carried her, too, even if she was so bloody tall. I could still have carried her for a short distance, but not fast, and not too far.

The woman shoved her clutch purse under one arm and took the unconscious woman's feet. We got moving a little awkwardly, but we managed to get a rhythm and Cassandra took us to the women's rest room. Or I should say, lounge. The front part had a couch and a lighted vanity. It was white and black, with a mural on the wall that was from a woodcut that I knew, entitled "Demon-Lover." The demon in this version looked suspiciously like Jean-Claude, and I doubted it was accidental.

We laid Karen on the black couch. The woman who was helping dampened some paper towels without being asked and brought them back. I laid them against Karen's forehead and neck. "Thanks."

"Is she going to be all right?" the woman asked.

I didn't answer, because that all depended on Damian. "What's your name?"

The woman smiled almost shyly. "Anabelle, Anabelle Smith."

I smiled up at her. "Anita Blake. This is Cassandra." I realized I didn't know her last name. Jean-Claude always called his wolves by only their first names, like a pet. "I'm sorry. I don't know your last name."

"Cassandra is fine." She shook Anabelle's hand. They smiled at each other.

"Should we report what happened to the police?" Anabelle asked. "I mean that vampire was going to force himself on her. That's illegal, right?"

Karen stirred on the couch, moaning.

"Yeah, it's illegal," I said.

Anabelle raised an interesting point. I could report it to the cops. If a vampire acquired three complaints against him or her, you could get a death warrant issued, if you got the right judge. I would talk to Jean-Claude and Damian first, but if they didn't give me the answers I wanted, maybe I should go to the cops. I shook my head.

"What are you thinking?" she asked.

"Nothing worth sharing," I said.

The bathroom door opened. Raina walked in wearing a cream-colored dress as short as my own. The dark hose and stiletto high heels made her legs go on forever. She wore a fur jacket in a dusty red, probably fox. She was the only shape-shifter I'd met who wore real fur that wasn't her own.

She'd pulled her auburn hair on top of her head in a soft bun with loose strands of hair curled artfully around her face and neck.

Karen chose that minute to regain consciousness. I wasn't sure she was going to like her wake-up call. I knew I didn't.

I stood. Cassandra moved in front of me and a little to one side, not blocking me, but closer to the danger than I was. I wasn't used to anyone guarding me. It felt odd. I could take care of myself. That was the point, wasn't it?

"What's happening?" Anabelle asked.

Karen was looking around, eyes going wide again. "Where am I?"

"Anabelle, can you sit with Karen, please?" I smiled when I asked, but I didn't take my eyes from Raina. The door had closed behind her, and there wasn't enough room to maneuver, not really. If Cassandra could hold her for a even a few seconds, I could get the gun out, but somehow I didn't think Raina had come to fight. I think she'd have worn different shoes.

Anabelle sat on the couch and literally held Karen's hand. But she was watching the rest of us. Hell, it might be a better show than what was outside.

"What do you want, Raina?" I asked.

She gave a wide smile with her lipsticked mouth, baring small, even white teeth. "It's the ladies' room, isn't it? I came to powder my nose. And to see how our frightened guest is doing." She took two steps into the room, and Cassandra moved in front of her, blocking her way.

Raina stared down at her. "You forget yourself, wolf." Her voice held a low edge of growl.

"I forget nothing," Cassandra said.

"Then stand aside," she said.

"What did you mean by *our guest?*" I asked.

She smiled at me. "I am Jean-Claude's partner in this little enterprise. Didn't he tell you?" From the look on her face, she knew the answer and was enjoying it.

"I guess it slipped his mind," I said. "Why aren't you part of the show then?"

"I'm a silent partner," she said. She pushed past Cassandra, body brushing the smaller woman. She knelt by the couch. "How are you feeling, my dear?"

Karen stammered, "I just want to go home."

"Of course you do." She glanced up and smiled. "If one of you would help me get her to her feet, there's a cab waiting to take her anywhere she wants to go at the club's expense. Or did you want to ride home with your friends?"

Karen shook her head. "They aren't my friends."

"So wise of you to realize that," Raina said. "So many people put their trust in the wrong people.'' She stared at me while she said the last. ''And they get hurt, or worse.''

Anabelle had moved away from Raina. She was staring at all of us, clutching her purse. I don't think she understood everything we were saying, but she obviously was not having a good time. One good deed and she was already being punished.

''Can you stand? Why don't you help me?'' Raina asked Anabelle.

''No, let Cassandra help you,'' I said.

''Afraid I might eat your newfound friend?''

I smiled. ''You'll eat anything that can't get away. We all know that.''

Her face tightened, anger flashing through her amber brown eyes. ''In the end, Anita, we will see who eats what.'' She helped the woman to stand.

Cassandra whispered, ''Jean-Claude told me to guard you.''

''Make sure she gets into a cab that really is going to take her home. Then you can follow me around for the rest of the evening, okay?''

Cassandra nodded. ''Jean-Claude won't like it.''

''I'm not too happy with him right now, either,'' I said.

''A little help here,'' Raina said.

Cassandra sighed, but she took Karen's other arm, and they helped her through the door. When the door closed behind them, Anabelle let out a long sigh. ''What is going on?''

I turned to the lighted mirror, leaning my hands on the vanity top. I shook my head. ''It's too long a story, and the less you know, the safer you'll be.''

''I have to confess I have an ulterior motive.'' I watched her through the mirror, and she looked embarrassed. ''I didn't just help out of the goodness of my heart. I'm a reporter, freelance. A quote from the Executioner would really put me on the map. I mean I could name my price, especially if you explained what just happened here.''

I bowed my head. ''A reporter. Not exactly what I needed tonight.''

Anabelle came up behind me. ''It was real on the dance floor, wasn't it? That vampire—Damian, right? He was really going to do her, right there, as part of the show.''

I watched her face in the mirror. She was vibrating with eagerness. She wanted to touch me. You could see her hands fluttering, nervous. It was a big story if I corroborated it. It would serve Jean-Claude right if I did.

Something went through Anabelle's eyes. Some of the brightness leaked away.

Several things happened almost simultaneously. Anabelle jerked my purse, the strap broke, she took a step back, and drew a gun from an inner-pants holster under her vest. The door opened, and three laughing women entered. The women screamed.

Anabelle looked at the door for just a heartbeat. I drew a knife and turned. I didn't try and walk those two steps to her. I dropped to one knee and lunged my body like a line with the knife as the point. The knife entered her upper stomach. The gun moved towards me. I used my left hand to sweep the arm away. The shot went wild, cracking the mirror. I shoved the knife upward, under her sternum, shoved it until the hilt met flesh and bone, and jerked the blade up and sideways.

Her hand convulsed on the gun and another shot hit the carpeted floor. The silencer made each shot seem muffled, almost anticlimactic.

She sank to her knees, eyes wide, mouth opening and closing. I ran my hand down her arm and took the gun from her. She blinked at me, eyes unbelieving, then she fell abruptly as if her strings had been cut. She twitched twice and died.

Edward was at the door, gun out, pointed. He stared from me to the fresh corpse. He took in the knife still protruding from her chest, the gun with silencer in my hand. He relaxed, pointing the gun at the floor. ''Some bodyguard I turned out to be, letting you get dusted in the ladies' room.''

I stared up at him. I felt numb, distant with shock. ''She almost got me,'' I said.

''But she didn't,'' he said.

I heard men's voices shouting, ''Police! Everybody stay where they are. We'll check it out.''

''Shit,'' I said softly and with feeling. I laid Anabelle's gun by her body and sat back on the carpet. I wasn't sure I could stand right then.

Edward holstered his gun and moved back from the door to join the crowd that was pushing forward to see the show. Just another part of the anonymous throng. Yeah, right.

I sat there beside the corpse and tried to think of something to tell the cops. I wasn't sure the truth was an option I could afford right now. I began to wonder if I was going to see the inside of a jail tonight. Watching the blood soak the front of Anabelle's vest, it seemed likely.

17

I was sitting in a straight-backed chair in Jean-Claude's office at Danse Macabre. My hands were cuffed behind me. They hadn't let me wash the blood off my right hand, and it had dried to a nice tacky substance. I was used to having dried blood on me, but it was still uncomfortable. The uniformed officers had taken the other knife and found the Seecamp in my purse. They had not found the big knife in the spine sheath. It had been a sloppy search to have missed a knife longer than my forearm, but the uniform that did it had at first assumed that I was another victim. It had shaken him to find out that the pretty little woman was a murderer. Oh, excuse me, alleged murderer.

The office had white walls, black carpet, a desk that looked like carved ebony. There was a red lacquer screen with a black castle done high on top of a black mountain. There was a framed kimono on the far wall, scarlet with black and royal blue designs. Two smaller frames held fans: one white and black with what looked like a tea ceremony painted on it, the other blue and white with a flock of cranes. I liked the cranes best, and I'd had plenty of time to make a choice.

One of the uniforms had remained in the room with me the entire time. They'd drunk coffee and not offered me any. The younger uniform would have uncuffed me, but his partner had pretty much threatened to beat the shit out of him if he did it. The partner was grey-haired with eyes as cold and empty as Edward's. His name was Rizzo. Looking at him, I was glad I'd put the gun on the floor before he came into the room.

Why, you may ask, wasn't I at the police station being questioned? Answer: The media had bayed us. Four uniforms had been enough to control traffic and keep the media from mobbing anyone—until they smelled a breaking story. Suddenly, there were cameras and microphones everywhere, like mushrooms after a rain. The uniforms had called for backup and barricaded the murder scene and the office. Everything else had fallen to the cameras and microphones.

There was a homicide detective standing over me—looming, actually. Detective Greeley was just under six feet tall, so broad-shouldered he looked like a big square. Most black people aren't truly black, but Greeley was close. His face was so dark it had purple highlights. His close-cropped greying hair looked like wool. But black, white, or brown, his dark eyes were neutral, secret, cop eyes. His gaze said he'd seen it all and hadn't been impressed by any of it. He certainly wasn't impressed by me. If anything, he looked bored, but I knew better. I'd seen Dolph get the same look right before he pounced on someone and tore their alibi apart.

Since I didn't have an alibi, I wasn't worried about that. I'd told my story before they read me my rights. After Greeley mirandized me, all I'd said was that I wanted a lawyer. I was beginning to sound like a broken record, even to me.

The detective pulled a chair around so he was sitting facing me. He even hunkered down trying not to be so intimidating. ''Once we get a lawyer in here,'' Greeley said, ''we can't help you anymore, Anita.''

He didn't know me well enough to call me by my first name, but I let it go. He was pretending to be my friend. I knew better. Cops are never your friends if they suspect you of murder. Conflict of interest.

''It sounds like a clear-cut case of self-defense. Tell me what happened, and I'll bet we can do a deal.''

''I want my lawyer,'' I said.

''Once we involve a lawyer, the deal goes out the window,'' he said.

''You don't have the authority to make a deal,'' I said. ''I want my lawyer.''

The skin around his eyes tightened; otherwise he looked the same, unmoved. But I was pissing him off. Couldn't blame him.

The door to the office opened. Greeley looked up, ready to be angry at the interruption. Dolph walked inside, flashing his badge. His eyes gave the briefest of flicks to me, then settled solidly on Greeley.

Greeley stood up. ''Excuse me, Anita. I'll be right back.'' He even managed a friendly smile. He was putting so much effort into the act, it was almost a shame I wasn't buying it. Besides, if he was really being friendly, he'd have taken the cuffs off.

Greeley tried to get Dolph to step outside, but Dolph shook his head. ''The office is secure. The rest of the club isn't.''

''What's that supposed to mean?'' Greeley said.

''It means your murder scene, complete with victim, is being flashed on national television. You ordered that no one was to talk to the press, so they've been speculating. Vampires run amok is the choice rumor.''

''You want me to tell the media that a woman attached to a police squad is being charged with murder?''

''You have three witnesses that all say Ms. Smith pulled her gun first. That it was self-defense.''

''That's something for the assistant district attorney to decide,'' Greeley said.

Funny how when he was talking to me he could make a deal. Now that he was talking to another cop, suddenly the ADA was the only one who could make a deal.

''Call them,'' Dolph said.

''Just like that,'' Greeley said. ''You want to cut her loose?''

''She'll make a statement after we get her and her lawyer down to the station.''

Greeley made a rude sound in his throat. ''Yeah, she's real hot for her lawyer.''

''Go talk to the press, Greeley.''

''And tell them what?''

''That vampires aren't involved. That it was just bad timing that the murder happened at Danse Macabre.''

Greeley glanced back at me. ''I want her here when I get back, Storr. No disappearing act.''

''We'll both be here.''

Greeley glared at me, all his anger and frustration filling his eyes for a second. The friendly mask was gone. ''Make sure you are. The brass may want you in on this, but this is a homicide case, *my* case.'' He shoved a finger at Dolph, not quite touching him. ''Don't fuck with it.''

Greeley pushed past him and shut the door firmly. Silence thick enough to walk on filled the room.

Dolph pulled a chair up in front of the desk, next to me, and sat facing me. He clasped his big hands together and stared. I stared back.

''The three women say Ms. Smith pulled her gun first. She ripped your purse off, so she knew where your gun was,'' he said.

''I flashed it a little too much tonight. My fault.''

''I heard about you joining the show out there. What happened?''

''I had to police the show a little. The woman didn't want to play. It's illegal to use preternatural powers to coerce anyone into doing something they don't want to do.''

''You aren't a policeman, Anita.''

It was the first time he'd ever reminded me of that. Usually, Dolph treated me like one of his people. He'd even encouraged me to simply say I was with his squad so people would assume I was a detective.

''You kicking me off the squad, Dolph?'' My stomach was tight as I asked. I valued working with the police. I valued Dolph and Zerbrowski and the rest of the guys. It would hurt more than I wanted to admit to lose all that.

''Two bodies in two days, Anita, both of them normal humans. That's a lot of explaining at headquarters.''

''If they'd been vamps or some other creepie-crawlie, everyone would look the other way, is that it?''

''Picking a fight with me isn't your best bet right now, Anita.''

We stared at each other for a second or two. I looked away first, and nodded. ''Why are you here, Dolph?''

''I handle the media a lot.''

''But you're letting Greeley talk to the press.''

''You've got to tell me what's going on, Anita.'' His voice was quiet, but I knew by the tightness around his eyes, the way he held his shoulders, that he was angry. I guess I couldn't blame him.

''What do you want to hear, Dolph?'' I asked.

''The truth would be nice,'' he said.

''I think I need a lawyer first.'' I wasn't going to spill my guts just because Dolph was my friend. He was still a cop, and I had killed someone.

Dolph's eyes narrowed. He turned to the uniform still leaning against the wall. "Rizzo, go get some coffee, black, for me. What do you want in yours?"

Coffee was coming. Things were looking up. "Two sugars, one cream."

"Get some for yourself, Rizzo, and take your time."

Officer Rizzo pushed away from the wall where he'd been leaning. "You sure about this, Sergeant Storr?"

Dolph looked at him, just looked at him.

Rizzo held his hands out in a sort of push away gesture. "I don't want Greeley riding my ass about leaving you two alone."

"Get the coffee, Officer Rizzo. I'll take any heat that comes down."

Rizzo left, shaking his head, probably at the stupidity of plainclothes detectives. When we were alone, Dolph said, "Turn around."

I stood up and offered him my hands. He uncuffed me, but didn't pat me down again. He probably assumed Rizzo had done it. I didn't tell him about the knife they missed, which would piss him off if he found it later, but hey, I couldn't let the cops confiscate all my weapons. Besides, I didn't want to be unarmed tonight.

I sat back down, resisting the urge to rub my wrists. I was heap-big-vampire-slayer. Nothing could hurt me. Yeah, right.

"Talk to me, Anita."

"Off the record?" I asked.

He stared at me, eyes flat and unreadable, good cop eyes. "I should say no."

"But," I said.

"Off the record, tell me."

I told him. I changed only one thing: that an anonymous call had alerted me to the contract on me. Other than that, it was the absolute truth. I thought Dolph would be happy, but he wasn't.

"And you don't know why someone would put a contract out on you?"

"For that kind of money, with a time limit on it, no."

He stared at me, as if trying to decide how much truth I was telling him. "Why didn't you tell us about the anonymous phone call earlier?" He put a lot of stress on the word *anonymous*.

I shrugged. "Habit, I guess."

"No, you wanted to hotdog it. Instead of hiding out, you came here and played bait. If the hitter had used a bomb, you could have gotten a lot of people hurt."

"But she didn't use a bomb, did she."

He took a deep breath and let it out slowly. If I hadn't known better, I'd have said he was counting to ten.

"You got lucky," he said.

"I know."

Dolph stared at me. "She nearly did you."

"If those women hadn't come in when they did, I wouldn't be talking to you now."

"You don't seem worried."

"She's dead. I'm not. What's to worry about?"

"For that kind of money, Anita, there'll be someone else tomorrow."

"It's after midnight, and I'm still alive. Maybe the contract will be canceled."

"Why the time limit?"

I shook my head. "If I knew that, I might know who put the hit out on me."

"And if you find out who put the money up, what will you do?" he asked.

I stared at him. Off the record or not, Dolph was still the ultimate cop. He took his job very seriously. "I'll turn the name over to you."

"I wish I believed that, Anita, I really do."

I gave him my best wide-eyed, innocent look. "What do you mean?"

"Can the little girl routine, Anita. I know you too well."

"Fine, but you and I both know that as long as the money is out there, hitters will keep coming. I'm good, Dolph, but no one's that good. Eventually, I'll lose. Unless the money goes away. No contract, no more hitters."

We stared at each other. "We can put you in protective custody," Dolph said.

"For how long? Forever?" I shook my head. "Besides, the next hitter might use a bomb. You want to risk your people? I don't."

"So you'll hunt the money man down and kill him."

"I didn't say that, Dolph."

"But that's what you're planning," he said.

"Don't keep asking the question, Dolph. The answer won't change."

He stood, hands gripping the back of the chair. "Don't cross the line with me, Anita. We're friends, but I'm a cop first."

"I value our friendship, Dolph, but I value my life and yours more."

"You think I can't handle myself?"

"I think you're a cop, and that means you have to play by the rules. Dealing with professional hitters, that can get you killed."

There was a knock on the door. "Enter," Dolph said.

Rizzo came in with a round tray and three slender black china mugs. There were little red coffee stirrers in each one. Rizzo glanced from Dolph to me. He stared at my uncuffed hands but didn't say anything. He sat the tray on the desk far enough from me that I couldn't have grabbed him. Officer Rizzo looked like a twenty-year man, and he was still treating me like a very dangerous person. I doubted that he'd have turned his back on Anabelle. If she hadn't grabbed my purse, she could have shot me in the back. Oh, I'd have seen it in the mirror, but I'd have never gotten my gun out in time. I'd never have let a man, no matter how friendly or how helpful, come up behind me like that. I'd made the same mistake with Anabelle that people made with me. I'd seen a small, pretty woman and underestimated her. I was a female chauvinist piglet. It had nearly been a fatal flaw.

Dolph handed me the mug that held the lightest-colored coffee. It was too much to hope that the cream would be real, but either way it looked wonderful. I'd never met coffee that wasn't wonderful. It was just a matter of how wonderful it was. I took a hesitant sip of the steaming liquid and made appreciative 'mmm' sounds. It was real coffee and real cream.

"Glad you like it," Rizzo said.

I looked up at him. "Thank you, Officer."

He grunted and moved away from us to lean against the other wall.

"I talked to Ted Forrester, your pet bounty hunter. The gun in your purse is registered to him." Dolph sat back down, blowing on his coffee.

Ted Forrester was one of Edward's aliases. It had stood up to police scrutiny once before when we ended up with bodies on the ground. He was, as far as the police knew, a bounty hunter specializing in preternatural creatures. Most bounty hunters stayed in the Western states where there were still substantial bounties on shapeshifters. Not all of them were particularly careful that the shapeshifter they killed was really a danger to anyone. The only criteria some states had was that after death, the body was medically certified as a lycanthrope. A blood test was sufficient in most cases. Wyoming was thinking of changing its laws because of three wrongful death suits that had made it all the way to their state supreme court.

"I needed a gun small enough to fit in the purse but with stopping power," I said.

"I don't like bounty hunters, Anita. They abuse the law."

I sipped coffee and stayed quiet. If he knew just how much Edward abused the law, he'd have locked him up for a very long time.

"If he's a good enough friend to bail your ass out of this kind of trouble, why haven't you mentioned him before? I didn't know he existed until that last trouble you had with those shapeshifter poachers."

"Poachers," I said and shook my head.

"What's wrong?" Dolph asked.

"Shapeshifters get killed, and its poaching. Normal people get killed, and it's murder."

"You sympathizing with the monsters now, Anita?" he asked. His voice was even quieter, so still you might have mistaken it for calm, but it wasn't. He was pissed.

"You're mad about something other than the body count," I said.

"You're involved with the Master of the City. Is that how you keep getting all that inside info on the monsters?"

I took a deep breath and let it out. "Sometimes."

"You should have told me, Anita."

"Since when is my personal life police business?"

He just looked at me.

I looked down into my coffee mug, staring at my hands. I finally looked back up. It was hard meeting his eyes, harder than I wanted it to be. "What do you want me to say, Dolph? That I find it embarrassing that one of the monsters is my boyfriend? I do."

"Then drop him."

"If it were that easy, trust me, I'd do it."

"How can I trust you to do your job, Anita? You're sleeping with the enemy."

"Why does everyone assume I'm sleeping with him? Doesn't anybody but me date people and not have sex?"

"I apologize for the assumption, but you got to admit a lot of people are going to assume the same thing."

"I know."

The door opened, and Greeley came back inside. His eyes took in the handcuffs being gone, the coffee. "You have a nice chat?"

"How'd your statement to the press go?" Dolph asked.

He shrugged. "I told them Ms. Blake was being questioned in connection with a death on the premises. Told 'em that no vamps were involved. Not sure they believed me. They kept wanting to speak to the Executioner. Though most of them were calling her the Master's girlfriend."

That made me flinch. Even with a career of my own, I was going to end up being Mrs. Jean-Claude in the press. He was more photogenic than I was.

Dolph stood. "I want to take Anita out of here."

Greeley stared at him. "I don't think so."

Dolph set his coffee on the desk and went to stand next to the other detective. He lowered his voice, and there was a lot of harsh whispering. Greeley shook his head. "No."

More whispering. Greeley glared at me. "All right, but she comes down to the station before the night is over or it's your ass, Sergeant."

"She'll be there," Dolph said.

Rizzo was staring at all of us. "You're taking her out of here, but not to the station house?" It sounded accusatory even to me.

"That's my decision, Rizzo," Greeley said. "You got that?" His voice growled the words. Somehow Dolph had pulled rank, and Greeley didn't like it. If Rizzo wanted to make himself a convenient target for that anger, fine.

Rizzo faded back against the wall, but he wasn't happy about it. "I got that."

"Get her out of here," Greeley said. "Try the back. But I don't know how you'll get past the cameras."

"We'll walk through," Dolph said. "Let's go, Anita."

I set my mug on the desk. "What's up, Dolph?"

"I got a body for you to look at."

"A murder suspect helping with another case. Won't the brass get mad?"

"I cleared it," Dolph said.

I looked at him, eyes wide. "How?" I asked.

"You don't want to know," he said.

I looked at him. He stared back. I finally looked away first. Most of the time, when people said I didn't want to know, it meant just the opposite. It meant I probably needed to know. But from a handful of people, I'd take their word for it. Dolph was one of those people. "Okay," I said. "Let's go."

Dolph let me wash the dried blood off my hands, and we went.

18

I'm not a big one for idle chatter, but Dolph makes me seem loquacious. We drove down 270 in silence, the hiss of the wheels on the road and the thrum of the engine the only sounds. Either he'd turned off his radio or nobody was committing crimes in Saint Louis tonight. I was betting the radio was off. One of the good things about being a detective on a task force is you don't have to listen to the radio all the time, because most of the calls aren't your problem. If Dolph was needed somewhere, they could always beep him.

I tried to hold out. I tried to make Dolph talk first, but after nearly fifteen minutes, I broke. ''Where are we going?''

''Creve Coeur.''

My eyebrows raised. ''That's a little upscale for a monster kill.''

''Yeah,'' he said.

I waited for more; there wasn't any more. ''Well, thanks for enlightening me, Dolph.''

He glanced at me, then back to the road. ''We'll be there in a few minutes, Anita.''

''Patience has never been my strong suit, Dolph.''

His lips twitched, then he smiled. Finally, he laughed, a short, abrupt sound. ''I guess not.''

''Glad I could lighten the mood,'' I said.

''You're always good for a laugh when you're not killing people, Anita.''

I didn't know what to say to that. Too close to the truth, maybe. Silence settled over the car, and I left it alone. It was an easy, friendly quiet this time, tinged with laughter. Dolph wasn't mad at me anymore. I could stand a little silence.

Creve Coeur was an older neighborhood , but it didn't look it. The age showed in the large houses set in long, sloping yards. Some of the houses had circular drives and servants' quarters. The few housing developments that had crept in here and there didn't always have big yards, but the houses had variety, pools, rock gardens. No cookie cutter houses, nothing déclassé.

Olive is one of my favorite streets. I like the mix of gas stations, Dunkin'

Donuts, custom order jewelry stores, Mercedes-Benz dealerships, and Blockbuster Music and Video. Creve Coeur isn't like most ritzy areas, at war with the peons. This part of the city has embraced both its money and its commerce, as comfortable buying fine antiques as taking the kiddies through the drive-up line at Mickey-D's.

Dolph turned on a road sandwiched between two gas stations. It sloped sharply, making me want to use the brake. Dolph didn't share this desire, and the car coasted down the hill at a nice clip. Well, he was the police. No speeding ticket, I guess. We sped past housing developments that branched off the road like true suburbia. The houses were still more distinct, but the yards had shrunk, and you knew that most of what you were driving past had never had servants' quarters. The road climbed just a touch, then evened out. Dolph hit his turn signal while we were still in the shallow valley. A tasteful sign said Countryside Hills.

Police cars clogged the narrow streets of the subdivision, lights strobing the darkness. There was a huddle of people being held back by uniformed police, people clutching light coats over their jammies or standing with robes tied tight. The crowd was small. As we got out of the car, I saw a drape twitch in a house across the street. Why come outside when you can peek from the comfort of your own home?

Dolph led me through the uniforms and the twist of yellow Do-Not-Cross tape. The house that was the center of attention was one story with a brick wall as tall as the walls of the house forming an enclosed courtyard. There was even a wrought iron gate to the curved entrance, very Mediterranean. Except for the courtyard, the house looked like a typical suburban ranch. There was a stone path and square, rock edged beds full of rosebushes. Floodlights filled the walled garden, lending every petal and leaf its own shadow. Someone had gone way overboard on the in-ground lighting.

"You don't even need a flashlight in here," I said.

Dolph glanced at me. "You've never been here then?"

I met his eyes and couldn't read them. He was giving me cop eyes. "No, I've never been here. Should I have been?"

Dolph opened the screened door without answering. He led the way in, and I followed. Dolph prides himself on not influencing his people, letting them come in cold and make their own conclusions. But even for him, he was being mysterious. I didn't like it.

The living room was narrow but long with a TV and video center at the end of it. The room was so thick with cops there was barely room to stand. Every murder scene gets more attention than it needs. Frankly, I wonder if more evidence is lost with all the traffic than is found with all the busy hands. A murder can make a cop's career, especially that jump from uniform to plainclothes. Find *the* clue or *the* evidence, shine at the critical time, and people notice. But it's more than that. Murder is the ultimate insult, the last worst thing you can do to another human being. Cops feel that, maybe more than the rest of us.

The cops parted before Dolph, eyes shifting to me. Most of the eyes were male, and after the first glance, almost all of them did the full body look. You know the look. The one that if the face and top match, they just have to see if the legs are as good as the rest. It works in reverse, too. But any man that starts at my feet and ends with my face has lost every brownie point he ever had.

Two short hallways led straight off the living room at right angles, a dining room directly off of the first room. An open door revealed carpeted stairs leading to a finished basement. Cops were traveling up and down the stairs like ants, with bits of evidence in plastic baggies.

Dolph led me down one of the hallways, and there was a second living room with a fireplace. It was smaller and more boxlike, but the far wall was entirely brick, which made it seem warmer, cozier. The kitchen showed to the left through an open doorway. The top half of the wall was a pass-through, open like a window so you could work in the kitchen and still talk to people in the living room. My father's house had a pass-through.

The next room was obviously new. The walls still had that raw paint look of fresh construction. Sliding glass doors made up the left-hand wall. A hot tub took up most of the floor space. Water still clung in beads to its slick surface. They'd finished the hot tub before they'd painted the room. Priorities.

A hallway so roughed out it still had that heavy plastic they put down for workers to walk on led away from the tub. There was another larger bathroom, not quite finished, and a closed door at the end of the hall. The door was carved, new wood, light-colored oak. It was the first closed door I'd seen inside the house. That was kind of ominous.

Except for the cops, I hadn't seen a damn thing out of place. It looked like a nice upper-middle-class house. A family kind of house. If I'd walked straight into carnage, I'd have been all right, but this long buildup had tightened my stomach, filled me with dread. What had happened in this nice house with its new hot tub and brick fireplace? What had happened that needed my kind of expertise? I didn't want to know. I wanted to leave before I saw some new horror. I'd seen enough bodies already this year to last a lifetime.

Dolph put his hand on the doorknob. I touched his arm. "It's not kids, is it?" I asked.

He glanced over his shoulder at me. Normally, he wouldn't have answered. He'd have said something cryptic like, "You'll see in a minute." Tonight, he said, "No, it's not kids."

I took a deep breath through my nose and let it out slowly through my lips. "Good." I smelled damp plaster, fresh cement, and underneath that, blood. The scent of freshly spilled blood, faint, just behind the door. What does blood smell like? Metallic, almost artificial. It isn't really much of a smell all by itself. The smell won't make you sick, it's what goes with it. We all know in some ancient part of ourselves that blood is the thing. Without it, we die. If we can steal enough of it from our enemies, we steal their lives. There's a reason that blood has been associated with almost every religion on the planet. It's primal stuff, and no matter how sanitized we make our world, part of us still recognizes that.

Dolph hesitated, hand still on the doorknob. He didn't look at me while he spoke. "Tell me what you think of the scene, then I have to take you back for a statement. You understand that."

"I understand," I said.

"If you're lying to me, Anita, about any of this, tell me tonight. Two bodies in two days takes a lot of explaining."

"I haven't lied to you, Dolph." At least not much, I added in my head.

He nodded without turning around and opened the door. He went in first and turned so he could watch my face as I entered the room.

"What's wrong, Dolph?" I asked.

"See for yourself," he said.

All I could see at first was pale grey carpet and a bureau with a large mirror against the right-hand wall. A cluster of cops blocked my view of the rest of the room. The cops stepped aside at a nod from Dolph. Dolph never took his eyes from me, my face. I'd never seen him so intent on my reaction before. It made me nervous.

There was a body on the floor. A man, spread-eagled, pinned at wrists and ankles with knives. The knives had black hilts. He lay in the middle of a large red circle. The circle had had to be large so the blood didn't leak out and spoil it. Blood had soaked into the pale carpet, spread across it like a red ruin. The man's face was turned away from me. All I could see was short blond hair. His chest was bare, so slick with blood it looked like a red shirt. The knives held him in place. They hadn't been what killed him. No, what had killed him was a gaping hole in his lower chest just below the ribs. It was like a red-lined cave big enough to plunge both hands into.

"They took his heart," I said.

Dolph looked at me. "You know that from the doorway?"

"I'm right, aren't I?"

"If you were going to take his heart out, why not go straight down?"

"If you wanted him to survive, like heart surgery, you'd have to break the ribs and go down the hard way. But they wanted him dead. If all you want is the heart, going under the ribs is easier."

I walked towards the body.

Dolph moved ahead of me, watching my face. "What?" I said.

He shook his head. "Just tell me about the body, Anita."

I stared at him. "What is your problem tonight?"

"No problem."

It was a lie. Something was up, but I didn't press it. It wouldn't have done me any good. When Dolph decides not to share information, he doesn't share, period.

There was a king-size bed with purple satin sheets and more pillows than you knew what to do with. The bed was rumpled as if it had been used for something other than sleeping. There were dark stains on the sheets, nearly black.

"Is that blood?"

"We think so," Dolph said.

I glanced at the body. "From the murder?"

"When you're finished looking at the body, we'll bag the sheets and get them down to the lab."

A subtle hint to get on with the job. I walked towards the body and tried to ignore Dolph. That was easier than it sounded. The body sort of stole the show.

The closer I got, the more details I could see, and the more I didn't want to see. Under all that blood was a nice chest, muscular but not too much of a good thing. The hair was cut very short, curly and blond. There was something naggingly familiar about that head. The black daggers had silver wire curled around them. They'd been shoved to their hilts in the flesh, bones had broken when they'd been driven in. The red circle was definitely blood. Cabalistic symbols ran round the inside of the circle, traced in blood. I recognized some of them, enough to know that we were dealing with some form of necromancy. I knew the symbols that stood for death and the symbols that watched against it.

For some reason, I didn't want to enter the circle. I walked carefully around the edge of it until I could see the face. With my back leaning against the wall I stared into the wide eyes of Robert the vampire. Monica's husband. The soon-to-be daddy.

"Shit," I said softly.

"You know him?" Dolph asked.

I nodded. "Robert. His name's Robert." The death symbols made sense if you were going to sacrifice a vampire. But why? Why like this?

I took a step forward and hit the circle. I stopped dead. It was like a million insects crawled and swarmed over my body. I couldn't breathe. I stepped back off the blood line. The sensation stopped. I could still feel it like a memory on my skin, in my head, but I was okay now. I took a deep breath, let it out slowly, and stepped forward again. It wasn't like hitting a wall. It was more like hitting a blanket, a drowning, suffocating, maggot-crawling blanket. I tried to walk forward, tried to move past the circle, and couldn't. I staggered back from it. If the wall hadn't been there, I'd have fallen.

I let myself slide down until I was sitting with my knees tucked up. My toes were inches from the circle. I did not want to touch it again.

Dolph walked through the circle like it wasn't there and knelt beside me, part of him still in the circle. "Anita, what's wrong?"

I shook my head. "I'm not sure." I stared up at him. "It's a circle of power, and I can't cross it."

He glanced back at his own body partially inside the circle. "I can."

"You're not an animator. I'm not a witch, and I don't know a lot of official magic, but some of the symbols are either death symbols or maybe symbols of protection from the dead." I stared up at him, my skin still shivering from trying to cross the line. A new horror spread through my mind. "It's a spell to both contain and keep out the dead, and I can't cross it."

He stared down at me. "What exactly does that mean, Anita?"

"It means," said a female voice, "that she didn't create the circle."

19

A woman stood just inside the door. She was tall, slender, dressed in a purple skirt suit with a white man-tailored shirt. She walked into the room with an eagerness that made me knock about ten years off her age. She looked thirty, but she wasn't. Twenty-something and full of herself. Probably around my own age, but there was a shiny newness to her that I'd lost years ago.

Dolph stood, offering me a hand up. I shook my head. "Unless you want to carry me, I can't stand yet."

"Anita, this is Detective Reynolds," he said. He didn't sound entirely happy about it.

Reynolds walked around the edge of the circle as I had, but she was coming for a better view of me. She ended up on the opposite side from Dolph. She stared down at me, smiling, eager. I stared up at her, skin still jumping from trying to force my way past the circle.

She leaned down and whispered, "You're flashing the room, dear."

"That's why the underwear matches," I said.

She looked surprised.

There was no way for me to stretch my legs out without touching the circle again, so if I wanted to quit flashing the room, I had to stand up. I held my hand up to Dolph. "Help me up, but whatever you do, don't let me fall into that thing."

Detective Reynolds took my other arm without being invited, but frankly, I needed the help. My legs felt like spaghetti. The moment she touched me, the hair on my body stood at attention. I jerked away from her and would have fallen into the circle if Dolph hadn't caught me.

"What's wrong, Anita?" Dolph asked.

I leaned into him and tried to breathe slowly and evenly. "I can't take anymore magic right this moment."

"Get her a chair from the dining room," Dolph said. He didn't speak to anyone in particular, but a uniform left the room, probably to get the chair.

Dolph picked me up while we waited. Since I couldn't stand, it was hard to protest, but I felt like a damn fool.

''What's on your back, Anita?'' Dolph asked.

I'd forgotten about the knife in the spine sheath. I was saved from having to answer by the uniform bringing one of the straight-backed chairs into the room.

Dolph eased me into the chair. ''Did Detective Reynolds try a spell on you?''

I shook my head.

''Someone explain what just happened.''

An unhealthy flush crept up Reynold's pale neck. ''I tried to read her aura, sort of.''

''Why?'' Dolph asked.

''Just curious. I've read about necromancers but never met one before.''

I looked up at her. ''If you want to do any more experiments, Detective, ask first.''

She nodded, looking younger, more unsure of herself. ''I am sorry.''

''Reynolds,'' Dolph said.

She looked at him. ''Yes, sir.''

''Go stand over there.''

She glanced at both of us and nodded. ''Yes, sir.'' She walked over to stand by the other cops. She tried to be nonchalant about it, but she kept looking over at us.

''Since when do you have a witch on the payroll?'' I asked.

''Reynolds is the first detective ever with preternatural abilities. She got her pick of assignments. She wanted to join our squad.''

I was happy to hear him call it ''our'' squad. ''She said I didn't draw the circle. Did you really think I'd done that?'' I pointed at the body.

He stared down at me. ''You didn't like Robert.''

''If I killed everyone I didn't like, Saint Louis would be littered with bodies,'' I said. ''Why else did you drag me down here? She's a witch. She probably knows more about the spell than I do.''

Dolph stared down at me. ''Explain.''

''I raise the dead, but I'm not a trained witch. Most of what I do is just,'' I shrugged, ''sort of natural ability. I studied basic magic theory in college, but for only a couple of classes, so if you want feedback on a detailed spell like this one, I can't help you.''

''If Reynolds hadn't been here, what would you have suggested we do?''

''Find a witch to undo the spell for you.''

He nodded. ''Any thoughts on who or why?'' He jabbed his thumb behind his back at the body.

''Jean-Claude made Robert a vampire. That's a strong bond. I think the spell was to prevent him from knowing what was happening.''

''Could Robert have alerted his master from this far away?''

I thought about that. I wasn't sure. ''I don't know. Maybe. Some master vampires are better at telepathy than others. I'm not sure how good Jean-Claude is with other vampires.''

''This setup took a while,'' Dolph said. ''Why kill him like this?''

''Good question,'' I said. I had a nasty idea. ''It's a weird way to do it, but this might be a challenge to Jean-Claude's control over his territory.''

"How so?" Dolph had his little notebook out now, pen poised. It was almost like old times.

"Robert belonged to him, and now somebody's killed him. Could be a message."

He glanced back at the body. "But who is the message meant for? Maybe Robert pissed someone off, and it was personal. If it was a message for your boyfriend, why not kill him at Jean-Claude's club? That's where he worked, right?"

I nodded. "Whoever did this couldn't have pulled off something so elaborate at the club, with other vampires around. No way. They needed privacy. They might have needed the spell just to keep Jean-Claude or some other vamp from riding to the rescue." I thought about it. What did I really know about Robert? Not much. I knew him as Jean-Claude's flunkie. Monica's boyfriend, now husband. A soon-to-be daddy. Everything I knew about him was through other people's perceptions of him. He'd been killed in his own bedroom, and all I could think of was that it was a message for Jean-Claude. I was thinking of him like a flunkie because Jean-Claude treated him that way. Because he wasn't a master vampire, no one would want to kill him for his own sake. Geez, I was actually thinking of Robert like a disposable commodity. We could always make more.

"You've thought of something," Dolph said.

"Not really. Maybe I've been hanging around vampires too long. I'm beginning to think like one of them."

"Explain," Dolph said.

"I assumed that Robert's death was connected to his master. My first thought was that no one would kill Robert for his own sake, because he wasn't important enough to kill. I mean, killing Robert won't make you Master of the City, so why do it?"

Dolph looked at me. "You're beginning to worry me, Anita."

"Worry, hell," I said, "I'm beginning to scare me." I tried to look at the murder scene fresh, not like a vampire. Who would go to this much trouble to kill Robert? I didn't have the faintest idea. "Except for this being a challenge to Jean-Claude's authority, I have no idea why anyone would kill Robert. I guess I don't really know that much about him. It could be one of the hate groups, Humans First or Humans Against Vampires. But they'd have to have some heavy magical know-how, and either group would stone a witch as fast as stake a vampire. They consider them both devil spawn."

"Why would the hate groups single out this vampire?"

"His wife's pregnant," I said.

"Another vampire?" Dolph asked.

I shook my head. "Human."

Dolph's eyes widened just a fraction. It was the most surprise I'd ever seen from him. Dolph, like most cops, doesn't ruffle easily.

"Pregnant? And the vampire is the father?"

"Yes," I said.

He shook his head. "Yeah, that might earn him a starring roll on the hate group hit parade. Tell me about vampire reproduction, Anita."

''First, I need to call Jean-Claude.''

''Why?''

''Warn him,'' I said. ''I agree this probably is something personal to Robert. You're right. Humans First especially would kill him in a heartbeat, but just in case, I want to warn Jean-Claude.'' I had another thought. ''Maybe that's why someone wanted me dead.''

''What do you mean?''

''If they want to harm Jean-Claude, killing me would be a good way to do it.''

''I think half a million dollars is a little steep for bumping off someone's girlfriend.'' He shook his head. ''That kind of money is personal, Anita. Someone's afraid of you, not your toothy boyfriend.''

''Two hired killers in two days, Dolph, and I still don't know why.'' I stared up at him. ''If I don't figure this thing out, I'll be dead.''

He touched my shoulder. ''We'll help you. Cops are good for some things, even if the monsters won't talk to us.''

''Thanks, Dolph.'' I patted his hand. ''Did you really believe Reynolds when she said I could have done this?''

He straightened, then met my eyes. ''For a second, yes. After that, it was a matter of listening to my detective. We hired her so she could help out on the preternatural stuff. It would be stupid to ignore her on her first case.''

Not to mention demoralizing, I thought. ''Okay, but did you really think I was capable of doing that?'' I motioned towards the body.

''I've seen you stake vamps, Anita. I've seen you decapitate them. Why not this?''

''Because Robert was alive while they carved open his chest. Until they removed his heart, he was alive. Hell, when they took his heart, I'm not sure how long he might have lived. Vampires are strange when it comes to death wounds. Sometimes they linger.''

''Is that why they didn't take his head? So he'd suffer more?''

''Maybe,'' I said. ''Jean-Claude needs to be told, in case it is a threat,'' I repeated.

''I'll have someone call.''

''You don't trust me to tell him?''

''Leave it alone, Anita.''

For once I did what he asked. Even a year ago I wouldn't have trusted anyone dating a vampire. I'd have assumed they were corrupt. Sometimes, I still assumed that. ''Fine, just call him now. Be bad if Jean-Claude got wasted while we were debating who should warn him.''

Dolph motioned one of the uniforms over. He scribbled something in his notebook, tore the page out, folded it, and handed it to the uniform. ''Take this to Detective Perry.''

The uniform left, note in hand.

Dolph glanced back at his notes. ''Now, tell me about vampire reproduction.'' He stared at what he'd written in his notebook. ''Even saying that sounds wrong.''

''Newly dead males often have leftover sperm from before death. That's the most common. Doctors recommend you wait six weeks before sex after you've become a vampire, sort of like after a vasectomy. Those babies are usually healthy. Being fertile is a lot rarer in older vamps. Frankly, until I saw Robert and his wife at a party, I didn't know vamps as old as he is could make babies."

"How old was Robert?"

"A century and some change."

"Can female vamps get pregnant?" he asked.

"Sometimes with the newly dead it happens, but the body spontaneously aborts or reabsorbs the baby. A dead body can't give life." I hesitated.

"What?" Dolph asked.

"There have been two reported cases of an older female vampire giving birth." I shook my head. "It wasn't pretty, and it certainly wasn't human."

"Did the babies survive?"

"For a while," I said. "The case that's the best documented was from the early 1900s. Back when Dr. Henry Mulligan was trying to find a cure for vampirism in the basement of Old Saint Louis City Hospital. One of his patients had given birth. Mulligan thought it was a sign that life was returning to her body. The baby had been born with a full set of pointed teeth and been more cannibal than vampire. Doctor Mulligan carried a scar on his wrist from the delivery until the day he died, which was about three years later when one of his patients crushed his face."

Dolph stared down at his notebook. "I write it all down. But frankly, this is one bit of information I hope I never have to use. They killed the baby, didn't they?"

"Yes," I said. "Before you ask, the father was not mentioned. The implication is that the father was human and may even have been Dr. Mulligan himself. Vampires can't make babies without a human partner, as far as we know."

"Nice to know humans are good for something besides blood," he said.

I shrugged. "I guess." Truthfully the thought of giving birth to a child with severe Vlad syndrome scared the hell out of me. I never planned on having sex with Jean-Claude, but if it ever came up, we were definitely taking precautions. No spontaneous sex, unless it included a condom.

Something must have shown on my face, because he asked, "Penny for your thoughts."

"Just glad I have high moral standards, I guess. Like I said, until I saw Robert and his wife, I thought a vampire over a century was sterile. And considering the length of time you'd have to keep the vamp's body temperature up"—I shook my head—"I don't see how it could be accidental. But they both claimed it was. She hasn't even gotten their amnio results back yet."

"Amnio test for what?" he asked.

"Vlad syndrome," I said.

"Is she healthy enough to stand up under this kind of news?" he asked.

I shrugged. "She looked fine, but I'm no expert. I'd say she shouldn't be told over the phone, and she probably shouldn't be alone. I just don't know."

"Are you friends with the wife?"

I shook my head. "No, and don't even ask. I am not going to hold Monica's hand while she cries over her dead husband."

"All right, all right, it's outside your job description. Maybe I'll let Reynolds do it."

I glanced at the young woman. She and Monica probably deserved each other, but . . . "Jean-Claude might know who Monica's friends are. If he doesn't, I know of one. Catherine Maison-Gillete and Monica work together."

"Monica is a lawyer?" Dolph said.

I nodded.

"Great," he said.

"How much are you telling Jean-Claude about this?" I asked.

"Why?" Dolph asked.

"Because I want to know how much I can tell him."

"You don't discuss ongoing homicide cases with the monsters," he said.

"The victim was his companion for over a century. He's going to want to talk about it. I need to know what you're telling him so I won't let something slip by accident."

"You don't have a problem withholding information from your boyfriend?"

"Not on a homicide. Whoever did this is at the very least a witch, and maybe something scarier. It's probably one of the monsters, one way or another. So we can't tell the monsters all the details."

Dolph looked at me long and steady, then nodded. "Keep back the heart and the symbols used in the spell."

"He'll have to know about the heart, Dolph, or he'll guess. Head or heart, there isn't a lot else that'll kill a century-old vamp."

"You said you'd withhold information, Anita."

"I'm telling you what will wash and what won't, Dolph. Keeping back the heart from the vamps won't work because they'll guess. The symbols, fine, but even there, Jean-Claude's going to have to have to wonder why he didn't feel Robert die."

"So what *can* we withhold from your boyfriend?"

"The exact symbols used in the spell. The knives." I thought about it for a moment. "How they got the heart out. Most people will still go through the ribs to tear out a heart. They see all the hospital shows on TV and they don't think about doing it differently."

"So if we get a suspect, we ask how'd you get the heart out?"

I nodded. "The crazies will start talking about stakes. Or be vague."

"Okay," he said. Dolph looked at me. "If anyone hated the monsters, I thought it was you. How can you date one of them?"

I met his eyes this time, not flinching. "I don't know."

He closed his notebook. "Greeley's probably wondering where I took you."

"What did you whisper to him? I would have bet money that he'd have held on to me."

"Told him you were a suspect in another murder. Said I wanted to watch your reaction."

"And he bought that?"

Dolph glanced back at the body. "Close to the truth, Anita."

He had me there. "Greeley didn't seem to like me very much," I said.

''You'd just killed a woman, Anita. Tends to give a bad first impression.''

He had a point. ''Do I need to have Catherine meet us down at the station?'' I asked.

''You're not under arrest,'' Dolph said.

''I'd still like Catherine to meet us at the station.''

''Call her.''

I stood.

Dolph touched my arm. ''Wait.'' He turned to the other cops. ''Everybody wait outside for a minute.'' There were some glances, but no one argued, they just went. They'd all worked with Dolph before, and no one present outranked him.

When we were alone behind closed doors, he said, ''Give it up.''

''What?''

''You've got some kind of freaking blade down your back. Let's see it.''

I sighed and reached under my hair to the hilt. I drew the knife out. It took a while. It was a long knife.

Dolph held out his hand. I handed it to him.

He balanced it on his open hands and gave a low whistle. ''Jesus, what were you planning to do with this?''

I just looked at him.

''Who frisked you at the club?''

''Rizzo's partner,'' I said.

''Have to have a talk with him.'' Dolph looked up at me. ''Be a bad thing to miss on someone who might use it. Is it the only weapon he missed?''

''Yep.''

He stared at me. ''Lean on the bureau, Anita.''

My eyebrows raised. ''You're going to pat me down?''

''Yeah.''

I thought about arguing but decided not to. There were no more weapons to find. I leaned on the bureau. Dolph laid the knife on the chair and searched me. If there'd been anything to find, he'd have found it. Dolph was thorough in everything he did, methodical. It was one of the things that made him a great cop.

I looked at him in the mirror without turning around. ''Satisfied?''

''Yeah.'' He handed the knife back to me, hilt first.

I must have looked as surprised as I felt. ''You're giving it back to me?''

''If you'd lied to me about it being your last weapon, I'd have kept it and everything I found.'' He took a deep breath and let it out. ''But I won't take your last weapon, not with a contract out on you.''

I took the knife and resheathed it. It was a lot harder putting it back than getting it out. I finally had to use the mirror to sort of direct me.

''I take it it's a new weapon?'' Dolph asked.

''Yeah.'' I flipped my hair out over the sheath and presto, you couldn't see it. I was really going to have practice with it more. It was too good a hiding place not to use more often.

''Any other impressions of the scene before I take you back?''

''Was there forced entry?''

''No.''

"Someone he knew then," I said.

"Maybe."

I glanced at Robert's still form. "Could we finish this discussion in another room?"

"This one bother you?"

"I knew him, Dolph. I might not have liked him, but I knew him."

Dolph nodded. "You can finish telling me all about it in the nursery."

I looked at him. I could feel myself going pale. I was not up to seeing what Monica would have done with a nursery. "You're developing a mean streak, Dolph."

"Can't seem to get past the fact you're dating the Master of the City, Anita. Just can't shake it."

"You want to punish me because I'm dating a vampire?"

He looked at me, a long searching look. I didn't look away. "I want you to not date him."

"You're not my dad."

"Does your family know?"

I did look away then. "No."

"They're Catholic, aren't they?"

"I am not going to have this discussion with you, Dolph."

"You need to have it with someone," he said.

"Maybe, but not with you."

"Look at him, Anita. Look at him, and tell me you could sleep with that."

"Drop it," I said.

"I can't."

We stared at each other. I was not going to stand here and explain my relationship with Jean-Claude to Dolph. It wasn't any of his business. "Then we have a problem."

There was a knock on the door. "Not now," Dolph said.

"Come in," I said.

The door opened. Goody. Zerbrowski walked in. Even better. I knew I was grinning like an idiot, but I couldn't seem to stop. The last time I'd seen him had been the day he got out of the hospital. He'd been nearly gutted by a shapeshifter, a wereleopard the size of a pony. His attacker had been not a lycanthrope but a shapeshifting witch. That was why Zerbrowski wasn't turning furry once a month. The witch had clawed him up horribly. I'd killed it. I'd held my hands over his stomach and pressed his intestines back into his body. I still had the scars from the same monster.

Zerbrowski's hair is normally curly and a mess, black going grey. He'd cut it short enough that it stayed in place. Made him look more serious, more grown-up, less like Zerbrowski. His suit was brown and looked like he'd slept in it. His tie was medium blue and matched nothing that he was wearing.

"Blake, long time no see."

I couldn't help myself; I walked over and hugged him. There are benefits to being a girl. Though, before Richard came into my life, I might have resisted the urge. Richard was bringing out my feminine side.

Zerbrowski hugged me awkwardly, laughing. "I always knew you wanted my body, Blake."

I pushed away from him. "You wish."

He eyed me up and down, eyes glittering with laughter. "If you dress up like that every night, I might leave Katie for you. If that skirt was any shorter, it'd be a lamp shade."

Even with the teasing, I was glad to see him. "How long have you been back on full duty?"

"Not long. I saw you on the news with your boyfriend."

"News?" I said. I'd forgotten about the media blitz Jean-Claude and I had walked through.

"He sure was pretty for a dead guy."

"Shit."

"What?" Dolph asked.

"It was national media, not just local."

"So?"

"My father doesn't know."

Zerbrowski laughed. "He does now."

"Shit."

"I guess you'll have that talk with your father after all," Dolph said.

There must have been something in Dolph's voice or my face, because the humor faded from Zerbrowski's face. "What's up, you two? You look like someone stepped on your puppy."

Dolph looked at me. I looked at him. "Philosophical differences," I said finally. Dolph didn't add anything. I hadn't really expected him to.

"Okay," Zerbrowski said. He knew Dolph well enough not to pry. Me alone, he'd have bugged the hell out of me, but not Dolph.

"One of the nearest neighbors is a serious right-wing vampire hater," he said. That got our attention.

"Explain," Dolph said.

"Delbert Spalding and his wife Dora sat on the couch, holding hands. She offered me iced tea. He objected to me saying that Robert had been murdered. Said you couldn't kill the dead." Zerbrowski dug a wrinkled notebook out of his suit pocket. He flipped some pages, tried to smooth the page down, gave up, and quoted. "Now that someone has destroyed that thing, the woman should abort that monster she's carrying. I don't believe in abortion normally, but this is abomination, pure abomination."

"Humans Against Vampires, at the very least," I said, "Maybe even Humans First."

"Maybe he just doesn't like living next door to a vampire," Dolph said.

Zerbrowski and I looked at him.

"Did you ask Mr. Spalding if he belonged to either of the hate groups?" Dolph asked.

"He had HAV's newsletters scattered on his coffee table, gave me one."

"Great, " I said, "evangelizing hatemongers."

"HAV doesn't advocate this kind of violence," Dolph said.

The way he said it made me wonder what mailing list Dolph was on. I shook my head. I wouldn't believe the worst of him just because he didn't like me dating the walking dead. A few months back, I'd have felt the same way. "Humans First does," I said.

"We'll find out if Mr. Spalding is a member of Humans First," Dolph said.

"You also need to find out if the Spaldings have any magical talent," I said.

"How?" Dolph said.

"I could meet them, be in the same room with them. To be sure, I might have to touch them, shake hands."

"I shook Mr. Spalding's hand," Zerbrowski said. "It was like shaking anybody else's hand."

"You're a great cop, Zerbrowski, but you're almost a null. You could shake the grand high pooh-bah's hand and not get more than a twinge. Dolph's a complete null."

"What's a null?" Dolph asked.

"A magical null. Someone who has no magical or psychic ability. It's what let you cross the blood circle and kept me out."

"So you're saying *I* have some magical ability?" Zerbrowski asked.

I shook my head. "You're a tiny bit sensitive. Probably one of those people who get hunches that turn out to be right."

"I get hunches," Dolph said.

"I'll bet your hunches are based on experience, years of police work. Zerbrowski will make a leap of logic that makes no sense, but proves to be true. Am I wrong?"

They looked at each other, then at me, then both nodded. "Zerbrowski has his moments," Dolph said.

"You want to come shake the Spaldings' hands?" Zerbrowski asked.

"Detective Reynolds can do it. It's one of the reasons you brought her on board, right?"

They looked at each other again. Zerbrowski grinned. "I'll get Reynolds and go back over." He stopped at the door. "Katie's been after me to invite you over for dinner, meet the kids, a real domestic affair." He stared at me with his brown eyes guileless behind dark-rimmed glasses. "I was going to tell you to bring Richard, but if you're dating Count Dracula now, guess that'd be awkward." He stared at me, asking without asking.

"I'm still seeing Richard, you pushy son of a bitch."

He smiled. "Good. Bring him over a week from Saturday. Katie'll fix her famous mushroom chicken."

"If I was only dating Jean-Claude, would the invitation still include my boyfriend?"

"No," he said. "Katie's a little nervous. I don't think she'd be up to meeting Count Dracula."

"His name's Jean-Claude."

"I know." He shut the door behind him, and Dolph and I were alone with the body once more. The night was not looking up.

''What are we hunting for, Anita?'' I was actually relieved that Dolph was talking business. I'd had enough personal chitchat to last the night.

''More than one murderer.''

''Why?''

I looked up at him. ''I don't know if there's enough humans in the world to pin a vampire to the floor like that. Even if it was other vampires or shapeshifters, it'd take more than one. I'd say two beings with abnormal strength to hold, and a third to put in the knives. Maybe more to hold, maybe more to do the spell. I don't know, but at least three.''

''Even if they were vampires?'' Dolph asked.

I nodded. ''Unless one vamp was strong enough to have mind control over Robert.'' I looked down at the body, careful not to touch the circle. I forced myself to stare at what had been done to him. ''No, once they started putting knives in him, I don't think any mind control would work. A human, yeah, they could have done this to a human and made him smile while they did it, but not another vamp. Did any of the neighbors see or hear anything? I mean the Spaldings may be involved, so they'd lie, but someone had to see or hear something. He didn't go quietly.''

''They say no,'' Dolph said. He said it like he knew some or all of them had lied. One of the things cops learn first is that everyone lies. Some people to hide things, some people just for the hell of it, but everyone lies. Assume that everyone is hiding something, it saves time.

I stared at Robert's face, his mouth half-open, slack. There were rubbed marks at each corner of his mouth, a slight reddening. ''Did you notice the marks by his mouth?''

''Yes,'' Dolph said.

''And you weren't going to mention them to me?''

''You were a suspect.''

I shook my head. ''You didn't really believe that. You're just playing all the details close to your chest, like always. I get tired of putting the pieces together when you've already done it.''

''So, what do you make of the marks?'' he asked, his voice neutral.

''You know damn well what I make of them. He may have been gagged while they did this to him. The neighbors really might not have heard anything. But that still doesn't say how the killers got into the house. If vampires were involved, they couldn't cross the threshold without an invitation. Robert wouldn't have invited strange vamps into his house, so someone with them had to be known, or human, or at least not vampire.''

''Could a human cross the threshold and invite vampires inside?''

''Yes,'' I said.

Dolph was making notes, not looking at me. ''So we're looking for a mixed group, at least one vamp, at least one not vamp, at least one witch or necromancer.''

''You got that last from Reynolds,'' I said.

''You disagree?''

''No, but since I'm the only necromancer in town, it has to be outside talent.''

The moment I said it, I realized that outside talent was in town now. Dominic Dumare.

"John Burke couldn't do it?"

I thought about that. "John's a vaudun priest, but this isn't voodoo. I don't know if his knowledge of the arcane stretches this far. I also don't know if he's powerful enough to have done this, even with the knowledge."

"Are you powerful enough?"

I sighed. "I don't know, Dolph. I'm sort of new at necromancy. I mean, I've raised the dead for years, but not this formally." I motioned at the body. "I've never seen a spell like this."

He nodded. "Anything else?"

I hated dragging Dominic into it, but it was too bloody big a coincidence that a powerful necromancer hits town and a vamp gets taken out with necromancy. If he was innocent, I'd apologize. If he wasn't innocent, it was a death penalty case.

"Dominic Dumare is a necromancer. He just got into town."

"Could he have done this?" Dolph asked.

"I only met the man once, Dolph."

"Give me an opinion, Anita."

I thought about the feel of Dominic in my head. His offer to teach me necromancy. The big thing was that killing Robert and leaving the body for us to find was stupid. Dominic Dumare didn't strike me as a stupid man.

"He could have. He's a vampire's human servant, so it gives you two of your mixed group."

"Did the vampire know Robert?"

I shook my head. "Not to my knowledge."

"You got a number where we can reach Mr. Dumare?"

"I can call our night secretary and get it for you."

"Great." Dolph stared down at his notes. "Is Dumare your best suspect?"

I thought about that. "Yeah, I guess he is."

"You got any proof?"

"He's a necromancer, and this was done by someone with knowledge of necromancy." I shrugged.

"The same reason we suspected you," Dolph said. He almost smiled when he said it.

"Point taken," I said. "Prejudiced little me."

Dolph closed his notebook. "I'll take you down for your statement then."

"Fine. Now can I call Catherine?"

"There's a phone in the kitchen."

Zerbrowski opened the door. "The wife's here, and she's pretty hysterical."

"Who's with her?" Dolph asked.

"Reynolds."

Through the open door, I heard a woman talking, just below the level of screaming. "Robert, my husband, dead? He can't be dead. He can't be dead. I have to see him. You don't understand what he is. He isn't dead." The voice was coming closer.

"She's doesn't need to see this, Anita."

I nodded. I walked out the door and closed it tightly behind me. I couldn't see Monica yet, but I could hear her. Her voice rising, growing thinner with panic. "You don't understand. He isn't really dead."

I was betting that Monica wouldn't take my word for Robert being well and truly dead. I guess if it was Jean-Claude lying in there, I wouldn't, either. I'd have to see for myself. I took a deep breath and walked forward to meet the grieving widow. Damn. This night just kept getting better and better.

20

The hospital room was soft mauve with paintings of flowers on the wall. The bed had a mauve bedspread and pink sheets. Monica lay in the bed hooked up to an IV and two different kinds of monitors. A strap across her belly monitored the contractions. Gratefully, the lines had gone flat. The other monitor was the baby's heartbeat. The sound had scared me at first; too fast, like the heart of a small bird. When the nurses assured me the heartbeat was normal, I relaxed. After nearly two hours, the frantic beat had become a comforting sound like white noise.

Monica's auburn hair was plastered in wet tendrils to her forehead. Her careful makeup was smeared across her face. They had been forced to give her a sedative, though it wasn't great for the baby. She had fallen into a light, almost feverish sleep. Her head turned, eyes flicking behind her lids, mouth working, caught in some dream, a very bad dream probably, after the night she'd had. It was almost two o'clock, and I still had to go to the station and make my statement to Detective Greeley. Catherine was on her way to take my place at Monica's bedside. I'd be glad to see her.

I had little crescent nail marks on my right hand. Monica had clung to it like it was all that was holding her together. At the worst of the contractions, when it looked like Monica would lose her baby as well as her husband, her long, painted nails had bitten into me, and only when blood trickled down my hand in fine crimson lines did a nurse say something. When Monica calmed down, they had insisted on messing with the wounds. They'd used the cartoon bandages they kept for the babies, so that my hand was covered in Mickey Mouse and Goofy.

There was a television on a shelf on the wall, but I hadn't turned it on. The only sounds were the whirr of air circulating through the vents and the baby's heartbeat.

A uniformed cop stood outside the door. If Robert had been killed by a hate group, then Monica and the baby were possible targets. If he'd been killed for personal reasons, Monica might know something. Either way, she was in danger. So they'd put a guard on her. Fine with me, since all I had left was a knife. I was really missing my guns.

The phone on the bedside table rang, and I flung myself out of the chair, scrambling for it, terrified that it would wake Monica. I cupped the receiver against my mouth and spoke quietly while my pulse pounded. "Yes?"

"Anita?" It was Edward.

"How did you know where I was?"

"All that matters is that if I can find you, so can someone else."

"Is the contract still on?"

"Yes."

"Damn. What about the time deadline?"

"Expanded to forty-eight hours."

"Well, shit. Aren't *they* determined."

"I think you should go underground for a while, Anita."

"You mean hide?"

"Yeah."

"I thought you wanted me to be bait."

"If you stay out as bait, we need more bodyguards. The werewolves and vamps are monsters, but they're still amateurs. We're professionals, it's what gives us our edge. I'm good, but I can't be everywhere."

"Like following me into the women's john," I said.

I heard him sigh. "I let you down."

"I was careless, too, Edward."

"So you agree?"

"To hiding? Yeah. You got some place in mind?"

"As a matter of fact, I do."

"I don't like the tone in your voice, Edward."

"It's the most secure place in town and has built-in bodyguards."

"Where?" That one word sounded suspicious even to me.

"Circus of the Damned," he said.

"You have got to be out of your freaking mind."

"It's the Master's daytime retreat, Anita. It's a fortress. Jean-Claude's sealed up the tunnel we came through to get Nikolaos. It's secure."

"You want me to spend the day bedded down with vampires. I don't think so."

"You going back to Richard's house?" Edward asked. "How safe are you going to be there? How safe will you be anywhere above ground?"

"Dammit, Edward."

"I'm right, and you know it."

I wanted to argue, but he *was* right. The Circus was the most secure place I knew. Hell, the place had dungeons. But the idea of voluntarily sleeping there made my skin crawl.

"How can I rest surrounded by vampires, even friendly ones?"

"Jean-Claude's offered you his bed. Before you get mad, he'll sleep in his coffin."

"That's what he says now," I said.

"I'm not worried about your virtue, Anita. I'm worried about keeping you alive. And I'm admitting that I can't keep you safe. I'm good. I'm the best money can buy, but I'm only one person. One person, no matter how good, isn't enough.''

That was scary. Edward admitting that he was in over his head. I never thought I'd live to see it. Come to think of it, I almost hadn't.

''Okay, I'll do it, but for how long?''

''You hide out, and I'll check some things. If I don't have to guard you, I can do more.''

''How long?''

''A day, maybe two.''

''What if whoever it is finds out I'm at the Circus?''

''They might try for you,'' Edward said. His voice was very matter-of-fact when he said it.

''And if they do?''

''If you, a half dozen vampires, and almost that many werewolves can't handle the action, then I don't think it matters.''

''You're just comforting as hell.''

''I know you, Anita. If I was any more comforting, you might refuse to hide.''

''Twenty-four hours, Edward, then I want another plan. I am not going to hide at the bottom of a hole and wait for people to kill me.''

''Agreed. I'll pick you up after you make your statement to the cops.''

''Where do you get your information?''

He laughed, but it was harsh. ''If I know where you'll be, so does someone else. Might ask your cop friends if they have a spare vest.''

''You mean a bulletproof vest?''

''Couldn't hurt.''

''Are you trying to scare me?''

''Yes.''

''You're doing a good job.''

''Thanks. Don't come out of the police station until I come in and get you. Avoid being in the open if you can.''

''You really think someone else will try to hit me tonight?''

''We're planning for worst-case scenarios from now on, Anita. No more chances. I'll see you then.'' He hung up before I could say anything else.

I stood there holding the phone, scared. In all the panic with Monica and her baby, I'd almost forgotten that someone was trying to kill me. Probably not a good thing to forget.

I started to hang the phone up, but dialed Richard's number instead. He answered on the second ring, which meant he'd been waiting up. Damn.

''Richard, it's me.''

''Anita, where are you?'' His voice sounded relieved, then cautious. ''I mean, are you coming back here tonight?''

The answer was no, but not for the reasons he feared. I told him what had happened, the shortest possible version.

''Whose idea was it that you stay with Jean-Claude?'' There was a hint of anger in his voice.

"I am not staying with Jean-Claude. I am staying at the Circus."

"And the difference is what?"

"Look, Richard, I am too tired to argue with you about this. Edward suggested it, and you know he likes Jean-Claude even less than you do."

"I doubt that," he said.

"Richard, I did not call you to fight. I called to tell you what's happening."

"I appreciate the call." I'd never heard him sound so sarcastic. "Do you want your clothes?"

"Damn, I hadn't even thought about that."

"I'll bring them to the Circus."

"You don't have to do that, Richard."

"You don't want me to?"

"No, I'd love to have my stuff, and not just the clothes if you get my drift?"

"I'll bring it all."

"Thanks."

"I'll pack a bag for myself."

"Do you think that's a good idea?"

"I've stayed at the Circus before. Remember, I used to be one of Jean-Claude's wolves."

"I remember. Should you ask Jean-Claude's permission before you invite yourself over?"

"I'll phone first. Unless you don't want me there tonight." His voice was very quiet.

"If it's okay with Jean-Claude, it's fine with me. I could use the moral support."

He let out a breath like he'd been holding it. "Great. Great, I'll see you there."

"I have to give a statement to the cops about the incident at Danse Macabre. It could take a couple of hours, so don't rush."

"Afraid Jean-Claude will hurt me?" He was quiet for a moment. "Or are you afraid I'll hurt him?"

I thought about that. "Worried about you."

"Glad to hear it," he said, and I could hear him smile.

The reason I was worried about Richard is he wasn't a killer. Jean-Claude was. Richard might start a fight, but Jean-Claude would finish it. I didn't say any of this out loud. Richard wouldn't have appreciated it.

"I'm looking forward to seeing you tonight," he said.

"Even at the Circus?"

"Anywhere. Love you."

"Love you, too."

We hung up. Neither of us had said good-bye, a Freudian slip, perhaps.

I was betting that Richard and Jean-Claude would find something to fight about, and I was really too tired to mess with it. But if I'd told Richard to stay away, he would have assumed I wanted to be alone with Jean-Claude, which was certainly not true. So they'd have their little fight. Frankly, I had my own fight all picked out, one involving me, Jean-Claude, and Damian. They'd broken the law at Danse

Macabre, broken it enough that with the right judge, I might have gotten a warrant of execution on Damian. We could have one great big glorious knock-down, drag-out fight.

I wondered where everybody would sleep, and with who.

21

Circus of the Damned is a combination of traveling carnival, circus, and one of the lower rungs of hell. Out front, fanged clowns dance above the lights that spell the name. Posters stretch the sides of the building, proclaiming, "Watch zombies rise from the grave. See the Lamia—half-snake, half-woman." There is no trickery at the Circus, everything advertised is absolutely real. It is one of the few vampire tourist attractions that welcome children. If I'd had a kid, I wouldn't have brought the little tyke near the place. Even I didn't feel safe.

Edward had picked me up outside the police station, just like he said he would. My statement had taken three hours, not two. The only reason I got out that soon was Bob, Catherine's husband and fellow lawyer, had finally told them to charge me or let me go. Truthfully, I thought they might charge me. But I had three witnesses saying the killing was self-defense, witnesses that I'd never met before tonight. That helped. The DA usually didn't charge on self-defense cases. Usually.

Edward took me into the Circus through a side door. There were no lights to mark it as special, but there was also no doorknob on the outside of the steel reinforced door. Edward knocked. The door opened, and in we went.

Jason closed the door behind us. I had missed him earlier at Danse Macabre. I certainly would have remembered the outfit. He was wearing a sleeveless plastic shirt, molded to his body. The pants were half crinkly blue cloth that looked like colored foil, with oval plastic windows, exposing his thigh, calf, and as he turned, one buttock.

I shook my head, smiling. "Please tell me Jean-Claude didn't make you wear that out where people could see you."

Jason grinned at me and turned so he flashed his butt at me. "Don't you like it?"

"I'm not sure," I said.

"Discuss fashion later, in a more secure place," Edward said. He glanced at the door to our right that led into the main part of the Circus. It was never locked, though it had a sign above the door about authorized personnel only. We were standing in a stone room with an electric light dangling from the ceiling. It was a storage area. A third door was set in the far wall. Behind it was a stairway and the nether regions where the vampires stayed during the day.

"I'll be underground, literally, soon enough, Edward."

Edward looked at me for a long moment. "You promised to hide out for twenty-four hours. No going outside for any reason. Don't even go into the main part of the Circus when it's open to the public. Just stay downstairs."

"Aye, aye, Captain."

"This isn't a joke, Anita."

I tugged at the bulletproof vest I'd put over my dress. It was too large for me, hot, and uncomfortable. "If I thought it was funny, I wouldn't have worn this."

"I'll bring you some armor that fits when I come back."

I met his pale blue eyes and saw something I'd never seen before. He was worried.

"You think they're going to kill me, don't you?"

He didn't look away. He didn't flinch. But what I saw in his face made me wish he had. "When I come back tomorrow, I'll have help with me."

"What kind of help?"

"My kind."

"What does that mean?"

He shook his head. "Twenty-four hours means that you hide until dawn tomorrow, Anita. With luck, I'll have a name for us, and we can kill him. Don't be careless while I'm gone."

I wanted to say something casual, joking, like "I didn't know you cared," but I couldn't. I couldn't joke staring into his serious eyes.

"I'll be careful."

He nodded. "Lock the door behind me." He went outside and Jason locked the door.

Jason leaned against the door for a second. "Why does he scare me?"

"Because you're not stupid," I said.

He smiled. "Thanks."

"Let's get downstairs," I said.

"Nervous?"

"It's been a long night, Jason. No games."

He pushed away from the door and said, "Lead the way."

I opened the door to the stone stairway, which led downward. It was wide enough for us to walk abreast. In fact, there was almost room for a third, as if the stairway had been built for wider things than human bodies.

Jason closed the door with a resounding thunk. It made me jump. He started to say something, but the look on my face stopped him. Edward's parting comments had unnerved me. If I didn't know better, I'd have said I was scared. Naw.

Jason walked down the steps ahead of me, exaggerating his walk just a touch to show off his derriere.

"You can cut the peep show," I said.

"You don't like the view?" He leaned against the wall, hands pressed behind him, showing off his chest.

I laughed and walked past him, clicking my nails down his shirt. It was solid and hard as a beetle's carapace. ''Is that as uncomfortable as it looks?''

He fell into step beside me. ''It's not uncomfortable. The ladies at Danse Macabre liked it a lot.''

I glanced at him. ''I bet they did.''

''I like flirting.''

''No joke.''

He laughed. ''For someone who doesn't flirt, you have a lot of guys after you.''

''Maybe because I don't flirt,'' I said.

Jason was quiet as we walked to the bend in the stairs. ''You mean because you're a challenge, they keep coming around?''

''Something like that.''

I couldn't see around the bend of the stairs. I hated not being able to see around corners. But this time I was invited; I hadn't come to kill anybody. The vamps tended to be a lot friendlier when you weren't trying to kill them.

''Is Richard here yet?''

''Not yet.'' He glanced back at me. ''Do you think it's a good idea to have them both here at the same time?''

''No,'' I said, ''absolutely not.''

''Well, at least we all agree it's a bad idea,'' he said.

The door at the bottom of the stairs was iron bound, made of a heavy, dark wood. It looked like a portal to another time—a time when dungeons were in vogue, and knights rescued ladies fair or slaughtered a few peasants and no one minded, except maybe the peasants.

Jason drew a key out of his pants pocket. He unlocked the door and pushed. It opened on well-oiled hinges.

''Since when did you get a key?'' I asked.

''I live here now.''

''What about college?''

He shrugged. ''It doesn't seem very important anymore.''

''You plan on being Jean-Claude's lap-wolf forever?''

''I'm having a good time,'' he said.

I shook my head. ''I fight like hell to stay free of him, and you just give in. I don't understand that at all.''

''You have a college degree, right?'' he asked.

''Yeah.''

''I don't. But here we both are, ending up in the same place.''

He had me there.

Jason motioned me through the door with a low flourish that had imitation Jean-Claude written all over it. Jean-Claude made it seem courtly and real. Jason meant it for a joke.

The door led into Jean-Claude's living room. The ceiling stretched up into darkness, but silken drapes hung in black and white folds that formed cloth walls on three sides. The fourth side was bare stone, painted white. A white stone fireplace looked original, which I knew it wasn't. The mantlepiece was black-veined white marble. A silver fireplace screen hid the hearth. There were four chairs in black and silver grouped around a wood and glass coffee table. A black vase sat on the table filled with white tulips. My high heels sank into the thick, black carpet.

There was one other addition to the room that stopped me in my tracks. A painting hung above the fireplace. Three people dressed in the style of the 1600s. The woman wore white and silver with a square bodice showing quite a bit of décolletage, her brown hair styled in careful ringlets. She held a red rose loosely in one hand. A man stood behind her, tall and slender, with dark gold hair in ringlets over his shoulders. He had a mustache and a Vandyke beard, so dark gold they were almost brown. He wore one of those floppy hats with feathers and was dressed in white and gold. But it was the other man who made me walk towards the painting.

He was seated just behind the woman. He was dressed in black with silver embroidery and a wide lace collar and lace cuffs. He held a floppy black hat with a single white feather and a silver buckle across his lap. Black hair fell in ringlets over his shoulders. He was clean shaven, and the artist had managed to capture the sinking blue of his eyes. I stared at Jean-Claude's face painted hundreds of years before I was born. The other two were smiling. Only he was solemn and perfect, dark to their lightness. He was like the shadow of death come to the ball.

I knew Jean-Claude was centuries old, but I'd never had such obvious proof, never had it shoved in my face. The portrait bothered me for another reason. It made me wonder if Jean-Claude had lied about his age.

A sound made me turn. Jason had slumped into one of the chairs. Jean-Claude stood behind me. He'd taken off his jacket and his curling black hair spilled across the shoulders of his crimson shirt. The shirt cuffs were long and tight at the wrist, held by three antique jet beads just like the high neck of the shirt. Without the jacket to distract the eye, the pale oval of skin framed by the red cloth gleamed. The cloth covered his nipples but left his belly button bare and drew the eye to the top of his black pants. Or maybe it just drew me. It was a bad idea to be here. He was just as dangerous as the assassin, maybe more. Dangerous in ways I had no words for.

He glided towards me in his black boots. I watched him walk closer like a deer caught in headlights. I expected him to flirt or ask how I liked the painting. Instead, he said, "Tell me of Robert. The police said he was dead, but they know nothing. You have seen the body. Is he truly dead?"

His voice was thick with concern, worry. It caught me completely off guard. "They took his heart."

"If it is only a stake through the heart, he might survive if it was removed."

I shook my head. "The heart was taken out completely. We couldn't find it in the house or the yard."

Jean-Claude stopped. He slumped suddenly into one of the chairs, staring at nothing, or nothing I could see. "Then he is truly gone." His voice held sorrow the way it sometimes held laughter, so that I felt his words like a cold, grey rain.

"You treated Robert like dirt. Why all this weeping and wailing?"

He looked at me. "I am not weeping."

"But you treated him badly."

"I was his master. If I had treated him kindly, he would have seen it as a sign of weakness. He would have challenged me and I would have killed him. Do not criticize things that you do not understand." There was anger in that last sentence, enough to brush heat along my skin.

Normally, it would have pissed me off, but tonight . . . "I apologize. You're right. I don't understand. I didn't think you gave a damn about Robert unless he could further your power."

"Then you do not understand me at all, *ma petite*. He was my companion for over a century. After a century, I would mourn even an enemy's passing. Robert was not my friend, but he was mine. Mine to punish, mine to reward, mine to protect. I have failed him."

He stared up at me, eyes gone blue and alien. "I am grateful to you for seeing to Monica. The last thing I can do for Robert is to tend his wife and child. They will want for nothing."

He stood suddenly in one smooth motion. "Come, *ma petite*. I will show you to our room." I didn't like the *our*, but I didn't argue. This new, improved, emotional Jean-Claude had me confused.

"Who are the other two in the painting?"

He glanced at it. "Julianna and Asher. She was his human servant. The three of us traveled together for nearly twenty years."

Good. He couldn't give me some bullshit about the clothing being costumes now. "You're too young to have been a Musketeer."

He stared at me, face carefully blank, giving nothing away. "Whatever do you mean, *ma petite*?"

"Don't even try. The clothing is from the 1600s, around the time of Dumas's The Three Musketeers. When we first met, you told me you were two hundred and ten. Eventually, I figured out you were lying, that you were closer to three hundred."

"If Nikolaos had known my true age, she might have killed me, *ma petite*."

"Yeah, the old Master of the City was a real bitch. But she's dead. Why still lie?"

"You mean why am I lying to you?" he said.

I nodded. "Yeah, that's what I mean."

He smiled. "You are a necromancer, *ma petite*. I would have thought you could judge my age without my help."

I tried to read his face and couldn't. "You've always been hard to read; you know that."

"So glad I can be a challenge in some area."

I let that go. He knew exactly how much of a challenge he was, but for the first time in a long time, I was bothered. Telling a vamp's age was one of my talents, not an exact science to be sure, but one I was good at. I'd never been off by this much. "A century older, my, my."

"Are you so sure that it is only a century?"

I stared at him. I let his power beat across my skin, rolled the feel of it around in my head. "Pretty sure."

He smiled. "Do not frown so, *ma petite*. Being able to hide my age is one of my talents. I pretended to be a hundred years older when Asher was my companion. It allowed us freedom to wander through the lands of other masters.''

''What made you stop trying to pass for older?''

''Asher needed help, and I was not master enough to help him.'' He looked up at the portrait. ''I . . . humbled myself to gain him aid.''

''Why?''

''The Church had a theory that vampires could be cured by holy items. They bound Asher with holy items and silver chains. They used holy water on him, drop by drop, trying to save his soul.''

I stared up at that handsome, smiling face. I'd been bitten by a master vampire once upon a time and had the wound cleansed with holy water. It had felt like a red-hot brand was being shoved into my skin, like all the blood in my body had turned to boiling oil. I had vomited and screamed and thought myself very brave for not passing out altogether. That had been one bite mark, one day. Having what amounted to acid dripped on you until you died was in the top five ways not to go out.

''What happened to the girl, Julianna?''

''She was burned as a witch.''

''Where were you?''

''I had taken a ship to see my mother. She was dying. I was on my way back when I heard Asher's call. I could not get there in time. I swear by all that is holy or unholy that I tried. I rescued Asher, but he never forgave me.''

''He's not dead?'' I asked.

''No.''

''How hurt was he?''

''Until I met Sabin I thought Asher's scars the worst injury I'd ever known a vampire to survive.''

''Why did you hang the painting if it bothers you this much?''

He sighed and looked at me. ''Asher sent it as a present, to congratulate me for becoming Master of the City. The three of us were companions, almost family. Asher and I were true friends, both masters, both of near equal power, both in love with Julianna. She was devoted to him, but I had her favor as well.''

''You mean a ménage à trois?''

He nodded.

''Asher doesn't hold a grudge?''

''Oh, no, he holds a grudge. If the council would allow it, he would have come with the picture and had his revenge.''

''To kill you?''

Jean-Claude smiled. ''Asher always had a strong sense of irony, *ma petite*. He petitioned the council for your life, not mine.''

My eyes widened. ''What did I ever do to him?''

''I killed his human servant; he kills mine. Justice.''

I stared back up at the handsome face. ''The council said no?''

''Indeed.''

''You have any other old enemies running around?''

Jean-Claude gave a weak smile. ''Many, *ma petite*, but none in town at the moment.''

I looked up at those smiling faces. I didn't know quite how to phrase it, but said it anyway. ''You all look so young.''

''I am physically the same, *ma petite*.''

I shook my head. ''Maybe young isn't the word I want. Maybe naive.''

He smiled. ''By the time this painting was made, *ma petite*, naive was not a word that described me, either.''

''Fine, have it your way.'' I looked at him, studying his face. He was beautiful, but there was something in his eyes that wasn't in the painting, some level of sorrow or terror. Something I had no word for, but it was there just the same. A vampire may not wrinkle up, but living a couple of centuries leaves its mark. Even if it's only a shadow in the eyes, a tightness around the mouth.

I turned to Jason, who was still slumped in the chair. ''Does he give these little history lessons often?''

''Only to you,'' Jason said.

''You never ask questions?'' I asked.

''I'm just his pet. You don't answer questions for your pet.''

''And that doesn't bother you?''

Jason smiled. ''Why should I care about the painting? The woman's dead, so I can't have sex with her. Why should I care?''

I felt Jean-Claude move past me, but couldn't follow with my eyes. His hand was a blur. The chair clattered to the floor, spilling Jason with it. Blood showed at his mouth.

''Never speak of her again in such a manner.''

Jason touched the back of his hand to his mouth and came away with blood. ''Whatever you say.'' He licked the blood off his hand with long slow movements of his tongue.

I stared from one to the other of them. ''You are both crazy.''

''Not crazy, *ma petite*, merely not human.''

''Being a vampire doesn't give you the right to treat people like that. Richard doesn't beat people up.''

''Which is why he will never hold the pack.''

''What's that supposed to mean?''

''Even if he swallows his high morals and kills Marcus, he will not be cruel enough to frighten the rest. He will be challenged again and again. Unless he begins slaughtering people, he will eventually die.''

''Slapping people around won't keep him alive,'' I said.

''It would help. Torture works well, but I doubt that Richard would have the stomach for it.''

''I couldn't stomach it.''

''But you litter the ground with bodies, *ma petite*. Killing is the best deterrent of all.''

I was too tired to be having this conversation. ''It's 4:30 in the morning. I want to go to bed.''

Jean-Claude smiled. ''Why, *ma petite*, you are not usually so eager.''

''You know what I mean,'' I said.

Jean-Claude took a gliding step towards me. He didn't touch me, but he stood very close and looked at me. ''I know exactly what you mean, *ma petite*.''

That brought heat in a rush up my neck. The words were innocent. He made them sound intimate, obscene.

Jason righted the chair and stood, licking the blood off the corner of his mouth. He said nothing, merely watched us like a well-trained dog, seen and not heard.

Jean-Claude took a step back. I felt him move, but couldn't follow it with my eyes. There had been a time only months ago that it would have looked like magic, like he'd just appeared a few feet away.

He held his hand out towards me. ''Come, *ma petite*. Let us retire for the day.''

I'd held his hand before, so why was I left standing, staring, like he was offering me the forbidden fruit that once tasted would change everything? He was nearly four hundred years old. Jean-Claude's face from all those long years ago was smiling down at me, and there he stood with almost the same smile. If I'd ever needed proof, I had it. He'd struck Jason down like a dog he didn't much like. And still he was so beautiful, it made my chest ache.

I wanted to take his hand. I wanted to run my hands over the red shirt, explore that open oval of flesh. I folded my hands over my stomach and shook my head.

His smile widened until a hint of fang showed. ''You have held my hand before, *ma petite*. Why is tonight any different?'' His voice held an edge of mockery.

''Just show me the room, Jean-Claude.''

He let his hand drop to his side, but he didn't seem offended. If anything, he seemed pleased, which irritated me.

''Bring Richard through when he arrives, Jason, but announce him before he comes. I don't want to be interrupted.''

''Anything you say,'' Jason said. He smirked at us, at me, a knowing look on his face. Did everyone and their wolf believe I was sleeping with Jean-Claude? Of course, maybe it was a case of the lady protesting too much. Maybe.

''Just bring Richard to the room when he comes,'' I said. ''You won't be interrupting anything.'' I glanced at Jean-Claude while I said the last.

He laughed, that warm touchable sound of his that wove over my skin like silk. ''Even your resistance to temptation grows thin, *ma petite*.''

I shrugged. I would have liked to argue, but he'd smell a lie. Even a run-of-the-mill werewolf can smell desire. Jason wasn't run-of-the-mill. So everyone in the room knew I was hot for Jean-Claude. So what?

''*No* is one of my favorite words, Jean-Claude. You should know that by now.''

The laughter faded from his face, leaving his blue, blue eyes gleaming, but not with humor. Something darker and more sure of itself looked out his eyes. ''I survive on hope alone, *ma petite*.''

Jean-Claude parted the black and white drapes to reveal the bare, grey stones that the room was made of. A large hallway stretched deeper into the labyrinth. Torchlight gleamed beyond the electricity of the living room. He stood there, back-lit against the flame and the soft modern lights. Some trick of light and shadow plunged half his face into darkness and brought a pinprick glow to his eyes. Or maybe it wasn't a trick of the light. Maybe it was just him.

"Shall we go, *ma petite*?"

I walked into that outer darkness. He didn't try to touch me as I moved past him. I'd have given him a brownie point for resisting the urge, except I knew him too well. He was just biding his time. Touching me now might piss me off. Later, it might not. Even I couldn't guarantee when the mood would be right.

Jean-Claude moved ahead of me. He glanced back over his shoulder. "After all, *ma petite*, you do not know the way to my bedroom."

"I've been there once," I said.

"Carried unconscious and dying. It hardly counts." He glided down the hall. He put a little extra sway to his walk, somewhat like Jason had done on the stairs, but where it had been funny with the werewolf, Jean-Claude made it utterly seductive.

"You just wanted to walk in front so I'd have to stare at your butt."

He spoke without turning around. "No one makes you stare at me, *ma petite*, not even me."

And that was the truth. The horrible truth. If in some dark part of my heart I hadn't been attracted to him from the beginning, I'd have killed him long ago. Or tried to. I had more legal vampire kills than any other vampire hunter in the country. They didn't call me the Executioner for nothing. So how did I end up being safer in the depths of the Circus of the Damned with the monsters than above ground with the humans? Because somewhere along the line, I didn't kill the monster I should have.

That particular monster was gliding up the hallway ahead of me. And he still had the cutest butt I'd ever seen on a dead man.

22

Jean-Claude leaned one shoulder against the wall. He'd already opened the door. He motioned me inside with a graceful sweep of his hand.

My high heels sank into the deep, white carpet. White wallpaper with tiny silver designs graced the walls. There was a white door in the left-hand wall near the bed. The bed had white satin sheets. A dozen black and white pillows were grouped at the head of the bed. A fan of black and white drapes fell from the ceiling, forming a partial canopy over the bed. The black lacquer vanity and chest of drawers still sat in opposite corners. The wallpaper and the door were new. Guess which bothered me more.

"Where does the door go?"

"The bathroom." He closed the outer door and walked past me to sit on the edge of the bed. There were no chairs.

"A bathroom. That wasn't here last time," I said.

"Not in its present form, but it was here just the same."

He leaned back on his elbows. The movement strained the cloth of his shirt, exposing as much skin as the shirt would allow. The line of dark hair that started low on his belly peeked just above the cloth.

The room was getting warmer. I undid the velcro fastenings on the bulletproof vest and slid it over my head. "Where do you want me to put this?"

"Anywhere you like," he said. His voice was soft and more intimate than the words themselves.

I walked around to the far side of the bed, away from him, and laid the vest across the satin sheets.

He lay back against the sheets, his black hair framing his pale face to perfection. Warmer, it was definitely getting warmer in here.

"Mind if I freshen up?"

"Whatever I have is yours, *ma petite*. You should know that by now."

I backed into the door and opened it with a feeling of relief. I closed the door without really looking at the bathroom. When I looked up, I let out a silent *wow*.

The room was long and narrow. It had a double sink and mirrors with round white lightbulbs edging it. The sinks were black marble with white veins running through. Every faucet, every metal edge, gleamed silver. The floor was black carpeting. A half wall of silver and mirrored panels hid the black stool against a black wall. Another half wall graced the other side. Then there was the bathtub. Three marble steps led up to a black bathtub, big enough for four people. The faucet was a silver swan with outspread wings. There was no way to take a shower, which was my preferred method, and the swan was a bit much, but other than that, it was lovely.

I sat down on the cool marble edging. It was nearly five in the morning. My eyes burned from lack of sleep. The adrenaline rush of nearly getting killed had long since faded. What I wanted was to be comforted, held, yes, sex was in there somewhere, but that wasn't my highest priority tonight. I think both Richard and Jean-Claude would say it was never my highest priority, but that was their problem. Okay, it was our problem.

If it had been Richard stretched out on the bed in the next room, I would have jumped him tonight. But it wasn't Richard, and once Richard got here, we'd be sleeping in Jean-Claude's bed. Seemed pretty tacky to have sex for the first time in your other boyfriend's bed. But it wasn't just the boys suffering from sexual tension, I was drowning, too.

Was Richard right? Was the fact that Jean-Claude wasn't human the only thing keeping me out of his bed? No. Or at least I didn't think so. Out of Richard's bed? The answer, sadly, was yes, maybe.

I freshened up and couldn't help checking myself in the mirror. The makeup had faded a little, but the liner still made my large, dark eyes stand out in dramatic contrast. The blush was almost gone, and the lipstick had long ago vanished. I had lipstick in my purse. I could freshen that at least. But freshening my lipstick was like admitting I cared what Jean-Claude thought of me. I did care. That was the truly scary part. I did not put on more lipstick. I walked back into the bedroom as is, let him make of it what he would.

He was leaning on one elbow, watching me as I came through the door. "*Ma petite*, you are beautiful."

I shook my head. "Pretty, I'll give you, but not beautiful."

He cocked his head to one side, sending a wave of hair over one shoulder. "Who told you you were not beautiful?"

I leaned against the door. "When I was a little girl, my father would come up behind my mother. He would wrap his arms around her waist, bury his face in her hair, and say, 'How is the most beautiful woman in the world today?' He said it at least once a day. She would laugh and tell him not to be silly, but I agreed with him. To me, she was the most beautiful woman in the world."

"She was your mother. All little girls think that of their mother."

"Maybe, but two years after she died, Dad remarried. He married Judith, who was tall and blond and blue-eyed, and nothing like my mother. If he had really believed my mother was the most beautiful woman in the world, why did he marry some Nordic ice princess? Why didn't he marry someone small and dark like my mother?"

"I don't know, *ma petite*," he said quietly.

"Judith had a daughter only a couple of years younger than me. Then they had Josh together and he was as blond and blue-eyed as the rest of them. I looked like a small dark mistake in the family photos."

"Your skin is almost as pale as mine, *ma petite*."

"But I have my mother's eyes and hair. My hair isn't brunette, it's black. A woman asked Judith once in front of me if I was adopted. Judith said, no, I was from her husband's first marriage."

Jean-Claude slid off the bed. He moved towards me, and I had to look at the floor. I wanted badly to be held, to be comforted. If it had been Richard, I'd have gone to him. But it wasn't Richard.

Jean-Claude touched my cheek and raised my face until I had to look at him. "I have lived for over three hundred years. In that time, the ideal of beauty has changed many times. Large breasts, small, thin, curved, tall, short, they have all been the height of beauty at one time or another. But in all that time, *ma petite*, I have never desired anyone the way I desire you." He leaned towards me, and I didn't move away. His lips brushed mine in a gentle kiss.

He took that one last step to press our bodies together, and I stopped him, one hand on his chest, but all I met was bare skin. The slickness of his cross-shaped burn scar met my fingertips. I moved my hand and found his heart beating against my palm. Not an improvement.

He drew back, a breath, and whispered into my mouth, "Tell me no, *ma petite*, and I will stop."

I had to swallow twice before I could speak. "No."

Jean-Claude stepped away from me. He lay back on the bed as he had earlier, propped on his elbows, his legs from the knees hung off the bed. He stared at me, daring me to come join him, I think.

I wasn't that stupid. There was some dark part of me that was tempted. Lust has less logic than love, sometimes, but it's easier to fight.

"I have played the mortal for you these many months. I thought in March when you held my naked body, when you shared blood with me, that it would be a changing point for us. That you would give in to your desire and admit your feelings for me."

A burning wash of color crept up my face. I had no good excuse for the foreplay that got out of hand. I was weak, so sue me. "I gave you blood because you were dying. I'd have never done it otherwise. You know that."

He stared at me. It wasn't vampire tricks that made me want to look away. It was a raw honesty that I'd never seen in his face before. "I know that now, *ma petite*. When we returned from Branson, you threw yourself into Richard's arms as though he were a lifeline. We continued to date, but you drew away. I felt it and did not know how to stop it."

He sat up on the bed, hands clasped in his lap. A look of frustration and confusion passed over his face. "I have never had another woman deny me, *ma petite*."

I laughed. "Oh, your ego isn't big."

"It is not ego, *ma petite*, it is the truth."

I leaned against the bathroom door and thought about that one. "No one in almost three hundred years has ever said no to you?"

"You find that so hard to believe?"

"If I can do it, so can they."

He shook his head. "You do not appreciate how very harsh your strength of will is, *ma petite*. It is impressive. You have no idea how impressive."

"If I'd fallen into your arms the first time we met, or even the dozenth time we met, you'd have bedded me, bled me, and dumped me."

I watched the truth of my words fill his face. I hadn't realized until this moment how much control he kept over his facial expressions, how it was the lack of reaction that made him seem more otherworldly than he was.

"You are right," he said. "If you had giggled and fawned over me, I would not have given you a second glance. Your partial immunity to my powers was the first attraction. But it was your stubbornness that intrigued me. Your flat refusal of me."

"I was a challenge."

"Yes."

I stared into his suddenly open face. For the first time, I thought I might see the truth in his eyes. "Good thing I resisted. I don't like being used and tossed aside."

"Once you were only a challenge, something to be conquered. Then I became intrigued by your growing powers. I saw possibilities that I could use you to strengthen my position if only you would join with me."

Something like pain passed over his face, and I wanted to ask if it was real. If any of this was real, or if it was only another act. I trusted Jean-Claude to do whatever it took to stay alive. I didn't trust him to tell the truth sitting on a stack of Bibles.

"I saved your ass enough times. I'm your declared human servant. What more do you want?"

"You, *ma petite*." He stood, but didn't come closer. "It is no longer challenge or the promise of power that makes me look to you."

My pulse was suddenly thudding in my throat, and he hadn't done a damn thing.

"I love you, Anita."

I stared at him, my eyes growing wide. I opened my mouth, closed it. I didn't believe him. He lied so easily, so well. He was the master of manipulation. How could I believe him now? "What do you want me to say?"

He shook his head, and his face fell back into its normal lines. That beautiful perfection that was what passed for ordinary. But I knew now that even this was a mask, hiding his deeper emotions.

"How did you do that?"

"After several centuries of being forced to school your face into pleasant, unreadable lines, you lose the knack of anything else. My survival has depended on my expression more than once. I wish you understood the effort that little display of humanity cost me."

"What do you want me to say, Jean-Claude?"

''You love me a little, that I am sure of.''

I shrugged. ''Maybe, but a little isn't enough.''

''You love Richard a lot, don't you?''

I met his eyes and wanted to lie, to save his feelings, but those kinds of lies hurt more than the truth. ''Yeah.''

''Yet, you have not made your choice. You have not told me to leave the two of you to matrimonial bliss. Why is that?''

''Last time we had this talk, you said you'd kill Richard.''

''If that is all that is stopping you, *ma petite*, have no fear. I will not kill Richard merely because you go to his bed and not mine.''

''Since when?'' I asked.

''When I threw my support to Richard, Marcus became my enemy. That cannot be changed.'' He leaned his shoulder against the dark wooden bedpost closest to me. ''I had thought to petition another pack. There is always an ambitious alpha male out there somewhere. Someone who would like his own pack but either through sentimentality or lack of strength is doomed to play second forever. I could kill Richard and bring someone else in to kill Marcus.''

I listened to his plan told so matter-of-factly. ''What changed your mind?''

''You.''

''Come again?''

''You love him, *ma petite*. You truly love him. His death would destroy something inside of you. When Julianna died, I thought I would never feel for anyone again. And I didn't, until I met you.''

''You won't kill Richard because it would hurt me?''

''Oui.''

''So I could tell Richard when he gets here that I've chosen him, and you would let us go off, get married, whatever?''

''Isn't there one hurdle to your marriage besides myself?'' he asked.

''What?''

''You must see him change into wolf form.'' Jean-Claude smiled and shook his head. ''If Richard was human, you would meet at the door with a smile and a yes. But you fear what he is. He is not human enough for you, *ma petite*.''

''He isn't human enough for himself,'' I said.

Jean-Claude raised his eyebrows. ''Yes, Richard runs from his beast, as you have run from me. But Richard shares a body with his beast. He cannot outrun it.''

''I know that.''

''Richard is still running, *ma petite*. And you run with him. If you were secure that you could accept him, all of him, you would have done it by now.''

''He keeps finding excuses not to change for me.''

''He fears your reaction,'' Jean-Claude said.

''It's more than that,'' I said. ''If I can embrace his beast, I'm not sure he'll be able to accept me.''

Jean-Claude cocked his head to one side. ''I do not understand.''

''He hates what he is so badly. I think if I can accept his beast, he won't . . . he won't love me anymore.''

''Being able to embrace his beast would make you what . . . perverse?''

I nodded. ''I think so.''

''You are trapped on the horns of a nasty dilemma, *ma petite*. He will not make love to you or marry you until you have seen and accepted his beast. Yet if you accept it, you fear he will turn from you.''

''Yeah.''

He shook his head. ''Only you could choose two men in one human lifetime that are this confusing.''

''I didn't do it on purpose.''

He pushed away from the bed. He stopped two small steps from me, staring down. ''I tried to play the mortal for you, *ma petite*. But Richard is much better at being human than I am. I have not been truly human for so very long. If I cannot be the better man, let me be the better monster.''

My eyes narrowed. ''What's that suppose to mean?''

''It means, *ma petite*, that Jason told me of what happened this afternoon. I know how close you and Richard came.''

How much had the lycanthropes been able to hear? More than I was comfortable with, that was for sure. ''I just love being spied on.''

''Do not be flippant, *ma petite*, please.''

It was the please that got me. ''I'm listening.''

''I told you once that if Richard could touch you and I could not, it would not be fair. That is still true.''

I pushed away from the door. He'd stepped over the line. ''Are you asking me to let you touch me where Richard touched me?''

He smiled. ''Such righteous indignation, *ma petite*. But have no fear. Forcing myself upon you in such a way would smack of rape. I have never been interested in such things.''

I took a step back, putting a little space between us. Unless I was really angry, it was never good to get that close. ''So, what are you saying?''

''You have always forbidden me to use vampire tricks, as you call them, with you.'' He held a hand up before I could say it. ''I do not mean bespelling you with my eyes. I am not even sure that is possible anymore. I cannot be human, *ma petite*. I am a vampire. Let me show you that has pleasures beyond humanity.''

I shook my head. ''No way.''

''A kiss, *ma petite*, that is all I ask. A chaste kiss.''

''And the catch is?'' I asked.

His eyes were solid, sparkling blue. His skin glowed like alabaster under lights.

''I don't think so,'' I said.

''If you were truly sure of Richard, I would leave you to him. But does the fact that I love you not earn me so much as a kiss?'' He glided towards me. I backed up, but the door was right there, and there was nowhere to go.

He was like a living sculpture, all ivory and sapphire, too beautiful for words. Too beautiful to touch. His hands smoothed over my forearms, along my hands. I gasped. Power rushed along my skin in a smooth wash, like air dancing over my body.

I must have tensed up because Jean-Claude said, ''It will not hurt, that I promise.''

''Just a kiss,'' I whispered.

''Just a kiss,'' he whispered. His face lowered towards mine. His lips brushed mine, gently, slowly. The power flowed across his lips into my mouth. I think I stopped breathing for a second. My skin felt like it was melting away and I would sink into his body, into that shining power.

''Looks like I got here just in time.'' It was Richard in the doorway.

I shoved my hand into Jean-Claude's chest and pushed him away hard enough for him to stumble. I was gasping for air like I'd been drowning. My skin pulsed and beat with the power that still crawled over me, into me.

''Richard,'' I whispered. I wanted to say that it wasn't what it looked like, but I couldn't get enough air.

Jean-Claude turned, smiling. He knew exactly what to say. ''Richard, how good of you to join us. How did you get past my wolf?''

''It wasn't that hard.''

I stared at both of them. I was still having trouble breathing. It felt like every nerve in my body had been touched all at once. The line between pleasure and pain was damn narrow, and I wasn't sure which side this went on.

The light was seeping away from Jean-Claude, leaving him pale, lovely, almost human.

Richard stood directly inside the door. His eyes glowed not with inner light but with anger, an anger that made his eyes dance, tightened the muscles across his shoulders and down his arms so that the effort showed from across the room. I'd never been so aware of how physically large he was. He seemed to fill more space than he should have. The first skin-prickling rush of his power swirled over me.

I took a deep, shaking breath and started walking towards him. The closer I got, the thicker the power, until about six feet from him, it was like stepping into a nearly solid mass of pulsing, vibrating energy.

I stood there, trying to swallow my heart back into my throat. He was dressed in jeans and a green flannel work shirt with sleeves rolled over his forearms. His hair fell loose round his shoulders in a wavy mass. I'd seen him like this a hundred times, but suddenly it was all different. I had never been afraid of Richard, not really. Now, for the first time, I saw that there was something to fear. Something swam behind his eyes, his beast, he called it. It was there now just behind those true, brown eyes. A monster waiting to be set loose.

''Richard,'' I said and had to cough to clear my throat, ''what's wrong with you?''

''Tomorrow is the full moon, Anita. Strong emotions aren't good right now.'' Rage thinned his face, made those lovely cheekbones high and tight. ''If I hadn't interrupted, would you have broken your promise to me?''

''He still doesn't know what kind of hose I'm wearing,'' I said.

Richard smiled, some of the tension easing away.

''Too smooth for garters,'' Jean-Claude said. ''Panty hose, though they could be crotchless, of that I am not sure.''

Richard snarled.

I glanced back at Jean-Claude. ''Don't help me.''

He smiled and nodded. He'd leaned his back on one of the bedposts, fingers playing over the bare skin of his chest. It was suggestive, and he meant it to be. Damn him.

A low, bass growl brought my attention back to Richard. He stalked towards the bed as if each movement hurt. The tension sang through the building power. Was I going to get to see him change here and now? If he changed, there'd be a fight, and for the very first time, I was worried for Jean-Claude's safety, as well as Richard's.

''Don't do this, Richard, please.''

He was staring past me at Jean-Claude. I didn't dare look behind to see what mischief the vampire was doing; I had my hands full with the werewolf in front of me.

Something flickered across his face. I was sure Jean-Claude had done something behind my back. Richard made a sound more animal than human and rushed for the bed. I didn't move out of the way. I stood my ground, and when he was even with me, moving past me, I threw my body into him and threw him in a nearly perfect shoulder roll. His momentum did the rest. Maybe if I'd let go of his arm, we could have avoided the rest, but I made the classic mistake. I didn't think Richard would really hurt me.

He grabbed the arm that was holding him and flung me across the room. He was flat on his back and didn't have much leverage, and that was all that saved me. I was airborne for just a second and rolled along the carpet when I hit. The world was still spinning when my hand went for the knife. I couldn't hear anything but the blood rushing in my own head, but I knew, I knew he was coming.

He touched my arm, rolled me over, and I laid the silver blade against his neck. He froze, bent over, trying, I think, to help me stand. Richard and I stared at each other from inches away. The anger was gone from his face. His eyes were normal, as lovely as ever, but I kept the knife against the smooth skin of his neck, dimpling it so he knew I meant business.

He swallowed carefully. ''I didn't mean to hurt you, Anita. I am so sorry.''

''Back off,'' I said.

''Are you hurt?''

''Back off, Richard. Now!''

''Let me help you.'' He bent closer, and I pressed the blade in hard enough to draw a trickle of blood.

''Let go of me, Richard.''

He let go and moved slowly away. He looked puzzled and hurt. He touched the blood at his neck as if he didn't know what it was.

When he was out of reach, I let myself sag against the carpet. Nothing was broken, of that I was sure, and I wasn't bleeding. If he'd thrown me into a wall with that much force, it would have been a different story. I'd been dating him for seven months, nearly slept with him more than once, and in all that time, I hadn't fully appreciated what I was playing with.

"*Ma petite*, are you all right?" Jean-Claude was standing at the foot of the bed. He was watching Richard closely as he moved towards me.

"I'm all right, I'm all right." I glared up at him. "What did you do behind my back to piss him off?"

Jean-Claude looked embarrassed. "I did tease Monsieur Zeeman. Perhaps I even wanted a fight. Jealousy is a foolish emotion. How was I to know you would not move out of the way of a charging werewolf?"

"I don't back up, not for anyone." I almost laughed. "Though next time, maybe I'll make an exception."

"I didn't mean to hurt you," Richard said. "But seeing you together like that . . . Knowing you're with him isn't the same thing as having it rubbed in my face." His anger had vanished the moment he'd hurt me. Horror at what he'd done, fear for my safety, sanity returning in a rush.

"We were only kissing, Richard, nothing else, no matter what he wants you to believe."

"I was suddenly so jealous. I'm sorry."

"I know it was an accident, Richard. I'm just glad there wasn't a wall closer."

"I could have hurt you badly." He took a step towards me, hands reaching, and stopped himself. "And you want me to let the beast loose enough to kill. Don't you understand how hard I fight to control it?"

"I understand better than I did a few minutes ago," I said.

"Your bags are in the hallway. I'll bring them in, then I'll go." This was the look I'd been dreading. This crushed, puppy dog look. The anger had been easier to deal with, if more dangerous.

"Don't go."

They both looked at me.

"Jean-Claude staged this." I held a hand up before he could protest. "Oh, I know you enjoyed yourself, but you still wanted Richard to see us together. You wanted to pick a fight. You wanted to show me he was as much a monster as you are. You succeeded on all counts beautifully. Now, get out."

"You are throwing me out of my own bedroom?" He looked amused.

"Yeah." I stood up and was only a little wobbly on the high heels.

Jean-Claude sighed. "I am to be relegated forever to my coffin then, to never know the joy of your company for my slumber."

"You don't go to sleep, Jean-Claude. You die. Maybe I lust after your warm, breathing body, but I'm not up to the full package yet."

He smiled. "Very well, *ma petite*. I will leave you and Monsieur Zeeman to discuss the last few minutes. I would ask one thing."

"And that is?" I asked.

"That you not make love in my bed when I cannot join you."

I sighed. "It would be pretty tacky to make love with Richard in your bed. I think you're safe on that one."

Jean-Claude glanced at Richard. His eyes seemed to take in every inch of him, lingering on the open wound at his neck, though maybe that was just my imagination. "If anyone could withstand the temptation, it is you, *ma petite*." Jean-

Claude looked at me, his face unreadable. ''I am sorry you were nearly hurt. I did not mean for that to happen.''

''You always have good intentions,'' I said.

He sighed, then smiled. He glanced at Richard. ''Perhaps I am not the better monster, after all.''

''Get out,'' I said.

He left, still smiling. He closed the door behind him, and I was left with his power dancing over my skin, the feel of his lips and hands on my body. It was only a kiss. Foreplay. But even the rush of adrenaline, of nearly being thrown into a wall, couldn't chase away the aftereffects.

Richard stood staring at me, as if he could sense the power somehow. ''I'll go get the bags,'' he said. He could have said so many things, but that was safest.

He went to get the bags, and I sat down on the bed. Richard could have killed me. Jean-Claude would never have lost control like that. I wanted Richard to embrace his beast, but maybe, just maybe, I didn't understand what that meant.

23

I sat on the edge of the bed, waiting for Richard to come back into the room. My skin was jumping from Jean-Claude's parting gift. Only a kiss, and Richard had nearly torn into Jean-Claude and me. What would Richard have done if he'd caught us doing something truly lascivious? It was better not to find out.

Richard set my suitcase and both bags inside the door. He went out and came back with his small overnight bag.

He stood there, just inside the door, staring at me. I stared back. Blood still trickled down his throat from where I'd cut him. Neither of us seemed to know what to say. The silence grew until it was so thick it began to have weight.

''I'm sorry I hurt you,'' he said. ''I've never lost control like that before.'' He took a step into the room. ''But seeing you with him . . .'' He held out his hands, then let them fall to his sides, helplessly.

''It was only a kiss, Richard. That's all.''

''It's never only a kiss with Jean-Claude.''

I couldn't argue that.

''I wanted to kill him,'' Richard said.

''I noticed.''

''You're sure you're all right?''

''How's your neck?'' I asked.

He touched the wound and came away with fresh blood. ''Silver blade, it won't heal immediately.'' He came to stand in front of me, looking down, so close that the legs of his jeans nearly brushed my knees. It was almost too close. The lingering brush of Jean-Claude's power made my skin ache. Richard's nearness made it worse.

If I stood up, our bodies would touch, he was that close. I stayed sitting, trying to swallow the last bits of Jean-Claude's kiss. I wasn't sure what would happen if I touched Richard now. It felt almost like whatever Jean-Claude had done reacted to Richard's body. Or maybe it was me. Maybe I was becoming that needy. Maybe my body was tired of saying no.

"Would you really have killed me?" Richard asked. "Could you have plunged that blade home?"

I stared up at him and wanted to lie to the sincerity in his eyes, but I didn't. Whatever we were doing with each other, whatever we meant to each other, it couldn't be based on lies. "Yes."

"Just like that," he said.

I nodded. "Just like that."

"I saw it in your eyes. Cold, dispassionate, like someone else was looking out. If I was sure I could kill coldly, it wouldn't scare me so much."

"I wish I could promise you that you wouldn't enjoy it, but I can't."

"I know that." He stared at me. "I couldn't kill you. Not for any reason."

"It would destroy something in me to lose you, Richard, but my first reaction is to protect myself at all costs. So, if we ever have another misunderstanding like we did tonight, don't help me up, don't come close to me, until I'm sure you're not going to eat me. Okay?"

He nodded. "Okay."

The energy rush that Jean-Claude had given me was fading, calming. I stood up, and Richard's body touched mine. I felt an instant rush of warm energy that had nothing to do with the vampire. Richard's aura enveloped me like a breath of warm air. His arms slid behind my back. I slid my hands around his waist and laid my cheek against his chest. I listened to the deep throbbing of his heart, running my hands over the softness of the flannel shirt. There was a measure of comfort in Richard's arms that simply wasn't there when Jean-Claude held me.

He ran his hands through my hair, putting one on either side of my face. He pulled me back until he could see my face. He bent towards me, lips parted. I stretched on tiptoe to meet him.

A voice said, "Master."

Richard turned with me still in his arms, so we could see the door. Jason crawled across the white carpet, dripping crimson drops as he moved.

"My God, what happened to you?" I asked.

"I happened to him," Richard said. He walked over to the crawling man.

"What do you mean, you happened to him?"

Jason abased himself at Richard's feet, face pressed to the carpet. "I'm sorry."

Richard knelt and raised Jason to a sitting position. Blood ran down his face from a cut above his eyes. It was deep and would need stitches.

"You threw him into a wall?" I asked.

"He tried to stop me from reaching you."

"I can't believe you did this."

Richard looked up at me. "You want me to be pack leader. You want me to be alpha. Well, this is what it takes." He shook his head. "You should see your face. You look so damned outraged. How can you want me to kill another human being and be upset by a little rough and tumble?"

I didn't know what to say. "Jean-Claude said that killing Marcus wouldn't be enough. That you'd have to be willing to terrorize the pack to rule it."

"He's right." Richard wiped the blood off Jason's face. The cut was already beginning to close. He put his bloody fingers into his mouth and licked them clean.

I stood there, frozen, staring, like an unwilling witness to a car crash.

Richard bent close to Jason's face. I thought I knew what he was going to do, but I had to see it to believe it. He licked the wound. He ran his tongue over the open wound like a dog will do.

I turned away. This couldn't be my Richard, my safe, comforting Richard.

''You can't stand to watch, can you?'' he asked. ''Did you think that killing was the only thing I had refused to do?''

His voice made me turn back.

There was a smudge of blood on his chin. ''Watch it all, Anita. I want you to see what it takes to be alphic. Then you tell me if it's all worth it. If you can't stomach it, don't ever ask me to do it again.'' The look in his eyes made it a challenge.

I understood challenges. I sat on the edge of the bed. ''Go to it. I'm all yours.''

Richard brushed the hair on one side, exposing the wound on his neck. ''I am alpha and I feed the pack. I spilled your blood, and now I give it back to you.'' The warm rush of his power spilled through the room.

Jason stared up at him, his eyes rolled almost to white. ''Marcus doesn't do this.''

''Because he can't,'' Richard said. ''I can. Feed on my blood, on my apology, my power, and never stand against me again.'' The air was so thick with power it was hard to breathe.

Jason rose on his knees and put his mouth over the wound, tentatively at first, as if afraid he'd be turned away or hurt. When Richard didn't say anything, Jason pressed his mouth to the open wound and drank. His jaw muscles worked, his throat swallowed. One hand slipped behind Richard's back, one hand on his shoulder.

I walked around them until I could see Richard's face. His eyes were closed, his face peaceful. He must have felt me watching him, because he opened his eyes. There was anger there, anger at me, partly. It wasn't only about killing Marcus, it was about giving up pieces of his humanity. I hadn't understood that, not until now.

He touched Jason's shoulders. ''Enough.'' Jason pressed himself harder against the wound, like a nursing puppy. Richard pulled him forcibly off of his neck. A hicky had already spread around the wound.

Jason lay back, half-cradled in Richard's arms. He licked the edges of his mouth, getting the last drops of blood. He giggled and rolled away from Richard, to kneel on the floor. He rubbed his face along Richard's leg. ''I've never felt anything like that. Marcus can't share power like that. Does anybody else in the pack know you can share blood?''

''Tell them,'' Richard said. ''Tell them all.''

''You really are going to kill Marcus, aren't you?'' Jason asked.

''If he gives me no other choice, yes. Now, go, Jason, your other master is waiting.''

Jason stood, and almost fell. He righted himself, rubbing his hands down his legs and arms as if he was bathing in something I couldn't see. Maybe it was the warm, ruffling power that he tried to tie around himself. He laughed again. ''If you'll feed me, you can hit me into a wall anytime.''

''Get out,'' Richard said.

Jason got out.

Richard was still kneeling on the floor. He looked up at me. ''Do you understand now why I didn't want to do this?''

''Yes,'' I said.

''Maybe if Marcus knows I can share blood, my power, he'll back down.''

''You're still hoping not to kill him,'' I said.

''It's not only the killing, Anita. It's everything that goes with it. It's what I just did with Jason. A hundred things, none of them very human.'' He looked at me, and there was a sorrow in his brown eyes that I had never seen before.

I understood suddenly. ''It isn't the killing exactly, is it? Once you take over the pack by blood and brute force, you have to keep the pack with blood and brute force.''

''Exactly. If I could force Marcus out somehow, if I could make him back down, then I'd have room to do things differently.'' He came to stand in front of me, his face eager. ''I've brought nearly half the pack either to my side or at least to be neutral. They aren't backing Marcus anymore. No one's ever divided a pack like this without deaths.''

''Why can't you split into two packs?''

He shook his head. ''Marcus would never allow it. The pack leader gets a tithe from every member. It would cut not just his power but his money.''

''You getting money now?'' I asked.

''Everyone's still tithing to Marcus. I don't want the money, and it's just one more fight. I think tithing should be abolished.''

I watched the light in his face, the plans, the dreams. He was building a power base of fairness and boy scout virtues with creatures that could rip out your throat and eat you afterwards. He believed he could do it. Watching his handsome, eager face, I almost believed it, too.

''I thought you could kill Marcus and that would be it. But it won't be, will it?''

''Raina will see to it that I'm challenged. Unless I put the fear of *me* into them.''

''As long as Raina is alive, she'll be trouble.''

''I don't know what to do about Raina.''

''I could kill her,'' I said.

The look on his face was enough.

''Just kidding,'' I said. Sort of. Richard wouldn't agree with the ultimate practicality, but if he was going to be safe, Raina had to die. Cold-blooded, but true.

''What are you thinking, Anita?''

''That maybe you're right and the rest of us are wrong.''

''About what?''

''Maybe you shouldn't kill Marcus.''

Richard's eyes widened. ''I thought you were angry with me for *not* killing Marcus.''

"It's not killing Marcus. It's endangering everybody by not killing Marcus."

He shook his head. "I don't see the difference."

"The difference is that killing is a means to an end, not an end in itself. I want you alive. Marcus gone. The pack members that follow you safe. I don't want you to have to torture the pack to keep your place. If we can accomplish all that without you having to kill anyone, I'm okay with that. I don't think there's an option that doesn't involve killing. But if you can come up with one, I'll support you."

He studied my face. "Are you telling me that you think I shouldn't kill now?"

"Yeah."

He laughed, but it was with more irony than humor. "I don't know whether to yell at you or hug you."

"I affect a lot of people that way," I said. "Look, when we went to rescue Stephen, you should have called a few people. Gone into the situation from a position of strength, with three or four lieutenants at your back. There is a compromise between playing Sir Lancelot and being Vlad the Impaler."

He sat down on the edge of the bed. "Being able to feed power through my blood is a rare talent. It's impressive, but it won't be enough. I'd have to have some major scary stuff to get Marcus and Raina to back down. I'm powerful, Anita, really powerful." He said it like it was simply the truth, no ego, no pride. "But it's not that kind of powerful."

I sat down beside him. "I'll do anything I can, Richard. Just promise me you won't be careless."

He smiled, but it didn't reach his eyes. "I won't be careless if you'll kiss me."

We kissed. The taste of him was warm and sure, but underneath it was the sweet salt of blood, and Jason's aftershave. I drew away from him.

"What's wrong?"

I shook my head. Telling him I could taste other people's blood in his mouth was not going to be helpful. We were going to work so he didn't have to do things like that. It wasn't his beast that would steal his humanity, it was a thousand smaller things.

"Change for me," I said.

"What?"

"Change for me, here, now."

He stared at me, as if trying to read something in my face. "Why now?"

"Let me see all of you, Richard, the whole package."

"If you don't want Jean-Claude sharing the bed, you don't want a wolf in bed with you, either."

"You wouldn't you be trapped in wolf form until morning, you said so earlier."

"No, I wouldn't," he said softly.

"If you change tonight, and I can accept it, we can make love. We can start planning the wedding."

He laughed. "Can I kill Marcus before I have to kill Jean-Claude?"

"Jean-Claude promised not to hurt you," I said.

Richard went very still. "You've already talked to him about this?"

I nodded.

''Why wasn't he angry with me?''

''He said he'd step aside if he couldn't win me, so he's stepping aside.'' I didn't add the part about Jean-Claude loving me. Save it for later.

''Call your beast, Richard.''

He shook his head. ''It isn't just my beast, Anita. It's the lukoi, the pack. You have to see them, too.''

''I've seen them.''

He shook his head. ''You haven't seen us at the lupanar. Our place of power. We're real there, no pretense, not even to ourselves.''

''I've just told you that I want to marry you. Did you pick up on that?'' I asked.

Richard stood. ''I want to marry you, Anita, more than almost anything in the world. I want you so badly my body aches with it. I don't trust myself to be here tonight.''

''We've managed to stay chaste so far,'' I said.

''By the skin of our teeth.'' He picked up his overnight case. ''The lukoi call sex the killing dance.''

''So?''

''We use the same phrase for battles of succession.''

''I still don't understand the problem.''

He stared at me. ''You will. God help us both. You will.''

There was something so sad, so wistful about him suddenly, that I didn't want to let him go. Tomorrow he'd face Marcus, and just because he'd agreed to kill didn't mean he could. When the moment came, I didn't trust him not to flinch. I didn't want to lose him.

''Stay with me, Richard. Please.''

''It wouldn't be fair to you.''

''Don't be such a frigging boy scout.''

He smiled and gave a very bad Popeye imitation, ''I am what I am.'' He closed the door behind him. I didn't even get to kiss him good-bye.

24

I woke to darkness and someone bending over me. I couldn't really see, but I felt something in the air above me like a weight. My hand slid under the pillow and came out with the Firestar. I shoved the gun into whoever it was, and they were gone like a dream. I slid off the bed, pressing my back against the wall, making myself as small a target as possible.

A voice came out of the darkness. I aimed for it, straining my ears for sounds of more intruders.

"It's Cassandra. The light switch is above you. I'll stay right here while you turn on the lights." Her voice was low, even, the sort of voice you used for crazy people, or people who had guns pointed at you.

I swallowed past my pulse and scooted my back up the wall. I swiped my left hand up the wall until it hit the switch plate, then I knelt back down, fingers touching the switch. When I was as far down as I could get and still turn on the light, I hit it. Light flared. There was a moment of dazzling blindness while I hunkered on the floor, gun pointed blindly. When I could see, Cassandra stood near the foot of the bed, hands out to either side, staring at me. Her eyes were a little too wide. The lace on her Victorian nightgown fluttered with her breath.

Yes, Victorian nightgown. She looked delicate, doll-like. I'd asked her last night if Jean-Claude picked out the gown. No, she'd picked it out. Each to their own.

She stood on the carpet, frozen, staring. "Anita, are you all right?" Her tone said she didn't think so.

I took a deep breath and pointed the gun at the ceiling. "Yeah, I'm all right."

"Can I move?"

I stood, holding the gun at my side. "Don't try to touch me when I'm in a sound sleep. Say something first."

"I'll remember that," she said. "May I move?"

"Sure. What's up?" I asked.

"Richard and Jean-Claude are outside."

I checked my watch. It was one o'clock in the afternoon. I'd had nearly six hours of sleep. Or would have had if Cassandra and I hadn't talked for an hour. I hadn't had a sleep-over in years, and frankly, girl or no, she was still a lycanthrope that I'd met only that night. It felt strange to trust her at my back as my bodyguard. I've never been too fond of sleeping with strangers. It's not sexual. It's plain suspicion. Being deeply asleep is as helpless as most of us get.

''What do they want?''

''Richard said he has a plan.''

I didn't need to ask what plan. There was only one thing on his mind the day of the full moon: Marcus.

''Tell them I'm getting dressed first.'' I went for my suitcase. Cassandra padded to the door. She opened it only a crack, speaking softly. She closed it firmly behind her and came back to me. She looked puzzled. In the nightgown with a puzzled frown on her face, she looked about twelve.

I knelt by the suitcase, clothes in my hands, looking up at her. ''What now?''

''Jean-Claude said not to bother getting dressed.''

I stared at her for a heartbeat. ''Yeah, right. I'm getting dressed. They can just bloody well wait that long.''

She nodded and went back to the door.

I went for the bathroom. I stared at myself in the mirror. I looked as tired as I felt. I brushed teeth, took care of necessities, and wished for a shower. It would have helped wake me up. I could have run a bath, but I wasn't sure the boys would last that long. Besides, a bath was something I did to get ready for bed, not for waking up. I needed something stimulating, not something soothing.

Richard had a plan, but Jean-Claude was with him. That meant that the vampire had helped come up with the plan. It was a scary thought.

Tonight Richard would fight Marcus. He could be dead by tomorrow. The thought made my chest tight. There was a pressure behind my eyes that had more to do with tears than anything else. I could live with Richard off somewhere. It would hurt if he wasn't with me, but I'd survive. I might not survive his death. I loved Richard. I really loved him. I didn't want to give him up. Not for anything.

Jean-Claude was being a perfect gentleman, but I didn't trust it. How could I? He always had a dozen different reasons for everything he did. What was the plan? The quicker I dressed, the quicker I'd find out.

I'd pretty much just grabbed stuff out of the suitcase. You can mix and match almost all the clothing I own. Dark blue jeans, navy blue polo shirt, white jogging socks. I hadn't dressed to impress anyone. Now that I was a little more awake, I wished I'd chosen something a little less practical. Love makes you worry about stuff like that.

I opened the door. Richard stood by the bed. The sight of him stopped me in my tracks. His hair was brushed until it fell like a frothy mass around his shoulders. He was wearing nothing but a pair of silky undershorts, royal purple. They were slit high on each side, giving glimpses of his thighs as he turned towards me.

When I could close my mouth and talk, I said, ''Why are you dressed like that?''

Jean-Claude leaned one shoulder against the wall. He was wearing a black ankle-length robe edged with black fur. His hair mingled with the fur collar until it was hard to tell where one blackness ended and the other began. His pale neck and a triangle of his chest showed almost perfectly white against the fur.

''You look like you've just stepped out of two different porno movies. Cassandra said something about a plan. What's the plan?''

Richard glanced at Jean-Claude. They exchanged a look between them that said better than words that they'd been plotting behind my back.

Richard sat on the edge of the bed. The shorts clung a little too close for comfort and I had to look away, so I looked at Jean-Claude. Not comforting, but at least most of him was covered.

''Do you remember some months ago, before Christmas, when we accidently set off some sort of magical energy in your apartment?'' Jean-Claude asked.

''I remember,'' I said.

''Monsieur Zeeman and I believe that the three of us could share power, become a triumvirate.''

I looked from one to the other. ''Explain.''

''There is a link between myself and wolves. There is a link between you, my little necromancer, and the dead. Lust and love have always held a magical energy. I can show you individual spells that can use the link between vampire and their animal, between necromancer and vampire. We should not be surprised that there is power between us.''

''Make your point,'' I said.

Jean-Claude smiled. ''I believe we could call up enough power to back down a certain Ulfric. I know Marcus. He will not fight if he believes he has no hope of winning.''

''Jean-Claude's right,'' Richard said. ''If I can shine with enough power, Marcus will back down.''

''How do you know we can even call this whatever-it-is up again?'' I asked.

''I have done some research,'' Jean-Claude said. ''There are two cases of master vampires who could call animals, who then made one of those animals in were-form a sort of human servant.''

''So?''

''It means that there is a chance of my being able to bind you both.''

I shook my head. ''No way, no vampire marks. Been there, done that, didn't like it.''

''There were no marks on either of you in December,'' Jean-Claude said. ''I think it will work without any now.''

''Why are the two of you dressed like that?''

Richard looked embarrassed. ''It was all I brought. I thought we were going to be sharing the bed last night.''

I motioned at the shorts. ''Those would not have helped us stay chaste, Richard.''

Heat crept up his face. ''I know; sorry.''

''Tell me there is no lingerie in your suitcase, *ma petite*.''

''I never said there wasn't.'' Ronnie had talked me into an outfit just in case I gave in to Richard. She was willing for me to bed him before the wedding if it would knock Jean-Claude out of the running.

''Who'd you buy it for?'' Richard asked quietly.

''You, but don't distract me. Why the nice jammies?''

''Richard and I have made an attempt or two on our own to call the power. It does not work with only the two of us. His dislike of me has rendered it useless.''

''Is this true, Richard?''

He nodded. ''Jean-Claude says we need our third; we need you.''

''What's with the clothes?''

''Lust and anger were what drew the power the first time, *ma petite*. We have our anger. We are missing our lust.''

''Wait just a damn minute.'' I stared from one to the other of them. ''Are you saying we become a ménage à trois?''

''No,'' Richard said. He stood up. He walked towards me in his little shorts, flashing the room. ''No sex, I promise you that. Even for this, I wouldn't have agreed to sharing you with him.''

I ran my fingertips down the silk of his shorts, lightly, almost like I was afraid. ''Then why the costumes?''

''We're running out of time, Anita. If this is going to work, it's got to work fast.'' He gripped my arms, his hands warm on my skin. ''You said you'd help me with a plan. This is the plan.''

I drew away from him slowly and turned to Jean-Claude. ''And what do you get out of it?''

''Your happiness. No wolf will challenge Richard if we are a true triumvirate.''

''My happiness, right.'' I studied his calm, lovely face, and had an idea. ''You tasted Jason, didn't you? You tasted the power that he sucked off of Richard, didn't you? Didn't you, you son of a bitch?'' I walked towards him as I talked, fighting an urge to hit him when I got there.

''What of it, *ma petite*?''

I stood right in front of him, throwing the words into his face. ''What do you gain from all this? And don't give me crap about my happiness. I've known you too long.''

His face was at its mildest, its most disarming. ''I would gain enough power that no master vampire, short of the council itself, would dare challenge me.''

''I knew it. I knew it. You don't do anything without a dozen ulterior motives.''

''I benefit in exactly the same way Monsier Zeeman benefits. We would both secure our power bases.''

''Fine, what do I get out of it?''

''Why, Monsieur Zeeman's safety.''

''Anita,'' Richard said softly. He touched my shoulder.

I whirled to face him. My angry words died at the look on his face. So serious, so solemn.

He gripped my shoulders, one hand cupping the side of my face. ''You don't have to do this if you don't want to.''

''Do you understand what he's suggesting, Richard? We would never be free of him.'' I touched his hand where he held my face. ''Don't tie us to him like this, Richard. Once he gets a piece of you, he never lets go.''

''If you really believed he was evil, you would have killed him a long time ago and been free of him.''

If I didn't do this, and Richard died tonight, would I be able to live with it? I leaned into him, pressing my face against his chest, breathing in his scent. No. If he died and I could have saved him, I'd never be rid of the guilt.

Jean-Claude came to stand near us. ''It may have been one of those freakish accidents that cannot be duplicated under controlled conditions, *ma petite*. Magic is often like that.''

I turned my face and looked at him, cheek still pressed to Richard's bare chest, his arms wrapped around my back. ''No vampire marks on either of us, right?''

''I promise. The only thing I would ask is that none of us back away. We need a true idea of how much power we can call. If it is not much, then it is moot, but if it is as I believe, then it will solve a great many problems.''

''You manipulative bastard.''

''Is that a yes?'' he asked.

''Yes,'' I said.

Richard hugged me. I let his arms hold me, comfort me, but it was Jean-Claude's eyes I met. There was a look on his face that was hard to describe. The devil must look like that after you've signed on the dotted line and given away your soul. Pleased, eager, and a little hungry.

25

"You and Monsieur Zeeman have a nice visit. I will take my turn in the bathroom, then join you."

Just hearing him say it out loud made me want to refuse. But I didn't. "Are you sure this isn't just your elaborate way of forming us into a ménage à trois?"

"Would I be so devious?"

"Yeah."

He laughed, and the sound shivered over my skin like an ice cube dropped down my spine.

"I will leave you two alone." He brushed past us into the bathroom.

I stalked after him and caught the door before it could close. He looked at me through the opening. "Yes, *ma petite*?"

"There better be something under that robe besides skin."

He smiled wide enough to show just a hint of fang. "Would I be so crude, *ma petite*?"

"I don't know."

He nodded and closed the door.

I took a deep breath and turned to face the other man in my life. Richard's clothes lay folded on my suitcase. He moved towards me. The shorts were slit high enough that I could see almost a clear line from foot to waist.

If we were truly alone, I would have gone to him. What should have been romantic was suddenly chokingly awkward. I was very aware of the sounds of running water from the bathroom. Jean-Claude planned to join us. Sweet Jesus.

Richard still looked scrumptious with his hair falling across one eye. He had stopped moving closer. He finally shook his head. "Why is this suddenly so awkward?"

"I think the biggest reason is in the bathroom getting ready to join us."

He laughed and shook his head again. "It doesn't usually take us this long to be in each other's arms."

"No," I said. At this rate, we were going to be staring at each other like high school kids at a dance when Jean-Claude came back out.

"Meet me halfway," I said.

Richard smiled. "Always." He walked to meet me. The muscles in his stomach rippled as he moved.

I was suddenly sorry that I was wearing jeans and a polo shirt. I wanted him to see me in the lingerie I'd bought. I wanted his hands to run over the silk and my body underneath.

Richard and I stopped inches away from each other, neither one touching. I could smell his aftershave faintly. I was close enough to feel the warmth of his body. I wanted to run my hands over his bare chest. I wanted to run my hands down the front of those silk shorts. The thought was so real I crossed my arms to keep my hands busy.

Richard leaned over me. He ran his lips over my eyebrows, kissed my eyelids ever so gently. He reached my mouth, and I rose on tiptoe to meet him. He slid his arms around me.

I fell against him, my hands searching his body, my mouth pressing against his. He bent and slid his arms under my butt, lifting me until our faces were even. I broke the kiss and started to say, "Put me down," but staring at his face from an inch away, I couldn't say it. I wrapped my legs around his waist. He braced his legs to catch his balance. I kissed him, and the first brush of power broke over me in a line of skin-prickling, belly-tickling warmth.

Richard made a small sound in his throat that was more growl than moan. He knelt on the floor with me still riding him, and when he took me to the floor, I didn't stop him. He raised his upper body over me, bracing with his arms, his lower body pressed against me. When he stared down at me, his eyes had gone wolfish. Something must have shown on my face because he turned his head so I wouldn't see.

I raised up underneath him, grabbed a handful of his thick hair, and turned his head back to me none too gently. Whether it was the pain or something else, he turned back with a snarl. I didn't flinch. I didn't look away.

Richard lowered his face towards mine, and I lay back on the floor. His mouth hovered over mine. There was a brush of warmth as our mouths met, as if I was tasting his energy, his essence.

The bathroom door opened. The sound froze me, making my eyes slide towards the open door. Richard hesitated for a second, mouth uncertain above mine, then he kissed the edge of my chin, running his lips down my neck.

Jean-Claude stood in the doorway, dressed in black silk pajamas. The long-sleeved top was unbuttoned so that it fanned around his naked upper body as he moved. The look on his face, in his eyes, panicked me.

I patted Richard's shoulder. He'd worked his way to the base of my neck and was nuzzling the collar of my polo shirt, as if he'd put his face inside the shirt. He raised those startling amber wolf eyes to me, and the only thing I could read on his face was desire, almost a hunger. His power breathed along my skin like a line of hot wind.

My pulse thudded against the skin of my throat until I thought it would burst the skin. "What's wrong with you, Richard?"

"Tonight is the full moon, *ma petite*. His beast calls to him." Jean-Claude padded across the carpet towards us.

"Let me up, Richard."

Richard went to his hands and knees, leaving me to squirm out from under him. I stood, and he knelt in front of me, wrapping his arms around my waist. "Don't be afraid."

"I'm not afraid of you, Richard." I stared at Jean-Claude.

Richard ran his hands down my ribs, fingers digging into the flesh as if he were massaging my back. It brought my attention back to him. "I would never hurt you willingly. You know that."

I did know that. I nodded.

"Trust me now." His voice was soft and deep, with a roll of bass to it that wasn't normal. He started pulling my shirt out of my pants. "I want to touch you, smell you, taste you."

Jean-Claude padded around us, not coming any closer. He circled us like a shark. His midnight blue eyes were still human, more human looking than Richard's.

Richard raised my shirt free of my pants, pushing it back until he exposed my stomach. He ran his hands over my bare skin and I shuddered, but it wasn't sex, or not only sex. That warm, electric power of his flowed from his hands across my skin. It was like having a low-level current tracing over me. It didn't quite hurt, but it might if it didn't stop. Or it might feel very good, better than anything else. I wasn't sure which thought scared me more.

Jean-Claude stood just out of reach, watching. That thought scared me, too.

Richard put his hands on either side of my exposed waist, holding the shirt up, draped over his wrists.

Jean-Claude took that last step, pale hand outstretched. I tightened up, fear overriding the remains of desire. He let his hand fall back without touching us.

Richard licked my stomach, a quick, wet motion. I stared down at him, and he stared back with brown eyes. Human eyes. "I won't let anything happen to you, Anita."

I didn't know what it had cost him to swallow his beast back down inside, but I knew it hadn't been easy. There were many lesser lycanthropes who could not go back once they started to change. It would have been more reassuring if his true brown eyes hadn't held a darkness all their own. But it wasn't his beast, it was something more basic, more human: sex. Even lust doesn't cover that look in a man's eyes.

Jean-Claude was standing behind me. I could feel him. Without touching me at all, I could feel his power, like a cool, seeking wind. He brushed his face against my hair. My heart was beating so loudly I couldn't hear anything but the thundering of my own blood in my head.

Jean-Claude brushed my hair to one side. His lips touched my cheek and his power burst over me in a quiet rush, cool as a wind from the grave. It flowed through me, seeking Richard's warmth. The two energies hit, mingled inside me. I couldn't breathe. I felt that thing inside me that could call the dead from the grave—magic, for lack of a better word—I felt it coil and flare against them both.

I tried to pull away from Richard, but his fingers dug into my ribs. Jean-Claude's arms tightened around my shoulders. ''Build the power, do not fight it, *ma petite*.''

I fought the panic, my breath coming in quick gasps. I was going to hyperventilate and pass out if I couldn't get a handle on it. I rode the power and my own fear, and I was losing.

Richard's mouth bit gently at my stomach. His mouth sucking my skin. Jean-Claude's lips touched my neck, nibbling gently. His arms cradled me against his chest. Richard was a growing warmth at my waist. Jean-Claude like some cool fire at my back. I was being eaten from both ends like a piece of wood going up in flames. The power was too much. It had to go somewhere. I had to do something with it or it was going to burn me alive.

My legs buckled, and only Richard's and Jean-Claude's hands on me kept me from falling. They lowered me to the floor, still cradled in their arms. My shoulder touched the ground, then my hand, and I knew what I could do with the power. I felt it surge through the ground, seeking, seeking the dead. I rolled onto my stomach. Jean-Claude's hands were on my shoulders, his face brushing mine. Richard's hands were under my shirt touching my back, roaming higher, but it was all secondary. I had to do something with the power.

I found the dead I needed, and it didn't work. The power continued to build until I would have screamed if I could have gotten enough air. A step, an ingredient, something was missing.

I rolled onto my back, staring up at both of them. They stared down at me. Jean-Claude's eyes had gone solid, midnight blue. They both leaned towards me at once. Richard went for my mouth, Jean-Claude went for my neck. Richard's kiss was almost a burning. I could feel the brush of fangs as Jean-Claude fought not to bite me. Temptation was everywhere. Someone's hand was under my shirt, and I wasn't sure whose it was anymore. Then I realized it was both of them.

What was one thing I needed for raising the dead? Blood. I must have said it out loud: ''Blood.''

Jean-Claude raised up, staring at me from inches away. His hand was just below my breast. I'd grabbed his wrist without thinking about it. ''What, *ma petite*?''

''Blood to finish it. We need blood.''

Richard raised his face up like a drowning man. ''What?''

''I can give you blood, *ma petite*.'' Jean-Claude leaned into me. I stopped him with a hand on his chest, at the same time that Richard put a hand on his shoulder. The power poured over us in a searing wash, and I was seeing white spots.

''You won't use me to sink fangs into her for the first time,'' Richard growled it at him. His anger fed the magic and I screamed.

''Give me blood, or get off me.'' I held up my own wrist between them. ''I don't have a knife, someone do it.''

Richard leaned over me. He swept his hair back from one side of his neck. ''Here's your blood.''

Jean-Claude didn't argue. He leaned into him, lips drawn back. I watched in a sort of slow motion as he bit the side of Richard's neck. Richard tensed, a hiss of breath as the fangs sank home. Jean-Claude's mouth sealed over his skin, sucking, throat working.

The power roared through me, raising every hair on my body, creeping through my skin until I thought I'd come apart. I sent it all outward to the dead that I'd found. I filled them up and still there was too much power. I reached outward, outward, and found what I was looking for. The power left us in a cool, burning, rush.

I lay gasping on the floor. Jean-Claude lay on my left, propped on one elbow. Blood stained his lips, trickling down his chin. Richard lay on his stomach to my right, pinning my arm underneath his cheek. His chest rose and fell in great gasps, sweat glistening along his spine.

The world was gold-edged, almost floating. Sound returned slowly, and it was like I was listening down a long tube.

Jean-Claude licked the blood from his lips, wiping a shaking hand across his chin, licking the hand clean. He lay down beside me, one hand across my stomach, his head cradled on my shoulder. His bare chest and stomach lay across my arm. His skin was almost hot, feverish. He'd never felt like that before. His heart pounded against my skin like a captive bird.

His hair fell against my face. It smelled of some exotic shampoo and of him. He gave a shaky laugh and said, "It was glorious for me, was it good for you, *ma petite*?"

I swallowed, and was too tired to even laugh. "Trust you to know just what to say."

Richard raised himself up on his elbows. Blood trickled down his neck where two neat fang marks showed. I touched the bite mark, and my fingers came away stained crimson.

"Does it hurt?" I asked.

"Not really." He grabbed my wrist, gently, licking the blood off my fingers, sucking them clean.

Jean-Claude's strangely warm hand caressed my stomach under my shirt. He undid the button of my pants.

"Don't even think it," I said.

"Too late, *ma petite*." He bent and kissed me. I could taste the metallic sweetness of Richard's blood on his tongue. I rose up to meet him, pushing at his mouth. I'd asked for the blood, not either of them. The truth was, we weren't done with the bloodletting today. Whatever I'd called from the grave had to be put back. That would take blood, fresh blood. The only question was who would donate it and how would it be gathered. Oh, one more question, how much blood would we need?

26

Jean-Claude's fingertips slid along the edge of my pants. Richard grabbed his wrist. Anger flared from both of them, and that shared power flickered to life.

"You won't use this as an excuse to get into her pants, either," Richard said. His voice was thick and dark with more than anger. His hand tightened on Jean-Claude's wrist.

Jean-Claude balled his hand into a fist and bent his arm at the elbow. Concentration and anger touched both their faces. I could feel the trembling effort through their chests. Their anger prickled along my skin. It was too soon to do all this shit over again. "You can arm-wrestle later, boys, we've got to go see what I raised from the dead."

There was a fraction of hesitation, then they both looked down at me. Their arms were still straining against each other. Richard's face showed the effort. Jean-Claude's face had gone blank and curious, as if it was no effort to hold off a werewolf. But I could feel the fine trembling through his body. Illusion was all with Jean-Claude. With Richard it was all nerve endings and reality.

"What did you say, *ma petite*?"

"She said she raised the dead," Richard said.

"Yep, so get off me. You can fight later, but right now, we need to check on what I did."

"*We* did," Jean-Claude said. He eased away from Richard, and after a second, Richard released his hand.

"What we did," I said.

Richard stood, the muscles in his bare legs moving under the skin, and it was hard not to touch them, feel the movement of him. He offered me a hand up.

"Give me a minute," I said.

Jean-Claude stood as if drawn to his feet by strings. He offered me a hand, too.

They stood glaring at each other. Their anger played through the air like invisible sparks. I shook my head. I seemed to be more worse for wear than either of them, poor human that I was. I'd have actually taken a hand up, which was rare for me. I sighed, got my feet under me, and stood without help from either of them.

''Behave yourselves,'' I said. ''Can't you feel what's in the air? Anger works just fine to call whatever it is, so stop it. We may have to do it again to lay to rest what we've already called from the grave.''

Jean-Claude looked instantly relaxed, at ease. He gave a low bow. ''As you like, *ma petite*.''

Richard rotated his neck, trying to loosen his shoulders. His hands were still balled into fists, but he nodded. ''I don't understand how what we did called zombies.''

''I can act as a focus for other animators. It's a way to combine powers and raise an older zombie or more than one or two zombies. I don't know how to do anything else but raise the dead, so when you shoved that much power in my face . . .'' I shrugged. ''I did what I know how to do.''

''Did you raise all of Nikoloas's old cemetery?'' Jean-Claude asked.

''If we're lucky,'' I said.

He put his head to one side, puzzled.

Richard looked down at himself. ''Can I get some pants on?''

I smiled. ''Seems a shame,'' I said, ''but yeah.''

''I will fetch my robe from the bathroom,'' Jean-Claude said.

''Help yourself,'' I said.

''No comment about how it is a shame that I am getting dressed?''

I shook my head.

''Cruel, *ma petite*, very cruel.''

I smiled and gave him a little bow.

He returned the smile, but there was a challenge to his eyes as he walked towards the bathroom.

Richard was sliding into his jeans. I watched him zip them up and button them into place. It was fun just to watch him dress. Love makes the smallest movements fascinating.

I walked past him, towards the door, leaving him to put a shirt on if he was going to. The only way to ignore him was to just not look. The same theory worked with Jean-Claude most of the time.

I walked to the door. My hand was reaching for the knob when Richard grabbed me from behind, lifting me off my feet, carrying me back from the door.

My feet were literally dangling off the ground. ''What the hell are you doing? Put me down.''

''My wolves are coming,'' he said, as if that explained everything.

''Put me down.''

He lowered me enough for my feet to touch the floor, but his arms stayed wrapped around me, as if he was afraid I'd go for the door. His face was distant, listening. I heard nothing.

A howl echoed up the corridor and raised the hairs on my arms. ''What's going on, Richard?''

''Danger,'' he almost whispered it.

''Is it Raina and Marcus?''

He was still listening to things I could not hear. He pushed me behind him and went to the door, still shirtless, wearing nothing but his jeans.

I ran for the bed and the weapons. I got the Firestar out from under the pillow. ''Don't go out there empty-handed, dammit.'' I dragged the Uzi out from under the bed.

A chorus of howls went up. Richard flung the door open and raced down the hallway. I called his name, but he was gone.

Jean-Claude came out of the bathroom in his black, fur-lined robe. ''What is it, *ma petite*?''

''Company.'' I slipped the Uzi's strap across my chest.

The sounds of snarling wolves came distant. Jean-Claude ran past me, the long robe flying out behind him. He ran like a dark wind. When I got out to the corridor, he was nowhere in sight.

I was going to be the last one there. Dammit.

27

Running full tilt towards a fight was not the best way to stay alive. Caution was better. I knew that, and it didn't matter. Nothing mattered but getting there in time. In time to save them. *Them.* I didn't dwell on that; I ran, the Firestar gripped tightly in my right hand, the Uzi in my left. I was running like an idiot, but at least I was armed.

A roaring shout thundered off the walls ahead. Don't ask me how, but I knew it was Richard. I didn't think I could run any faster. I was wrong. I spilled into the open, breath coming in throat-closing gasps, not looking left or right. If someone had had a gun, they could have blown me away.

Richard stood in the middle of the room, a zombie held at arm's length above his head. A wolf the size of a pony had pinned another zombie to the floor, savaging it. Stephen stood at Richard's back in human form, but crouched and ready to fight. Cassandra stood back from them. She turned to me as I skidded into the room. There was a look on her face that I couldn't quite read, and didn't have time to puzzle over.

Jean-Claude was at the far left, away from the werewolves. He was staring at me, too. I couldn't read his face, but he was in no danger. He hadn't waded into the zombies. He knew better. Richard didn't.

The room had been a narrow rectangle, but the far wall had blasted outward, scattering rubble across the floor. It looked like the zombies had crawled out from behind the wall. A graveyard that I, at least, hadn't known was there.

The dead stood in front of the ruins. Their eyes shifted to me as I saw them, and I felt the weight of their gaze like a blow to my heart.

The fear for everyone's safety was gone, washed away in a rush of anger. ''Richard, put it down, please, it won't hurt you. Call Jason off the other one.'' It had to be Jason unless there was another werewolf down here. And if it was someone else, where was Jason?

Richard turned his head to look at me, the zombie, once a human male, still held effortlessly above his head. ''They attacked Jason.''

''They wouldn't have done anything without orders. Jason jumped the gun.''

"They didn't attack us," Cassandra said. "They started pouring out of the wall. Jason changed and attacked them."

The giant wolf had opened the zombie's stomach and was tearing at intestines. I'd had enough. "Grab the wolf," I said. The zombie under him locked its arms around the wolf's forequarters. The wolf sank teeth into the corpse's throat and tore it out in a spurt of dark fluid and flesh.

The rest of the zombies, somewhere between sixty and eighty, surged toward the wolf. "Let him up, Jason, or I'll show you what it's like to be attacked by zombies."

Richard bent his elbow and tossed the zombie away from him. The body tumbled through the air and landed in the mass of waiting zombies. They fell like bowling pins, except that these bowling pins got to their feet, though one lost an arm in the process.

Richard crouched by his wolves. "You're attacking us?" He sounded outraged.

"Pull your wolf off my zombie and it stops here."

"You think you can take us?" Cassandra said.

"With this many dead, I know I can," I said.

Stephen's face crumpled, almost like he'd cry. "You'd hurt us."

Shit, I'd forgotten. I was their lupa now. I'd threatened to kill Raina if she hurt Stephen again, and here I was about to feed him to zombies. There was a logic gap somewhere.

"If I'm supposed to protect you all, then you have to obey me, right? So Jason gets the fuck off my zombie or I beat the hell out of him. Isn't that pack protocol?"

Richard turned to me. There was a look on his face I'd never seen before: anger and arrogance, or something close to it. "I don't think Jason really expected you to demand his obedience. I don't think any of us did."

"Then you don't know me very well," I said.

"*Mes amies*, if we kill each other, won't Marcus be pleased."

We all turned to Jean-Claude. I said, "Stop." All the zombies stopped at once like a freeze frame. One tumbled to the floor, caught in midshuffle, rather than take that last partial step. Zombies were terribly literal.

The giant wolf tore another piece out of the zombie. The dead man made a small involuntary cry. "Drag Jason off of it now, or we are going to do this dance. Fuck Marcus. I'll worry about it later."

"Off of him, Jason, now," Richard said.

The wolf reared back, tearing at the zombie's arm. Bone cracked. The wolf worried the arm like a terrier with a bone. Blood and thicker fluids flew in a spray.

Richard grabbed the wolf by the scruff of the neck, jerking it off its feet. He grabbed the front of its furry throat and turned it to face him. The muscles in his arms corded with the effort. The wolf's claws scrambled in the air while it strangled. The massive claws raked Richard's bare skin. Blood flowed in thin crimson lines.

He threw the wolf across the room into the waiting dead. "Never disobey me again, Jason, never!" His voice was lost in a growling that turned into a howl. He threw back his head and bayed. The sound rose from his human throat. Cassandra and Stephen echoed him. Their howls filled the room with a strange, ringing song.

I realized then that Richard might avoid killing Marcus, but he'd never control the lukoi without brutality. He was already casual about it. Almost as casual as Jean-Claude. Bad sign or good sign? I wasn't sure.

Jason scrambled out of the dead. He turned pale green wolf eyes to me, as if waiting for something. "Don't look at me," I said, "I'm pissed with you, too."

Jason stalked towards me on paws bigger across than my hands. The fur at his neck rose in a prickling brush. His lips curled back from his teeth in a silent growl.

I pointed the Firestar at him. "Don't do it, Jason."

He kept coming, each step so stiff and full of tension that it looked robotic. He gathered his body, legs squirming into position for a leap. I wasn't going to let him finish the movement. If he'd been in human form, I'd have aimed to wound, but in wolf form, I wasn't taking any chances. One scratch and I'd be alpha female for real.

I sighted down the barrel and felt that quietness fill me. I felt nothing while I stared down the gun at him. Nothing but a cool, white emptiness.

"Stop it, both of you!" Richard growled. He walked towards us. I kept my eyes on the wolf but had a peripheral sense of Richard moving closer.

He kept coming, easing himself between Jason and me. I had to aim the gun skyward to keep from pointing it at his chest. He stared at me, his face thoughtful. "You won't need the gun." He knocked the great wolf to the floor with his fist. The wolf lay stunned. Only the rise and fall of its chest showed it was still alive.

When he turned back to me, his eyes were amber, and no longer human. "You are my lupa, Anita, but I am still Ulfric. I won't let you do to me what Raina has done to Marcus. I lead this pack." There was a hardness to his voice that was new. I'd discovered his male ego at last.

Jean-Claude laughed, a high, delighted sound that made me shiver. Richard hugged his bare arms as if he felt it, too.

"Don't you realize by now, Richard, that *ma petite* is either your equal or your master? She knows no other way to be." He came to stand by us. He looked amused as hell.

"I want her to be my equal," Richard said.

"But not within the pack," Jean-Claude said.

Richard shook his head. "No, I mean . . . No, Anita is my equal."

"Then what are you bitching about?" I said.

He glared at me with his alien eyes. "I am Ulfric, not you."

"Lead, and I'll follow, Richard." I stepped close to him, almost touching. "But lead, Richard, really lead, or get out of the way."

28

''*As amusing as* this is,'' Jean-Claude said, ''and believe me, *ma petite*, Richard, it is amusing. We do not have time for this particular argument, not if Richard stands any hope of not being forced to kill tonight.''

We both glared at him, and he gave that graceful shrug that meant everything and nothing. ''We must call the magic again, but this time, Richard needs to try and pull some of it into himself. He needs to do something that would impress his pack. This,'' he motioned to the zombies, ''though impressive, looks too much like Anita's work.''

''You've got a suggestion, I take it.''

''Perhaps,'' he said. His eyes turned very serious then, the humor dying away until his face was lovely and blank. ''But first, I think I have a question or two for you, myself, *ma petite*. I think it is not only Richard that you are emasculating today.''

''What are you talking about?'' I asked.

He cocked his head to one side. ''Perhaps you honestly do not know?'' He sounded surprised. ''There is a small hallway to the right. Look inside it.''

I could see the archway at the top of the hall, but the zombies filled the space, hiding the rest from view. ''Move forward,'' I said. The zombies moved like a single organism, their dead eyes watching my face as if I were all that mattered. To them, I was.

The zombies moved like a shambling curtain. I could see the smaller hallway now, and the figures waiting inside. ''Stop,'' I said. The zombies stopped as if I'd hit a switch.

Liv, the blond bouncer from Danse Macabre, stood just inside the smaller hallway. She was still dressed in her violet body suit. Her extraordinary violet eyes stared at me, empty, waiting. My pulse thudded in my throat. There were other figures behind her.

Richard said softly, ''This isn't possible.''

I didn't argue with him. It would have been too hard.

"Bring them out, *ma petite*, let us see who you have called from their coffins." His voice was warm with the beginnings of anger.

"What's eating you?"

He laughed, but it was bitter. "I threatened my people with this, but you said nothing. You did not tell me you could truly raise vampires like any other zombie."

"I've only done it once before."

"Indeed," he said.

"Don't get all pissy on me."

"I shall get pissy if I want to," he said. "These are my people, my companions, and you have them walking around like puppets. I find that most disquieting."

"So do I," I said. I looked back at the vampires. Liv, who had been so animated last night, stood there like a well-preserved zombie. No. No, I'd never have mistaken her for a zombie. I could feel a difference. But there she stood, that muscular body waiting for my next order. There were others behind her. I couldn't see how many. Too many.

"Can you put my vampires back, *ma petite*?"

I continued to look at Liv, avoiding Jean-Claude's eyes. "I don't know."

He touched my chin, turning me to face him. He studied my face, eyes searching, as if some hint of truth might show through. I let anger fill my face, anger was always a great thing to hide behind.

"What did you do with the last vampire you raised, *ma petite*?"

I pulled away from him. He grabbed my arm unbelievably fast. Too fast to see. What happened next was simply automatic. He held my right upper arm, but I could still bend at the elbow and point the Firestar at him. The Uzi in my left hand pointed at him, too. He could have crushed my arm before I fired one gun, but not both. But for the first time, staring down the barrel of a gun at him was problematic. The sash of his robe had come loose and I could see a triangle of pale flesh. I could see where his heart would be. I could blow his heart out his back and sever his spine. And I didn't want to do it. I didn't want to splatter that beautiful body all over the wall. Damn.

Richard came closer. He didn't touch either of us. He just stared from one to the other. "Is he hurting you, Anita?"

"No," I said.

"Then should you be pointing a gun at him?"

"He shouldn't be touching me," I said.

Richard's voice was very mild. "He just finished touching you a lot more than this, Anita."

"Why are you helping him?"

"He helped me. Besides, if you kill him over something small and stupid, you'll never forgive yourself."

I took a deep breath and let it out. Some of the tension eased with the breath. I lowered the Uzi.

Jean-Claude released my arm.

I pointed the Firestar at the floor and looked at Richard. There was something in his eyes, even the wolf's amber eyes, that was all too human. Pain. He knew how much Jean-Claude meant to me. It was there in his eyes. That one comment said that he understood my relationship with the vampire, maybe better than I did.

I wanted to apologize to him, but I wasn't sure he'd understand what it was for. I wasn't even sure I could explain it. If you love someone, truly love them, you should never cause them pain. Never fill their eyes with something so close to grief.

"I'm sorry I got mad at you earlier. You want what's best for the pack, I know that."

"You still think I'm a fool to want a bloodless coup," he said.

I stood on tiptoe and kissed him gently. "Not a fool, just naive, terribly naive."

"Very touching, *ma petite*. And I do appreciate your interference on my behalf, Richard, but these are my people. I promised them certain freedoms when they joined me. I ask again. Can you put them back as they were?"

I turned to Jean-Claude, one hand still balancing against Richard's chest. "I don't know."

"Then you had better find out, *ma petite*."

It sounded too much like a threat for my taste, but . . . there was a figure behind Liv the bouncer that I couldn't take my eyes off of. I walked towards the waiting vampires. I opened my mouth, but no sound came out. My stomach clenched into a hard lump, my chest was tight. I finally said it: "Willie McCoy, come to me."

Willie walked out from behind the tall blond vampire. He was wearing the same chartreuse suit he'd had on at Danse Macabre. His brown eyes seemed to see me, but they were empty of that spark that was Willie. He wasn't home. It was like watching a puppet moving, and I was the puppet master. I tasted something bitter at the back of my throat. My eyes were hot and tight. I wasn't sure if I was going to throw up or cry first.

I stopped him about two feet from me. Close enough that I couldn't pretend or wish it away. I swallowed hard, and tears hot enough to scald ran down my face. "I didn't want to know this," I whispered.

Jean-Claude came to stand beside me. "Willie," he said, his voice vibrated through the room. Willie's body thrummed to the sound like a tuning fork struck. "Willie, look at me."

The blank, familiar face turned slowly towards his master. Something flickered through the eyes for a moment; something moved that I had no name for.

"This has possibilities," Jean-Claude said.

"Willie," I said, "look at me." My voice wasn't nearly as impressive as the vampire's, but Willie turned to me.

"No," Jean-Claude said, "look at me, Willie."

Willie hesitated.

"Willie," I said, "come to me." I held out a hand and he took a step towards me.

Jean-Claude said, "Stop, Willie, do not go to her."

Willie hesitated, almost turning to Jean-Claude.

I concentrated on that curl of power inside of me, that thing that allowed me to raise the dead and let it wash over me, flow out of me. I called Willie's body to me and nothing Jean-Claude could do would get him to turn away from me.

Richard said, "Stop it, both of you. He isn't a doll."

"He isn't alive, either," I said.

"He deserves better than this," Richard said.

I agreed. I turned to Jean-Claude. "He's mine, Jean-Claude. They're all mine. When night falls, they will be yours again, but their empty shells are mine." I stepped close to him, and that swirl of power lashed out.

He took a hissing breath and backed up. Holding his hand as if I'd struck him.

"Never forget what I am and what I can do. No more threats between us, ever, or it will be the last threat."

He stared at me, and for just a second, there was a flash of something I hadn't seen before: fear. Fear of me for the first time. Good.

Willie stared at me with empty, waiting eyes. He was dead, well and truly dead. Tears flowed down my face, tight and hard. Poor Willie, poor me. He wasn't human. All these months of being his friend and he was dead. Just dead. Damn.

"What happened to the first vampire you raised, *ma petite*? Why didn't you put it back into its coffin?" A thought slid behind his eyes. I watched the idea form, and fall from his lips. "How did Monsieur Bouvier get the lower half of his body melted away?"

Magnus Bouvier had been Serephina's mortal servant. It had been his job to keep me near Serephina's coffin until she rose to finish me off. I scrubbed at my face, trying to get rid of the tears. Always ruins the effect when you cry. "You know the answer," I said. My voice sounded strained and small.

"Say it aloud, *ma petite*, let me hear it from your own lips."

"I feel like I'm missing part of this conversation," Richard said, "What are you two talking about?"

"Tell him, *ma petite*."

"The vampire grabbed Magnus around the waist and held on. I'd planned on it slowing him down, nothing else. I got to the door and ran outside. The sunlight hit the vampire and it burst into flames. I expected Magnus to go back inside, but he didn't. He kept coming, dragging her into the light." Saying it fast didn't make it any better.

I stood in the middle of the dead I had called, hugging myself. I still had dreams about Serephina. Still saw Magnus reaching out to me, begging me to save him. I could have shot him and never lost a moment's sleep, but burning him alive was torture. I didn't do torture. Not to mention that Ellie Quinlan had already risen as a vampire, which made her legally alive. I'd killed them both, and it hadn't been pretty.

Richard was looking at me, a look of something close to horror on his face. "You burned the man and the vampire alive?" I watched the brown in his eyes swim back to the surface. The entire shape of the eye changed while I watched. It looked almost like it should hurt. If it did hurt, he never showed it.

"I didn't plan it, Richard. I didn't want it to happen, but I would have done anything to escape Serephina. Anything."

"I don't understand that."

"I know," I said.

"There is no shame in surviving, *ma petite*." I turned to Jean-Claude. There was no shock on his face. It was lovely and unreadable as a doll's.

"Then why can't I read your face right now?"

Life flowed back into his face, filled his eyes, moved behind his skin until he was there, staring at me. The look in his eyes wasn't what I expected. Fear was still there and surprise, but underneath was worry.

"Better?" he asked.

"Yes." I frowned. "What's worrying you?"

He sighed. "All honesty is eventually punished, but not usually this quickly."

"Answer me, Jean-Claude."

His eyes went past me to the werewolves waiting at Richard's back. "No one must speak of what has happened here, not to anyone."

"Why not?" Richard asked.

"It would embarrass *ma petite*."

"That's true," I said, "but that's not what you mean. You don't mind embarrassing me. Hell, this story would make a great threat for all your vampires. It'd scare the hell out of them."

"That, *ma petite*, is the point."

I sighed. "Stop being obtuse and just tell us."

"I do not want this," he waved at the vampires, "coming to the attention of the vampire council."

"Why not?" Richard and I asked together.

"Put simply, *ma petite*, they will kill you."

"I'm your registered human servant," I said, "you said you did that to keep me safe."

"For this they will come and see for themselves, *ma petite*. Whoever they send will know instantly that you do not bear my marks. You are my servant in name only. That will not be enough for them. Without any binding between us, they will not trust you."

"So they'll kill her, just like that?" Richard asked. He moved closer to me as if he'd touch me, but his hands hesitated above my shoulders.

Without looking at him, I said, "One story about burning people alive and you don't want to touch me. You prejudiced little werewolf, you." I tried to keep my voice light but a harsh edge crept in.

His hands gripped my shoulders tightly. "It really bothers you, what you did, doesn't it?"

I turned to see his face, his hands still on my shoulders. "Of course it bothers me. I didn't just kill Magnus, I tortured him to death. Ellie Quinlan didn't deserve to be burned alive." I shook my head and tried to step away from him. He slid his arms across my back, holding me gently against him.

"I'm sorry you had to do it." He touched my hair with one hand, the other still against my back. "Your eyes are haunted by it, by what you did. Don't take this wrong, but it makes me feel better to see that pain in your eyes."

I pushed away from him. "Did you think I could kill someone by torture and feel nothing?"

He met my eyes but it seemed like it was an effort. "I wasn't sure."

I shook my head.

Jean-Claude took my left hand; the other was still holding the Firestar. He turned me to face him. He raised my hand towards his lips as he bowed slowly towards me. He spoke as he moved, "There is nothing that you could ever do that would make me not desire the touch of your body." He kissed my hand. His lips lingered a little longer than was polite. His tongue licked across my skin, and I pulled away.

"It scares you that I can raise vampires like this."

"Perhaps, *ma petite*, but I have frightened you for years and yet you are still here."

He had a point. I stared at Willie. "Let's see if we can put everyone back where they belong." I hoped I could do it. I wanted Willie back, even if it was only a lie. He walked, he talked, it was still Willie. Or maybe, I just wanted it to be Willie. Maybe I needed it to be Willie.

29

''Take me to the coffin room,'' I said.

''Why?'' Jean-Claude asked. There was something in the way he said that one word that made me stare at him.

''Because I asked.''

''How would my flock feel if I allowed the Executioner to enter their private chamber while they slept helpless?''

''I'm not going to kill anybody today, not on purpose.''

''I do not like the way you said that, *ma petite*.''

''Uncontrolled power is unpredictable, Jean-Claude. All sorts of unpleasant things can happen. I need to see where the vampires will be resting. I want to try and put them back in a controlled manner.''

''What sorts of unpleasant things?'' Richard asked.

It was a good question. Since I was pretty much flying blind, I didn't have a good answer. ''It takes less power to put back than it does to raise. If we just call it up wild and try to will them back . . .'' I shook my head.

''You could extinguish their life force,'' Cassandra said.

I looked at her. ''What did you say?''

''You're going to put them back in their coffins as you would a zombie, but with a zombie you will it to be dead again, correct?''

I hadn't really thought of it that way, but she was right.

''If you will the vampires back in their coffins, you're in effect willing them dead again like a zombie, right?''

''Yeah.''

''But you don't want them permanently dead.''

My head was beginning to hurt. ''No, I don't want them permanently dead.''

''How do you know so very much about necromancy, Cassandra?'' Jean-Claude asked.

''I have a master's degree in magical theory.''

''That must be useful on a résumé,'' I said.

''Not in the least,'' she said, ''but it might be useful now.''

"Did you know your newest pack member was so well-educated, Richard?" Jean-Claude asked.

"Yes," he said, "it's one of the reasons I gave her permission to move here."

"Permission to move here?" I said. "Why did she need your permission?"

"A werewolf has to get the permission of the local pack leader before they can enter a new territory. If they don't, it's considered a challenge to his authority."

"Did she have to ask your permission or Marcus's?"

"Both," Cassandra said. "Most werewolves won't come near Saint Louis while this power struggle is going on."

"Why did you come, then, my wolf?" Jean-Claude asked.

"I liked what I heard about Richard. He's trying to bring the pack into the twentieth century."

"Did you come planning to be his lupa?" I asked. Yes, a little twinge of jealousy had reared its ugly head.

Cassandra smiled. "Maybe, but the job's filled. I came here to avoid fighting, not to start it."

"You have come to the wrong place, I fear," Jean-Claude said.

She shrugged. "If I waited until the battle was over and it was safe, I wouldn't be worth much, would I?"

"You came to fight at Monsieur Zeeman's side?"

"I came because I agree with what he's trying to do."

"You don't approve of killing?" I asked.

"Not really."

"Why, Richard, you have found a kindred spirit," Jean-Claude said, smiling, and far too pleased.

"Cassandra believes in the sanctity of life; a lot of people do," Richard said. He wouldn't look at me.

"If she's a better match for you than I am, I won't stand in your way."

He turned to me, a look of astonishment on his face. "Anita . . ." He shook his head. "I'm in love with you."

"You'd get over it," I said. My chest was tight with the offer, but I meant it. Richard and I had a basic fundamental difference of opinion. It wasn't going away. One of us was going to have to compromise, and it wasn't going to be me. I couldn't quite meet Richard's eyes, but I didn't take it back.

He stepped in front of me, and all I could see was his bare chest. There was a scratch just below his left nipple, blood drying on his skin in darkening strings. He touched my chin, raising my face until I met his eyes. He studied my face like he'd never seen it before.

"I would never get over losing you, Anita. Never."

"Never's a long time to tie yourself to a killer."

"You don't have to be a killer," he said.

I stepped away from him. "If you're hanging around me waiting for me to soften up and become this good little girl, you might as well leave now."

He grabbed my arms, pulling me against his body. "I want you, Anita, all of you." He kissed me, arms locked behind my back, raising me up against him.

I slid my hands behind his back, Firestar still in one hand. I pressed my body against his hard enough to know he was happy to see me.

We came up for air, and I pulled back, but not out of his arms, half-laughing. I caught a glimpse of Jean-Claude standing to one side. The look on his face wiped the smile from my lips. It wasn't jealousy. It was hunger. Desire. Watching us together had excited him.

I drew back from Richard and found blood on my hands. It was hard to tell on the navy blue shirt but there were wet spots where I'd pressed myself against the bloody scratches. Some of the wounds were deep enough that they were still seeping blood.

Richard was looking at Jean-Claude, too, now. I stepped away from Richard, holding up the bloody hand. I walked towards the vampire, and his eyes stayed on the fresh blood, not on me. I stopped less than a foot from him, my hand held out in front of his face.

''Which would you rather have right now, sex or blood?''

His eyes flicked to my face, back to my hand, then to my face. I watched the effort it took for him to keep eye contact. ''Ask Richard which he would rather have just after he changes into a wolf, sex or fresh meat?''

I glanced back at Richard. ''What's your choice?''

''Just after the change, meat.'' He said it like I should have known the answer.

I turned back to the vampire. I slid the Firestar into the front of my pants, and moved the bloody hand towards his lips.

Jean-Claude grabbed my wrist. ''Do not tease me, *ma petite*. My control is not boundless.'' A tremor ran through his arm and down his hand. He looked away, eyes closed.

I touched his face with my right hand, turning him back to face me. ''Who says I'm teasing?'' I said softly. ''Take us to the coffin room.''

Jean-Claude searched my face. ''What do you offer me, *ma petite*?''

''Blood,'' I said.

''And sex?'' he asked.

''Which would you rather have, right this minute?'' I stared at him, willing the truth in his face.

He gave a shaky laugh. ''Blood.''

I smiled, and pulled my wrist away. ''Remember, it was your choice.''

A look passed over his face that was a mixture of surprise and irony. ''Touché, *ma petite*, but I am beginning to have hopes that this will not be the last time I am given the choice.'' There was a heat to his voice, his eyes, just standing this close to his body, that made me shiver.

I glanced back at Richard. He was watching us. I expected to see jealousy or anger, but all I could read in his eyes was need. Lust. I was pretty sure that Richard's choice right this minute would be sex, but the thought of a little blood thrown in didn't seem to worry him. In fact, it seemed to excite him. I was beginning to wonder if the werewolf and vampire shared similar tastes in foreplay. The thought should have scared me, but it didn't. That was a very, very bad sign.

30

The last time I'd been in the coffin room under Circus of the Damned, I'd come to slay the current Master of the City. I'd come to slay every vampire in the place. My, how things had changed.

Track lighting in solid white fixtures clung to the walls, casting soft halos of light on each of seven coffins. Three of the coffins were empty, their lids propped open. All of the coffins were modern, new, roomy. They were all a rich varnished oak, stained nearly black. Silver handles graced the wood. The satin linings of the open coffins were different colors; white, blue, red. The coffin with the red interior held a sword in a specially made side sheath: a freaking two-handed sword as long as I was tall. A pair of the ugliest fuzzy dice I'd ever seen were suspended from the white satin coffin. It had to be Willie's. The blue satin held a small extra pillow. Standing over the coffin, the smell of herbs rose musty, vaguely sweet. I touched the small pillow and found it filled with dried herbs. "Herbs for sweet dreams," I said to no one in particular.

"Is there some purpose to you handling their personal belongings, *ma petite*?"

I looked at him. "What keepsakes do you have in your coffin?"

He just smiled.

"Why all the same coffins?"

"If you came in here to kill us, where would you start?"

I looked around at the identical coffins. "I don't know. If someone comes in, they can't tell who's the oldest or who's the Master of the City. It covers your ass but endangers the rest."

"If someone comes to kill us, *ma petite*, it is to everyone's benefit if the oldest are not killed first. There is always a chance that one of the older ones could awaken in time to save the rest."

I nodded. "Why the extra-wide, extra-high interiors?"

"Would you want to spend eternity on your back, *ma petite*?" He smiled and came to stand beside me, leaning his butt against the open coffin, arms crossed over his chest. "There are so many other more comfortable positions."

I felt heat rise up my face.

Richard joined us. ''Are you two going to exchange witty repartee or are we going to do this?'' He leaned on the closed end of the coffin, forearms resting on it. There was a bloody scratch on his right upper arm. He seemed at home. Jason, still furry and big enough to ride, padded over the stone floor, nails clicking. The wolf's head was high enough that it licked Richard's bloody arm while still on all fours. There were moments when I felt Richard was too normal to fit into my life. This wasn't one of them.

''Yeah, we're going to do it,'' I said.

Richard stood, running his fingers through his thick hair, getting it out of his face, and showing his chest off to good advantage. For the first time, I wondered if he'd done it on purpose. I searched his face for that edge of teasing that Jean-Claude had, that knowledge that even that simple movement touched me. There was nothing. Richard's face was guileless, handsome, empty of ulterior motives.

I exchanged glances with Jean-Claude. He shrugged. ''If you do not understand him, do not look to me. I am not in love with him.''

Richard looked puzzled. ''Did I miss something?'' He stroked under the wolf's throat, pressing the head against his chest. The wolf made a high whimpering sound of pleasure. Glad to be back in the pack leader's good graces, I guess.

I shook my head. ''Not really.''

''Why are *we* here?'' Stephen asked. He was as close to the door as he could get and not be outside the room. His shoulders were hunched. He was scared, but of what?

Cassandra stood near Stephen, inside the room, closer to us. Her face was bland, unreadable except for a certain wariness around the eyes. They both wore jeans with oversized shirts. Stephen's was a man's pale blue dress shirt. Cassandra had an oversized T-shirt a dull pine green with a wolf's head done large with huge, yellow eyes.

''What's wrong, Stephen?'' Richard asked.

Stephen blinked and shook his head.

''We all heard Anita tell Jean-Claude she'd need more blood, fresh blood,'' Cassandra said. She looked at me while she finished the thought. ''I think Stephen's worried where the fresh blood's coming from.''

''I'm not into human sacrifice,'' I said.

''Some people don't consider a lycanthrope human,'' Cassandra said.

''I do,'' I said.

She looked at me, judging my words. Some lycanthropes could tell if you were lying. I was betting she was one of them. ''Then where are you going to get the blood?''

It was a good question. I wasn't sure I had a good answer. ''I don't know, but it won't take a death.''

''Are you sure?'' she asked.

I shrugged. ''If it takes a death to put them back, they're dead. I'm not going to kill anybody else to bring them back.'' I looked at the three waiting vampires after I said it. Liv, Willie, and surprisingly, Damian. Raising the vampires was impressive enough, raising one as powerful as Damian was downright scary. He wasn't a master vampire, never would be, but he'd have frightened me in a fair fight. Now he stood dressed only in the green lycra pants and the pirate sash. His upper body gleamed like muscled marble under the glow of the lights. His green eyes stared at me with a patient waiting that only the truly dead can manage.

"You are shivering, *ma petite*."

"We raise the power again, then we need blood." I looked at Jean-Claude and Richard. "If Richard has to fight Marcus tonight, I'm not sure he should be the one who supplies this round of blood."

Jean-Claude cocked his head to one side. I expected him to say something irritating, but he didn't. Maybe even a very old dog could learn new tricks.

"He is not sinking fangs into you," Richard said. Anger made his brown eyes dark and sparkling, he was lovely when he was angry. That aura of energy flared around him, close enough to creep down my bare skin.

"You can't donate twice this close together, with Marcus waiting for you," I said.

Richard grabbed me by the upper arms. "You don't understand, Anita. Feeding is like sex to him."

Again, I half-expected Jean-Claude to chime in, but he didn't. I had to say it. Damn. "It won't be the first time he's done it, Richard."

Richard's fingers dug into my arms. "I know that. I saw the fang marks on your wrist. But remember, you weren't under any mind control that time."

"I remember," I said. "It hurt like hell."

Richard drew me to him with his hands still holding only my upper arms, drew me to tiptoe as if he'd drag me to his face. "Without mind control, it's like rape, not the real thing. It'll be real this time."

"You're hurting me, Richard." My voice was calm, steady, but the look on his face scared me. The intensity in his hands, his face, his body, was unnerving.

He eased down, but didn't take his hands away. "Take blood from Jason or Cassandra."

I shook my head. "That might work or it might not. If the blood comes from one of us, I know it'll work. Besides, should you be offering up other people's blood without asking them first?"

Doubt slid behind his eyes, and he let me go. His long hair fell forward, hiding his face. "You say you've chosen me. That you're in love with me. That you don't want to have sex with him. Now, you tell me you want him to feed off of you. That's as bad as sex." He stalked the room, pacing around the waiting vampires, swinging back in an agitated stride that filled the room with a warm, creeping power.

"I didn't say I wanted to feed him," I said.

He stopped in the middle of the room, staring at me. "But you do, don't you?"

"No," I said, and it was true. "I've never been interested in that."

"She speaks the truth," Jean-Claude said at last.

"You stay out of this," Richard said, pointing a finger at him.

Jean-Claude gave a small bow and fell silent. He was behaving himself far too well. Made me nervous. Of course, Richard was having enough of a fit for both of them.

"Then let me feed him again."

''Isn't it sexual for you, too?'' I asked.

Richard shook his head. ''It was you I was looking at, Anita, not him. A little pain is fine.''

It was my turn to shake my head. ''Are you truly saying that letting him sink fangs into my body would bother you as much as sinking . . .'' I let the thought die unspoken. ''I see donating blood as the lesser evil, Richard. Don't you?''

''Yes,'' he hissed. His power was filling the room like warm, electric water. I could almost reach out and grab it.

''Then what are you bitching about?'' I said. ''We wouldn't have done it the first time, but you wanted me to do it. You wanted us to do it.'' I stalked towards him, finally angry myself. ''You don't want to kill Marcus, fine, but this is the price. You want enough power to cow the rest of the pack without losing your humanity, great, but that kind of power isn't free.'' I stood in front of him, so close that his power danced over my skin like fine needles, like sex that rode that edge between pleasure and pain.

''It's too late to back out now. We are not going to strand Willie and the others because you're getting cold feet.'' I took that last step, putting our bodies so close together that a deep breath would have made them touch. I lowered my voice to a whisper, though I knew everything in the room would still hear me. ''It isn't the blood that bothers you. What bothers you is that you enjoyed it.'' I lowered my voice until it was almost a movement of lips with only a breath of sound. ''Jean-Claude isn't just seducing me, he's seducing us.''

Richard stared down at me, and the look in his true brown eyes was lost, hopeless. A little boy who's discovered the monster under the bed is actually real, and it's screwing Mommy.

Jean-Claude's power eased through the room, mingling with Richard's electric warmth like a cool wind from the grave. We both turned and looked at the vampire. He was smiling ever so slightly. He undid his robe and let it fall to the floor. He glided towards us, wearing nothing but his silk pajamas and a knowing smile. His own power making his long hair flare round his face like a small wind.

Richard touched my shoulders and even that chaste touch sent a line of warm, shivering energy along my skin. The power was there for the calling, just below the surface. We didn't need all the sexual charades.

Jean-Claude reached a pale hand out towards me. I met his hand with mine, and that one touch was enough. That cool, burning power flowed over me, through me, into Richard. I heard Richard gasp. Jean-Claude started to move forward, like he'd press his body against mine. I held him away from me with the hand that was entwined in his, straight-arming him. ''It's here, Jean-Claude, can't you feel it?''

He nodded. ''Your power calls to me, *ma petite*.''

Richard's hands slid over my shoulders, his face brushing my hair. ''Now what?''

''We ride the power this time, it doesn't ride us.''

''How?'' Richard whispered.

Jean-Claude looked at me with eyes that were deep as any ocean and as full of secrets. ''I believe *ma petite* has a plan.''

"Yeah," I said, "I have a plan." I looked from one to the other of them. "I'm going to call Dominic Dumare and see if he knows how to put vampires back in their coffins." Dominic had been cleared of Robert's murder. He had an airtight alibi. He'd been with a woman. Even if he hadn't been, I might have asked for his help. I wanted to save Willie more than I wanted to revenge Robert.

A strange expression crossed Jean-Claude's face. "You, asking for help, *ma petite*? That is unusual."

I drew away from both of them. We could get the power back, I was pretty certain of that. I looked at Willie's empty face and the fuzzy dice hanging from his coffin. "If I make a mistake, Willie's gone. I want him back."

There were times when I thought that it wasn't Jean-Claude who had convinced me that vampires weren't always monsters. It was Willie and Dead Dave, ex-cop and bar owner. It was a host of lesser vampires that seemed, occasionally, like nice guys. Jean-Claude was a lot of things; nice was not one of them.

31

Dominic Dumare showed up wearing a pair of black dress slacks and a black leather jacket unzipped over a grey silk T-shirt. He looked more relaxed without Sabin looking on, like an employee on his day off. Even the neatly trimmed Vandyke beard and mustache seemed less formal.

Dominic walked around the three vampires I'd raised. We'd moved back out into the rubble-strewn main area, so he could see the zombies and the vampires all at once. He paced around the vampires, touching them here and there. He grinned at me, teeth flashing in his dark beard. "This is marvelous, truly marvelous."

I fought the urge to frown at him. "Forgive me if I don't share your enthusiasm. Can you help me put them back the way they were?"

"Theoretically, yes."

"When people start using the word *theoretically*, it means they don't know how to do something. You can't help me, can you?"

"Now, now," Dominic said. He knelt by Willie, staring up at him, studying him like a bug under a bioscope. "I didn't say I couldn't help. It's true that I've never seen this done. And you say you've done this before." He stood up, brushing off the knees of his pants.

"Once."

"That time was without the triumvirate?" Dominic asked.

I'd had to tell him. I understood enough about ritual magic to know that if we withheld how we'd gotten this much power, anything Dominic helped us come up with wouldn't work. It would be like telling the police it was a burglary when it was really a murder. They'd be trying to solve the wrong crime.

"Yeah, the first time was just me."

"But both times in daylight hours?" he asked.

I nodded.

"That makes sense. We can only raise zombies after the souls have flown. It would make sense that vampires can only be raised during the day. When darkness falls, their souls return."

I wasn't even going to try and argue about whether or not vampires had souls. I wasn't as sure of the answer as I used to be.

''I can't raise zombies during daylight hours. Let alone vampires,'' I said.

Dominic motioned at all the waiting dead of both kinds. ''But you did it.''

I shook my head. ''That's not the point. I'm not supposed to be able to do it.''

''Have you ever tried to raise normal zombies during daylight hours?''

''Well, no. The man who trained me said it wasn't possible.''

''So you never tried,'' Dominic said.

I hesitated before answering.

''You have tried,'' he said.

''I can't do it. I can't even call the power under the light of the sun.''

''Only because you believe you can't,'' Dominic said.

''Run that by me again.''

''Belief is one of the most important aspects of magic.''

''You mean, if I don't believe I can raise zombies during the day, I can't.''

''Exactly.''

''That doesn't make sense,'' Richard said. He leaned against one of the intact walls. He'd been very quiet while I talked magic with Dominic. Jason, still in wolf form, lay at his feet. Stephen had cleared some of the broken stones and sat beside the wolf.

''Actually,'' I said, ''it does. I've seen people with a lot of raw talent that couldn't raise anything. One guy was convinced it was a mortal sin so he just blocked it out. But he shone with power whether he wanted to accept it or not.''

''A shapeshifter can deny his power all he wants, but that doesn't keep him from changing,'' Richard said.

''I believe that is why lycanthropy is referred to as a curse,'' Dominic said.

Richard looked at me. The expression on his face was eloquent. ''A curse.''

''You'll have to forgive Dominic,'' Jean-Claude said. ''A hundred years ago, it never occurred to anyone that lycanthropy could be a disease.''

''Concern for Richard's feelings?'' I asked.

''His happiness is your happiness, *ma petite*.''

Jean-Claude's new gentlemanly behavior was beginning to bug me. I didn't trust his change of heart.

Cassandra said, ''If Anita didn't believe she could raise the dead during daylight hours, then how did she do it?'' She had joined in the metaphysical discussion like it was a graduate class in magical theory. I'd met people like her in college. Theorists who had no real magic of their own. But they could sit around for hours debating whether a theoretical spell would work. They treated magic like higher physics, a pure science without any true way of testing. Heaven forbid the ivory tower magicians should actually try out their theories in a real spell. Dominic would have fit in well with them, except he had his own magic.

''Both occasions were extreme situations,'' Dominic said. ''It works on the same principle that allows a grandmother to lift a truck off her grandchild. In times of great need, we often touch abilities beyond the everyday.''

''But the grandmother can't lift a car at will, just because she did it once,'' I said.

''Hmm,'' Dominic said, ''perhaps the analogy is not perfect, but you understand what I am saying. If you say you do not, you are merely being difficult.''

That almost made me smile. ''So you're saying that I could raise the dead in daylight if I believed I could.''

''I believe so.''

I shook my head. ''I've never heard of any animator being able to do that.''

''But you are not merely an animator, Anita,'' Dominic said. ''You are a necromancer.''

''*I* have never heard of a necromancer that could raise the dead in broad daylight,'' Jean-Claude said.

Dominic shrugged gracefully. It reminded me of Jean-Claude. It takes a couple hundred years to make a shrug pretty. ''I don't know about broad daylight, but just as some vampires can walk around during the day, as long as they are sufficiently sheltered, I believe the same principle would apply to necromancers.''

''So you don't believe Anita could raise the dead at high noon out of doors, either?'' Cassandra said.

Dominic shrugged again. Then he laughed. ''You have caught me, my studious beauty. It may well be possible for Anita to do exactly that, but even I have never heard of such a thing.''

I shook my head. ''Look, we can explore the magical implications later. Right now, can you help me figure a way to put the vampires back without screwing them up?''

''Define screwing them up,'' Dominic said.

''Do not joke, Dominic,'' Jean-Claude said. ''You know precisely what she means.''

''I want to hear it from her lips.''

Jean-Claude looked at me and gave a barely perceptible shrug.

''When darkness falls, I want them to rise as vampires. I'm afraid if I do this wrong, they'll just be dead, permanently.''

''You surprise me, Anita. Perhaps your reputation as the scourge of the local vampire populace is exaggerated.''

I stared at him. Before I could say something that sounded like bragging, Jean-Claude spoke. ''I would think what she has done today is proof enough of how very much she deserves her reputation.''

Dominic and the vampire stared at each other. Something seemed to pass between them. A challenge, a knowledge, something. ''She would make an amazing human servant if only some vampire could tame her,'' Dominic said.

Jean-Claude laughed. The sound filled the room with echoes that shivered and danced across the skin. The laughter swept through my body, and for the briefest moment, I could feel something touch me deep inside where no hand belonged. In another context Jean-Claude might have made it sexual; now it was simply disturbing.

''Don't ever do that again,'' Richard said. He rubbed his bare arms as if he were cold or trying to erase the memory of that invasive laughter.

Jason trotted over to Jean-Claude, to butt his head against the vampire's hand. He'd liked it.

Dominic gave a little bow. "My apologies, Jean-Claude, you have made your point. If you wished to, you could cause the damage that my master caused by accident at your office."

"My office," I said. Personally, I didn't think that Jean-Claude could cause damage with just his voice. I'd been in situations where if he could have done it, he would have. No sense telling Dominic that, though.

Dominic gave an even lower bow in my direction. "Your office, of course."

"Can we cut the grandstanding?" I said. "Can you help us?"

"I am more than willing to try."

I walked up to him, picking my way over the broken stones. When I was standing as close as was polite and maybe an inch or so more, I said, "These three vampires are not an experiment. This is not some graduate study in magical metaphysics. You offered to teach me necromancy, Dominic. I think you're not up to the job. How can you teach me when I can do things you can't? Unless, of course, you can raise vampires from their coffins?"

I stared into his dark eyes the entire time I spoke, watching the anger narrow his eyes, tighten his lips. His ego was as big as I'd hoped. I knew he wouldn't disappoint me. Dominic would do his best for us now. His pride was at stake.

"Tell me exactly how you called the power, Anita, and I will build you a spell that should work—if you have the control to make it work."

I smiled at him, and I made sure it was just this side of condescending. "You come up with it, I can pull it off."

He smiled. "Arrogance is not a becoming trait in a woman."

"I find it a very becoming trait," Jean-Claude said. "If it's deserved. If you had just raised three vampires from their daytime rest, wouldn't you be arrogant, Dominic?"

His smile widened. "Yes, I would be."

Truth was, I didn't feel arrogant. I was scared. Scared that I'd screwed Willie up and he would never rise again. I felt bad too, about Liv and Damian. It wasn't a matter of liking them or not; I didn't mean to do it. You shouldn't extinguish someone's life force by accident. If I felt half as secure as my words to Dominic, why did my stomach hurt?

32

Dominic, Cassandra, and I came up with a spell. The part of the plan that was my idea was very simple. I had put zombies back in their graves for years. I was good at it. As far as I was able, I was going to treat this like just another job: laying the dead to rest, nothing special. Lay the zombies first, worry about the vamps later.

I had Cassandra fetch one of my knives and a wrist sheath from the bedroom. If I'd been acting as a focus for another animator, I wouldn't have let him sink teeth into me, so why did the blood have to come from Jean-Claude drinking it? It didn't, or I didn't think it did. Dominic agreed with me, but he wasn't a hundred percent sure. So zombies first. They'd be the practice. If the knife didn't work, we'd go to fangs, but what little normalcy was left to me, I was going to cling to.

I'd sent Stephen for a bowl to hold the blood. He'd returned with a small, golden bowl. I wondered if the size was deliberate, to encourage me not to spill too much blood. For a werewolf, Stephen didn't seem to like blood very much. The bowl was polished to a shine so bright it almost glowed. The inside showed the dimpled blows of hammer work. Beaten gold, and I knew as soon as I touched it, it was old. Why does everyone think you have to have something special to hold the blood? Tupperware would have worked.

We stood in the rubble-strewn room where the zombies waited, patient as only the dead can be. Some of the eyes that watched me were sunken like the blind eyes of dead fish, a few skulls were empty, and even without eyes, they all seemed to be looking at me.

I stood, knife strapped to my left wrist, facing them. Richard stood to my left, Jean-Claude to my right. They weren't touching me, by my request.

Dominic had asked for enough details of the first triumvirate that I'd been embarrassed. He agreed with me that the power was probably there without us having to crawl all over each other. Agreeing to that alone earned him brownie points. After all, the plan was to raise the magic tonight in front of the whole pack. I didn't really want to be having sex in front of that many strangers. All right, it wasn't exactly sex, but it was close enough that I didn't want an audience.

The glow was fading. Staring at the partially rotting zombies, it was hard to regain the mood. "My zombies usually hold together better than this," I said.

"If you had pulled this much power from two other necromancers, the zombies would be better," Dominic said.

"Perhaps it was the lack of control," Jean-Claude said.

I turned and looked at him. "I think Dominic means that some of the power that raised them was taken from a dead man."

"Do you believe I am a dead man, *ma petite*?"

I stared into that lovely face and nodded. "The vampires I raised are just corpses. Whatever you are, it's a form of necromancy. Necromancy only works when you start with a dead body."

He cocked his head to one side. "I hear your words, *ma petite*, but I do not think you believe them, not completely."

I shook my head. "I don't know what I believe anymore."

"Actually," Dominic said, "I don't believe it matters that Jean-Claude is a vampire. I think it is more that neither he nor Richard know anything of raising the dead. That is your talent alone. I think with practice, you could channel the power into perfect zombies, but in a way, Jean-Claude is right. The wildness of it, the lack of control, made the zombies less perfect."

Something must have shown on my face, because he said, "You had too many things to control to pay attention to all the details. I think you instinctively let the zombies go, because it was the part you were most sure of. You have excellent instincts."

"Thanks, I guess," I said.

He smiled. "I know time is growing short. As we can see from Jean-Claude's presence, not all vampires sleep until full dark. I fear that if one of the vampires passes its waking hour, that he or she will be lost. But I would ask Anita to do one thing for me that has nothing to do with her problem, but everything to do with mine."

"What problem?" I asked

"Sabin," Jean-Claude said.

Dominic nodded. "Sabin's time is running short."

"Sabin, the vampire at the club?" Cassandra asked.

"Yeah," I said. "What do you need, Dominic? Make it quick, and I'm your girl."

Dominic smiled. "Thank you, Anita. Concentrate on one of your zombies. Try to bring it closer to perfection."

I frowned at him.

"Heal one of your zombies, *ma petite*."

"You can't heal the dead," I said, "but I can make them more lifelike."

Dominic nodded. "That would do very nicely."

"I usually do that during the initial rush of power. I've never tried to fiddle with my dead once they were raised."

"Please try," Dominic said.

"We could raise the power between the three of us, then try it," I said.

Dominic shook his head. ''I am not sure what that would do to the spell. I think it would be taking a great risk with your companions.''

I stared at him for a heartbeat or two. ''You'd risk leaving Sabin to rot to save our friends?''

''You asked for my help, Anita. I think you are not a woman who asks for help often. It would be poor payment of such a compliment if I let you risk your friends for mine. If you can heal your dead cold, as it were, so be it. If you cannot, we will proceed to save these three vampires.''

''A very honorable sentiment,'' Jean-Claude said.

''There are moments when honor is all that is left,'' Dominic said.

The vampire and the man seemed to have a moment of near perfect understanding. A wealth of history, if not shared, then similar, passed between them. I was odd woman out.

I looked to Richard and we had our own moment of perfect understanding. We valued our mortal life span. The fatalism in Dominic's voice had been frightening. How old was he? I could usually tell with a vampire, but never with a human servant. I didn't ask. There was a weight of years in Dominic's brown eyes that made me afraid to ask.

I looked at Jean-Claude's lovely face and wondered if I would be as honorable, or would I have risked anyone, everyone, to heal him? To see Jean-Claude dead would be one thing, but rotted away like Sabin . . . It would be worse than death in many ways. Of course, Sabin was dying. Powerful as he was, he couldn't hold himself together forever. Or maybe he could. Maybe Dominic could sew him up in a big sack, like the gloves the vampire wore on his hands. Maybe Sabin could go on living even after he'd been reduced to so much liquid. Now that was a hideous thought.

I stared at the standing dead. They looked back. One of the zombies was almost intact. Grey skin clung to the bones, more like clay than flesh. One blue eye stared at me. The other eye had shriveled like a raisin. It reminded me of what had happened to Sabin's eye.

It would make more sense to say I touched the eye and healed it. Or that I thought at it and smoothed the flesh like clay. It wasn't like that. I stared at the zombie. I touched that spark inside me that allowed me to raise the dead. I drew that part of me outward, coaxed it like feeding a small flame, and threw it outward into that one zombie. I whispered, ''Live, live.''

I'd watched it before, but it never ceased to amaze me. The flesh filled out, plumping, smoothing. A warm flesh tone spread like heat across the grey skin. The dry, strawlike hair grew and curled, brown and soft. The dead eye blew up like a small balloon, filling the socket. Two good eyes looked back at me. Even the tattered clothing mended itself. He wore a vest with a gold watch chain. His clothes were a hundred years or more out of date.

''I am most impressed,'' Dominic said. ''If you changed his clothes, he could pass for human.''

I nodded. ''I make great zombies, but that won't help your master.''

''Call one of the vampires from the coffin room.''

''Why?'' I asked.

Dominic drew a small silver knife from a sheath at his back. I hadn't known he had a weapon. Careless of me.

"What are you going to do with that?" Jean-Claude asked.

"With your permission, I will cut one of the vampires and ask Anita to heal the wound."

Jean-Claude considered the request, then nodded. "A small cut."

Dominic bowed. "Of course."

The vamps could heal a small cut on their own eventually. If I couldn't heal it, no harm done. Though I wasn't sure the vampires would agree with me.

"Anita," Dominic said.

I called, "Damian, come to me."

Jean-Claude raised his eyebrows at my choice, I think. If he expected me to call Willie, he didn't understand. Willie was my friend. Even dead, I didn't want to see him cut up.

Damian had tried to mind-rape a woman tonight at the club. Let him get cut up just a little.

Damian walked in, staring until he found me. His face was still blank and empty. Emptier than sleep, empty as only death can make it.

"Damian, stop."

The vampire stopped. His eyes were the greenest I'd ever seen. Greener than Catherine's, more cat than human.

Dominic stepped in front of Damian. He stared at the vampire. He laid the silver blade against the pale cheek and pulled the point downward, sharply.

Blood flowed down that perfect paleness in a thin crimson wash. The vampire never reacted, not even to blink.

"Anita," Dominic said.

I stared at Damian, no, Damian's shell. I flung power at him, into him. I willed him to live. That was the word I whispered to him.

The blood slowed, then stopped. The cut knit together seamlessly. It was . . . easy.

Dominic wiped the blood away with a handkerchief he'd drawn from his jacket pocket. Damian's pale cheek was flawless once more.

It was Cassandra who said it first, "She could heal Sabin."

Dominic nodded. "She just might." He turned to me with a look of triumph, elation. "You would need the power of your triumvirate to raise Sabin during his daylight slumber, but once raised, I think you could heal him."

"A shallow cut is one thing," I said. "Sabin is a . . . mess."

"Will you try?"

"If we can put these three vamps back unharmed, yeah, I'll try."

"Tomorrow."

I nodded. "Why not?"

"I cannot wait to tell Sabin what I have seen here today. He has been without hope for so long. But first, we must put your friends back. I will help you all I can."

I smiled. "I know enough of magic, Dominic, to know that all you can do is advise from the sidelines."

''But it will be very good advice,'' he said with a smile.

I believed him. For Sabin's sake, he wanted us to succeed. ''Okay, let's do it.'' I held my hands out to Richard and Jean-Claude. They took my hands dutifully enough, and it was pleasant holding their hands. Both of them were warm and lovely, but there was no instant magic. No spark. I realized that in some strange way, the sexual interplay took the place of the ritual. Rituals aren't absolutely necessary to most magic, but they serve as a way to focus, to prepare yourself for the act of casting a spell. I had no blood circle to walk. I had no sacrifice to kill. I had no paraphernalia to use. All I had was the two men standing in front of me, my own body, and the knife at my wrist. I turned away from both of them.

''Nothing's happening,'' I said.

''What do you expect to happen?'' Dominic asked.

I shrugged. ''Something. I don't know.''

''You are trying too hard, Anita. Relax, let the power come to you.''

I rotated my shoulders, trying to ease the tension. It didn't work. ''I really wish you hadn't reminded me that some of the vamps could rise before dark. It's late afternoon, and we're underground. It could already be too late.''

''Thinking like that is not helpful,'' Dominic said.

Jean-Claude walked up to me, and even before he touched me, there was a rush of power like a spill of warmth over my skin. ''Don't touch me,'' I said.

I felt him hesitate behind me. ''What is wrong, *ma petite*?''

''Nothing.'' I turned to face him. I held my hand just above his bare chest and that line of warmth traveled from his skin to mine. It was as if his body breathed against me. ''Do you feel that?''

He cocked his head to one side. ''Magic.''

''Aura,'' I said. I had to fight an urge to glance at Dominic, like looking to a coach to see if this was the play he wanted. I was afraid to look away, to lose that thread. I held my hand out to Richard. ''Walk towards me, but don't touch me.''

He looked puzzled but did what I asked. When my hand was just above his skin, that same line of warmth came up, like a small, captive wind. I could feel their energy breathing against my skin, one to each hand. I closed my eyes and concentrated on the sensation. There. I could feel a difference, slight, almost indiscernible, but there. There was a prickling, almost electric tremble to Richard. Jean-Claude was cool and smooth. All right, we could touch auras, so what? Where did that get us?

I pressed my hands suddenly forward, through the energy, against their bodies. I forced that energy back into them, and got a gasp from both of them. The shock of it ran up my arms and I bowed my head, breathing through the rush of power. I raised my face up to meet their eyes. I don't know what showed on my face, but whatever it was, Richard didn't like it. He started to take a step back. I dug fingernails into his stomach just enough to get his attention.

''Don't break the connection.''

He swallowed. His eyes were wide and there was something close to fear in them, but he stayed put. I turned to Jean-Claude. He didn't look scared. He looked as calm and controlled as I felt.

''Very good, Anita.'' Dominic's voice came soft, low. ''Combine their power as if they were simply two other animators. You are acting as focus. You've done that before. You've laid the dead to rest a thousand times. This is only one more time.''

''Okay, coach,'' I whispered.

''What?'' Richard said.

I shook my head. ''Nothing.''

I stepped back from them slowly, hands extended towards them. The power trailed between us like two ropes. There was nothing to see, but from the look on Richard's face, we all felt it. I unsheathed the knife and picked up the golden bowl without looking down, my gaze on the two of them. There was a difference between this and combining with other animators, there was lust. Love. Something. Whatever it was, it acted like fuel, or glue. I had no words for what it was, but it was there when I looked at them.

I held the gold bowl in my left hand, knife in the right. I walked back to them. ''Hold the bowl for me, one hand apiece.''

''Why?'' Richard asked.

''Because I said so.''

He looked like he wanted to argue. I laid the flat of the blade against his lips. ''If you question everything I say, it spoils my concentration.'' I took the knife away from his mouth.

''Don't do that again,'' he said, voice soft, almost harsh.

I nodded. ''Fine.'' I held my wrist over the empty bowl and drew the knife down the skin in one sharp movement. Blood welled out of the cut, falling in thick drops, splashing down the sides and bottom of the gleaming gold bowl. Yes, it did hurt.

''Your turn, Richard.'' I kept my wrist over the bowl; no need to waste the blood.

''What do I do?''

''Put your wrist over the bowl.''

He hesitated, then did what I asked. He put his arm over the bowl, hand balled into a fist. I turned his hand over to expose the underside of his arm. I steadied his hand with my still bleeding hand. The bowl wavered where his free hand was still holding it with Jean-Claude.

I looked up at his face. ''Why does this bother you more than Jean-Claude tasting you?''

He swallowed. ''A lot of things don't bother me when I'm thinking about sex.''

''Spoken like someone with only one X chromosome,'' I said. I drew the knife down his skin in one firm bite, while he was still looking at my face. The only thing that kept him from pulling away was my hold on him.

He didn't struggle after that initial surprise. He watched his blood splash into the bowl, mingling with mine. The bottom of the bowl was hidden from sight, covered in warm blood. I released his hand and he held his bleeding wrist over the bowl.

''Jean Claude?'' I said.

He held his own slender wrist out to me without being asked. I steadied his wrist as I had Richard's. I met his dark blue eyes but there was no fear there, nothing but perhaps a mild curiosity. I cut his wrist and the blood welled crimson against his white skin.

His blood splashed into the bowl. It was all red. Human, lycanthrope, and vampire. You couldn't tell who was who by just looking. We all bleed red.

There still wasn't enough blood to walk a circle of power around the sixty or so zombies. There was no way short of a true sacrifice to get that much blood. But what I had in my hands was a very potent magic cocktail. Dominic thought it would be enough. I hoped so.

A sound brought my attention away from the blood, and the growing warmth of power.

Stephen and Jason were crouched near us, one in human form, one wolf, with nearly identical looks in their eyes: hunger.

I looked past them to Cassandra. She was standing her ground, but her hands were balled into fists, and a sheen of sweat gleamed on her upper lip. The look on her face was near panic.

Dominic stood smiling and unaffected. He was the only other human in the room.

Jason growled at us, but it wasn't a real growl. There was a rhythm to the noise. He was trying to talk.

Stephen moistened his lips. "Jason wants to know if we can lick the bowl?"

I looked at Jean-Claude and Richard. The looks on their faces were enough. "Am I the only one in this room not lusting after the blood?"

"Except for Dominic, I fear so, *ma petite*."

"Do what you have to do, Anita, but do it quick. It's full moon, and fresh blood is fresh blood," Richard said.

The two other vamps I'd raised shuffled towards me. Their eyes still empty of personality, like well-made dolls.

"Did you call them?" Richard asked.

"No," I said.

"The blood called them," Dominic said.

The vampires came into the room. They didn't look at me this time. They looked at the blood, and the moment they saw it, something flared in them. I felt it. Hunger. No one was home, but the need was still there.

Damian's green eyes stared at the bowl with the same hunger. His handsome face thinned down to something beastial and primitive.

I licked my lips and said, "Stop." They did, but they stared at the freshly spilled blood, never raising their eyes to me. If I hadn't been here to stop them, they might have fed. Fed like revenants, animalistic vampires that know nothing but the hunger and never regain their humanity or their minds.

My heart thudded into my throat at the thought of what I'd almost loosed upon some unsuspecting person. The hunger wouldn't have differentiated between human and lycanthrope. Wouldn't that have been a fine fight?

I took the bloody bowl, cradling it against my stomach, the knife still in my right hand.

''Do not be afraid,'' Dominic said. ''Lay the zombies to rest as you have a thousand times over the years. Do that and that alone.''

''One step at a time, right?'' I said.

''Indeed,'' he said.

I nodded. ''Okay.''

Everyone but the three vampires looked at me as if they believed I knew what I was doing. I wished I did. Even Dominic looked confident. But he didn't have to put sixty zombies back in the ground without a circle of power. I did.

I had to watch my step on the rubble-strewn floor. It wouldn't do to fall and spill all this blood, all this power. Because that's what it was. I could feel Jean-Claude and Richard at my back like two braids of a rope twisting inside me as I moved. Dominic had said that I would be able to feel both of the men. When I'd asked for specifics about how I would be able to feel them, he had gone vague. Magic was too individualistic for exactness. If he told me one way and it felt another, it would have made me doubt. He'd been right.

I stirred the knife through the blood and flung blood on the waiting zombies with the blade. Only a few drops fell on them, but every time the blood touched one, I could feel it, a shock of power, a jolt. I ended in the center of the once walled room, surrounded by the zombies. When the blood touched the last one, a shock ran through me that tore a gasp from my throat. I felt the blood close round the dead. It was similar to closing a circle of power, but it was like the closure was inside me, rather than outside.

''Back,'' I said, ''back into your graves, all of you. Back into the ground.''

The dead shuffled around me, positioning themselves like sleepwalkers in a game of musical chairs. As each one reached its place, it lay down, and the raw earth poured over them all like water. The earth swallowed them back and smoothed over them as if a giant hand had come to neaten everything up.

I was alone in the room with the earth still twitching like a horse thick with flies. When the last ripple had died away, I looked out of the blasted wall at the others.

Jean-Claude and Richard stood at the opening of the wall. The three werewolves clustered around them. Even Cassandra had knelt on the ground beside the wolf that was Jason. Dominic stood behind them, watching. He was grinning at me like a proud papa.

I walked towards them, my legs a touch rubbery, and I stumbled, splashing blood down the side of the bowl. Crimson drops fell onto the swept earth.

The wolf was suddenly there, licking the ground clean. I ignored it and kept walking. Vampires next. Everyone moved to let me pass as if they were afraid to touch me. Except for Dominic. He crowded almost too close.

I felt his own power crackle between us, shivering over my skin, down the ropes of power that bound me to Richard and Jean-Claude.

I swallowed and said, ''Back up.''

''My apologies.'' He moved back until I couldn't feel him quite so tightly. ''Good enough?''

I nodded.

The three vampires waited with hungry eyes. I sprinkled them with the cooling blood. They twitched when the blood touched them, but there was no rush of power. Nothing. Shit.

Dominic frowned. ''The blood is still warm. It should work.''

Jean-Claude moved closer. I could feel it without turning around. I could feel him coming down the line of power between us like a fish being reeled in. ''But it is not working,'' he said.

''No,'' I said.

''They are lost then.''

I shook my head. Willie was staring at the bowl of blood. The look was feral, pure hunger. I'd thought that the worst thing that could happen would be for Willie to simply lie down in his coffin and be truly dead. I was wrong. Having Willie crawl out of his coffin craving nothing but blood, knowing nothing but hunger, would be worse. I would not loose him, not yet.

''Any bright ideas?'' I asked.

''Feed them the blood in the bowl,'' Dominic said, ''but hurry before it grows colder.''

I didn't argue; there was no time. I wiped the knife on my jeans and sheathed it. I'd have to clean it and the sheath later, but I needed my hands free. I dipped my fingertips into the blood. It was still warm, but barely. The eyes were still brown as they followed my hand, but it wasn't Willie looking out of them. It just wasn't.

I lifted the gold bowl to Willie's mouth and said, ''Willie, drink.'' His throat moved, swallowing furiously, and I felt that click. He was mine again. ''Stop, Willie.''

He stopped, and I took the bowl away from him. He didn't grab for it. He didn't move at all. His eyes were blank and empty above his bloody mouth. ''Go back to your coffin, Willie. Rest until nightfall. Back to your coffin to rest.''

He turned and walked back down the hallway. I'd have to trust he was going back to the coffin. I'd check later. One down, two to go. Liv left like a good little puppet. The blood was getting pretty low by the time I raised it to Damian's lips.

He drank at it, his pale throat swallowing. The blood passed down his throat and something brushed me. Something that wasn't my magic. Something else. Damian's chest rose in a great breath like a man struggling back from drowning. And that something thrust me backwards, cast out my power, turned it back on me. It was like a door slammed, but it was more than that. A force thrust at me, hit me, and the world swirled around. My vision was eaten away in greyness and white spots. I heard my own heartbeat impossibly loud. The thudding chased me down into the darkness, then even that was lost.

33

I woke, staring up at the white drapes above Jean-Claude's bed. There was a damp washcloth folded over my forehead and voices arguing. I lay there for a few seconds, just blinking. I couldn't remember how I'd gotten here. I remembered the sensation of being cast out of Damian. I'd been cast out like an intruder, something to be protected against. The force that touched me hadn't been evil. I'd felt evil before, and that wasn't it. But it certainly hadn't been a beneficent force, either. More neutral, maybe.

The voices were Jean-Claude and Richard. The argument was about me. Big surprise.

''How can you let her die when you could save her?'' Richard asked.

''I do not believe she is dying, but even if she was, without her permission, I will never again invade her mind.''

''Even if she was dying?''

''Yes,'' Jean-Claude said.

''I don't understand that.''

''You don't have to understand it, Richard. Anita would agree with me.''

I brushed the rag from my head. I wanted to sit up, but it seemed too much effort.

Richard sat down on the bed, taking my hand. I wasn't sure I wanted him to, but I was still too weak to stop him.

Jean-Claude stood behind him, watching me. His face was blank and perfect, a mask.

''How do you feel?'' Richard asked.

I had to swallow before I could speak. ''Not sure.''

Dominic walked into view. He had, wisely, stayed out of the argument. Besides, he was already a vampire's human servant. What was he going to say? That the mark was evil, or that it was no big deal. Lies either way.

''I am very glad to see you awake.''

''It thrust me out,'' I said.

He nodded. ''Indeed.''

''What thrust her out?'' Richard asked.

Dominic looked at me.

I shrugged.

''When the power that animates the vampire returned and found Anita still inside the body, the power cast her out.''

Richard frowned. ''Why?''

''I shouldn't have been there.''

''Did the soul return as you touched it?'' Jean-Claude asked.

''I've felt the brush of a soul before, that wasn't it.''

Jean-Claude looked at me.

I looked back.

He was the one who looked away first.

Richard touched my hair where it had gotten wet from the rag. ''I don't care if it was a soul or the bogeyman. I thought I'd lost you.''

''I always seem to survive, Richard, no matter who else dies.''

He frowned at that.

I let him. ''Is Damian all right?'' I asked.

''He seems to be,'' Jean-Claude said.

''What were you two arguing about?''

''Dominic, could you leave us now?'' Jean-Claude asked.

Dominic smiled. ''Gladly. I am eager to speak with Sabin. Tomorrow, you and Richard can raise him, and you, Anita''—he touched my face lightly—''can heal him.''

I didn't like him touching me, but there was almost a reverence in his face. It made it hard to yell at him.

''I'll do my best,'' I said.

''In all things, I think.'' With that, he bid us a good day and left.

When the door closed behind him, I repeated my question. ''What were you two arguing about?''

Richard glanced behind at Jean-Claude, then back to me. ''You stopped breathing for a few seconds. No heartbeat, either. I thought you were dying.''

I looked at Jean-Claude. ''Tell me.''

''Richard wanted me to give you the first mark again. I refused.''

''Smart vampire,'' I said.

He shrugged. ''You have made yourself very clear, *ma petite*. I will not be accused of forcing myself upon you again. Not in any sense.''

''Did someone do CPR?''

''You started breathing on your own,'' Richard said. He squeezed my hand. ''You scared me.''

I drew my hand out of his. ''So you offered me to him as his human servant.''

''I thought we'd agreed to be a triad of power. Maybe I don't understand what that means.''

I wanted to sit up but still wasn't sure I could do it, so I had to be content with frowning up at him. ''I'll share power with you both, but I won't let Jean-Claude mark me. If he ever forces himself on me again, I'll kill him.''

Jean-Claude nodded. ''You will try, *ma petite*. It is a dance I do not wish to begin.''

''I'm going to let him mark me before I leave for the pack tonight,'' Richard said.

I stared up at him. ''What are you talking about?''

''Jean-Claude can't come tonight. He isn't a member of the pack. If we're joined, I can still call the power.''

I struggled to sit up, and if Richard hadn't caught me, I'd have fallen. I lay cradled in his arms, digging fingers into his arms, trying to make him listen to me. ''You don't want to be his servant for all eternity, Richard.''

''The joining of master and animal is not the same as between master and servant, *ma petite*. It is not quite as intimate.''

I couldn't see the vampire over Richard's broad shoulders. I tried to push myself up, and Richard had to help me. ''Explain,'' I said.

''I will not be able to taste food through Richard, as I could through you. It is a minor side effect, but in truth one I miss. I enjoyed tasting solid food again.''

''What else?''

''Richard is an alpha werewolf. He is an equivalent power to mine in some ways. He will have more control over my entering his dreams, his thoughts. He would be able to keep me out, as it were.''

''And I couldn't,'' I said.

He looked down at me. ''Even then, before you had explored your powers of necromancy, you were harder to control than you should have been. Now,'' he shrugged, ''now I am not sure who would be master and who would be servant.''

I sat up on my own. I was feeling just a tad better. ''That's why you didn't mark me while you had the chance and Richard to take the blame. After what I did today, you're afraid that I'd be the master and you'd be my servant. That's it, isn't it?''

He smiled softly. ''Perhaps.'' He sat on the bed on the other side of Richard. ''I have not worked for over two hundred years to be Master of my own lands to give up my freedom to anyone, even you, *ma petite*. You would not be a cruel master, but you would be an exacting one.''

''It's not pure master and servant. I know that from Alejandro. He couldn't control me, but I couldn't control him, either.''

''Did you try?'' Jean-Claude asked.

That stopped me. I had to think about it. ''No.''

''You simply killed him,'' Jean-Claude said.

He had a point. ''Would I really be able to order you around?''

''I have never heard of another vampire choosing a necromancer of your power as human servant.''

''What about Dominic and Sabin?'' I asked.

''Dominic is no match for you, *ma petite*.''

''If I agreed to the first mark, would you do it or not?'' I asked.

Richard tried to hug me to his chest, but I moved away. I had to put both arms down to prop myself up, but I was sitting on my own.

Jean-Claude sighed, looking down at the floor. ''If we truly joined, no one could stand against us. That much power is very tempting.'' He looked up suddenly, letting me see his eyes. Emotions rolled across his face. Excitement, fear, lust, and finally, just weariness. ''We could be bound together for all eternity. Bound together in a three-way struggle for power. It is not a pleasant thought.''

''Jean-Claude told me that he would not be my master,'' Richard said. ''We would be partners.''

''And you believed him?'' I said.

Richard nodded, looking terribly earnest.

I sighed. ''Jesus, Richard, I can't leave you alone for a minute.''

''It is not a lie, *ma petite*.''

''Yeah, right.''

''If it's a lie,'' Richard said, ''I'll kill him.''

I stared at him. ''You don't mean that.''

''Yes, I do.'' Something moved through his brown eyes, something low and dark and inhuman.

''Once you decide to kill someone, it becomes easier to kill others, doesn't it?'' I said.

Richard didn't flinch or look away. ''Yes, it does, but that's not it. I won't be anyone's servant. Not Jean-Claude's, not yours, not Marcus's, not Raina's.''

''Do you understand that once you're bound to him, that hurting him can hurt you? Killing him can kill you?''

''I'd rather be dead than trapped.''

I watched the absolute certainty in his eyes. He meant it. ''You'll kill Marcus tonight,'' I said.

Richard looked at me, and an expression passed over his face that I'd never seen before, a fierceness that filled his eyes and sent his power shivering through the room. ''If he doesn't back down, I'll kill him.''

For the first time, I believed him.

34

There was a knock on the door. Richard and Jean-Claude spoke at the same time. ''Enter.'' ''Come in.'' They stared at each other as the door opened.

Edward walked in. His cool blue eyes took in the three of us at a glance. ''What happened to you?''

''Long story,'' I said. ''It wasn't the assassin if that's what you're worried about.''

''I wasn't. Your wolves are guarding my backup. They wouldn't let me bring him in without somebody's approval.'' He looked at Jean-Claude and Richard. ''They weren't absolutely clear on whose permission I was supposed to get.'' He didn't smile while he said it, but I knew him well enough to see the shadow of humor on his face.

''This is my home,'' Jean-Claude said. ''It is my permission that is needed.''

I slid to the edge of the bed and found I could sit up. The movement put me between the two men. Richard hovered close to help me if I fell onto my face. Jean-Claude just sat there, not touching me, not offering to. In many ways, he understood me better than Richard did, but then he'd known me longer. I was sort of an acquired taste.

Jean-Claude stood up. ''I will go escort your guest in.''

''I better go with you,'' Edward said. ''Harley doesn't know you, but he'll know what you are.''

''What's that supposed to mean?'' I asked.

''If a strange vampire walked up to you in this place and said follow me, would you do it?''

I thought about that. ''Probably not.''

Edward smiled. ''Neither would Harley.''

Edward and Jean-Claude left to fetch Edward's friend. I tried standing while they were gone, just to see if I could do it. I always like to meet new people, especially new hired muscle, on my feet.

Richard tried to help me, and I pulled away. I had to grab for the wall to keep from falling.

''I was trying to help,'' he said.

''Don't try so hard.''

''What is the matter with you?''

''I don't like being helpless, Richard.''

''You aren't superwoman.''

I glared at him. ''I fainted, for God's sake. I never faint.''

''You didn't faint,'' he said. ''Whatever it was threw you out of Damian. I was still tied to you when it happened, Anita. I felt it brush me.'' He shook his head, hugging his arms to his chest. ''You didn't faint.''

I leaned my back against the wall. ''It scared me, too.''

''Did it?'' He came to stand in front of me. ''You don't seem scared.''

''Are *you* scared about joining with Jean-Claude?''

''That bothers you more than me killing for the first time tonight, doesn't it?''

''Yeah.''

The door opened before we could continue the conversation. It was just as well. We'd found something else we disagreed on. Letting someone tie themselves to my mind, my soul, frightened me a lot more than killing someone.

The man that followed Edward didn't look that impressive. He was slender, only a couple of inches taller than Edward. He had curly brownish red hair receding in a soft circle to nearly the middle of his head. He slouched even when he walked, and I couldn't tell if it was habit or some sort of spinal problem. Brown T-shirt over black corduroy pants, and sneakers. Everything looked like it had come from the Salvation Army. He wore a patched leather aviator's jacket that might have been original World War II issue. Under the jacket, I got a glimpse of guns.

He was wearing a double shoulder holster so that he had a 9 millimeter under both arms. I'd seen holsters like it, but never knew anyone who actually wore one. I thought they were mostly for show. Very few people are equally good with both hands. There was a crisscross of straps beneath the T-shirt that I didn't understand, but I knew it was for carrying something lethal. He had a duffel bag in one hand, crammed full and big enough to carry a body in. He wasn't even straining. Stronger than he looked.

I met his eyes last. They were pale and greyish green with lashes so gingery red they were almost invisible. The look in the eyes was the emptiest I'd ever seen in another human being. It was as if when he looked at me, he wasn't seeing me at all. It wasn't like he was blind. He saw something, but I wasn't sure what he saw. Not me. Not a woman. Something else. That one look was enough. I knew that this man walked in a circle of his own creation. Saw a version of reality that would send the rest of us screaming. But he functioned, and he didn't scream.

''This is Harley,'' Edward said. He introduced us all, as if it was an ordinary meeting.

I stared at Harley's pale eyes and realized that he scared me. It had been a long time since another human being frightened me just by entering a room.

Richard offered his hand, and Harley simply looked at it. I wanted to explain to Richard why he shouldn't have made the gesture, but I wasn't sure I could.

I did not offer to shake hands.

"I found out the name of the money man behind the attempts on your life," Edward said. He said it without preamble.

Three of us stared at him. Harley, disquietly, kept staring at me. "What did you say?" I asked.

"I know who we have to kill."

"Who?" I asked.

"Marcus Fletcher. The head of our local werewolf pack." He smiled, pleased with himself, on the effect the news was having on Richard.

"You're sure?" Richard said. "Absolutely sure?"

Edward nodded, studying Richard's face. "Does he hate you enough to kill Anita?"

"I didn't think so." Richard turned to me, the look on his face stricken, horrified. "My God, I never dreamt he'd do something like this. Why?"

"How well would you have fought tonight with *ma petite* dead?" Jean-Claude asked.

Richard stared at him so obviously overwhelmed by the dastardliness of what Marcus had done that I wanted to pat his head and tell him it was all right. I nearly get killed twice and I wanted to comfort him. Love is just plain stupid sometimes.

"It's all so convenient," Edward said, with a happy lilt to his voice.

"What do you mean?" Richard asked.

"He means you are supposed to kill him tonight, Richard, so we don't have to," I said.

"I just can't believe that Marcus would do something so . . ."

"Evil," I suggested.

He nodded.

"It would seem more Raina's sort of idea than Marcus's," Jean-Claude said.

"It's twisted enough for her," I said.

"Marcus could have said no," Richard said. He ran his hands through his hair, combing it back from his face. His handsome face was set in very stubborn lines. "This has got to stop. He'll do anything she asks, anything, and she's crazy."

My eyes flicked to Harley. I couldn't help it. He caught my look and smiled. I didn't know exactly what he was thinking, but it wasn't pleasant and it wasn't pretty. Having Harley as backup made me wonder if I was on the right side.

"Edward, can I talk to you a minute in private?" I didn't want to be this obvious, but Harley was bothering me that much.

I walked away from the others and Edward trailed behind. It was kind of nice to walk across the room, lower my voice, and know the person I was whispering about wouldn't hear me. Both Jean-Claude and Richard would.

Edward looked at me, and there was that same touch of amusement to him, as if he knew what I was going to say and thought it was a hoot.

"Why does he keep looking at me?"

"You mean Harley?"

"You know damn well who I mean," I said.

"He's only looking, Anita. No harm."

"But why me?"

"You're a girl maybe?"

"Stop it, Edward. Whatever he's thinking, it isn't sex, and if it is, I don't want to know the details."

Edward stared at me. "Ask him."

"What?"

"Ask him why he's staring at you."

"Just like that?"

He nodded. "Harley will probably get a kick out of it."

"Do I want to know?" I asked.

"I don't know. Do you?"

I took a deep breath and let it out slowly. "You're stringing me along here, Edward. What's the deal?"

"If something happens to me during the fighting, Harley needs at least one other person that he'll mind."

"Mind?"

"He's absolutely reliable, Anita. He'll stay at my back, never flinch, and kill anyone I tell him to, but he's not good without specific orders. And he doesn't take orders from just everybody."

"So you designated me?"

Edward shook his head. "I told him to pick someone in the room."

"Why me?"

"Ask him."

"Fine." I walked back towards the others, and Edward followed me. Harley watched us like he was seeing other things. It was too damned unnerving.

"Why are you staring at me?" I asked.

His voice was quiet, as if he never yelled. "You're the scariest motherfucker in the room."

"Now I know you can't see."

"I see what's there," he said.

"What the hell is wrong with you?"

"Nothing."

I tried to think of a better question and finally asked, "What do you see when you look at everybody in the room?"

"The same thing you see: monsters."

"Why do I think the monsters I see in the room aren't the same ones you see?"

He smiled, a bare upturning of lips. "They may look different, but they're still monsters. They're all monsters."

He was a card-carrying, rubber-room-renting psychotic. By the time most people got to the point where they weren't seeing reality, they were so far gone that there was no going back. Sometimes drug therapy helped, but without it, the world was a frightening, overwhelming place. Harley didn't look frightened or overwhelmed. He looked calm.

"When you look at Edward, he always looks the same to you. I mean you recognize him?"

Harley nodded.

"You'd recognize me," I said.

"If I make an effort to memorize you, yes."

"That's why you were staring."

"Yes," he said.

"What happens if Edward and I both go down?"

Harley smiled, but his eyes shifted to one side as if something low to the ground and rather small had run across the room. The movement was so natural that I looked. Nothing.

"Harley," I said.

He looked back at me, but his eyes were just a little higher up than my face should have been. "Yes," he said, his voice so quiet.

"What happens if Edward and I are both killed?"

Harley stared at me. His eyes shifted to my face for just a second, as if the fog had cleared. "That would be bad."

35

There would be no backing down for Marcus tonight. He had to die, one way or another. Richard wasn't arguing anymore. But there was still the chance that Raina would lead a revolt of the other lukoi. Their loyalty was divided enough for a war, even with Marcus dead. Jean-Claude came up with a solution. We'd put on a better show. A better show than Raina and Marcus? He had to be kidding. Richard agreed to let Jean-Claude costume him up for the night. As his lupa, that meant I had to get dressed up, too.

Jean-Claude took Richard off to dress him. He sent Cassandra with a white cardboard clothes box to me. She was supposed to help me change, she said.

I opened the box and all that was in it was a pile of black leather straps. I kid you not. I drew it out of the box and it didn't improve. ''I don't know how to get into this, even if I was willing to.''

''I'll get Stephen,'' Cassandra said.

''I don't want to undress in front of Stephen.''

''He's a stripper,'' she said. ''He dressed me last night at Danse Macabre, remember.'' She patted my hand. ''He'll be a perfect gentleman.''

I sat down on the bed and scowled at the door. I was not wearing this crap.

An hour later, Stephen and Cassandra were turning me in front of the bathroom mirrors so I could see myself. It had been embarrassing at first having a man help squeeze me into the thing, but Cassandra was right. Stephen was not only a perfect gentleman, he simply didn't seem to be moved at all by the fact that I was mostly naked. It was like having two girlfriends help me. One just happened not to be a girl.

The top was mostly a leather bra with lining for comfort. It was one of those that lifted and showed your cleavage to absolute best advantage. But it was tight and held in place. Nothing was falling out. My cross was visible, though. I taped it. I'd peel the tape when I left the Circus. Werewolves on the menu tonight, not vamps.

The bottom was sort of leather shorts, except that where the shorts stopped, straps took over. I wouldn't be caught dead or alive in something like this, not even to make a good show of things for Richard, except that there were extras.

Two leather sheaths covered my upper arms, complete with a knife apiece. The knives were high quality, high silver content. If the hilts were a little elaborate for my taste, the balance was good, and that's what counted. Two more sheaths covered my lower arms with two more knives, smaller, balanced more for throwing, though they both had hilts and weren't true throwing knives. The bulge under Harley's T-shirt had been throwing knives, the real McCoy, slender and innocent looking until you saw them used.

There was a leather belt around the top of the shorts that my Browning's shoulder holster fit on nicely. Edward had bought me a new Browning. It wasn't my very own gun, but it was still nice to have. Harley had fished a clip-on holster for the Firestar out of his duffel. The small clip-on rode to one side of my waist for a cross draw.

The straps down my legs had small silver loops, sheaths, two more knives, one on each thigh. No knife sheaths below the knees because boots came with the outfit. Jean-Claude had finally gotten me out of my Nikes. The boots were soft black suede with heels only a touch higher than I would have liked. A tiny stoppered vial fit in small loops just below the top of each boot. I held one up to the light, and knew what it was. Holy water. A nice gift from my vampire boyfriend, heh?

I stared at myself in the mirror. "How long has Jean-Claude been planning this outfit?"

"A little while," Stephen said. He was kneeling by me, tugging the straps into place. "We all had a running bet that he'd never get you to wear it."

"Who's we?"

"His flunkies." Stephen stood up, stepped back, and nodded. "You look amazing."

"I look like a biker slut from hell meets soldier of fortune pinup."

"That, too," Stephen said.

I turned to Cassandra. "Be honest."

"You look dangerous, Anita. Like somebody's weapon."

I stared in the mirror, shaking my head. "Somebody's sex toy, you mean."

"A dominatrix maybe, but nobody's toy," Cassandra said.

Why didn't that make me feel better?

Cassandra had insisted on helping me with my makeup. She was a great deal more skilled at it than I. Years of practice, she'd said. My hair was tight and curling, falling just below my shoulders now. It needed a cut. But for tonight, the hair was perfect. The face was still pretty. Makeup is a wonderful thing. But the outfit stripped away the pretense. I looked like what I was: something that would kill you before it would kiss you.

We walked out of the bathroom and found Edward and Harley waiting for us. They had brought two straight-backed chairs to sit on the white carpet, facing the bathroom door. I froze as Edward stared at me. He didn't say a word, just sat there with a sort of half-smile on his face.

"Well, say something, dammit."

"I would say it isn't you, but in a way, it is."

I took a deep breath. "Yeah."

Harley stared at me with vacant eyes. He was smiling, but not at the outfit. Smiling at some internal music or vision that only he could perceive.

There was a long leather coat on the bed. "One of the vampires dropped it off," Edward said. "Thought you might want something to cover up with until the big unveiling."

"You're enjoying this, aren't you?"

"I'd feel better if I could guard your back."

"You're going to do that with a rifle from the closest hill, remember."

"Night vision and scope, fine, but I can't kill them all from a distance."

"You couldn't kill them all if you were johnny on the spot, either," I said.

"No, but I'd feel better."

"Worried about me?"

He shrugged. "I'm your bodyguard. If you die under my protection, the other bodyguards will make fun of me."

It took me a second to realize he was making a joke. Harley looked back at him with an almost surprised look. I don't think either of us heard humor from Edward much.

I walked towards Edward. The leather made that little creaking sound it makes. I stopped in front of him, legs a little apart, staring down at him.

He widened his eyes a little. "Yes."

"I can't imagine anyone making fun of you, Edward."

He touched one of the leather straps. "If I went around dressed like this, they might."

I had to smile. "You probably would be dressed like this if you were going to be down in the clearing with us tonight."

He turned pale blue eyes to me. "I've worn worse than this, Anita. I'm a fine actor when I have to be." The humor drained away from his face, leaving something feral and determined behind. Edward would still do things that I wouldn't, still had fewer rules than I did, but in some ways, Edward was a mirror for me. A warning of what I was becoming, or maybe a preview.

Richard would have said it was a warning. I hadn't made up my mind yet.

There was a knock on the door. Richard came in without waiting for an invitation. He was scowling, but the grumpy look faded when he got a good look at me. His eyes widened. "I was going to come in and complain about my outfit." He shook his head. "If I complain, will you just shoot me?" A smile spread across his face.

"No laughing," I said.

The smile got wider. His voice was a little choked, but he managed, "Wonderful. You look wonderful."

There are only two things you can do when you're dressed like *Barbie Does Bondage*; you can be embarrassed or you can be aggressive. Guess what my choice was.

I stalked towards him, putting a little extra sway into my walk. The boots made it easier, somehow, giving just the right roll. I put into my eyes, my face, what the outfit promised: sex, violence, heat.

The humor faded from Richard's face, replaced by an answering heat and a hesitation, like he wasn't exactly sure we should be doing this in public.

He was wearing black leather pants with soft suede boots that were almost a match to my own. His hair had been slicked back, tied off with a black ribbon. His shirt was silk and a vibrant blue, somewhere between turquoise and royal. It looked splendid against his tanned skin.

I stopped just in front of him, legs apart. I stared up at him, defying him to think it was funny. I put a finger to his lips, trailing my fingertip down his cheek, his neck, caressing the edge of his collarbone, tracing the skin until it vanished down the buttoned front of his shirt.

I stalked to the bed, fetching the leather coat. I threw it over one shoulder so that it trailed down like a limp body, not hiding much of the outfit. I opened the door and stood for just a moment framed in it. "Coming?" I said. I walked away without waiting for an answer. The look on his face was enough. He looked like I'd hit him between the eyes with a sledgehammer.

Great. Now all I had to do was try the outfit out on Jean-Claude, and we could go.

36

The May woods were a warm, close darkness. Richard and I stood outside the barn where Raina shot dirty pictures. The pack meeting place was among the trees around the farmhouse. There were so many cars that they were parked on every bit of spare ground, some so close to the woods that they touched the trees.

There may have been a full moon up there somewhere, but the clouds were so thick, the darkness so complete, that it was like standing inside a cave. Except this cave had movement. A small oozing wind trailed through the thick, night-darkened leaves. It was like some invisible giant trailed fingertips through the trees, bending them, rattling the leaves, giving movement to the night that made my shoulders tight. It was like the night itself was alive in a way that I'd never seen before.

Richard's hand was warm and slightly moist. He'd dampened that creeping energy so that it wasn't uncomfortable to touch him. I appreciated the effort. His leather cloak whispered as he moved closer. It was tied across his chest, covering only one shoulder. The cloak, combined with the full sleeves of the brilliant blue shirt, made the whole outfit seem antique.

Richard pulled on my hand, bringing me against his body, into the circle of his arms, the brush of the leather cloak. The clouds slid apart and suddenly we were bathed in a thick, silver glow. Richard was staring outward. He seemed to be listening to something that I couldn't hear. His hands convulsed around my hands, an almost painful squeeze. He stared down at me as if just remembering I was there.

He smiled. "Can you feel it?"

"What?"

"The night?"

I started to answer, no, then stopped. I looked around at the hurrying woods, the feeling of movement. "The woods seem more alive tonight."

His smile widened, a brief flash of teeth, almost a snarl. "Yes."

I tried to pull away, but his hands tightened. "You're doing it," I said. My heart was suddenly thudding in my throat. I'd thought to be afraid of a lot of things tonight, but not of Richard.

"We're supposed to share power. That's what I'm doing. But it has to be my power, Anita. The pack won't be impressed with zombies."

I swallowed past my beating heart and forced myself to stand very still. Made myself return the grip of his hands. I hadn't thought what it would mean. I wasn't going to be in charge. Not my power but his. I was going to be fuel for his fire, not the other way around.

"It's Jean-Claude's mark," I said. "That's what's doing it."

"We hoped it would work this way," Richard said.

And I knew that the *we* he was referring to didn't include me. "How does it work?"

"Like this." That trembling energy broke over his skin like a rush of warmth. It plunged through his hands into my hand. It rode like a wave over my body, and everywhere it touched, the hair and skin of my body raised and shivered.

"Are you all right?"

"Sure," but my voice was a breathless whisper.

He took me at my word. Some barrier went down, and Richard's energy crashed into me like a fist. I remembered falling, and the feel of Richard's arms around my waist, catching me, then it was like I was elsewhere. I was everywhere. I was over there in the trees, staring at us with eyes that tried to turn and see me, but I wasn't there. It was like the wind that opened inside me when I walked a cemetery, except it wasn't power that was spreading outward. It *was* me. I flashed through a dozen eyes, brushed bodies, some furred, some still skinned. I hurried outward, outward, and touched Raina. I knew it was her. Her power lashed out like a shield, casting me away from her, but not before I felt her fear.

Richard called me back, though call implies a voice. I slipped back inside myself in a rush of curling golden energy. I could see the color behind my eyes, though there was actually nothing to see. I opened my eyes, though I wasn't a hundred percent sure that they'd been closed. That golden energy was still there, swirling inside, along my skin. I curled my hands over Richard's shoulders and felt an answering energy in him.

I didn't have to ask what I had just experienced. I knew. It was what it meant, at least for someone as powerful as Richard, to be alpha. He could fling his essence outward and touch his pack. It was how he kept the werewolf from changing form two days ago. It was how he could share blood. Marcus couldn't do it, but Raina could.

Jean-Claude's power, even my own power, never felt so alive. It was like I was drawing energy from the trees, the wind, like being plugged into a vast battery, as if there was enough magic to go on forever. I had never felt anything like it.

"Can you run?" Richard asked.

The question meant more than just the words, and I knew that. "Oh, yeah."

He smiled, and it was joyous. He took my hand and flung us into the trees. Even if he'd been human, I couldn't have kept up with Richard in a dead run. Tonight, he didn't run so much as flowed into the woods. It was like he had sonar telling him where every branch, every tree root, every fallen trunk would be. It was like the trees moved away from him like water, or maybe moved into him like something else that I had no words for. He pulled me with him. Not just with his hand, but with his energy. It was like he'd entered me and tied us together somehow. It should have been intrusive and frightening, but it wasn't.

We spilled into the great clearing and Richard's power filled it, flowed over the lycanthropes like a fire springing from one dry branch to another. It filled them and made them turn to him. Only Marcus, Raina, Jamil, Sebastian, and Cassandra were untouched. Only they kept him out by force of will. He swept everyone else before him, and I knew that part of what let him do that was me. Distant as a dream or a half-remembered nightmare, was Jean-Claude, down that twisting power that was almost buried under Richard's shining light.

I felt every movement. It was like the world was suddenly crystalline, almost like the effect from an adrenaline rush, or shock, where everything seems carved and hard-edged and terribly, frightfully clear. It was like being dipped in reality, as if anything else would forever be a dream. It was almost painful.

Marcus sat in a chair that had been carved from rock so long ago the edges were rounded with weather and hands and bodies. I knew that this clearing had been the meeting place for the lukoi for a very long time.

Marcus wore a brown satin-lapeled tux. The shirt was of gold cloth, not gold lamé, but the real deal, as if they'd melted down jewelry and beaten him out a shirt. Raina curled on the edge of the stone chair. Her long auburn hair was done in an elaborate swirl of soft curls on top of her head, down along her face. A gold chain cut across her forehead with a diamond the size of my thumb in it. More diamonds burned like white fire at her throat. She was absolutely naked except for a sprinkling of gold body glitter, done thick enough on her nipples to make them seem metallic. A diamond anklet glittered on her right ankle. Three gold chains rode low on her hips, and that was it.

And I'd complained about my outfit.

''Welcome, Richard, Anita,'' Marcus said. ''Welcome to our happy family.'' His voice was deep and thick. It flowed with its own edge of power, but it wasn't enough. It would never be enough. Richard could have worn his jeans and T-shirt, and still he would have won them over. There are things beyond clothing that make a king.

''Marcus, Raina.'' Richard released my hand slowly, and as he pulled away, the tie remained. It was a shadow of the way I'd bound Richard and Jean-Claude's auras to me, but more. He took a few steps away to stand a little in front of me. I could feel him like a large, shimmering *thing*. His energy was amazing. The closest thing I'd ever felt was the power of a Daoine Sidhe, a fairie of the highest court.

''You naughty boy,'' Raina said. ''You've made her one of us.''

''No,'' Richard said, ''she is what she always has been: herself.''

''Then how can you ride her power? How can she ride yours?'' Raina pushed away from the chair, stalking along the ground in front of it, pacing like a caged animal.

''What have you done, Richard?'' Marcus asked.

''She is my mate.''

"Raina, test it," Marcus said.

Raina smiled, most unpleasant, and stalked over the open ground. She swayed, transforming walking into a seductive dance. I felt her power tonight. Her sex rode the air like the threat of lightning, prickling along the skin, drying out the mouth. I felt every male watch her, even Richard. I didn't resent it. Hell, I watched her. She was magnificent in her sheer, naked lust. It was like sex for Raina was power, literally.

I slipped off the long, black coat and let it fall to the ground. There was a collective gasp from the human throats. I traced my hands over the bare skin of my waist, trailing down my leather-clad thighs. I laughed. A loud, joyous bark of noise. It was Raina. I was riding her power, dancing along the edge of her energy.

I stalked towards her, not waiting, but meeting her in the middle of the circle. We moved around each other, and I could match her dance. I pulled her aura of sex and violence into me, pulled it like a hand reaching inward and stealing bits of her. Fear widened her eyes, brought her breath faster.

She knew how to protect herself against another werewolf, but my brand of power was just different enough that she didn't know what to do with me. I'd never done anything like this before, didn't understand exactly what I was doing, until Raina backed off. She didn't run back to Marcus, but the shine was gone. She slunk back with her tail between her legs, and I could taste her inside my mind like I'd licked her skin.

I turned back to Richard and stalked towards him in the high-heeled boots. I felt every man watching. I knew it. I wrapped it around me and threw it all back into Richard. He stood almost frozen, his dark eyes filled with a heat that was part sex, part energy, part something else. And for the first time, I understood that something else. I heard that music, felt it dance inside my body.

I grabbed the leather cloak and pulled him down to me. We kissed and it burned, as if more than flesh was mingling. I released him abruptly, and my eyes didn't go to his face but fell lower. Without touching him, I knew he was hard and ready. I could still feel the pack, distant, but touchable. Jason's great wolf head brushed my thigh. I dug my fingers into that thick fur and knew that if Richard and I made love, the pack would know it. Here tonight, they'd be along for the ride. It wouldn't just be sex. It would be magic. And it didn't seem shameful or pagan or wrong.

"You can't let them do this," Raina said.

Marcus pushed himself to his feet. He seemed tired. "No, I don't suppose I can." He looked at Raina, naked, beautiful, fearful. "But it is not your blood that will be spilled tonight, is it, my love?" The irony was thick enough to walk on, and for the first time, I realized that Marcus knew what Raina was, maybe had always known.

Raina went to her knees in front of him, hands clutching at his legs. She rubbed her cheek along his thigh, one hand smoothing perilously close to his groin. Even now, it was what she knew best. Sex and pain.

He touched her hair gently. He stared down at her, and the naked tenderness on his face made me want to look away. It was a terribly intimate look, more intimate than sex, more powerful. The fool loved her.

If he hadn't been paying to kill me, I'd have felt sorry for him.

Marcus stepped away from Raina. He began walking across the clearing. His power opened like a door, flowing like electric water across the wolves, across me. He undid his tie, opened the first few buttons of his shirt. ''No more preliminaries, Richard. Let us do this.''

''I know you tried to have Anita killed,'' Richard said.

Marcus stopped in midmotion. His small, sure fingers hesitated. Surprise chased across his face, then changed into a smile. ''You have surprised me twice tonight, Richard. Let's see if you can make it three.''

''I will kill you tonight, Marcus; you know that.''

Marcus shrugged out of his jacket. ''You can try.''

Richard nodded. ''I'd planned on giving you the chance to just leave.''

''I tried to have your mate killed. You can't leave me alive now.'' He undid the cuffs of his shirt.

''No, I can't.'' Richard undid the cloak's tie, letting it fall to the floor. He pulled his shirt out of his pants and slid it over his head in one quick movement. The moonlight made shadows on the muscles of his arms and chest. I suddenly didn't want him to do it. I could shoot Marcus, and it would all be done. Richard would never forgive me, but he'd be alive. They wouldn't kill each other with power. They'd use claws and teeth for the killing. All Richard's trembling, eager power wouldn't keep him from getting his throat ripped out.

37

Richard turned to me, wearing only the leather pants and the boots. Marcus had asked that they not strip down, said something about saving an old man's dignity. Bullshit. There was something in the air that I didn't like, as if Marcus had known what was coming and he was ready.

"As acknowledged Ulfric, Marcus gets to choose the form we fight in," Richard said.

"What form did he choose?"

Richard raised his hand in front of my face. "Touch my hand."

He made it sound so serious for such a small request. I touched the back of his hand lightly.

"Grip my palm, Anita."

I wrapped my fingers around the lower part of his hand. Before I could look to his face or ask a question, I felt it. Energy welled up his hand like oil up the wick of a lamp. His skin flowed under my hand. I felt the bones lengthening. I felt his body give as if the boundaries that confined him to skin and bone and flesh had dissolved. It felt almost like he would scatter himself outward like I'd done earlier, but it wasn't his essence that was reaching outward. It was his body.

He held up his other hand, and I took it. I locked my fingers in his and felt his bones grow across my skin, watched claws form as his flesh flowed like clay. Distant as a scream, I knew I should have been scared or sickened. The power flowed down his shifting hands to my hands, flowing between us like cool fire.

He stopped when his hands were human claws with talons that could have ripped me apart. The power didn't stop abruptly; it wasn't like turning off a switch. It was like turning off a faucet, slowing the flow down to a trickle, a drop, then nothing.

I was on my knees and hadn't remembered getting there. Richard knelt in front of me, hands still clasped in mine. It took me two tries to be able to talk. "How can you stop like that?"

He drew his newly formed hands carefully out of my hands. I shivered as the tips of his claws trailed over my skin.

''Controlling the change is what separates the sheep from the wolves,'' he said.

It took me a second to realize he'd made a joke. He leaned into me and whispered, ''If I lose control in the fight, or if I'm losing, I'll shift completely. I want you to come touch me, if I ask you.''

''Why?''

His breath was warm against my cheek. He wrapped his arms around me, held me in the circle of his body, claws playing along the leather straps of the outfit. ''I want you to feel the rush of power. I want you to know what it can be like between us.'' His arms tightened. ''If I'm losing, you can ride the power and use it to get my wolves out of here. The others will kill anyone they think is disloyal.''

I pushed away enough to see his face. ''How can I use the power to do that?''

''You'll know.'' He kissed my forehead ever so gently. ''Save them, Anita. Promise me.''

''I promise.''

He stood, my hands slipping over his body as he got to his feet. I caught one of his hands. My hand slid down the long, curved claw. It was as hard and solid and unreal as it looked. I'd felt his body shift, and yet, staring up at Richard's handsome face and those monstrous hands, it was jarring. Still, I held on. I didn't want to let him go.

''Careful of the claws, Anita. I'm not in human form anymore.''

He meant that a scratch might make me furry, might not. Hard to tell. But it was enough to make me let go. No matter how good Richard felt, I wasn't ready to throw humanity completely behind me.

Richard stared down at me, and there was a world in his eyes of things unsaid, things undone. I opened my mouth, closed it. ''Do you have this much control over every body part?''

He smiled. ''Yes.''

I was so scared I couldn't speak. I'd made my last joke. The only thing left was truth. I raised up, putting my hands on his legs for support and kissed the back of his hand. The skin was still as soft, still smelled and tasted like Richard, the bones underneath felt like someone else.

''Don't get killed.''

He smiled. There was a sadness in his eyes that was bottomless. Even if he won this fight, it would cost him dearly. Murder, that's how he would see it. No matter how justified. Moral high ground is dandy, but it'll get you killed.

Raina kissed Marcus good-bye, pressing her body so tightly against him, it was like she was trying to walk through him, part him like a curtain and slip inside.

She pushed him away with a rich, throaty laugh. It was the kind of laughter that made you turn your head in bars. A joyous, slightly wicked sound. Raina stared across the clearing at me, the laughter still sparkling in her eyes, on her face. One look was enough. She was going to kill me if she could.

Since I was pretty much thinking the same thing about her, I gave her a little nod and a salute. We'd see who was dead come morning. It might be me, but somewhere on the lists of the dead would be Raina. That I could almost promise.

Marcus raised his clawed hands over his head. He turned in a slow circle.

"Two alphas fight for you here tonight. One of us will leave this circle alive. One of us will feed you tonight. Drink of our blood, eat of our flesh. We are pack. We are lukoi. We are one."

Jason threw his head back and howled, so close to me that I jumped. Furred throats echoed him, human throats joining the chorus. I stood alone among the pack and did not join in. When the last echo faded off in the rolling, wooded hills, Marcus said, "Death between us then, Richard."

"I offered you life, Marcus. You chose death."

Marcus smiled. "I suppose I did."

Marcus jumped straight at him, no feinting, no practice, just a blur of speed. Richard rolled to the ground, up and away, coming to his feet. Three thin lines bled across his belly. Marcus didn't give him a chance to recover. He covered the distance between them like a bad dream. I couldn't even keep track of it with my eyes. I'd seen lycanthropes move before, and I'd thought they were fast, but Marcus was breathtaking.

He slashed Richard, forcing him back towards the edge of the clearing where Raina stood. Richard wasn't being hurt, but the flurry of attacks forced him backwards, kept him from attacking. I needed to ask a question. I looked down at Jason. He turned pale wolf eyes to me.

"If anyone else helps Marcus, it's cheating, right?" It felt vaguely stupid talking to something that looked like an animal, but the look in those eyes wasn't animal. I wasn't sure it was human, but it wasn't animal.

The wolf nodded its head. Awkwardly.

Richard's back was almost within Raina's reach. Jamil, the black werewolf from two nights ago, had joined her. Sebastian was already at her side. Shit.

"If they cheat, can I shoot them?"

"Yes," Cassandra joined us, walking up through the pack like a warm, prickling wind. I got the first real brush of her power and knew she could have been lupa if she wanted to be.

I pulled the Browning out, and it felt odd in my hands, as if I didn't need it. I was channeling more of the pack than I knew if I didn't want my gun. A dangerous amount more. I wrapped my fingers around the butt of the Browning, digging my hand around it, remembering the feel of it. The sensory memory brought it back to me, pushed some of the glow of power away.

I didn't see a weapon, but Richard's back was to Raina and Sebastian. I raised the Browning, not aiming, not yet. I yelled, "Behind you."

I saw Richard's back spasm. He collapsed to his knees. Everything slowed down, carved in crystal. Sebastian's hand moved with a flash of silver blade. I was already aiming at him. Marcus's claw drew back for a downward swipe at Richard's unprotected throat. I pulled the trigger and turned the gun towards Marcus, but it would be too slow, too late.

The top of Sebastian's head exploded. I had a fraction of a second to wonder what ammunition Edward had put in the gun. The body started to fall backwards. Marcus's claw came sweeping down, and Richard drove his hand under the arm, into Marcus's upper stomach. Marcus stopped, froze for a second, as the claws dug into his stomach, up under his ribs. Richard's hand went into Marcus's body past the wrist.

I kept the Browning pointed at Raina in case she got any ideas about picking up the knife.

Marcus drove his claws into Richard's back. Richard tucked his face and neck against the other man's body, protecting himself from the claws. Marcus shuddered. Richard broke away from him, bringing his bloody hand out of Marcus's chest. He tore the still-beating heart out of his chest and flung it to the wolves. They fell on the morsel with small yips and growling.

Richard collapsed to his knees beside Marcus's body. Blood poured down his lower back where the knife had gone in. I walked to him, the gun still pointed at Raina. I knelt, still keeping a bead on her. ''Richard, are you all right?'' It was a stupid thing to ask, but what else was I supposed to say?

''Put up the gun, Anita. It's over.''

''She tried to kill you,'' I said.

''It's over.'' He turned his face to me, and his eyes were already gone. His voice fell towards a growl. ''Put it away.''

I stared up at Raina and knew if I didn't kill her now, I'd have to kill her later. ''She'll see us dead, Richard.''

Richard's hand was suddenly there, faster than I could see. He hit my hand, and the gun went spinning. My hand was numb. I tried to back away, but he grabbed me, wrapping his clawed hands around my upper arms. ''No more killing . . . tonight.'' He threw back his head and howled. His mouth was full of fangs.

I screamed.

''Ride the power, Anita. Ride it or run.'' His hands convulsed around my arms. I backpedaled, dug my heels in, and tried to get loose. He collapsed on top of me, too hurt for the struggle, too far gone to fight the change. His power roared over me, into me. I couldn't see anything but the glow of power behind my eyes. If I could have breathed, I'd have screamed again, but there was nothing but the force of his power, and it spread outward from him like a rock in water. The waves touched the pack, and where it touched, fur flowed. Richard shifted and took everyone with him. Everyone. I felt Raina struggle next to us. I felt her fight it. Heard her shriek, but in the end she fell to the ground and changed.

I held onto Richard's arms, and fur flowed under my hands like water. Muscle formed and shifted, bones broke and reknit. My lower body was trapped underneath him. Clear liquid gushed from his body, pouring over me in a near scalding wave. I screamed and struggled to get out from underneath him. And the power rode me down, filled me up, until I thought my skin wouldn't hold, couldn't hold it.

Finally, he rose off me, not a wolf, but man-wolf, covered in fur the color of cinnamon and gold. His genitalia hung large and full underneath him. He stared at me with amber eyes and offered me a clawed hand as he rose on two slightly bent legs.

I ignored the hand and scooted backwards. I got to my feet, a little unsteady, and stared. The wolf form was actually taller than his human shape, about seven feet, muscled, and monstrous. There was nothing left of Richard. But I knew how good it had felt to let loose the beast. I had felt it rise out of him like a second mind, soul, rising upward, outward, filling him, spilling out of his skin.

My body was still tingling with the brush of his beast. I could feel the thick softness of his fur under my fingertips like a sensory memory that would haunt me.

Marcus's very human-looking body lay on the ground at Richard's feet. The scent of fresh blood ran through him, ran through them all. I felt it thrill through my body. I stared down at the dead man and wanted to go down to my knees and feed. I had a strong visual image of tearing flesh, warm viscera. It was a memory. It jerked me back a step.

I stared at the man-wolf. I stared at Richard and shook my head. "I can't feed. I won't."

He spoke, but it was twisted and guttural. "You're not invited. We will feast, then hunt. You can watch. You can join the hunt, or you can go."

I backed away slowly. "I'm going."

The pack was creeping closer, gigantic wolves mostly, but here and there were man-wolves, watching me with alien eyes. I couldn't see the Browning that Richard had knocked from my hand. I drew the Firestar and started to back away.

"No one will hurt you, Anita. You are lupa. Mate."

I stared into the cool eyes of the nearest wolf. "Right now, I'm just food, Richard."

"You refused the power," he said.

He was right. In the end, I'd panicked and hadn't gotten the full dose. "Whatever." I eased through the wolves, but they didn't move. I walked out, brushing through fur like wading through a fur coat factory. Every brush of breathing, living animal scared me. Panic climbed at my throat, and I still had enough glow left to know that my fear excited them. The more scared I got, the more I smelled like food.

I kept the gun ready, but I knew if they went for me, I was dead. There were too many of them. They watched me walk. They stubbornly refused to move, forcing me to brush their furred bodies. I realized they were using me for a sort of appetizer, my fear to spice their food, the brush of my human body to flavor their chase.

When I passed the last furred body, the sound of tearing flesh brought my head around. I couldn't stop myself in time. Richard's muzzle was raised skyward, slick with blood, throwing down a piece of meat that I tried not to recognize.

I ran. The woods that I'd glided through with Richard's help suddenly became an obstacle course. I ran, and tripped, and fell, and ran some more. I finally got back to the parking lot. I had driven because nobody but me was going home tonight. They'd stay here and have a moonlight jamboree.

Edward and Harley had watched all of it from a nearby hill with night scopes. I wondered what they thought of the show.

38

Edward made me promise to go back to the Circus for one more night. Marcus was dead, so there was no more money, but if someone else had taken the contract, they might not know that yet. It would be a shame to get killed after all the effort we'd put in to save me. I walked all the way down the damn stairs to the iron-bound door before I realized I didn't have a key, and nobody was expecting me.

The clear liquid that had gushed out of Richard's body had dried to a sticky, viscous substance somewhere between blood and glue. I needed a bath. I needed clean clothes. I needed to stop seeing Richard's mouth while he ate pieces of Marcus. The harder I tried not to flash on it, the clearer the image got.

I banged on the door until my hands stung, then I kicked it. No one came. "Shit!" I screamed at no one and everyone. "Shit!"

The feel of his body on top of mine. His bones and muscle sliding on top of me like a bag of snakes. The warm rush of power, and that moment when I had wanted to drop to my knees and feed. What if I had swallowed the power whole? What if I hadn't backed off? Would I have fed on Marcus? Would I have done that and enjoyed it?

I screamed wordlessly, smacking my hands into the door, kicking it, beating on it. I collapsed to my knees, stinging palms pressed against the wood. I leaned my head against the door and cried.

"*Ma petite*, what has happened?" Jean-Claude stood behind me on the stairs. "Richard is not dead. I would feel it."

I turned and pressed my back against the door. I wiped at the tears on my face. "He's not dead, not even close."

"Then what is wrong?" He came down the steps like he was dancing, too graceful for words, even after an evening spent with shapeshifters. His shirt was a deep, rich blue, not quite dark enough to be navy, the sleeves were full, with wide cuffs, the collar high but soft, almost as if it were a scarf. I'd never seen him in blue of any shade. It made his midnight blue eyes seem bluer, darker. His jeans were black and tight enough to be skin, the boots were knee-high, with a trailing edge of black leather that flopped as he moved.

He knelt beside me, not touching me, almost like he was afraid to. "*Ma petite*, your cross."

I stared down at it. It wasn't glowing, not yet. I wrapped my hand around the cross and jerked, snapping the chain. I flung it away. It fell against the wall, glinting silver in the faint light. "Happy?"

Jean-Claude looked at me. "Richard lives. Marcus is dead. Correct?"

I nodded.

"Then why the tears, *ma petite*? I do not think I have ever seen you cry."

"I am not crying."

He touched my cheek with one fingertip and came away with a single tear trembling on the end of his finger. He raised it to his lips, the tip of his tongue licked it off his skin. "You taste like your heart has broken, *ma petite*."

My throat choked tight. I couldn't breathe past the tears. The harder I tried not to cry, the faster the tears flowed. I hugged myself, and my hands touched the sticky gunk that covered me. I held my hands away from my body like I'd touched something unclean. I stared at Jean-Claude with my hands held out in front of me.

"*Mon Dieu*, what has happened?" He tried to hug me, but I pushed him away.

"You'll get it all over you."

He stared at the thick, clear gunk on his hand. "How did you get this close to a shapeshifting werewolf?" An idea flowed across his face. "It's Richard. You saw him change."

I nodded. "He changed on top of me. It was . . . Oh, God, oh, God, oh, God."

Jean-Claude pulled me into his arms. I pushed at him. "You'll ruin your clothes."

"*Ma petite*, *ma petite*, it's all right. It is all right."

"No, it's not." I sagged against him. I let him wrap me in his arms. I clutched at him, hands digging into the silk of his shirt. I buried my face against his chest and whispered, "He ate Marcus. He ate him."

"He's a werewolf, *ma petite*. That's what they do."

It was such an odd thing to say, and so terribly true, that I laughed—an abrupt, almost angry sound. The laughter died in choking, and the choking became sobs.

I held onto Jean-Claude like he was the last sane thing in the world. I buried myself against him and wept. It was like something deep inside me had broken, and I was crying out bits of myself onto his body.

His voice came to me dimly, as if he had been speaking for a long time, but I hadn't heard. He was speaking French, softly, whispering it into my hair, stroking my back, rocking me gently.

I lay in his arms, quiet. I had no more tears left. I felt empty and light, numb.

Jean-Claude smoothed my hair back from my forehead. He brushed his lips across my skin, like Richard had done earlier tonight. Even that thought couldn't make me cry again. It was too soon.

"Can you stand, *ma petite*?"

"I think so." My voice sounded distant, strange. I stood, still in the circle of his arms, leaning against him. I pushed away from him gently. I stood on my own, a little shaky, but better than nothing.

His dark blue shirt was plastered to his chest, covered with werewolf goop and tears. "Now we both need a bath," I said.

"That can be arranged."

"Please, Jean-Claude, no sexual innuendo until after I'm clean."

"Of course, *ma petite*. It was crude of me tonight. My apologies."

I stared at him. He was being far too nice. Jean-Claude was a lot of things, but nice wasn't one of them.

"If you're up to something, I don't want to know about it. I can't handle any deep, dark plots tonight, okay?"

He smiled and gave a low, sweeping bow, never taking his eyes off me. The way you bow on the judo mat when you're afraid the person may pound you if you look away.

I shook my head. He *was* up to something. Nice to know that not everyone had suddenly become something else. One thing I could always depend on was Jean-Claude. Pain in the ass that he was, he always seemed to be there. Dependable in his own twisted way. Jean-Claude dependable? I must have been more tired than I thought.

39

Jean-Claude opened the bedroom door and stepped inside, ushering me through with a sweep of graceful hands. The bed stopped me. There'd been a change of bedding. Red sheets covered the bed. Crimson drapes formed a half canopy over the nearly black wood. There were still a dozen pillows on the bed and they were all screaming, brilliant red. Even after the night I'd had, it was eye-catching.

"I like the new decor, I guess."

"The linens needed to be changed. You are always complaining that I should use more color."

I stared at the bed. "I'll stop complaining."

"I will run your bath." He went into the bathroom without a single joke or risqué comment. It was almost unnerving.

Whoever had changed the sheets had also removed the chairs that Edward and Harley had used. I didn't want to sit on the clean sheets still covered in whatever the hell I was covered in. I sat down on the white carpet and tried not to think. Not thinking is a lot harder than it sounds. My thoughts kept chasing each other, like a werewolf chasing its tail. The image tore a laugh from my throat, and on the end of it a sound like a sob or a moan. I put the back of my hand against my mouth. I didn't like that sound coming out of me. It sounded hopeless, beaten.

I was not beaten, dammit, but I was hurt. If what I felt had been an actual wound, I'd have been bleeding to death.

The bathroom door opened at long last. A puff of warm, moist air flowed around Jean-Claude. He had taken off his shirt, and the cross-shaped burn scar marred the perfection of his chest. He held his boots in one hand, a towel as scarlet as the sheets in the other.

"I washed up in the sink while the tub filled." He walked barefoot across the white carpeting. "I'm afraid I used the last clean towel. I will fetch you more."

I took my hand away from my mouth and nodded. I finally managed to say, "Fine."

I stood before he could offer to help me up. I didn't need any help.

Jean-Claude moved to one side. His black hair lay in nearly tight curls across his pale shoulders, curled from the humidity of the bathroom. I ignored him as much as it was humanly possible and walked inside.

The room was warm and misty, the black marble tub full of bubbles. He offered me a black lacquer tray from the vanity top. Shampoos, soap, bath crystals, and what looked like oils were grouped on the tray.

''Get out so I can undress.''

''It took two people to dress you tonight, *ma petite*. Won't you need help getting undressed?'' His voice was utterly bland. His face so still, his eyes so innocent, it made me smile.

I sighed. ''If you get the two straps in back, I think I can manage the rest. But no monkey business.'' I held my hands over the bra because one strap would loosen it. The other strap, as far as I could tell, was the pivot point for the rest of the outfit.

His fingers moved to the top strap. I watched him in the fogged mirror. The strap came unbuckled, and the leather gave with a small sigh. He moved to the second strap without so much as an extra caress. He undid it and took a step back. ''No monkey business, *ma petite*.'' He backed out of the room, and I watched him go like a phantom in the mist-covered mirrors. When the door was shut, I started on the rest of the straps. It was like peeling myself to get the goo-soaked leather off.

I put the tray of bath accessories on the tub edge and slipped into the water. The water was hot, just this side of too hot. I sank into it up to my chin, but I couldn't relax. The gunk clung to my body in patches. I had to get it off me. I sat up in the tub and started scrubbing. The soap smelled like gardenia. The shampoos smelled like herbs. Trust Jean-Claude not to buy a name brand from the grocery store.

I washed my hair twice, sinking under the water and coming up for air. I was scrubbed and virtuous, or at least clean. The mirrors had cleared and I had only myself to stare at. I'd washed off all the careful makeup. I smoothed my thick, black hair back from my face. My eyes were enormous and nearly black. My skin so pale, it was almost white. I looked shocked, ethereal, unreal.

There was a soft knock on the door. ''*Ma petite*, may I come in?''

I glanced down at myself. The bubbles were still holding. I drew a pile of them a little closer to my chest and said, ''Come in.'' It took a lot of effort not to hunch down in the water. I sat up straight, trusting in the bubbles. Besides, I would not huddle. So I was naked in a tub of bubble bath. So what. No one can embarrass you unless you let them.

Jean-Claude came in with two thick, red towels. He closed the door behind him with a small smile. ''We wouldn't want to let the hot air out.''

I narrowed my eyes but said, ''I guess not.''

''Where do you want the towels? Here?'' He started to lay them on the vanity.

''I can't reach them there,'' I said.

''Here?'' He laid them on top of the stool. He stood there, staring down at me, still wearing nothing but the black jeans. His feet were startlingly pale against the black carpet.

''Still too far away.''

He sat down on the edge of the tub, placing the towels on the floor. He stared down at me as if he could will the bubbles away. ''Is this close enough?''

''Maybe a little too close,'' I said.

He trailed fingertips over the bubbles at the edge of the tub. ''Do you feel better now, *ma petite*?''

''I said no sexual innuendo, remember.''

''As I remember, you said no sexual innuendo until after you were clean.'' He smiled at me. ''You're clean.''

I sighed. ''Trust you to be literal.''

He trailed his fingers in the water. He turned his shoulder enough that I could see the whip scars on his back. They were slick and white, and I suddenly had an urge to trace them with my fingers.

He turned back to face me. He wiped his wet fingers across his chest, trailing shining lines of moisture across the flat slickness of the burn scar, down along his belly. His fingers played with the line of dark hair that vanished into his pants.

I closed my eyes and let out a sigh.

''What is the matter, *ma petite*?'' I felt him leaning over me. ''Are you faint?''

I opened my eyes. He had leaned his entire upper body across the tub, right arm on the far rim, the left near my shoulder. His hip was so far over the water that if I'd touched his chest, he'd have fallen in.

''I don't faint,'' I said.

His face leaned down over mine. ''So glad to hear it.'' He kissed me lightly, a brush of lips, but even that small movement made my stomach jerk.

I gasped and pushed him away. He fell into the tub, going completely under, only his feet sticking out. He landed on my naked body, and I screamed.

He came up for air, his long, black hair streaming around his face, across his shoulders. He looked as surprised as I'd ever seen him. He crawled off me, mainly because I was shoving at him. He struggled to his feet. Water streamed down his body. He stared down at me. I was huddled against the side, staring up at him, pissed.

He shook his head and laughed. The sound filled the room, played along my skin like a hand. ''I have been a lady's man for nearly three hundred years, Anita. Why is it only with you that I am awkward?''

''Maybe it's a hint,'' I said.

''Perhaps.''

I stared up at him. He stood there, knee deep in bubble bath. He was soaking wet and should have been ridiculous, but he wasn't. He was beautiful.

''How can you be so damn beautiful when I know what you are?''

He knelt in the water. The bubbles covered his waist, so he looked naked. Water trailed down his chest in fine beads. I wanted to run my hands over him. I wanted to lick the water off his skin. I drew my legs to my chest and locked my arms around them, not trusting myself.

He moved towards me. The water sloshed and curled around my naked body. He stayed kneeling, so close that his jeans brushed my huddled legs. The feel of him in the water, that close, made me hide my face against my knees. The pounding of my heart gave me away. I knew he could taste my need on the air.

"Tell me to go, *ma petite*, and I will go." I felt him lean over me, his face just above my wet hair.

Slowly, I raised my face.

He placed a hand on the tub edge, one arm on either side of me, bringing his chest dangerously close to my face. I watched the water bead on his skin, the way that he sometimes watched blood on mine: a need almost too overwhelming to deny, an urge so complete that I didn't want to say no.

I unclenched my arms from my knees and leaned forward. I whispered, "Don't go." I touched hands to his waist, tentative, as if it should burn, but his skin was cool under the slickness of water. Cool and smooth to the touch. I glanced up at his face and knew that there was something close to fear on my own face.

His face was lovely, and uncertain, as if he didn't know what to do next. It was a look I never thought to see on Jean-Claude's face when I was naked in his arms.

I kept my eyes on his face as I moved my mouth towards his stomach. I ran my tongue over his skin, a quick, tentative movement.

He sighed, eyes fluttering shut, body almost sagging. I pressed my mouth against his skin, drinking the water off of him. I couldn't reach his chest. I moved to my knees, hands steadying me against his slender waist.

The air was cool against my naked breasts. Kneeling had bared them. I froze, suddenly unsure. I wanted desperately to see his face and was afraid to look up.

His fingertips brushed my shoulders, sliding down the wet skin. I shivered and glanced up. The look on his face caught my breath in my throat. Tenderness, need, amazement.

"You are so beautiful, *ma petite*." He put his fingertips to my lips before I could protest. "You are beautiful. On this I do not lie."

His fingers moved across my lips, down my chin. He slid his hands to my shoulders, down my back, in slow, teasing lines. His hands stopped on either side of my waist, mirroring my hands on his own waist.

"Now what?" My voice was a little breathless.

"Whatever you like, *ma petite*."

I massaged my hands against his waist, feeling the flesh underneath, feeling him under my hands. I spread my hands wide, splaying my fingers tense against his skin, dragging my hands up his ribs.

He kneaded his fingers into my waist, pressing his hands against my ribs. He inched his hands upward along my sides. Strong fingers pressed into my skin just enough to make me sigh. He stopped with his thumbs below my breasts. His touch was feather light, almost not touching at all. But that one small brush of his skin against my breasts made my body react, tightening, nipples hardening. My body wanted him. Wanted him so badly that my skin felt large and aching with the thought of it.

My own hands were pressed against his chest. I realized that he was still mirroring me, waiting for me to move.

I stared up into his face. I searched that beauty, those dark eyes. There was no pull to them, no power, except the thick black line of his lashes, and the rich color like the sky just before darkness swallows the world when you think all is black, but there in the west is a shade of blue, dark and rich as ink. Beauty had its own power.

I slid my hands up his chest, fingers brushing across his nipples. I stared at his face while I did it, heart pounding in my throat, breath coming too fast.

His hands slid upward, cupping my breasts. The touch of his hands made me gasp. He scooted lower in the water, still touching me. He bent over my breasts and laid a gentle kiss on them. He licked the water off my skin, lips working gently.

I shuddered and had to steady myself on his bare shoulders. All I could see was his long, dark hair bent over me. I caught sight of us in the mirrors. I watched his mouth close over my breast, felt him take me into his mouth as far as he could. Fangs pressed against my breast. For a second I thought they would sink into my flesh, draw blood in a fine hot line, but he drew back. He dropped to all fours in the water, which made me taller, allowed me to look down into his face.

There was no uncertainty in his face now. His eyes were still lovely, still human, but there was a knowledge in them now, a growing darkness. Sex, for want of a better word, but that look in a man's eyes is too primitive for vocabulary. It's the darkness we all have inside of us, peeking out. That part of us that we trap in our dreams and deny in daylight hours. He stayed crouched in the water with that feral light in his eyes, and I went to him.

I kissed him, light, a brush of lips. I flicked my tongue along his lips and he opened his mouth for me. I cupped his face between my hands and kissed him, tasted him, explored him.

He came up out of the water with a sound between a moan and a cry. His arms locked behind my back and he rolled us in the water like a shark. We came up gasping. He pushed away from me to lean against the far edge of the tub. I was breathing so hard I was trembling. My pulse thudded at the back of my throat. I could taste it on my tongue, almost roll the beating pulse in my mouth like candy. I realized it wasn't just my heart I was hearing. It was Jean-Claude's.

I could see the pulse in his neck like something alive and separate, but it wasn't only my eyes that could see it. I could feel it like it was my own. I had never been so aware of the blood coursing through my body. The pulsing warmth of my own skin. The thick pumping of my heart. My life thundering inside me. Jean-Claude's body pulsed in time to mine. It was like he was riding my pulse, my blood. I felt his need, and it wasn't just sex, but for the first time, I understood it wasn't just the blood, either. It was all of me. He wanted to warm himself in my body, like holding hands to a flame, gathering my warmth, my life, to him. I felt his stillness, a depth of quiet that nothing living could touch, like a still pool of water hidden away in the dark. In one crystalline moment, I realized that, for me, this was part of the attraction: I wanted to plunge my hands into his stillness, into that quiet place of death. I wanted to embrace it, confront it, conquer it. I wanted to fill him up with a burning wash of life, and I knew in that moment that I could do it, but only at the price of drinking in some of that still, dark water.

"My deepest apologies, *ma petite*, you have almost undone me." He sank into the water, leaning against the edge of the tub. "I did not come here to feed, *ma petite*. I am sorry."

I felt his heartbeat going away from me, pulling away from me. My pulse slowed. The only heart thudding in my ears was my own.

He stood, water dripping down his body. "I will go, *ma petite*." He sighed. "You rob me of my hard-won control. Only you can do that to me, only you."

I crawled through the water towards him and let the darkness fill my eyes. "Don't go," I said.

He watched me with a look that was part amazement, part amusement, part fear, as if he didn't trust me—or didn't trust himself.

I knelt at his feet, running my hands up the soaked cloth of his jeans. I dug my nails lightly into the cloth over his thighs and stared up at him. My face was dangerously close to places I had never touched before, not even with my hands. This close, I couldn't help noticing that he was stretched hard and firm under the tight, heavy cloth. I had a terrible urge to lay my cheek over his groin. I ran my hand lightly over him, barely touching. That small touch brought a soft groan from him.

He stared down at me like a drowning man.

I met his eyes. "No teeth, no blood."

He nodded slowly. He tried twice before he found his voice. "As my lady wishes."

I laid my cheek across him, feeling him firm and large against my skin. I felt his whole body tense. I rubbed my face against him like a cat. A small sound escaped him. I looked up. His eyes were closed, his head thrown back.

I grabbed the waistband of his jeans and used it to pull myself to my feet. Water ran down my body, suds clung to my skin.

His hands encircled my waist, but his eyes went lower. He met my gaze and smiled. It was the smile he always had. That smile that said he was thinking wicked little thoughts, things you'd only do in the dark on a dare. For the first time, I wanted everything that smile promised.

I tugged at his jeans. "Off."

He unsnapped the jeans carefully. He peeled the wet cloth away from his body. If there'd been underwear, I never saw it. The jeans ended up on the carpet. He was somehow suddenly nude.

He was like carved alabaster, every muscle, every curve of his body pale and perfect. Telling him he was beautiful was redundant. Saying golly gee whiz seemed too uncool. Giggling was out. My voice came small and strangled, hoarse with all the words I couldn't find. "You're not circumcised."

"No, *ma petite*. Is that a problem?"

I did what I'd wanted to do since I first saw him. I wrapped my fingers around him, squeezing gently. He closed his eyes, shuddering, steadying his hands on my shoulders. "Not a problem," I said.

He pulled me against him suddenly, pressing our naked bodies together. The feel of him hard and firm against my stomach was almost overwhelming. I dug fingers into his back to keep my suddenly weak knees from giving out.

I kissed his chest. I rose on tiptoe and kissed his shoulders, his neck. I ran my tongue along his skin and tasted him, rolling the scent of him, the feel of him in my mouth. We kissed, a nearly innocent brush of lips. I locked my hands behind his neck, arching my body against him. He made a small sound low in his throat.

He slid down my body, arms locked behind my back, holding me against him as he left my arms and left me standing, staring down at him.

He licked my stomach with quick, wet flicks of his tongue. His hands played along my buttocks, teasing. He licked back and forth where stomach ended and lower things began. His fingers slid between my legs.

I gasped. "What are you doing?"

He rolled his eyes upward, mouth still pressed low on my stomach. He raised his face just enough to speak. "You may have three guesses, *ma petite*," he whispered. He put a hand on each of my thighs and spread my legs wider. His hand slid over me, exploring me.

My mouth was suddenly dry. I licked my lips and said, "I don't think my legs will hold."

He ran his tongue down my hip. "When the time comes, *ma petite*, I will hold you." He kissed his way down my thigh. His finger slid inside of me. My breath fell outward in a sigh.

He kissed the inside of my thighs, running his tongue, his lips along my skin. The feel of his fingers between my legs tightened my body, and I could feel the beginnings of something large and overwhelming.

He stood, hand still between my legs. He bent and kissed me, long and slow. The movement of his hand matched his mouth. Slow and lingering, teasing along my body. When his fingers plunged inside me, I cried out, shuddering against him.

He left me standing in the water, alone and shivering, but not from cold. I couldn't even think enough to ask where'd he gone. He appeared in front of me with a condom in his hand like he'd plucked it from the air. He traced the foil down my body.

I touched him while he unwrapped it. I held him in my hands and felt the velvet smoothness of him. The skin was unbelievably soft. He drew himself gently out of my hands with a shaking laugh.

When he was ready, he picked me up, hands on the backs of my thighs. He pressed himself against me without entering, rubbing himself where his hand had touched. I whispered, "Please." He spread my legs and eased inside of me. Slowly, so slowly as if he were afraid he'd hurt me, but it didn't hurt.

When he was sheathed inside me, he looked at me. The look on his face was haunting. Emotions flowed over his face. Tenderness, triumph, need. "I have wanted this for so long, *ma petite*, so very long." He eased in and out, slowly, almost tentatively. I watched his face until the play of emotions was too much, too honest. There was something like pain in his eyes, something that I didn't even come close to understanding.

The movements of his hips were still slow, careful. It was amazing, but I wanted more. I brought my mouth up to his and said, "I won't break." I pressed my mouth to his hard enough to feel the press of fangs.

He went to his knees in the water, pressing me against the side of the tub. His mouth fed at mine, and there was a small, sharp pain. Sweet copper blood filled my mouth, filled his mouth, and he plunged inside of me, hard and fast. I watched him in the mirrors. Watched his body coming in and out of mine. I gathered him in my arms, in my legs. I held him to me, feeling his body plunging inside of mine. Felt his need.

Someone was making a high moaning sound, and it was me. I wrapped my legs around his waist. The muscles in my lower abdomen spasmed, tightened.

I pressed my body against Jean-Claude as if I would climb through him, into him. I grabbed a handful of his long hair and watched his face from inches away. Watched his face while his body pumped into mine. The emotions were gone. His face was almost slack with need. Blood spilled down the corner of my mouth, and he licked it away, his body tightening against me.

He slowed the rhythm of his body. I felt the effort strain through his arms and back. He slowed. Every time he thrust into me, it was like I could feel it into the middle of my chest. As if he'd grown impossibly large within me. My body spasmed around him, tightened like a hand. He cried out, and his body lost its rhythm. He plunged inside me faster, harder, as if he would meld our bodies together, weld us into one flesh, one body. A wave of pleasure burst over me in a skin-tingling, body-sweeping rush. It burst over me like a rush of cool flame, and still he was not done. Every thrust of his body reached inside of me and caressed things that should never have been able to be touched. It was as if his body could reach the places his voice could touch, as if it were more than his body that plunged inside of me. The world became for a moment a shining whiteness, a melting thing. I dug fingers into Jean-Claude's back. Noises fell from my mouth that were too primitive for screams. When I realized I was drawing blood on his back, I scratched my own arms. I hadn't asked what he thought about pain.

I cuddled around him, letting him hold the full weight of my body. He climbed up the edge of the tub, lifting me out of the water. He crawled on all fours to the raised area around the tub with me hanging onto him. He lowered his body and I moved away from him. He slid out of me and was still as hard and ready as when he had started.

I looked at him. ''You didn't come.''

''I have not waited this long to end it so quickly.'' He lowered himself in a sort of push-up and ran his tongue down one of the scratches on my arm. He rolled his tongue around his lips. ''If you did this for my benefit, I appreciate it. If you did it to keep from damaging me, it was not necessary. I do not mind a little pain.''

''Me, either.''

He slid his body across mine. ''I noticed that.'' He kissed me slowly. He lay beside me, then scooted until he was lying on his back and I was almost back in the tub.''I want to watch you move, *ma petite*. I want you above me.''

I straddled his waist and slid slowly over him. It was deeper from this angle, sharper somehow. His hands moved up my body, over my breasts. He lay back underneath me. His long, curling, black hair was almost completely dry. It fanned out around his face in a thick, soft wave. This was what I wanted. Seeing him like this. Feeling him inside me.

''Move for me, Anita.''

I moved for him. I rode his body. He tightened inside me, and I gasped. I watched us in the mirrors. Watched my hips swaying above him.

"*Ma petite*," he whispered, "look into my eyes. Let it be between us as it always could have been."

I stared into his dark blue eyes. They were lovely, but they were just eyes. I shook my head. "I can't."

"You must let me inside your mind, as you let me inside your body." He spasmed inside of me, and it was hard to think.

"I don't know how," I said.

"Love me, Anita, love me."

I stared down at him and did. "I do love you."

"Then let me in, *ma petite*. Let me love you."

I felt it like a drape being pulled away. I felt his eyes, and they were suddenly drowning deep, an endless midnight blue ocean that somehow managed to burn. I was aware of my body. I could feel Jean-Claude inside my body. I could feel him like a brush of silk inside my mind.

The orgasm hit me unexpectedly, opened my mind to him more than I'd planned. Flung me wide open and falling into his eyes. He cried out underneath me, and I realized I could still feel my body, feel my hands on his chest, feel my pelvis riding him. I opened my eyes and for a dizzying second I saw his face go slack, that moment of total abandon.

I collapsed on top of him, trailing my hands down his arms, feeling his heart pound against my chest. We lay quietly for a few moments, resting, holding each other, then I slid off him, curling beside him.

"You can't hold me with your eyes anymore. Even if I let you, I can still break the hold at any time."

"Yes, *ma petite*."

"Does that bother you?"

He lifted a lock of my hair, running it between his fingers. "Let us say it does not bother me as much as it might have a few hours ago."

I raised up on one elbow so I could see his face. "Meaning what? That now that I've had sex with you, I'm not dangerous?"

He stared up at me. I couldn't read his eyes. "You will always be dangerous, *ma petite*." He raised upward, bending at the waist, bringing his lips against mine in a gentle kiss. He moved back from me just enough to speak, propping himself on one arm. "There was a time when you would have taken my heart with stake or gun." He took my hand in his and raised it towards his mouth. "Now you have taken it with these delicate hands and the scent of your body." He kissed the back of my hand ever so gently. He lay back, drawing me with him. "Come, *ma petite*, enjoy your conquest."

I held my face back, avoiding a kiss. "You aren't conquered," I said.

"Nor, *ma petite*, are you." He ran his hands up my back. "I am beginning to realize that you will never be conquered, and that is the greatest aphrodisiac of all."

"A challenge forever," I said.

"For all eternity," he whispered. I let him draw me down into a kiss, and part of me was still not sure if I'd done a good thing or a bad thing. But just for tonight, I didn't care.

40

I woke surrounded by bloodred sheets, naked, and alone. Jean-Claude had kissed me good-bye and gone to his coffin. I didn't argue. If I'd awakened to him cold and dead beside me . . . Let's just say I'd had all the shock I could handle from my boyfriends for awhile.

Boyfriend. That was a word for someone who walked you to your class. It didn't seem the right word after last night. I lay there, clutching the raw silk sheets to my chest. I could smell Jean-Claude's cologne on the sheets, on my skin, but more than that, I could smell him. I cuddled that scent to me, rolled in it. He said he loved me and for a time last night, I believed him. In the light of day, I wasn't so sure. How stupid was it to half-believe the vampire loved me? Not nearly as stupid as half-loving him. But I still loved Richard. One night of great sex didn't change that. I think I had hoped it would. Lust may die that easily, but love doesn't. True love is a much harder beast to kill.

There was a soft knock on the door. I had to reach under two red pillows before I came out with the Firestar. I held it at my side and said, ''Come in.''

A man entered the room. He was tall, muscular, with hair shaved on either side, the back left in a long ponytail.

I pointed the gun at him and clutched the sheets to my chest. ''I don't know you.''

His eyes went wide; his voice shook, ''I'm Ernie, I'm supposed to ask if you want breakfast.''

''No,'' I said. ''Now, get out.''

He nodded, eyes on the gun. He hesitated in the doorway, even staring down the barrel of a gun. I made a guess.

''What did Jean-Claude tell you to do?'' It was amazing how many people were more afraid of Jean-Claude than of me. I pointed the gun at the ceiling.

''He said I was to be at your disposal, anything you want. He said I was to make that very clear to you.''

''It's clear. Now, get out.''

He still hesitated.

I'd had enough. "Ernie, I am sitting here naked in a bed, and I don't know you. Get out or I'm going to shoot you on principle." I aimed the gun at him for dramatic emphasis.

Ernie ran for it, leaving the door open. Great. Now I had the choice of walking to the door naked and closing it, or draping a king-size sheet around me and stumbling to the door and closing it. Sheet. I was sitting on the edge of the bed, with the sheet in front of me and most of my backside not covered, gun still clutched in one hand, when Richard appeared in the doorway.

He was dressed in jeans, white T-shirt, jeans jacket, and white tennis shoes. His hair foamed around his face in a mass of golden brown waves. A claw had caught him across the face, leaving angry red welts that chased across the entire left side of his face. The injury looked days old. It had to have happened after I left last night.

He had my leather coat in one hand and the Browning in the other. He just stood there in the doorway.

I sat on the bed. Neither of us said anything. I wasn't slick and sophisticated enough for this. What do you say to boyfriend A when he finds you naked in the bed of boyfriend B? Especially if boyfriend A turned into a monster the night before and ate someone. I bet Miss Manners didn't cover this at all.

"You slept with him, didn't you?" His voice was low, almost soft, as if he was trying very hard not to yell.

My gut tightened. I was not ready for this fight. I was armed, but I was naked. I would have traded the gun for clothes in a hot second.

"I would say it's not what it looks like, but it is." My attempt at humor did not work.

He strode into the room like an approaching storm, his anger riding before him in a crackling wave. The power poured over me and I wanted to scream.

"Stop leaking all over me."

It stopped him, almost literally in midmotion. "What are you talking about?"

"Your power, aura, it's raining all over me. Stop it."

"Why? Does it feel good? Until you panicked last night, it felt good, didn't it?"

I shoved the Firestar under the pillow and stood, clutching the sheet to me. "Yeah, it felt good until you shapeshifted on top of me. I was covered in that clear gunk, thick with it." The memory was new enough that I shuddered and looked away from him.

"So you fucked Jean-Claude. Oh, that makes perfect sense."

I looked at him and felt an answering anger. If he wanted to fight, he'd come to the right place. I held up my right hand. It was covered in a wonderful multi-colored bruise. "You did this when you knocked my gun away."

"There'd been enough killing, Anita. No one else had to die."

"Do you really think that Raina is just going to let you take over? No way. She'll see you dead first."

He shook his head, his face set in stubborn lines. "I am Ulfric now. I'm in control. She'll do what I say."

"Nobody bosses Raina; not for long. Has she offered to fuck you yet?"

''Yes,'' he said.

The way he said it stopped me, brought my breath up short. ''Did you, after I left?''

''It would serve you right if I had.''

I couldn't meet his eyes on that one. ''If you make her lupa, she'll let it go. She just doesn't want to lose her power base.'' I forced myself to look up, to meet his eyes.

''I don't want Raina.'' Something passed over his face so raw, that it brought tears to my eyes. ''I want you.''

''You can't want me now, not after last night.''

''Is that why you slept with Jean-Claude? Did you think it would keep you safe from me?''

''I wasn't thinking that clearly,'' I said.

He laid the coat and the gun on the bed. He gripped the end of the bed. The wood groaned under the strength of his hands. He jerked back from it as if he hadn't meant to do it. ''You slept with him in this bed. Right here.'' He put his hand over his eyes as if he was trying to erase an image inside his head.

He screamed wordlessly.

I took a step towards him, hand out, and stopped. How could I comfort him? What could I say to make this better? Not a damn thing.

He jerked at the bottom sheet, tugging it until it came loose. He grabbed the top mattress and pulled it off the bed. He grabbed the bottom of the bed and lifted.

I screamed, ''Richard!''

The bed was antique solid oak, and he tossed it on its side like it was a toy. He pulled the bottom sheet off. The silk tore with a sound like skin peeling back. He was on his knees with the butchered silk in his hands. He held his hands out to me and the sheets fell away like blood.

Richard got to his feet, a little unsteady. He caught himself against the bed and took a step towards me. The Firestar and the Browning were somewhere on the floor in the welter of red silk and tossed mattress.

I backed away until I hit the corner, and I had nowhere else to go. I was still clutching the sheet around me like it was some kind of protection.

I held out a hand towards Richard, as if that would help. ''What do you want from me, Richard? What do you want me to say? I'm sorry. I am sorry that I hurt you. I'm sorry that I can't handle what I saw last night. I'm sorry.''

He stalked towards me, not saying anything, hands balled into fists. I realized that I was afraid of Richard. That I wasn't sure what he'd do when he reached me, and I wasn't armed. Part of me felt like I deserved to be hit at least once, that I owed that to him. But after seeing what he'd done to the bed, I wasn't sure I'd survive it.

Richard grabbed the front of the sheet, balling it in his fist, jerking me against him. He used the sheet to raise me to tiptoe. He kissed me. For a second I froze. Hitting, yelling, that I'd expected, but not this.

His mouth bruised against my lips, forcing my mouth open. The moment I felt his tongue, I jerked my head back.

Richard put a hand on the back of my head like he'd force me to kiss him. The rage in his face was frightening.

"Not good enough to kiss now?"

"I saw you eat Marcus last night."

He let me go so suddenly I fell to the floor, stumbling over the sheet. I tried to get to my knees, but my legs had tangled. The sheet slipped over one breast. I struggled to cover myself. Embarrassed at last.

"Two nights ago, you let me touch them, suck them. Now I can't even see them."

"Don't do this, Richard."

He went to all fours in front of me, so we'd be on eye level. "Don't do what? Don't be mad that you let the vampire fuck you?" He crawled forward until our faces were almost touching. "You fucked a corpse last night, Anita. Did it feel good?"

I stared at him from inches away, not embarrassed anymore. Instead, I was getting pissed. "Yeah, it did."

He jerked back from me like I'd hit him. His face crumpled, and his eyes searched the room frantically. "I love you." He looked up suddenly, eyes wide and pain-filled. "I love you."

I kept my eyes very wide so the tears in them wouldn't fall out and run down my cheeks. "I know, and I'm sorry."

He turned away from me, still kneeling. He slapped his hands against the floor. He pounded his hands into the floor over and over until blood smeared on the white carpet.

I got to my feet. I hovered over him, afraid to touch him. "Richard, Richard, don't, please don't." The tears fell and I couldn't stop them.

I knelt beside him. "You're hurting yourself. Stop it!" I grabbed his wrists, held his bleeding hands in mine. He stared at me, and the look on his face was raw, human.

I touched his face, gently tracing the claw marks. He leaned into me, tears spilling down his cheeks. The look in his eyes held me immobile. His lips brushed mine, soft. I didn't flinch, but I didn't kiss him back, either.

He moved back from me, just enough to see my face clearly. "Good-bye, Anita." He got to his feet.

I wanted to say so much, but none of it would help. Nothing would make it better. Nothing would erase what I'd seen last night or how it had made me feel. "Richard . . . I . . . I'm sorry."

"So am I." He walked to the door. He hesitated with his hand on the doorknob. "I'll always love you."

I opened my mouth, but no sound came. There was nothing left to say but, "I love you, Richard, and I am sorrier than I know how to say."

He opened the door and stepped through it without looking back. When the door closed behind him, I sat on the floor, huddled in the silk sheet. I could smell Jean-Claude's cologne on the silk, but I could smell Richard now, too. His after-shave clung to the sheets, to my mouth.

How could I let him go like this? How could I call him back? I sat on the floor and did nothing, because I didn't know what to do.

41

I called Edward's answering service and left a message. I couldn't stay where I was. I couldn't stay here staring at the wrecked bedroom and remembering Richard's wounded eyes. I had to get out. I had to call Dominic and tell him I wasn't coming. The triad of power didn't work without at least two of us on the spot. Jean-Claude was in his coffin and Richard was out of the picture. I wasn't sure what would happen with our little triumvirate now. I didn't see Richard standing around watching me grope Jean-Claude, if I wasn't groping him, too. I couldn't blame him on that.

Strangely, the thought of him sleeping with Raina still made me see green. I had no right to be jealous of him now, but I was. Go figure.

I dressed in black jeans, a black, short-sleeved blouse, and a black blazer. I had to work tonight, and Bert would kick a fit about me wearing black. He thought it gave the wrong image. Screw him. Tonight, black fit my mood.

The Browning in its shoulder holster, Firestar in the Uncle Mike's sidekick holster, a knife on each arm, and a knife down my spine. I was ready for work.

I was going to give Edward ten more minutes, and then I was out of there. If there was still an assassin lurking around, I'd almost have welcomed him or her.

There was a knock on the door. I sighed. "Who is it?"

"Cassandra."

"Come in."

She opened the door, caught one sight of the wrecked bed, and grinned. "I've heard of rough sex, but this is ridiculous." She was wearing a long, white dress that fell nearly to her ankles. White hose and white canvas flats completed the outfit. She looked light and summery with her long hair trailing down her back.

I shook my head. "Richard did it."

The smile left her face. "He found out you slept with Jean-Claude?"

"Does everyone know?" I asked.

"Not everyone." She walked into the room, shutting the door behind her. She shook her head. "Did he hurt you?"

"He didn't hit me, if that's what you mean, but I feel pretty shitty."

Cassandra walked to the bed, staring up at it. She grabbed the edge of the frame. She pulled with one hand and steadied with the other. She pulled several hundred pounds of wood and metal around like it was nothing. She settled the bed gently to the carpet.

I raised an eyebrow. ''That was impressive.''

She smiled, almost shyly. ''One of the fringe benefits of being a lycanthrope is that you can pretty much lift anything you want.''

''I see the appeal of that.''

''I knew you would,'' she said. She started picking up the pillows and ripped sheets. I joined her. ''We should probably put the mattress back first,'' she said.

''Okay. You need help?''

She laughed. ''I can lift it, but it's awkward.''

''Sure.'' I grabbed the other side of the mattress.

Cassandra came up beside me, lifting the mattress with her left hand. A look passed over her face. ''I am sorry.''

''I meant what I said about you and Richard earlier. I want him to be happy,'' I said.

''That's very flattering. I like you, Anita. I like you a lot. I wish I didn't.''

I had time to frown at her, then her delicate fist came out of nowhere, a blur of speed that smashed into my face. I felt myself fall backwards. I smashed into the floor and couldn't save my head from that extra smack against the carpet. It didn't hurt. I didn't feel a damn thing when blackness closed over me.

42

I rose out of the darkness slowly, dragging upwards like being awakened from deep sleep. I wasn't sure what woke me. I couldn't remember going to sleep. I tried to roll over and couldn't. I was suddenly very awake, eyes wide, body straining. I'd been tied up before; it was one of my least favorite things. I had a few moments of pure panic. I bucked against the ropes that tied me at the wrists and ankles. I fought, pulling until I realized that the knots were getting tighter as I struggled.

I forced myself to lie very still. My heart pounded in my ears so loudly that I couldn't hear anything else. My wrists were tied over my head at an angle sharp enough to squeeze my shoulder blades and put strain all the way down to my wrists. Even raising my head the little bit I needed to see my ankles was painful. My ankles were tied together to the foot of an unfamiliar bed. I rolled my head back and saw the rope that tied my wrists to the head of the bed. The rope was black and soft, and if I had to guess, I'd say it was woven silk. It looked like something Jean-Claude might have lying around in a closet somewhere. I considered it for only a split second, then reality stepped into the room, and my heart stopped for just a second.

Gabriel came to the foot of the bed. He was wearing black leather pants so tight they looked poured on, and high black boots that rode his thighs all the way up, with straps at the top to hold the soft leather in place. He was naked from the waist up, a silver ring through his left nipple and another through the edge of his belly button. More silver marched up his ears to the curve, glittering as he walked around the bed. His long, thick black hair fell across his face, framing his pale, storm grey eyes. He walked around behind the headboard, out of sight, then slowly back into frame.

My heart had started beating again. It was beating so hard I was going to choke on it. They'd taken the Browning and Firestar, holsters and all. The wrist sheaths were gone. I tensed my back and could still feel the back sheath. When I put my head back, I didn't feel the knife's handle. I guess I was grateful they hadn't stripped me to get the sheath. The way Gabriel was circling the bed, I was betting we'd get to that.

I tried to talk, couldn't, swallowed, and tried again. ''What's going on?'' My voice sounded amazingly calm. Even to me.

A woman's laugh, high and rich, filled the room. But of course, it wasn't a room. We were at the farm where they made dirty movies. The room I was tied in had only three walls. The lights hung above me were dead, not on yet.

Raina stalked into sight on high, spiked heels the color of blood. She was wearing what looked like a red leather teddy that left most of her long legs and hips bare. ''Hello, Anita, you're looking well.''

I took a deep breath in through my nose and let it out slowly. My heart slowed a bit. Good. ''You should talk to Richard before you do anything drastic. The position of lupa just opened up today.''

She cocked her head to one side, puzzled. ''What are you talking about?''

''She slept with Jean-Claude.'' Cassandra came to stand on the edge of the fake room, back to the wall. She looked like she'd always looked. If she felt uncomfortable having betrayed me to Raina, it didn't show. I hated her a lot for that.

''Aren't you going to sleep with both of them?'' Raina asked.

''Hadn't planned on it,'' I said. Every time I opened my mouth and nobody touched me, I got a little calmer. If Raina had done this to get me out of the way, then she didn't need to go any further. If it was revenge for Marcus, I was in deep shit.

Raina sat down on the end of the bed near my feet. I tensed when she did it; I couldn't help myself. She noticed and laughed. ''Oh, you are going to be a lot of fun.''

''You can be alpha female. I don't want the job,'' I said.

Raina sighed, running her hand along my leg, massaging the muscle in my upper thigh, almost absently like you'd pet a dog. ''Richard doesn't want me, Anita. He thinks I'm corrupt. He wants you.'' She squeezed my thigh until I thought she was going to grow claws and tear out the muscle. She forced a small sound out of my throat before she stopped.

''What do you want?''

''Your pain.'' She smiled when she said it.

I turned my head to Cassandra. There had to be someone sane in this room. ''Why are you helping them?''

''I am Sabin's wolf.''

My eyes narrowed. ''What are you talking about?''

Raina crawled up on the bed, lying beside me, insinuating her body against mine, one finger tracing over my stomach. It was an idle gesture, as if she wasn't really concentrating. I didn't want to be here when she started concentrating.

''Cassandra was a plant from the very beginning, weren't you dear?''

Cassandra nodded, coming to stand beside the bed. Her hazel eyes were calm, too calm. Whatever she was feeling was there behind that pretty face, carefully controlled. The trick was, was there anything behind that face that could help me?

''Dominic, Sabin, and I are a triumvirate. We are what you and Richard and Jean-Claude could have been.''

I didn't like her using the past tense. ''You're the woman he gave up fresh blood for?''

''I believe in the sanctity of life. I thought I valued that above all. Watching Sabin's golden beauty rot away has convinced me otherwise. I will do anything, *anything* to help him recover.'' Something like pain crossed her eyes and she looked away. When she looked back, her face was forcibly blank, the effort trembling down her hands. She noticed and hugged her hands to her arms. She smiled, but it wasn't a happy smile. ''I have to make it up to him, Anita. I am sorry that you and yours have become entangled in our problems.''

''How am I caught up in it?''

Raina slid her arm over my stomach, putting her face very near mine. ''Dominic has a spell to cure Sabin of the rotting disease. A transfer of magical essence, you might say. All he needed was exactly the right donor.'' She leaned in so close that only my turning my head kept our lips from touching. She whispered against my skin, breath warm, ''A perfect donor. A vampire who shares Sabin's powers exactly, a perfect match, and a servant, either alpha werewolf, or necromancer, bound to that same vampire.''

I turned and looked at her. I couldn't help it. She kissed me, pressing her mouth against mine, trying to force her tongue inside. I bit her lip hard enough that I tasted blood.

She jerked back with a startled scream. She put her hand to her mouth and stared down at me. ''That is going to cost you dearly.''

I spit her blood at her. It spattered along my chin. It was a stupid thing to have done. Making her angrier was not helpful, but watching the blood drip down her lovely face had almost been worth it.

''Gabriel, entertain Ms. Blake.''

That got my attention. Gabriel slid onto the bed, folding himself against me as Raina had done on the other side. He was taller, six feet, so he didn't fit quite as well, but what he lacked in matching size he made up for in technique. He straddled my body and leaned over me in a sort of push-up, bringing his mouth close and closer. He licked my bloody chin, one quick flick of his tongue. I jerked my head away.

He grabbed my chin with one hand, forcing me to look at him. He held my chin like a vise, fingers digging in when I struggled. The strength in his fingers was enough to crush my jaw if he squeezed. He licked the blood off my chin and lips in slow, lingering licks.

I screamed, then mentally cursed myself. This was what they wanted. Panic would not help. Panic would not help. I kept repeating it over and over until I stopped pulling at the ropes. I would not lose it, not yet, not yet.

Cassandra crawled up on the bed. I could only see her white dress out of the corner of my eye. Gabriel still held me immobile.

''Let go of her face so she can look at me.''

Gabriel glanced at her and hissed.

A low, rolling growl trickled out from behind her lips. "I'm in the mood for a fight tonight, kitty, don't make it easy for me."

"Aren't you expected at the ceremony?" Raina said. "Doesn't Dominic need you there for it to work?"

Cassandra reared back, and the voice that came was low and fell from her human lips with effort. "I will speak with Anita before I go, or I will not go."

Raina came to stand on the other side of the bed. "You'll never find another master vampire who matches your master as perfectly as Jean-Claude. Never. You'd jeopardize his one chance at a cure?"

"I will do as I wish on this one thing, Raina, for I am alpha. When Richard is gone, I will lead the pack. Do not forget that."

"That wasn't our bargain."

"Our bargain was that you would kill the Executioner before we arrived in town. You failed."

"Marcus hired the best. Who knew she would be so hard to kill?"

"I did, the first time I met her. You are always underestimating other women, Raina; it is one of your weaknesses." Cassandra leaned towards Raina. "You tried to kill Richard before Dominic could use him in the spell."

"He was going to kill Marcus."

Cassandra shook her head. "You panicked, Raina. You and Marcus. Now Marcus is dead, and you can't hold the pack. Too many of them hate you. And many of them love Richard, or at least admire him."

I wanted to ask where Jean-Claude and Richard were, but I was afraid I knew. A ceremony, sacrifice, but they needed Cassandra to make it work. I didn't want her to rush off.

"You were Dominic's alibi," I said. "Not that I'm complaining, but why am I still alive?"

Cassandra looked down at me. "Gabriel and Raina want you on film. If you would give me your word that you would seek no revenge against any of us for the deaths of your two men, then I would fight to see you go free."

I started to open my mouth and promise.

She waved a finger in front of my mouth. "No lies, Anita, not between us."

"Too late for that," I said.

Cassandra nodded. "True, and that grieves me. Under other circumstances, we might have been friends."

"Yeah." Of course, that made it hurt all the more. Nothing rubs salt in the wounds like betrayal. Richard could probably compare notes with me right now.

"Where are Richard and Jean-Claude?"

She stared down at me. "Even now you think you can save them, don't you?"

I would have shrugged, but I couldn't. "It was a thought."

"You were a lure and a hostage for the two men," Cassandra said.

Gabriel had settled on top of me, body pressing along the length of my body. He was heavy. You never noticed how heavy a man was when you were enjoying yourself. He had sunk down, so that his feet trailed off the bed, and he could fold his arms across my chest. His chin rested on his arms, and he stared at me like that, like he knew he had all day, all night, all the time in the world.

''I am very surprised that you broke up with Richard today, Anita,'' Raina said. ''We sent him a lock of your hair with a note saying we'd send a hand next. He came alone and told no one, as we had said to do. He really is a fool.''

It sounded like something Richard would do, but it surprised me, anyway. ''You didn't get Jean-Claude to hand himself over for a lock of my hair.''

Raina moved where I could see her better and smiled down. Her lip was already beginning to heal. ''Very true; we didn't even try. Jean-Claude would have known we meant to kill you, regardless. He'd have come with all his vampires, all the wolves that are loyal to him. It would have been a bloodbath.''

''How did you get him then?''

''Cassandra betrayed him. Didn't you, Cassandra?''

Cassandra just looked at us. ''If Richard hadn't broken with you, you might have been able to cure Sabin. Seeking your aid was originally only an excuse to enter Jean-Claude's territory, but you were more powerful than Dominic first thought. You surprised us by bearing none of the vampire's marks. You were supposed to be part of the sacrifice, but without at least the first mark, it will not work.''

Hurrah for me. ''You saw me heal Damian's cut and the zombie. I can heal Sabin. You know I can, Cassandra. You saw it.''

She shook her head. ''The sickness has moved inside Sabin. His brain is going. If you had cured him today, it would be moot. But he must be sane for the spell to work. Even one more day might be too late.''

''If you kill Richard and Jean-Claude, I won't have the power to heal Sabin. If Dominic came here planning to sacrifice all three of us, then the spell must need all three of us to work.''

Something flickered across her face. I was right. ''Dominic's not sure it will work without a human servant in the loop, is he?''

Cassandra shook her head. ''It has to be tonight.''

''If you kill them both and it doesn't cure Sabin, you've destroyed the only real chance he has. Our triumvirate can cure him. You know it can.''

''I know no such thing. You would promise me the moon itself if you thought it would save you all.''

''That's true, but I still think we can cure him. If you kill Richard and Jean-Claude, the chance is gone. Let us at least try. If it doesn't work, you can sacrifice them tomorrow. I'll let Jean-Claude give me the first mark. We'll either cure Sabin tomorrow or we'll be the perfect sacrifice for Dominic's spell.'' I willed her to listen to me. To believe me.

''Will Sabin be able to read his part of the spell tomorrow night?'' Raina asked. She moved in very close to Cassandra. ''Once his brain is rotted away, there will be nothing left to do but lock him in a box with crosses on it. Hide him away.''

Cassandra's hands balled into fists. A fine trembling ran through her body. Raw fear showed on her face.

Raina turned to me almost conversationally. ''Sabin won't die, you understand. He'll melt down into a little puddle of slime, but he won't die. Will he, Cassandra?''

''No,'' Cassandra almost shouted. ''No, he won't die. He'll just go insane. He'll still have all the powers of the triumvirate, but he'll be mad. We'll have to lock him away and pray that Dominic's spells can hold his power in check. If we can't hold his powers prisoner, the council will force us to burn him alive. Only that would be sure death.''

''But if you do that,'' Raina said, ''you and Dominic will die, as well. All those vampire marks dragging you down to hell with him.''

''Yes,'' Cassandra said, ''yes.'' She stared at me, anger and helplessness in her face.

''Am I supposed to feel sorry for you?'' I asked.

''No, Anita, you're just supposed to die,'' she said.

I swallowed hard and tried to think of something useful. It was hard to do with Gabriel lying on top of me, but if I didn't think of something, we were all dead.

Cassandra startled as if someone had touched her. A prickle of energy swept over my body from her, raising goose bumps where it touched. Gabriel ran his fingertips over the skin of my arms, making the gooseflesh stay just a little longer.

''I must go,'' Cassandra said. ''Before the night is over, you may wish you were being sacrificed.'' She looked from Gabriel to Raina. ''A slit throat would be quicker.''

I agreed with her, but I wasn't sure what to say. We were discussing different ways to kill me. None of them seemed particularly good choices.

Cassandra stared down at me. ''I am sorry.''

''If you're really sorry,'' I said, ''untie me and give me a weapon.''

She smiled wistfully. ''Sabin has ordered me not to.''

''You always do what you're told?'' I asked.

''On this one thing, yes. If you'd watched Jean-Claude's beauty rot before you, you'd do anything to help him.''

''Who're you trying to convince, me or you?''

She swayed slightly, and I felt the roll of power out of her body and along mine. Gabriel licked my arm.

''I must go. The circle will be closed soon.'' She stared down at me, at Gabriel running his tongue up my arm. ''I am truly sorry, Anita.''

''If you're looking for forgiveness, pray. God may forgive you; I won't.''

Cassandra stared down at me for another heartbeat. ''So be it. Good-bye, Anita.'' She ran in a blur of white, like a fast-forward ghost.

''Good,'' Raina said, ''now we can set up the lights and make some test shots.'' The lights sprang into a dazzling brightness.

I closed my eyes against the glare.

Gabriel moved up my body, and I opened my eyes. ''We were going to strip you naked and tie you spread-eagled, but Cassandra wouldn't let us. But now she's too busy with the spell.'' He put a hand on either side of my head, pinning some of my hair. ''We did makeup on your face while you were out. We can make the body makeup part of the show. What do you think?''

I tried to think of anything useful. Anything at all. Nothing came to mind. He leaned over me, bringing his face close and closer. He opened his mouth enough to show fangs. Not vampire fangs but small leopard fangs. Richard had told me once that Gabriel spent too much time in animal form so he didn't come completely back anymore. Great.

Gabriel kissed me, lightly, then harder, forcing his tongue in my mouth. He drew back from me. "Bite me." He kissed me, then raised his lips back just enough to whisper, "Bite me."

Pain excited Gabriel. I didn't want him more excited, but with his tongue halfway down my throat, it was hard not to give him what he wanted. He ran his hand over my breasts, squeezing hard enough to make me gasp. "Bite me, and I'll stop."

I bit his lip. I bit him until he pulled back, the flesh straining between us. Blood poured from his mouth to mine. I let go and spit blood into his face. He was close enough that it splattered in a red rain.

He laughed, wiping his fingers on the bloody lip, putting them in his mouth, sucking the blood off of them.

"Do you know how I became a wereleopard?" he asked.

I looked at him.

He slapped me lightly, casually. Starbursts exploded across my vision. "Answer me, Anita."

When I could focus, I asked, "What was the question?"

"Do you know how I became a wereleopard?"

I didn't want to play this game. I didn't want to participate in Gabriel's idea of pillow talk, but I didn't want to be hit again, either. It wouldn't take much for him to knock me unconscious. If I ever woke up again, I would be in worse shape than I was now. Hard to believe, but true.

"No," I said.

"I've always liked pain, even when I was human. I met Elizabeth. She was a wereleopard. We fucked, but I wanted her to change while we did it. She said she was afraid she'd kill me." He leaned over me. Blood dripped from his lip in slow, heavy drops.

I blinked, turning my face, trying to keep the blood out of my eyes.

"I almost died."

I had turned my head completely to the side, while his blood dropped on the side of my face. "Was the sex worth it?"

He leaned down and began to lick the blood off my face. "Best sex I ever had."

A scream started in my throat. I swallowed it, and it hurt going down. There had to be a way out of this. There had to be.

A man's voice said, "Lie on top of her like you're going to do for the shot, and let's get some light readings."

I realized that there was a crew here. A director, a cameraman, a dozen people scurrying around, not helping me.

Gabriel drew a knife out of his high, black boot. The hilt was black, but the blade had a high silver sheen. I watched that knife, couldn't help myself. I'd been scared before, but not like this. The fear burned at the back of my throat, threatened to spill out in screams. It wasn't the sight of the blade that frightened me. A moment ago I'd have done anything to have him cut the ropes. Now I would have given anything for him not to cut the ropes.

Gabriel put his hand on my stomach and slid one knee between my tied legs. There wasn't a lot of give. I was grateful. He twisted his upper body and reached downward with the knife. I knew what he was going to do before I felt the ropes give at my ankles. He cut my feet loose and collapsed his lower body against me at almost the same time. No time to struggle, no time to take advantage. He'd done this before.

He wiggled his hips against me, spreading my legs wide enough that I could feel him against me through the jeans. I didn't scream, I whimpered and hated it. My face was pressed into his naked chest just above his pierced nipple. His chest hair was coarse, scratchy against my cheek. His body covered me almost completely. They couldn't have seen much more than my hands and my legs from the camera.

I had a very strange idea. "You're too tall," I said.

Gabriel had to raise up a little to look down at my face. "What?"

"The camera will never see anything but your backside. You're too tall."

He crawled backwards, raising himself in a little push-up position. He looked thoughtful. He turned around without getting off of me. "Frank, can you see her at all?"

"Nope."

"Shit," Gabriel said. He stared down at me, then smiled. "Don't go anywhere. I'll be right back." He slid off me.

With my feet free, I could sit up. My hands were still above my head, but I could huddle against the headboard. It was an immense improvement.

Gabriel, Raina, and two men in scruffy clothes were talking in a huddled group. I caught snatches of the conversation. "Maybe if we hang her from the ceiling?" "We'll have to change the room setup for that."

I had bought some time, but time for what? There was a long table near the room. My weapons were on it, laid in neat lines like props. Everything I needed was right there, but how could I get to it? Raina wasn't going to hand me a knife so I could cut myself loose. No, Raina wouldn't, but maybe Gabriel would.

He walked towards the bed, moving as if he had more muscles, more something, than a human did. He moved like a cat, if a cat could walk on two legs.

He knelt on the bed and started untying the rope from the headboard, but leaving my wrists bound.

"Why not cut the rope?" I asked.

"Frank got pissed that I cut the first one. This is real silk. It's expensive."

"Nice to know that Frank's fiscally responsible."

Gabriel grabbed my face, forcing me to meet his eyes. "We're going to change the room and tie you standing up. I'm going to fuck you until you go with me inside you, then I'm going to change and I'll rip you apart. You may even survive like I survived."

I swallowed and spoke very carefully. "Is that really your fantasy, Gabriel?"

"Yes."

"Not your best fantasy," I said.

"What?"

"Raping me while I'm helpless isn't your idea of hot sex."

He grinned, flashing fangs. "Oh, yes it is."

Don't panic. Don't panic. Don't panic. I leaned into him, and he released my face so I could do it, but he jerked the rope up tight, making sure my hands stayed in sight. He had definitely done this before.

I forced myself to lean into his naked chest, my tied hands pressed against his skin. I leaned my face towards him and whispered, "Don't you want a blade inside you while you do it?" I touched the silver ring in his nipple, pulled on it until the flesh bowed outward and he gave a little gasp.

"Don't you want the feel of silver burning up inside you while you're shoving yourself inside of me?" I went up on my knees so our faces would be closer together. "Don't you want to know I'm trying to kill you while you fuck me? Your blood pouring over my body while you fuck me, isn't that your fantasy?" I whispered the last against his lips.

Gabriel had gone very, very still. I could see the pulse in his throat thudding against the skin. His heart beat fast and hard against my hands. I jerked the ring out of his nipple and he let out a low moan. Blood trickled down his chest. I raised the ring, and he let the rope go so I could move my hands. I raised the bloody ring between our lips, almost as if we'd both kiss it.

"You'll only have one chance to fuck me, Gabriel. One way or another, Raina will see me dead tonight. You'll never get another chance at me."

The tip of his tongue curled out and caught the ring, licking it from my fingers. He rolled it in his mouth and brought it back out, clean and free of blood. He held it out to me on the tip of his tongue. I picked the ring off and wrapped my fingers around it.

"You just want me to give you a knife," he said.

"I want to shove a silver blade so deep inside you that the hilt bruises your flesh."

He shuddered, breath escaping in a long sigh.

"You'll never find anyone else like me, Gabriel. Play with me, Gabriel, and I'll be the best sex you ever had."

"You'll try and kill me," he said.

I slid my fingers along the top of his leather pants. "Oh, yeah, but have you ever really been in danger of dying since that first time with Elizabeth? Since she shape-shifted underneath you, have you ever feared for your life during sex? Did you ever ride that thin, shining line between pleasure and death again?"

He turned away from me, not meeting my eyes. I touched his face with my bound hands, turned him back to me. "Raina hasn't let you, has she? Just like she won't let you tonight. You're alpha, Gabriel, I can feel it. Don't let her steal this from you. Don't let her steal *me* from you."

Gabriel stared at me, our bodies touching, faces close enough to kiss. "You'll kill me."

"Maybe, or you'll kill me."

"You might survive," he said, "I did."

''Are you still fucking Elizabeth, now that you survived?'' I kissed him softly, running my teeth along his skin.

''Elizabeth bores me.''

''Would you bore me, Gabriel? If I survive, would you be boring?''

''No,'' he whispered. I knew I had him, just like that. I either had the beginnings of a brilliant plan, or I'd bought myself some time, some options. It was an improvement. The real question was how much time did Jean-Claude and Richard have? How long until Dominic cut them open? If I couldn't get there in time, I didn't want to get there at all. If they both died, I almost wanted Gabriel to finish me. Almost.

43

They kept me tied to the bed, but Gabriel slipped the knives back in the wrist sheaths. He held the big knife that went down along my spine up to the light. I thought he wouldn't give it back, but in the end, he swept my hair to one side and slipped it into the sheath.

"Don't cut the ropes until I'm in the shot. I want the camera to know why you're scared. Promise not to spoil it."

"Give me a gun and I'll wait until you're on top of me to pull the trigger."

He smiled and waved a finger in my face like you'd scold a child. "Uh, uh, uh. No rough stuff."

I took a deep breath and let it out. "Can't blame a girl for trying."

Gabriel laughed, high and nervous. "No, can't blame you for trying."

We had lights, camera, all we needed was action. Gabriel had wiped the blood off his chest and put the silver ring back into his flesh. We were starting over for the camera. They'd even cleaned the blood off my mouth and freshened the makeup. It was the young woman, Heidi, the lycanthrope that did the makeup. Her eyes were too wide. Her hands shook when she touched me.

She whispered as she dabbed at my face. "Be careful when he kisses you. He ate a girl's tongue out once."

"Can you get me a gun?"

She shivered, eyes rolling white and panicked. She shook her head. "Raina'd kill me."

"Not if she's dead."

Heidi shook her head over and over and backed off the bed.

Most of the rest of the crew walked out. When the director realized they were going to lose too many people to run things, he offered bonuses. Big bonuses, and a few people stayed. The rest left. They didn't do snuff films. They wouldn't watch Gabriel kill me, but they wouldn't stop it, either. Maybe one of them would call the police. It was a nice thought, but I didn't pin any hopes on it.

Power rushed over me in a skin-prickling wave. It tugged at something low and deep in my body. The sensation was gone almost as soon as it came, but a smell lingered over my skin like I'd walked through somebody's ghost. I smelled Richard's aftershave. Richard was trying to tell me something, either on purpose or because he was being driven by fear. Either way, time was running out. I had to save them. I had to. There was no other choice. Saving them meant bringing Gabriel in close enough to kill him. Close to me. A mixed blessing at best.

''Get on with it,'' I said.

''You are terribly eager for someone who's about to die a truly horrible death,'' Raina said.

I smiled. I made the smile everything Gabriel wanted it to be, confident, dangerous, sexual. ''I don't plan to die.''

Gabriel's breath sighed outward. ''Let's do it.''

Raina shook her head and stepped back out of the shot. ''Fuck her, Gabriel, make her cry out your name before you kill her.''

''My pleasure,'' he whispered. He stalked onto the floor of the fake bedroom.

I unsheathed a wrist knife and cut the rope that held me to the headboard. My wrists were still bound. I watched him while I turned the blade to cut between my hands. He could have jumped me then, but he didn't. He glided around the bed while I cut my hands loose.

He ended on his knees beside the bed, staring at me. I backed away from him, knife in my right hand. I was going to get off the damn bed.

Gabriel crawled up on the bed as I crawled off it. He mimicked my movements but made them graceful and painfully slow. He shimmered with contained energy. He wasn't doing a damn thing but crawling across a bed, but the promise of violence and sex rode the air like lightning.

He was faster than me. His reach was almost twice mine. He was certainly stronger than I was. The only thing I really had going for me was the fact that I planned on killing him as quickly as possible, and he planned on raping me first. It meant I was willing to do things he wasn't. At least at first. If it wasn't over quickly, I was sunk.

I dropped to one knee and braced myself, with a blade in each hand. He wanted to come in close. He even wanted to be hurt, so no feinting, no trying each other's skill. I'd make him come to me, and I'd cut him up.

Power curled inside my stomach. It burst over me in a wave of sensations. The smell of the summer woods was so strong it was choking. For a second, I couldn't see the room. I had a glimpse of somewhere else, chaotic bits and pieces like a jigsaw puzzle thrown across the ground. I came away with three thoughts; fear, helplessness, and need.

My vision cleared to Gabriel frowning down at me. ''What is wrong with you, Anita? Did Cassandra hit you a little too hard?''

I shook my head and took a shaky breath. ''Are you all talk and no bite, Gabriel?''

He smiled, a slow, lazy grin that showed his fangs. He was suddenly there. I slashed out without thinking, pure reaction, no thought. He leaped away, and blood seeped down his stomach in a thin, crimson line.

He rubbed his fingers in the blood slowly, sensuously, then licked them with long, slow tongue movements. Playing for the camera. He crawled onto the bed and wrapped the white sheets around his body, rolling in them until he was tangled. He leaned over backwards, exposing his neck. Almost within reach of me. ''Come play, Anita.''

It was tempting, and it was meant to be, but I knew better. I'd seen Richard rip sheets earlier like they were paper. ''I'm staying here, Gabriel. You're going to have to come to me.''

He rolled onto his stomach. ''I thought I'd get to chase you. This isn't any fun.''

I smiled. ''Come closer, and it'll be a lot of fun.''

He rose onto his knees. The sheets were smeared with blood as he crawled out of them. Gabriel was just suddenly there, too fast for me to see it. He was by me and past me before I could react.

I fell back on my butt, trying desperately to keep him in sight. But he stood there, just out of reach. A second later, a sharp pain ran through my right arm. I glanced, and found bleeding claw marks on my upper arm.

He raised one hand in front of his face, and claws sprang out from under his fingernails. ''Meow,'' he said.

I tried to swallow my beating heart and couldn't. This meant that even if he didn't kill me, a month from now I might be sprouting fur.

It wasn't a scream that you could hear with your ears. It wasn't a sound. I had no words for it, but I felt Richard scream inside me. His power poured over me, and down that long line I felt Jean-Claude. Something tight and painful held him down. I tried to get to my feet and stumbled.

''What's wrong, Anita? I didn't hurt you that badly.''

I shook my head, and got to my feet. He wasn't going to come to me. Richard was growing desperate. I reached outward with that flare of power and I could feel Dominic's spell. He'd been shielding it somehow, but he couldn't hide from me. The spell was growing. The time of sacrifice was coming. I didn't have time for Gabriel to play with me. ''Stop playacting, Gabriel, or don't you want me?''

His eyes narrowed. ''You're up to something.''

''You bet. Now, fuck me, Gabriel, if you've got the balls for it.''

I put my back to the wall and hoped it would be enough, and knew it wouldn't be. I threw a thread of power back to Richard, hoping he'd get the hint and not interrupt for the next few minutes. If he distracted me at the wrong time, it would be all over.

Gabriel stalked in front of me, daring me to come out from the wall and get him. I did what he thought I would do. I tried for him and he just wasn't there. It was like trying to cut air.

He slashed out with one hand and sliced the back of my left hand open. I slashed at him with my right hand, trying to hold onto the left-hand knife. He hit the hand again, not with claws but backhanded. My hand spasmed, and the knife went spinning.

His body hit mine full out, slamming me to the floor. I shoved the right-hand knife into his stomach before my back hit the ground. But shoving the knife in meant I took the full force of the fall. It stunned me for a heartbeat. A heartbeat was all he needed.

He ran his hands under my arms, not trying to pin them, but forcing them up away from the knife in his stomach. He pinned me to the floor with his body. I expected him to draw out the blade, but he didn't. He pressed the hilt against my body and pushed. He shoved the blade into him up to the hilt and kept pressing. The hilt bruised against my stomach and he ground it into both of us.

He shuddered over me. He raised his upper body off me, pinning me with his lower body, snuggling it between my legs so I could feel him, hard and firm. He pulled the blade out in a burst of crimson and plunged it downward so fast my arms were only halfway up to protect my face when the blade bit into the carpet. He drove the blade hilt deep into the plywood floor, so close to my head that it pinned my hair on one side.

He undid the button on my jeans. He wasn't even trying to control my hands, but I only had one knife left. If I lost it, I couldn't kill him. We were about to find out just how good my nerves were.

Richard's power flowed over me again, but it wasn't the same. It was less frantic, more as if he was trying to whisper something to me, offer me something. Then I realized what it was. The first mark. Jean-Claude and Richard, for it was they, couldn't do it now without my permission. I was too powerful to be forced, at least psychically.

Gabriel kept my legs pinned with his hips and grabbed the front of my jeans, fingers pointing outward, away from my body. His claws sprang out through the cloth, and he ripped upward, slicing the cloth nearly to my pubic bone.

I screamed and let Richard do me. Better the monster you know than the monster about to go down your pants. A line of warmth ran through my body. It had been even simpler when Jean-Claude did it on his own, once upon a time. Even knowing what it was, it didn't feel like much.

But I felt better instantly; clearer-headed, more . . . something. Gabriel hesitated on top of me. "What the hell was that?" The skin of his bare arms was prickled with gooseflesh. He'd gotten a taste of the power.

"Didn't feel a thing," I said. I tugged on the knife in the floor, pulling at it. Gabriel ripped my jeans in both hands, and they split down the middle, leaving nothing between him and me but my panties and his leather pants. I was at a bad angle for the knife and it was only halfway out when he slid his hand down my panties.

I screamed. I screamed, "Richard!"

The power flowed over me. With Jean-Claude, I had watched his burning blue eyes enter me. With Richard as focus, there was nothing to see, but smells, the forest, his skin, Jean-Claude's perfume. I could taste them both in my mouth like drinking two strong wines one mouthful after another.

Gabriel's hand froze down the front of my body. He was staring down at me. "What did you just do?" His voice was a whisper.

"Did you think raping me would be easy?" I laughed, and it unnerved him. I saw something close to fear in his storm grey eyes. He'd moved his hand. Not having him down my underwear was too big an improvement for words. I never wanted him to touch me like that again. Never.

I had two choices. I could bluff and hope I could run, or I could reinitiate sex and kill him. The second mark didn't give me that much more power. In fact, it gave the boys more pull on my power than the other way around. So, sex it was.

"What's wrong?" Raina asked out of camera range.

"Gabriel's getting cold feet," I said. I raised up on my elbows. The knife he'd shoved in the floor held my hair pinned, and I kept raising up, tearing a hunk of my hair out. It was a small pain, but I knew it would appeal to Gabriel. It did.

I was sitting up with my legs on either side of his thighs. He picked me up, hands sliding over my undies, cupping my buttocks. He leaned back on his knees, supporting my weight. He watched me, and I saw something slide through his eyes, felt it tremble through his hands. For the first time, he thought I really might kill him, and it turned him on. Fear was the rush.

He kissed the side of my face gently. "Go for the last knife, Anita. Go for it." He leaned into me while he said it, biting gently down my face. I felt the pressure of his fangs down my jawline, onto my neck. He set his teeth into the side of my neck, bearing down, hard and harder, a slow, building pressure. His tongue licked across the skin.

I didn't go for the knife. I ran my hands through his thick hair, pulled it back from his face. His teeth continued to press into my skin. His hands slid inside my underwear, cupping my bare buttocks. I stiffened, then forced myself to relax. This would work. It had to work.

I traced my fingers along his face. His teeth bit in enough to draw the first faint blood. I gasped, and his claws dug into me. I ran my fingers along either side of his face, tracing his cheeks, his eyebrows. He came up for air, eyes wide and unfocused, lips half-parted. I caressed his face and pulled him in for a kiss. I traced his thick eyebrows. As he kissed me, he closed his eyes, and I put my thumbs over his eyelids. His eyelashes fluttered against my skin. I shoved my thumbs into both eyes, digging, trying to shove my thumbs into his brain and out the other side.

Gabriel reared back, shrieking. His claws ripped up my back. I gasped but didn't have time for screaming. I drew the big knife from the back sheath.

Raina screamed instead.

I shoved the blade under Gabriel's ribs. I shoved it into his heart. He tried to fall backwards, but my weight pinned his knees, so his back bowed backwards, but he didn't fall. I shoved the blade through him. I felt the tip of it burst out the other side.

Raina was suddenly there, grabbing me by the hair, flinging me off him. I flew through the air, smashed into the fake wall, and kept going. The wall splintered. I lay on my stomach, relearning how to breathe. My pulse was so loud in my head, I was deaf for a few seconds. My body stopped being numb in stages, and let me know it was scraped and bruised, but nothing was broken. It should have been. Two marks and I was suddenly Anita the human battering ram. When it happened the first time, I hadn't appreciated it. Now I did. I wasn't hurt badly, hurrah, but I still had to get past Raina. Everybody else would fold and run for cover if she were dead. Question was, how to get her there?

I looked up and realized I was right next to the prop table with my guns on it. Were they loaded? If I went for them and they weren't, Raina was going to kill me. Of course, if I just lay here and bled, she'd kill me anyway.

I heard her high heels coming my way. I pushed to my knees, my feet, and went for the table. She still couldn't see me through the partial wall, but she could hear me. She rushed up her side of the wall in those ridiculous high heels.

I grabbed for the Firestar and rolled over the table as I moved. I ended on my back, staring up as she leapt over the table. I hit the safety with my thumb and pulled the trigger. The gun exploded in my hand and took her in the upper stomach. The bullet seemed to slow her in midmotion, and I had time for another shot, higher up in the chest.

Raina collapsed to her knees, honey brown eyes wide with shock. She reached out one hand, and I scooted backwards, still on my butt and lower back. I watched her eyes go, that light sliding away. She slumped over on her side, her long hair spilling like auburn water across the floor.

The crew had hightailed it. Only Heidi was crouched by the wall, crying, covering her ears as if afraid to leave or stay.

I got to my feet, using the prop table for support. I could see Gabriel's body now. Blood and clear fluid flowed down his face from his eyes. His body still hadn't fallen. It knelt in a strange parody of life, as if he would open his eyes and it would all be pretend.

Edward came in through the covered door. He had a shotgun at his shoulder. Harley followed at his side with a machine gun. He surveyed the room and finally came back to me. ''Is Anita in this room?''

''Yes,'' Edward said.

''I can't recognize her,'' Harley said.

''Hold your fire. I'll go find her for you.'' He walked towards me, eyes taking it all in.

''How much of this blood is yours?'' he asked.

I shook my head. ''How'd you find me?''

''I tried to return your message. Nobody knew where you'd gone. Then nobody knew where Richard had gone, or Jean-Claude, or Raina.''

I felt Richard scream through me and I didn't fight it this time, I let the scream come out my mouth. If Edward hadn't caught me, I would have fallen. ''We've got to get to Jean-Claude and Richard. Right now!''

''You can't even walk,'' he said.

I grabbed his shoulders. ''Help me, and I'll run.''

Edward didn't argue; he simply nodded and slid one arm around my waist.

Harley handed my knives and the Browning to Edward. I was inches away, but he didn't try to touch me. He looked past me as if I wasn't there. Maybe, for him, I wasn't. I cut the legs of my jeans off, which left me in nothing but underwear and Nikes from the waist down, but I could run now, and we needed to run. I could feel it. I could feel the power growing on the summer night. Dominic was preparing the blade. I could taste it. I prayed as we ran. Prayed that we'd be in time.

44

We ran. I ran until I thought my heart would burst, jumping trees and dodging things in the dark only half-felt and not seen at all. Branches and weeds raked my legs in thin scratches. A branch caught my cheek and sent me stumbling. Edward caught me. Harley said, ''What is that?''

There was a bright, white glow through the trees. It wasn't fire. ''Crosses,'' I said.

''What?'' Harley asked.

''They've hung Jean-Claude with crosses.'' As the words left my mouth, I knew they were the truth. I ran towards the glow. Edward and Harley followed.

I spilled out to the edge of the clearing with them at my back. I raised the Browning without thinking about it. I had a second to take it all in. Richard and Jean-Claude were bound so thick with chains that they could barely move, let alone escape. A cross had been thrown around Jean-Claude's neck. It glowed like a captive star, resting on the folds of chain. Someone had blindfolded him as if afraid the glow would hurt his eyes. Which was odd, since they meant to kill him. Considerate murderers.

Richard was gagged. He'd managed to work one hand free, and he and Jean-Claude were touching fingertips, straining to retain that touch.

Dominic stood over them in a white ceremonial robe. The hood was thrown back, his arms wide, holding a short sword half the length of my body. He held something dark in his other hand. Something that pulsed and seemed to live. It was a heart. Robert the vampire's heart.

Sabin sat in Marcus's stone chair, dressed as I'd seen him last, hood up, hiding in the shadows. Cassandra was a shining whiteness on the other side of the circle of power, forming the last point of a triangle with her two men. My two men lay bound on the ground.

I pointed the Browning at Dominic and fired. The bullet left the gun. I heard it, I saw it, but it didn't go near Dominic. It didn't seem to go anywhere. I blew my breath out and tried again.

Dominic stared at me. His dark-bearded face was calm, totally unafraid. ''You are of the dead, Anita Blake, neither you, nor anything of yours may pass this circle. You have come only to watch them die.''

''You've lost, Dominic, why kill them at all, now?''

''We will never find what we need again,'' the necromancer said.

Sabin spoke, his voice thick, awkward, as if talking was hard. ''It must be tonight.'' He pushed to his feet and shoved the hood back. His flesh was almost completely gone, only straggles of hair and raw, putrefying tissue were left. Dark liquid oozed from his mouth. Maybe he didn't have one more night of sanity. But that wasn't my problem.

''The vampire council has forbidden any of you to fight each other until Brewster's Law is either passed or voted down. They'll kill you for disobeying them.'' I was half guessing on this, but I'd been around enough masters of the city to know how very seriously they took disobedience. The council was, in fact, the biggest, baddest, master of the city around. They would be less forgiving, not more.

''I will take that chance,'' Sabin said, every word careful, showing the effort it took to speak.

''Did Cassandra tell you about my offer? If we can't cure you tomorrow, I'll let Jean-Claude mark me. Tonight you only have part of what you need for the spell. You need me, Sabin, one way or another, you need me.'' I didn't tell them I was already marked. They obviously hadn't felt it. If they knew I was already marked, all I could offer was to die tonight with the boys.

Dominic shook his head. ''I have searched Sabin's body, Anita. Tomorrow will be too late. There will be nothing to save.'' He dropped to his knees beside Richard.

''You don't know that for sure,'' I said.

He laid the still-beating heart on top of Richard's bare chest.

''Dominic, please!''

It was too late for lies. ''I'm marked, Dominic. We're the perfect sacrifice. Open the circle, and I'll come inside.''

He looked at me. ''If this is true, then you are all far too dangerous to trust. The three of you together without the circle would overwhelm us. You see, Anita, I have been part of a true triumvirate for centuries. You have no dreams of the power you can touch. You and Richard are more powerful than Cassandra and I. You would have been a force to be reckoned with. The council itself might have feared you.'' He laughed. ''They may forgive us for that alone.''

He spoke words that curled power over me.

I walked to the edge of the circle and touched it. It was like my skin tried to crawl off my bones. I fell forward and slid down something that couldn't be there. Jean-Claude shrieked. It hurt too much for me to scream. I lay curled by the circle, and even when I breathed, I could taste death, old, rotting death in my mouth.

Edward knelt by me. ''What is it?''

''Without your other parts, you do not have the power to force this circle, Anita.'' Dominic got to his feet, raising the sword two-handed for a downward blow.

Dolph had passed the circle earlier in the room where they had taken Robert's heart. I grabbed Edward's shirt. "You pass the circle. Now. And kill that son of a bitch."

"If you can't, how can I?"

"You're not magic, that's how."

It was one of those rare moments when you understand how great trust can be. Edward knew nothing about the ceremony, yet he didn't argue. He accepted what I said, and simply did it. I wasn't a hundred percent sure it would work, myself, but it had to.

Dominic brought the sword down. I screamed. Edward crossed the circle like it wasn't there. The sword bit into Richard's chest, pinning the beating heart to his body. The pain of the blade drove me to my knees. I felt it enter Richard's body. Then I felt nothing, like a switch had been turned off. Edward's shotgun blast took Dominic in the chest.

Dominic didn't fall. He stared at the hole in his chest and then at Edward. He pulled the sword out of Richard's chest and slid the still-beating heart off it. He faced Edward with the sword in one hand and the heart in the other. Edward fired again, and Cassandra leapt on his back.

Harley crossed the circle then. He grabbed Cassandra around the waist and pulled her off of Edward. They fell, rolling to the ground. A gun sounded, and Cassandra's body jerked, but her dainty fist came up and smashed downward.

Edward fired the shotgun until Dominic's face vanished in a spray of blood and bones, and he fell slowly to his knees. His outstretched hand spilled the heart onto the ground beside Richard's terribly still body.

Sabin levitated upward. "I will have your soul for that, mortal."

I ran my fingers over the circle and it was still there. Edward started to turn the shotgun towards the vampire. The naked heart pulsed and shimmered in the cross's glare.

"The heart, shoot the heart!"

Edward didn't hesitate. He turned and shot the heart, exploding it into so much meat. Sabin hit him a second later and he went flying. He ended up very still on the ground with Sabin on top of him.

I pushed my hand forward. It met empty air. I fired two-handed at Sabin as I walked towards him. I put three shots into his chest, forcing him to his feet, back from Edward.

Sabin raised a hand in front of his skeletal face, almost a pleading gesture. I stared down the barrel of the gun into his one good eye and pulled the trigger. The bullet took him just above the crumbling remains of his nose. It made a nice big exit wound like it was supposed to, spattering blood and brains on the grass. Sabin collapsed backwards onto the grass. I fired two more shots into his skull until it looked like I'd decapitated him.

"Edward?" It was Harley. He was standing over Cassandra's very still, very dead body. His eyes searched wildly for the one person he recognized.

"Harley, it's me, it's Anita."

He shook his head, as if I was a buzzing fly. "Edward, I still see monsters. Edward!" He raised the machine gun at me, and I knew I couldn't let him fire. No, it was more than that, or less. I raised the Browning and fired before I'd had time to think. The first shot sent him to his knees. "Edward!" He squeezed off a round of fire that went inches above the men's heads. I fired another into his chest, and put one through his head before he fell.

I approached him, gun at the ready. If he'd twitched, I'd have shot him again. He didn't twitch. I knew nothing about Harley except he was genuinely crazy and very good with weapons. Now I'd never know because Edward didn't volunteer information. I kicked the machine gun out of Harley's dead hand and went for the others.

Edward was sitting up, rubbing the back of his head. He watched me walk away from Harley's body. "Did you do it?"

I faced him. "Yes."

"I've killed people for less."

"So have I," I said, "but if we're going to fight, can we unchain the boys first? I don't feel Richard anymore." I couldn't say the word *dead* out loud, not yet.

Edward got to his feet, a little shaky, but standing. "We'll fight later."

"Later," I said.

Edward went to sit by his friend. I went to sit by my lover and my other boyfriend.

I holstered the Browning, slipped the cross off Jean-Claude's neck, and threw it spinning into the woods. The darkness was suddenly velvet and intense. I bent to undo his chains and one of the links went spinning by my head.

"Shit," I said.

Jean-Claude sat up, sweeping the chains down his body like a sheet. He slipped off the blindfold last. I was already crawling to Richard. I'd seen the sword pierce his heart. He had to be dead, but I searched for the big pulse in his neck, and I found it. It beat against my hand like a weak thought, and I slumped forward with relief. He was alive. Thank you, God.

Jean-Claude knelt on the other side of Richard's body. "I thought you could not bear his touch, that is what he told me before they gagged him. They were afraid he would call his pack to aid him. I have already called Jason and my vampires. They will be here soon."

"Why can't I feel him in my head?"

"I am blocking it. It is a fearful wound, and I am better practiced at dealing with such things."

I pulled the gag from Richard's mouth. I touched his lips gently. The thought of how I'd refused to kiss him earlier that day bit at me. "He's dying, isn't he?"

Jean-Claude broke Richard's chains, more carefully than his own. I helped him clear them from Richard's limp body. Richard lay on the ground in the bloodstained white T-shirt I'd last seen him in. He was just suddenly Richard again. I couldn't imagine the beast I'd seen. I suddenly didn't care. "I can't lose him, not like this."

"Richard is dying, *ma petite*. I feel his life slipping away."

I stared up at him. "You're still keeping me from feeling it, aren't you?"

"I am protecting you." There was a look on his face that I didn't like.

I touched his arm. His skin was cool to the touch. "Why?"

He turned away.

I jerked him hard, forced him to look at me. "Why?"

"Even with only two marks, Richard can try and drain us both to stay alive. I am preventing that."

"You're protecting us both?" I asked.

"When he dies, I can protect one of us, *ma petite*, but not both."

I stared at him. "You're saying that when he dies, you're both going to die?"

"I fear so."

I shook my head. "No. Not both of you. Not all at once. Dammit, you're not supposed to be able to die."

"I am sorry, *ma petite*."

"No, we can share power just like we did to raise the zombies, the vampires, like we did tonight."

Jean-Claude slumped suddenly downward, one hand on Richard's body. "I will not drag you to the grave with me, *ma petite*. I would rather think of you alive and well."

I dug my fingers into Jean-Claude's arm. I touched Richard's chest. A shuddering breath ran up my arm from him. "I'll be alive, but I won't be well. I'd rather die than lose you both."

He stared at me for a long second. "You do not know what you are asking."

"We are a triumvirate now. We can do this, Jean-Claude. We can do this, but you have to show me how."

"We are powerful beyond my wildest dreams, *ma petite*, but even we cannot cheat death."

"He owes me one."

Jean-Claude flinched as if in pain. "Who owes you?"

"Death."

"*Ma petite* . . ."

"Do it, Jean-Claude, do it. Whatever it is, whatever it takes. Do it, please!"

He slumped on top of Richard, head barely raised. "The third mark. It will either bind us forever, or kill us all."

I offered him my wrist. "No, *ma petite*, if it is to be our only time, come to me." He lay half on Richard's body, arms open for me. I lay in the circle of his arms, and realized when I touched his chest there was no heartbeat. I turned and stared into his face from inches away. "Don't leave me."

His midnight blue eyes filled with fire. He swept my hair to one side and said, "Open for me, *ma petite*, open for us both."

I did, sweeping my mind open, dropping every guard I'd ever had. I fell forward, impossibly forward, down a long, black tunnel towards a burning blue fire. Pain cut the darkness like a white knife, and I heard myself gasp. I felt Jean-Claude's fangs sink into me, his mouth sealing over my flesh, sucking me, drinking me.

A wind swept through the falling darkness, catching me like a net before I touched that blue fire. The wind smelled of growing earth and the musty scent of fur. I felt something else: sorrow. Richard's sorrow. His mourning. Not of his death, but of my loss. Dead or alive, he'd lost me, and among his many faults was a loyalty that went beyond reason. Once in love, he was a man to stay there, regardless of what the woman did. A knight errant in every sense of the word. He was a fool, and I loved him for it. Jean-Claude I loved in spite of himself. Richard I loved because of who he was.

I wouldn't lose him. I wrapped his essence like winding myself in a sheet, except that I had no body. I held him in my mind, my body, and let him feel the love, my sorrow, regret. Jean-Claude was there, too. I half-expected him to protest, to sabotage it, but he didn't. That blue fire spilled upward through the tunnel to meet us, and the world exploded into shapes and images that were too confusing. Bits and pieces of memory, sensations, thoughts, like three separate jigsaw puzzles shaken and tossed into the air, and every piece that touched formed a picture.

I padded through the forest on four feet. The smells alone were intoxicating. I sank fangs into a dainty wrist, and it wasn't mine. I watched the pulse underneath a woman's neck and thought of blood, warm flesh, and far-off and distant sex. The memories came fast, then faster, flowing like some sort of carnival ride. Blackness gained on the images, like ink filling water. When the darkness ate everything, I floated for an impossible second, then went out like a candle flame. Nothing.

I didn't even have time to be scared.

45

I woke in a pastel pink hospital room. A nurse in a matching pink smock smiled down at me. Fear pumped like fine champagne. Where was Richard? Where was Jean-Claude? What I finally managed to ask, was, "How did I get here?"

"Your friend brought you." She motioned with her head.

Edward sat in a chair by the far wall, leafing through a magazine. He looked up and our eyes met. His face gave away nothing.

"Edward?"

"My friends call me Ted, Anita, you know that." He had that good ol' boy smile that could only mean he was pretending to be Ted Forrester. It was his only legal identity that I'd ever met. Even the cops thought he was this Ted person. "Nurse, can we have a few minutes alone?"

The nurse smiled, looked curiously from one to the other of us, and left, still smiling.

I tried to grab Edward's hand and found my left hand was taped to a board and stuck with an IV. I grabbed at him with my right hand, and he held it. "Are they alive?"

He smiled, a mere twitch of lips. "Yes."

A relief like I'd never known flowed through my body. I collapsed back against the bed, weak. "What happened?"

"You came in suffering from lycanthrope scratches and a very nasty vampire bite. He almost drained you dry, Anita."

"Maybe that's what it took to save us."

"Maybe," Edward said. He sat on the edge of the bed. His jacket gaped enough to flash his shoulder holster and gun. He caught me looking. "The police agree that the monsters might hold a grudge. There's even a cop outside your door."

We weren't holding hands now. He stared down at me and something very cold passed over his face. "Did you have to kill Harley?"

I started to say yes, but I stopped myself. I replayed it in my mind. Finally, I looked up at him. "I don't know, Edward. When you were knocked out, he couldn't see you anymore. I tried to talk to him, but he couldn't hear me. He started to raise the machine gun.'' I met Edward's empty blue eyes. ''I shot him. You saw the body. I even put one through his head. A coupe de grace.''

''I know.'' His face, his voice gave nothing away. It was like watching a mannequin talk, except that this mannequin was armed and I wasn't.

''It never occurred to me not to shoot, Edward. I didn't even hesitate.''

Edward took a deep breath through his nose and let it out through his mouth. ''I knew that's what had happened. If you'd lied to me, I'd have killed you.'' He walked away to stand at the foot of the bed.

''While I'm unarmed?'' I tried to make light of it, but it didn't work.

''Check your pillow.''

I slid my hand under and came up with the Firestar. I held it in my lap, laying it on my sheet-covered legs. ''What now?''

''You owe me a life.''

I looked up at that. ''I saved your life last night.''

''Our lives don't count, we'd back each other up, no matter what.''

''I don't know what you're talking about then.''

''Occasionally I'll need help, like Harley. Next time I need help, I'll call you.''

I wanted to argue because I wasn't entirely sure what mess Edward would drag me into, but I didn't. Looking into his empty eyes, holding the gun he'd put under my pillow, I knew he'd do it. If I refused his bargain, his trade as it were, he'd pull down on me, and we'd find out once and for all who was better.

I stared down at the gun in my hands. ''I've already got the gun out; all I have to do is point.''

''You're injured. You need the edge.'' His hand hovered near the butt of his gun.

I laid the gun on the sheets beside me, and looked at him. I lay back on the pillows. ''I don't want to do this, Edward.''

''Then, when I call, you'll come?''

I thought about it for another brief second, then said, ''Yeah, I'll come.''

He smiled, his Ted (good ol' boy) Forrester smile. ''I'll never find out how good you really are until you draw down on me.''

''We can live with that,'' I said. ''By the way, why the invitation to come monster hunting now? And don't tell me it's about Harley.''

''You killed him, Anita. You killed him without thinking about it. Even now, there's no regret in you, no doubt.''

He was right. I didn't feel bad about it. Scary, but true. ''So you invited me to come play because I'm now as much of a sociopath as you are.''

''Oh, I'm a much better sociopath,'' he said. ''I'd never let a vampire sink his fangs into my neck. And I wouldn't date the terminally furry.''

''Do you date anyone, ever?''

He just smiled that irritating smile that meant he wasn't going to answer. But he did. ''Even Death has needs.''

Edward dating? That was something I had to see.

46

I got out of the hospital with no permanent scars. That was a switch. Richard had touched the wounds Gabriel gave me, his face very serious. No one had to say it out loud. In a month, we'd know. The doctors offered to put me in one of the shapeshifter halfway houses (read prisons) for the first-time furry. It has to be voluntary, but once you sign yourself in, it's almost impossible to sign yourself out. I told them I'd take care of it myself. They scolded me, and I told them to go to hell.

I spent the night of my first full moon with Richard and the pack, waiting to see if I was going to join the killing dance. I didn't. Either I'd gotten incredibly lucky or just as a vampire can't catch lycanthropy, neither could I. Richard wouldn't have much to do with me after that. I can't blame him.

I still love him. I think he still loves me. I love Jean-Claude, too. But it's not the same kind of love. I can't explain it, but I miss Richard. For brief moments in Jean-Claude's arms, I forget. But I miss Richard.

The fact that we are both bound to Jean-Claude doesn't help. Richard has accidentally invaded my dreams twice. Having him that close to me is too painful for words. Richard fought it, but he finally agreed to let Jean-Claude teach him enough control so that he doesn't leak all over both of us. He talks to Jean-Claude more than he talks to me.

The triumvirate is useless. Richard is too angry at me. Too full of self-loathing. I don't know how he's doing with the pack. He's forbidden anyone to speak of pack business with me, but he hasn't chosen a new alpha female.

Willie McCoy and the rest of the vampires I accidentally raised seem fine. Big relief there. Monica's baby is due in August. Her amnio came back clean. No Vlad syndrome. She seems to think I'm her friend now. I'm not, but I help out sometimes. Jean-Claude is playing the good master and taking care of her and the baby. Monica keeps talking about me babysitting. I hope she's kidding. Auntie Anita, she calls me. Gag me with a spoon. Funnier still, is Uncle Jean-Claude.

My dad saw me on television in Jean-Claude's arms. He called and left a very worried message on my answering machine. My family are devout Catholics. There is no such thing as a good vampire to them.

Maybe they're right. I don't know. Can I still be the scourge of vampire kind when I'm sleeping with the head bloodsucker?

You bet.